Praise for

Elin Hilderbrand's
The Perfect Couple

"A quintessential summer read."   —*People*

"Readers can open Hilderbrand's latest with complete confidence that it will deliver everything we expect: terrific clothes and food, smart humor, fun plot, Nantucket atmosphere, connections to the characters of preceding novels, and warmth in relationships evoked so beautifully it gets you right there...Sink into this book like a hot, scented bath...a delicious, relaxing pleasure. And a clever whodunit at the same time."   —*Kirkus Reviews*

"Hilderbrand throws enough curveballs to keep readers guessing, but not too many, maintaining the breezy pace her novels are known for. The mystery element is new, but *The Perfect Couple* is classic Hilderbrand."
                                                   —*Booklist*

"A sizzling summer read fans won't want to miss."
                                                   —*Bustle*

"A fantastic and clever whodunit that keeps readers in suspense throughout the entire book."   —*Bookreporter*

"Secrets begin to come out as the families and local police officers realize that no couple is as perfect as they might seem."   —*Good Housekeeping*

The Perfect Couple

ALSO BY ELIN HILDERBRAND

The Beach Club

Nantucket Nights

Summer People

The Blue Bistro

The Love Season

Barefoot

A Summer Affair

The Castaways

The Island

Silver Girl

Summerland

Beautiful Day

The Matchmaker

Winter Street

The Rumor

Winter Stroll

Here's to Us

Winter Storms

The Identicals

Winter Solstice

Winter in Paradise

Summer of '69

The Perfect Couple

A Novel

Elin Hilderbrand

Little, Brown and Company

New York   Boston   London

Copyright © 2018 by Elin Hilderbrand

Hachette Book Group supports the right to free expression and the value of copyright. The purpose of copyright is to encourage writers and artists to produce the creative works that enrich our culture.

The scanning, uploading, and distribution of this book without permission is a theft of the author's intellectual property. If you would like permission to use material from the book (other than for review purposes), please contact permissions@hbgusa.com. Thank you for your support of the author's rights.

Little, Brown and Company
Hachette Book Group
1290 Avenue of the Americas, New York, NY 10104
littlebrown.com

The publisher is not responsible for websites (or their content) that are not owned by the publisher.

Printed in the United States of America

Originally published in hardcover by Little, Brown and Company, July 2018
First Back Bay paperback edition, February 2019
First Little, Brown and Company mass market edition, June 2019

10 9 8 7 6 5 4 3 2 1

For Chuck and Margie Marino
There's no such thing as a perfect couple, but
you come pretty close.
Forever love xo

The Perfect Couple

Saturday, July 7, 2018,
5:53 a.m.

THE CHIEF

A phone call before six on a Saturday morning is never a good thing, although it's not unheard of on a holiday weekend. Too many times to count, Chief Ed Kapenash of the Nantucket Police Department has seen the Fourth of July go sideways. The most common accident is a person blowing off a finger while lighting fireworks. Sometimes things are more serious. One year, they lost a swimmer to the riptide; another year, a young woman did a backflip off the bow of a speedboat and hit the water in a way that left her paralyzed. There are generally enough drunk-and-disorderlies to fill a sightseeing bus, as well as dozens of fistfights, a handful of which are so serious that the police have to get involved.

When the call comes in, Andrea and the kids are fast asleep. Chloe and Finn are sixteen, an age the Chief escaped easily with his own children, he now realizes. Chloe and Finn—who are properly the children of Andrea's cousin Tess and Tess's husband, Greg, who died in a boating accident nine years ago—are proving to be more of a challenge. Finn has a girlfriend named Lola Budd, and their young love is turning the household upside down. Finn's twin sister, Chloe, has a summer job working for Siobhan Crispin at Island Fare, Nantucket's busiest catering company.

The Chief and Andrea have divided their concerns

about the twins neatly down the middle. Andrea worries about Finn getting Lola Budd pregnant (though the Chief, awkwardly, presented Finn with a giant box of condoms and a rather stern directive: *Use these. Every single time*). The Chief worries about Chloe getting into drugs and alcohol. The Chief has seen again and again the way the food-and-beverage industry leads its unsuspecting employees into temptation. The island of Nantucket has over a hundred liquor licenses; other, similar-size towns in Massachusetts have an average of twelve. As a summertime resort, the island has a culture of celebration, frivolity, excess. It's the Chief's job to give the annual substance-abuse talk the week before the high-school prom; this year, both Finn and Chloe had been in attendance, and afterward, neither of them would so much as look at him.

He often feels he's too old for the enormous responsibility of raising teenagers. And impressing them is most certainly beyond him.

The Chief takes his phone out onto the back deck, which looks west over protected wetlands; his conversations here are private, overheard only by the redwing blackbirds and the field mice. The house has a great view of sunsets but not, unfortunately, of the water.

The call is from Sergeant Dickson, one of the best in the department.

"Ed," he says. "We have a floater."

The Chief closes his eyes. Dickson had been the one to tell the Chief that Tess and Greg were dead. Sergeant Dickson has no problem delivering disturbing news; in fact, he seems to relish it.

"Go ahead," the Chief says.

"Caucasian female by the name of Merritt Monaco. Twenty-nine years old, from New York City, here on Nantucket for a wedding. She was found floating facedown just off the shore in front of three-three-three Monomoy Road, where the wedding is being held. The cause of death appears to be drowning. Roger Pelton called it in. You know Roger, the guy who does the expensive weddings?"

"I do," the Chief says. The Chief is in Rotary Club with Roger Pelton.

"Roger told me it's his MO to check on each wedding site first thing in the morning," Dickson says. "When he got here, he said he heard screaming. Turns out, the bride had just pulled the body out of the water. Roger tried CPR but the girl was dead, he said. He seemed to think she'd been dead for a few hours."

"That's for the ME to determine," the Chief says. "Three-three-three Monomoy Road, you said?"

"It's a compound," Dickson says. "Main house, two guest cottages, and a pool house. The name of the property is Summerland."

Summerland. The Chief has seen the sign, though he has never been to the house. That stretch of Monomoy Road is the stratospherically high-rent district. The people who live on that road generally don't have problems that require the police. The houses have sophisticated security systems, and the residents use discretion to keep any issues under wraps.

"Has everyone else been notified?" the Chief asks. "The state police? The ME?"

"Affirmative," Dickson says. "The Greek is on his way to the address now. He was here on island last night, lucky for us. But both Cash and Elsonhurst are on vacay until Monday and I'm at the end of a double, so I don't know who else you want to call in. The other guys are kind of green—"

"I'll worry about that in a minute," the Chief says. "Does the girl have family to notify?"

"I'm not sure," Dickson says. "The bride was so upset that I told the EMTs to take her to the hospital. She needed a Xanax, and badly. She could barely breathe, much less speak."

"The paper will have to leave this alone until we notify next of kin," the Chief says. Which is one small piece of good news; the last thing the Chief wants is Jordan Randolph from the *Nantucket Standard* sniffing around his crime scene. The Chief can't believe he missed the 911 call on the scanner. Over the years he has developed an uncanny filter where the scanner is concerned; he knows, even in his sleep, what deserves his attention and what he can let pass. But now he has a dead body.

They have to assume foul play by law, although here on Nantucket, violent crime is rare. The Chief has been working on this island for nearly thirty years and in all that time, he has seen only three homicides. One per decade.

Roger Pelton called it in. The Chief has heard Roger's name recently. *Really* recently, at some point in the past couple of days. And a *compound* in Monomoy—that rings a bell too. But why?

He hears a light tap on the window, and through the glass slider, he sees Andrea in her nightshirt, holding up a cup of coffee. Chloe is moving around the kitchen behind her, dressed in her catering uniform of white shirt and black pants.

Chloe is awake already? the Chief thinks. At six o'clock in the morning? Or did she get home so late last night that she fell asleep in her clothes?

Yes, he thinks. She worked a rehearsal dinner the night before. Then it clicks: Chloe told the Chief that the rehearsal dinner and the wedding were being held in Monomoy and that Roger was the wedding coordinator.

It's the same wedding. The Chief shakes his head, even though he knows better than anyone that this is a small island.

"Was the woman you found *staying* at the compound where the wedding is taking place today?" the Chief asks.

"Affirmative," Dickson says. "She was the maid of honor, Chief. I don't think there's going to be any wedding."

Andrea, possibly recognizing the expression on the Chief's face, steps out to the deck, hands Ed his coffee, and disappears inside. Chloe has vanished. She has probably headed upstairs to shower for work, which will now be canceled. News like this travels fast; the Chief expects that Siobhan Crispin will be calling at any moment.

What else did Chloe say about that wedding? One of the families is British, the mother famous somehow—an actress? A theater actress? A playwright? Something.

The Chief takes the first sip of his coffee. "You're still on-site, correct, Dickson? Have you talked to anyone other than the bride and Roger?"

"Yeah, I talked to the groom," Dickson says. "He wanted to go with the bride to the hospital. But first he went inside one of the guest cottages to grab his wallet and his phone and he came right back out to tell me the best man is missing."

"Missing?" the Chief says. "Is it possible we have *two* people dead?"

"I checked the water, down the beach, and out a few hundred yards in both directions with my field glasses," Dickson says. "It was all clear. But at this point, I'd say anything is possible."

"Tell the Greek to wait for me, please," the Chief says. "I'm on my way."

Friday, July 6, 2018,
9:15 a.m.

GREER

Greer Garrison Winbury thrives on tradition, protocol, and decorum but on the occasion of her younger son's wedding, she is happy to toss all three out the window. It's customary for the bride's parents to host and pay for their daughter's nuptials, but if that were the case with Benji and Celeste, the wedding would be taking place in a church at the mall with a reception following at TGI Fridays.

You're a terrific snob, Greer, her husband, Tag, is fond of saying. Greer fears that this is true. But where Benji's wedding was concerned, she *had* to intervene. Look what she'd endured when Thomas married Abigail Freeman: a *Texas* wedding, with all of Mr. Freeman's oil money on grand, grotesque display. There had been three hundred people at the "welcome party" at the Salt Lick BBQ—Greer had hoped to live her whole life without ever patronizing a place called the Salt Lick BBQ—where the suggested dress code was "hill-country casual," and when Greer asked Thomas what that could possibly mean, he'd said, *Wear jeans, Mom.*

Wear *jeans* to her elder son's wedding celebration? Greer had opted for wide-legged ivory trousers and stacked Ferragamo heels. Ivory had turned out to be a poor choice, as the guests of this welcome party had all been expected to eat pork ribs with their fingers. Shrieks of joy had gone up when there had been a surprise appearance by a country singer named George Strait, whom everyone called "the King of Country." Greer still can't imagine how much it must have cost Mr. Freeman to hire the King of Country—and for an event that wasn't even part of the usual nuptial schedule.

As Greer drives the Defender 90 (Tag had it rebuilt and shipped over from England) down to the Hy-Line ferry to pick up Celeste's parents, Bruce and Karen Otis, she sings along to the radio. It's B. J. Thomas's "Hooked on a Feeling."

This weekend, Greer is *effectively* the bride's mother as well as the groom's, for she is 100 percent in charge. She hasn't encountered one iota of resistance from anyone, including Celeste herself; the girl responds to all of Greer's suggestions with the exact same text: Sounds good. (Greer despises texting, but if one wants to communicate with Millennials, one must abandon old-fashioned notions like expecting to speak on the phone.) Greer has to admit, it has been far easier to get her way with the color scheme, the invitations, the flowers, and the caterer than she ever anticipated. It's as if this were her own wedding, thirty-two years later...minus her overbearing mother and grandmother, who insisted on an afternoon reception in the sweltering garden of Swallowcroft, and minus a fiancé who insisted on a stag party the night before the wedding. Tag had gotten home at seven o'clock in the morning smelling of Bushmills and Chanel No. 9. When Greer had started weeping and demanding to know if he'd actually had the gall to sleep with another woman the *night before his wedding,* Greer's mother took her aside and told her that the most important skill required in marriage was picking one's battles.

Make sure they're ones you can win, her mother had said.

Greer has tried to remain vigilant where Tag's fidelity is concerned, although it has been exhausting with a man as charismatic as her husband. Greer has never found hard evidence of any indiscretions, but she has certainly had her suspicions. She has them right up to this very minute about a woman named Featherleigh Dale, who will be arriving on Nantucket from London in a few short hours. If Featherleigh is silly and careless enough to wear the silver-lace ring with the pink, yellow, and blue sapphires—Greer knows exactly what the ring looks like because Jessica Hicks, the jeweler, showed her a picture!—then Greer's hunch will be confirmed.

Greer encounters traffic on Union Street. She should have left more time; she *cannot* be late for the Otises. Greer has yet to meet either of Celeste's parents in person and she would like to make a good impression and not leave them to wander forlornly around Straight Wharf on this, their first trip to the island. Greer had worried about hosting a wedding so close to the Fourth of July, but it was the only weekend that worked over the course of the entire summer and they couldn't put it off until autumn because Karen, Celeste's mother, has stage 4 breast cancer. No one knows how much time she has left.

The song ends, traffic comes to a dead stop, and the sense of foreboding that Greer has successfully held at bay until now fills the car like a foul smell. Usually, Greer feels unsettled about only two things: her husband and her writing, and the writing always sorts itself out in the end (declining book sales aside, although, really, it's Greer's job to *write* the mysteries, not sell them). But now she worries about...well, if she has to pinpoint the exact locus of her dismay she would say it is Celeste. The ease with which Greer has been able to take control of this wedding suddenly seems suspect. As Greer's mother used to say, *Things that seem too good to be true usually are.*

It's as if Celeste doesn't *care* about the wedding. At all. How had Greer ignored this possibility for four months?

She had reasoned that Celeste was (wisely) deferring to—or placing extreme confidence in—Greer's impeccable taste. Or that Celeste's only agenda was getting the wedding planned as expediently as possible because of her mother's illness.

But now, other factors come into focus, such as the stutter Celeste developed shortly after the date was set. The stutter began with Celeste repeating certain words or short phrases, but it has become something more serious, even debilitating—Celeste trips over her *r*'s and *m*'s and *p*'s until she grows pink in the face.

Greer asked Benji if the stutter was creating problems for Celeste at work. Celeste is the assistant director at the Bronx Zoo and she is occasionally called upon to give lectures to the zoo's visitors—mostly schoolchildren during the week and foreigners on the weekends—so Celeste has to speak slowly and clearly. Benji replied that Celeste rarely stuttered at work. Mostly just at home and when she was out socially.

This gave Greer pause. Developing a stutter at twenty-eight could be attributed to…what? It was a *tell* of some kind. Greer had immediately used the detail in the novel she was writing: the murderer develops a stutter as a result of his guilt, which grabs the attention of Miss Dolly Hardaway, the spinster detective who is the protagonist of all twenty-one of Greer's murder mysteries. This is well and fine for Greer, who tends to mine every new encounter and experience in her fiction, but what about in real life, for Celeste? What is going on? Greer has the feeling that the stutter is somehow connected to Celeste's imminent marriage to Benji.

There's no time to think any further because suddenly traffic surges forward and not only does Greer move swiftly into town, she also finds a parking spot right in front of the ferry dock. She still has two minutes to spare.

What magnificent luck! Her doubts fade. This wedding, this union of two families on the most festive of summer weekends, is clearly something that's meant to be.

KAREN

Viewed from a distance, Nantucket Island is everything Karen Otis dreamed it would be: tasteful, charming, nautical, classic. The ferry passes inside a stone jetty, and Karen squeezes Bruce's hand to let him know she would like to stand and walk the few feet to the railing now. Bruce places an arm across Karen's back and eases her up out of her seat. He's not a big man but he's strong. He was the Pennsylvania state champion wrestler at 142 pounds in 1984. Karen first set eyes on him sitting in the Easton Area High School pool balcony. She was swimming the butterfly leg for the varsity relay team, which routinely practiced during lunch, and when she climbed out of the water, she spied Bruce, dressed in sweatpants and a hooded sweatshirt, staring at an orange he held in his hands.

"What is that guy doing?" Karen had wondered aloud.

"That's Bruce Otis," Tracy, the backstroker, had said. "He's captain of the wrestling team. They have a meet this afternoon and he's trying to make weight."

Karen had wrapped a towel around her waist and marched up the stairs to introduce herself. She had been well endowed even as a high-school sophomore and was pretty sure the sight of her in her tank suit would take Bruce Otis's mind off the orange and his weight and anything else.

Bruce holds Karen steady and together they approach the railing. People see them coming, take note of the scarf wrapped around Karen's head—she can't bring herself to do wigs—and back up a few steps to make a respectful space.

Karen grips the railing with both hands. Even that is an effort but she wants a good view for their approach. The houses that line the water are all enormous, ten times the size of Karen and Bruce's ranch on Derhammer Street in Forks Township, Pennsylvania, and these houses all have gray cedar shingles and crisp white trim. Some of the homes have curved decks; some have stacked decks at nifty angles like a Jenga game. Some have lush green lawns that roll right up to stone walls before a thin strip of beach. Every home flies the American flag, and all are impeccably maintained; there isn't a dumpy or disheveled renegade in the bunch.

Money, Karen thinks. Where does all the money come from? She is seasoned enough to know that money can't buy happiness—and it certainly can't buy health— but it's still intriguing to contemplate just *how much money* the people who own these houses must have. First off, these are *second* homes, so one must account for the first home—a brownstone in Manhattan or a brick mansion in Georgetown, an estate on the Main Line or a horse farm in Virginia—and then factor in the price of waterfront property here on this prestigious island. Next, Karen considers all of the furnishings such houses must contain: the rugs, the sofas, the tables and chairs, the lamps, the pencil-post beds, the nine-thousand-thread-count Belgian sheets, the decorative pillows, the Jacuzzi bathtubs, the scented candles next to the Jacuzzi bathtubs. (Celeste has educated Karen beyond the world of Yankee Candle; there are apparently candles that sell for over *four hundred dollars*. Celeste's future sister-in-law, Abby, gave Celeste such a candle as an engagement present, and when Celeste told Karen that a Jo Malone pine-and-eucalyptus candle sold for $470, Karen hooted. That was nearly as much as Bruce had paid for his first car, a 1969 Chevy Nova!)

Then, of course, there's the staff to pay: landscapers, house cleaners, caretakers, nannies for the children. There are the cars—Range Rovers, Jaguars, BMWs. There must be sailing and tennis lessons, monogrammed seersucker dresses, grosgrain ribbons for the hair, a new pair of Topsiders each season. And what about the food such houses must contain? Bowls of peaches and plums, cartons of strawberries and blueberries, freshly baked bread, quinoa salad, ripe avocados, organic eggs, fat-marbled steaks, and steaming, scarlet lobsters. And butter. Lots and lots of butter.

Karen also factors in all of the dull stuff that no one likes to think about: insurance, taxes, electricity, cable TV, attorneys.

These families must have fifty million dollars each, Karen decides. At least. And how does someone, anyone, make *that much money?* She would ask Bruce but she doesn't want to make him feel self-conscious. Meaning she doesn't want to make him feel any *more* self-conscious; she knows he's already sensitive about money—because they don't have any. Despite this, Bruce will be the best-dressed man at the wedding, Karen is certain. Bruce works in the suit department at Neiman Marcus in the King of Prussia Mall. He gets a 30 percent discount on clothes plus free alterations. He has managed to keep his wrestler's physique—strong shoulders, tapered waist (no beer belly for him!)—and so he cuts an impressive silhouette. If he were two inches taller, a store vice president once told him, he could work as a model.

Bruce is almost like a woman in the way he loves fine clothes. When he brings home something new (which is fairly often, a fact that used to confuse Karen, as they don't really have the money for new clothes or the money to go anywhere he might wear them), he likes to give

Karen a fashion show. She sits on the edge of the bed—lately, she lies *in* the bed—while Bruce gets dressed in the bathroom and then emerges, one hand on hip, and sashays around the room like it's a fashion runway. It cracks Karen up every time. She has come to understand that this is why he buys new suits, shirts, ties, trousers, and socks—to give Karen joy.

And because he likes to look good. Today, for their arrival, he's wearing a pair of pressed black G-Star jeans and a black-and-turquoise paisley Robert Graham shirt with contrasting grasshopper-green cuffs, a pair of zebra-striped socks, and black suede Gucci loafers. It's hot in the sun. Even Karen, who is always cold now thanks to the chemo, is warm. Bruce must be roasting.

A lighthouse swathed in an American flag comes into view, and then Karen sees two church steeples, one a white spire, one a clock tower with a gold dome. The harbor is filled with sailboats of all sizes, power yachts with tiered tuna towers, cigarette boats, cabin cruisers.

"It's like a movie set," Karen says, but her words get carried away on the sea breeze and Bruce doesn't hear her. She can see from the expression on his face that he's as mesmerized as she is. He's probably thinking that they haven't been anywhere this enchanting since their honeymoon thirty-two years earlier. She was eighteen years old then, just out of high school, and after the cost of the wedding clothes and a ceremony at the courthouse, they had $280 left for a weeklong getaway. They bought a case of wine coolers (they're out of fashion now but, oh, how Karen had loved a cold raspberry Bartles and Jaymes back then) and a bunch of snack food—Bugles, Cool Ranch Doritos, Funyuns—and they'd climbed into Bruce's Chevy Nova, popped in his *Bat Out of Hell* eight-track, and taken off for the coast, both of them singing at the top of their lungs.

They had reached the Jersey Shore points early on but neither of them had felt compelled to stop. The shore had been the beach of their youth—class trips, a family vacation to Wildwood every summer—and so they had continued going north to New England.

New England, Karen remembers now, had sounded very exotic.

They ran low on gas in a town called Madison, Connecticut, exit 61 off I-95, that had a leafy main street lined with shops, like something out of a 1950s sitcom. When Karen got out of the car to stretch her legs at the filling station, she had smelled salt in the air.

She said, "I think we're near the water."

They had asked the gas-station attendant what there was to see in Madison, Connecticut, and he directed them to a restaurant called the Lobster Deck, which had an uninterrupted view of the Long Island Sound. Down the street from the Lobster Deck, across from a state park with a beach, was the Sandbar Motel and Lodge; a room cost $105 for the week.

Karen knows she's not worldly. She has never been to Paris, Bermuda, or even the West Coast. She and Bruce used to take Celeste to the Pocono Mountains on vacation. They skied at Camelback in the winter and went to the Great Wolf Lodge water park in the summer. The rest of their money they saved for Celeste to go to college. She had shown an interest in animals at an early age, and both Bruce and Karen had hoped she would become a veterinarian. When Celeste's interests had instead run toward zoology, that had been fine too. She had been offered a partial scholarship at Miami University of Ohio, which had the best zoology department in the country. "Partial scholarship" still left a lot to pay for—some tuition, room, board, books, spending money, bus tickets home—and so there had been precious little left over for travel.

Hence, that one trip to New England remained sacred to both Karen and Bruce. They are even further in the hole now—nearly a hundred thousand dollars in debt, thanks to Karen's medical bills—but there was no way they were going to miss making the trip to Nantucket. On their way home, once Celeste and Benji are safely on their honeymoon in Greece, they will stop in Madison, Connecticut, for what Karen is privately calling the Grand Finale. The Sandbar Motel and Lodge is long gone, so instead, Bruce has booked an oceanfront suite at the Madison Beach Hotel. It's a Hilton property. Bruce told Karen he got it for free by accepting Hilton Honors points offered to him by the store's general manager, Mr. Allen. Karen knows that all of Bruce's co-workers have wondered how to help out their favorite sales associate, Bruce in Suits, whose wife has been diagnosed with terminal cancer, and while this is slightly mortifying, she does appreciate the concern and, especially, Mr. Allen's generous offer to pay for their hotel. Madison, Connecticut, has taken on the paradisiacal qualities of a Shangri-la. Karen wants to eat lobster—with butter, lots and lots of butter—and she wants to watch the honey lozenge of the sun drop into the Long Island Sound. She wants to fall asleep in Bruce's arms as she listens to waves lap the shore, their daughter successfully married.

The Grand Finale.

Last August, Karen learned that she had a tumor on her L3 vertebra. The breast cancer, which she'd believed she'd beaten, had metastasized to her bones. Her oncologist, Dr. Edman, has given her a year to eighteen months. Karen figures she has until at least the end of the summer, which is an enormous blessing, especially when you consider all the people throughout history who have died without warning. Why, Karen could be crossing Northampton Street to the circle in downtown Easton and get hit by a car, making the cancer diagnosis irrelevant.

Celeste had been gutted by the news. She had just gotten engaged to Benji but she said she wanted to postpone the wedding, leave New York, and move back to Easton to take care of Karen. This was the exact opposite of what Karen wanted. Karen encouraged Celeste to move *up* the wedding, rather than postpone it.

Celeste, always obedient, did just that.

When Dr. Edman called last week to say it appeared the cancer had spread to Karen's stomach and liver, Karen and Bruce decided to keep the news from Celeste entirely. When Karen leaves on Monday morning, she will say good-bye to Celeste as if everything is just fine.

All she has to do is make it through the next three days.

Karen can still walk with a cane but Bruce has arranged for a wheelchair to glide her gracefully down the ramp and onto the wharf. Greer Garrison Winbury—or, rather, Greer Garrison; people rarely call her by her married name, according to Celeste—is supposed to be waiting. Neither Karen nor Bruce has met Greer, but Karen has read two of her books: her most recent, *Death in Dubai,* as well as the novel that launched Greer to fame in the early nineties, *The Killer on Khao San Road.* Karen isn't much of a book critic—she has dropped out of three book groups because the novels they choose are so grim and depressing—but she can say that *The Killer on Khao San Road* was fast-paced and entertaining. (Karen had no idea where Khao San Road was; turned out it was in Bangkok, and there were all kinds of elaborate details about that city—the temples, the flower market, the green papaya salad with toasted peanuts—that made the book just as transporting as watching the Travel Channel on TV.) *Death in Dubai,* however, was formulaic and predictable. Karen figured out who the killer was on page fourteen: the hairless guy with the tattooed mustache. Karen could have written a more suspenseful novel herself with just *CSI: Miami* as background. Karen wonders if Greer Garrison, the esteemed mystery writer who is always named in the same breath as Sue Grafton and Louise Penny, is coasting now, in her middle age.

Karen has carefully studied Greer's author photo; both of the books Karen read featured the same photo, despite a nearly twenty-five-year span between publication dates. Greer wears a straw picture hat, and there is a lush English garden in the background. Greer is maybe thirty in the photo. She has pale blond hair and flawless pale skin. Greer's eyes are a beautiful deep brown and she has a long, lovely neck. She isn't an overtly beautiful woman, but she conveys class, elegance, regality even, and Karen can see why she never chose to update the picture. Who wants to see age descend on a woman? No one. So it's up to Karen to imagine how Greer might look now, with wrinkles, some tension in the neck, possibly some gray in the part of her hair.

There is a crush of people on the wharf—those disembarking, those picking up houseguests, tourists wandering the shops, hungry couples in search of lunch. Because the cancer has invaded Karen's stomach, she rarely feels hungry, but her appetite is piqued now by the prospect of lobster. Will there be lobster served over the wedding weekend? she had asked Celeste.

Yes, Betty, Celeste had said, and the nickname had made Karen smile. *There will be plenty of lobster.*

"Karen?" a voice calls out. "Bruce?"

Karen searches through the crowd and sees a woman—blond, thin, maniacally smiling, or maybe the smile only looks maniacal because of the face-lift—moving toward them with her arms wide open.

Greer Garrison. Yes, there she is. Her hair is the same

pale blond, and expensive-looking sunglasses—Tom Ford?—are perched on the top of her head. She's wearing white capri pants and a white linen tunic, which Karen supposes is very chic and summery although she herself always prefers color, a result of having worked in the gift shop at the Crayola factory in Easton for so many years. In Karen's opinion, Greer's look would be more interesting if the tunic were magenta or goldenrod.

Greer swoops down to hug Karen in her wheelchair without confirmation that she is, in fact, Karen Otis, which gives Karen the uncomfortable feeling that she and Bruce stick out so badly that there can be no mistaking them. Or maybe Celeste has shown Greer pictures.

"So wonderful to meet you finally," Greer says. "And on such a happy occasion. I'm thrilled you could make the trip."

Karen realizes that she is prepared to dislike Greer Garrison and take offense at everything she says. *Of course* Karen and Bruce made the trip! Their only daughter, their pride and joy, is getting *married!*

Karen needs to adjust her attitude, and fast. She needs to abandon her petty jealousy, her feelings of inferiority, her embarrassment because she and Bruce aren't wealthy or sophisticated. Mostly, Karen needs to abandon the anger she feels. This anger isn't caused by Greer specifically, by any means. Karen is angry at everyone who isn't sick. Everyone except Bruce. And Celeste, of course.

"Greer," Karen says. "It's so nice to meet *you*. Thank you for having us. Thank you for…*everything*."

Bruce steps forward and offers Greer his hand. "Bruce Otis," he says. "It's a pleasure, ma'am."

"Ma'am?" Greer says. She laughs with her head thrown back, her neck—still lovely but indisputably aged—exposed. "Please don't call me that, you make me feel a thousand years old. Call me Greer, and my

husband is Tag, like the game. After all, we're going to
be family!"

Family, Karen thinks as Bruce helps her into the backseat of Greer's car, which looks exactly like what people
drive in across the savannas of Africa on the Travel
Channel. They head up a cobblestoned street. Each cob-
blestone the car goes over is a punch to the gut for Karen,
but she grits her teeth and bears it. Bruce, sensing her
pain as if it's his own, reaches a hand between the seats to
comfort her. The comment about family might have
been a throwaway, but it holds undeniable appeal. Karen
and Bruce are low on family. Karen's father died of a
heart attack when Karen was pregnant with Celeste; her
mother put the house in Tatamy on the market and
ended up marrying Gordon, the listing real estate bro-
ker. Then, when Celeste was in kindergarten, Karen's
mother was diagnosed with a rare myeloma and died six
months later. Gordon is still a real estate agent in the area
but they hardly ever hear from him. Bruce's younger
brother, Bryan, was a state trooper in New Jersey; he was
killed in a high-speed chase. After Bryan's funeral,
Bruce's parents moved to a retirement community in
Bethlehem, where they both died of old age. Karen and
Bruce have always clung to each other and Celeste; they
are a small, insular cluster of three. Karen somehow
never imagined that Celeste would provide them with a
whole new family, and certainly not one as esteemed as
the Winburys, who not only have a summer estate on
Nantucket but also an apartment on Park Avenue in New
York City and a flat they keep in London for when Tag
takes business trips or Greer misses "home." Karen can't
help but feel a secret thrill at the thought of a new family,
even though she won't be around to enjoy it.

Greer points out Main Street, a certain restaurant she likes that serves an organic beet salad, a store that sells the red pants that all of the gentlemen will be wearing tomorrow. They've ordered a pair for Bruce, Greer says, tailored precisely to the measurements he sent them (this is news to Karen). Greer points out the boutique where she bought a clutch purse that matches her mother-of-the-groom dress (though the dress itself she bought in New York, of course, she says, and Karen nearly says that of course she bought her mother-of-the-bride dress at Neiman Marcus in the King of Prussia Mall using Bruce's discount but decides this will sound pathetic) and a shop that specializes in nautical antiques where Greer always buys Tag's Father's Day presents.

Bruce says, "Do you have a boat, then?"

Greer laughs like this is a silly question, and maybe it is a silly question. Maybe everyone on this island has a boat; maybe it's a practical necessity, like having a sturdy snow shovel for Easton winters.

"We have three," she says. "A thirty-seven-foot Hinckley picnic boat named *Ella* for puttering over to Tuckernuck, a thirty-two-foot Grady-White that we take to Great Point to fish for stripers, and a thirteen-foot Whaler, which we bought so the kids could get back and forth to Coatue with their girlfriends."

Bruce nods like he approves and Karen wonders if he has any earthly idea what Greer is talking about. Karen certainly doesn't; the woman might as well be speaking Swahili.

How will Karen and Greer be related once the kids are married? Karen wonders. Each will be the mother-in-law of the other's child but no relation to each other, or at least not a relation that has a name. In many instances, she suspects, the mothers of two people getting married dislike each other, or worse. Karen would like to think that she and Greer could get to know each other and find kinship and become as close as sisters, but that would only happen in the fantasy world where Karen doesn't die.

"We also have kayaks, both one-person and two-person," Greer says. "Tag loves the kayaks more than the boats, I think. He may love the kayaks more than the boys!"

Bruce laughs like this is the funniest thing he's ever heard. Karen scowls. Who would joke about something like that? She needs a pain pill. She rummages through her wine-colored Tory Burch hobo bag, which was a present from Bruce when she finished her first chemo protocol, back when they were still filled with hope. She pulls out her bottle of oxycodone. She is very careful to pick out a small round pill and not one of the three pearlescent ovoids, and she throws it back without water. The oxy makes her heart race, but it's the only thing that works against the pain.

Karen wants to admire the scenery but she has to close her eyes. After a while, Greer says, "We'll be there in a jiffy." Her British accent reminds Karen of Julie Andrews in *Mary Poppins. Jiff-jiff-jiffy,* Karen thinks. Greer drives around a traffic circle, then puts on her blinker and turns left. With the sudden movement of the car, the oxy kicks in. Karen's pain subsides and a sense of well-being washes over her like a golden wave. It's by far the best part of the oxy, this initial rush when the pain is absorbed like a spill by a sponge. Karen is most certainly on her way to becoming addicted if she isn't already, but Dr. Edman is generous with medication. What does addiction matter at this point?

"Here we are!" Greer announces as she pulls into a white-shell driveway.

SUMMERLAND, a sign says. PRIVATE. Karen peers out the window. There's a row of hydrangea bushes on either side of the driveway, alternately fuchsia and periwinkle, and then they drive under a boxwood arch into what Karen can only think of as some kind of waterfront utopia. There's a main house, stately and grand with crisp white-and-green awnings over the windows. Opposite the main house are two smaller cottages set amid landscaped gardens with gurgling stone fountains and flagstone paths and lavish flower beds. And all of this is only yards away from the water. The harbor is right there, and across the flat blue expanse of the harbor is town. Karen can pick out the church towers she saw from the ferry. The Nantucket skyline.

Karen has a hard time finding air, much less words. This is the most beautiful place she has ever been. It's so beautiful it hurts.

Today is Friday. The rehearsal at St. Paul's Episcopal Church is scheduled for six o'clock and will be followed by a clambake for sixty people that will include a raw bar and live music, a cover band that plays the Beach Boys and Jimmy Buffett. There will be a "small tent" set up on the beach to shelter the band and four rectangular tables of fifteen. And there will be lobster.

The wedding is Saturday at four o'clock, and it will be followed by a sit-down dinner under the "big tent," which has a clear plastic roof so that the guests can see the sky. There will be a dance floor, an eighteen-piece orchestra, and seventeen round tables that seat ten guests each. On Sunday, the Winburys are hosting a brunch at their golf club; this will be followed by a nap, at least for herself, Karen thinks. On Monday morning, Karen and Bruce will leave on the ferry, and Celeste and Benji will fly from Boston to Athens and from there to Santorini.

Stop time, Karen thinks. She doesn't want to get out of the car. She wants to stay right here, with all of those sumptuous plans still in front of her, forever.

*   *   *

Bruce helps Karen down out of the car and hands over her cane, and in the time it takes for this to happen, people pop out of the main house and appear from the cottages as though Bruce and Karen are visiting dignitaries. Well, they *are,* Karen thinks. They are the mother and father of the bride.

She knows they are also something of a curiosity because they are poor and because Karen is sick, and she hopes all of them will be gentle with their appraisals.

"Hello," Karen says to the assembled group. "I'm Karen Otis." She looks for someone she recognizes, but Greer has vanished and Celeste is nowhere to be found. Karen squints into the sun. She has met Benji, Celeste's betrothed, only three times, and all she can remember of him, thanks to chemo brain, is the cowlick that she had to keep herself from smoothing down every ten seconds. There are two young, good-looking men in front of her, and Karen knows that neither of them is Benji. One is in a snappy cornflower-blue polo and Karen smiles at him. This young man steps forward, hand extended.

"I'm Thomas Winbury, Mrs. Otis," he says. "Benji's brother."

Karen shakes Thomas's hand; his grip is nearly enough to turn Karen's bones to powder. "Please, call me Karen."

"And I'm Bruce, Bruce Otis." Bruce shakes Thomas's hand and then the hand of the young man standing next to Thomas. He has very dark hair and crystalline-blue eyes. He's so striking that Karen can hardly keep from staring.

"Shooter Uxley," the young man says. "Benji's best man."

Shooter, yes! Celeste has mentioned Shooter. It isn't a name one forgets, and Celeste had tried to explain why Shooter was the best man instead of Benji's brother,

Thomas, but the story was puzzling to Karen, as though Celeste were describing characters on a TV series Karen had never seen.

Bruce then shakes the hands of two young ladies, one with chestnut hair and freckles and one a dangerous-looking brunette who is wearing a formfitting jersey dress in a color that Karen would call scarlet, like the letter.

"Aren't you hot?" the Scarlet Letter asks Bruce. With a slightly different inflection, it would sound as though the girl were hitting on Bruce, but Karen realizes she's talking about Bruce's outfit, the black jeans, the black-and-turquoise shirt, the loafers, the socks. He looks sharp but he doesn't exactly fit in. Everyone else is in casual summer clothes—the men in shorts and polo shirts, the ladies in bright cotton sundresses. Celeste had told Karen no less than half a dozen times to remind Bruce that the Winburys were preppy. *Preppy,* that was the word Celeste insisted on using, and it sounded quaint to Karen. Didn't that term go out of style decades ago, right along with *Yuppie?* Celeste had said: *Tell Mac-Gyver, blue blazers and no socks.* When Karen had passed on this message, Bruce had laughed, but not happily.

I know how to dress myself, Bruce had said. *That's my job.*

A tall, silver-haired gentleman strides across the lawn and walks down the three stone steps into the driveway. He's dripping wet and wearing a pair of bathing trunks and a neoprene rash guard.

"Welcome!" he calls out. "I'd open my arms to you but let's wait until I dry off for those familiarities."

"Did you capsize again, Tag?" the Scarlet Letter teases.

The gentleman ignores the comment and approaches Karen. When she offers her hand, he kisses it, a gesture that catches her off guard. She's not sure anyone has ever kissed her hand before. There's a first time for everything, she thinks, even for a dying woman. "Madame," he says. His accent is English enough to be charming but not so much that it's obnoxious. "I'm Tag Winbury. Thank you for coming all this way, thank you for indulging my wife in all her planning, and thank you, most of all, for your beautiful, intelligent, and enchanting daughter, our celestial Celeste. We are absolutely enamored of her and tickled pink about this impending union."

"Oh," Karen says. She feels the roses rising to her cheeks, which was how her father always described her blushing. This man is divine! He has managed to set Karen at ease while at the same time making her feel like a queen.

There's a tap on Karen's shoulder and she turns carefully, planting her cane in the shells of the driveway.

"B-B-Betty!"

It's Celeste. She's wearing a white sundress and a pair of barely there sandals; her hair is braided. She has gotten a suntan, and her blue eyes look wide and sad in her face.

Sad? Karen thinks. This should be the happiest day of her life, or the second-happiest. Karen knows Celeste is worried about *her,* but Karen is determined to forget she's sick—at least for the next three days—and she wants everyone else to do the same.

"Darling!" Karen says, kissing Celeste on the cheek.

"Betty, you're here," Celeste says, without a trace of stutter. "Can you believe it? You're *here.*"

"Yes," Karen says, and she reminds herself that she is the reason that the whole wedding is being held now, during the busiest week of the summer. "I'm here."

Saturday, July 7, 2018, 6:45 a.m.

THE CHIEF

He pulls up to 333 Monomoy Road right behind state police detective Nicholas Diamantopoulos, otherwise known as the Greek. Nick's father is Greek and his mother is Cape Verdean; Nick has brown skin, a shaved head, and a jet-black goatee. He's so good-looking that people joke he should quit the job and play a cop on TV—better hours and more money—but Nick is content being a damn good detective and a notorious ladies' man.

Nick and the Chief worked together on the last homicide, a drug-related murder on Cato Lane. Nick spent the first fifteen years of his career in New Bedford, where the streets were dangerous and the criminals hardened, but Nick doesn't subscribe to the tough-guy shtick; he doesn't use any of the strong-arming tactics you see in the movies. When Nick is questioning persons of interest, he is encouraging and empathetic; he sometimes tells stories about his *ya-ya* back in Thessaloníki who wore an ugly black dress and uglier black shoes every day after his grandfather passed. And the results he gets! He says the word *ya-ya* and people confess to everything. The guy's a magician.

"Nicky," the Chief says.

"Chief," Nick says. He nods at the house. "This is sad, huh? The maid of honor."

"Tragic," the Chief says. He's dreading what he's going to find inside. Not only is a twenty-nine-year-old woman *dead,* but the family and guests have to be questioned, and all of the complicated, costly wedding preparations have to be undone without destroying the integrity of the crime scene.

Before the Chief left his house, he went upstairs to find Chloe to see if she had heard the news. She had been in the bathroom. Through the closed door, the Chief had heard the sound of her vomiting.

He'd knocked. "You okay?"

"Yeah," she said. "I'm fine."

Fine, the Chief thought. Meaning she'd spent her postshift hours on the beach drinking Bud Light and doing shots of Fireball.

He had kissed Andrea good-bye in the kitchen and said, "I think Chloe was drinking last night."

Andrea sighed. "I'll talk to her."

Talking to Chloe wasn't going to help, the Chief thought. She needed a new job—shelving books at the children's library or counting plover eggs out on Smith's Point. Something that would keep her out of trouble, not lead her right to it.

The Chief and Nick walk past the left side of the main house onto the lawn, where an enormous tent has been erected. They find the guys from forensics inside the tent, one bagging, one photographing. Nick heads down to the beach to check out the body; the Chief sees that the girl has been left just shy of the waterline but she'll need to be moved to the hospital morgue as soon as possible on this hot a day. Inside the tent, there is one round table surrounded by four white banquet chairs. In the middle of the table is a nearly empty bottle of Mount

Gay Black Barrel rum and four shot glasses, two of them on their sides. There's half a quahōg shell that served as an ashtray for someone's cigar. A Romeo y Julieta. Cuban.

One of the forensics guys, Randy, is bagging a pair of silver sandals.

"Where did you find those?" the Chief asks.

"Under that chair," Randy says, pointing. "Connor has a picture of them. Size eight Mystique sandals. I'm no shoe salesman, but I'm guessing they belonged to the deceased. We'll confirm."

Nick returns. "The girl has a nasty gash on her foot," he says. "And I noticed there's a trail of blood in the sand."

"Any blood on the sandals?" the Chief asks Randy.

"No, sir," Randy says.

"Took off her shoes, cut her foot on a shell, maybe," Nick says.

"Well, she didn't die of a cut on her foot," the Chief says. "Unless she swam out too far and couldn't get back in because of the foot?"

"That doesn't sound right," Nick says. "There's also a two-person kayak overturned on the beach, one oar a few yards away lying in the sand. No blood on the kayak."

The Chief takes a breath. The day is still; there's no breeze off the water. It's going to be hot and buggy. They need to get the body out of here, pronto. They need to start their questioning, try to figure out what happened. He remembers what Dickson said about the best man being missing. Hopefully that situation has resolved itself. "Let's go up to the house," he says.

"Should we divide and conquer?" the Greek asks.

"I'll take the men, you take the women," the Chief says. Nick works wonders with the women.

Nick nods. "Deal."

As they're approaching the steps of the front porch, Bob from Old Salt Taxi pulls up in the driveway and a kid in his twenties climbs out. He's wearing Nantucket Reds shorts, a blue oxford, a navy blazer, and loafers; he has a large duffel in one hand and a garment bag in the other. His hair is mussed and he needs a shave.

"Who is this guy?" Nick asks under his breath.

"Late to the party," the Chief says. He waves to Bob as Bob reverses out of the driveway.

The kid gives the Chief and Nick an uneasy smile. "What's going on?" he asks.

Nick says, "You part of the wedding?"

"Best man," the kid says. "Shooter Uxley. Did something happen?"

Nick looks to the Chief. The Chief nods ever so slightly and tries not to let the relief show on his face. One mystery is solved.

"The maid of honor is dead," Nick says.

The bags hit the ground, and the kid—Shooter Uxley; what a name—goes pale. "What?" he says. "Wait...*what?*"

Initial questioning, Roger Pelton, Saturday, July 7, 7:00 a.m.

The Chief meets Roger Pelton in the driveway. The two men shake hands, and the Chief grips Roger's arm in a show of friendship and support. Roger has been married to Rita since the Bronze Age, and they have five kids, all grown. Roger has been running his wedding business for over ten years; before that, he was a successful general contractor. Roger Pelton is as solid a human being as God has ever put on this earth. He was in Vietnam too, the Chief remembers, where he received a Purple Heart and a Bronze Star. He's an unlikely candidate to be Nantucket's most in-demand wedding planner, but he has a gift for it that has resulted in a booming business.

Right now, Roger looks *shaken*. His face is pale and sweaty; his shoulders are drooping.

"I'm sorry about this, Roger," the Chief says. "It must have come as a terrible shock."

"I thought I'd seen it all," Roger says. "I've had brides turn around halfway down the aisle; I've had grooms not show up; I've caught couples having sex in church bathrooms. I've had mothers of brides slapping mothers of grooms. I've had fathers who refused to pay my bills and fathers who tipped me five grand. I've had hurricanes, thunderstorms, heat waves, fog, and, once, hail. I've had brides vomit and faint; I even had a groomsman eat a mussel and go into anaphylactic shock. But I've never had anyone die. I met the maid of honor only briefly so I can't give you any information other than that she was Celeste's best friend."

"Celeste?" the Chief says.

"Celeste Otis is the bride," Roger says. "She's pretty and smart, but on this island I see a lot of pretty and smart. More notably, Celeste loves her parents and she's kind and patient with her future in-laws. She's humble. Any idea how rare humility is when you're dealing with Nantucket brides?"

"Rare?" the Chief asks.

"Rare," Roger says. "I hate that this happened on her wedding day. She was a complete mess."

"Let's try to figure out what happened," the Chief says. "I'm starting with you because I know you have work to do." The Chief leads Roger over to a white wrought-iron bench tucked under an arbor that is dripping with New Dawn roses and they both sit down.

"Tell me what you saw when you got here," the Chief says. "From the beginning."

"I pulled in about quarter to six," Roger says. "The

rental company was supposed to leave seventeen rounds and a hundred and seventy-five folding chairs. I wanted to double-check the numbers, see how the dance floor settled, make sure there hadn't been any after-hours partying. Standard stuff."

"Understood," the Chief says.

"As soon as I got out of my car, I heard screaming," Roger says. "And I realized right away that it was Celeste. I thought something had happened to her mother." Roger pauses. "Celeste's mother, Karen Otis, is very sick— cancer. Anyway, I could tell just from the kind of scream that someone was dead. It had that *urgency*. So I go charging out to the front of the house and there's poor Celeste trying to pull her friend out of the water by the arms. One look at her, I knew the girl was dead, but I helped Celeste drag her up onto the beach and then I tried to revive her."

"CPR?"

"I tried," Roger says. "I...tried. But she was dead when I found her, Ed. That much I know."

"So why bother with CPR, then?"

"I thought maybe. I had to try *something*. Celeste was begging me to save her. *You have to save her,* she said. *You have to save her!*" Roger drops his head in his hands. "She was dead. There was no bringing her back."

"Then you called 911?"

"I had dropped my phone in the driveway so I used Celeste's phone," Roger says. "The paramedics came in six minutes. They tried CPR as well. Then the police came. Sergeant Dickson. Together, he and I knocked on the front door of the house."

"And who answered? Who did you tell?"

"Greer Garrison, the groom's mother. She and her husband, Tag Winbury, own the house. Greer was already awake. She was holding a cup of coffee."

"She was? You're sure about that?" the Chief says.

"She was awake but didn't hear Celeste screaming and didn't notice you pulling a body out of the water in front of her house? With all of those giant windows, she didn't notice? She didn't hear the sirens or see the lights when the paramedics arrived?"

"Apparently not. She had no idea anything was wrong when I knocked."

"When you told her, what did she do?"

"She started to shake," Roger says. "Her coffee spilled. Dickson had to take it from her."

"So it's fair to say she seemed shocked and upset?" the Chief says.

"Oh yes," Roger says. "Mr. Winbury came to see what the ruckus was and I told him as well. He thought we were kidding."

"Kidding," the Chief says.

"Everyone reacts differently, but the first emotion is, of course, shock and disbelief. Celeste was still screaming. She went into one of the guest cottages to wake up Benji— he's the groom—and he tried to calm Celeste down but she was beyond helping. She was...well. Sergeant Dickson told the EMTs to take her to the ER." Roger shakes his head. "I feel for her. It's supposed to be the happiest day of her life and instead...her best friend..."

The Chief flashes back to the day he found out Tess and Greg were dead. He had gone right to the beach to find Andrea. Sometimes, in the dark of night, he can still hear the sound Andrea made when he told her that Tess was gone.

"There is nothing worse than the sudden, unexpected death of a young person," the Chief says.

"Amen," Roger says. "Anyway, while the family gathered inside, I made phone calls—the caterers, the church, the musicians, the Steamship Authority, the photographer, the chauffeur. I called everyone." Roger looks at his watch. "And I hate to say this, but I have two other weddings today."

The Chief nods. "We'll get you out of here. I just wanted to ask if you noticed anything odd or peculiar or suspicious or noteworthy about the bride or the groom or the family or any of the guests. Did anything or anyone strike you?"

"Just one thing," Roger says. "And it's probably nothing."

Probably nothing is usually something, the Chief thinks.

"What's that?" he asks.

"Celeste..." Roger says. "She had her purse and her overnight bag out on the beach. And she was fully dressed. She was wearing her going-away outfit, the one she was supposed to wear on Sunday."

"And you're wondering..."

"I'm wondering why she was wearing it this morning. I'm wondering why she had her purse and her overnight bag. I'm wondering why she was awake at quarter to six in the morning, dressed that way, on the beach."

"We'll ask her," the Chief says. "It does seem odd." He thinks about what Roger is telling him. "Maybe she and the groom had decided to elope at the last minute?"

"I thought that too, but her parents are here...her mother...something about that doesn't feel right to me. But she's such a good kid, Ed. I'm sure there's a logical explanation. It's probably nothing."

Initial questioning, Abigail Freeman Winbury, Saturday, July 7, 7:15 a.m.

Nick's choices with the women are sparse. The bride, Celeste, has gone to the hospital; the mother of the groom, Greer Garrison, is busy on the phone contacting guests to relay the tragic news; and the mother of the bride, who is quite sick, is still in bed. It's unclear if she has even learned what's happened.

This leaves Abigail Freeman Winbury—Abby— who is the bridesmaid and the wife of the groom's brother.

Abby is short with auburn hair cut bluntly at the shoulders. She has brown eyes and freckles. She is cute, Nick thinks, but not beautiful. When she walks into the formal living room where Nick is doing the questioning—it has glass doors that close, sealing it off from the hallway, the stairs, and the rest of the house—she is holding her breasts up with her hands. Nick blinks. It's okay; he has seen stranger things.

"Hi, Abby, I'm Nick Diamantopoulos, a detective with the Massachusetts State Police. Thank you for talking with me."

Abby lets go of her breasts to shake his hand. "Just so you know, I'm pregnant. Fifteen weeks along. I had an amnio a few days ago, and the baby's fine. It's a boy."

"Oh," Nick says. That, at least, explains why she was holding her breasts. Right? Nick doesn't have children, and he has never been married, but his sister, Helena, has three kids and what Nick remembers from Helena's pregnancies is that a certain amount of personal dignity goes out the window. Helena, who had always been rather private and discreet about her body and its functions, had complained about her aching (and then leaking) breasts as well as the frequency with which she had to pee. "Well, congratulations."

Abby gives Nick a tired but victorious smile. "Thank you," she says. "It'll be the first Winbury heir. That's important, I guess, to British people."

Nick says, "I have some water here, if you'd like any. I'm sure you must be pretty shaken up."

Abby takes a seat on the sofa and Nick sits in a chair opposite her so he can face her. "My stomach has been funny for weeks," she says. "And this news is so terrible. I can't believe it's real. This feels like a movie, you know? Or a dream. Merritt is dead. She's *dead*." She pours herself a glass of water but doesn't drink. "So do we know ... is the wedding *canceled?*"

Nick says, "Yes, I believe so." That's what he overheard Greer saying on the phone, he's pretty sure. That they're canceling the wedding.

"Okay," Abby says, but she sounds a little deflated. "I figured. I mean, Merritt is Celeste's best friend, her only friend, really, and she's dead." Abby shakes her head as if to clear it. "Obviously the wedding is canceled. I don't know why I even asked. You must think I'm some kind of monster."

"Not at all," Nick says. "I'm sure it's come as a shock."

"Shock," Abby says. "The wedding is a big deal— very expensive, you know, for Tag and Greer—and Celeste's mother isn't well and I just wasn't sure if ... if maybe they would just go through with it anyway. But of course not. Of *course* not. Please don't tell anyone I asked."

"I won't," Nick says.

"So ... what *happened?*" Abby asks. "You're a detective? Do you think someone *killed* Merritt? Like a *murder?*"

"By law, with unattended deaths, we have to rule out foul play," Nick says. "So I'm going to ask you some questions. Easy questions. Just answer as honestly as you can."

"Of course, of course. I just ... I can't believe this. I can't believe this is happening. I mean, intellectually my mind knows it's happening, but my heart is resisting. She's *dead*."

Nick says, "Tell me what you know about Merritt."

"I'm not really the best person to ask," Abby says. "I only just met her in May. We had a little bachelorette weekend here and it was the three of us—me, Celeste, and Merritt."

"That's all?" Nick says. "Nobody else?"

"Well, Tag and Greer were here. Greer kind of arranged it, just like she arranged the rest of the wedding. So my in-laws were here, but, like...no other *women*. It's kind of weird? Celeste doesn't have a lot of close female friends. When I got married, I had eleven bridesmaids. Some from St. Stephen's, some from UT. I was president of the Tri Delts, that was my sorority. I could have had thirty bridesmaids. But Celeste had only Merritt, who was a friend she met in New York. Merritt does PR for the zoo where Celeste works."

"Merritt worked in public relations," Nick says. "And Celeste, the bride, works at a *zoo,* you say?"

"Celeste is the assistant director of the Bronx Zoo," Abby says. "She knows a ton about animals, like genus and species and mating rituals and migration patterns."

"Impressive."

"And she's only twenty-eight, which I guess is unusual in that world. Merritt discovered her, in a sense. She chose Celeste as the face of the entire Wildlife Conservation Society. Celeste's picture is in the zoo brochure, and Merritt's big dream was to get Celeste's face on a billboard, but Celeste said no to that. Celeste is pretty conservative. They're a funny match, actually—Celeste and Merritt—like the Odd Couple. *Were* a funny match. Sorry." Abby mists up and waves a hand in front of her face. "I can't let myself get worked up about this because of the baby. I've had four miscarriages..."

"I'm sorry to hear that," Nick says.

"But *poor* Celeste. She must be *devastated*."

Nick leans forward to make eye contact with Abby. "The best way we can help Celeste now is to figure out what happened to her friend. When you say that Celeste and Merritt were like the Odd Couple, what do you mean?"

"Oh, just that they were opposites. Like, complete opposites."

"How so?"

"Well, start with their looks. Celeste is blond and fair, and Merritt had dark hair and olive skin. Celeste goes to bed early and Merritt likes to stay up late. Merritt has a second job—*had*, sorry—a second job as an influencer."

"Influencer?" Nick says.

"On social media?" Abby says. "She has something like eighty thousand Instagram followers who are all just like her—beautiful urban Millennials—and so Merritt gets perks for building brand awareness with her posts. She gets free clothes, free bags, free makeup; she eats at all of these hot new restaurants, goes to velvet-rope clubs, and works out at La Palestra for free, all because she features them on her Instagram account."

"Nice work if you can get it," Nick says.

"I know, right?" Abby says. "Merritt is...*was* a social media *goddess*. But Celeste doesn't even have a *Facebook* account. When I heard that, I couldn't believe it. I thought *everyone* had a Facebook account. I thought people were, like, given one at birth."

"I'm with Celeste," Nick says. He once dated a woman who tried to get him to set up a Facebook profile but the idea of reporting his whereabouts, his activities, and, worst of all, the company he was keeping didn't appeal to him. Nick is a confirmed bachelor; he plays the field. Facebook would be a liability. Speaking of which... "What about boyfriends? Did Merritt have a boyfriend that you know of?"

Abby gives him an uneasy look. One of the reasons Nick is so successful with women is that he has learned to listen not only to what they *are* saying but also to what they're *not* saying. It's a talent taught to him by his mother, his *ya-ya,* and his sister. Abby sustains eye contact long enough that he thinks she's trying to tell him something, but then she shakes her head. "I couldn't say for sure. You'd have to ask Celeste."

"Abby?" Nick says. "Do you know something you're not telling me?"

Abby takes a sip of water, then looks around the room as though she's never been there before. It's not a room that appears to get much use. The walls and trim are impeccably white, as are the half-moon sofa and modern egg-shaped chairs. There are three paintings on the wall, bright rainbow stripes—one diamond, one circle, one hexagon—and there are sculptures that look like Tinkertoys made out of steel and wooden spheres. There's a black grand piano; the top is covered with framed photographs. On a low glass table sits a coffee-table book about Nantucket, which seems redundant to Nick. If you want to see Nantucket, go outside. You're here.

"She came to the wedding alone," Abby says. "Which tells me that either she didn't want to be tied down or she had set her sights on someone who would already be at the wedding."

Ahhh, Nick thinks. Now they're getting somewhere. "Someone like who?"

"That's another way they're opposite!" Abby says. "Benji is Celeste's first real boyfriend. And Merritt…well, she's been with a bunch of people, I'm pretty sure."

"But no one seriously?" Nick asks. He senses Abby trying to change the subject. "If you ladies went out on the town for a bachelorette party, you must have shared some confidences, right?"

"And also?" Abby says. "Their parents. Celeste is super-close to her parents. Like, *abnormally* close. Well, that might be unfair to say because her mother has cancer. Let me restate: Celeste is very close to her parents, whereas Merritt hasn't talked to her parents in six or seven years, I think she said."

This does succeed in capturing Nick's attention because of the next-of-kin issue. "Do you know where her parents live?"

"No clue," Abby says. "She's from Long Island but not one of the fashionable parts, not the Hamptons or anything. She has a brother, I think she said. Again, you'd have to ask Celeste."

"Let's go back to your previous statement," Nick says. "Do you think maybe Merritt was involved with someone who was attending the wedding and that's why she didn't bring a date?"

"Can I please use the ladies' room?" Abby asks.

"Excuse me?" Nick says. He's pretty sure she's using the bathroom break to wiggle out of answering the question—but then he remembers Helena. "Oh, yes. Certainly."

Saturday, October 22, 2016

CELESTE

Blair Parrish, the head herpetologist at the Bronx Zoo's World of Reptiles, is a hypochondriac. She's "sick" more often than can reasonably be believed. She calls in sick on a *Saturday*—by far the zoo's busiest day—and Celeste assigns Donner from the Aquatic Bird House to cover Blair's ten o'clock snake talk. Donner complains about it (he's an expert on Magellanic penguins and *literally* nothing else), so Celeste assigns Karsang from the Himalayan Highlands to cover Blair's one o'clock snake talk and then she, Celeste, covers the three o'clock snake talk even though handling snakes is her least favorite task at the zoo. Celeste's specialty is primates, but as the assistant zoo director—the youngest in the entire country—it's her job to keep the peace, maintain routine, and lead by example as a team player.

Celeste is experienced enough to know that the three o'clock talk in any area of the zoo can be a mixed bag. Ten o'clock talks are routinely the best; the kids are still fresh, the parents or caregivers bright-eyed and optimistic. One o'clock talks are nearly always a catastrophe; that's the only way Celeste can describe it to Merritt via their work phones without using profanity. At one o'clock the kids are either impatient for lunch or they've just eaten and they are high on sugar and often have sticky hands and faces. Three o'clock talks can go either way. It's usually made up of older children, as younger kids have gone home for their naps by then, and, in general, the older kids are, the better their behavior. However, the three o'clock talk is often populated by people who simply couldn't get their acts together early enough in the day to make the ten o'clock or the one o'clock.

Celeste enters the World of Reptiles at ten minutes to three. She isn't crazy about the smell of the place; it has a musty, lizardy stink that she knows will cling to her hair and clothes, and more than likely, she'll offend people on the bus ride home. As the assistant zoo director, Celeste wears regular business clothes instead of a uniform, but for this talk, she buttons an army-green zoo issued shirt over her black turtleneck and houndstooth pencil skirt, and because she feels weird wearing her good work shoes (suede kitten heels from Nine West that Merritt helped her pick out) into the World of Reptiles, she switches them out for her running shoes, which she keeps in her work locker for the commute. She looks ridiculous, she realizes, but the kids are coming to see the snakes, not her.

There's already one couple waiting for the snake talk to begin. Genus: *European,* Celeste thinks. Species: *Swedish? Norwegian?* Their natural habitat includes fjords and midnight sun, steam saunas, and lingonberry bushes. They're both tall and hearty and have bushy, straw-colored hair. The man has a prodigious beard; the woman wears rimless spectacles. They both wear Birkenstocks over thick woolen socks. The woman pulls a piece of jerky out of a fanny pack and hands it to the man, and Celeste thinks about reprimanding them. There's no eating in the World of Reptiles, and outside food and drink are forbidden throughout the zoo—but it's the last talk of the day and Celeste doesn't want to be a Debbie Downer.

A few minutes before three o'clock a man and woman walk in with a little girl. She's about seven, Celeste guesses (she has become proficient at pegging children's ages, often down to the month). The little girl has Shirley Temple curls, the kind you want to pull straight just for the sheer joy of watching them bounce back. The couple are giving off static and Celeste gathers from the set of the woman's jaw and from the angry whispers that are flying over the little girl's head that they're arguing. As Celeste reaches into the first tank to retrieve Molly the milk snake, she eavesdrops. The woman wants the man to meet "Laney and Casper" for dinner at Root and Bone tonight, but the man reminds her that he has promised to have dinner at his parents' apartment because his parents are leaving for Barbados on Monday and will then be in London through the holidays so he can't cancel or postpone.

The woman—her hair very blond with tinges of silver but intentional silver, not aged silver, which makes her look like she belongs in a science-fiction movie— says, "You act like a minion around your parents. It's pathetic to watch."

The little girl turns her face up. "Who's a minion, Mommy?"

Science-fiction Mother snaps, "I wasn't addressing you, Miranda. I'm trying to conduct an adult conversation with Benji."

Benji catches Celeste's eye and smiles apologetically. "This nice woman is going to teach us about snakes, Miranda," he says.

Miranda's eyes widen. The mother huffs and Celeste smiles indulgently as if to convey that she knows how tedious trips to the zoo can be. The things parents do for their children! The fighting couple are expensively dressed, lots of suede and cashmere, a nice watch on the man, ballet flats on the woman, and she carries some kind of designer bag. (Merritt would be able to identify not only the designer but also the year; she feels about bags the way that most men feel about Corvettes.) Genus: *Manhattan,* Celeste thinks. Species: *Upper East Side.* Their natural habitat includes doormen and cabs, private school and Bergdorf's.

It's a typical sighting here at the Bronx Zoo.

Just as Celeste is about to begin—she reviewed Blair's notes over her lunch break—a group of boys in their late teens wander in; they carry the unmistakable scent of marijuana smoke. Celeste raises her eyebrows. "Are you guys here for the snake talk?" she asks. It seems like they might have been lighting up elsewhere in Pelham Park and stumbled into the World of Reptiles by mistake.

"Yeah," the one wearing a fluorescent-orange knit hat says. "You've got an anaconda in here, right?"

"We do, but I don't handle him," Celeste says. "He's way too big."

"I have a big anaconda too," the boy says. "But you can handle it anytime."

Celeste smiles patiently. No wonder Blair is so prone to migraines.

Benji turns on the kid and says, "Hey. Respect the lady, please."

My hero, Celeste thinks. She doesn't want the situation to escalate so she says, "Let's get started. I'm Celeste Otis, the assistant zoo director, but today I'm wearing my World of Reptiles hat. And this is Molly, one of our two milk snakes. Milk snakes aren't venomous or otherwise dangerous to humans; however, they do closely resemble coral snakes, which *are* deadly. This resemblance, known as Batesian mimicry, is one of the ways the milk snake protects itself in the wild."

She moves point by point through Blair's spiel. *All*

snakes are cold-blooded. Does anyone know what that means? She smiles at Miranda's mother, but Miranda's mother is in silent-treatment mode, eyes drilling holes into the concrete somewhere over Celeste's shoulder, arms locked across her chest. She keeps sneaking sideways glances at Benji, as if willing him to notice just how angry she is, realize just how unfair it is that he won't go to dinner with Laney and Casper because he committed to his parents. Benji's attention, meanwhile, is fixed on Celeste. He listens as if every word she says is wildly fascinating. *Snakes shed their skins once a year and when they do, their eyes grow cloudy. Snakes smell with their tongues. Snakes don't have ears.*

Benji leans down to Miranda. "Isn't that crazy? Snakes don't have ears."

Miranda giggles.

"Some people think snakes are slimy," Celeste says. "But actually, their skin is dry and cool. Would anyone like to touch Molly?" Celeste holds Molly out to Miranda's mother, who backs up a couple of steps.

"No, thank you," she says.

"Oh, come on, Jules," Benji says. "Be a sport."

"I don't want to touch the snake," Jules says.

"There's no reason to be afraid," Celeste says. "Snakes have gotten a bad rap since biblical times, but Molly is quite lovely."

"I'm not *afraid,*" Jules says. "How dare you suggest such a thing."

"Whoa," the stoner in the orange hat says.

Celeste thinks of apologizing but she doesn't indulge bratty behavior in children and she won't indulge it in their parents either. To prove a point, she holds the snake out to Miranda. "Let's show Mommy how brave you are," she says.

Miranda eagerly reaches out a hand to stroke Molly.

"Look at that," Celeste says. "I think she likes you."

Jules storms out of the World of Reptiles.

Celeste sighs. She has a long-running joke with her boss, Zed, about fund-raising to build a cocktail lounge next to the cafeteria for parents like Jules. It would make all of their jobs a lot easier.

The Swedes must think the talk is over because they follow Jules out.

"Can we see a boa now?" the stoner asks.

Celeste brings out Bernie the boa and she wraps up her talk with a stroll past the poisonous snakes— the puff adder, the rattler, the pit viper, and, a perennial favorite, Carmen the cobra. Celeste taps on the glass, and Carmen rises up like a plume of smoke and unfurls her hood— and everyone takes a step back.

"That concludes our snake talk," Celeste says. "Enjoy the rest of your Saturday."

The stoners tap on the glass of Carmen's tank, trying to get her to strike, while Celeste heads to the utility sink to wash her hands. She finds Benji and Miranda lingering before Molly's tank, and in an attempt to make amends for provoking Jules, Celeste joins them.

"Molly just shed her skin this week," she says. "That's it right there." She points to the gray tube of skin, as delicate as filigree, still mostly intact.

Benji smiles. "Thank you for all this information. I'm sorry Jules stormed out. She's upset about something else."

"No worries," Celeste says. "I'm just filling in for the usual snake expert. My job is mostly administrative these days. It's fun to be hands-on, although I hardly expect real-world problems to vanish when one walks into the World of Reptiles."

"Do you have a card?" Benji asks. "I have a friend who sets up excursions for businessmen traveling to New York from overseas. I want to suggest he bring people here to the zoo."

"Like a field trip for adults?"

"Mostly they like casinos and strip clubs," Benji says. "I think this would be something new and different. Something educational."

"I have cards," Celeste says. "But they're in my office. You can call the zoo's main number and ask for me. My name is Celeste Otis. Or, if you'd like, you can put my direct line into your phone right now?"

"I'd love that," Benji says. He pulls out his phone. "Go ahead, I'm ready."

Saturday, July 7, 2018,
7:00 a.m.

Initial questioning, Abigail Freeman Winbury, Saturday, July 7 (continued)

While Abby is in the bathroom, Nick listens for voices from the rest of the house. He hears nothing and sees no one out the glass doors. This room is perfect for questioning; it's almost hermetically sealed off from the rest of the house. Sitting here with the sun streaming in and the hydrangeas visible out the window, you wouldn't know anything was wrong.

Abby comes back in, arms crossed over her chest in what Nick perceives as a defensive attitude. She knows or suspects something about Merritt's romantic life; Nick just needs to get her to spill the beans.

"Where were we?" he asks.

"I'm not sure?" Abby says.

"Why don't you tell me about last night," Nick says.

"Well, the first thing that happened," Abby says, "was that the rehearsal was canceled."

"Canceled?"

"I guess Reverend Derby—that's the Winburys' minister from New York—called to say his flight had been delayed and he wouldn't get to Nantucket until very late. I figured we would go to the church anyway and run through the ceremony with Roger, the wedding planner. But Celeste and Benji decided to cancel it altogether. It was almost as if..."

"As if what?" Nick says.

"As if they knew...they wouldn't be getting married," Abby says.

"What do you mean by that?"

Abby takes a sip of her water and trains her gaze on the front of the Nantucket coffee-table book. The cover is a photograph of the Rainbow Fleet rounding Brant Point Lighthouse during the Opera House Cup. "Nothing," she says.

"Was there any indication that this wedding might not happen?"

"No," Abby says.

"So, no rehearsal, then," Nick says. "But there was still a rehearsal dinner, right?"

"It was a beach picnic here," Abby says. "A clambake. There were raw clams and oysters, which I didn't eat because I'm pregnant and raw shellfish can carry listeria. It's in lunch meat also." Abby takes another sip of water and Nick struggles against his instinct to categorize Abby as painfully self-absorbed and utterly useless to this investigation. "There was chowder, boiled lobster, sausages, potatoes, corn bread. Different kinds of pie for dessert. Oh, and there were cheddar biscuits. I ate about twelve."

"Sounds delicious," Nick says with a tight smile. "The clambake was catered?"

"Catered, yes. By the same people who were supposed to do the wedding reception tonight. Island Fare."

"Was there alcohol served?"

Abby laughs. "This is the Winbury house. These people brush their teeth with vintage Dom Pérignon."

"Were people drinking heavily?"

"The picnic had a signature cocktail," Abby says. "It was a blackberry mojito with big fat ripe blackberries and fresh mint from Bartlett's Farm and lots of rum.

People were talking about how delicious they were. They were a gorgeous purple color and it was so hot last night that I'm sure they were hard to resist. And let's see . . . Greer was drinking champagne; she always drinks champagne at parties. But everyone else was into those mojitos. Oh, and there was a keg of Cisco beer too, so after a while the guys were drinking that."

"Did you notice Merritt drinking?" Nick asks.

"Not specifically," Abby says. "But I'm sure she was. She acts like one of the guys. *Acted;* sorry. She listened to the same music as the guys—by which I mean Tay-K, not Taylor Swift—and she doused her food with hot sauce. She knew every player on the Yankees roster. It was her thing—she wanted to act like a guy but look like a woman." Abby pauses. "I found it a little hard to take, honestly."

"These are exactly the kind of details I'm after," he says, and Abby smiles at the praise. "Tell me what happened during the picnic."

"After we ate, people gave toasts. Celeste's father went first. Mr. Otis's toast was all about Celeste's mom, which seemed strange, but he brought it back around to Celeste and Benji eventually. And then after that, Thomas gave a toast. Thomas, my husband, the groom's brother."

"And he's the best man?"

Abby huffs. "He's *not* the best man. Benji asked Shooter instead. Shooter Uxley."

"Shooter. That's right, that's right. Tell me about Shooter."

"How long do you have?" Abby asks.

"All day," Nick says.

"You know how some people are so charming and magnetic that they can get away with anything?"

"My cousin Phil," Nick says. "Six-foot-two Adonis. My *ya-ya*'s favorite. Everyone's favorite."

"Exactly," Abby says. "Shooter is this wedding's version of your cousin Phil."

Nick smiles. He likes Abby a little better. "So...after your husband, Thomas, did anyone else make a toast?"

"No. I thought maybe Tag would speak but he didn't, for some reason. And Merritt...you know, I don't remember seeing either Merritt or Tag during the toasts."

Nick makes a note: *MM not present at toasts.*

"Maybe she was in the restroom?" Nick says. "Did she reappear?"

Abby bites the corner of her lip. "Yes, yes," she says. "I saw her later. Thomas went over to bum a cigarette from her."

"Merritt smoked?" Nick says.

Abby shrugs. "When she drank, I guess. Like everyone else. Except for me now."

"What time did the party end?" Nick asks.

"The band stopped playing at ten. That's a law, which you probably know because you're in law enforcement." She winks at him and Nick starts to feel optimistic. They're building a rapport here and any second Abby is going to give him what he's looking for. *Come on, Abby!* "I was exhausted, but Thomas said he wanted to go to town with Benji and his friends. So then we had a fight."

"A fight?"

"He told me early in our marriage that the way to keep him happy was to give him freedom. He goes out with his friends, he takes guy trips, and the rest of the time, he's at work."

Sounds like a real prince, Nick thinks.

"And I told him now that I'm pregnant, he has to change his ways." Abby shrugs. "If he thinks I'm raising this baby alone, he has another think coming."

Nick feels like he's suddenly been thrust into the role of marriage counselor. "Did Thomas end up going out?"

"Yes," Abby says. "But I wasn't happy about it."

"So who went out and who stayed home?" Nick asks.

"I stayed home. Mrs. Otis, Celeste's mother, stayed home. And Greer stayed home. Tag and Mr. Otis had a drink in Tag's study, which is a big deal."

"Oh, yeah?" Nick says. "Why?"

Abby blows her bangs out of her eyes. "No one is allowed to set foot in Tag's study without an invitation. I've never been invited so I'm not sure what's so *magical* about it. I know he keeps really good scotch in there. Anyway, when he invited Mr. Otis for a drink in his study, it meant Tag was... accepting him as a part of the family, I guess. And I will point out, not that I care, but Tag never invited *my* father into the study for a drink."

"Did Merritt go into town?" Nick asks.

"I assume she led the charge," Abby says. "No, *wait!*" Abby's voice rises so dramatically that Nick nearly leaps from the chair. "Wait, wait, *wait!* I *saw* Celeste and Merritt out in the rose garden after the party broke up! Our bedroom window looks right over the garden and I saw them when I went to pull the shade. Merritt was *crying*. Celeste had her hands on Merritt's shoulders. They were talking. Then they hugged and Celeste walked toward the driveway and Merritt stayed in the garden." Abby looks at Nick in astonishment. "I totally forgot about that until just this instant. If I had remembered, I would have started out by telling you that."

Merritt and the bride in the rose garden. Merritt crying.

"In the scene you're describing, did it look like Merritt was upset and Celeste was comforting her, or did it look like they were arguing?" Nick asks.

"The first," Abby says. "I'm pretty sure Celeste went out with Benji, Thomas, and the others. But I couldn't say for sure about Merritt. I pulled the shade and went to bed."

Really? Nick thinks. Abby didn't seem to miss much, and wouldn't a former University of Texas sorority girl be naturally drawn to drama of this kind? She just described Merritt as "one of the guys," so wouldn't seeing Merritt *crying* make Abby very, very curious? "You didn't peek again?" Nick asks. "To see what happened? To see if Merritt was okay?"

Abby looks him dead in the eye. "I was bone-tired. I went to bed."

This is her reminding him, once again, that she's pregnant. He nods. "From the looks of things under the tent, there was some late-night partying. Is it possible that the people who went out came home and drank some rum?"

"Possible," Abby says.

"Do you have any idea who that might have been?" Nick asks.

Abby's face shuts down. It's as abrupt as a slamming door. "Nope."

She's lying, Nick thinks. This must have been when things got interesting.

"Was Merritt part of the group who had the night-cap?" he asks.

"I honestly have no idea," Abby says. She couldn't be less convincing.

Nick takes a sustaining breath. "When Thomas got back to your room, did you happen to notice what time it was? This is very, very important. Please think."

"It was late."

"Late like midnight?" Nick says. "Or late like four a.m.?"

"I didn't look at the clock. I didn't know..." Here, Abby tears up. "I didn't know this would *happen!*"

"Please don't get upset," Nick says. "Let me find you some tissues."

"I'm fine," Abby says. And then, almost to herself, she says, "I can't believe this is real. It's real. Merritt is *dead*."

"Abby, I have to ask: Did you hear anything else in the middle of the night? Did you hear anyone in the water? There was a two-person kayak down by the beach—"

Abby's head snaps up. "A kayak? That would be Tag's."

"You're sure?"

"Yes," Abby says. "Tag has two kayaks and he treats them like they're his babies. They're handmade by some guy in Alaska or wherever kayaks were invented. Tag has a one-person kayak and a two-person kayak and when he invites someone out on the two-person kayak, it's a really big deal, like an even bigger deal than when he invites you into his study to drink his thousand-year-old scotch."

"Since the kayak was out, would you guess Mr. Winbury was the one who used it?"

"Absolutely, yes," Abby says.

"No chance someone might have borrowed it without asking?"

"No chance," Abby says. "Tag keeps the kayaks locked up. I know this because...well, because Thomas and I have tried to use the two-person kayak without permission. We tried to guess the combination—we ran through every birthday, every anniversary, and we could not unlock those kayaks. Frankly, I can't believe a kayak was left out on the beach. That's a sure indication that something went very wrong last night. Tag isn't careless like that."

"Abby, would you say Mr. Winbury is a person with a lot of secrets?"

"*Everyone* in the Winbury family has secrets!" Abby says.

Nick holds his breath. He's afraid to move. *Come on, Abby,* he thinks. *Give me a little bit more.*

"I'm sure Tag has secrets," she says. "But I really like Tag and I admire and respect him and I want that feeling to be mutual. I'm pretty sure both he and Greer think I'm a failure because I haven't managed to give them a grandchild...but they don't know what I'm dealing with. Thomas is...and the pressure..." Abby stops, sniffs. "I'm sorry I'm crying. This can't be good for my baby. May I please be excused?"

Nick sighs. He was so close. But he can't push her, not in her present condition. He'll have to get his answers elsewhere. "Yes, of course. Thank you, Abby." He smiles at her as he lies and says, "You've been very helpful."

Friday, May 18–Saturday, May 19, 2018

TAG

He catches a brief glimpse of the friend on Friday evening when she and Celeste and Abby arrive from the city for the bachelorette weekend that Greer has arranged. Tag sees the friend from the back—long dark hair and a sweet little behind put on display in a tight sequined miniskirt. When she turns, he's treated to her profile. Pretty. Then she pivots at the hip, notices Tag checking her out, waggles her fingers at him, and offers a half smile.

"What's the friend's name?" Tag asks his wife later.

"Merritt Monaco," Greer says. "She's a brunette. Not your type."

Tag gathers his wife up in his arms, and as usual, she places both palms on his chest as if to push him away, but he holds her tight. Tag maintains—untruthfully—that he has no interest in brunettes. "You're my type," he says.

"Yeah, right," she says in an American accent, which she knows he can't resist. He kisses her neck. He'll introduce himself to the friend later.

The introduction comes the next morning. Tag is in the kitchen reading the weekend *Journal* and enjoying coffee and grapefruit and a poached egg on whole-grain toast after having gone for a five-mile run and then taken a soak in the hot tub. He feels clean and virtuous, nearly relaxed. His wife and future daughter-in-law left a short while ago to meet with the wedding caterers. He has forgotten all about the friend until she comes wandering into the kitchen. She's barefoot, wearing a tiny pair of cotton sleep shorts and a threadbare T-shirt. No bra. Tag can see the two pellets of her nipples through the material.

"Good morning," he says brightly.

She jumps, startled. Or maybe she's just pretending. She's too pretty to be an innocent. Her hand flies to her chest as she turns to him. Her hair is mussed.

"Good morning," she says, her voice froggy with sleep. Or maybe it's naturally gravelly. She collects herself and offers a hand. "You must be Mr. Winbury. How are you? I'm Merritt, as in the parkway."

"Call me Tag, please," he says. "As in hash."

This earns him a smile. Oh, the Millennials!

"Thank you for hosting us this weekend," she says. "It's a surprise luxury. Your house is sublime."

"I'm glad you're enjoying it," Tag says. "What did you girls get up to last night?"

"Dinner at Cru," she says. "Great oysters there."

"Agreed," Tag says.

"Then we went to the Afterhouse for caviar," Merritt says.

"Well, well," Tag says. Oysters and caviar. He assumes he was footing the bill.

"Then we went to Proprietors. Then to the Boarding House. Then to the Chicken Box. Then to Steamboat for pizza, since we were all starving. Then we caught an Uber home. Around two, I think? Early night."

Tag laughs. In New York, she's probably out every night until four. If she's anywhere close to Celeste's age, then she's still in her twenties.

"Is there coffee?" she asks.

Tag rises. He's wearing a waffle-knit cotton robe he snagged from the pool house to put on over his wet bathing suit, but now he wishes for regular clothes. The robe feels too feminine; it feels like a dress. "I'll get it for you," he says. "Please, sit and relax. How do you take it?"

"Black," she says.

Girl after his own heart. Tag pours her a cup of coffee. She takes the seat next to his chair and folds her legs up under herself. Cozy. If Greer saw this, she would not be amused, even considering Merritt is a brunette and therefore theoretically not Tag's type. But imagining Greer's reaction turns Tag on. He is most certainly going to hell.

He sits down and considers his half-eaten breakfast. "Can I fix you something to eat?" He is startled by his own offer of hospitality. If this were anyone but a desirable woman, he would go back to his newspaper.

She holds up a hand. "No, thank you."

"So, are there any stories you can share from last night?" he asks.

Merritt tilts her head and gives him a wry smile. "We were perfect angels," she says. "It was rather disappointing."

He laughs.

"Abby threw up on the way home," Merritt says. "Our Uber driver had to pull over on Orange Street."

"She overdid it?" Tag says. "Good for her."

"If you ask me, she's pregnant," Merritt says. "I got that vibe."

"Well," Tag says. "That would be good news." And it would. Thomas and Abby have been trying for a baby ever since they got married four years earlier. Conception isn't a problem. Abby has been pregnant four times that Tag knows of, but each time ended in a miscarriage and one of them necessitated a D and C at Lenox Hill

Hospital. However, Tag feels more disloyal discussing Abby's potential pregnancy than he does looking at Merritt's breasts. He changes the subject.

"So what do you do for work, Merritt-as-in-the-Parkway?" he asks.

She takes a deliberate sip of her coffee. "Officially, I handle PR for the Wildlife Conservation Society, which manages all four city zoos and the aquarium. That's how I met Celeste. The Bronx Zoo has the biggest chunk of our budget so I do all of their press releases and whatnot. And Celeste, you know, is a rising star at the zoo. It's not every day you see a woman as young as Celeste named assistant zoo director."

"Right," Tag says. He's very fond of Celeste and thinks her career is magnificent. Greer has been less enthusiastic. *Why does she have to run a zoo?* she said. *Why not a museum or a charitable foundation? Something ladylike?* However, Greer far prefers Celeste to Benji's former girlfriend, Jules. Jules Briar lived on Park Avenue, which was good, but the apartment and the money and the daughter, Miranda, were all from the first husband, Andy Briar, a director at Goldman Sachs, which was bad. Greer wanted Benji to find someone without quite that much baggage—and Celeste offers a clean slate. It's almost as though she spent her first twenty-six years in a convent. Benji is the only serious boyfriend she's ever had.

"And unofficially," Merritt says with a bit of a tease in her voice, snapping Tag back to the present conversation— *Unofficially,* he thinks, *she's a stripper. Or a high-end escort*—"I'm an influencer."

"An influencer?" he says.

"I do work on the side to promote certain brands and events," Merritt says. "So some of my clothes and shoes and bags are by designers I can't afford, but I get them for free as long as I post about them on my social media platforms. I stump for nineteen companies."

"That's impressive," Tag says. He can see how she would succeed as an influencer: She's young, beautiful, cool, sexy. And edgy. She's an interesting match for Celeste, who doesn't have an edgy thing about her.

"What do *you* do for work?" Merritt asks.

Tag laughs; he likes her directness. "I own a hedge fund," he says.

"Note the look of surprise on my face," Merritt says.

"It's terribly boring, I know," he says. "I started my career at Barclays in London but when the boys finished with primary school, we decided it would be best to move to New York." He does *not* mention that the majority of their wealth comes from Greer's family. The Garrisons owned the mills that produced over half the gin in Great Britain. And Greer's book royalties are nothing to sniff at either, although sales are steadily declining and Tag has been tempted to suggest she retire before she becomes a parody of herself. Her fan base is nearly down to no one but the devoted cat ladies.

It's as Tag is thinking about the typical cat lady— tucked away in her Cotswold cottage fixing a cup of tea and preparing to spend a rainy afternoon in an armchair with a tabby spread across her lap as she cracks open the latest exotically located Greer Garrison mystery—that he feels something touch his leg. It's Merritt's foot. She is running her toes up his shin as she sips her coffee and pretends to be gazing out the window at Nantucket Sound. Tag immediately gets an erection. He thinks about lifting up her flimsy T-shirt or, better still, tearing the damn thing in half so he can lick the hard points of her nipples until she groans in his ear. Where can he take her? Maybe if he opens his robe and shows her what she's done to him, she'll get down on her knees in front of him. Right here in the kitchen. Could they be that brazen?

As he starts to reach for the belt of his robe, Abby comes limping into the kitchen, one hand on her stomach and one on the back of her neck as though she's trying to hold herself together. When she sees Tag and Merritt, a startled look crosses her face, then something darker flickers through her expression. *What must this look like?* Tag wonders.

Abby has been raised right. She smiles. "Good morning," she says. "Sorry I slept so late. I am *not* feeling well at all."

"Coffee?" Tag asks.

Merritt stands up. "I'm going to try the outdoor shower," she says.

When Greer and Celeste return, the girls all head out to the pool in their bikinis. Tag would like to join them but he can't possibly do so without seeming like a perverted and pathetic old man. He decides instead to go out in the kayak. He waves as he strolls past the pool, taking one long, appreciative look at Merritt, who is wearing a black bikini with a complicated web of straps across the back. The bikini is possibly meant to reference bondage and inspire any man who looks upon the suit to wish for a pair of sharp scissors to snip the straps and get to the luscious body underneath. However, the suit, with its web, also reminds Tag of a spider. A black widow, he thinks. Merritt is dangerous. He needs to stay away.

Tag paddles out to the Monomoy Creeks, a series of waterways that meander through reeds and eelgrass, around floating islands and sandbars. It's peaceful here. The only sound is the plashing of his paddle against the surface of the water. Up above, an osprey soars, and in the distance, Tag spies sailboats, an approaching ferry, and Commercial Wharf. The sun is unseasonably warm for May. He is tempted to take his shirt off so he can get something vaguely resembling a suntan. He must be bewitched, he thinks, because he hasn't given two thoughts to a suntan since he lifeguarded at Blackpool Sands in the summer of 1981. He's fifty-seven years old, likely more than twice the girl's age. He tries to banish her from his mind and instead focus on everything he already has—a satisfying, if stodgy, career; a beautiful, accomplished wife; and two healthy sons, both of whom are finally starting to get the hang of adulthood. Tag has a five-bedroom prewar apartment on Park Avenue, a flat in London, and this spread on Nantucket. He and Greer first visited Nantucket in the summer of 1997, and with the trust that Greer inherited on her thirty-fifth birthday, they bought the land. It had been quite expensive even then, this remote island of fishermen and free spirits, but Greer had loved it and Tag had loved making Greer happy.

He has grown quite fond of this island, even though his life here now is more fraught. There's always something *happening*—a festival, a benefit, houseguests, a cocktail party, a new restaurant Greer insists they have to try, and, in a few weeks, a wedding for which they will host 170 people. But Tag's favorite way to experience the island is like this, right now—on the water, in his kayak. Nantucket's charm is most easily found offshore. Tag paddles all the way to the Great Harbor Yacht Club, then he turns around and heads for home. He wills himself to be strong enough for what awaits him there.

He has never quite mastered the art of getting out of the kayak and nearly always dunks himself in the process. This gives Greer much joy and himself a much-needed cooling-off so he is half guilty of facilitating the mishap. After he pulls the kayak up on the shore, he towels himself dry and checks his phone. There's a voice mail from his friend Sergio Ramone.

Tag finds Greer arranging flowers on the sunporch.

"Sergio called," he says. "He has two tickets to the Dujac Grand Cru wine-festival dinner tonight. The chef from Nautilus is doing the food and it's at some swanky house out on Quaise Pasture Road. I told him we'd take them. They're ridiculously expensive, but we deserve it."

"I can't go," Greer says.

"What?" Tag says. "Why not? You love Dujac. It's blue-chip terroir. Not Sonoma, not South Africa. These wines will be once-in-a-lifetime. You know how these French vintners are. If you show the proper appreciation, they can't help themselves—they open up the bottles they aren't supposed to, the really, really good stuff, the rare vintages that we'll never have the opportunity to taste again."

"I have to stay home and write tonight," Greer says. "My deadline is in thirty days and I'm dreadfully behind because of the wedding. Also, I had an idea while Celeste and I were out and I want to get it down before I forget."

"The dinner isn't until seven," he says. "Go write now and you'll be finished by six, in time for a shower and a dressing drink."

"I can't now," Greer says. "I'm busy."

"I'll arrange the flowers," Tag says. "You go write."

"You know it doesn't work like that, darling," she says.

He wants to strangle her. He should never have expected his wife to suddenly display a penchant for spontaneity. He knows it doesn't work like that; he knows Greer can't be prodded to write, that she has to listen to her internal muse, and the muse prefers the nighttime hours, a quiet, dark house, a glass of wine (ordinary wine, a fifteen-dollar bottle of chardonnay, for example, which will have nothing in common with the wine that will be served with this dinner).

"What the hell am I going to do?" Tag says. "I promised Sergio I'd take the tickets off his hands." If it were anyone else, Tag would call and renege, but Sergio is an esteemed criminal-defense attorney and he's also the friend who got Thomas into law school at NYU when there was no prayer of Thomas getting in on his own. And then Sergio angled to get Thomas a job at Skadden, Arps, the law firm where Thomas now works. Thomas, Tag has to admit, isn't the achiever the rest of them are; Tag suspects he'll quit law before he makes partner. But even so, Tag and Greer owe Sergio Ramone a lifelong debt of gratitude. Tag can't back out on these tickets. He can pay the $3,500 apiece and just not go, he supposes, but what a waste that would be. "Please, darling."

Greer stabs a peony into the vase. The peony is deep pink and resembles a human heart unfurling in desperation. Or possibly he's projecting. "Take one of the girls," she says.

Tag scoffs.

"I'm serious," Greer says. "Don't be a martyr for me. I won't like that one bit. Ask one of the girls."

"But isn't this supposed to be a bachelorette weekend?" Tag says.

"They partied last night," Greer says. "Unless I'm mistaken, they're planning on staying home tonight. But I'm sure you can talk one of them into it."

The girls, as Greer calls them, are in the casual dining area, reading magazines, snacking on chips and salsa. Merritt-as-in-the-Parkway, Tag is relieved to see, has covered herself properly, in white jeans and a navy cashmere sweater. Abby is resting her head on her arms on the table.

"Hello, ladies," Tag says. His stomach feels leaden; it's nerves. He knows how this is going to end. Greer too must know how this is going to end. She is the one he will hold responsible. She has suspected him of cheating for the entirety of their marriage, he knows, and now it feels like she is pushing him toward it. "I have an extra ticket to a very fancy wine dinner tonight and my wife feels she needs to stay home and write. Would any of you three like to go with me?"

"God, no." Abby groans.

"No, thank you," Celeste says sweetly. "I'm exhausted."

Merritt raises her face and looks him dead in the eye. His heart skips a beat.

Tag wears a jacket but no tie. Merritt wears a lavender dress with thin straps that crisscross her back and a pair of silver stiletto heels. It's the heels Greer chooses to comment on.

"You'll break your neck in those," she says.

"I'll be fine," Merritt says. "Years of practice."

"Well," Greer says in Tag's ear as she kisses him goodbye, "I believe Quaise Pasture is in for quite a shock."

Once they're in the Land Rover headed out the Polpis Road, Tag worries that Merritt will reach over and put her hand on his leg. Then he worries she won't. He has an erection simply from smelling her perfume and listening to her rummage through her clutch purse in the dark. He can't go inside in this state; he needs to talk himself down. He takes a deep breath. He worries there will be someone he knows at this dinner—and how will he explain who Merritt is? *My future daughter-in-law's best friend.* It sounds sleazy. It *is* sleazy. What will people think? They'll think...well, they'll think the obvious.

But then Tag calls upon one of his favorite sayings: *Perception is reality.* This situation can be translated in more than one way. Tonight, Tag will perceive this outing as innocent and fun and that is what it will become. He relaxes a little.

"Is this your first time on Nantucket?" he asks.

"Not at all," she says. "I've come with friends over the years, in college and then as a so-called adult."

"Where was college?" he asks.

"Trinity," she says. "In glamorous Hartford."

He has friends whose children went to Trinity but he doesn't dare ask if Merritt knows any of them; he's already self-conscious enough about how young she is. Or how old he is.

"Do you have siblings?" Tag asks.

"A brother," she says. "Married with kids and a mortgage."

"And where did you grow up?" Tag asks.

"On Long Island," she says. "Commack."

Tag nods. He and Greer have successfully avoided Long Island, though he does have a client with a house in Oyster Bay whom he visits on occasion and there was one long-ago rainy weekend in Montauk when the boys were small. He has never heard of Commack. "I always wanted a daughter," he says. "But Greer didn't. She's happy with the boys."

"Greer is lovely," Merritt says.

"Isn't she?" he says. "Anyway, now we have a daughter-in-law. Abby. And soon, Celeste."

"Celeste is a treasure," Merritt says. "I met her at a difficult time in my life. She saved me."

This statement seems to warrant a follow-up question, but it's too late. They've arrived. The house is, in fact, grand—it's all lit up from within, overlooking the sound but from a more dramatic vantage point than Tag's house. There are two unfamiliar cars in the driveway.

Tag parks, then smiles at Merritt. This is going to be innocent and fun. "Shall we?" he says.

The evening unfolds easily. There are ten diners, plus the French gentleman from the esteemed Dujac vineyard plus one of the sous-chefs from Nautilus plus two kitchen staff and two waitstaff. Tag doesn't know a soul. The other eight diners are all one group. They tell Tag it's their first time to Nantucket. They live in Texas.

"Where in Texas?" Merritt asks.

Tag steels himself to hear that they're from Austin and then to find out that they are best friends or business partners of Abby's parents, the Freemans.

"San Antonio," they say. "Remember the Alamo."

It quickly becomes obvious that Merritt knows nothing about wine, not even the basics. She doesn't know that cabernet sauvignons are from Bordeaux and that pinot noirs and chardonnays are from Burgundy. She doesn't know what terroir is. She has never heard of pinot franc; she has never heard of the Loire Valley. How can she be an influencer of culture when she doesn't have even a basic vocabulary of wine? What does she drink when she goes out?

"Cocktails," she says. "Gin, bourbon, vodka, tequila. Skinny margaritas are my go-to." She must see him grimace because she adds, "There used to be a place downtown, Pearl and Ash, that made a cocktail called Teenage Jesus, which was my particular favorite. Plus, the name."

Tag can't imagine drinking something called a Teenage Jesus. "What about when you have oysters? When you have caviar? Surely you must drink champagne."

"Prosecco," she says. "But only if someone presses it on me. It gives me a headache."

After his starter glass, a 2013 Chambolle-Musigny, goes down, he decides that Merritt's ignorance is fortuitous. She isn't the jaded, worldly woman he thought she was. He had convinced himself over the past few hours that she was at least thirty but now he fears she's closer to twenty-five. More than thirty years younger than he is.

After his second glass, a 2009 Morey Saint-Denis, he is loose. He will teach Merritt about wine. He will teach her how to roll the wine over her tongue. He will teach her how to identify black-cherry and tobacco notes in pinots, and lemon, mint, and clover in sauvignon blancs. He's excited by this mission, although her palate will be exposed to some of the finest wines in the world tonight, and this worries him. When you start with the best, the future offers only disappointment.

They stumble out of the house well past midnight, hand in hand. At one extremely saturated point during the evening, one of the Texas ladies turned to Merritt and said, "So how long have y'all been married?"

Without hesitation, Merritt said, "We're newlyweds."

"Congratulations!" the woman said. "Second marriage?"

Merritt winked. "How'd you guess?"

So when they leave, they are a couple, married by the incredible wine, the extraordinary food, the camaraderie of complete strangers. It's as if they have stepped out of their lives into another life where everything is new and anything is possible. When Tag opens the passenger door for Merritt, she turns to him and raises her face.

He kisses her once, chastely, on the lips.

"That's all I get?" she says.

Say yes, Tag thinks. *Be strong. Be true to Greer and the boys. Show some integrity, for God's sake.*

But.

Even that faintest touch of her lips sent a surge of electricity through him. Tag is pulsing with desire for her. He won't be able to stop himself from driving Merritt to the beach and making love to her, maybe more than once.

He is, ultimately, only a man.

Saturday, July 7, 2018, 8:30 a.m.

THE CHIEF

After interviewing Roger, the Chief has some choices for who to talk to next. There's the bride's father, who is in an upstairs bedroom with the bride's mother; Greer Garrison has requested that they not be disturbed until the last possible minute because of the mother's health. And the groom, Benjamin Winbury, asked permission to go to the hospital to check on Celeste. He promised to be back in an hour. So, as far as persons of interest go, that leaves the Chief with the groom's brother, Thomas; the groom's father, Thomas Senior, known as Tag; and this Shooter fellow, the best man. The Chief thinks the third option is the most promising.

Dickson said the best man was missing when he arrived on the scene, but then the guy turned up in a cab an hour later. He could have met a woman—or a man—last night and slept elsewhere. But the perplexing thing is that he had his luggage with him. It's almost as if he'd planned to leave and then changed his mind. There might be a plausible explanation for this, but the Chief can't come up with it himself. He will question Shooter.

The Chief finds Shooter standing behind the police tape at the edge of the beach, staring in the direction of the water. He has shed the blazer, removed his shoes, untucked his shirt.

"Hey there," the Chief says. Shooter turns. His expression

is one of fear, maybe, or alarm. The Chief is used to it. In thirty years, no one has been exactly *happy* to see him while he was on duty in the field. "Are you free to answer a few questions?"

"What about?" Shooter says.

"We're interviewing everyone who's part of the wedding. I understand you're the best man?"

"If you're going to ask me what happened to her, I really have no idea," Shooter says.

"I'd just like to get some background," the Chief says. "About the events of last night. Easy stuff."

Shooter nods. "I can handle that, I suppose."

"Great," the Chief says. He leads Shooter across the driveway to the white wrought-iron bench under the rose arbor where he talked to Roger. He sees police tape all around the cottage on the north side of the property, which was where the maid of honor was staying by herself. The Chief is fairly certain that if they can find the girl's phone, they'll have the answers they're looking for. The Chief has learned over the past decade that if you want to know the truth about a person, just look through his or her phone.

Shooter takes a seat and the Chief pulls his notebook out. He has only one question for Shooter. "So...where were you last night?"

"Last night?" Shooter says.

Just like that, the Chief knows a lie is coming. "Yes, last night," the Chief says. "The groom told my sergeant that you were missing. Until you pulled up in the cab, we thought maybe you were dead as well. But, thankfully, we were mistaken. Where were you?"

"I'm sorry I caused you to worry," Shooter says. "I was up at the Wauwinet."

"The Wauwinet Inn?" the Chief says.

"The restaurant, actually. Topper's? I'm friendly with the bartender there."

"And what's the bartender's name?"

"Name?" Shooter says. "Oh. Gina."

"The bartender at Topper's is named Gina. And you spent last night with Gina?"

"Yes," Shooter says.

"She lives up there?" the Chief asks. "At the Wauwinet?"

"Yes," Shooter says. "Staff housing."

"Had you *planned* to spend the night with Gina?" the Chief asks. "Because the groom seemed to think you'd spent the night in the cottage."

"I hadn't planned on it, no," Shooter says. "It was just a booty call. It was late, she texted, I went up there."

A booty call. The Chief thinks protectively of Chloe. He feels a hundred years old. "What time was that?"

"I'm really not sure," Shooter says.

"You can check your phone," the Chief says.

Shooter slips his phone out of the pocket of his Nantucket Reds shorts. He pushes some buttons and says, "I must have deleted the text."

"You must have deleted the text," the Chief says. "Tell me why you took your luggage. *All* of your luggage, from the looks of it."

"Right," Shooter says. His tone is cautious, and the Chief can practically see the shadowy interior of his mind where he's groping around for something solid to hold on to. "I took my luggage because I thought I might just stay up at the Wauwinet with Gina."

"But then this morning, quite early, I'd say, you showed back up here. So what happened?"

"I changed my mind," Shooter says.

"You changed your mind," the Chief says. He looks at Shooter Uxley. The kid is sweating, but then again, it's hot, even in the shade. "Would you mind giving me this Gina's cell phone number, please?"

"Her number?" Shooter says. "I'd rather not. I don't want her to get involved in this if we can help it."

"We can't help it," the Chief says. "Because Gina is your alibi."

"My *alibi?*" Shooter says. "Why do I need an *alibi?*"

"We have an unattended death," the Chief says. "And you were missing, then you showed back up. Now, maybe your story holds water. Maybe you did go up to the Wauwinet to hook up with Gina the bartender with all your luggage and maybe you did then decide you didn't like Gina that much or that the staff housing wasn't as nice as the Winburys' guest cottage. That's all feasible. But we have a twenty-nine-year-old woman dead, so I'm going to proceed with due diligence and check out your story. You can either give me the girl's cell phone—which I know you have because you said she texted you late last night—or I'll call the front desk of the Wauwinet and contact her that way."

Shooter gets to his feet. "Call the Wauwinet," he says. "I need to use the bathroom right now. My stomach is funny. I think it was the raw bar from last night."

"Go ahead," the Chief says. He's not stupid. He knows that Shooter will go into the cottage to "use the bathroom," but really he'll text Gina the bartender and ask her to corroborate his story.

The Chief waits until Shooter disappears into the cottage, then he takes out his phone and calls Bob from Old Salt Taxi. Bob, who dropped Shooter off here this morning, has been a friend of the Chief's for twenty-five years.

"Hey, Bob," the Chief says. "It's Ed Kapenash."

"Ed," Bob says. "Sorry I didn't stop to chat this morning. You looked like you were busy. What's going on? Word on the street is there was a murder."

Word on the street. Already? Well, it is a small island. "I can't get into it," the Chief says. "But you remember the kid you dropped off? I need to know where you picked him up. Did you pick him up at the Wauwinet?"

"The *Wauwinet*?" Bob says. "No. That real handsome kid in the red shorts and the blazer? I picked him up down at the Steamship. He had a ticket for the six-thirty slow boat this morning but I guess he missed it. And so he asked me to take him back to Monomoy. He said he was staying there."

"You're *sure* you picked him up at the Steamship dock?" the Chief says. "And not at the Wauwinet?"

"Sure I'm sure," Bob says. "I may not be getting any younger but I have yet to make a twelve-mile mistake. I picked that kid up on Steamboat Wharf. He told me he'd missed the six-thirty."

"Okay, Bob, wonderful, thanks. I'll talk to you." The Chief hangs up and takes a second to think. Shooter had a ticket for the early boat? With the wedding scheduled for this afternoon? Something is going on. And he flat-out lied about the Wauwinet.

Why?

A text comes in on the Chief's phone. It's from the funeral director, Bostic, saying he's on his way to collect the body—which is good news, considering the heat and the fragile state of everyone's nerves. Bostic will get the body ready for transfer to the medical examiner on Cape Cod. The Chief checks the time. If everything goes perfectly, they may have a report on the cause of death by early afternoon.

The Chief waits another few minutes for Shooter to emerge. By now, he must know he's been caught in a lie. The Chief strides across the shell driveway to the cottage that Shooter entered and knocks on the door. "Excuse me?" he says. "Mr. Uxley?"

No answer. He knocks harder. "Sir?"

The Chief tries the knob. The door is locked. He

forces the door, which feels extreme, but he wants Shooter Uxley to know he can't hide.

The cottage is empty. The Chief checks the little sitting room, the galley kitchen, the bedroom, and the bathroom—where the window is wide open.

Shooter Uxley is gone.

Friday, July 6, 2018,
4:00 p.m.

KAREN

She wakes up from her nap with the sun striping her bed and for one glorious instant, she feels no pain. She sits up without any help. It's as if Nantucket Island—the quality of the air, the rarefied seaside atmosphere—has cured her. She's going to be fine.

"B-B-Betty?"

Karen turns. Celeste emerges from Karen's bathroom wearing a ruffled sundress the color of a tangerine, a sunset, a monarch butterfly. It's bright and very flattering. Celeste may have the brain and temperament of a scientist, but she has the body of a bathing-suit model. She inherited Karen's breasts, which used to be her best feature, round and firm. But along with the breasts, Celeste may also have inherited the predisposition to cancer. Karen has made Celeste promise that as soon as she and Benji are married and Celeste has comprehensive health insurance, she will go to Sloan Kettering for genetic testing. And if necessary, she will get screened every year. Early detection is key.

"Hello, sweetheart," Karen says. "What are you doing here? Surely you have more important places to be? This is your time to shine."

"I was putting your t-t-toiletries away," Celeste says. "And now I can help you g-g-get ready."

Karen's eyes prick with tears. It is she who should be

helping Celeste, she who should be fussing over her daughter, the bride. But there is no denying that if Karen is to get dressed and make herself presentable, she will need help.

"Where's your father?" she asks.

"Swimming," Celeste says.

There's a stabbing pain in Karen's chest. It's jealousy. Bruce is swimming. Karen yearns to be with him, to feel the power of her four limbs. She had once been so strong; she remembers swimming the butterfly leg on her relay team, soaring from the water, arms stretched overhead, legs pumping behind. When she looks back at her life, she sees how much she has taken for granted.

Celeste is by her side. Karen takes a moment to look up at her face. Her eyes are sad, and Karen is concerned about the stutter, although she hasn't mentioned it because she doesn't want to make Celeste self-conscious for fear that the stutter will get worse. She knows that Benji and Celeste have whittled down their wedding vows so that all Celeste has to say is "I do."

"Is everything okay?" Karen asks.

"Yes, B-B-Betty, of course," Celeste says.

The nickname never fails to give Karen joy, even so many years later. She is Betty, for Betty Crocker, because Karen swears by the tattered, spiral-bound cookbooks she inherited from her own mother. Bruce, meanwhile, is Mac, for MacGyver, because he has a talent for unconventional problem-solving. The man can fix anything and prides himself on not having called a repairman in thirty years of marriage. Celeste gave them the nicknames when she was eleven years old and had outgrown Mommy and Daddy.

Karen strokes Celeste's forearm and Celeste adjusts her smile so that it seems almost real. She's pretending. But why? Is she feeling scared and anxious about Karen's illness? The decline has been significant, Karen knows, even in the two weeks since she last saw Celeste. Karen had dropped thirteen pounds as of a week ago and maybe another ten since then. Her stomach is compromised; she eats a bite or two of food per meal and forces down enough Ensure to keep up her strength. Her hair is nothing but gray fuzz, like one finds on a pussy willow. Her eyes are sunken, and her limbs tremble. It has probably come as a shock to Celeste.

But Karen isn't persuaded that she, Karen, is the reason for Celeste's pensive, faraway mood. It's something else, maybe the stress and pressure of being the center of attention. This wedding is huge; the setting is grandiose. Elaborate, expensive plans have been made, with Celeste and Benji at their center. It would be intimidating for anyone. When Karen married Bruce, there were six people in attendance at the Easton courthouse. She and Bruce celebrated afterward with a bottle of Asti spumante and a pizza from Nicolosi's.

Or maybe the problem isn't the wedding. Maybe it's Benji himself. Karen thinks back on her ill-advised visit to Kathryn Randall, the psychic.

Chaos.

"Darling," Karen says.

Celeste looks at her mother, and their eyes lock. Karen sees the truth in Celeste's clear blue irises: she doesn't want to marry Benji.

Karen needs to reassure Celeste that she's doing the right thing. Benji is a good man. He *adores* Celeste. He keeps her on the exact same pedestal that Karen and Bruce placed her on at the moment of her birth. That's really the wonderful thing about Benji: He loves their daughter the way she deserves to be loved. That...and he has money.

Karen would like to pretend that the money doesn't

matter, but it does. For over thirty years, Karen and Bruce have lived from paycheck to paycheck; 95 percent of their decisions have had to do with money: Should they buy organic fruit so Celeste wouldn't be exposed to a lot of pesticides? (Yes.) Should they drive the extra twenty minutes to Phillipsburg, New Jersey, for cheaper gas? (Yes.) Should they take Celeste to the orthodontist who allegedly had been accused of child molestation but who charged half as much as the reputable orthodontist? (No.) They had enough money to pay their mortgage and send Celeste to college, but any financial surprise—a leak in the roof, a raise in property taxes, a cancer diagnosis—was enough to sink them. Karen doesn't want Celeste to have to live that way. She has a college degree and a good job at the zoo, but Benji can give her everything. And everything is what she deserves.

As Karen opens her mouth to assure her daughter that she *is* doing the right thing, Bruce comes into the room with a navy-and-white-striped beach towel wrapped around his waist. Karen feasts her eyes on her husband—to her, he's every bit as beautiful as he was on the pool balcony so many years ago. His shoulders are defined by rippling muscles; his chest is smooth and broad. They have never had money for gym memberships; Bruce does old-fashioned calisthenics—sit-ups, push-ups, and pull-ups—in their bedroom every morning before work. He has been outside for less than an hour and already his skin has a healthy golden glow. Karen always envied the Mediterranean blood he'd inherited from his mother. He would go outside to mow the lawn and come back a bronzed god.

"Both my girls!" he says. "What a surprise!"

"D-D-Did you get the Reds, Mac?" Celeste asks. "For t-t-tomorrow?"

"Yes," Bruce says. He pulls a pair of pants out of the closet; they are the color of dusty bricks. "I don't see what the big deal is. It's certainly not the style. Is it the color? Mrs. Winbury, Greer, told me they would fade with every washing. It sounds like I'm going to need to spring for the dry cleaner."

"N-N-No, you should wash them," Celeste says. "That's the idea. The m-m-more they f-f-fade, the c-c-cooler they are."

"That makes no sense," Bruce says. "Did you happen to notice the black jeans I had on earlier? Sleek as a panther."

"The Reds are d-d-different, though," Celeste says.

"It's a Nantucket thing, darling," Karen says to Bruce. She thinks she gets it; the older and more worn the pants, the more authentic they are. The sleek-as-a-panther look, shiny and new, doesn't work on Nantucket; the preferred aesthetic is a careless appearance: faded pants, frayed collars, scuffed penny loafers. Bruce won't understand this but Karen gives him a look that implores him to just get with the program. The last thing they want to do is make a fuss and embarrass Celeste.

Bruce catches Karen's eye and seems to read her mind. "I'll do as you tell me, Bug." He throws on a T-shirt, then takes Celeste's hand and Karen's hand so that they form a human chain. But every chain has a weak link, and in their case, it's Karen. She's leaving them behind. The agony of this is exquisite. There is nothing more terrible, she has decided, than the ferocity with which humans can love.

"I came in to help B-B-Betty get ready," Celeste says. "The p-p-party starts in a little while."

"What about the rehearsal?" Bruce says. "Aren't we all going to the church?"

"Reverend D-D-Derby's flight from New York was d-d-delayed so we decided to scrap the rehearsal," Celeste says.

Karen is relieved. She isn't certain she would have made it through both the rehearsal and the party. Bruce, however, seems miffed.

"How are we supposed to practice our walk?" he says.

"We don't have to p-p-practice," Celeste says. "We link arms, we walk. Slowly. You hand me off to B-B-Benji. You k-k-kiss me."

"I wanted to practice," Bruce says. "Practice doing it without crying. I figured since today was the first time, I'd cry, but then tomorrow it would be old hat and maybe I wouldn't cry. Maybe. But I wanted to practice."

Celeste shrugs. "We d-d-decided not to d-d-do it."

Bruce nods. "All right. I'll help your mother. You go relax, Bug. Have a glass of wine."

"Find Benji," Karen says. "The two of you could probably use some alone time before all this begins."

"But I want to stay here," Celeste says. "With b-b-both of you."

Bruce helps Karen in and out of the shower.

Celeste helps Karen put on a soft white waffle-knit cotton robe with a light terry-cloth lining—there are two in every guest room, Celeste tells her, laundered after each use by Elida, the Winburys' summer housekeeper— and then Celeste rubs her mother's arms, back, and legs with Greer Garrison's favorite lotion, La Prairie White Caviar Illuminating and Moisturizing Cream, also in every guest room. The lotion is like none Karen has ever used before; it's rich, luscious even. Karen's skin drinks it in.

Bruce helps Karen get dressed. She is wearing a silk kimono over black leggings and a pair of Tory Burch ballet flats from two seasons ago that Bruce plucked off the sale rack for pennies.

"Style," Bruce says. "And comfort."

Karen looks in the mirror. She's swimming in the kimono. She tugs on the belt.

"Lipstick, B-B-Betty," Celeste says. She dabs at Karen's lips with the nub of Karen's old standby, Maybelline's New York Red. It's the only lipstick Karen has ever worn. Or ever will wear.

"I'd say you're ready," Bruce says. "You look stunning."

"I just want to use the toilet real quick," Karen says. This, at least, she can still do without help. She closes the door to the bathroom. She needs an oxycodone. Two, actually, because so much is expected of her. She'll be introduced to dozens of people she doesn't know and wouldn't care about except that some of these people will remain in Celeste's life long after Karen is gone, and Karen is determined that every single one of those people will remember her, Celeste's mother, as a "lovely woman."

Karen can't find her oxy. The pill bottle was in her Vera Bradley cosmetic bag along with her lipstick and a Revlon mascara that was rendered useless when she lost her eyelashes. Where…Karen tries not to panic but those pills are the only thing keeping her going. Without them, she will curl up in bed in a fetal position and howl with pain.

Karen's gaze sweeps the gleaming marble, glass, and mirrored surfaces of the guest bathroom. There's Karen's toothbrush in a silver cup. There's the miraculous body cream. Karen pulls open the little drawers, hoping that maybe Celeste tucked her things away so that she would feel at home.

And yes—in the third drawer, there are her pills. Oh, thank you! It seems like an unusual place to put them, but maybe Celeste didn't want the summer housekeeper to stumble across them and be tempted. Karen thinks about chastising Celeste for pawing through her things. Everyone deserves a modicum of privacy, a secret or two. But mostly, Karen feels an overwhelming relief that is nearly as powerful as the pills themselves. She taps two oxy into her palm, fills the silver cup with water, and swallows.

GREER

She checks her e-mail to review the timetable that Siobhan the caterer sent her and, unfortunately, she sees a new e-mail from Enid Collins, Greer's editor at Livingston and Greville, with the subject line URGENT.

This makes Greer laugh. Enid is seventy-seven years old. She has eleven grandchildren and one great-grandchild and she still marks up Greer's manuscripts with a red pencil. Never once in the twenty-two years that Enid has been editing Greer's novels has she ever used the word *urgent*. Enid believes strongly in letting ideas marinate—for days or weeks or months. There's nothing Enid despises more than a rush.

Greer checks the e-mail even though the definition of *urgent* is transpiring right outside the window of Greer's sitting room: the rental people are setting up chairs, the band is doing a sound check, and sixty people are due to descend on Summerland for the rehearsal dinner, among them Featherleigh Dale.

Dearest Greer, the e-mail begins (Enid composes all of her e-mails as formal letters).

I'm sure you will understand how it pains me to tell you

this, since I have long been a champion of your work, your very first champion, if you remember.

Yes, Greer does remember. She was out of her mind with boredom when she was pregnant with Thomas—Tag was at the office day and night back then—and so she'd started writing a murder mystery set in the sixth arrondissement of Paris entitled *Prey in the Saint-Germain-des-Prés*. She had sent it off to Livingston and Greville, the publishing house that brought out the mysteries Greer most enjoyed herself, and, lo and behold, she received a letter of interest from an established editor named Enid Collins who said she would like to publish the book and might Greer be able to meet and discuss terms of payment and editorial changes? This had launched the Dolly Hardaway murder mystery series, the most successful of which, *The Killer on Khao San Road,* was made into a movie that had somehow attained that elusive thing known as cult status.

But since we have been bought by Turnhaute Publishing Group, my autonomy has been greatly diminished.

Is it really the fault of the corporate Goliath of Turnhaute, fondly known as Turncoat, Greer wonders, or is Enid being pushed out because of her advanced age? Her driver's license will be the next thing taken, Greer supposes.

My editorial director, Mr. Charles O'Brien, also read your manuscript and he has deemed it "unacceptable." He has asked me to let you know you have a fortnight to rewrite it entirely. He suggests you use an alternate exotic locale, one you can describe with more "colorful detail" than what he calls the rather "pale" version of Santorini you present here. I'm sorry to be so blunt and to bear this dreadful news, my darling Greer. But a fortnight makes your new due date July 21, and I felt it best to be direct in light of that looming deadline.

With best wishes,
Enid Collins

Hell and damnation, Greer thinks. Her twenty-first manuscript has been…*rejected,* then? Who *is* this Charles O'Brien and what does *he* know? Charlie, old Chuck, an Irishman. Greer can't bring to mind an Irish writer she has ever admired. She has always despised Joyce, pretentious sod, writing in code and asking his readers to follow the twists and turns of his demented mind. She finds Wilde predictable, Swift histrionic, Beckett inscrutable, Stoker overrated, and Yeats dull.

Her cell phone pings. It's Benji. Roger has questions about the seating chart. Where are you?

In my sitting room. Witnessing the end of my career.

What had old Chuck O'Brien said about the book? Pale. He had called Greer's description of Santorini *pale* and suggested Greer use a different exotic locale.

It *has* been over thirty years since Greer set foot on Santorini. She chose it only because back in August when Benji proposed to Celeste, he mentioned he would like to honeymoon there. Greer's own memories of the place were brilliant. She recalled stark limestone cliffs and a red beach, colored by iron deposits; robust, bushy-haired Greek men selling freshly caught fish in woven baskets; she remembered the deep aquamarine of the Aegean Sea, whitewashed churches with cobalt-blue domes, the winding streets of Oia, the seafood restaurants where the water practically lapped onto one's feet and everyone was offered the same wine, a lovely, crisp white that was made on the east side of the island. Greer and Tag had chartered a catamaran, and Tag had sailed them around while Greer sat under a canopy wearing a floppy straw hat and Jackie O. sunglasses. They had swum into the beaches from the boat and paid the cabana boys two drachmas for chaises and an umbrella.

Greer had left the island with recipes for garlicky tzatziki, grilled chicken with lemon and fresh oregano, and of course her famous lamb souvlaki.

She had been dismayed to find, upon researching Santorini 2018 via the internet, that Oia is now home to a Jimmy Choo boutique and that the donkey ride from the port up to Fira has been given a one-star rating on Trip-Advisor. Greer had adored the donkey ride.

If she is very honest with herself, she will admit that the novel did feel a bit thin on plot, a bit slapdash, a bit "phoned in," as it were. The key to a good whodunit is a murderer who is hiding in plain sight. Her character with the newly acquired stutter is, perhaps, underdeveloped. She remembers thinking when she handed the novel in, *Well, that wasn't so bad.* She had delivered a seventy-five-thousand-word manuscript on time, despite planning a wedding to rival Prince Harry's, and she hadn't pulled her hair out or been committed to an insane asylum.

Things that seem too good to be true usually are.

Can she rewrite the novel in a fortnight? (No one but the British—scratch that—no one but *Enid Collins* still uses the term *fortnight*.)

She isn't sure. She'll have to wait and see how the weekend goes.

She clicks out of Enid, clicks out of e-mail entirely. Thinking about the unpleasant reality of her work life has provided a distraction, at least, from the even more unpleasant reality of the present moment. Featherleigh Dale will be arriving in less than an hour. Featherleigh is the rare party guest who sees fit to show up exactly on time. She does this, Greer suspects, so that she can have some private moments with Tag. Tag is ready for every occasion half an hour early and Greer is always half an hour late. It is a cunning and perceptive woman indeed who notes this habit and takes advantage of it, as Featherleigh does.

Greer changes into her party outfit—a sleek ivory silk jumpsuit by Halston, vintage, that looks like something Bianca Jagger might have worn to Studio 54. It's one of the most fabulous pieces Greer owns. She had the trousers temporarily shortened so that she might wear the jumpsuit barefoot in the sand, showing off her toenails, which have been painted pale blue. Her mother-of-the-groom dress for tomorrow is proper—which is to say, matronly—and so tonight, Greer is going to emphasize her youthful, fun, carefree side. (Tag might say she abandoned this side of herself in the nineties and he might be partially correct, but she is reasserting it tonight.) For the first time since primary school, she is going out in public with her hair down, all the way down, straight and loose on both sides of her face. She always wears her hair up or back, normally in a chignon, sometimes in a tight ballerina bun, occasionally braided for casual occasions. When she exercises, which is infrequently, she wears her hair in a ponytail. She never allows herself to wear it like this—like a hippie, or something worse.

But it's sexy. She looks younger.

When she goes into the kitchen, Tag whistles. "You'd better get out of here before my wife sees you. She's quite formidable, with her hairpins and her diamonds."

Greer grins at him. She doesn't do this enough, she realizes. Tag always gets the worst of her: her laser focus, her inflexibility, her condescension, her acerbic tongue. She used to love that she could be herself in front of him, but now it feels like all he gets is the negative, unpleasant, unflattering aspects of Greer Garrison; the sweet, gentle, caring parts of her she saves for others— her sons, certainly, but also virtual strangers, such as her fans, waiters at restaurants, and retail girls in shops. Greer is nicer to Tita at the Nantucket post office than she is to her own husband.

She stands before him, raises her face, lowers her eyelids, purses her lips.

"Darling," he says. "You look gorgeous. No, I take that back. You look *hot*." He kisses her, and his hands cup her behind.

The doorbell rings. *That,* Greer thinks, *will be Featherleigh.*

It isn't a question of *if* Tag has slept with Featherleigh Dale, it's a question of how many times, how recently, and how far things went between them emotionally. Featherleigh Dale is the much younger sister of the late Hamish Dale, who was Tag's closest friend at Oxford. To hear the stories, Featherleigh used to come visit the boys at school when she was merely eight years old and would accompany them first to the pub and then to the Nosebag, where they would reward Featherleigh's patience with cheddar scones and lime posset. They also used her as a lure for young female students who thought it adorable that Hamish and Tag were minding a little sister.

Hamish was killed six years earlier in a gruesome car crash on the M1. Greer and Tag and Thomas and Benji flew to London for the funeral and became reacquainted with Featherleigh, who was then all grown up and living in Sloane Square, working in the fine carpet division of Sotheby's. As far as Greer knows, nothing happened between Tag and Featherleigh at the reception following Hamish's funeral, although certainly cards were exchanged because after that, Featherleigh Dale started to appear at nearly every social event the Winburys attended. She had shown up at a graduation party for Thomas's law-school roommate held at the Carlyle Hotel in New York, and that was when Greer grew suspicious. What were the chances that Featherleigh Dale would be at that party? Featherleigh claimed she had bumped into Thomas at a club downtown a few days earlier and that *he* had invited her. Ha! Preposterous!

The next time they had run into Featherleigh Dale had been when Tag and Greer took Thomas and Abby to Little Dix Bay in Virgin Gorda over the Christmas holidays. Featherleigh had appeared on an enormous yacht belonging to some Saudi Arabian sheikh who was quite definitely gay.

Somehow, Featherleigh had insinuated herself into Greer's life as well. When she left Sotheby's, she started her own business as a personal shopper who matched antiques with private homes in London. Featherleigh was too smart to come to Greer first. Instead, she started finding pieces for Greer's London neighbor Antonia. When Antonia mentioned that she had gotten a hard-to-find Kano School Japanese screen from Featherleigh Dale, Greer had said, *Oh! I know Featherleigh*. And the next thing Greer knew, Featherleigh was calling her about this Morris chair and that Biedermeier walnut commode.

Now Featherleigh is as much a part of Greer's life as she may or may not be of Tag's. There was no question about whether or not to invite her to the wedding. They had to.

And there was no surprise in Featherleigh's response. Despite Greer's fierce wish that Featherleigh would decline, she had responded yes. For one. She would be attending alone.

Will she be wearing the silver-lace ring with the sapphires? Greer wonders. The ring is meant to be worn on the thumb. When Jessica Hicks, the jewelry designer, told

Greer this, Greer had thought she'd misunderstood. Who wears a ring on her thumb? Only gypsies, so far as Greer knows. It sounds like a trend—but of course, no one adores a trend more than Featherleigh. She had moved to Sloane Square only because it was where a young Diana Spencer once lived. And what about Featherleigh's penchant for cold-shoulder dresses, which Donna Karan helped make popular in 1993? Greer can too easily picture Featherleigh waltzing right into Greer's home with the ring on her thumb. Greer hopes she can keep her composure while she admires the ring and asks Featherleigh where she got it.

She will then watch Featherleigh Dale squirm.

An hour into the rehearsal dinner (a bit of a misnomer, as the rehearsal was canceled due to Reverend Derby's travel delay), Greer is enjoying herself immensely. She is floating between the front lawn and the beach in her bare feet with a glass of champagne in her hand that one of the adorable girls who work for the caterer is in charge of keeping filled.

Greer asks the girl her name.

"Chloe," she says. "Chloe MacAvoy."

"Don't be a stranger, Chloe!" Greer says. A steady stream of champagne is the key to Greer staying relaxed.

It's a glorious night. There's a light breeze off the water, and the sky looks like a blue ombré silk scarf as the sun descends, setting the Nantucket skyline aglow. The band is playing songs by James Taylor, Jimmy Buffett, the Beach Boys. Greer tries to manage her time among all of the guests arriving and the major players— Benji, Celeste, the wedding party, and Mr. and Mrs. Otis. Mrs. Otis—Karen—looks lovely in an embroidered kimono. She leans on her cane for a few minutes talking with Tag's interminably boring colleague from work and then, just as Greer feels she must swoop in and save the poor woman—with so little time left, Karen has none to waste on Peter Walls—Bruce leads Karen over to a chair at the edge of the action. She will sit and receive visitors like a queen. As she should.

Benji is talking with Shooter and the four Alexanders from Hobart—Alex K., Alex B., Alex W., and Zander. Greer is fond of Benji's Hobart friends—all of them have spent long weekends here at Summerland—but no one has captured Greer's heart quite as much as Shooter. Shooter Uxley is the son of a Palm Beach real estate scion and his mistress. Shooter's mother got pregnant with the sole intention of eliciting a marriage proposal, but it never came. The father had five other children by two wives and he was senile enough to let one of his older sons oversee his will, which cut Shooter and his mother out entirely. Shooter had somehow managed to produce the tuition for his last year at St. George's, but after graduation he had been forced to find a job. That he has turned himself into such a success is a testament to his intelligence, his charm, and his perseverance.

Greer sips her champagne and wanders to the raw bar, where Tag is sucking down oyster after oyster, dripping shellfish liquor onto his bespoke pink shirt, tailored for him at Henry Poole. Despite how much Tag loves New York, he trusts only Savile Row tailors, and yet he seems to think nothing of defiling said shirts in the name of a good bivalve. He would stay here all night if Greer let him.

"You should take a plate of those over to the Otises," Greer says. "Karen is sitting and Bruce is stationed at her side like the Swiss Guard."

"Do they eat oysters, do you think?" Tag asks.

Good question. Celeste confided that Mrs. Otis is

excited about having lobster—there had been some confusion with the term *clambake*—because she, Karen Otis, hasn't eaten lobster since her honeymoon more than thirty years earlier. Greer tried to hide her shock. At the end of every summer on this island, it was all Greer could do not to feel weary of lobster, after having lobster rolls at Cru, the lobster spaghetti from the Boarding House, lobster fritters and tartlets and beignets and avocado-toast-with-lobster at every cocktail party she attends. But, of course, Karen Otis lives a vastly different life. Greer informed Siobhan Crispin, the caterer, that the mother of the bride was to be offered as much lobster as she wanted and that all uneaten lobsters should be cracked and the meat stashed in a bag in the fridge of the main house in case Mrs. Otis craved a midnight snack.

"Just offer, please," Greer says to Tag. "Take some of the shrimp with cocktail sauce and lemons—they'll like that."

"Good idea," Tag says. He leans over to kiss her. "You're very thoughtful."

"And hot," she reminds him.

"Hottest woman here," Tag says. "Not that I've noticed another soul."

"Have you seen Featherleigh?" Greer asks. This will not seem like a loaded question, because in all this time, Greer has never confronted Tag with her suspicions.

"I caught a glimpse," Tag says. "She looks god-awful."

"Does she?" Greer says, although she knows the answer is yes. Greer sought Featherleigh out immediately after dealing with the last-minute party logistics, and although it's ungracious, Greer will say that the twenty pounds (at least) that Featherleigh has gained and Featherleigh's bad haircut and her even worse dye job and her reddened nose are the best things about this wedding weekend so far.

Greer had checked both of Featherleigh's hands—she was not wearing the ring. Greer had found herself almost *deflated* by this; she had been ready for a confrontation. Instead, Greer had no choice but to be civil.

"Featherleigh Dale, you're a sight for sore eyes."

The corners of Featherleigh's mouth had pulled down unattractively. "Thank you for having me," she'd said. She had then proceeded to detail the horror of her travel. No money for a first-class ticket so she was squished in coach. The flight from New York to Nantucket was overbooked, everyone was obnoxious, there was no decent food at the airport, she'd had a Nathan's hot dog and the thing was as shriveled as a mummy's pecker. She finds Nantucket damp, just look at her hair, the place she booked is an *inn,* not a hotel, so there's no room service, no fitness center, no spa, and the pillowcases are decorated with tulle flowers, they're honestly the most hideous things she's ever seen, how she's supposed to lay her head on something like that she has no idea, but the inn was the only place available because she'd waited until the last minute. She wasn't going to come at all because she was so low on funds, but then she hoped the trip would help snap her out of her funk.

"Funk?" Greer asked, wondering if this litany was ever going to end.

"My business went belly-up," Featherleigh said. "And I've been through a devastating breakup"—*Aha!* Greer thinks. *So it's over with Tag?*—"which is why I have this bad dye job and I look like an absolute hippo. It's been all vodka and fish and chips and takeout vindaloo for me. I'm forty-five years old, I'm not married, I have no children, I have no job, I'm under investigation—"

"A devastating breakup?" Greer said, backing up to the only one of Featherleigh's complaints that she cared about. "I didn't realize you were seeing anyone special."

"It was on the down-low," Featherleigh said. Her eyes filled with tears. "He's married. I knew he was married, but I thought..."

"You thought he would leave his wife for you?" Greer asked. She had gathered Featherleigh up in a hug, mostly to put an end to the tears—nothing kills a party like somebody weeping—and said, "Men never leave their wives, Featherleigh. You're old enough to know better. Is it anyone I know?"

Featherleigh had sniffed and shaken her head against Greer's shoulder. Greer eased away, suddenly concerned about mascara on her ivory silk jumpsuit. Would Featherleigh cry about her breakup with Tag to Greer? Was she capable of that kind of insidious deception?

"And why," Greer asked, "are you under investigation?"

"For fraud," Featherleigh admitted glumly.

So clearly she *was* capable of deception. And that would explain the absence of the ring.

"When was this breakup?" Greer had asked. "Recently?"

Featherleigh's bottom lip trembled. "May," she said.

May? Greer thought. She's positive Jessica Hicks said that Tag had bought the ring in June. But Greer supposes she could have been mistaken; she should have asked Jessica to forward the receipt to her e-mail, but Greer had been so stunned, so seized with angst, that she had hurried out of the store without proper follow-up.

After writing twenty-one novels in the persona of Miss Dolly Hardaway, Greer had cultivated the mind-set of a detective. Once her head cleared of all this champagne and excitement, she would go back over the events of May with a fine-tooth comb. See what nits she could pick.

"Go get yourself a drink," Greer had said. "It certainly sounds like you could use one."

* * *

Greer's seating chart is brilliant, she thinks, except that the seat of honor, the seat next to Benji, is empty. Where is Celeste? She's sitting with her parents, naturally, playing nanny to both Karen and Bruce. Celeste cracks the claws of her mother's lobster and pulls the snowy meat from it with the slender silver pick, just as Greer taught her. She pries the tail meat free and cuts it into bite-size pieces, then identifies the cups of melted butter. Because this is an Island Fare clambake, every traditional element has been given a sophisticated twist. There are three kinds of melted butter for the lobster: regular, lime, and chili pepper. There are two types of corn bread, one with whole sweet corn kernels and one with pork cracklings. There are also feathery-light buttermilk biscuits made even more savory by the addition of aged English cheddar. Alongside the standard grilled linguica are house-made lamb sausages, another offering to please the Brits. In the center of every table is a pinwheel of Bartlett's Farm hothouse tomatoes drizzled with a thick, tangy blue cheese dressing and sprinkled with chopped green onions and crispy bacon.

Celeste goes through the same lobster routine with her father. Greer notices the tender attention Celeste pays to her parents. It's remarkable. It's envy-inspiring. Greer believes she did an impeccable job parenting her boys but she knows bloody well they would never treat her with this kind of loving, thoughtful care. The bond that Celeste has with her parents is special; anyone can see that. Maybe it's because her mother is dying—but somehow, Greer doesn't think that's the sole reason. Maybe it's because the Otises had Celeste when they were so young. Maybe it's because Celeste is an only child.

Maybe Greer should stop wondering.

Greer splits a biscuit in half. She'll allow herself two bites. She turns to Tag. "Do the boys love me, do you think?"

"Is that an actual question?" Tag asks.

Chloe appears at Greer's shoulder with yet another glass of champagne. Greer should stop drinking because following the question *Do the boys love me?* are a host of other questions. Does Tag love her? Does anyone else love her? Does anyone appreciate just how much hard work this wedding has entailed? It took money, yes, but also a good deal of time— hundreds of hours, if Greer added it up, on lists, phone calls, logistics. She essentially cannibalized her career because the wedding came first, her novel second—and some bloke named Chuck O'Brien has now called her on it. Can she write the novel all over again, or write a new novel start to finish in a fortnight? Maybe without the wedding as a distraction, yes.

Did Tag have an affair with Featherleigh that ended in May?

No more champagne. Greer has to stop. But the flute is such a pretty shape and the liquid is an irresistible platinum color; the bubbles wink at her seductively and she knows exactly how it will taste: cool and crisp, like an apple just plucked from the branch.

Celeste takes her seat next to Benji and for a moment, Greer relaxes. Everyone is in his or her proper place. "We should probably do the toasts now," Greer says. "Before people get antsy."

"I thought toasts were scheduled for after dinner but before dessert," Tag says. He checks his watch. "I have a quick call with Ernie at nine."

"What?" Greer says. "A call with Ernie at nine o'clock *tonight?"*

"It's the Libya deal," Tag says. "It'll be quick but I can't reschedule; Ernie is going to Tripoli in the morning. This deal is big, darling. Big, big." Tag kisses Greer and stands up, leaving an untouched lobster tail on his plate.

"Make it quick, quick," Greer says, trying to maintain her playful attitude. Her eyes flick across the tent to where Featherleigh is sitting; Greer placed her in social Siberia with Tag's work colleagues, among them the tedious Peter Walls. If Featherleigh follows Tag out, Greer will know there is no call to Ernie.

But Featherleigh stays put; she doesn't even seem to notice Tag leaving the party. Or actually, yes, she does. Her eyes trail him. Her expression holds longing, Greer thinks, except, really, her own judgment can't be trusted after so many glasses of champagne. But Featherleigh doesn't move. Instead, she lavishly butters a piece of corn bread and pops it into her mouth. Greer pushes her own plate away.

Bruce Otis, adhering to Greer's wishes if not the precise timetable, stands up and clinks his spoon against his water glass.

"Ladies and gentlemen, I'm Bruce Otis, father of the bride," he says. "I'd like to make a toast."

A murmur ripples through the crowd; the band stops playing and everyone quiets down. Greer is grateful. She isn't sure how much practice Mr. Otis has at speaking to a group this size but it's always easier when people are well behaved.

"When I met my wife, Karen, I thought I was the luckiest man alive. Boy, not man, because when I met Karen, I was only seventeen years old. But I knew I loved her. I could see myself growing old with her. Which is exactly what we've gone and done."

There is gentle laughter.

"And I know I speak for Karen when I say that our love for each other was so extraordinary that years went by when neither of us wanted children. We were so happy just being together. I would work all week, and every day at five o'clock the sun came out for me because I got to go home to this beautiful, extraordinary woman. On Saturdays we used to run our errands. We would go to the post office to mail packages or check our box, and the line was always extra-long on Saturdays, but you know what? I didn't care. I could wait an hour. I could wait all day... because I was with Karen." Bruce's voice starts to crack and Greer can see tears shining in his eyes and she realizes that he's using this toast as a way to pay tribute to his wife. It's brilliant; Karen deserves this and more. She deserves a *cure* or a cutting-edge clinical trial that puts her into remission for ten years, or even five years—at least then she might be able to meet her future grandchildren. Celeste has confided to Greer that she sends a hundred dollars from each of her paychecks to the Breast Cancer Research Foundation without Karen's or Bruce's knowledge. Greer was so moved by this that she sat down at her desk that very evening and wrote the organization a $25,000 check without telling Celeste or Benji or even Tag. The charitable acts that count the most, Greer believes, are those done without anyone knowing. But she had wanted very badly to send a note with the check that said: *Please use this money to cure Karen Otis.*

Bruce clears his throat, regroups, and says, "And then, twenty-eight years ago, we had a baby girl. And man, nothing on this earth—and I mean *nothing*—prepares you for how much you love your kids. Am I right?"

There are some *Hear, hear*s from the audience. Greer feels a vague recognition. She loved her children. Loves them. It was different when they were small, of course.

"And Karen and I somehow lucked out and got this

beautiful, smart, *nice* little girl. She got a hundred percent on all her spelling tests. She was the one who scooped up a spider and carried it outside instead of squishing it with her shoe, and she was always digging in the backyard looking for snakes or salamanders and then putting them in a shoe box with grass and little dishes of drinking water. She was never ashamed or embarrassed of where she came from or *who* she came from, even though she outgrew us and the rest of Forks Township, Pennsylvania, a long time ago." Bruce raises his glass. "And so to you, Benjamin Winbury, I say from the heart: Take care of our little girl. She is our treasure, our hope, our light, and our warmth. She is our legacy. Here's to the two of you and your life together."

Greer wipes a tear from the corner of her eye with a napkin. She isn't normally sentimental, although anyone would have found that toast stirring.

Thomas stands up next and chimes on his own water glass. It's true perhaps that nothing in this world prepares you for how much you love your children, but Greer has always been a realist where her sons are concerned. She has a firm handle on their strengths and weaknesses. Thomas is the better-looking one; Benji inherited Greer's father's crooked nose, and no barber has ever been able to tame Benji's cowlick. But Benji is smarter and has been either blessed or cursed with a natural gravitas, so he has always seemed like the older brother.

For his toast, Thomas tells the story of when Thomas and Benji, ages eight and six, respectively, got lost at Piccadilly Circus and how Benji was the one who had saved them from abduction or worse. The story goes that Benji, against his brother's severe warnings, had approached a group of punk rockers and asked a girl with a bright pink Mohawk to help them find their mummy.

"He said the girl's hair was pretty," Thomas says. "He believed anyone with such pretty hair was sure to have deep reserves of cleverness and wisdom."

Greer laughs along with everyone else, although the story rubs her the wrong way for two reasons. First off, *she* was the one who had taken the boys to Piccadilly, where she had bumped into a woman named Susan Haynes, who sat on the ladies' auxiliary at Portland Hospital, a group Greer had been keen to join. Greer had become so engrossed in conversation with Susan that she had lost track of the boys. Her own children. When Greer surfaced from the conversation, she looked around and found the two of them had *vanished*.

Greer is also dismayed because this is the *exact same story* that Benji told when he had given the toast at Thomas's wedding four years earlier. Greer finds it terribly unimaginative for Thomas to recycle the very same story. Greer would like to give Tag a private look to see if he agrees, but he's . . . where? Still on the call with Ernie? Greer checks on Featherleigh. She's in her seat, gazing at Thomas with an insipid look on her face.

She's blotto, Greer thinks. She has three empty cups of the blackberry mojito punch in front of her.

As soon as the applause for Thomas's half-baked effort subsides, Greer slips discreetly into the house in search of her husband.

She skirts the kitchen, where the catering staff is plating dessert, an assortment of homemade pies: blueberry, peach, Key lime, banana cream, and chocolate pecan. She heads through the den toward the back stairs but stops when she hears a voice coming from the laundry room.

The laundry room? Greer thinks. She pokes her head in.

There's a girl with her back up against the stacked

washer and dryer, her face in her hands, sobbing. It's . . .
it's the *friend,* Celeste's friend, the maid of honor. Greer
blanks on the girl's name. It's . . . Merrill or Madison?
No, not quite. *Merritt,* she thinks. Merritt Monaco.

"Merritt!" Greer says. "What's wrong?"

When Merritt turns to see Greer, she gasps in surprise. Then she hurries to wipe away her tears. "Nothing," she says. "It's just . . . the excitement."

"It's overwhelming, isn't it?" Greer says. She feels a
wave of maternal concern for this girl who is neither
getting married like Celeste nor pregnant like Abby. But
still, the freedom! Greer wants to encourage Merritt to
savor her freedom because soon enough, certainly, it will
be gone.

"Come, let's get you a drink," Greer says. She beckons
Merritt forward, thinking she will lead the girl back out
to the party and find Chloe-with-the-champagne. Surely
Merritt's sadness is nothing a little Veuve Clicquot
can't fix.

"I'm fine," Merritt says, sniffing and trying to collect
herself. "I'll be out shortly. I need the ladies' room. I
should fix my face. But thank you."

Greer gives the girl a smile. "Very well. I'm on a mission to find my husband anyway. He seems to have disappeared." She turns to leave but not before catching the
glint of a silver ring on Merritt's thumb.

So it's true, Greer thinks. *All the fashionable girls are
wearing them now.*

Monday, October 24, 2016

CELESTE

Two days after giving Benji her direct line at the zoo, he calls—not to put her in touch with his friend who may or may not want to bring groups of foreign executives to the zoo but to ask her out to dinner. He wants to take her to the Russian Tea Room on Friday night.

"They've redone it since the eighties," he says. "It's supposed to be over the top now. Do you like caviar?"

"Um…" Celeste says. She has never had caviar, not only because it's expensive but also because she has seen sacs of fish eggs floating in aquarium water and…no, thank you.

"Or we could go down to the East Village and eat at Madame Vo's? It's Vietnamese. Would you prefer Vietnamese?"

Celeste nearly hangs up the phone. She chastises herself for giving this guy her number. He's an alien species—or, more likely, she's the alien. He's used to beautiful, sophisticated women like Jules, who probably grew up with caviar packed in her lunchbox. Celeste's rent on East One Hundredth Street is a bit of a stretch, so she rarely goes out to eat. Occasionally, she will meet Merritt for brunch or dinner. Many times, if Merritt is photographed eating at the restaurant or if she posts photos of the food online at #eatingfortheinsta, the meal will be comped. Usually, however, dinner for Celeste is the salad bar at the corner bodega or takeout from the cafeteria at the zoo and, yes, Celeste does know how pathetic that is, but only because Merritt has told her.

"Vietnamese sounds great!" Celeste says, manufacturing as much enthusiasm as she can about a cuisine she knows nothing about.

"Okay, Madame Vo's it is, then," Benji says. "I'll come pick you up?"

"Pick me *up*?" Celeste says. Her block—which is too far north to properly qualify as the Upper East Side, though too far south to be called Harlem—is relatively safe but neither sexy nor fetching. There's a laundromat, the bodega, a pet groomer.

"Or we can meet there?" Benji says. "It's on East Tenth Street."

"I'll meet you there," Celeste says, relieved.

"Eight o'clock?" Benji says.

"Sounds good," Celeste says, and she hangs up the phone to call Merritt.

First, Merritt screams, *You have a date!*

Celeste's face contorts into an expression halfway between a smile and a grimace. She *does* have a date, and it feels good, because normally, when Celeste and Merritt talk, the only person who has exciting news, or news of any kind, is Merritt. Merritt's romantic life is so populated that Celeste has a hard time keeping the men straight. Presently, Merritt is dating Robbie, who's the daytime bartender at the Breslin on Twenty-Ninth Street. He's tall and pale with bulging biceps and an Irish accent. *What's not to love about Robbie?* Celeste wondered after Merritt dragged Celeste down to a Saturday lunch at the Breslin so she could meet him. Why didn't Merritt stay with him?

For one, Merritt said, Robbie was an aspiring actor. He was constantly going on auditions, and Merritt felt it was only a matter of time before he was cast in a TV pilot that got picked up, at which point he'd move to the West Coast. It wasn't a good idea to get too attached to anyone not firmly rooted in New York, Merritt said. However, Celeste knew that Merritt was afraid to commit because of a truly heinous situation she'd found herself in the year before she and Celeste met.

The man's name was Travis Darling. Travis and his wife, Cordelia, owned a PR firm called Brightstreet where Merritt had worked right out of college. She had been handpicked for her job as publicity associate from a pool of over a thousand applicants, and both Travis and Cordelia saw Merritt as a rising PR star, the next Lynn Goldsmith. Merritt's life had become completely intertwined with the lives of the Darlings. She accompanied them to dinner at least once a week; she hung out at their brownstone on West Eighty-Third Street; she went skiing with them in Stowe and joined them for beach weekends in Bridgehampton.

Travis had always been Merritt's champion. He asked questions about Merritt's personal life, encouraged her interest in fashion; he remembered her college roommates' names. He sought out her opinion because she was young and had a fresh perspective. He would sometimes rest his hand on her shoulder when he was standing behind her desk, and he forwarded her racy jokes from his personal e-mail. When Merritt was out to dinner with Travis and Cordelia, he would pull out her chair. If they were waiting at the bar to be seated, he would usher her forward with his hand on her back. Merritt noted these things but she didn't protest. After all, Cordelia was *right there*.

But then.

It was summer and Merritt was spending a weekend in the Hamptons with the Darlings. On Saturday afternoon, the three of them were lying on the beach when a call came in from a client, a supermodel who had just had an altercation with a flight attendant. Words had been exchanged and a fellow passenger had leaked the story—which cast the supermodel in a very unflattering light—to the press. It was a publicity situation that could easily escalate into a publicity nightmare. Cordelia had to go back to the city to deal with the fallout.

I'll go with you, Merritt had said. *You'll need help.*

I have Sage, Cordelia said. Sage Kennedy was a brand-new hire. Merritt had sensed Sage's ambition and professional envy immediately; Sage wanted to be the next Merritt. Sage was too young and broke to spend summer weekends away, but now that would work in her favor. When Merritt insisted she was more than happy to go back to the city, Cordelia said, *You stay here and enjoy. I'll see you Monday.*

Had Merritt been uneasy about staying in the house with Travis alone? Not really. By that point, Merritt had been working for Brightstreet for three years. If Travis were going to make a pass at her, she figured, it would have happened already.

But late that afternoon, as Merritt was rinsing the sand off her feet at the outdoor hose before going into the house, Travis came up behind her and, without a word, untied the string of her bikini top. Merritt had frozen. She was petrified, she told Celeste, but she'd decided to laugh it off as a prank. She grabbed the strings and started to retie them but Travis stopped her. He took both of her hands, pulled her to him, and started kissing the back of her neck. Into her ear he whispered, *I've been waiting so long for this.*

"I was trapped," Merritt told Celeste. "I could have

pushed him away but I was afraid I'd lose my job. I was afraid he'd tell Cordelia that I was the one who took off my top. So I let it happen. I let it happen."

The affair lasted seven torturous months. Merritt lived in mortal fear of Cordelia finding out, but Travis assured Merritt there was nothing to worry about. His wife, he said, was frigid and possibly even a lesbian and she wouldn't have cared even if she did find out.

Deep down, she wanted this to happen, Travis said. *One of the reasons she wanted to hire you was that she knew I thought you were hot.*

As it turned out, Travis was gravely mistaken about what Cordelia wanted. Cordelia hired a private investigator, who followed both Merritt and Travis, accessed their phone records and text messages, then presented Cordelia with all the proof she needed, including, somehow, 8-by-10 glossies of Merritt and Travis showering together in Merritt's apartment.

Cordelia had swiftly taken the company from Travis, as well as their investments and their brownstone. She fired Merritt and set out to shred Merritt's reputation professionally and personally—and by then, Cordelia's friends were Merritt's friends. Travis forsook Merritt as well. She called and begged him to tell Cordelia the truth: that he had started the affair and he had given her no choice but to be complicit. Travis had responded to her calls and texts by filing a restraining order against her.

Merritt had been suicidal in the aftermath, she confided to Celeste. On bad days she stared at a bottle of hoarded pills—Valium, Ambien, Xanax. On good days, she looked for jobs in other cities, but it turned out Cordelia's tentacles reached all the way to Chicago, DC, Atlanta. Merritt didn't get so much as a callback. Every

once in a while Cordelia would text her, and each time
Merritt saw Cordelia's name on her phone's screen, she
thought that maybe, just maybe, Travis had come clean
and told Cordelia that the affair had been his fault, that
he had coerced Merritt, then basically blackmailed her.
But the texts were always the exact opposite of apologies.
One said: If I thought I could get away with it, I would
kill you.

But then, one miraculous day, Merritt received a text
from Sage Kennedy, who, Merritt knew, had summarily
taken her position in the company. The text said: Cordelia has sold the brownstone on Eighty-Third Street and is
relocating Brightstreet to LA. Thought you would want to
know.

At first, Merritt didn't believe it. She was wary of Sage
Kennedy. But when Merritt checked *Business Insider,* she
saw it was true. She wondered if maybe Travis had
preyed on Sage Kennedy after Merritt left. She was
afraid to ask, though she did text Sage back to thank her
for the information. She had, essentially, been set free.

Soon thereafter, Merritt found a job in PR with the
Wildlife Conservation Society, and although she took a
pay cut, she was grateful for the fresh start. She introduced herself to Celeste in her first weeks of work by saying, "You're the best-looking, most normal person who
works at any of our zoos. Please let me use photos of you
in the literature."

Celeste had been stupefied by Merritt's blunt honesty.
"Thanks," she said. "I think." They had gone to lunch
together in the zoo's cafeteria, and over tuna fish sandwiches, a friendship was forged. Merritt credited Celeste
with "saving" her, although Celeste saw it as the other
way around. Celeste had been bound and determined to
move out of Forks Township and make it in New York
City on her own, but even she had been confounded by

just *how* on her own she actually was. The city was home to ten million people and yet Celeste had a hard time meeting anyone outside of work. She had two sort-of friends on her block: Rocky, who worked at the bodega, and Judy Quigley, who owned the pet-grooming business.

Rocky had taken Celeste on a date to the Peruvian chicken place on Ninety-First Street but then he confessed that although he liked Celeste and thought she was very, very pretty, he had neither the time nor the money for a girlfriend. Mrs. Quigley was a pleasant woman and she and Celeste shared a love of animals but it wasn't like they were ever going to go out for cocktails.

Merritt was the New York City friend of Celeste's dreams. She was fun, sophisticated, and plugged in; she knew *everything* that was happening for Millennials in the city. She told Celeste that her experience with Travis Darling had jaded her, but all Celeste saw was her tender heart. Merritt was remarkably patient, kind, and maternal when it came to Celeste, and she knew that Celeste could handle her pulsing, frenetic world only in small bites.

"I don't know what to do," Celeste says to Merritt now. "Benji came to the zoo with his girlfriend and his girlfriend's *daughter.* He and the girlfriend were arguing and then I noticed him staring at me. Then he asked for my card. *For a friend,* he said, and I believed him. I gave him my direct line. So do you think he broke up with his girlfriend already? He wants to take me to Madame Vo's, which is all the way down on Tenth Street. It's Vietnamese."

"Madame Vo's is on everyone's list because SJP eats there," Merritt says. "But I don't like the way they seat twos. It feels like you're on a date with the couples on either side of you."

"Should I cancel?" Celeste says. "I should probably cancel."

"No!" Merritt says. "Don't you dare cancel! I'm going to help you. I'm going to transform you. We are going to make this Benji fall in love with you in only one date. We are going to make him propose."

"Propose?" Celeste says.

Later, Merritt comes over to Celeste's apartment and she uses Celeste's laptop to Google Benji—Benjamin Garrison Winbury of New York City. In a matter of seconds they discover the following: Benji attended the Westminster School in London, then went to high school at St. George's in Newport, Rhode Island, and college at Hobart. Now he works for Nomura Securities, which further Googling discloses is a Japanese bank with a headquarters in New York. He sits on the board of the Whitney Museum and the Robin Hood Foundation.

"He's twenty-seven years old," Merritt says. "And he sits on two boards. That's impressive."

Celeste's anxiety ramps up. She has met several board members of the conservancy; they're all wealthy and important people.

Merritt scans through images of Benji. "The mother has resting-bitch face. The father is kind of hot, though."

"Merritt, stop," Celeste says, but she peers over Merritt's shoulder at the screen. She expects to see pictures of Benji with Jules and Miranda, but if those pictures existed, they've all been expunged. There is a photo of Benji with friends in a restaurant raising cocktails and one of him posing on the bow of a boat. There's a picture of Benji with a guy who must be his brother at a Yankees game, and in the picture Merritt is referring to, Benji poses with a refined older couple, the mother cool and blond, the father silver-haired and grinning. There's Benji hoisting a tropical drink under a beach umbrella and one of him in a helmet sitting astride a mountain bike.

"Girlfriend is gone, I'd say," Merritt remarks. "Thoroughly scoured from his feed. Let's check Instagram—"

"I don't want to check Instagram," Celeste says. "Help me find something to wear."

Celeste meets Benji outside Madame Vo's at exactly eight o'clock on Friday. Merritt advised Celeste to show up ten minutes late but Celeste is always prompt—it's a compulsion—and Benji is already waiting, which is, she decides, a good sign. Celeste has borrowed a dress from Merritt; it's a rose-gold Hervé Leger bandage dress that Celeste knows retails for well over a thousand dollars. Merritt was given it for free to wear to the opening of a new club, Nuclear Winter, in Alphabet City, and when Merritt is photographed in something as much as she was in this dress that night, she can never wear it again. Celeste is also wearing Merritt's shoes—Jimmy Choo stilettos—and she's carrying Merritt's gold clutch purse. The only things she's missing are Merritt's wit, charm, and confidence. Celeste calls upon advice her parents have been giving her since she was old enough to understand English: *Be yourself.* It's wonderfully old-fashioned and possibly ill advised. Celeste has always been herself, but that hasn't won her any popularity contests. Genus: *Girl Scientist.* Species: *socially awkward.*

"Hi," she says to Benji as she steps out of her Uber.

"Wow," Benji says. "I almost didn't recognize you. You look—wow. I mean, wow." Celeste blushes. Benji is taken aback, maybe even awestruck, and it doesn't seem like an act. Celeste is unsure whether to kiss him or hug him and so she just smiles and he smiles back, looking into her eyes.

Then he holds the door to the restaurant open and ushers Celeste inside. "Are you hungry?" he asks.

Benji is nice. Celeste didn't think there were any nice guys living in New York. The men she sees on the subway and on the street all seem to leer at her breasts or swear under their breath if she's taking too long with her MetroCard. The men at the zoo are no prizes. Darius, who took Celeste's job in primates when she got promoted, has confessed that he spends nearly half his paycheck on internet porn. Mawabe, who works with the big cats, is addicted to the video game Manhunt; he offers to teach Celeste to play it every time they have a conversation. The problem with people from the zoo in general is that they relate better to animals than to humans, and that's true for Celeste as well.

When Benji tells Celeste that he works for the Japanese bank Nomura, she pretends this is brand-new information. "You mean to tell me you're just another soulless private-equity guy?" she says, hoping it sounds like she is subjected to dates with such guys every weekend.

He laughs. "No, that would be my father." He then explains that he heads Nomura's strategic-giving department, so it's his job to give money away to meaningful causes.

"Eventually, I'd like to run a large nonprofit. Like the Red Cross or the American Cancer Society."

"My mother has breast cancer," Celeste blurts out. Then she bows her head over her crispy spring rolls. She can't believe she just said that, not only because it's the world's most depressing topic but because she hasn't discussed her mother's cancer with anyone.

Benji says, "Is she going to be okay?"

Well, that's the question, isn't it? Celeste's mother, Karen Otis, had stage 2 invasive ductal carcinoma that reached her lymph nodes, necessitating eighteen rounds of chemo and thirty rounds of radiation *after* her double mastectomy. She rang the bell at St. Luke's for her final treatment back in July and she isn't supposed to have a follow-up appointment for six months. But she was experiencing back pain so she'd gone to see her doctor this week. He ordered an MRI, one that Karen nearly refused because it was so expensive and Bruce and Karen were already loaded down with medical bills for treatments that weren't covered by Bruce's modest health insurance. However, Bruce insisted they do the test. When he talked to Celeste about it on the phone, he quoted a song by the Zac Brown Band. "'There's no dollar sign on peace of mind,'" he said. "'This I've come to know.'"

Celeste figures they must play this song on the Neiman Marcus Pandora, because she hasn't known her parents to like any song recorded after 1985.

The results of the MRI should be back on Monday.

Celeste raises her eyes to Benji's, his brown to her blue. Brown is a dominant gene. Benji's DNA, she is sure, is composed of only dominant genes. She's not sure what to say. Her mother's cancer is a private matter, and Celeste's entire relationship with her parents is too intense to explain to most people.

"I don't know?" Celeste says. She raises her voice at the end so that she sounds more hopeful than maudlin. She doesn't want Benji feeling sorry for her. This is one reason why Celeste doesn't like talking about Karen's illness. Also, she doesn't want to hear anyone else's inspiring story about a sister-in-law who went through *exactly the same thing* and is now running ultramarathons. Celeste doesn't mean to be ungenerous in her thoughts, but she has come to the chilling conclusion that we are all alone in our bodies. Irrefutably, immutably alone. And hence, no one's story offers hope. Either Karen will survive the cancer or it will metastasize and she will succumb to it. The only people Celeste can tolerate discussing Karen's treatment with are Karen's doctors. Celeste believes in science, in medicine. She has secretly been donating a hundred dollars a week to the Breast Cancer Research Foundation. "She's okay now. For the time being." Celeste is too superstitious to say her mother has beaten it, and she refuses to call her mother a survivor. Yet.

"Thank you for telling me," Benji says.

Celeste nods. He understands her, maybe? He senses the agony lurking behind her metered answers? He seems perceptive the way so few men—so few *people*—are. Celeste picks up a spring roll and dips it into the vinegary sauce. "These are really good."

"Wait until you taste the *pho,*" he says. He takes a sip of his beer. "So, tell me about the zoo," he says, and Celeste relaxes.

Benji insists on taking Celeste home in a taxi, which seems quaint. He asks the driver to wait while he walks Celeste to the door of her apartment building. She feels a huge relief that there will be no quandary about whether to invite Benji up and if she does invite him up about how far to let things go. Merritt believes in sleeping with a guy on the first date, but Celeste feels very much the opposite. She would never, ever.

Ever.

Benji tells her he would like to see her again. The following night, if she's free, he has tickets to see *Hamilton.*

Celeste gasps. Everyone in this city wants to see *Hamilton.*

Benji laughs. "Is that a yes?"

Before she can answer, he's kissing her. Celeste starts out feeling self-conscious about the taxi driver who is waiting, but then she surrenders. *There is nothing in the world that is quite as intoxicating as kissing,* Celeste thinks. She lets herself get lost in Benji's lips, his tongue. He tastes delicious; his mouth is both soft and insistent. His hands are on her face, then her neck, then one hand travels to her hip. Before she can guess what will happen next, he pulls away.

"I'll see you tomorrow night," he says. "I'll call with details in the morning." With that, he goes down the stairs and by the time Celeste's head clears, his taxi has pulled away.

They go to see *Hamilton*. It turns out that Benji's father is one of the original investors and has house seats, which are first-row center of the first balcony. Benji has seen the musical five times but he doesn't tell her this until afterward, when they're sitting at Hudson Malone, dipping jumbo shrimp into cocktail sauce, and Celeste has to admit, she would never have known. He had seemed as enraptured as she was.

Benji says he would like to see her Sunday and Celeste suggests a walk in Central Park. The park is a place she feels comfortable, nearly has a sense of ownership. She runs the reservoir any chance she can get and in the summer lies out on a towel in North Meadow. She loves Poet's Walk and the Conservatory Pond, but her favorite spot is surely a place Benji hasn't experienced before. She meets him south of Bethesda Fountain where a group of roller skaters congregates on weekends. There's a motley crew of characters—Celeste has come to recognize most of the regulars—who skate in an oval around a boom box that plays classic rock songs.

When Benji arrives, they're skating to "Gimme Three Steps," by Lynyrd Skynyrd.

"I didn't think anyone roller-skated anymore," Benji says. "This is like something out of 1979."

"I come here all the time," Celeste says. "I think I like it so much because this is the music my parents listen to."

"Oh, yeah?" Benji says. "Are they big Skynyrd fans?"

"All classic rock," Celeste says. "They especially love Meat Loaf." As Celeste watches the skaters, she thinks about being a little girl sitting in the backseat of their Toyota Corolla while her parents cranked up the volume on their cassette of *Bat Out of Hell*. They loved all the songs, but their favorite was "Paradise by the Dashboard Light." When the song got to the middle section with Meat Loaf and Mrs. Loud, Karen would sing the woman's part, and Bruce would sing the man's part, and at the end of the song they would belt out the lyrics together with so much gusto that Celeste got swept away. Her parents, in those moments, had seemed the most glamorous couple in the world. Celeste fully believed that if they had shared their car-singing with the wider world, they would be famous.

The roller-skating song changes to "Stumblin' In," by Suzi Quatro and Chris Norman, and Celeste gets lightheaded. It's *eerie;* this song is a particular favorite of her parents, and it's not a song that's played on the radio anymore. Celeste is stunned. She turns to Benji, overcome. How can she explain that this song so strongly evokes her parents, it's as if Betty and Mac are standing right there? Benji makes the slightest movement of withdrawal but Celeste can't possibly leave the skaters until this song is over. She sings along softly under her breath and Benji seems to understand. He stays patiently at her side. The next song is "Late in the Evening," by Paul Simon, which is also on Bruce and Karen's comprehensive playlist, but Celeste realizes that enough is enough. She takes Benji's hand and they stroll toward Bethesda Fountain.

After the park, Celeste and Benji sit at the Penrose and drink beer and watch football. When the game is over, Celeste asks Benji if he wants to grab a pizza and go back to her apartment but Benji says he likes to be in bed early on Sundays so that he's fresh and ready for the week ahead. Celeste says she understands and a part of her is relieved because it once again delays the question of what she and Benji will do once they're alone together. But a part of her is disappointed. She really enjoys Benji's company; he's easy to be with, he's funny, he tells stories about growing up in London and his family's immigration to New York City but he never sounds like he's bragging even though it's clear he's a member of the elite. He listens well too. He encourages Celeste to talk by asking good questions and then giving her lots of time to answer.

But she has probably bored him to death. And freaked him out by wanting to listen to old-people music in the park.

"I do have a question before we leave," Celeste says.

Benji covers her hand with his hand.

She can't believe she's being so bold. It's none of her business, but if Benji is giving her the brush-off and she might never see him again, she might as well ask this question.

"Shoot," he says.

"What happened with your girlfriend?" Celeste asks. "And her daughter?"

Benji sighs. "Jules?" he says. "We broke up. I mean, obviously. But it wasn't your fault. Things had been bad for a long time…"

"How long had you dated?" Celeste asks.

"Just over a year," Benji says.

Celeste exhales. Not as long as she had feared. "I guess I'm mostly worried about her daughter," Celeste says. "She seemed so attached to you."

"She's a great kid," Benji says. "But she has a father and two really involved uncles who live only a few blocks away, and when I broke things off with Jules, I told her I would be available if Miranda ever needed me." He stares at Celeste. "It says a lot that you would ask about Miranda."

His gaze is so intense that Celeste casts her eyes down to the scarred bar. "What about Jules?" Celeste says. "Did she take it okay?"

"Not at all," Benji says. "She threw her shoes at me. She screamed. She smashed her phone and that made her cry. She's in love with her phone."

"So many people are," Celeste says.

"That was part of the problem. She couldn't be present; she was self-absorbed; she wasn't a kind or thoughtful person. She called herself a stay-at-home mom but she never spent time with Miranda. She went to Pilates class, got her nails done, and met her friends for lunch, where they all engaged in competitive non-eating. The only reason we were even at the zoo that day was that I insisted. Jules was hung over from the night before and all she wanted to do was take a nap and a bubble bath before she met her friends Laney and Casper for dinner at some overrated restaurant where she would order a salad and eat two pieces of lettuce and half a fig. That trip to the zoo put it all in perspective."

"I just wondered," Celeste says. "I wasn't trying to steal you away or break you up."

Benji laughs and slaps money on the bar. "Let me walk you home," he says.

He kisses Celeste good-bye outside her apartment

building and the kissing becomes so heated that Celeste wants to ask him to come upstairs. But he pulls away and says, "Thanks for a great weekend. I'll talk to you later."

Celeste watches him take the steps two at a time, wave, then disappear down the dark street.

When she gets upstairs, she sends Merritt a text: I blew it.

How? is Merritt's response. What happened?

Celeste sends a series of question marks. A few seconds later, her phone rings. It's Merritt, but Celeste declines the call because suddenly she is too sad to speak. She should have canceled the date on Friday, she thinks. Because what she has learned over the course of this weekend is that she *is* lonely and life is nicer when there's someone to talk to. To kiss. To bump knees and hold hands with. Celeste was pretty sure from the start that she was an alien species, but it's disheartening to have it proved true.

He'll talk to her later. Yeah, right.

On Monday, as she is in her office reviewing the following summer's special programming—they're getting a gray-shanked douc langur from Vietnam, which makes Celeste think of Madame Vo's with Benji across the table—there's a knock on her door. It's a quarter after two and Celeste suspects it's Blair from the World of Reptiles saying she has to go home because she has a migraine setting in and can Celeste please cover her three o'clock snake talk, which also makes Celeste think about Benji.

"Come in," Celeste says halfheartedly.

It's Bethany, her assistant, holding a vase of long-stemmed pink roses.

"These are for you," Bethany says.

* * *

The next day, Celeste's father calls to say that Karen's MRI came back fine.

"Really?" Celeste says. It's not beyond her parents to lie to her about this.

"Really," he says. "Betty is as fit as a fiddle."

On Thursday night, Benji takes Celeste to a movie at the Paris Theater. The movie is French with subtitles. Celeste falls asleep as soon as it starts and wakes up at the end credits, nestled in Benji's arm.

On Friday, Benji takes Celeste to dinner at Le Bernardin, which is nine courses of seafood. About half the courses press at Celeste's boundaries. Sea urchin custard? Kampachi sashimi? She imagines telling her parents that Benji spent nine hundred dollars on a dinner that included sea urchin, kampachi, and sea cucumber, which is not a vegetable but an animal. There is wine with every course and Celeste gets tipsy. That night, she invites him upstairs.

She is nervous. Before Benji, there have been only two other men, one of whom was the TA in her Mechanisms of Animal Behavior class in college.

The next day, Merritt texts: So???????

Celeste deletes the text.

Merritt texts again: Come on, Celeste. How was our Benji in the sack?

Fine, Celeste texts back.

That bad? Merritt says.

Good, Celeste says. Which is true. Benji was very considerate, very aware of Celeste's desires—what felt good, what she liked. Maybe he was too aware. But that hardly seems like something to complain about.

Uh-oh, Merritt says.

* * *

There are dinners in SoHo, the Village, and the Meatpacking District. There is takeout Indian food and sushi and Vietnamese, now a favorite, that they eat at Celeste's apartment while watching *The Americans*. There is brunch at Saxon and Parole, where Benji introduces Celeste to the phenomenon of the bloody mary bar. She loads her glass up with a little of everything: celery, carrots, peppers, housemade pickles and pickled onions, bacon, fresh herbs, beef jerky, olives, and spirals of lemon and lime. Then, when her glass is accessorized like an eighty-year-old woman who is wearing every piece of jewelry she owns, she snaps a photo and sends it to Merritt, who responds ten seconds later: *Are you at Saxon and Parole?*

There's a reading at the Ninety-Second Street Y by a writer named Wonder Calloway, who reads a story about a woman Celeste's age who treks to the base camp of Everest with a man she loves but who does not love her in return. The man suffers from altitude sickness and has to turn back. The woman has to decide whether to stop or keep going. Celeste is moved by the story and by the whole idea that literature can be relevant to *her* life and *her* feelings. She never felt that way when reading *anything* in high school. At the end of the reading, Benji buys Celeste a copy of Wonder Calloway's short stories and Wonder autographs it. She smiles at Celeste and asks her name, then writes *To Celeste* in the book. Celeste is thrilled but also a little chagrined. The experiences Benji is showing her, while extraordinary, are messing with her head. She knows she is fine just as she is—she has a college education and a good job—but each date shows her all the ways she has yet to grow.

She reads the short stories on her commute to work and by the end of the week, she's finished and she asks

Benji for another book. He gives her *The Night Circus* by Erin Morgenstern. She loves it so much she reads it any chance she can get. She reads *Small Great Things* by Jodi Picoult and *The Nightingale* by Kristin Hannah. Benji gives her a list of books he's loved and together they go to Shakespeare and Company.

There's a new Burmese place on Broome Street that Benji wants to try and Celeste says, "Burmese?" She didn't even realize Burmese food warranted its own restaurant, but she should know by now that Benji seeks out far-flung cuisines—East African, Peruvian, Basque. He compares it to Celeste's love of exotic animals. She can talk all day about the Nubian ibex and he can talk about momos.

The Burmese restaurant has only ten seats, all of them taken, so they get their order to go and Benji says, "Since we're close, we might as well go to my place."

"You live nearby?" Celeste asks. Benji has referred to his apartment only as being downtown—but everyone lives downtown compared to Celeste. She has wondered why she has never been invited to Benji's apartment. After she finished reading *Jane Eyre,* she joked that Benji must be hiding a crazy wife in his apartment. He bristled at this. "It's nothing special," he said. "You won't like it."

If it's yours, I'll like it, Celeste thought, but she hadn't wanted to push. He obviously had his reasons.

Now, Benji leads Celeste into a high-rise luxury building in Tribeca, right next to Stuyvesant High School, and after greeting the doorman and the man behind the front desk, they get into the elevator and Benji presses the button that says 61B.

The sixty-first floor, Celeste thinks. Her building is a

six-floor walk-up and she lives on the fifth floor in the rear.

Celeste's ears pop on the way up and Benji is uncharacteristically quiet. The elevator fills with the scent of the Burmese food, but Celeste's appetite is quelled by a sudden case of nerves.

The elevator doors open and Celeste steps *into* an apartment. She's confused for a second.

"So, wait," she says. She turns around. Yes. The elevator has opened up right into Benji's apartment.

Benji takes Celeste's hand. She is fixated on the elevator. An elevator into his apartment. Did she know places like this existed? Yes, she has seen it in the movies. If she lived here, she might be tempted to press the elevator button just so she could experience its arrival *solely for her,* even when she didn't have to go anywhere.

The apartment has been professionally decorated and it's immaculately clean. There are black leather sofas, deep royal-blue club chairs, a colorful kaleidoscope of a rug, an enormous flat-screen TV, and, on either side of the TV, shelving that is crisscrossed on the diagonal, which is one of the coolest things Celeste has ever seen. She didn't even know diagonal bookshelves existed, but now all she wants in the world, other than an elevator that opens up into her apartment, are diagonal bookshelves and books to put on them.

There's a gourmet kitchen, which is sleek and gleaming except for a wide, rough-hewn wooden bowl filled with fruit: pineapple, mangoes, papayas, limes, kiwis. The fruit in that bowl probably costs as much as everything in Celeste's apartment. She feels a sudden hot shame about the futon she uses as a bed, covered with a quilt her mother bought from an Amish market in Lancaster, and about her Ikea side tables and the lamps she took from her parents' house, the bases of which are mason jars filled with beans. She cringes when she thinks of the vintage zoo posters that she had framed at great expense (they had been ninety dollars apiece and she had blanched) and the rainbow candles her mother made out of melted crayons.

Benji says something about showing her around and she mutely follows him into the bedroom, where there is a floor-to-ceiling window that looks out on uptown. All of Manhattan is rolled out before them, colorful and twinkling—and one of those lights, just one dim bulb a hundred-plus blocks up and to the east, is in Celeste's apartment window.

She presses her hands against the window, then removes them; she doesn't want to leave prints.

"You hate it," Benji says.

"How could you possibly think that?" she asks. "It... it... defies my humble vocabulary."

"My parents pay for it," Benji says. "They offered it to me and I couldn't say no. I mean, I guess I could have said no, but you'd have to be crazy to turn a place like this down."

Part of Celeste agrees, of course, but another part of her stands in righteous opposition. She thinks of Rocky, who rents a studio apartment in Queens; he rides the N/R train into the city at five o'clock each morning to run the bodega. At night, he takes classes at Queens College. He's studying to be a teacher. There's nobility in that, Celeste sees, a nobility and an ethic that's missing when one lives in an apartment that could easily cost seven or eight thousand dollars a month, paid for by one's parents.

"This building has a gym," Benji says. "And it has a pool. You can use the pool this summer. You can kiss North Meadow good-bye."

I don't want *to kiss North Meadow good-bye!* Celeste thinks stubbornly. But she knows she's being silly.

"We should appreciate this place while we can," Benji says. "My parents are threatening to buy me a brownstone uptown."

A brownstone uptown, Celeste thinks sardonically. Of course; the next logical step.

"East Seventy-Eighth Street," she murmurs in spite of herself. When she first moved to Manhattan, before she met Merritt, she used to spend her weekends wandering the Upper East Side, looking in windows, admiring leaded-glass transoms and iron fretwork. The block between Park and Lexington on Seventy-Eighth Street had been her very favorite. She used to gaze at the fronts of the homes and wonder just what lucky people lived there.

People like Benji.

"I'll tell them to look only on East Seventy-Eighth Street," Benji says. "Now let's eat."

Celeste spends all week feeling uneasy about Benji's privilege. She can't exactly claim to be blindsided, she knew it existed, but now that the extent of his wealth and advantage has been fully revealed, her view of him is tinged, ever so slightly, with distaste.

But then Benji informs her that on the last Sunday of every month, he volunteers at a homeless shelter in the basement of his parents' church on the Upper East Side. He asks Celeste if she would like to come. It entails serving the guests a hot supper, then making up the cots and staying overnight. Benji would be in a room with the men and Celeste with the women.

"It's not everyone's cup of tea," he says.

"I'll do it," Celeste says.

At Benji's suggestion, Celeste dresses casually, in sweatpants and a T-shirt. She helps chop vegetables for soup, and during the meal, she pours coffee. All of the guests want sugar in their coffee, lots of sugar; the pockets of Celeste's pants bulge with packets. One of the male guests starts calling her Sugar Girl. Benji hears him and says, "Hey there, Malcolm, slow your roll. She's *my* Sugar Girl." This makes everyone laugh. Benji has an easy rapport with the guests and knows many of them by name—Malcolm, Slick, Henrietta, Anya, Linus. Celeste tries to be respectful, to pretend she's working at a restaurant for paying guests, but she can't help wondering what circumstances life threw at these people that they ended up here. With one stroke of bad luck, she supposes, it could be her. Or her parents.

After dinner, Celeste makes up fourteen cots with sheets and blankets. She doles out one flat pillow per guest. Benji had told her that the guests go to bed early—even though TV is allowed until ten—because being homeless is cold and exhausting. Most of the women lie down right away. Celeste has brought her toiletries in a plastic bag and she goes to the bathroom to brush her teeth and wash her face. It's kind of like living in the college dorms, but she suspects Benji is right: this isn't for everyone. Celeste can't imagine Merritt here in a million years and his ex-girlfriend Jules even less so. She feels proud of herself for being a good person, then decides that the pride means she's not so good after all.

She kisses Benji chastely in the hallway between the men's dorm and the women's dorm.

"Are you going to be okay?" he asks.

"Yes, of course," she says.

"I wish I could be with you," he says. He kisses her again.

Celeste crawls onto her cot. The sheets smell like industrial-strength bleach, and the pillow is no more effective than a cocktail napkin. She stuffs her winter coat under her head.

She falls asleep listening to the other women snore. She misses her mother.

Merritt sends a text in the middle of the following week: How's everything with the boyfriend?

Boyfriend. The term gives Celeste pause—but there's no denying it. Celeste and Benji like each other. They're a couple, doing couple things. They're boyfriend and girlfriend. They're happy.

And then Celeste meets Shooter.

Saturday, July 7, 2018,
9:30 a.m.

NANTUCKET

Marty Szczerba (Skuh-*zer*-ba) is the head of security at the Nantucket Memorial Airport. It's a town job and comes with full benefits, which nearly makes up for the ball-breaking stress of his job in the summer.

June and July are foggy months. In the early summer on Nantucket, warm, moist air flows over the colder water. The moist air cools to its dew point and a cloud forms at the water's surface. This is fog. Marty wishes the town had a budget allocation for a program in Fog Awareness because cutesy T-shirts and mugs that display the slogan FOG HAPPENS don't seem to be getting the message across. Fog *happens*. It will happen to *you*, Mr. Millionaire from Greenwich, Connecticut, and to *you*, Ms. Billionaire from Silicon Valley. Your flight will be delayed or canceled if the ceiling drops below two hundred feet. You will miss your connection, and your day's plans—board meeting, daughter's graduation from Duke, rendezvous with your lover at the Hotel Le Meurice in Paris—will have to be canceled.

On Saturday, July 7, Marty sits down at his desk for his hot breakfast from Crosswinds, the excellent airport diner—a perk of the job he has greatly appreciated since his wife of thirty-one years, Nancy, died—to look over his choices on Match.com. Finding an age-appropriate woman who wants to live year-round on Nantucket has proven to be something of a challenge. Marty has been on three dates in the past six months, but not one of the women has looked a single thing like her profile picture, which has thrown the integrity of the website into question for Marty. His assistant, Bonita, is a thirty-three-year-old single woman and she keeps telling Marty to use Tinder.

"Swipe right," she always says. "Guaranteed action."

It has become a joke between them; Marty isn't after "action." What he would like is a meaningful relationship, a leading lady for his second act. It's just when he is, for the first time, seriously considering Tinder—*could* he swipe right, just once?—that a phone call comes in from the chief of police. They have found a body floating out in Monomoy and there's a person of interest—the name the Chief gives Marty is Shooter Uxley—on the run.

Marty writes down the name and a description of the guy—late twenties, dark hair, wearing Nantucket Reds shorts, blue oxford shirt, navy blazer, and loafers. Good-looking, the Chief says. Marty laughs because this description fits any of a hundred guys in the airport at any given moment over the summer. He shovels in a bite of scrambled eggs and home fries, clicks out of his dating website, and goes downstairs to talk to the state police.

Lola Budd has shocked every adult in her life by excelling at her job on the ticket desk at Hy-Line Cruises. Lola's aunt Kendra, who has been her legal guardian since her mother overdosed and her father went to jail, told Lola she was too young and *too immature* to handle such a job. Lola Budd has exhibited some uneven behavior both at home and at school, but she convinced her aunt that if she took on a job with a lot of responsibility, she would rise to the challenge. She wants to eventually attend the hospitality school at UMass and she feels a summer job that involves a lot of interfacing with the public will give her an advantage.

She has been at the job for three weeks now and she absolutely loves it. Unlike school, which she believes is a waste of time, this job makes her feel adult, relevant. She is doing something meaningful, facilitating travel between Nantucket and Hyannis, which is to say, between a summer fantasyland and the real world.

Lola especially likes her job on frenetic days like today, the Saturday after the Fourth of July, when the line is 117 people long. This boat, the 9:15, is sold out. Every boat today and all of the boats tomorrow are sold out. To get tickets for you, your wife, and your three kids back to America today, you basically had to make that your New Year's resolution and execute on January second.

The woman who works at the station next to Lola's, a sixty-year-old Nantucket native named Mary Ellen Cahill, has a sign in front of her computer terminal that says: BAD PLANNING ON YOUR PART DOES NOT CONSTITUTE AN EMERGENCY ON MY PART. Although Lola agrees with this sentiment, she finds the most satisfying parts of the job are when she can be a hero, when she can arrange for a last-minute ticket to appear out of thin air, when she can fix a snafu. Mr. and Mrs. Diegnan meant to book the last boat back on Friday, not Thursday, even though the ticket Susan Diegnan was showing clearly said Thursday, which was the day before. *No problem!* Lola would switch the Diegnans to the Friday boat, free of charge. Lola loves calling a name off the waiting list and seeing joy and relief flood someone's face.

This particular day, however, there will be no faces filled with relief, and Lola has nothing to offer but a manufactured expression of sympathy. "I'm sorry, sir. I don't have a boat ticket available until Monday at four oh five. You may want to check with the Steamship Authority. Their car ferries accommodate far more passengers." Today there will be people swearing in front of and *at* Lola. Today there will be people calling the Hy-Line a "Mickey Mouse operation" and a "dog-and-pony show."

A dog-and-pony show? Lola thinks. *What even* is *that?*

In job training, Lola was taught to accept all comments with calm reserve. The worst thing she can do is react with anger or indignation, thereby engaging the disgruntled customer.

"I have a problem," a puffy-faced pregnant woman says. She's sweating, carrying a toddler, and she has another child, perhaps five years old, clinging to her leg. "I was holding my ferry tickets for two adults and two children, and I set them down for a second and when I picked them back up I had only one adult and two children, which means someone stole one of my ferry tickets."

Lola nods. She has yet to be confronted with accusations of ticket theft, but if it was going to happen, she thinks, then it was going to happen today. On the other side of her counter is a mob of desperate people.

"Have you checked with your husband?" Lola asks. "Is it possible he took his ticket without you realizing it?"

"Of course I checked with my husband!" the woman says. "He doesn't have it. I was in charge of the tickets and he was in charge of handling the luggage, which really means sneaking in one final beer at the Gazebo because he has a crush on the bartender. The one with the…" She gives Lola a good approximation of the eye-roll emoji. "You know how men can be."

One of the things Lola has learned on this job is *how men can be*. Before, Lola knew only how boys could be. She has had a boyfriend for nine months, two weeks, and five days. His name is Finn MacAvoy and Lola loves him like crazy, it's true love forever, et cetera, and she presumes they'll end up getting married. Finn lost both his parents in a sailing accident and so he and Lola are both in the same situation—virtual orphans.

But Lola would be lying if she said she hasn't been amazed by the power she seems to exert over certain men. She has been propositioned by some and blatantly ogled by others. It's common for a pale, chubby, balding married dude to confront Lola and find himself tongue-tied. What had he meant to ask her? He can't recall.

And that's how men can be.

Lola feels bad for the pregnant woman (Aunt Kendra worries about Lola getting pregnant, but this job is effective birth control), but there is nothing she can do.

"I'm sorry," Lola says. "I don't even have one extra seat on this boat. The next seat I do have available is on Monday at four oh five."

"But I had the ticket!" the woman shrieks. "I paid for it! And someone stole it!"

"Unfortunately, we have no way to prove that," Lola says. "You might have dropped it accidentally and someone else might have picked it up. You do have your hands full."

"But my mother is sick!" the woman says. "She's in the hospital with shingles. We have to get off today. It's a medical emergency."

Lola remembers to breathe. It's astonishing the lies people will fabricate when they're desperate. Lola wants to quietly tell this woman that her best bet for getting off the island is to pretend she's going into labor. She will be taken to the mainland in a medical helicopter and her husband can use the one remaining adult ferry ticket.

"I'm sorry," Lola says. "And I'll have to ask you to step aside so I can help the next customer."

The next customer swears she has a reservation under

the name Iuffredo but Lola doesn't see it on her computer. "Could it be under a different name?" she asks.

"I have the reservation number somewhere," Ms. Iuffredo says. She rummages through her purse.

The phone rings. Lola looks down at her console. It's the emergency line, one that can't be ignored. Lola picks it up.

"Hello, Hy-Line Cruises. This is Lola Budd speaking. How may I help you?"

There's a split-second pause, then a man's voice. "Lola Budd? Oh, that's right. I forgot you worked there. Lola, this is Chief Kapenash. May I talk to your supervisor, please?"

"Oh, hi, Chief!" Lola says. The Chief is Finn's uncle and legal guardian. He is a very important person on Nantucket. He's the Chief. Of. Police. Lola has the distinct impression that the Chief doesn't like her, doesn't *approve* of her. He probably wishes Finn were dating someone like Meg Lyon, a three-sport athlete with good grades and squeaky-clean behavior. But now the Chief will witness Lola Budd in her new persona as a responsible, competent Hy-Line Cruises employee. "My supervisor isn't here right now. It's just me, Mary Ellen, and Kalik and we have a boat leaving in eight minutes so everyone is really busy. Gracie should be back soon, though. Would you like me to leave her a—"

"Eight minutes?" the Chief says. "Put Mary Ellen on the phone, please."

"She's with a customer," Lola says.

"Put her on the phone, Lola," the Chief says. "This is an emergency."

Marty Szczerba talks to Brenner, the state policeman on duty at the airport, and gets more details about the potential murder. The body they have is a twenty-nine-year-old New York City woman who came to Nantucket to be the maid of honor in her best friend's wedding.

The news lands like a punch to Marty's gut because his very own daughter, Laura Rae, is getting married in September and her maid of honor, Adi Conover, is like a second daughter to Marty. Because Marty's wife, Nancy, is gone, Marty has been the one planning the wedding with Laura Rae. They hired Roger Pelton to help—Marty and Roger go way back, as Roger's daughter Heather and Laura Rae played softball together in high school—and out of curiosity plus some kind of hunch, Marty asks Brenner the state policeman if Roger Pelton was doing the wedding.

"Roger Pelton?" Brenner says. "He's the one who called it in. But I'm pretty sure he's been cleared."

Cleared? Marty thinks. Of course Roger has been *cleared*. He certainly didn't murder anyone! Marty tells Brenner to call over to Blade, the private helicopter service, as well as the private plane hangar ASAP. There's no way a person of interest would escape Nantucket via a commercial flight. The TSA are too assiduous; they're bulldogs. They don't let peanut butter through, much less a person of interest.

Brenner says he'll handle the private services, and Marty alerts the TSA and the policeman on duty inside security, then he goes back upstairs to his desk to call Roger Pelton.

"I heard about the body," Marty says. "I'm so sorry, Roger."

"I can't...I don't think..." Roger sounds choked up. "I can't describe what it was like, pulling that poor girl out of the water. The bride was the one who found her floating, her best friend, her maid of honor. The bride was... well, she was hysterical and she's such a sweet, sweet kid. Her big day ended before it even began, and in complete tragedy."

"Aw, jeez, Roger," Marty says. He eyes his breakfast, which has now grown cold. He pushes the plate away. "Who's this person of interest on the lam? This Shooter Uxley?"

"On the *lam?*" Roger says. "Shooter?"

"The Chief called a little while ago," Marty says. "They're looking for someone named Shooter Uxley."

"He's the best man," Roger says. "Real gregarious kid, strong handshake. He went out of the way to notice the details. He's in event planning himself, I guess. I have twenty weddings this month alone and I can't remember anyone—but that guy I really liked."

"Well, he's missing," Marty says. "He was about to be questioned by the police and he escaped through a bathroom window."

"That doesn't look good," Roger says. "I guess you never know."

"Ain't that the truth," Marty says. And then he says good-bye, hangs up, and gets back to the job.

When Mary Ellen Cahill gets off the phone with the Chief, she hands Lola a slip of paper that says *Shooter Uxley*.

"He's not in the computer," Mary Ellen says. "So he would have been a walk-in. He's six feet tall, dark hair, wearing a blue blazer."

"That narrows it down," Lola says.

"My guess is he took the Steamship," Mary Ellen says. "I hope he took the Steamship. We're too busy for a murder suspect today."

Lola looks at the name again. Shooter Uxley. She pulls out her phone, which is expressly forbidden on the job, and finds him instantly on Facebook. He's as handsome as Tom Brady. And then Lola figures it out.

"Hold the boat!" she shouts. She tears out from behind the counter and goes charging out of the office and down the dock. George, the steward, is just about to fold up the gangplank.

"Lola." George winks at her. He has a crush on her, she knows, which will work to her advantage.

"I need to get on that boat," she says. "And as soon as I get on, I need you to find a policeman and send him right behind me."

"Whoa!" George says. "You buggin'?"

"Trust me, Georgie. This is an urgent matter. A life-and-death matter. Let me on the boat, then find a policeman."

"Seriously?"

"Seriously," Lola says.

She wants to go charging through the cabin but she maintains her calm. The stolen ticket. The movie-star handsome Shooter Uxley stole a ticket from the pregnant woman and went sauntering onto the boat. Lola scans the faces. She sees old people, sunburned people, men wearing Nantucket Reds; she sees yellow Labs, crying babies, Boston terriers, women who have had a lot of plastic surgery. She sees a kid in a Spider-Man costume. She sees a shirtless guy in a pair of American-flag trunks, passed out and snoring.

Lola Budd feels a hand on her arm. She turns to see a policeman standing with Fred Stiftel, one of the captains.

"Young lady," the policeman says. "What's going on?"

Lola glances around the cabin. Her eye snags on a

face in line at the bar. He has his sunglasses on but she recognizes the set of his jaw and the dark, floppy forelock. Blue shirt, navy blazer.

"There he is," Lola says to the policeman. She keeps her voice normal and her eyes trained on the person of interest. "Shooter Uxley. He's right there."

The officer approaches Shooter Uxley, who drops his beer. In the ensuing commotion, he tries to run but it's too crowded, there's nowhere to go, and the policeman easily pins Shooter's arms behind his back and cuffs him. He informs Shooter that he is a person of interest in an ongoing investigation and that he will be detained until the police release him from questioning. Everyone on the boat is watching. There's a low-level hum beneath a general hush.

It's just like on TV! Lola thinks. In this case, the hero is her! Lola Budd!

She can't wait to text Finn and tell him about it. The Chief will *have* to like her now.

Friday, July 6, 2018, 8:30 p.m.

KAREN

Bruce brings her a cup filled with a pale, fizzy liquid garnished with two blackberries.

"What is this?" she asks. "Not the punch? I don't think I can handle the punch."

"Not the punch," Bruce says. "It's a wine cooler, hand-crafted by yours truly. More cooler than wine, but I tasted it and I think you'll approve."

Karen takes a sip and is transported back to her youth. Her husband is the most thoughtful man on earth. "Thank you, baby," she says.

He kisses her full on the lips, and even after so many years, something inside of Karen stirs. "Anything for you," he says. "And I do mean anything."

At the table, Karen eats half a lobster tail. Each butter-drenched bite makes her moan with pleasure. Never in her life has anything tasted so divine.

Bruce tries to cajole her into tasting his biscuit. He pulls it apart so she can see the fluffy layers, but she demurs. The lobster was enough, more than enough.

Bruce chimes his spoon against his water glass as he holds it aloft. The tent grows quiet. Karen hopes this goes well. Bruce has had at least three cups of the punch.

Bruce says, "Ladies and gentlemen, I'm Bruce Otis, father of the bride."

His face radiates pride. He loves the title and Karen has to admit, she does too. The last time either of them were people of distinction, she thinks, was when they were in high school. She swam the butterfly leg on the four-hundred-meter relay team, and anyone who isn't impressed by that has never tried to swim a hundred yards of butterfly, much less swim it fast. And Bruce, of course, won the state wrestling title.

Karen gazes down at the table and closes her eyes to listen. *We would go to the post office to mail packages or check our box, and the line was always extra-long on Saturdays, but you know what? I didn't care. I could wait an hour. I could wait all day…because I was with Karen.* Karen embeds these words deep within herself. She has been loved in her life, deeply and truly loved. She has been known and understood. Is there anything more she is supposed to want?

But following her gratitude is…guilt. She hasn't told Bruce about the three pearlescent ovoid pills mixed in with her oxy. The pill is an unpronounceable compound that she bought illegally off the internet from a website she stumbled across when she Googled *euthanasia*. She e-mailed with a person named Dr. Tang who used to be an anesthesiologist, licensed in the state of Utah, and now provides terminally ill patients with drugs—for a price—so that people like Karen can end their lives with dignity.

The three pills cost twelve hundred dollars, eleven hundred of which Karen withdrew from her own personal checking account, money she had stashed away from working at the Crayola factory gift shop—her "mad money," as her mother used to call it. The other hundred dollars she stole from Bruce's wallet in five- and ten-dollar increments. She justifies the act because, unlike Bruce, she does not have a penchant for expensive clothes. She has never spent a frivolous dollar in her life, and she certainly isn't now. These pills will put her down instantly, saving both Bruce and Celeste the anguish, mess, and expense of her natural demise.

If she told Bruce, he would understand, she thinks. In thirty-two years of marriage, they have always viewed the world the same way. But what if he *doesn't* understand? Euthanasia is a topic that taps into deeply personal views of dignity and fear but, mostly, spirituality. Karen is afraid of pain, yes, she's afraid of the cancer eating her up from the inside. Bruce is afraid of being left alone, but he might also be afraid for her soul. She has no idea. They haven't been big church people, though they identify loosely as Catholic and celebrate all the holidays. They had Celeste baptized at St. Jane's in Palmer Township, back when Karen's mother and Bruce's parents were still alive. But Karen hasn't set foot in St. Jane's for years and years. Bruce has always seemed to be on the same page as Karen—she doesn't know what she believes in; she just tries to be a good person and hopes for the best. But what if Bruce secretly holds the tenets of the Catholic Church to be absolute and believes that suicide will automatically assign Karen to hell?

Karen hasn't talked to Bruce about life after she's gone because he refuses to acknowledge the inevitable—which, she supposes, is better than him accepting it too readily. As the assembled guests raise their glasses to Celeste and Benji, Bruce gazes down on Karen with an expression so filled with tenderness, with love and awe, that Karen can barely meet his eyes. Her ardor matches his own, but she is a realist. Cancer has made her a realist.

She has, for example, come to terms with the likelihood that Bruce will remarry. She wants him to. It won't be the same, she knows. He will always love her first, last, and best. The new wife will be younger—not as young as Celeste, Karen hopes—and she will add a new vitality to Bruce's life. Maybe the new wife will have a job that provides money for traveling, real traveling— national parks, cruises, bicycle tours of Europe. Maybe Bruce will take up yoga or watercolor painting; maybe he'll learn to speak Italian. Karen can imagine these possibilities without jealousy or anger. That's how she knows it's time for her to go.

After dessert, she and Bruce dance to one song, "Little Surfer Girl." Karen has always loved this song even though she has never been anywhere near a surfboard. She heard her father sing it once, in the car, when she was a little girl and that was all it took. Her father's happiness and his carefree falsetto had been contagious. Bruce knows about this memory and so he croons in Karen's ear. They are dancing—shuffling, really— among the other guests. No one is staring at them, she hopes, or taking photos or marveling that a woman so sick can still dance.

When the song is over, everyone claps. The band, it seems, is calling it a night. The evening is drawing to a close.

Celeste appears out of nowhere. "D-D-Did you have fun, B-B-Betty?"

"So much fun," Karen says. "But I'm exhausted."

She feels Bruce's hand against her back; even the light pressure is excruciating. The oxy is wearing off, leaving her nerve endings to glint like shattered glass. She needs one more oxy before she falls asleep.

"We have a big day tomorrow," Bruce says.

Celeste says, "T-T-Tag is really looking forward to

having a drink with you in his st-st-study. A drink and a Cuban cigar. He's been t-t-talking about it all week."

"He has?" Bruce says. "News to me."

"I'll get B-B-Betty up to b-b-bed," Celeste says.

"No, no, darling," Karen says. "You go have fun. It's the night before your wedding. You should go out with your friends."

Celeste gazes across the yard to where Benji and Shooter are filling up cups of beer at the keg. Shooter looks up, then jogs over. Karen is embarrassed at how handsome she finds him. He's as good-looking as the teen idols from her era—Leif Garrett, David Cassidy, Robby Benson.

"Mrs. Otis," he says. "Can I get you anything? I happen to know where the caterers stashed the extra lobster tails."

This makes Karen laugh despite the knives starting to twist in her lower back. How darling of Shooter to remember that Karen likes lobster, even though the days when she might have enjoyed a midnight snack are gone.

"We're going to bed," Karen says. "But thank you. Please take my daughter out on the town."

"I need my b-b-beauty sleep," Celeste says.

"You're beautiful enough as it is," Shooter says. "You couldn't get any more beautiful."

Karen looks at Shooter and notes the expression on his face: tenderness. Celeste inspires it in people, she supposes.

"I couldn't agree more," Karen says.

"The defense rests, then," Bruce says. He kisses Celeste's forehead, then nudges her gently toward Shooter. "Go have fun, darling."

"But Mac, T-T-Tag wants—"

"Your father will go find Tag for a drink," Karen says. "I'm perfectly capable of getting myself to bed."

Shooter takes Celeste's arm but she pulls away to give Karen one more hug and a kiss on each cheek. This is an echo of how Karen kissed Celeste good night when she was growing up. Does Celeste realize this? Yes, she must. Karen would like Celeste to come upstairs, tuck her in, read her something, even if it's just an article from the issue of *Town and Country* on the nightstand, and then lie with her until she falls asleep, just as Karen used to do with Celeste. But she will not be a burden. She will allow—indeed, encourage—Celeste to pursue her new life.

Bruce turns to Karen. "Let me just walk you upstairs."

"I'll be fine," Karen says. "Go find Tag now so you can come up to me sooner. I'd prefer that."

Bruce kisses her on the lips. "Okay. Just one drink, though."

Karen takes her time on her way to her room upstairs. She wants to experience the house at her own pace. She wants to touch the fabrics, sit in the chairs to judge their comfort; she wants to smell the flower arrangements, read the titles of the books. She has never been in a house like this, one where every piece of furniture has been professionally chosen and arranged, where the clocks tick in unison and the paintings and photographs are lit to advantage. The other homes Karen has visited in her lifetime have all been variations of her own—corner cabinets to display the wedding china, sectional sofas, afghans crocheted by maiden aunts.

Karen wanders into the formal living room and stops immediately at a black grand piano. The top of the piano is down flat and it's covered with framed photographs. The frames themselves strike Karen initially—the majority look like real silver and others are burled wood—and then she looks at the photographs. All of them seem to have been taken on Nantucket over the years. In the one that Karen studies first, Benji and Thomas are teenagers. They're standing on the beach in front of this house with Tag and Greer behind them. Tag looks then like Benji does now—young and strong with a wide smile. Greer's expression is inscrutable behind her sunglasses. She wears white capri pants with red pompoms dangling from the hems. *That's a playful touch,* Karen thinks. In her next life, she will own such pants.

When she goes to pick up the next photo, she hears someone cough. Karen is so surprised she nearly throws the photograph over her shoulder. She turns to see a woman curled up in one of the curvy modern chairs, like an egg in a cup. The woman is so still that Karen would guess she's asleep except that her eyes are wide open. She has been here all along, watching Karen.

"I'm sorry," Karen says. "You frightened me. I didn't see you."

The woman blinks. "Who are you, then?" she asks.

"I'm Karen Otis," Karen says. "Celeste's mother. The bride's mother."

"The bride's mother," the woman says. "Yes, that's right. I noticed you earlier. Your husband gave that lovely toast."

"Thank you," Karen says. She suddenly feels very weak. This woman has a British accent; she must be a friend of Tag and Greer's—nearly everyone here is. Karen remembers her vow to shine. "And what's your name?"

"Featherleigh," the woman says. "Featherleigh Dale. I live in London."

"Very nice," Karen says. She should excuse herself for bed but she doesn't want to appear rude to this Featherleigh. Why do the British give their children last names for first names? Winston. Neville. And Greer. When Karen first heard Celeste say the name Greer, Karen had thought it was a man. And this practice is catching on in America, she's noticed. She used to shake her head in wonder at the children who would come through the Crayola factory gift shop. Little girls named Sloane, Sterling, Brearley. Boys named Millhouse, Dearborne, Acton. And what about Celeste's maid of honor, Merritt? *Like the parkway,* Karen heard her say, though Karen has no idea what that means. "I just took a detour on my way to bed. But I should really excuse myself. It was nice to meet you, Featherleigh. I suppose I shall see you tomorrow."

"Wait!" Featherleigh says. "Please, can you stay another couple of minutes? I'm too drunk to get back to my inn right now."

"Would you like me to go find Greer?" Karen asks. She's only asking to be polite. The mere prospect of hunting down Greer is exhausting.

"No!" Featherleigh says. "Not Greer."

Something in her tone catches Karen's attention.

Featherleigh lowers her bare feet to the ground and leans forward. "Can you keep a secret?"

Karen nods involuntarily. She can keep a secret, yes. She is keeping a secret from her husband and her daughter, the secret of the three pearlescent ovoid pills, the secret of her intentions, and that is surely a bigger secret than whatever this Featherleigh wants to disclose.

Featherleigh says, "I've been involved with a married man. But he broke things off with me in May and I can't seem to recover."

"Oh dear," Karen says. What she thinks is *Serves you right!* Karen cannot abide adulterers. She doesn't like to judge but she can say with certainty that if any woman had pursued Bruce and managed to ensnare him in an affair, her life would have been destroyed. She and Bruce are lucky, she knows, in that they're both true blue. This isn't to say that Karen has never felt jealous. Bruce would sometimes talk about the housewives who came into his department looking to buy their husbands a suit, and Karen would wonder what the women looked like and if they flirted with Bruce more than he let on. There had been one period—right after Celeste left for college— when Bruce had come home from work singing unfamiliar country music songs and acting strangely distant, and Karen thought that maybe...maybe he'd met someone else. She finally asked him about it. He very bluntly said that he was just upset about Celeste being away. He was finding it more challenging than he expected. Karen admitted that she was taking it harder than she'd expected too, and they ended up crying together and then making love in the kitchen, which was something that hadn't happened since Celeste was born.

"I think the truth might interest you," Featherleigh says. "Maybe, maybe not."

Karen can't stand to hear it. "Stop," she says. "Please, just stop." Karen holds her hand aloft, as though she can swat the words away. She backs out of the room.

The words swarm her as she climbs the stairs. *I think the truth might interest you. I've been involved with a married man.* Karen badly needs an oxy and her bed. Why, oh why, did that woman choose Karen to confess to? How could Featherleigh's adulterous relationship possibly matter to *Karen?* She knows no one here! Featherleigh was clearly quite drunk, and drunk people, in Karen's experience, love nothing more than to confess. Featherleigh would have told anyone. It serves Karen right for snooping around.

When Karen finally reaches the top of the stairs, she's

disoriented. Is her room to the right or the left? She steadies herself with her cane and thinks, *The right.* When she turns right, it's the last door on the left. But at that instant, the door Karen thinks is hers opens and Merritt "as in the parkway" steps out. Merritt is the same young woman Karen thought of as the Scarlet Letter when she'd first arrived before she realized that it was Merritt, Celeste's maid of honor. Celeste adores Merritt, thinks she hung the moon, and while Karen is thrilled that Celeste has found a real friend, she can't help thinking Merritt is a little fast.

Fast. Now Karen sounds like her own mother, or even her grandmother. Who uses the word *fast* to describe a woman? No one. At least, not in the past forty years. Karen is sure Merritt must be very nice, otherwise Celeste would not be so fond of her. Tonight, Merritt is wearing black.

"I…" Karen says. Now she is really and truly confused. This house has more rooms than a hotel. "I think I've gotten turned around somehow? I thought that was *my* room."

"Oh, it is your room, Mrs. Otis," Merritt says. "I was just looking for Celeste. You don't know where she is, do you?"

"Celeste?" Karen says. "Why, she was outside when last I saw her. She's planning on going out with Benji."

"Okay," Merritt says. She seems to be in a tremendous hurry; she sidles her way past Karen and heads down the stairs. "Thank you, Mrs. Otis. Good night."

"Good night," Karen says. She stands in place, staring at the bedroom door. Looking for Celeste? In Bruce and Karen's room? What on earth for? Why not look for Celeste in *Celeste's* room, which is down the hall on the left? Clearly that Featherleigh woman has written her filthy graffiti on the walls of Karen's mind because all she can think is that she's going to open the bedroom door and find Bruce inside and then she will have to ask why Merritt and Bruce were in the bedroom alone together.

Hadn't Merritt been flirting with Bruce earlier that day? *Aren't you hot?*

Karen turns the knob and swings open the door. The room is dark and empty.

Karen exhales. She props her cane against the nightstand and sits on the bed. She waits for her heart to stop racing.

Saturday, July 7, 2018,
10:20 a.m.

Initial questioning, Greer Garrison Winbury, Saturday, July 7, 10:20 a.m.

After Nick finishes writing notes from his interview with Abby, he pulls on a pair of latex gloves and enters the cottage where Merritt Monaco was staying. He has gotten in ahead of forensics, which is how he prefers it.

"Tell me a story," he whispers. "What happened?"

The cottage has been decorated with a feminine sensibility, in pastels and florals. It's probably meant to evoke an English garden, though to Nick it feels cloying and overwrought; it's like walking into a Crabtree and Evelyn.

The living area appears untouched; Nick doesn't see a thing out of place. He moves into the bedroom, where the air-conditioning has been turned up so high, the room is like a meat locker. Nick has to admit, it feels good, nearly delicious after the oppressive heat outside. The bed is made, and Merritt's suitcase is open on the luggage rack with her shoes underneath. Her bridesmaid dress—ivory silk with black embroidery—hangs alone in the closet. Nick enters the bathroom. Merritt's cosmetics are lined up on the lower glass shelf—she is clearly a fan of Bobbi Brown—and her hairbrush and flat iron are on the upper glass shelf. Toothbrush in the cup.

She was nice and neat, Nick thinks.

A quick check of Merritt's cosmetic bag reveals eyeliners, mascaras, lipsticks, and powder, but nothing more.

Hmmpf, Nick thinks. He's looking for something, but what? He'll know it when he sees it.

On the dresser, Nick finds an open clutch purse that contains a driver's license, a gold American Express card, seventy-seven dollars in cash, and an iPhone X. He studies the license: *Merritt Alison Monaco, 116 Perry Street, New York, New York.* She's a beautiful woman, and young; she just turned twenty-nine. It's such a shame.

"I'm going to do right by you," Nick says. "Let's figure this out."

He picks up the iPhone X and swipes across. To his enormous surprise, the phone opens. *Whaaaaa...* He didn't think there was a Millennial alive who left her phone unsecured. He feels almost cheated. Does this woman have *nothing* to hide?

He scrolls through her texts first. There is nothing new today, and yesterday there's one text from someone named Robbie wishing her a belated "Happy Day of American Independence"; he hopes she's well. The day before that, Merritt sent a text to someone named Jada V., thanking her for the party. Attached is a photo of fireworks over the Statue of Liberty.

The call log is ancient as well—by *ancient,* Nick means nothing within the past twenty-four hours. Friday morning there was a call placed to a 212 number but when Nick calls that number from his own phone, he gets the switchboard for the Wildlife Conservation Society. Merritt had probably been checking in at work.

The scant offerings on Merritt's phone lead Nick back to Abby's comment that Merritt might have set her sights on someone who was already at the wedding. She wouldn't have to call or text anyone if she could talk to him in person.

Nick puts the clutch purse down where he found it and pokes around a little longer. A journal left lying around is too much to hope for, Nick knows, but what about a joint, a condom, a doodle on a scrap of paper with the name of the person she was involved with? She's too attractive for there not to have been *someone*.

He finds nothing.

The mother of the bride is still in her bedroom, and the bride herself still at the hospital. Nick finds Greer Garrison, mother of the groom, on her phone in the kitchen. She has obviously just told someone the awful news and is now accepting condolences.

"Celeste is devastated," she says. "I can't imagine her agony." She pauses. "Well, let's not get too far ahead of ourselves…we're all still in shock and"—here, Greer raises her eyes to Nick—"the police are trying to figure out what happened. I believe I'm the next to be interrogated, and so I really must hang up, I'm afraid. Love to Thebaud." Greer punches off her phone. "Can I help you?" she asks Nick.

She looks fairly put-together, considering the circumstances, Nick thinks. She's dressed in white pants and a beige tank; there is a gold cross on a thin gold chain around her neck. Her hair is sleek; she's wearing lipstick. Her expression is guarded. She knows her task is about to be interrupted and she resents it.

Nick says, "Ms. Garrison, I'm Detective Nick Diamantopoulos with the Massachusetts State Police. I'll need you to put away your phone."

"You're *Greek?*" she says, tilting her head. She's probably trying to reconcile the name with his black skin.

He smiles. "My mother is Cape Verdean and my father is Greek. My paternal grandparents are from Thessaloníki."

"I'm trying to write a novel set in Greece," she says. "Problem is, I haven't been there in so long, I seem to have lost the flavor of the place."

As much as Nick would love to talk about the Aegean Sea, ouzo, and grilled octopus, he has work to do. "I need to ask you some questions, ma'am."

"I don't think you understand my predicament here, Detective," she says. "This is *my* wedding."

"*Your* wedding?"

"I planned it. I have people to call. All of the guests! People need to know what's happened."

"I understand," Nick says. "But to find out exactly what *did* happen, I require your cooperation. And that means your undivided attention."

"You do realize I have a houseful of people?" Greer says. "You do realize that Celeste's mother has terminal *breast* cancer? And that Celeste has been taken to the hospital? I'm waiting to hear from Benji about how she's doing."

"I'll make this as fast as possible," Nick says. He tries to ignore the phone, although he would like to take it from her. "Would you please come with me to the living room?"

Greer stares at him with reproach. "How dare you order me around *in my own house*."

"I'm very sorry about that, ma'am. Now, please." He walks down the hall and hopes she follows him. He hears her rustling behind him so he stops at the entrance of the living room and lets her walk in first. He closes the door tightly behind them.

Greer perches on the edge of the sofa, leaning forward as though she might spring to her feet and escape at any moment. Her phone is in her lap, buzzing away.

"Can you please tell me what you remember *after* the rehearsal dinner ended?" Nick says. "Who went where?"

"The young people went out," Greer says. "The old people stayed home. The exception was Abigail, my daughter-in-law. She's pregnant. She stayed home."

"But both the bride and groom went out? Who else?" Nick pulls out his notepad. "Merritt? Did she go out?"

"Do you know what I do for a living, Detective?" Greer asks. "I write murder mysteries. As such, I am intimately familiar with procedure, so I appreciate that you have to ask these questions. But I can tell you exactly what happened to Merritt."

"Can you?" Nick says. "Exactly?"

"Well, not exactly," Greer says. "But the gist is fairly obvious, is it not? The girl drank too much or she took pills and then she decided to go for a swim in her dress and she drowned."

"You'll agree," Nick says, "that as viable as that explanation might be, it leaves some unanswered questions."

"Such as?"

"I've interviewed one witness who says she's fairly certain that Merritt *didn't* go out. So if she stayed home, where and what was she drinking? Did anyone see her? Did anyone talk to her? I just walked through the cottage where Ms. Monaco was staying. There was no alcohol in the cottage—no bottles, no empties, nothing. And no pills, no prescription bottles. As a fiction writer, you must know that it's difficult, when one is drinking and popping pills, to get rid of all incriminating evidence. Also, Ms. Monaco had quite a nasty cut on her foot. How did that happen? When did that happen?"

"Don't look for drama where there is none," Greer says. "There's a term for that in literature. It's called a *red herring*. The term was coined in the early 1800s by hunters who would throw a kipper down behind their trail to divert the wolves."

Nick almost smiles. He wants to dislike her but there's

something about her he admires. He has never met a published author before, and it's true—if she is a seasoned mystery writer, she might be able to help them. "That's good to know," he says. "Thank you."

"I came across Merritt at the end of the rehearsal dinner," Greer says. "She was hiding in the laundry room. She was crying."

"Crying?" Nick says. He remembers that Abby also said Merritt had been crying, out in the rose garden. "Did she tell you what was wrong?"

"She did not," Greer says. "And I didn't press; it wasn't my place. But I think it was clear she was feeling left out. Her best friend was getting married. Celeste was the center of attention and Merritt was at the wedding alone. Maybe she was depressed. I have no idea. But I can say that she was very upset, which only solidifies the argument that she drank too much, maybe took some pills, and went for a swim. Maybe she drowned accidentally or maybe it was intentional."

"Suicide?" Nick says.

"Is that impossible?" Greer asks. "It's not something one likes to think about, of course. But..."

"Let's get back to you," Nick says. "What did *you* do when the party ended? You and Mr. Winbury stayed home, is that right?"

"I don't see why what Tag and I did is relevant," Greer says.

"You're a mystery writer," Nick says. "So you're familiar with the term *alibi*?"

Greer raises an eyebrow at him. "Touché," she says. "Yes. My husband and Mr. Otis, the bride's father, had a drink in Tag's study and then they must have gone outside to smoke a cigar because when Tag came to bed, he smelled like smoke."

"We found a cigar stubbed out on a table under the

tent. One cigar. Would you guess that cigar belonged to your husband?"

"I would guess," Greer says, "but I couldn't be sure."

"What kind of cigars does your husband smoke, Ms. Garrison?"

"He smokes Cuban cigars," Greer says, "but more than one kind. Cohiba. Romeo y Julieta. Montecristo. I hardly see how the cigar is relevant to what happened to Ms. Monaco."

"We aren't sure it is relevant," Nick says. "Right now, we're just trying to figure out who was where after the party broke up. It appears a handful of people were out under the tent smoking and drinking, and we're trying to identify who exactly was there. Did Mr. Winbury say where he'd been when he came to bed?"

"I didn't ask where he'd been because I knew where he'd been. Here, on the grounds."

"What time did Mr. Winbury come to bed?"

"I have no earthly idea. I was asleep."

"You were asleep but you noticed that Mr. Winbury smelled like cigar smoke?"

"That's correct," Greer says. "I woke up just enough to know Tag was coming to bed and that he smelled like cigar smoke but not enough to bother checking the time."

"And you didn't wake up again until the morning?"

"That's correct. I woke up on my own at half past five."

"And, Ms. Garrison, what time did you retire? Did you go to bed right after the party was over?"

"No, I did not."

"What did you do after the party? While Mr. Winbury and Mr. Otis were in the study?"

"I sat down at my computer. I was writing. I have a deadline looming."

"I see. And where did you do this writing?"

"On my laptop," Greer says. "In my sitting room."

"And does that desk face a window?"

"Yes, it does."

"Did you notice any activity out the window?"

"I did not."

Nick pauses. Is it likely she didn't see *anything* out the window? No lights? No shadows?

"And what time did you finish writing?" he asks.

"I finished at eleven fifteen," she says.

"You're sure about that?"

"Yes," Greer says. "I made myself stop because I didn't want to be tired today."

"So after you finished writing, you went to bed. Say, eleven thirty?"

"Around then, yes."

Something about Greer Garrison's answers bothers him. They're too neat, too crisp. It's as though she has thought them through in advance. Nick takes a gamble.

"Would you bring me to the computer, please, Ms. Garrison?" he asks.

"I don't see why that's necessary."

"I would like to see it."

"Well, then, I shall go fetch it for you."

"No, you misunderstood me," Nick says. "I would like you to bring me *to* the computer."

"That's an unreasonable request," Greer says.

I've got her, he thinks.

"It's an unreasonable request for you to bring me to the computer but not for you to bring the computer to me? Because there's something you want to delete or hide on the computer?"

"Not at all," Greer says.

"Fine, then bring me to the computer. Please, Ms. Garrison."

She stares at him for a beat, then she rises.

Nick follows Greer down the hall. They step through an arched doorway into an anteroom—there's a niche built into the wall that holds an enormous bouquet of hydrangeas and lilies—and Greer opens a door. There's a sitting room with a sofa, a love seat, antique tables, and a desk that faces out a window. The view out the window is of the side yard—of a fence and the top of the pool house. Through a connecting door, Nick sees the master bedroom. There's a king bed made up with white sheets and a comforter and an assortment of pillows, all of them neatly arranged. A cashmere blanket embroidered with the word *Summerland* is draped on the diagonal across the corner of the bed. Nick blinks. Greer found the time to make her bed so artfully after she found out Merritt was dead—or before? But at that moment, a woman pops out of the master bath holding a bucket and a roll of paper towels. The housekeeper.

"You'll excuse us, please, Elida?" Greer says.

Elida nods and scurries away.

"Does Elida live here?" Nick asks.

"She does not," Greer says. "She works seven to five. Today she came a bit earlier because of the wedding."

Nick follows Greer over to a simple mahogany desk, gleaming as though just polished. On the desk are a laptop, a legal pad, three pens, a dictionary, and a thesaurus. There's a Windsor chair at the desk and Nick takes a seat and turns his attention to the computer. "So this here, *A Slayer in Santorini,* is the piece you were working on last night?"

"Yes," Greer says.

"It says you closed it at twelve twenty-two a.m. But you told me eleven fifteen."

"I stopped writing at eleven fifteen. I closed the document at twelve twenty-two, apparently."

"But you said you went right to bed. You said you went to bed around eleven thirty."

"I did go to bed," Greer says. "But I had difficulty falling asleep, so I had a drink."

"Of water?"

"No, a *drink* drink. I had a glass of champagne."

"So sometime between eleven fifteen and twelve twenty-two a.m. you went to the kitchen for a glass of champagne?"

"Yes."

"And did you notice any activity then?"

Greer pauses. "I did not."

"You didn't see anyone?" Nick says.

"Well, on my way back to my room I saw my daughter-in-law, Abby. She was going to the kitchen for water."

"She was?"

"Yes."

"Why didn't she get water from the bathroom?"

"She wanted ice, is my guess. She's pregnant. And it was a warm night."

"Did you and Abby have a conversation?"

"A brief one."

"What did she say to you?"

"She said she was waiting for Thomas to get home. He had gone out with Benji and the others."

Ah, yes. Nick recalls that Abby was annoyed that Thomas had decided to go out. "Anything else?"

"Not really, no."

"Did you see anyone else?"

"No."

"And after you got your champagne, you returned to your bedroom to sleep?" Nick asks.

"That's right."

Nick pauses to scribble down notes. She lied to him

ten minutes ago; there's no reason to believe another word she says.

"Let me switch gears here. We found a two-person kayak overturned on your beach. Do you own such a kayak?"

"It belongs to my husband," Greer says. She cocks her head. "It was left overturned on the beach, you say?"

"Yes. Does that seem odd to you?"

She nods slowly. "A bit."

"And why is that?"

"Tag is fanatical about his kayaks," Greer says. "He doesn't leave them just lying about."

"Is it possible that someone else used the kayak?"

"No, he keeps them locked up. If the two-person kayak was left out then he must have taken someone out on the water. If he were going out alone, he would have taken his one-person kayak."

"Any idea who he might have taken out?"

Greer shakes her head. She looks far less confident than she did a moment ago, and Nick feels her losing her grip on the explanation she had so neatly written in her mind.

"I suppose you'll have to ask my husband that," she says.

Wednesday, May 30-Tuesday, June 19, 2018

TAG

He takes Merritt's number but makes no plans to see her again. It's a one-and-done, a weekend fling, which is how he likes to keep things with other women. There have been half a dozen or so over the course of his marriage, one- or two-night stands, women he never sees or thinks of again. His behavior has nothing to do with how he feels about Greer. Or maybe it does. Maybe it's an assertion of power, of defiance. Greer entered the marriage with more money and higher social standing. Tag has always felt a touch inferior. The prowling around is how he balances the scales.

When he gets back to New York, two things happen. One is that Sergio Ramone calls. Tag considers letting the call go to voice mail. He fears that Sergio has learned that he took Merritt to the wine dinner and he's calling to express his disapproval. But then Tag reminds himself that taking Merritt to the dinner was done with Greer's blessing.

"Hello," Tag says. "Sergio, how are you?"

It turns out that Sergio is calling for a very different reason. His contact at Skadden, Arps has told Sergio that there's grumbling within the litigation department about Thomas Winbury. He isn't pulling his weight, apparently. He takes long lunches and unscheduled vacation days. He often leaves work at five o'clock when other associates stay until nine or ten at night. At his last review, he was given a warning, but he's shown no improvement. There's talk of letting him go.

Tag sighs. Thomas has always put in just enough work to get by. Abby's family is so wealthy that Tag suspects Thomas *wants* to get fired. He'll work for Mr. Freeman in the oil business. He'll move to Texas, which will break Greer's heart.

"Thanks for the heads-up, Sergio," Tag says. "I'll have a talk with him." He hangs up before Sergio can ask him how the wine dinner was and then he swears at the ceiling.

A few nights later, Thomas and Abby come for dinner at Tag and Greer's apartment. Greer has made a leg of lamb and the apartment is redolent with the smell of roasting meat, garlic, and rosemary, but as soon as Abby enters the apartment, she covers her mouth with her hand and bolts for the bathroom.

Thomas shakes his head. "I guess she's gone and ruined the surprise," he says. "We're pregnant again."

Greer reaches out for Thomas, but they all know to limit their reaction to cautious optimism.

Tag shakes Thomas's hand, then pulls him in for a hug and says, "You'll make one hell of a father." No sooner are the words out of his mouth than Tag doubts their veracity. *Will* Thomas make a hell of a father? He needs to buckle down at work, start setting an example. Tag nearly brings Thomas into his study to tell him as much, but he decides, in the end, to let the occasion be a happy one, or as happy as it can be with a woefully sick Abby. He'll talk to Thomas another time.

That night, Tag can't sleep. He slips from bed and goes into his study. His three home studies—the one in New York, the one in London, and the one on Nantucket—

are sanctuaries dedicated to Tag's privacy. No one enters without permission except the cleaning ladies.

Tag takes out his phone and scrolls for Merritt's number. She answers on the third ring. "Hey, Tag."

Her voice brings it all back. There is noise in the background, voices, music—she's out somewhere. It's two o'clock in the morning on a Wednesday night. Tag should not be pursuing this.

"Hey yourself," he says. "I hope I didn't wake you."

She laughs. "I'm downtown at this speakeasy thing. It looks like a laundromat but there's a secret door, a code word, and voilà, you enter the underworld. Do you want to come join me? I'll tell you how to get in."

"No, thank you," Tag says. "I just called to tell you your instincts were correct. Abby *is* pregnant. She and Thomas told us tonight at dinner."

"Who?" Merritt says.

"Abby. Abby, my daughter-in-law. She was with you during Celeste's bachelorette weekend. You said—"

"Oh, that's right," Merritt says. "Abby. Yeah, I'm not surprised."

Tag feels like a fool. He should hang up. He's going to see Merritt in a few weeks at the wedding and it would be best if their dalliance were a thing of the past. But there is something about this girl. He can't leave it alone.

"Where did you say your apartment is?" he asks. "I think I've forgotten."

Tag sees Merritt the next day after work, and the day after that, and on Saturday he tells Greer he's going to run in Central Park but instead he goes to Merritt's apartment. After sex, they walk down the street to a really good sandwich place and order lunch and sit side by side and talk and laugh—and in the middle of it, Tag realizes that he is losing control of the situation. What is he doing? Anyone might see him here with this girl.

He walks Merritt back to her apartment and she pulls him in by the front of the shirt. She wants him to come inside. And he wants to, oh, does he want to. He agrees, but just for a minute, he says.

She has turned him into a teenager again. His desire is so intense, so relentless, it frightens him. He can't remember wanting anyone or anything as much as he wants this girl. His feelings for Greer seem almost quaint by comparison.

Merritt is twenty-eight years old, nearly twenty-nine. She has a lukewarm relationship with her brother and she doesn't speak to her parents at all. This, Tag can't understand.

"What do you do on Thanksgiving?" he asks. "Christmas?"

She shrugs. "Last year, Thanksgiving was Chinese food and a movie. On Christmas, I flew to Tulum for a yoga retreat."

Tag senses a hole inside of Merritt, an emotional hole, which he knows is very, very dangerous. He needs to end this thing now, while there is still time to recover before the wedding. But the attraction grows stronger. Soon, he thinks only of Merritt—when he's working, when he's exercising, when he and Greer are eating dinner at Rosa Mexicano. Greer is consumed with finishing her novel and planning Benji's wedding. She is so focused on these two projects that she doesn't notice any change in Tag. She doesn't see him, she doesn't hear him, and sex is out of the question. She jokes that they'll have a second honeymoon once Benji and Celeste are on their first honeymoon. But Tag knows that once the wedding is over, Greer will collapse, exhausted, or she'll go into a funk because there's nothing left to look forward to.

He schedules a drinks meeting with clients at the bar at

the Whitby Hotel and he asks Merritt to go sit at this bar without letting on that she knows him. She does exactly as he asks, wearing a slinky black dress and five-inch stilettos, and Tag excuses himself from his clients for a moment. He follows Merritt into the ladies' room, where they lock the door and have shockingly hot sex. When Tag walks out, he is so intoxicated he doesn't care who sees him.

Later, he chastises himself for being reckless. He asks himself what he's doing.

She is given tickets to see Billy Joel at Madison Square Garden. Will he go with her?

"I can't," he says. "It's too risky."

"Please," she says. "They're second-row seats."

"That's the problem," he says. "If they were nosebleed seats, I wouldn't worry about seeing anyone I know."

"Fine, then," she says. "I'll take Robbie."

"Who's Robbie?"

"My on-again, off-again," Merritt says. "He's the day-time bartender at the Breslin."

Tag is addled by news of Robbie's existence, although what did he expect? Naturally, there's a Robbie. He wouldn't be surprised if there were half a dozen Robbies. The thought is so dispiriting that the next day finds Tag at the bar of the Breslin at lunchtime, ordering the rabbit terrine and a scotch egg—at least it's a good place—from a big Irish hunk. Robbie. He has six inches and forty pounds on Tag, plus he's twenty-five years younger. This is who Merritt *should* be dating. Not only is Robbie a bartender, he's an aspiring actor—and idle chitchat reveals that he's just been cast in a pilot. Tag hates Robbie with a bloodred passion; he leaves him an absurdly large tip.

The night of the concert, Tag is agitated. He imagines Robbie putting his shovel-size hands on Merritt's waist and swaying to the music behind her. He's so unsettled by this vision that he tells Greer he isn't hungry for dinner; he might have a sandwich in his study later.

He sends Merritt a text: Let me know when the concert is over. I'll meet you at your place.

Twenty fraught minutes later, he receives a text back: K.

K. Has there ever been a less satisfying response in the short history of texting? Tag thinks not.

Eleven o'clock comes and goes, eleven thirty. Tag succumbs to his hunger and heads to the kitchen for a ham sandwich. He sees a light on in their bedroom. He opens the door to find Greer wearing her tailored blue pajamas. Her hair is in a bun held up with a pencil and her reading glasses are perched on the end of her nose. There's a glass of chardonnay to the right of her laptop. She's in the middle of a scene, he can tell, but she looks up and smiles.

"Shall we go to bed, then?" she asks.

Yes, Tag thinks. *Say yes.* Look how elegant his wife is, how productive, how ingenious. She's absolutely everything he could ever want in a woman.

"I need to keep going," Tag says. "Ernie and I are putting that Libya deal together. It's going to be huge. He'll be at the office first thing in the morning and I have to have the numbers waiting for him."

Greer shuts off her computer. "Well, I'm calling it a night." She raises her face for a kiss. "Don't stay up too late."

"You know I won't," Tag says. "Love you, darling."

He waits until twelve thirty and when there is still no text from Merritt, he sneaks out of the apartment, hails a taxi, and goes down to Perry Street. He stands outside her building and buzzes her apartment, but there's no answer.

Then he hears her laugh. He looks down the street to spy Merritt and Robbie on approach. They are walking close together but not touching. Tag tries to hurry down the steps of the building before she sees him…but it's too late.

"Tag?" she says.

He's caught. It's nearly one in the morning; there is no way to play this off as casual. He's a worldly, successful man standing in front of a girl's apartment building like some schlub in a rom-com; if Greer could see him now, she would find him so absurd she might even laugh. But the sight of Merritt sends a surge of adrenaline through Tag. He feels enough passion to kick Robbie the lickspittle to the curb despite his size advantage and then carry Merritt up the stairs over his shoulder. She's wearing a white crocheted sundress and dangling earrings and her hair is up. She's as fetching as any woman he's ever seen.

"I need to talk to you," he says.

"Okay," Merritt says. She looks up at Robbie. "Robbie, this is Tag. Tag, Robbie."

Tag extends a hand automatically. Robbie says, "Weren't you in for lunch the other day? At the Breslin?"

Tag shouldn't have left such a big tip. It would have been impossible to forget.

"Were you?" Merritt says. She looks amused. She now understands the power she has over him. He has made such a mess of things, he thinks. He should have just gone to the concert.

Merritt's birthday is June 18. She wants to do something special. She wants to go away with Tag. Tag considers this request. Where would they go? To Paris? Rome? Istanbul? Los Angeles? Rio de Janeiro? He does some research on Istanbul but decides flying overseas is impractical and risky, even if they do so separately. He books a hotel room in New

York instead, at the Four Seasons downtown. He worries a bit because before he and Greer moved to New York, they used to stay at the Four Seasons in midtown, and they like to stay at Four Seasons when they travel. But it's a brand he trusts and it's only one night and the hotel is all the way down by the Freedom Tower, which isn't a neighborhood that anyone he knows frequents after five o'clock.

The weekend before Merritt's birthday, Tag and Greer are on Nantucket. Greer has a three-hour meeting with Roger Pelton, the wedding planner. Tag goes for a ride in the kayak, then he drives into town to get lunch—he loves the soft-shell crab sandwich from Straight Wharf Fish— and while he's at it, he decides to buy Merritt a present. He has been trained by Greer to understand that the only acceptable present for a birthday or anniversary is jewelry. He walks into the Jessica Hicks boutique thinking he will get earrings or a choker, but when he describes the young woman he's buying for—he pretends the gift is for his daughter-in-law, Abby, who is pregnant with their first grandchild—Jessica shows him the silver ring with the lace pattern embedded with the multicolored sapphires.

"It's meant to be worn on the thumb," Jessica says.

"The *thumb*?" Tag says.

"Trust me," Jessica says. "It's a thing."

Tag buys the thumb ring and leaves the store feeling a sense of giddy anticipation. The ring is beautiful; Merritt will love it, he's certain.

His happiness is a thing.

On the eighteenth, Tag gets to the hotel early. He has had a bouquet of expensive roses delivered to the room as well as champagne. He sets the box from Jessica Hicks between the flowers and the ice bucket. Everything is as it should be, but he can't relax. Something about this scenario makes him feel like a run-of-the-mill cheat. He's a stereotype, a middle-aged man sleeping with one of his daughter-in-law's friends because his wife is busy and distracted and he needs to boost his self-esteem.

He waits in the room for Merritt to arrive but she texts to say she's at the salon getting a bikini wax and she'll be late. He's a bit turned off by her frankness. Is it necessary to tell him she's getting *waxed*? It feels inelegant.

He decides to go down to the bar for a drink. A real drink.

As soon as he walks into the bar, he locks eyes with a man, then he realizes with horror that the man is his son Thomas. Before Tag can think better of it, he ducks behind a pole. He waits a few seconds, not breathing, his heart skidding to a near stop as he waits for Thomas to confront him and ask what he's doing there. What should Tag say? Meeting a client for drinks, of course, and then when the client doesn't materialize, Tag can pretend to be annoyed and skip out to make a phone call.

He waits. Nothing happens. Tag saw Thomas, but is it possible that Thomas didn't see Tag or saw him but somehow didn't register the face as that of his father?

Enough time passes that Tag decides to take action. He peers around the column. Thomas is staring into his highball glass. He looks miserable. As much as Tag realizes the urgency of him leaving the bar while he can, he's arrested by his elder son's demeanor. He thinks back to the phone call from Sergio. Thomas is leaving work early; Thomas is taking unscheduled vacations. And now here he is having a drink at a hotel bar at the far tip of Manhattan, which isn't anywhere close to his office. Tag wants to sit down next to Thomas and ask him what's going on.

Maybe he's been fired?

Maybe Abby lost the baby?

If it's either of those, Tag will find out soon enough. He

needs to get out of the bar undetected. He turns and hurries out, hoping Thomas won't recognize him from behind. He goes back up to the room for his bag and texts Merritt.

Something came up. Room 1011 is yours for the night. There's champagne and a little gift for you. But I have to take a raincheck. Sorry about that. Happy birthday, Parkway.

Tag takes a taxi back uptown and walks into his apartment to find Greer in her yoga clothes, folded over in child's pose on the living-room rug. She looks up and beams. "You're home!" she says.

And just like that, the spell is broken. Tag is finished fooling around. He is back to being a dutiful husband, a steadfast father, and an expectant grandfather. Merritt calls in tears; she leaves messages, sends texts. She calls him a bastard, she tells him to stick a fork in his eye, only that's not how she phrases it.

She calls Tag's office and speaks to Miss Hillery, Tag's very proper, very British secretary, who is so devoted to Tag that she followed him over from London.

"A Ms. Parkway called?" Miss Hillery says, handing Tag the message slip. "She said it's urgent."

"Thank you, Miss Hillery," Tag says with what he hopes is a carefree smile. He closes the door to his office and collapses at his desk. Merritt calling him at the office is one step away from Merritt calling the apartment or—because Tag knows Celeste might naively give Merritt the number—calling Greer's cell phone.

Well, she's going to get what she wants. Tag calls Merritt back.

"Tag?" she says.

"What on God's green earth are you *doing?*" he asks. "You can't call me here."

"I'm pregnant," she says.

Saturday, July 7, 2018,
12:00 p.m.

NANTUCKET

By midmorning, the entire island is buzzing with news of the Murdered Maid of Honor. Marty Szczerba calls his daughter, Laura Rae, initially just to hear the sound of her voice and to reassure himself that she is okay, but then he asks about Adi Conover—is *she* okay?—and Laura Rae says, "Yes, Dad, obviously. What's wrong with you?" Marty ends up spilling the whole story, or what he knows of it. Laura Rae tells her fiancé, Ty, who works for Toscana Excavating and who is as tight-lipped as they come. But Ty swings by his mother's house for a second breakfast and he tells her the story. Carla, Ty's mother, volunteers at the Hospital Thrift Shop Saturdays at noon and she proceeds to tell every single person who walks in the door.

Finn MacAvoy gets a text from his girlfriend, Lola Budd, saying I caught a murder suspect! Finn is at Cisco Beach giving surfing lessons to a group of overprivileged eight-year-olds who all want to be John John Florence. Finn casually flings out the content of Lola's text. "My girlfriend caught a murder suspect," he says.

The next thing Finn knows, he is surrounded by the young surfers' mothers, and they're all talking about someone called the Murdered Maid of Honor and they ask Finn if the police had caught the guy and who it was and Finn is sorry he ever opened his mouth.

* * *

Finn's twin sister, Chloe MacAvoy, has taken to her bed despite the fact that it's a hot, sunny summer Saturday and work that day has been canceled. Work has been canceled because Merritt Monaco, the maid of honor in the Otis-Winbury wedding, is dead. Roger Pelton found her floating just off the beach earlier that morning.

Siobhan had called to tell Chloe about the death herself instead of having Donna, the waitstaff manager, do it because Siobhan is that kind of owner. She takes responsibility for her employees.

"Chloe," she said. "The wedding has been canceled. Merritt Monaco, the maid of honor, passed away overnight."

"Passed away?"

"She died, Chloe," Siobhan said. "She's dead. She drowned out in front of the house last night."

"But..." Chloe said.

"That's all we know for now," Siobhan said. "The police are working on it."

The police? Chloe thought. She had seen Uncle Ed out on the deck on his phone a short while earlier, but Uncle Ed was always on the phone.

Chloe had hung up with Siobhan and closed her eyes. Chloe had been kept far away from death since she was seven years old, when Uncle Ed and Auntie came to tell her and Finn that their parents were dead. Both of them at once, killed in a sailing accident. Chloe hadn't really gotten it then; she had been too young. What did she know of death at age seven? Not one thing. Her parents' death has gotten much worse for Chloe as she's grown older. Now she knows what she's missing. She has no father to treat her like a princess; she has no mother to rebel against. She does have Uncle Ed and Auntie and they are strong, reliable, capable caregivers... but they aren't her parents. Whenever Chloe thinks about her father playing "Please Come to Boston" on his guitar or her mother painting a rose on Chloe's cheek, she feels unbearably sad.

She texted Blake, a girl who worked with her, Merritt, the maid of honor, is dead.

Blake texted back, I know. I heard there was a lot of blood.

Chloe ran to the bathroom to throw up. After the rehearsal dinner the night before, Chloe had a few beers with Blake and Geraldo. Geraldo is twenty-four years old, from El Salvador, and he always provides Chloe and Blake with postshift alcohol.

Uncle Ed had knocked on the door. "You okay in there?"

"Fine," Chloe said. She wanted to ask Uncle Ed about Merritt but she couldn't handle the conversation right that second. She cursed Geraldo.

Now, back in bed, Chloe revisits the events of the party. Most jobs go the same way. Chloe and her co-workers show up early in their immaculate black pants and crisp white shirts, showered, fresh-faced, ready to serve. Because she is only sixteen, Chloe can't serve alcohol, although this rule gets bent all the time. Nearly the first thing that happened at this rehearsal dinner was that Greer Garrison, the mother of the groom, asked Chloe for a refill of champagne. Chloe told Ian, the bartender, that *he* needed to serve Ms. Garrison but Ian was three-deep and he told Chloe to find Geraldo. But Geraldo wasn't around and Greer Garrison sang out for a refill again with a pointed look at Chloe, so Chloe grabbed the Veuve Clicquot from the cooler and discreetly filled Ms. Garrison's glass.

Chloe didn't notice much else about the actual festivities other than the guests growing drunker and drunker. There was a blackberry mojito punch and the guests were inhaling it. Chloe cleared a bunch of half-empty punch cups with mint leaves and whole fat blackberries trapped among the melting ice; she brought them to the kitchen, where she found Geraldo manning the kitchen trash. He picked up the cup with the most punch and drank it.

"Ew," Chloe said. "Someone else's mouth was on that. Also, if Siobhan sees you doing that, she'll fire you."

"Siobhan just left," Geraldo said. "She has four other events tonight. She won't be back."

"Donna, then," Chloe said, but they both knew Donna wasn't strict at all. If she saw Geraldo drinking, she would do no more than roll her eyes.

"Try it," Geraldo said.

"No," Chloe said.

"Just try it," Geraldo said.

Chloe had never been good at resisting peer pressure. Plus, the drink was a delicious-looking purple color. Chloe drank half a cup without letting her lips touch the rim. The drink was so fruity and minty that she could barely taste the alcohol, but almost instantly she felt lighter, more relaxed.

She fell into the habit of sneaking a few sips of punch whenever she cleared. She wasn't getting drunk, she didn't think; if anything, the punch was making her more perceptive. Chloe wanted to be a writer like Greer Garrison. But she didn't want to write murder mysteries; she wanted to write a blog about fashion and lifestyle, what was new, what was *hot*. The great thing about this wedding in particular was how attractive and stylish everyone was. Chloe had mentally snapped pictures of at least four outfits, including the outstanding jumpsuit that Greer Garrison was wearing. She looked *amazing* and she was in her *fifties!*

When Chloe was heading back to the kitchen—there was a British woman at table 4 who demanded more biscuits—she smelled smoke, and as Greer had decreed there was to be *absolutely no smoking* anywhere on the premises, Chloe decided the biscuits could wait and she went in search of the source. She had found the maid of honor on the side porch, smoking a cigarette and ashing into the lace hydrangea bush below.

Chloe was about to open her mouth to let her know smoke was blowing into the house when a man walked up the outside steps of the side porch. It was the groom's father. He took a drag off the maid of honor's cigarette and he leaned his elbows on the railing next to her.

Chloe should have gone back to work. If the father of the groom, who owned this house, sanctioned the smoking, then it must have been okay. But Chloe stayed plugged in right where she was. The maid of honor was cooler than cool. She wore a stretchy black tank dress with straps that crisscrossed and a very low dip in the back and a leather-and-crystal choker that Chloe thought could have come from Van Cleef and Arpels or could have been purchased at a flea market in Mumbai; it was impossible to tell, which was what made it cool.

"You have to get rid of it," the father of the groom said.

"I can't," the maid of honor said.

"You can," the father of the groom said.

"I won't."

"Merritt, you don't want a baby."

Chloe pressed her lips together.

"I *don't* want a baby," Merritt said. "But I do want you. I want *you,* Tag, and this is your baby. It's my connection to you."

"I could call your bluff," Tag said. "How do I know the baby is mine? It could just as easily be Robbie's."

"I haven't slept with Robbie since last year," Merritt says. "And nothing happened a few weeks ago. You saw to that, didn't you?"

"How can I be sure you're really pregnant? How do I know you haven't gotten rid of it already? Here you are *smoking*. If you're so set on having the baby, why not start taking care of it?"

"It's none of your business what I do," Merritt said.

"Either it is or it isn't," Tag said. He flicked the cigarette into the lace hydrangea. "Make up your mind."

"Tag…"

"We are going to get through this wedding," Tag said. "And when you leave on Sunday, I'll write you a check. But then that's it, Merritt. This is over." Tag disappeared from Chloe's view—down the stairs, she imagined, and back to the party.

"I'll tell Greer!" Merritt called out after him.

There was no response and Merritt dissolved into tears. Chloe had the urge to comfort her, but at the same time she was thinking, *What a scandal*. The maid of honor was pregnant with the father of the groom's baby! He wanted her to get rid of it; she wanted to be with him. He wanted to pay her off; she threatened blackmail.

"Chica!" Geraldo was gesturing from down the hall, and Chloe hurried toward him. She needed to get back to work.

Despite what she had witnessed, or maybe because of it, Chloe continued to sneak drinks. It didn't seem to be affecting her work performance. She served the clambake, cleared the clambake; she half listened to the toasts. She served dessert and then cleared dessert. People started to dance. Chloe looked for Merritt, the maid of honor, but didn't see her. Tag, meanwhile, was dancing with Greer.

The party was coming to an end. The band played its final song and Chloe switched into what she thought of as turbo-clear mode. Anything not nailed down was going back to the kitchen. There had been champagne toasts, so there was a slew of slender flutes, which were more difficult to transport than punch cups because of their high center of gravity. Chloe tried to be mindful. It was dark, the terrain was uneven, and she had had no small amount of punch herself. She was carrying a full tray of flutes with varying levels of champagne remaining. Chloe was debating whether she should start drinking the champagne—Veuve Clicquot was very expensive, she knew—and she was also thinking of a musical instrument she had once seen that was nothing more than a collection of water glasses filled to different levels that some dude played with one wetted finger when the toe of her clog caught the raised lip where the lawn met the beach. The tray went flying; the glasses shattered. The sound was one from the recurring nightmares of servers everywhere. Chloe cringed. She willed the tray to fly back up into her hands like a film in reverse, the glasses restored to whole. She was relieved that the party was ending and no one seemed to have noticed her display of utter gracelessness.

But then a voice came from out of the darkness. "Here, let me help."

Chloe looked up from the wreckage. It was Merritt, the maid of honor, in her cool black dress.

"You don't have to," Chloe said. "It's my fault."

"Could have happened to anyone," Merritt said. "*Would* have happened to me, I assure you, if I'd been brave enough to do this job at your age."

Chloe stared at Merritt for a second. She was intrigued and embarrassed now that they were face-to-face. Chloe knew Merritt's secret but Merritt didn't know that Chloe knew. If Merritt had realized Chloe knew that she was pregnant with the groom's father's baby, she would have been... what? Angry that Chloe eavesdropped? Mortified by the example she was setting? Chloe kept her face down so as not to give anything away in her expression. She picked the bigger shards out of the grass. They clinked on the tray.

"What's your name?" Merritt asked.

"Chloe MacAvoy."

"Where do you live, Chloe?"

"Here," Chloe said. "On Nantucket. Year-round."

Merritt sighed. "Well, then, you're the luckiest girl in the world."

"Where do you live?" Chloe asked.

"I live in New York City," Merritt said. "I work in PR there and I do some influencing stuff on Instagram."

"Oh." Chloe swallowed. "Really? What's your name? I'll follow you."

"At Merritt—two *r*'s, two *t*'s—Monaco, like the country. Can you remember that? I'd be honored if you followed me, Chloe. I'll keep an eye out and follow you back."

"You will?" Chloe said. She felt insanely flattered— Merritt was an *influencer!*—even as she knew she should *not* put Merritt on any kind of pedestal. If she ever got into the position Merritt was in, Auntie and Uncle Ed would be *extremely disappointed*. Still, she couldn't help but feel a bit of starstruck awe. "I love your dress. Do you mind telling me who it's by?"

Merritt looked down as if to remind herself what she was wearing. "Young, Fabulous, and Broke," she said. "Which describes me." Her smile faded. "Well, two out of three, anyway."

* * *

Once the glass was all picked up and Merritt had hurried off to find Celeste, Chloe wanted to finish cleaning up and leave. She presented the tray of broken glass to Donna, who frowned but then said, "Happens to the best of us, kid."

Geraldo said, "Let's get out of here, chica."

Chloe had to go to the bathroom. Badly. Siobhan didn't like them to use the restrooms unless it was an absolute emergency, and this definitely qualified. There was a powder room designated for guests, and now that most of the guests had left, it was unoccupied.

When Chloe emerged a few minutes later, she turned left down the hall toward what she thought was the front door and freedom. But the hall led her into a living room.

"Hey," a voice said.

Chloe peered into the room but saw no one. Then, from a chair that looked like a scoop of vanilla ice cream, a woman sat up. It was the woman who had been so rude about the cheddar biscuits and had sent Chloe in search of more. *And see that they're warm!*

"Hello?" Chloe said.

"Can you bring me a bottle of something, doll face?" the woman said. "Whiskey? Vodka? Some of that champagne Greer was drinking?"

"Uh..." Chloe said. "The party is over, actually."

"The *official* party is over," the woman said. She had a bad dye job, blond turning a rust color at the part. "Now is the *after*-party and as I've run dry, I need your help."

"I'm only sixteen," Chloe said. "I can't serve alcohol. It's against the law."

The woman laughed. "Ha! What if I give you a hundred pounds? Or, wait, a hundred...what do you Yanks call them? Bucks!"

A hundred bucks? It was tempting. Chloe knew how easy it would be to pluck a bottle from the boxes waiting to go back out to the catering truck. But she thought of Merritt. One wayward decision might lead to another, she feared.

"I'm sorry," Chloe said. "I have to get home."

"Sweetie, *please,*" the woman said. "I'm desperate. I would have bet my last shilling that Tag Winbury kept scotch in every room, but I can't find a drop. And you *are* the catering help, aren't you? So it's your job to bring me what I want."

"I'm sorry," Chloe said. "I'm off the clock. I'm leaving now." She gave the woman what she hoped was a professional smile and turned around. She headed back the way she'd come and zipped out the side door of the house. Because, really, how much could she be expected to deal with in one night?

Saturday, July 7, 2018,
12:30 p.m.

THE CHIEF

He has to drive from Monomoy to the station, where they're holding Shooter Uxley. He has two state policemen back at the scene to make sure nothing is tampered with and no one else flees. He could use two more guys, quite honestly. Nantucket just isn't equipped for a murder during a busy holiday weekend. That is the stark truth.

The Chief inhales through his nose and exhales through his mouth, his takeaway from the stress management course he's required to attend every three years. He'll question Shooter himself and that will likely shed some light on things. He'll hear from the ME about an exact cause of death. If he still hasn't figured out what happened, he has the father, the brother, and the groom himself.

But frankly, the Chief likes the best man for this. Why else would he *run?* Then again, after he'd disappeared last night, why would he come *back?* What is going *on* here?

The Chief talked to Nick briefly before he left the compound. Nick said the mother of the groom, Greer Garrison, the mystery writer, had misled him about her timetable. Intentionally, he thinks.

I didn't like the way our interview went, Nick said. *It had a funny smell.*

* * *

The Chief calls home. Andrea answers. "How's it going?"

"Oh, fine," Ed says. Andrea will know he means the exact opposite. He wants to tell Andrea that Finn's girlfriend, Lola Budd, was the one who ended up finding their main suspect. It's a good story and it will hearten Andrea to know that Lola has had a chance to shine, but there isn't time to get into it now.

"How's Chloe?" the Chief asks. "Is her stomach feeling any better?"

"Not sure," Andrea says. "She's locked herself in her room."

"No locked doors," Ed says. This has been a rule since back when his own kids, Kacy and Eric, were growing up.

"You come home and tell her that," Andrea says. "Because I've tried and she won't budge. She's upset about the girl. The Murdered Maid of Honor, everyone is calling her now."

"*Everyone?*" Ed asks. "Is it that bad already? People talking? People giving this story a name? We aren't even sure she was murdered. Not sure at all."

"It's a small island, Ed," Andrea says. She pauses, and he realizes she has just lobbed his favorite line right back at him. "Would it be awful if while you were out solving this murder, I went to the beach?"

He's *investigating* a murder, not solving anything. "Go to the beach," he says. "But please be careful."

"You're sweet," Andrea says. "Love you."

He hangs up just as a call comes in from Cape Cod Hospital.

"This is Ed Kapenash," he says.

"Chief, it's Linda." Linda Ferretti, the medical examiner. "Prelims indicate our girl died by drowning around three a.m. The blood work shows someone slipped her a mickey, or maybe she self-medicated. A barbiturate seems to be the culprit. The cut on her foot was the source of all that blood but it was just a surface wound. She has one fingerprint-size bruise on her wrist; my best guess is someone yanked her or pulled on her arm. There are no other signs that she was strangled or smothered and then dumped. She either took pills or was given something. She went out for a swim, passed out, drowned. Could have happened in a bathtub."

"Okay," the Chief says. "What was her blood alcohol content?"

"Low," Linda says. "Point zero-two-five."

"Really?" the Chief says. "You're sure?"

"Surprised me too, at first," she says. "The contents of her stomach were minimal. Either she didn't eat much last night or, what I think is more likely, she vomited up what she did eat."

"What makes you think that?" the Chief asks.

"She was pregnant."

"You're *kidding*," the Chief says.

"Wish I was," Linda says. "Very early stages. My guess is she was six or seven weeks along? She might not even have realized it."

"Wow," the Chief says.

"The plot thickens," Linda says.

The Chief hangs up and his phone rings again. This time it's the Nantucket hospital.

"This is Ed Kapenash," he says.

"Chief, it's Margaret from the ER."

"Hey, Margaret," the Chief says. "What's up?"

"We have the bride from that wedding," Margaret says. "Kind of strange? She says she wants to talk to the police here at the hospital rather than at the house. Her fiancé came to check on her. They had words, then he stormed out."

"Keep her there, Margaret," the Chief says. "I'll send the Greek the instant he's free."

"The Greek?" Margaret says. "My nurses will be thrilled."

The Chief smiles for the first time that day. "Thanks, Margaret," he says, then he turns into the station.

They are holding Shooter Uxley in the first interview room. When the Chief enters, Shooter is fast asleep with his head on the table. The Chief watches him for a second and listens to him snoring. Whatever anxiety he might be feeling is clearly overridden by exhaustion.

Didn't sleep much last night, buddy? the Chief wonders.

Mr. Uxley has taken off his blazer and untucked his shirt. The Chief looks at his paperwork: Michael Oscar Uxley. New York driver's license, Manhattan address, West Thirty-Ninth Street. Also from New York City, like the deceased. He wonders if Uxley was the father of Ms. Monaco's baby.

The Chief nudges his arm. "Hey there, wake up. Mr. Uxley, sir?"

Shooter groans and raises his head. He seems disoriented for a second, then he straightens up.

The Chief says, "In case you've forgotten, I'm Chief Kapenash, Nantucket Police. You put on some nice moves out there."

Shooter blinks. "I want a lawyer," he says.

Thursday, June 22-Friday, June 23, 2017

CELESTE

She doesn't meet Shooter until she and Benji have been together for nine months. Shooter is Benji's best friend—so why does it take so long? Well, Shooter is busy. He owns and operates a company called A-List, which provides American retreats for foreign businessmen. What this means essentially is that Shooter has made a career—lucrative, Benji says—out of partying. He takes executives from Asian and emerging Eastern European countries and shows these gentlemen (for his clientele is 100 percent male) an old-fashioned American good time. Much of the "work" is centered in Manhattan. The executives are fond of the long-established steak houses—Smith and Wollensky, Gallagher's, Peter Luger's; they like the *Intrepid* and Times Square; they like the clubs, especially the gentlemen's clubs on Twelfth Avenue. Shooter also spends a lot of time in Las Vegas. He is, Benji says with a straight face, a Vegas regular. He divides his time between the Aria Sky Suites and the Mandarin Oriental. Shooter himself plays only craps; in prep school at St. George's, he ran a late-night dice game, and that was the source of his nickname.

"You all gambled in high school?" Celeste asks Benji. She herself has never been to a casino, but if she went, she would steer clear of the craps table. The name alone.

"Shooter made it impossible to resist," Benji says. "I always lost, but it was fun."

When Shooter isn't "working" in Manhattan or Las Vegas, he is at the Kentucky Derby, the Masters, the Super Bowl, the Indy 500, Coachella, or Mardi Gras. He is sunning in South Beach or skiing in Aspen. Wherever you wish you could be on any given weekend, Shooter is there with a group of his executives.

On the weekend of June 23, however, Shooter is coming to Nantucket with Benji and Celeste. Celeste is excited to finally meet him. She's also glad he's coming because this is Celeste's first time to Nantucket, her first time to any summer resort, and it's her first time spending the weekend with Tag and Greer, Benji's parents. Celeste met Tag and Greer on three previous occasions. The first was a dinner at Buvette, then a few weeks later there was Sunday church at St. James's followed by dim sum in Chinatown. The third occasion was a dinner at the Winburys' apartment on Park and Seventieth to celebrate Benji's twenty-eighth birthday.

The Winburys are less intimidating than Celeste expected. Tag is gregarious and charismatic; Greer is high-strung and a bit imperious until her second glass of champagne, when she relaxes into someone quite funny and warm. They are wealthy beyond Celeste's wildest imagination but as she strove to seem cultured and well bred, they strove to seem down-to-earth, and they all met in the middle. Neither of the elder Winburys flinched when Celeste announced that her father sold suits at the mall and her mother worked in the gift shop at a crayon factory. Greer asked several questions about Karen's health that revealed her concern without seeming phony or overbearing. They made Celeste feel comfortable. The Winburys made her feel *acceptable,* which she found a pleasant surprise.

Despite this, staying with them for a long weekend on Nantucket is a daunting prospect and Celeste is glad for Shooter's presence to take some pressure off her.

They are leaving late afternoon on Thursday and returning on Sunday evening. Celeste has taken Friday off work, her first vacation in a year and a half; the last time was when she took a week to care for Karen after her double mastectomy. They are flying from JFK on Jet-Blue. The flight is only forty minutes long but it's another source of anxiety for Celeste. She has never been on an airplane. Benji couldn't believe it when she told him.

"Never been on a *plane*?"

She tried to explain to him that she grew up sheltered, more sheltered than the most sheltered person he knows. She knows that *sheltered* makes it sound like Bruce and Karen were trying to keep Celeste from the evils of the wider world, but the truth was that Bruce and Karen didn't have the money to explore the world beyond their own neat pocket of it. They didn't have relatives in Duluth or St. Louis to visit, and when Celeste came home from school in sixth grade asking to go to Disney World, Bruce arranged for a Saturday excursion to Six Flags in New Jersey. Over spring break in college, when everyone at Miami of Ohio went to Daytona or the Bahamas, Celeste took the bus home to Easton. There had been no junior year abroad. After college, there had been New York City, her job at the zoo, her life right up until meeting Benji. When would she have boarded a plane?

Celeste is so concerned about arriving at JFK in a timely fashion that she forgoes public transportation and springs for an Uber from the zoo. It's $102. Celeste ignores the tight knot of dread in her gut as she adds this expense to the many others this weekend away has incurred. She needed a whole new summer wardrobe—two bikinis, a cover-up, three sundresses to wear out at night, shorts and flip-flops, and a straw bag. She needed a pedicure and a fresh haircut. She needed sunscreen and a hostess gift for Greer.

"What do you get for a woman who has literally everything?" Celeste asked Merritt.

"Bring her really good olive oil," Merritt said. "It's more interesting than wine."

Celeste bought a forty-two-dollar (gulp) bottle of olive oil at Dean and DeLuca. Transporting the olive oil to Nantucket cost her another twenty-five dollars in checked-bag fees.

Celeste goes through airport security, a soul-shredding experience where she has to stand barefoot among strangers and put her drugstore toiletries on display in a clear plastic bag for others to comment on. The woman behind her points to Celeste's Noxzema and says, "I thought they stopped making that in the eighties."

As Celeste is walking to the gate, she gets a text from Benji. Accident on 55th Street, midtown at a standstill, I may miss the flight. You go, I'll meet you there tomorrow.

Celeste stops and rereads the text. I'll just wait and go with you tomorrow, she texts back. But she imagines undoing all the steps she has just taken only to reiterate them tomorrow. Unchecking her bag, Ubering back to Manhattan, rebooking her ticket for a Friday.

Just go now, Benji texts. Please. It'll be fine. Shooter will take good care of you.

When Celeste gets to the gate, there is a man in jeans and a white linen shirt who breaks into a grin when he sees her.

"You're as pretty as he said." The man offers his hand. "I'm Shooter Uxley."

"Celeste," she says. "Otis." Celeste shakes Shooter's

hand and tries to manage the emotions careening around inside of her. Ten seconds ago she was despondent about having to get to Nantucket and endure an entire night and half the next day without Benji. Now, however, her insides are swooping and dipping like a kite. Shooter is ... well, the first word she thinks of is *hot,* but she has never described anyone that way and so she switches to *handsome.* Objectively handsome; his handsomeness is a matter of fact, not opinion. He has dark hair with a forelock that falls over one of his blue eyes. Celeste's eyes are also blue, but blue eyes look better on Shooter with his dark hair. But what Celeste is responding to is more than Shooter's looks. It's his gaze, his grin, his energy—they grab her. Is there a better way to describe it? She's in thrall. This, she thinks, is love at first sight.

But no! It can't be! Celeste loves Benji. They have just started saying it. The first time was five days earlier, Sunday evening, as they drove back to the city from a visit with Celeste's parents in Easton. Benji had met Bruce and Karen and seen the modest house on Derhammer Street where Celeste grew up. Celeste had shown Benji her elementary school, her high school, the Palmer pool, downtown Easton, the Peace candle, the Free Bridge, and the Crayola factory. They had supper with Karen and Bruce at Diner 248. Celeste had thought about making a reservation somewhere more refined—Easton had a crop of new restaurants; Masa for Mexican, Third and Ferry for seafood—but Celeste and her parents had always celebrated family milestones at the diner, and to go anywhere else would feel phony. They all ate vegetable barley soup and turkey clubs, and Karen, Bruce, and Celeste split the Fudgy Wudgy for dessert as usual and Benji gamely tried a bite. After supper, they drove back to the house and said their good-byes at the curb. Bruce and Karen waved until Celeste and Benji turned the corner and Celeste shed a few tears as she always did when she left her parents. Benji said, "Well, now I've seen Easton. Thank you."

Celeste had laughed and wiped tears from the bottom of her eyes. "You're very welcome. It's not Park Avenue or London, of course..."

"It's a sweet little town," Benji said. "It must have been a nice place to grow up."

Celeste flinched at this assessment; something about his tone sounded patronizing. "It was," she said defensively.

Benji reached over to squeeze her knee. "Hey, I'm sorry. That came out wrong. I liked Easton, and your parents are true gems. Real salt of the earth."

They're people, Celeste had thought. Good, honest, hardworking people. She had never understood the phrase *salt of the earth,* but it sounded like something you said about someone you knew was beneath you. To make the moment even more humiliating, Celeste started to cry again and Benji said, "Wow, I'm making things worse. Please don't cry, Celeste. I love you."

Celeste shook her head. "You're just saying that."

"I'm not," Benji said. "I've been wanting to say it for weeks, months even, but I've been afraid because I wasn't sure you felt the same way. But believe me, please, when I say I love you. I love you, Celeste Otis."

She had felt emotionally goosed. He *loved* her. He loved *her.* Celeste didn't know what to say, and yet it was clear Benji was waiting for a response. "I love you too," she said.

"You do?" he asked.

Did she? Celeste thought back to the first time she met Benji, how wonderful he had been with Miranda, how exasperated with glamorous Jules. She thought of the flowers and the books and the restaurants and his mind-boggling apartment and the homeless shelter. She thought about the ease she felt in his presence, as though the world had only good things to offer. She thought about how much his opinion mattered to her. She wanted to be good enough for him.

"Yes," she said. "I do."

If Celeste loves Benji, then what is happening now, with Shooter? Celeste knows her parents' story by heart: Karen came marching up the pool steps and introduced herself to Bruce, who was sweating off water weight and staring at his orange. Karen had stuck out her hand and said, *I admire a man with willpower.* And those, apparently, were the magic words, because they both knew instantly that they would get married and stay together forever.

I wasn't even hungry after that, Bruce said. *I threw my orange away, I made weight, I won my match, but it barely mattered. All I wanted was a date with your mother.*

That's how love works, Karen said.

Does love work only one way? Celeste wonders. She has spent the past nine months carefully, cautiously getting to know Benjamin Winbury and has just decided to call that experience love. But only five days later, she's pretty sure she has made a mistake. Because in meeting Shooter, Celeste has been swallowed whole by the world. *Goner,* she thinks. *I'm a goner.*

No. She is a scientist. She believes in reason. What she's feeling now is as ephemeral as a shooting star. Soon enough, it will fade away.

"The old boy isn't going to make this flight," Shooter says. "He gave me very strict orders to take care of you."

"That won't be necessary," Celeste says. "I can take care of myself."

"Can you?" Shooter says. His eyes flash with blue sparks. Celeste can't look directly at him, then she decides that she's being silly, of course she can look at him, and she does. The bottom drops out of her stomach, *whoosh!* He is so painfully attractive. Maybe she just needs to build up a tolerance. Even the best-looking men in the world—George Clooney, Jon Hamm—might seem run-of-the-mill if you looked at them long enough. "What seat are you in?"

"One-D," she says.

"I'm in twelve-A," Shooter says. "I'm going to ask them to give me Benji's seat."

"I'm not a senior vice president from Prague," Celeste says. "You don't have to babysit me."

"You've been dating my best friend for nine months," Shooter says. "I want to get to know you. Hard to do from eleven rows away, don't you agree?"

"Agreed," Celeste concedes.

They sit side by side in the front row of the plane. Shooter lifts Celeste's carry-on into the overhead compartment, then asks if she would prefer the window or the aisle. She says aisle. She realizes most people who have never flown before might want to sit at the window but Celeste is terrified. Shooter waits for her to sit down and then he sits. He's a gentleman, but then so is Benji. Benji is the ultimate gentleman. Benji stands whenever Celeste leaves the table to go to the ladies' room and he stands when she gets back. He holds doors, he carries a handkerchief, he never interrupts.

Shooter pulls a flask out of his back pocket and hands it to Celeste. She eyes the flask. It's alcohol, she assumes, but what kind? She is far too cautious a person to drink without asking. But in the moment, she doesn't feel like being cautious. She feels like being daring. She accepts the flask and takes a swig: It's tequila. Celeste drinks tequila only when she's with Merritt, although personally she thinks it tastes like dirt. This tequila is smoother than most, but even so it singes her throat. However, an instant later the tension in her neck disappears and her jaw loosens. She takes another slug.

"I carry that because I hate flying," Shooter says.

"You?" Celeste says. "But don't you fly all the time?"

"Nearly every week," he says. "The first time I flew, I was eight years old. My parents were sending me to summer camp in Vermont." He leans his head back against the seat and stares forward. "Every time I fly I have an atavistic reaction to the memory of that day. The day I realized my parents wanted to get rid of me."

"Were you a very naughty child, then?" she asks. She sounds exactly like Merritt, she realizes.

"Oh, probably," Shooter says.

Celeste hands Shooter back the flask. He smiles sadly and takes a slug.

Later, Celeste will think back on the twenty hours she spent on Nantucket with Shooter alone as the kind of montage they show in movies. Here's a shot of the airplane bouncing and shaking during turbulence and Shooter raising the window shade in time for Celeste to see bolts of lightning on the horizon. Here is Shooter taking Celeste's hand, Celeste imagining her parents' reaction when they are informed that Celeste has died in a plane crash. Here is the plane landing safely on Nantucket, passengers cheering, Shooter and Celeste executing a perfect high-five. Here are Shooter and Celeste climbing into a silver Jeep that Shooter has rented. The sky has cleared, the top of the Jeep is down, and Shooter takes off down the road while Celeste's blond hair blows behind her. Here is Elida, the summer housekeeper, meeting Shooter and Celeste at the front door of the Winbury property, known as Summerland, and informing them that Mr. and Mrs. Winbury have also been detained in New York but that they should make themselves at home; she, Elida, will return in the morning.

Here is Celeste acting nonchalant when she enters the house. It's a palace, a summer palace, like the monarchs of Russia and Austria used to have. The ceilings are soaring, the rooms are open, bright, airy. The entire thing is white—white walls, white wainscoting, whitewashed oak floors, a kitchen tiled in white with pure white Carrara marble countertops—with stunning bursts of color here and there: paintings, pillows, fresh flowers, a wooden bowl filled with lemons and Granny Smith apples. Celeste would say she can't believe how glorious the house is, with its six bedrooms upstairs and master suite downstairs; with its uninterrupted views of the harbor; with its glass-walled wine cellar off the casual "friends'" dining room; with its dark rectangular pool and Balinese-style pool house; with its two guest cottages, tiny and perfect, like cottages borrowed from a fairy tale; with its round rose garden in the middle of a koi pond, a garden that can be accessed only by a footbridge. Shooter gives Celeste the tour—he has been coming to Summerland since he was fourteen years old, over half his life—and hence his attitude is charmingly proprietary. He tells Celeste that he used to have a terrific crush on Greer and had near Oedipal dreams about killing Tag and marrying her.

"Essentially becoming my best friend's stepfather," he says.

Celeste shrieks. "Greer?" Celeste likes Greer, but it's hard to imagine her as the object of teenage lust.

"She was so beautiful," Shooter says. "And she doted on me. She was more my mother than my own mother. I think she would probably write both of her sons out of the will and leave this place to me if I asked her nicely."

Celeste laughs, but she's beginning to believe that Shooter might have the ability to disrupt primogeniture and overturn dynasties.

Here is Shooter pouring Celeste a glass of Greer's wine and opening one of Tag's beers for himself. Celeste feels like they're teenagers throwing a party while their parents are away. Here is Shooter opening a can of cocktail peanuts, then paging through the Nantucket phone book and making a call behind closed doors. Here are Celeste and Shooter clinking wine glass to beer bottle as they sit in Adirondack chairs and watch the sun go down. Here is Shooter going to the front door, paying the delivery boy, and bringing a feast into the kitchen. He has ordered two lobster dinners complete with corn, potatoes, and containers of melted butter.

Celeste says, "I thought it was pizza."

Shooter says, "We're on Nantucket, Sunshine."

Here are Celeste and Shooter after dinner and after several shots of Tag's absurdly fine tequila headed to town in a taxi to the Chicken Box, which is not a fast-food restaurant but rather a dive bar with live music. Here are Celeste and Shooter dancing in the front row to a cover band called Maxxtone who play "Wagon Wheel," followed by "Sweet Caroline." Here are Celeste and Shooter pumping their fists in the air, chanting "Bah-bah-bah!" and "So good! So good! So good!" Here are Celeste and Shooter stumbling out of the Chicken Box and into another taxi that takes them back to the summer palace. It's one thirty in the morning, which is later than Celeste has stayed up since she pulled all-nighters in college, but instead of going to bed, she and Shooter wander out to the beach, strip down to their underwear, and go for a swim.

Here is Celeste saying, "I'm so drunk, I'll probably drown."

"No," Shooter says. "I would never let that happen."

Here is Shooter floating on his back, spouting water out of his mouth. Here is Celeste floating on her back, staring at the stars, thinking that outer space is a mystery but not as much of a mystery as the universe of human emotion.

Here are Celeste and Shooter wandering back inside the house, wrapped in navy-and-white-striped towels that Shooter swiped from the pool house. They linger in the kitchen. Shooter opens the refrigerator. Elida has clearly provisioned for the weekend; the inside of the Winburys' refrigerator looks like something from a magazine shoot. There are half a dozen kinds of cheese, none of which Celeste recognizes, so she picks them up to inspect: Taleggio, Armenian string cheese, Emmentaler. There are sticks of cured sausage and pepperoni. There is a small tub of truffle butter, some artisanal hummus, four containers of olives in an ombré stack, from light purple to black. There are slabs of pâté and jars of chutney that look like they were mailed directly from India. Celeste checks the labels: Harrods. Close enough.

"Okay, can I just say?" Celeste puts a hand on Shooter's bare back and he turns to face her. The two of them are illuminated by the fluorescent light of the fridge and for a second Celeste has the sense that she and Shooter are curious children peering into a previously undiscovered world, like the young protagonists in a C. S. Lewis novel.

"Yes?"

"In my house growing up, if I wanted a snack? There was a tub of Philadelphia cream cheese. And I spread it on Triscuits. If my mother had been to the Amish farmers' market, there was sometimes pepper jelly to put on top." Celeste knows she must be deeply and profoundly drunk because she never, ever shares details about her life growing up. She feels like a fool.

"You are such a breath of fresh air," Shooter says.

Now Celeste feels even worse. She doesn't want to be a breath of fresh air. She wants to be devastating, alluring, irresistible.

But wait—what about Benji?

It's time to go to bed, she thinks. This is what she always suspected happened when one stayed up too late; reputations were shredded, hopes and dreams destroyed. What had Mac and Betty always told her? *Nothing good happens after midnight.*

"And also?" Celeste says. "If I held the refrigerator door open for this long? I would have been scolded for wasting energy."

"Scolded?" Shooter says.

"Yes, scolded." She tries to frown at him. "I'm going to bed."

"Absolutely not," Shooter says. He regards the contents of the fridge, then grabs the truffle butter. A rummage through the cabinet to the left of the fridge—*he docs know where everything is,* Celeste thinks, *just like he owns the place*—produces a long, slender box of . . . bread sticks. Rosemary bread sticks. "Come sit."

Celeste joins Shooter in the "casual" dining room off the kitchen, where they watch the glass cube of the wine cellar glow like a spaceship. Shooter opens the box of bread sticks and the butter.

"Prepare yourself," he says. "This is going to be memorable. Have you ever had truffle butter?"

"No," Celeste says. She knows that truffles are mushrooms—pigs dig them out of the ground in France and Italy—but she can't get too excited about mushroom butter. Nothing about it sounds appetizing. Still, she is hungry enough to eat just about anything—the lobster dinner seems like days ago—so she accepts a reed-thin bread stick with a dollop of butter on the end.

She bites off the bottom of the bread stick and the flavor explodes in her mouth. She whimpers with ecstasy.

"Pretty good, huh?" Shooter says.

Celeste closes her eyes, savoring the taste, which is unlike anything she has ever eaten. It's rich, complex, earthy, sexy. She swallows. "I can't believe how ... *good* ... that is."

Here are Shooter and Celeste eating rosemary bread sticks with truffle butter until the butter is gone and only a few bread-stick stubs rattle around in the box. It was a deceptively simple snack but Celeste will never, ever forget it.

Here are Celeste and Shooter wandering upstairs. Celeste is sleeping in "Benji's room," which is decorated in white, beige, and taupe, and Shooter is sleeping at the far end of the hallway in "guest room 3," which is done in white, navy, and taupe. Celeste checks the other guest rooms; they're nearly identical and she wonders if people new to the house like herself ever wander into the wrong room accidentally. She gives Shooter a feeble wave.

"I guess I'll call it a night."

"You sure about that?" Shooter says.

Celeste thinks for a second. *Is* she sure about that? They have pressed to the edge of a platonic relationship; there's nothing left they can do while maintaining their innocence other than maybe go down to the game room and play Scrabble.

"I'm sure about that," she says.

"Sunshine," Shooter says.

She looks at him. His eyes hold her hostage; she can't

look away. He's asking her without saying anything. They are the only ones here. No one would ever know.

Amid the battle going on in her mind—her fervent desire versus her sense of right and wrong—she thinks of the age-old philosophical question: If a tree falls in the forest and nobody's there to hear it, does it still make a sound? That question, Celeste realizes, isn't about a tree at all. It's about what's happening right here, right now. If she sleeps with Shooter and it remains unknown to anyone but the two of them, did it even really happen?

Yes, she thinks. She would never be the same. And she hopes that Shooter wouldn't be the same either.

"Good night," she says. She kisses him on the cheek and retreats down the hall.

Here are Shooter and Celeste the next morning riding two bikes from the Winburys' fleet of Schwinns into town to the Petticoat Row Bakery, where they get giant iced coffees and two ham and Gruyère croissants, which ooze nutty melted cheese and butter as they pick them apart on a bench on Centre Street. Here is Shooter buying Celeste a bouquet of wildflowers from a farm truck on Main Street, a pointless, extravagant gesture because Tag and Greer's house is set among lush gardens and the house is filled with fresh flowers. Celeste reminds him of this and he says, "Yes, but none of those flowers are from *me*. I want you to look at this bouquet and know just how besotted I am with you."

Besotted, she thinks. It's a peculiar word, old-fashioned and British-sounding. But Benji is the British one, not Shooter. Somewhere in all the sharing of last night, Celeste learned that Shooter is from Palm Beach, Florida. Shooter was shipped off to summer camp at age eight and to boarding school a few years after that.

Shooter's father died when Shooter was a junior at St. George's.

"And that was when the wheels fell off the bus," Shooter said. "My father had been married twice before and had other kids and those other Uxleys swooped in and claimed everything. My one brother, Mitch, agreed to pay my final year of tuition at St. George's but I had no discretionary income so I started running a dice game at school. There was no money for college so I moved to DC, where I worked as a bartender. Eventually I found a high-stakes poker game where I met diplomats, lobbyists, and a bunch of foreign businessmen. Which led me to my present venture."

"What happened to your mother?" Celeste asked.

"She died," Shooter said. Then he shook his head and Celeste knew not to ask anything further.

Besotted. What does he mean by that, exactly? There's no time to ponder because he's leading her down the street toward the Bartlett's Farm truck. He buys three hothouse tomatoes and a loaf of Portuguese bread.

"Tomatoes, mayonnaise, good white bread," he says. "My favorite summer sandwich."

Celeste raises a skeptical eyebrow. She was raised on cold cuts—turkey, ham, salami, roast beef. Her parents may have struggled with money but there was always meat piled high on her sandwiches.

Celeste changes her tune, however, when she is sitting poolside in one of her new bikinis and Shooter brings her his favorite sandwich. The bread has been toasted golden brown; the slices of tomato are thick and juicy, seasoned with sea salt and freshly ground pepper, and there is exactly the right amount of mayonnaise to make the sandwich tangy and luscious.

"What do you think?" he asks. "Pretty good, huh?"

She shrugs and takes another bite.

* * *

They are lying side by side on chaises in the afternoon sun, the pool cool and dark before them. The pool has a subtle waterfall feature at one end that makes what Celeste thinks of as water music, a lullaby that threatens to put her to sleep in the middle of a very important conversation. She and Shooter are picking the best song by every classic rock performer they can think of.

"Rolling Stones," Shooter says. "'Ruby Tuesday.'"

"'Beast of Burden,'" Celeste says.

"Ooooooh," Shooter says. "Good call."

"David Bowie," Celeste says. "'Changes.'"

"I'm a 'Modern Love' guy," Shooter says.

Celeste shakes her head. "Can't stand it."

"Dire Straits," Shooter says. "'Romeo and Juliet.'" He reaches his foot over to nudge her leg. "Wake up. Dire Straits."

She likes the song about roller girl. *She's making movies on location, she don't know what it means.* Celeste is sinking behind her closed eyelids. Sinking down. What is the name of that song? She can't . . . remember.

Celeste wakes up to someone calling her name.

Celeste! Earth to Celeste!

She opens her eyes and looks at the chaise next to hers. Empty. She squints. Across the pool she sees a man in half a suit—pants, shirt, tie. It's Benji. Benji is here. Celeste sits up. She straightens her bikini top.

"Hey there," Celeste says, but the tone of her voice has changed. Her heart isn't in it.

"Hey," Benji says. He moves Shooter's towel aside and sits on Shooter's chaise. "How are you? How has it been?"

"I'm fine," Celeste says. "It's been . . . fine."

Celeste tries to think of details she can share: lobster dinner, "Sweet Caroline," swimming in her bra and panties under the stars way past her bedtime, truffle butter, a tree falls in the forest?

No.

A bike ride with the morning sun on her face, a bouquet of snapdragons, cosmos, and zinnias, tomato sandwiches?

The name of the song comes to her.

" 'Skateaway,' " she says.

"Excuse me?" Benji says.

Celeste blinks rapidly. Her field of vision is swimming with bright, amorphous blobs, as though she's been staring at the sun.

Friday, July 6, 2018, 11:15 p.m.

KAREN

She takes an oxy, brushes her teeth, and puts on a night-gown only to take the nightgown off right before she slides into bed. The sheets are Belgian, Celeste said, seven-hundred-thread-count cotton, which is the very best. The bed is dressed in a white down comforter, an ivory cashmere blanket, these white cotton sheets with a scalloped edge, and a mountain of pillows, each as soft as a dollop of whipped cream. Karen places them all around her and sinks in. It's like sleeping on a cloud. Will heaven be like sleeping in one of Summerland's guest beds? She can only hope.

She drifts off, her pain at bay.

She wakes up with a start—*Celeste! Celeste!* She reaches an arm out to feel for Bruce but the other side of the bed is cool and empty. Karen checks the bedside clock: 11:46. Quarter to twelve and Bruce hasn't come to bed yet? Karen feels annoyed at first, then hurt. She realizes her naked body is no longer appealing, but she had thought maybe something would happen tonight. She wants to feel close to Bruce one more time.

She struggles to catch her breath. She was having a dream, a nightmare, about Celeste. Celeste was...some-where unfamiliar...a hotel with unnumbered floors, different levels, some of which led to dead ends; it was a confusing maze of a place. Celeste kept calling out but Karen couldn't get to her. Celeste had something to tell her, something she needed Karen to know.

Celeste doesn't want to marry Benji, Karen thinks. That is the stark truth.

Involuntarily, the psychic's word comes to her: *Chaos.*

Part of Karen believes Celeste should go through with the wedding anyway. So she isn't madly in love with Benji. Possibly she feels only a fraction of what Karen feels for Bruce, or possibly it's a different emotion altogether. Karen wants to tell Celeste to make the best of her situation, a situation any other young woman would kill to find herself in. Celeste and Benji don't have to be a perfect couple. Really, there is no such thing.

But then Karen stops herself. It is only the most selfish of women who would encourage their daughters to marry people they don't love. What Karen must do—now, she realizes, *now*—is give Celeste permission to back out. There are 170 people descending on Summerland tomorrow for a wedding unlike any other; over a hundred thousand dollars has been spent on these nuptials, perhaps even twice that. But no amount of money or logistics is worth a lifetime of settling. Karen must find Celeste now.

Finding Celeste, however, suddenly seems arduous. Will a phone call suffice? Karen picks up her cell phone and dials Celeste's number. The call goes to voice mail.

This is the universe telling Karen that a phone call will *not* suffice. Celeste turns her phone off when she goes to bed; she must be asleep.

Gingerly, Karen lowers her feet to the floor and stands. She finds her cane and hoists herself up. The oxy is still working; she feels strong and steady with purpose. She wraps herself in the robe and ventures out into the hallway.

If Karen's memory serves, Benji's room, where Celeste is staying alone tonight, is the second door on the left.

The hallway has subtle lighting along the baseboard so Karen can see where to plant her cane as she pads down the hall. When she reaches the door, she taps lightly. She doesn't want to wake the whole house up but neither does she want to interrupt anything.

There is no answer. Karen presses her ear to the door. In their house on Derhammer Street, the doors are hollow-core. Here they are true, solid wood, impossible to hear through. Karen eases the door open.

"Celeste?" she says. "Honey?"

The room is silent. Karen gropes for the switch and turns on the light. The bed is made up just as Karen's is—comforter, cashmere blanket, a host of pillows. Celeste hasn't gotten home yet, then. Or maybe she decided to join Merritt in the cottage so they can stay up gossiping and giggling on Celeste's last night as a single woman. But somehow Karen doubts that. Celeste has never been a gossiper or a giggler. She never had close girlfriends growing up, which used to worry Karen, even as she loved being Celeste's closest confidante.

Karen gazes upon the white silk column wedding dress hanging on the back of the closet door. It's a dress from a dream, ideally suited to Celeste's simple tastes and her classic beauty.

But ... she won't be wearing it tomorrow. Karen sighs, turns off the light, and closes the door.

As Karen heads back down the dark hallway, she feels a growing irritation. Where *is* everyone? Karen has been left all alone in this house. She wonders if this is what it feels like to be dead.

Stairs are tricky with a cane. Karen decides she feels strong enough to leave her cane behind. She takes the stairs slowly, gripping the rail, and thinks about the leftover lobster tails stashed in the fridge. The idea of them is enticing but she can't make herself feel hungry. The only thing she craves right now is a meaningful conversation with her daughter, and her husband's body next to her in their bed.

Karen hears distant voices and she smells smoke. She tiptoes along, reaching out for the wall when she needs to steady herself. She hears Bruce's voice. When she turns the corner, she can see two figures out on a deck—not the main deck but a horseshoe-shaped deck off to the right, one Karen hasn't noticed before. She wedges herself behind a sofa and peers behind the drapes. Bruce and Tag are sitting on the edge of this deck, smoking cigars and drinking what she thinks must be scotch. She can hear their voices but not what they're saying.

She should either go back to bed or find her daughter. But instead, Karen quietly cranks open the window. In a fine house like this one, the crank is smooth. The window opens silently.

Tag says, "There hasn't been anyone serious before this. Just casual stuff, when I was traveling. A woman in Stockholm, one in Dublin. But this girl was different. And now I'm trapped. She's pregnant and she's keeping the baby. She says."

Bruce shakes his head, throws back a swallow of scotch. He must be very, very drunk after an evening of mojitos, champagne, and now scotch. At home, all Bruce ever drinks is beer—Bud Light or Yuengling. When Bruce speaks, his words are slurred. "So whaddaya go' do, then, my friend?"

"I'm not sure. I need her to listen to reason. But she's stubborn." Tag studies the lit end of his cigar, then looks at Bruce. "So, anyway, now I've told you my war story. How about you? Have you ever stepped out on Mrs. Otis?"

"Naw, man," Bruce says. "Not like that."

Karen takes a deep breath. She should *not* be eavesdropping; this is a conversation between men, and now she has heard Tag confess he has gotten someone pregnant—probably that Featherleigh woman!—and what a mess *that* will turn out to be! Karen feels a little better about the last-minute canceling of the wedding. The Winbury family isn't at all what she thought.

"But I did have a crush on this chick once," Bruce says. "A real intense crush."

Karen is so shocked she nearly cries out. The pain is instant and rude. A crush? A *real intense crush?*

"Oh yeah?" Tag says.

"Yeah, yeah, yeah," Bruce says. *He's drunk,* Karen reminds herself. He hasn't had this much to drink maybe ever. He is probably making up a story to impress Tag Winbury.

"She worked with me at Neiman Marcus," Bruce says. "At first we were all business. In fact, I didn't even like her that much. She was uppity. She came to my store from New York City, from Bergdorf Goodman, where she worked in shoes."

Bergdorf's. Shoes. Yes, Karen vaguely recalls someone... but who was it?

"Oh yeah?" Tag says again.

"Then we became friends. We'd take our dinner break together. She had a different perspective on the world and it was... I don't know... refreshing, I guess, to talk to someone who had been places and done things. This was right after Celeste left for college, and I'm not going to lie, it was like a midlife crisis for both me *and* Karen. Karen hates to shop, *hates* to spend money on frivolous things, but she started going to all these trunk shows, Tupperware parties, something called the Pampered Chef. And I took on more night shifts so that I could be with this other woman."

Karen feels her heart pop, like a tire sliced by a granite

curb, like a balloon drifting into a thorny rosebush. There's a concussion in her chest. She can't believe she's hearing this. Now, in her final days, she is learning that the man she has spent her whole life loving once harbored feelings for another woman.

Karen tries to calm herself. A crush is nothing. A crush is harmless. Hasn't Karen herself had crushes on people—the young man who worked in the produce section of Wegman's, for example? She used to give him a little wave and if he waved or smiled back she would float through the store, sometimes so giddy that she would buy treats she shouldn't have—white chocolate Magnum bars, for example.

"Did you two ever..." Tag asks.

"No," Bruce says. "I thought about it, though. It was a confusing time in my life. I can't tell you how much it turned my whole world upside down. I had spent my entire life feeling like one person and then suddenly I felt like someone else."

"Tell me about it," Tag says. "What was her name?"

"Robin," Bruce says. "Robin Swain."

Karen does gasp—loudly—but neither Tag nor Bruce hears her. They just puff away on their cigars. Karen feels her insides turn to liquid. She has to sit down. She frantically tries to arrange the drapes back as she found them and she clambers out from behind the sofa. She should go back to her room. She can't have Bruce finding her here. If he knew she had been eavesdropping he would...vaporize.

Robin Swain. No. Please, God, no.

She can't make it back up the stairs. She sits on the sofa but feels too exposed. She would slide down to the floor but she'll never be able to get back up. She looks around the room in a wild panic. Suddenly, she hates the house, its luxurious furnishings, the ostensible kindness of the

Winburys, which now seems like a masked cruelty. Why on earth would Tag ask Bruce *such a heinous question?*

Why would Bruce give such an answer?

Robin Swain.

What did Bruce *mean* by that?

But Karen knows what he meant. And that's why she's reacting this way. She knew there was something unusual about Bruce's friendship with Robin. But of course it was inconceivable, unthinkable. It made no sense.

Karen steadies herself. *Bruce is drunk,* she thinks. He made up a story for Tag, out of machismo. He used Robin Swain's name because it was the first that came to mind. Karen shouldn't put any stock in what she just heard. She should go to bed. She manages to make her way back to the entry hall and climbs the stairs.

Once in her room, she takes an oxy. She takes two. Then she climbs into bed, still in her robe. She's shivering.

An intense crush on Robin Swain. They shared dinners; Bruce worked nights so they could be together. A confusing time in his life. A midlife crisis.

Well, yes, Karen thinks. This *is* confusing.

Robin Swain is a man.

It was September, right after Celeste left for college. Karen and Bruce had rented a U-Haul and driven her all the way across Pennsylvania and nearly all the way across Ohio to Oxford, which was only five miles from the Indiana border. They had helped her move into her dorm room in Hahne Hall, they had met her roommate, Julia, and Julia's parents. Karen and Bruce had attended the opening address by the college president and then they returned with Celeste to her room, both Bruce and Karen at loose ends, unsure of how to say good-bye. Eventually, Celeste decided to go to dinner at the Kona Bistro with Julia and her parents; she had left

Karen and Bruce alone in her room. Karen had thought about simply moving in or renting an apartment down the street, and she's sure Bruce did too.

Neither of them had said much on the drive home.

A week or two later, Bruce had come home talking about a new colleague, Robin Swain. He was a man about Bruce's age who had transferred in from the shoe department of Bergdorf's. Robin had grown up in Opelika, Alabama, and had started college at Auburn but hadn't finished. He'd always wanted to go to New York City so he saved his money and bought a bus ticket. He was first hired at Bergdorf's to work in the stockroom.

Initially, Bruce complained about Robin. He might have come from a small town, but working in Manhattan had given him an attitude. He disparaged the King of Prussia store, the mall, the entire Delaware Valley. It was nowhere near as sophisticated as New York City, he said. The area was permanently stuck in 1984, back when the Philadelphia sports teams were good and perms were in fashion and everyone listened to Springsteen. Robin himself listened to country music.

But over the course of a few weeks, Karen noted a shift. Bruce started to talk more favorably about Robin. One of the shirts that Bruce came home to model for Karen was something that Robin had picked out for him. Now that Karen thinks back, *that* was when Bruce's sock fetish started. Robin loved flashy socks, and soon after, Bruce adopted the affectation; he wore rainbow socks, zebra socks, socks printed with the likeness of Elvis. He bought a CD called *When the Sun Goes Down* by Kenny Chesney and started singing the song all the damn time. *Everything gets hotter when the sun goes down.*

One night, Bruce invited Robin home for dinner. This had struck Karen as a bit strange. She and Bruce rarely had guests for dinner, and the town of College-ville, where Robin was renting an apartment, was over an hour away. It was impractical. If Bruce wanted to have dinner with Robin, he should do so at the mall.

But Bruce had insisted. He had instructed Karen what to cook—her Betty Crocker pot roast with potatoes and carrots, a green salad (*not* iceberg lettuce, he said), and snowflake rolls. He would pick up wine on the way home, he said.

Wine? Karen had thought. They never, ever drank wine with dinner. They drank ice water, and Bruce, occasionally, a beer.

When Bruce and Robin walked in, they had been laughing at something, but they sobered up when they saw Karen. Robin was tall, wearing an expensive-looking blue blazer, a white shirt, navy pants, a brown leather belt with a silver H buckle. He wore light blue socks patterned with white clouds, which Bruce proudly showed off to Karen by lifting Robin's pants at the knee. Robin had a receding hairline, brown eyes, a slight Southern drawl. Had Karen thought *gay* when she saw him? She can't remember. Her overarching emotion at dinner was jealousy. Bruce and Robin talked between themselves—about the merchandise, about the clientele, about their co-workers. With each change of topic, Robin tried to include Karen, but maybe Karen's responses were so frosty that he stopped trying. She hadn't meant to be unkind to Robin but she had felt blindsided by his presence. Her mind kept returning to the sight of Bruce lifting Robin's pant leg at the knee. The gesture had seemed so familiar, nearly intimate.

She had chalked up her conflicting emotions to the fact that Celeste had left and now it was just Karen and Bruce, and Bruce had gone out and found a friend at work. Which was fine. After all, Karen had friends at the Crayola factory gift shop. She was friends with nearly everyone! But there was no one special, no one she would invite home to dinner, no one she would talk to and laugh with and in so doing make Bruce feel irrelevant.

After dinner, Bruce had suggested Robin help him with the dishes so that Karen could put her feet up. When had Karen *ever* put her feet up? Never, that's when. But she knew how to take a hint. She bade Robin good-bye and Bruce a good night and she had stormed upstairs to lie angrily on the bed and listen to the two men washing and drying the dishes and finishing the wine and then stepping out onto the back porch to talk about heaven knows what.

Karen feels the oxy gripping her by the shoulders, then there is a great release as the pain falls away.

Bruce had an intense crush on Robin. A man. *It was a confusing time,* he said. *Suddenly I felt like someone else,* he said.

To Karen, it's a nuclear confession. Her husband, her state champion wrestler, her hungry wolf in bed had had feelings for another man, feelings he obviously isn't comfortable acknowledging because to Tag, he changed Robin's gender to female.

Robin worked at Neiman Marcus only through the holidays that year. By the time Celeste returned to Oxford after Christmas break, Robin had been transferred to the Neiman Marcus flagship store in Dallas. Had Bruce been upset? Heartbroken, even? If so, he'd hid it well.

Bruce had a secret, an intense crush. He never acted on it; this, Karen believes.

And Karen has a secret of her own: the three pills in the bottle, among the oxy.

Karen issues Bruce a silent pardon—it *had* been a confusing time. And, as Karen had wanted to tell Celeste, there is *no such thing* as a perfect couple.

Karen will tell Celeste this in the morning. She closes her eyes.

Saturday, July 7, 2018,
12:45 p.m.

NANTUCKET

Nick "the Greek" Diamantopoulos is driving from 333 Monomoy Road to the Nantucket Cottage Hospital, where he is finally going to talk to the bride. She wants to be interviewed *at the hospital,* and Nick hopes this means she has real information. He's eager to find out, but when he rolls around the rotary, he catches the scent of Lola Burger through his open window and the smell is too much to resist. One thing about Nantucket, Nick thinks, the food is top-notch. Even the burger joints. Nick pulls into takeout parking and races inside to charm Marva, the hostess, who scores him a medium-rare Lolaburger (aged cheddar, onion compote, foie gras dipping sauce) with a side of fries. Nick leaves Marva a nice big tip and she says, "Don't be a stranger, Greek man. Come back and see me!"

Nick hops back in his car, stuffing fries in his mouth.

At the hospital, the Greek is greeted by a trio of nurses—Margaret, Suzanne, and Patty. Nick has been on dates with both Suzanne and Patty—nothing serious, just fun. He smiles at all three and says, "Where am I going and what do I need to know?"

Patty links her arm through his and leads him down the hall to an exam room. "She came in early this morning and we treated her for hysteria slash panic attack, meaning we took her vitals and gave her some Valium to calm her down. She slept for a little while. I wish there were something more we could do. Her best friend drowned out in front of the house? And Celeste found her? On her wedding day?"

"Wedding was canceled," Nick says. "Obviously."

"Obviously."

"The deceased was the maid of honor," Nick says.

"That's what Celeste told me," Patty says. She gives a dry laugh. "Maybe she didn't like the dress."

Nick shakes his head. He can't make a joke at Merritt's expense. He just can't.

"What happened when the groom showed up here?" he asks.

"That was about an hour ago. Seemed like a nice guy. He was worried about Celeste and he expected to take her home. He was in her room for about ten minutes, then he left. And she asked to speak to you."

"Okay, Patty. Thank you. It's okay if I question her in here?"

"Sure," Patty says. "One strange thing? Celeste came with a bag packed. I'm just not sure what to make of that. When I asked her about it, she started to cry, so I let it be."

"Okay," Nick says. That *is* strange, but there's probably an explanation.

"My shift ends at three," Patty says. "Call me if you want to get together tonight."

The idea is tempting, but he knows he won't relax until he cracks this case. Hopefully the bride has the answer.

"Will do," he says.

He finds Celeste in a hospital gown, lying back on the examining table. When she sees him, she sits up. "Are you the police?"

"State police detective Nick Diamantopoulos," he says. "I'm very sorry about your friend."

Celeste nods. "You're here to take my statement."

"I am," Nick says. "It's a tragedy, what happened to Merritt."

"She's dead?" Celeste says. "Is she…I mean, she's dead, right?"

Nick takes a seat in the chair at the foot of the examining table. The fries start to churn in his stomach. "I'm sorry, yes. She's dead."

Celeste bows her head and cries softly. "It's all my fault."

"Excuse me?"

"It's my fault. I knew something bad would happen. I thought it would be my mother but it wasn't—it was Merritt. She's dead!"

"I'm very sorry," Nick says again. "I know you have a lot to deal with right now."

"You *don't* know," Celeste says. "You have no idea."

Nick takes out his notepad. "The best way to help Merritt is to help me figure out what happened to her. She was your best friend, your maid of honor. She confided in you, right?"

Celeste nods.

"And here's the funny thing about weddings," Nick says. "They bring together people who don't know each other. I've interviewed two people already but neither of them really knew Merritt. So you are a key part of this investigation."

Celeste takes a deep breath. "I'm not sure I want to break Merritt's confidence. Other people are involved. Other people I care about."

"I understand," Nick says. His sympathy is genuine, but he is a sapper looking for land mines. "Why don't you just tell me what you know and we'll see if it's relevant."

Celeste stares at him.

"I have someone who witnessed you and Ms. Monaco in the Winburys' rose garden after the party ended," Nick says. "This person said Ms. Monaco was crying and you were comforting her. Do you want to tell me what that was about?"

Celeste blinks. "Someone saw us in the *rose garden?*" she says. "Who?"

"I can't tell you that," Nick says. "What you tell me here is confidential. That's true for everyone."

"I hear you saying that, but..."

"But what?" Nick says. She's scared to tell him what she knows—but why? "My understanding is that Ms. Monaco was estranged from her parents and there's a brother somewhere but no one knows where. So she doesn't have any family here to advocate on her behalf. That leaves me—and you—to find out what happened. Do you understand the magnitude of that responsibility, Celeste?"

"She was...going through a tough breakup," Celeste says. "With a married man. She was very upset about it."

Nick nods. He waits.

"I told her to end it. Back when I found out, which was only a few weeks ago, I told her to end it and she said she would, but she didn't. And then he ended it."

"The married man?"

"Yes," Celeste says. "And that was why she was crying."

Nick writes on his notepad: *Married man.* Then he scans his other notes and he thinks about Merritt's cell phone. She had just gone through a breakup but there were no calls or texts, either coming in or going out. Except for the one from Robbie wishing her a belated "Happy Day of American Independence" and hoping she was doing well.

"Is the married man named Robbie, by any chance?"

Celeste's eyes widen. "How do you know about Robbie?"

"I'm a detective," Nick says. "Is Robbie the married man?"

"No," Celeste says. "Robbie is her...was...I don't know, her friend. A guy friend. A past boyfriend, but not anymore."

"Celeste, was the married man that Merritt was involved with at the party last night?"

The barest movement of the head forward. Almost involuntary, it seems.

"Is that a nod?"

"It's Tag," Celeste whispers. "Tag Winbury, my father-in-law."

Boom, Nick thinks.

Once the name is out, the rest flows more easily, as though a plug has been pulled.

Merritt and Tag hooked up two months ago during Celeste's bachelorette weekend. They saw each other in the city, Celeste isn't sure when or where. As recently as the Fourth of July, Merritt said the relationship was over. It wasn't a big deal, according to her.

"But I talked to her after the rehearsal dinner. She was upset. I encouraged her to come into town with us but she said she wouldn't be any fun. She wanted to stay home and mope, she said. Get it out of her system so she would be good to go today." Celeste pauses. "For the wedding."

"Was the last time you saw Merritt alive in the rose garden?" Nick asks.

"No," Celeste says. "I saw her when we got back from town."

"You did?" Nick says. "Where was she?"

"She was at a table under the tent with Tag," Celeste

says. "And Thomas, Benji's brother. Thomas came with us into town. We went to the back bar at Ventuno but when we got to the Boarding House, his wife, Abby, called and told him to come home. When we got back, he was sitting under the tent with Tag and Merritt... and a friend of the Winburys named Featherleigh Dale."

Nick writes down the names: *Merritt, Tag, Thomas, brother, and a person—woman?—named Featherleigh Dale.*

"Do you know Featherleigh Dale?" Nick asks.

"Not really," Celeste says. "I just met her last night. She's from London."

"And was she also staying at the Winbury house?"

"No."

"But she was there last night?"

"Yes," Celeste says.

"What time was it when you saw Merritt under the tent with Tag?"

"We left town when the bars closed, at one," Celeste says. "So maybe one thirty?"

"And when you saw Merritt with Tag," Nick says, "were you concerned?"

"I was preoccupied..." Celeste says.

"That stands to reason," Nick says. "After all, you were supposed to get married today."

"It's no excuse." Celeste bows her head. "I was preoccupied and I didn't persuade Merritt to come to bed. If I had done that, she would be alive. This is my fault."

Nick needs to keep his bride focused. "Celeste, what were Tag and Merritt and Thomas and...Featherleigh doing under the tent? Drinking? Smoking?"

"Drinking shots," Celeste says. "Of some special rum Tag gets in Barbados. Tag had a cigar. They looked happy. Merritt looked *happy,* or happier, anyway. They tried to get me to join them but Benji and Shooter had gone to bed and I wanted to get some sleep…"

"Understandable," Nick says. "You were getting married the next day."

Again, Celeste shakes her head. It's the mention of the wedding that seems to set her back, so Nick decides not to do it again.

"As I was saying good night to everyone, Abby called down from an upstairs window," Celeste says. "She wanted Thomas to come to bed. And I did hesitate a bit then because I thought it would be bad for Tag and Merritt to be alone together. Honestly, I thought they might rekindle their…" She stops, pinkens. "I thought they might hook up."

Nick nods. "Okay."

"But Featherleigh was there and she showed no intention of leaving. She made a comment that it was morning in London and she had just gotten her second wind." Celeste swallows. "I kissed Merritt good night and I squeezed her hand and looked her in the eye and I said, *Are you okay, my friend?* And she said, *Hey, your stutter is gone.* Because I had a stutter for a few months, actually. Anyway, I figured she was sober enough to notice that, she would be fine. So I went up to bed."

"Did you hear anything outside after that?" Nick asks. "Did you hear anyone in the water? There was a two-person kayak left out on the beach. There was blood in the sand and Merritt had a cut on her foot. Do you know anything about that?"

"Kayak?" Celeste says. She sits up, swings her feet to the floor, and starts to pace. "Did Tag take Merritt out in the kayak? Do you know if that happened?"

"I don't," he says. "I'm working with the Nantucket Police on this. The Chief will question Mr. Winbury about the kayak. The important thing is you didn't *hear* anything?"

"No," Celeste says. "But the house has central air and Benji's bedroom—the room where I was staying—faces the driveway, not the water."

"And this morning... you're the one who found Ms. Monaco, is that correct?"

"Yes," Celeste says.

"You were up early," Nick says. "Why is that?"

Celeste bows her head and starts to shake.

Nick turns to see a yellow paisley duffel bag in the corner of the room. He remembers what Patty said. "And you had a bag packed? I guess I don't understand why you were down at the beach at five thirty in the morning with your bag." Although Nick does understand, or he thinks he does.

When Celeste looks up, tears are streaming down her face. "Is there any way we can be finished for now?"

Nick scans his notepad. This was not your typical wedding. The maid of honor was sleeping with the groom's father. Nick will call the Chief and have him question the father; Nick would likely lose his cool with the guy. He's beginning to have emotions about this case, which is never a good thing.

But then Nick thinks about Greer Garrison. Which of Greer's answers had Nick found suspicious? All of them, really. She had seemed bloodless, soulless, unaffected, and... unsurprised. And she had intentionally not told Nick about going to the kitchen for a nightcap. Greer writes murder mysteries. *If anyone would be able to plot a murder and get away with it,* Nick thinks, *it would be her.*

Right?

If she knew about this affair, she would be a prime suspect.

But Nick can't leave any stone unturned here. Featherleigh Dale was at the table after both Celeste and Thomas left. Featherleigh might be able to say for sure if Tag took Merritt out in the kayak.

Nick writes on his notepad: *Find Featherleigh Dale!*

The sound of Celeste crying brings Nick back to the present.

"We can be finished," Nick says. "For now." He gets to his feet. The poor kid. It's pretty clear she's going through more than just her best friend dying. "I'll send Patty back in."

Saturday, July 7, 2018,
2:00 p.m.

THE CHIEF

Shooter Uxley wants to lawyer up, which is his right, although any cop in America will tell you the same thing: It doesn't look good. Why lawyer up if you have nothing to hide? The Chief tries to point this out to Shooter gently, without making his true motivation known, his true motivation being that they need answers, and fast.

Keira, the Chief's assistant, informs the Chief that before he went off duty, Sergeant Dickson was able to locate and speak to Ms. Monaco's brother, Douglas Monaco, of Garden City, New York, and that Mr. Monaco said he would contact his parents and would, when the time came, make the necessary arrangements for the body.

"How did he sound?" the Chief asks. "Did he have any questions?"

"He was shocked," Keira says. "But he hadn't talked to her since last Christmas and he said his parents hadn't spoken to her in years. They had a falling-out."

"Did he ask you what happened?" the Chief says.

"He didn't," Keira says. "He just thanked me for letting him know and gave me his contact information."

"Good," the Chief says. The last thing he needs now is aggressive, upset family members demanding more intensive police work. And yet the complete opposite of that feels sad, even though it makes his job easier. "You can release the name, age, and the hometown—use New York City—to the press and tell them the matter is under investigation. No further comment."

"Also?" Keira says. "Sue Moran from the chamber of commerce called. She's concerned."

"About what?"

"Weddings on Nantucket generate over fifty million dollars, she said. A Murdered Maid of Honor is extremely bad for business, she said. She wants us to try to keep the wedding angle quiet."

"Fine," the Chief says. "We'll try. But you might want to remind her that it's a small island."

Uxley chooses a local attorney, Valerie Gluckstern. The Chief knows Val well, and while she's not his favorite lawyer on this island, neither is she his least favorite. She started out as a trust and estate attorney and switched to criminal defense six or seven years ago, once there were enough wealthy and connected lawbreakers to keep her in business. Val is willing to relax certain rules because they live thirty miles out to sea and big-city procedure doesn't always apply.

For example, instead of wearing a suit and heels, Val shows up at the station wearing a beach cover-up, a straw hat, and flip-flops.

"I came right from the beach," Val says, and in fact she has sand breading the backs of her legs. "My brother is here with his four kids and his pregnant wife. I wasn't exactly unhappy to be called away." She cocks an eyebrow at the Chief. "Do you ever have houseguests, Ed?"

"Not if I can help it," he says.

"Wise man," Val says. She looks around. "Where's the Greek? I thought he was investigating this case."

That explains Val's prompt arrival more than the houseguests, the Chief thinks. Every woman on this island will jump through hoops of white fire for the Greek.

"He's interviewing a witness at the hospital," the Chief says.

Val nods. "Let me talk to my client."

"He tried to run," the Chief says. "It doesn't look good, Val. You should let him know that."

"Let me talk to my client," Val says again.

While Val is in with Shooter, Ed checks his phone. He sees a text from Nick that says, We need to find a wedding guest named Featherleigh Dale, and the Chief curses under his breath. Here he's liking Shooter Uxley for this and now there's a new person of interest? The Chief calls the Winbury house to speak to Greer.

"We're looking for someone named Featherleigh Dale," he says.

"Yes," Greer says. She sounds unsurprised.

"Do you have any idea where we might find her?" he asks.

"She's staying at an inn," Greer says. "Let me check which one. I have it written down." A moment later she comes back to the phone. "The Sand Dollar Guest House, on Water Street."

"Thank you." The Chief hangs up and dispatches one of his patrolmen to the Sand Dollar to bring this Featherleigh Dale in for questioning.

Nick calls on his way from the hospital to the compound. "Talked to the bride," he says. "She was a gold mine."

"What did she give you?" the Chief asks.

"Our maid of honor wasn't exactly honorable," Nick says. "She was sleeping with the groom's father, Tag Winbury."

The Chief closes his eyes. He's so hungry, he's seeing stars—then he remembers that Andrea packed him a lunch: turkey BLT, two ripe, cold plums, a thermos of chilled cucumber-coconut soup. He loves his wife. As soon as he gets off with Nick, he'll eat.

"I talked to Linda Ferretti, the ME," the Chief says. "Victim was seven weeks pregnant."

Nick sucks in his breath and the Chief feels a renewed sense of purpose. This woman's death was no accident. They have a real situation on their hands.

"She was pregnant with Winbury's kid," Nick says. "I wonder who knew. Celeste didn't tell me that. I . . . I don't think she knew. I wonder if Greer Garrison knew.

"I dispatched Luklo to go pick up Ms. Dale at her inn," the Chief says. "How is she involved?"

"She was sitting under the tent late last night with Merritt, Tag, and Thomas, the groom's brother. The brother, Thomas, went up to bed, leaving Merritt, Tag Winbury, and Featherleigh Dale. She should have something to tell us."

"Yes, we need the Dale woman," the Chief says. "Now that we know what we know. So why am I talking to Shooter Uxley? Why did he run? Where is he in all of this? Why did he, of all people, lawyer up?"

"I guess we'll find out," Nick says. "Who's his attorney?"

"Valerie Gluckstern."

"I like Val," Nick says. "And she likes me."

"Let's hope that works in our favor and we can get the kid to talk," the Chief says. "After I'm finished with Uxley, I'll talk to the father."

"I'll talk to this Dale woman," Nick says. "Once we find her. And, hey, if you need help swaying Val Gluckstern, let me know."

"Thanks, Prince Charming," the Chief says.

Saturday, August 12-Monday, August 21, 2017

CELESTE

She takes a week's vacation from the zoo in August, coordinating with Benji's vacation, and the two of them go to Nantucket.

Merritt says, "You do know how lucky you are, right? Having a rich boyfriend with a huge waterfront home on Nantucket?"

"Right," Celeste says uneasily. She doesn't want anyone—even Merritt—to think she is after Benji for his money. The money makes things nicer and easier. They can go to dinner whenever and wherever they want, they go to concerts and sit in the front row, Benji always treats her to taxis and sends her bouquets of beautiful, exotic flowers, and occasionally she will come home to find he has delivered a box of Pierre Hermé macarons to her doorstep (she had never tasted a macaron before meeting Benji; now, they're one more expensive habit that she's developed). Celeste enjoys these aspects of their relationship—she would be a liar if she denied it—but her favorite things about Benji are that he's kind, thoughtful, solid, steady, and even-keeled.

Despite all this, she had been thinking, right before plans for the vacation were made, of breaking up with him. She likes him but she has been consistently misrepresenting her feelings because she does not love him.

She loves Shooter Uxley.

She has tried to talk herself out of it. How can she love Shooter when she spent only one day with him? After Benji belatedly arrived that weekend in June, Shooter left the island, claiming a work emergency. That Sunday afternoon, once Celeste was back in her own apartment, Shooter had sent her a text that said, I couldn't stay and watch the two of you together.

So, Celeste thought, Shooter had felt it too. He had felt that strong, unmistakable *thing,* that animal attraction. Celeste uses the phrase purposefully because she's a scientist and may understand better than most how human beings are at the mercy of their biology. Celeste thinks of a male lion establishing dominance in a pride or the blue-footed booby showing the female his blue feet by dancing. The natural world is filled with such rituals that can be documented and categorized but ultimately not explained. Celeste can't control her urges or her feelings any better than hyenas or aardvarks; however, she *can* control her behavior. She has no intention of leaving Benji for his best friend. But she knows it's not fair to stay with him when she doesn't love him.

She needs to break it off.

She will break it off, she decides, after they get back from Nantucket.

Saturday, Sunday, Monday: Celeste and Benji lie by the pool, swim in the harbor, eat the finger sandwiches and cubes of melon that Elida brings them on a tray for lunch. In the late afternoon, they go to 167 Raw to buy fresh tuna and swordfish steaks, then they go to Bartlett's Farm for corn, summer squash, greens for salad, a home-made peach pie. In the mornings, they wander the shops in town. At Milly and Grace, Celeste tries on four dresses, and Benji, unable to decide which he likes best on her, buys her all four. That night, Benji takes Celeste out to Sconset to eat at a candlelit table in the garden of the Chanticleer. At the center of the garden stands a carousel horse, and Celeste finds herself staring at the horse throughout dinner.

This week, Shooter is in Saratoga Springs, New York, with a group of tech executives from Belarus; they have gone to see the races. Celeste knows this because Benji keeps her constantly informed about Shooter's whereabouts; Benji shows her every picture Shooter sends him, like a proud uncle. Sometimes he says, jokingly, "I'm boring, but here's my exciting friend." Celeste smiles mildly; she glances at the photos but can't bring herself to focus on Shooter's face. What good would it do? She never responded to Shooter's text. She can't have a secret line of communication with him; she knows where that would lead.

Celeste tears her eyes away from the carousel horse and thoughts of Saratoga and wills herself to be happy. She likes Benji. She cares about Benji.

As she watches Benji sip his wine, she imagines Shooter at the betting window, track pencil behind his ear. She imagines him in the grandstand or the elevated suite with fancy free hors d'oeuvres and scantily clad cocktail waitresses, where only the most important people in the world are allowed to sit. She imagines Shooter's horse pulling ahead on the outside. Shooter has picked the winner again. He high-fives the Belarusians.

"Do you want dessert?" Benji asks. "Celeste?"

Tuesday and Wednesday: Celeste is tan. Celeste is relaxed. Celeste is growing more comfortable with Benji's parents. One morning, she runs five miles with Tag. The following afternoon she goes to a photography exhibit on Old South Wharf with Greer, and afterward,

Celeste suggests they get an Italian ice at the little shop next to the gallery.

"My treat," Celeste says. The ices cost only ten dollars but Celeste leaves the cute red-haired teenager behind the counter a five-dollar tip. Tag and Greer are so generous that it makes Celeste want to be generous on her own scale.

They sit on a bench on the wharf to enjoy their ices in the sun and Greer says, "So, how are things going with you and Benji?"

Celeste isn't sure what Greer is asking. "Everything is fine," she says.

"Tag and I are heading back to the city tomorrow," Greer says. "My friend Elizabeth Calabash's son is getting married at the Plaza."

"Oh," Celeste says. She savors the taste of her passionfruit ice and thinks of how, before she met Benji, she would have stuck to something safe like lemon or raspberry. "That's nice."

"I think Benji would like some alone time with you," Greer says. "Nothing quashes romance like having one's parents around."

"I enjoy your company," Celeste says. It's true. With the elder Winburys in residence, there is a family atmosphere at the house. There are times it feels like she and Benji are siblings. Celeste's greatest dream is that her parents might someday see Nantucket. She tries to describe it in her phone calls, but she can't do it justice, and there are things she knows they won't understand—dining at nine o'clock at night in a garden with a carousel horse, paying seventeen hundred dollars for a photograph, or even passionfruit Italian ice.

Thursday and Friday: Tag and Greer leave late on Thursday. Benji apologizes to Celeste, but he has committed to playing in the member-guest golf tournament at the Nantucket Golf Club, which will eat up most of Friday.

"No problem," Celeste says. She has a new book— *Mrs. Fletcher* by Tom Perrotta—and she looks forward to the time alone. It's not supposed to be this way, she knows.

"I've arranged for a surprise," Benji says. He kisses Celeste. "Shooter is coming."

Celeste blinks and pulls back. "What?" she says. "I thought he was in Saratoga."

"He was," Benji says. "But he has a couple of days free so I asked him to come."

Celeste has no idea what kind of expression crosses her face. Is it one of alarm? Fear? Panic?

"I thought you liked Shooter," Benji says.

"Oh, I do," Celeste says. "I do."

At seven o'clock on Friday morning, Benji pulls away in Tag's Land Rover with his golf clubs in the back. Celeste stands on the front porch and waves until he's gone. Then she steps inside to the entrance hall and studies herself in one of Greer's antique mirrors. She is blond and blue-eyed, pretty but not beautiful, or maybe beautiful but not extraordinary. Is there something she's not seeing? Something inside of her? She likes animals, the environment, the natural world. This has always set her apart, made her less desirable rather than more so. When she was growing up, she was always reading the encyclopedia or *National Geographic,* and when she wasn't doing that, she was collecting snakes and salamanders in shoe boxes and trying to re-create their natural habitat. She wasn't interested in boy bands or wearing friendship bracelets or roller-blading or shopping for CDs and hair clips at the mall, just as now she doesn't care about gender politics or social media or bingeing on Netflix or going to barre class or who wore what to the Met Ball. She is atypical. She is weird.

Shooter is coming. She's not sure what to do. Proceed as normal? She changes into her bathing suit, grabs her new book, and goes out to the pool.

When she wakes up with the book splayed open on her chest, she finds Shooter sitting on the next chaise with his elbow on his knee, his chin in his hand, staring at her.

No, she's dreaming. She closes her eyes.

"Sunshine."

Opens her eyes.

"Hi," he says. He grins. "Benji called to say you needed looking after."

"I don't," she snaps. She refuses to flirt with him. She refuses to be *complicit* in this. It's as though Benji is *trying* to lose her, handing her off to Shooter once again. "You should have stayed in Saratoga."

"You're sexy when you're stern," Shooter says. "And I was happy to come, I wanted to come. All I've wanted since I left the last time was to see you again."

"Shooter," she says.

"You must think I'm a real bastard," he says. "Going after my best friend's girl. People write songs about this very scenario, Celeste—Rick Springfield, the Cars. And do you know why? Because it happens. It happens all the time."

"But why *me?*" Celeste says. It's amazing enough that she won the devotion of Benjamin Winbury, but to have Shooter's attention too seems so inconceivable that she wonders if it's a trick or a joke. Men like Benji and Shooter should be chasing after women like Merritt. Merritt is an influencer; she has power, clout, and she knows everyone. She is connected, savvy, witty, a social genius. Celeste, meanwhile, writes e-mails to other zoo administrators about improving the orangutan habitat.

"Because you're real," Shooter says. "You're so normal

and down-to-earth that you're exotic. There is no pretense with you, Celeste. Any idea how rare that is these days? And I had such a good time with you here. I haven't enjoyed a woman's company that much ever before in my life. It's like you cast a spell on me. When Benji asked me to come, I didn't think twice."

"Benji is my boyfriend," Celeste says. "Nothing is going to happen between you and me."

Shooter gives her a laser stare with his sapphire-blue eyes. "Hearing you say that makes me like you even more. Benji is the better choice."

Benji is *the better choice!* Celeste thinks. She wonders if Shooter is motivated by envy. He wants what Benji has—his parents, his pedigree, and now his girlfriend. Probably that's it. Celeste turns her eyes back to her book, hoping Mrs. Fletcher can save her.

"Put your shorts and flip-flops on," Shooter says. "I'm taking you somewhere."

"Where?" Celeste says.

"I'll meet you out front," he says.

Shooter has rented a silver Jeep. He tells Celeste he asked for the exact same one they had before, and when Celeste sits in the passenger seat, she does indeed feel a strong sense of familiarity, like this is their car, like they belong in it.

Shooter drives out to the Surfside Beach Shack. "I was wrong about the tomato sandwich," he says. He climbs out of the Jeep and returns a few moments later with a cardboard box that holds two sandwiches wrapped in foil and two drinks. "These are the best sandwiches on the island, possibly the world." They proceed all the way to the end of Madaket Road, cross a small wooden bridge, and enter what looks like a seaside village from another era. The houses are teensy-tiny beach shacks with funky architectural details: a suspended deck that joins two roof-lines, a slant-roofed tower, a row of round porthole windows. These are nothing like the elegant castles out in Monomoy. These are like beach cottages for elves, and they all have funny names: Duck Inn, It'll Do, Breaking Away.

"They're so small," Celeste says. "How do people actually live in them?"

"The best living is done outside," Shooter says. "And look at the location—they're right on the water."

Celeste nearly points out that the Winburys' house is right on the water, but she understands the inherent charm of these homes. There are brightly striped towels draped over railings and hibachi grills on the decks; the "front yards" are sand and a tangle of *Rosa rugosa* bushes. How idyllic life would be out here. You spent all day at the beach, rinsed off under the outdoor shower, grilled a striped bass that you had caught yourself surf-casting a hundred yards away. At night, your neighbors wandered over to share an ice-cold beer or a gin and tonic while you all gazed up at the stars and listened to the pounding surf. Rainy days would mean cards, board games, or a good paperback mystery read in a comfortable old chair.

Shooter crouches down to let some of the air out of the Jeep's tires; Celeste watches him from her perch in the passenger seat. She studies the back of his neck, the shape of his ears. When he works on the back tires she trains her eyes on him in her side-view mirror. He looks up, catches her, blows her a kiss. She wants to scowl, but instead, she smiles.

Celeste and Shooter drive up over the dunes. The stark natural beauty of Smith's Point is staggering. There's a long stretch of pristine beach in front of them with the ocean to the left and dunes carpeted in eelgrass to the right. Beyond those dunes is the flat blue surface of Nantucket Sound.

Shooter is taking it slow—five miles an hour—so he can easily reach over to the glove compartment, grazing Celeste's knee with the back of his hand as he does so. He pulls out a guide to eastern shorebirds.

"For my zoologist," he says.

Celeste wants to correct him—she isn't *his* anything—but she becomes instantly enthralled by the guidebook. She has always loved ornithology, although it requires more patience than she has been naturally gifted with to pursue as a specialty. Still, she loves to visit the World of Birds and talk to Vern, their resident ornithologist. Vern has sighted over seven thousand of the world's ten thousand bird species, a life list that puts him in a very elite category of bird-watcher. Vern's best stories often aren't about the birds themselves but rather about the travels he has undertaken in order to see them. When he was only eighteen, he hitchhiked from Oxford, Mississippi, to the Monteverde Cloud Forest in Costa Rica to see the resplendent quetzal. He has been to Gambia to see the African gray hornbill and to Antarctica to see the Adélie penguin.

Right away, Celeste points out the sandpiper and the American oystercatcher with its signature orange beak. Shooter laughs and says, "You delight me." He drives out to the tip of Smith's Point—Celeste sees the much smaller island of Tuckernuck across a narrow channel—and then he curves around to the far side of the point. He sets up a camp—a chair for each of them, an umbrella for shade, towels, and a small table, where he lays out their lunch. He shucks off his polo shirt. Celeste tries not to notice the muscles of his back.

"Watch this," he says. He wades out into the water a few feet and then he must drop off a ledge or a shelf because suddenly he is in up to his chest. He lifts his hands in the air, and the water whooshes him down the shore. "Yee-haw!" he cries out. About forty yards down, he climbs out of the water and jogs back to Celeste. "It's a natural water slide," he says. "You have to try it."

Celeste can't resist. Her parents took her to Great Wolf Lodge every summer of her growing up; she has never met a water slide she didn't love. She wades in, her feet feeling for the edge of the shelf. Then she jumps in and the current carries her down the coastline.

It's exhilarating! It's hilarious! Celeste hasn't laughed or enjoyed herself this much since she was a child with her father, going down Coyote Canyon.

"How did you know this was here?" she asks Shooter, breathless.

Shooter says, "It's my business to know the secrets of every universe."

"I want to go again," Celeste says.

The film montage starts once more: Here are Celeste and Shooter riding the current down the beach again and again and again, whooping like rodeo cowboys. Celeste can't get enough; the water is swift, powerful, alive. Shooter gives up first, and finally Celeste declares she is going only one more time. Here are Shooter and Celeste eating their sandwiches—a crab, shrimp, and scallop "burger," topped with avocado, bacon, lettuce, tomato, and a creamy dill and smoked-pepper aioli. And to drink they have fresh watermelon limeades. It's the most delicious lunch Celeste has ever eaten. Is this hyperbole? She doesn't think so, though she realizes the sandwich and the drink are only part of it. The swimming is also part of it, the sand, the view...and Shooter. Celeste is so exhausted after eating that she spreads out a towel and lies facedown. Shooter follows suit, and when Celeste wakes up, his leg is touching hers. Celeste doesn't want to move, but move she must.

* * *

At five o'clock, when they drive off the beach, Celeste's skin is tight from the sun, and her blond hair is stiff with salt. She figures she must look a fright, but when she catches a glimpse of herself in the side-view mirror, what she sees is a young woman who is happy. She has never, in her life, been *this* happy.

"Hey, Sunshine?" Shooter says.

"Please don't," she says. She doesn't want him to say anything that's going to ruin it. She doesn't want him to make any declarations. She doesn't want him to try to name what is happening. They both know what's happening.

Shooter laughs. "I was just going to ask if you wanted to stop at Millie's on the way home? Get a margarita?"

"Yes," she says.

As soon as Shooter pulls into the parking lot at Millie's, his phone starts to ping, and so does Celeste's. Shooter cocks an eyebrow at her. "Check our phones?" he asks. "Or ignore them?"

Ignore them, Celeste thinks. But out of habit, she glances at her display. There are three texts from Benji.

I'm back.

Where are you guys?

Hello?

Celeste feels like she's suspended in midair. What should she do? She wants to go into Millie's with Shooter, order a margarita, maybe knock legs with him under the bar.

But that kind of misbehavior is beyond her.

"We need to go," she says.

Back at Summerland, Benji is on the deck, wearing a coat and tie. He has a bottle of vintage Veuve Clicquot chilling in an ice bucket. He stares pointedly at Shooter.

"You're late," he says.

"Late?" Celeste says. "Were you expecting us earlier? I thought you were golfing."

Shooter says, "Sorry, man, I lost track of time."

Something passes between Benji and Shooter. Celeste is afraid to ask what's going on.

"Should I shower?" Celeste says.

"Yes," Benji says. He kisses her. "Wear the new pink dress. We're going out."

Celeste goes upstairs to shower and change. She puts on a green dress instead of the pink, a small but important defiance. She hates when Benji tries to control her; she knows he thinks he's the Professor Henry Higgins to her Eliza Doolittle. But he's not. She's an intelligent adult; she can pick her own dress.

She is suddenly in an incredibly foul humor. She doesn't even want to go to dinner.

She peers down at the deck from her bedroom window. The champagne remains in the ice bucket—but Benji and Shooter are gone.

There is a whisper of a noise and Celeste turns to see a slip of paper slide under the bedroom door. She freezes. She hears footsteps retreating. After a few moments pass, she tiptoes over to pick up the paper. It says: *In case you have any doubts, I'm in love with you.* The handwriting is unfamiliar. It's not Benji's.

Celeste clutches the note to her chest and sits on the bed. This is either the most wonderful or the most horrible thing ever to happen to her.

"Celeste!"

Benji is calling up the stairs for her. Celeste crumples the note. What should she do with it? She reads it one more time, then she flushes it down the toilet.

"Coming!" she says.

* * *

Shooter has changed into Nantucket Reds, a white shirt, a double-breasted blue blazer, and a captain's hat that Celeste had noticed hanging on a hook in the Winburys' mudroom but that she assumed was just a prop of sorts.

"Nice hat!" Celeste says. Shooter doesn't crack a smile.

Benji leads Celeste out to the end of the Winburys' dock, where a boat is waiting. It's *Ella,* the Winburys' Hinckley picnic boat. It's so sleek and beautiful with its gleaming wood and pristine navy-and-white cushioned benches that Celeste is afraid to climb aboard. Shooter gets on first and offers his hand to Celeste. She wants to squeeze his hand to let him know she got his note and she feels the same way— but she is afraid of Benji noticing.

She and Benji settle in the back while Shooter takes the wheel. Benji opens the champagne, fills two waiting flutes, and hands one to Celeste.

"Cheers," he says.

"Cheers," Celeste says. She clinks glasses with Benji and forces herself to make eye contact with him. Every second is a struggle to keep her gaze off Shooter in the captain's chair. "Is Shooter not having any?"

"Shooter is not having any," Benji says. "He's our skipper tonight."

"Where are we going?" Celeste asks.

"You'll see," Benji says.

Celeste leans back in her seat but she can't relax. Shooter is at the wheel in that ridiculous hat; it's almost as if Benji has set out to humiliate him. But maybe she's over-reacting. Maybe Shooter offered to drive the boat; maybe he likes it. It is a stunner of an evening, the air clear and mild, the water of the harbor a mirror that reflects the rich golden light of the sun behind them. Other boaters wave as they pass. One gentleman calls out, "Beautiful," and Benji calls back, "Isn't she?" and kisses Celeste.

Celeste says, "I'm sure he was talking about the boat."

"The boat, you, me, this incredible night," Benji says.

Right, Celeste thinks. From a distance, they must seem like the most fortunate, privileged couple in the world. No one would ever guess Celeste's private torment.

She sips her champagne. Benji wraps his arm around her and pulls her in close. "I missed you," he says.

"How was golf?" she asks. He doesn't answer, which is just as well.

They dock at the Wauwinet Inn. Shooter is surprisingly skilled with the ropes and knots, making Celeste wonder at his other hidden talents. Playing the harmonica? Shooting a bow and arrow? Skiing moguls? He secures the boat and then helps Celeste up onto the dock. Benji climbs up behind Celeste and checks his watch. "We'll be back at nine o'clock," he tells Shooter.

"Wait a minute," Celeste says. Her heart feels like it's being squeezed. She turns to Shooter. "Aren't you coming to dinner?"

Shooter smiles but his blue eyes are as flat as eyes in a painting. "I'll be here when you're finished," he says.

Celeste wobbles in her wedge heels. She's unsteady in heels on a good day, never mind on a dock under the present circumstances. Benji takes her arm and leads her down the dock to the hotel.

When they are out of earshot, Celeste says, "I don't get it. Why isn't Shooter coming to dinner?"

"Because I want to have a romantic dinner with my girlfriend," Benji says. For the first time since she has known him, he sounds petulant, like one of the cranky children who are at the zoo past their nap time. This show of unexpected attitude provokes Celeste.

"So, what, you just *hired* him to drive the boat? He's our *friend,* Benji. He's not your servant."

Benji says, "I should have realized you would find this scenario unjust. But when I told Shooter my plans to bring you up here, he offered. He's going to grab dinner in the bar."

"By himself?" Celeste says.

"It's Shooter," Benji says. "I'm sure he'll make some friends."

Dinner at Topper's is an extraordinary experience, with attention given to every detail. Drinks are brought on a tiered cocktail tray; Benji's gin and tonic is mixed at the table with a glass swizzle stick. The bread basket features warm, fragrant rosemary focaccia, homemade bacon-and-sage rolls, and twisted cheddar-garlic bread sticks that look like the branches of a tree in an enchanted forest. Under other circumstances, Celeste would be committing all this to memory so she could describe it for her parents later, but she is preoccupied with the one sentence written on the note that was slipped under her door. *In case you have any doubts, I'm in love with you.*

Their appetizers arrive under silver domes. The server lifts both domes at once with a theatrical flourish. The food is artwork—vegetables are cut to resemble jewels; sauces are painted across plates. Benji ordered a wine that is apparently so rare and amazing, it made the sommelier stammer.

Celeste doesn't care. Shooter's absence is more powerful than Benji's presence. She does a desultory job on her appetizer—summer vegetables with stracciatella cheese—then excuses herself for the ladies' room.

On her way, she walks past a window that opens onto
an intimate enclave that has five seats at a mahogany bar,
a television showing the Red Sox game, and a handful of
tables with high-backed rattan chairs. The bar has a
clubby, colonial British feel that is a little cozier and more
casual than the dining room.

Shooter is sitting at the bar alone, drinking a martini.

Celeste stares at Shooter's back and does a gut check.
Talk to him or leave him be? *Talk to him!* She will tell
him she feels the same way, and then later they can make
a plan to be together without hurting Benji. But before
Celeste sets foot in the bar, a woman appears. She's wearing black pants, a black apron, a white shirt open at the
collar. *Oh, she's the bartender,* Celeste thinks with relief.
She's quite attractive, with short, dark, bobbed hair,
cat's-eye glasses, and dark red lipstick. She approaches
Shooter and he gives her a hug, then pulls her into his lap
and starts tickling her. She shrieks with laughter—
through the closed door, Celeste can just barely hear it—
and just as Celeste's emotions are curdling into hurt and
rage, the bartender stands up, straightens her apron, and
gets back to work.

Celeste slams into the ladies' room, startling a woman
applying her lipstick at the sink.

When Celeste returns to the table, Benji stands up. *He is
a gentleman,* she thinks. And she will never have to
worry about him.

Between dinner and dessert—they have ordered the
soufflé, which takes extra time to prepare—Benji pulls
something out of his coat pocket. It's a small box. Celeste
stares at the box almost without seeing it.

She realizes she knew this was coming.

"I didn't go golfing today," Benji says. "I flew back to

the city to pick up a little something." He opens the box to reveal the most insanely beautiful diamond ring Celeste has ever seen.

She bobs her head at the ring once, as if being formally introduced to it.

"Will you marry me, Celeste?" Benji asks.

Celeste's eyes fill with tears. Not only did *she* know this was coming but Shooter did too. And yet he *still* took her to Smith's Point, *still* showed her how to ride the current, *still* bought her a birding book, *still* called her Sunshine, and *still* made her feel like she was, in fact, the brightest light in the sky. And then he slipped that note under her door.

In case you have any doubts.

He didn't mean in case Celeste had any doubts about him. He meant in case Celeste had any doubts about marrying Benji.

I'm in love with you.

Shooter is a gambler. He's throwing the dice to see if he can win. It's a game to him, she tells herself. His feelings aren't real.

With her napkin, she blots the tears that drip down her cheeks. She can't look at Benji because if she does, he'll see they are tears of confusion, but right now he must be assuming—or hoping—that they are tears of overwhelmed joy.

The whole thing is a mess, a giant, emotionally tangled mess, and Celeste has half a mind to stand up and walk out on both men. She will get herself home, back to Easton, back to her parents.

Celeste thinks of Shooter pulling the sexy, bespectacled bartender into his lap, his wicked grin, his fingers tickling the other woman's ribs. Celeste would have a miserable life with Shooter. Her feelings for him are too strong; they would be her undoing. A better, wiser choice is to marry

Benji. Celeste will continue to be who she has always been: The center of someone else's universe. Beloved.

"Yes," Celeste whispers. "Yes, I will marry you."

When Benji and Celeste arrive back at the boat, Shooter is waiting. He has the gleam of a martini or three in his eyes. His hair is mussed; there is a smudge of the bartender's red lipstick on his cheek.

In case you have any doubts, I'm in love with you.

"So how'd it *go?*" Shooter asks with corny enthusiasm. *It might have been more like five martinis,* Celeste thinks. Shooter's words are slurred. Benji will have to drive the boat home.

Celeste holds out her left hand. "We're engaged."

Shooter locks eyes with her. *You lost,* she thinks, gloating for a second. But then she corrects herself. They both lost.

"Well," he says. "Congratulations."

Benji insists that Celeste call her parents on the boat ride home, but strangely, they don't answer. It's even stranger when Benji tells her that he spoke to both Bruce and Karen earlier in the week, told them his intentions, asked for their blessing. They were over the moon, he says.

Celeste leaves a message on the answering machine asking them to call her back. She doesn't hear from them at all on Saturday. When she calls again on Sunday morning, her father answers, but something is wrong. Her father is crying.

"Daddy?" Celeste says. She holds out hope for one second that he's weeping sentimentally over news of the engagement.

"It's your mother," he says.

Saturday, July 7, 2018,
1:12 p.m.

NANTUCKET

As the day unfolds, news about the Murdered Maid of Honor spreads across the island. Because nobody knows what happened, everything and anything becomes a possibility.

A group of New York Millennial women having lunch and cocktails at Cru are told the news by their server, Ryan.

"As if being maid of honor isn't hard enough," says Zoe Stanton, a store manager at Opening Ceremony.

"Maid of honor," a PR associate named Sage Kennedy murmurs. A bell goes off in Sage's head. "What was the woman's name?"

"Not yet released," says Lauren Doherty, a physical therapist at the Hospital for Special Surgery.

Sage pulls her phone out despite her resolution not to use it at meals (unless she's dining alone). She is pretty sure she follows someone on Instagram who was serving as a maid of honor at a wedding on Nantucket this weekend.

She gasps. It's Merritt. Merritt Monaco.

Sage gets a chill that starts at her feet and travels up her spine to the base of her brain. Once upon a time, Sage and Merritt worked together at a PR firm called Brightstreet, owned by Travis and Cordelia Darling. Merritt had an extremely ill-advised affair with Travis

Darling and when Cordelia found out—well, Sage had never seen anyone so hell-bent on exacting revenge. She'd *cringed* as she listened to Cordelia bad-mouth Merritt to absolutely every single one of their clients, calling her *disgusting* names. Cordelia even contacted Merritt's parents. Her *parents,* as though Cordelia were the high-school principal and Merritt had been caught setting a fire in the cafeteria. With Merritt's dismissal, Sage's own position in the company improved; she was, essentially, given all of Merritt's responsibilities. Another girl might have delighted in the career-ending poor decisions of the person directly above her—but Sage just felt bad. She suspected that the affair had been Travis Darling's fault. He was creepy.

Sage had wanted to contact Merritt after the smoke cleared, but she was afraid of going behind Cordelia's back. When Cordelia announced that she was moving the business to Los Angeles, Sage took the sparkling reference and robust severance package and immediately found another job. She texted Merritt with news of Cordelia's departure, and Merritt had responded: Thanks for letting me know.

They hadn't become friends, by any means, but Sage kept a cyber-eye on Merritt. She followed her on Instagram under an account with a made-up name—which was strange, she realized, but less complicated than following, liking, and commenting as her real self. She found herself cheering Merritt on as she got a new job at the Wildlife Conservation Society and started stumping for Parker and Young, Fabulous, and Broke, as well as nearly every hot restaurant and club that opened south of Fourteenth Street.

There had been recent posts about Merritt's upcoming maid-of-honor duty this weekend on Nantucket. Earlier this week, Merritt had posted a photo of herself modeling her bridesmaid dress—it was antique-ivory silk with black embroidery on the bodice, meant to look like classic scrimshaw, which Sage thought was such a *cool idea*—with the caption: *Tonight I am Nantucket-bound. #MOH #weddingoftheyear #BFF.*

Had someone murdered *Merritt?*

Sage stared down at her lobster roll and her full glass of Rock Angel rosé, her appetite for lunch gone. Who would want to kill Merritt?

Cordelia, she thinks. She sips her rosé for fortitude and wonders if it's remotely possible that Cordelia came to Nantucket, somehow infiltrated the wedding festivities— maybe dressing up as one of the catering crew—and got to Merritt that way. Absurd? Only happens in the movies? Normally, Sage would think that, but she will forever be haunted by the vitriol she had seen emanating from Cordelia Darling in the days following her discovery of the affair.

Cordelia is in Los Angeles, Sage tells herself. There is no reason for her to celebrate the Fourth of July week on Nantucket; the West Coast has its own beaches.

Sage puts her phone away and smiles at her friends. It might not even be Merritt, she thinks. She follows Lauren's gaze out the open sides of the restaurant. The vista is nothing short of spectacular: sparkling blue harbor, sailboats, seagulls, the bluffs of Shawkemo in the distance. How could anything bad ever happen here?

The Murdered Maid of Honor is all anyone is talking about across town at the Greydon House on Broad Street. Heather Clymer, who is staying with her husband, Steve, in room 2, has just gotten back from the Hospital Thrift Shop, where she heard the whole story from one of the volunteers. Heather brought the story back to the Greydon

House, where it spread like a virus: the maid of honor in a big, fancy wedding out in Monomoy was found early that morning floating in the harbor, and both local and state authorities suspect foul play.

Laney and Casper Morris are standing by the hotel's front desk and are just about to head down the street to the Nantucket Whaling Museum when they hear the news. Laney digs her fingernails into Casper's forearm.

"Ouch," Casper says. He's already a bit irritated with Laney for making him go to the Whaling Museum on such a gorgeous, sunny day, the final day of their vacation. They should be headed to the beach! The Whaling Museum isn't going anywhere; they can tour it when they're old.

"A big, fancy wedding out in Monomoy?" Laney says. She pulls Casper back into their elegantly appointed room, where Casper collapses on the bed, grateful for the delay in their day's agenda. "The maid of honor was found floating. She's dead. You know whose wedding that is, right? Out in Monomoy?"

"Benji's?" Casper guesses. He knows this is the right answer; it's basically all Laney has been talking about this week because Laney's best friend is Jules Briar, Benji's ex-girlfriend. Casper isn't a big fan of Jules and he knows the friendship wears on Laney as well, but she and Jules have known each other since first grade at Spence and some habits are hard to break. Jules somehow discovered that Benji was getting married this weekend on Nantucket, and when Jules learned that Laney and Casper would be on the island as well, she implored Laney to keep an eye out and report back. Jules is insanely jealous of Benji's fiancée, *whom he had met when Benji and Jules took Miranda to the zoo!*

Laney had done exactly as Jules asked. Last night, when they were standing in line at the Juice Bar, Laney had seen Shooter Uxley, Benji's best friend, outside of Steamboat Pizza. He was with a blond woman. Laney took a picture of Shooter and the blonde and texted it to Jules.

Jules responded immediately. That's her! That's zoo woman! Benji's fiancée!

They texted back and forth about why the fiancée—Celeste Otis, her name was; Jules had done the requisite stalking—was getting pizza with Shooter instead of Benji. Then they texted about how much they missed Shooter. He had been so much fun.

Now Laney says, "The maid of honor was killed. Poor Benji!"

"Maybe Benji did it," Casper says, and then he laughs because Benjamin Winbury is one of the nicest guys to ever walk the planet, so nice that Casper used to give him a hard time for making the rest of the male population look bad. And, too, Casper has had his own murderous thoughts about some of Laney's friends; the subject of their present conversation ranks at the top of the list.

"If it were the bride who had died," Laney says, "I would have suspected Jules."

"Damn straight," Casper says.

Laney sighs. "It's sobering, you know. Thinking someone our age could die just like that."

Casper reaches out to his wife. "Hey," he says. "Don't let it get to you. We don't know what happened."

"Life is so short." Laney smiles at Casper. "Forget the Whaling Museum," she says. "Let's go to the beach."

Benjamin Winbury is sequestered in his father's study with his father and his brother.

Intellectually, Benji understands that Merritt is dead, that she drowned out front, but he can't quite come to terms with this new reality. His mind won't switch over to *Merritt is dead*. He is stalled, stuck, in *Merritt is alive and the wedding will go ahead as scheduled at four o'clock*. His tuxedo is hanging up in the closet, and in the breast pocket of the jacket are the rings, which Benji was going to hand over to Shooter along with Shooter's best-man gift, a pair of monogrammed cuff links. He still has things to check off on his to-do list, such as setting up a boat trip and a spa day for Celeste once they get to Santorini, but now his procrastination doesn't matter. The wedding has been canceled.

Of course the wedding has been canceled. There was no question of going forward with a wedding when Celeste's best friend was found dead.

Benji is experiencing a host of very confusing emotions. He is upset, shocked, and horrified just like everyone else. And yet also mixed in there are anger and resentment. It's his *wedding day!* His parents have gone to enormous effort and expense to make this wedding unforgettable and now it's *all for naught*. But aside from the predictable shallow complaint that the happiest day of Benji's life has turned out to be tragic and chaotic, there is a deeper sadness that he won't be entering into a lifelong commitment with the woman he loves beyond all comprehension.

He has been influenced enough by Celeste that he now occasionally thinks in wildlife metaphors. Celeste is like a rare butterfly that Benji was somehow able to capture. That comparison is, no doubt, inappropriate on many different levels, but that's how he thinks of her in his private mind where no one can judge him, that she's like an exotic bird or butterfly. If he takes that imagery further, then marrying her is akin to putting her in a cage or pinning her to a board. She was supposed to be *his*.

What Merritt's death has brought to light, however, is that Celeste belongs only to herself.

She was the one who found Merritt. With Roger's help, Celeste pulled Merritt's body from the water. She was hysterical, beyond talking to, beyond consoling. She couldn't breathe, and Roger and the paramedics had wisely decided to take Celeste to the hospital where they could get her calmed down.

Benji waited two hours before he went to see her in order to give her time and space to process what had happened, but when he arrived to pick her up, their conversation had not gone the way he expected it to.

She had been in bed, woozy from the Valium, her eyelids fluttering open when he walked in the room. He sat at her bedside, took her hand, and said, *I'm so sorry.*

She shook her head and said, *It's my fault.*

For reasons he could not explain, this answer had unleashed a mighty fury within him. He thought Celeste was blaming herself for having an oceanfront wedding, for asking Merritt to be her maid of honor, for bringing her here to Nantucket. And Benji's response to this came flying out: *She was lucky to be here, lucky she had a friend like you, she didn't deserve you, wasn't worthy of you, Celeste. And furthermore, she probably did this to herself! You told me once that she stockpiled pills and considered suicide, so what's to say that's not what this is? She orchestrated this to ruin our big day!*

Celeste had closed her eyes and Benji thought the sedative had reclaimed her but then she spoke. *I can't believe you just said that. You blame Merritt. You think this is her fault. Because you've never liked her. You thought she was a bad influence. But she was my* friend, *Benji. She was the friend I'd been looking for my entire life. She accepted me, she loved me, she took care of me. If I hadn't met Merritt*

*when I did, I might have left New York. I might have gone
back to Easton and worked at the zoo in Trexlertown. I
might never have met you. You blame Merritt because you
can't imagine a scenario where maybe someone in your
house, someone in your family, made a very, very grave mistake. You think your family is beyond reproach. But you're
wrong.*

What are you talking about? Benji asked.

You'll find out soon enough, Celeste said. *But right now
I'd like you to leave. I want to talk to the police. Alone.*

What? Benji said. *What about your parents? Do they
even know? They were still in their room when I left.*

I've called my father, Celeste said. *Now, please, go.*

Benji had been incredulous, but he could see by the
set of her jaw that she was serious.

Benji stood to go. He knew there was no point broach-
ing the topic of getting married in Greece or reschedul-
ing the wedding for August. Merritt's death had changed
things. He'd lost Celeste.

Now he's left to pace Tag's study, asking the same question over and over again of his father and brother.

"What *happened?*" Benji had gone to bed after they
all got back from town last night. But Thomas and Tag
stayed up. "Right?" Benji asks. *"Right?"*

"Right," Tag says. "It was Thomas, myself, Merritt,
and Featherleigh."

"What were you guys doing?" Benji asks.

Thomas shrugs. "Drinking."

"Drinking what?" Benji asks. "Scotch?"

"Rum," Tag says. "I just wanted to finish my cigar,
enjoy the evening. I was sitting in peace with your
brother until Merritt and Featherleigh joined us."

"Where did they come from?" Benji asks.

"They'd clearly met at the party and hit it off," Tag says. "They came out of the house chatting like soul sisters. Like Thelma and Louise."

"Abby called me up to bed shortly after those two sat down with us," Thomas says. He holds up his palms. "I literally have *nothing* to do with this. I barely knew Merritt. But she had that look. You know the look? She was trouble."

"Amen," Tag whispers.

"Did Merritt seem really drunk?" Benji asks. "Did it seem like she was on something?"

"You need to relax, bro," Thomas says. "The police will sort this out."

The police, Benji thinks. That's why the three of them are holed up in his father's study; they're waiting to be questioned by the police. The study smells like tobacco and peat and it's filled with antiques—sextants, barometers, prints of long-ago British naval victories. Most men find Tag's study intriguing; Benji finds it obnoxious. Although, under the circumstances, it makes a serviceable bunker, and Benji could use a drink.

"Pour me a Glenmorangie?" he asks his father.

"Before you talk to the police?" Tag asks. "Is that wise?"

"Nantucket Police, intimidating bunch," Thomas says. "I'll pour it." He heads over to the bar. "If they suspected Benji, they would have questioned him first."

"Suspected *me*?" Benji says. This isn't something that has crossed his mind. "Why would they suspect me?" At that moment, there's a knock on the study door, and Benji's heart somersaults in fear. *Do* the police suspect him?

Tag strides across the room to open the door. His

father looks respectable in a white polo shirt and a pair of dark madras shorts, but Benji and Thomas are still in the gym shorts and T-shirts they slept in.

It's Reverend Derby at the door. All three Winbury men exhale a sigh of relief. The reverend embraces Tag.

"I came to see if I can help," the reverend says.

Benji can't handle any talk of God right now. He isn't in the mood to hear that this was part of God's plan, nor does he want to debate the question of whether it was a suicide and what that might mean for Merritt's soul.

"What's going on out there?" Tag asks Reverend Derby. "Is there any news?"

"No one has said anything directly to me," the reverend says. "But I overheard someone saying that the medical examiner found a sedative in the young woman's bloodstream. She must have gone swimming for some reason and then just passed out."

A sedative, Benji thinks. *Bingo.* Merritt took an Ambien and went into that well-documented twilight state where her brain was shutting down though her body was still awake. She went out for a late-night swim and she drowned.

Reverend Derby claps Benji on the shoulder. "How are you holding up, young man?"

Benji shrugs. He sees no point in lying to Reverend Derby. He is like part of the family, as close as an uncle. Most of Benji's memories of him are secular. Reverend Derby comes each year to the Winburys' anglicized Thanksgiving; he goes with Tag to Yankee games; he has spent many weekends here on Nantucket; he attended Thomas's and Benji's graduations from high school, college, grad school. Having Reverend Derby around always lent the family a certain moral authority, although none of the four Winburys is particularly religious. Or Benji isn't. He understands he can't speak for anyone else's interior life, but his life has been so blessed—up to this point—that he has had no *need* for religion.

"I'm mostly concerned for Celeste," he says. "This has blindsided her."

Reverend Derby looks at him with his watery blue eyes but knows better than to speak. He lifts his hand from Benji's shoulder. "I'm going to give you your privacy. Just know I'm here if you need me."

Tag shakes Reverend Derby's hand as he shows him the door.

Thomas says, "Scotch."

Benji and Thomas are each a drink and a half in when there's another knock at the door. Again, Tag stands to answer. Again, Benji's heart reacts like a pit bull straining on a chain.

It's Benji's mother.

"May I come in?" she asks Tag. Her voice is arch. Benji knows she doesn't like the way Tag guards the privacy of his study. It makes her suspicious, she says.

Tag holds the door open and extends a hand. Greer walks in. She, too, is dressed appropriately, in a pair of white pants and a linen tank the color of whole-wheat bread. Her hair is up in a chignon and she is wearing lipstick. Celeste would be offended, Benji suspects, that Greer saw fit to put on lipstick this morning, but Greer is a certain kind of British woman who wouldn't want the strangers in the house—the police, the forensics experts, the detective—to see her without makeup, no matter the circumstances.

"Mom?" he says. He believes in his mother's ability to somehow make this situation bearable.

"Oh, Benny," she says. She uses his long-abandoned childhood nickname. It hits the right note; he knows she loves him. She squeezes him so tightly he can feel her bones and her beating heart. When she pulls away, she looks right at him and he can feel her trying to shore him up. If anyone's hopes and dreams have been razed as much as his by the wedding going up in smoke, it's Greer's. And yet she seems to be processing the turn of events with mournful dignity, exactly as she should.

"Have you talked to the Otises?" he asks. "Celeste said she called her father."

"They haven't emerged from their room," Greer says. "I had Elida deliver a tray with lunch, but I'm sure they're too upset to eat much." She eyes the tumblers of scotch on the coffee table. "Have you boys eaten anything?"

"No," Benji says.

"I could eat," Thomas says.

Greer looks at him sharply. "Well. There are sandwiches in the kitchen."

"What's going on, exactly?" Tag asks. "We're still waiting to speak to the detectives."

"I had my interview with the fellow from the state police," Greer says. "I daresay, he has it in for me—"

"For *you*?" Benji says.

Greer waves a hand. "I'm not sure what they're thinking. The Nantucket Chief just called to ask what inn Featherleigh is staying at."

"Featherleigh?" Thomas says. "What the hell does *she* have to do with anything?"

"Well," Tag says, "she *was* the last person to see Merritt."

"Was she?" Greer asks.

"She was?" Thomas says.

Tag turns away from all of them and goes to pour his own scotch at the bar cart. "I believe so," he says, looking into his glass before drinking. "Yes."

"Wasn't Featherleigh with you?" Greer asks. She sounds more interested than accusatory. "Didn't you take her out for a ride in the kayak?"

"Featherleigh?" Thomas says. "Why would Dad take Featherleigh out for a ride in the kayak? She's hardly the seafaring type."

"I didn't take Featherleigh out in the kayak," Tag says.

"You didn't?" Greer says.

"I didn't," Tag says.

"You took *someone* out for a kayak," Greer says. "The kayak, the two-person kayak, was left overturned on the beach. With only one oar. And we all know nobody else used it."

Benji sinks into one of the leather club chairs and throws back what's left of his scotch. He doesn't like where this is headed. Here is his nuclear family, his parents and his older brother. They are the Winburys, a very fortunate group, not only because of their money, position, and advantages, but also because, by the standards of today, they are "normal." A happy, normal family; a family, he would have said, without secrets or drama.

But now he's not so sure.

He speaks to the room. "Who did you take out in the kayak, Dad?" He thinks back to what Celeste said, that someone in his family had made a very, very grave mistake.

Benji stands up. "Dad?"

Tag is facing the bar cart. He has one hand on his glass and one hand wrapped around the neck of the Glenmorangie. Greer is watching him. Thomas is watching him. They're all waiting for an answer.

His voice is barely a whisper but his words and tone are clear.

"Merritt," he says. "I took Merritt out in the kayak."

KAREN

Karen wakes up with a start. The sunlight is pouring through the windows, bright and lemony. She was supposed to be up at eight thirty to help Celeste get ready, but she can tell it's much later than that. She reaches over to check her phone. It's half past noon.

Karen shrieks and sits up in bed. Bizarrely, there's no pain. No pain? Her last oxy was late last night, but still, that was twelve hours ago. On a normal day, her nerve endings are screaming after seven or eight hours.

"Bruce?" she calls out. His side of the bed is empty but—she reaches out a hand—still warm.

She hears him retching. He's in the bathroom. The blackberry mojitos and the scotch must have caught up with him. The toilet flushes, the water runs, and then Bruce comes into the bedroom. He looks smaller, she thinks. And ten years older.

He comes to sit next to her on the edge of the bed.

"Karen," he says. "The wedding has been canceled."

"Canceled?" she says. Somehow, she already knew this, but how? She tries to piece together the events of the night before. Celeste had wanted to stay home but Bruce and Karen had encouraged her to go out. They wanted her to enjoy herself.

Celeste!

Karen had had a bad dream—she was trying to find Celeste but couldn't get to her. And then came the revelation: Celeste didn't want to marry Benji. Karen had tiptoed down to Celeste's room; it had been empty. She had gone downstairs. She had overheard the strange, awful conversation between Bruce and Tag.

Robin Swain.

Karen shakes her head. Last night, the confession

about Robin Swain had seemed so devastating, but this morning, her shock and horror have vanished, just like her pain. Human beings experience all kinds of crazy and unexpected emotions while they are alive. Robin Swain was nothing more than a tiny blip on the screen of their distant past.

"Celeste doesn't want to marry Benji," Karen says.

"No, Karen," Bruce says. "That's not it."

But that is *it,* Karen thinks. She has never once said this, but she does believe she is naturally closer and more in tune with Celeste than Bruce is. Celeste is Bruce's little girl, no doubt about that, but he doesn't understand Celeste's mind like Karen does.

"Merritt died, Karen," Bruce says. "Celeste's friend Merritt. The maid of honor. She died last night."

Karen feels like her head is going to topple right off her neck and onto the floor. *"What?"* she says.

"They found her floating in the harbor this morning," Bruce says. "She drowned."

"She *drowned?*" Karen says. "She drowned last *night?*"

"Apparently so," Bruce says. "I was with Tag and then I came to bed. You were asleep when I came in. That was pretty late, but it must have happened afterward."

"Oh no," Karen says. She is aghast, really and truly aghast. Merritt was so young, so beautiful and confident. "How...what..."

"She drank or took drugs, I guess," Bruce says. "And then she went swimming. I mean, what other explanation is there?"

"Where's Celeste?" Karen asks.

"The paramedics took her to the hospital," Bruce says. His eyes fill with tears. "Celeste was the one who found her."

"No! No, no, no!" Their poor, sweet daughter! Karen fears Celeste doesn't have the strength to deal with this.

She is too fragile, too gentle and kind. This had been true even in adolescence, *especially* in adolescence. Other people's daughters had been drinking and smoking, secretly going on the pill or being fitted for diaphragms. Celeste had stayed home with Bruce and Karen watching *Friday Night Lights*. That had been their favorite show, so much so that Tim Riggins and Tami Taylor felt like friends of the family, and, often, Bruce, Karen, and Celeste would look at one another over their morning cereal and say, "Clear eyes, full hearts, can't lose." Celeste volunteered at the Lehigh Valley Zoo in Trexlertown on the weekends. Bruce would drop her off and Karen would pick her up. Karen would nearly always find Celeste with the lemurs or the otters, either feeding them or scolding them like naughty children. Karen used to have to yank her out of there. On Saturday nights, they would go to Diner 248 and then to the movies. Celeste would often see kids from school in groups or on dates and she would wave and smile, but she never seemed embarrassed to be seen with her parents. She was always even-keeled and content, as though she simply preferred to be with Bruce and Karen. Mac and Betty.

"And so now the wedding has been canceled," Karen says.

"Yes," Bruce says. "And the police are conducting an investigation."

"Does the girl have family?" Karen asks.

"Not much, I guess," Bruce says. "She hasn't spoken to her parents in seven years."

Seven years? Karen thinks. She's nearly as upset about that as she is about Merritt's passing. And yet, Karen could tell from the girl's demeanor that no one had been looking out for her, not even from afar.

So now there will be no wedding. Karen understood

this last night, but she had thought the reason would be different. She thought Celeste would call it off.

And then Karen's visit to the psychic comes flooding back in vivid detail.

The psychic's studio was in downtown Easton, half a block from the Crayola factory; Karen used to pass it all the time on her way to and from work. She had looked at the sign with only mild curiosity. KATHRYN RANDALL, PSYCHIC: INTUITIVE READINGS, ANGEL WHISPERER. Kathryn Randall was such a pretty name, such a normal, field-of-daisies name; this had been part of what triggered Karen's interest. Her name wasn't Veda or Krystal or Starshower. It was Kathryn Randall.

Karen visited Kathryn Randall two days after she received news of her metastases. She wasn't looking for Kathryn to predict *her* future—she would live for weeks, months, a year, and then she would die—but she had to know what life held for Celeste.

Kathryn's "studio" was just a normal living room. Karen sat on a gray tweed sofa and stared at Kathryn's diploma from the University of Wisconsin. She handed Kathryn a photograph of Celeste and said, "I need to know if you have any intuitive thoughts about my daughter."

Kathryn Randall was in her mid-thirties, as pretty as her name, with long light brown hair, flawless skin, a calming smile. She looked like a kindergarten teacher. Kathryn had studied the photograph for a long time, long enough for Karen to grow uncomfortable. She was thrown by the conventional surroundings. She had expected silk curtains, candles, maybe even a crystal ball, something that suggested a connection to the supernatural world.

Kathryn Randall closed her eyes, and she started to talk in a slow, hypnotic voice. Celeste was an old soul, she said. She had been to the earth before, more than once, which accounted for her serenity. She didn't ever feel the need to impress. She was comfortable with who she was.

Kathryn stopped suddenly and opened her eyes. "Does that sound right?"

"It does," Karen said, growing excited. "It really does."

Kathryn nodded. "She'll be happy. Eventually."

"Eventually?" Karen said.

A concerned look passed across Kathryn's face, like a breeze rippling the surface of a pond. "Her romantic life..." Kathryn said.

"Yes?" Karen said.

"I see chaos."

"Chaos?" Karen said. Here she had thought Celeste's love life was rock solid. She was engaged to Benjamin Winbury. It was a real-life fairy tale.

Kathryn offered a weak smile. "You were right to come to me," she said. "But there's nothing either one of us can do about it."

Karen had paid the thirty-dollar fee and left. Chaos. *Chaos?*

After that, Karen had avoided walking by Kathryn Randall's studio. She started parking in the lot on Ferry Street, even though it was farther away.

Now, Karen's mind starts to grind. Kathryn Randall was correct about chaos. The wedding has been canceled. Merritt is dead. She drank or took pills, Bruce said, then drowned.

Pills, Karen thinks, and she suddenly feels as nauseated as she did after her first round of chemo. Karen had caught Merritt coming out of this very bedroom last night. Merritt had said she was looking for Celeste, but that sounded like a fabrication. She hadn't been looking for Celeste; she had been looking for pills. Had she gotten as far as the third drawer in the bathroom? Had she found the bottle of oxy and the three pearlescent ovoids mixed in? Had she been curious about those pills and taken one to see what happened?

The notion is too appalling for tears. It is a dense, dark, soul-destroying thought: Not only is Merritt dead but it's Karen's fault.

She needs to check her pills.

She can't check her pills.

If she checks her pills and finds one or more of the pearlescent ovoids missing, what will she tell Bruce? Celeste? The police?

Her thoughts are a soundless scream.

She can't continue another second not knowing. Karen gets to her feet. Her pain is still at bay, which is impossible, she knows. She hasn't taken an oxy in nearly twelve hours, so something else is at work in her body. The shock.

Bruce falls back on the bed, his eyes open. He is there but not there, which is just as well. Karen closes the bathroom door, locks it. She sits on the toilet and slides open the third drawer. She takes out the bottle of pills.

She clutches the bottle in her fist.

Then she lays out a clean white washcloth and empties all of the pills onto it. She stares at the pile, smooths them out.

One, two…three pearlescent ovoids, present and accounted for. And then, for good measure, she counts the oxy. All there.

The rush of relief Karen feels nearly knocks her unconscious. She sways; splotches appear in her vision.

Karen staggers back to lie down on the white bed. The shape of her body is still imprinted in the sheets and blankets, like a snow angel. She fits herself back in like a piece of a puzzle and closes her eyes.

Saturday, July 7, 2018, 2:47 p.m.

THE CHIEF

He's prepared to give Valerie Gluckstern one hour with Shooter Uxley, but after only twenty minutes, she tells the Chief that her client is ready to answer questions.

In the interview room, the Chief sits down across the table from Shooter and Val. The Chief feels infinitely better since eating his lunch but he needs to come up with something here because Barney from forensics called to say they found nothing in the shot glasses, on the cigar, or in the bottle of rum.

"Are you sure?" the Chief asked. "There has to be *something* in one of the glasses."

And Barney, who did not like having his expertise questioned, had sworn at the Chief and hung up.

"My thinking has changed substantially from this morning," the Chief says. He knows Nick likes to ease into things, build a rapport, and allow information to flow organically, but the Chief isn't feeling it. A girl is dead, this guy made a run for it, and the Chief wants answers. Now.

"Mr. Uxley is prepared to answer all your questions, as I said," Val says. "He has nothing to hide."

The Chief stares at the kid. He's too damn good-looking to pity, although he seems pretty shaken up.

"Tell me where you were coming from this morning," the Chief says.

Shooter spreads his fingers out on the table in front of him and stares at them as he speaks. "The Steamship," he says.

"What were you doing at the Steamship?" the Chief asks.

"I was trying to leave the island," Shooter says.

"But you missed the boat?" the Chief says.

"I didn't miss the boat," Shooter says. "I just changed my mind."

"You changed your mind," the Chief says. "You'd better start explaining yourself, son." The Chief looks at Val. "Your client lied about being at the Wauwinet. He lied about his alibi. Then he tried to board the Hy-Line with a stolen ticket. Now I'm hearing that he was at the Steamship this morning to board the six-thirty boat, presumably without anyone's knowledge, since the groom told Sergeant Dickson he was missing. The ME put the time of death on the girl between two forty-five and three forty-five. She was dead, and then he decided to flee. On the basis of these facts alone, I have probable cause to hold you for murder one."

"You do not," Val says.

The Chief turns to Shooter. "You'd better cough up one hell of a believable story."

Shooter taps his fingers one by one, starting with his left pinkie, proceeding all the way to his right pinkie, and then going back again.

Val puts a hand on his forearm. "Tell the Chief what you told me," she says. "It's okay."

"I left the Winbury compound early this morning," Shooter says. "I walked all the way to the rotary and caught a cab down to the Steamship. I was going to the Steamship because…" He hesitates, looks at Val. She nods. "Because I was running away with the bride."

Running away with the bride, the Chief thinks. *This was one hell of a wedding.*

"I'm in love with Celeste and she said she was in love with me," Shooter says. "Last night a bunch of us went out after the party and Celeste and I peeled off to get some pizza and I asked her to run away with me." He pauses, looks down at the table, takes a deep, shaky breath, then continues. "I told her that I would take care of her, that I would love her forever. All she had to do was meet me at the Steamship at six o'clock this morning. We were going to hop on the six-thirty slow boat to Hyannis, rent a car, drive to Boston, fly to Las Vegas, and get married ourselves."

Val says, "Mr. Uxley waited at the Steamship for Miss Otis until six thirty-five." She turns to Shooter. "Is that accurate?"

"When I saw the ferry pulling out, when I heard the foghorn, I knew she wasn't coming," Shooter says. "I had figured there was a fifty-fifty chance she'd be there. When she didn't show, I thought she'd decided to marry Benji. So I took a taxi back to the house. Because I was the best man. And there was going to be a wedding after all."

"That's when I saw you?" the Chief asks.

"And you told me Merritt was dead." He shakes his head. "You know, Celeste was afraid to follow through with our plan because she thought something bad would happen if we did it." He swallows. "I'm sure she's blaming herself."

"Why didn't you tell me this in the first place?" the Chief asks. "Instead of coming clean, you lied to me, then you ran off. You understand the light that puts you in? Why should I believe a word you say?"

"I was rattled," Shooter says. "I thought I was coming

back to a wedding and instead, you tell me that Merritt is *dead?* I couldn't add our drama on top of that. Celeste would have had to corroborate my story, and I wanted to protect her from that. And I didn't want the Winburys to know. I was agitated and confused and I figured it would be easier to just say I'd been with Gina. I didn't think you'd actually check it out. Then, once I knew I'd been caught in a lie, I figured my only course of action was to bolt." Shooter looks at the Chief. "I realize I handled this poorly. But I didn't kill Merritt."

"Did Merritt know the two of you were running away?" the Chief asks. "Do you think Celeste confided in her?"

"We agreed not to tell anyone," Shooter says. "We were going to make a clean break for it, get off the island, then tell everyone later. Celeste wasn't even going to say anything to her parents. So, no, I do not think she confided in Merritt."

The interview room is quiet for a second. The Chief is combing back through the story. Does it make sense? Does it have any holes? Nick is a strong believer in intuition when it comes to questioning. The story may make sense, but do you believe the guy?

Yes, the Chief thinks. He recalls Roger saying that when Celeste found the body, she had a bag packed. She was headed to meet Shooter and she...what? Caught a glimpse of something in the water as she was leaving? It wasn't impossible.

She had a bag packed. For that reason, and that reason alone, the Chief is going to choose to believe Mr. Uxley.

He stands up and nods at Val. "You two are free to go," he says. He has to move on—and quickly—to Tag Winbury and the Dale woman, whoever *she* is.

August 2017

CELESTE

Her mother's cancer has metastasized to her bones. There are tumors on her spine. The cancer isn't curable. They can, however, do another course of chemo, which will buy her a year to eighteen months.

Benji's response to the news is to pull Celeste closer and hold her tighter. They are now engaged, and this has inspired him to become the spokesperson for *we*. He wants Karen to get a second opinion at Mount Sinai. His parents know "influential people" who sit on the board of directors. They'll be able to get Karen an appointment with the "best doctors, the very best doctors."

Celeste resents Benji's involvement. She and her parents are an insular unit: Mac, Betty, and Bug. *They* are the *we*. It feels like Benji is horning in with his connections and his optimism. In Benji's world, every problem has a solution, thanks to who the Winburys know and how much money they have.

Celeste says, "My parents can't *afford* to get a second opinion at Mount Sinai. My father's insurance was maxed out long ago."

"I'll pay for it," Benji says.

"I don't *want* you to pay for it!" Celeste says. "My mother has a doctor she likes and trusts. Dr. Edman at St. Luke's—which is a real hospital, by the way, not just some clinic in a strip mall."

"Okay, I get it," Benji says, though Celeste knows exactly what he's thinking. He's thinking that St. Luke's isn't as good as Mount Sinai. How could it possibly be as good when it isn't in New York City and Tag and Greer don't know anyone who sits on the board? "I'm only trying to help."

"Thank you," Celeste says as sincerely as she can. "I'm very upset and I want to handle this my own way."

Because Celeste is just back from her Nantucket vacation, she can't take any more time off; it's the end of summer and the zoo is simply too busy. But in the middle of her first week back, Celeste rents a Zipcar and drives out to see her parents after work. When Celeste reaches the house on Derhammer Street, she finds her mother sitting at the kitchen table with a coloring book for adults and a deluxe set of sixty-four pencils. Celeste walks in, and she holds up the page she's been working on. It's a mandala.

"Not bad, huh?" Karen says. She has colored the mandala in shades of green, blue, and purple.

"Pretty," Celeste says, but her voice is shaky and her eyes well up. Karen has worked at the Crayola factory gift shop for over a decade. Some people sniff at what they see as a menial job selling boxes of crayons, but Karen has always taken pride in it. *I bring color into children's lives,* she says.

Karen stands up and lets Celeste hug her. "I'm going to win this battle," she says.

"You're not supposed to call it a battle," Celeste says. "I read that somewhere. It's a violent word and some survivors find it offensive."

Karen scoffs. "Offensive?" she says. "So what am I supposed to call it?"

"A journey," Celeste says.

"Bullshit," Karen says. Celeste blinks in surprise; her mother never swears. "It's a battle."

They go for a quick dinner at Diner 248 and make a point of ordering the Fudgy Wudgy, though Celeste and Bruce manage only one bite apiece and Karen doesn't have any. Karen makes a big fuss over Celeste's diamond ring: It's the most beautiful ring she has ever laid eyes on. It's the biggest diamond she has ever seen. *A full four carats! And set in platinum!*

Celeste says, "I'm thinking of postponing the wedding. I'm thinking of quitting my job and moving home until you get better."

"Nonsense," Karen says. Her voice is sharp and loud, and people at nearby tables turn their heads. The three Otises sit in silence for a second; they aren't people who draw attention to themselves.

Celeste knows better than to say anything further. Her mother has spent Celeste's entire life claiming that no mortal man would ever be good enough for Celeste, but that's because she didn't have the imagination to dream up someone like Benjamin Winbury, a real-life Prince Charming. Celeste's future will be blessed. She will never have to worry about money the way that Bruce and Karen did.

Celeste looks at Mac and Betty sitting across from her in the booth the way they always do, her father's arm draped across her mother's shoulders, her mother's hand resting on her father's thigh. Celeste envies them. She doesn't want money; she wants what they have. She wants love.

In case you have any doubts...

"If anything," Karen says in a lower voice, "I was thinking you might get married sooner. Maybe in the spring or early summer."

...I'm in love with you.

Sooner? Celeste thinks.

She nods. "Okay," she whispers.

Shooter has disappeared back into his own life—steak houses, downtown clubs, the U.S. Open with clients, Vegas with clients to draft fantasy-football teams. Benji shows Celeste the pictures but she barely gives them a glance. She can't think about Shooter; she can't *not* think about Shooter. Part of her suspects her desire for Shooter is what caused Karen's cancer to spread. Celeste knows life doesn't work like that but she still gets the nagging sense that the two things are connected. If she stays with Benji, if she marries Benji, Karen will get better. If they get married in the spring or early summer, Karen will live forever.

Celeste drops five pounds, then ten. Merritt expresses envy and tells Celeste how wonderful she looks.

Celeste is irritable at work. She finally loses her temper with Blair the hypochondriac. One more missed day and Blair will be fired, Celeste says. Blair threatens a lawsuit. She has *legitimate reasons* for calling in sick. Celeste, in a rare fit of rage, tells Blair she needs to stop with the *bullshit,* and the next thing Celeste knows, she's getting called into Zed's office for a lecture on professional attitude, appropriate workplace language, blah-blah-blah.

Greer summons Benji and Celeste to the Winbury apartment for dinner. She has made something called a cassoulet. Celeste is her dutiful self and replies that it sounds good, but in fact, Celeste is annoyed. She has no idea what cassoulet is. She hates constantly being confronted with these erudite dishes—can't Greer just make meat loaf or sloppy joes like Betty?—and it turns out that cassoulet has duck, pork skin, and, worst of all, *beans* in it. Celeste manages two bites. Her lack of appetite goes largely unnoticed, however, because Greer's real motivation isn't to feed Celeste and Benji but rather to let them know that she would like to plan their wedding. They can have the entire thing at Summerland on Nantucket the weekend after the Fourth of July.

Benji reaches for Celeste's hand under the table. "Would that be okay with you?" he asks.

"We don't want you to feel railroaded," Tag says. "My wife can be a bit forceful."

"I'm just trying to help," Greer says. "I want to offer my support and our resources. I hate to think of you having to plan a wedding while your mother is so sick."

Celeste nods like a marionette. "Sounds good," she says.

At first, Celeste stutters only when she's talking about the wedding. She has a problem with the word *caterer;* it's a stuttery word all by itself. Then *reverend,* then *church.* People pretend not to notice but the stutter grows gradually worse. Benji finally asks about it and Celeste bursts into tears. She can't c-c-control it, she says. Soon, all hard consonants give her trouble.

But not at work.

Not on the phone with Merritt.

Not alone in her apartment when she's reading in bed. She can read entire passages from her book aloud and not trip up once.

Celeste holds out hope that a big, elaborate wedding on Nantucket will prove to be a logistical impossibility—it's too last-minute, every venue must already be booked—and so either the wedding will be postponed indefinitely or they can plan something smaller in Easton, something more like her parents' wedding, a ceremony at the court-house, a reception at the diner.

But apparently, Greer's influence and her pocketbook are mighty enough to make miracles happen. Greer enlists Siobhan at Island Fare, arranges for Reverend Derby to do the service at St. Paul's Episcopal, finds a band and an orchestra, and hires Roger Pelton, Nantucket's premier wedding coordinator—not that Greer can't handle it all herself, but she does have a novel to write and it would be silly to have a resource like Roger on the island and not use him.

The wedding is set for July 7.

Greer asks Celeste what she would like to do about bridesmaids.

"Oh," Celeste says. This obviously isn't something she can ask Greer to handle. "I'll have my friend Merritt Monaco." Merritt will be a good maid of honor; she knows all the rules and traditions, although Celeste shudders when she thinks about the bachelorette party Merritt might plan. Celeste will have to talk to her about that.

She notices Greer is still looking at her expectantly.

"And who else?" Greer asks.

Who *else?* Her mother? Nobody ever asks her mother to be a bridesmaid; Celeste knows that much. She doesn't have a sister or any cousins. There are no suitable choices at work—Blair is now not speaking to Celeste; Bethany is her *assistant,* so that's too weird; and the rest of the staff are men. There is Celeste's roommate from college, Julia, but Celeste's relationship with Julia was utilitarian rather than friendly. They were both scientists, both neat and respectful, but they parted ways after college. There is Celeste's one social friend from college, Violet Sonada, but Violet took a job at the Ueno Zoo in Tokyo. Is there anyone from high school? Cynthia from down the street had been Celeste's closest friend but she dropped out of Penn State with a nervous condition and Celeste hasn't talked to her since. Merritt has a bunch of people she knows in the city, but Celeste can barely remember who is who.

She is a social misfit and now Greer will know it.

"Let m-m-me think ab-b-bout it," Celeste says, hoping Greer will assume there are too many young women to choose from and Celeste will need to whittle the list down.

But Greer, of course, sees the humiliating truth. It's because she's a novelist, Celeste supposes. She is perceptive to a fault; it's almost as if she reads minds.

"I shouldn't get involved," Greer says, "but I do think Abby would love to serve as a bridesmaid."

Celeste perks up immediately. Abby! She can ask Abby Winbury, Thomas's wife. She's the right age; she is appropriately girly; she has probably been a bridesmaid twenty times before. Celeste relaxes even as she realizes that the Winburys are providing for her once again.

Celeste tells Benji that she's asking Merritt to be her maid of honor and Abby to be her bridesmaid and Benji gets a crease in his brow.

"Abby?" he says. "Are you sure?"

The nice thing is that Celeste doesn't have to hide anything from Benji. "I c-c-couldn't think of anyone else," she says. "You're marrying the most socially awkward g-g-girl in New York."

Benji kisses her. "And I couldn't be happier about it."

"So what's wrong with Ab-b-by?" Celeste asks.

"Nothing," Benji says. "Did she say yes?"

"I was p-p-planning on e-mailing tomorrow f-from work," Celeste says.

Benji nods.

"What?" Celeste says. Abby would be filling a glaring gap. And besides, as Thomas's wife, wouldn't Abby be insulted *not* to be asked? It's true, Abby can sometimes be a bit off-putting—she was a sorority girl at the University of Texas and she has retained some shallow cattiness, and she is presently obsessed with getting pregnant—but she is family.

"I get the feeling Thomas and Abby are on the rocks," Benji says.

Celeste gasps. "What?"

"Thomas is always taking trips alone," Benji says. "And going out with his friends after work. Not to mention his obsession with the gym."

"Oh," Celeste says. She knows Benji is right. They have met Thomas and Abby for dinner a few times and Thomas is always the last to arrive, often straight from the gym, still in his sweaty workout clothes. Abby won't even let him kiss her unless he's showered, she says. He has to shower before sex, and sex is kept to a schedule since they are trying to conceive. But why try so hard for a baby if you're not planning on staying together?

"I'm not asking Thomas to be my best man," Benji says.

"W-W-What?" Celeste says. This shocks her even more than the news of Thomas and Abby's supposed marital discord. "But he's your b-b-brother."

"Something is going on with him," Benji says. "And I want to distance myself from it. I'm having Shooter serve as my best man."

"Shooter?" Celeste says.

"I've already asked him," Benji says. "He was so happy. He teared up."

He teared up, Celeste thinks. *So happy.* "What are you g-g-going to tell T-T-Thomas?"

"I'll tell Thomas he can be an usher," Benji says. "Maybe."

Saturday, July 7, 2018,
3:30 p.m.

GREER

At half past three, when all of the guests have been called and all of the friends and relatives back in England have been notified about the tragedy and all of the wedding preparations have been summarily undone— except for those that are part of the "crime scene"— Greer takes a moment to peek out the window at the second cottage, the one where Merritt was staying. It's wrapped in police tape like a tawdry present, although the forensics men have left and no one is there to stop Greer from entering. She would love to go in and poke around, but she fears the Winburys are in enough trouble as it is; she can't afford to cause any more.

Tag took Merritt out in the kayak.

Merritt, not Featherleigh.

Greer needs to speak to Tag alone but he said he had to make a phone call, probably to Sergio Ramone, who is not only a friend but a brilliant criminal-defense attorney. Greer isn't sure even Sergio can get Tag out of this mess. He took the girl out on the kayak and she shows up in the morning dead. Drowned in the harbor. Greer retreats to the master suite and perches on the sofa at the end of the bed, waiting for Tag, although she expects him to be led from the house in handcuffs the instant the police figure out this affair was going on.

The boys handled the news badly. Benji exploded. "Did you kill her, Dad? Did. You. Kill. Her?"

"No," Tag said. "I took her out on the kayak, yes, I did. But I brought her back to shore safely."

He sounded like he was telling the truth. His inflection and tone were full of calm conviction, but Greer now knows he's been lying to her for a long time— maybe for the entirety of their marriage—so how would she know for sure?

Thomas hadn't said anything at all. Possibly he, like Greer, had been too stunned to speak.

The ring that Greer thought Tag had bought for Featherleigh he'd bought for Merritt. Greer had seen the ring on Merritt's thumb—she had *seen* it!—but she had one thing so firmly lodged in her brain that there hadn't been room for any other possibilities.

The ring had been Tag's only misstep. Greer had gone in to see Jessica Hicks, the jeweler, about wedding bands. Greer thought it would be a nice touch for Benji and Celeste to have rings fashioned by a Nantucket jeweler. The instant Greer entered the shop, Jessica's brows had shot up. She said, *Did your daughter-in-law not like the ring, then?*

Daughter-in-law? Greer had said.

The one who's pregnant? Jessica said. *Did she not like the ring?*

The ring? Greer had said.

Your husband came in . . . Jessica said.

Oh, right! Greer had said enthusiastically, although a bad feeling had started to seep through her. Tag had said nothing about getting a present for Abby. And Tag wasn't known for thoughtful gestures where the kids were concerned; he left that to Greer.

He told me about it but we've been so busy he hasn't had a chance to show it to me, Greer said. *And he wouldn't do a proper job describing it anyway. What did it look like?*

Silver-lace pattern, Jessica said, *embedded with multicolored sapphires. Like this one. It's meant to be worn on the thumb.* Jessica had then shown Greer a ring that sold for six hundred dollars. So it wasn't a fortune, wasn't like a trip to Harry Winston for diamonds, but Greer had been near certain she would never see Abby wearing that ring.

Tag steps into the bedroom, closes the door behind him, and locks it.

"Greer," he says. He holds his hands up as if she might strike him.

She would like to strike him. What has he *done?* The girl dead, the wedding canceled, their marriage, their life…

And yet all Greer can think to say is "I thought you were having an affair with Featherleigh."

Tag's eyes widen. "No," he says.

"No," Greer says. "It was Merritt."

"Yes," he says.

Greer nods. "If you want me to help you, you had better tell me everything. Everything, Tag."

It started the night of the wine dinner, he says. They were both drunk, very drunk, and she came on to him. They slept together; it was unremarkable, regrettable. He thought that would be it but then he bumped into her again in the city, by accident, at a hotel bar, and she invited him to her apartment. He's not sure why but he said yes. And then there was another time or two, but he finally demanded she leave him alone.

"You bought her gifts?" Greer says.

"No."

"Tag."

He sighs. "A trinket. It was her birthday a few weeks ago. That was when I ended it. She wanted to go away together. I said no. She persisted. I booked a room at the Four Seasons downtown..."

The Four Seasons? Every detail pierces her.

"She was late showing up and in the minutes that I was waiting, I came to my senses. I left the hotel and went home to you."

"So how many times did you screw her?" Greer asks. "Sum total."

"More than five, less than ten," Tag says.

Greer feels ill. She can see the allure, she supposes. Merritt was attractive; she was young, free, unfettered. Merritt had the whiff of a rebel about her. Who wouldn't want to shag Merritt? What makes Greer want to vomit on her shoes is the thought of her own self while all of this was going on those six, seven, eight times. What had Greer been doing? Was she writing her perfectly mediocre novel or was she planning their son's wedding? Whatever she was doing, she wasn't paying attention to Tag. She hadn't given Tag a minute's thought.

"And that was it?" Greer says. "Nothing more? You had an affair, you broke it off. She was upset about it. I saw her crying during the rehearsal dinner, in the laundry room, of all places. So when you talk to the police, you'll tell them she was emotionally overwrought and that she threatened suicide if you didn't leave me. You took her out on the kayak to try and talk some sense into her. You delivered her back to shore; you came to bed. She drowned herself."

"Well," Tag says.

"Well what?"

"It's a bit stickier than that," Tag says. He clears his throat. "She was pregnant."

Greer closes her eyes. Pregnant.

"You're going to the gallows," she says.

Tag's face crumples; Greer has landed the poison dart right between his eyes. The girl was pregnant. *Pregnant* with a Winbury bastard child. The thought is hideous, and yet it feels utterly predictable. Thomas Winbury the elder, known to most as Tag, has taken the family down. His poor judgment, his base urges, and his weak character have desecrated the Winbury name. He has committed murder, and he will be caught.

Greer can think ill of Tag all she likes, but in the end, she knows, she will say and do whatever she needs to do to protect him.

There's a knock on the bedroom door.

It's Thomas.

"The chief of police is back," Thomas says. "He'd like to talk to you next, Dad."

Tag looks to Greer. She nods but is afraid to say a word in front of Thomas. Tag should stick to the story they came up with. She tries to convey this with her eyes but Tag hangs his head like a guilty man. Greer would like to go into the questioning with him. Let her talk, let her present the argument. She, after all, is the storyteller.

But that, of course, won't be possible. Tag got into this mess without her; he will have to go it alone.

Greer is exhausted. It's nearly four o'clock, the hour the ceremony was to take place.

She lies down on the bed. She is so tired she could sleep until morning. Maybe she *will* sleep until morning.

Merritt Monaco. She was twenty-nine years old. Pretty, but unoriginal. That was who Tag was screwing.

Disgust courses through Greer's veins. She is hardly naive; she has written scenarios this nefarious and more

so. There wasn't one original thing about it—a charming, rich, powerful older man with an indifferent wife
seduced or was seduced by a young, beautiful, silly girl.
It practically described the history of the entire world—
from Henry VIII with Anne Boleyn to an American
president with his impressionable intern. But it feels
brand-new, doesn't it? Because it is happening to Greer.

Pregnant.

When Tag is charged with murder, the papers will
have a field day. Their wealth and the fact that Greer
writes murder mysteries will make the story positively
irresistible. The *New York Post* will cover it, then the
British tabloids. Greer will be cast as an object of pity;
her fans will either cringe or rage on her behalf. The
thought is horrifying—so many middle-aged women
writing indignant Facebook posts or penning sympathetic letters. Thomas's and Benji's lives will be ruined.
They'll become social outcasts. Thomas will be fired;
Benji will be asked to resign from his charitable boards.

Greer sits up. She can't sleep. She needs a pill.

She goes into the master bathroom and eyes Tag's
sink—his razor, his shaving brush, his tortoiseshell
comb. She couldn't bear to walk into this bathroom and
find Tag's side empty. They have been together too long,
endured too much.

Greer opens her medicine cabinet, and as she does so,
she gets a peculiar feeling of déjà vu, as though she
watched herself go through these exact motions a short
time ago—and so a part of her knows that when she
looks, her sleeping pills will be missing.

Wait, she thinks. *Wait just a minute!*

The pills were prescribed by her GP, Dr. Crowe. Dr.
Crowe is doddering, nearly senile; he has been Greer's
"woman doctor" since she moved to Manhattan. The
pills are "quite potent," as Crowe likes to remind her,

some cousin to the quaaludes everyone was taking in the seventies. "Quite potent" isn't just some humble-brag; the pills knock Greer out immediately and lock her in an obsidian casket for a full eight hours. Greer doesn't keep her sleeping pills in a prescription bottle but rather in a round enamel box decorated with a picture of a young Queen Elizabeth II. Greer received the box as a present from her grandmother on the occasion of her eleventh birthday.

The Queen Elizabeth box always sits in the same spot on the same shelf and Greer knows why it's gone. Or at least she suspects she does.

She closes the medicine cabinet and stares at herself in the mirror. She needs to think this through. But there's no time. She needs to talk to the Chief immediately. She needs to save her husband, that bastard.

Saturday, July 7, 2018,
4:00 p.m.

NANTUCKET

Marty Szczerba is sitting at the bar at the Crosswinds restaurant in the Nantucket airport finally eating his lunch. He likes the Reuben, loves the coleslaw; he has gained thirty pounds since Nancy died, which isn't helping in his quest for a new girlfriend. A not-unattractive woman in her early to mid-forties suddenly takes the seat next to his. She points at his sandwich and says, in a posh English accent, "I'm having what this chap's having. And a glass of chardonnay. A large glass."

Marty fumbles with his knife and fork in an attempt to flag down Dawn, the bartender, who is watching Wimbledon on the TV in the corner. "Dawn, this young lady would like to place an order."

While Dawn takes the order for the Reuben, the coleslaw, and the large chardonnay, Marty sneaks a better look at his new neighbor. She is blond, or blondish, in halfway decent shape, with laugh lines around her mouth and fingernails painted cherry red. She is dressed in a strapless army-green jumpsuit type of thing that Marty knows is meant to be stylish. It gives him a good view of her chest and arms. She's a bit puffy, but Marty is hardly sculpted himself.

"I'm Marty Szczerba," he says, holding out his hand.

"Featherleigh," she says. "Featherleigh Dale." She takes his hand and offers a smile, then her chardonnay arrives. She lifts the glass to Marty and says, "I can't wait to get off this island. The past twenty-four hours have not been kind to me."

Marty wishes he had a glass to cheers her with, but he's still on the clock. He, too, has had one hell of a day, beginning and ending with the case of the Murdered Maid of Honor and the runaway person of interest. It turned out the guy they were looking for was caught by a local teenage girl who works for the Hy-Line. Marty is glad the guy isn't still at large but he bristles at being bested by some kid who found him by using Facebook. That's cheating, is it not? Marty would have benefited from a little glory. He has been considering asking out Keira, the chief of police's assistant, but she's in her thirties and goes to barre class every day and is, likely, looking for more of a hero than Marty can currently claim to be.

"So you're just visiting?" Marty says. "Where do you live?" He knows better than to get his hopes up about anyone from off-island; he still has two years left until retirement, although after that, he'll be ready to go. Laura Rae and Ty will be happily married, maybe even starting a family, and Marty will become an annoyance. He hopes this Featherleigh says she lives in Boston. How perfect would that be? He gets two free round-trip tickets to Boston on Cape Air per month. He envisions himself and Featherleigh strolling around the Public Garden hand in hand, stopping in at the Parish Café on Boylston for lunch. They'll have cocktails down at the Seaport. Boston is a great city for people in love. They can ride the swan boats! Have high tea at the Four Seasons! Go to a Sox game! And in two years, when Marty is ready to retire, his relationship with Featherleigh will be established enough to take it to the next level.

"London," she says. "I have a flat in Sloane Square,

although I fear it'll belong to the bank by the time I get home."

London, Marty thinks as his dreams deflate. That's too far away. But it wouldn't be a bad place to visit Featherleigh for a casual, no-strings-attached fling. Marty has never been to London, which is something he needs to remedy, especially since his Match.com profile boasts that he loves to travel.

"And what do you do for a living?" Marty asks.

Featherleigh takes a long sip of her wine, then sets her elbow on the bar and rests her head in her hand to regard him. "I sell antiques to rich people," she says. "What do you do, Marty?"

Marty straightens up a little. "I'm head of security here at the airport."

"Well," she says, "that's a very prestigious job, isn't it?" The way she pronounces the word *prestigious* in her English accent sounds so lovely, Marty grins.

"He's the top gun," Dawn chimes in.

Marty silently thanks Dawn for the backup even though he feels somewhat mortified that she's eavesdropping on his first attempt at a pickup since 1976. He bobs his head yes, then wonders if Featherleigh is making fun of him. After all, it's not like he's the head of security at Heathrow. *That would be a hellish nightmare of a job,* Marty thinks. Flights from all over the world converging. How would he ever keep track of the potential threats? And yet somehow those chaps do it, day in and day out.

"In the summer, Nantucket is the second-busiest airport in the state," Marty says. "Only Logan is busier."

"Logan?" Featherleigh says.

"The airport in Boston," he says.

"Ah, right," Featherleigh says. "Well, I'm flying standby to JFK on JetBlue." She checks her phone. "I really hope

I get on." She winks at Marty. "You don't have any pull, do you?"

"With the airlines?" Marty says. "No."

This admission sends Featherleigh right into the electronic abyss of her phone. She sips her large glass of chardonnay, then starts scrolling. Marty regards the second half of his Reuben, the cheese now cold and congealed, and his coleslaw, which has grown soupy. Before he loses Featherleigh entirely to the seductive allure of Instagram, he says, "So what was so bad about your stay?"

Featherleigh sets down her phone and Marty feels a childish triumph. "I couldn't begin to explain."

"Try me."

"I came all the way from London for a wedding. Now, mind you, I had no interest in attending the wedding, but this man I've been seeing was going to be there so I said yes."

Marty hears the phrase *man I've been seeing* and what's left of his enthusiasm flags. Even someone not-gorgeous-but-okay-looking like Featherleigh has found someone. *Where are all the half-decent-looking-but-not-attached women?* Marty wonders. *Tell me!*

"And then, for reasons too awful to explain, the wedding was canceled—"

"Wait a minute," Marty says. "Were you going to the wedding out in—" At that moment, Marty's phone starts ringing and a discreet check of his screen shows that it's the chief of police. Marty has to take the call. He holds a finger up to Featherleigh. "Excuse me one moment," he says. He relishes the opportunity to show Featherleigh that he really *is* sort of important. "What can I do for you, Chief?" he says.

"We're looking for someone else now," the Chief says. "And we have good reason to believe she's at the airport, trying to fly standby. Female, early forties, blondish hair, name is Featherleigh Dale."

Marty's mouth falls open and the phone nearly slips from his hand but he manages to compose himself and offer Featherleigh a smile.

"I'm on it, Chief," he says.

TAG

He shakes hands with the chief of police and tries to strike the appropriate tone: mournful yet strong, concerned yet guilt-free. When Greer woke up Tag, jostling his shoulder and saying, "Celeste's friend Merritt, the friend, the maid of honor, Tag, she's dead. She drowned out front. She's dead. The paramedics are here and the police. Celeste found her floating. She's dead. Jesus, Tag, wake *up. Do* something," he'd thought he was ensnared in a bad dream. It had taken several long seconds for Tag to realize that Greer was real and that what she was saying was true.

Merritt had drowned. She was dead.

Not possible, he thought. He had dropped her off on the beach after the kayak ride. She had stormed off— upset, yes, but still very much alive.

On solid ground. He'd thought she'd gone to bed.

Tag isn't sure what the police know.

Do they know about the affair?

Do they know about the pregnancy?

They'll find out Merritt was pregnant as soon as they

hear from the medical examiner, but will they learn about the affair? Whom did Merritt tell? Did she tell Celeste? Did Celeste tell the police? Tag's first instinct upon hearing the hideous news was to find Celeste and remind her that the future of the Winbury family rested with her discretion. But Celeste had been taken to the emergency room to be treated for anxiety and she hasn't returned to the house—which is, Tag suspects, a bad sign.

Tag leads the Chief to his study. Benji walked out after Tag admitted that it had been Merritt he'd taken on the kayak, and Thomas vamoosed as well. But both of his sons know better than to say a word to the police, Tag is confident of this. Their well-being is contingent on *his* well-being.

Tag says to the Chief, "Can I offer you a drink?"

The Chief lifts a hand. "No, thanks."

Tag settles in the chair behind his desk and offers the Chief one of the two chairs facing the desk. This makes Tag feel in control of the situation, as if it were Tag who invited the Chief in for a chat and not the other way around. *Perception is reality,* Tag thinks. Why *not* put the Chief in the hot seat?

"What have you got?" Tag asks.

"Excuse me?" the Chief says.

"A young woman is dead," Tag says. "And it happened on my property, or very nearly. Now, maybe it was an accident. Maybe Merritt had too much to drink and drowned. But if you have any evidence that something else is going on, then I deserve to know about it." Tag hardens his gaze. "Don't I?"

"No," the Chief says. "You don't."

Tag opens his mouth to say—to say what? It doesn't matter because the Chief leans forward in his chair and says, "When did you last see Ms. Monaco?"

Tag blinks. His instinct is to lie—of course his instinct is to lie!—because the truth is too incriminating.

"I saw her last night," Tag says.

The Chief nods. "At what time?"

"I couldn't say."

"All right," the Chief says. "Where were you when you last saw her?"

"I was...out back."

"Can you be more specific, please?" the Chief says. "What were the circumstances surrounding the last time you saw Ms. Monaco?"

Tag takes a moment. He has had all day to consider various answers to this question, but now he's floundering.

If he lies, they'll catch him, he thinks. And he is innocent. Where Merritt's death is concerned, he is innocent.

"We were out back under the tent, drinking," he says. "A group of us. Myself, my son Thomas, a friend of the family named Featherleigh Dale, and Ms. Monaco."

"And how would you describe Ms. Monaco's mood at that time?" the Chief asks.

Tag thinks about this. He had bidden Bruce Otis good night and had planned to go to bed—but Thomas had arrived back from town by himself. Abby had called and insisted Thomas come home; when he'd gone up to check on her, however, she'd been asleep.

"Or she was pretending to be asleep," Thomas said. "It's like she's trying to catch me at something."

"*Catch* you at something?" Tag said. He flashed back to the evening he ended things with Merritt, when he saw Thomas sitting alone at the bar at the Four Seasons. And so instead of going to bed, Tag grabbed a bottle of good rum from the bar in his study. As his favorite auntie, Mary Margaret, used to say, *When you don't know what else to do, get drunk.* Tag would have a heart-to-heart with Thomas; it was long overdue.

"Come on out to the tent with me," Tag said.

Thomas had needed no further enticement. He set up one of the round tables meant for the reception and brought over four folding chairs—thinking, Tag supposed, that the others might join them when they got back from town. Tag had just been pouring the shots when Merritt and Featherleigh appeared out of the shadows. It was almost as though they'd been lying in wait. Tag was spooked to see Merritt but she'd offered him an apologetic smile and Tag thought he'd seen acquiescence in her eyes. She would do as he asked: Take the money, end the pregnancy, walk away. He knew she didn't want a baby.

"Would you ladies care for a nightcap?" Tag asked.

"Answer to my prayers," Featherleigh said.

Merritt hadn't spoken, although she did take a seat next to Tag, and when he set a shot in front of her, she didn't protest.

He had been a little uncomfortable about how chummy Merritt suddenly seemed to be with Featherleigh Dale. What were *they* doing together? And why was Featherleigh still at the house? She was staying at an inn downtown. She had waited until the last minute to book and so she ended up in a real dump, as Greer described it; maybe that was why she was hesitant to leave.

"Merritt seemed to be in fine spirits," Tag says to the Chief. "I mean, I guess. I really didn't know her well."

"Didn't you?" the Chief asks.

Tag's gut twists. Now is the time to ask for an attorney. He had considered calling Sergio Ramone the second he found out Merritt was dead, but in his mind, hiring an attorney is as good as admitting you're guilty. And Tag didn't kill her.

He didn't kill her.

"I had nothing to do with Ms. Monaco's death," he says. "Not one thing."

"Were you having an affair with Merritt Monaco?" the Chief asks.

"I was," Tag says. "But I ended things weeks ago."

"Did Ms. Monaco tell you she was pregnant with your baby?"

"She *said* she was..."

"Okay, then," the Chief says. He leans forward in the chair. "I'm going to guess that when you heard that news, you weren't too happy. I'm going to guess you would have gone to great lengths to keep that news quiet."

Tag sinks into himself. Could he throw himself on the mercy of the Chief, maybe appeal to him man to man? One look at the Chief tells Tag that the guy is honorable. He's wearing a gold wedding band. He has probably been married twenty-five or thirty years and never so much as glanced at another woman.

"I *would* have gone to great lengths to keep that news quiet," Tag admits. "If I were even certain the baby was mine. Merritt was seeing other men. There's an Irish bloke named Robbie who bartends at the Breslin in New York City. It might have been Robbie's baby."

"But she told you it was yours," the Chief says. "Doesn't matter if it was Robbie's. She was threatening *you*. She was threatening to expose your affair. I'm sure that must have been scary for you, especially this weekend, when you were surrounded by family and friends. Your son's getting married; seems pretty unfair for her to choose this time to air your dirty laundry."

Tag hears the phony sympathy in the Chief's voice, even as his words ring true: It *was* unfair.

"I told Merritt that after the wedding I would write her a check. I wanted her to terminate the pregnancy." He holds up his hands. "That's bad, I know. But it's a far cry from killing her."

The Chief stares at him.

"Do you really think I'd be daft enough to drown a woman I was sleeping with, a woman who claimed to be pregnant with my child, and leave her to wash up in front of my house on the morning of my son's wedding? I wasn't that desperate. I was worried, definitely, but I wasn't desperate and I didn't kill anyone."

"You did take Ms. Monaco out for a ride on your kayak, though, correct? The kayak we found on the beach? Your wife and your daughter-in-law both said you're the only person who uses the kayaks."

"Yes," Tag says. "Yes, I did."

"Even though it was the middle of the night," the Chief says. "Did that not seem like a desperate measure to you? Reckless, at the very least?"

"She said she needed to talk to me," Tag says. "Away from everyone, away from the house."

"And what happened while you were out on this kayak ride?"

"I was paddling for an island beach out by Abrams Point but it was dark and I was having a difficult time finding it," Tag says. "And when we were out in open water, in the middle of nowhere, the kayak tilted to the right and I heard a splash. Merritt had jumped off." Tag leans forward. "You have to understand, Merritt was unhinged. She was hormonal, emotional, mentally unstable. She admitted that the only reason she wanted to keep the baby was that it gave her leverage over me. Then she leaped off the boat like a crazy person. I had to paddle back around and haul her up by the wrist."

"By the wrist?" the Chief says.

"Yes," Tag says. "And as soon as she was back up in the kayak, I paddled like hell for home. She got out on the beach and headed off. I thought she was going to bed."

"You didn't tie the kayak up," the Chief says. "You left

it overturned on the beach. Which I understand is out of character for you."

"It was unusual," Tag says. "But I worried that if I hung around to tie up the kayak, she would reappear, there would be more drama, she would raise her voice, people would hear us." Tag drops his head into his hands. "I just wanted her to leave me alone."

"Exactly," the Chief says. "You just wanted her to leave you alone." He puts his hands on the desk and leans forward. "The medical examiner found a heavy-duty sedative in Ms. Monaco's system. So let me tell you what I think. I think you were pouring the girl shots and you slipped her a mickey. Then you invited her out for a kayak and you accidentally on purpose capsized and she never made it back to the boat. Or maybe you did as you say, and you pulled her up by the wrist. Maybe you let her pass out on the kayak and then you dumped her off closer to shore so that it looked like she went for a swim and drowned."

"No," Tag says. "That is *not* what happened. I didn't drug her and I didn't dump her anywhere."

"But you do admit you were the one pouring the shots," the Chief says. "Right?"

"Right, but—"

"Did she have anything else to drink?" the Chief asks.

"Water," Tag says. "Water! Featherleigh went to the kitchen at some point…" Now Tag can't recall if it was before or after Thomas went upstairs. Before, he thinks. Thomas can vouch for him. But no…no, it was after. Definitely after. "And Featherleigh brought out a glass of ice water."

"Really," the Chief says. He makes a note on his pad.

"Yes, really," Tag says. This suddenly seems like the detail that will save him. He had been wary when Merritt asked for the water because it seemed to indicate she was

concerned about her health—or the health of the baby—
and then Tag realized that he hadn't actually witnessed
Merritt doing either of the shots he'd poured. He wondered if she'd thrown them over her shoulder. Featherleigh had been only too happy to fetch water for her new
best friend, and while she was gone, Merritt told Tag she
needed to talk to him alone. "Featherleigh brought Merritt a glass of water. Merritt drank the whole thing."

"She drank the whole thing?" the Chief says. "Nobody
else had any?"

"Correct," Tag says. He relaxes back into the chair.
Maybe Featherleigh slipped Merritt a mickey, or maybe
they popped pills earlier in the night. Featherleigh is a
wild card. Tag would have categorized her as harmless
but it's not beyond her to have accidentally wreaked this
kind of havoc.

"There wasn't a water glass on the scene," the Chief
says.

"No?" Tag says. This doesn't make sense. "Well, I'm
telling you, Merritt drank a glass of ice water. Featherleigh got it from the kitchen." Tag glowers at the Chief,
which feels risky, but he is through being intimidated.
He didn't drug Merritt and he didn't kill her. "I think
you need to talk to Featherleigh Dale."

"I think you need to stop telling me how to run my
investigation," the Chief says. He barely raises his voice
but his tone is stern nonetheless. He's a local guy. He
must resent men like Tag with their showcase homes
and their shaky morals. "I have one more question."

Tag is seeing spots in his peripheral vision, the first
sign of a tension headache. "What is it?"

"Ms. Monaco had quite a nasty cut on her foot," the
Chief says. "And there were traces of Ms. Monaco's blood
in the sand on the beach out front. Do you know anything about this?"

"Nothing," Tag says. "She didn't have a cut on her foot when she was under the tent. You can ask Featherleigh! Ask Thomas! So... she must have cut it when she got back on land. Which is proof I delivered her safely!"

The Chief says, "It's not 'proof' of anything. But thank you for your answers." He stands and Tag stands as well, though his legs are weak and watery.

"I think it's pretty obvious Merritt took some pills because she was upset, and then she wandered back into the water and drowned," Tag says. "You could simply conclude that her death was an accident. It would be easier on everyone—her family, her friends, my son, and Celeste."

"I could conclude it was an accident," the Chief says. "And you're right—it would probably be easier on everyone, including my police department. But it wouldn't necessarily be the truth. And in my job, Mr. Winbury, I seek the truth. Which obviously isn't something you'd understand."

"I resent that," Tag says.

"Oh, well," the Chief says. But then, to Tag's relief, he heads for the door. "I'll let you know if I need anything else."

"So we're finished?" Tag asks.

"For now," the Chief says.

Sunday, June 10, 2018

CELESTE

Benji is away on his bachelor-party weekend. Shooter arranged for complete debauchery: Thursday afternoon they landed in Vegas, where they went to their penthouse suite at Aria and gambled until dawn. Friday brought a double bill of race-car driving and gun club. Saturday they drove to Palm Springs to golf and have a thousand-dollar-a-head steak dinner at Mr. Lyons. And today, Sunday, they are to fly home.

Before he left, Benji tried to apologize in advance. "There will probably be strippers," he said. "Or worse."

"Hookers and b-b-blow," Celeste says, and she kisses him good-bye. "Or p-p-performing lesb-b-bians. I really d-d-don't want to know any d-d-details. Just have f-f-fun."

"Should I be happy that you're not protesting this trip," Benji asks, "or concerned?"

"B-B-Be happy," Celeste says.

Celeste spent Friday and Saturday night in Easton with her parents. Her mother was finished with treatment; there was nothing they could do now but be grateful for each new day. Karen was feeling pretty good, so the three of them took a walk around the neighborhood and then went for an early dinner at the diner.

Celeste had brought her wedding dress at her father's behest.

He said, "You might want to try it on for your mom."

"B-B-But why?" Celeste said. "You g-g-guys are still c-c-coming, right? To Nant-t-tucket?"

"Just bring it, please," Bruce said.

And so, once her mother was settled at home on Saturday night, Celeste tried on the wedding gown. She put on her white silk shantung kitten heels and her pearl earrings. She didn't bother with hair or makeup but that hardly seemed to matter. Karen beamed; her eyes were shining; she clasped her hands to her heart. "Oh, honey, you're a *vision*."

Thank you, Bruce had mouthed from across the room.

Celeste had twirled and tried to smile.

Now, Sunday morning, Celeste drives back to the city to meet Merritt for lunch at a place called Fish on Bleecker Street.

"I want oysters," Merritt had said to Celeste over the phone. "And I don't want to see anyone I know. I have to talk to you."

When Celeste gets to Fish, Merritt is already there with a bloody mary in front of her. She's breaking peanuts between her thumb and forefinger and throwing the shells on the floor. Fish has the atmosphere of a dive bar, but there are yards of crushed ice upon which rest piles and piles of oysters. The Yankees game is on TV. The bartender wears a T-shirt that says SEX, DRUGS, AND LOBSTER ROLL.

"Hey," Celeste says, taking the stool next to Merritt. She plants a kiss on Merritt's cheek and orders a bloody mary as well. She feels she deserves a little hedonism.

She has been performing her daughterly duties while Benji has been on a three-day bender.

"Hey yourself," Merritt says. "Have you heard from Benji?"

"No," Celeste says. "I asked him not to call me." Her mood is suddenly buoyant, her tongue nimble. Her stutter all but disappears when she's alone with Merritt.

"Seriously?" Merritt says.

"Seriously," Celeste says. "I wanted him to enjoy himself and not worry about checking in with the future wife."

"Relationship goals," Merritt says.

Celeste takes a sip of her bloody mary; the alcohol and spice go right to her head. She considers telling Merritt that the reason she asked Benji not to call was that she didn't want to hear any news about Shooter—what Shooter had planned, what Shooter was doing, what funny thing Shooter said. Celeste is almost to the finish line. The wedding is four weeks away, but still she's afraid she'll get tripped up by her irrational heart. Every day she thinks about calling the wedding off.

Celeste takes another sip of her bloody while Merritt peruses the oyster list on the blackboard. It would be such a relief to confess her feelings to Merritt. That's what best friends are for, right? Technically Celeste is being a bad friend by *not* telling Merritt. And yet Celeste fears naming her feelings. She's afraid if she says the words aloud—*I'm in love with Shooter*—something very bad will happen.

Merritt orders a dozen oysters. She's in a West Coast mood, she says, so six Kumamotos and six Fanny Bays; Celeste has agreed to taste one of each in an attempt to cultivate a taste for the little buggers. Genus: *Crassostrea*. Species: *gigas*.

Merritt takes an exaggerated breath and says, "Please don't judge me."

"I would never," Celeste says. "What's going on?"

Merritt holds out her hand. "I'm so nervous, I'm actually shaking."

"Just tell me," Celeste says. She's used to Merritt's theatrics. They're one of the reasons Celeste loves her.

"I've been seeing someone," Merritt says. "It started a few weeks ago and I thought it was a casual fling, but then the guy called me up and since then it's gotten more serious."

"Okay?" Celeste says. She doesn't understand what the big deal is.

"He's married," Merritt says.

Celeste shakes her head. "I thought you learned your lesson with Travis Darling."

"Travis was a predator," Merritt says. "This guy I really like. The problem is . . . promise you won't kill me?"

"Kill you?" Celeste says. She can't figure out what Merritt is going to tell her.

"It's your future father-in-law," Merritt says. Her head falls forward but she turns to give Celeste a sidelong glance. "It's Tag."

Celeste is very proud of herself: She doesn't scream. She doesn't hop off her stool, leave the bar, and get back on the subway uptown. Instead, she sucks down the rest of her bloody mary and signals the bartender for another.

It's Tag. Merritt and . . . Tag.

Celeste has been hanging out with Merritt for too long, she thinks, because she isn't shocked. She can all too easily picture Merritt and Tag together. "Did it start when he took you to the wine dinner?"

"A little before that," Merritt says. "I noticed him checking me out the Friday night of your bachelorette weekend while we were out front waiting for the taxi.

And so on Saturday morning, I did an exploratory mission to see if he was actually interested, and he was."

"Have you *slept* with him?" Celeste asks. Tag is an attractive guy, and very alpha, which is how Merritt likes her men. But Celeste can't imagine having *sex* with him. He's older than her father.

"Are you really twenty-eight years old?" Merritt asks. "Of course I slept with him."

"Ugh," Celeste says. "I'm sorry, but—"

"I figured it would be a one-night stand," Merritt says. "He asked for my number but I never thought he'd use it. But then, a week and a half later, he called me at two o'clock in the morning."

"Oh, jeez," Celeste says. Her mind starts traveling the predictable path: *What is Tag thinking? He's such a creep! Such a stereotypical male douchebag!* Up until this very moment, Celeste had liked him. It's heartbreaking to discover he's preying on her friend, a woman the same age as his children. Does he do this all the time? He must! And what about Greer? Celeste would never have guessed she would ever have occasion to feel sorry for Greer Garrison, but she does now. She understands the biological impulse behind Tag's actions: he is still virile, still seeking to spread his seed and propagate the species.

But come on!

"Come on!" Celeste says.

Merritt cringes at the outburst.

"Sorry," Celeste says. She dives into the second bloody mary. "I'm sorry. I won't judge you. But p-p-please, Merritt, you have to end it. Tomorrow. Or better still, t-t-tonight."

"I don't think I can," Merritt says. "I'm in it. He's got me. My birthday is next week and I asked him to take me away. I think he's considering it."

"You're a g-g-grown woman," Celeste says. She winces; her stutter is back. Of course it's back! Celeste went from feeling relaxed to feeling like she just stepped off the Tilt-a-Whirl at the carnival with a stomach full of fried dough. "He hasn't *got* you. You can exercise free will and walk away."

"He's all I think about," Merritt says. "He's in my blood. It's like I'm infected." The oysters arrive and Merritt absentmindedly douses half of them with hot sauce. "Do you have any idea what that feels like?"

In my blood. Infected.

Yes, she thinks. *Shooter.*

"N-N-No," she says.

Against her better judgment, Celeste stays with Merritt at Fish all afternoon. Celeste has a Cobb salad, Merritt a tuna burger with extra wasabi. They order a bottle of Sancerre, and then—because Celeste is very slowly processing the news and Merritt is experiencing some kind of high at finally sharing it—they order a second bottle.

"Sancerre is a sauvignon blanc that comes from the Loire Valley," Merritt says. "Tag taught me that our first night together."

"Great," Celeste says. She is patient as Merritt gradually reveals the particulars of her relationship with Tag. They meet at her apartment. They once went out for sandwiches. Tag paid, pulled her chair out, emptied her trash. Tag is refined, he's mature, he is smart and successful. She knows it's cliché but she is a sucker for his British accent. She wants to eat it, take a bath in it. Tag is jealous of Robbie. He showed up outside Merritt's apartment building in the middle of the night because he was so jealous.

"Does he ever t-t-talk about Greer?" Celeste asks. She pours herself another glass of wine. She is getting drunk. Their food has been cleared and so Celeste attacks the bowl of peanuts.

"Sometimes he mentions her," Merritt says. "But we tend to stay away from the topic of family."

"Wise," Celeste says.

Merritt tells Celeste that, just a few days earlier, Tag asked Merritt to show up at a hotel bar where he was meeting clients for drinks. They had sex in the ladies' room, then Merritt left.

It's like a scene from a movie, Celeste thinks. Except it's real life, her real best friend and her real future father-in-law. She should be *horrified!* But in an uncharacteristic twist, she is almost relieved that Merritt is doing something even worse than she is. She's in love with Benji's best friend. But she has exercised willpower. Willpower, she now understands, is an endangered species. Other people conduct wildly inappropriate affairs.

"I have to get home," Celeste says, checking her phone. "Benji lands in twenty minutes and he's c-c-coming over for dinner."

"You can't tell Benji," Merritt says.

Celeste gives her friend a look. She's not sure what kind of look because her face feels like it's made of Silly Putty. The air in the bar is shimmering. Celeste is *so* drunk.

"Obviously not," she says.

Merritt pays the bill, and Celeste, for once, doesn't protest or offer to pay half, nor does she refuse when Merritt presses thirty dollars in her hand and puts her into a cab headed uptown. It's bribe money, and Celeste deserves it.

Somehow, she makes it up the stairs and into her apartment. She can't imagine sobering up enough to have dinner with Benji, but if she cancels he'll think she's upset about his weekend away.

She *cannot* tell him about Merritt and his father. She can't let anything slip. She has to act as though everything is fine, normal, status quo.

She sends Merritt a text. End it! Now! Please!

Then she falls asleep facedown on her futon.

She wakes up when she hears her apartment's buzzer. The light coming through her sole bedroom window has mellowed. It's late. What time? She checks her bedside clock. Quarter after seven. That will be Benji.

She hurries to the front door and buzzes him in, then she rushes to the bathroom to brush her teeth and splash water on her face. She's still drunk but not as drunk as she was and not yet cotton-mouthed or hung over. She's even a little hungry. *Maybe she and Benji can walk down to the Peruvian chicken place,* she thinks. It's Sunday night, so Benji will sleep at home and Celeste can be in bed by ten. She has two all-school field trips coming to the zoo tomorrow; it's the curse of June.

Celeste is immersed in these mundane thoughts when she opens the door, so what she sees comes as a complete shock.

It's not Benji.

It's Shooter.

"Wait," she says.

"Hey, Sunshine," he says. "Can I come in?"

"Where's B-B-Benji?" she asks, and an arrow of pure red panic shoots through her. "D-D-Did something happen?"

"He took a cab straight home from JFK," Shooter says. "Didn't he call you?"

"I d-d-don't know," Celeste says. She hasn't checked her phone since...since before getting in the taxi to come home.

Shooter nods. "Trust me. He called you and left a message saying he wanted to go home to bed. There wasn't much left of old Benji when we got off the plane."

"Okay," Celeste says. "So what are you d-d-doing here?"

"Can I come in, please?" Shooter asks.

Celeste checks behind Shooter. The stairwell is its usual gray, miserable self. She thinks to feel embarrassed about her apartment—Shooter lives in some corporate condo in Hell's Kitchen, but even that must put her place to shame.

She isn't supposed to care what Shooter thinks.

"Fine," she says. She's doing a good job at sounding nonchalant, even a bit irritated, but her insides are flapping around like the Bronx Zoo's hysterical macaw Kellyanne. Benji has been diminished by his bachelor adventure, and Shooter doesn't look so hot either. His hair is messy and he's wearing a New York Giants T-shirt, a frayed pair of khaki shorts, and flip-flops. He looks younger to Celeste, nearly innocent.

She steps aside to let him in, then she closes the door behind him.

"So how was the bachelor party of the century?" she asks.

Instead of answering, Shooter kisses her, once, and it feels exactly the way Celeste dreamed it would: soft and delicious. She makes a cooing sound, like a dove, and Shooter kisses her again. Their mouths open and his tongue seeks out hers. Her legs start to quiver; she can't believe she is still standing. Shooter takes her head in his hands; his touch is gentle but the electricity, the heat, the desire between them is crazy. Celeste had no idea her body could respond to another person like this. She's on fire.

Shooter's hands travel down Celeste's back to her ass. He pulls her against him. She wants him so badly she could weep. She hates that she was right. She had known if this ever happened, she would become delirious and lose control of her senses.

Don't stop, she thinks. *Don't stop!*

He pulls away. "Celeste," he says. His voice is husky. "I'm in love with you."

I'm in love with you too, she thinks. But she can't say it, and suddenly her good sense kicks in the way it should have a few moments ago. *This is wrong! It's wrong!* She is engaged to Benji! She will not debase that, she will *not* cheat on him. She will not *cheat* on him. She will not be like Merritt or Tag. They may think that the intensity of their desire justifies their actions, but that is morally convenient. Celeste isn't religious but she does have an immutable sense of right and wrong and she also believes—though she would never say this—that if Merritt and Tag continue, something bad will happen. Something very bad.

This will not be the case for Celeste. She can't falter like this or her mother will die. She's sure of it.

"You have to leave," Celeste says.

"Celeste," he says.

"Leave," she says. She opens the door. She feels faint. "Shooter. Please. *Please.*"

He stares at her for a long moment with those hypnotic blue eyes. Celeste clings to the small piece of herself that knows this is the right action, the only possible action.

Shooter doesn't press. He steps out, and Celeste shuts the door behind him.

Saturday, July 7, 2018,
5:15 p.m.

NANTUCKET

Nick has just heard from the Chief: His interview with Featherleigh Dale is suddenly *very important*. Tag Winbury, the father, is still a person of interest but the Chief isn't convinced he did it.

"He admitted he took the girl out in the kayak," the Chief said. "He said she jumped off, on purpose, and he yanked her back up by the *wrist*, which is consistent with the ME's report. He admitted to pouring the shots, so a reasonable explanation is he slipped a mickey into one of the shots, but forensics found nothing in the bottle or the shot glasses. He didn't know about the cut on her foot. He said she must have cut it after they got back to dry land. We need to check with Featherleigh about the cut. And Tag said Merritt drank a glass of water that Featherleigh Dale got from the kitchen."

"Water?" Nick said. "There wasn't a water glass at the scene."

"Exactly," the Chief said. "So maybe he's lying. Or maybe..."

"Someone got rid of the water glass," Nick said. The mother, Greer Garrison, had been in the kitchen at some point, getting champagne. Nick still has a feeling she's hiding something. "If Greer knew about the affair..."

"And the baby..." the Chief said.

"Maybe *she* slipped a pill into the drinking water,"

Nick said. "And then went back and cleared the glass. Ran it through the dishwasher on the power-scrub cycle. But how would she know Merritt would then go for a swim?"

"Maybe the father and mother are in it together," the Chief said.

"Both of them?" Nick said. "The night before their son's big wedding? A wedding they're paying for?"

"Another thing," the Chief said. "Tag Winbury is a smart guy. If he'd used the kayak ride to drown our girl, he would have made damn sure he locked the kayak up when he got back. Right? To cover his tracks?"

"Are we overthinking this?" Nick asked. "Was it just an accident?"

"Be thorough with Featherleigh," the Chief said.

"You know me," Nick said. "I'm a bloodhound."

Nick is waiting in the interview room when they bring Featherleigh Dale in. He hears her squawking a bit out in the hallway: She's going to miss her flight to JFK. She needs to get back to London. Luklo swings open the door to the interview room and ushers Ms. Dale inside. Nick stands.

He and Featherleigh Dale regard each other.

She says, "Well, you're a tasty morsel, aren't you?"

Luklo smirks and Nick extends a hand. "Ms. Dale, I'm Nick Diamantopoulos, a detective with the Massachusetts State Police. I just have a few questions and as soon as we're through here, assuming we're satisfied with your answers, I'll have Officer Luklo get you back to the airport and on your way."

"If I had known the detective would look like you," Featherleigh says, "then I would definitely have committed a crime."

"If you'll just have a seat," Nick says.

Featherleigh wheels in her roller bag and sets a handbag bursting with *stuff*—a paperback novel, a hairbrush, an open bag of pretzels, which spill all over the floor—on top of the suitcase, then she grabs a smaller clutch purse from within the bag and brings it with her to the table, where she proceeds to put on fire-engine-red lipstick.

Nick waits for her to get settled and thinks, *This woman is too disorganized to kill anyone, even accidentally*. But maybe he's wrong. Featherleigh Dale is in her midforties. She's a bit chunky, she has hair halfway between blond and red—it looks like she changed her mind in the middle of a dye job—and she's wearing what looks like a jumpsuit issued by the air force in 1942, minus the sleeves.

"Can I get you anything to drink?" Nick asks.

"Not unless you have a decent chardonnay," she says. "You interrupted my lunch."

Nick takes a seat. "Let's get started, Ms. Dale—"

"Feather," she says. "My friends call me Feather."

"Feather," Nick says, and he nearly smiles. There used to be a transvestite prostitute on Brock Avenue in New Bedford named Feather. He pauses to remind himself that this is serious business and he needs to be thorough. "Let's start with how you know the Winburys."

Featherleigh, now Feather, waves a hand. "Known them forever," she says.

"Meaning?"

"Meaning, let's see... Tag Winbury went to Oxford with my older brother, Hamish, may he rest in peace, so I've known Tag since I was a kid. I reconnected with the family at my brother's funeral, and after that, our paths kept crossing. I own a business finding antiques for people like Greer, people who have more money than God and don't mind plunking down thirty thousand quid for a settee. I found her some salvaged windows from a church in Canterbury. Those went for ten thousand quid *apiece* and I'm pretty sure she's still got them in storage."

"So you have a business relationship with the Winburys, then," Nick says.

"And personal," Feather says. "We're friends."

"Well, yes," Nick says. "You came over from London for the wedding. How well do you know Benji and Celeste?"

"I know Benji a little bit," Feather says. "Celeste not at all. Just met her last night. Her and her friend. Shame what happened."

"What happened?" Nick says.

Feather's eyes widen. "Have you not heard? The bride's friend, Merritt, *drowned*. The maid of honor. I thought that was why you had questions."

"No, right, it is, I do," Nick says. Her disarray is throwing him off his stride. "I meant, what happened last night? You were part of the group that sat out under the tent drinking rum, correct?"

"Mount Gay Black Barrel," Feather says. "Out of Barbados. You know, I've been to the estate where it's made. I love the stuff."

"Who exactly was sitting at the table with you?" Nick asks.

"Tag, Thomas, myself, and Merritt," Feather says. Then she adds gravely, "The deceased."

"So you say you just met Merritt last night," Nick says. "How did that come about?"

"It came about the way those things do at a party," Feather says. "I noticed her right away. She was pretty and stylish and she had natural confidence. I love confidence." Feather beams at Nick. "*You* have natural confidence. I can see it. It's a very attractive trait in a man."

"So you noticed her from afar," Nick says. "Were you properly introduced?"

"Not until later," Feather says. "Much later, in fact—after the party was over."

Nick makes a note and nods. He senses Feather needs only the slightest encouragement to keep talking.

"I was desperately seeking another drink. The young kids went into town—bride, groom, best man, Thomas—but no one thought to invite old Feather, and I just wasn't ready to go back to my inn. I tried to wrangle a bottle of booze out of the catering help but that didn't work, so I went on a hunt."

"A hunt," Nick says.

"I was stealthy," Feather says. "Because I knew if Greer saw me, she would put me right into a taxi."

"Oh, really?"

"Greer doesn't like me, doesn't *approve* of me. She's old money, landed gentry, grew up on a manor called Swallowcroft, went to Wycombe Abbey, all of that. And she suspects I'm after her hubby. Ha!" Feather hoots. "He's way, *way* too old for me."

Nick needs a verbal leash for this woman so she doesn't go wandering off, although he makes a note: *Greer suspected Feather + Tag???* "Back to how you met Merritt…"

"So I was sneaking around a bit, tiptoeing, dodging behind bushes, harder than it looks because of motion-detector lighting. I figured if I could get to the pool house, I would find alcohol." Feather taps a finger against her temple. "Clever bit of sleuthing on my part there. Anyway, I stumbled across the maid of honor sitting in Greer's rose garden. She was crying."

"Crying?"

"I asked if she was all right. Yes, she said. Then I asked if there was anything I could do. No, she said. I

was surprised because I'd pegged her for naturally confident and then there she was, like a little girl on the playground whose friends had all forsaken her. So I asked if
she wanted to join in my caper."

"Caper," Nick says.

"Hunting for booze in the pool house," Feather says.
"And she said yes and came with me."

"Then what?" Nick says.

"We opened the gate, we selected a couple of chaise
longues, I slid the glass doors to the pool house open, and
voilà—full bar! I made a couple of Grey Goose and ton-
ics and brought them out. Merritt said she didn't want
hers, her stomach was feeling funny, and that was just
fine by me. I had them both."

"Did Merritt stay with you?" Nick asks.

"Yes, she stayed. We talked. Turned out we had a lot
in common."

"Did you?"

"We were both involved with married men," Feather
says. "I mean, *what* are the chances of that?"

Not so slim, Nick wants to say, but he needs to tread
carefully here. Feather seems to be genuine but he has
been at this long enough to suspect it might be an act.

"Did Merritt say anything about the man she was
involved with?" he asks.

"Only that he was married," Feather says. "And was
apparently a real bastard. Pursued her, pursued her, pursued her...then dropped her like a hot potato. Won't
leave his wife, no way, nohow. And I'll tell you, that all
sounded much too familiar."

"But Merritt didn't say who the man was?"

"She didn't tell and neither did I," Feather says. "We
were there to commiserate, not confess."

"Did she say if the man she was seeing was *at* the
wedding?" Nick asks.

"*At* the … no. She lives in Manhattan. Why would … are you thinking she was seeing a married man at the wedding and he was the one who killed her?"

Nick needs to redirect. "What happened when you left the pool house?"

"We decided to walk back to the main house," Feather says. "And we happened across Tag and Thomas and their bottle of Black Barrel."

"Did they seem surprised to see you two?" Nick asks.

Feather tilts her head. "Did they? I don't remember. Tag asked if we were up for a nightcap. We said yes."

"So you're sitting around under the tent drinking rum and what happens?" Nick asks.

"What do you think happens?" Feather asks. "We get drunk." She pauses. "Drunk*er*."

"Was Merritt drinking?"

"I assume so?" Feather says. "Don't quote me on that because, remember, she had a queasy stomach. After a while, Thomas's wifey called him upstairs and I figured the party was breaking up. But Tag is a night owl and he seemed game to keep going awhile longer and Merritt asked for water. I got it for her, actually."

"You got Merritt a glass of water?" Nick says.

Feather nods.

"Did you put ice in the water?" Nick asks.

Feather's eyes roll skyward, as if the answer to that question is written on the ceiling. "I can't recall. I'm sorry. Is that important?"

"Did anything else happen while you were inside getting the water?" he asks. "Did you see anyone? Do anything?"

Feather nods. "I took a piss."

"You went to the bathroom," Nick says. "Was that before you poured the water? Or after?"

Feather stares at him. "After," she says. "I left the

water on the counter. I mean, I didn't bring it into the loo with me."

"But you didn't see anyone else in the kitchen?" Nick asks.

"No."

"Did you hear anyone?"

"No," Feather says. "Fan was on. In very posh houses, you know, they don't listen to one another tinkle."

"No one followed you in from outside?" Nick asks.

"No," Feather says.

"And when you brought Merritt the water, did she drink it?" Nick asks.

"Drank it down like she'd eaten a pound of rock salt."

"Do you remember *clearing* her glass?" Nick asks. "Because the water glass wasn't on the table this morning. But the shot glasses were."

Feather shakes her head. "I've got no memory of clearing the glass or not clearing the glass. If I had to guess, I'd say I left it there, thinking the housekeeper would get it in the morning."

Nick makes a note: *Housekeeper?*

"And how did the party finally break up?" Nick asks.

"We ran through the bottle of rum," Feather says. "Tag said he was going to his study for another. Right after he left, Merritt said she was going to bed. So I was in the tent by myself for a while…then I decided I'd better skedaddle. I didn't want to stay up late drinking with just Tag."

"Why not?"

"It wouldn't look good," Feather says. "If Greer caught us…" Feather pauses. "I'm terrified of that woman."

"Are you?"

"Everyone is terrified of her," Feather says. "She says one thing but you can just tell by looking at her that in her mind she's thinking something else. Novelists are notorious liars, you know."

"Are they?" Nick asks.

"Aren't they?" Feather says. "They lie for a living. They make up stories. So it stands to reason that this tendency runs over into their personal lives."

Nick is intrigued by this answer. "Did you see Greer around at all, even for an instant, after the party? Did you see her in the kitchen pouring herself a glass of champagne?"

"No," Feather says. She gasps. "Why? Do you think Greer had something to do with what happened?"

"You didn't see her?" Nick asks.

Feather shakes her head.

"Did you see Merritt again that night?"

"No," Feather says.

"So the last time you saw Merritt was when she left the tent saying she was going to bed."

"Correct."

"At any point during the night, did Merritt cut her foot?" Nick asks.

"Cut her *foot*?" Feather says. "No."

"Was she wearing shoes when you were doing your stealthy hunting?"

"Yes," Feather says. "Silver sandals. Gorgeous. Merritt said she had gotten them for free from the company and I asked if she could get me a pair for free and she asked what size I wore and I said ten and a half and she said, 'Done.'" Feather's eyes start to water. "She really was a lovely girl."

"Yes," Nick says. "I'm sure she was." He writes: *No cut. Sandals.* He knows there were silver sandals on the scene, under the tent, which Merritt must have left behind when she went for the kayak ride. Nick finally feels like he can see what happened last night...except for a few critical details.

"Okay, so when you...skedaddled, where did you go? Did you call a taxi and go back to your inn?"

"Mm-hmm," Feather says.

"I'm sorry," Nick says. "I need you to give me a yes-or-no answer."

Feather hesitates.

Okay, then, Nick thinks. *Here it is.* "Feather?"

"Yes," she says. "Yes, I did."

"And what time was that?" Nick asks.

"Couldn't tell you."

"But it was late," he says.

Feather shrugs.

Nick locks eyes with Feather and gives her his best smile. Nick's sister, Helena, calls this smile "the kill," because it usually gets him whatever he's after. And Feather succumbs to it. She cocks an eyebrow.

"Are you single?" she asks. "Because if you are, I could be convinced to stay another night."

"Did you call the taxi right away?" Nick asks. "Or did you stay in the tent? Or did you do something else?"

"Something else?" Feather says.

"The manager of your inn," Nick says, "told our officer that you returned to the hotel at quarter past five this morning. And we have a time of death for Ms. Monaco somewhere between two forty-five and three forty-five. Working backward, then, she likely entered the water between two thirty and three thirty. Now, if you didn't reach your inn until quarter after five..."

"The manager is mistaken," Feather says. "It was earlier than five. Hours earlier."

"But you said only a moment ago that you didn't know what time it was," Nick says.

"Well, I can bloody well tell you it was earlier than five o'clock!" Feather says.

"We can easily check the security cameras," Nick says.

Feather hoots. "*That* place does *not* have security cameras!" she says. "You're trying to *trick* me!"

"They had a break-in last year," Nick says. "Nothing was taken, but Miss Brannigan, who runs the inn, was understandably skittish, so she installed cameras." Nick closes his notebook, grabs his pen, and stands. "I'll send Officer Luklo out to request the camera footage."

He turns, wondering how many steps away he'll get.

Two steps, as it turns out.

"Wait," Feather says. "Just wait."

"Do you want to change your answer?" Nick says.

"Yes," Feather says. "Do you have a cigarette?"

"Quit five years ago," Nick says. "Saved my own life. It's a filthy habit."

"Filthy," Feather agrees. "But sometimes nothing else will do."

"I have to agree with you there," Nick says. He sits back down. "I do sometimes bum one when I've been drinking bourbon."

"You're human, then," Feather says. She tears up. "And I'm human too."

"That's exactly right," Nick says. "You're human and human beings make mistakes and act in all kinds of ways we shouldn't." He pauses and very slowly opens his notebook. "Now, why don't you tell me what happened. You didn't call a taxi, did you?"

"No," Feather says. "No, I didn't. I went into the house and fell asleep."

Nick drops his pen. "Fell *asleep?*"

"More like passed out," Feather says.

"You expect me to believe that?" Nick says.

"It's the truth," Feather says.

Nick stands up. "You were one of the last people to see Merritt Monaco alive. Unless you can come up with a taxi driver who will vouch for picking you up before two forty-five, I have you at the scene at the time of death. You were also the one who brought Ms. Monaco the water, which was the last thing she consumed before she died. Do you know what kind of trouble that puts you in, Ms. Dale?"

"I stayed at the Winburys' house," Feather says, "because I was waiting for someone."

"Waiting for who?" Nick says. He tries to sort through the major players. Mr. Winbury having an affair with Merritt. Shooter Uxley in love with the bride. Who was Featherleigh Dale waiting for in the middle of the night?

Feather's full-on crying now.

Nick can't decide which way to go. Should he raise his voice and play the bully? *No,* he thinks. That only works on TV. In real life, what works is patience and kindness.

Nick grabs the box of tissues they keep in the interview room for just this sort of occasion. He puts it on the table, plucks out a tissue, hands it to Feather, then eases down into his seat.

"Who were you waiting for, Feather?" he asks, as gently as he can. "Who?"

"Thomas," Feather says.

Thomas? Nick thinks. *Who's Thomas?* Then he remembers: Thomas is Benji's brother.

"Thomas Winbury?" Nick says. "Are you involved with Thomas Winbury...romantically?" *Married man,* he thinks. *Tag...way, way too old... They were there to commiserate, not confess.*

"Was," Feather says. "But then he broke things off in

May"—she stops to pluck another tissue out of the box and blow her nose—"when his wife got pregnant. He said he couldn't see me anymore. He told me not to come to the wedding. He said if I came to the wedding, he'd kill me. Those were his exact words."

Nick's thoughts are hopping now. Like father, like son. Thomas was involved with Feather but broke it off when he found out Abby was pregnant. Thomas tells Feather not to come to the wedding. Threatens her. Maybe he thinks she'll tell Abby about the affair.

"Do you think Thomas *meant* it?" Nick says. "People say 'I'm going to kill you' all the time. Too much for my taste. Or do you think...do you think he actually tried to kill you?"

There was nothing in the shot glasses, nothing in the bottle.

The water glass.

"Let's go back," Nick says. "When you went into the kitchen to get water for Merritt, you said everyone was still back at the table, correct?"

Feather pauses. "Yes."

"And there was no one in the kitchen?" he asks. "You're sure you didn't see Greer? I know you're terrified of her but you can tell me the truth."

"No," Feather says. "I did not see Greer."

"And you used the restroom after you poured the water?" Nick says. "How long were you in the bathroom?"

"Couple minutes?" Feather says. "The usual amount of time. But I did try to primp a bit as well."

"So let's say five minutes. Sound fair?"

"Fair."

Plenty of time for Thomas to sneak in and drop a mickey in the water glass—or for Greer to do the same.

But, Nick thinks, *Merritt wasn't poisoned, just sedated.* Which leads Nick back to the father, Tag Winbury. Tag could have doctored the water before he took Merritt out on the kayak. Then, when she "fell overboard," she would have been more likely to drown.

What about the cut on her foot?

Maybe she cut it on a shell on the ocean floor when she fell off the kayak? But there was blood in the sand. If Feather is telling the truth and Merritt was wearing sandals earlier in the night, then she must have cut her foot after she got back from the kayak ride. Could she have cut her foot on the beach before climbing into the kayak? But there was no blood in the kayak.

Unless Tag had washed it off.

But if he was going to do that, why not tie the kayak back up?

Aaarrgh! Nick feels the answer is *right there* . . . he just can't see it.

He smiles at Feather again and says, "I'll be back in two shakes."

Nick steps outside the interview room to call the Chief.

"Talk to Thomas, the brother," he says.

KAREN

A knock at the door wakes Karen up. Karen looks over to Bruce and finds him asleep and snoring aggressively.

Another knock. Then a voice: "Betty? Mac?"

It's Celeste. Karen swings her feet to the floor and carefully stands up. She still feels no pain, which is odd.

She opens the door to see her sad, beautiful daughter standing before her, wearing the pale pink dress with the rope detail that she was supposed to travel in tomorrow. She's holding her yellow paisley duffel bag.

"Oh, my poor, poor Bug," Karen says. She gathers Celeste up in her arms. "I am so sorry, sweetheart. So, so sorry about Merritt."

"It's my fault," Celeste says. "She died because of me."

Karen recognizes this response as an opening for a longer conversation. She glances back at Bruce. He's still sawing logs, as they say; she knows she should wake him up—he will want to see Celeste—but she senses that Celeste needs a confidante, and there are some things that men just don't understand.

Karen grabs her cane, steps out into the hallway, and closes the bedroom door behind her. "Where shall we go?"

Celeste leads her to the end of the hall where there is a glassed-in sunporch that is quiet and unoccupied. Karen negotiates the one step down holding on to Celeste's arm. Celeste leads Karen over to a sofa with bright yellow-orange cushions the color of marigolds.

Karen takes a moment to admire the room. The floor is herringboned brick covered with sea-grass area rugs. The perimeter of the room is lined with lush potted plants—philodendron, ferns, spider plants, a row of five identical topiary trees trimmed to look like globe lamps. From the ceiling hang blown-glass spheres swirling with a rainbow of color. Karen becomes mesmerized for a second by the spheres; they look as delicate as soap bubbles.

Celeste follows her gaze and says, "Apparently these were an obsession of Greer's the year she wrote *A Murder in Murano*. Murano is an island near Venice where they make glass. I had to look it up when Benji told me that."

"Oh," Karen says. The room has enormous windows that look down over the round rose garden. "There is no end to the wonders of this house."

"Well," Celeste says, but nothing follows and Karen can't tell if she's agreeing or disagreeing. She sits next to Karen on the cheerful sofa. "I decided last night that I wasn't going to marry Benji."

"I know," Karen says.

"How?" Celeste whispers. "How did you know?"

"I'm your mother," Karen says. She could tell Celeste about the dream with the strange hotel and how, in that dream, Celeste was lost. She could tell Celeste that she woke up so certain marrying Benji was the wrong thing for Celeste to do that she got out of bed and went looking for her, but she had found Bruce and Tag instead and learned something she could have lived the rest of her days without knowing. She could even tell Celeste about her visit to the psychic, Kathryn Randall, who had predicted that Celeste's love life would enter a state of chaos ... *But there's nothing either one of us can do about it.*

Instead, Karen lets those three words suffice. She is Celeste's mother.

It's suddenly clear that Karen's remaining time on earth matters. There are so many moments of her life that will be overlooked or forgotten: locking her keys in her car outside of Jabberwocky in downtown Easton, having her credit card declined at Wegman's, peeing behind a tree at Hackett's Park when she was pregnant with Celeste, beating her best time in the two-hundred-meter butterfly in the biggest meet of the year against Parkland when she was a senior, nearly choking on a cherry Life Saver during a game of kickball when she was ten years old, sneaking out to the eighth hole of the Northampton Country Club with Bruce during her prom. Those moments had seemed important to Karen at the time but then they vanished, evaporating to join the gray mist of her past.

However, what Karen says to Celeste here and now

will last. Celeste will remember her words for the rest of her life, she is sure of this, and so she has to take care.

"When you met Benji," Karen says, "we were very excited. Your father and I have been so happy together... we wanted you to find someone. We wanted you to have what we have."

Celeste lays her head in Karen's lap, and Karen strokes her hair. "Not everyone is like you," Celeste says. "Not everyone gets that lucky on the first try... or ever."

"Celeste," Karen says. "There are things you don't know..."

"There are things *you* don't know!" Celeste says. "I tried to make myself love Benji. He's a good person. And I understood it was important to you and Mac that I married someone who could take care of me financially—"

"Not just financially," Karen says, although she realizes she and Bruce are probably guilty as charged. "Benji is strong. He comes from a good family—"

"His family," Celeste says, "isn't what it seems."

Karen gazes out the window at the serene expanse of the Nantucket harbor. Maybe Celeste already knows that Tag Winbury's mistress has a baby on the way. It makes either perfect sense or no sense at all that a family as wealthy and esteemed as the Winburys have a second narrative running deep underneath the first, like a dark, murky stream. But who is Karen to judge? Only a few hours ago, she feared *she* had caused Merritt's death.

"So few families are," Karen says. "So few *people* are. We all have flaws we try to hide, darling. Secrets we try to keep. *All* of us, Celeste."

"I made it to the night before the wedding," Celeste says. "Before that, I thought if I acted on my true feelings, something bad would happen. Then I told myself that was silly. My actions don't influence the fate of others. But Merritt died. She *died,* nearly as soon as I made the decision. She was the only real, true friend I've had in my life other than you and Mac, and now she's gone forever. Forever, Mama. And it's my fault. I did this to her."

"No, Celeste—"

"Yes, I did," Celeste says. "One way or the other, I did."

Karen watches the tears stream down her daughter's face. Karen is curious—and more than a little alarmed—that Celeste keeps insisting Merritt's death is her fault. Did Celeste *do* something to her? Did she *not* do something? It can't be a good idea for Celeste to be carrying on about how it's her fault when the house is crawling with police.

"What do you mean by that, darling?" Karen asks. "Do they know what happened?"

"I think she took pills," Celeste says. "I think she did it to herself. She was in a bad relationship, a bad *situation* ... and I was emphatic about her breaking it off for good, but she said she couldn't. I found her crying in the rose garden last night."

"You did?"

"She wanted to know why love was so hard for her, why she couldn't get it right. And I hugged her and kissed her and told her it was going to be fine, she just needed to move on. But you know what I should have done? I should have told her that I couldn't get it right either. That love is hard for everybody." Celeste takes a breath. "I should have told her I didn't love Benji. But I couldn't even say the words in my own mind, much less out loud to another person. She was my best friend and I didn't tell her."

"Oh, honey," Karen says.

"Early this morning I went outside to look at the water one last time because I knew I was leaving this view behind for good. And I saw something floating."

"Celeste," Karen whispers.

"It was Merritt," Celeste says.

Karen closes her eyes. They are both quiet. Outside, birds are singing and Karen can hear the gentle lapping of the waves on the Winburys' beach.

Celeste says, "I'm not going to marry Benji. I'm going to take a trip, by myself maybe. Spend some time alone. Try to process what happened."

"I think that's wise, darling," Karen says. "Let's go tell your father."

Bruce is still asleep in bed, though his noisy breathing has quieted. His hair is standing on end, his mouth hangs open, and even from so far away, Karen can smell his night-after whiskey breath. His left hand, the one with the wedding band, is resting on his chest, over his heart. *Their love is real,* Karen thinks. It's strong but flexible; it's unfussy and unvarnished. It has thrived in the modest house on Derhammer Street, in the front seat of their Toyota Corolla, in the routine of their everyday— breakfast, lunch, dinner, bedtime, repeat, repeat, repeat. It has endured long workweeks, head colds, snowfalls and heat waves, meager pay raises and unexpected bills; it endured the deaths of Karen's parents, Bruce's brother, Bruce's parents, and the smaller losses of Celeste's toads, lizards, and snakes (each of which required a burial). It endured through construction on Route 33, a school-teacher strike when Celeste was in fourth grade, the Philadelphia Eagles losing season after season after season despite Bruce's impassioned ranting at the TV (and finally winning it all this past year when, quite frankly, both Bruce and Karen had stopped caring about football); it endured the sad day the Easley family moved away and took their dogs Black Bean and Red Bean, who at the time were Celeste's best friends, with them. It survived the Pampered Chef parties thrown by women who all secretly thought they were better than Karen, it survived Bruce's bizarre friendship with Robin Swain, and it will survive this tragic weekend.

We would go to the post office to mail packages or check our box, and the line was always extra-long on Saturdays, but you know what? I didn't care. I could wait an hour. I could wait all day … because I was with Karen.

While Celeste gently jostles Bruce's shoulder to wake him up, Karen slips into the bathroom and locks the door behind her. She opens the third drawer, finds the bottle of pills, picks out the three pearlescent ovoids, and flushes them down the toilet.

Karen's pain is gone. She feels stronger than she has in weeks, months even. It makes no sense, and yet it does.

Karen can't go anywhere just yet. She needs to see what will happen next.

GREER

She catches the Chief on his way out of Tag's study.

"There's something I think you should know," she says.

The Chief barely seems to hear her. He's looking at his phone. "If you'll excuse me," he says. He reads his screen, then says, "Your son Thomas is … where? I'll need to talk to him next."

Greer can't believe he's brushing her off. She deliber-ated about her best course of action: Tell him about the pills or not? Yes, she decided, for a couple of reasons. She will tell him about the pills and they will finally be able to put all this to rest.

"I haven't seen Thomas," Greer says. "But Chief Kapenash, sir, there's something I must tell you."

The Chief finally seems to notice her. They are standing in the hallway; God only knows who's listening. Tag is in his study. He might have his ear pressed up against the door. Greer wonders if she should have discussed her decision with him first. He has always been good at seeing a problem from every possible angle and ensuring that a strategy won't backfire. Many times, when Greer needed help with the plot in one of her mysteries, she would consult Tag and he would nearly always come up with a creative answer. Those were some of Greer's favorite moments in her entire marriage—lying in bed with Tag, her head resting in the crook of his arm as she explained her characters and their motivations while Tag asked provocative questions. He praised her imagination; she gushed over his insightful solutions. Character development required a humanist like Greer, but plotting often benefited from the mind of a mathematician. Greer had felt, in those instances, like part of a team.

Oh, how she hates him! For an instant, she wishes she'd married someone mediocre, uninspiring. *Wealthy* and uninspiring—her third cousin Reggie, for example; posh accent and not an original bone in his body.

"Shall we go into the living room?" Greer asks the Chief. She turns on her heel, not waiting for an answer.

The Chief follows her into the living room and Greer closes the door behind him. She doesn't bother with sitting. If she sits, she thinks, she might lose her nerve.

"I forgot to tell the detective something," she says.

The Chief's expression hardens into all business. He's

not a bad-looking man, Greer thinks. He has a gruffness that she finds sort of appealing, nearly sexy. And he's age appropriate. This is what Tag has done; now Greer has to appraise candidates for future romantic interludes. Would the Chief be interested in her?

Never, she decides.

The Greek, maybe, Nick, if he were in the mood for an older woman. Greer flushes, then she notices the Chief looking at her expectantly.

"I didn't forget, exactly," Greer says. She wants to clarify this. "It's something I only just remembered."

The Chief nods almost imperceptibly.

"I went to bed whenever, midnight or so, but I couldn't sleep. I was wound up."

"Wound up," the Chief says.

"Excited about the wedding. I wanted everything to go well," Greer says. "So, as I told the detective, I got up and went to the kitchen to pour a glass of champagne."

"Yes," the Chief says.

"Well, what I forgot to tell the detective—meaning what I didn't remember at *all* until just a little while ago—is that I brought my sleeping pills to the kitchen. My intention was to take a pill with water before I drank my champagne."

"What kind of pills were they?" the Chief asks.

"I'd have to call my physician in New York to be sure," Greer says. "They're quite potent, put me to sleep instantly and knock me out for eight hours straight. Which was why, in the end, I decided *not* to take a pill. I needed to be up early this morning. So I hoped the champagne would do the trick by itself, and that was, in fact, what happened. But when I looked for the pills a few moments ago in my medicine cabinet, where I keep them, they weren't there. And that's when I recalled bringing them to the kitchen. I checked the counter next to the refrigerator plus every shelf, every drawer, every possible hiding place. I asked my housekeeper, Elida. She hasn't seen them."

"Were they in a prescription bottle?" the Chief asks. "Were they marked?"

"No," Greer says. "I have a pillbox. It's an enamel box with a painting of Queen Elizabeth on the top."

"So who would have known that the pills inside were sleeping pills?" the Chief asks.

"The sleeping pills and the pillbox were something of a family joke," Greer says. "My husband obviously knew. And the children."

"Would Ms. Monaco have known they were sleeping pills?" the Chief says.

Greer knows she can't hesitate here, even for a second. "Oh, yes," Greer says. "I offered Merritt a sleeping pill from the box the last time she stayed with us, in May." This answer wouldn't pass a polygraph, she knows. The truth is that Greer had offered Merritt aspirin for the headache she had after the wine dinner but never a sleeping pill. "So I think we can conclude what happened."

"And what's that?" the Chief says.

"Merritt took a sleeping pill," Greer says.

The Chief says nothing. It's infuriating; the man is impossible to read, even for Greer, who can normally see people's agendas and prevailing emotions as though she were looking into a clear stream.

"She helped herself to my pills," Greer says. "Then she went for a swim, maybe thinking she would cool down before slipping into bed. And the pill knocked her out. It was an accident."

The Chief pulls out his pad and pencil. "Describe the pillbox again, please, Ms. Garrison."

He's bought it, she thinks, and relief blows through her like a cool breeze. "It's round, about four centimeters in diameter, cherry red with a portrait of the queen on the top," she says. "The top is hinged. It flips open."

"And how many pills inside?" the Chief asks.

"I couldn't say exactly," Greer says. "Somewhere between fifteen and twenty-five."

"The last time you remember seeing the pillbox, it was in the kitchen," the Chief says. "There's no chance you brought it back to your bedroom?"

"No chance," Greer says. Her nerves return, multiplied, quivering.

"So you know there's no chance you brought the pills back to your bedroom," the Chief says, "and yet you didn't remember bringing the pills into the kitchen when you talked to the detective. I guess I'm questioning how you can be so certain."

"I keep the pills in only one place," Greer says. "And they weren't there. If I had brought the pills back to my room, they would have been where I always keep them."

"No guarantees of that," the Chief says. He clears his throat. "There are a couple of reasons why I don't think Merritt took a pill of her own volition."

Of her own volition, Greer thinks. Oh, dear God. They'll suspect Tag of drugging the girl, of course. Or they'll suspect Greer herself.

"But wait..." Greer says.

The Chief turns away. "Thank you for the information," he says. "Now I'm going to find your son Thomas."

Tuesday, July 3–Friday, July 6, 2018

CELESTE

Tuesday at work, she makes a list of things that might take the place of love.

Security, financial
Security, emotional
Apartment

After the honeymoon, Celeste is moving into Benji's apartment in Tribeca. Together they surveyed Celeste's studio to see what would make the trip downtown. Not her futon, not her yard-sale furniture, none of her dishes or pots and pans, not her shower curtain or bathroom rug, not the pair of mason-jar lamps filled with beans. When Celeste said that she wanted to bring the rainbow candles her mother made, Benji said, "Just bring the candle Abby gave you if you want a candle." The candle he was referring to was a Jo Malone pine-and-eucalyptus luxury candle that Abby gave Celeste as an engagement present. Celeste does love the way it smells but once she found out how much it cost, she knew she could never, ever light it.

Celeste immediately decided she would bring her mother's candles despite Benji's obvious opinion that they weren't as good as a department-store candle. Celeste would set them on the mantel!

Benji told Celeste that he contacted a real estate agent

at Sotheby's who is searching for a brownstone on East Seventy-Eighth Street, specifically on the block between Park and Lexington. Celeste tries to imagine herself living on that block, owning a home on that block. Would that be as good as love?

Shooter has the condo in Hell's Kitchen. The condo has nothing in it but a mattress and a TV, Benji has told her. Shooter is never there.

Family

Tag, Greer, Thomas, Abby, Abby's future baby, assorted aunts, uncles, and cousins in England.

Shooter has even less family than Celeste. Shooter has no one.

Nantucket

This is, perhaps, the strongest competition for love. Because Celeste has never felt about a place the way she feels about Nantucket. She tries to ignore that her most romantic storybook times there have been with Shooter. She could easily go to the Chicken Box with Benji; she could take Benji out to Smith's Point and show him the natural water slide. On Nantucket, she will always have a beach to walk on, a path to run, a farm to provide heirloom tomatoes and corn on the cob, a boat to putter around the harbor in, cobblestoned streets to stroll in the evenings. Celeste yearns to experience Nantucket at every time of year. She wants to go to the Daffodil Festival in the spring, wear a yellow sweater, make a picnic of cold roast chicken and deviled eggs and asparagus salad, and cheer as the antique-car parade passes by. She wants to go in the fall when the leaves change and the cranberries are harvested and the high-school football team is playing at home. She wants to go at Thanksgiving, swim in the Turkey Plunge, watch the tree-lighting on Friday night, eat scallops just harvested from the sound. She wants to go in the dead of winter during a blizzard when Main Street is blanketed with snow and not a soul is stirring.

Shooter won't be able to give her Nantucket the way that Benji can.

Celeste can't come up with anything else, so she rolls back up to *Security, financial.* Celeste will have health insurance. Celeste will be able to shop for groceries at Zabar's, Fairway, Dean and DeLuca. She will be able to buy expensive salads, bouquets of fresh flowers—every day if she wants! Orchids if she wants!—boxes of macarons, bottles of Veuve Clicquot, *cases* of Veuve Clicquot! She will be able to buy hardcover books the day they come out and get orchestra seats for the theater. They'll be able to take trips—to London, certainly, but also to Paris, Rome, Shanghai, Sydney. They'll be able to go on safari in Africa, maybe even hike to see the silverback gorillas in Uganda, a dream so far-fetched that Celeste has put it in the same category as space travel. She will shop with Merritt at Opening Ceremony, at Topshop, at Intermix. She'll try things on without checking the price tag. It's inconceivable. It doesn't seem real.

How will it work? Celeste asked Benji. *M-M-Money, I m-m-mean. Once we're m-m-married?*

I'll put your name on my accounts, Benji said. *We'll get you an ATM card, a checkbook. Once I turn thirty-five, I'll have access to the trust from my Garrison grandparents, so there will be that money as well.*

Celeste has wondered since then how much money is in the Garrison trust. A million dollars? Five million? Twenty million? What is the amount that takes the place of love?

What about m-my salary? Celeste had asked.

Keep it for yourself, Benji said.

Celeste earns sixty-two thousand dollars a year, but Benji makes that sound like a quarter she found on the sidewalk. She supposes that, to him, it is.

Celeste's assistant, Bethany, walks into her office without knocking and Celeste scrambles to hide the list. What would Bethany think if she saw it? What kind of woman has to make a list of reasons she's happy to be marrying Benjamin Winbury?

"Celeste?" Bethany says. Her expression is uneasy, as though she suspects she interrupted something.

"Mmm?" Celeste says.

"Zed wants to see you in the conference room," Bethany says.

"Conference room?" Celeste says. She was supposed to meet with Zed in his office because tomorrow starts a two-and-a-half-week vacation that includes her wedding and honeymoon and she needs to delegate the work on her desk.

Bethany shrugs. "That's what he said."

The door to the conference room is closed and when Celeste swings the door open she sees a dozen golden balloons and, in the center of the table, a round bakery cake ringed with icing flowers and the words *Congrats, Celeste!* A cheer goes up and Celeste looks around at her zoo colleagues: Donner, Karsang, Darius, Mawabe, Vern, even Blair from reptiles.

Celeste tears up. A shower! Her co-workers have thrown her a bridal shower, complete with balloons, cake, a few bags of chips, and a wrapped present. Celeste can't believe it. This isn't *that* kind of office and these aren't *those* kind of co-workers. They obviously know Celeste is getting married, and she knows that Blair feels her long-ago migraine was responsible for Celeste and Benji meeting in the first place. Three of Celeste's co-workers are actually making the trip to Nantucket—Bethany, Mawabe, and Vern—but because it's the Fourth of July week, all of the reasonably priced hotels were sold out, so the three of them are arriving Saturday at noon and leaving on the nine-thirty fast boat. Celeste is touched that the three of them are making the trip—to drive from the city and take the boat requires more effort than she thought they'd make—but Celeste is also a bit nervous about their arrival. Benji exacerbated Celeste's concern when he said, "I can't imagine Mawabe and Vern in the same room as my mother."

Although Benji's sentiment echoed Celeste's own feelings, she took umbrage. "Why not?" she said. "It would be g-g-good for your mother to realize people like Mawabe exist. I'm just sorry B-B-Blair isn't coming." She paused. "B-B-Bethany is normal. Sort of."

"Sort of," Benji conceded.

Now, Bethany comes forward holding out the gift. Celeste assumes Bethany selected the gift and everyone else chipped in, but some people—like Darius—probably have yet to pay their share.

"What c-c-could it be?" Celeste asks. She unwraps the box and lifts off the top to find a simple white apron with *Mrs. Winbury* embroidered in black on the front.

Mrs. Winbury. Celeste's heart sinks.

"I love it," she says.

Her stutter is so debilitating and so unpredictable that she and Benji have had to tailor their wedding vows with Reverend Derby so that all Celeste has to say is "I do."

But even those two words present a challenge.

It's Wednesday, the Fourth of July. Benji and Shooter, Thomas and Abby, and Tag and Greer are already up on Nantucket. But Celeste had to work through Tuesday, and Merritt has a can't-miss fireworks party tonight. Celeste's parents aren't due to arrive until Friday. Celeste decides she will fly to Boston with Merritt on Thursday morning and then Uber to the Cape and take the fast ferry across to Nantucket.

Celeste calls Merritt at three o'clock on Wednesday afternoon. "I c-c-can't do it," she says.

"What?" Merritt says. "What do you mean?"

What *does* she mean? She means she can't marry Benji. She knows she's making a mistake. She's in love with Shooter. It's a physical condition, an affliction. It is, as Merritt said, in her blood. Celeste feels like she's standing on a cliff. If Shooter were here right now by her side, willing to hold her hand and never let go, she would jump.

But he's not. He's on Nantucket, executing the best-man duties with his usual flair.

"I c-c-can't say my vows," Celeste says. "I st-st-st…" She can't force it out. *Stutter* is, ironically, the hardest word.

"I'll be right there," Merritt says.

Merritt stands before Celeste and says, "Do you, Celeste Marie Otis, take Benjamin Garrison Winbury to be your lawfully wedded husband? To have and to hold, to bug and to pester, to scream at and screw, until death do you part?"

Celeste smiles.

"Say it," Merritt says.

"I d-d-do," Celeste says. She winces.

"Pretend it's a different word," Merritt says. "Pretend it's *dew* like on a leaf in the morning or *due* like your rent. I think you're just psyching yourself out."

Dew, like on a leaf in the morning, Celeste thinks.

"I dew," she says.

The corners of Merritt's mouth lift.

"Again," she says.

"I d-d-do," Celeste says. "I mean, I dew."

"Just like that," Merritt says. She glances at her phone. "I have to go. We'll practice more tomorrow. And Friday."

"Okay," Celeste says. "Merritt—"

Merritt holds up a hand. "You don't have to thank me," she says. "You're my best friend. I'm your maid of honor."

"No," Celeste says. "I mean, yes, thank you. B-B-But what I want to know is, d-d-did you end things with Tag?"

"No," Merritt says. "He ended things with me."

Once Celeste is on Nantucket, she becomes a marionette operated by Greer and Roger Pelton, the wedding planner. Roger is like a kind and supremely capable uncle. He goes over the three-day schedule with Celeste— where she needs to be, what she needs to do, what she will be wearing; the outfits are lined up in the closet. Thursday afternoon, Greer has scheduled Celeste for a massage, a mani-pedi, and an eyelash extension.

"Eyelash extension?" Celeste says. "Is that n-n-necessary?"

"No," Roger says. "I'll call R. J. Miller and cancel that part of the appointment."

"Thank you," Celeste says.

"The most important part of my job," Roger says, "is protecting my brides from their mothers and mothers-in-law."

Celeste loves how Roger refers to her as "my bride." She pretends she's marrying Roger, and this lightens her mood. Temporarily.

Celeste keeps one eye trained on Shooter at all times, like she's a spy or a sniper. Their gazes meet and lock, and

Celeste dissolves inside. He's trying to tell her something without speaking—but what? Celeste craves the looks, even though they're ruining her. When Shooter isn't looking at her, when he's joking with Merritt or Abby or Greer, she feels sickeningly jealous.

Celeste's parents arrive. Celeste worries that, like Benji, the Winburys will think Karen and Bruce are "the salt of the earth" and will patronize them, possibly without their even realizing it.

But Greer is fine with Celeste's parents, and Tag is better than fine. Celeste wants to hold a grudge against Tag, but he is so gracious and charming with her parents that she can feel only gratitude toward him. She'll confront her anger and disappointment later, after the wedding.

The rehearsal dinner unfolds exactly as it should. Other people are drinking the blackberry mojito punch. Celeste has one sip of Benji's and decides to stick to white wine. She doesn't have time to keep track of Shooter; she's too busy meeting this person and that person: a friend of Tag and Greer's from London named Featherleigh, a business associate of Tag's named Peter Walls, neighbors from London, neighbors from New York, Benji's lacrosse coach from St. George's, and the four Alexanders—blond and preppy Alexander, Asian Alexander, Jewish Alexander, who is engaged to a black woman named Mimi who is a Broadway dancer, and the Alexander known as Zander, who is married to a man named Kermit.

Celeste feared her parents would be shy and overwhelmed but they are holding their own and Betty looks better than Celeste anticipated. She walks with a cane and Celeste knows she's on a mighty dose of painkillers, but she appears happy, nearly radiant. She is far happier about this wedding than Celeste is.

Celeste makes a deal with God: *I will go through with this if You just please keep my mother alive.*

There are passed hors d'oeuvres, each one more creative and delicious-looking than the next, although Celeste is far too anxious to eat. She sips her wine but it has little effect. Her body is numb. The only thing that matters is Shooter. Where is Shooter? She can't find him. Then he will appear, brushing past her elbow; even the slightest touch lights her up. She has thought back on the kissing in her apartment only a few thousand times since it happened. How did she have the willpower to refuse him? She is in awe of herself.

Her father stands to give a toast. It's about Betty first, and Celeste's eyes well with tears. Then it's about Celeste and Bruce says, *And so to you, Benjamin Winbury, I say from the heart: Take care of our little girl. She is our treasure, our hope, our light, and our warmth. She is our legacy. Here's to the two of you and your life together.* And everyone clinks glasses and drinks.

Thomas stands to speak next, and Celeste leans over to Benji and says, "I thought Shooter was giving the toast."

"He didn't want to," Benji says.

"What?" Celeste says.

"He told me he didn't want to speak tonight," Benji says. "He'll give a toast tomorrow, after we're married."

Tomorrow, Celeste thinks. *After we're married.*

Celeste doesn't want to go out; she has done enough pretending for one night. She wants to go to bed. Honestly, she would like to sleep as she did when she was a child: right between Mac and Betty.

Her mother senses something is wrong. Celeste can tell by the emphatic way Betty insists that Celeste go out to be with her friends, be with Benji.

I'll be with Benji the rest of my life! Celeste thinks. Her time with her mother is dwindling; the sand is running through the hourglass more quickly now, at the end. But Celeste knows her mother will be happier if she goes out.

Besides, Shooter is going. And Merritt—Celeste needs to keep an eye on Merritt. However, when they are all piling into cars, Merritt is missing.

"Wait a minute," Celeste says. She climbs out of the Winburys' Land Rover and runs across the driveway to the second cottage. She pokes her head in but the lights are off; Merritt isn't there.

"Celeste," Benji says. "Come on!"

"I have to find Merritt," she says. She tries to remember the last time she saw Merritt. It was during the dinner, obviously, but Celeste had to meet and mingle with so many people that she didn't get to spend any time with her one true friend. And Merritt didn't give a toast, even though she'd intimated that she might. *Please,* Celeste thinks, *don't let her be with Tag.* But that has to be it. Where else could she be? She is always the one leading the charge when it comes to continuing the fun.

Celeste tears through the house checking each room— the kitchen, the formal dining room, the casual dining room, the powder room, even the glowing cube that is the wine cellar. She goes down the hall and checks the alcove outside Greer and Tag's room but she doesn't have the courage to knock on their bedroom door or on the door to Tag's study. She scurries down to poke her head into the white living room, even though she has never once set foot in there. She sees a figure in one of the chairs and she's so startled, she cries out.

"It's just me," someone with a British accent says. It's that Featherleigh woman. "Are you looking for someone?"

"My friend Merritt?" Celeste says. "Maid of honor? Black dress?"

"If you bring me a bottle of whiskey, I'll tell you where she is."

"Excuse me?" Celeste says. She has been told that Featherleigh is an old friend of the family but Celeste can't imagine Greer abiding this kind of rudeness. "Have you seen Merritt? I'm sorry, I need to find her."

"I'm the one who's sorry, love," Featherleigh says. "I noticed her earlier, quite an attractive girl, but I haven't seen her in hours."

"Okay, thank you," Celeste says, hoping she doesn't now seem rude by rushing out. What is Featherleigh doing in the living room, anyway? Certainly Greer didn't offer to let her *sleep* there?

Celeste sails through the laundry room and out the side door, hurrying toward the pool house. She hears coughing and can just barely make out the shadow of a figure bent over in the rose garden. It's Merritt.

"Merritt!" Celeste says. She crosses the arched footbridge over the koi pond into the rose garden. Merritt is spitting into the grass. "Are you *sick?*"

Merritt straightens up and wipes her mouth. There are tears running down her face. "The oysters aren't agreeing with me."

Celeste reaches out to embrace her friend. "You poor thing," she says. "Let me walk you back to your cottage. I'm going to tell the rest of them to go to town without me. I didn't want to go anyway."

"No," Merritt says. "No, you go, please, or I'll feel guilty. I just need some air." She tries to smile at Celeste but then she starts crying again. "Only I could mess up a gorgeous night like this."

"Stop it," Celeste says. "Weddings are stressful."

"Especially this one," Merritt says. She holds out her left hand. "You see this ring?" Merritt points to a silver band on her thumb. "He gave me this for my birthday."

"Tag did?" Celeste whispers. She takes hold of Merritt's hand and studies the ring. It's set with tiny multicolored stones. It's very pretty, but Merritt has a lot of cool jewelry, some of it given to her for free by various fashion labels.

"It's a *ring*," Merritt says. "He could have given me anything for my birthday—a book, a scarf, a bracelet. But he gave me a *ring*."

"Yes, well." Celeste is pretty sure Tag meant the ring to be a token of his fondness, nothing more, but he might have chosen something a little less emotionally charged. Just then, Celeste hears the Land Rover's horn and she knows Benji is losing patience; she has been gone much longer than she intended. "I love you. You know that, right? And when you leave here Sunday, you never have to see Tag Winbury again. I promise I won't make you attend any family functions."

"I wish it were that easy," Merritt says. She takes an exaggerated breath. "There's something I have to tell you."

The car horn sounds again. Celeste feels annoyed at Benji's impatience, but she knows he has a caravan of people waiting on her. "I have to scoot," she says. "Come with us."

"I can't," Merritt says. "I don't feel well. I'm just going to hang around here, maybe go to bed."

"Before midnight?" Celeste says. "That would be a first." She gives Merritt another hug. "Tomorrow we'll find time to talk, I promise. I don't care if a church full of people have to wait."

Merritt gives a small laugh. "Okay."

They are a party of twelve, and town is crowded with holiday revelers. There's a line to get into the Boarding House; the Pearl is at maximum capacity, as is Nautilus. The Club Car piano bar is an option, but Thomas announces that one *ends* at the Club Car; one never starts there. Asian Alexander's wife is wearing stilettos and doesn't want to risk walking down to Straight Wharf or Cru.

Celeste looks to Benji, waiting for him to make an executive decision. As it is, they are spilling off the corner of India and Federal into the street.

"Let's go to the back bar at Ventuno," he says.

Everyone agrees. It's nearby, it's open-air; they'll go for one drink, then reassess.

Somehow Celeste gets sifted to the back of the group, probably because she's literally dragging her feet. She doesn't see the point of yet another drink. If anything, she needs food. She was so busy worrying about Mac and Betty and getting them set with their lobsters that she hadn't eaten anything.

"I'm starving," she says to herself.

"You and me both."

Celeste turns to see Shooter at her right shoulder.

She looks for Benji. He's up front, talking to Mimi the Broadway dancer.

"He's occupied," Shooter says. "Let's go get pizza." He grabs her hand.

"I can't," Celeste says. She's afraid to look at him, so she stares down at her feet in her jeweled sandals. Her toes are painted a color called Sunshine State of Mind to match her dress tonight. She does leave her hand in his, however, for a few forbidden seconds.

"We'll come right back," Shooter says. He whistles sharply, and Benji spins around. "I'm taking your bride to get a slice. Back in ten."

Benji waves, then turns again to Mimi—and Kermit, who has joined their conversation.

He couldn't care less.

"Okay," Celeste says. "Let's go."

There's a line outside Steamboat Pizza and a steady stream of cars unloading from the late ferry. Celeste feels weirdly exposed and she distances herself half a step from Shooter. She has dreamed of being alone with him but now that it's happening, she's tongue-tied. Across the street she sees a woman with long jet-black hair wearing suede booties with shorts—suede booties in July; even Celeste recognizes that as a no-no—and the woman looks like she's pointing her phone at Celeste and Shooter. Taking a picture? Celeste turns her back. She wants to make a joke about the care and feeding of the bride but she can't manage small talk and, apparently, neither can Shooter.

"Follow me," he says.

He gets out of line, which is fine—Celeste wouldn't have been able to eat anything in front of him anyway—and starts walking down the street toward the ferry dock. Celeste follows, bobbing and weaving, skirting groups of teenagers, dodging couples with strollers, stopping short so an elderly couple can pass.

She doesn't ask Shooter where they're going. She doesn't care. She would follow him anywhere.

They cross the Steamship Authority parking lot, Shooter striding ahead, and then he cuts to the right of the terminal building and turns to check that she's behind him. He waits for her, places a hand on her back, and ushers her to a bench at the edge of the dock. The view is over the working part of the harbor. It's not glamorous, but it's still pretty. Everything on Nantucket is pretty.

They sit side by side, their thighs touching, and then Shooter wraps his arm around Celeste's shoulders. She suddenly feels the effect of the wine she drank earlier. She acts impulsively; she doesn't care who sees. She buries her face in Shooter's chest and inhales the scent of him. He is *all she wants*.

"Run away with me," he says.

She takes a breath to say, *Yeah, right*—but he stops her.

"I'm serious, Celeste. I'm in love with you. I know it's wrong, I know it's unfair, I know all of our friends will hate us, especially my own best friend—hell, my brother, because Benji is by every standard my brother. I don't care. I do care, but I care about you more. I have never felt this way about anyone before. My feelings for you are tragic; they're Shakespearean—I'm not sure which play, some combination of *Hamlet* and *Romeo and Juliet,* I think. I want you to sneak out of the house and meet me here, right here, at six fifteen tomorrow morning. I'll have two tickets on the six-thirty ferry. The boat gets to Hyannis at eight thirty, which is also our scheduled reveille tomorrow, so by the time people realize we're both gone, we'll be safely on the mainland."

Celeste nods against his chest. She's not agreeing, but she wants to hear more; she wants to imagine this escape. The anxiety that has been squeezing her heart loosens its grip. She gets a clear breath.

"You can say no. I expect you to say no. And if you do say no, I'll show up at the altar tomorrow right next to Benji like I promised. I will give a sweet, meaningful toast with the appropriate amount of humor and at least one line about how Benji doesn't deserve you. I will ask for one dance with you and when that dance is over, I'll give you a peck on the cheek and let you get on with the rest of your life. With him."

Celeste exhales.

"If you come with me, I will buy four tickets to Las Vegas—one for me, one for you, two for your parents. And I will marry you by the end of the day tomorrow. Or we can move more slowly. But I need you to know that I am serious. I'm in love with you. If you don't feel the same way, I will still go to my grave feeling grateful for every second I have had with you. If nothing else, you proved that the heart of Michael Oscar Uxley is not made of stone."

Michael Oscar Uxley, she thinks. She realizes with shock that she has never asked his real name.

"Yes," she says.

"What?"

She raises her face. She looks into Shooter's blue eyes...but what she sees is her parents in profile from the backseat of their old Toyota. They are turned toward each other, singing along to "Paradise by the Dashboard Light." *Do you love me, will you love me forever?* Celeste is eleven years old, she knows all the words too, but she doesn't dare sing because the two of them sound so... *good* together.

Then she flashes back to before they were Mac and Betty to her, before they were even Mommy and Daddy, back to when they were just ideas: love, security, warmth.

Celeste is young, only one or two years old. They are playing a game called Flying Baby. Bruce has Celeste by one hand and Karen has her by the other. They swing Celeste between them until Bruce calls out, "Flying," and Karen calls out, "Baby!" And they lift Celeste up off the ground. For one delicious moment, she is suspended in midair, weightless.

Finally, she thinks of her parents as teenagers—her mother in her red tank suit, her father in his sweatpants and hoodie staring at the orange. The moment their eyes meet, the moment their hands touch. That certainty. That recognition. *You. You are the one.*

This is what it feels like.

Nothing, as it turns out, can take the place of love.

"Yes," she says.

Saturday, July 7, 2018,
5:45 p.m.

THE CHIEF

He finds Thomas in the kitchen, scarfing down a turkey sandwich. Next to the sandwich plate is a highball glass of scotch, three-quarters full.

"Mr. Winbury?" the Chief says.

"Thomas," he says, wiping his hands hastily on a napkin and then extending one to the Chief. "Mr. Winbury is my father."

"I have a few questions," the Chief says.

"You've talked to just about everyone else," Thomas says. "I don't know that I'd have much to add."

"Please," the Chief says. He's too low on patience to deal with the runaround. "Follow me." He heads down the hall and around the corner to the living room. Thomas has abandoned the sandwich but brought the scotch, and the Chief can't blame him. Thomas takes a seat on the sofa, crosses his ankle over his knee, and sinks back into the cushions like a man without a care in the world, and the Chief closes the door.

"Events of last night?" the Chief asks. "After the party?"

"Back bar at Ventuno, Boarding House. I left after one drink. My wife called to say she wanted me home. Pronto."

"What did you do at home?"

"Went up to see Abby. She was asleep so I went down-stairs for a drink."

"Did anyone join you?"

"My father."

"Anyone else?"

"No."

"Are you sure about that?"

Thomas's eyebrows shoot up, but it's acting. He's a man pretending to remember something. The Chief is surprised he doesn't snap his fingers.

"Oh! After a while, Merritt joined us, as well as a friend of my parents' named Featherleigh Dale. She's an antiques dealer from London, here for the wedding."

"Why was Featherleigh Dale at the house so late?" the Chief asks. "Is she staying here?"

"No. I'm not sure why she was still around."

"You're not?"

"I'm not."

The Chief lets the lie sit there for a moment, stinking.

"The four of you sat under the tent drinking rum, is that right?"

"Yes, sir."

"Who was the first to leave the tent? Was it you?"

"It was. My wife called down. I had pushed my luck by then already, so I went up to bed."

"Do you have any idea what time that was?"

"Around two, I think."

"I need you to focus here. Do you remember Feather-leigh Dale going into the kitchen for water? A glass of water for Ms. Monaco?"

Thomas shakes his head, but then says, "Yes."

"When Featherleigh went in to get the water, do you recall how long she was gone?"

"Five minutes. Maybe a bit longer."

"Did you have any of the water?"

"No, sir."

"Do you remember anyone else having any of the water? Even a sip?"

"I was there to drink rum, sir," Thomas says. "I don't remember much about the water."

Somewhere in the house, the clock strikes six. The Chief is dying to get home, take off his shoes, crack open a beer, hug his wife, talk to Chloe. This day has lasted five years, but that's the way it is with murder cases. He's sure that, back at the station, his voice mail is filled with messages from insistent reporters. When this is all over, he's going to need another stress-management class.

"Let me switch gears. Does your mother have a pillbox?"

"Excuse me?"

"Does your mother have a box where she keeps her..."

"Her sleeping pills?" Thomas says. "Yes. It's round. It has a picture of Queen Elizabeth on it."

"Would you say this pillbox is well known to members of your family?"

Thomas laughs. "Oh, yes. My mother's pillbox is infamous. It was a gift from her grandmother."

"And would you say that everyone in your family is aware that it holds *sleeping* pills?"

"Yes. And she won't share them. I asked for one once and she told me I couldn't handle it."

"Really," the Chief says. Greer claimed she offered Merritt one of the sleeping pills. So they were "too strong" for her son but she gave one to a houseguest? Does that seem likely?

No, it does not.

"Did you see the pillbox in the kitchen last night?"

"No," Thomas says. "Why? Was it left out?" He sits up straighter. "Do you think Merritt took one of my mother's sleeping pills?"

"You didn't see the pillbox?" the Chief asks. "You didn't *touch* the pills?"

Thomas slaps his knee. "I most certainly did not. But *Merritt* must have seen my mother's pills and taken one—or even two—not realizing how potent they are. And then she went for a swim." He stands up. "I think everyone will be fine with this being called an accidental death. There's no reason to manufacture any more drama. This little inquisition has produced enough anxiety as it is—"

"We're not finished here," the Chief says. He waits while Thomas reluctantly sits back down. "Do you know anything about a cut on Merritt's foot?"

"A cut?" Thomas says. "No. But if she did cut her foot, maybe she went into the water to rinse it."

This isn't something the Chief has considered. She did have quite a nasty gash on her foot. It's possible she rinsed it off in the water to avoid tracking blood into the Winbury house. The only place they'd seen blood was in the sand.

"Also, Merritt had been drinking," Thomas says.

The Chief doesn't respond to this. It's interesting that Thomas is so eager to offer up theories about what happened. The Chief has been at this long enough to know that that is how a guilty person acts.

"What is your relationship with Ms. Dale?" the Chief asks.

"My...I already told you, she's a friend of my parents."

"And that's it? You don't have a personal relationship with her?"

"Not really," Thomas says. "No."

"My colleague with the Massachusetts State Police

interviewed Ms. Dale," the Chief says. "She told him that she had been romantically involved with you but that you broke things off in May when your wife got pregnant. Is that true?"

"No!" Thomas says.

"One of you is lying," the Chief says.

"Featherleigh is lying. She's a pathological liar, in fact. She's being investigated for fraud in her antiques business. Did she tell your colleague *that*? She tried to pass off a fake George the Third gilt-wood table to what she thought was a naive client. So, clearly, she lies as a general practice."

"That seems like pretty specialized knowledge to have about your parents' friend," the Chief says.

"My mother told me about it."

"Your mother? So if I ask Greer right now if she told you about Featherleigh's fraud charges and what exactly they were, she'll say yes."

Thomas nods. His expression is confident except for three tense lines high on his forehead.

The Chief stands up. "All right. I'll go talk to your mother."

"Wait," Thomas says. He collapses against the back of the sofa. "We did have a brief fling. Me and...Ms. Dale. Featherleigh."

"How brief?" the Chief asks.

Thomas throws up his hands. "Not brief, exactly. But sporadic." He pauses. "Several years."

The Chief sits back down. "So you've been romantically involved with Ms. Dale for several years?"

"On and off," Thomas says. "And like she told you, I ended things in May."

"Did it upset you that Ms. Dale chose to attend the wedding?"

"Of course it upset me," Thomas says. "I want her out

of my life. My wife is pregnant, I need to focus on her and on getting my career back on track. This thing with Featherleigh, well, it ran amok. She was blackmailing me."

"Blackmailing you?" the Chief says.

Thomas picks up his scotch and throws half of it back. The Chief feels a mixture of triumph and shame. He has gotten people to break down and talk before and it always feels satisfying on the one hand—like cracking a safe, almost—and vaguely obscene on the other. This guy has been hiding something for *years* and now he's coming clean. So many crimes, and especially murders, are committed by people with dark motivations like Thomas. Thomas likely had no intention of killing anyone; he just wanted to keep the secret of his love affair safe.

"I hooked up with her initially after her older brother, Hamish, died. Hamish was a school friend of my father's. I went to the funeral with my parents—this was before I met Abby—and at the reception afterward, Featherleigh and I got drunk and things happened. After that, I saw her whenever I was in London or she was in New York. Then I met Abby. I told Featherleigh I couldn't see her anymore and she went off the deep end."

"How so?"

"Abby came with my family to Virgin Gorda over the Christmas holiday the first year we were together. Featherleigh must have found out because she showed up on Virgin Gorda with a client of hers from Abu Dhabi who had a gigantic yacht. And then another time, right after I finished law school, Featherleigh made a surprise appearance at my classmate's graduation party. She walked right into Bemelmans Bar at the Carlyle Hotel in New York and told everyone *I'd* invited her there."

"Why didn't you just correct the misperception then?"

"Because...well...there *had* been times that I'd seen Featherleigh since I'd been with Abby. And that's where I messed up. I didn't make a clean break. I didn't keep Featherleigh firmly in my past. The first time I wasn't sure if things were going to work out with Abby and me, so when Feather called and told me she had a suite at the Gramercy Park Hotel, I went. Then, after Abby had her second miscarriage—which was a really bad one—she was weepy and depressed, really difficult to be around. She felt like a failure. I felt like a failure. We started to fight. There wasn't a conversation we could have that didn't lead right back to the pregnancies. Sex was out of the question. It was a tough time. And Featherleigh capitalized on that. She magically appeared in New York and then in *Tampa, Florida,* where I was assisting on a case. She sent me a first-class plane ticket to Paris and then, a few months later, to Marrakech. Then, of course, it turned out she was charging her clients the price of my plane tickets, thinking they wouldn't notice. But of course they did and they dragged Featherleigh to court, which killed her business and depleted her savings and caused her to do something stupid, like try to pass off a fake George the Third gilt-wood table as genuine."

The Chief nods. He has his guy. He can feel it. "The blackmail?" he says.

"The blackmail," Thomas says. He throws back the rest of his scotch and the Chief wishes for the bottle, anything to keep him talking. "It started back in January of this year. I wanted to break things off. And Feather told me if I did, she would tell Abby what we'd been doing. So I had to keep on." Thomas presses his fingers into his eye sockets. "I started failing at work. I was trying to get Abby pregnant and trying to keep Featherleigh from running her mouth. Then, in May, Abby got pregnant and the pregnancy seemed strong and viable and I just made a decision that I wasn't going to let Featherleigh Dale control me any longer. The fraud charges helped because I figured even if she did contact Abby, she would have zero credibility."

"But even so, you must have been upset that Ms. Dale was attending your brother's wedding."

"I asked her not to come," Thomas says. "I pleaded and begged."

"And threatened," the Chief says. "Ms. Dale said that you said if she showed her face on Nantucket, you would kill her. Did you say that?"

Thomas nods. "Yes. Yes, I did."

"Did you drop one of your mother's sleeping pills into the glass of water Featherleigh brought to the table, thinking she would be the one to drink it? Did you think *she* might take a swim and drown or get behind the wheel of a car and have an accident? Did you do that, Thomas? Because after what you've told me, I would understand if you did."

Thomas starts to cry. "I've made such a mess of things."

The Chief breathes all the way out, maybe for the first time since he woke up this morning. "I'll need you to come down to the station and sign a statement. You have the right to an attorney."

Thomas sniffs, shakes his head. "I think you've misunderstood. I've made a mess of things but I didn't drug anyone. I didn't see my mother's pills. I didn't touch the glass of water. And you'll forgive me, but it would take a hell of a lot more than a measly sleeping pill to kill Featherleigh Dale."

"So you..." the Chief says. "You didn't..."

Thomas shakes his head again. "I wanted Featherleigh to disappear. But I didn't put anything in anyone's water. I didn't see or touch my mother's sleeping pills and

Featherleigh is still very much a threat to me." Thomas offers the Chief a sad smile. "That is the truth."

The Chief calls Andrea and tells her he's on his way home.

"Did you figure out what happened?" Andrea says.

"Not quite," the Chief says. "We uncovered a bunch of ugly secrets, don't get me wrong, but we can't quite link any of them to the death of the young woman." He thinks of Jordan Randolph at the *Nantucket Standard*. He's going to have questions. Everyone is going to have questions. "How's Chloe?"

"She's upset," Andrea says. "She told me she bonded with the maid of honor at the rehearsal dinner."

"Bonded?" the Chief says. "What does that mean?"

"I tried to get more out of her but she said she wanted to talk to you. I told her you were very busy—"

"No, no, it's fine," the Chief says. He wonders if the answers he's been looking for are under his own roof. "I'll be there in a few minutes."

The Chief knocks on Chloe's bedroom door.

"Come in," she says.

She's lying on her bed reading a book about turtles. Is that right? *Turtles All the Way Down,* the cover says. The Chief has no idea what that means but he's glad she's reading. Her phone is plugged in on the nightstand and it buzzes and blinks with incoming messages—Instagrams, he supposes, or Snapchats, or whatever has replaced Instagram and Snapchat. Nick would probably know.

"Hey," he says with what remains of his good humor. He closes the door behind him and takes a seat on her bright blue fuzzy chair. The chair reminds the Chief of

Grover from *Sesame Street,* but at least it's comfortable. "Auntie said you wanted to talk?"

Chloe nods, sets the book down, sits up. She isn't wearing any makeup, which is unusual. Her face is maturing into beauty, a beauty she inherited from her mother. Tess wasn't much older than Chloe is now when the Chief first met her, Andrea's beloved younger cousin, a cousin as close as a sister.

"There are two things I want to tell you," Chloe says. "About last night."

"Go ahead," the Chief says.

"I was eavesdropping during the party," Chloe says. "I overheard a conversation between the maid of honor and the father of the groom. I think they were...involved. I know they were. She was pregnant with his baby. He wanted her to get rid of it. He said he would write her a check. She said she wanted to keep the baby because it was a link to him. She said she would tell Greer. Greer is his wife."

The Chief nods and tries not to let any emotion show on his face. He's appalled that this particular storyline managed to make its way to Chloe.

"You haven't told anyone that, I hope," the Chief says. "That's volatile information."

"I haven't told a soul," Chloe says softly. "I was waiting for you to get home."

After dealing with one liar after another all day long, the Chief is heartened to know he recognizes the truth when he hears it.

He takes a deep breath. "What's the other thing?"

"The other thing happened when I was clearing," Chloe says. "It was after the dessert, after the toasts, and I had a tray of champagne flutes I was taking back to the kitchen. I wasn't watching where I was going and I tripped and fell and the glasses all broke."

Broken glass, the Chief thinks. "Where did this happen?" he asks.

"At the place where the beach meets the lawn. Over by the left side of the house if you're standing with your back to the water."

The Chief writes this down.

"The maid of honor helped me clean up," Chloe says. "And she was really cool. She asked my name and where I was from, and when I told her I was from Nantucket, she said I was the luckiest girl in the world." Chloe's voice gets thick and she wipes at her eyes. "I can't believe she's *dead.* She was a person I talked to *last night.*"

"Sometimes things happen that way," the Chief says. "There's a good chance she took pills, maybe drank too much—"

"She wasn't drunk," Chloe says. "Not even a little bit. She seemed like the most sober person at the party."

"I just want you to realize, Chloe, that every single decision you make—who your friends are, who you date, whether you decide to smoke or drink—has a consequence. I think that Merritt, ultimately, was the victim of her own poor choices."

Chloe stares at the Chief for a second and he can see she resents his using Merritt's death as a public service announcement—but this is nothing if not a teachable moment. Chloe reaches for her phone and the Chief knows he's lost her. Andrea is better at dealing with Chloe; he always ends up sounding like the gruff uncle who also happens to be the chief of police.

"One other question, Chloe," he says, though he's sure she wants nothing more than to be rid of him. "Did Merritt *cut* herself when she was helping you clean up the glass?"

"Cut herself?" Chloe says. She looks up from her phone. "No. Why?"

"Just wondering," the Chief says. "Are you sure the two of you picked up every bit of glass?"

"It was dark," Chloe says. "We did the best we could. I was worried, actually, that Greer would find a piece of glass we missed and I would get in trouble for it today. But I guess they had bigger things to worry about."

The Chief stands up.

"Wait, can I show you one more thing?" Chloe says. She holds her phone up and scoots to the edge of the bed. The Chief takes a seat next to her. "Merritt is an influencer, so I started following her on Instagram last night when I got home. This was her last post."

The Chief accepts the phone from Chloe and puts on his reading glasses. He has never looked at Instagram before, and he sees it's nothing more than a photograph with a caption. In this instance, the photo is of two young women posing on the bow of the Hy-Line fast ferry. Their hair is windblown, and Nantucket is visible behind them in the background—the harbor, the sailboats, the gray-shingled fisherman cottages of the wharves, the steeples of the Unitarian and Congregational churches. The blond— Celeste, the bride, the Chief realizes—looks nervous; there's a hesitation in her smile. The brunette, Merritt, however, is beaming; she is luminous, giving the moment everything she has. *She's a good actress,* the Chief thinks. There's no hint or clue that she was pregnant with the baby of a married man and that he wanted nothing to do with her. The caption of the photo reads: *Goin' to the chapel… wedding weekend with the BEST FRIEND a woman could ask for. #maidofhonor #bridesmaid #happilyeverafter.*

"Hashtag happily ever after," Chloe says. "That's the part that kills me. Isn't that the saddest thing you've ever seen?"

"Just about," the Chief says, handing the phone back to Chloe. "Just about."

* * *

The Chief changes into casual clothes and looks longingly at the cold blue cans of Cisco beer in his fridge—but he can't relax yet. He has arranged to meet Nick back at the station to go over everything one last time.

"Don't worry about dinner," he tells Andrea. "I'll have Keira order us something."

"I hate murder investigations," Andrea says, lifting her face for a kiss. "But I love you."

"And I love you," he says. He gives his wife a kiss, a second kiss, a third kiss. He thinks about letting Nick wait.

The Chief and Nick meet in an interview room back at the station. Keira, the Chief's assistant, has ordered a kale Caesar and a couple of artisanal pizzas from Station 21 so they can have a little dinner.

Nick takes a lusty bite of the shrimp and pancetta pizza. "This isn't bad," he says. "Normally I stay away from anything called 'artisanal.' I like my food real."

"Chloe said Merritt didn't cut herself when she helped clean up," the Chief says. "But she may have cut herself after the kayak ride. The place Chloe said she dropped the tray is right near the path Merritt would have taken to get back to her cottage."

"That could explain why Merritt went in the water," Nick says. "I mean, you'd rinse a cut at the water's edge, but you wouldn't go all the way in."

"Unless the water felt nice," the Chief says. "It *was* a hot night."

"And I'm guessing the maid of honor didn't care for the heat," Nick says. "The A/C in her bedroom was cranked to ten. It was practically snowing in there."

"But that doesn't tell us who slipped her the sleeping pill," the Chief says.

"She might have taken one herself," Nick says. "After all, we know she was upset."

"Doesn't that seem reckless?" the Chief asks. "Taking a sleeping pill when she's pregnant?"

"The father said she jumped off the kayak way out in the middle of the harbor, right? That's the definition of reckless. Her frame of mind was reckless, sounds like."

The Chief stabs a piece of kale in the round foil container in front of them. "I'm not liking this as an accident. There are two people who wanted Merritt to go away—Tag Winbury and Greer Garrison. And one person who wanted Featherleigh Dale to go away—Thomas Winbury."

"Calling it an accident would be easier on Merritt's family," Nick says. "And the bride."

"We don't work for her family," the Chief says. "We work for the Commonwealth of Massachusetts. And beyond that, we work in the name of justice for the citizens of this great country. Do *you* think it was an accident? Really?"

"No," Nick says. "I like the mother."

The Chief munches a crouton. "Funny. I like the father. Tag Winbury sees his wife's sleeping pills, drops one in Merritt's water glass. He then takes her out in the kayak and eliminates both his problems—no mistress, no baby. What's your angle?"

"Greer finds out about the affair and the baby and *she* drops a sleeping pill in the water, hoping Merritt will drink it and that Tag will take Merritt out in the kayak. Or maybe, *maybe,* Greer is trying to kill her husband. Maybe Greer slips him a mickey hoping he'll go out in the kayak and never return." Nick picks up a piece of the sausage pizza. "Yes, I do realize how far-fetched that sounds."

"It would be different, maybe, if we had that water glass," the Chief says.

Nick cocks his head. "Does it seem odd to you that the water glass was cleared from the table but the shot glasses remained? Someone took *only the water glass* inside. Or someone came out and cleared *only the water glass.*"

The Chief shakes his head and picks up his own piece of pizza. He can't believe that Chloe is the one who dropped the tray of glasses. Shard of glass on the lawn, cut foot, maid of honor goes into the ocean to wash it off, dead maid of honor. It's not Chloe's fault; no one on earth would think that. But if Chloe hadn't dropped the tray, would Merritt still be alive? Yes, if she hadn't taken a sleeping pill or been slipped a sleeping pill and then gone into the water, she *would* be alive. Limping down the aisle of the church, maybe. But alive.

"The fact is, we don't have enough evidence to charge anyone," Nick says.

The Chief knows Nick is right. "Tomorrow we'll call the brother back and tell him we concluded it was an accident. She took a sleeping pill, she went for a nighttime swim, she drowned."

"There were so many secrets in that house," Nick says. "I can't believe one of them didn't cause this."

The Chief raises his cup of coffee. "To the deceased," he says.

Nick touches his cup to the Chief's. "May she rest in peace."

Saturday, July 7, 2018,
6:55 p.m.

NANTUCKET

The Nantucket Standard—www.ackstandard .net—Saturday, July 7, 2018

Nantucket Police Department Rules Drowning Death Accidental

8:12 p.m.

The Nantucket Police Department, in conjunction with the Massachusetts State Police, has ruled the death of Merritt Alison Monaco, 29, of New York, New York, early this morning, an accident. Ms. Monaco was on Nantucket to serve as an attendant at a wedding on Saturday. She is survived by her parents, Gary and Katherine Monaco, of Commack, New York, as well as a brother, Douglas Monaco, of Garden City, New York. Ms. Monaco was employed by the New York Wildlife Conservation Society and has served as their director of public relations since 2016.

Chief Edward Kapenash of the Nantucket Police Department said, "We have investigated the case and determined Ms. Monaco's death was an accident. We thank the entire Nantucket community for their cooperation and encourage locals and visitors to the island alike to exercise extreme caution in and around the water."

Marty Szczerba gets an alert from the *Inky* on his phone: The maid of honor out in Monomoy apparently drowned accidentally. It sounds suspicious to Marty, and it also feels a bit anticlimactic—after the person of interest trying to escape on the Hy-Line and the dramatic removal of Featherleigh Dale from the Crosswinds restaurant, it turns out the death was *accidental*?

Huh, Marty thinks.

Then Marty realizes this means Featherleigh Dale isn't a murder suspect and thus might be interested in a little romance. Marty can't see himself pursuing anything like a one-night stand, but a drink might be nice.

He decides to call the police station to ask Keira if she knows if Featherleigh was brought back to the airport or taken to stay at an inn overnight.

"Hey, Keira," Marty says when she answers. "This is Marty Szczerba. I have a question for you."

"Hey, Marty," Keira says. Just the sound of her voice reminds Marty that he still harbors a terrific crush on Keira. "I have a question for *you*. When are you ever going to ask me out?"

Marty blinks. The phone grows warm in his hand. *Featherleigh who?* he thinks. "How about tonight?" he says.

Celeste texts Benji to let him know she's taking a taxi back from the hospital.

I'll just come get you! Benji says.

Please don't, Celeste responds. Three dots appear and then a second text comes through. We can talk when I get back.

Benji feels suddenly hot and prickly, uncomfortable in his own skin for the first time in his life. How he longs to shed his identity at this moment. He no longer wants to be a Winbury. Celeste has obviously learned about Merritt and Tag. They were having some kind of affair, some kind of *something*—Benji couldn't bear to press for details—but he has a feeling his father is to blame for Merritt's death.

His own father.

You think your family is beyond reproach, Celeste had said. *But you're wrong.*

Benji meets Celeste out in the driveway but she gives him a hollow look and says, "I need a minute, please, Benji. I have to talk to my parents."

He says, "Your parents aren't the priority right now, Celeste. I'm your fiancé. We were supposed to get *married* today."

She walks right past him and into the house, and it's all Benji can do not to follow behind her like a puppy dog.

Instead, he heads to the kitchen and watches Thomas pile a plate high with sandwiches and potato salad and summer fruit that the caterer had dropped off earlier that afternoon as scheduled—it was supposed to be the pre-wedding lunch—and when Thomas notices Benji staring at him, he says, "What? I'm hungry, and my wife is pregnant and needs food."

Benji says in the calmest voice he can manage, "Is this Dad's fault? Was he *screwing* her?"

"Sounds like it," Thomas says matter-of-factly. He notices the look of disgust that crosses Benji's face. "Oh, don't be such an altar boy, Benny."

Altar boy? Benji thinks. Does it make him an *altar boy*

to expect his father to be a man of character and integrity, to not cheat on their mother with someone Benji's age, someone who also happened to be *Celeste's best friend?* "Did you *know* about this?" Benji asks.

"Not really," Thomas says. "But I saw Dad in the bar at the Four Seasons downtown a few weeks ago and he hid from me. I figured *something* was going on." Thomas blinks. "Now I know what that something was."

Benji shudders. The Four Seasons downtown? It was like *that,* like an affair from a novel or a movie? Thomas disappears down the hall with his plate before Benji can ask what *Thomas* had been doing at the Four Seasons downtown.

He doesn't want to know.

Benji loiters at the mail table at the bottom of the stairs until he hears Celeste leaving her parents' room, then he races to the second floor and catches her right before she enters her/his/their bedroom. His bedroom that she was using as a bridal suite that will become their bedroom in this house.

"Celeste."

She turns. "I need to lie down," she says.

"I understand you're tired," he says. He lets her enter the room, follows her, then closes the door behind them.

"Benji," she says.

Her wedding dress is hanging on the closet door; it's as unsettling to him as a headless ghost. "You're not going to marry me," he says. "Are you? Like at all, ever?"

"No," she says. "I'm sorry, Benji, I'm not."

Benji's entire body goes numb. He nods but he feels like his head is being pulled by a string. Celeste! He wants to talk her out of it. He wants to explain that she shouldn't judge him by his family's actions. He's not his father. He's not his brother. He's a good, true person and he will love her forever.

But he stops himself. Every single thing that Benji has comes from his parents—the money, the apartment, the education, the advantages. To denounce his family, to deny his unconditional love for them, would be disingenuous, and Celeste would recognize it as such. He has taken the privilege for granted for twenty-eight years, and now he has to accept the shame.

"What are you going to do?" he asks.

"I'm not sure," she says. "Maybe take a trip. Maybe not."

"I know it seems inconceivable right now," Benji says, "but you will get past this. I don't mean to say you'll ever stop missing Merritt..."

"Benji," Celeste says, and Benji clamps his mouth shut. He sounds like an ass. "My decision doesn't have anything to do with Merritt."

"It doesn't?" he says.

She shakes her head. "It has to do with me."

She doesn't want to marry him.

He would like to say this comes as a complete shock, a wrecking ball out of nowhere—but it doesn't.

"Your stutter is gone," he says.

She smiles, sadly at first, but then with a touch of relief—or triumph. "Yes," she says. "I know."

As Benji is walking back to the first cottage—he needs to hide; he can't bear to see either of his parents—he spies Shooter walking down the driveway.

Shooter. Benji has completely lost track of him, of time, of everything. Shooter looks like he's just survived a shipwreck. He's unshaven, his blue oxford is rumpled and untucked, he has his navy blazer crushed under one arm, and his mouth is hanging open as he stares at his phone.

"You look even worse than I feel," Benji says, trying

for the jocular tone they normally use with each other. "Where have you been?"

"Police station," Shooter says. He follows Benji into the first cottage, then goes straight to the fridge and flips the top off a bottle of beer. "Want one?"

"Sure," Benji says.

"Listen, there are some things you need to know," Shooter says.

"Spare me, please," Benji says. "I've heard too much already."

Spare me, please. I've heard too much already.

Shooter lets that comment sink in. He was finally released from the police station; in the end, they had nothing to hold him on except impeding an active investigation. They issued him a ticket for three hundred dollars, which he paid in cash. Val Gluckstern had offered him a ride back to Summerland, but he said he wanted to walk. He needed to clear his head.

He hadn't been sure how much he would need to explain. Maybe everything. Maybe nothing. He wanted very badly to talk to Celeste but he was afraid. He had spilled the beans to the police, which already felt like a betrayal. He was afraid Celeste would be angry, but he was more afraid she would deny that she had ever intended to run away with him.

As he was walking down the Winburys' white-shell driveway between the rows of hydrangeas and under the boxwood arch, his phone pinged. It was a text from an unfamiliar 212 number. Shooter had clicked on the text more out of habit than anything else.

It was a picture of Shooter and Celeste standing outside Steamboat Pizza. They weren't touching, though they were very close together—too close, probably. Shooter clicked on the photo and zoomed in. Celeste was looking in the vague direction of the camera and Shooter was looking at Celeste, his expression one of naked desire, longing, covetousness.

The photo is chilling, a threat. Did someone else know their plans? Who took it? Who sent it?

Shooter stopped dead in his tracks. He texted back: Who is this?

To which there was no response. Shooter ran through the possibilities. The 212 area code was Manhattan. And whoever this was either had been across the street or knew someone who was.

The implications were obvious, right? Someone was trying to scare him. If the photo was being sent to Shooter, it had probably also been sent to Benji. But Benji knew that Shooter and Celeste had gone to get pizza. It wasn't as if someone had sent a picture of Shooter and Celeste a few minutes later, sitting on the bench by the Steamship terminal. That would have been harder to explain.

Okay, fine. Honestly, Shooter was too tired for games. He proceeded under the boxwood arch and bumped right into Benji.

Spare me, please. I've heard too much already.

"I ran away from the police this morning," Shooter says. "They wanted to question me and I told them I had to use the john and then I slipped out the bathroom window."

"Shut up," Benji says.

"I'm serious."

Benji says, "I hope you told them you didn't want to talk to the police because of what happened to your mother."

Shooter takes a long pull off his beer. Benji is the only person who knows about Shooter's mother, Cassandra. She became addicted to heroin after Shooter's father died, but she had happened to OD during one of Shooter's rare visits home. He was twenty-one years old, working as a bartender in Georgetown, and he gave Cassandra a fifty-dollar bill. She had spent it on smack. Shooter had woken up in the morning to find his mother dead. And, yes, he had blamed himself. He had basically begged the Dade County police to arrest him, but they had far too much experience with overdoses to blame anyone but the user herself.

"I hopped on the Hy-Line and they caught me, cuffed me, brought me to the police station. I hired a lawyer. She sat with me while I gave my account of last night."

Benji barely reacts. It's as if he expects these kinds of theatrics from Shooter. Either that or he's not really listening. "They found something in Merritt's bloodstream," Benji says. "Pills."

"Really," Shooter says. "How is Celeste taking it?"

Benji shoots up off the sofa. "How is Celeste *taking* it?" he says. "Well, let's see, she was so hysterical that she spent half the day in the emergency room. And yet she seems to have gained a certain clarity. She doesn't want to marry me. At all. Ever."

Shooter is suddenly very alert, despite his profound exhaustion. What is Benji going to say next?

"She says it has nothing to do with what happened to Merritt. It has to do with *her*. She doesn't want to marry me—not next month, not next year, not on a beach in Aruba, not at city hall in Easton, Pennsylvania. She doesn't want to marry me. When was she going to tell me this? Was she going to stand me up at the altar? Oh, and guess what else. Guess what else. Just guess."

Shooter doesn't want to guess, which is okay because Benji isn't waiting for an answer.

"Her stutter is gone! Completely gone! She decides she's not going to marry me and her speech impediment disappears."

Her stutter was gone last night, Shooter thinks. If Benji had paid attention, he would have realized that. When Celeste and Shooter left the bench next to the Steamship terminal, they had gone back to get pizza, and when Shooter asked Celeste what she wanted, she said, "Slice of pepperoni and a root beer, please." Her words had been as clear as the peal of church bells on a summer morning.

"Did she say anything else?" Shooter asks. His plan of running away with Celeste was incredibly cowardly, he sees now. Because this—Benji's reckoning—wasn't anything Shooter wanted to witness.

"Anything *else?*" Benji says. "She didn't need to say anything else. She destroyed me." He winds up and throws his beer bottle across the room, where it hits the wall and shatters. Benji puts his hands over his face. He makes a choking noise and Shooter realizes he's crying.

Shooter Uxley has envied Benjamin Winbury since the day they met at the St. George's School freshman year, and although Shooter has always longed to have something, anything, that Benji couldn't have, all that comes to mind now are the infinite kindnesses that Benji has shown him: The day after Shooter's mother died, Benji skipped his economics midterm at Hobart and flew down to Miami. During their senior year at St. George's, when Shooter was so destitute that he organized an illegal dice game, it was Benji who had encouraged people to come and gamble. Benji had been a prefect, he could have gotten in trouble, lost his position, faced suspension, but none of that had been as important to him as giving Shooter the opportunity to make enough money to stay at school.

Benji had picked Shooter over his own brother to be his best man.

Benji had always believed in Shooter and continues to believe in him, even as Shooter came *this close* to stealing his bride away.

Celeste has done her part. She has broken things off. This is how things should go. Let Benji deal with the breakup and let Celeste deal with losing Merritt. After some time passes, Shooter and Celeste can be together. *How much time will that be?* he wonders. He is, by nature, a very impatient person. He wants to start his life with Celeste today.

He decides he will keep the picture of himself with Celeste. It arrived like an anonymous gift from the universe; when Shooter looks at it, he will remember that he finally has something in his life worth waiting for. He will remember that she said yes.

Shooter stands up. He reaches out for Benji, hugs him tight; he absorbs the shudders of Benji's sobs.

He says nothing.

Saturday, July 7, 2018,
8:00 p.m.

GREER

There's a knock on Greer's bedroom door and she stands.

"Yes?"

Elida, the housekeeper, enters the room. It's way past time for Elida to leave. Even with the wedding, she was supposed to be gone by three so she could attend the ceremony at four. But here she is, quietly and steadfastly doing her job.

"Elida," Greer says, and tears rise in her eyes. What does it say that in her household she can only trust two people: her younger son and her housekeeper?

From behind her back, Elida produces Greer's pillbox.

"What?" Greer says. Her novelist mind immediately wonders if *Elida* had anything to do with Merritt's death. Perhaps Elida learned about the affair and the baby and poisoned the girl out of fealty to Greer. That would be an unexpected upstairs-downstairs twist. "Where did you find this?"

Elida says, "In Mr. Thomas's room. In the trash."

In Thomas's room, in the trash. In the *trash*? Thomas knows how much Greer cherishes this pillbox. She can't believe he would throw it away. Greer takes the box from Elida. There are still pills inside; she can hear them.

"Thank you, Elida," Greer says. "You can go home."

Elida slips out of the room. Greer returns the pillbox

to its rightful place in the medicine cabinet. Then she marches upstairs.

As Greer approaches Thomas's bedroom door, she hears yelling. This is hardly surprising; Greer would very much like to yell herself. She quickly realizes the voices she's hearing belong to Thomas and Abby.

Greer's first thought is that yelling can't be good for the baby, but then she recalls that her greatest rows with Tag were when she was pregnant. Her hormones had turned her into a lunatic with pendulum swings between elation and despair. The worst row—when Greer was bored out of her mind, pregnant with Thomas, and Tag was at work every night until ten and on business trips across Europe every weekend—had actually resulted in Greer picking up a pen and writing her first novel, *Prey in the Saint-Germain-des-Prés*.

Greer sighs. Thoughts of her first novel lead her to thoughts of her twenty-first novel, due in thirteen days. Well, it won't get done now, and no one will blame her. Her husband's pregnant mistress was found dead outside her house on the morning of her son's wedding. Greer gets a pass.

Greer stands just outside the bedroom door, where she can hear distinct words and phrases. She loathes eavesdropping; she's going to insist they pipe down. The last thing anyone else in this house needs to hear is Thomas and Abby's marital squabbling.

But then Greer hears Abby say, "I've known about you and Featherleigh for years, since Virgin Gorda, since Tony Berkus's graduation party at the Carlyle Hotel! Amy Lackey told me she saw you with a trashy-looking woman at L'Entrecôte in Paris on a weekend you told me you were visiting your parents in London. I've read all your texts and e-mails and picked through your credit card bills, including the British Airways Visa Signature card you think I know nothing about!"

Greer stops herself from knocking just in time. Thomas and Featherleigh? *Thomas?* Featherleigh is fifteen years his senior. Surely that can't be right?

"I told you, I broke it off," Thomas says. "I broke it off for good in May, as soon as we found out about the baby."

Wait! Greer thinks. *Featherleigh told Greer that she had broken up with a married man in May.*

It's a disheartening discovery indeed that Thomas seems to have inherited Tag's questionable morals, setting Abby up to be just like Greer, a generation later.

Thank God Benji is a Garrison, through and through.

"There is no breaking it off for good when it comes to you and Featherleigh," Abby says. "Look at last night! I *saw* you with her under the tent. I saw you! And I knew what was going to happen. You were going to appease me by coming upstairs, and then as soon as I was asleep, you were going to screw her in the pool house!"

"You're crazy," Thomas says. "I came upstairs and Featherleigh *left,* Abby. She left for her inn or her guest-house. I don't even know where she was staying, that's how little I cared—"

"She did *not* leave!" Abby says. "I sneaked downstairs while you were in the bathroom brushing your teeth and I heard her in the powder room humming 'The Lady in Red.' She wasn't going anywhere. She was lying in wait for you."

At that instant, Greer figures it out.

She hurries back down to her bedroom and finds her cell phone.

She sends a text to both Thomas and Abby. It says: Lower your voices. Everyone can hear you.

* * *

Thomas has been having a years-long affair with Featherleigh, and Elida found the pillbox in Thomas's bedroom. In the trash.

Well.

Tag is the plotter, not Greer, but after twenty-one murder mysteries, she has learned a thing or two about motivation. Greer saw Abby last night when she went to the kitchen to pour herself the final glass of Veuve and *left her pills on the counter.* Abby had either snatched the pills up then or noted their existence. Much later, she went down to see if Featherleigh had left. She overheard Featherleigh humming in the powder room and must have decided to put the old girl to sleep...to keep her from fooling around with Thomas.

And who could blame her?

Abby dropped a pill in Featherleigh's drink, only the drink had gone to the wrong person. It had somehow gone to Merritt.

The police have ruled Merritt's death accidental—and an accident it indeed was. Abby may not even realize she's to blame, and Thomas will never put two and two together. The secret resides with Greer, and with Greer it will remain until her death.

The future of the Winbury family depends on it.

Saturday, July 7, 2018,
2:47 a.m.

NANTUCKET

Nantucket Island holds her people's secrets.

When Merritt Monaco and Tag Winbury get back from the kayak ride, Merritt is soaking wet and crying. Tag is a man struggling with both fury and feelings of tenderness. Merritt staggers off down the beach, and Tag kicks over the kayak, bringing up a spray of wet sand. He considers going after Merritt but instead heads up to the house. She can't be reasoned with right now; he'll have to postpone further talks until after the wedding.

Merritt turns her face just enough to see Tag scurry for the safety of his home base. She can't believe how craven and heartless he has turned out to be. Only a few weeks ago, she found him standing outside her apartment building like a lovesick teenager; now, he is someone else entirely.

Merritt wrenches the silver ring off her thumb and throws it into the water, then immediately regrets it. This is another childish gesture on her part. The first was jumping off the kayak when they were hundreds of yards offshore. Merritt was like any other woman who went to desperate measures to gain her lover's attention.

There had been one moment when Merritt had believed she would drown. She was so tired, so lethargic, her limbs were too leaden to swim, and she'd nearly sunk to the harbor floor like a stone.

Tag had grabbed her by the wrist and hauled her back up onto the kayak. He had been even angrier then than he was when they started out.

It was a fling, he said, *for* fun, *for a* release, *for* escape. *Nothing more, Merritt. Nothing more!*

You were obsessed with me, she said, but her words had been garbled and he didn't understand her. If he had understood her, he would have denied it, but Merritt knows he was obsessed, captivated, enraptured. For hours, days, weeks, he thought of nothing but her.

The problem is it didn't last. The obsession, such as it was, vanished as capriciously as it had arrived. Merritt longs to inspire a more substantial feeling, a real feeling— like what Benji and Celeste feel for each other.

Benji and Celeste are the perfect couple. Merritt wants what they have more than she wants anything else in this world.

It's very late, and Merritt can barely keep her eyes open. She could lie down on the beach right now and sleep until morning, but if she does that, she is sure to wake up to Greer standing over her with a disapproving glare.

Merritt stumbles back up toward the flagstone path that leads around the house to the second cottage. She indulges in a fantasy that Tag is waiting inside the cottage for her or that he has left a note or a rose cut from the garden on her pillow. Anything.

Merritt cries out. There is a rude, sharp pain. She lifts her foot and pulls a shard of glass from her soft instep. She's at the edge of the lawn, where the cute young girl dropped the tray of champagne flutes.

There is blood everywhere. Merritt stumbles back into the sand. Now there's sand in the cut. She will have to rinse it and hop back up to the path.

Salt water is supposed to cure everything, but Merritt doesn't expect the sting. She looks down to see a plume of blood rise and she cries fresh tears. That girl, the niece of the Nantucket police chief, had gazed at Merritt with such wide-eyed awe; she had no idea what kind of mess Merritt had made of her life.

She's pregnant. And alone.

It's okay, Merritt thinks. She will raise the child by herself; she will hardly be the first woman to do so. Maybe she will write a blog: *Millennial Influencer Turned Unwed Mother.* Merritt's eyes drift close. Rousing herself feels like pulling on a rope to get out of a deep, dark hole—but she does it. When she opens her eyes, she sees a glint of silver on the ocean floor a few yards away.

Her ring.

Yes, she thinks. She should get the ring. It's the only present Tag will ever give her. She will save it for her baby. The baby will no doubt be a girl, and long after Merritt has moved on to the next man and the man after that, she will whisper to her daughter, *This is a ring your father gave me. Your real father.*

Merritt wades in and bends down to grab the ring but she kicks it accidentally and she has to wait for the sand to settle before she can find it again. She is unreasonably sleepy, too sleepy to stand, and so she spreads her arms and legs out and she floats. She opens her eyes underwater.

Where is the ring?

There it is. She sees it.

Like love, she thinks, *it is just beyond her reach.*

ACKNOWLEDGMENTS

I want to start by thanking Detective Sergeant Tom Clinger of the Nantucket Police Department for meeting with me to run through procedure. Because of the nature of the novel and its timetable, I had to make changes that would not happen in a real investigation. Rest assured, Tom gave me good information. His mother, Marie, should be quite proud!

Thank you to my brother, the NOAA/NWS meteorologist Douglas Hilderbrand, who explained in detail how fog happens. He also advocates for people being "weather ready"—and after this past year, I'm with him.

Cindy Auris: You get all credit for introducing me to Meat Loaf back in the 1970s. I've been trying to get "Paradise by the Dashboard Light" into a novel for eighteen years and I've finally done it!

My editor, Reagan Arthur, *yet again* edited this book with sheer brilliance. I tell you the woman is always right, and she *is* always right. For any aspiring writers out there who think a novel like this comes easily and on the first try, I am here to tell you it is hard work, mind-bending work, that requires revision after revision after revision. I am fortunate to have an incredibly intelligent, thoughtful, and clear-eyed sensibility like Reagan's to guide me to my final draft.

To my agents, Michael Carlisle and David Forrer of

Inkwell Management: I love you both beyond words. You are my people.

To my publicist, Katharine Myers: You are a kind, gentle, and patient woman, the calm eye in the hurricane of my public life, and I want to say, in equal parts, thank you for all you do and I'm sorry for the chaos and the "enormous changes at the last minute" that are my trademark.

To Tayler Kent: Thank you for continuing in the tradition of great nannies for the Cunningham children. I couldn't have written this novel without you doing the things I was too busy to do and doing it with style, a sense of fun, and unwavering competence.

To my friends, the women in my barre class at Go Figure, and the parents I have sat next to in the football stadium, on the basketball court, by the baseball diamond: Thank you for giving me a community worth bragging about. Special thanks to Rebecca Bartlett, Debbie Briggs, Wendy Hudson, Wendy Rouillard, Elizabeth and Beau Almodobar, Chuck and Margie Marino, John and Martha Sargent, Heidi and Fred Holdgate (Fred was a huge help with all details Nantucket airport–related), Evelyn and Matthew MacEachern, Mark and Gwenn Snider and the entire staff at the Nantucket Hotel, Dan and Kristen Holdgate, Melissa and Angus MacVicar, Jana and Nicky Duarte, Linda Holliday and Dr. Sue Decoste, Paul and Ginna Kogler, the Timothy Fields big and small, Manda Riggs, David Rattner and Andrew Law, West Riggs (who helped me choose the Winburys' boats), Helaina Jones, Marty and Holly McGowan, Scott and Logan O'Connor, Liza and Jeff Ottani (parents of my favorite child Kai), Sheila and Kevin Carroll (parents of my other favorite child Liam), Carolyn Durand of Lee Real Estate, who showed me one of her gorgeous properties in Monomoy so I could better describe the Winburys' home. Thank you to Cam Jones for the inside intel on St. George's School, and to Julia Asphar, about Miami of Ohio.

Thank you to my mother, Sally Hilderbrand; to my siblings, especially my stepsister Heather Osteen Thorpe, the very best friend I have in this world; and to Judith and Duane Thurman, who have been second parents to me for more than thirty years.

Always, at the end of this page, I thank my children. It is such a bittersweet year for me as my eldest, Maxwell, heads off to college in the fall. I sold my first novel, *The Beach Club,* in the spring of 1999 when I was pregnant with Maxx, and so his life and my career have run parallel. Maxx Cunningham: I am so proud of you and all you've accomplished, but let me tell you, the best is yet to come, and I can't wait to see it. To Dawson: You are my well-adjusted middle child, possibly the most beloved person on the entire island of Nantucket, and, yes, you do take up 90 percent of my parenting energy but I wouldn't change a thing about you (this might be hyperbole...look it up). To Shelby: You are my hero—at age twelve, already a "strong and independent woman"—and I strive every day to be even half the mother that you deserve.

In closing, I want to acknowledge and send love, strength, and clarity to each and every breast cancer survivor who reads this book. Thank you to the hardworking wonder-folks at the Breast Cancer Research Foundation and to my medical oncologist, Dr. Steven Isakoff, who continues to keep me healthy, four years after my initial diagnosis. It's a journey or it's a battle—you pick what you want to call it—but someday soon, we are going to triumph. We are all going to call ourselves survivors.

ABOUT ELIN HILDERBRAND

Elin Hilderbrand is a graduate of the Johns Hopkins University and the Iowa Writers' Workshop. She has lived on Nantucket for twenty-five years and is the mother of three teenagers. *The Perfect Couple* is her twenty-first novel.

A TIME
FOR TRUMPETS

THE AMERICAN SOLDIER
Staff Sgt. Joseph Arnaldo, New Bedford, Mass.

THE
UNTOLD
STORY OF
THE BATTLE OF
THE BULGE

A
Time
for
Trumpets

Charles B. MacDonald

Perennial
An Imprint of HarperCollinsPublishers

Photographs are courtesy of the United States Army and the individuals pictured (or their relatives) with the exception of the following: German photographs courtesy *Bibliothek für Zeitgeschichte*, Günter von der Weiden, and the Still Picture Branch, National Archives: Strong, Williams, de Guingand, and preparing to execute Skorzeny's men, Imperial War Museum; Vandenberg, Smithsonian Institution; and the ENIGMA machine, National Security Agency.

First Quill edition published 1997.

Reprinted in Perennial 2002.

Designed by Bernard Schleifer

Library of Congress Cataloging-in-Publication Data

MacDonald, Charles Brown, 1922-1990.
   A time for trumpets: the untold story of the battle of the bulge/
Charles B. MacDonald.
      Bibliography: p.
      Includes index.
      1. Ardannes, Battle of the, 1944-1945. I. Title.
D756.5.A7M26   1984   940.54'21   84-9043
ISBN 0-688-15157-4

   08 09 10 QW 20 19 18 17

For my brother, Rae,
his wife, Nannie,
and theirs,
and for the American soldiers and airmen
who fought in the Ardennes.

Contents

CONTENTS

BOOK IV: THE SHOULDERS

BOOK V: DAMS AGAINST THE TIDE

BOOK VI: THE ROAD BACK

A TIME
FOR TRUMPETS

Prologue

Located in western reaches of the Ardennes region of Belgium, the village of Bande had little distinction. It was just another farming village, lacking the narrow, winding, cobblestoned streets and mountain-like setting of so many villages and towns that help make the Ardennes a picture postcard region.

In early September, 1944, on either side of the main highway through the village—the Grand' Rue—stood a cluster of ten to twelve red brick buildings, mostly dwellings but some with small shops on the ground floor. One was the Café de la Poste. Along a winding side road up a gently sloping hill were other houses belonging mostly to farmers, as might be discerned from their attached barns and from compost heaps almost always located near the front door. At the top of the hill was a small church of drab gray native stone. Much of the nearby land was cultivated, but two or three miles away on every side were forests.

Since less than a thousand people lived in Bande, it was of insufficient importance for the German Army to station occupation troops in the village. The entire region fell under the jurisdiction of the *Kreiskommandant* in Bastogne, twenty-four miles to the southeast, and there was a detachment of *Feldgendarmerie* eight miles to the northwest in Marche. In a nearby forest, close to a hundred German soldiers lived in wooden barracks, their duty to guard Russian prisoners of war who worked in an ammunition depot.

During the first days of September, 1944, the exhilaration of impending liberation was in the air in Bande. Adding to the excitement, word spread among the villagers that a group of Belgian resistance fighters of the *Armée Secrète* had moved into a nearby wood. Such was the elation of approaching freedom after four long years of omnipresent German soldiers—their hobnailed boots, their imperious commands, their edicts, their requisitions, their unannounced knocks in the night that might mean a loved one seized for deportation—that some of the villagers defiantly displayed the black, red, and yellow Belgian flag. *A bas les Boches*!

Before daylight on September 5, men of the *Armée Secrète* attacked the German barracks at the ammunition depot. Three German soldiers died in the attack. The next day, the Germans surrounded the center of Bande along the Grand' Rue, ordered the inhabitants from their homes, and systematically put the torch to every building.

Two days later, on September 8, as troops of the American 9th Infantry Division approached, the last of the German soldiers hurriedly departed. As they left, some of them shook their fists at the obviously exultant inhabitants. "We'll be back!" they shouted.*

On September 16, 1944, the man who had plunged the world into the most devastating war in the history of mankind, Adolf Hitler, Chancellor of Germany and self-styled Führer, summoned a number of senior officers to his study. It was in a huge, underground steel-reinforced concrete bunker within the *Wolfschanze* (Wolf's Lair), Hitler's field headquarters in the swampy pine forest of Gorlitz in East Prussia. Those summoned had come to constitute a kind of household military staff. Among them was one of the few wearing the red stripes of the General Staff on their trews whose advice Hitler still sought and sometimes heeded, the head of the operations staff of the *Oberkommando der Wehrmacht*, or *OKW* (Armed Forces High Command), General Alfred Jodl.

The officers were waiting when Hitler entered the study, his shoulders sagging, his face drained of color, looking considerably older than his fifty-four years. Although he had recovered from most of the injuries incurred not quite two months before when conspirators within the army had tried to assassinate him by setting off a bomb, smuggled into a conference in a briefcase, he still had a ruptured right eardrum and a sometimes uncontrollable twitching of his right arm. He also had spells of dizziness and a persistent sinus headache. The Führer's voice had become hoarse (it would later be determined because of a benign growth on his vocal chords), and he sometimes had such severe stomach spasms that it was almost impossible for him to keep from crying out, an affliction (it would also be determined later) attributable to pills prescribed for flatulence by his personal physician, who was unaware that they contained strychnine and atropine. A steady diet of those pills had turned his skin yellow, as if he had jaundice, and that very morning, before calling the officers to his study, Hitler had had what was probably a mild coronary, the third in less than a week.

Taking a seat at his desk, Hitler asked Jodl to sum up the situation on the Western Front. Jodl first noted the strength of the opposing forces, which was heavily in favor of the Western Allies—Great Britain, France,

---

*Citations for all direct quotes are part of the bibliography.

and the United States. Of more than a million German casualties incurred over the last three months, said Jodl, almost half had been in the West.

The German troops, he went on, were continuing their withdrawal from southern France, and in northeastern France they were trying to form a new line based upon sturdy old forts dating from the Franco-Prussian War. In the north they were forming new lines along canals and rivers in the Netherlands or falling back from Belgium into the border fortifications, the West Wall. There was one spot of particular concern, added Jodl, referring to a convoluted, heavily forested region encompassing eastern Belgium and much of the Grand Duchy of Luxembourg, where the Americans were attacking and the Germans had almost nothing: the Ardennes.

At the word "Ardennes," Hitler sat erect and ordered Jodl to stop. A long pause followed.

"I have made a momentous decision," the Führer said at last, the firmness of his voice belying his weakened condition, his blue eyes alight with a fervor that nobody had seen since the attempt on his life. "I shall go over to the offensive, that is to say"—he slapped one hand down on a map that lay across his desk— "here, out of the Ardennes, with the objective, Antwerp!"

With those words, Adolf Hitler set in motion preparations for a battle that was to assume epic proportions, the greatest German attack in the West since the campaign of 1940 had brought down the Netherlands, Belgium, Luxembourg, and France in swift and ignominious defeat. It was destined to involve more than a million men and to precipitate an unparalleled crisis for the Allied armies. It was also to involve one of the most egregious failures in the history of American battlefield intelligence. Yet it was also to become the greatest battle ever fought by the United States Army.

It was cold. A damp, penetrating cold, typical for the Grand Duchy of Luxembourg in the second week of December.

Elise Delé and her son Jean plodded through heavy mist along a deserted highway that followed the west bank of the little Our River. To Elise, there was something almost eerie about returning to her village, Bivels, from which every living soul and even the pigs and cows had been evacuated. Yet she badly needed to get to her farmhouse on the steep slope overlooking the village, the house she had long shared with her husband, Mathias, until the Germans in October had taken him away. She had to get warmer clothes for herself and for Jean. Early that morning, December 10, with the approval of the civil authorities in Vianden (not quite two miles from Bivels), she and Jean had set out, Jean pulling a small cart in which to carry back their belongings.

They had passed the first house in the village and were approaching the second when two German soldiers appeared at the door. When they beckoned, Jean dropped the handle of the cart and ran. Elise ran, too, but the soldiers quickly overtook her; it was easier for a thirteen-year-old boy to get away than a woman of forty-one.

At the soldiers' order, Elise went with them across a temporary footbridge over the Our and up a sharp incline beyond to what appeared to be a low-level command post in a concrete bunker of the West Wall. There a young German officer asked what Elise knew about the American soldiers in and around Vianden.

She knew little. The Americans had a post halfway up the steep, cobblestoned main street of Vianden, she said, perhaps eighteen or twenty men. That was all. Those were the only Americans she had seen.

The questioning at an end, the officer appeared to be embarrassed by Elise's presence, as if he was at a loss to know what to do with her; but he refused her every entreaty to be allowed to return to Bivels. At last he put her with some soldiers in a truck heading east.

Elise had no idea where the soldiers were taking her, but when they turned onto a main road, she recognized it as that leading to the town of Bitburg, eighteen miles inside Germany. When they got to Bitburg, the truck stopped at the schoolhouse, and one of the soldiers told Elise to follow him inside. There another German officer questioned her, then sent her to stay in the house of a woman in the town.

The next morning, Elise told the woman she was worried about her son. The soldiers had left no guard, replied the woman. Why not just leave?

Elise was at first too frightened to take her advice. What would the soldiers do if they caught her?

For the better part of two days, Elise stayed in the woman's house. On the 11th, it began to snow, which increased her concern about Jean, and the next afternoon she finally made up her mind to go. As she left the house, she was struck with the change in the town. It was teeming with soldiers and military traffic, and some of the troops wore gray uniforms with black collars, which Elise knew to be the uniform of the SS.

She had traveled about half the distance of her return journey when she came upon two elderly men whom she knew from a village inside Germany opposite Bivels. They invited her to walk with them.

As they continued along the road, Elise began to notice a sharp increase in military traffic. Passing through a wood, she saw great stacks of military equipment piled on both sides of the road just inside the tree-lines. Not long after that, columns of artillery overtook them, some guns drawn by trucks, others by teams of horses. Each time that happened, she and her companions stepped off the road to get out of the way, but nobody paid them any attention. As they entered another wood, she saw row after row of what looked like small boats.

What was going on? Elise only vaguely remembered when the Germans had come in 1914 and had had little experience with the military other than in 1940, when the Germans had attacked across the Our and driven through Luxembourg and Belgium to the sea, and again just last September, when the Americans had come and made a brief attack across the Our not far from Bivels. On both those occasions, there had been a stream of traffic much like that she was seeing then. Did that mean the Germans were going to attack again? The thought made her all the more anxious to get back to her son.

When Elise and the two German men reached the village where the men lived, she rested in one of their homes; but as darkness fell the next day, December 13, she set out to cover the remaining distance to Bivels. Not far from some concrete pillboxes, she came upon entanglements of barbed wire. As she tried to work her way through, she activated a trip wire, and a mine exploded. Elise was terrified, but because she had been bending forward to negotiate the barbed wire, she was unharmed; and to her immense relief, the noise drew no fire from the pillboxes.

When at last she reached the point where the ground dropped sharply down to the Our, the valley was immersed in a dense fog. She dared not try the descent under those conditions. Lying down in the snow, she tried to sleep, but that was impossible. For what seemed like an eternity, Elise did her best to keep warm by chafing her hands and legs and stamping her feet.

An hour before midnight, the fog lifted. Ignoring the cold, she took off her shoes to cut down on noise and followed a path leading down to the river; but at the river, she saw that the footbridge which she had crossed earlier no longer existed.

Close to weeping from fright and despair, Elise followed the trace of the Our until at last she came to that part of Vianden which lay on the east bank, the only place where the little river diverged as a boundary between Germany and Luxembourg. Although the bridge connecting the two parts of the town had long been destroyed, there was an old man who called across the river to partisans of the Luxembourg underground. Elise knew the partisans helped the Americans to man their post and also occupied the ruins of a tenth-century castle at the top of the town, which in happier times was one of the attractions drawing swarms of tourists to Vianden.

Early in the morning of December 14, two young men from the underground came in a small boat to row Elise across the river. While they crossed, she told them what she had seen behind the German lines. It looked to her, she said, as if the Germans were coming back.

As the three made their way up the main street, the young men insisted on stopping at the Hotel Heintz where the Americans—men of the Intelligence and Reconnaissance (I&R) Platoon of the 28th Division's 109th Infantry—were billeted, to tell them what Elise had seen. Although Elise understood no English, it was obvious that what she had to say excited the Americans. They gave her coffee and something to eat, but like the German officers, the American officer who interrogated her (it was 1st Lt. Stephen Prazenka) refused to release her to look for her son. Instead, the Americans bundled her into a jeep and hurried her back to the town of Diekirch and into the high school, which served as a command post.

There another American officer wearing a red shoulder patch that looked a little like a square-cut bucket questioned Elise at length. Although the officer was calmer than the soldiers in Vianden, there was no doubt that what she had to say highly interested him. So much so, in fact, that he too declined her request to be allowed to find her son. She was soon in the cab of a truck that took her farther west, to the town of Wiltz and another headquarters that appeared to be even bigger and more important than the one in Diekirch.

Elise Delé had no way of knowing it, but a report of what she had to say was quickly on its way up the American chain of command. At headquarters of the VIII Corps in the Belgian town of Bastogne, a clerk jotted down an entry in the G-2 (intelligence) journal:

From 28th Div to MONARCH 2, Msg # 60, 142320 Dec 44:
The following is a preliminary interrogation of a Luxembourg woman who has been interrogated by the 28th Inf Div:
The woman reports that she had been given permission to go to Biewels [sic] where her home is to pick up clothes . . . while there a German reconnaissance patrol took her into custody. . . . [En route to Bitburg] she observed many trucks and horse-drawn vehicles, pontons, small boats, and other river-crossing materiel. In addition, she observed many artillery pieces, some of which were horse-drawn and others truck-drawn. She was again interrogated at Bitburg and while in this town she observed many troops in light gray uniform with black collars (SS troops). . . . She escaped at Bitburg . . . [and] went to Vianden where she was picked up and taken across the river . . . 28th Div considers the informant fairly reliable. . . . Woman's condition is highly nervous, [she] having stepped on a trip wire which detonated a mine. . . . Further check and interrogation is continuing and complete report will be submitted as early as possible.

A short time later, a digest of that message was on its way from Bastogne to the Belgian town of Spa, where at fifteen minutes before midnight on December 14, a corporal entered it into the G-2 journal of the First United States Army. The message said much the same as the one that had gone to the VIII Corps except that it erroneously identified the woman as German.

In Wiltz, in the meantime, the Americans provided Elise Delé with food and comfortable accommodations, but the next morning they refused to allow her to return to Vianden and sent her instead to Bastogne, whence they intended sending her on to Spa. As it turned out, she was destined to spend a long time in Bastogne—most of it taking refuge in a cellar.

BOOK

I

PLANS AND PREPARATIONS

CHAPTER ONE

The Decision, the Setting, and the Plan

By late summer of 1944, few other than a megalomaniac such as Adolf Hitler could have discerned any hope for the beleaguered National Socialist state that Hitler called the Third Reich. Like other German rulers before him, the Führer faced the dilemma of fighting a two-front war, east and west, however much he had tried to avoid it. After conquering France, he had attempted to lure the British into a separate peace; when that failed, he launched what was meant to be a lightning campaign of annihilation against the *Untermenschen* (subhumans) of Russia, whereupon, having "knocked from Britannia's hand the last 'continental sword' at Britain's disposal," he could effectively deal with the British. Yet that strategy too had foundered, on the reef of Russian nationalism and in the sea of Russia's vast expanses.

By late summer of 1944, the Allied armies that had come ashore on June 6 in Normandy and on August 15 in southern France controlled almost all of France, Belgium, and Luxembourg and stood little more than fifty miles from the Ruhr industrial region, whose mines, smelters, and factories were vital to the survival of the German war machine. In Italy, other Allied armies were close to breaking into the Po valley not far from the southern frontier of the Reich; and in the East, during the course of the summer, the Red Army had driven four hundred miles from deep inside White Russia to the Vistula River across from the Polish capital of Warsaw, an advance that conquered half of Poland and put Russian soldiers virtually on the frontier of East Prussia. Red Army troops had been in the Romanian capital of Bucharest for nearly a fortnight and were almost at the gates of the Bulgarian capital of Sofia. Their advances had forced German withdrawal from Greece and had precipitated the kind of defection of Germany's allies that had presaged collapse in World War I. Italy had long since given in and become a battleground; Bulgaria and Romania had defected, with Finland about to follow; and only the presence of German divisions kept Hungary from doing the same.

In five years of war the German armed forces had lost almost three and three-quarters of a million men, the elite of German manpower. Essential raw materials from Russia, the Balkans, Finland, and France were no longer to be had, and neutral Sweden was becoming increasingly reluctant to provide its iron ore to a nation that appeared about to collapse. Thousand-plane raids by Allied bombers on German cities had become commonplace.

Yet Adolf Hitler still saw hope. Or professed that he did.

For all the immense losses in battle, Germany had close to ten million men in uniform, including seven and a half million in the army and another ground combat force, a kind of Praetorian guard of the Nazi Party, the *Waffen-Schutzstaffel*, or SS. There were still others who could be committed to the fight: heretofore-deferred students, men with less than crippling physical defects, nonessential government workers, convalescents from the hospitals, sailors and airmen turned into foot soldiers, new classes made available for the draft simply by extending the age limit at both ends of the induction spectrum (to run from sixteen to sixty).

Nor was there concern, as there had been in 1918, about collapse of the home front. The police state had eliminated the internal Red threat—or at least driven it underground—so that not once during the war years had the ugly noise of street demonstrations reached Hitler's ears. And so ruthlessly had he dealt with the cabal of army officers who tried to kill him—for those most deeply involved, death by hanging on meat hooks, with motion-picture cameras recording the agony—that the chance of a recrudescent opposition was remote. So, too, the air raids and the demand of his enemies for unconditional surrender had cemented the will of the German people.

However damaging the thousand-plane raids, they had failed to prevent German industry from maintaining a remarkably high rate of production. Indeed, not until the late fall of 1944 was German production to reach a wartime peak. Smaller industries had been dispersed to the countryside or moved to the East, where the Russians had few big bombers. A new decree would put workers on a sixty-hour week, impressed foreign workers would be driven ever harder, and production of civilian goods would be drastically cut.

By those methods, German industry during the fall of 1944 was to produce a record million and a quarter tons of ammunition, three-quarters of a million rifles, a hundred thousand machine guns, and nine thousand artillery pieces. Only in tanks was production to decline, and that would be partially offset by record production of self-propelled assault guns from factories previously moved beyond the range of Allied bombers to Czechoslovakia. Hitler also put great store by a new weapon of which some models were already appearing: jet-propelled fighter aircraft three times faster than anything flown by Allied pilots. Once the new jets got into action in substantial numbers, Hitler maintained, they would sweep Allied planes from German skies.

What Hitler needed was time.

For all the crises on the Eastern Front, Hitler was still capable of gaining time there simply by utilizing the age-old process of trading it for space. Although Russian penetration onto the soil of the Reich in East Prussia would be a heavy psychological blow, there was nothing in East Prussia absolutely vital to German survival. (As the master strategist Alfred von Schlieffen had put it: Better an enemy in East Prussia than one on the Rhine.) At the Vistula the Red Army was still three hundred miles from any really critical objective, such as the capital, Berlin, or the coal fields and industry of Silesia. In any case the current Russian offensive had run its course, supply lines too taut to support another great lunge forward until well into the winter.

The Western Front was another matter, for there the Allied armies threatened the vital Ruhr. Yet hope Hitler could see on the Western Front as well. Like the Russians, the Allies had outrun their supply lines, and by ordering diehard holdouts in the French and Belgian ports even as the German armies fell back toward the frontier, he had ensured that for some time to come the Allies would still have to base their supplies on the Normandy beaches or on ports far from the front. There was also the factor of the border fortifications on the western frontier, the combination of concrete antitank obstacles (dragon's teeth), pillboxes, and bunkers known to the German soldier as *Westwall,* and to the Allied soldier as the Siegfried Line. No matter how dated those defenses, Hitler maintained that concrete in any form lent impetus to the defense; and besides, the terrain along the frontier was forbidding.

Space in the East, fortifications and inhospitable terrain in the West thus spelled time, but in the final accounting, time alone was not enough. To stand beleaguered on the defensive while his enemies gradually strangled him was no solution. He had to go over to the offensive, strike a blow that would change everything, prove decisive.

There was no hope for such a decisive blow in the East. The number of new and refitted divisions Hitler could muster for an offensive would simply be swallowed by the great distances and ingested by the Red Army's multitudes. Besides, there was no chance there for a separate peace, for Hitler saw Germany as the last bulwark against the forces of unholy communism, with which he could never traffic. By way of Japan, there had been indications that the Russian dictator, Joseph Stalin, might be willing to parley, but Hitler forbade any dickering with the *Untermenschen.* "Probing the Soviet attitude," he wrote the wife of his foreign minister, Joachim von Ribbentrop, "is like touching a glowing stove to find out if it's hot."

The situation in the West was a different matter. Not only were the distances shorter, the strategic objectives within acceptable range, and the opposing forces far less overwhelming in numbers. Hitler also saw a real possibility of inducing the Allies, for all their proud decrees about unconditional surrender, to accept a separate peace.

Never in history, as he perceived it, had war produced such strange bedfellows as the Western democracies and the Soviet Union. "Ultra-capitalist states on one side," he would tell his generals on the eve of his big offensive, "ultra-Marxist states on the other; on one side a dying empire—Britain; on the other side a colony, the United States, waiting to claim its inheritance." Each of the three, he said, was determined "either to cheat the others out of something or get something out of it." A great victory on the Western Front, Hitler declared, would "bring down this artificial coalition with a crash."

It was absurd for Anglo-American armies to fight a war which, if Germany were defeated, would allow the mucky fingers of communism to grub about in western Europe. Impossible strains among such strange bedfellows would surely develop, and already Hitler thought he detected them, including some in the Anglo-American alliance.

If he could destroy the British and Canadian armies, Britain would be unable to replace its losses, and Canada would hardly be inclined to send another contingent to the slaughter. In which case, would the United States be willing to continue the absurd fight alone? It was obvious that the survival of the United States of America itself was not at stake: And the enemy in the Pacific, Japan—not Germany—had sullied American honor at Pearl Harbor. If a catastrophic blow to the Allied armies should precipitate a separate peace, that would enable Hitler to turn a still powerful army and all Germany's resources to putting an end to the Red menace, thus fulfilling his ambition to destroy communism and the pagan Russian hordes utterly, to level Moscow and Leningrad, blotting their names forever from geography and history alike.

Had not Frederick the Great—who among all the military leaders of history was Hitler's idol, whose maxims were always on the tip of the Führer's tongue to silence the pessimist, invoke new sacrifice, or justify cruel discipline, and whose portrait hung behind the desk in Hitler's study in the Reichschancellery—faced vastly superior forces converging on his kingdom in the Seven Years' War? And had not Frederick, by engaging and defeating his enemies one by one, hung on until the historical accident of the death of the empress Elizabeth of Russia brought to the throne one of Frederick's admirers, Peter III, which split the coalition opposing him? Under intense adversity, would the unholy alliance of capitalism and bolshevism hold up any better? With the British and Canadian armies wiped out, would it not become obvious to the American people that their sons were dying to impose on western Europe the dictatorship of the proletariat?

As early as the last day of July, 1944, when the Allied armies were about to break out of their Normandy beachhead, Hitler, who to that point had adamantly refused to sanction any withdrawal—and replaced his commander-in-chief in the West, Field Marshal Gerd von Rundstedt, for proposing it—admitted to a few intimates that eventual withdrawal to the West Wall might be the only recourse. That would mean, in time, an offensive mounted from behind the protection of the West Wall, a decision which Hitler revealed to a select group on August 19. He planned, he said, to launch an offensive on the Western Front at the beginning of November when heavy fog and rain—poor campaigning weather—traditionally came to northwestern Europe, weather that would seriously interfere with the operations of the Allied air forces.

Not quite a fortnight later, on September 1, Hitler called to the *Wolfschanze* the man he had so recently removed from command, Gerd von Rundstedt, and asked him to return as commander-in-chief in the West. A wizened, venerable old soldier (he was almost seventy), von Rundstedt was to most Germans the paragon of all that was good and right about the German Officer Corps. Hitler disliked him intensely, partly because he was such an obvious exemplar of that elite corps with its plumy elegance, whose officers, Hitler knew, saw him in his role as supreme military commander as an imposter, and partly because Hitler also knew that in private conversations von Rundstedt referred to him mockingly by his rank in the Great War as "the Corporal." On the other hand, after having been relieved in France, von Rundstedt had demonstrated his loyalty by presiding over a Court of Honor to expel those officers associated with the attempt on the Führer's life. Besides, Hitler needed a proud figurehead around which the troops might rally. He needed, too, someone whose presence as commander-in-chief might lull Allied commanders, who would expect that such an experienced and capable old soldier would conduct his campaign according to accepted canons of the military art.

At the meeting in the *Wolfschanze*, Hitler treated von Rundstedt "with unwonted diffidence and respect," while the old soldier "sat there motionless and monosyllabic," but as a loyal German, von Rundstedt agreed to serve. He was to defend for as long as possible in front of the West Wall, then fall back on the fortifications for the decisive battle. Everything depended on that battle, Hitler stressed, for under the conditions existing in the Third Reich, there was insufficient strength to mount an offensive.

Having thus deceived his commander-in-chief, Hitler set about creating the conditions for his offensive. To his minister of propaganda, Josef Goebbels, he gave the assignment of combing the country for enough untapped manpower to create twenty-five new divisions, while others might later be culled from Finland and Norway. To assure von Rundstedt's holding the line, he accorded the Western Front priority on tanks coming off the assembly lines; but to create an armored force to

form the steel heart of the offensive, he ordered the four SS panzer divisions then fighting in the West to be pulled from the line and refitted,
without telling von Rundstedt why. To control the armor, he created a
new headquarters, the Sixth Panzer Army,* commanded by a hard-drink-
ing old crony from the early, street-brawling days of the Nazi Party, SS-
Obergruppenführer Josef ("Sepp") Dietrich.

Although von Rundstedt appealed for reinforcements from the new
formations, Hitler refused all but minimal help; for as he had anticipated,
the Allied armies had outrun their supply lines and would soon grind to a
halt. There was a spasmodic climax: an attempt with three airborne divisions to gain bridgeheads over the canals and sprawling rivers of the
Netherlands, including the Lower Rhine, and turn the flank of the West
Wall; but when that failed, the Supreme Allied Commander, General
Dwight D. Eisenhower, had no recourse for a time but to accept a slow,
grinding battle of attrition.

As Hitler began more detailed planning for his offensive, one factor
remained constant—the goal of destroying the British and Canadian armies, which were located in the far north, mostly in the Netherlands.
Although the British had seized the great Belgian port of Antwerp, German troops upon Hitler's specific order still held onto the banks of the
Schelde Estuary, which connects the port with the North Sea, and
thereby denied Allied ships the use of the harbor. Yet it could be expected that Antwerp would eventually be opened and serve as the principal port for Allied supplies. Since a drive to Antwerp would not only
deny the Allies the port but also trap the British and Canadian armies,
Antwerp was a strategic objective of the first order.

That objective ruled out launching the offensive against the Allied
south wing, for from the Vosges Mountains of Alsace or the hills of Lorraine in northeastern France the route to Antwerp was too long. The
shortest distance—no more than sixty miles—was in the north, along
the boundary between the American and British armies north of the old
Carolingian capital of Aachen, but there the multiple rivers and canals
posed serious obstacles to tanks. That left the Ardennes, a region that
had long fascinated Hitler, where German armies had attacked with
tremendous success in 1914 and again, at Hitler's personal instigation,
in 1940.†

At that point, Hitler had no way of knowing how strong the Allied
line might be in the Ardennes by the time his offensive was ready. Indeed, even as he reached his decision, there was considerable concern
about a drive by a corps of the American First Army through the Ar-

---

*Although Hitler sometimes referred to that headquarters as the Sixth SS Panzer Army, it
would officially be accorded the honorific only in the spring of 1945.
†But not also, as is often erroneously remarked, in 1870. That advance was from the Saar-
Palatinate through the Wissembourg Gap into Alsace.

dennes and into the contiguous region inside Germany known as the Eifel. There two American infantry divisions had crossed the frontier and penetrated a thinly fortified sector of the West Wall near and astride a high ridgeline, the Schnee Eifel, while a few miles to the south an armored division had crossed Luxembourg, penetrated the West Wall, and headed for the crossroads town of Bitburg. Not until September 17 were hastily assembled troops able to halt the drive at the Schnee Eifel, and even then the Americans retained control of the ridge. Only four days later would German pressure force the armored division to abandon its thrust on Bitburg and retire into Luxembourg.

On the other hand, Hitler might well expect that Allied commanders in 1944 would view the Ardennes much as their predecessors had in 1914 and 1940, as being too compartmented and too heavily forested to accommodate a major offensive. The Supreme Allied Commander in World War I, Marshal Ferdinand Foch, had called the Ardennes "an almost impenetrable massif," and one of his generals, Charles Lanrezac, reputedly said: "If you go into that death-trap of the Ardennes, you will never come out." If Dwight D. Eisenhower in 1944 held a similar view, he too would accord little credibility to the possibility of a German thrust through the Ardennes, so that an attack there could be expected to hit a weak point in the Allied line.

Some days before Hitler made his dramatic announcement at the *Wolfschanze* on September 16, he had directed his plans and operations officer, General Jodl, to study the possibility of an offensive in the Ardennes, and he himself had pored over the results. Opposite the Ardennes, inside Germany, dense forests in the Eifel region provided a ready cloak for the assembly of an attacking force; and however restrictive the terrain, German armies had demonstrated in 1940 that mobile forces could negotiate the Ardennes swiftly.

From the frontier, the route through the Ardennes to the strategic objective of Antwerp was little more than a hundred miles as the Messerschmitt flew, and a drive to Antwerp through the Ardennes would trap not only the British and Canadians but also the American First and Ninth Armies around Aachen—fully half the Allied forces on the Continent—a prize as alluring as that gained in the dash to the sea in 1940. Any coalition that lost half its field strength would surely collapse. At the very least the offensive would eliminate the immediate threat to the Ruhr, thus enabling Hitler to draw on the Western Front for troops to meet the next big lunge by the Red Army.

Although Hitler was aware that he could muster no such power as he had employed in 1940, particularly in the air, he saw methods of overcoming that. It would certainly be November before the new and refitted divisions were ready, and by choosing a period of prolonged bad weather, he would assure that his panzer divisions were well on the way to Antwerp before clearing weather enabled the Allied planes to operate. So, too, he expected to be in Antwerp (it would take a mere week to get there, he said) before Eisenhower could mount a major riposte, for Eisenhower first would have to determine the extent of the offensive, and in responding to such a strategic threat to forces of three nationalities— so Hitler reasoned—the armies of a democratic alliance would require decision at the political level. That too would take time.

At the *Wolfschanze* on September 25, Hitler spelled out in more detail what he had in mind. The artillery preparation was to be massive, followed by infantry assault to achieve a swift penetration and enable a first wave of panzer divisions to begin a rapid drive to seize bridgeheads over the Meuse River, a major military obstacle defining the western and northern reaches of the Ardennes. Quick seizure of bridgeheads over the Meuse was essential for continuing the thrust to Antwerp. At that point, a second wave of panzer divisions was to be committed, while infantry divisions followed and peeled off north and south to protect the flanks of the penetration.

The *Schwerpunkt* (main effort) of the offensive was to be delivered by the four SS panzer divisions of the Sixth Panzer Army, a manifestation of Hitler's faith in the loyalty and ability of the SS units, which even as late as the fall of 1944 were made up in large measure of volunteers. (Naming the SS for the *Schwerpunkt* was also a slap at the army, whose officers had tried to kill him.) The main effort was to be supported by army panzer divisions under another recently created headquarters, the Fifth Panzer Army, commanded by a successful and trusted general brought from the Eastern Front, Hasso von Manteuffel; while infantry divisions under the Seventh Army, commanded by General der Panzertruppen Erich Brandenberger, were to protect the south flank of the penetration. The offensive would require a minimum of thirty divisions, a third of them armored, and Hitler expected the Luftwaffe to support the offensive with more than a thousand planes.

While charging Jodl and his operations staff with devising a detailed plan of operations, the Führer also ordered them to draw up a comprehensive cover and deception plan; for, as Hitler emphasized, secrecy was basic to the plan. Everybody let in on the plan, including clerks and typists, was to sign a pledge of secrecy upon pain of death. Field commanders, including Field Marshal von Rundstedt himself, who was to be the overall commander, were to be brought in only as time, detailed planning, and assembly of forces required.

Hitler may have forgotten that he himself had already been less than discreet about his intentions when, three weeks earlier, on September 4, the Japanese ambassador to Berlin, Baron Hiroshi Oshima, had called at the *Wolfschanze* in company with the German foreign minister, von Ribbentrop, for another of what had come to be periodic conferences. Probably because Japan was Nazi Germany's only ally with muscle, Hitler had long been candid with the Japanese ambassador, yet as the defeats in the field multiplied, he had become uncharacteristically defensive.

When Oshima expressed some concern about the perils facing Germany, Hitler assured him that he still had ample resources for restoring the situation.

> When the current replenishment of the air forces is completed—said Hitler—and the new army of more than a million men, which is now being organized, is ready, I intend to combine the new units with units to be withdrawn from all possible areas and to open a large-scale offensive in the West.

The news astounded Oshima. When? he asked. To which Hitler replied: "After the beginning of November."

A few days later, Baron Oshima reported the conversation to his government in Tokyo where, as in Berlin, nobody was aware that since mid-1941 the United States had been intercepting and decrypting Japanese diplomatic wireless (radio) traffic, a process known by the code-name MAGIC. By means of MAGIC, Oshima's report that Hitler was planning "a large-scale offensive in the West" to start sometime "after the beginning of November" was on the desks of intelligence officers in the Pentagon in Washington almost as soon as it reached the desks of the foreign office in Tokyo.

In Julius Caesar's time, the Ardennes region of what was to become Belgium and Luxembourg constituted the most extensive forest in all Gaul; but over the centuries, as the region passed under the control of one ruler after another, including Charlemagne, much of the land was cleared by agriculture and animal husbandry, so that by the start of the twentieth century only about half of it was still wooded. The most extensive stands that remained were in the east, close to the borders with Germany, almost all of them coniferous, stately firs harvested from time to time for timber, then replanted in orderly rows.

Between the two world wars the Ardennes became a haven for tourists, its countryside dotted with picturesque villages with narrow streets and here and there abbeys and castles, or the ruins of them, a place where tourists partook of the region's renowned venison, wild boar, and marvelously succulent cured ham. A westward extension of the high plateau of the Eifel, so deeply etched through the centuries by serpentine streams that it appears to be less plateau than mountains, the Ardennes presents a rugged face scarred by deep gorges and twisting stream valleys. It has the shape of a big isosceles triangle with an eighty-mile base along the frontiers, extending from an ill-defined point in the north near the Belgian town of Eupen (fourteen miles south of Aachen) to the vicinity of Luxembourg City, the capital of Luxembourg, in the south. Although part of the region protrudes westward beyond the Meuse River, so deep and broad is the cut of the Meuse that for military purposes the region can be said to end there, some sixty miles from the base of the triangle.

As the most extensive stands of forest are close to the German frontier, so too is the most forbidding terrain. For almost the entire length of the frontier, the terrain poses a major obstacle to military movement.

In the north rises the Hautes Fagnes (High Marshes), in effect a ridgeline whose crest marks the highest elevation in the Ardennes (2,777 feet). It is an almost trackless moor covered with forest or peat bogs, the latter providing the source of medicinal waters for the thermal baths of Aachen and of Spa, the Belgian resort whose name long ago passed into English as a synonym for thermal watering places.

Southeast of the Hautes Fagnes, in Belgium's easternmost reaches, dense forests mark the frontier to the vicinity of a road center, St. Vith. Because American troops who attacked there in September held onto the nearby prominent feature just inside Germany, the Schnee Eifel, that ridgeline in the fall of 1944 constituted a part of the obstacles to be faced by any attacker from the east.

The little Our River, which rises in eastern Belgium, becomes a major obstacle as it crosses into Luxembourg, where it marks the frontier and flows through a gorge whose almost clifflike sides are covered with firs. The roads leading west toil upward to a high ridge which American troops, familiar with the Shenandoah Mountains of Virginia, called the "Skyline Drive." Behind that ridge lies another gorge cut by the Clerve and Sûre Rivers. After absorbing the waters of the Clerve, the Sûre drains southeastward to the frontier, where it absorbs the Our and forms the border with Germany (the Germans call it the Sauer) until it joins the Moselle River northeast of Luxembourg City at roughly the southern terminus of the Ardennes.

Along the entire stretch of the Ardennes near the frontier, only one corridor at all conducive to military movement exists, a sector some five miles wide beginning at the northern end of the Schnee Eifel. Taking its name from the village of Losheim, just inside Germany, it is known as the Losheim Gap. The term "gap" is relative, for even though it lacks extensive forest along the frontier, a belt of woodland two miles thick has to be crossed before gaining more open country a few miles deeper into Belgium, and the hills are steep, the valleys deep. Nevertheless, as the Kaiser's armies entered the Ardennes in 1914, a force heavy in horse cavalry pushed through the Losheim Gap in advance of the main body and quickly reached the Meuse. The same thing happened in 1940 when a panzer division under an obscure general, Erwin Rommel, passed through the Losheim Gap to gain the Meuse by nightfall on the third day of attack.

From the high ground along the frontier the terrain slopes gradually downward toward the west, losing some of its convulsive nature except for tortuous meanderings of streams through deep valleys in the extreme north and south. In the center, around Bastogne, the true nature of the region as a plateau is readily discernible, no more of an obstacle to military movement than is always present in a gently rolling landscape. Beyond the little Ourthe River, roughly two-thirds of the distance to the Meuse, the same rolling hills prevail, for the most part, the rest of the way to the Meuse. The Meuse itself follows a south-north course before swinging northeast at the town of Namur. After washing the industrial wastes of one of Belgium's principal cities, Liège, it finally resumes a northward course through the Netherlands to the sea.

The roadnet for such a pastoral region was extensive, although the roads usually twisted and turned in conformity with the stream valleys and in many places passed through thick forests or sharp defiles where they might be readily blocked. As an added obstacle, at every crossroads or road junction stood either a closely knit town or village or at least a collection of stone farm buildings, which almost always constricted the width of the road. Although most of the railroads had been put back into service for military traffic by late 1944, the repairs ended some miles short of the German frontier, and without connections to lines inside Germany, railroads in the Ardennes would have little bearing on the fighting to come.

Not so across the frontier in the Eifel. There, in countryside even more heavily forested than that of the Ardennes, the Germans in preparing for the onset of World War I had constructed a number of rail lines feeding from marshalling yards at Cologne in the north and Koblenz in the south and from other crossings of the Rhine River in between. Since the distance between the Rhine and the western frontier is only about forty-five miles, trains moving along those spur lines have relatively short hauls. The lines lead to towns that are also road centers: Bitburg in the south; Prüm and Gerolstein in the shadow of the Schnee Eifel; and Gemünd and Schleiden in the north. Although the sole arterial line runs along the valley of the Moselle on the southern periphery of the region to the old Roman outpost town of Trier, spur lines lead north from marshalling yards at Trier to Bitburg and the other road centers within the Eifel.

There are no cities in the Eifel and few in the Ardennes. Except for Liège on the northern periphery and Luxembourg City and Arlon to the south, there are only the picturesque villages and an occasional town with a population of two to five thousand. Yet those towns pull together a number of roads and then release them in various directions. So St. Vith near the frontier, Malmédy in the north, and Bastogne and Houffalize in the center would become critical features in any military advance.

The people of Luxembourg reflect a fierce independence befitting a region that has been a separate entity, although not always autonomous, since the tenth century. Of Germanic descent, they speak a dialect, Letzemburgesch, which to the American soldier sounded like German.

The population of the Belgian Ardennes is composed primarily of French-speaking Walloons, but in the northeastern corner most are ethnic Germans, reflecting the fact that before the Treaty of Versailles, the easternmost province, Eupen-et-Malmédy, had long been a part of Germany. In late 1944, in such border towns as Eupen and St. Vith, shop signs were in old German script and almost all the people spoke German. Many—even a majority—might be loyal to Belgium, but the American soldier did not trust them. Almost every home had a photograph of a father or son in German uniform, and few American soldiers bothered to reason that ethnic Germans in regions conquered by the German Army had no choice but to serve the Fatherland.

Situated not far from the North Sea, the Ardennes has a harsh, wet climate, with rainfall averaging 35 to 40 inches a year. Some of the heaviest rains come in November and early December, so saturating the soil that any movement off the roads is difficult; and with them comes the fog or mist that sometimes fails to clear before midday and reappears again in late afternoon. Snow sometimes accumulates up to a foot in depth—deeper in the drifts—and cold, raw winds sweep the heights.

As American intelligence officers would consistently note, the Ardennes presented little attraction for anybody except (they might have added) a tourist. Surely it proffered nothing of strategic importance to German armies forced back on their homeland in desperate straits.

Yet that was reckoning without the fact that by way of the Ardennes it was just over a hundred miles, as the Messerschmitt flew, to Antwerp.

Although Hitler had specifically directed that his offensive be made through the Ardennes, Alfred Jodl and his planning staff studied various alternatives, eventually settling on five, only one of which involved that part of the Ardennes which Hitler had specified, and even that failed to name Antwerp as the objective. As proposed by the planners, that operation would consist of two prongs: a main effort passing through the Ardennes and then turning north, where it would meet a thrust launched from the vicinity of Aachen—a shallow double envelopment which could be expected to trap not the British and Canadians but just the American First and Ninth Armies. Proposing the alternative plans may have been simply a logical procedure for men with General Staff–trained minds; on the other hand, the plan for a shallow envelopment may have been a subtle attempt by Jodl to modify Hitler's grandiose scheme, to reduce it to the dimensions a trained and experienced military planner such as Jodl recognized as within German capabilities.

If such a ploy it was, it failed. The effect was not to lessen Hitler's ambition but to increase it, for he liked the idea of supplementing the

Ardennes thrust with a second prong originating near Aachen; and on Antwerp as an objective, he was immovable.

As finally worked out by Jodl and his staff, the offensive was to be launched along a sixty-mile front from Monschau in the north, some twenty miles southeast of Aachen, whence led the only lateral road across the Hautes Fagnes, to the medieval town of Echternach in the south, downstream from the juncture of the Our and Sûre Rivers. Sepp Dietrich's Sixth Panzer Army, comprising the *Schwerpunkt*, was to attack along a front extending from Monschau to a point within the Losheim Gap, with a panzer division debouching from the gap to follow the path of Erwin Rommel's division in 1940, bypassing opposition, and quickly gaining and crossing the Meuse. (Jodl dug from the archives a copy of the 1940 plan.) Dietrich was to pass south of Liège, cross the Meuse upstream from the city, then head for Antwerp while anchoring his northern flank on the considerable obstacle of the Albert Canal.

On Dietrich's left, General von Manteuffel's Fifth Panzer Army was to attack through and south of St. Vith, cross the Skyline Drive, jump the Meuse upstream from the bend in the river at Namur, and then wheel northwest, bypassing the Belgian capital, Brussels, and protecting the Sixth Panzer Army's southern flank. Erich Brandenberger's Seventh Army, made up primarily of infantry, was to attack on either side of Echternach, and while advancing westward was to peel off divisions to block to the south.

Forty-eight hours after the offensive in the Ardennes began, the Fifteenth Army, composed of infantry reinforced by a panzer and a *Panzergrenadier* (mechanized) division, was to be prepared to attack from the vicinity of Aachen. The basic objective was to pin down American divisions and prevent them from reinforcing in the Ardennes; but if all went well, the attack was to continue southward to reach the Meuse near Liège and trap the Americans around Aachen. Although Hitler spoke grandly of yet another attack in Alsace to tie down American divisions there, plans for that attack, like that by the Fifteenth Army, remained indefinite. So did a suggestion that Army Group H, which defended in the Netherlands, might drive through the Canadians to link with the Sixth Panzer Army at Antwerp, thereby constricting the trap around the Allied armies. Nobody said anything about how the Germans were going to liquidate the more than a million Allied troops who would presumably be trapped.

Accepting the plan, Hitler continued his deception by giving it a codename, Operation *WACHT AM RHEIN* (Watch on the Rhine), designed to provide a defensive rather than offensive connotation. The next day the head of the *OKW*, Field Marshal Wilhelm Keitel, issued a general order to all commanders on the Western Front asserting that for the mo-

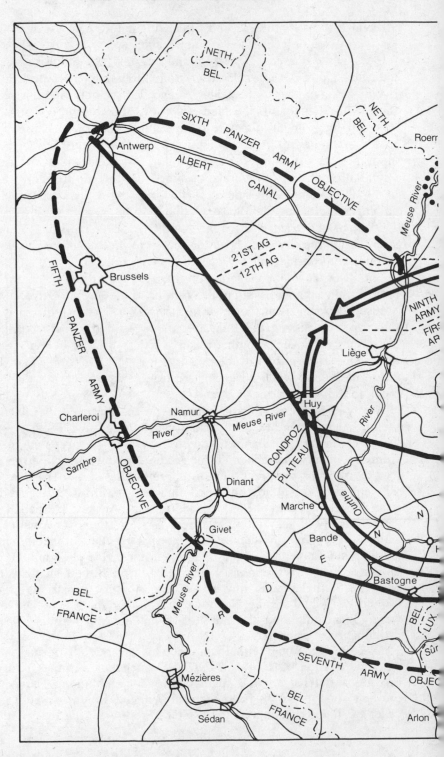

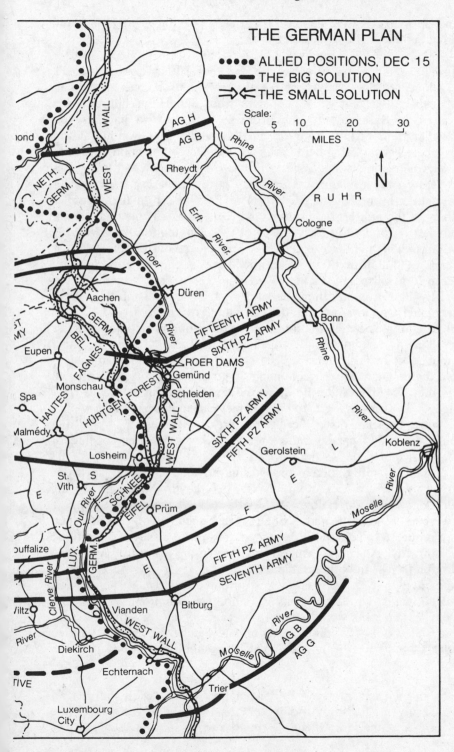

THE GERMAN PLAN

•••••• ALLIED POSITIONS, DEC 15
— — — THE BIG SOLUTION
⇒⇐ THE SMALL SOLUTION

Scale:
0   5   10   20   30
        MILES

N

AG H
AG B

Rhine
River

RUHR

mond

NETH.
GERM.
WEST
WALL

Rheydt

Erft

River

Cologne

Roer

Aachen   Düren

GERM.

River

Bonn

FIFTEENTH ARMY

SIXTH PZ ARMY

Rhine

EST
MY

Eupen

BEL.

FAGNES

ROER DAMS

Gemünd

River

Monschau

Schleiden

Spa

HAUTES

HÜRTGEN FOREST

SIXTH PZ ARMY

Malmédy

WEST WALL

FIFTH PZ ARMY

Gerolstein

Koblenz

L

Losheim

St.
Vith   S

SCHNEE

Our River

EIFEL

Prüm

E

F

Moselle River

E

ouffalize

LUX.

GERM.

Clerve River

I

E

FIFTH PZ ARMY

SEVENTH ARMY

Viltz

Vianden

Bitburg

WEST WALL

River

AG B

AG G

River

Diekirch

Moselle

TIVE

Echternach

Trier

Luxembourg
City

ment no German offensive was possible, that the saving of the Fatherland depended upon unyielding defense.

During the afternoon of the same day that Hitler approved Jodl's plan, October 21, he received at the *Wolfschanze* someone he held in special respect, a blond giant of a man who, like Hitler himself, was Austrian: Otto Skorzeny. It was Skorzeny who in 1943 had rescued Hitler's friend and erstwhile ally, Benito Mussolini, from a mountaintop in Italy where he was being held in the wake of Italy's defection; and only a few days before the visit to the *Wolfschanze*, Skorzeny had led a successful raid on the seat of the Hungarian government in the Citadel in Budapest to prevent Hungary's defection. Possibly as an indication of something of the Führer's admiration and trust, Skorzeny may have been the only person briefed in early stages of the planning for *WACHT AM RHEIN* from whom Hitler exacted no written pledge of secrecy.

Wearing the uniform of an SS major, Skorzeny entered Hitler's study and received a warm handshake. "Well done, Skorzeny!" exclaimed the Führer. He had promoted him, he said, to Obersturmbannführer (lieutenant colonel) and awarded him the German Cross in Gold.

After hearing Skorzeny's account of the operation in Budapest, Hitler began a lengthy recitation of *WACHT AM RHEIN*. "One of the most important tasks in this offensive," he said at last, "will be entrusted to you and the units under your command." Skorzeny was to form a special brigade that would precede the attacking armies and seize bridges over the Meuse. The troops were to wear American uniforms, which would enable small detachments to "cause the greatest confusion" by cutting communications and passing false orders. "I know," Hitler concluded, "you will do your best."

A few days later, Skorzeny was dismayed to come upon an order signed by a senior officer of the *OKW*. At the top were the words: "Secret Commando Operations." Units throughout the army, the order read, were to "send in the names of all English-speaking officers and men who are prepared to voluntarily apply for transfer for a special operation" under Skorzeny. All units were also to turn in any captured American vehicles, uniforms, and other equipment.

Skorzeny was livid. Such a widely distributed order was bound to fall into Allied hands. To Skorzeny his operation was compromised from the start, but his superiors would agree to no cancellation lest Hitler himself learn of the gaffe. "It's idiotic," commented Reichsführer-SS Heinrich Himmler, "but it has been done. We cannot hold up your operation now."

Scion of an aristocratic old Prussian family from Mecklenburg, Karl Rudolf Gerd von Rundstedt disdained Nazism and Adolf Hitler. Yet like many another of the senior generals anxious to circumvent the Treaty of

Versailles and restore German military strength, he had pledged himself to the *Fahneneid*, the ancient oath passed down from the Teuton knights requiring every soldier to obey the Emperor unto death, an oath with which Hitler, like the kaisers before him, bound his officers.

Having enlisted in an infantry regiment as an ensign at the age of seventeen, von Rundstedt by the fall of 1944 had been soldiering for more than half a century. Joining the General Staff after the Great War, he had worked hard to dispel the paralysis that the machine gun had engendered, insisting on increased fire support and mobility for the infantryman. Although he believed fervently in the supremacy of the state over the army and despised politics, in 1938 he so disagreed with Hitler's policies—which he considered to be leading to full-scale war at a time when Germany was grossly unprepared for it—that in company with a dozen other top generals he resigned. With the invasion of Poland in 1939, he nevertheless accepted a recall to duty and commanded army groups with distinction in Poland, Belgium, France, and Russia before becoming commander-in-chief on the Western Front.

Von Rundstedt was, to many of his compatriots, the prototype of the Prussian officer, stiff, formal, utterly dedicated to his profession. Some saw him as "excessively modest, too reserved," a man who "led a simple life and was indifferent to money or possessions," one who was "affable to inferiors" and "extravagantly polite to women." He smoked too much and enjoyed an occasional drink. Like most German officers of his time, he had learned the language of the courts; he liked the French and when in France, "chose to speak in French with visiting dignitaries."

By the fall of 1944, von Rundstedt's advanced age was showing. The skin on his face was wrinkled like crepe paper, and even as Hitler recalled him once again to duty, he had been taking the cure at Bad Tölz. Establishing his headquarters in Ziegenberg Castle, in the Taunus Hills east of the Rhine near Bad Nauheim, he made few visits to the troops, a practice far different from the old days. Many of his associates saw the noble old man for what Hitler intended him to be—a figurehead.

Among them was one of his three army group commanders, Field Marshal Walter Model of Army Group B, who was destined to be the tactical commander for Hitler's ambitious offensive. A man of humble origins, in no sense of the nobility, Model had early tied his career to Hitler's. As von Manteuffel put it: "His manner was rough, and his methods were not always acceptable in the higher quarters of the German Army, but they were both to Hitler's liking." He was one of only a few among the thoroughly cowed officer corps who still dared to speak his mind to the Führer and occasionally carried his point. Stockily built, Model found it hard to look the stiff, formal Prussian, but with the aid of a monocle, he managed it.

In Russia, Model had established a reputation as a "lion of defense," and in August, 1944, when Hitler needed a lion of defense on the Western Front, he made him commander of Army Group B and at the same time, briefly, commander-in-chief in the West. To some, Model appeared not only ardent but fanatical. When a commander in Normandy insisted that the remnants of his division be pulled from the line for a rest, Model said: "My dear Bayerlein, in the East our divisions take their rest in the front line. And that's how things are going to be done here in the future." And when Model learned that Field Marshal Friedrich Paulus had surrendered to the Russians at Stalingrad, he was appalled. "A field marshal," said Model, "does not become a prisoner. Such a thing is just not possible." (He would eventually take his own life rather than surrender.)

Sixteen years von Rundstedt's junior, Model treated the old man with due respect, but he ran his army group with little reference to Ziegenberg Castle. Von Rundstedt, for his part, conscious of the peculiar position in which Hitler had placed him (about the only authority left to him, he was to note, was "to change the guards in front of my own headquarters"), accepted Model's deference as his due but made no effort to interfere with Model's trading on his prerogative as bearer of a marshal's baton to deal directly with Hitler. Relations between the two were "correct but not cordial."

As October passed its midpoint, von Rundstedt at Ziegenberg Castle and Model at his headquarters in a former sanitarium for alcoholics near Krefeld, northeast of Aachen, received summonses to send their chiefs of staff to the *Wolfschanze*. Neither knew why, but both assumed for a taste of Hitler's choler, for the Americans had finally captured Aachen, the first German city of appreciable size to fall. Von Rundstedt nevertheless instructed his chief of staff, General der Kavellerie Siegfried Westphal, to seize the occasion to press his repeated unanswered pleas for reinforcements to prevent a breakthrough beyond Aachen to the Rhine.

Arriving at the *Wolfschanze* on the morning of October 22, General Westphal and Model's chief of staff, General der Infanterie Hans Krebs, first had to sign the pledge required of those let in on Hitler's secret: To guard it or be shot. Following the Führer's daily situation conference, all but fifteen of the participants were asked to leave, whereupon Hitler himself took the floor. To the surprise of Westphal and Krebs, he said not a word about the fall of Aachen. Instead, he unfolded an astounding plan: *WACHT AM RHEIN.*

As Westphal and Krebs listened in stunned silence, Hitler outlined the forces that were to be employed. There were to be thirty divisions: eighteen infantry and twelve panzer or *Panzergrenadier* divisions. To Westphal and Krebs, such largesse was heady news, but their enthusiasm cooled when Hitler told them that von Rundstedt's command would have to provide nine of the divisions, including six panzer divisions. Those would have to be pulled from the line in sufficient time to be refitted with replacements in men and equipment before the offensive. For general fire support, there were to be five motorized antiaircraft regiments, twelve artillery corps, and ten rocket projector brigades. There would also be additional general support troops, such as engineer and signal battalions, and the Luftwaffe was to provide at least 1,500 planes, including 100 of the new jets.

Although Hitler said that he wanted to attack early in November, it would be impossible to assemble all the troops by that time, so that the offensive was to begin on November 25, a date, his meteorologists had promised him, that assured inclement weather with poor visibility to conceal the buildup. In the meantime, he intoned, there was to be no let-up in the defensive battle, yet not one of the formations intended for *WACHT AM RHEIN* was to be committed to bolster the defense. With that, Hitler dismissed his generals, ordering them to return to their headquarters and draw up detailed operational plans.

When Westphal reported back to his chief, von Rundstedt was appalled. While admitting that Hitler's choice of the Ardennes for the offensive represented "a stroke of genius," he saw the plan as far too ambitious. As he was to put it later, "all, absolutely all conditions for the possible success of such an offensive were lacking." Even to hold on along the frontier while the men and supplies for the offensive were readied would be problem enough, for there were clear indications that the Americans were preparing new drives in both north and south, the First and Ninth Armies in the Aachen sector and the Third Army in Lorraine. If the German armies should reach and cross the Meuse, which von Rundstedt seriously doubted they could do, both flanks would be highly vulnerable; and to expect to advance all the way to Antwerp without encountering a major counterblow was crediting the Allied commanders with a languor and a dearth of resources they had yet to exhibit. About all Hitler's plan could be expected to achieve, in von Rundstedt's view, was a salient or bulge in the line, costly and indecisive, like those Ludendorff had forged during the Great War.

It was with considerable relief that von Rundstedt learned that Hitler's fair-haired boy, Walter Model, shared his misgivings. "This plan," Model said, when General Krebs presented it to him, "hasn't got a damned leg to stand on."

Without consulting each other, both commanders adopted the same method of trying to whittle down the grandiose scope of their Führer's plan by devising an alternative more in keeping with the reality of German resources. To both, Antwerp as an objective was out of the question. Von Rundstedt proposed a drive through the Ardennes to cross the Meuse between Liège and the bend at Namur for a juncture with a simultaneous attack launched from the north, thereby trapping the Americans around Aachen in a double encirclement. Model proposed instead a single encirclement with all the forces committed through the Ardennes, then driving north.

On October 27, von Rundstedt went to Model's headquarters to discuss Hitler's proposal and his and Model's suggested alternatives. The three army commanders who were to be involved—Sepp Dietrich, Hasso von Manteuffel, and Erich Brandenberger—also participated in what was their first initiation into the secret brotherhood in which they were to serve as potentates. After several hours of discussion, von Rundstedt directed Model to resolve the differences between their two plans. Conscious that the two commanders needed to present a united front if they were to have any power of persuasion with Hitler, Model prepared a final plan almost identical to von Rundstedt's.

As the commander of the Fifth Panzer Army, General von Manteuffel, put it, it was a matter of the "grand slam"—Hitler's plan—versus the "little slam"—von Rundstedt and Model's. (Von Manteuffel was an avid fan of contract bridge.) In time, the generals came to refer to them as the "Big Solution" and the "Small Solution." Since the Small Solution was virtually the same as that proposed earlier by General Jodl, its chances of getting past the Führer were predictably thin.

That failed to deter the old soldier and the ardent young Nazi commander from joining forces to do battle. In the first place, they sensed an ally in Alfred Jodl. In the second, although well aware that Hitler as supreme dictator had debased, broken, and even executed many of their compatriots while they and most of the others in the officer corps had looked on benignly, they were also aware that there were few field marshals of their stature and proven loyalty left to do the Führer's bidding. They were in a position to risk the Führer's fury.

They sensed Jodl's thinking when on November 2 a courier brought a written copy of Hitler's plan with a covering note from Jodl. In the note, Jodl wrote that Antwerp as the objective was "unalterable," but he added, "although from a strictly technical standpoint, it appears to be disproportionate to our available forces." He continued: "In our present situation, however, we must not shrink from staking everything on one card."

The next day, when Jodl followed up the written instructions by visiting Model's headquarters, he faced the combined protests of von Rundstedt, Model, and von Manteuffel—whom von Rundstedt had personally invited to be present. Von Manteuffel—as von Rundstedt intended—carried the weight of the argument, a fresh voice in the controversy. "General," he said to Jodl, "I think under your plan that we can reach the Meuse—but only if certain conditions are met." Every man, every tank, every plane, every gallon of gasoline, every round of ammunition as promised by Hitler would have to be on hand when the movement began, and the attack by the Seventh Army to protect the south flank would have to be materially strengthened. As von Manteuffel's statement inferred, he saw no possibility of an advance beyond the Meuse on Antwerp.

Jodl had thus heard another advocate of the Small Solution, but he had his orders. The Führer's plan, he replied, was "irrevocable." A week later, on November 10, the issue appeared to be closed when Hitler signed a formal operational directive specifying an offensive exactly as he himself had originally envisaged it.

Yet the man with over a half century of honorable service in the uniform of his country continued to protest, striving to spare the troops whose trust he bore the sure debacle he envisaged if Hitler persisted in his plan. Along with Model, von Rundstedt proposed yet another Small Solution: an attack from the north with some of the divisions scheduled for *WACHT AM RHEIN* into the northern flank of the American Ninth Army, which on November 16, along with the First Army, had begun a major offensive in the Aachen sector but had failed to achieve a breakthrough. That posed a chance to destroy some fourteen American divisions, which would have been weakened by their offensive, thereby setting up conditions conducive to a big German offensive to be mounted later on the order of the one Hitler had in mind.

Hitler saw through the gambit. "Preparations for an improvisation," Jodl replied in Hitler's name, "will not be made." Yet when it became apparent that the target date of November 25 was unrealistic and Hitler agreed to delay until December 10, von Rundstedt vowed to continue to try to effect a change. He saw a chance when Hitler called him and Model to a conference at the Reichschancellery in Berlin on December 2. Pleading preoccupation at the front, he sent his chief of staff, Westphal, to represent him, a form of protest not to be lost on Hitler; but he also sent two whom he hoped still might persuade Hitler to reconsider: von Manteuffel, who obviously stood high in the Führer's regard or he would not have brought him as a relatively junior general from the Eastern Front for such a major assignment in the offensive; and Hitler's old crony, Sepp Dietrich.

Nobody, including von Rundstedt, thought highly of Dietrich, but he was a favorite of Hitler's, and to his military colleagues he had already made clear the derision he felt for the job assigned him and the Sixth Panzer Army:

> All Hitler wants me to do is to cross a river, capture Brussels, and then go on and take Antwerp! And all this in the worst time of the year through the Ardennes where the snow is waist deep and there isn't room to deploy four tanks abreast let alone armored divisions! Where it doesn't get light until eight and it's dark again at four and with re-formed divisions made up chiefly of kids and sick old men—and at Christmas!

Von Manteuffel and Dietrich constituted von Rundstedt's big artillery, his fortress guns detailed to fire a final, decisive salvo. Yet the rounds fell short. Dietrich failed to speak at all, and von Manteuffel achieved only some minor changes, mostly of a tactical nature. Hitler nevertheless threw a sop to his faithful Nazi, Walter Model, by changing the codename to that used by Model in his plan for a Small Solution: *HERBSTNEBEL* (Autumn Mist). That was all.

What the field commanders failed to recognize—or to accept—was the desperation that lay behind Hitler's plan, a desperation reinforced by the Führer's megalomania and his distrust of his generals, whose ineptitude and disloyalty, he was convinced, were responsible for bringing Nazi Germany to the brink of destruction. From the day his generals tried to kill him, he had been convinced that he and he alone could save Germany, that some divine providence had spared him for that role, and that the way to do it was to exploit the dissensions he deemed inherent in the misalliance of his adversaries and to "continue this battle until, as Frederick the Great said, one of our damned enemies gets too tired to fight any more."

Destroying ten or fourteen or twenty American divisions around Aachen would not do it. He had to create conditions in which one nation could blame the other for the debacle that engulfed its troops, to sow mutual distrust, to deal such a blow that the people of Britain, Canada, and America would demand that their leaders bring their boys home. Surely, at some point—at that point—the Western democracies would realize that it was Adolf Hitler who had long been fighting their battle for them, the battle to keep the pagan Communist hordes out of civilized Europe.

Hardly had Hitler dismissed the four commanders on December 2 than he ordered preparations to begin for a move from the *Wolfschanze* to underground concrete chambers amid the wooded Taunus Hills little more than a mile and a half up a winding road from Ziegenberg Castle. From there—the *Adlerhorst* (Eagle's Aerie)—he personally would direct his grand offensive, as he had done from the same place for his triumph in 1940, under a design little altered from the one he had had in mind that day in September when he had slapped the map on his desk and first announced his decision: "Here, out of the Ardennes, with the objective, Antwerp!"

CHAPTER TWO

The Deception and the Intelligence Apparatus

Adolf Hitler and his intelligence chiefs considered that they had the most secure enciphering system for wireless communications in the world. It was impossible, they were convinced, to break its codes.

It consisted of a machine that looked like a bulky portable typewriter in a varnished wooden case measuring 7 by 11 by 13 inches. The letters on the keyboard were arranged like those on a typewriter, but there the similarity ended. There were no numbers or punctuation marks, and on a deck behind the keyboard, the twenty-six letters of the alphabet appeared in alphabetical order in three rows. When an operator punched a letter on the keyboard, one of the letters on the deck lit up but never the letter the operator punched; and if the operator punched the same letter another time, yet another different letter lit up.

As the operator worked, an assistant wrote down the letters as they appeared on the deck, and what he put down looked to be merely a jumbled collection of meaningless letters. The assistant then transmitted the jumble of letters in Morse code by wireless. Equipped with the same type of machine, the operator for whom the message was intended typed the jumbled letters onto his keyboard, whereupon they appeared on the deck in the same order in which the original operator had typed them and spelled out a meaningful message.

Like almost any transmission by wireless, the jumbled message could be intercepted. Yet it could be decoded, in theory, only by someone equipped with the same type of machine, and even then the decoder would have to know what particular setting the sender had used on his machine that day, for there were literally millions of possible settings. By late 1944, the Germans were changing the settings at least once a day, and there were different settings each day for each of the services that

39

used the machine: the army, the navy, Luftwaffe, SS, Gestapo, and such civilian services as the *Reichsbahn* (German State Railroads).

The machine was known as the Enigma, named after the *Enigma Variations* in which the British composer Sir Edward Elgar described his friends in musical cipher. A Dutchman invented and patented it in 1919, but when he was unable to build a marketable machine, he sold the patents to a German engineer and inventor, Artur Scherbius. As successfully designed and developed by Scherbius, the machine was intended for commercial use to protect business secrets. By the time Hitler came to power in the early 1930s, the Enigma had been vastly improved. The reforming and expanding Wehrmacht adopted the machine as its basic enciphering device and continued to increase its capabilities and complexity while retaining its compactness and portability, which made it ideal for use in the field.

As Hitler began his preparations for *WACHT AM RHEIN*, it was apparent that somehow the Western Allies were obtaining German secrets, but so convinced was Hitler of the security of the Enigma—and as a dictator, so obsessed about traitors—that he attributed the leaks to some spy within his inner circle of advisers. Yet for something so vital as *WACHT AM RHEIN*, he could take no chances. He forbade transmission by telephone, telegraph, or wireless of any information that could in any way be connected with the offensive, including the supposedly deceptive codename he himself had coined. Anything dealing specifically and identifiably with the offensive had to be transmitted by officer courier, the Gestapo on his tail; and all else had to be justified by another codename, *ABWEHRSCHLACHT IM WESTEN* (Defensive Battle in the West), which was already in use for the fighting around Aachen.

To justify to foe and uninitiated friend alike the massing of men and supplies, the German command pointed to the imminent American offensive to be launched from positions near Aachen toward the Rhine and the industrial region of the Ruhr. The first paragraph of almost every movement order contained the words "in preparation for the anticipated enemy offensive." When the Sixth Panzer Army, for example, had completed its organization and its SS panzer divisions were refitted and prepared to move west of the Rhine, an entry in the War Diary of von Rundstedt's headquarters (known as *Oberbefehlshaber WEST*, or *OB WEST*) read: ". . . there can be no doubt that the enemy will commit maximum strength and maximum matériel to force the breakthrough to the Rhine. Our own defensive measures must be attuned to this. . . . Hence the Commander-in-Chief WEST will order the transfer of Sixth Panzer Army to the OB WEST theater on 7 November. . . ."

Then the Sixth Panzer Army moved, not into the Eifel whence it was to launch its attack, but onto the open plain near Cologne at which the Americans were to aim their November offensive; and there the Germans intentionally bungled their security, parading their preparations before the eager eyes of Allied intelligence. Not until three days before the offensive was to begin would the Sixth Panzer Army make the move of some thirty-five miles into the Eifel, and then only at night.

For the Fifth Panzer Army, which had seen its first commitment in control of a few panzer brigades in a futile counterattack in September against the Third U.S. Army's south flank in Lorraine, there was the problem of disengaging from the front in Lorraine and moving north for some apparent purpose not associated with the offensive. Since such a move could hardly escape Allied notice, von Manteuffel's headquarters appeared in late October in the line near Aachen, where it assumed command of two corps already committed. The Americans were obviously going to employ armor in their coming offensive; it was wholly logical for the Germans to oppose them with a headquarters schooled in the use of armor.

The shift of the Fifth Panzer Army served an added purpose in that it halved the sector then held by General Brandenberger's Seventh Army, which to that point had been responsible for both the Aachen sector and the Eifel. Von Manteuffel's entry into the line left Brandenberger responsible only for the Eifel, a reality to which Allied intelligence was long accustomed. Who might suspect that the Seventh Army had a new mission?

As the target date for the German offensive approached, it became essential to pull von Manteuffel and his headquarters back from the line in preparation. To mislead the enemy, the headquarters of the Fifteenth Army, which had been responsible for the sector opposite the British in the Netherlands, secretly relieved the headquarters of the Fifth Panzer Army and assumed an alias, *Gruppe von Manteuffel*, in the process getting into a proper position for mounting an attack in support of *WACHT AM RHEIN*. In the Netherlands, the headquarters of the Twenty-fifth Army, which took over from the Fifteenth Army, called itself the Fifteenth Army, while a bogus headquarters calling itself the Twenty-fifth Army pretended through false wireless traffic to be assembling west of the Rhine near the assembly area of the Sixth Panzer Army. When pulled from the line, von Manteuffel and his headquarters hid behind the innocuous name of *Feldjägerkommando z.b.V.* (Military Police Command for Special Assignment).

There was less complexity in relieving Field Marshal Model and his Army Group B of some of their responsibilities, for any intelligence officer would recognize that in commanding a front extending from the North Sea across the Netherlands into Germany and thence south almost to the Moselle River—more than 150 airline miles—Army Group B was overextended. Without unusual provisions for secrecy, a new headquarters, Army Group H, assumed control of the front in the Netherlands, leaving Model responsible only for the Aachen sector and—most importantly—the Ardennes-Eifel.

*   *   *

As those shifts took place, Field Marshal von Rundstedt's problem was to halt the American attacks, or at least to contain them sufficiently so that they would not jeopardize the German offensive. There was some space to be traded for time in the south, where on November 8 the Third U.S. Army began to attack from the vicinity of Metz aimed at gaining the German frontier and penetrating the West Wall in the Saar-Palatinate, that corner of Germany lying in the angle between the Moselle and the Rhine. Nor was there particular concern about the First French and Seventh U.S. Armies that had driven up from southern France, for even should those armies get through the forbidding Vosges Mountains, the broad moat of the Rhine would bar the way. The critical sector was in the north.

There von Rundstedt gained some respite in that once the Allied attempt to jump the canals and rivers of the Netherlands with airborne troops failed, the British commander, Field Marshal Sir Bernard L. Montgomery, had to turn his attention to clearing the seaward approaches to Antwerp. Failing to clear the sixty-mile approach to Antwerp from the sea when the port fell without a fight in early September had been one of the more serious tactical lapses of the campaign, and Hitler's order to build a strong defense along the banks of the Schelde Estuary a most prescient reaction.

As the Allied attack began in mid-October, the Germans opened dikes that industrious Dutchmen through the years had erected to keep out an antagonistic North Sea, and it took the Allied soldiers—mostly Canadians—almost a month to battle through mud, muck, and flood before the last German soldier fell back from the banks of the Schelde. Even then minesweepers required three weeks to cleanse the channel, so that not until November 28—three months after the British took Antwerp—was the first supply ship to drop anchor in the port.

Around Aachen, von Rundstedt had neither leeway nor respite. As the First and Ninth U.S. Armies began their offensive there on November 16, the jump-off line was in some places no more than six miles from the little Roer River, the only obstacle remaining before the open plain comprising the last twenty-five miles to Cologne and the Rhine.

To be sure, the American command had aided von Rundstedt during October and early November by attacking with inadequate strength to clear a vast stretch of woodland south and southeast of Aachen, an extension of the forests of the Ardennes and the Eifel known as the Hürtgen Forest. As the Americans attacked, they ignored the fact that on the upper reaches of the Roer River the forest concealed two big dams, the Schwammenauel and the Urftalsperre. Should the Germans blow the dams, they could produce a single destructive flood wave in downstream lowlands where the Roer marks the start of the Cologne Plain, or by calculatedly releasing the waters slowly, a flood that might last for two weeks or more to prevent crossings of the Roer or trap any force that had jumped the river.

Those dams thus were of critical importance to von Rundstedt, for even should his defense falter in front of the Roer, he could still gain at least two weeks on behalf of Hitler's offensive by manipulating the waters of the river. Conversely—and unknown to von Rundstedt—the American command was belatedly to become aware of the importance of the dams. Just three days before the German offensive began, the First Army was to mount an attack to seize them, an event that was to have an effect on Hitler's offensive far out of proportion to the number of American troops involved.

In the end, the German defense held. It was a remarkable achievement, accomplished as part of a resurgence that some Germans, in remembrance of World War I's Miracle of the Marne, referred to as the "Miracle of the West." Lashed by Hitler's ambition and regimented by the rigorous discipline of the police state, Nazi Germany and its army during the fall of 1944 demonstrated a resilience not unlike that of the giant Antaeus in Greek mythology, who regained his strength whenever he touched Mother Earth.

During the last half of 1944, the German Army refitted the skeletons of thirty-five divisions that had been stripped of flesh on either the Eastern or Western Front and built fifteen new divisions. With a salaam to the German people (*das Volk*), Hitler traded on national pride by calling them *Volksgrenadier* (people's infantry) divisions, an honorific previously reserved for infantry divisions that had performed with extraordinary ability and valor.

In selecting that name, Hitler drew an unanticipated intelligence bonus. Only recently he had issued a public decree calling for a levy of the rank and file of the German people to flock to the defense of the Fatherland. He called that force the *Volksturm*, and both the Supreme Allied Commander, General Eisenhower, and the commander of the 12th Army Group, Lt. Gen. Omar N. Bradley, who was responsible for the Ardennes, confused the two, seriously underestimating the capabilities of what they termed the new *Volksturm* divisions.

Some of the new and refitted divisions had to be returned to the Eastern Front and some helped hold the line in the West, but others joined the four SS panzer divisions as part of the Führer's strategic reserve. Without Hitler's knowledge, von Rundstedt used a few of the divisions to relieve others temporarily so that they might be pulled from the line for quick rehabilitation before the offensive, but few of them stayed in the line for long. With Hitler's approval, some of the newly formed general support artillery and rocket units were employed at some length, in the process eating into ammunition reserves stockpiled for the Ardennes but at the same time gaining battle experience. So, too, ten to twenty thousand men who might have helped fill the strategic reserve had to fight as individual replacements in the defensive battles. Yet in the end, of twenty-eight divisions specifically designated for the offensive, only an SS panzer division, a *Volksgrenadier* division, and two panzer divisions were never able to get out of the line for the refitting necessary for participating in the offensive. The process of getting the others ready, plus two reinforced brigades, nevertheless pushed forward Hitler's target date another five days, to December 15.

That the soldiers making up the new and refitted divisions bore little resemblance to the well-trained, thoroughly indoctrinated, splendidly equipped troops that had swept out of the Ardennes in 1940 was obvious to all. It was only with moderate hyperbole that General Dietrich, who had a reputation for grousing, complained of divisions filled mainly with "kids and sick old men"; but even though under the new decrees sixteen- and seventeen-year-olds were liable for service, few below the age of seventeen were actually assigned to army combat units, although there were many under that age and even younger who served as volunteers or quasi-volunteers in the SS divisions. So, too, even though men through age sixty were theoretically liable for service, few of anywhere near that age were actually called, and seldom did a man over forty-five find himself in a combat unit. The principal weakness of the troops was a lack of training for those men only recently called up and for the thousands upon thousands hastily transferred from the navy, the Luftwaffe, and rear echelon assignments. Yet the numbers at least—a total of more than 250,000 for the first wave—were impressive, and there was still a residue of considerable size of combat veterans and hard-nosed noncommissioned officers to infuse flint into the new and refitted formations.

In equipment, the most serious shortage was motor transport. Even the best-equipped divisions had no more than 80 percent of the vehicles called for under their tables of equipment, and one *Panzergrenadier* division had sixty different types of motor vehicle. Providing spare parts for such a fleet would have been a nightmare, but there were few spare parts for vehicles in any case. Another panzer division, the *Panzer Lehr* (so named because it had originally been a training demonstration division), had only enough half-tracks to transport one of its *Panzergrenadier* battalions; the others had to use trucks or bicycles.

On the other hand, the amount of artillery the army managed to amass was impressive. There were nine of the new artillery units, known as *Volksartillerie* corps, each equipped with fifty to a hundred pieces, and seven of the new rocket, or *Volkswerfer*, brigades, each with more than a hundred rocket projectors; and both types of units were fully motorized. The difficulty with those and other corps and army artillery units was that the guns were of varying caliber and even manufacture—there were, for example, more than a smattering of French and Russian pieces. That complicated ammunition supply. The total of all general support artillery and rockets was 1,900 pieces, a powerful array, and that was in addition to artillery organic to the divisions. Much of the divisional artillery was horse-drawn, but the German soldier had long been accustomed to that.

While the Eastern Front and other parts of the Western Front starved through the fall for want of armored vehicles, Hitler allotted to Army Group B and the strategic reserve 2,168 tanks and assault guns (German statistics always lumped the two together). Most of the assault guns were a lightly armored, self-propelled, high-velocity 75mm. piece, which was an effective antitank weapon as well as a superb weapon for supporting infantry in the attack.

Since some 700 tanks and assault guns had to be held, at least for a time, with the Fifteenth Army for the projected attack in support of *WACHT AM RHEIN*, that left approximately 970 for the opening wave of the offensive and around 450 for the follow-up force. Hitler's beloved SS panzer divisions had priority on those. The total numbers available fell short of the 2,500 that had participated in the Blitzkrieg through the Ardennes in 1940, but it was a powerful force nevertheless.

As expected, it was in tactical aircraft that the Germans were weakest. Despite Hitler's early prediction of at least 1,500 fighter-bombers, the commander of the Luftwaffe, Reichsmarshal Hermann Goering, could promise only a thousand and was actually able to deliver only a few more than that, and those in driblets except on one spectacular occasion. That figure bore no comparison with the two thousand available in 1940.

Those forces were all that Hitler could muster for an offensive in the sixth winter of the war. Given the condition of the Third Reich by that time and the vast superiority in men, weapons, and equipment of its enemies, to assemble even that much while still fighting on two fronts was an exceptional achievement. That the numbers were no fewer was attributable in large measure to the defensive stand of a presumably defeated German soldier who had regained his strength upon touching Mother Earth, and to the performance of his leaders, the old soldier Gerd von Rundstedt and the lion of defense Walter Model.

Transporting the attack divisions to their assembly areas and accumulating and transporting the ammunition, rations, and fuel that they would need in the opening days of the offensive was another remarkable achievement. By Hitler's order, the assignment went to General Jodl's chief, the head of the *OKW*, Field Marshal Keitel. Under a head of state less unorthodox than Adolf Hitler, an officer in Keitel's post would have been in the forefront of the strategic and tactical planning for the offensive; but Hitler himself had all but usurped that role, and Keitel was not a man to press his prerogatives with his Führer. (Some made a pun on his name, calling him *Lakaitel*, meaning "Little Lackey.") Yet the head of the *OKW* was an efficient administrator, and he brought to the logistical assembly for the Ardennes that not unworthy talent.

The workhorse of the buildup was the *Reichsbahn*. By 1944 the state railroad system was so thoroughly tied in with the Wehrmacht that it was in essence an adjunct of the military. Ever since the swift and massive concentration for the Franco-Prussian War in 1870, which had astounded the world, the German General Staff had looked to the railroads as the basic instrument for strategic concentration, which explained the creation of spur lines into the Eifel before the Great War. In preparation for the Ardennes offensive, engineers reinforced the pillars and supports of all the rail bridges over the Rhine lest some lucky hit by an Allied bomb should send an entire bridge crashing into the water.

A lucky hit it probably would have been, for Allied airmen considered bridges of any kind to be one of the most difficult of targets. Ringed with multiple batteries of flak guns, the bridges over the Rhine were doubly inaccessible, and throughout the fall of 1944, as official priority focused on other targets, Allied airmen made no concentrated effort to take out the Rhine bridges.

For the trains themselves and the marshalling yards there was no such immunity. Yet darkness and rain or a sky heavily overcast were all elements basic to Hitler's entire plan. Each train carried its own antiaircraft guns, which tended to keep the *jabos*, as the Germans called Allied fighter-bombers, at high and usually ineffective altitudes; and the cabs of locomotives had long been plated with armor to cut down on casualties from strafing among engine crews. For the final run across the Rhine into the Eifel, engineers timed their movement for an overnight trip, and if anything untoward intervened, there were a number of tunnels in which to hide until bad weather or nightfall came again. Laborers were so organized for quick repairs at the marshalling yards that seldom, even after a heavy air attack, did bomb damage interfere with operations for longer than forty-eight hours. The fact that through much of the fall Allied airmen made German oil production rather than transportation their number one target also helped the railroads.

The campaign against oil had its effect, although not nearly to the extent that Allied analysts perceived. By stringent rationing, by drawing on stockpiles, and by taking extraordinary measures to bring oil from Hungary (except for synthetic oil plants, the only source remaining), Keitel managed to meet the anticipated requirement of not quite five million gallons, but about half of that would still be on the east bank of the Rhine as the offensive began. There was no intent to rely on captured Allied stocks of gasoline—any such stocks would be a bonus—for sufficient supplies were on hand. Yet that was not to say that there would be no problems in getting fuel forward to the troops who needed it.

In trying to keep the offensive secret, moving the German fighter aircraft westward, however few in numbers, posed a special problem. Any careful observer of the air scene during the early weeks of autumn could have discerned that the Luftwaffe had virtually abandoned close air support for the Western Front in order to concentrate its available aircraft for defense of the industrial centers. Since Allied air attacks against the homeland continued without let-up, any move of fighter aircraft back to the West would appear to be odd. In the event, Reichsmarshal Goering failed in his attempt at secrecy, but how the Allied command reacted to the failure was another matter.

Toward the end of the first week of December, corps commanders who were to be involved in the offensive were at last let in on Hitler's secret, and on the 10th, the division commanders. Late the next afternoon, von Rundstedt, Model, von Manteuffel, and approximately half the corps and division commanders (the others were to be called in the next day) gathered at von Rundstedt's headquarters in Ziegenberg Castle. Ordered to divest themselves of their side arms and briefcases, they boarded a bus, which began a circuitous tour in darkness and rain through the countryside lasting half an hour and ending finally at the *Adlerhorst*, actually a three-minute ride from Ziegenberg Castle.

Dismounting, the generals passed between a double row of armed SS guards, standing rigidly to attention, and descended into a deep underground conference room. As they sat down around a large square table, an SS guard assumed a position behind each chair, glowering with a ferocity that made at least one of the generals, Fritz Bayerlein, fear even to reach for his handkerchief.

Entering with Keitel and Jodl, Hitler took a seat at a long narrow table at one end of the room. He was, von Manteuffel noted, "a broken man, with an unhealthy color, a caved-in appearance." His hands trembled, and to von Manteuffel, who had seen him less than a fortnight earlier, he appeared to have aged even in that short time: "His body seemed still more decrepit, and he was a man grown old, completely overworked and tired."

Yet when Hitler began to speak, his appearance changed. A kind of fire came into his eyes, and as his speech gathered momentum, he grew ever more forceful. For more than two hours he harangued his audience, speaking extemporaneously of German history, German destiny, the glories of Frederick the Great, the absolute necessity for *Lebensraum* for the great German people, the virtues of what he called the preventive war he had begun in 1939, the necessity for a nation to display not only toughness, stubbornness, and endurance but also daring, "to make it clear to the enemy that whatever he would do he will never be able to count on a capitulation, never, never, never!" People had doubted him over Austria, over Czechoslovakia, over France, but he had triumphed, and he would triumph again. It was then that he began his tirade about the strange bedfellows the war had aligned against Germany—"Ultra-capitalist states on one side; ultra-Marxist states on the other." A great victory would "bring down this artificial coalition with a crash."

The next day, as Hitler briefed his second set of generals, he granted his commanders a minor concession: a twenty-four-hour postponement for last-minute preparations at the front. *Null-Tag* (literally, Zero Day), the jump-off date, was set for Saturday, December 16. There was to be no further postponement.

The naming of a final target date set in motion a plan previously worked out in meticulous detail for a three-day movement to forward assembly areas, a plan based in large measure on the secrecy achieved in preparation for a number of German offensives in World War I and for the concentration in 1940. Although the troops were to be told nothing of what they were about to do until the night before the jump-off, the *Volksdeutsch* (ethnic Germans from Alsace and other border regions) had already been combed from the combat units lest they go over to the enemy with some small but revealing knowledge of what was to come. Troops marched only by night, taking cover by day in forests and cooking only with charcoal fires. Special security detachments prowled in search of anybody who violated camouflage discipline. Patrolling on the existing front line was restricted to the most trusted soldiers lest somebody who had observed more than he should might desert. There was to be no increase in artillery fires above the norm.

Those troops not already in the line—a few of the *Volksgrenadier* divisions had already relieved units not scheduled for the offensive—were allowed to advance at first no closer than twelve miles toward the front, then to move progressively forward over the last two nights, first to a line six miles from the front, then two. In concern for the noise created by tanks and in recognition of their mobility, the restraining line for panzer units was farther to the rear. On the last two nights, as tanks and artillery pressed closer to the front, troops covered the roads with straw to muffle the sound, and planes flew low over American positions in hope of concealing or at least disguising the noise.

To eighteen-year-old Pvt. Helmut Stiegeler, the snow and the cold reminded him that Christmas was only a short time away. "Our thoughts wandered to our folks back home, no one talked to the other, and silently we marched along, unaware of what was ahead of us." The next night, the night before the jump-off, Stiegeler and other men of the 12th Volksgrenadier Division's engineer battalion at last learned what they were to do. After an evening meal of sweet rice with plums, "each group was given a bottle of booze, and off we went."

Meanwhile, for all the efforts at secrecy, there had been yet another lapse in security at the governmental level when on November 15 the Japanese ambassador, Baron Oshima, was invited to confer with Foreign Minister von Ribbentrop at Sonnenberg, sixty miles east of Berlin. During the conversation, Oshima asked about the offensive in the West that

Hitler had told him would be launched sometime "after the beginning of November." Had there been any change in that intention?

Although von Ribbentrop was evasive about details and timing, he confirmed that Hitler still intended to take the offensive in the West. Then, again, it might be the East.

There were some, suggested Baron Oshima, who believed that the big German offensive in 1918 had hastened Germany's defeat, that without it the war might have ended differently. Would it not be "a wise plan for Germany to fight a war of attrition?"

"Absolutely not!" rejoined von Ribbentrop. "The Chancellor believes that we cannot win this war by defense alone and has reiterated his intention of taking the offensive right to the bitter end."

In reporting that conversation to Tokyo, Baron Oshima sneered at the possibility of a German offensive. It was, he said, "one of the instances in which truth from the mouth of a liar reaches the highest pinnacle of deceptiveness"; but a few days later he changed his view. Thinking back to his earlier conversation with Hitler, he notified Tokyo that he believed "we may take at face value" the intent of the German leadership to mount an offensive, for "a Germany whose battle lines have contracted virtually to the old territory of Germany . . . will have no choice but to open a road of blood in one direction or another." And probably, he added, in the West.

As always, those two messages from Oshima to his government were soon on the desks of intelligence officers in the Pentagon.

"He who defends everything," Frederick the Great used to admonish his generals, "defends nothing." During the fall of 1944 the Supreme Allied Commander, General Eisenhower, had sixty-five infantry, airborne, and armored divisions with which to cover a front extending from the North Sea to Switzerland, a distance, not counting local twistings and turnings, of over five hundred miles. Had he divided the front equally among his divisions, each would have been responsible for just over seven miles, which would have constituted a fairly cohesive linear defense. Yet what if the enemy should penetrate the line; where was the reserve to eliminate the penetration? Besides, nobody won wars by defense alone. The problem was how to gain sufficient strength for an attack.

Eisenhower's solution was to concentrate his forces within two sectors where the terrain was most conducive to advance: one concentration south of the Ardennes pointed toward the Saar industrial region; the second, and larger, north of the Ardennes pointed toward the Ruhr. To make those concentrations possible, he employed only minimal forces to defend the other sectors, particularly in Alsace and the Ardennes. Even so, Eisenhower was unable to hold out a reserve.

As the alignment developed, the British 21st Army Group with the

First Canadian and Second British Armies under Field Marshal Montgomery was in the far north, mainly in the Netherlands. To the far south, the 6th Army Group, commanded by Lt. Gen. Jacob L. Devers, had the Seventh U.S. and First French Armies, mainly in Alsace. The American 12th Army Group, under General Bradley, was in the center: the Ninth Army north of Aachen, the First Army around and south of Aachen, and the Third Army in Lorraine.

While the First Army's greatest concentration was in the vicinity of Aachen, its commander, Lt. Gen. Courtney H. Hodges, was also responsible for the Ardennes. The assignment fell in turn primarily to the VIII Corps, which had to cover a front extending from the Losheim Gap in the north to a point southeast of Luxembourg City in the south, a distance of about sixty miles. Since the VIII Corps had only three infantry divisions, that meant a defensive frontage for each division of about twenty miles, more than double the length of front normally assigned a division to defend. In the northern reaches of the Ardennes, from the Losheim Gap to the vicinity of Monschau, the southernmost division of the V Corps held a front of similar length, so that only four divisions were responsible for the entire eighty-mile front through the Ardennes.

The Allied deployment reflected what became known as Eisenhower's "broad front strategy," which was actually nothing more than a version of an age-old, time-tested practice of advancing in parallel columns. Yet to Eisenhower's chief British subordinate, Field Marshal Montgomery, it was anathema. In late summer and through the autumn, Montgomery insisted that the Allied command possessed neither the strength nor the logistical resources to support two major drives into Germany. He wanted the entire front to go on the defensive except in the sector north of the Ardennes, where he wanted to concentrate sufficient strength and sufficient logistical support to launch and sustain a juggernaut all the way to Berlin.

It was a proposal not without reason or merit, but Montgomery—who was inclined to argue his proposals in imperious tones—weakened it by insisting that the entire attacking force, to be composed of British, Canadians, and Americans, be under his command; indeed, that he be designated as overall ground commander for the entire Western Front. To American generals, the proposal appeared to reek of personal ambition, an attempt to usurp a portion of Eisenhower's prerogative as Supreme Commander, a position that had gone to an American for the basic reason that the United States would be furnishing the preponderance of forces. ("Monty's suggestion is simple," Eisenhower confided at one point; "give him everything, which is crazy.")

Yet there were other reasons why Eisenhower turned Montgomery down. There was no way, his logistical planners told him after detailed study, that the existing resources could be reallocated to make it possible to sustain an offensive all the way to Berlin. The basic problem was the lack of ports close to the front, a problem to which Montgomery himself had contributed by failing to clear the banks of the Schelde Estuary once Antwerp fell with its port facilities intact. There was also a possibility that the German armies were less nearly finished than seemed apparent from the overwhelming defeat inflicted on them in France, that they might muster reserves to deal telling blows to any thrust whose flanks would be exposed for several hundred miles. Eisenhower himself had seen, at a place in North Africa called Kasserine Pass, the damage supposedly defeated German forces could wreak.

It was a serious difference of opinion, one replete with rancor. German agents may well have passed some word of it to Berlin, thereby contributing to Hitler's belief that a grand offensive in the West stood a chance of splitting the Anglo-American alliance. Yet for all the rancor, the fact was that it was nothing more than a difference of opinion between a commander and a subordinate, albeit the two senior field commanders of the two principal powers in the Allied coalition; but those were two powers that had achieved a degree of cooperation and coordination never before known in coalition warfare. Although serious differences of opinion and such human failings as national chauvinism and personal antagonism well might recur under the impact of severe adversity at the front, would even the spectacle of the two senior commanders coming to blows be sufficient to wreck such a close-knit coalition?

The exchanges between Eisenhower and Montgomery over strategy and command occurred at a time of heady optimism, an optimism reflected in intelligence reports at every level. In late August, for example, the G-2 at Eisenhower's Supreme Headquarters, Allied Expeditionary Force (SHAEF), Maj. Gen. Kenneth W. D. Strong, had written: "Two and a half months of bitter fighting, culminating for the Germans in a blood-bath big enough even for their extravagant tastes, have brought the end of the war in Europe within sight, almost within reach." It was a view the Supreme Commander himself fully shared. "The defeat of the German armies is complete," he noted a few days later in the course of dictating an office memorandum, "and the only thing now needed . . . is speed."

At headquarters of the First U.S. Army, the G-2, Col. Benjamin A. Dickson, saw political upheaval within Germany or insurrection within the Wehrmacht as likely to hasten the end of the war. The commander of the First Army, General Hodges, had sent General Bradley a bronze bust of Hitler taken from a house in the Belgian border town of Eupen and told the commander of the 12th Army Group that, given ample ammunition and an additional division, the First Army would "deliver the original in thirty days." However much Hodges jested, the incident reflected the prevailing state of mind.

Only one among the G-2s in the senior commands sounded a note of caution. At headquarters of the Third U.S. Army, Col. Oscar W. Koch (pronounced Kotch) remarked that for all the debacle that had befallen the enemy, "his withdrawal, though continuing, has not been a rout or mass collapse." All indications pointed to the fact that the Germans were determined "to wage a last-ditch struggle in the field at all costs." The enemy, he noted, was "playing for time," and weather and terrain would soon be on his side.

Yet Koch's was a lone voice, and despite the stiffening of resistance in the lowlands of the Netherlands, at Aachen, in the Hürtgen Forest, and in the rolling hills of Lorraine, the optimism was slow to dissipate. Meeting in Washington in October, the Allied body charged with directing the conduct of the war, the Combined Chiefs of Staff—made up of the service chiefs of both Britain and the United States—still saw hope of an early victory. They wanted Eisenhower to institute extraordinary measures to assure victory before the year 1944 came to an end: shift the strategic air offensive from all but the most immediately remunerative targets; employ all troops and stockpiles of supplies without regard for withholding reserves; and make use of a heretofore super-secret proximity fuse (VT or POZIT) that exploded an artillery shell by radio impulse in the air just short of the target, thereby sharply increasing the lethal fragmentation effect of the burst.

Eisenhower himself at that point urged caution. The approaches to Antwerp still had to be cleared, he told the U.S. Army's chief of staff, General George C. Marshall, and the port facilities of Antwerp were essential to the final battle. Eisenhower nevertheless saw the possibility of taking the Ruhr before the end of the year or at least of gaining a bridgehead over the Rhine.

Those were the goals of the American offensive that opened near Aachen on November 16, but after almost a month of fighting and a cost to two American armies of 125,000 casualties (killed, wounded, missing, and so-called nonbattle casualties), the American troops were gazing not at the fabled Rhine but at an obscure, flood-threatened Roer only six miles beyond the line from which they had started. Furthermore, they were powerless to cross the little river until somebody got around to doing something about the dams upstream.

The fact that German troops who in September had appeared thoroughly beaten had fought back with such determination and relative success, the Allied commanders attributed to German stubbornness, to blind faith in the Führer, to devotion to the home soil, and, most of all, to the solid generalship of Gerd von Rundstedt. There were other contributing factors: abominable weather, constricted terrain, the West Wall, some few continuing logistical problems on the Allied side. Yet nobody saw in the stalwart German stand any grand design that might threaten the survival of the Allied armies.

Indeed, Allied intelligence officers perceived the heavy fighting as contributing to the possibility of a sudden German collapse. Even before the November offensive began, Eisenhower's G-2, General Strong, noted that the Germans were losing the equivalent of a division every few days and were being forced to shift meager reserves hither and yon as one threat subsided and another arose. "The dwindling fire brigade," wrote Strong, "is switched with increasing rapidity and increasing wear and tear from one fire to another." When the Germans failed to react with a strong counterattack against the American offensive that opened near Aachen on November 16, the First Army's G-2, Colonel Dickson, considered that they had lost any opportunity for a decisive blow and saw the possibility of large-scale surrenders leading to the collapse of the German state.

As late as December 12, only four days before the Germans were destined to emerge from the mists and snows of the Eifel into the Ardennes, the report of the 12th Army Group's G-2, Brig. Gen. Edwin L. Sibert, noted: "It is now certain that attrition is steadily sapping the strength of German forces on the western front and that the crust of defenses is thinner, more brittle and more vulnerable than it appears on G-2 maps or to troops in the line." At about the same time, Field Marshal Montgomery's G-2, a don from Oxford University, Brig. E. T. Williams, was declaring: "The enemy is in a bad way . . . his situation is such that he cannot stage a major offensive operation."

"Gentlemen," Secretary of State Henry L. Stimson reputedly stated in 1929 when abolishing a small State Department–funded cryptanalysis branch known as the Black Chamber, "do not read one another's mail." Yet the remark failed to deter the Signal Intelligence Section of the army's Signal Corps and the navy's Office of Naval Intelligence from trying to read the mail of potential enemies, particularly that of the Japanese, which led to the remarkable achievement of MAGIC. On the other hand, that attention to one aspect of the dirty work of spying failed to carry over into the field of battlefield intelligence.

In the United States Army, seldom did an officer consciously pursue a career in battlefield intelligence. The 12th Army Group's G-2, General Sibert, for example, got into intelligence simply because somebody flagged his file after he served a tour of duty as military attaché in Brazil; and the First Army's G-2, Colonel Dickson, was a reserve officer who when called to active duty in 1940 drew an assignment in intelligence only because he was proficient in French and German. Seldom did G-2s move on to high command; those gems went to chiefs of staff and to plans and operations officers, the G-3s. The G-2 and his counterpart at regimental and battalion level (S-2) held one rank below that of the G-3 or S-3, and before war came, they often drew lowly extra duties such as club officer or command historian.

In the British Army, by contrast, intelligence was a prestigious field.

Eisenhower's G-2, General Strong, for example, planned a role in intelligence from his days as a cadet at the Royal Military Academy at Sandhurst, where he became fluent in French, German, and Italian. Following a prewar tour as an assistant military attaché in Berlin, he headed the German Section of the War Office, then served successively as chief of intelligence of the Home Forces and of Allied Force Headquarters in the Mediterranean.

That was not to say that American intelligence officers were incapable. As with any group of staff officers, their abilities varied; but almost to a man they encountered the antipathy of other members of their staffs arising from the long-established low estate of the intelligence officer. (General Sibert said he often heard the remark: "I wonder what is wrong with him that he is in G-2.") For Colonel Dickson at the First Army's headquarters, the situation was compounded by a personality conflict with a strong-willed chief of staff, Maj. Gen. William B. Kean—who, many said, virtually ran the First Army (the staff called him Captain Bligh)—as well as between himself and the G-3 section.

Benjamin Abbot ("Monk") Dickson got his nickname from childhood playmates in Washington, D.C., who dubbed him "Monkey"; his older brother shortened it to "Monk," calling him that when the two were at West Point, and it stuck. He was a handsome man, over 6 feet, 3 inches tall, angular, mustached; and at thirty-seven years of age he maintained the same weight (190 pounds) at which he had played on the football team at the Military Academy. In the classroom Dickson displayed a photographic memory, a talent that was to serve him well in the profession he eventually entered. He graduated from West Point in one of the accelerated classes during World War I and served in the American Expeditionary Force in Siberia; but after assessing the chances of promotion in the postwar army as poor, he resigned, earned a degree in mechanical engineering from the Massachusetts Institute of Technology, and went into the warehouse business in Philadelphia.

Having maintained a reserve commission, he returned to active duty as a captain in 1940 and soon rose to become a corps G-3 in North Africa, where he gained a reputation as a pessimist, which stuck with him even though events at Kasserine Pass proved his point. He also gained the confidence of his commander, General Bradley, who took him along to England when forming the staff of the First Army; but when Bradley, after the invasion of Normandy, moved up to command the 12th Army Group, a readymade staff was waiting, so that Dickson, Kean, and the others were left behind.

Going beyond the usual resentment of one headquarters for the next senior headquarters, the First Army's staff officers saw their counterparts at the 12th Army Group as Johnny-come-latelys, lacking their own battlefield experience, and some on occasion played on their past association with General Bradley to bypass his staff and deal directly with the general. None resented his counterpart at the 12th Army Group more than did Dickson, for Edwin Sibert was a career artilleryman who had never served in intelligence until to his surprise he was plucked from an artillery command with an infantry division in the United States to become G-2 at headquarters of the European Theater, which was essentially an administrative and logistical headquarters. On the basis of experience in North Africa and Normandy, Dickson viewed Sibert's job—and his rank—as rightfully his. Although Dickson later denied that he held any animosity for Sibert, his contemporaries saw it otherwise; one remarked that he "hated Sibert and the latter reciprocated."

Whether for that reason or for some other, coordination between the G-2 sections of the First Army and the 12th Army Group was minimal. Except when specifically asked, Dickson never visited headquarters of the 12th Army Group, and when he wanted to consult a G-2 at a higher level, he went to Brigadier Williams at headquarters of the 21st Army Group. Under the American staff system, there was no chain of command among intelligence staffs: Dickson served his commander, Sibert his; and even though Dickson served at a subordinate level, Sibert had neither command nor technical jurisdiction over him.

To Monk Dickson's associates in intelligence at higher levels, he was a volatile man, a pessimist, an alarmist. It was sufficient, for example, whenever Dickson learned that the Russians had lost contact with a division on the Eastern Front, for him to list it in the enemy's order of battle in the West. At times he might have several divisions listed in the West that other intelligence officers knew to be elsewhere. They called them "Monk's shrubbery." Although the practice caused no real harm, it contributed to the view of Dickson as an alarmist, a man who sometimes had to be sat on.

At an operational level—army group and below—prisoners of war constituted a basic source of intelligence. American intelligence officers considered themselves particularly adept at gleaning information from German prisoners, for they might employ as interrogators refugee German Jews whose appearance belied their race but whose knowledge of Germany enabled them to gain a prisoner's confidence and ask penetrating questions. Thus the intelligence officers saw no reason to question what they learned from prisoners during much of the fall of 1944, and since most of those who surrendered were dregs, their morale low, the interrogations tended to reinforce the view that Germany would be unable for long to continue the fight. So, too, did the capture of prisoners from such special units as so-called stomach battalions, composed of men with digestive problems who required a special diet. Did not the very existence of those units indicate that the Third Reich was running out of manpower?

In France and Belgium, civilians had also been a basic source of intelligence, but with the crossing of the German border, information from civilians had virtually ceased to exist. It was much the same story with special agents from the Washington-based Office of Strategic Services (OSS), who had found it relatively easy to penetrate the lines in France but who had little success inside Germany.

Furthermore, relations between the First Army's headquarters and the OSS were strained. In Normandy, Colonel Dickson had found the OSS agents to be individualistic, their demands on the army's communications too heavy; and he had convinced General Hodges to kick them out, with the exception of a small section under Capt. Stuyvesant Wainwright that engaged in counterespionage and antisubversion. ("I don't want a man from OSS," Dickson reputedly declared, "nor a dwarf, nor a pygmy, nor a Goddamned soul.") In the office of the OSS detachment at headquarters of the 12th Army Group, some wag placed under a picture of Hitler the caption: "He fools some of the people some of the time but he fools Dickson all of the time."

The strain increased when somebody at the First Army's headquarters wrote a parody of a prisoner-of-war report, allegedly representing an interrogation of Hitler's latrine orderly. Finding it amusing, Captain Wainwright sent it to his OSS superiors at the 12th Army Group, where everybody missed the point and took the parody seriously. An order was soon on the way to the First Army to fly the prisoner back to SHAEF for further questioning, much to the subsequent embarrassment of the OSS.

In the long run, it probably made little difference that the First Army had only one small section of OSS operatives, for those located at headquarters of the 12th Army Group had every license to operate in the First Army's sector and beyond it into enemy territory. Yet not a single OSS agent penetrated the line and entered the Eifel before the enemy's offensive began.

Another basic source of battlefield intelligence was aerial reconnaissance, including that conducted by artillery observation aircraft. Despite many days of inclement weather in the month preceding the German offensive, seldom were all reconnaissance aircraft grounded. During that month of November, the 67th Tactical Reconnaissance Group of the IX Tactical Air Command, which supported the First Army, flew 361 missions, of which two-thirds were considered successful. Yet seldom were missions flown over the region that was to prove critical, the Eifel, for the basic concern was the sector in the north between the Roer River and the Rhine. Although there were many requests for reconnaissance over the Eifel, air officers assigned them low priority, and when weather was marginal, pilots usually elected to fly over the presumably more important region to the north. In the critical last five days before the German attack, pilots of the 67th Tactical Reconnaissance Group flew only three missions over the Eifel, all three on December 14 over Trier.

Partly because a portion of the Eifel lay in the projected zone of advance of the Third Army and partly because airfields of the reconnaissance group of the XIX Tactical Air Command, which supported the Third Army, were better situated than those of the IX Tactical Air Command's reconnaissance group for missions over the Eifel, the commander of the Third Army, Lt. Gen. George S. Patton, Jr., gained approval for pilots of the 10th Tactical Reconnaissance Group to include the Eifel in their coverage. The reports of that group were thus added to the accumulated knowledge of what was going on in the Eifel, as were the reports of the pilots of fighter-bombers flying attack missions and those of two available night fighter squadrons, although neither of those squadrons had more than ten P-61 night fighters, so that their contribution was limited.

At corps and army headquarters, there were Signal Radio Intelligence Companies that constantly monitored the enemy's voice radio communications, usually at division level and below. By that monitoring or by radio directional finding, the companies often picked up the shift of German divisions. Yet German radio security was in general excellent, and those companies discerned "absolutely no indication" of what was about to happen in the Ardennes.

Yet another source of operational intelligence was the front line itself, where outposts day after day looked across at the enemy and where patrols almost every night probed the line. Many an American soldier who gazed out on the Eifel in those days would later recall reports he had submitted that, in his opinion, should have told his superiors that something was afoot; but in most cases he was unaware of the various sieves the information he provided had to pass through. Before ever reaching the First Army, the word he passed back went through S-2s at battalion and regiment and G-2s at division and corps. Each in his turn evaluated the message, reflecting in the process his own preconceptions, his own appreciation of the enemy situation, so that in the end many a front-line soldier's report failed to go much beyond the regimental level, and when it did, it might be deflated by an S-2's or a G-2's observation about it. When on December 12, for example, a front-line regiment reported hearing tanks, the division G-2 noted: "No confirmation, may have been tracked vehicles."

At the optimum, operational intelligence worked in two ways: up and down. Subordinate units passed up such information as they gleaned and deemed important, while G-2s at higher commands passed information back down, in the process taking advantage of their broader knowledge as evaluated and correlated from more diverse sources. One of those sources was strategic intelligence, and in that field the Allied command had a special capability.

"A sonnet written by a machine," wrote a brilliant young British mathemetician, Alan Mathison Turing, "will be better appreciated by another machine." Turing was a person with "the unpredictable way-wardness of genius"—he once changed all his money into silver, melted it down into ingots, buried them, and never could recall where he had left them. As war came to Europe in 1939, young Turing (described as having "long hair, rumpled and dirty clothes"), a graduate of Cambridge University and of the Institute of Advanced Studies at Princeton University, was a member of a team made up primarily of Cambridge dons assembled for the specific purpose of attacking the German enciphering machine, the Enigma. The dons proceeded on a variation of Turing's theory of the sonnet: A riddle created by a machine can best be solved by another machine.

Turing and his colleagues worked under the cover of a technically nonexistent Government Code and Cipher School. It was based in a modest though architecturally flamboyant pseudo-Tudor–Gothic mansion known as Bletchley Park, located in Buckinghamshire outside the grimy railway-junction town of Bletchley some fifty miles northwest of London. Most of the work took place in Hut 6, one of several temporary wooden buildings erected on the grounds of the estate.

The work at Hut 6 received strong assistance from Polish crypt-analysts, who in the years before the war had enjoyed a modest success in breaking some of the ciphers of the early Enigma machines by means of a machine they called the "Bombe," a combination of six Enigmas joined together. As war neared, the Poles turned over both to the British and to the French a Polish-constructed copy of the Enigma along with plans and drawings of the Bombe.

By the spring of 1940, Turing and his colleagues had built the first of what was destined to be a series of ever more complex machines designed to attack the Enigma. It was "a large copper-coloured cupboard" about 6 feet tall, "which on first glance looked like an oriental goddess." They called it the Mark I Heath Robinson, after a satirical British cartoonist who drew weird, fanciful machines supposedly capable of extraordinary feats; but they usually referred to it by the original Polish name, the Bombe.

It was a forerunner of the computer yet not a true computer, for it worked on electromechanical rather than electronic principles and had no memory. Once wireless interceptors picked up an enemy signal, it was copied onto a tape and fed into the Bombe, which proceeded at a speed far beyond that of the human mind to determine which of the more than a million keys or variations of them had been used to encipher the message.

For all the miraculous ability of the Bombe, it had to have extensive human help. That was where the cryptanalysts came in, for through long months of working with Enigma intercepts and creating a vast databank of intercepted signals, they had discerned certain patterns in the transmissions. They had early learned, for example, that the letter punched by the operator never showed up in the encoded message as the same letter; thus X or Y or whatever could represent only one of twenty-five letters, not one of twenty-six. They had also learned to capitalize on the laxity of the German operators, many of whom after setting the machine and closing it, selected as the day's key the three letters that were visible in windows on the lid, and the operators dutifully repeated the key at the start of every message they transmitted. Constant repetition of the key could in time mean something in regard to the overall code.

Over a long period of time the cryptanalysts became familiar with the various headquarters making the transmissions, thereby ascertaining the call sign of the sender and usually the call sign of the recipient, for the traffic between the various headquarters was fairly constant. By directional radio finding, they could also determine the geographical location of both sender and recipient. Even though call signs changed daily, the German operator had only so many for his own headquarters and for those with which he communicated, so that in time the cryptanalysts could develop a catalogue of call signs and geographical locations for various headquarters.

So, too, the cryptanalysts could capitalize on the fact that military units were usually required to transmit situation reports at much the same time each day, and those usually contained standard opening phrases, such as "Morning report from Seventh Army," or "Evening report from Fliegerkorps II." From the hour of transmission and from the standard phrases, the cryptanalysts might determine the code letters used that day for the hour and the standard phrase.

By feeding all those clues and more into the Bombe, the cryptanalysts usually provided enough information for the amazing machine to turn the clues swiftly into a break of the day's code. From that point it was simple for the Bombe to decipher all intercepted signals enciphered in that particular code.

Wireless intercept stations in various parts of Britain fed one signal after another to Bletchley Park, literally thousands every day. They went to Hut 6, where the Bombe deciphered them. Then messengers passed them to one of two other huts—if army or air force messages, to Hut 3; if naval intercepts, to Hut 5. The material that emerged from those two huts as translated and interpreted messages was known by the codename ULTRA.

A staff of more than a hundred manned each hut, working in shifts around the clock, filling in missing letters or words (for seldom was an intercept perfectly received), translating the messages, and from a vast collection of data recorded on index cards providing interpretation of the message, which to differentiate the interpretation from the message was always carefully labeled "comment." Many of the people who did the work were in uniform, but most who filled in the letters and words and did the translating were civilian dons highly proficient in German and accustomed to the painstakingly slow functioning of the pedagogue. Beginning in 1942, Americans joined the staff, most of them lawyers in uniform.

By late 1944, deciphered, reconstructed, and translated messages, reinciphered in Allied codes and known as flimsies, were going in abundance from Hut 3 directly over special communications links to more than fifty Allied air and ground headquarters, including Eisenhower's SHAEF, all three army groups under Eisenhower's command, all army headquarters, and all major air commands, down to and including tactical air commands. There the information was received by small sections known as Special Liaison Units, or SLUs, which in British practice usually consisted of an officer and two or three men, but which in American practice were usually slightly larger.

The number of people within the headquarters privy to the ULTRA material—indeed, to the very fact that there was such a thing as ULTRA—was sharply limited, usually to the commanding general, his chief of staff, and his G-2. Information provided by ULTRA was not to be reported in G-2 summaries, periodic reports, or intelligence estimates unless it could be truthfully ascribed to some other source.

A specially designated officer in Hut 3 determined which headquarters got which flimsy, but that was usually a decision involving only major commands, such as SHAEF or the Allied command in Italy. Which headquarters got what appeared in code letters at the top of the flimsy: for the 12th Army Group, for example, WM; for the First Army, YK; and the list of code letters was usually long, for if it was considered to be of interest to Eisenhower's headquarters, it was considered to be of interest to all commands under Eisenhower.

The volume of flimsies reaching an SLU was large but seldom overwhelming, and Bletchley Park provided an indication of a flimsy's importance by assigning it a number of Zs from one to five. Although the identification or location of enemy units as obtained through ULTRA might be posted on a special situation map maintained by the SLU, a flimsy had to be destroyed within twenty-four hours of receipt. Heads of the SLUs were nevertheless permitted to make notes so long as they bore no identifiable relation to the original source material. That provided at least a modicum of institutional memory, as did the comments often provided with a message by Bletchley Park.

Since all commanders receiving ULTRA information knew that the data came from the enemy's own messages, none was inclined to discount it. ULTRA had, after all, given fairly explicit warning of the enemy's counterattack in Normandy designed to cut off Allied spearheads that had broken out of the beachhead.

In most headquarters, procedures for passing ULTRA information to the commander were much the same. Each morning the head of the SLU or his representative briefed the commander and senior members of his staff along with the comparable air commander (the commander of the

Ninth Air Force, for example, with General Bradley; the commander of the IX Tactical Air Command with General Hodges). Commanders and all of the few other officers cleared for ULTRA were free to visit the ULTRA room at any time, and whenever a message came in labeled with five Zs, the head of the SLU had to take it personally to the commander, no matter what time of day or night.

The only exception to those procedures was at headquarters of the First Army, where the G-2, Colonel Dickson, insisted on presenting the ULTRA briefing himself, a briefing from which he excluded the head of his SLU, Lt. Col. Adolph G. Rosengarten, Jr. For a time Dickson merely employed the raw messages, but in the weeks before the start of the German offensive, he began to use a briefing paper prepared by Rosengarten. Although Dickson resisted having the ULTRA officer from the IX Tactical Air Command, Lt. Col. James D. Fellers, attend, he had to bow to pressure from the commander of the IX Tactical Air Command, Maj. Gen. Elwood R. ("Pete") Quesada.

As the German Army fell back on the frontier in early fall, the volume of wireless traffic decreased, for there the telephone took over many of the chores of communication. Yet Hitler's order forbidding transmission by wireless of any information that might be connected with the impending offensive had little additional effect on the number of intercepted messages pouring into Bletchley Park, certainly not enough of a reduction to indicate that anything untoward was afoot; for if day-to-day functions and operations were to continue, the German Army, and particularly the Luftwaffe and the *Reichsbahn*, had to use wireless. So, too, wireless was a basic means of conveying the disinformation that the Germans wanted the Allies to hear.

Thus all that was really missing was any reference to an offensive in the Ardennes, and interceptors and cryptanalysts continued to handle around fifty messages a day dealing with the Western Front. What those messages had to tell Allied intelligence chiefs and their commanders in the weeks immediately preceding the German offensive was considerable.

CHAPTER THREE

What Did the Allies Know?

On September 27, 1944, Bletchley Park deciphered a message from Operational Headquarters of the *Waffen-SS* dated September 18, directing that all SS units on the Western Front be pulled from the line for rest and refitting, beginning with the 1st, 2d, 9th, and 12th SS Panzer Divisions, the 17th SS Panzergrenadier Division, three separate heavy (Tiger) tank battalions, and headquarters troops of the 1st SS Panzer Corps. All were to be assigned to "the staff of Sixth Panzer Army, the setting up of which has been ordered under Oberstgruppenführer Sepp Dietrich."

That there was a nine-day delay between the sending of the German message and Bletchley Park's deciphering it was probably attributable to cryptographic difficulties, for a delay of that length was unusual. The deciphered message went out in late afternoon of the 27th to General Eisenhower's headquarters and all subordinate commands down to and including armies and tactical air commands. Four days later, on October 1, the SHAEF G-2, General Strong, noted in his weekly intelligence summary that the Germans were withdrawing armor from the line in an apparent effort to provide a panzer reserve north of the Ardennes. Strong made no mention of specific divisions nor of the Sixth Panzer Army.

Throughout October, ULTRA provided further details about the withdrawals. In mid-October, for example, a message from Field Marshal Keitel revealed that the Sixth Panzer Army was to be the *OKW* reserve, which meant that neither Field Marshal Model nor Field Marshal von Rundstedt had control over it; it was a *strategic* reserve for the *Führerhauptquartier*, Hitler's headquarters.

Other messages located assembly areas for the divisions, mostly east of the Rhine in Westphalia, just north of the Ruhr, or dealt with the training areas where the divisions were to refit. Still others told of difficulties in releasing certain units from the line, noted altered withdrawal schedules, and revealed that the SS panzer divisions were to be brought to full strength. A further message revealed that Hitler himself had or-

62

dered the withdrawals and the creation of the Sixth Panzer Army. Yet another revealed a certain urgency: headquarters of the 1st SS Panzer Corps was to join the Sixth Panzer Army by October 20 "at latest. Longer delays by corps could not be permitted."

Throughout the month, neither General Strong nor any other Allied intelligence officer in intelligence summaries, periodic reports, or estimates of enemy intentions made mention of the Sixth Panzer Army. Strong first named it at the end of the first week in November, citing a German deserter as the source of the information; and at the same time Strong remarked that the Fifth Panzer Army had disappeared from the line in Lorraine, which, unknown to Strong at the moment, was the first step in the move of General von Manteuffel's headquarters to the Aachen sector.

What preoccupied Strong, Sibert, Dickson, and the other intelligence chiefs was what the Germans intended to do with the SS panzer divisions. Was it counterattack, or spoiling attack?

General Sibert at the 12th Army Group expressed the generally held view that it would be counterattack, to be launched once the First and Third U.S. Armies achieved a breakthrough toward the Rhine and the Ruhr. General Strong believed that whatever action the Germans took, it would occur in November, which was what the MAGIC intercept of Baron Oshima's report of his conversation with Hitler had indicated: an offensive in the West sometime "after the beginning of November." Nobody mentioned that the SS panzer divisions constituted—as ULTRA had reported—not a reserve for Model or von Rundstedt but for *OKW*, for Hitler.

In early November, ULTRA began to provide evidence of a hurried move of German fighter aircraft to the West. Beginning on the 8th, the Luftwaffe command in the Netherlands sent the first of a series of messages dealing with the expected arrival of fighter groups at airfields in its sector. The messages displayed an air of haste and secrecy in regard to "the special contingency known to you."

On November 16, in a message from a higher Luftwaffe command ordering daily reports on the serviceability of all aircraft, the sender used the term *"Jägeraufmarsch,"* which the officials in Hut 3 considered to be worth a comment. In a military context, the comment read, *Aufmarsch* "denoted the assembly of forces for a planned operation," a term which the Germans had used in that sense when describing "the Allied dispositions on the eve of D-Day." Other messages meanwhile told of a buildup of fighter aircraft at fields inside Germany close to the front, and by November 23 it was clear that the hurried *Jägeraufmarsch*—whatever it was for—was complete.

Neither at Bletchley Park nor at any Allied air or ground headquarters on the Continent did anybody divine the purpose behind the *Jägeraufmarsch*. Years later it would be clear that the haste reflected

Hitler's original intention of launching his offensive before the end of November, but nobody on the Allied side could discern that at the time nor even why the Germans moved the planes at all.

In the new locations, the aircraft still might intercept Allied bombers raiding German cities or they might support a German counterattack when the American armies broke through toward the Rhine. When the transfers produced no increase in the paltry amount of air support the German ground troops were receiving, support of the expected German counterattack appeared to be the answer.

Nor did the fact that the bulk of the transfers ended on November 23 provide any clue, and nobody saw any particular significance in a revelation by ULTRA early in December of the creation of a new headquarters, *Jagdführer Mittelrhein* (Officer Commanding Fighters, Central Rhineland), although it was soon obvious from strength reports to that headquarters that it controlled the newly transferred aircraft. Any Allied attempt to determine the meaning of the shifts was all the more difficult because in most cases, in keeping with Hitler's stringent security plan, the German commanders and operators who sent the messages Bletchley Park deciphered knew little or nothing of the purpose themselves.

Starting in early November, troops of the Sixth Panzer Army began to transfer to the west bank of the Rhine. Duly noting the moves, Allied intelligence officers began a guessing game as to the exact location of the assembly areas. The game was essentially meaningless, for all deduced that the assembly areas were in the vicinity of Cologne, a location from which the SS divisions might readily counterattack a thrust toward the Ruhr.

Noting that the enemy had apparently created or rebuilt at least five SS panzer or panzer divisions and five parachute divisions during September and October, a "truly colossal effort," General Strong at SHAEF concluded that the Germans intended "a final showdown before the winter," and deemed it logical that they would use their newly created reserve against an Allied drive in the north. General Sibert at the 12th Army Group continued to think much the same, while Colonel Dickson at the First Army saw the possibility of a spoiling attack from positions northwest of Aachen to drive down both banks of the Meuse River, a maneuver not unlike the Small Solution proposed to Hitler by von Rundstedt and Model, although Dickson presupposed no accompanying drive through the Ardennes.

By November 20, almost all were of one mind: The Sixth Panzer Army's mission was to counterattack once the American armies crossed the Roer River, probably with the help of the Fifth Panzer Army, whose arrival in the Aachen sector they had quickly spotted, for three divisions of that army were behind the Roer River in a position to assist the Sixth Panzer Army. It was a few days later before they picked up the bogus headquarters, *Gruppe von Manteuffel*, but when they did so they saw through a part of the German deception by identifying the arrival of headquarters of the Fifteenth Army. At that point they concluded that von Manteuffel controlled two armies, the Fifth Panzer and the Fifteenth, and ULTRA, at least, learned that the Fifth Panzer Army had moved out of the line. The German attempt through false wireless traffic to conceal the Fifteenth Army's relief in the Netherlands by the Twenty-fifth Army failed utterly.

Meanwhile, ULTRA was continuing to feed the intelligence officers a steady diet of intercepted messages, mainly dealing with troop movements by rail and related requests for air protection. In a message sent with high priority, Model's Army Group B in early November asked the Luftwaffe for fighter protection for the unloading of troop trains in the vicinity of Cologne. That was the first of more than thirty similar intercepted and decoded messages over the weeks remaining before the German attack, always originating with Army Group B. Although many requests were for protection in the north near Cologne, most (sometimes communicated with "almost shrill urgency") were for the Rhine crossings between Bonn, just beyond the northern reaches of the Eifel, and for Koblenz, at the confluence of the Moselle River with the Rhine, whence the main rail line along the southern periphery of the Eifel ran along the Moselle to Trier. From any of those rail crossings of the Rhine, trains might use the spur lines into the Eifel; and in the last days before Hitler's deadline, most requests were for protection in the vicinity of Koblenz, well away from the sector in the north where Allied eyes were focused. At the same time, the Luftwaffe was ordering subordinate commands to fly counter-reconnaissance screens to keep allied aircraft away from the marshaling yards at Koblenz and Trier.

Of greater interest, many of the requests were for aerial protection of railheads inside the Eifel. On December 2, for example, Army Group B wanted fighter cover not only for Trier but for Wittlich, Gerolstein, and Bitburg, all deep inside the Eifel. In a request for protection on December 3, Army Group B named the ground units involved in the movements: the 326th Volksgrenadier Division at Gerolstein, in the shadow of the Schnee Eifel (and not far from Monschau, where the division subsequently attacked); the 62d Volksgrenadier Division at Wittlich, due east of Bitburg (and a relatively short march from St. Vith, where that division attacked); and the *Führer Begleit Brigade*, an armored brigade built around Hitler's inner palace guard and never before employed at the front, at Cochem on the main rail line along the Moselle. On December 7, Army Group B wanted fighter cover for virtually the entire Eifel. And all the while, none of the planes providing cover either for the rail movements or the railheads came from those airfields so recently reinforced with additional fighter aircraft.

With some exultancy, the cryptanalysts with the help of their ingenious Turing engine began early in November to break the codes of the

Reichsbahn. Of some eight hundred trains used to move the German attack force into position, ULTRA picked up signals on almost half, clearly indicating a massive movement toward the Western Front.

On occasion, the messages revealed intense urgency: on November 10, about a week after the movements began, the Director-General of Transport insisted that the Sixth Panzer Army order all units "to ensure punctual transport," for it would be "impossible to make up any delays once they had occurred" because "all formations already [were] being moved at highest possible tempo." The day before, he noted with some agitation, the 2d SS Panzer Division had fallen thirty-six hours behind schedule, the *Panzer Lehr Division*, twenty-four, and the 12th SS Panzer Division, twelve. Maintaining the tight schedules was clearly of major importance: Even a twelve-hour delay was reason for concern.

Even as ULTRA was reporting rail movements and requests for their aerial protection, reconnaissance and fighter pilots of the IX and XIX Tactical Air Commands were picking up many of the movements. Despite the bad weather that Hitler counted on—and got—and despite the tendency of the pilots to concentrate on regions to the north where ground intelligence officers expected the enemy to strike, there was many an indication of buildup in the Eifel.

In fairly clear weather on November 18 and 19, for example, pilots reported heavy rail movements at various points in the Eifel: at Gemünd, near the Roer River dams; at Gerolstein; and at Bitburg. Marshaling yards at Koblenz and Trier were aswarm with activity. Pilots reported trains loaded with tanks, ambulances, and other vehicles, hospital trains, troop trains. Sometimes there were truck convoys marked with white square panels in an apparent effort to simulate American convoys. A few pilots reported what looked to be piles of equipment alongside the roads just inside the treelines.

In the first two weeks of December the weather proved even more restrictive, but there was continued evidence of buildup nevertheless. Many sightings were again in or near the Eifel: at Koblenz, Prüm, Gemünd, Münstereifel (a few miles east of Gemünd), Gerolstein, Trier. Despite having only a few Black Widow planes each, the two American night reconnaissance squadrons also turned in considerable evidence of buildup: columns of what looked to be vehicles with dim-out lights, which would indicate truck convoys, on many of the roads west of the Rhine, and in some places irregular patches of shielded lights away from the roads, which might indicate troop assembly areas. One pilot reported a battery of searchlights turned on briefly near Kaiserslautern, which was well south of the Moselle River in front of the Third Army, but—it might have been noted—only a few miles by rail from the Eifel.

On November 24, ULTRA began to decipher what became a series of requests from Army Group B—some betraying "an increasingly urgent note"—for aerial reconnaissance missions that when viewed in the context of a German counterattack in the north near Cologne made little sense. The first asked for reconnaissance of the region around Eupen and Malmédy, which was the most direct route from the Eifel to the American supply center of Liège and for American reinforcements moving south into the Ardennes; and also of roads along the Prüm-Houffalize axis, which was one of the most direct routes, via St. Vith, into and through the Ardennes. On December 3, Army Group B again asked for reconnaissance of the area around Eupen and Malmédy: "Are forces being brought up in Monschau area and what forces? Where are troop movements and concentrations and tank assemblies?"

Beginning on November 29 there were odder requests still: for aerial reconnaissance of crossings of the Meuse River from Liège past the bend in the river at Namur and upstream for fifty-five miles past Dinant to Givet. A few days later the Luftwaffe gave that assignment to a special detachment of jet aircraft, and night reconnaissance also began. Reconnaissance was "to be forced through at lower level if weather prevents high level flight." On December 3, a message said that reconnaissance of the bridges over the Meuse was "of the greatest urgency." And five days later, on the 8th: "A good photo of Mass [Meuse] crossings from Maastricht to Givet still with priority over other tasks." As late as December 14, demands for those photos and for others of the road center of Ciney a few miles short of the Meuse were still coming in. What could crossings of the Meuse River in the Ardennes, far from the German concentration near Cologne, have to do with a German counterattack near Cologne?

ULTRA revealed all those things; and more too. For every request for reconnaissance of the region around Eupen and Malmédy, there were at least three more for reconnaissance around Aachen and repeated requests for aerial protection for trains unloading in the vicinity of Cologne. Reconnaissance pilots reporting rail movements and possible truck convoys in the Eifel were also reporting movements farther north that well might be deduced to feed a buildup near Cologne, and railheads and marshaling yards other than those in or close to the Eifel were also busy.

So, too, on December 11, Bletchley Park deciphered a message from Field Marshal von Rundstedt:

> Large scale attack against Western Germany might begin in very near future. Allies would probably try to seize Rhine crossings by air landings on large scale. Most important therefore that defense at Rhine bridges should be in constant state of readiness. . . . *Wehrkreis* [county] commanders to report by 18th whether all preparations for defense of Rhine crossings made.

In response to concerns about the thinness of the front in the Ardennes as expressed by the commander of the VIII Corps, Maj. Gen. Troy H. Middleton, General Eisenhower and General Bradley visited Middleton on November 8, lunched with him at his headquarters in a Belgian Army caserne in Bastogne, then toured lower headquarters near the front. They left at the end of the day well aware of widely spaced positions; but since the Germans, like the Americans, appeared to be using the sector to give depleted divisions a rest and new ones a taste of combat experience, they entertained no real concern for what Bradley would later call a "calculated risk." Besides, Bradley had already sent a newly arrived 9th Armored Division to the Ardennes in October to serve Middleton as a reserve.

One of Bradley's subordinates, the commander of the Third Army, General Patton, was less sanguine. On November 24 he wrote in his diary that "the First Army is making a terrible mistake in leaving the VIII Corps static, as it is highly probable that the Germans are building up east of them."

That entry no doubt reflected a growing concern on the part of Patton's G-2, Colonel Koch, he who had never been so optimistic about the condition of the German forces as were his intelligence colleagues in other commands. Since the southern portion of the Eifel was an extension of the Third Army's projected zone of advance, Koch paid it special attention; it was at his suggestion that Patton had obtained approval for reconnaissance aircraft supporting the Third Army to reconnoiter over the Eifel. Koch was particularly concerned about the threat that would accrue to the Third Army's north flank should the Germans emerge from the Eifel into the Ardennes. By December 9, he was sufficiently worried to invite his commander to a special intelligence briefing.

As Koch put it to Patton, the enemy had at least thirteen divisions out of the line, including six panzer or SS panzer divisions and at least four parachute divisions. Koch had also learned—presumably from ULTRA—that three divisions had left Scandinavia for the Western Front. Although most of the armor was in the north near Cologne, the 2d Panzer and 12th SS Panzer Divisions had recently been reported moving south. By Koch's reckoning, the enemy had four *Volksgrenadier* divisions in the line opposite the First Army's VIII Corps, two panzer divisions with a total of 105 tanks in immediate reserve, and three *Volksgrenadier* divisions nearby. Considering what the VIII Corps had in the line, the German concentration was greater, comparatively, than it was opposite the rest of the First Army or the Third Army. Koch concluded that the Germans intended either to shift the reserve forces in the Eifel north or south to meet American threats, to use them to try to lure American divisions away from the main attack, or "to launch a spoiling or diversionary offensive."

A short silence followed Koch's presentation, then discussion began. Nothing was to be allowed to interfere with the Third Army's plan for a renewed offensive on December 19, Patton declared at the end, but the staff was to begin "limited outline planning" to meet any threat that might emerge from enemy action in the Ardennes. "We'll be in a position," said Patton, "to meet whatever happens."

The next day, December 10, Colonel Koch put his concern in writing. Strongly impressed by the withdrawal of German divisions from the line, particularly panzer divisions, at a time when the enemy's defensive need was so great, he predicted that the Germans probably intended "to mount a spoiling offensive in an effort to unhinge the Allied assault on *Festung* [Fortress] *Deutschland*." Yet three days later he weakened his earlier warning about the Ardennes by falling into line with the view prevailing among his intelligence associates: that the enemy was planning a counterattack with the Sixth Panzer Army in the north.

At headquarters of the First Army, Colonel Dickson was also becoming concerned. One event that set him worrying was the capture in late November by troops of the Ninth Army of an order issued on October 30 by the 86th Corps, which called on all units of the corps to screen for men who had "a knowledge of the English language and also the American dialect," and who might volunteer for "a special unit" the Führer had ordered "for employment on reconnaissance and special tasks on the western front." The order also directed that "captured U.S. clothing, equipment, weapons and vehicles" were to be collected as "equipment of the above troops." Otto Skorzeny's fear that the Allies would obtain a copy of that order had come to pass.

In several informal discussions with Dickson, the head of the First Army's SLU (ULTRA), Colonel Rosengarten, recalled the German offensive through the Ardennes in 1940 and noted that "desperate men are likely to take desperate measures." Possibly as a result of those discussions, Dickson prevailed on his commander, General Hodges, to ask General Bradley for two divisions to back up the line in the Ardennes. No, said Bradley, he had none to spare.

On December 8, Monk Dickson presented to Hodges a map labeled "Study of Enemy Armored Reserves" on which the head of his G-2 target section, Lt. Col. Clarence M. Mendenhall, had tabulated German troop and armor concentrations, as well as stockpiles of ammunition and bridging equipment based on information gathered from all intelligence sources. Mendenhall had labeled each location priority "Red Bomb" (one), "Blue Bomb" (two), or "Brown Bomb" (three). Those labeled Red and Blue Bombs were troop concentrations close to railheads or rail junctions through which troops and supplies were known to pass. Of a total of fifty-three targets, twenty-nine were in the sector north of the Eifel, twenty-six of which were labeled Red Bomb; in the Eifel, some as far back as the Rhine, there were twenty-four, ten of them labeled Red Bomb. Priority clearly was in the north.

Convinced that Allied bombing of the enemy's railroads had been at random and never sufficiently concentrated to knock out all lines in a given area at once, Dickson wanted all the targets hit in a concentrated offensive by medium and heavy bombers. When General Hodges approved, as did the commander of his supporting tactical air command, General Quesada, the request went forward to the commander of the United States Strategic Air Forces in Europe, General Carl Spaatz, who controlled the heavy bombers. It came back disapproved: "Targets unremunerative."

By December 10, Dickson had become convinced that the Germans were going to make a move somewhere soon. He was scheduled to go on a long-delayed four-day leave to Paris the next day (although still subject to the return from leave of the G-3, Brig. Gen. Truman C. Thorson), and even though he had no concern about leaving his intelligence duties to the "deft, sure hand" of his deputy, Col. William Silvey, he considered the German buildup so threatening that before departing, he wanted to convey "a solemn warning." On the 10th, he issued G-2 Estimate No. 37, on which he had worked at considerable length—a document he and others would later claim should have been sufficient to alert the Allied command to the offensive in the Ardennes.

In the estimate, Dickson used the terms "all-out counterattack" and "all-out counteroffensive" interchangeably, although technically they are two different things. "An extremely intelligent PW," he noted, "stated that every means possible is being gathered for the coming all-out counteroffensive." Morale among recently captured prisoners of war had "achieved a new high," as "expressed by attempts to escape and avowed eagerness . . . to rejoin the battle for Germany." With a jibe at Adolf Hitler, who often boasted of success in military operations based on his intuition, Dickson wrote that "von Rundstedt, who obviously is conducting military operations without the benefit of intuition, has skillfully defended and husbanded his forces and is preparing for his part in the all-out application of every weapon at the focal point and the correct time to achieve defense of the Reich west of the Rhine by inflicting as great a defeat on the Allies as possible."

Among enemy capabilities, Dickson mentioned as "current" continuing to defend along the line of the Roer River with particular attention to the Roer River dams, which the enemy recognized as "a tactical ace." When American troops crossed the Roer, a second capability would be likely: "a concentrated counterattack with air, armor, infantry, and secret weapons at a selected focal point at a time of his own choosing." It was "plain" that the enemy's strategy was "based on the exhaustion of our offensive to be followed by an all-out counterattack with armor, between the Roer and the Erft [a small stream midway between the Roer and the Rhine]." The "continual building up of forces to the west of the Rhine" pointed "consistently to his staking all on [that] counteroffensive."

The focal point, wrote Dickson, was "between Roermond and Schleiden." Roermond, which lay within the sector of the 21st Army Group, is twenty-two miles north of Aachen; Schleiden is within the northern reaches of the Eifel near the Roer River dams, almost due east of Monschau. That placed the focal point well north of the Ardennes.

To deduce from that prediction that Dickson anticipated an offensive out of the Eifel into the Ardennes would be to strain credulity. Although he noted that the enemy's armored reserve appeared "to be quartered in houses and barns along the railroads generally in a semi-circle from Düsseldorf to Koblenz [thereby placing some of it in the Eifel] with Cologne as a center point," his only specific reference to the Ardennes was to remark "a definite pattern for the seasoning of newly-formed divisions in the comparatively quiet sector opposite VIII Corps prior to their dispatch to more active fronts." He did note the presence in back-up positions in the Eifel of the 2d and 116th Panzer Divisions but believed they were being readied to counterattack to deny the First Army capture of the Roer River dams, which may have been the reason he extended the likely sector for enemy action as far south as Schleiden.

At General Bradley's headquarters in a drab brownstone office building belonging to the Luxembourg State Railways, across a cobblestoned Place de Metz from the Luxembourg City railroad station, Edwin Sibert was also beginning to have some concern about the Ardennes. In late November, as he and General Bradley had driven through the region en route to visit Field Marshal Montgomery's headquarters in northern Belgium, they had both remarked the absence of troops and installations behind the lines. When they discussed the possibility of a German thrust through the Ardennes, Bradley said that "when anyone attacks, he does it for one of two reasons. Either he is out to destroy the hostile forces or he's going after a terrain objective." Neither, said Bradley, could be attained in the Ardennes. Yet even should the Germans attack there, it was hardly likely that they could make "decisive progress" through such "broken, relatively roadless country"; and if they tried, "we could chew them up."

Hardly had Bradley and Sibert returned to Luxembourg City when a disturbing ULTRA intercept reached Sibert's desk. It was the first order to the Luftwaffe to reconnoiter crossings of the Meuse River from Liège to Givet, with reconnaissance "to be forced through at lower level if weather prevents high level flight." So concerned was Sibert that he sent his deputy, Col. William H. Jackson, to SHAEF and thence to London to visit the top British intelligence agencies to see if he could get any additional information. Jackson departed on December 1 but soon cabled that he could find out nothing more.

On December 10, the terrain expert in Sibert's G-2 section, Maj. Ralph Ingersoll—in civilian life, a prominent newspaperman—asked Sibert to come to his office, where on a wall map he pointed out detraining areas in the vicinity of Bitburg. Instead of just moving inexperienced or recuperating divisions in and out of the Eifel, said Ingersoll, the Germans might be building up there by a stratagem of moving three divisions in and two out while hiding the extra one.

The theory impressed Sibert enough for him to relate it to General Bradley, who promptly asked the Supreme Commander, General Eisenhower, for a newly arriving armored division as an additional reserve for the Ardennes; but Eisenhower said no. He needed the new division for reinforcing the Seventh Army to help it support renewal of the Third Army's offensive. Furthermore, there was some concern that if the Germans struck other than in the north, it might be in Alsace, where Allied lines were also thin and such French cities as Metz and Nancy were within easy reach.

For all the rising interest in the Ardennes, Sibert believed any threat there to be minimal compared to the buildup of German armor in the north near Cologne. Even on that score, Sibert thought that Monk Dickson in his G-2 Estimate No. 37 was exaggerating. Indeed, he found Dickson's latest assessment so pessimistic that when General Strong telephoned from SHAEF to complain and to urge that Sibert "get Dickson straightened out," Sibert agreed something should be done. Strong was also concerned about "Monk's shrubbery," for Dickson had bolstered his pessimistic case by naming some German units identifiable only through ULTRA (that was a no-no) and known in fact to be located on other fronts.

Lacking either technical or command supervision over Dickson, Sibert chose to counter Dickson's alarm by issuing a more sober report himself. That he failed to telephone Dickson or to ask for a conference appeared to say something about the state of relations between the two.

By chance, that was the point at which the G-2 section, in response to criticism that its intelligence summaries were dull and therefore seldom read, chose to call in the newspaperman Ralph Ingersoll to dress them up. Ingersoll's first rewrite was of G-2 Summary No. 18, which Sibert issued on December 12, the summary in which Sibert remarked that attrition was eating heavily into German strength and that the front was more brittle and vulnerable "than it appeared on G-2 maps or to troops in the line." The "deathly weakness" of the infantry divisions, "plus the inevitability" that the enemy had fewer and fewer replacements, the report continued, made it "certain that before long he will utterly fail in his current attempt to withdraw and arrest his tactical reserve so that he will be forced to commit at least part of his panzer army to the line." The report concluded: "With continuing Allied pressure in the south and in the north, the breaking point may develop suddenly and without warning."

The ideas, the opinions were Sibert's, based on his own beliefs and on Kenneth Strong's recent report stressing heavy German losses; but it was unfortunate, Sibert was to remark years later, that that was the first report to be dressed up by Ingersoll. He "stressed the optimistic picture, so it looked a lot better than it should." Whatever the case, G-2 Summary No. 18 was to haunt Edwin Sibert for the rest of his life.

In the offices of SHAEF's G-2 section in the Trianon Palace Hotel at Versailles, General Strong was still optimistic because of the continuing high level of German attrition, yet he mentioned that until the Sixth Panzer Army was committed, "We cannot feel really satisfied." Noting continuing troop movements in the Eifel, he remarked that "the procession is NOT yet ended."

Although Strong saw the troop movements in the Eifel as just that—a procession, troops passing through—he nevertheless joined those who were directing increased attention toward the Eifel and the Ardennes. For "at least a fortnight" before the German attack began, he called attention at morning briefings conducted by the chief of staff, Lt. Gen. Walter Bedell Smith, to three possible uses of the reserve panzer divisions. They could go to Russia; counterattack an Allied penetration; or "stage a relieving attack through the Ardennes." As was the custom, he presumably listed the possibilities in descending order of probability, and as General Smith was to recall, Strong also suggested that the relieving attack might be made in Alsace.

It may have been Strong's growing concern that prompted General Eisenhower, as he motored through the Ardennes on December 7 on the way to a conference with Montgomery, to remark that the Allied command might be in for "a nasty little Kasserine." It was definitely Strong's concern that prompted Bedell (pronounced Beedle) Smith to urge Strong to go to Luxembourg City and alert General Bradley.

Strong made the visit during the first week of December at the time when General Sibert was also beginning to look with some anxiety at German activity in the Eifel. Strong talked first with Sibert, then spent more than half an hour with Bradley, who told him that he was "aware of the danger" but that he had "earmarked certain divisions to move into the Ardennes area should the enemy attack there." If so, he told nobody else about it and issued no directive. In any event, those at Bradley's headquarters in Luxembourg City looked on Kenneth Strong as a worrywart.

Bradley had by that time already spoken again about the possibility of a German strike in the Ardennes with the commander on the ground, a reserve infantry officer and former dean of Louisiana State University,

Troy Middleton. Bradley saw an attack in the Ardennes as "only a remote possibility," at most a spoiling attack involving four to six divisions. If it should happen, Middleton was "to make a fighting withdrawal, all the way back to the Meuse River if necessary." (Middleton never told his division commanders that.) He was to locate no major gasoline or supply depots within the area to be given up. (Bradley never told Courtney Hodges that.) As Middleton withdrew, Bradley was to order armored divisions to hit the enemy's flanks. (Bradley never alerted any division to that role.)

If Middleton continued to harbor any particular concern, it could hardly have been as a result of any warning from his intelligence officer, Col. Andrew R. Reeves. In a report on December 9, Reeves estimated the enemy opposite the VIII Corps to consist of four infantry divisions with a total strength of 24,000 men. That, if correct, meant that the enemy's line was almost half as thin as that of the widely stretched VIII Corps. "The enemy's present practice," wrote Reeves, "of bringing new divisions . . . to receive front line experience and then relieving them out for commitment elsewhere indicates his desire to have this sector of the front remain quiet and inactive."

Both Reeves and Middleton could, of course, read the intelligence reports sent down from higher echelons, and they must have remarked the difference in tone between that from Dickson of the First Army on December 10 and that from Sibert of the 12th Army Group on the 12th. In any event, it was obvious that higher command expected nothing to happen on the front of the VIII Corps, for Middleton received an order, as a corollary of the attack by the First Army to seize the Roer River dams, to stage a feint near his southern boundary in Luxembourg in hope of drawing enemy strength from the north.

The assignment went to the 23d Special Troops, a deception unit equipped with such devices as sonic gear to simulate heavy motor traffic and inflatable rubber tanks. Assuming the guise of the 75th Infantry Division, which was actually en route from England to the Continent, the men of the detachment wore the division's shoulder patch and marked their vehicles as if they belonged to the 75th Division. Radio traffic simulating a division headquarters and supporting units went out intentionally in an easily broken code. Proceeding for five days, the so-called rubber duck operation showed up on German situation maps for a while as a question mark; but by December 15, von Rundstedt's headquarters had decided that no new division existed, and the question mark disappeared. The only ones genuinely fooled were the Americans, for at headquarters of the VIII Corps, they read reports from the front of increased enemy radio and vehicular traffic as a response to the deception operation, and some troops of the 4th Infantry Division in the line in Luxembourg were later to wonder why the 75th Division never came forward to help them.

Middleton nevertheless still nursed a considerable concern. To the commander of the Ninth Army, Lt. Gen. William H. Simpson, who stopped by Bastogne on December 5 after a conference with General Bradley in Luxembourg City, he confided "in strong terms" that he was convinced the Germans had altered their practice on his front. "Whereas previously the Germans had been unloading troops in the rear area, bringing some up to the front line and then moving them to other sectors," he thought at that point that they were pretending to do the same thing but "were actually building up a large force in the rear area."

To subordinates, at least, Middleton displayed no such concern, as exemplified on December 10 when he heard from the commander of the 2d Infantry Division, Maj. Gen. Walter M. Robertson, who at the time was responsible for that part of the front which included the Schnee Eifel. On the 8th and the 9th, the 2d Division's outposts had reported intense enemy activity, including heavy motor traffic. By the 10th, the activity had slackened, leading Robertson's G-2, Lt. Col. Donald P. Christensen, to conclude that one unit had replaced another in the line and that "the relief is now complete."

Yet Robertson was still worried, not necessarily about any broad German plan but about his own front, for the troops on the Schnee Eifel might be trapped by German drives around both ends of the ridge. That night as he talked in his office in St. Vith with his chief of staff, he telephoned Middleton, who declined a request for aerial reconnaissance the next day. "Go back to sleep, Robbie," he said. "You've been having a bad dream."

The corps commander whose responsibility included the northern portion of the Ardennes, Maj. Gen. Leonard T. ("Gee") Gerow of the V Corps, was preoccupied throughout much of November with an attack in the Hürtgen Forest, and later—as the date for the enemy's offensive approached—with the attack to take the Roer River dams. Gerow's G-2, Col. Thomas J. Ford, noted that prisoners were reporting the presence of SS troops "in towns close to the front," but he presumed they were "possibly surveying the new Roer River defense line."

The 2d Division's G-2, Colonel Christensen, whose division was to be relieved in the Schnee Eifel sector to carry the main weight of the attack for the dams, was more concerned. He expected the Germans to react to the American attack with local counterattacks, but also envisaged the possibility of "a major counterattack" just south of the dams. Christensen had in mind a counterattack with two panzer divisions, for it seemed "probable" that two were located several miles east of the dams.

Considering Gerow's own strength in that sector—three infantry divisions, a combat command of armor, and a cavalry reconnaissance squadron—the possibility of a counterattack by two panzer divisions was hardly to be taken lightly. Such a counterattack, Gerow believed, posed the greatest threat to his south wing, where one of his divisions (like those of the VIII Corps) was spread thin along a twenty-mile front southeastward from Monschau to the Losheim Gap, and where the attacking 2d Division would be depending for support of its attack upon a single road running through a dense forest close behind the front. That prompted Gerow to designate a fall-back position in that sector should it be required. He chose a stretch of high ground that would come to be known as the Elsenborn Ridge.

In the mineral resort town of Spa, at the First Army's headquarters in the Grand Hôtel Britannique—which twenty-six years before had served the same purpose for von Hindenburg and Ludendorff—Monk Dickson—his trip to Paris again delayed by General Thorson's failure to return because of bad flying weather—was becoming not only concerned but agitated. He learned on the 14th that "many PWs" were saying an offensive was soon to begin, probably "between the 17th and 25th of December," while others spoke of "the recapture of Aachen as a Christmas present for the Führer." There were further reports of heavy reinforcements pouring toward the front in the general area between Düren and Trier, which encompassed the entire Eifel.

That night, during a staff meeting held in General Hodges's office—it had once been von Hindenburg's—Dickson suddenly slapped the situation map in the area between Monschau and Echternach. "It's the Ardennes!" he exclaimed.

Yet Courtney Hodges and Dickson's compatriots on the First Army's staff knew Monk Dickson as an impetuous man. (In September, he had burst into Hodges's sleeping van with a monitored radio report saying von Rundstedt had ordered army troops to disarm the SS and appealed to the German people to join him in obtaining an honorable peace, which when checked turned out to be an American "black propaganda" broadcast designed to confuse the German people.) Indeed, a basic reason for the conflict within the staff was the G-3 section's failure except on rare occasions to listen to Dickson. On the night of December 14, nobody paid much attention to his outburst.

As evidenced by Dickson's next G-2 periodic report, issued the following morning, he himself saw no reason to put his impetuosity on record. The enemy, he assumed, "was resorting to his attack propaganda to bolster morale of the troops," although, he cautioned, it was possible that "a limited scale offensive will be launched for the purpose of achieving a Christmas morale 'victory' for civilian consumption." As for the Ardennes, he remarked only that the VIII Corps had reported that "an abrupt change of routine of enemy personnel opposite 9th Armored Division strongly suggests that new troops may have arrived in that area," to which he—or a subordinate—commented: "Very likely a recently arrived

Volksgrenadier Division coming in to relieve 212 Volksgrenadier Division."

With that, Dickson finally set off for his four-day leave in Paris. Before he went, he may have seen the message that arrived in the headquarters from the VIII Corps shortly before midnight on the 14th: It told of "a German woman" who had come through the lines and spoken of seeing "many horse-drawn vehicles, pontoons, small boats, and other river-crossing equipment," as well as "many artillery pieces, both horse-drawn and carried on trucks," in the vicinity of Bitburg.

The observations were not those of a German woman but of Elise Delé. Reproducing the report for transmission to subordinate commands, somebody added the comment: "A very interesting report. Build-up of troops has been confirmed by Tac/R [aerial reconnaissance] and PW statements. However, presence of large numbers of engineers with bridging equipment suggests preparation for offensive rather than defensive action."

Word went out to the 28th Division to investigate with ground patrols, but that was all.

As Monk Dickson left for Paris, all the other senior intelligence officers were at their posts. None expressed any new concern for the Ardennes, although one whose remarks had gone unnoticed by the others—Lt. Col. Anthony Tasker, a British officer serving as G-2 of the First Allied Airborne Army—had for two weeks been pointing toward the Ardennes as a likely spot for the anticipated German strike. Making his predictions at daily headquarters briefings, he pointed particularly to the thinly held sector on and near the Schnee Eifel. Yet headquarters of the First Allied Airborne Army was out of the line in England and, not being engaged in operations, was publishing no intelligence estimates; and since Tasker had no intelligence input that the other commands lacked, who would have paid any attention anyway?

There was clearly no concern at headquarters of the 21st Army Group. Field Marshal Montgomery's chief of staff, Maj. Gen. Francis ("Freddie") de Guingand, was on leave in England, and Montgomery himself had written General Eisenhower for permission to spend Christmas in London with his son. In Luxembourg City, General Bradley was getting ready to depart on the morning of the 16th for Versailles, where he was to participate in a conference at SHAEF's main headquarters on a critical shortage of American infantry replacements. In Spa', the First Army's commander, General Hodges, during the afternoon had received a "visiting galaxy" of professional baseball players (including Frankie Frisch, Bucky Walters, Dutch Leonard, and Mel Ott) and had then conferred for an hour with the commander of the VIII Corps, General Middleton. Since he had a bad head cold, he retired early in his requisitioned villa, Le Bocqueteau, atop a ridge two miles outside Spa in a community of expensive villas known as Balmoral. After returning from Spa to Bastogne, General Middleton also went off early to his sleeping van.

At Versailles on the 15th, an Allied air commanders' conference heard Eisenhower's G-3, Maj. Gen. Harold R. ("Pinky") Bull, report that the First Army's attack on the Roer River dams had failed to provoke a reaction from the enemy's panzer reserve and that on the VIII Corps front there was "nothing to report." Eisenhower's air intelligence officer, Air Commodore C. M. Grierson, then rose to relate that the Luftwaffe had continued to move fighter aircraft westward but that the shifts were "defensive" only.

At Bletchley Park, somebody put into the file a flimsy deciphered and sent to headquarters on the Continent on December 12: "Jadg Corps II aware 11 hours [December] 10th that all SS units were observing wireless silence."

Colonel Dickson at headquarters of the First Army had come closer than anybody to predicting what was about to happen in the Ardennes. Yet despite his brief impetuous outburst—"It's the Ardennes!"—Dickson, too, represented part of a general intelligence failure. Yet ULTRA and many another intelligence source had provided a lot of information that, properly interpreted and mixed with other material, should have told Eisenhower, Bradley, Hodges, Middleton, and Gerow what was about to hit them.

What ULTRA had failed to do was to be specific, to say exactly why Hitler was shifting fighter aircraft westward and building a large reserve with panzer and SS panzer divisions as its core. Allied commanders had come to expect ULTRA to be specific, to tell them not only what but when and where. When neither ULTRA nor their other intelligence sources told them those things, they failed to penetrate Hitler's masterful deception scheme to parade the assembly of the Sixth Panzer Army in the north while preparing secretly to attack in the Ardennes.

Only toward the end had Strong, Sibert, and Dickson, with some help from Koch of the Third Army, begun to pay attention to the Ardennes, to become aware of the move of enemy units into the Eifel. Yet even then they expressed no conviction—with the exception of Dickson's outburst—that the Germans intended a major blow in the Ardennes. It would represent, as Walter Bedell Smith was to remark later, "a dying gasp. No Goddamned fool would do it." In no way did the intelligence officers alert their commanders to a threat in the Ardennes serious enough or imminent enough to warrant any change in Eisenhower's offensive plans north and south of the region. To skitter and react with nervous defensive moves to every possibility open to the enemy is tantamount to surrendering all initiative.

The fact was that throughout the autumn and up to the last, almost all the intelligence specialists were assessing German intentions with three propositions in mind:

- First, that von Rundstedt, a capable old soldier, was in full charge on the Western Front. Had not the sturdy German defense all through the fall reflected the steady hand of an experienced commander acting according to time-tested and long-accepted tactics and principles? That gave verisimilitude to the theory, which even a doubting Oscar Koch finally accepted, that the German armor would be used sanely and rationally to counterattack the impending Allied drive toward the Rhine and the Ruhr.
- Second, so hardpressed was von Rundstedt both north and south of the Ardennes, partly as a result of having pulled divisions from the line to form a reserve, that he was finally having to shift divisions in either direction to counter upcoming American offensives. That accounted for the rail and motor traffic in the Eifel.
- Third, as General Sibert reported on December 12, German losses had been so great that the front was more brittle and more vulnerable than it appeared to be, and the enemy—as Brigadier Williams so forcibly noted—was in no condition to mount a major offensive. A general belief that the Germans were desperately short of fuel for tanks and planes fed that assumption. One intercepted message after another told of crippling fuel shortages. Who could have guessed that those messages told in fact of a desperate effort to accumulate enough fuel to launch a major offensive?

The enemy could still do something—the feeling was—but not much.

The basic failure was to have neglected to look beyond Gerd von Rundstedt to Adolf Hitler and to have recognized the desperation that motivated the Führer. The great German military theorist Carl von Clausewitz, in his famous treatise *On War*, written while he headed the *Kriegsakademie* early in the nineteenth century, had spelled it out:

> When the disproportion of power is so great that no limitation of our own object can ensure us safety from a catastrophe, or where the probable duration of the danger is such that the greatest economy of forces can no longer bring us to our object, then the . . . forces will, or should, be concentrated in one desperate blow. . . . He who is hard pressed . . . will regard the greatest daring as the greatest wisdom—at most, perhaps, employing the assistance of subtle stratagem.

Allied intelligence officers had committed the most grievous sin of which a G-2 is capable. They "had looked in a mirror for the enemy and seen there only the reflection of their own intentions."

CHAPTER FOUR

The Last Few Hours

The heavy drain of the long war had forced the German Army early in 1944 to reduce the strength of its infantry division from just over seventeen thousand men to just under thirteen thousand and to cut one of the battalions from each of three infantry regiments, although a so-called Fusilier battalion under division control was normally employed like a seventh infantry battalion. At slightly over fourteen thousand men, the American division had a thousand more men and nine infantry battalions. To make up, in part, for the cuts, the Germans vastly increased individual automatic weapons, especially a machine pistol known as the *Schmeisser*, whose high cyclic rate of fire made a kind of emetic or *b-r-r-r-r-r-p* sound so that the American soldier called it a "burp gun."

In most other aspects of armament, the two divisions were roughly similar. The individual American rifle, the M-1, was semi-automatic; that of the German, a bolt-action piece. Light air-cooled machine guns were comparable, except that the German piece had a much higher cyclic rate of fire, which produced such rapid fire that the German soldier called it the *"Hitler-Säge* (Hitler's Saw)." The Americans had a heavy water-cooled machine gun dating from World War I, which the Germans had abandoned. The Americans also had another weapon dating from the Great War, the Browning Automatic Rifle, called the BAR (pronounced as if spelling it). Basic mortars were similar: the American, a 60mm. and an 81mm.; but on the American side there were limited numbers of a much more powerful weapon, the 4.2-inch chemical mortar, designed for firing chemical shells but effective with high explosive and white phosphorus. Both sides had individual antitank rockets employing a shaped charge: the Germans a one-shot *Panzerfaust* and the Americans a bazooka, named for a makeshift musical instrument played by a hillbilly radio comedian, Bob Burns.

The crew-served American antitank weapon, a towed 57mm. piece, was little better than a pea-shooter against German tanks, while the German division had eighteen self-propelled 75mm. assault guns, normally used as close support for attacking infantry but effective against tanks. As a kind of assault gun, each American infantry regiment had six towed short-barreled 105mm. howitzers in a Cannon Company. Both divisions had three medium (105mm.) artillery battalions and one heavy battalion (150mm. for the Germans, 155mm. for the Americans) for a total of forty-eight howitzers.

To provide increased direct fire support for the infantry and better antitank defense, it had become standard practice by the fall of 1944 to attach to each American infantry division a tank battalion and a tank destroyer battalion. The tank battalion had a company (thirteen) of lights and three companies (fifty-three) of mediums; and some recently arrived battalions had an assault gun platoon with six tanks equipped with a 105mm. howitzer. The tank destroyer battalion had either a towed 3-inch gun (so-designated because it was a copy of a naval weapon) or a 76mm. (same as a 3-inch) or 90mm. self-propelled gun.

Those attachments made the American infantry division considerably stronger in men and firepower than the German *Volksgrenadier* division and at least the equal of the German *Panzergrenadier* division, which had organic medium tank and tank destroyer battalions and a contingent of half-tracks for transporting its grenadiers. Since the American division had a wealth of motor vehicles, plus the attached tanks and tank destroyers, it was as mobile as the *Panzergrenadier* division.

Neither the *Panzergrenadier* nor the parachute division had had to take the sharp reductions imposed on the *Volksgrenadiers*, so that both types of divisions still had nine battalions of infantry. The parachute divisions were considered to be elite, and in months long past they had been made up almost entirely of volunteers; but after heavy losses in an airborne assault on Crete in 1941, Hitler had become disenchanted with airborne troops. Airborne training virtually ceased, and among the parachute infantry in the Ardennes, few had any parachute training. The name parachute division had become nothing more than an honorific.

The German panzer and SS panzer division had a panzer regiment with two tank battalions and a self-propelled tank destroyer battalion. Most of the divisions in the Ardennes had around 130 tanks and tank destroyers combined. The *Panzergrenadiers* of both types of divisions— four battalions in the army division, six in the SS division—were supposed to ride in half-tracks. Only one of three artillery battalions in the army division and one of four in the SS division was self-propelled. The army division had thirteen thousand men, the SS division, twenty thousand. And all the SS divisions were beefed up with an attached tank or tank destroyer battalion, a *Nebelwerfer* (rocket) battalion, and a heavy 170mm. artillery battery.

Most American armored divisions had three tank battalions equipped with a total of 177 medium tanks, a self-propelled tank destroyer battalion, three medium artillery battalions (all self-propelled), and three battalions of armored infantry (one of the war's great misnomers, for when battle was joined, the armored infantryman fought outside his half-track with no more protection than any other foot soldier). Two divisions—the 2d and 3d Armored—were different, having been organized under an earlier table of organization with more tanks but fewer infantry than the other armored divisions.

Both sides had general support artillery, plus such specialized units as signal, quartermaster, ordnance, engineers, and the like; but in those specialized units, the Germans were at a dual disadvantage in numbers and quality. Such a basic item as tank recovery vehicles, for example, was in critically short supply, and several engineer battalions had never erected a bridge before. The American units, on the other hand, were at full strength, thoroughly trained and experienced in the field. American engineer battalions, trained in addition to their engineer duties to fight as infantry, were to prove to be a hidden reserve.

The one major German advantage was the quality of German tanks *vis-à-vis* those of the Americans. The Americans still had seventy-seven light tanks in their armored divisions and still used the light tank as a basic weapon in cavalry reconnaissance units, but its armor was absurdly thin and its 37mm. piece of no value except for firing canister against enemy infantry. The standard American tank was the 33-ton Sherman, most still equipped with a short-barreled 75mm. gun, although some had an improved long-barreled 76mm. high-velocity piece. By December 1944, the Sherman would have to be considered almost obsolescent, its only advantage over German tanks being a greater rapidity of fire (as a result of a gyrostabilizer and power traverse) and somewhat greater mobility. Like German tanks, it used regular gasoline rather than Diesel and was thus readily put to the torch: Some crewmen called it, after a popular cigarette lighter, the "Ronson." No American heavy tank had yet reached the battlefield.

The workhorses of the battlefield for the panzer and SS panzer divisions were medium tanks: the 27-ton Mark IV, a mainstay for the entire war, which mounted a long-barreled 75mm. gun; and the 47-ton Mark V Panther, which also mounted a 75mm. gun but had much thicker armor than either the Mark IV or the Sherman. Although the Sherman fought on equal terms with the Mark IV, it could knock out a Panther only with a shot to the side or rear.

The Germans also had behemoths, a 63-ton Mark VI Tiger and a 68-ton Royal or King Tiger, both of which were heavily armored and mounted a deadly high-velocity 88mm. gun. Although reports from American soldiers would indicate that the Tiger was omnipresent, only about 150 of them were to fight in the Ardennes, employed in separate battalions usually attached to a panzer or SS panzer division. The only American weapon that could consistently be counted upon to knock out a

Tiger was the tank destroyer equipped with a 90mm. gun, which had been developed originally as an antiaircraft weapon. A Tiger advancing with machine guns blazing or 88 blasting was a near-paralyzing sight.

The Ardennes was at once the nursery and the old folks' home of the American command. New divisions came there for a battlefield shakedown, old ones to rest after heavy fighting and absorb replacements for their losses.

In the north, covering Monschau, was the 102d Cavalry Group, a light force equipped with armored cars, light tanks, and a few self-propelled 75mm. assault guns. From Monschau southeast to the Losheim Gap and the boundary with the VIII Corps, the 99th Infantry Division, which had been in the line for five weeks but had yet to mount an attack, held a front approximately twenty miles long. Like almost all American divisions arriving in Europe in the fall of 1944, the 99th had been raided for replacements and shortly before shipping overseas, filled its ranks with men transferred from ground units of the Army Air Forces, from antiaircraft units, and from the Army Specialized Training Program (ASTP), the last an ill-starred experiment to provide technical training in colleges and universities for men with high IQs. (The program was sharply cut back as battlefield losses mounted.)

For long, only a cavalry reconnaissance squadron had held the five-mile width of the Losheim Gap. After repeated requests for reinforcement from the commander of the 2d Division, General Robertson, to whom the cavalry was attached, headquarters of the 14th Cavalry Group had arrived on December 11 to assume control of that squadron and brought with it a second squadron. That such a small force was entrusted with defending the critical Losheim Gap demonstrated the complacency with which American commanders viewed the possibility of a German offensive in the Ardennes. Yet other commanders on the ground were concerned. The 99th Division protected its right flank next to the gap with its only reserve infantry battalion, and the 2d Division placed one of its two reserve infantry battalions on its left flank close to the gap. The only other deference to the gap as a historic *débouché* was provided by the commander of the VIII Corps, General Middleton, who placed eight of his thirteen corps artillery battalions in positions from which they could fire either into the Losheim Gap and or in the sector around the Schnee Eifel.

Since early October, the 2d Division had held an eighteen-mile front that included the Schnee Eifel and extended southwest beyond the ridge almost to the Luxembourg border. To free the 2d Division for the First Army's attack on the Roer River dams, the 106th Infantry Division, fresh off the boats and flush with new men, mostly from the ASTP, began taking over on December 10.

In late November, the veteran 28th Infantry Division, having lost five thousand men in bloody fighting in the Hürtgen Forest, replaced another division that had been resting in the Ardennes, taking over a twenty-five-mile front along the Our River all the way south to the juncture of the Our and the Sûre. In effect, the 28th held nothing more than an outpost line.

With the arrival of the 9th Armored Division in late October as a reserve for the VIII Corps, General Middleton in order to provide the men with some battle experience, used the armored infantry battalion from one of the three combat commands to hold just over two miles of the 28th Division's front, intending to rotate the battalion with others. The tanks of that battalion's combat command were kept in reserve a few miles to the rear. Although the 9th Armored Division's other two combat commands were in reserve farther to the rear, one began to move on December 13 to provide an armored reserve for the attack to take the Roer River dams.

On December 7, the veteran 4th Infantry Division, having incurred almost as many casualties in the Hürtgen Forest as the 28th Division, took over the rest of the line—some twenty miles from the vicinity of Echternach to the boundary with the Third Army southeast of Luxembourg City. Since the southern boundary of the German offensive was to be a few miles south of Echternach, only a portion of the 4th Division was destined to become involved in the fighting.

In addition to the thirteen general support artillery battalions of the VIII Corps, General Gerow of the V Corps had just over six battalions concentrated near his southern boundary to support the attack on the Roer River dams. Thus there were 228 artillery pieces in addition to the 276 organic to divisions that would be capable of firing at some point within the Ardennes. It was an impressive assembly, yet far fewer than those available to the attacker. Middleton also was to have the support of an engineer combat group of four battalions and another of three battalions operating in rear areas of the VIII Corps under control of headquarters of the First Army. In the entire VIII Corps, there were 182 self-propelled tank destroyers and 242 medium tanks; they would be considerably outnumbered.

The men who manned the foxholes in the Ardennes knew that in comparison to attacking, they had it good. When not in their holes, they had warm, dry places to sleep in: houses, cellars, or bunker-type squad huts made from logs of the big fir trees, covered with sandbags. Some had heating from stoves mostly taken from nearby villages. Except in the most exposed positions, the troops almost always had hot food, and they could attend religious services back at battalion or regimental headquarters. From time to time, a man got to go on a forty-eight-hour pass to regimental or divisional rest camps well to the rear, where he could take a shower, sleep on a cot, buy a watered beer, have coffee and doughnuts dispensed by smiling American girls in Red Cross uniforms, see a movie, or, on rare occasions, a USO show, and, even more rarely, find a whorehouse where you had to stand in line, but what the hell?

There was, nevertheless, a war on. The Germans shelled with mortars and artillery, got nervous when a new division moved in and sent combat patrols to find out what was going on. The battalion S-2 was forever demanding that companies send out patrols to nab a prisoner, to determine what the enemy was up to; and to cover the great gaps in the line (sometimes up to a mile or more between units), contact patrols had to operate on a fairly regular basis. So porous was the line that German soldiers whose homes were in the eastern corner of Belgium sometimes slipped through to spend a night with their wives or girlfriends in St. Vith or nearby villages, and German agents mingled with the GI patrons of bars and cafés in the bigger towns. On occasion a German patrol might hit an installation in the rear of the line, a battalion headquarters or a supply point, lay mines on roads, or sometimes string a strand of heavy wire across a road within American lines so that the driver of a fast-moving jeep with windshield down might be decapitated.

On one occasion a German patrol ambushed three medical officers—a lieutenant colonel and two majors—killed them, and stripped them of their uniforms. A few days later, in the reserve positions of the 9th Armored Division's Combat Command B, as three officers were going to their mess hall, they passed three medics, a lieutenant-colonel and two majors, who were escorting three women wearing nylons and heavily veiled. The two parties exchanged salutes, but as the armored officers sat down to their meal, almost as one they did a double take. What was it about those medical officers? They had red crosses on their helmets and on the brassards on their arms, but something was wrong. No American medic ever carried a weapon, yet all three had .45-caliber pistols strapped to their waists. And nylons? What woman in wartime Luxembourg had nylons?

The three officers dashed outside, their weapons at the ready, but they were too late. Nobody was to be seen.

As *Null-Tag* finally approached, senior German commanders had no more faith in the Führer's grand design than when they had first heard of it. Individually, without consulting one another, neither von Rundstedt, Model, nor von Manteuffel made any plans for operations beyond the Meuse. Although von Manteuffel, at least, hoped to gain bridgeheads over the river just in case Hitler "had more forces hidden up his sleeve," he was convinced that that was the only way the offensive might continue toward Antwerp, for if by some strange good fortune the German armies should reach the Meuse without encountering "strong enemy forces," those forces would surely be lying in wait on the other side of the river.

Nor did Sepp Dietrich display any greater optimism. In conjunction

with his chief of staff, Brigadeführer der Waffen-SS Fritz Kraemer, a
General Staff–trained officer for whom von Rundstedt and Model had
arranged appointment in order to afford the Sixth Panzer Army professional tactical and strategic direction, Dietrich had drawn up a plan, with
the tacit consent of von Rundstedt and Model but without the knowledge
either of General Jodl or Hitler, to alter the Führer's dictate. Instead of
passing south of Liège and crossing the Meuse west of the city, the Sixth
Panzer Army was to cross on both sides of the city. That would put Dietrich in position to implement the Small Solution. Should it come to that.

Hitler for some reason became suspicious, for on the eve of the offensive, after nightfall on December 15, he telephoned Model. "There will
be no deviation by the panzer units east of the Meuse toward the north,"
he admonished. "The Sixth Panzer Army must keep clear of the covering
front to be built up between Monschau and Liège. Do not let Dietrich
become involved in the fighting along his northern flank." To which
Model replied, *Jawohl, mein Führer*, and shortly telephoned back to say
he had given the instructions to Dietrich. "All the efforts of Army Group
B," said Model, "will be directed toward the thrust to Antwerp."

As for the other army commander, General Brandenberger, whose
Seventh Army was to secure the southern flank of the penetration, there
was no way he could be optimistic. To attack and then to defend more
than eighty miles of up-and-down Ardennes countryside from Echternach
to the Meuse River at Givet, he would have only four infantry divisions,
no tanks, and a mere handful of tank destroyers and assault guns. An
earlier hope of taking Luxembourg City had to be abandoned, but even
with that modification, Brandenberger's appeared to be an impossible assignment.

Despite the presence to the south of the Third U.S. Army and its
commander, George Patton, for whom German generals had immense
respect, Hitler showed less concern about the south flank than about the
north. Enlarging on an idea originally suggested by Model, Hitler on December 8 suddenly developed a new interest in parachute troops. He
wanted a battalion of just over a thousand paratroopers to drop behind
Monschau astride the only north–south road leading across the moors of
the Hautes Fagnes, there to block American reinforcements from the
north until Dietrich's troops could arrive to erect a solid defensive shoulder. Making the link-up was to be the assignment of a special task force
equipped with twenty-one experimental *Jägdtigers* (tank destroyers), 82-
ton monsters mounting an awesome 128mm. gun, the mainstay of German antiaircraft defenses, on a Tiger chassis.

The airborne attack fell to a veteran paratrooper who had fought on
Crete, a man of the old Catholic aristocracy, Col. Graf (Count) Friedrich
August von der Heydte. To assemble the troops, Hitler ordered commanders of all parachute regiments to send a hundred of their best soldiers, which predictably set in motion the game long practiced in every

army of getting rid of misfits and incompetents. Yet when men of von der Heydte's old unit, the 6th Parachute Regiment, learned of the mission, some 250 of them took off and reported to their former commander, who somehow managed to convince his superiors to allow him to hold onto them.

At that point, von der Heydte had only a few days left in which to prepare his rag-tag force, few of whom had ever made even a practice parachute jump; and the man to whom von der Heydte was to be responsible, Sepp Dietrich, was less than cooperative. When von der Heydte reported at his headquarters near Münstereifel, Dietrich had been drinking heavily. Since a parachute drop would alert the enemy, declared Dietrich, it would have to be made only a few hours before the ground attack started, which would mean a night drop.

Von der Heydte pointed out that to jump at night into a region of forests and moors with such inexperienced troops as he possessed would be suicidal, but Dietrich refused to budge. Don't worry, Dietrich assured him. The paratroopers would have to hold for only a few hours before the big *Jägdtigers* reached them.

The commander of another special force, Otto Skorzeny, already concerned that the order requesting volunteers for his mission had surely fallen into Allied hands, had encountered little to encourage him in his assignment of penetrating the American line with German soldiers masquerading as Americans. From the first he was concerned that soldiers wearing the enemy's uniform would be violating International Laws of War and subject, if captured, to execution; but legal counsel assured him that the laws permitted wearing enemy uniforms as a *ruse de guerre*, forbidding only fighting while wearing them. His men could wear their German uniforms underneath and take off the American ones before opening fire. (That, Skorzeny knew, was claptrap.)

Skorzeny also recognized that it would be impossible to create a cohesive brigade, which was the size unit he considered necessary, out of random volunteers in the short time available. Only with difficulty did he persuade Jodl to give him two infantry battalions and a company of tanks. Those were to be the core of the 150th Panzer Brigade of 3,300 men.

The response to the call for volunteers who spoke American "dialect" left Skorzeny in dismay. Only ten, mostly former merchant seamen, spoke perfect English with some knowledge of American slang. Another 125 had a fair command of English, and about 200 others had learned a little English in school. A few could say yes and no. That was all.

The quest for American uniforms and equipment was at least as discouraging. Although Skorzeny asked for twenty American tanks, he got two, one of which quickly broke down with transmission trouble. Skorzeny had to make do with twelve Panthers camouflaged to look like Shermans, sufficient only, Skorzeny ruefully observed, to "deceive very young American troops seeing them at night from very far away." Of ten armored cars received, six were British, but in any case they soon broke down. There were about fifteen American trucks and thirty jeeps.

The first consignment of uniforms turned out to be British. When a consignment of American field jackets arrived, they had a big triangle—indicating prisoner of war—painted on the back. There were a few American mortars and antitank guns but no rounds for them and possibly enough M-1 rifles to arm half the brigade but with limited amounts of ammunition. It was soon obvious that Skorzeny would be able to disguise only those men in a commando company who were to spread confusion in the American rear, and even those would lack much of the paraphernalia that American soldiers usually wore and carried.

Skorzeny also had another security scare. Although his troops were sealed in their training area at Grafenwöhr, near Nuremberg, so wild were the rumors circulating among them as to their mission that Skorzeny was sure some word would leak to Allied intelligence. Yet how to stop the rumors? Skorzeny decided at last to let them fly, the wilder the better.

A few days later, when Skorzeny was visiting at Grafenwöhr, a lieutenant assigned to the commando company asked to speak with him privately. "Sir," said the young officer, "I believe I know the real objective of the brigade." Skorzeny bristled. Had somebody talked? But the lieutenant quickly continued: "The brigade is to go straight to Paris and capture Allied headquarters!" He himself wanted to help; he had lived in Paris and spoke French fluently. Although he recognized that Skorzeny had probably already drawn up a plan, he had some ideas he hoped Skorzeny would consider. After slipping through the lines in American uniforms, the men would rendezvous at the Café de la Paix on the Place de l'Opéra, and from there proceed to capture or assassinate General Eisenhower and his staff.

As far as Skorzeny could make out, the lieutenant had based his reckoning on the codename Skorzeny had chosen for the operation: *GREIF*. It meant a mythical bird, but in another sense the word could mean "Grasp." "Well," said Skorzeny, "go and think it all over very carefully and work out the details. We'll have a further talk—but mind you, keep as silent as the grave."

By the time night fell, Skorzeny reckoned, almost every man in the camp believed he knew what the mission was: Kill Eisenhower.

Aside from spreading confusion in the American rear, Skorzeny's mission was to seize three bridges over the Meuse in the zone of the Sixth Panzer Army between Liège and the bend in the river at Namur. Once *Volksgrenadier* divisions had broken the American line, which Skorzeny assumed would be accomplished before the end of the first day, he was to send three task forces (two of which would have twelve tanks each) through the darkness, bypassing opposition, and seize the bridges before the Americans could blow them. Jeeps carrying drivers and riders disguised as Americans were to lead the way.

One of Skorzeny's three task forces was to accompany another special group, a beefed-up *Kampfgruppe* (battle group) of the 1st SS Panzer Division known as the *Liebstandärte Adolf Hitler* (Hitler's Own), a division which traced its origins to Hitler's first bodyguard, initially organized by Sepp Dietrich. The commander of the *Kampfgruppe* was SS-Lt. Col. Joachim Peiper, who at age nineteen had become an officer candidate in the SS, and except for a brief stint on the staff of Reichsführer-SS Himmler had spent the next ten years with the *Liebstandärte Adolf Hitler* and stood high in Hitler's personal favor. (Possibly reflecting the SS distaste for names of biblical origin, Peiper had come to prefer to spell his first name "Jochen.")

The moment the *Volksgrenadiers* achieved a breakthrough, *Kampfgruppe Peiper* was to drive through the northern reaches of the Losheim Gap toward the bridge over the Meuse at Huy, midway between Liège and Namur. Over a route specially chosen because it had fewer bridges than the others—at some points, Peiper was later to complain with considerable justification, a route "more fit for bicycles" than for tanks—Peiper was to dash for Huy without regard for his flanks, avoiding likely opposition, and where possible bypassing it if encountered. In the interest of speed, the armored spearhead of Peiper's column could hardly be expected to burden itself with large numbers of prisoners of war, but whether they were to be cared for by troops following later in the column or just what was to be done with them would in time become a matter of major importance and tragedy.

As each German soldier marched to his jump-off position in the Eifel and on the evening of December 15 learned for the first time what he was to do, reactions varied widely. Some received the news stoically, much like Private First Class Stiegeler whose group "was given a bottle of booze, and off we went." Others doubted that anything substantial could be accomplished: Had they not lived on promises ever since the retreat from Normandy? Where were the miracle weapons the official communiqués promised? Many of those transferred from rear echelon posts and from the navy and the Luftwaffe were depressed. At a time when the war was practically over, why should they have to fight and probably die for a lost cause?

Thousands received the news with resignation. In the 2d SS Panzer Division, for example, 1st Lt. Erich Heller and his young officer friends, all of whom had fought in Normandy, "agreed that the war was virtually lost," but even so, they "had no idea of not doing their duty." The people at home were taking terrible punishment from the bombers, yet they were holding firm, doing what was expected of them. As soldiers at the front, could they do less?

For some, it was, in any case, a battle for survival, for if Germany lost the war, the people would be, at best, enslaved. If not, why the demand for unconditional surrender? Why the Morgenthau Plan to abolish German industry and turn the country into a pastoral, agricultural land?

Still others saw the possibility of achieving something that might alleviate postwar Germany's fate. A sergeant in *Kampfgruppe Peiper,* Karl Wortmann, thought they would succeed, "not necessarily a great victory but gaining as much territory as possible to embarrass the Americans and demonstrate success to the German people." A regimental commander in the 12th Volksgrenadier Division, Col. Wilhelm Osterhold, intended to lead his troops as capably as possible, "perhaps in the process achieving something that might lessen the harsh treatment that was in store for Germany."

Thousands more received the news with enthusiasm. As one German officer wrote in his diary: "There is a general feeling of elation; everybody is cheerful." Pvt. Klaus Ritter and his young friends in the 18th Volksgrenadier Division were "euphoric . . . in four weeks they would actually be in Paris!"

For many, faith in the Führer's ability to set matters right remained, and since all news came through a controlled press, they had no real knowledge of how grim was Germany's plight. Countless numbers among them welcomed the chance at battlefield booty: to feast on American rations, to smoke cigarettes with real tobacco in them ("A choice between Camels and Chesterfields!"), to get a pair of the good leather boots the *Ami* wore. Others welcomed retribution: a chance to pay back the *Ami* for the destruction of German cities, for the bombing of civilians, to chase him forever from German soil.

In the SS panzer divisions, morale was highest of all. Noted one SS trooper to his sister:

> I write during one of the great hours before we attack . . . full of expectation for what the next days will bring. Everyone who has been here the last two days and nights (especially nights), who has witnessed hour after hour the assembly of our crack divisions, who has heard the constant rattling of Panzers, knows that something is up . . . we attack and will throw the enemy from our homeland. That is a holy task!

On the back of the envelope, he scribbled: "Ruth! Ruth! Ruth! WE MARCH!"

A member of an old Virginia family, Walter Melville Robertson had received a commission in the infantry from West Point in 1912. Seeing no overseas duty during World War I, he served the usual between-wars assignments, mostly with infantry regiments at isolated U.S. posts in the West and Southwest, but he also served as an instructor at the Command

and General Staff College and at the Army War College. Early in 1940, he went to Fort Sam Houston, just outside San Antonio, Texas, to join one of the U.S. Army's more renowned regular units, the 2d Infantry Division, with which Robertson's destiny was long to be linked. Possibly because he and his wife had no children, the 2d Division became a kind of family to him. Mild-mannered and soft-spoken, he had the reddish hair and florid complexion of an Irishman and also "a temper when tested too far." No drinker, something of a loner, he seldom mingled socially with his officers, but they had deep respect for his ability as a commander.

Robertson first commanded a battalion in the 9th Infantry, then the regiment itself, then the 23d Infantry, whereupon he became assistant division commander and finally assumed command of the division. Under his command, the 2d Division came ashore on OMAHA Beach the day after D-Day. At fifty-six, Robertson was a few years older than most division commanders.

When at the end of the first week of December Robertson went to headquarters of the V Corps in Eupen to receive the order for the attack on the Roer River dams, one aspect of the plan of attack troubled him deeply. Approaching the dams from the south, he would have at first only one road over which the entire division would have to advance and also depend upon for supply. It ran from the town of Büllingen north through Krinkelt and Rocherath, two villages so close together that they appeared to be one (American troops called them the "twin villages"), thence for six miles through a dense fir forest to the first objective, a road junction known as Wahlerscheid and marked by a customshouse, a farmhouse, concrete dragon's teeth, and a thick cluster of pillboxes of the West Wall. The enemy strongpoint sat astride one of the wide gaps in the defensive line of the 99th Division. *(See map, Chapter Eight, p. 164.)*

For almost the entire distance, the road ran behind and almost parallel with the 99th Division's positions along the German frontier, from one to three miles away. If the Germans should penetrate the 99th Division's extended line and cut the road at any point along the nine miles from Büllingen to Wahlerscheid, whatever portion of Robertson's troops had passed over the road would be trapped. There would be no way out except on foot, for there was not even a trail leading westward except for a dirt track from Krinkelt-Rocherath through the village of Wirtzfeld, thence over a meandering course to the town of Elsenborn, and for more than half a mile the track ran along a stream bottom with soil of such consistency that not even a jeep could negotiate it.

Once troops of the 106th Division began to take over on the Schnee Eifel, Robertson's engineer officer, Lt. Col. Robert W. Warren, put his 2d Engineer Battalion to work to improve that track to make it passable at least for one-way traffic. Yet that would merely alleviate Robertson's problem, not solve it, for the track through Wirtzfeld was near the start of what would be the division's lone supply route, so that a cut along the wooded six-mile stretch north of Krinkelt-Rocherath might still trap the division. So, too, would an enemy thrust into Krinkelt-Rocherath, and there were two fairly good roads leading into the twin villages through frontier forests from German positions.

A heavy snowstorm was pelting the northern reaches of the Ardennes and the Eifel when Robertson's troops began to move from the Schnee Eifel region to assembly areas in and near a Belgian Army caserne close behind the 99th Division's front, Camp Elsenborn. In an effort to achieve surprise, there was no patrolling to pinpoint the enemy's defenses before the troops of the leading 9th Infantry began to march north from Krinkelt-Rocherath into the fir forest soon after daylight on December 13.

There was at first no enemy, but the going was slow. Although the storm had passed, warming weather made the snow heavy, and because the road was known to be mined and at intervals blocked by felled trees, the men had to plow through the forest on either side, sometimes grappling through growths of wet young firs, at other times subjected to falling snow from towering branches of the bigger ones. By the time the column neared the enemy-held road junction around noon, everybody was drenched.

The hope for surprise quickly vanished. A hundred yards in front of the pillboxes the forest cover ran out, and the first men to emerge from the woodsline drew a blast of fire from rifles and automatic weapons, while mortar and artillery shells exploded in the treetops and threw a lethal shower of fragments onto the forest floor. In some places rows of barbed-wire entanglements six to ten deep barred the way to the pillboxes, and the snow hid a veritable quilt of deadly antipersonnel mines.

That first day, the men of the 9th Infantry made not a dent in the German position, and night brought with it a numbing cold that froze the men's wet uniforms almost stiff. Through the night patrols probed without success to try to find a weak spot in the defenses, while most of the men tried to keep warm by painfully etching some kind of cover from the frozen earth. It was a miserable pattern that would be long repeated, and all the while medical jeeps formed a steady procession back down the forest road, laboriously swept of mines by the engineers.

Meanwhile, a few hundred yards to the southeast of Wahlerscheid, three of the 99th Division's battalions attacked down into deep ravines and up precipitous wooded hillsides in an effort to pin down other enemy troops and prevent them from reinforcing at Wahlerscheid or pushing through the forest to cut the lone supply route. In almost every case on the first day, German fire stopped those men, too, and the cold night was just as painful for them as for the men of the 2d Division. Over the next two days those men nevertheless wrenched gains of a few hundred yards from the stubborn defenders and the hostile forest.

Several miles to the north, beyond Monschau, an untried infantry division, the 78th, attacked southeastward in support of the 2d Division's attack over rolling, open ground dotted with villages and pillboxes, the northern prong of what the corps commander, General Gerow, hoped would become a double envelopment converging on the dams. Gains were painfully slow, but one battalion managed on the first day to advance a mile and a half to seize two villages, and on the next, a company slipped past defended pillboxes to take a third.

Then the Germans began to counterattack. By late afternoon of the third day, the company in the forward village still held, but its position was precarious; and after nightfall a prisoner provided the disturbing news that a previously unidentified 326th Volksgrenadier Division was assembled nearby.

Back at Wahlerscheid, as dusk approached on the second day, December 14, ten men slithered unnoticed by the Germans under one barbed-wire entanglement after another until all the rows were behind them, and in their wake other men cut a four-foot gap through the wire. Yet the men had no communications with their company headquarters, where some confusion existed because the company commander had just been wounded and evacuated. The men of the patrol had long since retired before word of what they had accomplished reached the battalion commander, Lt. Col. Walter M. Higgins, Jr.

When the next night came—December 15—and the 9th Infantry was as far as ever from cracking the defenses at Wahlerscheid, Higgins decided to try to exploit the little gap in the wire. Soon after dark, an eleven-man patrol, guided by one of the men who had helped forge the gap the night before and equipped with a sound-powered telephone, moved through the gap. Around 9:30 P.M., the patrol leader whispered into the telephone. The patrol had surrounded a pillbox and the Germans seemed unaware that anything was going on.

That was all Higgins needed. Within minutes, first one company then another was plodding single file, following a band of white tape through the gap in the wire. When another battalion quickly followed, the assault began. The men moved swiftly, blowing the doors of pillboxes with explosive charges, killing or capturing the occupants, prodding sleepy Germans from their foxholes, and capturing seventy-seven in one sweep at the customshouse. With Wahlerscheid at last in hand, a second regiment, the 38th Infantry, was soon moving forward to help exploit the breach.

Elsewhere on the Ardennes front, in the final hours before the Germans were to doff their cloak of deception, all remained relatively quiet, but there were a few last-minute indications that something untoward might be stirring. Late on the 15th, the 4th and 106th Divisions each took two prisoners, all of whom stated that they had been told a big attack was coming. Yet two were deserters who said they put little store by what they were told, for they had been promised big things before and nothing happened. Another impressed his interrogators, but he was so heavily sedated because of wounds that detailed questioning had to be delayed. The fourth, an ethnic Pole, was eager to talk. Interrogated at a regimental headquarters, he said the Germans would attack sometime between December 16 and Christmas "in a large-scale offensive, employing searchlights against the clouds to simulate moonlight." But the 106th Division's G-2, Lt. Col. Robert P. Stout, delayed reporting that information to the VIII Corps until he could talk personally with the prisoner.

For several nights, outposts of the 106th Division had been reporting the noise of tracked vehicles, and on the 15th, Colonel Stout noted that the night before there had been the "sound of vehicles all along the front after dark—vehicles, barking dogs, motors." A prisoner, Stout added, had said that "soldiers who come under the category of 'Volkliste III' [one of the categories of Volksdeutsch]" had been withdrawn from the front, but Stout made no effort to read significance into the information.

A few miles to the south, outposts of the 28th Infantry Division reported that there appeared to be new and more disciplined troops opposing the division. The soldiers had fresh uniforms, including overcoats, and outside the pillboxes there was "much saluting and double-timing of guards."

A few more miles to the south, the G-2 of the 4th Infantry Division, Lt. Col. Harry F. Hansen, told his commander, Maj. Gen. Raymond O. Barton, that there were "large enemy formations in Bitburg." Although Barton had no thought of a big enemy offensive, he did assume that the Germans might stage a large raid, possibly to seize General Bradley's headquarters in Luxembourg City. With that in mind, he sent Hansen to talk with General Sibert, but Sibert discounted the idea. Barton nevertheless ordered all men who were in rest centers farther back than regimental headquarters to return to their units, and on the 15th he assembled his regimental commanders to discuss counterattack plans.

On both the 14th and 15th, worried civilians from villages and towns near the Our River began to turn up in the town of Diekirch, several miles back. The Germans were up to something, said the civilians, though they knew not what. "Don't worry," Americans from a Counter-Intelligence Corps detachment in Diekirch told them; "Jerry will never come back." Unconvinced, the civilians either continued to make their way farther from the front or looked up friends and relatives with whom to stay in Diekirch.

Around midnight on the 14th, in response to the information imparted by Elise Delé, a patrol from the 28th Division's 109th Infantry crossed the Our River at Vianden and crept warily up the high ground beyond. The men investigated one pillbox after another, all of which the Germans had long occupied, but they found not a man in any of them. What did that mean?

On the 28th Division's north wing that night, Pfc. John B. Allard, a nineteen-year-old member of Company F, 112th Infantry, volunteered

for a patrol also mustered in response to the information from Elise Delé.
Having recently learned that his twin brother in another regiment of the
division was missing and presumed dead, Allard had made a point of
becoming "a more active participant in combat patrol activities." Led by
1st Lt. Donald Nikkel, the twelve-man patrol slipped past German outposts across the Our from the village of Ouren, surrounded a pillbox, and
seized it without a fight. While two men escorted twenty prisoners to the
rear, the others stayed in the pillbox all the next day while watching with
concern as one German formation after another arrived and settled down
in nearby woods.

When night came on the 15th, Allard and other members of the patrol
started back; but in every direction they came upon German troops,
back-tracked, then tried again. In the end, they decided to brave it and in
the darkness walked straight through a bivouac where Germans were
sleeping in two-man tents. In some of the tents, candles were glowing.
After wading the icy Our, Allard and the others reported what they had
seen to their company commanders, but as they headed for their cellars,
dawn of December 16 was only a few hours off.

In late afternoon of December 15, a farmer named Nikolaus Manderfeld left the village of Afst in the Losheim Gap to walk a little over half a
mile along a snow-covered trail leading to the settlement of Allmuthen.
One of only ten farmers whom the Americans had allowed to stay in Afst
to care for the *bêtes*, as the locals called their pigs and cattle, Manderfeld's home was in Allmuthen, but neither Americans nor Germans occupied that little settlement. Manderfeld wanted to check his house to see
if all was well.

Manderfeld was almost there when three German soldiers emerged
from behind it, their machine pistols at the ready. One with binoculars
around his neck demanded to know what Manderfeld was doing there.
Accepting his explanation, they asked what he knew about the American
positions. There were a few Americans in Afst, he said, and maybe about
forty in the next village of Krewinkel.

"Tomorrow," said the soldier with the binoculars, "the heavies'll start
firing again. We'll begin the final offensive. By the day after tomorrow,
we'll be in Liège. In four days Antwerp will be ours!"

That night, after Manderfeld returned to Afst and was sitting by the
stove in the house where he and all the other men were staying, he told
his friends what had happened, but nobody believed him. Klaus Manderfeld always was a great one for tall stories.

Had Nikolaus Manderfeld spoken to the American soldiers in Afst, he
might have found a more receptive audience, for the Americans were
indeed concerned. The night before, the pattern of enemy behavior had
abruptly changed. For long weeks the enemy had appeared to be nervous

at night, firing flares and occasionally letting go with a burst from a machine gun or a burp gun; but the night before, there had been not a single flare and the darkness was eerily silent. So, too, an accustomed parade of putt-putting V-1 buzz bombs passing overhead en route toward Liège and Antwerp came to an end.

It was the same on the night of the 15th as 2d Lt. Max L. Crawford led an eight-man patrol from Troop C, 18th Cavalry Reconnaissance Squadron, to set up an ambush in Allmuthen and try to grab a prisoner. At first the men circled the cluster of farmhouses, attached barns, and manure piles at a distance, then, hearing nothing suspicious, they moved to a trail junction across from one of the houses. While three men took up positions across the trail from the house at an open shed filled with hay, others deployed closer to the trail junction, and Lieutenant Crawford and Cpl. John Banister took cover alongside the attached barn. From inside the house, the two heard low voices and a muffled cough.

The patrol had been in position only a short time when a group of about thirty Germans, some pulling a sled loaded with something and all talking unconcernedly, approached the trail junction. According to Crawford's instructions, the men were not to fire if badly outnumbered, but when several of the Germans began to walk toward the hay shed, Pvt. Richard King, armed with a Thompson submachine gun, considered that he had no choice. The Germans were almost on top of him as he fired.

Considering that the little patrol "didn't have the chance of a snowflake in hell," Crawford's second-in-command, Sgt. David Herzog, yelled to take off. Most of the men made it, scrambling back to a rendezvous point previously agreed upon, but the Germans captured one man and were so close to Crawford and Banister that they dared not move. For more than two hours they flattened themselves against the side of the barn while soldiers passed in and out of the house, sometimes so near it seemed to Crawford and Banister they could have reached out and touched them. It was close to midnight before they dared try to escape, and however carefully they set their feet down in the snow, it seemed as if they were moving like elephants and that the loud crunching noises would surely give them away.

At long last, they were far enough from the house to make a run for it. Getting back to Afst close to one o'clock in the morning, Lieutenant Crawford reported to the squadron's S-2 what had happened. No patrol, said Crawford, had ever run into that much enemy activity in Allmuthen.

That same night of December 15, at the southern terminus of the Skyline Drive in Diekirch, a glamorous German-born film star, Marlene Dietrich, heading a USO troupe, performed to the raucous applause of hundreds of GIs. She went to bed as soon as possible after the performance, for she had to get up early the next morning to travel north to the sector of the 99th Infantry Division, where she was to make informal appearances at several regimental rest camps close behind the front.

Within the Eifel on December 15, German intelligence officers took a last look at the American side of the line. The only possible trouble spot appeared to be in the extreme north near Monschau, where on the 13th an apparently small-scale American attack had begun. That might pose problems for the northernmost unit in the offensive, the 272d Volksgrenadier Division, which had been hit by the northern prong of the American attack. The other division that was to attack at Monschau, the 326th Volksgrenadier Division, had just arrived in an assembly area for the jump-off and was thus unaffected by the American attack.

Otherwise, the American front appeared much the same as it had for some days: the 4th, 28th, and 99th Divisions and the recently arrived 106th Division, which German intelligence had quickly identified. The 2d Division presumably had moved to a reserve position and thus would probably have to be reckoned with at some point during the offensive but not right away. Possibly because the 2d Division had removed all unit markings from its vehicles and all of its distinctive big Indianhead shoulder patches before beginning its attack, and possibly too because three battalions of the 99th Division had also been involved in the attack, the Germans had failed to discern the presence of the 2d Division at Wahlerscheid. They still expected to encounter in that sector only the thinly spread 99th Division.

At most, the Germans believed the Americans had about 370 tanks in the entire Ardennes, and they felt fairly sure that the 12th Army Group had no major reserves. Yet from agents they had learned that the 82d and 101st Airborne Divisions had assembled in northern France, where they were presumably resting after a long stay in defensive positions in the Netherlands following participation in the Allied airborne operation in September. The bars in Rheims and surrounding towns were filled at night with rowdy paratroopers.

In assembly areas close behind the front that night, commanders read out a message from Field Marshal von Rundstedt and endorsements from Field Marshal Model and the appropriate army commander to their men. Von Rundstedt's message said:

> Soldiers of the West Front!! Your great hour has arrived. Large attacking armies have started against the Anglo-Americans. I do not have to tell you anything more than that. You feel it yourself. WE GAMBLE EVERYTHING! You carry with you the holy obligation to give everything to achieve things beyond human possibilities for our Fatherland and our Führer!

At von Rundstedt's headquarters in Ziegenberg Castle, the keeper of the *OB WEST* War Diary made a final entry for the day at midnight: "Tomorrow brings the beginning of a new chapter in the Campaign in the West."

BOOK

II

THE
FIRST
DAY

CHAPTER FIVE

In Front of St. Vith

Scion of one of the oldest of the hereditary nobilities of Prussia, Hasso Eccard von Manteuffel was, at forty-seven, young for an army command and at 5 feet, 2 inches, and 120 pounds, hardly of the physique to inspire awe in subordinates. When he was a cadet-officer candidate at the age of fourteen at the Berlin-Lichterfelde Academy, they had to remove a portion of his rifle barrel to enable him to manipulate it in drill. At last old enough for military service in 1916, he served on the Western Front as a lieutenant of infantry, where he was wounded slightly by shrapnel.

Long an avid and expert horseman, von Manteuffel transferred after the war to the cavalry and became enthused over the possibilities of armor as espoused by a young major, Heinz Guderian. He joined the Inspectorate General of Armored Forces soon after Guderian in 1934 became its chief of staff. Then, as later, von Manteuffel (like Gerd von Rundstedt) was apolitical, "in the true Prussian tradition."

Although von Manteuffel saw Hitler's attack on Russia as a mistake, he volunteered for front-line service, commanded a *Panzergrenadier* battalion, and soon replaced the fallen commander of his regiment. During the unsuccessful drive on Moscow, he performed with such distinction that he gained promotion to colonel and received the Knight's Cross to the Iron Cross.

As the German retreat began in heavy snows and below-zero cold, von Manteuffel ran afoul of his army commander, Colonel-General Walter Model. Model ordered von Manteuffel to make an attack, but hardly had it begun before von Manteuffel called it off: the snow was so deep his men could barely move. Outraged, Model went to von Manteuffel's headquarters and threatened court-martial, but the division commander defused the issue by sending von Manteuffel with the advance party for the division's impending transfer to France. By the time von Manteuffel saw Model again, the diminutive soldier—his friends called him "*Kleiner*" ("Little")—had commanded a division in North Africa and had returned to the Eastern Front to lead an elite panzer division, *Grossdeutschland*. He so impressed Adolf Hitler in the process that the Führer summoned him to the *Wolfschanze* to jump him past corps command to the rank of General der Panzertruppen and command of the Fifth Panzer Army on the Western Front.

In October, 1944, as the Fifth Panzer Army shifted to the command of Army Group B, von Manteuffel with some trepidation reported to Field Marshal Model's headquarters near Krefeld. Entering Model's office, he saluted and noted with relief that Model returned the salute. "You remember our conversation in 1941?" asked Model. "Now we two have the same task; we are good friends."

More than anybody other than Hitler himself, von Manteuffel put his imprint on the way the big offensive was to begin. As part of the unsuccessful effort to talk Hitler out of the Big Solution, he found an opportunity, when he saw Hitler at the Reischschancellery on December 2, to convince the Führer to make changes. Rather than a two- to three-hour artillery preparation, he argued that a short, concentrated preparation would accomplish much the same effect while lessening the enemy's alert. Rather than attack at 10 A.M., which would leave little more than six hours of daylight for the first day's operation, he wanted the artillery preparation to begin well before daylight at 5:30 A.M., followed a half hour later by a ground assault assisted by artificial moonlight to be created by bouncing the light of giant searchlights off the clouds. ("How do you know you will have clouds?" asked Hitler. Responded von Manteuffel: "You have already decided there will be bad weather.")

Having donned the uniform of a colonel of infantry and spent a night in a pillbox overlooking the Our River, von Manteuffel had personally determined that outposts of the American 28th Division's 110th Infantry pulled back from the river at night. He thus proposed no artillery fire along the river, so that the assault troops could begin crossing while the artillery was hitting American positions a mile or so beyond on the Skyline Drive. Since he also discerned that the positions of the 28th Division's 112th Infantry, which were on the German side of the Our, were widely spaced, he asked authority to forego an artillery preparation there so that troops might infiltrate between and in rear of the American positions before the hour of attack.

To all those proposals, Hitler agreed.

Split seconds before 5:30 A.M. on Saturday, December 16, an American soldier from Company K, 110th Infantry, manning an observation post atop a concrete water tower along the Skyline Drive in the village of Hosingen, telephoned his company commander. In the distance on the German side of the Our, he could see a strange phenomenon: countless flickering pinpoints of light. Moments later both he and his company commander had the explanation. They were the flashes of German guns,

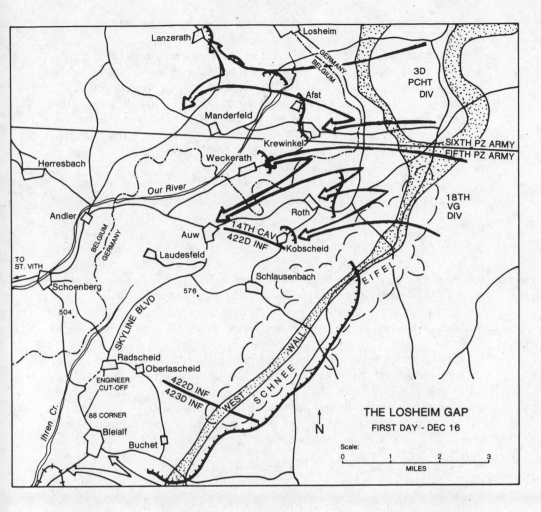

Lanzerath
Losheim
GERMANY
BELGIUM
3D
PCHT
DIV
Afst
Manderfeld
Krewinkel
SIXTH PZ ARMY
FIFTH PZ ARMY
Weckerath
Herresbach
Our River
18TH
VG
DIV
Roth
Andler
BELGIUM
GERMANY
Auw
14TH CAV
422D INF
Kobscheid
TO
ST. VITH
Laudesfeld
Schlausenbach
Schoenberg
576
EIFEL
504
SKYLINE BLVD
Radscheid
Oberlascheid
ENGINEER
CUT-OFF
422D INF
423D INF
WEST WALL
SCHNEE
Ihren Cr.
88 CORNER
Bleialf
Buchet

THE LOSHEIM GAP
FIRST DAY - DEC 16

Scale:
0   1   2   3
MILES

N

for at Hosingen, along the rest of the Skyline Drive, and at many another point along what had been the quiet front in the Ardennes, the morning darkness suddenly came alive with a maelstrom of bursting shells.

No experienced mechanized cavalry commander—least of all a stickler for spit-and-polish and soldiering by the rules such as Col. Mark A. Devine, Jr.—would have viewed the positions of the 18th Cavalry Reconnaissance Squadron with anything less than dismay. Devine and headquarters of the 14th Cavalry Group had assumed responsibility for the cavalry squadron on December 11. To defend the Losheim Gap, the roughly eight hundred men had had to sacrifice the one genuine asset of lightly armed mechanized cavalry: mobility. They instead occupied little fixed islands of defense, mainly in widely separated farm villages, most of them built in depressions—"sugar bowls," the troops called them—

providing some relief from the raw winds that swept the heights but affording little advantage for military defense.

To compound Devine's problems, one of his three troops (at 145 men, a troop was about 40 men smaller than a rifle company) had been detached to strengthen defenses at the other end of the Schnee Eifel. On the other hand, Devine had the assistance of twelve towed 3-inch guns and two reconnaissance platoons of the 820th Tank Destroyer Battalion, as well as the self-propelled 105mm. howitzers of the 275th Armored Field Artillery Battalion, attached to the 106th Division but detailed to support of the 14th Cavalry Group.

In large measure, the positions occupied by the cavalrymen reflected those prepared originally by units of the 2d Division, which upon first arriving in October had had no cavalry attachment. Thus the stronger positions—if any could be called strong—were in the south close to the Schnee Eifel, blocking roads leading from the Losheim Gap into the rear of the Schnee Eifel, for holding those roads was critical to maintaining the positions on the high ridge. All the roads led by one route or another to the upper valley of the Our River, and thence down the valley to the village of Schoenberg, where a road coming around the south end of the Schnee Eifel joined up. From Schoenberg, St. Vith is only six miles to the west.

Unknown to the cavalrymen, the boundary between the Sixth Panzer Army to the north and the Fifth Panzer Army ran through the southern portion of the Losheim Gap. That was designed to provide running room for *Kampfgruppe Peiper* and the rest of the 1st SS Panzer Division in the bid for a swift drive to the Meuse, while at the same time affording General von Manteuffel just enough space for swinging a pincer around the north end of the Schnee Eifel.

The southernmost unit of the Sixth Panzer Army, the 3d Parachute Division, intent on opening up routes for the tanks, thus hit, for the most part, the north portion of the 14th Cavalry Group's positions, where the little islands of defense consisted of only two to four towed tank destroyers and a few riflemen and machine gunners from one of the reconnaissance platoons of the attached tank destroyer company. Most of the other cavalry positions were in the path of two regiments of the 18th Volksgrenadier Division, supported by the bulk of the division's artillery and reinforced by a battalion of forty 75mm. assault guns and as many self-propelled tank destroyers, equipped with long-barreled 75s. The *Volksgrenadiers* were seeking access to the valley of the Our and the road to Schoenberg, there to link with their division's third regiment coming around the other end of the Schnee Eifel.

Just before 5:30 A.M. on December 16, men on outpost duty in the villages in the Losheim Gap saw the same kind of spectacular flickers of light on the horizon as had the soldier on the water tower atop the Skyline Drive. Moments later followed a bombardment from artillery, rockets, and mortars such as no one in the 18th Cavalry Reconnaissance Squadron had experienced before. Amid the thunder the troops could make out the distinctive screeching sound of rockets (the Americans called them "Screaming Meemies") from the *Nebelwerfer*, a multiple-barreled, electrically fired rocket launcher.

Yet little of the shelling hit the villages in the southernmost reaches of the Losheim Gap, the villages of Weckerath, Roth, and Kobscheid. That reflected the fact that German patrols had found an undefended area of more than a mile between Weckerath and Roth, and at the last minute General von Manteuffel decided to eschew an artillery preparation there while sending a column through the gap to gain a leg on the march to the valley of the Our. A battalion of *Volksgrenadiers* was soon pushing unhindered in the darkness toward the village of Auw, whence the road continued to the Our. There was also another road from Auw leading south atop the first ridgeline behind the Schnee Eifel, a road which troops of the 2d Division had named "Skyline Boulevard."

Hardly had the artillery fire lifted elsewhere and passed on to targets farther to the American rear than German searchlights flicked on, providing a kind of eerie moonlight made the more effective by reflection off the snow. It was a new and in some ways disturbing experience for the men in the Losheim Gap, but they soon realized that the illumination helped them at least as much as it did the attackers.

At Kobscheid, as at all the cavalry posts, the defenses had been heavily reinforced with .50-caliber machine guns taken from the squadron's armored cars. Those and other weapons manned by two platoons of cavalry opened fire just as the Germans reached barbed wire encircling the village. Throughout the day the fight at Kobscheid eddied back and forth, but for the most part the cavalrymen held their own.

Not so at Roth, which sat astride the most direct route to the Our. The Germans needed Roth to move reinforcements and supporting guns for the foot column that had already bypassed the village, so that from the start the *Volksgrenadiers* attacking Roth had strong support from assault guns. Consisting of a lone platoon of cavalry, the few men of Troop A's headquarters under Capt. Stanley E. Porché, and two of the virtually immobile towed 3-inch tank destroyers, the defenders of Roth were hard-pressed from the start. Although Colonel Devine tried to send a platoon of light tanks to help, the tankers found the road blocked by those *Volksgrenadiers* who had slipped past Roth. By late morning, hope for Captain Porché and his men was fading.

At Weckerath, only a few men from headquarters of Troop C were in the village, but a troop of light tanks quickly arrived to help. From the village, the crews of the light tanks could see what looked to be about fifteen tanks—they were either assault guns or tank destroyers—accompanied by a battalion of infantry marching through the gap between Weckerath and Roth. Although the tanks opened fire, as did 75mm. assault guns on a ridgeline farther back, the Germans plodded on. The pincer around the northern end of the Schnee Eifel was moving methodically into place, and there was little the cavalrymen could do about it.

At Krewinkel, the next village to the north, where a platoon of cavalry and a platoon of attached reconnaissance troops had been jolted by the opening artillery barrage, the men watched incredulously through the eerie half-light created by the searchlights as a column of men from the 3d Parachute Division marched down the road, talking, whistling, singing as if they were on a hike. The commander of the little garrison, 1st Lt. Kenneth Ferrens, waited until the Germans were almost atop the outer coils of wire before he gave his men the signal to fire.

The first fusillade wreaked terrible damage on the German column, but those men who survived quickly dispersed and pressed the attack. About fifty got inside the village, where fighting raged at close quarters; but the Americans, firing from dug-in positions and from a sturdy stone church and schoolhouse, had the advantage. "Surrender, Americans," yelled some of the Germans. "You are surrounded!"

Full light of day was still to come when the Germans began to withdraw. One man among the last to leave shouted toward Lieutenant Ferrens's command post: "Take a ten-minute break, soldier. We'll be back." To which Ferrens responded: "And we'll be waiting for you—you son of a bitch!"

In the meantime, Troop C's executive officer, 1st Lt. Aubrey L. Mills, had made it through a hail of small-arms fire into Krewinkel with a halftrack loaded with ammunition. As Lieutenant Ferrens had promised, the defenders were thus ready and waiting when German paratroopers wearing white camouflage suits made a second assault. Some got into the lower, eastern fringe of the village, but that was all. At least one hundred and fifty Germans died in the two assaults; miraculously, only two Americans were wounded and one killed, Lieutenant Mills. Having continued past Krewinkel a few hundred yards to the next village of Afst, Mills had just started back when he took a bullet between the eyes.

At Afst, which was the only other village occupied by the cavalrymen, the glow from the enemy's searchlights also provided a first view of attacking Germans for Lieutenant Crawford and the men of his platoon. Like Ferrens, Crawford waited until the white-suited Germans were close to the outer wire before signaling his men to fire. Not one German got inside the wire before the leaders whistled withdrawal, leaving behind thirty dead.

At the drab settlement of Lanzerath, near the northern extremity of the Losheim Gap on the forward slope of a high ridgeline, Susanne ("Sanny") Schür lived with her parents in a house on the eastern edge of the village, overlooking a wide valley toward the pillboxes of the West Wall and the German village of Losheim. When twelve American soldiers came to stay in the Schür household, digging an emplacement for a machine gun in the garden, Sanny slept at night between her mother and father, concerned that the soldiers might molest her. An attractive young woman of twenty-five, she found it baffling that nobody ever made a pass at her. The soldiers were always polite and would never let her carry heavy loads. She warmed their rations for them, and they gave some to her and her parents. (Sanny particularly liked the K-ration cheese, which had little slivers of bacon in it.)

When the German shelling began before daylight on December 16, Sanny and her parents retreated to the cellar. Most of the Americans joined them, then as the shelling continued, the men who had been manning the machine gun in the garden also came to the cellar. The shelling had stopped and some time had passed when the door at the top of the cellar stairs opened and another American appeared. He said something to the other soldiers (Sanny understood no English), and they hurried upstairs.

When Sanny went to get her father a cup of coffee, she found all the soldiers gone. They had obviously left in a hurry, for they had abandoned much of their equipment, including their radio.

Sanny had just returned to the cellar when she heard heavy footsteps overhead. Mounting the stairs, she opened the door warily to find an irate SS-trooper. Why had she allowed the Americans to fire a machine gun from her garden? Noticing the American radio, he grabbed it and smashed it against the wall. When he stormed out of the house without searching it, Sanny hastily gathered all the American equipment and hid it under the potatoes in the cellar. In the process, she came upon a note addressed to her by one of the soldiers:

> This is just a present for being so nice to us during our stay here. I am sorry we couldn't have stayed longer. I will remember your kindness and good luck to you, also to your mother and father.

[signed] Russell.

> PS: If I ever come back through here, I will stop to see you.

Sanny Schür had witnessed the departure of part of Lanzerath's tiny garrison, a squad of reconnaissance troops and the crews of two 3-inch guns of the 820th Tank Destroyer Battalion. Others who witnessed the swift withdrawal were men of the Intelligence and Reconnaissance (I&R) Platoon of the 99th Division's 394th Infantry, who just a few days earlier had occupied log-covered foxholes in a copse of fir trees atop a hill just north of Lanzerath only a few hundred yards up the slope from the Schürs' house.

"If they can't sign off on the phone," said Pfc. William J. Tsakanikas, to his platoon leader, 1st Lt. Lyle J. Bouck, Jr., as the half-tracks towing

the guns disappeared, "they might at least wave goodbye as they leave."
To Tsakanikas and Bouck, the departure from Lanzerath looked like a
bug-out, yet even if it was, Bouck, at least, was inclined to afford the
crews some compassion, for so vulnerable were towed antitank guns (no
matter the caliber) that their first shot was often their last.

It was, indeed, a bug-out; but at 9:30 A.M. the cavalry commander,
Colonel Devine, made it legal by ordering all the towed 3-inch guns to be
pulled back to the vicinity of his headquarters in Manderfeld, for at two
other villages near Lanzerath, the crews of six of the towed tank destroyers were under siege from overwhelming numbers of paratroopers. Although most of the men got away, they managed to save only two of the
guns.

The crisis in the Losheim Gap was all the more alarming for Mark
Devine because he was frustratingly aware that he had been able to
achieve no defensive coordination with the 106th Division. When he first
arrived on December 11 to assume responsibility for the sector, he had
learned from the commander of the 18th Cavalry Reconnaissance Squadron, Lt. Col. William F. Damon, Jr., that the 2d Division had prepared a
plan, in case the Germans came around the north end of the Schnee Eifel
through the Losheim Gap, to counterattack with a reserve infantry battalion supported by attached tanks. Although Devine had gone promptly
to the 106th Division's command post in St. Vith to try to affirm the
continued existence of that plan, the division commander, Maj. Gen.
Alan W. Jones, and his staff were too preoccupied with the myriad details of getting their division into the line to be bothered with a counterattack plan. It was, after all, a quiet sector, and nothing was likely to
happen. Once the problems of relieving the 2d Division had been dealt
with, there would be time enough to coordinate with the attached cavalry.

Thus frustrated, Devine put his staff to work on a plan of his own to
be executed should something happen before he could coordinate with
the 106th Division. He decided on a fighting withdrawal from the original
positions in the villages to a ridgeline marked by his headquarters village
of Manderfeld, and from there, if required, to a second ridgeline two
miles behind Manderfeld. He intended bringing forward the 32d Cavalry
Reconnaissance Squadron, which had only recently arrived and was then
well to the rear in the town of Vielsalm, repairing its light tanks and other
vehicles. As the 32d Cavalry counterattacked, he would pull the 18th
Cavalry back. The commander of the 32d Cavalry, Lt. Col. Paul Ridge,
and his staff reconnoitered possible routes for the proposed counterattack, while Devine's staff worked to get the plan ready for distribution on
the morning of December 16.

Because the opening artillery barrage knocked out all wire communications to the forward posts and German jamming made radio communi-

cations difficult, Devine at first had little information about what was happening, and he was not one to go forward under fire to find out for himself. He nevertheless assumed the peril sufficient to order Colonel Ridge to bring his 32d Cavalry forward.

After ordering the tank destroyers in northern reaches of the Losheim Gap to fall back, Devine alerted the cavalrymen in the villages in front of Manderfeld to be ready to withdraw at 11 A.M., by which time he hoped the 32d Cavalry would have arrived. The response from Kobscheid and Roth was less than encouraging. From Kobscheid came word that it would be impossible to withdraw during daylight, but the troops probably could hold and escape after dark. From Captain Porché in Roth there was even less hope. A last radio message soon emerged: enemy self-propelled guns were "seventy-five yards from CP, firing direct fire. Out." Of a garrison of ninety men at Roth, three were killed and eighty-seven surrendered.

When Colonel Devine asked General Jones by telephone for help, Jones replied that he culd provide nothing "at this time." In which case, said Devine, he had no choice but to fall back to the Manderfeld Ridge, whereupon he hoped to counterattack with the 32d Cavalry Reconnaissance Squadron. The fact that Devine might be able to counterattack eased concern for the Losheim Gap at headquarters of the 106th Division. At any rate, in St. Vith, they had troubles enough of their own.

When the withdrawal from Weckerath, Krewinkel, and Afst began, so close was the enemy that it was a shoot-out in the tradition of stagecoaches beset by Indians in the Wild West. The cavalrymen clambered aboard any vehicle that could move: jeeps, half-tracks, armored cars, light tanks, holding on with one hand so they could shoot with the other. Because of the cold and lack of any opportunity to warm transmissions and engines in advance, the vehicles could make only about ten miles an hour. At that agonizingly slow pace, they had to run a gauntlet of Germans on both sides of the road.

Two light tanks led the way, machine guns blazing, while men clinging to the lurching vehicles fired their individual weapons. Although most of the Germans took cover, they fired repeatedly, while some stood erect waving their arms and shouting for the Americans to surrender. The last man to leave Afst, Lieutenant Crawford, fired a bazooka to prevent a self-propelled gun from charging the rear of the column. Despite the German fire, not a man was killed and only one wounded.

At Kobscheid, the two platoons held throughout the afternoon. Soon after nightfall, the remaining sixty-one men sabotaged their vehicles, broke into three groups, and slipped out of the village to a rendezvous point in a wood lot a few hundred yards away. Over the next three days, bumping into and shying away from German columns and shaking German patrols that followed their tracks in the snow, they made their way to St. Vith.

As the main body of the cavalry began to dig in on the Manderfeld Ridge, it was obvious from patrol reports that the Germans were pushing around both flanks. To cover the southern flank, Devine sent a troop of the 32d Cavalry to Andler, a village affording entry to the valley of the Our. To seal the northern flank and reestablish contact with the 99th Division, he sent another troop of the 32d Cavalry with the assault guns of the 18th Cavalry, formed as a task force under Maj. James L. Mayes, driving up the road along the crest of the Manderfeld Ridge toward Lanzerath. The task force reached a road junction half the distance to Lanzerath but there ran into a battalion of the 3d Parachute Division supported by self-propelled guns and some of the towed 3-inch guns captured earlier from the Americans. There was no getting past them.

With the Germans moving unchecked around the north flank, Devine saw no hope of holding the Manderfeld Ridge. Around 4 P.M. he asked the 106th Division for permission to withdraw to the next ridgeline two miles behind Manderfeld while continuing to anchor his south flank at Andler, which would still deny the Germans access to the road down the valley of the Our in rear of the Schnee Eifel. General Jones approved.

To Devine, it seemed inexplicable that the Germans made no effort to interfere with the withdrawal. The reality was that except at Andler, the 14th Cavalry Group had ceased for the moment to be of concern either to the 18th Volksgrenadier Division or to the 3d Parachute Division. The *Volksgrenadiers* had yet to reach Andler, and when they got there, they were to turn away from the cavalrymen to push down the valley road to Schoenberg. Meanwhile the paratroopers, however belatedly, were busy accomplishing their mission of opening routes for the 1st SS Panzer Division.

That night, as the cavalrymen dug in on their new position without contact with the enemy, their commander, Colonel Devine, went to St. Vith to talk with General Jones and try to get help. Jones said he was too busy at present to speak with him but told him to stick around the command post until he found the time. Devine was still waiting when daylight came. That he stayed without raising any kind of a fuss was out of character, for to at least one who knew Devine well, he seemed like "a volcano about to erupt"; and to wait all night in St. Vith displayed an odd complacency for a colonel with long years of service who had to be aware that his command was in serious peril.

Operating essentially with a single cavalry reconnaissance squadron, the 14th Cavalry Group had done about all that could have been expected from such a light force. The cavalrymen had sounded the alarm and delayed the enemy, which were the roles of cavalry on defense. They had done their job, moreover, with minimal casualties and in a sector where the attacker outnumbered the defender far more heavily than anywhere else on the first day of the offensive. Nevertheless, at the end of the day the failure to hold the original positions posed a critical peril for the 106th Division.

The most immediate peril came from the battalion of *Volksgrenadiers* that had infiltrated the gap between Weckerath and Roth and headed for Auw, where only a company of the 81st Engineer Combat Battalion, the 106th Division's organic engineers, barred the way. Since the village was at the end of the enemy's infiltration route, it drew a heavy bombardment in the German artillery preparation. Tumbling from sleeping bags, the engineers hurried to the cellars, there to find the local inhabitants—the village was inside Germany—already dressed and taking cover, which prompted some of the men to recall having seen a young woman the night before going from house to house. When the shelling ended and nothing else happened, the company commander, Capt. Harold M. Harmon, turned out his road work details as usual; but only one platoon had departed beyond recall when in mid-morning German small-arms fire erupted.

Some of the engineers dashed for previously prepared defensive positions, others for the houses. They were making a good fight of it until German assault guns appeared and began a brutal and systematic fire. Just before German grenadiers closed in, one American platoon and men of the company headquarters made a run for it, some in jeeps, some on foot, heading for the next village of Andler.

For the remaining platoon, the escape route led across an open field, so there was little hope of getting out unless somebody somehow could distract the enemy's attention. Cpl. Edward S. Withee made that job his. "I'll stay," he said. "Get going." Armed with a Thompson submachine gun, Withee began a steady fire while the rest of the men raced across the open ground to safety. When all had escaped, Withee somehow managed to surrender.

Although the Germans had yet to gain Andler and access to the valley of the Our, they already possessed at Kobscheid and Auw entrée to two roads leading in behind the Schnee Eifel. From Kobscheid a farm track led to the village of Schlausenbach and headquarters of one of the 106th Division's regiments; and from Auw a road ran along the top of the ridgeline immediately behind the Schnee Eifel: Skyline Boulevard.

There was obviously nothing the 14th Cavalry Group could do at that point to help the 106th Division block its north flank except to try to hold at Andler. That Troop B, 32d Cavalry Reconnaissance Squadron, was preparing to do; but on the ridgeline extending to the northwest, which constituted the 14th Cavalry Group's third delaying position, there was less resolve.

Lacking direction from Colonel Devine, who was still in St. Vith, some commanders were looking for excuses to continue to retire. One of those was the commander of the 32d Cavalry's Troop A, 1st Lt. Robert B. Reppa, who was concerned that his little force stood all alone on the north end of the new defensive line and that he had no contact with anybody. Although he asked for authority to move north to join the troops of the 99th Division in the village of Honsfeld, he had yet to receive it when he decided to act on his own. He and his men reached Honsfeld shortly after 9 P.M., there to find a captain from the 99th Division organizing a defense of the village with men from a regimental rest center and anybody else who happened into the village. Reppa might have done better to have stayed where he was.

To break past the Schnee Eifel and take the road center of St. Vith, General von Manteuffel had two *Volksgrenadier* divisions under the 66th Corps. To ensure close coordination for the pincers carrying out the dual envelopment of the Schnee Eifel, he insisted that the corps commander, General der Artillerie Walter Lucht, make one division responsible for both prongs.

General Lucht chose to give the assignment to the 18th Volksgrenadier Division, primarily because that division had been holding the line there since late October and thus had some familiarity with the terrain. He also directed the 62d Volksgrenadier Division, newly rebuilt from remnants of a division destroyed on the Eastern Front, to attack alongside the 18th Volksgrenadier Division's southern flank, take a bridge over the Our River at the customs post of Steinebrück, five miles southeast of St. Vith, and support the 18th Volksgrenadier Division's drive on St. Vith. Except for the assault guns and tank destroyers that were mostly with the pincer moving around the north end of the Schnee Eifel and a battalion of assault guns with the 62d Volksgrenadier Division, neither division had any armor. All the Fifth Panzer Army's tanks were either farther south making the main effort against the Skyline Drive or in reserve with restrictions on their use imposed by Field Marshal Model. Because von Manteuffel needed the roads funneling through St. Vith to broaden the base of his drive to the west, he nevertheless insisted that the town be taken on the first day of the offensive.

When a military force first attacks, then stops the attack and shifts to the defensive, the positions it assumes usually reflect the positions reached as the attack came to an end. As those defenses are already prepared, a relieving force arriving later finds it easier, especially if the enemy is close, simply to occupy the old positions and make only minor adjustments. That is particularly true if the positions embrace some terrain feature that higher command insists must be retained in the same strength with which it had been held before—such as the Schnee Eifel.

When the 2d Division took over in the vicinity of St. Vith in early October, it assumed responsibility from the two divisions it relieved of two salients into the West Wall, one atop the densely forested, often fogenshrouded Schnee Eifel, the other some seven miles to the southwest

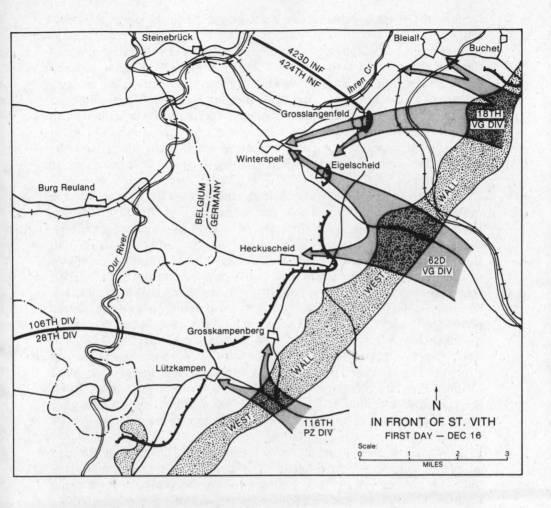

near the village of Grosskampenberg. The salient near Grosskampenberg was on open ground, dominated by pillboxes on higher ground still held by the Germans, so exposed that movement to or within the positions by daylight was impossible; and even in a sector where both sides were inclined to live and let live, the Germans were nervous lest the Americans exploit that partial penetration of the West Wall. They threw in frequent mortar and artillery concentrations and probed the positions with strong patrols.

After tolerating the situation for almost a month, the division commander, General Robertson, convinced his corps commander, General Middleton, to allow him to blow up the captured pillboxes and retire to positions prepared in advance a few miles to the rear. Having accomplished that at the start of November, the division's southernmost regiment from that point held a well-prepared although elongated line in the

vicinity of Grosskampenberg and a village a little to the north, Heckhuscheid.

Yet despite those adjustments, the regiment's line still reflected something of the original dispositions. The new positions covered two relatively minor roads leading west, while on the regiment's north wing, a
major road leading to the crossing of the Our River at Steinebrück and
on to St. Vith was the responsibility of what could only be described as an
outpost. Astride that road at the hamlet of Eigelscheid stood 130 men of
the regiment's cannon company, operating not in their normal role as
infantry fire support with towed short-nosed 105mm. howitzers, but as
infantrymen.

The outpost at Eigelscheid was all the more vulnerable because to the
north, the main positions of the next regiment, atop the Schnee Eifel,
were almost four miles away. In between were to be found only the division's reconnaissance troop (50 men) and an attached troop of the 18th
Cavalry Reconnaissance Squadron (145 men). In addition, at the village
of Bleialf, guarding the south flank of the positions on the Schnee Eifel,
was a provisional (meaning makeshift) battalion composed of an antitank
company, a platoon of a cannon company operating as infantry, a rifle
platoon, and an I&R platoon. The grand total came to about 350 men.

The principal points of entry into what was to become the 106th Division's sector, all of which funneled into St. Vith, were thus barred in less
strength than any other part of the overextended line: the cavalry in the
Losheim Gap defending the route around the north of the Schnee Eifel;
the makeshift battalion at Bleialf astride the principal route around the
south end of the high ridge; and a cannon company fighting as infantry
astride the road leading to the Our at Steinebrück.

In rear of the two regiments on the Schnee Eifel, the roadnet afforded
an enemy coming around either or both ends of the ridgeline an opportunity for not one but two envelopments. From the village of Auw in the
Losheim Gap, there was the road running south along a relatively high
ridgeline to Bleialf—Skyline Boulevard—thus affording a route for a
shallow envelopment. From Andler in the Losheim Gap there was the
road following the trace of the Our River to link with a road from Bleialf
at Schoenberg, thus affording a route for a deeper envelopment. The
only major road leading to St. Vith ran through Schoenberg, and the
entire division, including all of its artillery battalions, had a river at its
back.

Atop the Schnee Eifel, the defensive positions were well prepared,
the product of two months' work by the men of the 2d Division. Almost
all foxholes had log cover, and the troops had dry sleeping quarters either
in pillboxes or in squad huts constructed from logs. Yet that was about all
that could be said for the positions except that they were on dominating
ground. Even that advantage was largely negated by a dense coniferous

forest covering the entire ridge, which sharply limited both observation and fields of fire.

As with the salient in the West Wall near Grosskampenberg, the commander of the 2d Division, General Robertson, was unhappy with the salient on the Schnee Eifel, and early in November he had asked permission to withdraw the two regiments to the open ridgeline carrying the Auw–Bleialf road, Skyline Boulevard. His corps commander, General Middleton, agreed, but neither General Hodges nor General Bradley would approve on the grounds that the positions on the Schnee Eifel represented a penetration of the West Wall that might later be exploited in any general advance toward the Rhine. Neither of those commanders nor any of their senior staff officers chose to have a first-hand look at the ground.

Despite their denial, Robertson made up his mind that should the two regiments on the Schnee Eifel be threatened with envelopment, he would pull them back to Skyline Boulevard. Yet the fact that Robertson was planning to move to Skyline Boulevard, which would still be subject to envelopment, rather than behind the Our River, was an indication that he was not thinking in terms of any major enemy offensive, and he made no effort to construct alternate positions, nor did the 2d Division prepare a plan of withdrawal.

The division did prepare a counterattack plan based on the possibility of a limited enemy thrust around one end or the other of the Schnee Eifel. In that event, Robertson intended to employ an infantry battalion that he held in reserve well to the rear at the village of Born, just north of St. Vith, and possibly a second infantry battalion held in reserve near Steinebrück, plus an attached medium tank battalion, the division engineer battalion, and attached antiaircraft half-tracks. That force appeared to be adequate for any contingency, for as the letter of instructions outlining the plan put it, "a major offensive in this sector is not probable."

That there was nevertheless concern about the whole area, including the Losheim Gap, was reflected in General Middleton's placing the bulk of his corps artillery in positions from which to fire into some part of the sector. Seven of those battalions were brigaded under headquarters of three artillery groups, while the eighth, the 275th Armored Field Artillery Battalion, was attached to the 106th Division for support of the 14th Cavalry Group. Forward observers from all the battalions maintained observation posts in the line and all charted prearranged concentrations on points of likely trouble; the 275th Armored Field Artillery Battalion, for example, registered two hundred concentrations that might be called for by number within the Losheim Gap.

The eight battalions represented a powerful reinforcement. On the other hand, the firing positions of three of them were east of the Our River behind the Schnee Eifel and thus shared one of the weaknesses inherent in the 106th Division's positions—a river at their back. If the enemy should achieve a major penetration, support from the corps artillery battalions would be short-lived, for few commanders would risk the loss of big corps guns, not only 105mm. howitzers but also 155mm. and 8-inch guns and howitzers.

Despite the support inherent in the presence of the corps artillery, the defensive positions inherited by the 106th Division—and particularly the positions of the two regiments on the Schnee Eifel—were an invitation to disaster, the only possible rationalization being that nothing ever happened in the Ardennes. Small wonder that General Jones and his regimental commanders were upset. Yet there was little they could do about it, for in order to conceal and facilitate the 2d Division's relief and movement to the attack on the Roer River dams, the relief had to be accomplished man for man, gun for gun, with the 2d Division leaving its heavier weapons in place in exchange for those of the 106th Division.

Like many divisions that had failed to get overseas before American battlefield casualties began to mount, the 106th had undergone several levies on its trained troops. During the year of 1944, the division had to relinquish more than seven thousand men, representing 60 percent of enlisted strength. In their place, arriving only a short time before the division embarked for shipment overseas, were 1,200 men from the ASTP, 1,100 from training as air cadets, 1,500 from other divisions not yet scheduled for overseas, and 2,500 from various disbanded small units, mostly service troops. That the 106th Division was not the only division to go through that debilitating process afforded scant comfort.

Like most veteran divisions in Europe, the 2d Division by that time had accumulated weapons well in excess of normal issue, particularly machine guns, and when men of the 106th Division had no machine gun to exchange, the men of the 2d Division took their extra weapons with them. Although the 2d Division left its extensive telephone lines intact— a line ran to almost every squad—those were of little use to incoming troops who lacked the large numbers of sound-powered telephones that over the months the 2d Division had seized from the Germans. Unlike the 2d Division, the 106th Division had no attached tank battalion, and its attached tank destroyers were not self-propelled but towed. The lack of tanks, in particular, was a serious, even crippling, disadvantage.

Division headquarters was set up in a former hospital, St. Joseph's Kloster, run by a Catholic order in St. Vith. The Germans had used it as a hospital, but the 2d Division later put a tarpaulin over the large Red Cross on the roof. There General Robertson and his staff briefed General Jones and his. At Robertson's order, an officer was to remain behind at each battalion and regimental headquarters, and a senior noncommissioned officer with each company to spend the first night with the new units. For a division that was to jump off in the attack the morning after its last regiment was relieved from its defensive positions, that was about all that men and commanders of the 2d Division could be expected to do for the newcomers.

Except to tell the men for God's sake take off those neckties, and in at least one case, to assure a worried soldier: No, you don't stand guard at right shoulder arms. And to tell each and all how lucky they were. It was a quiet sector, a little mortar and artillery fire, an occasional patrol, but that was all. A piece of cake.

For men thus assured, the artillery barrage that began at 5:30 A.M. on December 16 was a jolting experience, even though the artillery available to the German 66th Corps was considerably less than elsewhere along the front. Atop the Schnee Eifel, the shells ripped into the big fir trees, sending branches crashing to the forest floor, but since the positions were sturdy and covered with logs, few casualties resulted. At the same time, heavy shelling hit the villages behind the ridgeline, particularly Schlausenbach and Buchet, sites of the command posts of the two regiments on the Schnee Eifel. Shelling was also heavy on the two villages barring major roads, Bleialf and Eigelscheid. It was heavy, too, on road junctions in the rear, including Schoenberg and St. Vith, which took a pounding from big railway guns. Telephone lines at the front went out early, including those to supporting artillery battalions, and the units of the 106th Division had had little experience using radios.

As in the Losheim Gap, nowhere along the entire extended line of the 106th Division did the Germans take advantage of the artillery preparation to close quickly with the defenders. On the Schnee Eifel, that was by design. All that the 18th Volksgrenadier Division planned there were a few thrusts during the course of the day by strong patrols to conceal the fact that in order to free troops for the pincer movements north and south, nothing more than the division's field replacement battalion of two hundred men had been left to face the Schnee Eifel. Although General von Manteuffel had considered that the Americans might respond to his attack by driving down the eastern slopes of the Schnee Eifel to cut off his spearheads, he concluded in the end that an inexperienced division would hardly react that way.

Men of the 422d and 423d Regiments on the Schnee Eifel handily repulsed such patrols as tried to climb the steep slope, and when the day came to an end, they considered that they had done their job well. The 2d Division troops had warned them that when a new division entered the line, the Germans would react with strong patrols, and that was what they thought had happened.

At Bleialf, there was no such misplaced confidence, for a half hour after the artillery fire lifted, a battalion of *Volksgrenadiers* struck the village. The impetus of that thrust threw back the bulk of the provisional battalion, while other Germans advancing up a railway cut at the southern edge of the village severed contact with the attached troop of the 18th Cavalry.

Telephoning General Jones in St. Vith, the commander of the 423d Infantry, Col. Charles C. Cavender, asked for return of his 2d Battalion, which had been held at Born as the mainstay of the division reserve. Jones refused. It was too early in the fight to part with half his little reserve. Left with no other choice, Cavender assembled a makeshift counterattacking force built around his Service Company (the regimental supply troops), a company of the 81st Engineer Battalion, every man who could be spared from Headquarters Company, and the remainder of Cannon Company, all fighting as infantry. With help from supporting artillery and a brace of towed 3-inch guns from the 820th Tank Destroyer Battalion emplaced on a hill overlooking Bleialf, that conglomerate force penetrated the village and in house-to-house fighting retook all the houses except for a few on lower ground near the railroad.

A few hundred yards to the south, against the men of Troop B, 18th Cavalry Reconnaissance Squadron, the German attack began in earnest just as it was getting light. By mid-morning, with the help of supporting artillery, the cavalrymen had the situation in hand but were running low on ammunition. Four men in an armored car commanded by Sgt. Wade H. Bankston managed to work forward from troop headquarters in Winterscheid, a thousand yards to the rear, and distribute a resupply of ammunition just before the Germans struck again; but when ammunition began to run low a second time, German fire made it impossible to get forward with more. By radio, the troop commander, Capt. Robert G. Fossland, reported his situation to Colonel Cavender, to whose regiment the cavalrymen were attached. In a rare display of concern for an impossible situation, Cavender responded: "If you can't hold, you may withdraw."

Under covering fire from three armored cars, all three cavalry platoons fell back, bringing their wounded and their equipment with them. Reaching Winterscheid, they began preparing an all-around defense of the village, out of contact with men of the 424th Infantry in Bleialf and those of the division's reconnaissance troop to the southeast in the village of Grosslangenfeld. As troopers began to drift into Winterscheid, the cavalrymen soon learned that the 106th Reconnaissance Troop—little larger than a platoon—had gone to pieces under the first impact of the enemy attack.

In the sector of the 424th Infantry to the southwest, the 62d Volksgrenadier Division attacked with two regiments abreast with the main effort directed at Eigelscheid and the road to Steinebrück while a supporting attack not quite two miles to the south aimed at high ground marked astride its crest by the village of Heckhuscheid. It was at

Heckhuscheid that the first Germans appeared, just as a misty dawn was beginning to break.

The positions of the 3d Battalion at Heckhuscheid had the shape of an inverted L (⌐), with Company L holding a cluster of houses on a hillock at the angle (a road junction) and other positions on a reverse slope extending to the north, while Company K extended the line from the cluster of houses into Heckhuscheid. The Germans quickly seized the cluster of houses, from which they were able to provide supporting fire for an assault against the rest of Company L's position. The assault forced the men of Company L back to the next ridgeline, where they held until the battalion's reserve company counterattacked and restored the position. Among some two hundred German prisoners were a battalion commander and his reconnaissance officer.

Subjected to heavy fire from *Nebelwerfers*, Company K in Heckhuscheid nevertheless repulsed several attacks and in the process captured a wounded German officer. On his person the company commander, Capt. Richard J. Comer, found a map case containing a document that looked to be of considerable importance. It was an order from the G-3 of the 46th Corps, "Subject: Undertaking GREIF," and it told of Germans operating in American uniforms, explaining how they were to identify themselves to other Germans. Comer rushed it to the rear. By early afternoon it was in the hands of the division G-2, Colonel Stout.

A few hundred yards south of Heckhuscheid, near Grosskampenberg, a misty day had fully dawned when the first Germans struck the 424th Infantry's other forward battalion. Those Germans were from the 116th Panzer Division, spilling over from that division's thrust against a neighboring regiment of the 28th Division. The Germans passed diagonally across the front of the battalion's flank, which enabled the men on that flank to exact a heavy toll. Because the German objectives appeared to be a road leading from Lützkampen, in the 28th Division's sector, into the rear of the 424th Infantry, and a bridge over the Our at the village of Burg Reuland, the battalion commander, Lt. Col. Leonard Umanoff, covered his open flank by positioning his reserve company astride the road.

Hardly had that company moved into position when five Mark IV tanks appeared. Small-arms fire forced the tank commanders to close their turrets, a 57mm. antitank gun knocked out one, and Pvt. Gilbert E. Thomas stopped another with a bazooka. When the other three fell back, that ended the threat to the 424th Infantry's right flank.

Meanwhile, the critical spot for the 424th Infantry was at Eigelscheid on the road to Steinebrück, where the commander of the 62d Volksgrenadier Division, Col. Frederich Kittel, was hoping for a swift penetration, whereupon he intended to commit a battalion on bicycles to seize St. Vith in a *coup de main* and there, he hoped, capture trains loaded with gasoline. As Kittel soon learned, it was a plan far too ambitious for the inexperienced troops involved. Even had it succeeded, they would have found no gasoline stocks in St. Vith, for the closest American railhead to the town was ten miles away.

Soon after daylight, the little band of defenders in Eigelscheid saw a mass of Germans in a long skirmish line on the skyline at a road junction a few hundred yards to the front. To the American soldiers, the inexperience of the German troops seemed apparent, for they stood erect, advanced in bunches, and fired their weapons wildly without regard for specific targets. They also appeared to be either drunk or doped, and the men of Cannon Company could hear their leaders swearing and shouting: "*Marschiert schnell! Schnell!*" ("Move quickly! Quickly!").

The commander of Cannon Company, Capt. Joseph Freesland, called for round after round of artillery fire from the supporting 591st Field Artillery Battalion. With each concentration, the German line would waver, but amid shouting and blowing of whistles, the men re-formed and continued forward. One man with a bugle exhorted the troops with bugle calls until American fire cut him down. Fire from four heavy .30-caliber and three .50-caliber machine guns the men had borrowed from the regiment's reserve battalion strongly augmented the fire of the company's carbines and M-1s.

Early in the fighting, Captain Freesland raced by jeep to the regimental headquarters in a village to the rear to ask for help from the reserve battalion located near Steinebrück only to learn that since General Jones had designated that battalion as part of the division reserve, the commander of the 424th Infantry, Col. Alexander D. Reid, could release it only with Jones's approval. As with Colonel Cavender of the 423d Infantry, the answer was no. By the time Freesland got back to his company, the situation had markedly deteriorated. With the collapse of the 106th Reconnaissance Troop at Grosslangenfeld, just over a mile to the north, another German force was advancing on Eigelscheid from that direction, and along the main road appeared four self-propelled 75mm. assault guns.

Again Freesland rushed back to the regimental headquarters. That time Colonel Reid told him that the assistant division commander, Brig. Gen. Herbert T. Perrin, had arrived at Winterspelt, the first village behind Eigelscheid. Perhaps Perrin could prevail upon General Jones to release the reserve battalion.

When Perrin heard Freesland's story, he took it on his own to call forward a rifle company from the reserve, Company C, which despite German shelling was soon on the march to join Cannon Company in Eigelscheid. Not long before noon, Perrin gained Jones's approval to move up the rest of the battalion; but by the time those companies got to Winterspelt, the defenses of Eigelscheid were about to collapse and Winterspelt itself was under attack from German troops moving up a dirt track from Grosslangenfeld.

At Eigelscheid, the commander of a detachment of 57mm. antitank guns, Staff Sgt. Rocco P. DeFelice, although wounded, brought the fire of one of his guns to bear on the four German assault guns. He knocked out two before fire from one of the others demolished his frail piece.

By that time, the *Volksgrenadiers*, by sheer weight of numbers, were beginning to break into the houses. When Captain Freesland ordered one of his platoons on the southern fringe of the village to fall back, the platoon leader, 2d Lt. Crawford Wheeler, told his men to obey, but he himself refused to budge. "Somebody's got to stay here and do the job," he shouted. The last anybody saw of Wheeler, one of the assault guns was firing point-blank into his position.

In the end, there was no holding Eigelscheid. Early that afternoon, in a sudden snow squall, the survivors of Cannon Company (eleven men were wounded and twenty-six were missing) made a fighting withdrawal along with the men of Company C back to Winterspelt to join the rest of the 1st Battalion, augmented by a company of the 81st Engineer Battalion. There the men prepared to stand, just two miles by way of a winding, rapidly descending road in front of the important bridge over the Our River at Steinebrück.

Except at Eigelscheid, the 424th Infantry's defenses were intact and the enemy's ambitious plan for a swift thrust to St. Vith thwarted, but the augury for the morrow was less than good. The 591st Field Artillery Battalion had fired over 2,600 rounds, which was about all the artillerymen had on hand, and soon after nightfall, astride the road to Steinebrück, troops of the 62d Volksgrenadier Division renewed their attack, striking hard at Winterspelt.

A crisis was thus developing close to the south flank of the 106th Division. Yet it had nowhere near such perilous connotations for the survival of the division as the crisis that had evolved on the north flank with the withdrawal of the 14th Cavalry Group. There the command post of the 424th Infantry at Schlausenbach, the regiment's direct support field artillery battalion, and the division's general support 155mm. howitzer battalion all were in immediate peril. And unless the northern pincer of the 18th Volksgrenadier Division could be blunted, both regiments on the Schnee Eifel soon might be trapped.

Only recently promoted to the rank of colonel at age thirty-two, George L. Descheneaux, Jr., was one of the youngest regimental commanders in the United States Army. With the start of the enemy's artillery preparation early on December 16, Descheneaux awoke in the house where he was billeted and hurried next door to his command post in the village's tiny *gasthaus* beside a little stream running through the valley.

So, thought Descheneaux, that ethnic Pole the men of Company E had captured the day before had not been nuts. He had said the Germans were going to attack before Christmas, and from the weight of shells falling on Schlausenbach, he knew what he was talking about.

By 8:30 A.M. there were reports of Germans infiltrating up a wooded draw between Kobscheid and Auw in the direction of Schlausenbach, then another report of fifty Germans in white camouflage suits on high ground between Schlausenbach and Auw. Patrols dispatched from the regimental reserve, Company L, soon returned with two defiant prisoners.

In addition to the command post, Descheneaux was concerned about his supporting artillery, for both his own direct support battalion, the 589th, and the general support howitzers of the 592d were emplaced a mile or so from Schlausenbach along either side of Skyline Boulevard near the hamlet of Laudesfeld. They thus were vulnerable to any German push down the road from Auw. When the company of the 81st Engineer Battalion at Auw folded in mid-morning, it was obvious that those artillery battalions would soon be under attack unless Descheneaux could do something about it. Employing his reserve, Company L, as a nucleus, Descheneaux added portions of his Antitank and Cannon Companies, fighting as infantry but supported by Cannon Company's howitzers, and ordered the force to retake Auw and block access to Skyline Boulevard.

Even as the men were assembling, three German assault guns (the Americans took them to be tanks) began to push south from Auw along the little road inappropriately christened a boulevard. From a previously prepared outpost along the road, a bazooka team hit the first gun, and a howitzer from Battery A, 589th Field Artillery Battalion, also hit it with a round of direct fire, setting the gun on fire. The other two assault guns fell back along the road to a point where the lay of the land hid them from view.

The action produced momentary relief for the men and howitzers of the 589th Field Artillery Battalion, but there was ample evidence that German patrols were operating in woods near the firing positions, and an enemy force blocked the only exit—little better than a logging road—for Battery C's pieces. As nightfall approached, the howitzers were in obvious peril, and the general support 155mm. pieces soon might be no better off.

Colonel Descheneaux's little counterattack, which began around 2 P.M., even as the artillerymen first engaged the assault guns, was making some progress when Descheneaux had to call it off. Because Germans were pressing up the wooded draw leading to Schlausenbach, he was forced to establish a defensive line to protect his headquarters. That left nobody to block for the artillery.

Early on the morning of December 16, General Jones ordered half his division reserve, the 2d Battalion, 423d Infantry, commanded by Lt. Col. Joseph P. Puett (the battalion that was located at Born and whose services Jones had denied the commander of the 423d Infantry), to move by truck to St. Vith and await instructions. As Puett waited in the division headquarters, Jones and his staff were discussing, sometimes heatedly, whether to pull the two regiments off the Schnee Eifel and back to Skyline Boulevard. At one point, Jones telephoned the corps commander to raise the issue. (General Middleton was to say later that he was concerned that if the two inexperienced regiments began to withdraw, they "might go half-way to Paris.") Jones decided finally to leave the regiments in place.

Shortly after midday, General Jones told Colonel Puett to proceed to Schoenberg and sent a radio truck with him so that Puett could report what he found when he got there. At the village, Puett saw vehicles from the 14th Cavalry Group streaming through, but the word was that a troop of cavalry was still at Andler, thus blocking the road that led down the valley of the Our to Schoenberg. Reporting all that to Jones, Puett told him also that he had heard from the 589th Field Artillery Battalion, which needed help.

Well after nightfall, around 7:30 P.M., Jones radioed Puett to go to Skyline Boulevard and help the 589th and 592d Field Artillery Battalions to displace. Having by that time released his other reserve infantry battalion for commitment at Winterspelt, Jones wanted to maintain some flexibility with Puett's battalion and told Puett "not to get heavily engaged." Yet by denying Puett mobility, Jones virtually ensured that that would happen; once Puett reached the artillery battalions, he was to release his trucks for return to the rear.

As commander of a reserve battalion, Colonel Puett had made a point of reconnoitering as many roads as possible in the division's sector and in the process had discovered the existence of a corduroy (log) road leading up a steep incline through a fir forest. Known as the Engineer Cut-Off, it had been constructed by engineers of the 2d Division to bypass the junction of Skyline Boulevard with the Schoenberg-Bleialf road, which was under enemy observation and frequently shelled (the troops named it "88 Corner"). Calling in a platoon leader, 2d Lt. Oliver B. Patton, Puett told him to go by jeep by way of the Engineer Cut-Off to Skyline Boulevard, locate the artillery battalions, and return to guide Puett's battalion forward.

With a driver and two other men, Patton reached the Engineer Cut-Off, but as the jeep bounced over the logs in the darkness Patton heard what sounded like tanks approaching and shouts in German. Patton ordered his driver to turn the jeep off the road as if it were wrecked, and everybody hid in the woods while what appeared to be several tanks (they would have been either assault guns or tank destroyers) drove by with German infantry accompanying them.

Once the Germans had passed, the men pulled the jeep from the ditch, pushed it to get it started again, and continued on their way. Locating the positions of the 589th Field Artillery Battalion, they picked up a guide to ensure that they would find their way back again and returned without difficulty to Schoenberg. (The German vehicles and soldiers Patton and his men encountered on the Engineer Cut-Off apparently constituted a patrol and may have subsequently established a roadblock at 88 Corner.) By midnight, Puett's battalion had reached the artillery positions, where Puett found that Jones's order not to get heavily engaged was like telling a man to take a swim but not get very wet.

Early in the evening, from his command post at the *gasthaus* in Schlausenbach, George Descheneaux asked General Jones for authority to pull back his northernmost battalion from the Schnee Eifel to form a new line blocking to the north between the Schnee Eifel and Schlausenbach. Not until a little after 11 P.M. did Jones grant that authority, so that it was midnight before the battalion began to move. By that time, Colonel Puett's battalion had arrived. Soon a line was forming, consisting of two battalions and Company L and extending from the Schnee Eifel past Schlausenbach and across Skyline Boulevard.

That line, thin as it was, conceivably might block envelopment of the Schnee Eifel from the north along the road from Kobscheid to Schlausenbach or along Skyline Boulevard—the shallow envelopment—but along the principal approach to Schoenberg from the north—the road following the trace of the Our and the possible route for a deeper envelopment—the only defenders were the hundred or so men of Troop B, 32d Cavalry Reconnaissance Squadron, at Andler. If that little force collapsed, or if the conglomerate force that had retaken Bleialf at the other end of the Schnee Eifel should fold, the way to Schoenberg and its critical bridge over the Our River would be open. And once the Germans got to Schoenberg, anybody and anything still on the east bank of the Our River would be trapped.

While attending the University of Washington, Alan Walter Jones earned a commission as a second lieutenant of infantry through the ROTC and entered the army in 1917; he elected to stay on after the Great War and between wars went through all the appropriate service schools. He had commanded the 106th Infantry Division (nicknamed the "Golden Lions" from a shoulder patch depicting a yellow lion's head) since the division's formation in the spring of 1943.

A stockily built man with full, rounded face, jet-black hair, heavy eyebrows, and a thin mustache, Jones had just turned fifty when he brought his Golden Lions into the line. Outwardly calm, he was a person who seldom revealed his emotions. Yet because he was sharply conscious that he had never been responsible before for men's lives in combat, the ill-chosen, overextended positions he had inherited troubled him far more than they had apparently disturbed General Robertson. Jones also had an intense personal concern. His only son, 1st Lt. Alan W. Jones, Jr., was on the staff of one of Colonel Cavender's battalions, and Alan's wife, Lynn, back in Washington, D.C., was pregnant with her first child.

Almost from the start of the German artillery preparation on December 16, General Jones was convinced that what was hitting his division was something big. What else could explain the reports from the 28th Division to the south and the 99th Division to the north of similar heavy barrages?

Yet for a long time Jones did little in reaction to the crisis. Having denied one of his two reserve infantry battalions to Colonel Cavender for use at Bleialf, it was almost noon before he authorized the battalion near Steinebrück to move to Eigelscheid and Winterspelt and after midday before he sent Colonel Puett's battalion to Schoenberg. The last two decisions may both have been made easier by the fact that at 11:20 A.M. the corps commander, General Middleton, attached to the 106th Division a battalion of corps engineers, the 168th, a part of which was soon in St. Vith, so that even after committing two infantry battalions, Jones still had a small reserve. In the meantime, Jones had denied Colonel Devine's plea for help in the Losheim Gap, for what had he to send?

Around midday, the commander of the First Army, General Hodges, at Middleton's request, released to the VIII Corps the 9th Armored Division's Combat Command B, which had only recently left the corps to serve as a reserve in the attack on the Roer River dams. Since the combat command was in an assembly area twelve miles north of St. Vith near the village of Faymonville, and was already on one-hour alert for possible commitment in support of the attack on the dams, its men and armored vehicles could have been in St. Vith in less than two hours; but General Middleton wanted to learn more of the enemy situation before committing what constituted one of only two armored combat commands available to him as reserves. Although he attached the 9th Armored Division's CCB to the 106th Division, it was to remain in its assembly area and be committed only with Middleton's approval.

Darkness was approaching when the combat command's liaison officer, 1st Lt. Raymond L. Lewis, arrived back from a mission to the 2d Division to find the headquarters in a schoolhouse on the edge of Faymonville astir with the news of the attachment. He left promptly to travel the few miles to the village of Ligneuville, where his commander, Brig. Gen. William H. Hoge, was enjoying an early dinner with a friend, Brig. Gen. Edward W. Timberlake, commander of the 49th Antiaircraft Artillery Brigade, in one of the more charming old inns in the Ardennes, the Hôtel du Moulin, long renowned for its cuisine.

Grimy from a day on the road, young Lewis reluctantly interrupted the dinner to tell General Hoge that General Middleton wanted him to telephone. As Hoge left to make the call, General Timberlake invited Lewis to sit down and eat. As far as Lewis was concerned, the hotel was still renowned for its cuisine, for the chef had done things with U.S. Army ground beef that Lewis had never known a mess sergeant to do.

After putting CCB on a ten-minute alert, General Hoge left at 6 P.M. for St. Vith, arriving at General Jones's headquarters in the St. Joseph's Kloster a half hour later. On the ground floor it was pandemonium— noncommissioned officers and clerks running about, junior officers arguing in loud voices. Going upstairs, he found Jones in his office, remarkably composed.

Jones wanted Hoge to move his combat command into the Losheim Gap at Manderfeld, arriving there at dawn the next day to counterattack and erase the enemy penetration threatening the positions on the Schnee Eifel. In the meantime, Jones wanted a platoon of self-propelled tank destroyers at St. Vith immediately to protect his headquarters.

Hardly had Hoge left the headquarters than Jones received a telephone call from General Middleton. He was sending more help, said Middleton. A combat command of the 7th Armored Division was to arrive at St. Vith at 7 A.M. the next morning, December 17, and the entire division was to follow.

With Jones when he received that news was the assistant G-2 of the VIII Corps, Lt. Col. William H. Slayden, whom Middleton had sent to the 106th Division as an adviser until the division could become acclimated. Slayden knew that the 7th Armored Division was at least sixty miles away in the Netherlands. Whereas the head of the ponderous column might conceivably reach St. Vith by seven o'clock the next morning, it would be long hours before an entire combat command could arrive, and longer than that before the combat command would be ready to attack. Yet Slayden kept his views to himself. Both Middleton and Jones had attended more service schools and studied far more logistical tables than he had. Who was he, a lieutenant colonel, to say that his corps commander, a major general, was, at best, abysmally misinformed?

When Jones heard the news that he was soon to get a second combat command of armor—and, in time, an entire armored division—he felt as if somebody had removed a sack of lead from his back. Although he recognized that the principal crisis he faced involved the two regiments on the Schnee Eifel, he was also seriously concerned about the Germans at Winterspelt, who were apparently bearing down on the crossing of the Our River at Steinebrück. Yet at that point, he had the means to deal with both. It would be better, he decided, to use the 9th Armored Division's CCB at Winterspelt, thereby freeing the narrow streets of St. Vith of that combat command's host of tanks and other vehicles. That in turn would allow unfettered passage of the combat command of the 7th Armored Division through St. Vith and out on the road to Schoenberg to the relief of the troops on the Schnee Eifel.

At the schoolhouse in Faymonville, General Hoge was about to end his briefing of his commanders for the move to the Losheim Gap and Manderfeld when a call came through from St. Vith informing him of Jones's change of plan. The greater distance involved, Hoge decided, dictated that his command get on the road immediately. His subordinate commanders hastened back to their units to pass the word along.

As the evening wore on in the St. Joseph's Kloster, Alan Jones, for all his relief over the morrow's promised help, began to question his decision to leave the two regiments up on the Schnee Eifel. At some time late in the evening, he decided to propose withdrawal. He soon had the corps commander on the telephone for a conversation that was destined to have a major impact on the outcome of the battle in front of St. Vith.

Ralph G. Hill, Jr., was a captain in command of a detachment of three other officers and five enlisted men detailed to serve, once the U.S. Army entered Germany, as a military government for a *Wehrkreis*. Hill and his detachment had arrived in eastern Belgium in September at a time when it appeared that American troops were about to penetrate well beyond the German frontier. When the drive ended atop the Schnee Eifel, he and his detachment assumed responsibility for handling relations with Belgian civilians in and just north of the Losheim Gap. On the order of the commander of the first division to occupy defensive positions north of the gap, Hill evacuated some ten thousand civilians from the region, leaving behind only some four hundred inmates and attendants of an asylum for geriatric patients in the division headquarters town of Bütgenbach, and around two hundred farmers, who were to care for the *bêtes*.

When the 99th Division assumed responsibility for the area in November, the division commander, Maj. Gen. Walter E. Lauer, found the lowing of the cattle upsetting (two hundred men were unable to keep them all milked on schedule) and ordered Hill to get rid of them. Since driving the animals westward would tie up military traffic for days, the only solution appeared to be slaughter.

Hill had the Belgian farmers set up twelve butchering stations, and when American supply trucks had delivered their loads in Bütgenbach, the Belgians reloaded the empty trucks with meat, which the drivers delivered to towns and cities to the rear. There the civilian authorities, if notified in advance, would be happy to provide men to unload it. Yet in order to notify the civilian authorities, Hill needed a reliable communications system.

Carrying a flashlight and a field telephone, he went across the street from the house where he was billeted in the town of Büllingen and descended the stairs into the cellar of the post office. There he found an underground telephone cable and a long row of terminal points. Connecting his field telephone to each in turn, he finally got a response:

"*Bonn hier.*" He had reached a female operator in the German city of Bonn alongside the Rhine.

When the woman learned she was talking to an American soldier in Büllingen, she thought it hilarious. Where did her switchboard indicate his call was originating from, Hill asked. When she said Spa, Hill disconnected her and as soon as possible sent a man to Spa. Once the man located the terminus of the cable and convinced civilian authorities to run a line to headquarters of the First Army in the Hôtel Britannique, Hill had the communications network he needed. To make it more comprehensive, he arranged for lines to be run to headquarters of the 99th Division in Bütgenbach and to headquarters of the 2d Division (later the 106th) in St. Vith.

On December 16, Ralph Hill faced another day of supervising the butchering of cattle and arranging for receiving and shipping the meat. When he tried to place a telephone call to Eupen through the 99th Division's switchboard, the operator told him the line was out, cut by "paratroopers." Talking to the signal officer, he learned that the line had gone out before daylight, that the officer had sent out a trouble-shooting crew that failed to return, and that a second crew had found the men of the first dead in a ditch. When the signal officer learned that Hill had a line to Spa and thence to Eupen (headquarters of the V Corps), he was elated and quickly put such a load on Hill's little switchboard that Hill had to ask him for operators to help.

If the 99th Division was having communications problems, thought Hill, perhaps the 106th Division was too. When that proved to be the case, Hill immediately handled a call from General Jones to General Middleton. As it turned out, lines from the two divisions to their respective corps headquarters were in and out throughout the day, but by seven o'clock that evening both were in again and Hill let the 99th Division's operators go.

It was late in the evening when the 106th Division's line to the VIII Corps at Bastogne went out once more, and a call came through Hill's switchboard for MONARCH 6 (codename for Middleton). Hill connected it and listened in. It was General Jones, talking in riddles in case the Germans were tapping the line, about his regiments on the Schnee Eifel. He thought it would be wise to withdraw his "two keys [regiments] from where they are because they are very lonely." He knew, Jones continued, that he would have "two big friends [combat commands] to rescue them in the morning," but he thought it would "be wise to prevent a scissors working on them."

Middleton responded that Jones was the commander on the ground. "You know how things are up there better than I do," he said.

At that moment, a call came into the switchboard from the 99th Division. Since the departing operators had taken their telephones with them, leaving Hill with only one, he disconnected Jones and Middleton momentarily to tell the caller he would get back to him when the line was free; but he quickly reconnected Jones and Middleton. That brief period—only seconds—may have been the time when Middleton added, "but I agree it would be wise to withdraw them."

When Jones put down the telephone, he was convinced either that Middleton wanted him to leave his regiments in place or that he was putting the onus of the decision entirely on him. "Well, that's it," he said to one of his staff. "Middleton says we should leave them in." A short while later that decision appeared to be confirmed when Jones saw an order from Middleton—issued earlier in the day but just arrived—directing no withdrawals unless positions became totally untenable and designating a line not far behind the existing front that was to be held "at all costs." Jones apparently failed to note that that line in his sector was the west bank of the Our River, well behind the Schnee Eifel.

Meanwhile at Bastogne, when General Middleton put down his phone, he turned to a member of his staff. "I just talked to Jones," he said. "I told him to pull his regiments off the Schnee Eifel."

That night the 106th Division's G-2, Colonel Stout, noted in his periodic report: "The enemy is capable of pinching off the Schnee Eifel area . . . at any time."

CHAPTER SIX

The Skyline Drive

For the Fifth Panzer Army's main effort, General von Manteuffel planned for two panzer corps to attack abreast. The 58th Panzer Corps, commanded by Generaloberst Walter Krüger, was to attack on either side of the border village of Ouren, on the Our River ten miles south of St. Vith. It would then cross the northern reaches of the ridgeline the Americans knew as the Skyline Drive and jump the Meuse River just downstream from the bend at Namur. The 47th Panzer Corps, commanded by General der Panzertruppen Heinrich Freiherr (Baron) von Lüttwitz, was to cross the Our a few miles farther south, jump the Skyline Drive, take the road center of Bastogne nineteen airline miles beyond the German frontier, and seize crossings of the Meuse upstream from Namur.

Each of the panzer corps had only two divisions, one panzer, one *Volksgrenadier;* but General von Manteuffel had two panzer units in reserve, the *Führer Begleit Brigade*, which had the strength of a little better than half a panzer division, and the *Panzer Lehr Division*. Von Manteuffel could commit the *Führer Begleit Brigade* only with the approval of his superior, Field Marshal Model; but as soon as General von Lüttwitz's 47th Panzer Corps put in a bridge behind its *Volksgrenadier* division, he intended to use the *Panzer Lehr* with that corps.

Originally a part of the Pennsylvania National Guard, the 28th Infantry Division, which had been fighting since Normandy and had incurred such losses in the Hürtgen Forest that people had begun calling its red bucket-shaped keystone shoulder patch the "Bloody Bucket," held such an elongated defensive front that each of the panzer corps was destined to strike little more than a regiment. In the north, Krüger's 58th Panzer Corps faced only some three thousand or so men of the division's 112th Infantry, while von Lüttwitz's 47th Panzer Corps faced the 110th Infantry. (The division's third regiment, the 109th Infantry, was to become involved with the supporting attack by the Seventh Army.) Thus the ratio of attacker to defender was roughly ten to one.

The Germans that Private First Class Allard and other members of the patrol from Company F, 112th Infantry, came upon on the night of December 15 while making their way back across the Our River near Ouren were from the 560th Volksgrenadier Division. Created from occupation troops in Denmark and Norway, the division had seen no combat and had had only limited training, and one of its three regiments had yet to arrive from Denmark. Its running mate, on the other hand, the 116th Panzer Division, known as the *Windhund* (Greyhound) Division, had a long, distinguished record on the battlefield, having fought in Normandy and having previously dealt the 112th Infantry a crippling blow in the Hürtgen Forest. The division was nearly at full strength in men and had close to a hundred tanks—mostly Panthers—and assault guns.

The positions held by the 112th Infantry constituted an extension of the line of the 106th Division and had the same basic weakness: a river at the back. Yet nothing ever happened in the Ardennes, so why relinquish ground within the pillbox belt of the West Wall dearly bought with American blood? Only two of the regiment's battalions were in the line—one in and around the village of Lützkampen, close to the flank of the 106th Division's 424th Infantry; the other a little to the southwest near the village of Sevenig. The third battalion occupied back-up defensive positions on the west bank of the Our but was, in essence, a reserve. Although the regiment had lost almost two thousand men in the Hürtgen Forest, the commander, Col. Gustin M. Nelson, considered the replacements to be well trained and highly motivated.

The 112th Infantry was defending the sector where General von Manteuffel had decreed that there should be no artillery preparation so that eighty-man shock companies might infiltrate up wooded draws between the widely spaced American positions, attack from flanks and rear, and strike swiftly for bridges over the Our (two at Ouren and two farther north). When the searchlights flicked on in the early morning darkness of December 16 and German artillery opened fire to north and south but not on the positions of the 112th Infantry, the men in the foxholes were left to wonder—however reverentially—why not them too?

In the darkness a small German force attacked mortar positions behind the 3d Battalion near Sevenig, but the mortarmen had well-prepared foxholes near their pieces and fought off the assault. Another force caught a platoon of Company L at breakfast, captured the kitchen, killed the platoon leader, and put the men to flight.

The first indication that Germans were moving in behind the 1st Battalion near Lützkampen came with word of the ambush of a kitchen truck returning from the front, but there was little other evidence of the enemy presence until approaching daylight revealed German troops marching in the open. When one of the shock companies came under devastating flanking fire from the 424th Infantry to the north, that part of the attack collapsed. As twenty-five Germans emerged from a wood to move past an exposed crossroads, small-arms fire killed four and the rest surren-

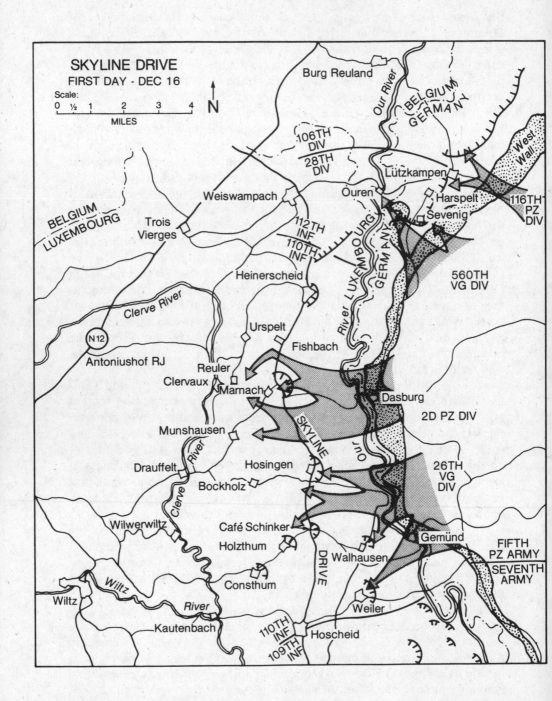

SKYLINE DRIVE
FIRST DAY - DEC 16

Scale:
0 ½ 1   2   3   4
MILES

N

Burg Reuland

Our River

BELGIUM
GERMANY

West Wall

106TH DIV
28TH DIV

Lützkampen

116TH PZ DIV

Weiswampach

Ouren

Harspelt
Sevenig

BELGIUM
LUXEMBOURG

Trois Vierges

112TH INF
110TH INF

560TH VG DIV

Heinerscheid

Clerve River

LUXEMBOURG GERMANY

River

N 12

Urspelt

Fishbach

Antoniushof RJ

Reuler
Clervaux
Marnach

SKYLINE

Dasburg

2D PZ DIV

Munshausen

Our

Drauffelt

River

Hosingen

Bockholz

26TH VG DIV

Wilwerwiltz

Clerve River

Café Schinker

Holzthum

DRIVE

Walhausen

Gemünd

FIFTH PZ ARMY

SEVENTH ARMY

Wiltz

Wiltz

Consthum

River

Weiler

Kautenbach

110TH INF
109TH INF

Hoscheid

dered. The battalion commander himself, Lt. Col. William H. Allen, manned a .50-caliber machine gun protecting an antitank gun near his headquarters. When he had exhausted his ammunition, a score of Germans lay dead and forty surrendered.

Meanwhile, a group of forty Germans had moved through the darkness toward the southernmost of the two bridges at Ouren. At close to 9:30 A.M., men of the 3d Battalion's Headquarters and Cannon Companies, having rushed to foxholes previously prepared for a close-in defense of Ouren, spotted them. "Get them when they cross the bridge!" yelled the personnel officer, Capt. William B. Cowan. The men thought at first that the Germans were prisoners on their way to the rear, but when it became obvious that they were armed, everybody heeded Cowan's order to fire. Some of the Germans fell on the bridge, others made it across a little farther, and only a few managed to get away. Somebody on the German side nevertheless reported overeagerly that the 560th Volksgrenadier Division had seized a bridge across the Our.

With the coming of daylight, German artillery and *Nebelwerfers* at last opened fire, but since the German troops were in and behind the American line, the artillerymen had to direct most of their fire well to the rear against American artillery positions and villages beyond the Our. American mortars and artillery at the same time caught Germans in the open or in the draws and exacted a heavy toll.

Shortly before noon, the commander of the 112th Infantry, Colonel Nelson, ordered his 2d Battalion to move from the west bank of the Our through Ouren and counterattack to clear the enemy from between the village and the 3d Battalion's positions. By nightfall, that sweep was complete and the positions abandoned by the platoon of Company L restored.

Also shortly before noon, the commander of the 116th Panzer Division, Generalmajor Siegfried von Waldenburg, decided to commit tanks to try to get his *Panzergrenadiers* moving. The first attempt ended in failure when fire from the adjacent 424th Infantry knocked out two tanks and three others fell back. Soon after that, the commander of the 58th Panzer Corps, General Krüger, informed that the *Volksgrenadiers* had taken one of the two bridges at Ouren, ordered von Waldenburg to end his try for the two bridges farther north and join in the fight to take Ouren itself. That was what halted the threat to the 424th Infantry's flank.

The dragon's teeth of the West Wall in front of the 3d Battalion's positions sharply restricted the routes available to the German tanks and made them ready prey for American guns. A second German attempt to get tanks forward failed when Pfc. Paul C. Rosenthal, the gunner in the crew of a towed 3-inch tank destroyer supporting the 424th Infantry, expending only eighteen rounds, knocked out five. A third try failed when the lead tank of a group of five set off a mine and the others turned back under fire from 57mm. antitank guns. A fourth and fifth attempt failed when towed guns of a company of the 630th Tank Destroyer Battalion, attached to the 112th Infantry but firing from dug-in positions on a ridge behind the Our, knocked out six. A final foray, by three German tanks equipped with flamethrowers, ended with another assist by towed tank destroyers supporting the 424th Infantry.

Since the report of a captured bridge at Ouren proved to be false, the only real success to which the 58th Panzer Corps might point at the end of the first day was a small bridgehead established by the *Volksgrenadiers* over the Our in an undefended sector downstream from Ouren. There the bridge had long been destroyed, its debris blocked the site, and felled trees and mines denied egress along the exit road on the far bank, so that there was little hope that German engineers could bridge the river swiftly. That meant that the two bridges at Ouren, although denied by American defenses against which the Germans had made few inroads, still constituted the most likely way for the 58th Panzer Corps to get past its first obstacle in the drive for the Meuse.

It had clearly been a less than rewarding day for Krüger's 58th Panzer Corps. Although the losses of the 116th Panzer Division were moderate, they included thirteen tanks and at least eighty men captured, and one of the leading shock companies had been wiped out by flanking fire from men of the 424th Infantry. The inexperienced *Volksgrenadiers* had lost close to a thousand men. Of greater importance, the 112th Infantry had delayed one of von Manteuffel's two main columns for twenty-four hours.

On the other hand, as night fell on December 16, the men of the 112th Infantry knew that their foe was still there and hardly likely to desist after only one day of attack. "Nobody able to sleep and no hot meals today," one man wrote in his diary. "This place is not healthy anymore."

Hurley Edward Fuller was known as a curmudgeon. A Texan, he had enlisted in the United States Army in 1916, the next year attended officer candidate school and obtained a commission as a second lieutenant of infantry, and went to France, where he fought in the bitter campaign in the Argonne Forest. Fuller was for long disenchanted by that experience, but he stayed in the army, where he established a reputation as a capable but irascible commander, a man with a cantankerous disposition. After commanding the 2d Division's 23d Infantry for a year and a half, he brought the regiment ashore in Normandy on D-Day plus 1 but lasted in combat only ten days before the soft-spoken but firm Walter Robertson relieved him of his command. Something about having maneuvered his regiment into an untenable position.

Still determined to fight, Fuller had gone to an old friend, Troy Middleton of the VIII Corps, also a veteran of the American Expeditionary Force, and asked for help. Although Middleton recommended to General

Bradley, then commanding the First Army, that Fuller be given another chance, Bradley was moved up to command the 12th Army Group and nothing came of Middleton's recommendation until November, when a vacancy developed in the command of the 110th Infantry. As the 28th Division had just been transferred to the VIII Corps, Middleton suggested to the division commander that Fuller fill the slot.

Assuming command of the 110th Infantry in late November, only a few days before turning fifty, Colonel Fuller moved the regimental command post from a farm village to the more comfortable locale of Clervaux. A charming old town set astride a bend in the Clerve River in a deep, narrow basin formed by the merging of four precipitous wooded gorges, the narrow streets, framed by houses and shops with sharply pitched roofs, were dominated by a château. Dating from the twelfth century and situated on a promontory near the eastern edge of town, the château, although small, had most of the usual attributes of a castle except a moat: two turreted towers, a massive stone entranceway with heavy wooden doors built to withstand siege, a cobblestoned interior courtyard, and dungeon-like cellars. Long a magnet for tourists, Clervaux had the hotels to go with it, thus making the town an ideal rest center for troops of the 110th Infantry and for other units of the 28th Division. Colonel Fuller established his headquarters in the Hôtel Claravallis in the western part of town near the railroad station.

Hurley Fuller made few changes in the dispositions of his troops from those of his predecessor, for what choice had he? The deep gorge of the Our River in front of his regiment was so forbidding that his division commander, Maj. Gen. Norman D. Cota, had elected to achieve such concentration as was possible on a twenty-five-mile front at either end of the line: in the north, where the 112th Infantry held a bridgehead beyond the Our River, and in the south, where the 109th Infantry constituted, in effect, a part of the defenses of Luxembourg City. That left the 110th Infantry responsible for fifteen miles of front in the center. And to add to the regiment's difficulty, Fuller had to furnish the division's sole infantry reserve, a battalion positioned a few miles behind the Clerve River near a principal highway leading to Bastogne.

Since manning a fifteen-mile line close alongside the Our with two battalions was an obvious impossibility, the regiment stationed squad-sized outposts near the river during the daytime and patrolled a mile or so of open slopes and steep-walled draws between the river and the Skyline Drive at night. So, too, with the available troops, a solid defensive line along the Skyline Drive was impossible. Instead, the regiment blocked each of five roads leading up from the valley of the Our and on to the west with a rifle company, garrisoning either a village astride the ridge road or a village just in front of or behind it. The two points of greatest concern were at Marnach, through which ran a principal road leading through Clervaux and on to Bastogne; and at Hosingen, roughly in the center of the regimental sector, through which another road led fairly directly to Bastogne.

Each of the two battalions ostensibly held out a reserve company, but both of those were also responsible for defending a village just behind the Skyline Drive through which other roads to the west also passed. In other villages there were only makeshift forces, consisting of the regimental antitank company deployed as infantry and such as was left of the two weapons companies once their heavy machine guns and 81mm. mortars had been parceled out to the rifle companies.

The wide frontage also forced the supporting 109th Field Artillery Battalion into the unusual tactic of widely separating its three firing batteries to enable at least one battery to reach a portion of the front. Even so, to ensure coverage for the entire front an attached battery from a corps artillery unit had to help out. Because of the distance between the infantry positions on the Skyline Drive and the enemy beyond the Our, the firing positions had to be established close behind the crest of the Skyline Drive in unusual proximity to the infantry.

Like the other regiments of the 28th Division, the 110th Infantry had received approximately two thousand replacements for the men lost in the Hürtgen Forest, mostly riflemen and machine gunners, the soldiers with whom combat always deals most harshly. On the assumption that the Ardennes front would remain quiet, Colonel Fuller intended rotating the reserve battalion from time to time with the forward battalions.

On the German side, during the three nights preceding the assault, one of the German Army's more experienced units, the 2d Panzer Division, which had taken heavy losses in Normandy but had retained a solid cadre of experienced noncommissioned officers and officers, made its move forward by the prescribed stages. Rebuilding of the division had started fairly early in the fall, so that the replacements were of better caliber than those reaching other divisions at the last minute. The division had eighty-six tanks, two-thirds of them the latest model Panthers, and twenty assault guns; but the chronic shortage of motor transport afflicted the division much as it did other units. The commander was a newcomer, Col. Meinrad von Lauchert, a seasoned campaigner of the Eastern Front whom General von Manteuffel had requested to replace a commander who lacked experience with armor.

Veteran of many a fight on the Eastern Front, the 26th Volksgrenadier Division—one of the infantry divisions that had earned its honorific in battle—had moved into the Eifel in October and had held a front almost as wide as that of the 28th Division. Defending in such a quiet sector had enabled the division commander, Col. Heinz Kokott, a dignified, soft-spoken man of scholarly mien, to re-equip and build up his division with little interference. By December, Kokott had some seventeen thousand men, considerably more than the recently formed *Volksgrenadier* divisions, but, like everybody else, short on motor transport.

The experienced *Panzer Lehr Division* was one of only a few divisions that even though earmarked for the Ardennes offensive, had been committed to help hold the line in advance of the offensive. In a counterattack role against the Third Army, the division had incurred heavy losses in both men and tanks. On the night of December 15, the division had only fifty-seven Mark IV and Panther tanks, although it had received some relief in the attachment of an assault gun brigade and two battalions of self-propelled tank destroyers. The division commander, Generalleutnant Fritz Bayerlein, a short, stocky man of forty-nine who reminded some people of an aggressive terrier, created a task force—an advance guard—composed of reconnaissance troops, two companies of *Panzergrenadiers*, and a company of Panthers, which he intended to commit early to exploit the gains of the 26th Volksgrenadier Division.

As dictated by General von Manteuffel, the troops were to make direct attacks on American positions at only two places, Marnach and Hosingen, in order to open the two principal roads leading west. Units not designated for those attacks were to practice what had become known in World War I as "Hutier tactics" (after a German general, Oscar von Hutier), whereby the troops advanced in small units avoiding prepared enemy positions, leaving them to be mopped up by other units coming later.

Since the 26th Volksgrenadier Division had become accustomed to putting outposts across the Our after dark and had learned that American troops withdrew their outposts at nightfall, supporting engineers started building a bridge at the village of Gemünd even before the artillery preparation began. Further north at Dasburg, in the sector of the 2d Panzer Division, that could not be done, for access to the site of the demolished bridge—the only site in the vicinity where a bridge might be built—was blocked by an electrically operated iron gate anchored in stalwart concrete stanchions, a part of the West Wall defenses, and the commander of the 600th Army Engineer Battalion which was to construct the bridge, Maj. Georg Loos, was unable to locate the key needed to operate the electrical mechanism. The only alternative was to demolish the gate with explosives, and lest the noise should give away what was happening, that could be done only after the artillery preparation began.

Meanwhile, two German soldiers carrying a radio had slipped past the American positions and made their way down a steep forested slope into the northern fringe of Clervaux. They sneaked past the château and holed up in a room in the rear of the Pharmacie Molitor, across from the Hôtel Central in the heart of town. From the pharmacy, they would have a good vantage point, once daylight came, for directing artillery fire on targets within Clervaux.

The pinpoints of light that the American observer atop the water tower in Hosingen reported at 5:30 A.M. on December 16 were the belch-

ings of 554 organic or attached artillery pieces and *Nebelwerfers* of the
67th Panzer Corps. As German patrols had long ago established the location of the American positions, the fire was markedly accurate on the
forward villages, while *Nebelwerfer* rockets cascaded into the narrow
streets of Clervaux, awakening the men quartered there on leave and
sending civilians scurrying for their cellars or for those of the old château.

The shelling also awakened the regimental commander, Colonel Fuller, and his executive officer, Lt. Col. Daniel B. Strickler, on the second
floor of the Hôtel Claravaliis. Strickler hurried into Fuller's room, No.
10. "What do you make of it?" asked Fuller. "All this big stuff," Strickler
responded, "is a sure sign we're in for a fight." Dressing hurriedly, both
officers rushed down to the operations room off the lobby of the hotel.
Every telephone line to the front-line units, they discovered, was out. So
was the line to division headquarters seven miles to the southwest in the
town of Wiltz.

Late on December 15, the commander of the 3d Battalion, 110th Infantry, Maj. Harold Milton, had directed a training mission to be conducted early the next morning for a section of 81mm. mortarmen.
Protected by a squad of riflemen from Company L, the mortarmen were
to move forward from the Skyline Drive and fire on a village just beyond
the Our River. The squad of riflemen had already moved out when the
German artillery preparation began. As it lifted, Major Milton canceled
the mission, and Company L's commander, 1st Lt. Bert Saymon, sent
two men in a jeep to tell the riflemen to return.

Reaching a crossroads atop the Skyline Drive marked by a lone building, the Café Schincker, the two men in the jeep told riflemen of one of
Company L's platoons defending the crossroads where they were going
and that they and the squad of riflemen would soon be returning. In
darkness and thick fog, the jeep continued to the east. A minute or so
later, the men at the crossroads heard a squeal of brakes and a burst of
small-arms fire. When they later saw shadowy forms moving past the
crossroads, they were unable to make out whether they were Germans or
their fellow riflemen on the way back. Lest they shoot their own men,
they held their fire.

At the Café Schincker crossroads and almost everywhere else, a heavy
ground fog early on December 16 helped the troops of the 26th Volksgrenadier Division get past the defensive positions atop the Skyline
Drive. Men of Company K in Hosingen could hear troops crossing the
highway to the north, but they could see nothing. South of Hosingen, the
Germans were almost on top of one of Company K's platoons before
the Americans spotted them; nobody from that platoon got away. Other
Germans surprised Battery C, 109th Field Artillery Battalion, in firing
positions behind Hosingen. Although the artillerymen lowered the muzzles of their howitzers and opened fire with fuses set for one or two sec-

onds, the Germans continued to attack, so that for a long time that battery would be fighting for its life and unable to provide any fire support for the infantry.

Also having crossed the Skyline Drive unimpeded, company-sized enemy forces got almost atop the villages of Holzthum and Consthum, on the reverse slope of the ridge below the Café Schincker crossroads, and were trying to slip past undetected when men of the 3d Battalion's reserve in Holzthum, Company L, and of the battalion headquarters in Consthum took them under fire. As heavy fighting erupted for both villages, it alerted men of a battery of the attached 687th Field Artillery Battalion just outside Consthum and enabled the artillerymen to set up a close-in defense bolstered by two half-tracks of an antiaircraft battalion, each with quadruple-mounted .50-caliber machine guns.

In at least one case, the fog worked against the Germans. Making out a large body of men approaching, the crew of another U.S. half-track with quad-50 machine guns was unable to determine at first whether they were Germans or Americans. When the approaching troops halted at the sight of the half-track, the crewmen assumed the worst. As they waved the men forward "in friendly fashion," the Germans decided that their own side had captured the half-track and advanced. They were within a hundred yards when the gunner pressed the button that fired the four machine guns in tandem. Close to a hundred Germans fell.

At the only positions of the 110th Infantry on the forward slope of the Skyline Drive, which the first German units were supposed to bypass, the Germans in fact stumbled onto the positions. There a detached platoon of Company I, protecting a battalion observation post behind the village of Wahlhausen, and the rest of Company I, at the village of Weiler, spotted the Germans in time to bring mortar and artillery fire to bear. Those Germans were destined to be pinned down for the rest of the day.

In the meantime, atop the Skyline Drive at Hosingen, which the Germans needed both as a principal route westward and as egress along the best road leading uphill from the bridge at Gemünd, somebody failed to press the attack in keeping with the importance of the objective. After overrunning the platoon of Company K south of the village, the Germans made only a feeble stab at the village itself. It was a lack of aggressiveness that as the day passed could hardly be ignored by the division commander, Colonel Kokott.

To the north, in the zone of the 2d Panzer Division, the leading battalion of *Panzergrenadiers* stumbled into an American minefield soon after crossing the Our River, which so delayed the advance that it was full daylight and the fog had thinned when the men drew up to the village of Marnach astride the Skyline Drive. Since Marnach with its entry to the road to Clervaux was not to be bypassed, the *Panzergrenadiers* began immediately to attack. Yet Company B and a platoon of towed guns of the 630th Tank Destroyer Battalion were on full alert and the attack failed. The defenders in the village nonetheless were soon uncomfortably aware that other Germans were bypassing Marnach on either side, heading down a steep slope toward Clervaux and the positions of their supporting artillery, Battery B, 109th Field Artillery Battalion.

In the Hôtel Claravallis, Colonel Fuller soon had radio contact with headquarters of his 1st Battalion and his supporting artillery, but so far away was headquarters of the 3d Battalion in Consthum that he was unable to get through, nor could he raise the division headquarters in Wiltz. Turning to his executive officer, Colonel Strickler, he told him to go to Wiltz and inform the division commander, General Cota, that his regiment was under heavy attack, then proceed to Consthum and stay there to oversee the defense of the regiment's south wing.

By 9 A.M. the telephone line to division headquarters was back in again, and through the division switchboard, Fuller was able to talk with Major Milton in Consthum. At about the same time, he received a radio call from Battery C, 109th Field Artillery, under siege in its firing positions behind Hosingen. The Germans had captured one of the battery's twelve howitzers, and even though the artillerymen were still fighting for the others, they needed help desperately.

Telephoning Cota in Wiltz, Fuller demanded (he was not the type of man to ask) release of his 2d Battalion from the division reserve. A big, blustery New Englander known as Dutch, who could be as strong-willed as anybody, Cota refused. It was too early, the situation not developed fully enough, for him to part with his lone infantry reserve. On the other hand, since reports reaching Cota from his other two regiments indicated that the 110th Infantry's situation was the most serious, he afforded Fuller two companies of medium tanks of the 707th Tank Battalion, long an attached fighting colleague of the 28th Division. (The third company was with the 109th Infantry; the company of lights with the 112th.)

Since the tanks were in a village alongside the Clerve River only two miles from Battery C's positions, a platoon was soon on the way. Reaching the nearby village of Bockholz without difficulty, the five tanks enabled the artillerymen to drive off their foe, retake their captured piece, and resume firing.

Two companies of tanks—thirty-four Shermans—was a considerable force, but in view of the multiple and widely spaced crises confronting the 110th Infantry, it could hardly be employed in the most advantageous fashion as a single unit. Faced with calls for help from almost every direction and under orders to give no ground anywhere, Colonel Fuller parceled out his newly obtained support piecemeal, a platoon here, half a platoon there. He kept one platoon in reserve in Clervaux and ordered two platoons to what he considered to be the most critical spot of all, Marnach, astride the German route to Clervaux.

The 1st Battalion commander, Lt. Col. Donald Paul, had already tried to help hardpressed Company B in Marnach by sending a strong patrol south from Company A, which was on the regiment's north flank in the village of Heinerscheid and had yet to come under attack. The patrol got only halfway to Marnach before running into Germans who were bypassing the village. Pinned to the ground for a while by small-arms fire, the men of the patrol finally managed to fall back just in time to help their company repel a first attack on Heinerscheid.

Colonel Paul then ordered his reserve, Company C, located with Cannon Company two miles southwest of Marnach on the reverse slope of the Skyline Drive at the village of Munshausen, to move to Marnach and clear Germans from the southern fringe of the village. The company, under Capt. Carrol Copeland, had already begun to march when Colonel Paul learned that Colonel Fuller had two platoons of medium tanks earmarked for Marnach. At Paul's request, those ten tanks headed for Munshausen to overtake and join Company C. The men of Company C had meanwhile come under heavy small-arms fire in which Captain Copeland was wounded; they pulled off road and were trying to advance cross-country. The tankers failed to spot them but nevertheless succeeded in reaching Marnach.

Once the southern edge of Marnach was clear of Germans, Colonel Paul had intended sending infantry and tanks together southward to sweep the enemy from the Skyline Drive and move into Hosingen, which he mistakenly believed had fallen. When Company C failed to reach Marnach, Paul ordered one of the tank platoons to retrace its steps, pick up the men of Company C, and help the infantry defend Munshausen. The other platoon of tanks, commanded by 1st Lt. Robert A. Payne, was to drive alone on Hosingen.

In the confusion nobody appeared to notice that those instructions left Company B in the critical village of Marnach without tank support. Indeed, Colonel Fuller, who sanctioned the drive on Hosingen, thought the other platoon had stayed in Marnach. When that platoon turned up in Munshausen, he was convinced that the platoon leader had bugged out.

Machine guns blazing, Lieutenant Payne and his tanks swept the two-and-a-half-mile stretch of the Skyline Drive between Marnach and Hosingen free of Germans—at least for a time—and found, with relief, that Company K still held Hosingen. Indeed, Company K and a company of the division's organic 103d Engineer Battalion, which was also in Hosingen, had stood virtually ignored while Germans eddied around them to north and south.

A mile south of Hosingen at the crossroads marked by the Café Schincker, in the meantime, men of the platoon of Company L defending the crossroads saw a jeep approaching at mid-morning from the east. Since that was the road taken before daylight by the jeep sent to recall the squad of riflemen scheduled to participate in the training exercise, the men waved to the occupants. In response, they drew a burst of fire from burp guns. Screeching around the corner onto the main road atop the Skyline Drive, the jeep raced up the road toward Hosingen, leaving the men at the crossroads agape; but they had time to note that the jeep bore Company L's markings on the bumpers.

Down at the Our River, German engineers were working hard to put in bridges, but it was a slow process. Because the bridges had to be stout enough to support big Panther tanks, the girders were heavy, and the terrain around the bridge sites was so confined by the deep river gorge that no heavy equipment could get forward to help. All had to be done by hand; furthermore, the Our, normally a placid stream, was swollen from rains and melting snow. During the morning the commander of the Fifth Panzer Army, General von Manteuffel, visited both sites. While lamenting the slow progress, he considered that the engineers were doing the best they could under the circumstances.

Shortly after 1 P.M., Major Loos's engineers finally completed the bridge for the 2d Panzer Division at Dasburg, whence ran the road to Marnach and Clervaux. The Mark IV and Panther tanks were nevertheless slow to cross, for a narrow, precipitous approach road on the east bank had a succession of hairpin turns that was hard for the ponderous tanks to negotiate. Only ten had crossed the span when the next tank in column took the last turn too short, crashed into one side of the bridge, and plunged into the water. Except for the driver, the crew escaped; but repairing the bridge consumed another two hours, so that it was late afternoon before tanks could begin crossing again. At about the same time, around 4 P.M., engineers of the *Panzer Lehr Division* completed a bridge downstream at Gemünd.

Throughout the afternoon, German pressure was intense almost everywhere except at Hosingen, and almost everywhere the American troops were running low on ammunition. As darkness approached, each little garrison was virtually surrounded, yet nowhere had they given in, although Company L in Holzthum held at that point only a few houses and a barn. On the other hand, the complexion of the battle was about to change, for with two bridges across the Our River, the Germans would soon have the added strength of tanks and other armored vehicles.

Additional firepower was first apparent on the forward slope of the Skyline Drive near Wahlhausen, where the lone platoon of Company I was holding at the former battalion observation post. Soon after it was fully dark, flak wagons with quadruple-mounted 20mm. guns joined the attack. Almost out of ammunition, the platoon leader, 1st Lt. Jack Fisher, radioed for artillery fire on top of his position. He got it, but that failed to stop the Germans. Only one of Fisher's men got away. Fisher himself, although captured, soon eluded his guards in the darkness and eventually made his way back to the battalion headquarters in Consthum.

The rest of Company I in the nearby village of Weiler was in little better shape than the detached platoon. Surrounded and virtually out of ammunition, the company commander, Capt. Floyd K. McCutchan, determined to break out after nightfall. He himself took charge of one group of fifty men while 1st Lt. Edward Jenkins led a second group of similar size.

Although the two groups were supposed to rendezvous at a designated point along the Skyline Drive, Jenkins and his men got diverted by an encounter with a German patrol, never reached the rendezvous point, and ended up the next day at a village still in American hands along the Clerve River. McCutchan and his group, meanwhile, waited in vain all night for Jenkins's arrival. The next day, they fought their way past one German force after another until at last they reached the road behind Consthum, where an ambulance driver told McCutchan that troops of the 3d Battalion still held the village. Turning over the wounded to the driver, Captain McCutchan and the thirty-five men still left to him plodded wearily up the road toward Consthum and back into the fight.

Meanwhile in Clervaux, Colonel Fuller early on the afternoon of the 16th rounded up sixty men of the 110th Infantry who had been on leave in the town and sent them to Reuler, a village just north of the Marnach road, there to protect the firing positions of Battery B, 109th Field Artillery. They arrived just in time to help half-tracks of the division's attached antiaircraft artillery keep the Germans from overrunning the battery. Yet it was obvious to all that the howitzers would soon have to displace or fall into German hands. Near nightfall they managed to get out and took up new firing positions alongside the Clerve River in the shadow of the château in Clervaux.

In late afternoon, Fuller again appealed to General Cota for release of his 2d Battalion from the division reserve, but again Cota refused. What about some two hundred men from other units of the division who, like the sixty of the 110th Infantry, had been on leave in Clervaux? Those, said Cota, Fuller could use.

Organized into a provisional company, those men and the few officers among them, armed only with rifles and carbines, began to dig in to block hairpin curves in the road from Marnach as it descended into Clervaux. The crews of two heavy .30-caliber machine guns soon joined them and after nightfall a platoon of 57mm. antitank guns. The little force was obviously makeshift and thin, but except for the platoon of Shermans in reserve, it was all Fuller had for defense of his headquarters town. For a last-ditch defense within the town itself, he ordered cooks, clerks, MPs, anybody who could be spared from his duties in the headquarters, to organize the old château as a strongpoint.

Defense it would be, for there could be no question of withdrawal. Early in the day, General Cota had passed on the order from the corps commander, General Middleton, directing all units to hold until their positions became "completely untenable." Even then, they were not to withdraw beyond a specified line, which in the 110th Infantry's sector included Marnach and thus Clervaux. Cota himself later in the day reinforced Middleton's order by admonishing everybody to hold at all costs.

Orders or no, the sorely pressed men of Company B in Marnach were close to going under. Their commander had been wounded early in the fighting and evacuated, so that the 1st Battalion's executive officer, Capt. James H. Burns, had assumed command.

An hour after nightfall, Burns reported by radio that the Germans were attacking again supported by half-tracks firing machine guns. That was the last word to come from the men who had so stoutly defended Marnach, but a continuing noise of firing from the village gave Colonel Fuller hope that some of them were still holding out. If only he could get his hands on his 2d Battalion, he might restore the position at Marnach and save Clervaux.

Around 9 P.M., General Cota telephoned Fuller. He was considering releasing the 2d Battalion, said Cota; if he did, what would Fuller do with it? He would attack, Fuller replied without hesitation, to relieve Marnach. And if that proved successful, he would continue south to Hosingen, where early that evening the Germans had at last launched a heavy attack against Company K.

OK, said Cota. He could have the battalion minus one rifle company, which Cota retained to protect the division headquarters.

As Fuller drew up his plans for an attack before daylight the next morning, he learned that Cota had ordered the 707th Tank Battalion's light tank company, which had spent the first day uncommitted by the 112th Infantry, to attack at daylight down the Skyline Drive to Marnach. That prompted Fuller to delay the 2d Battalion's attack an hour to coincide with the drive by the light tanks. At the same time, the medium tank platoon at Munshausen, along with a platoon of Company C's riflemen, was also to drive on Marnach.

As December 16 neared an end, the commander of the 47th Panzer Corps, General von Lüttwitz, had to accept that he had fallen well short of his first day's objective, crossings over the Clerve River. That was attributable in part to the delay in getting bridges installed across the Our; but even when the bridges were in, the *Panzer Lehr Division* was in for more delay when vehicles mired on the unpaved roads leading from Gemünd and blocked them. The failure was also attributable in part to the unsuccessful application of the Hutier tactics by units of the 26th Volksgrenadier Division, for except at Hosingen and at the Café Schincker crossroads, the *Volksgrenadiers* had been unable to avoid a fight. They were like a man who tries to sneak past a hornet's nest, only to find the hornets swarming at him so ferociously that he has to stop and try to destroy the nest. Nor had the Hutier tactics worked much better for the two *Panzergrenadier* regiments of the 2d Panzer Division.

The Germans had taken only three defended positions: Marnach, Weiler, and the position held by a single platoon of Company I near Wahlhausen. With the arrival of the 26th Volksgrenadier Division's reserve regiment, they finally mounted an attack at Hosingen, but there Company K and its engineer support were still strong. Only at Holzthum was another American force near caving in, so near, in fact, that the commander of Company L, Lieutenant Saymon, ordered his platoon at the Café Schincker crossroads to fall back to Holzthum to help, but the platoon was unable to break into the village and had to go instead to join the defenders at Consthum.

The fact that the Germans had failed to achieve their objective was also attributable to the intrepidity of the American soldier. With only two battalions supported for part of the day by two companies of medium tanks, the 110th Infantry had held off four German regiments and had nowhere been routed. That was around two thousand men versus at least ten thousand. And the men of the 110th Infantry had done it at times without normal artillery support, so hardpressed were two of the four supporting batteries. Considering the odds, nowhere on the first day of the German offensive was there a more remarkable achievement by the American soldier.

Yet how much more punishment could those men take? Hundreds dead, hundreds wounded, possibly more than a hundred captured, and the survivors all short of ammunition. There were hopes for the morrow, of course, when two-thirds of the reserve infantry battalion—about six hundred men—was to join the fight. What the American commanders could not know was that just before midnight, Mark IV tanks of the 2d Panzer Division—all resistance finally eliminated at Marnach—were beginning to assemble in the village, to be ready with the start of a new day to head downhill toward the little town of Clervaux and its two bridges over the Clerve River.

CHAPTER SEVEN

The Southern Shoulder

Erich Brandenberger and his Seventh Army were like poor relations from whom the patriarch of the family expects big things but to whom he provides little material assistance. Adolf Hitler expected the Seventh Army to protect the southern flank of his offensive all the way from the German frontier to the Meuse River, a distance of about eighty miles, and to do it with a parachute and three *Volksgrenadier* divisions dependent almost entirely on horse-drawn transport. Assuming the Seventh Army reached the Meuse and aligned its four divisions to hold equal portions of the south flank, that would mean a defensive sector for each division of twenty miles, which could hardly be considered much of a barrier to a counterattack from General Patton's Third Army to the south. Yet Hitler was paying scant heed to the south flank, for he was counting on surprise and speed to get the Fifth and Sixth Panzer armies across the Meuse before the Americans could counterattack, so that he expected the first American riposte only after his troops got beyond the Meuse. At that time, he figured, Eisenhower would be too concerned about stopping the forward thrust of the offensive to pay much attention to its flanks.

Hitler's senior field commanders saw it differently. They all were well aware of the tactical dictum that had emerged from the Great War and long been taught at the *Kriegsakademie,* a dictum with which American commanders were also familiar, for it had been taught too through the interwar years at the U.S. Army's Command and General Staff College at Fort Leavenworth, Kansas: The way to deal with an enemy penetration is to hold tight at the shoulders to deny any widening of the penetration and thus limit the force the enemy can project in his forward thrust. Once the lines are stabilized, cut off the penetration at its base.

Both Field Marshals von Rundstedt and Model urged Hitler to strengthen the Seventh Army, and General von Manteuffel made a last effort at the Reichschancellery on December 2 to get at least a *Panzergrenadier* division for Brandenberger, whose advance was crucial for the protection of his own south flank. But Hitler refused. Any additional unit given the Seventh Army would be either one less unit available to propel the two panzer armies swiftly over the Meuse or one less unit for the second wave he was counting upon to exploit the crossings of the Meuse all the way to Antwerp.

That left General Brandenberger—at fifty, a bald, bespectacled, paunchy man who was a conservative but experienced commander—with 2 corps headquarters, 4 divisions, 30 assault guns, 427 artillery pieces and rocket projectors, and no tanks, more a reinforced corps than a field army. In Brandenberger's view, the best he could hope to accomplish was to make a penetration with one corps on his south wing in the vicinity of the border town of Echternach and erect a defensive barrier about eight miles short of Luxembourg City. With the other corps he would penetrate close along the flank of the Fifth Panzer Army, gaining as much impetus as possible from that army's advance, and drive—if fortune smiled—as far as the region south of Bastogne, there to assume defensive positions facing south toward Arlon. Getting to the Meuse, Brandenberger reasoned, was chimerical.

On the other hand, as elsewhere in the Ardennes, the forces available to the Seventh Army, however limited, dwarfed the defensive strength immediately available to the opposing American units. Each of the two divisions of the 85th Corps next to the Fifth Panzer Army faced a single battalion (eight hundred men) of the 28th Division's 109th Infantry on the west bank of the Our River—seven battalions against one—while one of the two divisions of the 80th Corps faced an armored infantry battalion of the 9th Armored Division and the other a regiment of the 4th Division, the 12th Infantry, both of which held positions on the west bank of the Sûre River below the juncture of the Our and the Sûre.

Yet in that sector, as in few other places, there were some American reserves. With the arrival of the 60th Armored Infantry Battalion to gain battle experience, the 109th Infantry had been able to pull a battalion into reserve, and the 28th Division's commander, General Cota, had afforded the regiment a medium tank company of the 707th Tank Battalion and a company of towed tank destroyers. As a component of the 9th Armored Division's Combat Command A, the armored infantry battalion had the back-up of the combat command's medium tank battalion and a company of self-propelled tank destroyers. Although the commander of the 4th Division, General Barton, had two more regiments, both were holding elongated fronts farther south; and since Barton had no way of knowing German intentions, he would be reluctant to draw on those regiments until he determined the extent of the German attack. Barton also had a self-propelled tank destroyer battalion and a medium tank battalion, but in the wake of the hard fighting in the Hürtgen Forest, both were far under strength and even those vehicles that survived the forest fighting needed repairs and overhauls.

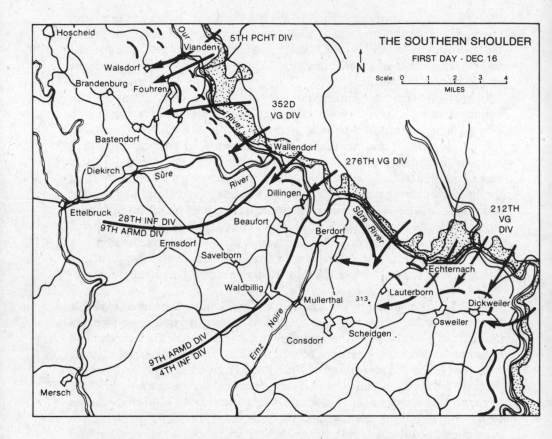

In artillery, the defenders were to have at first less than a fourth of the strength available to the Germans. The 109th Infantry had its usual light 105mm. howitzer battalion plus the 28th Division's general support 155mm. battalion, which Cota had allotted the regiment because of the possibility of a German move against Luxembourg City. The 60th Armored Infantry Battalion had an armored field artillery battalion with self-propelled 105mm. howitzers in support, and the 12th Infantry its usual 105mm. howitzer battalion. General Barton also had his organic 155mm. howitzers and two corps field artillery battalions, but those were positioned farther south, where the infantry's lines were even thinner than in the 12th Infantry's sector.

Of the two divisions of the 85th Corps commanded by General der Infanterie Baptist Kniess, the more ambitious assignment went to the 5th Parachute Division on the north wing. Hoping to benefit from the rapid advance expected of the *Panzer Lehr Division* just to the north, the paratroopers—in reality, mostly recently converted Luftwaffe ground troops—were to cross the Wiltz River, in effect, a southward extension of the Clerve, a goal expected to be reached by the end of the first day. They would then continue west, bypassing the 28th Division's headquarters town of Wiltz, and finally form blocking positions south of Bastogne.

The 352d Volksgrenadier Division was to cross the Our a little farther south, seize dominating ground in the angle formed by juncture of the Our and the Sûre, and push on toward the westward reaches of the Sûre and the towns of Diekirch and Ettelbruck. Having crossed the Sûre, the troops were to build defensive positions on the heights beyond. One of the newly formed 13,000-man *Volksgrenadier* divisions, made up mainly of converted airmen but with a sprinkling of shore-based sailors, the 352d had been holding the line in the Eifel for several weeks but had pulled back during the night of December 12 to prepare for the attack. (Which explained why nobody fired when Elise Delé set off a mine and why the patrol of the 109th Infantry that crossed the Our before daylight on the 15th at Vianden found nobody in the pillboxes.) Most of the Seventh Army's skimpy allotment of assault guns was with those two divisions.

Reflecting the greater ambition of the objectives assigned the 85th Corps over those assigned the Seventh Army's other corps, two-thirds of the artillery pieces and rocket projectors fired their preparation in the 109th Infantry's sector. Most of the fire hit headquarters towns and artillery positions in the rear, little of it against the forward infantry. So accurate was the shelling in Diekirch, where the regiment's reserve battalion was billeted, that men of the battalion's intelligence section went looking for an observer in their midst. As the story reached the troops—possibly apocryphal—they found a radio antenna erected over a cobbler's shop and inside, operating a radio set, "a good-looking blond." (Are all female spies blond and good-looking?) The word passed among the troops that "she was summarily shot."

Little of the snow that was present in northern reaches of the Ardennes was to be found that morning in central Luxembourg, for what had been snow farther north had fallen as rain and sleet there; but the same kind of heavy fog that obscured German movement elsewhere hugged the ground. (Although the Seventh Army had a few of the big searchlights used farther north, few American troops remarked on any effects.) In the fog and darkness, the Americans saw nothing of the Germans crossing the Our in assault boats; and at Vianden, engineers of the 5th Parachute Division were on top of the roadblock maintained outside the Hôtel Heintz before men of Lieutenant Prazenka's I&R Platoon awoke to their presence. Everybody in the little platoon was either killed or captured.

The German advance against the extreme northern wing of the 109th Infantry reflected orders to the paratroopers to sidestep opposition wherever possible. One column bypassed Company F, which was dug in on a ridge commanding a meandering road leading from Vianden, and toiled slowly toward the southern reaches of the Skyline Drive. Another force entered the undefended village of Walsdorf, a little over a mile behind Vianden, which prompted the 2d Battalion commander to commit a company to dig in facing the village. When the paratroopers began to emerge from Walsdorf in late afternoon, heading toward the 2d Battalion's headquarters village of Brandenburg, the commander of the 109th Infantry, Lt. Col. James E. Rudder, who had only recently taken over the regiment after having led a Ranger battalion ashore on D-Day in Normandy and later in the Hürtgen Forest, sent a company from the regimental reserve to help the headquarters troops hold Brandenburg.

The other of the 2d Battalion's forward units, Company E in Fouhren—almost due south of Vianden astride the principal highway leading down to the valley of the Sûre and thence to Diekirch—had more difficulty. Both the 5th Parachute Division and the adjacent 352d Volksgrenadier Division needed either that highway or a secondary road that also passed through the village. Paratroopers passing to the north, *Volksgrenadiers* to the south, soon isolated Fouhren, and Company E's radio failed. Paratroopers and *Volksgrenadiers* alike poked at the village through the day, but possibly because it lay on the interdivisional boundary, they made no coordinated assault. At the end of the day, Company E was still in place.

Volksgrenadiers passing south of Fouhren nevertheless posed a considerable threat, for they soon held two nearby undefended villages, one on the main highway leading down to the Sure valley, the other on a side road also providing access to the valley. Should they reach the valley road, they would cut the supply route to the 3d Battalion's positions in the angle formed by confluence of the Our and the Sûre. Having taken advantage of the fog, German patrols had already begun to fire on one of the batteries of the 108th Field Artillery Battalion alongside the valley road. Shortly after midday, Colonel Rudder committed a company from his reserve battalion, supported by a platoon of medium tanks, to drive the Germans from the two villages and later reinforced those with the final company of his reserve.

Among the last to be committed was Company B's Second Platoon, accompanied by two Sherman tanks. The platoon leader, 1st Lt. James V. Christy, had seen action before, but as was the case in all the rifle companies of the 109th Infantry, many of his men had only recently reached the front as replacements. One of those was Tech. Sgt. Stanislaus Wieszcyk, one of hundreds of noncommissioned officers combed from support units, given a few days of refresher training, and put into the infantry. Over Wieszcyk's protest ("Listen, Lieutenant, I got these stripes for running a consolidated mess hall at Camp Fannin, Texas!"), Christy had made him his platoon sergeant, second in command; either he did the job his stripes at that point called for or he would lose them.

By nightfall, the platoon and its two supporting tanks had advanced well along the road from the Sûre valley toward Fouhren. In the darkness, it was eerie moving forward with flashes of artillery fire lighting the night sky in seemingly every direction. The men were tired, hungry, and upset over the losses they had taken during the day. Lieutenant Christy "could sense the uneasiness of the soldiers."

The lead tank suddenly came to a halt. Going forward, Christy found the tank commander determined to proceed not another inch without riflemen in front of him to guard against antitank rockets from *Panzerfausts*. Turning to Sergeant Wieszcyk, Christy told him to get a squad out front. "The guys have had more than enough today," responded Wieszcyk. "They won't go."

The young lieutenant gulped, but he quickly turned to the commander of the tank. "How many men do you want in front of this tank to move it?" The tank commander said one good soldier would do. "You've got him!" said Christy. "Follow me."

With pounding heart, Lieutenant Christy stepped out in front of the Sherman and started walking into the darkness. He had gone only a short way and the tank had scarcely begun to rumble forward behind him when Christy made out a figure on his left. It was Wieszcyk. "OK, Lieutenant," said Wieszcyk, "you made your point." Close behind him was the entire First Squad.

Before digging in for the night, the two reserve companies made it to the fringes of the two villages, thereby blocking both roads leading to the valley of the Sûre but without dislodging the Germans from the villages. Company E remained isolated in Fouhren, and Colonel Rudder had committed the last of his infantry reserve.

Meanwhile, against the high ground in the angle formed by the confluence of the Our and the Sûre, German infantry, having crossed the Our unobserved in the fog and darkness, had attacked positions of the 3d Battalion early in the morning. As defensive positions went in the Ardennes, those were fairly compact: two rifle companies dug in on steep bluffs overlooking the Our and the third in reserve, while the battalion's right flank drew protection from the deep cut of the Sûre. To the waiting Americans, the attacking Germans appeared to be "fanatically hopped up"; many of them charged "wildly, screaming and firing their weapons until killed or wounded." Whether courage drunk from bottles or some other kind, it was undeniably courage and drew grudging admiration from the defenders, but it went for nought. In what General Brandenberger was later to call "very bloody fighting," the Germans made no dent in the 3d Battalion's line, while artillery fire observed from the forward positions pummeled them throughout the day along the banks of the Our, seriously interfering with attempts to put in a bridge just downstream from Vianden.

As the first day of the attack against the 109th Infantry came to an end, Colonel Rudder saw "no cause for alarm." While there was no doubt that the attack was in considerable strength, Rudder considered his regiment to be "in a good position" with "a distinct advantage of terrain." The Germans had yet to employ any tanks or assault guns, and Rudder still had the bulk of a company of medium tanks on hand. Although Company E remained isolated in Fouhren, isolation on the battlefield held few concerns for an officer with Rudder's background in the Rangers, and a renewal of the counterattack by his reserve battalion should remedy Company E's situation with the coming of a new day.

Men of the 9th Armored Division's 60th Armored Infantry Battalion held on a high plateau between the Sûre River in the north and a little stream known as the Ernz Noire (Black Ernz) in the south. With an eye to tourism, Luxembourg officials called the terrain to the south "*La Petite Suisse* (Little Switzerland)." The name denotes no great heights but instead spectacular sandstone rock formations in the deep gorge of the little Ernz Noire, formations carved by the elements over the centuries, sometimes isolated and looking like misshapen chimneys, elsewhere clustered like the ruins of some grotesque fortress. Except for the verdant forest cloaking the gorge, the officials might also have called it "*le Wild West*," for to many an American soldier familiar with the rock formations on the buttes and mesas of southwestern states, it looked like a setting for cowboys and Indians. The gorge lies some three to five hundred feet below the surrounding tableland, and in some places its walls are sheer cliffs.

Unlike the deep cut of the Sûre River, which afforded flank protection for the 109th Infantry's 3d Battalion, the gorge of the Ernz Noire did nothing to strengthen the armored infantrymen's positions, for three roads cut perpendicularly across it. One of them led directly into the rear of the American positions at Beaufort, where the battalion commander, Lt. Col. Kenneth W. Collins, had his headquarters in a castle dating from the twelfth century, that Victor Hugo, who spent time in the region as an exile, called "a vision." Farther up the gorge, the other two roads led toward firing positions of the 3d Armored Field Artillery Battalion. Furthermore, responsibility for the Ernz Noire belonged to the neighboring unit, the 4th Division's 12th Infantry, and as Colonel Collins knew, the 12th Infantry was so overextended that only a small outpost was in a position to block German movement up the gorge.

Collins also was considerably concerned about his north flank, for more than a mile separated his men from the closest positions of the 109th Infantry. To cover that gap—or at least to give the alarm—he had only a squad positioned in the settlement of Hogenberg, looking down on the German village of Wallendorf and the juncture of the Our and the Sûre, the spot where American armor in September had crossed and headed for Bitburg. Yet Collins's main positions were compact and located atop steep bluffs with good fields of fire into the valley of the Sûre.

Like both forward battalions of the 109th Infantry, the 60th Armored Infantry Battalion faced seven enemy battalions, an entire division, the 276th Volksgrenadier, recently arrived from Poland, where it had been rehabilitated after disastrous losses in Normandy. Most of the new men were young conscripts who had received adequate basic training, but they had neither tanks nor assault guns.

The division's objective was somewhat indefinite—merely to cross the Sûre, annihilate the Americans who stood in the way, and gain high ground to the southwest from which to constitute part of a blocking position to be formed by the 80th Corps facing in the direction of Luxembourg City. Just where that line was to be established depended upon how much ground the two divisions of the 80th Corps were able to gain, but they hoped to reach a point eight miles from Luxembourg City. Contrary to what the Americans were to perceive, the capital of Luxembourg was not an objective. Neither were the transmitters of Radio Luxembourg, one of Europe's most powerful stations, located just over halfway between the frontier and Luxembourg City at Junglinster, although to the American commanders both seemed likely targets.

Since the bulk of the Seventh Army's artillery supported the north wing of the attack, the preparation in the sector of the 60th Armored Infantry Battalion was less than awesome, about a thousand rounds, most of which fell on the battalion headquarters village of Beaufort and on the artillery positions farther back. Yet that was sufficient to knock out all telephone lines within the battalion.

The first Germans the armored infantrymen spotted early on December 16 appeared to constitute nothing more than patrols; but by late morning, that first impression had proven to be deceptive. When the fog lifted, the men could see swarms of Germans crossing the Sûre near Wallendorf and downstream near the village of Dillengen, just down the bluff from the foxholes of Company A. Supporting artillery took both sites under heavy fire, but still the Germans continued to cross.

The little outpost at Hogenberg was quickly overwhelmed, and the men of both forward companies were soon aware that the wooded draws leading to their positions were thick with Germans. Shortly before midday, an attack launched from the houses of Dillingen forced back a platoon of Company A, but the battalion's reserve company moved forward quickly from Beaufort to restore the line. As night fell, except for the outpost at Hogenberg, the 60th Armored Infantry's positions were intact. The battalion commander, Colonel Collins, nevertheless continued to worry about the possibility of the Germans moving up the roads from the Ernz Noire and isolating his companies and their supporting howitzers.

The commander of the Seventh Army, General Brandenberger, considered the 212th Volksgrenadier Division the most capable of his four divisions, which was why he assigned the division the task of anchoring the army's south flank and why he withheld one regiment as an army reserve. Burned out in fighting on the Eastern Front, the division had begun rebuilding in September around a cadre of experienced junior officers and noncommissioned officers and with conscripts judged to be better than average, including a considerable number of seventeen-year-olds. Yet the division had only four assault guns and the usual handicap posed by horse-drawn artillery.

As for the American 4th Infantry Division, having arrived in Luxembourg only at the end of the first week in December, it had had little time in which to reorganize and absorb replacements for the five thousand casualties incurred in the Hürtgen Forest. All rifle companies were still short by at least forty men, the size of a platoon, and they would have been even more understrength had not General Barton, concerned about a possible enemy raid on Luxembourg City, recalled the men who had been in rest centers to the rear.

The German artillery barrage that began at 5:30 A.M. on the 16th struck only the division's northernmost regiment, the 12th Infantry, and most of the shells fell on company and battalion command posts and artillery positions. While heavy and surprising for what was supposed to be a quiet sector, the preparation was hardly enough to create much alarm in old hands who had experienced German shelling since the early days in Normandy. It was nevertheless sufficient to knock out most telephone lines forward of the battalion headquarters (or else, as most men believed, German patrols deliberately cut them).

Concealed by the fog and darkness, the *Volksgrenadiers* crossed the Sûre on both sides of Echternach, a medieval town of some five thousand people (all previously evacuated) on the west bank of the Sûre almost at the center of the 12th Infantry's positions. Having defended the West Wall opposite the sector for several weeks, the *Volksgrenadiers* had plotted the American positions accurately and moved swiftly to encircle the outposts.

Southwest of Echternach, the Germans overran a squad-sized outpost each of Companies I and L, but the men in other companies managed to fall back on the main positions in the villages of Osweiler and Dickweiler, located in rolling, high farm country about a mile back from the Sûre. In Echternach itself, all three of Company E's rifle platoons in widely separated positions came under fire from Germans who had infiltrated nearby buildings, as did the company headquarters in a hat factory on the southern edge of town. At the village of Lauterborn, just over a mile behind Echternach, where Company G provided a back-up position along the main highway to Luxembourg City, all three of the company's squad-sized outposts were cut off, but to a man they were eventually to make their way to safety, some after wandering behind German lines for up to four days.

The effect of the German infiltration was far more damaging against the outposts of Company F. Three were located northwest of Echternach near the village of Berdorf, on a lip of high ground overlooking the Sûre, or just back from it in farm buildings, all held in platoon strength. The fourth, manned by an under-strength squad, was in the gorge of the Ernz Noire near the point where the first of the perpendicular roads crossing the gorge led to Beaufort. All four outposts fell, everybody either killed or captured except for two men from the outpost along the Ernz Noire and thirteen who had gone on a routine contact patrol. Four of those men were also captured later in the day, but the nine others eventually made their way out, some after playing cowboys and Indians with the Germans among the big rock formations in the valley of the Ernz Noire.

By late morning, the Germans had surrounded all five of the forward companies: Company I in Dickweiler, Company L in Osweiler, Company G in Lauterborn (which had the effect of cutting off Company E in Echternach), and what was left of Company F in a resort hotel a hundred yards outside Berdorf. Yet their presence still posed considerable difficulties for the Germans, for the American positions controlled every road leading into the 12th Infantry's sector except that up the valley of the Ernz Noire.

Shortly before noon, General Barton granted the regimental commander, Col. Robert H. Chance, authority to commit his reserve battalion and released to him a platoon of medium tanks of the attached 70th Tank Battalion and two platoons of the battalion's light tanks, rushed forward from assignment guarding Radio Luxembourg. Chance sent one company with some of the tanks marching on Berdorf to relieve the men of Company F in the nearby hotel and another with the rest of the tanks toward Lauterborn to relieve Company G.

The force advancing on Berdorf failed to make it, encountering strong resistance near the village and precipitating a fight that was destined to continue well into the night. The force moving on Lauterborn did better. Overcoming resistance on a hill just outside the village, it continued forward, and as night began to fall, reached a mill on the edge of Lauterborn. There the force rescued a small group of Americans who through the afternoon had undergone what had been, at best, an unnerving experience.

As the Germans advanced on Lauterborn, about forty of them captured fifteen Americans manning an outpost built around a 57mm. antitank gun. Continuing to advance, the Germans marched the Americans up the road in front of them, heading toward the millhouse that was occupied (although the Germans had no way of knowing it) by Company G's command group. Alongside the road outside the millhouse stood a low stone wall; as the prisoners passed behind the wall, they had cover, but the Germans were still in the open. The men of the command group opened fire. Armed only with rifles and a single BAR, the command group nevertheless managed to keep the Germans pinned to the ground until the relief force arrived.

At Osweiler and Dickweiler, the two forward companies of the 3d Battalion held their own. At Osweiler, the Germans fell back after making an assault that cost them fifty men, and even though twenty Germans managed later to get into a few of the houses, they pulled out after dark. At Dickweiler, the Germans made only a halfhearted effort against the village until late afternoon, by which time the battalion commander, Maj. Herman R. Rice, had sent fifteen men from his reserve company riding three medium tanks to the village. As two German companies attacked, everybody held his fire until the Germans were so close that the tank commanders feared their tanks might be hit by *Panzerfausts*. When at last the infantry company commander signaled fire, the effect was devastating. A German company commander and fifty of his men were killed; another company commander and thirty-five men surrendered; and the other survivors fell back in disorder.

A hundred yards east of Berdorf, the commander of Company F, 1st Lt. John L. Leake, had established his headquarters in the Parc Hôtel, built in the early 1930s when tourism was beginning to develop into a major industry in Luxembourg. As the hotel's brochures proclaimed, the Parc Hôtel occupied a *site isolé*—a high, open plateau only a few hundred yards from one of the more spectacular rock formations in the gorge of the Ernz Noire known as the *Ile du Diable* (Devil's Island)—and featured both *confort moderne* and *cuisine distinguée*. Since Leake and the members of his command group had to make do with U.S. Army victuals prepared by their own less than accomplished chefs, they could provide no testimony to the distinguished cuisine, but they could attest to the modern comforts of the beds and the plumbing, and the isolated site afforded excellent fields of fire.

Since all communication had failed, Lieutenant Leake had no early knowledge of the tragic fate of his outposts, located a mile from the hotel, but in the wake of the early morning shelling, he was markedly concerned about a lack of communications with his battalion headquarters and the artillery. Since his executive officer, 1st Lt. Richard McConnell, was planning to go to the rear to dispose of cash left over from paying the men, he urged McConnell to hurry back with the company's radio, an SCR*-300, which had been left for repair. McConnell was about ready to leave by jeep but was waiting for the first sergeant to complete the morning report when a soldier came running up. It was a man from the crew of a nearby 57mm. antitank gun. Did anybody know anything about a column of troops marching up the hill from the direction of the Hamm Farm?

*Signal Corps Radio

Almost simultaneously men manning an observation post on top of the hotel called down that they could see a column of troops approaching. Rushing to the roof, Lieutenant Leake saw Germans advancing, one file on either side of the road. At Leake's urging, Lieutenant McConnell and his driver took off in their jeep immediately, wheels spinning, under orders to report to battalion the approach of "a possible enemy patrol" and to hurry back with the SCR-300.

As Lieutenant Leake was soon aware, what he had seen was no German patrol but the vanguard of an entire battalion. The bulk of the battalion bypassed the Parc Hôtel and entered the unoccupied village of Berdorf, while the group seen from the observation post moved into a cluster of houses just short of the hotel and opened fire.

Inside, Leake, three other officers, and fifty-five men took refuge. Other than their rifles, they had only a few BARs, one .50-caliber machine gun, and little reserve ammunition. Such extra ammunition as the company had on hand was in a small shed in the garden, which was impossible to reach in the face of fire from the German-held houses. Two men who had been working in the shed were trapped there.

As the Americans took up firing positions at the hotel's windows, the Germans were unable to advance. Meanwhile, those in the village of Berdorf moved about freely until Company F's first sergeant, Gerveis Willis, placed a BAR in a window near the entrance to the hotel and opened fire on a crossroads at the edge of the village. Willis reckoned that he killed eight men before the Germans began to respect his marksmanship and avoid the crossroads.

Lieutenant McConnell had in the meantime reached battalion headquarters in a village a few miles back and found the company's radio fully repaired. Conscious of Lieutenant Leake's urgent need for the radio, he dismissed his other mission of getting rid of the excess money and with his driver, Cpl. John Mandichak, headed back for the Parc Hôtel. As they reached the crossroads in Berdorf, Germans at close range opened a hail of fire. Mandichak dived out his side of the jeep and ran into a barn, where he hid under a pile of hay until nightfall and then slipped away, the beginning of a seven-day odyssey that was eventually to bring him to safety in American lines. Diving out the other side of the jeep, McConnell ran into a house, but the Germans spotted him and he had to surrender.

A German sergeant took McConnell's bag of money, examined the contents, then handed it back with a smile. Having sold newspapers as a youth in Miami, McConnell had picked up some Yiddish and found that he could converse, after a fashion, with the sergeant. His company commander was with a German group that had just taken the Parc Hôtel, said the sergeant; he was sending the lieutenant there. At the point of a rifle, McConnell started up a straight, exposed road leading directly to the hotel's entrance.

When McConnell and his guard got within twenty-five yards of it, McConnell realized that the German sergeant was wrong. Those were American soldiers at the windows. "Don't shoot," McConnell shouted; "they'll shoot me." Since it was obvious to the German soldier, too, that Americans, not Germans, held the hotel, he used his prisoner as a shield and backed down the road to Berdorf.

At that point, the German sergeant saw a chance to use his prisoner to engineer surrender of the Americans in the hotel. Summoning his squad and with McConnell in the lead at the point of a gun, he headed up the road. As the group got close to the hotel, one of the soldiers yelled from a window: "Are all those your prisoners?" McConnell shouted back: "Hell, no. I'm the prisoner!"

Lieutenant Leake was momentarily at a loss to know what to do, but he made up his mind quickly and shouted his order to his men loud enough for McConnell to hear: "Pick your targets. It's just like shooting ducks in a gallery. Squeeze 'em off and don't waste ammo!"

McConnell understood, but for the benefit of the Germans, he shouted back: "Don't shoot!" Then he added: "And don't miss!"

At one of the windows, Cpl. Robert Hancock drew a bead on the German closest to McConnell. He "could see the lieutenant's shoulder and the Jerry's left pocket"—he held on the pocket.

At Lieutenant Leake's signal, everybody fired at once. The first volley dropped all but two of the Germans. Along with McConnell, those two— one of them the sergeant—ran behind a nearby building that shielded them from the hotel but exposed them to the two men from Company F who had been trapped in the supply shed. Each choosing a target, the two men fired, killing one German but only wounding the sergeant. (The man firing at the sergeant was new to the front and reluctant to kill any-body. He had consciously aimed at the sergeant's buttocks.)

"Now," said McConnell to the sergeant, "you had better give up." To which the sergeant responded: "I give up."

McConnell cradled the German in his arms, an act that presumably kept the Germans in nearby houses from opening fire, and took him into the hotel. There he and the others were careful to treat their prisoner with consideration, for they were all too conscious that before long, their roles might be reversed.

As the afternoon wore on, that appeared to be ever more likely, for even though the Germans in the nearby houses attempted no assault, German artillery pummeled the hotel, caving in the attic and part of the third floor, and there was no sign of a relief force coming to the rescue. Just after nightfall there was the sound of heavy firing on the far side of Berdorf, which indicated that somebody was trying to get through, but it eventually died away.

By early evening of December 16, the 12th Infantry continued to hold all its positions except those outposts overrun in the first German surge during the early morning fog and darkness, but it was clear that the Germans were continuing to build their strength. So intense was the pressure against Companies I and L at Osweiler and Dickweiler that the regimental commander, Colonel Chance, sent the last company of his reserve battalion to the 3d Battalion's command post to be ready to move to the two villages early the next day. The companies had no choice but to hold, for in mid-afternoon the 4th Division commander, "Tubby" Barton—as West Point classmates had long ago nicknamed him—had ordered that there was to be "no retrograde movement" in the 12th Infantry's sector.

However hardpressed the 12th Infantry, Barton was still hesitant to call on his other two regiments for help, for there was no guarantee that the German attack was not to expand. He nevertheless took the gamble of ordering his southernmost regiment to release its reserve battalion to move north early the next morning. He also directed much of the artillery supporting other parts of his front to shift to positions from which to fire in support of the 12th Infantry; and from the commander of the 9th Armored Division, he got the promise of a company of medium tanks to arrive the next morning from that division's CCA and augment his own badly depleted tank battalion. He also alerted the 4th Engineer Battalion and the 4th Reconnaissance Troop to be ready for commitment at an hour's notice.

On the German side, the commander of the Seventh Army, General Brandenberger, viewed the day's developments with some equanimity. Although he lamented the fact that American artillery fire had prevented installing even one bridge to enable his few assault guns to enter the fight (a mile to the north, the *Panzer Lehr Division* refused the use of its bridge, pronounced "too busy"), there were positive points as well. While it was true that the 5th Parachute Division had fallen far short of crossings over the Wiltz River, it was also true that each of the army's four divisions had penetrated the American front at one point or another, and Brandenberger perceived the failure to advance farther as attributable to his enemy's local reserves, all of which he assumed had been committed by the end of the day. At that point it was "a matter of making the breakthrough a thorough one before the enemy had a chance to bring up stronger reserves."

What Brandenberger could not know was that he was destined to meet a stronger reserve sooner than he anticipated. A few minutes before midnight, the commander of the VIII Corps, General Middleton, telephoned General Barton. At daybreak the next morning, said Middleton, a combat command of the 10th Armored Division was to leave an assembly area in the Third Army's sector only thirty-five miles from the 12th Infantry's positions. Barton was to have the use of that combat command.

CHAPTER EIGHT

The Northern Shoulder

When he spoke, it was as if he strained his words through gravel. The illegitimate son of a Bavarian servant girl, he was short and burly and looked like a man who depended for his livelihood on slaughtering pigs on a farm, which he did as a youth, or cutting meat at the butcher's, which he did after his discharge from the army at the end of the Great War until he joined the SS in 1928 and became Adolf Hitler's chauffeur and bodyguard. Five years later he organized and commanded the Führer's household troops, the *SS-Leibstandärte Adolf Hitler*, and in the summer of 1934 acted as chief executioner in Hitler's notorious purge of Nazi ranks, which became known as the Night of the Long Knives.

He commanded the *SS-Leibstandärte Adolf Hitler* as a regiment in France in 1940, then headed it as a brigade in Greece and finally in Russia as a division, renamed the 1st SS Panzer Division *(Leibstandärte Adolf Hitler)*. He was commanding an SS panzer corps in Normandy in the summer of 1944 when the cabal of army officers tried to kill the Führer. Hitler promptly made him head of a newly formed panzer army, but that command disintegrated in the defeat in Normandy and the retreat to the West Wall. Whereupon Hitler designated him to rebuild the SS panzer divisions, command the Sixth Panzer Army, and make the main effort in the offensive through the Ardennes.

While admitting the man's personal bravery, the German Army's generals despised him. His World War I rank of sergeant "attached to him perpetually in the minds of the aristocratic members of the German General staff." He was, said von Rundstedt, "decent, but stupid." To senior army commanders, he had at most the ability to command a division, which was why Model and von Rundstedt arranged to have the experienced and capable Fritz Kraemer assigned as his chief of staff. He was also sinister and ruthless: In Russia, when he learned that the Russians had murdered six of his troopers, he ordered all Russians captured over the next three days to be shot, and more than four thousand died.

By late 1944 he was drinking too much, seldom actually drunk but often close to it. By that time, also, he had come to decry his Führer's rash and clumsy interference with battlefield command, which explained his conniving to alter Hitler's plan for the Sixth Panzer Army's crossings of the Meuse so that if the offensive failed, his army would be in a position to implement the Small Solution.

Yet the man was careful to conceal his discontent from the Führer, and to Hitler none of his shortcomings mattered. He had been loyal since that night long ago in 1923 when Hitler had attempted to seize power in the *Feldherrnhalle* in Munich and failed. Hitler knew that the troops adored the man, that they would die for him; and Hitler was convinced that he, above all others, could be trusted.

That was why Hitler chose Sepp Dietrich as the one to lead the beloved SS panzer divisions to victory and save the Third Reich.

As befitted the force making the main effort, the Sixth Panzer Army was by far the strongest of the three armies attacking in the Ardennes. Dietrich had three corps headquarters, five parachute and *Volksgrenadier* divisions, four SS panzer divisions (counting attached separate tank and assault gun battalions, eight hundred tanks and assault guns), and more artillery and *Nebelwerfers* than the Fifth Panzer and Seventh Armies combined, an awesome one thousand pieces.

With two *Volksgrenadier* divisions, the 67th Corps was to attack on both sides of Monschau to get onto the Hautes Fagnes, the high moors just beyond the frontier, there to join von der Heydte's parachutists and the big *Jägdtigers* with 128mm. guns in blocking American reinforcements. South of Monschau, after a parachute and two *Volksgrenadier* divisions achieved penetrations, two SS panzer divisions of the 1st SS Panzer Corps were to make the main thrust in the vicinity of the twin villages of Krinkelt-Rocherath and through the northern reaches of the Losheim Gap. Two more SS panzer divisions under another SS panzer corps were to constitute a second wave, and most of Skorzeny's brigade was to operate in support of Dietrich's army.

Roads were, of course, vital to swift advance by the German armor. None of the roads in the sector to be traversed by the SS panzer divisions was ideal, but the planners designated five as adequate. Two emerged from the Losheim Gap, while the other three in the vicinity of Krinkelt-Rocherath crossed a broad expanse of high ground that the Americans called the Elsenborn Ridge. Since the network of through roads was so limited, it was vital that the SS panzer commanders adhere strictly to the routes assigned them, so vital that Hitler invoked his pet tactic of demanding compliance upon pain of death. To fail to obtain use of any of the five roads would impose a severe strain on the execution of the plan; to fail to gain as many as three could well be disastrous.

Not that anybody expected any difficulty, for all knew that their ad-

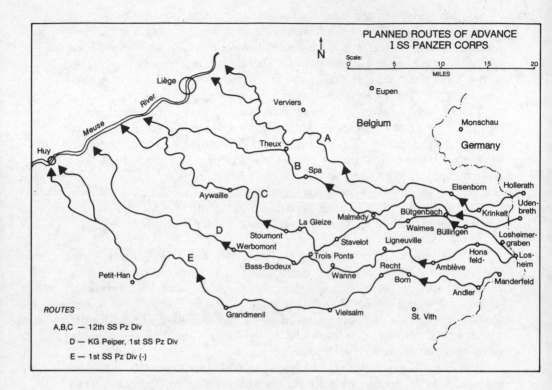

PLANNED ROUTES OF ADVANCE
I SS PANZER CORPS

ROUTES
A,B,C — 12th SS Pz Div
D — KG Peiper, 1st SS Pz Div
E — 1st SS Pz Div (-)

versary was inexperienced and vastly overextended. At either end of the Sixth Panzer Army's jump-off line, there was only a cavalry reconnaissance squadron and, in between, holding a twenty-mile front, the 99th Infantry Division. Even as the German troops crept through the snow and darkness on the night of December 15 to their attack positions, they and their commanders were still unaware that close behind the 99th Division was the 2d Infantry Division.

What Dietrich did soon learn was that two elements of his plan had already gone awry. One of the *Volksgrenadier* divisions that was supposed to attack at Monschau had been unable to break free from defensive positions farther north, so that the 67th Corps would have only a single division. Nor was there to be any help from von der Heydte's parachutists, at least not, as intended, before the attack started. Some of the trucks carrying the parachutists to the airfields from which their planes were to take off ran out of gasoline before they got there. By 10 P.M., when the planes were scheduled to take off, only 400 out of 1,200 parachutists had arrived. There would be no airborne attack that night.

Nowhere along the Ardennes front was the German artillery preparation more intense, more spectacular than in the sector of the Sixth Panzer

Army. To Cpl. Rudi Frübeiser of the 3d Parachute Division, it was "an earth-shaking inferno." To Tech. Sgt. Ben Nawrocki of the 99th Division's 393d Infantry, it seemed that "all hell broke loose . . . The ground shook." The operations officer of the 394th Infantry, Maj. William B. Kempton, called it "thunderous." For Pfc. Thor Ronningen of the 395th Infantry, who was asleep in a foxhole in Höfen, close to Monschau, it was "a terrifying experience to wake up to the crash of the artillery and the ear-splitting scream of the rockets. The ground shook like a bowl of Jell-O." And Maj. Günther Holz, commander of the 12th Volksgrenadier Division's tank destroyer battalion, said that "the earth seemed to break open. A hurricane of iron and fire went down on the enemy positions with a deafening noise. We old soldiers had seen many a heavy barrage, but never before anything like this."

In Höfen, the shelling crumbled many of the buildings, filling the streets with debris, and set some of the houses on fire, illuminating the foggy night with a lurid glow. Along the rest of the 99th Division's line, where most of the defensive positions were within or on the edge of fir forests, shells exploded in the treetops, knocking off big limbs and spraying the forest with jagged metal. Yet even though the overall effect was awesome, the damage to the defenders was minimal. Wire communications went out almost everywhere, but so widely spaced were the positions that many of the shells fell on undefended sectors, and elsewhere the men were well dug in, their foxholes roofed with logs.

At the road junction of Wahlerscheid, where the 2d Division was attacking, there was no shelling, for the Germans planned no attack in that sector. Nor was there any artillery fire on the town of Monschau. One of the most picturesque towns in all Germany, Monschau was in peacetime a favorite of honeymooners and—so the word went—of Adolf Hitler himself. Set in a deep gorge astride the upper reaches of the Roer River (at that point more like a mountain stream gurgling over a rock-strewn bottom), the town consisted of charming medieval buildings, their upper stories of white stucco and exposed wood framing ranged along cobblestoned streets little wider than sidewalks. Somebody—some said it was Model, others Hitler himself—had ordered that there was to be no shelling of Monschau.

The artillery was still firing when the big searchlights lit the sky with a milky glow. If the light helped the Germans in their attack, it also helped the Americans in their defense, particularly at three places where the attackers closely followed the artillery preparation. There were only three places where that happened along the entire front: against the 38th Cavalry Reconnaissance Squadron at Monschau; against a lone battalion of the 395th Infantry at Höfen; and against two battalions of the 393d Infantry dug in where two woods trails emerged from the forest almost due east of Krinkelt-Rocherath to join a highway following the trace of the

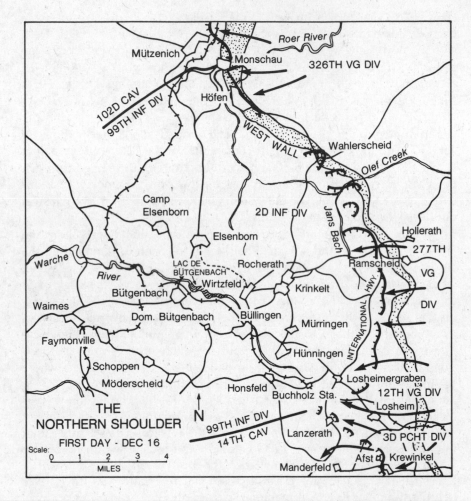

Map labels:

Roer River

Mützenich

Monschau

326TH VG DIV

102D CAV

99TH INF DIV

Höfen

WEST WALL

Wahlerscheid

Olef Creek

Camp Elsenborn

2D INF DIV

Jans Bach

Hollerath

Elsenborn

Warche

River

LAC DE BÜTGENBACH

Rocherath

Ramscheid

277TH

VG

Wirtzfeld

Bütgenbach

Krinkelt

DIV

Waimes

Dom. Bütgenbach

Büllingen

Faymonville

Mürringen

INTERNATIONAL HWY.

Schoppen

Hünningen

Möderscheid

Honsfeld

Buchholz Sta.

Losheimergraben

12TH VG DIV

THE NORTHERN SHOULDER

N

99TH INF DIV

14TH CAV

Lanzerath

Losheim

3D PCHT DIV

FIRST DAY - DEC 16

Scale:
0   1   2   3   4
MILES

Afst

Krewinkel

Manderfeld

Belgian-German frontier, a road the Americans called the "International Highway."

To Pfc. Bernie Macay, whose Company B, 393d Infantry, faced that highway, it seemed there were thousands of Germans. He and the men with him "could see them against the skyline as they came over the hill. It seemed like they were coming right at us and for some reason ignoring everybody else." At Höfen, the Germans approached "in swarms," moving forward at a slow, methodical walk; and at Monschau, men of the 38th Cavalry Reconnaissance Squadron saw shadowy forms plodding toward them. With a round in the chamber of every rifle and machine gun, and with 37mm. guns on the light tanks loaded with canister, the men waited for the Germans to reach the barbed wire in front of their positions.

As elsewhere in the Ardennes, the defensive line around Monschau was thin. The cavalry's strongest positions, including a line of fifty machine guns culled from jeeps and armored cars, were northwest of the town behind a railroad track. They had been emplaced there to deny access to the town of Mützenich, on high ground behind Monschau; for Mützenich more than Monschau was the key to access to the highway leading onto the Hautes Fagnes. Immediately north of Monschau, the defensive line swung to the other side of the railroad in order to deny entry to Monschau, while at the southern edge of the town, where a road cut across the deep gorge of the Roer, the cavalrymen had a roadblock backed up by light tanks. The squadron had direct support from the 62d Armored Field Artillery Battalion, and the pieces of two corps artillery battalions were within easy firing range.

At Höfen, the commander of the 3d Battalion, 395th Infantry, Lt. Col. McClernand Butler, had managed to hold only a single rifle platoon as a reserve. Even so, his line was thin, but having defended the town since early November, the men were well dug in and their fields of fire across ground rising steeply toward the positions were excellent.

Butler had the support of a battalion of the 99th Division's artillery; and two nights earlier, a company of towed guns of the 612th Tank Destroyer Battalion, attached to the 2d Division, had arrived in Höfen in order to be ready to provide support when the men of the 2d Division broke through at Wahlerscheid and fanned out to other objectives in front of Höfen. The crews dug in their twelve 3-inch guns and camouflaged them with bed sheets.

Despite the small size of the defending force, the Germans had no such numerical superiority as they had elsewhere in the Ardennes, primarily because of the failure of one of the two *Volksgrenadier* divisions to arrive but also because the other, the 326th Volksgrenadier Division, was depleted. One battalion had yet to arrive; another had been siphoned off the day before to help repel the attack by the 78th Division, a part of the attempt to take the Roer River dams; and yet a third, having briefly held the pillboxes at Wahlerscheid, had been relieved there the night before by the division's replacement battalion (less than an hour before the 2d Division's 9th Infantry carried the position) and would be unable to reach the line of departure for an attack before daylight on the 16th. Instead of two divisions with fourteen infantry battalions, there was thus a single division with only four battalions immediately available.

The Germans struck the cavalry on either side of the gorge of the Roer River in front and just to the north of Monschau. As a German set off a trip flare, the waiting defenders opened fire as one. When the cavalry commander, Lt. Col. Robert E. O'Brien, called on the commander of the 405th Field Artillery Group, Col. Oscar A. Axelson, for help, Axelson decided, even though the super-secret proximity fuse had yet to be released officially, that he would use it. The shells bursting in the air above the approaching Germans were terrifying and devastating. As

60mm. mortars fired illumination rounds, the cavalrymen could see the Germans falling back in "headlong retreat."

Exulting in that success, Colonel O'Brien was nevertheless conscious of the meager strength of a cavalry reconnaissance squadron and early asked for reinforcements. In response, the commander of the V Corps, General Gerow, sent the 146th Engineer Combat Battalion, whose men arrived soon after nightfall and began to dig in before Mützenich, the gateway to the road to the Hautes Fagnes and to Eupen, where Gerow had his headquarters.

At Höfen, meanwhile, the defenders waited as the men of two German battalions trudged up the steep hill toward their positions through the murky illumination of the artificial moonlight. They were less than two hundred yards from the American foxholes when "every weapon the battalion possessed opened fire" and "practically swept" most of the Germans away. Yet so persistent was the assault that in at least three cases, dying men pitched forward into the foxholes.

Only in the center of the elongated town at the seam between Companies I and K was there any German success. There some thirty or so got into the houses, but as the others fell back, harassed at every step by the towed tank destroyers firing high-explosive rounds, the infiltrators held on for less than an hour. When it was over, at least a hundred Germans were dead, possibly more, and nineteen captured. The contrast in American casualties was striking: four killed, four missing, seven wounded. If the Sixth Panzer Army was to break through at Monschau-Höfen and secure its northern flank on the high moors beyond, General Dietrich obviously would have to come up with greater strength for the 67th Corps.

Yet success or failure for the Sixth Panzer Army rested ultimately not with the 67th Corps but with the 1st SS Panzer Corps, a few miles to the south along the approaches to Krinkelt-Rocherath and a cluster of other frontier villages, and in the Losheim Gap. And there the Germans had the same great numerical superiority they possessed at most other places. Striking to gain access to two woods trails leading to Krinkelt-Rocherath, the entire 277th Volksgrenadier Division (built around remnants of an infantry division that had been virtually destroyed in Normandy) was destined to hit only three American battalions, while a little farther south the entire 12th Volksgrenadier Division was to hit but two battalions.

Once past the frontier forests and villages, in the process opening up routes for the SS panzer divisions, the two *Volksgrenadier* divisions were to cross the Elsenborn Ridge and swing northwest to block in the direction of the Hautes Fagnes. The task of opening other routes for the panzers farther south in the Losheim Gap fell to the 3d Parachute Division, which was then to follow *Kampfgruppe Peiper* closely but peel troops off to face north and protect Peiper's supply route.

On the American side, the commander of the 393d Infantry, Lt. Col. Jean D. Scott, who had been ordered to demonstrate by fire in support of the attack by the 2d Division and the 395th Infantry, seized the opportunity to better his positions. He decided to attack with a portion of his 3d Battalion to take a dominating forested hill, the Rath Berg (American troops called it "Rat Hill"), just off the battalion's north flank. The 3d Battalion had accomplished that handily; but the added defensive responsibility had absorbed all but a platoon of the reserve company.

Thus there was scant back-up for a line of foxholes extending more than two miles, all of the line inside dense fir forest except for a short stretch where the holes were on the fringe of the forest looking out over the International Highway. The foxholes constituted more a series of platoon strongpoints than a solid line, and the critical point was that at which the woods trail leading four miles back to Krinkelt-Rocherath joined the highway. Beyond the International Highway, the Germans still held the pillboxes of the West Wall, and open draws led up to the highway from German villages behind the pillboxes.

The critical junction of the woods trail and the highway was the responsibility of Company K under Capt. Stephen K. Plume. Yet the main thrust against Plume's company hit not there but along the woodsline a little to the south. There two battalions of Germans were almost on top of Company K's foxholes just as the artillery preparation lifted, and the outcome dramatically illustrated the advantage the Germans forfeited at most other places by failing to follow their artillery fire closely. Except for the platoon astride the woods road, the first rush overwhelmed all of Company K. If the men of the remaining platoon were to survive, they had to fall back, and Captain Plume ordered them to withdraw immediately to the company command post.

Because communications were out, it was close to 8 A.M. before the battalion commander, Lt. Col. Jack G. Allen, learned of Company K's fate. Since the collapse jeopardized Company L on the other side of the woods trail, Allen told that company to fall back to defend the battalion command post and soon directed Company I, a mile away atop Rat Hill, to do the same. The men of Company I had to fight to get there, but by noon a defensive position encompassing the battalion command post was forming, based in part on old positions dug when the battalion had a reserve company.

On the German side, the commander of the 1st SS Panzer Corps, Generalleutnant der Waffen-SS Hermann Priess, was markedly upset by the failure of the *Volksgrenadiers* to achieve a quick penetration so that the 12th SS Panzer Division (*Hitlerjugend*) could get going on the drive to the Meuse. Around noon, he ordered a battalion of *SS-Panzergrenadiers* to help, but that failed to carry the 3d Battalion's position. The *SS-Panzergrenadiers* did push down the woods trail as far as the deep cut of a creek called the Jans Bach, thereby succeeding in blocking the 3d Battalion's only road to the rear.

There was no question but that Colonel Allen and his men were fighting for their lives. The regimental commander, Colonel Scott, could send no help, for what had been his reserve battalion had moved on December 13 to help in the 395th Infantry's attack in support of the 2d Division; but early in the afternoon, the commander of the 99th Division, Maj. Gen. Walter E. Lauer, released a company from his only reserve, a battalion of the 394th Infantry, to go to Allen's assistance. Allen sent guides to the rear to lead the company forward over firebreaks, thereby avoiding the Germans on the road.

As night fell, the German pressure decreased, for German commanders had to reorganize their units in the face of heavy, even crippling losses. Before the attack, regiments of the 277th Volksgrenadier Division had been critically short of officers and noncommissioned officers— hardly a single front-line company had more than a single officer—and as those leaders tried to inspire their inexperienced troops by example, they had been among the first to fall. The Germans probably lost as many as three hundred men, for when a thaw came at last to the Ardennes in the spring, local inhabitants found the draws leading up to the International Highway thick with German bodies. American losses were also heavy, some three hundred either killed, wounded, or captured, three-fourths of them from Company K, including the commander, Captain Plume, who was captured.

Just to the south, Maj. Matthew L. Legler's 1st Battalion, 393d Infantry, underwent the same kind of numerically overwhelming assault as did the 3d Battalion. Yet most of Legler's positions were at the edge of the forest, overlooking the International Highway and generally open ground, so that the men of the 1st Battalion had an advantage not shared by their neighbors. With machine guns, mortars, and artillery, they exploited excellent fields of fire to exact a heavy toll. Not one German got inside the American positions, and within an hour the assault was at a halt.

Under strong pressure to obtain a quick penetration for the waiting tanks of the 12th SS Panzer Division the commander of the 277th Volksgrenadier Division, Col. Wilhelm Viebig, committed his reserve regiment. At 8 A.M., that regiment and the survivors of the other attacked behind a heavy concentration of artillery fire and rockets. Again many a German fell, particularly noncommissioned officers and the few junior officers who were herding the troops forward, but the sheer weight of numbers soon began to tell.

The first breakthrough came on the right where the International Highway entered the woods, and where, in order to cover the second woods trail leading back to Krinkelt-Rocherath, most of Company C's positions had to be within the forest with limited fields of fire. A half hour after the renewed assault began, two of Company C's platoons fell back, but the Germans failed to pursue their advantage, seemingly content merely to occupy the foxholes and loot them. An hour later, two of Company B's platoons also caved in.

At that point, Major Legler committed his reserve company to restore Company B's positions. Employing marching fire, the men retook most of the foxholes.

Yet Legler needed help to reoccupy Company C's positions. When he appealed to the regimental commander, Colonel Scott, all Scott could provide was the Mine Platoon from the Antitank Company, composed of a lieutenant and twenty-five men. When they reached the battalion command post, the operations officer, Capt. Lawrence H. Duffin, was waiting with thirteen men from the Headquarters Company. Taking command of the little force—less than a full-strength rifle platoon—Duffin led the men up the trail, soon to find Company C's command post under attack. Fixing bayonets, the men charged. They killed twenty-eight Germans, and the rest fell back to the foxholes they had captured earlier. With Company C's survivors, Captain Duffin formed a new line based on the command post.

By midday, the 1st Battalion, 393d Infantry, still maintained a fairly cohesive defense, but the battalion had lost four hundred men, more than half its foxhole strength. The Germans were nevertheless slow to continue the attack, a reflection of their own heavy losses.

With the coming of darkness, the Germans took advantage of the gaps they had forged on the flanks of both the 1st and 3d Battalions to send strong patrols—some composed of more than fifty men—to probe deep into the forest. Sometimes the Germans called out in English in an effort to trap the unwary. Sometimes they fired their burp guns wildly, seemingly on the offchance that they might hit somebody.

For men of both American battalions, it was a cold, miserable night. Anybody who slept did so only fitfully, and if anybody ate, he had only frozen C- or K-rations, for there could be no fires. Medical officers and aid men in both battalions tried to make the wounded as comfortable as possible, but both aid stations were overflowing. Through much of the day medics of the 1st Battalion had been able to take out most of their wounded by jeep, but nobody dared make the run after nightfall. Evacuation of the wounded from the 3d Battalion ended early when the Germans cut the woods trail at the Jans Bach.

Just to the south of Major Legler's battalion, the northernmost unit of the 394th Infantry, the 2d Battalion, had also become embroiled with the 277th Volksgrenadier Division but against nothing like the heavy odds faced by the two battalions of the 393d Infantry. All that the German division commander, Colonel Viebig, had left to throw against that battalion, located mostly within the woods alongside the International Highway, was the division's Fusilier Battalion.

The men of that battalion were slow to follow up the artillery preparation and paid the inevitable consequences. Mortar and artillery concentrations zeroed in earlier rained down on them, while machine gunners and BAR-men unleashed a torrent of small-arms fire. In less than half an hour, the Germans were falling back.

They tried again in mid-morning with the help of three assault guns, but a heavy concentration of fire from the 155mm. guns of the 99th Division's general support artillery battalion erupted around the vehicles and sent them scurrying to the rear. Some of the Fusiliers nevertheless worked their way within hand grenade distance of one of the platoons of Company E; but since all men of the platoon had overhead cover on their holes, the platoon leader, Tech. Sgt. Fred Wallace, called for artillery fire on top of the positions. Most of the Germans were killed, and such few as survived were quickly rounded up.

Except for occasional shelling, that was all that happened on December 16 to the 394th Infantry's 2d Battalion. The men were proud of their stand. All their positions were intact and the casualties few. Yet most were aware that something serious—they knew not what—was happening to their neighbors off either flank, and at the command post deep in the forest, the battalion staff had to cope with a special problem. Their commander had gone to pieces, cowering in a corner of one of the log huts, his head between his knees.

To anyone with a map, it would be obvious why the Germans made no major thrust against the 394th Infantry's 2d Battalion, for in rear of the battalion, the only passage through the forest was over firebreaks and muddy logging trails. But just a few miles farther south two paved roads and a railroad led into the 99th Division's positions, and there waited *Kampfgruppe Peiper*, the tank-heavy task force of the 1st SS Panzer Division, ready to begin the thrust on which Adolf Hitler's principal hope rode for quick seizure of crossings over the Meuse River. There, too, the entire 12th Volksgrenadier Division was to make the penetration and was to have some help from adjacent troops of the 3d Parachute Division. To defend against that formidable force, there were only two U.S. battalions of the 394th Infantry (one of them designated as the division reserve and short a company) and the regiment's I&R Platoon.

For the Germans, the two roads were crucial. The main road led up a gently rising incline from Losheim to an intersection with the International Highway at Losheimergraben, a crossroads settlement consisting of a customshouse and a few other buildings. It then passed through dense forest to open country and a cluster of villages and towns—Hünningen, Mürringen, Büllingen, and Bütgenbach—continuing westward to Malmédy and beyond. The other road, just south of the railroad, also had a connection from Losheim and ran through the Belgian frontier village of Lanzerath. From there it passed a cluster of buildings known as Buchholz Farm and a nearby railroad station, which American troops called Buchholz Station (actually, Losheimergraben Station), and on to the west by way of the village of Honsfeld. The main road through Losheimergraben was to be used by a column of the 12th SS Panzer Division; the other by *Kampfgruppe Peiper.*

Wilhelm Osterhold was a slight, wiry man with a black mustache, known among the troops of the 12th Volksgrenadier Division's 48th Regiment as one who believed that a regimental commander led his troops from the forward ranks. A career soldier, Osterhold had entered the army not to accommodate any military bent but in search of refuge from National Socialism. When Hitler and the Nazis came to power in the 1930s, Osterhold's father, a staunchly anti-Nazi representative in the Reichstag, had been arrested for distributing anti-National Socialist literature and sent to a concentration camp. That left a black mark against every member of the family, and the only way young Osterhold could see of evading it was to submerge himself in the army. It had proven to be a good choice, for Osterhold knew that on at least one occasion, Nazi authorities had raised questions about him, but by that time he had become an officer with a record, and his superiors covered for him.

Colonel Osterhold's 48th Regiment was to make the 12th Volksgrenadier Division's main effort, its first goal to seize the crossroads at Losheimergraben and open a path for a column of the 12th SS Panzer Division. Like other units of the division, Osterhold's regiment had lost heavily in late September after arriving hurriedly from the Eastern Front to halt the American drive near Aachen and in the process earning the honorific *Volksgrenadier* in the days when the name had some meaning. The replacements who had only recently joined the regiment were young and inexperienced, but hospital returnees who had fought in Russia had joined the ranks of veteran noncommissioned officers and junior officers.

For the assault, Osterhold had the support not only of all his division's artillery but also of two *Volksartillerie* corps. He also had fifteen 75mm. assault guns, while another regiment of his division was to make a supporting attack up the line of the railroad close by on the south.

To Colonel Osterhold, as to the other soldiers at the front that morning, the artillery preparation seemed awesome, but as he and his men soon discovered, it did little damage. To Osterhold, the fire plan appeared to have been drawn up far away in Berlin.

In a fan-shaped defense of the crossroads, the Americans of the 1st Battalion, 394th Infantry, got their first indication of the enemy's approach soon after the artillery fire lifted with the appearance in the diffused glare from the enemy's searchlights of a U.S. jeep on the road from Losheim. The jeep approached a concealed outpost containing a

57mm. antitank gun, but the crew of the antitank gun was so stunned to
see an American vehicle that nobody fired. Turning around, the jeep
raced back to Losheim, then reappeared a short time later preceding a
75mm. assault gun.

The crew of the antitank gun let the jeep pass but opened fire on the
assault gun. A first round knocked off a track, a second penetrated the
hull, and a third set the assault gun on fire. Only the commander, a
lieutenant, got out, and he was badly wounded. Men in positions a little
farther up the road killed the occupants of the jeep with small-arms fire.

Because the going was slow up steep wooded draws which the Germans had to use to reach other portions of the 1st Battalion's positions, it
was well into the morning before the defenders saw any of the enemy;
but when the Germans came, they came in strength. Two battalions of
the 48th Regiment hit the seam between two American companies in the
thick forest northeast of Losheimergraben; then one of the battalions
swung down the line of Company B's foxholes in the direction of the
crossroads, taking the positions in flank. With the attacking Germans was
Osterhold himself, frustrated because he was unable to establish radio
contact with his supporting artillery, and when he finally did get through
to call for fire, the artillery fell short on his other battalion, disrupting
that part of the attack.

The assault against Company B nevertheless continued, so that by
early afternoon the company had lost sixty men, including the leader of
an attached heavy machine-gun platoon, Tech. Sgt. Edward Dolenc, last
seen firing his machine gun with twenty or more Germans piled in front
of it. Because the other half of the German thrust had been disrupted by
the misdirected artillery fire, the men of Company C were free to try to
reestablish their neighboring company's positions, but with little success.
Night was falling when Colonel Osterhold and one of his battalions
reached the edge of the woods overlooking Losheimergraben. Osterhold
was reluctant to continue further without assured fire support from either
artillery or assault guns.

In the woods on the other side of Losheimergraben, what appeared to
be two platoons of Germans bounced off positions of Company A astride
the International Highway and worked their way toward the crossroads.
Only the men of Company D's 81mm. mortar platoon, their mortars dug
in around a farmhouse a hundred yards short of the crossroads, stood in
the way. The Germans were almost on top of one of the mortar positions
before the crew spotted them across a firebreak no more than fifteen
yards away.

Looking out from the mortar position, Pfc. Robert Newbrough saw a
German soldier holding a potato masher hand grenade, the first German
soldier Newbrough had ever seen close up. The German was "just as
startled" to see him, Newbrough decided, as he was to see the German.
Newbrough was debating what to do when his sergeant called by tele-

phone for the other mortars to fire almost on top of his position. Elevating the tubes to almost ninety degrees, the mortarmen in the other positions opened fire. Once the shells began to burst, the surviving Germans fled. Newbrough, as he put it, "didn't know where and didn't care."

As night came, the 1st Battalion still held most of its original positions, except for the penetration that had split Company B. Yet the commander, Lt. Col. Robert H. Douglas, doubted how much longer he could hold on. Along the main road leading from Losheim to Losheimergraben, he was disturbingly aware, he had only about fifty men left, a heterogeneous group from various units that had coalesced around a platoon leader, 1st Lt. Dewey Plankers. If the Germans launched a strong thrust up the highway, that little group would be hardpressed to stop it.

With the authority of the commander of the 394th Infantry, Col. Don Riley, Douglas early that evening called on four platoons from the 3d Battalion, ostensibly the division reserve, to dig back-up positions astride the highway behind Losheimergraben. Yet by usurping those platoons, Douglas raised the possibility of the men of the 12th Volksgrenadier Division taking him in the rear, for even before the *Volksgrenadiers* had hit his battalion, they had struck the supposedly reserve positions of the 3d Battalion off his flank; and even though the Germans had absorbed considerable losses, they were still there.

Constituting the 99th Division's only reserve, the 3d Battalion, 394th Infantry, commanded by Maj. Norman A. Moore, was located in and around the little rural railroad depot that the Americans called Buchholz Station. Because one of the rifle companies had been sent as a reserve for the 395th Infantry's attack (and was to be committed later on the 16th to help Colonel Allen's battalion of the 393d Infantry), Moore had only two rifle companies, one of which he established at Buchholz Station; for even though the battalion was supposed to be in reserve, nobody else was defending the line of the railroad, which ran through a deep cut in the forested hills along the frontier and was an obvious route of advance should the Germans attack.

Not that Moore or anybody else in the 3d Battalion was expecting an attack any more than anybody else in the 99th Division or elsewhere in the Ardennes. Indeed, on the morning of the 16th, once the unusual phenomenon of German shelling had passed and nothing else had happened other than the appearance of a strange luminous glow on the horizon, the men of Company L began to prepare for breakfast. Their company kitchen having arrived at the position only the night before, they were anticipating their first full hot meal in several days.

The chow line had yet to form when somebody noticed a group of just over fifty men walking through the fog along either side of the railroad track. Somebody shouted, Who were those guys? One man thought they might be men of the company's Weapons Platoon coming for breakfast, but he yelled at them anyway to halt. When someone in the approaching group began shouting orders in German, 1st Sgt. Elmer Klug fired with his carbine.

For the other men of Company L, that was all the signal they needed. Everybody within sight of the German column opened fire. The Germans scattered, some into the woods on either side of the railroad, others to the protection of a freight car on the tracks. Cpl. George F. Bodnar managed to fire four bazooka rockets into the freight car but was unable to get close enough to assess the results.

Constituting the advance guard of the leading battalion of the 12th Volksgrenadier Division's 27th Regiment, the Germans had obviously been surprised, but their commander quickly fed in reinforcements. For the rest of the morning, fighting around the station and in the adjacent woods raged at close quarters, while Major Moore brought up his remaining rifle company to help. Some of the Germans reached the roundhouse close to the station, whereupon Tech. Sgt. Savino Travalini, leader of the battalion's Antitank Platoon, fired enough rockets from a bazooka to flush them, then cut them down with fire from his rifle when they tried to escape.

As German pressure eased around noon, Company L's cooks prepared to serve the long-delayed breakfast, but shells from German mortars and artillery rained down in such numbers that the meal was soon forgotten. The men of the 3d Battalion, 394th Infantry, were to get nothing to eat that day.

When the early night of the Ardennes winter closed in around the little railroad station, American troops still held the station and positions on either side, thus blocking the nearby road leading from Lanzerath to Honsfeld and a woods trail leading from the station into the rear of the 1st Battalion's positions at Losheimergraben. Yet the defenses were flimsy at best, made the more so after the regimental commander authorized sending the four platoons—more than half the 3d Battalion's remaining riflemen—to back up the positions at Losheimergraben. That prompted Major Moore to abandon the railroad station in order to put greater strength on the Honsfeld road (meaning only two platoons) and the trail.

In the day's fighting, the Germans had lost at least fifty killed and thirty captured, about equal to American losses. Yet to the little cluster of Americans who remained, it was obvious that the Germans would be back. As far as they knew, unless a small band of men of the 394th Infantry's I&R Platoon was still holding out nearby on a wooded hillock overlooking the village of Lanzerath, they were all that stood in the way to prevent the Germans from turning the south flank of the 99th Division.

Lyle Joseph Bouck, Jr., was anticipating nothing special for his birthday, which was December 17, but he had taken note that it was an important one, his twenty-first. Only two others among the seventeen men in the I&R Platoon, which Bouck commanded, were younger. Yet Bouck already had six years of military service behind him. In his home town of St. Louis, he had enlisted in the National Guard at the age of fourteen, and at eighteen he had completed Officer Candidate School at Fort Benning and been commissioned a second lieutenant. After assignment to the 99th Division, he had attracted the attention of the 394th Infantry's intelligence officer, Maj. Robert L. Kris, who picked him to command the regimental I&R Platoon. Its combat mission was just what the letters I and R stood for: intelligence and reconnaissance, which meant, mainly, patrolling.

Six days earlier the regimental commander, Colonel Riley, had ordered Lieutenant Bouck to go with his platoon to the vicinity of Lanzerath and pick a defensive position to serve as an outpost for the 99th Division's south flank. There was nothing on that flank, Riley knew, but the 14th Cavalry Group with a single cavalry reconnaissance squadron in the line, and the sector, Riley also knew, was the historic Losheim Gap. Any force penetrating into the gap might turn north to trap not only the 394th Infantry but the entire 99th Division. A single I&R Platoon could hardly be expected to stop a strong thrust, but it could give the alarm.

What Bouck and his men found was a readymade outpost. Some two months earlier, before the 4th Division (which had made the attack that captured the nearby Schnee Eifel) had left for another assignment, a battalion of that division's 12th Infantry had dug the foxholes to protect a flank abutting on the Losheim Gap. To Lieutenant Bouck, it seemed an excellent position. The foxholes were covered with logs and looked out from the edge of a fir forest onto a field sloping down to the highway that passed through Lanzerath, an extension of the International Highway. Not only were there good fields of fire onto the highway but also onto a road junction a few hundred yards outside Lanzerath where a road branched off and led past Buchholz Farm to Honsfeld. When the weather was clear, you could look over the tops of the houses in Lanzerath into a wide valley beyond, where lay the village of Losheim and the dragon's teeth and pillboxes of the Siegfried Line.

So ideal was the position as an outpost that Colonel Riley ignored the fact that it lay just outside the 99th Division's southern boundary and told Bouck to occupy it. As Bouck and his men moved in, they established contact with the crews of the four towed guns of the 820th Tank Destroyer Battalion and their supporting reconnaissance troops, who constituted the 14th Cavalry Group's little strongpoint in Lanzerath. Although Bouck was aware that such a small force as his could hardly be expected to hold at length, he was pleased with the commanding nature of his position, and he congratulated himself that he and his men had managed to accumulate more weapons than normally allotted an I&R Platoon: To augment their M-1 rifles, they had scrounged several BARs,

two .30-caliber machine guns, and a .50-caliber machine gun mounted on
a jeep.

The night of December 15, Lyle Bouck was wary. Every night since
moving into the position, there had been strange noises rising from the
valley beyond as if heavy vehicles were moving about. Did that portend
what the intelligence officer, Major Kris, had warned him about, that
there might be a German reaction to the attack under way to seize the
Roer River dams? Taking no chances, he ordered every man to stay alert
throughout the night.

Bouck and all his men were thus awake when at 5:30 A.M. the valley
behind Losheim came alive with pinpricks of light on the horizon that
soon turned into flickers. There followed the thunder of what seemed to
be hundreds of guns, then the crash of shells on Lanzerath, and then right
on top of the I&R Platoon's positions. Despite their foxhole cover, the
men breathed with relief only after the barrage passed on beyond them in
the direction of Buchholz Farm. Not long after that the sky lit up with a
strange glow, made all the more eerie by a heavy fog.

A first cousin of Sanny Schür—in whose house some of the reconnaissance troops supporting the tank destroyers in Lanzerath lodged—Adolf
Schür lived with his parents and an older brother at the northern edge of
the village, just down the hill from the woodsline where six days earlier a
small group of Americans had moved in. At sixteen years of age, Adolf
was enjoying his friendship with the Americans in Lanzerath. They gave
him and his family good-tasting canned food, sugar, and real coffee, and
they taught him some English words. He was sure they were swear words
and vulgarities, for the soldiers laughed when he repeated them, but Adolf liked the attention that afforded him.

Early in the morning of December 16, when the shelling began, Adolf
took refuge with his family in the cellar; but when it had stopped, he
hurried upstairs eager to see what might happen. Not long after daylight,
he saw his American friends hitching their big guns to their half-tracks
and heading north out of the village. That must mean the Germans were
coming, but Adolf found it odd that the Americans would leave without
firing a shot.

There was no time to determine whether the little group of Americans
a hundred yards away at the woodsline on the hill was still there before
German soldiers came marching up the road through the village. There
was a line of men in the mottled uniforms of paratroopers on either side
of the road, their rifles slung from their shoulders, not at all as if they
expected trouble. A few dropped out of the column and entered the
Schürs' house, ostensibly looking for a drink of water, but when they
spotted the sugar and American rations that Adolf's mother was saving
for Christmas, they took them, then rejoined the column outside.

Up on the hill, after recovering from the jolt of seeing the crews of the tank destroyers fleeing, Lieutenant Bouck puzzled over why no German attack had followed the heavy artillery barrage. With three of his men, he went into Lanzerath and from the second story of a house, looked out over the valley toward Losheim. Despite the fog, he could make out streams of German troops marching up the road from Losheim in his direction.

Hurrying back to the hilltop position, Bouck radioed his regimental headquarters what he had seen and begged for artillery fire on the approaching Germans, but the officer with whom he spoke obviously thought Bouck was out of his mind. No artillery fire followed.

Turning to his men, Bouck told them to get ready to fight. In view of the apparent size of the German force, most of the men wanted to withdraw, but Bouck ordered them to hold. From their commanding position, Bouck believed, they could do heavy damage to the German column.

The men were in their foxholes, their weapons trained across a snow-covered field onto the road below, when the first Germans emerged from the concealment of the barn attached to Adolf's house. Bouck told the men to hold their fire. The first Germans, he reasoned, were probably an advance guard; he wanted to wait until the main body was in his men's sights.

A hundred had passed when there was a break in the column, then a group of three men alone. That, thought Bouck, would be the command group. His runner, Private Tsakanikas (one of the few men in the platoon who was younger than Bouck) drew a bead on the three, and Bouck was about to give the order to shoot when a blond-haired girl of about thirteen emerged from a house beyond the road. Running to the three figures, she pointed uphill toward the I&R Platoon's positions.

Lest the child be killed, Bouck hesitated. In that split second, one of the Germans yelled something, and the column of paratroopers dived for the ditches on either side of the road.

From the barn of his father's house, Adolf Schür was watching. "Goddamn!" he muttered. "Mother fucker! Son of a bitch!"

The predictable attack—by what turned out to be a battalion of the 3d Parachute Division's 9th Regiment—soon followed. To Bouck and his men, it seemed stupid. The paratroopers had no fire support except for some men firing from the ditches along the road, no mortars, no artillery; but still they tried to rush the hundred yards uphill across an open, snow-covered field to get at the American position. To many in the I&R Platoon it was a painful assignment to fire at them. They could see their faces, and they were only kids. The fire caught some of them trying to cross a barbed-wire fence bisecting the field and left them hanging on the wire.

All the while Lieutenant Bouck was appealing by radio to headquarters of the 394th Infantry for artillery support. An officer finally told him there would be no artillery; all the guns were preoccupied on other missions.

"What shall we do then?" asked Bouck.

"Hold," the answer came back, "at all costs!"

Bouck pondered what that meant. Hold until every man was dead?

Around noon a white flag appeared; the Germans wanted to evacuate their wounded. At Bouck's order, the men held their fire, but no sooner was the task completed than the Germans returned to the assault just as before, frontal assault up the steep hill, by that time littered with German corpses. From beyond the road light mortars coughed some support, but because of the overhead cover on the foxholes, the fire did little damage.

In the barn next to the Schürs' house, Adolf's brother, Eric, and his father, Christolf, came up from the cellar to join Adolf. Christolf had been a drummer in the Great War. "Now," he told his sons, "you can see what war is really like."

Atop the hill, Lieutenant Bouck was again on the radio to his regiment. He was reiterating the vain requests for artillery support when what sounded like an explosion in his ear knocked him to the ground. A burst of automatic fire had struck his radio, destroying it. Only stunned, Bouck recovered quickly.

Conscious that ammunition was running low, Bouck told Tsakanikas to take whoever wanted to withdraw and get out, but Tsakanikas refused to go without Bouck. "No," said Bouck, "I have orders to hold at all costs. I'm staying."

Bouck was nevertheless beginning to have his doubts, for his men had accomplished about all they could. For the better part of a day they had occupied what appeared to be a German battalion and had frustrated any advance in the direction of Honsfeld into the division's exposed flank. Given the growing shortage of ammunition, he could hold little longer in any case. He called for two men to go to the regimental headquarters and return either with ammunition and reinforcements or with authority to withdraw; but neither man made it.

Down the hill in Lanzerath, a German sergeant, Vince Kühlbach, protested against continuing to attack the Americans across the open field, and in gathering dusk fifty Germans assembled behind the Schür house and began advancing against the flank of the position. As the darkness thickened, the paratroopers were soon in among the foxholes, pulling the occupants out at gunpoint, clearing one foxhole after another. A burst from a burp gun into the foxhole that Bouck shared with Tsakanikas caught Tsakanikas in the right side of his face, blowing out his right eyeball and leaving it "hanging limply in the cavern where his cheek had been." Bouck himself was hit in the leg.

Downhill, Adolf Schür was struck by the sudden silence. Soon he saw Americans coming down past his house, their helmets gone, their hands above their heads. Then came the wounded, not many, only five or six. A German soldier and an American lieutenant were supporting one man whose face looked as if it had been blown away. Adolf watched in morbid fascination and followed the procession until the wounded and their guards went into the Café Scholzen.

Inside the little tavern, Bouck and Tsakanikas lay on the floor beneath a cuckoo clock hanging on the wall. They had been there for what seemed to Bouck a long time when the clock signaled midnight. It was December 17. He was twenty-one years old, thought Bouck; he had become a man.

Because American commanders had anticipated that the Germans would make some kind of riposte in response to the attack on the Roer River dams, their first reaction early on the morning of December 16 was that that was what was happening. At 8:30 A.M., the former commander of the 1st Infantry Division, Maj. Gen. C. Ralph Huebner, who was acting as deputy commander of the V Corps in anticipation of assuming command when General Gerow moved up to take command of a new army headquarters, visited General Lauer at headquarters of the 99th Division in the town of Bütgenbach, and the two agreed that that was the case. From a forward headquarters in the village of Wirtzfeld behind the twin villages of Krinkelt-Rocherath, the commander of the 2d Division, General Robertson, was at first unaware that anything untoward was happening other than the unusually heavy German artillery fire just before dawn; yet that, too, could have been a predictable reaction to the attack by Robertson's troops at Wahlerscheid.

The first indication Robertson had that the 99th Division might be in trouble came later in the morning in a roundabout way via a telephone call to Robertson's artillery commander, Brig. Gen. John H. Hinds. The caller identified himself as a captain on the 99th Division's staff and asked for loan of the battalion of towed tank destroyers that was attached to the 2d Division. Hinds thought it so strange that a junior officer should make the request and to him, the artillery commander, rather than to Robertson, that he reported the call immediately to Robertson. Concerned as he had been since the start of his division's attack lest the Germans cut the lone road leading to his attacking regiments, Robertson hurried with Hinds to the 99th Division's headquarters in an imposing villa in Bütgenbach.

What they found appalled them. The living room of the house was in tumult, crowded with enlisted men and officers, everybody seemingly trying to talk at once, and at one side of the room the division commander himself, General Lauer, playing a piano—as was his wont in times of crisis.

"Can't we go to your CP where we can talk?" Robertson asked above the din.

"This *is* my CP," replied Lauer.

As Robertson discerned the situation from Lauer, the Germans had attacked the 99th Division at several points, but Lauer insisted he had matters in hand. On the basis of the confusion at the command post, Robertson was inclined to think otherwise.

Robertson and General Hinds headed back for Wirtzfeld more concerned than ever about the 2d Division's lone supply route, and the thought struck Robertson that he had better begin considering withdrawal from the attack at Wahlerscheid. Yet his mission still was to exploit the capture of the pillboxes, and barring a change in orders, that had to have priority. To increase his forces for the exploitation, he directed the commander of his reserve regiment, the 23d Infantry, to begin moving his regiment forward. A battalion was soon on the way to a bivouac alongside the forest road a mile or so beyond the twin villages.

Before noon, Robertson learned that he was to lose the combat command of the 9th Armored Division that had been attached to his division to help in the drive for the Roer River dams. That, Robertson assumed, was a result of the German attack against the 106th Division in the 2d Division's old defensive positions near St. Vith, word of which reached Robertson through the corps commander, General Gerow.

Gerow, like Robertson, was worried. Early in the afternoon he asked the commander of the First Army, General Hodges, for authority to call off the 2d Division's attack and move the division back to the positions he had charted earlier on the Elsenborn Ridge. Obviously less concerned than Gerow about what might be developing, Hodges refused.

In mid-afternoon, Gerow telephoned Robertson, ordering him—apparently at General Lauer's request—to release the two remaining battalions of his reserve, the 23d Infantry, for attachment to the 99th Division. One battalion was to go to the village of Hünningen, a short distance behind the Losheimergraben crossroads and the positions of the 394th Infantry, there to occupy defensive positions that Lauer, in concern for the fragile nature of his division's south flank, had ordered dug long before. The other battalion was to move into the forest east of Krinkelt-Rocherath and at dawn on the 17th attack to restore the positions of Colonel Allen's 3d Battalion, 393d Infantry.

That General Lauer would ask the help of those two battalions told Robertson something of how serious Lauer's situation had become. He had almost decided to take it on himself to halt his division's attack and withdraw when he had a visit from Gerow's deputy, Ralph Huebner. Both were convinced that the 2d Division should withdraw. As Huebner departed, he told Robertson: "Go slow and watch your step; the overall situation is not good."

No division commander as experienced as Robertson was could have been unaware of the precarious position of his command. All three battalions of the 9th Infantry and two of the 38th were fighting at

Wahlerscheid—those of the 9th Infantry seriously depleted by the heavy fighting for the road junction—and the remaining battalion of the 38th Infantry was well forward in reserve. A battalion of the 23d Infantry was also forward, as were two battalions of the 2d Division's artillery, even more dependent than the infantry, should it come to withdrawal, on the single road leading back through the dense forest to Krinkelt-Rocherath. The 99th Division's 395th Infantry also depended upon that road for survival.

Hardly had Huebner left Robertson's command post than Robertson, without notifying General Gerow, telephoned the commanders of his two attacking regiments and told them to halt their attacks and hold where they were. Although he added an order to renew the attacks the next morning, he left the hour open, and the attacks were to be launched only on his specific command.

That done, Robertson went forward up the critical road to ensure that both regimental commanders fully understood what they were to do and that they alerted their battalions to begin planning for withdrawal. Then back in his headquarters in a farmhouse on the edge of Wirtzfeld, he and his chief of staff, Col. Ralph W. Zwicker, sat up well past midnight refining the withdrawal plan.

At the 99th Division's headquarters a few miles away in Bütgenbach, General Lauer exhibited far less concern. Lauer was exceedingly proud of the way his inexperienced troops had fought that day, and nowhere had there been a penetration in depth. At midnight, he reported personally by telephone to General Gerow that he had heard from all his units, and his "entire front was practically established on its original line—that the situation was in hand and all quiet." Yet his south flank, he added, did have him "considerably worried."

Lauer's report was far more optimistic than the actual situation justified and was particularly strange in that Lauer knew that men of the 394th Infantry's Company A had captured a copy of Field Marshal von Rundstedt's order telling his troops that their "great hour" had arrived: "WE GAMBLE EVERYTHING!" Lauer hardly could have continued to believe that his division was encountering a mere local reaction to the attack for the Roer River dams.

Admittedly, Lauer did have the added strength of the battalion of the 23d Infantry in the woods east of Krinkelt-Rocherath and of the other battalion moving into prepared positions at Hünningen. The battalion at Hünningen would help strengthen the division's southern flank, about which Lauer was so concerned. Although he knew nothing of the fate of the 394th Infantry's I&R Platoon outside Lanzerath, he knew he still had some troops near Buchholz Station, and not far away at Honsfeld the commander of the 394th Infantry's rest center was forming a provisional company from men who had been at the center to defend the village.

Thus there was at least a shield—albeit thin—covering the division's southern flank.

On the German side of the International Highway, the commanders were markedly disappointed with the results of the first day's fight. Most had expected that as early as 7 A.M.—and surely well before nightfall—columns of the 1st and 12th SS Panzer Divisions would have been well past the forward American positions on their way to the Meuse. Yet nowhere had there been a penetration sufficient for the panzers to exploit.

One man who was particularly concerned was Otto Skorzeny, whose special brigade was to follow the panzer divisions. Trying to go forward to Losheim to find out what was happening, he encountered roads so jammed with vehicles and horse-drawn artillery that he had to walk almost six miles to get there. Since it was obvious the day's objectives were out of reach, and since the success of Operation *GREIF* depended upon surprise and speed, he was tempted to call off the operation. Yet if the panzer divisions got through that night or early the next morning, he decided finally, there still might be a chance of reaching the Meuse, in which case his men's seizing the bridges "could be decisive."

For his part, the commander of the 1st SS Panzer Corps, General Priess, was fuming. Having already ordered a battalion of *SS-Panzergrenadiers* to try to achieve a breakthrough in the direction of Krinkelt-Rocherath, he told the commander of the 12th SS Panzer Division, Brigade-fuhrer der Waffen-SS Hugo Kraas, to commit two more battalions of *SS-Panzergrenadiers* supported by two companies of Mark IV tanks and two companies of Panthers. When Kraas protested the attachment of his tanks to the 277th Volksgrenadier Division, Priess relented and put Kraas himself in charge. From that point, the assignment of breaking through the forest to Krinkelt-Rocherath fell to the 12th SS Panzer Division with such help as the badly depleted 277th Volksgrenadiers might provide.

In front of Losheimergraben, the commander of the 12th Volksgrenadier Division, Generalmajor Gerhard Engel, exhorted the commander of his tank destroyer battalion, Major Holz, to bring his assault guns into play at the crossroads. At the same time an even more determined commander, Joachim Peiper, arrived on the scene a few miles to the south at Lanzerath.

Shortly before midnight, Peiper pushed his way into the Café Scholzen. On the dingy floor wounded Germans and Americans were sprawled against the walls. Under a cuckoo clock mounted on one wall slumped an American lieutenant holding a soldier who had lost part of his face and was bleeding profusely over the lieutenant's uniform. Other Germans seemed simply to have chosen the tavern as a place to sleep. What was the matter? Had everybody simply "gone to bed instead of waging war?"

Peiper was already in a foul mood. All day he had waited, his tanks and half-tracks using up precious gasoline in traffic jams, and still no penetration to spring his column loose. In the end he had simply plowed his way forward, ordering his tank commanders, if they had to, to run down the horse-drawn artillery that was clogging the roads. Then to arrive at the Café Scholzen and find that everybody appeared to have called off the war for the night.

Locating the commander of the 9th Parachute Regiment, Col. Helmüt von Hofmann, Peiper learned that he was delaying his attack until morning because the woods between Lanzerath and Honsfeld were heavily fortified, defended by at least a battalion, and the road was mined. Had he personally reconnoitered the American positions? demanded Peiper, uncaring that as a lieutenant colonel he was grilling a senior officer. Well, no, replied von Hofmann, but . . .

In disgust, Peiper demanded that the colonel reinforce him with one of his parachute infantry battalions. He was going through.

CHAPTER NINE

Reaction at the Top

At fifty-one years of age, Omar Nelson Bradley still had a touch of rural Missouri about him. He spoke with a high-pitched voice in a flat Midwestern accent. His hair was thinning and his ears protruded. To many, he had the air of a schoolteacher, as well he might, for his father had been one in Missouri and he himself had spent thirteen of his first twenty-three years of commissioned service teaching either in the ROTC, at West Point, or at The Infantry School.

It was at The Infantry School at Fort Benning that Bradley had first come into contact with a man who was destined to become the U.S. Army's chief of staff and to make an indelible imprint on the conduct of the war: George Catlett Marshall. Bradley's class of 1915 at West Point would be known as "The Class the Stars Fell On"—fifty-nine of them became general officers—and a number who received their stars, including Dwight D. Eisenhower and Omar Bradley, could attribute their accession in large measure to the fact that George Marshall recognized their talents.

On the morning of December 16, Omar Bradley awoke in his room in the Hôtel Alfa, looking out over the Place de Metz in Luxembourg City, to confront a dismal day: cold, damp, foggy. It came as little surprise when at breakfast in the hotel's plain ground-floor restaurant his aide, Lt. Col. Chester B. Hansen, told him that it would be impossible to fly to a scheduled appointment with General Eisenhower at SHAEF's main headquarters in Versailles. Yet Bradley considered the business to be discussed so significant that he determined to proceed by car. Indeed, in order to stress its importance, he planned to accompany his personnel officer, Brig. Gen. Joseph J. ("Red") O'Hare, on the first leg of a trip to Washington, where O'Hare was to press the War Department for more infantry replacements for the European Theater.

To get an early start on the four-hour drive, Bradley decided to forgo the usual nine fifteen situation briefing at his headquarters, but as it turned out, he missed nothing of significance. As his olive drab Cadillac sedan threaded through the fog-enshrouded streets of Luxembourg City and out onto an icy highway leading to Verdun and Paris, a briefing officer from the operations section was noting that there had been little change along any part of the front. That included the sectors of the First Army's V and VIII Corps. When a briefing officer from the intelligence section had his say, he noted that the 326th Volksgrenadier Division had been identified moving north through the Eifel, which, he added, "might be the answer to the numerous vehicular movements in the northern VIII Corps sector." Nobody yet knew anything of the portentous events already taking place in the Ardennes—searchlights, heavy artillery fire, ground attacks—which at one point were occurring little more than twenty miles away.

After a stop for lunch in a transient officers' mess at the Ritz in Paris, Bradley and his party went on to Versailles, reaching Eisenhower's headquarters in the Trianon Palace Hotel early in the afternoon. They found the Supreme Commander in a pleasant mood: He had learned earlier in the day of his promotion to the rank of General of the Army, which carried with it five stars, the equivalent of field marshal in other armies. He had also just had an enjoyable diversion, the wedding of his orderly, Mickey McKeough, to a soldier from the headquarters, Pearlie Hargreaves.

It was late afternoon—almost dusk—when a colonel from SHAEF's G-2 section tiptoed into the room where Eisenhower, Bradley, O'Hare, and several members of Eisenhower's staff were talking. He handed a note to Eisenhower's G-2, General Strong. Glancing at it, Strong interrupted the conference to say that the Germans had attacked at five points along the front of the VIII Corps. Although the attacks had begun early in the morning, there was as yet no word as to their size or extent.

As Strong moved over toward a situation map to indicate the points of enemy attack, Bradley found it impossible to believe that the enemy could be launching more than a spoiling attack with perhaps four to six divisions, designed to upset the First Army's attack for the Roer River dams and the Third Army's impending attack against the Saar industrial region south of the Ardennes. After all, only a few days earlier Bradley's G-2, General Sibert, had remarked on the "critical dilemma" faced by the German command, and even General Strong, who had warned of possible enemy action in the Ardennes, had spoken only of "a relieving attack."

A short while later a message arrived indicating that eight German divisions not previously identified on the Ardennes front were involved in the attacks. Recalling how Bradley on a number of occasions had wished for the Germans to come out of their pillboxes and fight in the open, Eisenhower's chief of staff, Bedell Smith, put a hand on Bradley's shoulder. "Well, Brad," he said, "you've been wishing for a counterattack. Now it looks as though you've got it."

"A counterattack, yes," replied Bradley, "but I'll be damned if I wanted one this big."

Yet Bradley was still unconvinced that the Germans were launching anything more than a spoiling attack. No, said Eisenhower, it was no spoiling attack. (Eisenhower, apparently through the MAGIC intercepts of Baron Oshima's messages, knew something Bradley did not know.) Calling for a situation map that showed two American armored divisions out of the line, the 7th Armored Division with the Ninth Army in the north and the 10th Armored Division with the Third Army in the south, Eisenhower said he thought Bradley should "send Middleton some help. These two armored divisions."

Still Bradley caviled. While agreeing that it would be prudent to shift the two divisions, to remove a division from the Third Army just as General Patton was preparing to launch a big offensive was bound to upset Patton. "Tell him," Eisenhower came back, "that Ike is running this damn war."

When Bradley got Patton on the telephone, Patton was indeed irate. It was nothing more than a spoiling attack, Patton insisted, and Troy Middleton could handle that himself. "I hate like hell to do it, George," Bradley responded, "but I've got to have that division. Even if it's only a spoiling attack as you say, Middleton must have help." That done, Bradley telephoned his staff in Luxembourg City with instructions to tell General Simpson of the Ninth Army to put the 7th Armored Division on the road. He also directed both Patton and Simpson to alert any other divisions that were out of the line for a possible move to the Ardennes.

Bradley and Eisenhower had dinner that night in Eisenhower's imposing requisitioned stone villa in nearby St. Germain-en-Laye, a villa earlier occupied by Field Marshal von Rundstedt. Afterwards, they "cracked a bottle of champagne" to celebrate Eisenhower's promotion and played five rubbers of bridge.

Shortly before eleven, as the two were at the point of retiring, they learned of a message just received in SHAEF's ULTRA room in an attic above the palace stables. Bletchley Park had intercepted and decrypted a signal ordering the German air command in the Netherlands, Jägdkorps II, to be prepared the next morning, the 17th, to "support the attack of 5 and 6 Armies." Eisenhower and Bradley could hardly have been unaware that that meant the Fifth and Sixth Panzer Armies.

After Bradley finally got to bed around midnight, he found it difficult to fall asleep, and when he did, he slept fitfully.

In an age of virtually instantaneous communications by telephone, telegraph, and radio, it was taking a surprisingly long time for information about the German offensive to reach Eisenhower's headquarters.

Except for the late night flash from Bletchley Park, there was, even more than eighteen hours after the start of the German artillery preparation, little to go on.

The artillery preparation itself was in large measure responsible. Almost everywhere the shelling knocked out telephone lines leading from front-line units, and even in experienced regiments, rear headquarters were often slow in the wee hours to realize that lines were out and switch on their radios. Add to that the time it took an officer to pass a message to a corporal or a sergeant for transmission to the message center, then the time it took the message to move up the chain of command: from battalion to regiment to division to corps to army to army group to SHAEF. So, too, as with intelligence reports, there was a process of selection: What was important enough to pass up the line? Although there was no problem with telephone lines at corps level and above, the two corps headquarters were slow to get solid information to pass along. And for some reason, neither Eisenhower nor Bradley deigned to pick up the telephone and talk directly with the senior commander most intimately concerned, Courtney Hodges of the First Army.

In early afternoon, the text of von Rundstedt's hortatory field order to the German troops, captured by the 99th Division's 394th Infantry, reached headquarters of the First Army, whence it passed quickly to headquarters of the 12th Army Group. It stopped there. Not until early the next morning were Eisenhower and Bradley in Versailles to learn of it, and then it was by means of an ULTRA intercept sent from Bletchley Park:

> Rundstedt on sixteenth informed soldiers of West Front that hour of destiny had struck. Mighty offensive armies faced Allies. Everything at stake. More than mortal deeds for Fatherland and Führer. A quote holy duty unquote.

No American commander on the Western Front had more concern for the men serving under him than did Courtney Hicks Hodges, commander of the First Army. He personally saw to it that towns behind the line were set aside as rest centers for the exclusive use of combat troops, where, by his direction, the men were to eat, drink, loaf, and "do whatever they wish within the limits of propriety." On at least one occasion, he told his jeep driver to halt while he got out to stand by the road as trucks sloshed past carrying bearded, grimy, bone-tired infantrymen of the 4th Division from the fighting in the Hürtgen Forest. As he watched, tears came to his eyes. "I wish," he said, "everybody could see them."

Hodges's concern may have stemmed from the fact that only he among all the senior U.S. commanders in Europe had seen war at the level where men do the dying. In charge of a machine-gun company in the grim Meuse–Argonne campaign of World War I, he had received the nation's second highest award for valor, the Distinguished Service Cross. So, too, only he among the senior commanders had served as an enlisted man. Having failed geometry in his plebe year at West Point, Hodges had joined the army as a private but had earned a commission only a year behind his former classmates at the Military Academy.

With gray hair and mustache (he was six years older than Bradley), Hodges looked more businessman than soldier. Georgia born, he was soft-spoken. He was also taciturn. Lacking personal eccentricities, he seemed essentially colorless, but both Bradley and Eisenhower thought highly of him. His only fault, it seemed to Eisenhower, was that "God gave him a face that always looked pessimistic." Bradley had "implicit faith in his judgment, skill, and restraint."

Hodges and Bradley had served together at the Army War College and on the faculty of The Infantry School (where Hodges, too, impressed George Marshall and where Bradley later succeeded Hodges as commandant). When Bradley commanded the First Army in the invasion of Normandy, Hodges was his deputy, serving with the sure knowledge that after Bradley moved up to command an army group, Hodges was to get the First Army. Inheriting Bradley's staff (with the exception of the G-1, Red O'Hare, whom Bradley took with him), Hodges made no changes, for he himself had helped select most of the officers.

Shortly before 7 A.M. on December 16, as Hodges—still bothered by a head cold—was preparing to sit down to breakfast in his requisitioned villa outside Spa, he received first word of enemy action in the Ardennes: German attacks against the cavalry in the Losheim Gap and "the heaviest artillery fire ever received in the 28th Division area." Hodges went quickly to his office in the Hôtel Britannique, where news of other attacks all along the line as far south as Echternach soon came in, some "in large patrol strength and others in battalion strength."

On the basis of the early reports, Hodges perceived the greatest threat to be against the 106th Division and in the Losheim Gap. Just before ten thirty, he directed General Gerow of the V Corps to release Combat Command B of the 9th Armored Division from attachment to the 2d Division and turn it over to Troy Middleton of the VIII Corps to be used to help the 106th Division. At noon, Hodges ordered the commander of the VII Corps in the vicinity of Aachen, Maj. Gen. J. Lawton Collins, to place a regiment of the 1st Infantry Division, which had recently come out of the line after fighting in the Hürtgen Forest, on six-hour alert for possible movement to the Ardennes. An hour later he told Collins to put the entire 1st Division on six-hour alert along with a combat command of the 3d Armored Division. Even so, when Gee Gerow telephoned to ask authority to call off the 2d Division's attack for the Roer River dams, Hodges said no. If the Germans were trying to divert that attack, why give them what they were after?

The news in early afternoon of the capture of von Rundstedt's order would seem to have made it clear that more than a spoiling attack was under way, even more so because the order bore an endorsement from the commander of the 12th Volksgrenadier Division, General Engel: "This call to arms to be made known to all soldiers without exception at once before beginning of attack." Yet that fact occasioned no particular alarm.

Hodges's junior liaison officers, whom he always maintained at the divisions to keep his headquarters informed, were reporting that even though some companies and battalions had given ground and some were isolated, there had been no major German penetration and nobody saw the situation as critical. (As late as 4:15 P.M., the 28th Division, which all along its extended front was under heavy attack, reported that "the situation for the division is well in hand.") Furthermore, in late afternoon Hodges received word from the 12th Army Group that he was to get the 7th and 10th Armored Divisions. Hodges was "neither optimistic nor pessimistic," but on the evidence he had received to that point, he believed not only that he could "handle" the attack but that it afforded an opportunity to inflict heavy losses on the enemy.

Nevertheless, before retiring for the evening, he ordered the 1st Division to send one of its regiments immediately to help the 99th Division, and by midnight the 26th Infantry was on the way. He had still to retire when a German plane strafed the road in front of his villa and dropped two bombs nearby.

Shortly after Hodges finally went to bed that night of December 16, word came through a radio intercept from the XXIX Tactical Air Command, which supported the Ninth Army, that planes were preparing to take off from airfields east of the Rhine near Paderborn to drop parachutists behind the First Army's lines. Somebody on Hodges's staff alerted the guard at the gatehouse in front of the villa to watch for parachutists and doubled the guard.

At two other headquarters buildings within Belgium, there was no such ambiguity. The V Corps was based in the Belgian Army's physical training institute on Bellmerin Strasse, Eupen; the VIII Corps had its headquarters in a red-tiled caserne in Bastogne that belonged to the Belgian Army. At both headquarters, the capture of von Rundstedt's order removed any doubt about what the Germans were up to. For the VIII Corps there was an additional indication with the 106th Division's capture of the order providing details of Skorzeny's Operation *GREIF*, and on the body of a fallen officer of the 116th Panzer Division someone found not only a copy of von Rundstedt's order but similar orders issued by Field Marshal Model and General von Manteuffel.

> *Model*: We will not disappoint the Führer and the Fatherland, who created the sword of retribution. Forward in the spirit of Leuthen!

> *Von Manteuffel*: Forward, march, march! In remembrance of our dead comrades, and therefore on their order, and in remembrance of the tradition of our proud Wehrmacht!

In passing along those orders and von Rundstedt's, the VIII Corps G-2, Colonel Reeves, noted: "These documents indicate the scope of the German offensive, and its importance becomes apparent from the impressive list of high-ranking German generals whose signatures appear thereon. The GRIEF operation appears to be a part of a large-scale offensive."

Gerow and Middleton also discounted the optimistic reports from some of their units, such as that from the 28th Division that all was "well in hand." Middleton was all the while getting full and candid reports from the inexperienced Jones of the 106th Division (who had yet to learn the old dodge that one's own command looks better if the enemy's successes appear to be less), and it was clearly obvious that something serious was happening in the Losheim Gap. Gerow, too, received cheerful reports, the 99th Division telephoning that "by 1130 hours we had practically restored our line to its former positions," but that failed to deter him from asking Hodges's permission to call off the 2d Division's attack and pull the division back to the Elsenborn Ridge.

At the headquarters of the 12th Army Group across from the railroad station in Luxembourg City, there was no such view of what the Germans were trying to accomplish. "The sudden attacks and seemingly overpowering array of six enemy divisions . . . should not be misinterpreted," wrote General Sibert. "The quality of divisions involved, the piecemeal efforts to launch small-scale attacks and the apparent lack of long range objectives would seem to limit the enemy threat." Sibert in fact saw the enemy's attack much as did his boss, General Bradley, back in Versailles, as "a diversionary attack" to disrupt the American attacks north and south of the Ardennes. "Until the magnitude of the enemy's attack increases in more cohesive action or until one or more elements of the Sixth SS [*sic*] Panzer Army are committed. . . ." Sibert concluded, "the day's events cannot be regarded as a major long term threat."

The key phrase was "piecemeal efforts." That looked to Sibert to be the case partly because of erratic reports from the front and partly because the inexperienced German troops were generally slow to follow up their artillery fire, so that there was no impression of one grand assault. Yet those attacks still occurred over an extended front, all the way from Monschau in the north to Echternach in the south. Should not that fact in itself have conveyed some meaning?

Whether the ex-journalist, Ralph Ingersoll, massaged that report or not, what it had to say was clear. The intelligence section at headquarters of the 12th Army Group was as yet unprepared to go back on its earlier miscalculation of what the enemy was capable of doing. General Sibert nevertheless put somebody to work trying to contact the First Army's G-2, Monk Dickson, on leave in Paris. The word finally got through to Dickson: Sibert suggested that he make his way as quickly as possible to Luxembourg City.

Among the German army commanders, there was disappointment that in the first day of the grand offensive they had gained considerably less than they had intended. Yet there was no despair. He who had expected the least, General Brandenberger, was the most optimistic: He considered that his Seventh Army was close to a breakthrough. For General von Manteuffel, the Fifth Panzer Army's gains "did not come up to expectations," but he hoped to make up for lost time by continuing to attack through the night. There was more concern in the Sixth Panzer Army, if not with the commander, General Dietrich, then with his more pragmatic chief of staff, General Kraemer. He thought the unexpectedly strong resistance from Monschau to Losheimergraben was predicated upon his enemy's expectation of rapid reinforcement from the north, and because the 326th Volksgrenadier Division had failed to break through at Monschau and von der Heydte's parachutists had failed to jump, there was nothing to keep those reinforcements from arriving.

In late afternoon, Kraemer himself telephoned von der Heydte, telling him it was vital for his parachutists to jump that night and block the highway leading south across the Hautes Fagnes. "Hold on as long as possible," Kraemer told him, "two days as a minimum, and do as much damage as you can to the reinforcements."

From the first, Friedrich von der Heydte had been concerned about the inexperience of his young parachutists and when he learned the background of the Luftwaffe crews that were to fly him to the drop zone, he was appalled. Although the crews belonged to the renowned "Stalingrad Squadron," which had flown supplies to Field Marshal Paulus's besieged troops at Stalingrad, the only man remaining who had actually flown those missions was the squadron commander. None of the others had ever dropped parachutists in a combat operation; none had ever flown a combat mission of any kind; and none had ever flown his Junkers 52 aircraft at night. Von der Heydte could see nothing ahead but disaster.

When most of the parachutists failed to reach the airfields on the night of December 15, von der Heydte hoped with some degree of fervor that the operation might be canceled. Headquarters of the Sixth Panzer Army quickly sent an investigating officer to conduct a formal inquiry into von der Heydte's failure to take off, and von der Heydte was clearly under suspicion of sabotaging the operation. (Was he not a cousin of the officer who had planted the bomb back in July in the plot to kill the Führer?) Yet General Kraemer's order to jump on the night of the 16th ended both the investigation and von der Heydte's fervent hopes of a cancellation.

Just before midnight, 112 Junkers 52s began to taxi to take-off positions on two airfields near Paderborn. By tradition, von der Heydte as commander was in the leading pathfinder plane and would jump first. He would be jumping with his right arm in a splint, hurt a few weeks before in an airplane accident in Italy.

As the planes took off and searchlights lit up one by one to guide them to and over the Rhine, von der Heydte began to have some hope that the inexperienced pilots and navigators might yet deliver his troops to the correct drop zone. In time, he could make out the trace of the front, distinguishable by the flash of artillery pieces and the light of smoldering buildings. As the planes flew over, there was no mistaking it, for to help maintain formation, the pilots were flying with their navigation lights on, and heavy antiaircraft fire erupted. When they were over the drop zone, the pathfinder planes dropped incendiary bombs to mark it, and von der Heydte—his right arm strapped to his side—dove into the night.

As he neared the ground a strong wind seized his parachute, and when he landed, the impact knocked him unconscious. When at last he came to his senses, he found himself alone. Taking a compass bearing, he began to walk toward the designated rendezvous, a road junction known as Belle Croix astride the north-south highway leading across the moors.

There he found 20 of his men—20 out of 1,200. Others were to turn up in time, but for the most part the planes had scattered the parachutists all the way from the Rhine to the Hautes Fagnes and some far to the north in the sector of the Ninth U.S. Army beyond Aachen.

In the *Adlerhorst* amid the forested hills of the Taunus, Field Marshal von Rundstedt made no effort to spare his Führer his own pessimistic evaluation of the first day's events. There was no question, he said, that the offensive had achieved total surprise, yet the main effort by the Sixth Panzer Army had failed to achieve a penetration. That meant a loss of at least a day, making it questionable whether the army could reach the Meuse.

The report infuriated Hitler. The weight of the Sixth Panzer Army's SS panzer divisions had yet to be felt, he said. Once they got going, they would "crush everything before them."

When the briefing was over, well after midnight—late nights were commonplace with the Führer—Hitler got on the telephone to the commander of Army Group G, General der Panzertruppen Hermann Balck, who was responsible for the front south of the Ardennes. Balck thought at first he was in for yet another diatribe admonishing him to hold fast, yield not a foot of ground, but he soon found that the Führer had something different to say.

Good old dependable Dietrich, said Hitler, had punched a hole in the Losheim Gap, and *Kampfgruppe Peiper* was poised for the march to the Meuse. Von Manteuffel was encircling the Schnee Eifel, already had tanks on the heights overlooking Clervaux, and would be on the way to Bastogne and the Meuse as soon as it was daylight. And the weather! The forecast was for more of the same—fog, drizzle, perhaps some light snow, but in any case, weather to keep Allied planes on the ground.

Despite himself, Balck, a hardened old soldier, became caught up in his Führer's enthusiasm.

"Balck! Balck!" Hitler exulted. "Everything has changed in the West! Success—complete success—is now in our grasp!"

The reality of what actually happened on that first day lay somewhere in between Hitler's elation and the incomprehension of Omar Bradley and Edwin Sibert of the 12th Army Group. Bradley and Sibert were finding it difficult to accept that the German blow in the Ardennes was a major offensive ("No Goddamned fool would do it!"), and Hitler was reading more into his armies' successes than was actually there.

In the far south, all four divisions of Erich Brandenberger's Seventh Army had crossed the Our and Sûre Rivers, which in view of the thin American positions was hardly to have been prevented; but unknown to Brandenberger, he was soon to be facing American reserves. At Marnach, von Manteuffel's tanks were indeed "on the heights overlooking Clervaux"; but everywhere else the 28th Division's 110th Infantry was still making a fight of it, and how soon von Manteuffel's two panzer corps could get across the Clerve River and on with the drive for Bastogne and the Meuse remained to be seen. So, too, the 28th Division's 112th Infantry was still holding firm.

From the American viewpoint, the most critical sector as night fell on December 16 was the Losheim Gap and the threatened encirclement of two regiments of the 106th Division on the Schnee Eifel. Yet there, too, it remained to be seen how long it would take von Manteuffel's *Volksgrenadier* divisions to gain St. Vith and open the roadnet in the vicinity, a roadnet critical for sustaining a broad-based advance to the Meuse. Since the cavalry at Monschau and the 99th Division at Höfen and along the International Highway had stopped the Sixth Panzer Army's *Volksgrenadier* divisions, the critical sector for the Germans, too, was the Losheim Gap; for in northern reaches of the gap, Joachim Peiper, as Hitler said, was genuinely "poised for the march to the Meuse."

Despite the fight put up by the men of the 99th Division, which, as von Rundstedt noted, had produced a delay of at least a day in the quest for the Meuse, chances for a breakthrough along the International Highway were good, particularly east of Krinkelt-Rocherath where the 12th SS Panzer Division was getting ready to take over the assignment. If the added weight of tanks could produce a quick breakthrough there, the

Germans would score a success they had no inkling of, for they would trap the 2d Division. The 12th SS Panzer Division would also be past the first big hurdle in a drive for the Meuse close along the flank of *Kampfgruppe Peiper* and the 1st SS Panzer Division.

Nevertheless, except in gaining total surprise, nowhere on December 16 had the Germans achieved any of their first day's goals. The soldiers whom Hitler saw as "the Italians" of the Allied side—how could a nation as heterogeneous as the United States of America, with its mixture of ethnic and racial types, field a capable fighting force?—had nowhere turned and run. When men in foxholes refuse to admit overwhelming odds, advance through or past them may be inevitable, but it is seldom either easy or swift.

BOOK

III

THE
PENETRATIONS

CHAPTER TEN

Kampfgruppe Peiper

Handsome, "well bred . . . dashing and resourceful," Joachim Peiper at a youthful twenty-nine brought to the Ardennes long months of combat experience in Russia, where he had risen from command of one of the 1st SS Panzer Division's *Panzergrenadier* battalions to command of the division's panzer regiment. He had been awarded Nazi Germany's highest award for valor, the Knight's Cross of the Iron Cross, and had earned the admiration of his troops for bravery, sangfroid, and ruthlessness. He personally led a night attack on the village of Pekartschina with flamethrowers mounted on his half-tracks and burned the village to the ground—other units of the division called Peiper's *SS-Panzergrenadiers* the "Blowtorch Battalion." In one drive, the panzer regiment under Peiper's command claimed 2,500 Russians killed and only 3 captured, which was testimony to the brutality, fanaticism, and mounting desperation that characterized the ideological, racist war in the East, at least as Peiper practiced it. Many of the men who came with Peiper to the Ardennes had also experienced that savagery.

Peiper received his orders for what his superiors called "the decisive role in the offensive" three days before the start of the attack from the commander of the 1st SS Panzer Corps, General Priess. In the course of the briefing, Priess passed along an order of the day from the Sixth Panzer Army's commander, General Dietrich, which reflected Hitler's exhortation to his senior commanders at the *Adlerhorst*. The offensive represented "the decisive hour of the German people" and thus was to be conducted with "a wave of terror and fright" and without "humane inhibitions."

As Peiper himself later recalled the order, the German soldiers were to be reminded of "the innumerable German victims of the bombing terror." He was also "nearly certain" that "it was expressly stated that prisoners of war must be shot where the local conditions of combat should so require it." Although that proviso was incorporated into the

197

Kampfgruppe's order for the attack, Peiper himself made no mention of it in his oral briefing to his commanders, for they "were all experienced officers to whom this was obvious."

The word to kill prisoners nevertheless reached almost all subordinate units. One company commander enjoined his men to "fight in the old SS spirit," and added: "I am not giving you orders to shoot prisoners of war, but you are all well-trained SS soldiers. You know what you should do with prisoners without me telling you that." A private recalled that not only were they to take no prisoners but "civilians who show themselves on the streets or at the windows will be shot without mercy." One non-commissioned officer urged his men to think of the thousands of German women and children buried in the rubble of German cities; then they would know "what you as SS men have to do in case you capture American soldiers." The offensive was aimed at "the murderers of our mothers, fathers, and children."

Serious questions were to arise later as to the methods through which those testimonials, including Peiper's, were elicited. On the other hand, it would be hard to maintain that all that was about to happen in abject violation of the basic rules of international warfare was the result of nothing more than spontaneous reaction to the pressures of the battlefield.

Kampfgruppe Peiper was a powerful force of approximately four thousand men. Peiper had seventy-two medium tanks, almost equally divided between Mark IVs and Mark Vs (Panthers), roughly the equivalent of one and a half American tank battalions. He also had five flak tanks; a light flak battalion with self-propelled multiple 20mm. guns; about twenty-five assault guns and self-propelled tank destroyers; an artillery battalion with towed 105mm. howitzers; a battalion of *SS-Panzergrenadiers*; around eighty half-tracks; a few reconnaissance troops; and two companies of engineers, although the column was supposed to move so rapidly that the engineers carried no bridge construction equipment. Attached to Peiper were one of Skorzeny's four-man teams disguised as Americans; one of Skorzeny's task forces with seven hundred men and twelve Panthers disguised to look like Shermans; and thirty 68-ton Mark VI (King Tiger) tanks of the 501st SS Heavy Panzer Battalion. Because the Tigers were slow and cumbersome, Peiper put them at the rear of his column, to be called forward once the advance reached more open country close to the Meuse.

The rest of the 1st SS Panzer Division was to proceed in three columns. Composed of the division's reconnaissance battalion, one was to follow Peiper in order to deal with any threat to resupply. Two others were to proceed through the lower portion of the Losheim Gap: one composed of the 2d SS Panzergrenadier Regiment (minus a battalion with Peiper), reinforced by the division's twenty remaining tanks and most of its twenty-two self-propelled tank destroyers; the other composed of the

1st SS Panzergrenadier Regiment with a few of the tank destroyers. The division commander, Col. Wilhelm Mohnke, his headquarters and support troops, and the bulk of the division's artillery were to bring up the rear. Should Peiper's column be held up, one of the other columns was to assume the mission of seizing the bridges over the Meuse.

As Peiper calculated it, his column would be about fifteen miles long and in the sharply compartmented terrain of the Ardennes, mostly road-bound. If he was to accomplish his mission of driving swiftly to the Meuse without regard for his flanks, he needed the heavy firepower of the Mark IVs and Panthers to the fore, intermixed with *SS-Panzergrenadiers* riding in half-tracks, who would be called upon as required to help the tanks. Peiper established his command group midway in the column, but he himself would usually be well forward in one of the leading half-tracks.

In Lanzerath in the early hours of December 17, it took the commander of the parachute battalion that Peiper had commandeered considerable time to roust his men from the houses where they had settled down for the night. Thus it was close to four in the morning before the leading vehicles of *Kampfgruppe Peiper*—two Panthers and three half-tracks—began the advance on the first objective of Honsfeld. Four Mark IV flak tanks, each equipped with a 37mm. cannon, and two flak wagons, with quadruple 20mm. pieces, were next in line, followed by more half-tracks transporting *SS-Panzergrenadiers* and tanks with paratroopers clinging to the decks. A company of paratroopers advanced on foot to provide flank protection as the column moved through woods between Buchholz Farm and Honsfeld.

Where were the mines and well-manned American defenses that Colonel von Hofmann had predicted? Peiper's leading vehicles encountered nothing, and only those vehicles well back in the column came under any fire from the two platoons of Company K, 394th Infantry, at the farm and in the nearby woods. The platoons quickly disintegrated under fire from the quad-20s on the flak wagons. One American remained: a radio operator hiding in the cellar of the farmhouse. He counted the German vehicles as they passed and reported the number by radio to his regimental headquarters; he got up to twenty-eight half-tracks and thirty tanks before the Germans rooted him out.

Just over a mile short of Honsfeld, a road from within the Losheim Gap joined the Lanzerath-Honsfeld road. As Peiper's lead tank reached the road junction, the driver came upon American vehicles heading into Honsfeld. He fell in behind one of them and followed.

In Honsfeld, the captain commanding the 394th Infantry's rest center had had a busy day. He first had to welcome Marlene Dietrich, who was supposed to entertain the troops, then hurriedly send her back. As the

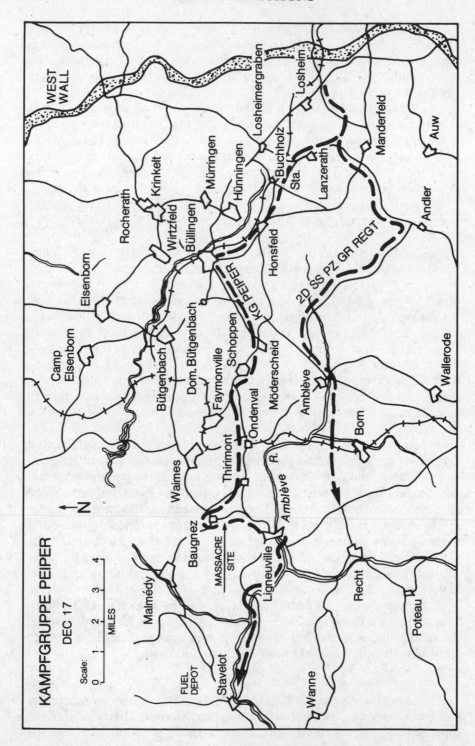

KAMPFGRUPPE PEIPER
DEC 17

Scale:
0   1   2   3   4
MILES

N

WEST WALL

Losheimergraben
Losheim
Manderfeld
Auw
Andler
Wallerode

Krinkelt
Mürringen
Hünningen
Buchholz
Sta.
Lanzerath

Rocherath
Wirtzfeld
Büllingen
Honsfeld

Elsenborn

2D SS PZ GR REGT

Camp Elsenborn

Bütgenbach
Dom. Bütgenbach
Faymonville
Schoppen
Ondenval
Möderscheid
Amblève
Bom

KG PEIPER

Waimes
Thirimont
Amblève R.
Ligneuville
Recht
Poteau

Baugnez
MASSACRE SITE

Malmédy

FUEL DEPOT
Stavelot
Wanne

situation everywhere along the front worsened, he used the men from the rest center, augmented by stragglers, to form a provisional company and placed them in positions behind a creek a few hundred yards to the east and south of the town. Two platoons of towed guns of the 801st Tank Destroyer Battalion backed up that line from the edge of the village. When two platoons of towed guns of the 612th Tank Destroyer Battalion arrived around three o'clock in the morning, borrowed from the 2d Division, the commander of the 801st's guns told the leaders of those two platoons to bed down for the rest of the night; he would direct them into firing positions at daylight.

Earlier, when Lieutenant Reppa and his troop of cavalry arrived from the Losheim Gap, Reppa checked in with the captain from the 99th Division, who asked him to be prepared to send out patrols the next morning but suggested his men bed down for the night in the village. Reppa did as he was told, but he sent an armored car commanded by Sgt. George Creel to take up a position just beyond the last house in Honsfeld along the road entering the village from the south (the direction of Lanzerath) and give the alarm should the Germans approach.

In the armored car close by the road, Creel and his crew through much of the pitch-black night saw nothing to disturb them. Now and then American vehicles approached, sometimes several traveling together, all fleeing from the Losheim Gap and continuing into Honsfeld and beyond. Most had their "cat's-eye" blackout lights on, but sometimes a soldier walked ahead of a vehicle with a flashlight to guide the way.

It was close to 5 A.M. and another American vehicle had just passed when Creel blinked in disbelief. Coming up the road was a lone soldier carrying a white handkerchief and guiding the "biggest damn tank" Creel had ever seen. The tank passed so close to the armored car—within three or four feet—that despite the darkness, Creel could make out a small black swastika on it. As the tank passed, Creel tried to fire, but a trailer attached to his armored car blocked his field of fire.

From farther down the road there was a sudden flurry of small-arms fire from the American infantrymen. It lasted less than a minute before the infantrymen broke for the rear, and crews of the tank destroyers joined them. Everybody was soon engaged "in a wild scramble, trying to separate themselves from an enemy that seemed to be all around them, yet was not visible." Creel and his crew took off on foot to try to warn Lieutenant Reppa but were unable to get into the center of the village.

The two leading Panthers of *Kampfgruppe Peiper* were soon past the first scattered houses of Honsfeld. As they entered the heart of the village, they came to an S-bend in the road—at that point more a street than a road—and a building on either side narrowly restricted passage. It took considerable backing and filling before the big tanks were able to get past. Three half-tracks—Peiper himself riding in one of them—followed closely.

Once past the S-bend, the German crews could make out jeeps, armored cars, light tanks, and towed tank destroyers parked beside almost every house. At the order of the commander of the advance guard, 1st Lt. Georg Preuss, machine gunners in the tanks and on the half-tracks opened fire, spraying the buildings and all the while continuing to advance. They reached the far edge of the little village with not a shot fired back at them.

Karl Wortmann was a big, strapping man, well over 6 feet tall and solidly built. He had enlisted in the *Waffen-SS* as a youth and was proud of his service. A noncommissioned officer, Wortmann was the aiming gunner for the 37mm. cannon on the third of four flak tanks closely following Peiper's lead tanks into Honsfeld. Early traces of a foggy daylight were bringing increased visibility when the first flak tank edged around the S-bend and past the buildings closely flanking it.

A U.S. antitank gun opened fire. The first round hit the flak tank, but it kept moving. A second round hit the second vehicle, immobilizing it. Bypassing the immobilized tank, the driver of Wortmann's flak tank continued to advance. Although the antitank gun fired a third time, it missed Wortmann's vehicle. Wortmann could see that the gun was firing from a barn concealed by a hedge. Taking aim with his 37mm. piece, he knocked it out with one round.

As small-arms fire erupted from the upper stories of houses into the open turrets of the flak tanks, gunners on flak wagons equipped with quad-20s returned the fire. It took some twenty minutes before the last of the Americans either fled or surrendered. Wortmann and his crew found the men who had manned the antitank gun hiding in the cellar next to the barn from which they had fired.

By that time, more half-tracks carrying *SS-Panzergrenadiers* and tanks with paratroopers on them were pouring into the village. Dismounting, the foot troops fanned out to clear any resistance that remained.

In one of the houses, Lieutenant Reppa was dozing in a chair. At the sound of the first German tanks passing, he snapped fully awake. "Those don't sound like ours," he said to his first sergeant, William Lovelock. The two rushed to a window just as a shell exploded and illuminated a German half-track passing outside.

Reppa's initial shock quickly turned to dismay that Sergeant Creel had failed to give any warning. Then Reppa determined to make a run for it, but first he had to send messengers to the houses where his other men had bedded down and tell them to do the same. He was briefing the messengers when a tank loaded with paratroopers stopped just outside the house. Jumping to the ground, the paratroopers headed for the door, their rifles and burp guns at the ready.

"*Heraus!*" a German commanded.

"We can't make it," Reppa muttered, half to himself. "We can't do a damn thing."

Going to the door, he opened it, threw up his hands, and shouted: "*Kamerad!*"

Variations of that scene were taking place all over Honsfeld. At the first fire from the German tanks and half-tracks, many men fled, some even managing to escape with their jeeps and other vehicles; but others, rudely awakened, saw their best chance of survival in surrender.

Just when the murder started and how widespread it was, nobody could say. But it happened.

Three houses from the center of the village on the road to Büllingen, an SS officer prodded eight sleepy Americans, barefoot and in their underwear, at gunpoint from the house, lined them up beside it, and mowed them down with a burp gun. From another house, five American soldiers emerged under a white flag. A group of German soldiers opened fire with rifles and burp guns, killing four and wounding the fifth, and as the wounded soldier cried for help, a tank ran over him and crushed him. From yet another house, four men carrying a large white flag tried to surrender, but a machine gunner in a German tank opened fire, killing all four.

Elsewhere, seventeen men from the 612th Tank Destroyer Battalion and an officer, 1st Lt. Laurens B. Grandy, kept up a steady fire for a time but eventually concluded that their situation was hopeless. When Grandy and one of the men emerged with half a tablecloth as a flag of surrender, a German soldier told them to have everybody leave his weapon and file out with hands overhead. All eighteen were standing in a row, hands raised, when a German noncommissioned officer jumped from a half-track, raised his burp gun, and killed the two men at the end of the row. One of the Americans took that as a signal to run: Staff Sgt. Billy F. Wilson fled to the back of the house, then dodged from one building to another to reach a field and the concealment of a hedgerow. Some four hours later he made his way to safety.

Pfc. William T. Hawkins was with a group of approximately a hundred men whom the Germans herded together after they had surrendered, many of them also from the 612th Tank Destroyer Battalion. They were standing in a closely packed group with hands overhead when German machine gunners opened fire, killing—it appeared to Hawkins—some twenty to thirty men. Then for some unexplained reason the firing abruptly stopped, and the survivors were soon marching down the road toward Lanzerath.

As about 250 prisoners plodded down one side of the narrow road, more of *Kampfgruppe Peiper's* tanks and half-tracks were moving forward. Some of the drivers of the vehicles veered toward the prisoners as if to run them down. Soldiers on the tanks swung at the prisoners with the butts of their rifles, knocking some men down. Still others took pot-shots with their rifles. If an American fell, the guards would let nobody help him. A machine gunner in one tank fired a few rounds into the air, then lowered his gun and killed two prisoners. An SS officer fired his pistol into the forehead of one of the men.

As those things happened, the Americans would dive for the ditches or jump behind trees, but their guards quickly prodded them out. In only one case did a guard intervene. He looked to be no more than eighteen; when an SS officer ordered him out of the way so he could take a shot at the prisoners, the young German refused, standing instead with his arms outstretched to protect the prisoners behind him. Frustrated, the officer went on his way.

By the time the column of prisoners reached Lanzerath, somebody had added two Belgian civilian men to the tail. As the last of the column was passing the Café Palm, just across the road from Adolf Schür's house, a soldier jumped from a passing tank, grabbed the two civilians, and forced them into a barn next to the Café Palm. Several shots sounded. An hour later, one of the men dragged himself across the road and into the Schür's barn, where Adolf found him.

Adolf helped the man into the kitchen, where Frau Schür bathed his wounds—he had been shot twice in the nape of the neck. The other man, he said, was dead. Although there were several German paratroopers in the kitchen, they made no objection to helping the civilian. An SS trooper came in later, seemingly intent on finishing the man off, but Christolf Schür protested vehemently, and the presence of the other soldiers appeared to intimidate the SS trooper. After a time, he left.

One more terrible deed remained to be done in nearby Honsfeld. Two nights later, after seventeen-year-old André Schroeder and the few other civilians still living in Honsfeld had repaired for the night to the staunchest cellar in the village, as was their custom, five SS troopers called down from the top of the stairs. They wanted somebody, they said, to show them the way to Büllingen. Although Schroeder volunteered to do it, the Germans spotted sixteen-year-old Erna Collas, whom everybody in Honsfeld considered to be the prettiest girl in the village. They insisted that she show them the way.

Erna went with the soldiers but never returned. In the spring, after the snows melted, they found her body in a shallow grave alongside the road to Büllingen, shot seven times in the back. There was no way of telling whether she had been raped.

After reaching the far edge of Honsfeld, Colonel Peiper sent a half-track to reconnoiter his assigned road leading west. The weather was turning warmer; most of the snow, except in the woods, was melting; and Peiper was concerned that the road, which showed on his map to be little more than a cart track, would not support his heavy vehicles. The reconnaissance confirmed his fears.

The alternative was to proceed northwest, to the town of Büllingen, which was on the route assigned to the 12th SS Panzer Division. Hearing the noise of battle from the direction of Losheimergraben, Peiper deduced that the tanks of that division had yet to get past the crossroads. He decided to take the chance of going to Büllingen, then turn back onto his assigned route before the other German column reached Büllingen. Not only was it a better road; Peiper had heard that there was American gasoline in Büllingen, and after all the delays and peregrinations of the day before, his vehicles were badly in need of fuel. That Hitler had decreed death to any commander impinging on the route of another held little concern for Peiper.

While waiting at the edge of Honsfeld for the column to close up, Peiper started a company of the paratroopers that he had appropriated in Lanzerath on the march to Büllingen in half-tracks accompanied by a single tank. He told the battalion commander to return with the rest of the paratroopers to his own regiment.

There would be little to prevent *Kampfgruppe Peiper* from taking Büllingen. A town with a normal population of two thousand people, it lay four miles behind the 99th Division's line at Losheimergraben and served as a center for troops supporting the division. Within recent days, it had also served those supporting the 2d Division, for Büllingen sat astride the main supply route for the troops who were attacking at Wahlerscheid. The service batteries of two of the 99th Division's artillery battalions were there. So was Capt. Ralph Hill's little Civil Affairs detachment with Hill's telephone connection in the basement of the post office, so helpful the day before to commanders of the 99th and 106th Divisions. Then there was the 2d Division's Quartermaster Company and a company of the division's organic 2d Engineer Battalion; and several hundred yards outside the town on either side of the road to Honsfeld, artillery observation pilots of both the 2d and 99th Divisions had turned the fields into airstrips for their frail little L-5 aircraft.

At the instigation of the commander of the V Corps, General Gerow, the First Army at midnight on December 16 released a battalion of combat engineers, the 254th, for attachment to the 99th Division, which sent the battalion to Büllingen to defend the town to the east (the direction of Losheimergraben) and to the south (the direction of Honsfeld). The first company arrived at 4 A.M.—the same time at which Peiper was starting his move from Lanzerath—and went into position just east of the town. Company B followed an hour later. As the men marched along the road toward Honsfeld, they came upon the airstrips and nearby the 924th Field Artillery Battalion's Service Battery, which was occupying a few isolated houses along the road. Rather than set up a defense close to those installations, the company kept going all the way to the far edge of a growth of scrub brush little more than a thousand yards short of Honsfeld. There the Americans began to dig in.

The third company arrived only at daybreak and stopped short of Büllingen to assume a reserve position on the road leading back to Bütgenbach—site of the 99th Division's headquarters—at a road junction marked by a manor house and several outbuildings that the Americans knew as Dom. Bütgenbach (dom. is a map abbreviation for *domaine*, meaning estate). A platoon of towed guns of the 612th Tank Destroyer Battalion was already in position there, a reserve for the two platoons that had gone on to Honsfeld.

As the engineers of Company B marched along the road toward Honsfeld, one man dropped out of the column to pound on the door of a house which served as a billet for the pilots of the 99th Division's L-5 planes. "The Germans are coming!" he shouted. Nobody questioned how he knew. While the pilots went to their planes and warmed up the motors, the crewmen loaded the detachment's gear onto trucks.

At the edge of the patch of scrub brush on a hill overlooking Honsfeld, the men of Company B, 254th Engineers, had had scant time to dig in when around 6 A.M. they heard tracked vehicles and German voices. They opened fire. In the darkness, the men could make out German soldiers piling off a tank and six half-tracks; they were the paratroopers that Peiper had sent ahead of his main column. The engineers repulsed a first assault and what appeared to be two more; but shortly after 7 A.M., as it was beginning to get light, twelve German tanks joined the attack. Lacking any defense against the tanks, the engineers broke. Some fell back toward Büllingen, others toward Dom. Bütgenbach.

While the main body of Peiper's force was still coming forward, Peiper dispatched two patrols along dirt tracks roughly paralleling the main road to Büllingen. Five tanks and several half-tracks went beyond the railroad connecting Honsfeld and Büllingen to come at Büllingen from the east. There they shot up the company of engineers that was defending near the railroad and continued into town.

The other patrol, consisting of a tank and several half-tracks, took a route to the left of the main road and approached the 99th Division's airfield just as the pilots were getting ready to take off. As the tank's machine guns opened fire, each pilot in turn took off in the direction of the tank, as if dive-bombing it (although they had no weapons), and so intimidated the gunner that all but one plane got away, that one left behind in the mud. Only then did the pilots of the 2d Division's planes realize that something was wrong and race for their airstrip. A sole pilot escaped in his plane.

When the commander of the 924th Field Artillery Battalion's Service Battery, Capt. James Cobb, learned what was happening, he was at his battalion's headquarters in Krinkelt. He raced back in his jeep to his command post along the road to Honsfeld and ordered twelve men under 1st Lt. Jack Varner to form a roadblock between the two airstrips. They had just gotten into position with two .50-caliber machine guns and two bazookas when a column of German vehicles with two tanks in the lead appeared along the main road from Honsfeld.

Sgt. Grant Yager hit the second tank with a rocket from a bazooka, and as the crew piled out, the machine gunners and other men with carbines opened fire, but the return German fire was deadly. At least two men were killed, and both the two-man machine-gun crews were wounded. Except for one of the machine gunners, Pfc. Deloise Rapp, who was wounded twice in one foot and played dead, and Lieutenant Varner, who was out of sight behind a hedgerow, the men surrendered. (Rapp eventually crawled to a basement, coming upon Lieutenant Varner in the process. Although Rapp was certain Varner could have escaped after nightfall, Varner refused to go without Rapp, who was unable to walk. Both were captured.)

As tanks and half-tracks plowed onto the 2d Division's airstrip, shooting up the remaining planes, the Germans permitted Sergeant Yager and two other men to administer first aid to one of the wounded, Pvt. Bernard Pappel, who had been hit in a leg and an arm. As they treated him, a German officer in a light-colored leather jacket began berating Yager in German, but when Yager was unable to understand, he turned away. It was so unusual for an SS officer to wear a light-colored jacket—SS jackets were always black—that numerous witnesses to Peiper's march were later to remark on it. The man was the commander of Peiper's *SS-Panzergrenadier* battalion, Maj. Josef Diefenthal.

When the column was ready to continue into Büllingen, the Germans ordered Yager and the two men with him onto the hood of a half-track. As it moved forward, the men heard a single pistol shot. "My God!" yelled one of the men with Yager. "They shot Pappel in the head."

Inside Büllingen, there was no fight.

Shortly after 7 A.M., the company of the 2d Division's engineers in the town received orders to mine the roads leading into Büllingen and to prepare all bridges for demolition, but they were still loading mines into their trucks when German tanks and half-tracks appeared—the German patrol that had come into the town from the east. Some of the engineers managed to get out of town, mostly along the road to Losheimergraben. There they joined men of the 254th Engineers who had escaped the fight just east of Büllingen and augmented the defenses of the battalion of the 23d Infantry that had moved the day before into Hünningen. Others hid in cellars, but over the next three days the Germans routed them from their hiding places.

The men of the 2d Division's Quartermaster Company in Büllingen were lining up for breakfast when those same five German tanks and accompanying half-tracks appeared. The Americans dived for basements, from which they could see an elderly man emerge from his house. Wearing a Nazi armband and carrying a burp gun, he gave every passing tank a Nazi salute, then directed them to the railroad station where there were large stocks of supplies.

At the station, the tanks shot up parked trucks and trapped some men of the 2d Division's Signal Company in the basement. To escape detection, the men had to strangle their little dog mascot, Queenie. Those men as well as almost all those of the Quartermaster Company and seven of the pilots and ground crewmen of the 2d Division's artillery aircraft managed to hide through the rest of the day and get out of town after nightfall.

Because the other artillery service battery in Büllingen was along the road to Bütgenbach, those troops escaped with most of their vehicles and equipment. So did Captain Hill and his Civil Affairs detachment; but most of the men of Captain Cobb's battery, including the commander himself, were either captured immediately or ferreted from cellars the next day. Of sixty-nine officers and men in the battery, only eleven got away.

At a big, treeless square in Büllingen that served in normal times as the cattle market, Peiper's tanks and half-tracks found the gasoline they were hoping for in a small depot only recently established by the 2d Division's Quartermaster Company. The Germans used captured Americans to help fuel their vehicles. When each vehicle was filled up, Peiper hurried it out of town to the southwest along the road leading back onto his assigned line of march.

A flank patrol of five Mark IVs took the road toward Bütgenbach, but at Dom. Bütgenbach the guns of the 612th Tank Destroyer Battalion opened fire, knocking out three of the German tanks. The others quickly turned back, and the American gunners, along with the company of engineers in position there, were left to wonder (albeit with considerable relief) why the foe had turned away from them.

So long was Peiper's column that even as the first vehicles left Büllingen, others were still far to the rear on the road from Honsfeld and even farther back in and beyond Lanzerath. They proved to be ready targets when in mid-morning the skies cleared enough to permit two squadrons of the 366th Fighter Group, assigned for the day to support the 99th Division, to attack. Pilots of the 389th Squadron bombed and strafed Peiper's column, sending vehicles scurrying for concealment. They subsequently claimed thirty German tanks and other vehicles destroyed; but like infantrymen making their estimates of enemy losses, seldom were the claims of pilots in the air justified by the reality on the ground. When the second squadron, the 390th, moved in to attack, a squadron of ME-109s appeared. Although the American pilots shot down seven German planes, they had to jettison most of their bombs while doing it.

*   *   *

Inside Büllingen, Karl Wortmann and the crew of his flak tank delighted in the booty. When the radio operator handed Wortmann a small rectangular wax-coated cardboard box, Wortmann was at a loss to know what was in it. Breakfast, said the radio operator. Wortmann found that hard to believe, but he watched the others and quickly learned how to get at the food. Cigarettes, too. Although Wortmann had never smoked, he was unable to resist taking along several cartons. Like the crews of many other vehicles, Wortmann and his men stashed every empty space in their flak tank with whatever they found: food, cigarettes, field jackets, gloves, boots.

There were to be reports later that in Büllingen, Peiper's men killed fifty American prisoners who had helped them fill their vehicles with gasoline. The reports were false. *Kampfgruppe Peiper* took about two hundred prisoners in and around Büllingen, and somebody murdered Private Pappel; but there was no repetition of the mass atrocities committed in Honsfeld. Since others were destined to happen later, who could say why?

In capturing Büllingen, *Kampfgruppe Peiper* had seemingly trapped the bulk of the 2d and 99th Infantry Divisions. Most of the men, most of the artillery pieces, and most of the supporting tanks and tank destroyers of the two divisions were located somewhere along or near the road leading northeast from Büllingen through the twin villages of Krinkelt-Rocherath and the forests near the road junction of Wahlerscheid. At that point there were only two ways out of the trap. Infantrymen might make it on foot through the forest over firebreaks and muddy logging trails; vehicles and artillery pieces just might make it over the farm track leading from Wirtzfeld, behind Krinkelt-Rocherath, to the little town of Elsenborn and nearby Camp Elsenborn. Yet for all the efforts of the 2d Division's engineers to improve that muddy lane, no one knew how long it would stand up under heavy traffic. What was more, if the Germans who had taken Büllingen continued on to Wirtzfeld and Krinkelt-Rocherath, they could roll up the two divisions from the flank. Or should they continue to Bütgenbach and then swing north up the road to Elsenborn, they could come in behind everybody, even men trying to get out of the forest on foot: two divisions and their attachments, possibly as many as thirty thousand men.

That was what Walter Lauer thought was about to happen. "The enemy," Lauer noted later, before Peiper's objectives had become clear, "had the key to success within his hands but did not know it."

Walter Robertson thought the same. Just a few minutes before 7 A.M. on December 17, from the 2d Division's forward headquarters in a house on the edge of Wirtzfeld, Robertson telephoned the commandant of the division's Special Troops, Lt. Col. Matt F. C. Konop. German tanks had broken through and were on their way to Büllingen, said Robertson. He wanted Konop to get every man and every gun he could put his hands on to form "a last ditch defense of the CP." Such unaccustomed agitation was there in Robertson's voice that for a brief moment Konop failed to recognize who was talking.

The minute Robertson hung up, Konop was on the phone to the various headquarters units, telling them to get cooks, clerks, jeep drivers, MPs, whoever, out to form a line on the southern fringe of Wirtzfeld in front of the command post. He tried to warn the Quartermaster Company in Büllingen, but the telephone line was out.

It was a fairly impressive little defensive force that Konop assembled. Aside from the heterogeneous collection of men from the division headquarters, there were others from the division artillery's command post, also located in Wirtzfeld. The presence of the division artillery commander, General Hinds, facilitated repositioning a battery of 105mm. howitzers and another of 155mm. howitzers so that they could fire on the approaches to Wirtzfeld from Büllingen. There were a few 57mm. antitank guns and four half-tracks equipped with quad-50 machine guns. Even so, the little force would have been no match for a determined armored thrust from Büllingen, which was what Robertson and everybody else thought was coming.

Not long after 8 A.M., the worst appeared about to happen. Five German tanks and several half-tracks—the force that had entered Büllingen from the east and driven to the railroad station—appeared out of the mist on the Büllingen road, where it crossed a ridgeline eight hundred yards outside Wirtzfeld. Just at that moment Konop's defense received a strong boost with the arrival of five self-propelled tank destroyers of the attached 644th Tank Destroyer Battalion. The destroyers quickly knocked out four of the tanks and a half-track and sent the other vehicles hurrying back into Büllingen.

After leaving Büllingen, Colonel Peiper halted his leading vehicles at a crossroads so that the column could close up. During the pause, a half-track reconnoitered a dirt track that led more directly than the main road to the next point on Peiper's route, the village of Möderscheid. Since the road appeared to be serviceable, Peiper took it and from Möderscheid proceeded northwest toward the village of Schoppen. On the way, the Germans captured the two-man crews of two ambulances, plus Staff Sgt. Henry R. Zach, two junior officers (1st Lt. Thomas E. McDermott and 2d Lt. Lloyd A. Iames), and six other Americans in a four-jeep convoy. They loaded some of the prisoners on their vehicles but made the four jeeps join the column.

About midway between Schoppen and the village of Faymonville at a little chapel, St. Hubert, Peiper found another side road that appeared promising and would enable him to avoid Faymonville and the adjacent fair-sized town of Waimes, where he might well run into opposition. It was little more than a country lane, but Peiper risked it, and his vehicles made it.

The lead tank was approaching the village of Ondenval when an American 6×6 truck appeared. The machine gunner in the tank fired, hitting the truck and sending it careening into a ditch, where it turned over on one side. As the tank passed by, the German gunner gave the truck another burst of fire, as did the gunners in several other tanks that followed.

Inside the cab of the truck, two American engineers huddled. Miraculously, the German fire hit neither man. When the noise of the German vehicles had passed, the two scrambled out, raced to a nearby railroad embankment, clambered to the other side, and began to run back south in the direction from which they had come.

That little episode marked the beginning of what was to prove a series of fateful encounters between *Kampfgruppe Peiper* and Americans of the 1111th Engineer Combat Group.

Just up the road from Ondenval in the schoolhouse in the center of Waimes was a forward hospital run by a platoon of the 47th Field Hospital. By early morning of December 17, the surgeons, nurses, administrative officers, technicians, and orderlies were aware that something unusual was happening at the front, for the rumble of artillery fire was almost constant and during the night the number of incoming patients markedly increased. In mid-morning, a sudden spate of patients hurriedly evacuated from a hospital run by another platoon of the 47th Field in Bütgenbach appeared, and close behind them the medical personnel of that platoon.

Orders soon arrived to transfer all patients to a hospital in Malmédy; then came orders for the platoon that had been in Bütgenbach to follow, but the hospital in Waimes was to continue to function. Throughout the rest of the morning, ambulances continued to arrive from the direction of Bütgenbach. Although busy with patients, at least one of the nurses, 2d Lt. Mabel Jessop, felt a gnawing anxiety. Were the Germans coming? Were she and the others in the platoon considered expendable? When it came time for lunch, she had trouble swallowing "the usual cold, tasteless mixture of canned hamburger and dehydrated potatoes."

As Peiper's column proceeded from Ondenval around midday over a winding back road to the village of Thirimont, Peiper rode in a half-track with the commander of the *SS-Panzergrenadiers*, Major Diefenthal. The leading tanks tried to go all the way through Thirimont along a dirt road that led directly to a principal north-south highway, N-23, which connected Malmédy with the little resort town of Ligneuville and thence with St. Vith. Peiper wanted to get to N-23 by the shortest route, for he needed to reach Ligneuville in order to pick up another road leading west. It was a back road, but by taking it he might avoid likely American strength on the highway that passed through Malmédy; and, in any case, that highway was assigned to the 12th SS Panzer Division.

Just beyond Thirimont, Peiper's luck with country lanes ran out: The lead tank bogged down at a ford where the little road crossed a small stream. The column thus had to swing northwest at Thirimont to pick up N-23 at a road junction known as Baugnez, then turn south to Ligneuville. Peiper himself had abandoned the lead vehicles at that point, having climbed down from Major Diefenthal's half-track to question an American soldier (Peiper spoke excellent English) who had been captured, along with his jeep, while he was trouble-shooting telephone lines.

Kampfgruppe Peiper was about to have its second brush with men of the 1111th Engineer Combat Group. They were two men—a sergeant and a private—sent out scouting in a jeep by their company commander from the 291st Engineer Combat Battalion in Malmédy, who had learned of a German breakthrough in the vicinity of Bütgenbach. The two had turned left at the Baugnez road junction in the direction of Waimes and Bütgenbach when something caught their eye down the hill to the south in the direction of Thirimont, from which a secondary road led up to the highway they were on.

Moving down the secondary road, they hid in the edge of a wood bordering the road to watch wide-eyed the scene below them. Tanks, tanks, half-tracks, and more tanks. Wary that at any moment they might be discovered, they waited long enough to count sixty-eight German vehicles, thirty of them tanks, then avoiding the highway by which they had come, took a winding back road toward Malmédy.

At one o'clock, the word finally came to the schoolhouse in Waimes: Evacuate immediately! Patients and surgical teams went first and within ten minutes were on their way toward the road junction at Baugnez, where their trucks and ambulances turned right onto Highway N-23 and proceeded down a steep hill into Malmédy.

The nurses were next, ten of them crowded into a single ambulance. The vehicle was nearing a point where a woods ran out and open fields led to the road junction of Baugnez when shells began to explode in the road ahead. As the driver pulled the ambulance to the side of the road, the nurses clambered out and into the ditch. Only then did they notice that there were six trucks also stopped, men taking cover in the ditch beside them.

More shells, so close that Lieutenant Jessop thought the gunners must surely know exactly where they were and expected "to be blown up with the next blast." As some of the men from the trucks began to crawl down the ditch toward Waimes, the nurses turned to follow, and as they turned they could see big German tanks entering the road below them and making for the junction at Baugnez.

The nurses were soon filthy with mud, drenched by the slush and snow. When two American trucks came along the road from the direction of Waimes, they waved them down frantically, told the drivers what had happened, climbed aboard, and headed back to the schoolhouse in Waimes.

Only scant minutes earlier, a long column of tanks, half-tracks, and trucks of the 7th Armored Division's Combat Command R (CCR) had passed through Malmédy, one of two march columns by which the 7th Armored Division was moving south at General Bradley's order to help the 106th Infantry Division near St. Vith. The last of CCR's vehicles had climbed the road out of Malmédy and past the Baugnez road junction when a small convoy of three serials transporting 140 men entered the other side of Malmédy. The convoy belonged to Battery B, 285th Field Artillery Observation Battalion.

The 285th Field Artillery Observation Battalion was one of those technical units that, however small, make important contributions to a modern army in the field. The men did mapping and surveying, but for the most part theirs was a sound-and-flash unit, whose mission was to detect the location of enemy mortars and artillery and pass that information to howitzer and gun battalions. The battalion had only a Headquarters Battery and two operational batteries, A and B. Seldom did the battalion function as a unit: Its two batteries were usually parceled out individually where needed.

Commanded by Capt. Leon T. Scarborough, Battery B had recently been operating near Aachen, and when the 7th Armored Division received the order to move south, so did Battery B. Even though the battery was not attached to the armored division, Captain Scarborough arranged for a slot in one of the division's two march columns and then left with a small billeting detail to precede the convoy and prepare for the battery's arrival at its new location.

Battery B's route led through Eupen, across the Hautes Fagnes to Malmédy, and on to the south. There were thirty-three vehicles in the convoy: jeeps, three-quarter-ton trucks, 6×6 trucks, and a command car. The vehicles were numbered B-1 to B-33.

Cpl. Ernest W. Bechtel was one of the men assigned to a 6×6, Number B-26, one of only a few that had no tarpaulin over the bed. As the men were loading, Bechtel spied his best friend, who was also a neighbor back in his home town in Pennsylvania, Cpl. Luke B. Swartz. He was standing with his head bowed just behind the next truck, B-25. "Hey," called Bechtel, "why don't you ride with me on B-26?"

"No," replied Swartz, "it's beginning to sleet. I'll ride on one of the trucks with a tarp." Besides, he went on, it was his last day anyway. "Ernie," he said, "I'll not be going home. Something terrible is going to happen to most of us today, but you'll be going back. Tell the folks back home I love them."

"What the hell are you talking about?" demanded Bechtel.

Without further word, Swartz climbed aboard B-25 just as the convoy got under way. Bechtel boarded B-26.

It was a cold, miserable ride through the murky early morning of December 17. On the way the column paused briefly for the men to search for German paratroopers, and shortly after midday, as the vehicles entered Malmédy, it was apparent to almost everybody that something unusual was happening. The narrow, winding streets of the town were jammed with military vehicles, most of them going in the opposite direction from that of Battery B's convoy and their drivers obviously in a hurry to get out of town. As the trucks neared the center of town, civilians began to run alongside, shouting *Boches! Boches!* and pointing in the direction Battery B was going.

When the lead vehicle of the convoy reached one of the last houses on the edge of Malmédy before N-23 began its ascent to Baugnez, the commander of the 291st Engineer Combat Battalion, Lt. Col. David E. Pergrin, came out of the house, flagged down the convoy, and talked to the 285th Field Artillery Observation Battalion's executive officer, Capt. Roger L. Mills, who was in command. There had been a German breakthrough near Bütgenbach, said Pergrin; it might be wise for the convoy to swing to the west along the 7th Armored Division's other march route.

Mills pondered the advice briefly. No, he decided; if he lost his position in the march column, it might be difficult to get back in. He would continue on N-23.

Seemingly inexorably, fate was drawing *Kampfgruppe Peiper* and that small American unit to a rendezvous at the road junction known as Baugnez. Had there been no boggy ford on the road leading west from Thirimont, *Kampfgruppe Peiper* would never have gone to Baugnez. Had Captain Mills heeded Colonel Pergrin's advice, there would probably have been only one American—a military policeman—at the road junction when *Kampfgruppe Peiper* got there.

At 12:45 P.M., two military policemen at the Baugnez road junction directed the last vehicle of the 7th Armored Division's CCR down N-23 and watched it disappear in the direction of Ligneuville. They had about an hour to wait before the next scheduled convoy appeared, that of the division's artillery. (They knew nothing about Battery B.) Since a single man could handle anything that passed in the meantime, one climbed into a jeep and headed down the road to Malmédy. The man left behind was Pfc. Homer D. Ford.

Most of Battery B's vehicles had begun the ascent toward Baugnez when the man in charge of the truck known as B-26, Sgt. James Barrington, became ill. As the driver brought the truck to a halt, Barrington staggered from the cab, vomiting. While two other trucks, B-27 and B-28, waited, the driver of B-26 searched for an aid station. It took ten minutes to find one and leave Sergeant Barrington there. (He was suffering from food poisoning.)

As the three trucks headed out of Malmédy, they came upon a group of men from the 291st Engineer Combat Battalion placing explosive charges against stately ash trees that lined either side of the road. "We're going to blow this row of trees," the engineers warned. "Once you're through, you can't return." Determined to catch up with the convoy, the men in charge of the three trucks told their drivers to keep moving.

As the trucks continued up the steep hill, the noise of heavy firing broke out: the *crump-crump* of big shells, the din of machine-gun fire. The lead driver slowed down. What was going on?

Only moments later, a jeep came roaring down the hill apparently out of control, but it came screeching to a halt just before colliding with B-26. An officer in the front passenger seat was bleeding profusely from a wound in the neck, and the driver was almost incoherent. All the men in B-26 could make out was the word "Krauts!"

By that time, shells had begun to burst alongside the highway nearby, and the noise of firing up ahead had become thunderous. It would be suicide to drive on. Somehow the drivers of all three trucks managed to turn around in the narrow road and head back toward Malmédy. The engineers, they noted with considerable relief, had yet to blow the trees across the road.

Back on the fringe of Malmédy, where Colonel Pergrin had the command post for his 291st Engineer Combat Battalion, the two men who had been scouting in the direction of Thirimont brought their jeep to an abrupt halt in front of the house. Pergrin found it hard to believe the story they told.

"There's a big Kraut column coming, Colonel! They've got tanks and half-tracks and armored cars, everything, and there's a hell of a lot of 'em. It looks like the whole German Army!"

Pergrin had barely gotten all the details of what the two men had to say when the noise of heavy shelling and machine-gun fire drifted down the hill south of Malmédy. "That little FAOB outfit," Pergrin said, half to himself, "has run smack into that Kraut column."

A small advance party, consisting of two vehicles and fifteen men (mostly route markers, who were to be dropped off at intersections to guide the way), had already disappeared down the road in the direction of Ligneuville when a round from a German tank fell just in front of the first vehicle of the main column, a command car in which Captain Mills

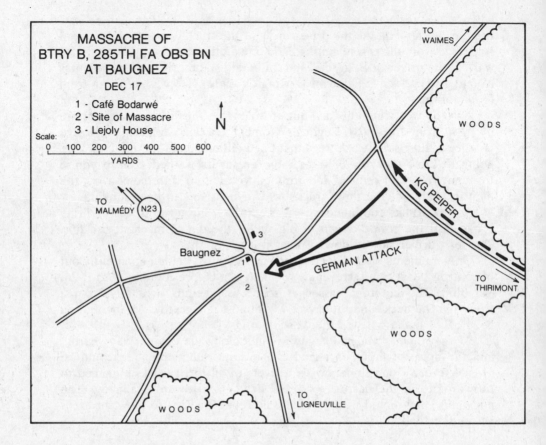

MASSACRE OF
BTRY B, 285TH FA OBS BN
AT BAUGNEZ
DEC 17

1 - Café Bodarwé
2 - Site of Massacre
3 - Lejoly House

Scale:
0   100   200   300   400   500   600
YARDS

N

TO
WAIMES

WOODS

KG PEIPER

TO
MALMÉDY   N23

Baugnez

3

1

2

GERMAN ATTACK

TO
THIRIMONT

WOODS

TO
LIGNEUVILLE

WOODS

was riding with Battery B's executive officer, 1st Lt. Virgil T. Lary, Jr. The driver braked to a precipitous stop, and the truck behind swerved as its driver applied the brakes.

At that moment, a jeep arrived from the direction of Ligneuville, an officer in the passenger seat. It swerved to a halt beside the first truck, but Staff Sgt. William H. Merriken and others in the truck shouted to the driver to keep moving. Go to Malmédy and get help! Gunning the motor, the driver careened down the road, dodging in and out of the vehicles of the convoy and through a hail of German fire at an incredible speed.

Round after round came from the German tanks, raking up and down the American column. Machine guns. Mortars. Several of the trucks exploded. Many crashed into the ditches on either side of the highway. The kitchen truck caught fire.

Battery B, 285th Field Artillery Observation Battalion, had met *Kampfgruppe Peiper*. Having spotted the American column while moving up the secondary road from Thirimont, the German tanks and half-tracks had veered off and charged across open fields toward N-23 and Baugnez, firing as they advanced.

Most of the men dived for cover in the ditches or behind vehicles, and many opened a futile fire with M-1s and carbines. A few ran for a nearby wood, but German fire cut them down. Cpl. Warren Schmitt ran to a little stream a few yards from the road, flopped down in the edge of the icy water, and pretended he was dead. Captain Mills and Lieutenant Lary both vaulted into a ditch. Everywhere there was firing and the heavy, raucous noise of churning tank treads.

Men in the vehicles near the tail of the column were unable to see what was happening. One thought the column had come upon German paratroopers; because a V-1 buzz bomb was passing overhead, several thought everybody was firing at that. But as the German tanks and half-tracks reached the highway, the rear vehicles, too, were caught up in the maelstrom. One of those vehicles was an ambulance with two medics from the 1st Division's 26th Infantry, Pvts. Roy Anderson and Samuel Dobyns, who had missed their unit's convoy as it moved to join the 99th Division and had tacked onto the tail of Battery B's column. A round from a German tank set the ambulance on fire.

At the road junction, as the Germans struck, Private Ford was still directing vehicles past. When three or four men from one of the trucks ran in Ford's direction, he motioned them to come with him and dashed behind one of the few buildings close by, a café run by Mme. Adèle Bodarwé. From there, Ford spotted a small shed and swiftly hid in it with the other men.

Inside the café, Madame Bodarwé watched the carnage in horror. Even though her son had been forced to serve in the German Army, she was a loyal Belgian. With her that morning was a farmer neighbor, Henri Lejoly, who was not necessarily pro-German but thought it well to side with whoever appeared to be in charge. He went to the door of the café and waved warmly to the Germans.

Firing was still rampant when an American jeep arrived driven by a German officer. It was Peiper. While questioning his American prisoner, he had heard the sound of firing up the hill and hurried forward. When he saw what was happening, he was annoyed, both because of the delay and because of the needless expenditure of ammunition against a helpless target—"those beautiful trucks, which we needed so badly, all shot up."

Only with difficulty did Peiper manage to stop the firing, and as it ceased, American soldiers emerged from the ditches, their hands in the air. The Germans herded them together roughly in small groups, many of them relieving the prisoners of rings, watches, cigarettes, and gloves. Almost every German soldier appeared intent on getting a pair of gloves.

Germans guarding one group wanted three men to drive the American trucks. Several said they could not drive; three others, Master Sgt.

Eugene L. Lacy and Cpls. Thomas J. Bacon and Ralph A. Logan, said
they could. The Germans ordered them to move three undamaged trucks
to the head of the column but there told them to dismount and join a
group of several other men standing in a line along the road. A German
with a pistol went down the line of men, putting the barrel first to one
man's forehead, then another's. He was going to shoot them all, he said,
because American planes were bombing his people. Standing nearby,
slightly wounded, Captain Mills intervened. The men, he insisted, were
to be treated honorably as prisoners of war. The German put away his
pistol.

By that time, Colonel Peiper had established control over his men,
and tanks and half-tracks began moving again down the hill in the direction of Ligneuville. One half-track stopped to pick up the ten men whom
the German had threatened to shoot. (They were subsequently left under
guard in Ligneuville and later marched into Germany.) Peiper left the
scene in Major Diefenthal's half-track.

Homer Ford, the military policeman, and the men who had hidden
with him in the shed, soon joined the ranks of prisoners. Henri Lejoly
pointed out their hiding place to the Germans.

In time, the Germans herded all the prisoners into a field to the west
of N-23, a hundred yards south of the road junction and the Café
Bodarwé. All told there were approximately 130: Of the 140 men making
up Battery B, a total of 64 (those who had left early with the battery
commander, the route markers, the men in trucks B-26, B-27, and B-28,
and the 10 who, however inexplicably, the Germans had sent on to Ligneuville) were safe; but the number of prisoners was augmented by men
from other units. Some had been taken earlier, such as the medics from
the two ambulances captured near Möderscheid, several MPs, and Sergeant Zach, Lieutenants McDermott and Iames, and others from the
four-jeep convoy. Others again, such as the two medics from the 26th
Infantry, Anderson and Dobyns, had simply happened on the scene. And
the MP who had been on duty at the road junction, Private Ford.

The Germans herded the men tightly together only sixty feet from the
highway, roughly in eight rows, hands above their heads. Some men
jostled briefly for position, for they disliked being in the front row. The
weather was damp and raw, the ground soggy underfoot with here and
there a patch of old snow. The men's hands grew numb from holding
them up and from the cold, for hardly anybody still had gloves.

Some of the men were uneasy, but the majority were complacent.
Although most recognized that their captors were SS troops, hardly anybody expected treatment different from what might be expected of regular troops. Quite obviously the Germans were merely waiting for trucks
with which to transport them to the rear, where they were destined to
pass the Christmas of 1944 as prisoners of war.

A German officer—later identified as Maj. Werner Poetschke, com-

mander of the 1st SS Panzer Battalion (perhaps conveniently so identified, for by that time he had been killed on another battlefield)—stopped
two Mark IV tanks and directed them into position covering the prisoners. Once they were in place, he ordered one of the commanders, Sgt.
Hans Siptrott, to open fire. Siptrott in turn ordered his assistant gunner,
Pvt. Georg Fleps, a twenty-one-year-old SS volunteer from Romania who
already had his pistol at the ready, to shoot.

Fleps fired. Standing beside Lieutenant Lary, Lary's driver collapsed
backward from the impact of the bullet, toppling men behind him in an
accordion action, so tightly were they all grouped. With the shot, the
prisoners began shouting and jostling, and at least two in the front rank,
Pfc. James P. Mattera and one of the medics, Dobyns, bulldozed their
way toward the rear. Some of the officers yelled for the men to stand fast
lest they provoke more shooting.

No provocation was needed. Private Kleps fired a second shot with his
pistol, killing a medical officer, 1st Lt. Carl R. Guenther; then somebody
shouted: "*Machen alle kaputt!* (Kill them all!)," and machine guns on
both tanks opened fire.

Those who survived the first deadly fusillade flung themselves to the
ground, burying their faces in the mud and trying to burrow under the
bodies around them. The firing continued, the machine guns raking back
and forth across the prostrate forms. There were screams, groans, cries of
agony "almost like a lowing."

To the men who still lived, it seemed that the firing went on for an
eternity. It actually lasted about fifteen minutes. Yet for a full two hours
afterward, men on passing German vehicles amused themselves by firing
a few bursts into the clump of bodies.

At long last, the cries and moans of the wounded died out and the
noise of German vehicles on the road faded away. To the survivors, the
silence was eerie. A few dared a glance to see whether any Germans were
left, but most kept their heads glued to the ground. The silence at last
ended with the sound of German voices and approaching footsteps. Engineers of the 3d SS Pioneer Company were moving into the field to finish
off anybody who might have survived.

Upon first reaching the field, the Germans stood "for a few minutes to
observe the Americans who were still moving or otherwise showing signs
of life." Then they fanned out to finish them off. One of the engineers
shot "four or five" with his pistol, making sure he put the muzzle only a
few inches from the man's heart. As he remarked later, "I was sure I
killed each man at whom I fired." Other Germans asked men to speak
up, promising medical treatment, and a few made the mistake of responding. One German allowed an aid man to minister to one of the
wounded, then killed them both. The medic, Dobyns, made a run for it,
which so surprised the Germans that he succeeded in covering twenty-five
to thirty yards before fire from a machine gun cut him down. Although

wounded four times, Dobyns was still alive, but the Germans presumed him dead and left him alone.

By that time, nobody still living could be unaware of what was going on. Each man tried desperately to control his breathing, not only to keep his body still but to prevent vapor from showing in the cold as he exhaled. To many a survivor it seemed that the pounding of his heart would surely give him away, and for some, no attempt to appear dead would suffice, for as the Germans systematically kicked them in the head or the groin, it was almost impossible to keep from reacting.

Shot in the calf and the foot, Lieutenant Lary recalled that a German came his way,

> shooting here and there. A bullet went through the head of the man next to me. I lay tensely still, expecting the end. Could he see me breathing? Could I take a kick in the groin without wincing? . . . He was standing at my head. What was he doing? Time seemed to stand still. And then I heard him reloading his pistol in a deliberate manner . . . laughing and talking. A few odd steps before the reloading was finished and he was no longer so close to my head, then another shot a little farther away, and he had passed me up.

Almost miraculously, others than Lary still lived. In the front row, Sgt. Kenneth Ahrens had been shot in the back, his uniform so soaked with blood that the Germans apparently had no doubt that he was dead. Sergeant Merriken, with two machine-gun bullets in his back and a pistol bullet in one knee, found himself amazed at how calm he was, but praying "that someone would survive and tell what the Germans had done." Then there was Cpl. Michael T. Sciranko, shot in an upper thigh; Cpl. Albert M. Valenzi, hit in both legs; the MP, Homer Ford, hit in an arm; the medic, Dobyns, shot four times; his buddy, Anderson, unwounded; Cpls. Theodore J. Paluch and Charles F. Apperman, also unwounded. Sergeant Zach was hit in the leg and the hip, and Pvt. John H. Cobbler, hit six times, somehow still survived.

As the executioners left the field and silence again descended, men began to venture a whisper, a soft, agonizing query to try to determine if they were alone or if somebody else was alive. Here and there somebody answered, and one human being gained courage from the proximity of another.

"They'll be back," said one man; "we've got to make a run for it." "No, no," urged another; "wait until dark." Lary was among those who wanted to wait until dark. Mattera was one of those who wanted to go, so traumatized by the cold, the shock, and the presence of death that he was convinced he would never escape detection a second time.

"Let's go!" shouted Mattera and rose to his feet "in slow motion, resembling a drunken man." However much Lary disagreed, he was one of those who took the cue, rose, and began to run.

Some twenty men tried it, most heading for the Café Bodarwé. "No," yelled Mattera, "head for the woods!" But few heeded him. Twelve men took refuge in the café. Lieutenant Lary headed there at first but at the last minute went for the shed behind it and covered himself with straw. Three other men fell to the ground some distance behind the café and played dead again. All the while Germans were firing machine guns, and Lary saw one man fall. When the Germans saw men enter the café, they set it on fire and as the Americans emerged to escape the flames, shot them down.

On the edge of Malmédy, the commander of the 291st Engineers, Colonel Pergrin, had decided at last to risk a look in the direction of Baugnez and headed there with his jeep and his communications sergeant, William Crickenberger, armed with a Thompson submachine gun. As they came within sight of the burning Café Bodarwé, they left the jeep and began walking. Off to the right, three men emerged from the woods: Sergeant Ahrens and Corporals Sciranko and Valenzi. All three were wounded and babbling incoherently. Helping the men to the jeep, Pergrin and Crickenberger hurried back to Malmédy, where so intense was the men's shock that it took Pergrin an hour and a half to get the story of what had happened. Once he had it, he rushed a message to General Hodges in Spa, telling both of the massacre and something of the size of the German force.

Up on the hill near the road junction, darkness turned out in the end to be the only salvation for those few who still survived and for those who had run but had yet to reach safety. A few still hiding among the dead crawled away, mostly to the woods, whence they somehow made their way down the hill into Malmédy. Four men, among them Sergeant Zach, hid in the smoldering ruins of the café, where they were rescued the next morning by an artillery officer passing in a command car.

Three men tried to take cover in a house along a dirt road behind the café, but the people inside bolted their doors and refused to let them in; the men hid behind the house until darkness came. After seeing that, Sergeant Merriken, his wounds almost incapacitating, crawled into a woodshed near the house. He had either dozed off or lost consciousness when he revived to see a figure crawling toward the shed. Arming himself with a piece of wood, he prepared for the worst; but it turned out to be Pfc. Charles E. Reding, who had braved the flames inside the café until the Germans left, then crawled away, the only survivor from the café.

Blood from Merriken's back wounds had dried, gluing his shirt to his back, and he had to drag his right leg like "a chunk of lead." But with the help of Reding, who was unhurt, the two crawled across fields and Highway N-23, and as daylight came, hid in a thicket. Late in the day an elderly farmer approached, spotted them, and signaled with his head and his eyes for the men to come to his house. There the man and his wife hid them through the night, at one time turning away a German patrol that knocked at the door. The next day the woman walked into Malmédy and returned with an ambulance and American aid men.

Others who made it were the medics Anderson and Dobyns; Corporal Paluch, who played dead behind the Café Bodarwé; and Homer Ford. So did Corporal Schmitt, so numb from hours of immersion in icy water that he could only crawl. And the man who had been wounded six times, John Cobbler, but he died later while being evacuated by ambulance from Malmédy.

Mattera eventually reached an outpost of the 291st Engineers on the edge of Malmédy. "Forget the password!" he shouted. "I'm from Lancaster County, Pennsylvania . . . outfit wiped out . . . the Germans are coming!"

To four sisters—Bertha, Ida, Marie, and Martha Martin—who lived in a farm house with their aging father, the appearance of a young American, "wild-eyed, blood-spattered," on the doorstep was a terrifying experience. He said his name was Lieutenant Lary. They sat him on a chair beside the kitchen stove and washed and bound his bloody foot. They thought he was going to die, but when he rallied in the warmth, Marie and a neighbor, Martha Marx, fashioned a crutch for him and practically carried him down the precipitous hill into Malmédy. They reached Colonel Pergrin's command post at three o'clock in the morning. When Pergrin heard Lary's story, the testimony of the sole surviving officer, he sent his assistant operations officer, 1st Lt. Thomas Stack, to Spa to describe the massacre personally to General Hodges.

Hodges immediately ordered his inspector general to begin an investigation. And his aide, Maj. William C. Sylvan, noted in his diary: "There is absolutely no question as to its proof—immediate publicity is being given to the story. General Quesada [commander of the IX Tactical Air Command supporting the First Army] has told every one of his pilots about it during their briefing."

At the Baugnez road junction, the Germans threatened to kill Henri Lejoly, despite his protestations that he was German, for Lejoly had seen what had happened; but they eventually let him go. What happened to Madame Bodarwé would never be determined. She simply disappeared, and her son, back from the wars, was never able to find her or her body.

Five nights after what came to be known as the Malmédy Massacre, a heavy snow fell, mercifully blanketing the bodies of the eighty-six dead (seventy-two in the field where the main massacre occurred) and temporarily concealing the evidence of the most heinous crime inflicted on American troops during the course of the war in Europe. The forty-three men who escaped that dreadful field that Sabbath afternoon would always wonder why they had been spared. So would those men of Battery B who missed the tragic rendezvous, such as Sergeant Barrington, Corporal Bechtel, and the others in vehicles B-26, B-27, and B-28. And Bechtel would long reflect on the premonition of his friend, Luke Swartz. For as Swartz had predicted, he had died in the "something terrible" that he had somehow discerned was about to happen to Battery B, 285th Field Artillery Observation Battalion.

CHAPTER ELEVEN

"The Damned Engineers"

As daylight waned on December 16, Otto Skorzeny sent three of his teams disguised as American soldiers to try their luck at penetrating the front. Four men rode in each jeep, which to Skorzeny was logical, for there were seats for four. Skorzeny failed to note that the Americans had so much transport that seldom did four ride in one jeep, and when it became known that Skorzeny's four-man teams were abroad, any jeep with four men in it aroused suspicions. At least one man who spoke English well, usually a former merchant seaman, rode with each German team, and if forced to communicate with the Americans, he tried to do all the talking.

Of Skorzeny's three large task forces, only one got started on the original mission of seizing bridges over the Meuse. Attached to *Kampfgruppe Peiper*, the force took position well back in the column, and to Peiper's disgust, displayed no inclination to do what it was supposed to do: move out in advance and make a quick dash for the bridge at Huy. Since Peiper had no command authority over the task force, there was nothing he could do about it. Because the other two task forces were to accompany the 12th SS Panzer Division, what they did depended on the progress of that division.

On December 17, Skorzeny sent another of his disguised teams with Peiper and six others to penetrate the line on their own. All probably got through, but how much they accomplished was another matter.

One of the few to cause any confusion—and that minimal—reached a road junction atop the Hautes Fagnes known as Mont Rigi. By the time a convoy of the 1st Division's 16th Infantry arrived during the afternoon of December 17, the Germans had changed the road signs, so that the convoy took not the most direct route to its destination at the town of Waimes but a roundabout route through Malmédy. As American MPs arrived at Mont Rigi, the Germans jumped into their jeep and raced away. The misdirection added about an hour to the convoy's driving time.

Although there was considerable cutting of telephone lines, no serious disruption of telephone service developed. The difficulties experienced by the 99th and 106th Divisions happened before any of Skorzeny's men went into action, probably the work of patrols from the attacking divisions or of civilians.

The first team to be captured was that which accompanied *Kampfgruppe Peiper*. Only half an hour after the team moved ahead to operate on its own, a military policeman stopped the jeep. When the men were unable to give the password, the MP detained them, and discrepancies in their uniforms and what they had in their pockets gave them away. They wore neither leggings nor combat boots, and only one had a regulation U.S. Army belt. Whereas American soldiers used specially printed invasion currency, the men had dollars and pounds, and all carried the German soldier's personal document, the *Soldbuch*. The night before they were to be shot as spies, American authorities permitted captured German nurses in a nearby cell to sing Christmas carols for them.

Just before dark on December 18, engineers manning a roadblock on the highway leading into Malmédy from the Baugnez road junction saw a jeep approaching. In it were what appeared to be four American soldiers and two more on the hood. As the jeep neared the roadblock, one of the soldiers on the hood jumped off and ran toward the roadblock. "They're Krauts!" he yelled. "The men in that jeep are Krauts!" When those inside the jeep opened fire, the other man on the hood jumped off. As the driver of the jeep tried desperately to turn around in the road, the engineers returned the fire. They killed one man who tried to run, and the other three surrendered. They had been bringing two prisoners to what they thought to be German-held Malmédy.

Two teams claiming to have reached the Meuse returned to German lines after only twenty-four hours, having accomplished nothing more than a look around; and a third team was to come near the river on Christmas Eve but would not live to tell about it. Yet another team reached the Meuse at a bridge midway between Huy and Namur. When the driver of the jeep failed to produce a valid trip ticket, an MP at a checkpoint before the bridge arrested the four occupants. They turned out to be wearing Nazi armbands beneath their field jackets and there were German weapons and explosives in the jeep.

The leader, Lt. Günther Schulz, talked freely. He gave the objective of the offensive in considerable detail and catalogued the role of Skorzeny's brigade. A principal goal, he said, was to penetrate SHAEF headquarters to assassinate General Eisenhower and other senior officers. Skorzeny himself, and some fifty men, were to rendezvous in Paris at the Café de la Paix on the Place de l'Opéra and proceed from there to

Versailles. (Was Schulz the lieutenant who had advanced that scheme to Peiper?)

To Americans in the Counter-Intelligence Corps, Skorzeny's reputation lent credence to what Schulz had to say. Early the next morning, December 18, a disturbed colonel on the SHAEF staff brought the information to General Eisenhower. Although Eisenhower scoffed, he soon discerned that the less he cooperated with security arrangements, the more men the Counter-Intelligence Corps detailed for his protection. He finally agreed to move from his villa in St. Germain-en-Laye to a house close to the headquarters in Versailles and gradually accepted the heavy guards, constant changing of routes to and from the headquarters, and other minor inconveniences. An officer who bore a remarkable resemblance to Eisenhower, Lt. Col. Baldwin B. Smith, moved into the villa in St. Germain and took the Supreme Commander's usual route to and from the headquarters each day. In Paris, a detail staked out the Café de la Paix without results.

General Bradley, too, had to endure the concern of his staff for his safety. His personal plane moved from a nearby civilian airfield to a secure military base across the frontier in France, and no longer could he travel in a sedan. Instead he rode in a jeep without general's stars on the bumper and with escort jeeps equipped with machine guns ahead and behind. His staff also insisted on obscuring the stars on his helmet. At the urging of the security officers, he used the rear entrance of the Hôtel Alfa and finally consented to move from his room at the front of the hotel to one at the back.

That there were Germans roaming about in American uniforms led to increased security checks everywhere. Many a soldier, including senior officers, found it insufficient to know the day's password: He also had to answer queries on such Americana as state capitals, who was the current husband of film star Betty Grable (it was band leader Harry James), who were "dem Bums" (the Brooklyn Dodgers baseball team), and what was the name of President Roosevelt's dog (Fala). As Skorzeny himself was later to note, his men set off "a real spy mania in the American back areas," but it resulted in nothing more than minor inconveniences and had little or no effect on operations.

Skorzeny's concern that his men might be treated as spies turned out to be real, for the American command paid no heed to the nicety, as presumed by Skorzeny's legal advisers, that it was acceptable to wear the enemy's uniform as a *ruse de guerre* so long as you did not actually fight in it. Eighteen of Skorzeny's men were captured; eighteen were shot.

A last gasp by one of Skorzeny's teams occurred on Christmas Eve, when four men in a jeep crashed through a checkpoint established on the road leading to a bridge over the Meuse at Dinant by men of the British 3d Royal Tank Regiment. A short distance beyond the checkpoint, the jeep hit a necklace of mines the British had emplaced to be pulled across the road should a vehicle refuse to stop. For a moment there was immense concern, for all four occupants were blown to pieces and all wore American helmets and overcoats. Relief prevailed when the guards found the four were wearing German uniforms underneath.

Combat Command B, 9th Armored Division, William Hoge commanding, began leaving its assembly area near Faymonville for St. Vith to help the 106th Division at 2 A.M. on December 17, two hours before Joachim Peiper started his thrust from Lanzerath. Had the orders that Hoge originally received held—to move into the Losheim Gap—the combat command would have left Faymonville at daybreak and at some point would have bumped into *Kampfgruppe Peiper.*

Even as it was, a small portion of Hoge's command was destined to have a brush with Peiper, for at the town of Ligneuville, down a steep slope from the Baugnez road junction, there was an ad hoc force made up of the company kitchens and supply trucks and also Service Company of CCB's 14th Tank Battalion. The combat command had been engaged in a crash program to install grousers on the tracks of its armored vehicles to widen the tracks and improve footing on muddy ground. The work had been completed except for two Shermans and a 105mm. assault gun, which were unable to accompany the combat command because their tracks had been removed in preparation for installing the grousers. Also in Ligneuville was General Timberlake's headquarters of the 49th Anti-aircraft Artillery Brigade, situated in the Hôtel du Moulin, at a curve in the road near the northern edge of town.

Because General Timberlake was in touch by radio with one of his big 90mm. firing batteries near Bütgenbach, he learned fairly early in the morning of a breakthrough in the 99th Division's sector. He ordered his men to pack and be ready to leave Ligneuville at short notice and subsequently ordered departure right after the noonday meal.

When the noise of cannon and machine guns erupted somewhere to the north of Ligneuville, the commander of the ad hoc force, Capt. Seymour Green, set off in his jeep toward the Hôtel du Moulin in hope of getting a better fix on the location of the firing. He was parked beside the road when a tankdozer (a Sherman equipped with a bulldozer blade) came down the hill at breakneck speed. "German tanks!" shouted the driver. "Captain, I was shot at by German tanks!"

The tankdozer had been on loan to the 2d Division, was returning to the 14th Tank Battalion in Ligneuville, and had just passed the Baugnez road junction when Peiper's advance guard began shooting up Battery B's convoy. That sent the operator dashing for Ligneuville.

Passing word to the kitchen and supply trucks to get out of town, Captain Green and his driver headed uphill toward the sound of the firing, while General Timberlake and his staff rushed from the Hôtel du Moulin to make their getaway. At a sharp curve in the highway above

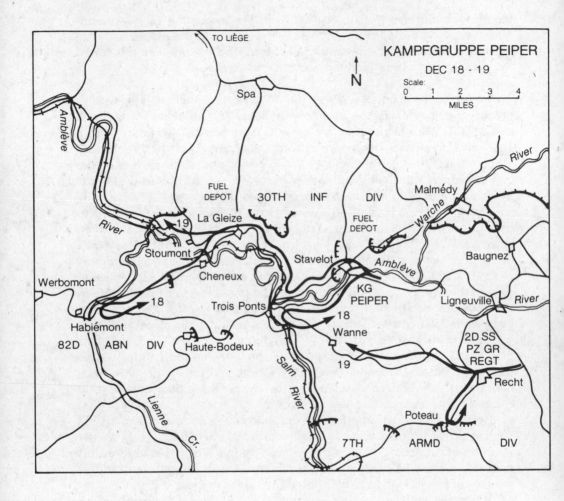

Ligneuville, Green told his driver to stop while he proceeded on foot. "If anything happens," he said, "go back."

As Green rounded the curve, he found himself practically face to face with a German tank. The sight so stunned him that he stood rooted to the spot. As the tank approached, Green threw away his carbine and raised his hands in surrender.

Continuing down the hill, the German column was in full sight of men of the 14th Tank Battalion's Service Company, who were working on the two Shermans and the assault gun on a hill overlooking the highway. The tankdozer joined them there, and when the first German tank appeared—a Panther commanded by Peiper's adjutant, 1st Lt. Arndt Fischer—a round from the 76mm. gun on the tankdozer sent it up in flames. As the driver of Peiper's half-track drove to cover behind a house, Peiper jumped down and helped bandage Lieutenant Fischer, who was badly burned.

Angered at the loss of an officer whom he considered a personal friend, Peiper grabbed a *Panzerfaust* and set out to destroy the American tank, but a round from a German tank knocked the tankdozer out before Peiper got to it. The German tanks also knocked out the immobile Shermans and the assault gun, but the encounter prompted Peiper to delay while he sent *SS-Panzergrenadiers* to clear the town. Peiper himself entered the Hôtel du Moulin, where he spent a half hour helping himself to food left behind by General Timberlake and his staff.

Peiper's goal at that point was to get onto a road just beyond Ligneuville that led west to the town of Stavelot. Although that would represent another encroachment on the 12th SS Panzer Division's assigned route, the road, however poor, was better than one assigned him farther south, and even though Peiper had lost radio contact with headquarters of his division, he assumed from the lack of noise of battle in Malmédy that the other division was still far behind. After Stavelot, he would return to his assigned route at Trois Ponts, so named from three bridges in and near the town at the juncture of the Amblève and Salm Rivers. From there he would proceed to Werbomont on the north-south Bastogne-Liège highway, which would put him past the worst of the Ardennes terrain and provide fairly easy going to the Meuse at Huy, only twenty-five miles beyond Werbomont.

Peiper himself had gone on his way when a Belgian farmer's wife, Mme. Marie Lochem, who was in her barn tending her cows, looked out to see just over twenty American soldiers marching up the street. A German sergeant, Paul Ochmann, culled eight of them to dig graves for three dead Germans. Once they had finished, Ochmann lined them up in a row. As Madame Lochem watched in horror, the sergeant shot one of the prisoners in the head, then another, and another, until all eight lay prone on the ground.

Seven of the men were dead, but the eighth, Cpl. Joseph P. Mass, received only a grazing wound. Throughout the rest of the afternoon he pretended to be dead. As it got dark, he crawled to a clump of trees, where in time a Belgian man brought him food and pointed the direction to St. Vith; but in trying to get there, Mass lost his way and was captured again.

From a window in the Hôtel du Moulin, the proprietor, sixty-nine-year-old Peter Rupp, a German by birth but a Belgian by loyalty, witnessed the executions and feared for the lives of fourteen other Americans held in the hotel, among them Captain Green. As Ochmann entered the hotel, Rupp confronted him. "Murderer!" he shouted. "You killed eight of them! I saw you put the pistol in their mouths!" The German sergeant hit Rupp in the jaw with his fist, knocking out two of his teeth.

A watching SS officer told Ochmann to kill all the prisoners and the old Belgian as well, and Ochmann was on the point of herding the prisoners out of the hotel when another officer countermanded the order. Immensely relieved, Rupp was nevertheless concerned that somebody else might do the prisoners in. Going down to the cellar, he came back with bottles of wine and cognac, which he passed to the German soldiers. In a short while, the prisoners were all but forgotten.

David Edward Pergrin studied civil engineering at Pennsylvania State College and at the same time earned a U.S. Army commission through the ROTC. Not quite six feet tall, he was broad-shouldered, solidly built (he played football at Penn State), and wore glasses. As a lieutenant colonel at the age of twenty-five, he took the 291st Engineer Combat Battalion overseas, where in England it became part of the 1111th Engineer Combat Group, commanded by a veteran of World War I, Col. H. Wallis Anderson, then led it on a variety of engineering tasks through the Normandy hedgerows and on into the Ardennes. Casualties had been remarkably light; one man lost both legs to a mine, but nobody had been killed.

As winter approached, the group commander, Colonel Anderson, assigned one of his three battalions the task of operating sawmills to provide timber for squad huts and other amenities at the front. Another drew the job of building and maintaining roads close behind the front just north of the Losheim Gap, while the third, Pergrin's 291st, served as security for Anderson's headquarters but at the same time operated some sawmills and did road maintenance as required. It was not without intention that the battalions of the 1111th Engineer Combat Group were deployed so as to provide a screening force for the First Army's headquarters town of Spa.

As befitted the role of security for group headquarters, Pergrin's battalion was closest to Anderson's command post in Trois Ponts. Pergrin's own headquarters was just up the hill to the west in the village of Haute-Bodeux. One company was farther west, at Werbomont. A second was billeted in one of the more imposing buildings in the Ardennes, the Château de Froid-Cour (built early in the twentieth century but in the style of a medieval castle), just outside the village of La Gleize, overlooking the scenic valley of the meandering Amblève River. The third was in Malmédy. The three companies of the 291st Engineers were thus either astride or near the central leg of the route that Peiper wanted to take in his quest to reach the Meuse River.

That line-up was destined to remain much the same despite the fact that on December 16, Company A, under Capt. James H. Gamble, began to move from Werbomont closer to the front, assigned to follow the advance of the 9th Armored Division's CCB to remove any demolitions the Germans might have implanted in the Roer River dams. One platoon was already forward, operating sawmills in the villages of Montenau and

Born, midway between Malmédy and St. Vith. Although Captain Gamble hoped to billet the rest of his company in Born, the place was so bulging with support troops of the 106th Division that he continued a few miles on to the village of Amblève, near the headwaters of the little river behind the Losheim Gap. There he found space for his command post in the schoolhouse and billets for his men in houses and barns close by.

Gamble and his men had passed from the French-speaking part of Belgium into the German-speaking part, and they disliked it. "The people of the village watched them unload in a silence as chill and gray as the stone houses." The atmosphere seemed heavy with a sense of foreboding, and there were rumors of a German breakthrough somewhere along the front.

The feeling of uneasiness spread that night through many of the men of the 291st Engineer Combat Battalion. Indeed, the day had begun with an unusual occurrence, four shells from big German railroad guns falling in Malmédy. Then, during the night, the telephone line between the battalion headquarters and the group headquarters went out, which was highly unusual that far behind the front; and when troubleshooters found the break, it was obvious that somebody had cut the line. A short while later, group headquarters passed along an alert disseminated by headquarters of the First Army to watch for German paratroopers. Through much of the night at Amblève, the guard on duty outside Captain Gamble's command post heard heavy traffic on the main road through the town. Had he left his post to check, he would have found vehicles of the 14th Cavalry Group pulling back from the Losheim Gap.

The coming of daylight brought considerably more concern. A platoon of Company B, leaving Malmédy to work on the road leading from the Baugnez junction east toward Bütgenbach, found a steady stream of American vehicles heading west, jeeps and trucks from rear echelon supply units, but also some artillery pieces and big antiaircraft guns. When the platoon leader, 1st Lt. Frank W. Rhea, Jr., arrived in his jeep to check on the platoon's work, the heavy traffic so disturbed him that he drove on in the direction of Bütgenbach to determine what was happening.

Rhea got as far as a road junction just short of Bütgenbach. From there he could hear the sound of small-arms and artillery fire and could see American fighter-bombers attacking some target out of sight beyond the hills. "What's going on here?" Rhea asked an MP on duty at the intersection. All hell had erupted before daylight, said the MP, and the Germans had broken through the 99th Division's lines.

Rhea hurried back to alert his company commander. On the way, he told his men to drop their roadwork and return to Malmédy. As the men passed the road junction at Baugnez, the town in the valley below them looked "like a giant anthill somebody had stirred with a stick." Vehicles were pouring in on two sides and out the other two.

*   *   *

In Amblève that morning, the man on radio duty in Company A's command post, Cpl. Albert C. Schommer, pulled back the blackout curtains and looked outside. Military vehicles of virtually every description were streaming through the village, and not far to the north Schommer could see American planes attacking. He called for 1st Sgt. William H. Smith to take a look.

Smith was so concerned that he jumped into a weapons carrier and drove off to see what he could find out. He returned around ten thirty to report to his company commander, Captain Gamble: "A whole column of German tanks [is] up there, headed in this direction. If we don't get out of here fast, we're not going to get out at all!" (Smith had seen *Kampfgruppe Peiper* on its way to Möderscheid, only a mile and a half from Amblève, and had no way of knowing that at Möderscheid, Peiper was to swing west away from Amblève.)

Although Gamble had no authority to pull back, the choice appeared to be between pulling back and being overrun. He made his decision, telling Sergeant Smith to have the men siphon gasoline from the equipment vehicles so there would be enough for those carrying troops, but he was relieved when a message arrived from Colonel Pergrin: Pull back to Werbomont.

The men were having some difficulty taking down a radio antenna installed on the roof of the schoolhouse when one of them raised a pair of binoculars. He let out a yell. At a road junction not over a mile to the southeast, there were several half-tracks, German soldiers milling about, and what looked to be three German tanks. The man had spotted not *Kampfgruppe Peiper* but one of the 1st SS Panzer Division's other columns. Whoever it was, it speeded Company A's withdrawal.

As the column stopped in Montenau to pick up the platoon operating a sawmill there, Captain Gamble learned that the platoon was desperate for gasoline. The platoon leader, 1st Lt. Archibald L. Taylor, had sent two men in a 6×6 to Malmédy to get more, but they had come back on foot telling of having been shot up by German tanks and their truck overturned alongside a railroad embankment near the village of Ondenval.

Company A, 291st Engineers, made it out, but barely. As Lieutenant Taylor's platoon, bringing up the rear, left Montenau, Germans of the 1st SS Panzer Division were coming in the other side; and as Company A tried to turn west, the little convoy ran into one of the most stifling traffic jams to beset the U.S. Army during the course of the war in Europe. Men of the 7th Armored Division with their tanks, half-tracks, trucks, and artillery were trying to get into St. Vith, and a lot of other people in their vehicles and some with their big guns were trying to get out. Only by using forest trails and logging roads was Company A able to bypass the traffic jam and make its way (albeit slowly) toward the west and in late evening of December 17 reoccupy its old billets in Werbomont.

*   *   *

When Lieutenant Rhea of Company B, 291st Engineers, returned to Malmédy from his reconnaissance toward Bütgenbach, he reported to his company commander, Capt. John T. Conlin, what he had learned. Conlin promptly telephoned Colonel Pergrin at his headquarters in Haute-Bodeux. Pergrin told him to begin setting up blocks on the roads leading into Malmédy, and he and his staff headed for the town. Although Malmédy was only thirteen miles away, it took forty-five minutes for Pergrin to get there, for almost all the way he was bucking the traffic of the march column of the 7th Armored Division that was heading for St. Vith by way of Trois Ponts.

When Pergrin did reach Malmédy, it was what Lieutenant Rhea had learned of the breakthrough near Bütgenbach that prompted him to warn Battery B, 285th Field Artillery Observation Battalion. Less than an hour after his unheeded warning, another convoy entered Malmédy: that of the 7th Armored Division's artillery. Convinced that the Germans were aiming for Malmédy, since as a road center it was an obvious military objective, Pergrin tried to talk the commander of the artillery's convoy into staying to provide support for the defense of the town; but the officer in charge insisted that his orders were to go to St. Vith, and he was not about to disobey orders.

The vehicles of one of the artillery battalions managed to inch through the congested streets to get onto the road to Stavelot and Trois Ponts, but it proved such a mammoth task that the convoy commander turned the rest of the vehicles around to go back to Eupen and from there get onto the march route. The delay thus imposed was destined to come close the next morning to bringing the 7th Armored Division's artillery into direct confrontation with *Kampfgruppe Peiper*.

As the artillery convoy pulled back from Malmédy, something akin to pandemonium was enveloping the town. An evacuation hospital, a replacement depot, quartermaster units, ordnance units, all began to pull out. Their vehicles added to the congestion already brought about by vehicles of withdrawing units passing through the town. Civilians joined the exodus with bicycles, pushcarts, wheelbarrows, children's wagons, anything in which to transport a few pitiful belongings.

If Colonel Pergrin was to have any hope of keeping the Germans out of Malmédy—indeed, of even delaying them appreciably—he had to have more than the 180 men of Company B and his headquarters, and the only sure way to get help was to call on the rest of his battalion. At that point he had no way of knowing where Captain Gamble's Company A was located in the course of withdrawing from Amblève, but he still had Company C in the Château de Froide-Cour at La Gleize. He promptly ordered that company to Malmédy, stressing that in the process the company was to drop off a squad to establish a roadblock at Trois Ponts and another at Stavelot. If the Germans took either town, they would cut off Malmédy from the west; and if they gained Stavelot, they would be only a short distance from the First Army's headquarters at Spa and even closer to a mammoth gasoline depot along a secondary road leading north from Stavelot to Spa.

That order dispatched, Pergrin made his reconnaissance toward the Baugnez road junction, in the course of which he picked up Ahrens, Sciranko, and Valenzi, and learned of the massacre at the road junction and something of the size of the German column. Unknown at first to Pergrin, the message he sent the First Army's headquarters telling of the massacre and the German column started a limited number of reinforcements heading for Malmédy. For again, if Malmédy should fall, the Germans would have access to roads over which to probe deep into the First Army's rear, not only to Spa but to Liège with its big supply installations.

The only troops at General Hodges's immediate disposal for reinforcing Malmédy quickly had been serving as a kind of palace guard for the First Army's headquarters. They consisted of two separate (nondivisional) infantry units—the 526th Armored Infantry Battalion and the 99th Infantry Battalion, the latter made up of Norwegian Americans and Norwegian citizens (escapees from occupied Norway, merchant seamen stranded in the United States after their vessels were lost) all of whom had volunteered to serve in the U.S. Army. He also had at hand a company of towed 3-inch guns of the 825th Tank Destroyer Battalion. Those three units were soon on their way to Malmédy, and upon arrival all were to come under the commander of the 99th Infantry Battalion, himself a Norwegian American, Lt. Col. Harold D. Hansen.

Early on the afternoon of December 17, a Belgian customs officer, twenty-six-year-old Nicolas Schugens, left by bicycle from the village of Wanne, just south of Stavelot, where he had been living temporarily, to go to a new customs assignment at the border point of Steinebrück. As he left Wanne, the local youths were getting ready for a football match with men of the Royal Air Force who manned a nearby radar post. Cycling through that part of Stavelot on the south bank of the Amblève River, he could see beyond a stone bridge over the stream into the main part of town, where American soldiers were strolling, some with Belgian girls in their Sunday best on their arms.

Near the bridge, Schugens turned south and began to pedal up a steep hill along a narrow, twisting road leading to Ligneuville. He had gone about two miles when he came upon an old man, who shouted that German tanks were coming. "Go to the devil," responded Schugens; "you're crazy." Not long afterwards, he came upon a *garde-champêtre* (rural policeman), who in considerable excitement told him the same thing. Again Schugens said he was crazy and continued on his way, but not without some wariness.

A short while later, Schugens stopped to listen. Was that the rumble of tanks? It seemed incredible. But then came the unmistakable sound of machine guns firing.

That was enough for Schugens. Turning his bicycle around, he took a short cut over a forest trail to Wanne. Because Schugens was in the customs service, he had avoided being drafted into the German Army when the Germans came in 1940, but he was not about to risk it again. Hurrying to his house, he gathered a few possessions and took off again on his bicycle, headed west, he knew not where.

As he left, he told the young men playing football that German tanks were coming. They said he was crazy and went on with their match.

Sgt. Charles Hensel commanded the twelve-man squad (plus a truck driver) from Company C, 291st Engineer Combat Battalion, that the company commander had designated to establish a roadblock at Stavelot. It was completely dark—around 6:30 P.M.—when Hensel and his men got there. Surprised to find great numbers of trucks, their headlights blazing, milling around the town (supply troops billeted there were pulling out), Hensel and his men crossed the bridge over the Amblève and began the steep ascent beyond, where Nicolas Schugens had passed on his bicycle just a few hours earlier. For a short distance there was a line of houses on the left of the road, but they ran out where the ground dropped off sharply toward the deep valley of the Amblève below.

Hensel stopped the truck at a sharp bend in the road, such a sharp bend that any vehicle would have had to slow down to negotiate it. A rocky escarpment bordered one side, and on the other, the drop to the valley of the Amblève was precipitous. Hensel put his men to work installing mines: They had no concern for American vehicles, for the word they had was that anything that came down the road would be German. Hensel placed a bazooka team just down the road from the mines, while one man, Pvt. Bernard Goldstein, went beyond the bend in the road to a small stone shed to serve as a lookout.

Goldstein had been there only a few minutes when he heard tracked vehicles approaching, obviously tanks inching their way slowly along in the darkness, and he could hear men speaking German. The tanks were only a few yards away when Goldstein stepped out into the road, his M-1 rifle at the ready. "Halt!" he commanded.

On the way up to Goldstein's position to guide a companion for Goldstein, Sergeant Hensel heard the incredible command. As paratroopers jumped off the tank and opened fire with rifles and burp guns, Hensel and the man with him dropped to the ground and fired a few rounds from their rifles; but when the tank opened up with its machine gun, they scurried back around the bend in the road. Goldstein clambered up the rocky hill to the west, while the bazooka team fired a rocket that by sheer luck damaged the German tank.

Hensel and his men waited at the roadblock for twenty minutes, but the Germans made no effort to continue. Although several men tried to get forward to look for Goldstein, German fire turned them back. When Hensel heard the tanks backing up the hill, he told everybody to mount the truck, and to prevent the Germans from realizing that he and his men were leaving, the truck coasted down the road to the bridge over the Amblève. Hensel intended making his stand there.

Incredibly, there was to be no need for a fight at the bridge right away. Bone-weary, the venturesome Joachim Peiper had ceased to be his usual volatile self. Had there been no delay in Ligneuville, Peiper would have reached the heights overlooking Stavelot before it got too dark for him to discern that the vehicles in the town were not moving in but pulling out. So, too, there would have been no roadblock manned by a handful of engineers at the canalized stretch of road above the town to add to the impression that Stavelot would be staunchly defended. As it was, Peiper assumed he was in for a fight, and before it started, he needed to give his men some rest. They had been on the road three days and nights almost without pause.

The delay afforded American commanders a few hours to do something about defending Stavelot. It also enabled the 7th Armored Division's artillery convoy to thread its way through the town and on to Trois Ponts and St. Vith.

When Sergeant Hensel and his men reached the bridge at Stavelot, a platoon of engineers was preparing it for demolition. It was probably a platoon of a company of the 202d Engineer Combat Battalion, which had recently arrived from the Third Army and, while resting, was attached temporarily to the 1111th Engineer Combat Group. With that platoon on hand and apparently in charge, Hensel decided to rejoin his own platoon in Trois Ponts.

The intrepid Private Goldstein found his way to the bridge around midnight, but the lieutenant in charge of the engineers sent him with another man as an outpost. The two ran into Germans in the last houses of the town. The other man was mortally wounded, and Goldstein took three bullets in his right hip and leg but eventually crawled back to the bridge.

Soon after midnight, the engineers attempted to blow the bridge, but the charges failed to go off. What they did not know was that among their midst were two of Skorzeny's men disguised as Americans who had done something to sabotage the attempt. (A patrol from a company of the 5th Belgian Fusilier Battalion, which was responsible for guarding the gasoline depot north of Stavelot, had become suspicious of those two men earlier in the evening; but since the Americans appeared to accept them without any concern, the Belgians said nothing.)

In the meantime, when the commander of the Norwegian battalion, Colonel Hansen, reached Malmédy, he agreed with Colonel Pergrin that even though Malmédy appeared to be the German objective, reinforcements should be sent to help the squad of engineers in Stavelot. They got a message to the 526th Armored Infantry Battalion to drop off a company there along with a platoon of towed tank destroyers; and around three o'clock on the morning of December 18, that little force, commanded by the 526th's executive officer, Maj. Paul J. Solis, moved into Stavelot.

Major Solis delayed another attempt to blow the bridge, for he intended putting a roadblock on the other side of the river. Two squads of infantry, a 57mm. antitank gun, and two towed tank destroyers were making their way up the steep hill beyond the Amblève when, shortly before daybreak, *Kampfgruppe Peiper*'s mortars and assault guns opened a preparation fire for the delayed attack on Stavelot. That fire prompted the men to fall back; but as the trucks towing the antitank pieces tried to turn around, direct fire from German tanks farther up the hill knocked out the towed tank destroyers and the trucks. The men who survived hurried back across the bridge.

As German paratroopers headed down the road for the bridge, three of Major Solis's 57mm. antitank guns sprayed the bridge and the approach with canister. The paratroopers took cover in houses near the bridge to await arrival of German tanks.

By that time the light was sufficient for the gunners of two remaining towed tank destroyers, commanded respectively by Sgts. Martin Hauser and Louis Calentano, and emplaced atop a knoll along the road from Malmédy, to make out German tanks descending the steep hill on the other side of the river. Each of the tank destroyers knocked out two German tanks, but other tanks made it to the bridge, where the 57mm. antitank guns were no match for them. Paratroopers and *SS-Panzergrenadiers* soon followed the tanks across the bridge.

At that point, the last vehicles of the 7th Armored Division's artillery convoy were passing through the town—antiaircraft half-tracks with quad-50 machine guns. They paused to give the American infantry a hand but soon pulled out to continue their march by way of Trois Ponts for St. Vith. So, too, the company of the 202d Engineers that had been resting in the town did a yeoman job of fighting for a while, but like the half-tracks, had no real commitment to defending the town and soon pulled out.

So overwhelming were the odds against Solis's lone armored infantry company that at 8 A.M., Solis ordered withdrawal. Most men and the two tank destroyers fell back along the road to Malmédy, but Solis himself, in a half-track, withdrew along the road to Spa. After a delay of more than twelve hours, much of it self-imposed, Peiper had his passage through Stavelot.

Equipped with British uniforms and weapons, the 5th Fusilier Battalion was the first unit of the Belgian Army to be formed after the country's liberation, drawn in large measure from men who had fought in the underground resistance. In early December, the battalion was attached to the First Army to be used primarily for guarding supply installations. One of the tasks assigned the 3d Company under Capt. Jean Burniat was to guard the American gasoline depot, which contained almost a million gallons, on the Stavelot-Spa road. The gasoline was in 5-gallon Jerricans stacked alongside the road, mostly just inside a forest, but some of it on open ground between the forest and the first houses of Stavelot.

As Solis approached the first stacks of Jerricans in his half-track, Lieutenant Detroz of the Belgian Army beckoned him. He and his platoon were the guards—and only defenders—of the depot, and Detroz was convinced that the Germans would soon go for the gasoline. Since the ground on one side of the road rose sharply and on the other dropped off sharply, Detroz suggested piling Jerricans across the road and setting the gasoline on fire. The Belgians and the men with Solis were soon secure behind a great wall of flame.

Although Colonel Peiper had no knowledge of that gasoline depot, a German flank patrol consisting of a few tanks and half-tracks, possibly attracted by the great clouds of smoke, climbed the road from Stavelot. The tanks tried to maneuver past the roadblock, but the sharply sloping ground, as Lieutenant Detroz had figured, prevented it. The patrol turned back.

Peiper's delay in front of Stavelot had afforded time for Colonel Anderson of the 1111th Engineer Combat Group to prepare a defense of what looked to be the next town on the route of the German armored column—his own headquarters town of Trois Ponts. As Anderson pulled his headquarters back, he left defense of Trois Ponts in the hands of his executive officer, Maj. Robert B. Yates. Around midnight on the 17th, Company C, 51st Engineer Combat Battalion, arrived and began preparing the two bridges in the town for demolition while a platoon of the 291st Engineers did the same at a bridge farther south. The engineers were aided by a 57mm. antitank gun of the 526th Armored Infantry Battalion and its crew when a half-track towing the gun threw a tread and had to fall out of the battalion's convoy.

Just before the highway from Stavelot reached Trois Ponts, it curved to the right to run through two railroad underpasses. At the exit of the second, the road came to a dead end before the Amblève River: There one either turned left to enter Trois Ponts over two of the three bridges that gave the town its name or right to follow the trace of the Amblève. Peiper wanted to turn left to pass through Trois Ponts and continue beyond to Werbomont.

By the time the leading tanks of *Kampfgruppe Peiper* moved out of Stavelot, the engineers at Trois Ponts had prepared their bridges for demolition, the two over the Amblève and Salm Rivers in Trois Ponts and the

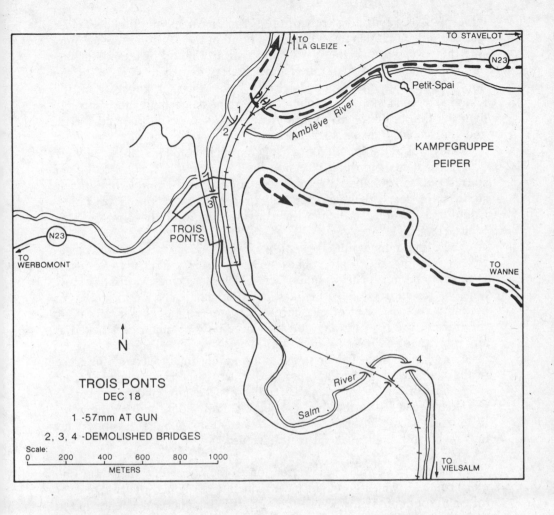

TROIS PONTS
DEC 18

1 -57mm AT GUN

2, 3, 4 -DEMOLISHED BRIDGES

Scale:
0   200   400   600   800   1000
METERS

third over the Salm River a mile south of the town as well, for by an unlikely but possible roundabout route, the third bridge might also provide access to the town. There was no time to prepare the two railroad underpasses for demolition; instead, a four-man crew—Buchanan, Higgins, Hollenbeck, and McCollum—positioned the 57mm. antitank gun on the road between the second underpass and the first bridge. When the leading German vehicle poked its nose beyond the second underpass, the crew was to fire, thereby providing time for the engineers to blow the two bridges. The men were aware that theirs was virtually a suicide mission. When somebody remarked that they had only seven rounds of ammunition, they said that if they failed to accomplish their mission with those seven rounds, they would have no need for any more.

It was just after eleven o'clock on December 18 when the lead vehicle of *Kampfgruppe Peiper*, a Panther, emerged cautiously from the second underpass. The four-man crew of the 57mm. antitank gun fired. So close was the range that there was little likelihood of their missing, but so puny was their weapon that there was also little likelihood of their knocking out a Panther. That first round nevertheless damaged a track on the tank—but not its 75mm. gun. With one round the tank knocked out the 57mm. piece and killed all four of the crew, but behind those intrepid men the first bridge went up in a great blast of dust, debris, and sound, and the second went up soon after.

There was at that point no way Joachim Peiper and his tanks could get into Trois Ponts from that direction, and for the first time since Peiper started out on his remarkable trek, despair engulfed him. No one understood more clearly than he how badly he needed to get into Trois Ponts. Could he have done so, Peiper was convinced he would have reached the Meuse that night.

Yet at that point a little rock-strewn river defied him. No major obstacle for infantry, the Amblève has such steep banks that it is an insurmountable barrier for tanks and other vehicles. If Peiper was to have any hope of reaching the Meuse, he somehow had to find another way of getting across the river or else face a serpentine, circuitous route along the trace of the river through terrain where passage might be blocked at any number of points.

Consulting a map, Peiper saw that along that road following the trace of the Amblève there was another bridge across the river, downhill from the village of La Gleize near the hamlet of Cheneux; and from there a secondary road led to the road connecting Trois Ponts and Werbomont. If he could seize that bridge—and if it was sturdy enough to support his tanks—he still might make it to the Meuse.

Although Peiper paid scant attention to the possibility, there was one more route by which he might have gained Trois Ponts: the bridge over the Salm south of the town. The job of destroying that bridge belonged to a platoon of Company A, 291st Engineers.

When Peiper began the attack early that morning, the 18th, he had been obsessed with the thought that he faced a major fight to get through Stavelot. In search of an alternate route, he sent a company of Mark IVs along a dirt road leading down the left bank of the Amblève to the village of Wanne (site of the football match the previous afternoon between locals and men of the RAF) and thence to Trois Ponts by way of the railroad station on high ground overlooking the town. Should Peiper be delayed further at Stavelot, those tanks still might secure passage at Trois Ponts.

As it turned out, the hope was vain, for by the time the Mark IVs reached the railroad station, Peiper's main column was approaching and the two bridges in Trois Ponts were already down. On the other hand, if the tanks gained the bridge over the Salm south of Trois Ponts, vehicles might follow a road from Wanne to that bridge and so enter Trois Ponts through the back door.

From a hiding place near the bridge, the noncommissioned officer in charge of the company of 291st Engineers, Sgt. Jean B. Miller, watched as the Mark IVs reached the railroad station. Since Miller had heard the blasts of the two bridges going up in Trois Ponts, he felt sure the Germans would make a try for his bridge. He had not long to wait.

Miller and his men watched from concealed positions as paratroopers who had ridden the tanks moved cross-country downhill toward the bridge. The Germans approached warily, while Miller waited with one hand on the key to the detonator. Some of the Germans began removing the mines that the engineers had implanted in the road in front of the bridge, while others examined the bridge for demolitions.

Still Miller waited. Some of his men, watching breathlessly from their hiding places, wondered what was wrong with their sergeant. It was only when several of the Germans were on the bridge and walking across that Miller finally turned the key. The bridge went up with a thunderous roar, taking several of the paratroopers with it. At that point there was no way for Peiper to get into Trois Ponts.

It was with considerable relief that Peiper learned soon after midday that his advance guard had found the bridge across the Amblève at Cheneux intact and strong enough to support his tanks. That would enable him to get out of the tortuous valley of the Amblève and back en route for the Meuse by way of Werbomont.

Yet he was reckoning once again without the seemingly ubiquitous American engineers.

When news that the German armored column had passed through Stavelot reached headquarters of the First Army, the commander of the IX Tactical Air Command, General Quesada, whose headquarters was in nearby Verviers, telephoned the commander of the 67th Tactical Reconnaissance Group, Col. George W. Peck. He wanted volunteers, said Quesada, to try to break through the low cloud cover and locate the German column. Two pilots, Capt. Richard Cassady and 2d Lt. Abraham Jaffe, were soon in the air in F-6 reconnaissance aircraft.

Since the Germans were obviously moving in or near the valley of the Amblève, Cassady and Jaffe concentrated their search there. To get under the cloud cover, they sometimes had to fly less than a hundred feet off the ground. Then suddenly both pilots spotted what they were after: a column of tanks and other vehicles stretching from La Gleize seemingly all the way back to and beyond Stavelot. To pin down the exact location, they made three runs over the column, and only during the last did the Germans recover enough from their surprise to fire at the planes.

Cassady and Jaffe promptly radioed the IX Tactical Air Command of their find, and Quesada ordered fighter-bombers of the 365th and 368th Fighter Groups to attack. In four-plane flights, sixteen P-47 Thunderbolts roared in, first making a bomb run with 500-pound bombs, then returning to strafe. Some planes worked the column as far back as Stavelot, there shooting up ten German tanks that appeared to be attacking the town.

For most of the German troops, it was an unaccustomed, terrifying experience, since even those with long service on the Russian front had seldom been exposed to attack from the air. Yet losses were few: only some of the smaller vehicles knocked out, a few men killed, a few wounded.

The attack seemingly at an end, the vehicles pulled out of their hiding places and resumed the march. The head of the column was across the bridge over the Amblève and entering Cheneux when sixteen more Thunderbolts broke through the low cover. Near the bridge two half-tracks went up in flames, many of the men in them killed or wounded, and a 500-pound bomb hit the front of a farmhouse, disabling a Panther that was passing on the road. The explosion also blew up a command car and the officers in it.

Peiper's flak tanks with their 37mm. guns and flak wagons with 20mm. pieces fought back, scoring hits on three planes and sending one careening out of control. The gunners could see it disappear over the wooded hills to the north, leaving behind a thick trail of smoke.

The American pilots, as usual, overestimated the damage they did, claiming thirty-two armored vehicles destroyed, which was a vast exaggeration. Peiper actually lost only a few half-tracks and lesser vehicles and the lone Panther at Cheneux. What was of greater importance to both sides was the delay imposed by the attack. The American planes were at it for the better part of two hours, and even after they went away, it took time to get the disabled Panther off the road at Cheneux so that the column could get moving again.

The American pilots had bought almost two and a half hours for men of Captain Gamble's Company A, 291st Engineers. It was time that the engineers needed badly.

Many years before, Wally Anderson as a lieutenant had pondered the moves of Pancho Villa along the Mexican border. As commander of the 1111th Engineer Combat Group, Colonel Anderson pondered the moves of Joachim Peiper. Like Peiper, he consulted a map. Where was the German column headed? Since the Germans had tried to get into Trois Ponts, they obviously intended to move westward along the road to Werbomont. Relegated at that point to the serpentine valley of the Amblève, the Germans, Anderson deduced, would seize the first opportunity to get out of the valley and back onto the Werbomont road.

Aware that the bridge over the Amblève near Cheneux could accommodate tanks, Anderson reasoned that the Germans would use it to gain egress from the valley, but it was too late to hope to destroy that bridge. Yet if the Germans used the bridge at Cheneux to get back onto the road to Werbomont, they would also have to cross another bridge on the way to Werbomont over the Lienne Creek near the hamlet of Habiémont. Although the Lienne is smaller even than the Amblève, it too is deeply incised and forms an effective barrier for vehicles, including tanks.

Colonel Anderson promptly radioed headquarters of Company A, 291st Engineer Combat Battalion, in Werbomont. Captain Gamble was to send a detail immediately to prepare the bridge over the Lienne for destruction.

Other than the men of the company headquarters, there were only about fifteen of Company A's engineers left in Werbomont; the rest were either at Trois Ponts or Malmédy or out hunting German paratroopers. A platoon sergeant, Staff Sgt. Edwin Pigg, assembled those men left and the necessary wire and TNT and loaded all onto the only available truck, one that had burned out its valves on the hurried trip back from Amblève the day before and could go no faster than ten miles an hour.

Because the truck moved so slowly, Sergeant Pigg and his detail did not reach Habiémont and the bridge over the Lienne until 3 P.M. An hour later they were busy wiring the bridge when a small convoy approached carrying Colonel Anderson and men of the group headquarters and those whom Colonel Pergrin had left behind in his headquarters in Haute-Bodeux. The First Army's engineer officer had ordered Anderson to fall back.

All the way from Trois Ponts the vehicles of that convoy had passed civilian refugees trudging along with little bundles of possessions. At one point, as the convoy was forced to slow down, someone knocked on the side of a command car in which Tech. Sgt. John L. Scanlan and another soldier were riding. It was an old man and an old woman. "Please, Monsieur," the man pleaded, "take us with you. We are Jewish. We lived through the Nazi occupation but we cannot stand any more." The two men shifted to one side of the seat and helped the old couple in.

Had it not been for the bombing by American planes, neither the old couple nor anyone else in that convoy would have escaped. The last vehicle passed the point where the road from Cheneux joined the Trois Ponts–Werbomont road no more than a half hour before Peiper's leading tank got there.

At just about the same time, the little band of Company A's engineers completed wiring the bridge near Habiémont. By that time they had a new commander, one of the company's officers, 1st Lt. Alvin Edelstein, who had arrived with Colonel Anderson's convoy. Although it was rapidly growing dark, the man charged with turning the detonator key, Cpl. Fred Chapin, could make out the first German tank as it rounded a curve not more than two hundred yards away. Others were close behind.

Seeing the Americans near the bridge, the gunner of the first tank opened fire. Although the round did no damage, it prompted Chapin to duck, and when he looked up, he was unable to spot Lieutenant Edelstein, who was to give the signal to blow the bridge.

When he finally saw him, the lieutenant was waving wildly as if to say Blow it! Blow it! Chapin turned the key and saw a "streak of blue lights, the heaving blast of dust and debris, and knew he had a good blow."

Joachim Peiper reputedly pounded one knee with his fist in sheer frustration and muttered: "The damned engineers! The damned engineers!"

Dwight D. Eisenhower, Omar N. Bradley, George S. Patton, Jr., in Bastogne

Bernard L. Montgomery

Courtney H. Hodges

The Enigma machine

Kenneth Strong

Edwin L. Sibert

E. T. Williams

**THE
INTELLIGENCE
CHIEFS**

Benjamin A. Dickson

Oscar Koch

William H. Simpson

Troy H. Middleton

Leonard T. Gerow

J. Lawton Collins

Hoyt S. Vandenberg

Pete Quesada

Panther tank (Mark V)

Sherman tank (M-4)

Walter M. Robertson

Walter E. Lauer

Alan W. Jones

Norman D. Cota

Raymond O. Barton

Robert W. Hasbrouck

Adolf Hitler

Alfred Jodl

Gerd von Rundstedt

Walter Model

Joseph Sepp Dietrich

Hasso von Manteuffel

Nebelwerfer

Antiaircraft half-track

Captured Tiger tank (Mark VI)

Erich Brandenberger

Hermann Priess

Walter Krüger

Heinrich von Lüttwitz

Friedrich von der Heydte

Otto Skorzeny

Joachim Peiper

Henri Lejoly

Victims at Baugnez

Lyle Bouck, Jr.

Long H. Goffigon

William D. McKinley

Derrill M. Daniel

David E. Pergrin

Marlene Dietrich

Bruce C. Clarke

Hurley E. Fuller

Elise Delé

Renée Lemaire

Wilhelm Osterhold

Karl Wortmann

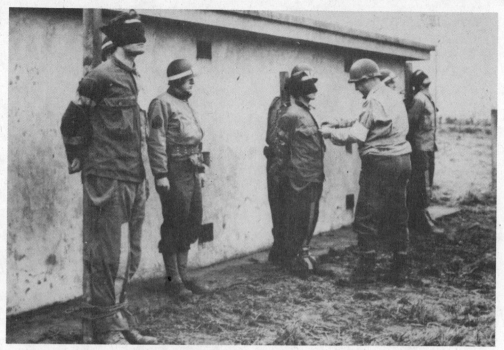

Preparing to execute prisoners of Skorzeny's Brigade

Gasoline depot near Stavelot

Matthew B. Ridgway

James M. Gavin

Anthony C. McAuliffe

Leland S. Hobbs

Maurice Rose

Samuel M. Hogan

Walter Bedell Smith

Francis de Guingand

Manton S. Eddy

Ernst Barkmann

Daniel B. Strickler

Léon Praile

Ernest Harmon

Creighton Abrams

William R. Desobry

Hal D. McCown

Gerhard Tebbe

Fritz Bayerlein

CHAPTER TWELVE

The Race for Bastogne: The First Phase

Behind blackout curtains, lights burned through the night of December 16 in almost every office in the Grand Hôtel Britannique in Spa alongside once well-kept lawns where guests come to take the cure of the mineral waters used to stroll down to a little rock-strewn river, the Vesdre, and the bandstand alongside it. Well before daylight, the commander of the First Army, General Hodges, was in his war room in what had once been an elegant suite.

Although immensely concerned, Hodges was still disinclined to accept that the enemy's attack was anything more than an attempt to thwart his drive on the Roer River dams, and when General Gerow telephoned just after 7 A.M. to ask again for permission to halt the 2d Division's attack on the dams and pull the division back, Hodges resorted to the device of the uncertain commander: Leave the decision to the man on the ground. Still unhappy about calling off the attack, he told Gerow to handle the situation as he saw fit.

Otherwise, Hodges could feel a certain comfort in that reserves were on the way: the 9th Armored Division's CCB and the entire 7th Armored Division to St. Vith; a battalion of combat engineers and a regiment of the 1st Division to help the 99th Division (the rest of the 1st Division would also be arriving soon); and the bulk of the 10th Armored Division to help north of Luxembourg City. Yet his relative peace of mind was short-lived, for first reports were soon in of *Kampfgruppe Peiper*'s breakthrough at Honsfeld. Hodges was quickly on the telephone to his colleague in the Great War and longtime friend, the commander of the Ninth Army, "Big Bill" Simpson. The 30th Infantry Division, Hodges knew, was out of the line just north of Aachen, and he needed it. Badly.

Shortly before noon on the 17th, the 30th Division's commander, Maj. Gen. Leland S. Hobbs, received a call telling him to get his division

261

on the road. "I don't know any details," said the chief of staff of the XIX Corps, "but you are going south. I think it is only temporary." To Hodges, it appeared that *Kampfgruppe Peiper* intended either to take Malmédy and swing northwest on Liège or to continue to the Bastogne-Liège highway and then turn north on Liège. In either event, he intended using the 30th Division to block a move on Liège.

General Hodges also telephoned headquarters of the 12th Army Group in an effort to reach General Bradley to ask for two airborne divisions—the 82d and 101st—which constituted the Supreme Commander's only reserve; but Bradley was out of touch, on the way back to Luxembourg City from his meeting with Eisenhower in Versailles. He was not expected back until late afternoon.

In the Trianon Palace Hotel in Versailles, Eisenhower's staff was also thinking about the two airborne divisions. While General Bradley was still en route back to his headquarters, the chief of the SHAEF planning staff, a British officer, Maj. Gen. John F. M. ("Jock") Whiteley, telephoned Bradley's chief of staff, Maj. Gen. Leven C. Allen, to remind him that the two divisions were available. "I'll put it up to Ike, if you wish," said Whiteley.

Although Allen was quick to say yes, there had been no word on General Eisenhower's decision when Bradley got back to his headquarters. He went immediately to the war room for a look at the situation map, which showed that the Germans had committed fourteen divisions. "Pardon my French," said Bradley, "but where in hell has this son of a bitch gotten all this strength?"

Yet even though Bradley referred to the offensive as "Rundstedt's all-out attack," he still looked on it with parochial vision. He still believed that it was deliberately designed to disrupt the First Army's attack for the Roer River dams and the impending offensive by the Third Army, and that if von Rundstedt could force the American command "to pull our strength" away from the Third Army's sector, "he will achieve his primary purpose." He saw the enemy's geographical objective to be Liège in an attempt to disrupt American supply and noted that the Ninth Army should be alert to the possibility of an attack to link with the main thrust on Liège (the Small Solution). To a suggestion that he move his headquarters back from Luxembourg City, Bradley responded: "I will never move backwards with a headquarters. There is too much prestige at stake."

Soon after Bradley's return, General Hodges called asking for the two airborne divisions. Bradley immediately put in a call to Eisenhower, but it was 7 P.M. before Eisenhower, reluctant to part with his last reserve, gave his permission. Everybody in Luxembourg City and Versailles agreed that the divisions should move to Bastogne, not with an eye to turning Bastogne into a bastion but in recognition that the road network there would afford multiple options. When Bradley told Hodges he was to get the divisions, Hodges already wanted to exercise an option: He needed only one division at Bastogne; the other he wanted to block Peiper at Werbomont.

In a venerable French Army barracks at Sissons, thirty miles southeast of Rheims, Maj. Gen. James M. ("Slim Jim") Gavin, at thirty-seven years of age the youngest commander of an American division, the 82d Airborne, had just returned from a performance for his troops by the Ballet Russe de Monte Carlo. He was sitting down to dinner at his headquarters when he received a telephone call from an old friend, the chief of staff of the XVIII Airborne Corps, Col. Ralph D. Eaton. Eisenhower's headquarters, said Eaton, "considered the situation on the Ardennes front critical," and the 82d and 101st Airborne Divisions were to move immediately to the Ardennes.

At General Hodges's request, the divisions were to be committed under the command of the XVIII Airborne Corps. Since the corps commander, Maj. Gen. Matthew B. Ridgway, was away in England (conducting a postmortem on the lengthy battle the two divisions had concluded not quite three weeks before in the Netherlands), as was the senior division commander, Maj. Gen. Maxwell D. Taylor, commander of the 101st Airborne Division (in Washington at Ridgway's behest to prod the War Department into increasing the strength of the airborne division), Gavin was to serve as acting corps commander.

Although some men from both divisions were on pass to Paris, they would be sent forward later. Since the 82d Airborne Division had had longer out of the line to recover from the fighting in the Netherlands, the division was to move first, shortly before dawn the next morning, December 18, and go to Bastogne. The 101st was to follow as soon as possible. In keeping with General Hodges's wish, it was to make for Werbomont.

The necessary orders issued, Gavin departed shortly before midnight to consult with Hodges in Spa. Aware that he might run into Germans, he and two members of his staff set out in darkness, fog, and light rain in an open jeep "prepared for any eventuality."

With the news that an airborne division was coming to Bastogne, the commander of the VIII Corps, Troy Middleton, could relax a little. As he was disturbingly aware early in the evening of December 17, the center of his front was falling to pieces, leaving him to wonder whether he or the Germans would be in Bastogne to welcome the airborne troops when they got there.

It was thus with additional relief that Middleton later in the evening saw the commander of the 10th Armored Division, Maj. Gen. William H. H. Morris, Jr., enter his headquarters in the Heintz barracks (named for a lieutenant from Bastogne who was killed in World War I). On the way north from the Third Army, the 10th Armored Division had already passed to Middleton's command under orders to counterattack the flank of the enemy's penetration north of Luxembourg City. Middleton changed that order. While the bulk of the division was to pursue its original mission, Morris's leading combat command, then bivouacked near Luxembourg City, forty miles from Bastogne, was to move as rapidly as possible the next day to Bastogne. To Middleton's immense concern, a race for Bastogne had developed, and he had precious little left to throw off the sled to the wolves.

Just how long it would be before General von Lüttwitz and his 47th Panzer Corps could get across the little Clerve River and begin traversing the fifteen remaining miles to Bastogne depended primarily upon the 28th Division's 110th Infantry, sorely pressed but still holding at the end of the first day's fighting along the Skyline Drive. It also depended, to a lesser degree, upon what happened to the division's other two regiments, the 109th Infantry to the south and the 112th Infantry to the north; for if the Germans could overrun or even bend back those regiments in the manner of the sweep of a windshield wiper, the 110th Infantry would be left to fight alone.

Whether the 109th Infantry could provide any help to the central regiment depended in turn upon the advance of the German 5th Parachute Division, the northernmost unit of the Seventh Army. For once past the first tier of villages behind the Our River, the paratroopers were to aim for Wiltz, where the 28th Division's commander, Dutch Cota, had his headquarters, only twelve miles from Bastogne. That advance would take place along the seam between the two American regiments, and at the seam, in the village of Hoscheid atop the Skyline Drive, there was only a small American force: a portion of the 110th Infantry's Antitank Company with three Shermans and the 707th Tank Battalion's assault gun platoon, six Shermans mounting 105mm. howitzers.

At two thirty on the morning of December 17, General Cota telephoned the commander of the 109th Infantry, Colonel Rudder, at his headquarters in the Hôtel Lieffrig in Ettelbruck. Earlier in the night, several German assault guns had crossed the Our on a weir near Vianden and with a parachute battalion had moved up a winding road toward the Skyline Drive and Hoscheid. That looked to Cota as if the Germans intended taking Hoscheid, then driving down the Skyline Drive to cut off Rudder's regiment. Cota ordered Rudder to send a platoon each of infantry and tanks to reinforce Hoscheid.

The tanks and the soldiers riding on them failed to make it, for the paratroopers had already cut the Skyline Drive south of Hoscheid. Stopped a half mile short of the village, the relief force could provide no help; Rudder eventually had to call it back to help a besieged battery of field artillery.

The tanks, assault guns, and men of the Antitank Company fighting as infantry nevertheless held throughout the day but at nightfall, almost out of ammunition, the foot troops climbed aboard the vehicles to make a run for it back to positions of the 687th Field Artillery Battalion and then to fall back with that battalion to Wiltz. The stand at Hoscheid had delayed the parachute division for a day, but at that point the paratroopers had split the two American regiments. From then on, the 109th Infantry would be totally involved in trying to prevent the Germans from expanding the southern shoulder of their penetration.

At the other end of the Skyline Drive, where the 112th Infantry's positions were on the German side of the Our River and where the Germans had failed on the first day to get a bridge over the river at Ouren, the Americans through the night could hear the noise of German tanks. A battalion of the 116th Panzer Division was moving into the village of Lutzkampen for renewed attack before daylight on the 17th. Through much of the night searchlights played against the clouds, keeping the American line in a kind of twilight and helping *Volksgrenadiers* and *Panzergrenadiers* to move into attack positions.

An hour before dawn, the searchlights went out, and German artillery and *Nebelwerfers* opened fire all along the two-battalion line. As the shelling lifted, eighteen tanks advanced from Lutzkampen. Although men of the 1st Battalion managed to stop most of the accompanying *Panzergrenadiers*, the tanks fired methodically into the foxholes with machine guns and cannon, broke through, and turned down the road toward Ouren, in the process cutting in behind the 1st Battalion's headquarters village of Harspelt.

Just before the artillery preparation began, in response to repeated pleas for help from the regimental commander, Colonel Nelson, a platoon of self-propelled tank destroyers from the 9th Armored Division's CCR had reached Harspelt. Those destroyers opened up on the German tanks at short range, knocking out four but in the process losing all but one gun.

As the surviving tanks continued toward Ouren, observers for the 112th Infantry's Cannon Company, whose 105mm. howitzers were just across the Our, spotted them only eight hundred yards away. The gunners depressed their pieces, bore-sighted them, and fired. With the second round, the first tank went up in flames. The German tanks quickly returned the fire, knocking out one of the howitzers; but the others continued to fire, eventually knocking out three more of the tanks and damaging two.

While the remaining tanks pulled back behind a rise in the ground,

American fighter-bombers appeared, also as a result of repeated calls for help from Colonel Nelson. That sent the German tanks scurrying for concealment in nearby woods. Although the time of the fighter-bombers over a cloud-shrouded battlefield was brief, the German tankers had become wary.

Again Nelson appealed to his division commander, General Cota, for help. The parent unit of the tank destroyers that had helped at Harspelt, the 9th Armored Division's CCR, was in reserve, Nelson knew, at Trois Vierges, only eight miles from Ouren. Although Cota passed along the request for the armor to the corps commander, General Middleton, that was the only reserve left to Middleton, other than three engineer battalions, to block the roads to Bastogne. Middleton said no.

Back on the heights beyond the Our, four more German tanks emerged from Lutzkampen and with help from *Panzergrenadiers* pushed much of the 1st Battalion back into woods near the positions of the 229th Field Artillery Battalion. In mid-morning, the tanks fired on the artillery pieces, but the American gunners used direct fire to turn them back. When infiltrating *Panzergrenadiers* took the gunners under fire later in the day, Colonel Nelson ordered the battalion commander, Lt. Col. John C. Fairchild, to move his howitzers to the other side of the Our.

The inexperienced *Volksgrenadiers* of the 560th Volksgrenadier Division, often advancing as they had done the first day in column or closely bunched, attacked the 3d Battalion in the village of Sevenig and nearby pillboxes. They captured a few of the pillboxes, but in a repeat of the first day's counterattack, the 2d Battalion crossed the Our from its reserve position and retook them.

As the day wore on, Colonel Nelson could take comfort in that most positions were still intact, but he was disturbingly aware that hundreds of Germans had infiltrated into the rear of his men, some of them firing with burp guns and rifles on his own command post in Ouren. The infiltrators had virtually surrounded his 1st Battalion; and although he had no reason to believe that the battalion had folded, he had lost radio contact with the commander, Colonel Allen, in Harspelt.

In mid-afternoon, Nelson sent his executive officer, Lt. Col. William F. Train, on a roundabout route to Wiltz, avoiding the embattled positions of the 110th Infantry, to report personally to General Cota on the regiment's condition. Nelson wanted Cota's authority to pull everybody back behind the Our. As it turned out, Cota was thinking the same thing, and even before Train arrived, he had gained General Middleton's approval. The only limiting proviso was that the two bridges over the river at Ouren be destroyed.

By the time the 3d Battalion began to withdraw early in the evening, the German infiltrators had occupied that part of Ouren lying on the east bank of the Our and had seized the bridge south of the village over which the 3d Battalion was supposed to withdraw. Suspicious, the battalion commander, Maj. Walden F. Woodward, sent a patrol to the bridge and learned that the Germans were there. Having earlier sent all his vehicles to the rear, Woodward led the infantry to a ford farther south and crossed, feet wet but safe.

On the west bank at Ouren, Colonel Nelson and the men of his headquarters departed under sporadic small-arms fire. Although a rear guard kept the Germans away from the bridge joining the two sections of the village until most of the troops had left, the Germans were too close for the Americans to think of preparing the bridge for demolition.

When Nelson reached Weiswampach, at the northern extremity of the Skyline Drive, he learned that a patrol had failed to contact the 1st Battalion to inform Colonel Allen of the withdrawal. Nelson was worried, for he knew that without orders, Allen would never fall back.

It was near midnight when a communications sergeant finally established intermittent radio contact with Allen's command post. Getting Allen on the radio, Nelson asked if he recognized his voice. When Allen said yes, Nelson told him: "Get all your boys together and visit Blue [3d Battalion] and then White [2d Battalion]." Considering the location of those two battalions, that could mean only one thing: Withdraw by way of Ouren. Allen said he understood.

The Germans had already forced one of Allen's companies back onto the adjacent 424th Infantry of the 106th Division, but Allen set out with the rest of the battalion. As the column neared the bridge linking the two sections of Ouren, Allen, like Woodward, sent a patrol to see if the Germans held the bridge. They did, reported the patrol, but with only half a squad.

Allen determined to bluff his way through, and even if he failed, he considered he could overwhelm six Germans. Ordering his men into a column of twos, he put an officer who spoke German in the lead. In the darkness just before dawn, with the officer shouting commands in German, the men marched in closed ranks across the bridge. Nobody challenged them, and nobody fired a shot.

For two days men of the 116th Panzer and 560th Volksgrenadier Divisions had fought to take the two bridges over the Our at Ouren, but once they held them, they discovered that neither bridge could handle even a tank the size of a Mark IV. Rather than delay the advance while reinforcing the bridges, the corps commander, General Krüger, arranged for his tanks and half-tracks to cross on the bridge of the neighboring 47th Panzer Corps at nearby Dasburg. The delay was of paramount concern to General von Manteuffel, who had been convinced that the 116th Panzer Division's route was the fastest way to the Meuse River.

During the night of the 17th and all through the 18th, as Krüger's divisions plodded across the Our, they gave the 112th Infantry a respite and an opportunity to dig in on a new position covering Weiswampach, roughly a thousand yards behind the Our. Throughout the day of December 18, men at the southern end of the position could see German tanks, half-tracks, and troops filing past. Howitzers of Cannon Company and the 299th Field Artillery Battalion harassed them but were unable to stop the procession.

When the infantry commanders found time to count noses, they learned that despite two days of heavy fighting, the 112th Infantry had emerged in relatively good shape. After having dealt the foe considerable losses, including a probable twenty-one tanks, the regiment still was an effective fighting force.

In mid-afternoon of December 18, Colonel Nelson received an order from General Cota by radio to withdraw through Trois Vierges, on the main St. Vith–Bastogne road, Highway N-12, and fight a delaying action back toward Bastogne. By that time, Nelson knew that the 9th Armored Division's CCR had left Trois Vierges and suspected that the Germans filing past his southern flank had moved in. He saw only two ways of getting to Highway N-12 on the Bastogne side of Trois Vierges. He could cut across the German route of advance between the Skyline Drive and Trois Vierges, which he saw as impossible without tanks or self-propelled tank destroyers; or he could circle well around Trois Vierges.

Notifying Cota that he intended bypassing Trois Vierges, Nelson led his regiment before daylight on December 19 to a point north of the town and was getting ready to swing around it when he received a radio message from the 28th Division's headquarters telling him to occupy a new line, essentially the old position he had just left near Weiswampach. Believing the staff at Wiltz to be out of touch with the situation and convinced at that point that he could accomplish neither mission, Nelson got into a jeep and rode a few miles to the north to the town of Vielsalm, where the commander of the 106th Division, General Jones, had shifted his headquarters from St. Vith.

Once Nelson explained the situation, Jones welcomed him with fervor, for Jones needed every man he could get, and as if by miracle, a commander had appeared who had at his disposal a complete regimental combat team—a company of engineers, a battalion of artillery, a few towed tank destroyers, and an entire regiment of infantry. "From now on," said Jones, "you are attached to the 106th Division, and I will take full responsibility."

Like the 109th Infantry, forced by the Germans back to the south, the 112th Infantry had been forced back to the north, no longer to be involved even peripherally in the struggle to keep the Germans away from Bastogne. From the start that job had belonged, in any case, almost entirely to Hurley Fuller and the 110th Infantry Regiment.

Between the hours of midnight, December 16, and daylight, December 17, much happened that was to have a telling effect on how well and how long the 110th Infantry could continue to do its job. (*See map, Chapter Seventeen, p. 355.*) Having finally gained control of two-thirds of the 2d Battalion from the division reserve, Colonel Fuller had ordered the battalion to counterattack at daylight, retake Marnach atop the Skyline Drive, and block the principal road into his headquarters town of Clervaux. Yet things were happening that were going to make that difficult.

The action began in Clervaux, the picturesque town astride a bend in the Clerve River whose bridges the 2d Panzer Division needed in order to get through the town onto a high plateau beyond and thence to Highway N-12, leading to Bastogne. Soon after midnight, assisted by the two Germans equipped with a radio who had slipped into the Pharmacie Molitor, German artillery and *Nebelwerfers* began to bombard the town. The shelling proved to be covering fire for German patrols, which entered the town in the darkness and began to harass the 110th Infantry's headquarters installations, including the men of Headquarters Company who were holed up in the old château. In reaction to the shelling and the patrols, Battery B, 109th Field Artillery Battalion—which had already displaced from its original firing positions to others near the château in Clervaux—had to displace farther to the rear. That put its howitzers out of range for supporting the counterattack.

Other German actions were to deny the counterattacking 2d Battalion all artillery support. Bypassing Company A's strongpoint on the Skyline Drive at Heinerscheid, a company of *Panzergrenadiers* attacked Battery A's firing positions behind the Skyline Drive, knocked out or captured three half-tracks of the 447th Antiaircraft Artillery Battalion, and overran the guns. The artillerymen saved not a single gun, nor was there any opportunity to spike them. By 4 A.M. Battery A had ceased to exist except for a few men who made their way out on foot.

The overrunning of Battery A and the displacing of Battery B left only Battery C, south of Clervaux at Bockholz, and Cannon Company, nearby at Munshausen, in position to deliver any fire in support of the 2d Battalion's counterattack. Yet both those units were preoccupied with providing support for the hardpressed strongpoints on and behind the central and southern portions of the Skyline Drive, and both were soon to come under strong German ground attack.

As men of the 2d Battalion (less one company) moved onto the ridge north of Clervaux before daylight, planning to get past Reuler and into Marnach, German tanks and half-tracks were already emerging from Marnach, aiming both for Clervaux and for the same high ground that the 2d Battalion occupied. So canalized was the road from Marnach to Clervaux that the commander of the 2d Panzer Division, Colonel Lauchert, decided to opt for a second route that led from the ridge north of the town, through a succession of hairpin turns, into the western end of the town near the railroad station and Colonel Fuller's headquarters in the Hôtel Claravallis. To get into Clervaux by the back door.

Hardly had the American infantry begun to advance than Company F on the left bumped head-on into German troops emerging in a skirmish line from a woods. It took the company the better part of two hours to drive those Germans back. At the same time, Company E ran into Germans in a draw close to Reuler. A stiff fight was going on there when Colonel Fuller radioed the battalion commander, Lt. Col. James R. Hughes, to send a platoon to block the Marnach-Clervaux highway. A platoon of Company E tried, but a single rifle platoon had no chance of stopping the tanks and half-tracks that were by that time clanking down the road toward Clervaux.

Part of the armored assistance Fuller was counting on in the counterattack on Marnach—a drive by the eighteen light tanks of the 707th Tank Battalion down the Skyline Drive from Heinerscheid—quickly ran afoul of German self-propelled guns. As the tanks neared the hamlet of Fishbach, not quite midway between Heinerscheid and Marnach, the guns knocked out eight of them, and *Panzerfausts* accounted for three more. Five other tanks escaped to the west, while the other two, although damaged, limped back to Heinerscheid and the perimeter defense of the 110th Infantry's Company A.

A second drive in support of the counterattack had slightly more success—that by a platoon of medium tanks commanded by 1st Lt. Raymond E. Fleig with a platoon of Company C's infantry riding on the decks. Repeating a maneuver executed the day before, the force moved from Munshausen northeastward on Marnach. The tanks and infantry reached the edge of Marnach and held a few houses against a swift riposte by German tanks and *Panzergrenadiers*, but since the little force clearly would be unable to retake the village without help, Colonel Fuller in mid-morning ordered it back.

Faint hope stirred for Colonel Fuller that same morning with the unexpected arrival of more tank support. Earlier, the corps commander, General Middleton, had ordered the 9th Armored Division's CCR at Trois Vierges to move to a reserve position closer to Bastogne and attached the combat command in place to the 28th Division; but it was not to be used without Middleton's approval. Yet the 28th Division's commander, General Cota, was so desperate for help that he exceeded his authority and sent a staff officer to commandeer a company of tanks from CCR's column: Company B, 2d Tank Battalion.

With seventeen Shermans, the commander, Capt. Robert L. Lybarger, reported to Fuller in Clervaux around 10:30 A.M. on the 17th. Fuller promptly sent a platoon to Heinerscheid to support Company A, another to Reuler to help Colonel Hughes's 2d Battalion, and the third to clear Germans from the eastern end of Clervaux. As on the first day of the offensive, Fuller was expending his armor in little increments, but under orders to hold at all costs everywhere, he saw no alternative.

Those platoons moving to Heinerscheid and Reuler were in for rude receptions. The platoon going to Reuler was entering the killing zone of the bulk of the 2d Panzer Division and soon paid the consequences: three out of five tanks knocked out in what was for the crewmen their first combat experience. The platoon going to Heinerscheid arrived just as an attack by the 116th Panzer Division's reconnaissance battalion, having crossed the Our at Dasburg, was nearing a climax. As Company A's defense collapsed, the platoon lost two tanks, but the other three managed to make their way to join the platoon at Reuler.

It was the lot of the men in those tanks to arrive just as the tanks and *Panzergrenadiers* of the 2d Panzer Division were mounting a climactic attack to clear the heights above Clervaux and get into town by the back door. As night was falling, the Germans drove the five surviving tanks and about two hundred infantrymen out of Reuler. At the same time, other German tanks in the nearby village of Urspelt were knocking out four of the five light tanks that had survived the early morning shootout on the Skyline Drive at Fishbach. Before fleeing with men of the 1st Battalion's headquarters, the crew of the fifth tank put a thermite grenade down the muzzle of its cannon.

The collapse at Urspelt left the Germans free to come in behind the men of Colonel Hughes's 2d Battalion, who were trying to make a stand on an open ridge between the two villages, and the infantrymen and their five tanks were soon surrounded. Convinced that the situation was hopeless, Colonel Hughes ordered the tanks to form a rear guard while the infantry tried to escape in the darkness in small groups. After allowing the infantry a reasonable time, the tankers were to blast their way out of the encirclement.

In the pre-dawn darkness of December 18, only about sixty of the infantrymen made it. The withdrawal was even more disastrous for the tanks. Moving cross-country, four either threw a track or bogged in the mud and had to be abandoned. The fifth, with men of the other crews clinging to the decks, made it to the Clerve, but in attempting to ford the river, mired in the soft bottom. It, too, had to be abandoned.

The back door to Clervaux was open.

South of Clervaux, at Munshausen, Bockholz, Holzthum, and Consthum behind the Skyline Drive, and at Hosingen and Hoscheid astride the high ridge, every American strongpoint was under heavy attack. Assisted by assault guns that had at last toiled up the muddy roads from the deep valley of the Our River, not only were troops of the 26th Volksgrenadier Division attacking the strongpoints but others were bypassing them and edging down back roads through thick forests to get at the bridges over the Clerve.

The first of the positions to be abandoned was that of Battery C, 109th Field Artillery Battalion, just outside Bockholz, where four assault guns joined the *Volksgrenadiers* that had given the battery such a difficult time the day before. Rather than suffer annihilation, the battery commander in mid-morning ordered withdrawal. Despite German fire, the artillerymen hitched their howitzers to their trucks and made a getaway, losing but two howitzers in the process and eventually occupying new firing positions on the other side of the Clerve.

At nearby Munshausen, Company C and Cannon Company were under attack all through the 17th with the Germans so close that the gunners had difficulty depressing their howitzers low enough to hit them. The companies were without the tank support they had had on the first day, for soon after Lieutenant Fleig's tank platoon withdrew from Marnach, Colonel Fuller ordered Fleig and the platoon of infantry that accompanied him to help out in Clervaux.

Learning in early afternoon of the heavy pressure at Munshausen, Fuller withheld the infantry platoon for the defense of his command post but sent Fleig and his tanks back to Munshausen. As the tanks moved up from the river valley toward the village, a *Panzerfaust* knocked out one, and when the others reached the fringe of the village, so many of the buildings were in flames that the tankers assumed no Americans remained. Two rounds from a bazooka, which the tank crewmen took to be from a *Panzerfaust*, convinced them.

In reality, the man firing the bazooka thought the tanks were German, and Company C and Cannon Company were in full control of Munshausen. They had been under attack by the 2d Panzer Division's reconnaissance battalion, which was providing flank protection for Colonel Lauchert's main drive, and late in the afternoon Lauchert afforded a company of Panthers to help. With that added strength, the reconnaissance battalion reached the center of the village, but as the company commander rode erect in the turret of the first Panther, an American rifleman shot him in the head. That took the spirit out of the attack, and the Germans fell back to the fringe of the village.

By that time, Cannon Company had lost two of its six howitzers, and near midnight the two company commanders agreed that unless they withdrew, everybody would be lost. Because the Germans were too close to hope to get the howitzers out, the men spiked them and broke into small groups to try to escape. Although there were still more than two hundred men, so thick were the Germans in the river valley that few made it.

When men of the 2d Panzer Division's reconnaissance battalion swarmed over Munshausen the next morning, they were impressed by the number of their comrades who had been shot through the head. There was no anger at that, merely admiration for those whom they were for long to speak of as "the sharpshooters of Munshausen." What did anger them was finding the body of one of their company commanders, Capt. Heinz Nowak. Something of a maverick, Nowak had endeared himself to his men. The night before, he had marched off alone into Munshausen "swinging a souvenir American bayonet like a baton." When his men found him, he was dead on a path near the church, the bayonet protruding from his throat.

Incensed, the men wanted to kill their American prisoners, but a sergeant intervened. The war would soon be over, he said, and "measures would be taken against those who mistreated prisoners of war."

At Hoscheid, the few men of Antitank Company with their tank and assault gun support, under attack all day on the 17th from paratroopers of the 5th Parachute Division, made their escape after nightfall. At nearby Holzthum in mid-afternoon, the few survivors of Company L— the company commander, Lieutenant Saymon, and forty men—slipped away to join the defenders of the adjacent village of Consthum.

Atop the Skyline Drive at Hosingen, Company K, Lieutenant Payne's platoon of Shermans, and Company B of the 103d Engineers were under heavy attack following the late arrival west of the Our of the 26th Volksgrenadier Division's reserve regiment. The continued American possession of Hosingen was so irksome to the commander of the 47th Panzer Corps, General von Lüttwitz, that he early sent the *Panzer Lehr Division*'s advance guard to help. He had to have unfettered passage through the village if the advance guard was to cross the Clerve downhill from Hosingen and exploit the gains of the 26th Volksgrenadier Division. So badly did he want the village that he told Colonel Lauchert to loan a few of his Panthers and Mark IVs of the 2d Panzer Division to assist the attack from the north.

Faced by such an overwhelming force, the defenders of Hosingen were doomed. By noon the village was surrounded, the men fighting desperately from the houses, Lieutenant Payne's five tanks dashing here and there in response to one threat from German tanks and assault guns after another. Although Company K's commander, Capt. Frederick Feiker, pleaded for artillery support, not a single battery was still within range. By nightfall the engineers were isolated in one part of the village, the infantry and three remaining tanks in a perimeter defense of Company K's command post in another; and ammunition was perilously low.

When Captain Feiker radioed his situation to his battalion commander, Major Milton, in Consthum, Milton told him to break into small groups and infiltrate out to join the remainder of the 3d Battalion in Consthum. So close were the encircling Germans, said Feiker, that that would be impossible. Not long after daylight on the 18th, all ammunition exhausted except for a few hand grenades and a few smoke rounds for nonexistent 60mm. mortars, Feiker asked Milton what he was to do. The decision, said Milton, was his.

Not long after that, a radio operator reported: "We've blown up everything there is to blow except the radio, and it goes next." The men in Hosingen, who had stymied superior forces for two days and into a third, at last surrendered. That they numbered little more than three hundred came as a surprise to their captors. That only seven had died in the prolonged fight came as almost as much of a surprise to the defenders themselves.

At Consthum, where the remnants of the 3d Battalion blocked two roads leading to the 28th Division's headquarters town of Wiltz, the defenders held under heavy pressure all through the 17th. During the morning of the 18th, the regimental executive officer, Colonel Strickler, who had been at Consthum almost from the start, obtained General Cota's approval to withdraw. While the battalion commander, Major Milton, got the men and three surviving tanks ready to pull out, Strickler left by jeep in a hail of bullets to determine whether a bridge over the Clerve at the village of Kaustenbach was still in American hands. It was not, but no Germans were there either, and the survivors of the fight at Consthum eventually made their way back to help defend Wiltz.

By that time, almost all the other bridges over the Clerve south of Clervaux belonged to the Germans. Soon after nightfall on December 17, men of the 26th Volksgrenadier Division seized intact a bridge at Drauffelt, downhill from Hosingen, another a mile downstream between Drauffelt and Wilwerwiltz, and a third at Wilwerwiltz. A day late, the *Volksgrenadiers* with the help of the *Panzer Lehr Division* could at last begin their role in the race for Bastogne.

In Clervaux on December 17, the first crisis arose around nine-thirty in the morning when Mark IVs and half-tracks approached along a steeply descending road from Marnach. Colonel Fuller promptly sent the platoon of five Shermans from the 707th Tank Battalion that he had held in reserve in the town climbing around three steep hairpin curves in the road at the edge of Clervaux to meet them. At a bend high above the rooftops of the town, the two forces met in a blaze of fire. The Americans lost three tanks, the Germans four, and the remaining tanks on both sides fell back.

Rather than returning to Clervaux, the two surviving American tanks turned left at the third of the hairpin curves along a road following the trace of the Clerve to the south, ostensibly to get more ammunition at the headquarters of their company. Whatever the reason, Colonel Fuller was to get no more help from them. Nor did he get much support from the platoon of tanks of the 9th Armored Division's CCR that he sent to help the infantry clear the Germans from the eastern end of Clervaux. There the platoon lost two tanks to German fire—one to a long-range shot from a German tank high above the town, the other to a *Panzerfaust*—and the remaining three withdrew without telling Fuller to their parent unit well

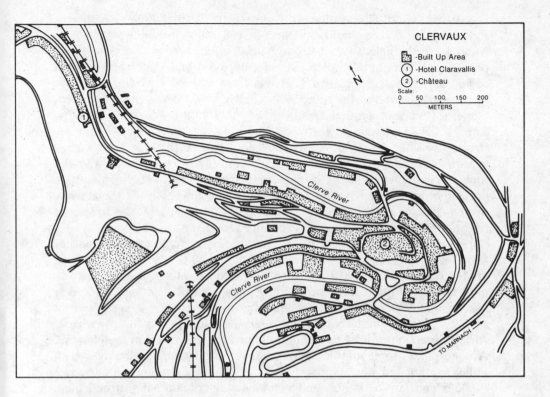

beyond the Clerve. Those were the only tanks of Company B, 2d Tank Battalion, to survive the company's baptism of fire.

The departure of those tanks was what prompted Fuller to order Lieutenant Fleig's tank platoon from Munshausen to Clervaux. To get there, Fleig had to take a roundabout route down to the valley of the Clerve and thence up the little road following the trace of the river to the lower of the steep hairpin curves above the town. As Fleig's lead tank reached the road junction, a Mark IV high up the road above Clervaux near an overlook, where in happier times hikers and tourists paused to look down on the picturesque rooftops of the town, opened fire. The infantrymen aboard the tanks dove for whatever cover they could find while the gunners of the two tanks slugged it out. The Sherman won, and the wreckage of the Mark IV formed a perfect roadblock for preventing any German vehicle from getting into Clervaux along the road from Marnach.

Because of that roadblock, German tanks made no new effort to enter Clervaux from that direction. Instead, several tanks assumed firing positions on high ground uphill from the destroyed Mark IV and from time to time threw direct fire into the town.

While Lieutenant Fleig and his tanks waited at the edge of town, the commander of the infantry platoon, 1st Lt. Jack D. Haisley, made his way to the Hôtel Claravallis and reported to Colonel Fuller. Although Fuller wanted Haisley and his men to help defend his command post, he wanted Fleig's tanks to go back to Munshausen, for by that time Company C and Cannon Company were hardpressed and Fuller had just received armored assistance for Clervaux from another source.

In early afternoon, in response to Fuller's continuing pleas for help, General Cota sent another small contingent from the 9th Armored Division's CCR, a platoon of self-propelled tank destroyers. When the destroyers reached the Hôtel Claravallis, Fuller directed them up the road toward Marnach to engage the German tanks that were firing into the town. A short while later, all five came racing back in such precipitate haste that at the first hairpin curve above the town one of them overturned. Picking up the crew, the others continued through the town and beyond the Clerve. Nobody in Clervaux saw them again.

By that time, most men of the provisional company formed earlier from men on leave in Clervaux and sent out along the Marnach road had gradually drifted back into the town, a kind of disintegration not uncommon among hastily formed provisional units where the individual soldier has no unit loyalty. Those men became caught up in the fight against steadily growing numbers of *Panzergrenadiers* infiltrating the town from various directions, and a few of them joined the defenders in the château. At one point, some of the Germans got within two hundred yards of Fuller's command post before Lieutenant Haisley's infantry platoon, a single 57mm. antitank gun, and several stragglers and MPs turned them back.

Throughout the afternoon, Fuller appealed time after time to General Cota for permission to withdraw any of his men and guns that could still get away to a new position behind the Clerve and so block the road leading to the St. Vith–Bastogne highway. Yet each time either Cota or his chief of staff, Col. Jesse L. Gibney, refused. Newly come to the 28th Division, Fuller was not yet a trusted member of the family, and who was to say whether his dolorous assessment of the situation was accurate?

Dutch Cota was nevertheless torn, for it was possible that he might be presiding over the demise of one of his proud regiments. On the other hand, he knew there was a race on for Bastogne, and his corps commander still insisted that he hold at all costs. Cota finally did agree to send Fuller Company G, which he had withheld when releasing the 2d Battalion from division reserve.

Not long after dark, around 6:30 P.M., Colonel Hughes radioed Fuller from his encircled position on the ridge north of Clervaux that six German tanks had bypassed him and were heading for Clervaux along the road leading into town from the rear. Again Fuller got Colonel Gibney on the telephone, but again Gibney refused permission to withdraw. Even as the two were talking, a staff officer ran into the room to tell Fuller that six German tanks were approaching the hotel. Fuller told that to Gibney. He would obey the order to hold, said Fuller, but as a Texan, he wanted Gibney to know that he was assigning him the same fate as befell the defenders of the Alamo.

At that moment three shells from German tanks exploded one after the other inside the ground floor of the hotel beneath the room from which Fuller was talking. What was that? asked Gibney. Fuller told him. When Gibney began to say something more, Fuller interrupted; he had "no more time to talk," he said brusquely, and rang off.

Fuller had just turned from the telephone when a blast of machine-gun fire tore into the ceiling of the room he was in, and tank fire continued to blast the ground floor. All lights went out. Going into the corridor, Fuller felt his way to his own room, No. 10, to get his carbine and overcoat. He was determined to get out some way and reconstitute as much of his regiment as he could put together on the other side of the Clerve.

As Fuller entered No. 10, he found ten men taking refuge there. Just at that moment a rocket from a *Panzerfaust* exploded into the room, wounding five of the men, including one who was blinded. By the light of German flares outside, Fuller hurriedly bandaged the man's eyes.

As Fuller was working, an MP entered. He had found a way out of the building, he said, if anybody wanted to take the chance. Fuller and the others, including the blinded man, all said yes. With the blinded man holding Fuller by the hand, the MP guided them across the hall to No. 12 and over to the only window in the room.

Someone had thrown a narrow iron ladder from the window across a twelve-foot space between the rear of the hotel and the landing of a fire escape built onto the side of a sheer cliff. (Had the men but known, in a short corridor off the main hall stood a large armoire hiding a door that led directly onto the fire escape.) With the blinded man still holding on, Fuller walked across the ladder to the landing, then up a few metal steps which soon gave way to steps carved out of the side of the cliff. The military policeman and eleven others followed.

At the top, Fuller, winded, paused briefly to catch his breath, then led the little group westward toward the village of Esselborn. There, he knew, one of the 2d Battalion's companies had once been billeted so that there still might be a telephone with which to contact Cota. He also hoped he might find Company G there, but in both cases his hopes were vain.

After rebandaging the blinded soldier's eyes, Fuller left him and another man whose wounds made it difficult for him to walk in the care of an unarmed soldier. With the rest, he set off again in the hope of finding some part of the 2d Battalion that had been fighting north of Clervaux.

Back at the Hôtel Claravallis, not long after Colonel Fuller made his escape, a switchboard operator put in a call to headquarters of the 28th Division. Germans were all over the command post, said the operator, and a tank had stuck its cannon inside the lobby of the hotel. Just as taught in communications training, the operator in a solemn voice said formally: "This switchboard is now closed."

By midnight of December 17, the fight by the center regiment of the division whose officers and men wore the bloody bucket shoulder patch was nearing an end. Yet some who somehow managed to get across the Clerve River were to fight again along Highway N-12—the St. Vith–Bastogne highway—and only the next day, December 18, was resistance to end in Hosingen and Consthum. So, too, there was still to be a fight by men of the 110th Infantry's Headquarters Company, holed up in the old château in Clervaux.

The order received by the commander of Headquarters Company, Capt. Claude B. Mackey, was to hold at all costs. For a little band of about eighty officers and men, armed only with carbines and M-1s plus a single .50-caliber machine gun, that was absurd. Yet it was the order Mackey had received and that was what he intended to do.

It was, Mackey might note, a romantic setting for a last stand: the ancient twelfth-century fortress with its thick stone walls, its turrets, and its firing apertures (designed for the crossbow but easily adaptable for a rifle or a carbine), perched atop a promontory commanding not only the entire town of Clervaux but also the two bridges over the winding Clerve River, the highway leading in from Marnach, and to some degree the open ridge to the north. The château's one weakness as a bastion was the lack of a moat; and whereas the massive wooden doors between the entrance towers may well have been a genuine obstacle to a medieval battering ram, they would pose no real obstacle to a twentieth-century tank.

Even before dawn on December 17, the Americans had to close the big doors leading into the inner courtyard and take to the apertures, for infiltrating *Panzergrenadiers* were making their presence felt with determined fire from rifles, burp guns, and machine guns. Sometimes the men opened the doors slightly to let in some American soldier seeking refuge, so that in time their numbers grew to 102, which included the regimental communications officer, Capt. John Aiken, Jr.

Since the château housed the regiment's message center, there was a half-track in the inner courtyard with a radio, an SCR-193, by means of which the men could maintain contact with the division command post in Wiltz. In the dungeon beneath, there were eighteen German prisoners of war and some seventy-five civilians, mostly elderly men, women, and children. Because the château housed Headquarters Company's kitchen, food and water were ample for all.

Sixteen-year-old Jean Servais, who had taken refuge in the château with his parents, found the siege a lark. Much of the time he roamed around watching the soldiers with fascination. During the height of the shelling, he came upon one soldier calmly playing a popular American

tune on a piano and paying no heed to the shells bursting nearby. At one of the apertures, he watched another soldier, cigarette dangling from his lips, his rifle equipped with a sniper-scope, calmly and deliberately squeeze off his rounds; before Jean turned away for some other diversion, the man hit four Germans, one of whom rolled like a heavy stone down the steep wooded slope just across the Clerve from the château.

Before daylight on December 18, a Sherman—from where and what unit, nobody inside the château knew—took up position in the outer courtyard. After daylight, as German tanks shoved aside the destroyed Mark IV on the road above the town and began descending the hill, the Sherman opened fire. From the road, the Sherman was difficult to spot, but somebody eventually picked it up. A first round merely scratched the armor plate, but a second entered between the turret and the hull, blowing off the gun. The Sherman's crew somehow survived and eventually reached safety beyond the Clerve.

The firing from inside the château still indicated clearly that only armored vehicles could make it through Clervaux with impunity. That no doubt contributed to the German decision to get rid of the troublesome hold-out. Fire from tanks and assault guns soon set a portion of the château to burning, and smoke billowed in the little courtyard. Considering the end to be near, Captain Aiken ordered the half-track and its radio destroyed with thermite grenades.

Around noon on the 18th, a German tank rammed the big doors blocking the entrance, poised there, and fired a round from its cannon. To Mackey and Aiken, there appeared to be no point in resisting any longer. They brought out a white flag.

As the Americans, the civilians, and the German prisoners all filed out, Jean Servais supported an American who had lost considerable blood from a wound in his cheek. Because of that, the Germans herded him together with the Americans. For Jean, the events had ceased to be fun. At the first opportunity, he slipped away.

The Race for Bastogne: The Second Phase

For the commander of the Fifth Panzer Army, Hasso von Manteuffel, the commander of the 47th Panzer Corps, General von Lüttwitz, and the German division commanders, the race for Bastogne took on added urgency during the evening of December 17 with news through an intercepted radio message that the Allied command had ordered two American airborne divisions to Bastogne. The way the German commanders figured it, the airborne troops would reach Bastogne during the night of the 18th or early on the 19th. That made the continued slow progress on the second day of the offensive all the more upsetting. Not only getting Bastogne but also reaching and crossing the Meuse River appeared to von Manteuffel "already imperiled."

Since the Fifth Panzer Army's primary goal was to cross the Meuse, the 2d Panzer Division in pursuit of that goal was to bypass Bastogne to the north. Yet if Bastogne could not be taken swiftly, it would tie down German forces needed elsewhere while at the same time affording the Americans a base from which to launch a counterattack that, as von Manteuffel put it, "could seriously endanger the German attack." Thus it was critical that the *Panzer Lehr Division*, with help from the 26th Volksgrenadier Division, beat the American reinforcements to Bastogne and thereby free the *Panzer Lehr* to join the 2d Panzer Division in the drive for the Meuse.

The commander of the *Panzer Lehr Division*, the feisty General Bayerlein, believed that General von Lüttwitz during December 17 had seriously jeopardized his chances of a *coup de main* at Bastogne. Von Lüttwitz had committed one of Bayerlein's *Panzergrenadier* regiments against the unyielding American defenders of Consthum. And he had also appropriated Bayerlein's advance guard, the special task force he had created for quickly exploiting the early gains—an armored reconnais-

sance company, two companies of *Panzergrenadiers*, and a company of Panthers—against the strongpoint at Hosingen. By late afternoon of the 17th both forces had incurred heavy casualties.

Once von Lüttwitz early in the evening of December 17 learned that the 26th Volksgrenadier Division had a bridge over the Clerve River at Drauffelt, he nevertheless moved swiftly to get the *Panzer Lehr* marching toward Bastogne. He ordered Bayerlein's advance guard pulled back from Hosingen and shifted immediately to the bridge at Drauffelt, to be followed by the division's previously uncommitted *Panzergrenadier* regiment. As the advance guard moved forward, Bayerlein reinforced it with fifteen Mark IV tanks, a company of engineers, and a battery of self-propelled artillery that had toiled through the traffic jams endemic on the muddy roads leading up to the Skyline Drive from the valley of the Our.

Von Lüttwitz was taking a chance that the forces of the *Panzer Lehr* and 26th Volksgrenadier Divisions could jointly use the bridge at Drauffelt and a steep, winding road leading from the river valley toward the St. Vith–Bastogne road, Highway N-12. As soon became evident early on December 18, to expect men moving basically on foot but with a mix of motor vehicles and horse-drawn transport to share a single narrow, muddy road with armored vehicles was to presume the millennium. Even the breakdown of a single vehicle meant a traffic jam of immense proportions until the vehicle could be shoved off the road. Bayerlein's armor was soon "flowing to the west not in a quiet, even stream but . . . irregularly from traffic congestion to traffic congestion, slowly and clumsily." The German commanders and the troops could only be thankful that for yet another day low clouds and a misty rain concealed them from Allied fighter-bombers. It was mid-afternoon before the armor could at last break free of the congestion.

To the north, at Clervaux, the 2d Panzer Division encountered no such difficulties, for the road through Clervaux belonged exclusively to the division. That was not to say there were no delays, for the hairpin curves on the approach to Clervaux and the narrow streets were tricky for the big tanks to negotiate, and until well into the day small-arms fire from the château made it difficult for anything other than tanks and assault guns to get through. Yet there was another route around the town to the north, and even before daylight on the 18th, advance elements of the 2d Panzer Division were on their way westward across the river, headed for Highway N-12.

On the American side, the commander of the VIII Corps, General Middleton, was running distressingly low on troops with which to slow the German advance. Late on the 17th, he at last agreed for General Cota to withdraw the 110th Infantry behind the Clerve with the idea of forming a new delaying line west of the river, but that approval came too late for Hurley Fuller and almost all the regiment except Colonel Strickler and the remnants of the 3d Battalion in Consthum. Those remnants, plus previously uncommitted Company G, were about all the 110th Infantry could still contribute as an organized force to further delay in front of Bastogne. Other than what remained of that embattled regiment, all that Middleton had left to throw into the fight were three engineer combat battalions, a separate (nondivisional) armored field artillery battalion, and the 9th Armored Division's Combat Command R.

It was precious little with which to delay three German divisions, including two panzer divisions, long enough to allow the 10th Armored Division's CCB and the airborne division to get to Bastogne. At best, Middleton knew, not until late afternoon of the 18th could the combat command reach the town, and it might be well into the night before the first airborne troops arrived, which meant that only the next day, the 19th, could he hope to get any of the airborne troops into the line.

Middleton sent one of the engineer combat battalions (the 44th) to help Cota at Wiltz, and the other two (the 35th and 158th) to form a screen of outposts in villages just beyond the eastern periphery of Bastogne. Earlier assigned to general support of the 28th Division, the armored field artillery battalion (the 58th) was to support all units in front of Bastogne. Having also earlier ordered the 9th Armored Division's CCR from Trois Vierges to an assembly area closer to Bastogne, Middleton toward evening on the 17th told the commander, Col. Joseph H. Gilbreth, to establish two roadblocks in an effort to stay the German advance.

As yet untested in battle, the 9th Armored Division's CCR had the usual components of a combat command: a battalion each of armored infantry, medium tanks, and armored field artillery, and a company each of self-propelled tank destroyers, armored engineers, and antiaircraft artillery (half-tracks mounting quad-50s). Yet the fighting had already drawn off a portion of Colonel Gilbreth's command: a platoon of tank destroyers to help the 112th Infantry near Ouren; another to help the 110th Infantry at Clervaux (although four of the five guns had come back); and a company of medium tanks appropriated by General Cota to help the 110th Infantry, of which only three survived.

At Middleton's order, Gilbreth was to establish one roadblock at a road junction known as Antoniushof, the meeting of the road from Clervaux with Highway N-12, and another at a junction known as Fe'itsch, where a secondary road from the valley of the Clerve at Drauffelt joined N-12 only eight miles from Bastogne. The terrain in the vicinity of the two junctions is unusual for the Ardennes—high and rolling, devoid of the deep ravines and heavy woods cover to be found in most other places, and it afforded ample fields of fire for armored vehicles. In a fairly straight line, the highway followed the crest of the high ground. Unfortunately for armor on the defensive, there were only two or three build-

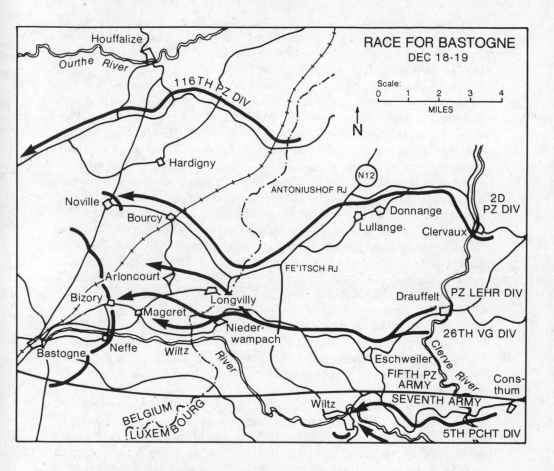

ings at each road junction and thus little cover or concealment for tanks and tank destroyers.

Task Force Rose at Antoniushof—named for the commander of Company A, 2d Tank Battalion, Capt. Lawrence K. Rose—consisted of Rose's company of Shermans, a company of the 52d Armored Infantry Battalion, and a platoon of armored engineers, while a battery of the 73d Armored Field Artillery Battalion was close enough to provide support. Unknown to Rose, another American unit was nearby: Company G, 110th Infantry, which General Cota had withheld when releasing the 2d Battalion from the division but had at last released early in the evening on the 17th to go to Clervaux.

Arriving after midnight in the village of Donnange (the 2d Battalion's former reserve position on a side road just off the main highway from Antoniushof to Clervaux), the men of Company G spotted the silhouettes of what looked to be German tanks on high ground just beyond the village. Because the company had no radio and thus no way of knowing what was happening in Clervaux, the commander, Capt. George N. Prestridge, decided to hole up for the night. To put some distance between his company and the possible German tanks, he pulled his men from Donnange to dig in behind the village.

At the other road junction, Fe'itsch, not quite four miles down N-12 in the direction of Bastogne, there would also be limited help from men of the 110th Infantry. A former commander of the regiment, Col. Theodore A. Seely, had arrived at the road junction. Having been slightly wounded in the Hürtgen Forest, Seely had refused evacuation but until his wound healed had remained at the division headquarters as an extra regimental commander while Colonel Fuller took over his regiment. When Cota lost contact with Fuller and his command post in Clervaux, he ordered Seely to "go find your regiment and take command of it."

At the Fe'itsch road junction, Seely found several junior officers from the regimental headquarters who had escaped from Clervaux and with them began to reconstitute a headquarters in a farmhouse a half mile behind the junction. When the armored task force that was to establish a roadblock at Fe'itsch arrived, Seely had ten officers and a hundred men, who took position on a flank of the task force.

Named after the commander of the 2d Tank Battalion, Lt. Col. Ralph S. Harper, the task force at Fe'itsch had Harper's remaining company of Shermans and a company of armored infantry. Except for a battery with Task Force Rose, the 73d Armored Field Artillery Battalion was in position to provide support.

Not quite three miles behind the road junction the commander of CCR, Colonel Gilbreth, established his headquarters in the village of Longvilly. To provide a screen for it, for his artillery battalion, and for a nearby 58th Armored Field Artillery Battalion, Gilbreth formed a small task force to occupy high ground north of the main highway between Fe'itsch and Longvilly. Commanded by the head of the 52d Armored Infantry Battalion, Lt. Col. Robert M. Booth, the task force had Booth's remaining line company, a platoon of light tanks, and a platoon of self-propelled tank destroyers.

As daylight came on December 18, that was the alignment facing the armor of the 2d Panzer Division coming up from the valley of the Clerve at Clervaux and the *Panzer Lehr Division* along with the bulk of the 26th Volksgrenadier Division toiling up from the valley at Drauffelt. With those defenders, plus a thin screen of engineers in the villages behind them, rested the chances of keeping the Germans out of Bastogne long enough for reinforcements to get there.

Just outside Donnange at daybreak on December 18, a man from the 109th Field Artillery Battalion, Sgt. Charles T. Johnson, who had been detailed along with a second lieutenant and a radio operator as a forward observer team for Company G, 110th Infantry, volunteered to go into the village and find an observation post to determine if the silhouettes the men had seen on the skyline the night before were indeed German tanks. With the team's jeep and radio operator, Johnson entered the village, then climbed the church steeple and peered through the mist with his binoculars. On the high ground not two hundred yards from where the men of Company G had dug in were four tanks. The U.S. Army, Johnson knew, had no tanks that big.

Sending the radio operator back to alert Company G, Johnson established radio contact with the fire direction center of his battalion and was getting ready to call for a fire mission when he looked back toward Company G's positions. Having learned of German tanks so near, Captain Prestridge was marching his men back to the protection of the houses in the next village of Lullange. Quick to spot the movement, the German tanks began firing, and the infantrymen broke into a run to gain the cover of the houses.

Climbing down from the steeple, Johnson found his radio operator waiting with the jeep behind a stone wall. They, too, raced back to Lullange.

The German tanks failed to follow the withdrawal, for their goal was the road junction at Antoniushof, but an hour later a company of *Panzergrenadiers* supported by mortars attacked Lullange. From an observation post in a house, Johnson was able to bring down effective artillery fire, and the attack collapsed.

During the action, Johnson was appalled at the conduct of his lieutenant. Lips trembling, his head in his hands, the officer cringed in a corner of the room.

With the support of assault guns, the Germans in late afternoon attacked again. Although Johnson moved immediately into his observation post, try as he might he was unable to raise the 109th Field Artillery Battalion on the radio. The instrument appeared to be dead.

They might as well fall back, said the lieutenant. A forward observer was no good without a radio.

It gradually dawned on Johnson that the terrified lieutenant had sabotaged the radio in order to have an excuse to fall back. Johnson refused to go, but the lieutenant drew his pistol and ordered him to join him. The officer was shaking, tears in his eyes. "My God," thought Johnson, "this is the kind of thing that happens in the movies!" Having no radio and facing a desperate man, Johnson decided to go along. If they made it out, he would turn him over to the MPs.

Dodging mortar shells, the two took off across an open field and after nightfall found Colonel Seely's command post near the Fe'itsch road junction. While Johnson waited, the lieutenant went inside, but when he failed to return, Johnson asked the sentry at the door what had happened. The colonel, said the soldier, had put the lieutenant under arrest.

* * *

Through the night of December 17, Hurley Fuller had gotten nowhere in his efforts to return to the east bank of the Clerve River and find his 2d Battalion. At every turn, he and the few men still with him ran into Germans or German tanks. By daylight, Fuller had become separated from everybody except a lieutenant, David Wright, but soon came upon fifty men of the 630th Tank Destroyer Battalion. They were trying to turn their jeeps and trucks around on a narrow woods trail in order to head south, for they too had run into Germans going the other way.

Fuller and Wright joined them, but hardly had they begun to move when the little column came under fire from German tanks. There was no way past, and Fuller detected German infantry trying to encircle them. He ordered the vehicles set on fire and led the little force—the size of a platoon—to a nearby hillock, where the men dug in. They held there through the afternoon, losing fifteen men to German fire. When night came, ammunition was so low that Fuller told the troops to break into small groups and try to escape.

Fuller himself, with Lieutenant Wright and three men, had gone about a mile when they stumbled upon a German assembly area in a wood. Although the Americans hid, one of them suddenly jumped up and began shouting, "*Kamerad!*" (He told Fuller later that a German was pointing a rifle at him.) Fuller and the others tried to run but without success, and in the melee somebody hit Fuller on the back of the head, knocking him unconscious.

Fuller came to to find he had a flesh wound from a bayonet in his stomach. Kicking him, his captors forced him to his feet, and along with Lieutenant Wright and the three men herded him to a battalion head-quarters. Once an interrogator had discerned his captive's rank, Fuller was soon on his way by truck to headquarters of the 2d Panzer Division on the other side of the Clerve in Bockholtz.

During the morning of the 18th, the 2d Panzer Division's reconnais-sance battalion felt out the positions of Task Force Rose at Antoniushof, and in early afternoon *Panzergrenadiers* and Mark IVs and Panthers at-tacked. Under direct fire from the big guns, Rose's armored infantrymen broke and fled in some confusion down Highway N-12 toward the Fe'itsch road junction. Fire from the tanks also forced the battery of field artillery to withdraw. That left only Captain Rose's Shermans and his assault gun platoon, and seven of the tanks (over a third of Rose's strength) were soon knocked out. Although Colonel Gilbreth asked per-mission to pull the remnants of Task Force Rose back to reinforce Task Force Harper at Fe'itsch, General Middleton refused.

Whether Rose could have made his way to Fe'itsch in any case was problematical. By the time night fell, he had had to relinquish the road junction itself, which afforded German tanks free passage in the darkness along N-12 to Fe'itsch. With or without orders, Rose finally decided to break out in another direction, toward the northwest and Houffalize, ten miles north of Bastogne. Five of the tanks and the assault guns made it; but near Houffalize, they ran into the 116th Panzer Division's reconnaissance battalion, which was moving forward after bypassing the 112th Infantry's positions near the frontier. Only a few of Rose's men escaped, eventually to make their way to Bastogne.

The end came even more quickly for Task Force Harper. In early darkness, *Panzergrenadiers* began to attack, reinforced a few hours later by Mark IVs and Panthers, which were equipped with new infrared night-sighting devices. It was no contest. Only three of the American tanks—or so it seemed to the Germans—offered any appreciable resistance, and when Colonel Harper was killed, the defense fell apart. The company of armored infantrymen broke first, but the surviving tanks soon followed, scurrying down the highway to Longvilly, where Colonel Gilbreth rallied them for defense of his headquarters.

Despite the collapse of Task Force Harper, Fe'itsch was not yet fully in German hands, for most of the stragglers from the 110th Infantry were still there. Shortly before dark, Colonel Seely had gained reinforcements, men from Captain Prestridge's Company G, who had been driven from Lullange. Even so, Seely had little hope of holding for long, and inside his command post in the farmhouse near the road junction, he had already told some forty officers and men to divide themselves into groups of three and four to be ready if necessary to pull out.

It would not be long before that time came. When a sentry came in to tell Seely that he could hear a tank approaching, Seely went outside. He could see nothing, for it was dark and a heavy fog had descended, but he could hear the tank. To Seely's accustomed ear, it was a Sherman, yet advancing so tentatively that Seely was convinced the driver was unfamiliar with it. Hurrying back inside the house, he yelled for attention. "There's a tank coming down the road," he shouted; "it's very close. It's an American tank but it's not an American driver. Go! Go! Go! Fast!"

Everybody dashed for the rear of the house. Most made it out windows and a back door, but not Seely himself. He, his operations sergeant, James M. Hanna, and the commander of the 109th Field Artillery Battalion, Lt. Col. Robert E. Ewing, were at the back of the group scrambling for the exits. They were opposite the door to the cellar when they heard the tank stop in front of the house. Seely yelled to the others to get into the cellar, and the three tumbled downstairs. For a moment, Seely congratulated himself on his foresight, for he and his companions had hardly started down the stairs when the tank put a round from its 75mm. gun through the center of the first floor.

On the other hand, Seely realized quickly that his decision had only short-term benefits. The single outside door of the cellar was open, and it faced the front of the house and the German-operated American tank. Seely still figured that in the foggy darkness he and the others might escape during a break in the German column; but that break never developed, for in the fog and darkness, the German vehicles were bumper to bumper.

In time, a half-track stopped directly in front of the house. Jumping down, a German soldier approached the door to the cellar, stuck his head in, and turned on a flashlight six inches from Colonel Seely's face. There was no possibility of escape.

Splitting up the three prisoners, the Germans put Seely on the hood of a half-track. As the column inched toward Longvilly, Seely took advantage of a pause, jumped off, and headed for a wood. Although bursts of fire followed him, he escaped without injury, but his freedom was to be short-lived. Groping through the dense fog, he bumped into the side of another German half-track.

Recaptured, Seely was to stay with that half-track for three days until a German company commander recollected that he had captured a senior officer and sent him to the rear. At headquarters of the 2d Panzer Division, his presence confused his interrogators. They had already captured one colonel, whom they had identified as the commander of the 110th Infantry, and they knew that two other regiments of the 28th Division, the 109th and 112th, were still intact. Thus they deduced, not without some logic, that Seely commanded the 111th Infantry, which, indeed, had been a part of the division before the U.S. Army adopted a triangular structure for its divisions. Seely said nothing to correct their error.

Colonel Gilbreth and the remnants of Task Force Harper in Longvilly were left in the meantime to wonder why the German tanks that had dealt such a blow at Fe'itsch failed to follow up their advantage, for through the night the Germans made no assault on Longvilly. The answer was that the 2d Panzer Division was not headed for Bastogne but for the Meuse. At a road junction a half mile outside Longvilly, the troops and vehicles of Colonel Lauchert's division turned off the main highway onto a road bypassing Bastogne to the north.

Whereas that turn spared the stragglers and headquarters troops in Longvilly, it trapped Task Force Booth, the small force that Gilbreth had established on high ground to screen Longvilly and his supporting artillery. Having lost radio contact with Gilbreth's headquarters, Colonel Booth during the night decided to try to save his little force by moving cross-country in hope of gaining American lines someplace, he knew not where. At seemingly every turn, the men and light tanks bumped into Germans. Although they managed to back off from those encounters, not quite three miles from the starting point at the village of Hardigny, a strong force of tanks and *Panzergrenadiers* cut the little task force to pieces. Eventually, in some cases after up to six days of wandering, some 225 men made their way into Bastogne.

In mid-afternoon of December 18, when the advance guard of General Bayerlein's *Panzer Lehr Division* and one of the *Panzergrenadier* regiments at last broke free of the traffic jam along the road leading up from the valley of the Clerve, Bayerlein, who was forward, split the column at the village of Eschweiler. He planned to take advantage of two roads leading toward Bastogne. Bayerlein sent the advance guard up the road on the left, while he himself moved with the *Panzergrenadier* regiment and fifteen Mark IV tanks on the right.

The road that Bayerlein was traveling led to the Fe'itsch road junction, but about a mile short of it Bayerlein took a back road leading directly toward Bastogne. As he made the turn, he could hear the sounds of fighting at Fe'itsch, and fiery tracer bullets gave the night "a fantastic aspect." Not long after 6 P.M., Bayerlein and his force drew up at the hamlet of Neiderwampach, less than six miles from Bastogne.

On the verge of victory in the race for Bastogne, Bayerlein pondered how to proceed from there. There were two choices. He could turn south to get onto a principal hard-surfaced highway leading from Ettelbruck and the valley of the Sûre River into Bastogne; or he could continue to the west along a side road to get onto the road from Fe'itsch and Longvilly to Bastogne at the village of Mageret, three miles from Bastogne. Because the side road was the more direct, because Bayerlein knew that American reinforcements would soon be arriving in Bastogne, and because he considered it unlikely that such a minor road would be defended, he chose the side route. Besides, civilians assured him the road was excellent. Nevertheless, concerned about its condition, he employed at first only a platoon of tanks and a company of *Panzergrenadiers*.

For a time, Bayerlein worried that he might have made a mistake, for the little road grew progressively worse until finally it was nothing but a muddy farm track. Yet for the most part his vehicles managed to traverse it, and at Mageret he found only a small detachment of the 158th Engineer Combat Battalion. Soon in control of the village, Bayerlein was preparing to head down the highway toward the goal of Bastogne when he received disturbing news. According to a Belgian man, a large American force with at least forty tanks and other vehicles, including artillery, had only a short time before passed through Mageret going in the direction of Longvilly.

If Bayerlein turned at Mageret to move into Bastogne, the American force would be in his rear. He had at that point only his *Panzergrenadiers*, a battery of artillery, and fifteen tanks, and much of that force still had to inch forward over the muddy track from Niederwampach. Did he dare turn his back on such a strong American force?

*   *   *

Preceding the main body of the 10th Armored Division's CCB, the commander, Colonel Roberts, reported into General Middleton's headquarters in Bastogne just before 4 P.M. on December 18. The Heintz Barracks was less bustling than usual, for at the direction of the commander of the 12th Army Group, General Bradley—with whom Middleton at that point had much better communications than with his immediate superior, General Hodges—Middleton had already started most of his headquarters troops moving to the rear, retaining only key staff officers and their assistants. He himself was determined to remain, despite admonitions from Bradley to the contrary, until he could brief Roberts and the commander of the airborne division.

Like most experienced armored commanders, Colonel Roberts, who had taught armored doctrine at the Command and General Staff College, was always wary of the way doughboy generals might employ armor. They had a tendency to use it in the fashion that helped bring the downfall of the French Army in 1940, not as a powerful massed force but in increments, often as infantry support. And Middleton—Roberts was aware—was a doughboy general.

Middleton's first question fulfilled all Bill Roberts's concerns: "How many teams can you make up?"

Reluctantly, Roberts responded: "Three."

Once Roberts had formed the three teams, said Middleton, he was to send one north of Bastogne on the Liège highway to the village of Noville; a second to the southeast to block the highway leading from Ettelbruck; and a third (in fact, the first to be formed) to what looked to be at the moment the most threatened point, Longvilly. However much Roberts disagreed with the splitting of his command, he conceded mentally that the corps commander knew more about the situation than he did.

Having had experience with wholesale retreat at Château-Thierry in May, 1918, Roberts wanted to know what he should do about stragglers. "Sir," he said, "I want authority to use those men." Middleton promptly agreed and the next morning issued an order specifically authorizing Roberts "to take over all or any part" of the 9th Armored Division's CCR "in case they show the slightest inclination to retire."

The force that Colonel Roberts sent to Longvilly was Team Cherry, named for Lt. Col. Henry T. Cherry, commander of the 3d Tank Battalion. Cherry had one of his own medium tank companies, two light tank platoons, a company of the 20th Armored Infantry Battalion, and a few reconnaissance troops, engineers, and medics.

It was Team Cherry that passed through Mageret on the way to Longvilly not long before General Bayerlein reached Mageret. Team Cherry had, in fact, not forty tanks—as the Belgian had told Bayerlein—but only seventeen mediums, ten lights, and no artillery. Whether the Belgian simply overestimated the American strength or deliberately misinformed Bayerlein was never determined, for the man was never identified. What mattered, in any case, was that the word of the American force made Bayerlein cautious and delayed even a probe toward Bastogne for six hours and a genuine attack considerably longer than that.

Roberts had yet to leave Middleton's headquarters in Bastogne when Middleton had another visitor, the commander of the 101st Airborne Division's artillery and, in General Taylor's absence, the acting division commander, Brig. Gen. Anthony C. McAuliffe. When McAuliffe left Camp Mourmelon, near Rheims, his orders were to go, not to Bastogne but, in accord with the wishes of General Hodges, to Werbomont. He had come by Middleton's headquarters only because he was some distance ahead of the trucks transporting his troops, had some time to spare, and welcomed a chance to find out the situation from Middleton.

What McAuliffe could not know was that when the commander of the 82d Airborne Division and acting commander of the XVIII Airborne Corps, General Gavin, reached the First Army's headquarters in Spa, he had found Hodges increasingly concerned about the threat posed by *Kampfgruppe Peiper*. Since Gavin's division was ahead of McAuliffe's, Hodges told Gavin to move to Werbomont to stop Peiper while the 101st Airborne Division went to Bastogne. Gavin got that word to his convoy, but it failed to reach McAuliffe's.

It did reach General Middleton, and he told McAuliffe. While it was still light, McAuliffe and his G-3, Lt. Col. Harry W. O. Kinnard, picked out an assembly area just west of Bastogne and sent a military policeman to a road junction to divert the march units of the 101st Airborne Division's convoy to Bastogne. Yet some of the march units had already passed the junction.

Acting commander of the division artillery because of General McAuliffe's change in roles, Col. Thomas L. Sherburne, at the head of the 101st Airborne Division's convoy, was becoming irritated by the accordion-like action of the 82d Airborne Division's convoy ahead of him. Fed up with the constant stop-and-go, stop-and-go, Sherburne paused at a crossroads northwest of Bastogne, wondering whether he might not gain time by detouring on a roundabout route to Werbomont by way of Bastogne. When a sergeant of military police told him that some hours earlier General McAuliffe and his party had turned toward Bastogne, Sherburne told the MP on duty at the crossroads to divert all march units of the 101st Airborne Division to Bastogne. By that chance development, the division was soon on its way to where the American command wanted and vitally needed it.

That was not to say that movement to the assembly area just outside Bastogne was swift. The trucks carrying men of the airborne division had to buck heavy traffic generated by service units withdrawing from Bastogne, and officers of those units, under orders to fall back, insisted on priority on the road. In the congestion, once a group of vehicles came to a halt, many a driver dozed off, so that in the end it took MPs moving up and down the column to awaken drivers and keep the traffic flowing in both directions.

First units of the 101st Airborne Division nevertheless began arriving in the assembly area near Bastogne around midnight on December 18. The men were cold and wet, having ridden in big cattle trucks through rain with no overhead cover and having left Camp Mourmelon so hurriedly that many lacked helmets, ammunition, some even weapons; and hardly anybody had overcoats or overshoes. They were to have little sleep and little time to prepare for the battle ahead of them, but what mattered was that they were there.

The advance guard of CCB's Team Cherry, commanded by 1st Lt. Edward P. Hyduke and composed mainly of light tanks and armored cars, reached the edge of Longvilly around 7 P.M. on the 18th. As far as Hyduke could make out, the village was jammed with men and vehicles of the 9th Armored Division's CCR. Rather than risk getting his vehicles intermingled with those of CCR, Hyduke halted his column and radioed Colonel Cherry, who came forward and went into Longvilly to talk with CCR's commander, Colonel Gilbreth.

Gilbreth was elated to learn of Team Cherry's arrival, for at that hour Task Force Harper was still holding at the Fe'itsch road junction and Gilbreth assumed Team Cherry would help. Colonel Cherry quickly squashed the idea; his orders, he said, were to go no farther than Longvilly.

Learning that Gilbreth had no plans other than to carry out his orders to hold at all costs, Cherry headed back to Bastogne to explain the situation to Colonel Roberts and get a decision as to where to position his command. He told Lieutenant Hyduke, in the meantime, to deploy the advance guard in fighting positions on the Bastogne side of Longvilly, thereby avoiding confusion with CCR. Hyduke chose positions on high ground along the highway near a roadside religious shrine, the grotto of St. Michael.

As Colonel Cherry passed back through Mageret, General Bayerlein and his tanks and *Panzergrenadiers* had just arrived. Although Cherry's jeep drew some small-arms fire, Cherry thought it was from trigger-happy American stragglers, picked up speed, and proceeded on his way. In Bastogne—where Colonel Roberts had yet to receive Middleton's order telling him to prevent CCR from retiring—Roberts told Cherry that should CCR withdraw, Cherry was to cover the withdrawal; but no matter what, Team Cherry was to hold.

When Cherry started back, he got no farther than the hamlet of Neffe, a half mile short of Mageret, where he had earlier established his headquarters in a nearby château. There he learned that at least a strong

German patrol was in Mageret. By radio, he ordered the commander of the armored infantry company with Team Cherry, Capt. William F. Ryerson, to send a patrol to open the road through Mageret.

Ryerson sent two squads of armored infantry in a half-track. Short of the first houses, the men dismounted and made their way on foot to a crossroads in the center of the village. There they determined that in fact at least three German tanks and a company of infantry were in the village, too much for two squads to think of tackling.

Just as the men were getting ready to pull out, they heard the noise of a tracked vehicle approaching from the rear. Were they to be trapped? After a breathless wait, they found it to be a self-propelled tank destroyer, which CCR's commander, Colonel Gilbreth, had sent to clear Mageret. Along with the tank destroyer, the two squads withdrew.

When Captain Ryerson radioed word on the enemy's strength to Colonel Cherry, Cherry ordered him to leave Lieutenant Hyduke's force as a rear guard and turn the medium tanks and armored infantry to clear the Germans from Mageret. That Ryerson prepared to do, but it was to be a difficult assignment, partly because an ugly situation was about to develop in Longvilly.

In late evening of December 18, Colonel Gilbreth faced a crisis. He had lost Task Force Rose and much of Task Force Harper, he had no contact with Task Force Booth and no way of knowing whether it still existed, his own field artillery battalion and the separate 58th Armored Field Artillery Battalion were under intermittent shelling from German tanks and assault guns and direct pressure from German patrols, and he himself and his headquarters were in what amounted to the front line, no place from which to direct a battle. Shortly before midnight, Gilbreth told his staff and headquarters troops to prepare to withdraw to Bastogne, while the combat troops (mainly the men, half-tracks, and tanks that had fallen back from the Fe'itsch road junction) were to stay behind to hold Longvilly and screen the artillery.

Word for the headquarters troops to withdraw went out in a grim setting. Pitch darkness, a clinging fog, German searchlights in the distance, fiery arcs of tracer bullets, eerie flickers of flares. There was shelling, the occasional chatter of burp guns from German patrols, and everywhere untold confusion. To many a man it looked like Armageddon, and somewhere just over a hill or two, maybe three, there was a place where he could escape it: Bastogne.

There was no way to confine word of the withdrawal to the few who were supposed to execute it, and for men who had just experienced the enemy's deadly power at the Fe'itsch road junction, it was easy to convince themselves that the order to fall back applied to them too. At the appointed hour for men of the headquarters to depart, seemingly every man, every vehicle, every gun in Longvilly converged on the western exit from the village. Soon there was panic, an ugly panic.

Somehow Colonel Gilbreth and his staff managed to stop it. Gilbreth "cut the column in the middle" and ordered that not another vehicle, not another man, including the headquarters troops, was to leave Longvilly until daylight. Yet in the meantime, those vehicles that had succeeded in getting out of the village added to the congestion already created on the narrow highway leading to Mageret by the presence of Team Cherry's half-tracks and tanks.

On the German side that night, the commander of the 47th Panzer Corps, General von Lüttwitz, unaware that American reinforcements had reached Bastogne but expecting them at any time, ordered an all-out attack to take the town at daylight the next morning, December 19. In keeping with General von Manteuffel's original plan, the 2d Panzer Division was to continue along its route, bypassing Bastogne, and because the 5th Parachute Division was lagging far behind and thus exposing the south flank of the panzer corps, a regiment of the 26th Volksgrenadier Division was to screen that flank. Every other force available to the corps was to drive for Bastogne. From Mageret and along the next road to the south, the *Panzer Lehr Division* was to make a two-pronged thrust against the town, while two regiments of the 26th Volksgrenadier Division marched north through Longvilly to gain the village of Bizory and pivot against Bastogne from the northeast and north.

Neither von Lüttwitz nor the commander of the *Volksgrenadiers*, Colonel Kokott, knew of the presence of Team Cherry along the Mageret-Longvilly road, and they thought the Germans held Longvilly. That was not the case, but neither did the Americans, for with the first traces of daylight, all that was left of the 9th Armored Division's CCR began a disorderly exodus onto the road to Mageret. Once on the road, the vehicles had no place to go, for on one side the ground dropped off sharply into a marsh and on the other it rose steeply. The only exit from the road, a steep, muddy farm track leading north to the hamlet of Arloncourt, was blocked by vehicles that had tried to get out that way during the night; and at Mageret, the Germans still held the village.

At daylight, the commander of Team Cherry's armored infantry company, Captain Ryerson, tried to execute his assignment of driving the Germans from Mageret. Because of the obstacles on either side of the highway, Ryerson had trouble getting tanks and half-tracks turned around to make the attack. Their job was made the more difficult by the crush of CCR's vehicles, which in some places jammed the highway by moving abreast of Ryerson's vehicles in the other lane of the two-lane road. Not until mid-morning was Ryerson able to get a small force headed for Mageret with a medium tank in the lead.

Some three hundred yards outside Mageret, the highway passed through a cut and at the far end of it swung left. As the leading tank reached that point, a German antitank gun knocked it out. The tank burst into flames, partially blocking the road.

Dismounting from the half-tracks, infantrymen tried to get past the burning tank, but small-arms fire from Mageret turned them back. Shells from two 105mm. assault guns slowed the firing for a while, but each time the infantry tried to advance, it increased again.

The infantry was still trying to make it when two half-tracks of the 482d Antiaircraft Artillery Battalion, attached to CCR, raced forward, their drivers obviously determined to get out no matter what. Team Cherry's infantrymen shouted for the half-tracks to stop, but the drivers paid no heed. Just as they reached the bend in the road, they spotted the burning tank. Seeing that they were about to crash, drivers and the other men on the half-tracks jumped clear. With the half-tracks wrecked against the remains of the tank, no vehicle was going to get through.

For much of the morning, the blocked American column escaped major interference from the Germans, for General von Lüttwitz's order to attack at daylight was unrealistic. During the night advance, troops had crossed and recrossed unit boundaries, and some order had to be established. So, too, the division commanders felt compelled to delay in order to bring up food and ammunition and to afford their men at least a few hours' rest.

It was late morning before Colonel Kokott got his two *Volksgrenadier* regiments on the move, one to cross the Mageret-Longvilly highway, the other to pass through Longvilly. Hardly had they begun to advance when they came under fire from Lieutenant Hyduke's force from Team Cherry on the high ground near the grotto of St. Michael, the only American force along the highway occupying a viable fighting position. It took three hours for Kokott to get an attack organized against Hyduke's force, but when it started he had help from a portion of the *Panzer Lehr Division,* for General Bayerlein was determined to deal with the armored force in his rear before committing himself to an all-out attack against Bastogne.

For all Bayerlein's concern about that armored force, he himself was at that point directing less than full attention to conduct of the battle. In a wood outside Mageret, his troops had found a platoon from an American field hospital, and among the staff, a "young, blonde, and beautiful" American nurse attracted Bayerlein's attention. Through much of December 19, he "dallied" with the nurse, who "held him spellbound."

When German artillery, *Nebelwerfers,* and tanks at last opened fire, they pummeled not only Lieutenant Hyduke's positions but the trapped convoy of American tanks, half-tracks, self-propelled artillery, armored cars, trucks, jeeps, and ambulances along the road between Longvilly and Mageret. Here and there vehicles were soon burning, sending up great clouds of black smoke. Crews of the tanks and self-propelled artillery tried to fight back, firing at German tanks at long range—and occasionally scoring a hit—but for the most part, the men and machines along the highway were helpless. Only along some short stretches of the road were there woods providing concealment, and only where the road passed through the cut near Mageret was there any protection from the enemy fire.

Lieutenant Hyduke, his men, armored cars, light tanks, and tank destroyers (he appropriated the lone surviving platoon of CCR's 811th Tank Destroyer Battalion) held near the grotto of St. Michael for a little more than an hour, in the process knocking out eight German tanks, but time finally ran out. Ordered by Colonel Cherry to fall back on the main body of Team Cherry, Hyduke had to order his remaining vehicles destroyed, for there was no way they could get past the double bank of vehicles along the constricted highway behind them.

As darkness fell, somebody managed to push aside the vehicles blocking the steep track leading north from the highway to Arloncourt, and most of the self-propelled artillery and a few other vehicles inched out along that route. Many men headed cross-country on foot (among them the forward observer from the 109th Field Artillery, Sergeant Johnson). The coming of darkness also enabled Ryerson's armored infantrymen at last to gain enough of a foothold at the edge of Mageret to afford access to a dirt road leading west in the general direction of Bastogne. Once tanks had shoved aside the wreckage that blocked the highway at the cut in the road, Ryerson was able to get most of the surviving tanks and other vehicles out by that route. He got most of the wounded out the same way.

Team Cherry and the 9th Armored Division's CCR paid dearly along the Mageret-Longvilly road. The effect when combined with earlier losses at Antoniushof and Fe'itsch was that CCR had virtually ceased to exist. Its armored field artillery battalion got none of its howitzers out, although the corps battalion, the 58th, lost only four pieces. Team Cherry lost 175 officers and men—a fourth of the command—7 light and 10 medium tanks and 17 half-tracks. Under the circumstances, it was incredible that any men or vehicles escaped.

To those casualties in the race for Bastogne would have to be added those incurred by the 28th Division's 110th Infantry and its attached and supporting units. And their losses were horrendous. The 110th Infantry lost 2,750 officers and men wounded, captured, and killed—virtually the entire regiment—and almost all its vehicles and the six howitzers of its Cannon Company. Company B of the 103d Engineers was wiped out. The 109th Field Artillery lost a hundred men, all the howitzers of one battery, and two of another. Except for nine medium tanks, most of them crippled, and five assault guns, the 707th Tank Battalion lost two entire companies of medium tanks, a company of lights, and most of the crews. So, too, the 630th Tank Destroyer Battalion lost most of its men and all but six of its towed guns, and a company of the 447th Antiaircraft Artillery Battalion was also virtually erased. CCR's Company B, 2d Tank Battalion, lost fourteen out of seventeen medium tanks and most of the crews.

It was impossible to ascertain with accuracy what the fight cost the Germans, but losses of forces on the attack almost always exceed those of forces on the defense. What mattered, in any case, was not the losses in men, machines, and guns but the loss in precious hours.

Had the 2d Panzer Division and the 26th Volksgrenadier Division crossed the Clerve River on the first day, December 16, the Germans would have captured Bastogne, and the *Panzer Lehr Division* would have been free to join the 2d Panzer Division in a drive to the Meuse with almost nothing in the way. Muddy roads, traffic jams, and difficulty in installing bridges across the Our River were partly responsible for the delay, but in the main the men of the 110th Infantry were responsible, both on the first day and the second. All of that accomplished by easily the most overextended regiment on the American front, a regiment that only a few weeks before had had its guts ripped out in the Hürtgen Forest.

Those delays, combined with that imposed by the 9th Armored Division's CCR, enabled American reinforcements to win the race for Bastogne. Yet even after the 10th Armored Division's CCB arrived, the Germans still might have seized the town had it not been for Team Cherry, which for all the "mischance and confusion" along the road between Longvilly and Mageret, had posed such a threat (real or imagined) that General Bayerlein had delayed the final thrust on Bastogne by his *Panzer Lehr Division*. Perhaps a minor accolade might be accorded the unidentified American nurse who diverted Bayerlein from focusing on his appointed task at a critical hour.

Even after the arrival of troops of the 101st Airborne Division in their assembly area just outside Bastogne around midnight of the 18th, the town was still in dire peril, for only a combat command of armor, a lightly armed airborne division, a few artillery battalions, and a few other small units were available for Bastogne's defense. In winning the race for Bastogne, the Americans had nevertheless forced General von Manteuffel to face a critical decision: Bastogne, the Meuse, or both? Much would hinge on that decision, and it was not von Manteuffel's alone to make.

CHAPTER FOURTEEN

The Defense of Wiltz

When General Cota late on December 17 obtained authority to pull the 110th Infantry behind the Clerve River, so little was left of the regiment that all Cota could hope to do was delay for a time at his headquarters town of Wiltz. But why Wiltz? What would a delay at Wiltz accomplish?

Holding Wiltz would block three minor roads that converged on the town: one climbing up from the valley of the Clerve at Wilwerwiltz; another meandering along a wooded, clifflike hillside high above the scenic trace of the little Wiltz River from the confluence of the Wiltz and the Clerve at Kautenbach; and a third entering the town from the south off the Ettelbruck-Bastogne highway. Since the Germans had roads north of Wiltz leading to Bastogne—of which Cota was surely aware by daylight of December 18—and since delaying at Wiltz would leave nobody for blocking the principal Ettelbruck-Bastogne highway, who needed those roads through Wiltz? Holding the town however long would do nothing to keep the Germans out of Bastogne.

It looked to be one of those decisions taken at any number of places in the early days of the German offensive that rested on nothing more logical than that American troops were there; ergo, American troops should stay until the Germans kicked them out. Why not let Wiltz go and instead defend the Ettelbruck-Bastogne highway? For anybody holding Wiltz, leaving that highway unprotected was, in any case, asking for disaster.

With a population of four thousand, Wiltz was, in essence, two towns: the first a picturesque quarter, set high on a ridgeline and dominated by a château dating from the thirteenth century that overlooked the deep-cut valley of the Wiltz; and the second a more prosaic quarter on low ground to the west, close along the river. The roads from Kautenbach and the Ettelbruck-Bastogne highway entered upper Wiltz; that from Wilwerwiltz, lower Wiltz.

Having released the 110th Infantry's Company G from the mission of defending the division's command post, Cota had left only a provisional battalion formed from headquarters and postal clerks, bandsmen, telephone linemen, drivers, MPs, whatever. Men of that battalion were digging in outside Wiltz during the morning of the 18th when the corps commander, General Middleton, sent help: the six hundred-man 44th Engineer Combat Battalion, commanded by Lt. Col. Clarion J. Kjeldseth. When Cota learned that the 10th Armored Division's CCB was moving up from the Third Army, he sent a liaison officer to the commander, Colonel Roberts, asking his help, in particular to block the Ettelbruck-Bastogne highway. Roberts replied, sorry; he had his orders to go to Bastogne.

From Wiltz, Cota sent two companies of the engineers beyond the little Wiltz River to block roads in the villages of Eschweiler and Erpeldange leading up from the valley of the Clerve, while the third company and the provisional battalion constituted a reserve. The other two roads were of no particular concern at the moment, for Colonel Strickler and what was left of the 110th Infantry's 3d Battalion were soon to withdraw from Consthum to help defend upper Wiltz.

Fire support was limited: six crippled Shermans and five assault guns of the 707th Tank Battalion, six towed guns of the 630th Tank Destroyer Battalion, a few half-tracks of the 447th Antiaircraft Artillery Battalion, and a few armored cars of the 28th Reconnaissance Troop. On the southeastern fringe of upper Wiltz were the 105mm. howitzers of the 687th Field Artillery Battalion, which had fallen back in stages from their original firing positions near the southern end of the Skyline Drive.

General Cota was actually preparing a party to which no German commander wanted to come. General von Lüttwitz of the 47th Panzer Corps had no interest in Wiltz other than to assure that nobody made a foray from the town into his flank, which was why he told the commander of the 26th Volksgrenadier Division, Colonel Kokott, to withhold a regiment to keep an eye on it. So, too, even though Wiltz lay in the zone of the Seventh Army's 5th Parachute Division, the commander of that division, Col. Ludwig Heilmann, had no designs on Wiltz. He wanted to move as fast as possible to blocking positions south of Bastogne, and that could best be achieved by bypassing Wiltz.

Around midday on December 18, it nevertheless appeared to the Americans that a battle for Wiltz was beginning with German attacks at Eschweiler and Erpeldange; but those attacks, which overran two of the towed tank destroyers, were actually a part of the *Panzer Lehr Division*'s efforts to get out of the valley of the Clerve and gain Bastogne. The attacks still forced American troops back to the Wiltz River, only a few hundred yards from the first buildings of lower Wiltz. Lest the sole remaining tanks and assault guns of the 707th Tank Battalion be lost, Cota

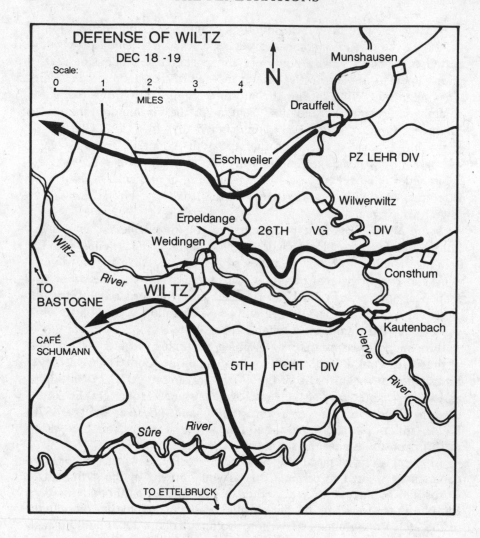

ordered withdrawal behind the Wiltz and the bridge destroyed; but for some reason, the bridge remained intact.

To the surprise of the defenders, the Germans failed to follow. As *Panzer Lehr*'s columns moved on, the regiment of the 26th Volksgrenadier Division assigned to guard the flank arrived. Yet, that regiment had no intention of attacking Wiltz and exerted so little pressure that early the next day, December 19, Cota ordered the engineers to push out again to Erpeldange, there to block the road from Wilwerwiltz with a little greater margin of safety than at the crossing of the Wiltz River on the very fringe of Wiltz. Seeing that move as a possible threat, the *Volksgrenadiers* attacked and drove the Americans a second time across the Wiltz River. That time the engineers blew the bridge.

*   *   *

Before daylight that morning, the 19th, General Cota sent his headquarters out of Wiltz to relocate ten miles to the rear in Sibret, southwest of Bastogne. A platoon of the 42d Field Hospital, which had been operating in the old château in upper Wiltz, also departed, taking most of the patients, but twenty-six were in such serious condition that the surgeons ruled they would have to be left behind. Several surgeons and technicians volunteered to remain with them. The provisional battalion also remained in Wiltz, and Cota himself departed only in late afternoon after Colonel Strickler and the remnants of the 110th Infantry's 3d Battalion had arrived from Consthum. Cota left Strickler in command at Wiltz.

By that time, a genuine attack against Wiltz was in the making. Not that the commander of the German parachute division, Colonel Heilmann, wanted it any more than before but because he was having trouble maintaining control of his regiments, whose commanders were as inexperienced in battle as were most of the troops. Rather than following orders to bypass defended villages, the paratroopers fought for them: They wanted loot and a warm place to pass the night. That was the basic reason why the parachute division was trailing its neighbors to the north; and partly by chance, the same thing happened at Wiltz.

Trying to get past the town, the parachute division's advance guard lost its way and in mid-afternoon of the 19th blundered into the firing positions of the 687th Field Artillery Battalion on the fringe of upper Wiltz. The artillerymen used direct fire from their howitzers to knock out assault guns accompanying the paratroopers, but in the process, they expended all their artillery rounds.

As night fell, the American battalion commander, Lt. Col. Max E. Billingsley, ordered withdrawal to a rendezvous point at a crossroads on the Ettelbruck-Bastogne highway four miles outside Wiltz, known from an inn located there as the Café Schumann crossroads. After assembling there, Billingsley intended displacing farther to the rear, for since he had no ammunition, there was no point in risking loss of his howitzers.

When the commander of the 110th Infantry's 3d Battalion, Major Milton, saw the howitzers leaving, he assumed that a prepared withdrawal plan was in effect. Unable to contact Colonel Strickler by radio to verify it, Milton told his force of about two hundred men to follow the artillery. They had reached a three-pronged road junction, where two roads from Wiltz join the Ettelbruck-Bastogne highway less than a mile from the Café Schumann crossroads, when a messenger from Strickler overtook them in a jeep. There had been no order to withdraw, the word was, and if Milton continued, he would jeopardize the rest of the garrison in Wiltz.

Milton sent word with the messenger that he would await instructions at the road junction. Having no further word after waiting more than an hour, he borrowed the only jeep remaining to the battalion, that of the artillery liaison officer, and went back to Wiltz and Strickler's headquarters.

There he learned that the defense of the town was collapsing. Ammunition was nearly exhausted, and on the heights east of upper Wiltz, a regiment of the 5th Parachute Division had made several dents in the line. Almost all the U.S. tanks and assault guns were either destroyed or immobilized, the crews of those few still functioning so exhausted that at every pause, they fell asleep. There had been no contact for hours with the 28th Division's headquarters at Sibret; and advance parties sent to assembly areas west of Wiltz to which the units in the town were to withdraw returned with word that German paratroopers held them. It began to look as if Wiltz was surrounded.

With that news, Strickler saw no hope of any orderly withdrawal. Instead, he told all commanders to try to pull back with their units intact. Should that prove impossible, they were to break into small groups and try to work their way westward. Move out, said Strickler, as soon as ready.

With two other officers of the 3d Battalion whom Major Milton had encountered at Strickler's headquarters, Milton began to make his way on foot back to his battalion at the road junction. On Strickler's orders, the battalion was to block the Ettelbruck-Bastogne highway until the units leaving Wiltz could get past. Executing that order presupposed the continued existence of the residue of his battalion.

Not long after Major Milton first left for Wiltz, the men of his battalion, having begun to dig in on either side of the Ettelbruck-Bastogne highway at the road junction, heard the sound of marching feet. Because Milton had said that the men were to fire only if attacked, the officers passed the word to hold fire. A platoon of German paratroopers, each man pushing a bicycle, paraded past.

When the Germans disappeared, the officers assembled the men on the highway with the idea of continuing to withdraw when heavy firing broke out in the direction of the Café Schumann crossroads. The men scurried for cover. When it became apparent that the firing was some distance away, they began to return to the road; but not all of them. At least half the men had decided to take off, to try to make their way out individually or in small groups.

As the officers were preparing to march the remaining men toward the Café Schumann crossroads, headlights blazed behind them along one of the roads from Wiltz, and a burst of machine-gun fire erupted. The firing came from an American armored car, which was leading a convoy of various types of American vehicles, all with headlights on. The men in the convoy were trying to brazen their way out. Having spotted three figures on the road, the machine gunners on the armored car had fired.

Moments later, the headlights picked up the clump of men from the

3d Battalion. Recognizing them as Americans, the driver stopped. After a hurried conference, the two groups joined forces, and the men of the 3d Battalion clambered aboard the vehicles. One who clung to the side of the armored car in the lead was the erstwhile commander of Company L, Lieutenant Saymon.

The three figures at which the armored car's machine gunner fired had in the meantime pulled themselves from the ditches: Major Milton and the two officers accompanying him. Arriving at the spot where Milton had left his men, they found nobody, and from the direction of the Café Schumann, they heard heavy firing. All that was left to do, the officers agreed, was to head west as best they could. Several days later, having picked up a few stragglers along the way, they arrived in Sibret.

The artillerymen of the 687th Field Artillery Battalion reached the Café Schumann crossroads not long after full darkness descended. After placing outposts on all four points of entry to the crossroads, the battery commanders were getting ready to feed their men, then continue the withdrawal.

At the outpost southeast of the crossroads on the Ettelbruck-Bastogne highway, small-arms fire erupted. The platoon of German paratroopers that had just marched past Major Milton's men had reached the crossroads. The paratroopers quickly deployed and attacked. Spread out in fields and woods around the crossroads with the vehicles and artillery pieces, few of the artillerymen got involved in the fight, for the attack centered on the crossroads itself, where the only Americans were the officers and men of the battalion headquarters inside the café.

As the firing began, the commander of Battery A, Capt. Norris D. McGinnis, whose howitzers were beyond the crossroads in the direction of Bastogne, told his men to pull out. At that point the battery had only three guns, which were destined to get out and eventually join the defenders of Bastogne. That was about all that was to be left of the 687th Field Artillery Battalion.

The fight for the crossroads was in full swing when up the road, in rear of the paratroopers, appeared the convoy of vehicles with headlights on. Stunned, the Germans at first held their fire, but when about half the vehicles had passed, they opened a blaze of fire. A *Panzerfaust* knocked out a half-track close behind two leading armored cars, blocking the road. Another knocked out a tank farther back in the column. Fire from burp guns and machine guns swept men from the vehicles "like autumn leaves before a strong wind." Most who survived the first fusillade dived for the ditches, but the ditches already belonged to the Germans.

Small-arms fire swept off most of the men clinging to the sides of the two leading armored cars, but as the machine gunners worked their weapons relentlessly, a few continued to hold on, including Lieutenant Saymon. After what seemed an eternity, the two armored cars finally broke free and were soon on their way toward Bastogne. Although hit in the left leg, Saymon was still holding on.

At the crossroads, the screams and moans of the wounded mingled with the sound of continued firing. Inside the café, officers of the battalion headquarters considered their situation hopeless, and if anything was to be done for the wounded, they would have to surrender. The operations officer, Maj. Edgar P. German, who spoke German, called for a cease-fire. The Germans complied.

As the officers had hoped, the Germans helped move the wounded into the café, but for a time there was a question whether the able-bodied would survive. Overhearing German conversations, Major German detected that the paratroopers were under orders to speed their attack, and handling a large body of prisoners would delay them. A sergeant was adamant that the prisoners should be shot, but before he could act, a captain arrived. There would be no killing of prisoners, he decreed.

In the melee, the 687th Field Artillery lost almost all its vehicles and all howitzers but the three of Battery A. As for the men, many melted into the darkness even as the surrender was taking place, and a few eventually made their way to safety. The Germans marched those who surrendered away from the crossroads and held them temporarily in a wood. From there, the men could hear renewed firing at the crossroads.

That was German fire directed at another column of vehicles trying to escape from Wiltz, made up primarily of men of the provisional battalion who had climbed aboard anything with wheels or tracks that could still function. As the men in that convoy soon learned, the Germans had by that time installed mines across the main highway at the three-pronged road junction and backed up the roadblock with paratroopers and machine guns.

When the leading half-track hit a mine, it blew up. The driver of the next vehicle, a half-track of the 447th Antiaircraft Artillery Battalion, its quad-50s blazing, drove deliberately into the minefield; that half-track, too, went up in a deafening explosion, but it got rid of the mines. As the paratroopers fled, the sacrifice made by the men in the half-track provided a safe path for the vehicles that followed.

The encouragement the rest of the men gained from that experience was short-lived, for just down the road was the Café Schumann crossroads. There the paratroopers had erected another roadblock amid the wreckage of American vehicles and the bodies of American and German dead. As the convoy approached, a *Panzerfaust* hit the first armored car at point-blank range. Turning over from the impact, the vehicle burst into flames, lighting the scene for German machine gunners so well that it was difficult for them to miss their concentrated target.

Yet the Germans were dealing with near-desperate men, and amid the pandemonium three dozen of them rushed forward from the rear of the

American column, firing and hurling grenades. The Germans fell back. Once a half-track cleared a passage through the wrecked vehicles, the convoy continued toward Bastogne.

Again the men's encouragement was to be short-lived. Only a few hundred yards beyond the crossroads, they came upon another road-block. Vehicles burned; men fell left and right. The few survivors threw themselves into the ditches, then took advantage of the darkness to crawl away, eventually to get far enough from the scene of the carnage to dare to rise and run. Many were destined to blunder into German positions or to come across German patrols; but some—nobody would ever know just how many—eventually made their way out.

The experiences of the men in those two convoys were much like those of all others who tried to get away from Wiltz that terrible night, for there was no denying the inevitable consequences of an ill-advised decision to fight a delaying action with no provision for keeping escape routes open. The last organized unit to attempt to leave, the 44th Engineer Combat Battalion, lost more than 160 men in the withdrawal; added to the casualties incurred inside Wiltz, that meant that the battalion had lost more than half its strength.

Every man who got out had his own personal odyssey: kindness from Belgian civilians whenever he dared enter a village, but mostly bitter cold, hunger, fear, lack of sleep, water-logged feet often leading to trench foot. Those few who turned south into the heavily wooded country along the Sûre River had the greater fortune, for the Germans had yet to push far to the south. Yet few men knew that, and since many had heard the names of only two places to their rear—Bastogne and Sibret—those drew them like lodestones, particularly Bastogne. For any number of men, heading for those places was their undoing, since those were the two towns for which the Germans were heading. It was only with fortitude, perseverance, guile, and a triple helping of luck that anybody got through.

One who did get through was the commander in Wiltz at the end, Dan Strickler. Before ripping a map off the wall in the command post and burning it, Strickler tore out the section depicting the region around Bastogne and thrust it inside his shirt. He also made sure he had a compass.

An hour before midnight, Strickler, the 28th Division's assistant G-3, Maj. Carl W. Plitt, and Strickler's driver, Cpl. Robert Martin, took off in Strickler's jeep. They had gone only a short distance in the direction of the Café Schumann crossroads when German mortars and machine guns opened fire. In trying to evade the fire, Martin drove the jeep into a ditch, and it was impossible to get it out. At that point, they had no alternative but to proceed on foot, moving north to get around the Café

Schumann crossroads, then to cross the Ettelbruck-Bastogne highway farther along, and head west for Sibret.

The trek that began with that decision turned out to be grueling and nervewracking. A crackling noise in the woods. Was it Germans? In one case, it turned out to be an American corporal, the division chaplain's assistant. Later other American soldiers emerged in ones or twos, mainly MPs, among the last to leave Wiltz, so that in little more than an hour Strickler's group increased from three to ten.

Reaching the Ettelbruck-Bastogne highway, the group paused for a long time to observe the pattern of German traffic before seizing a quiet moment to dash across. Avoiding roads and villages, the men plodded on through "mud, fields, streams, forests, underbrush, and over barbed-wire fences and stone walls." Whenever they paused to rest, most dropped off to sleep, then awoke trembling from the cold. They drank from streams, but there was nothing to eat.

As daylight neared, Strickler halted the men in a patch of woods overlooking a village. If daylight revealed no Germans, he intended sending someone into the village to find food. He was about ready to venture it when a man and a boy ran up from the village into the woods. The man explained that he was fleeing lest the Germans deport him as a laborer. The name of his village, he said, was Tarchamps.

Strickler, checking the map inside his shirt, realized that he and his group had covered over half the distance to Sibret. Considering that they had moved cross-country and in the dark, they were making remarkable progress.

While Strickler was questioning the civilian man, a German column roared by on the road below, assault guns with soldiers riding on the decks interspersed with captured American jeeps and trucks. Pulling deeper into the woods, Strickler insisted that the man and his son come along; he could trust nobody.

The little group sat out the daylight hours of December 20 in the woods. Although two other small groups of fleeing American soldiers stumbled upon the hideout, all agreed that their chances of escape were better in small groups than together.

Strickler's goal that night was to get across the major Arlon-Bastogne highway; but as he and his men reached the highway, German traffic was almost constant and every three hundred yards or so there was a listening post. In time they finally reached a point where the highway passed through a wood, and a slow, careful search revealed no listening post. Even so, Strickler decided to wait to cross until around 3 A.M. when the Germans might be less alert. Then all went well, except that there turned out to be a barbed-wire fence on the far side of the road and in the darkness, several men drew blood as they tugged frantically at their clothing to free themselves, expecting a German vehicle to appear at any moment.

Beyond the highway, at the first village, German armored vehicles were entering, and dogs emerged, barking furiously. At the next, which Strickler identified as Hollange, it appeared so quiet that he decided to risk an attempt to get food. While the others hid behind a haystack at the edge of the village, Strickler and his driver, Corporal Martin, approached a house.

As they neared, a farmer appeared at the door with a lantern. Asking in halting French for food, Strickler also asked if there were many German soldiers. As he raised the lantern for Strickler to have a look, Strickler saw the hallway full of sleeping Germans and in an adjoining room an officer sprawled across a bed.

"*Merci beaucoup*," said Strickler, and pretending nonchalance, he and Martin walked away. The farmer must have thought that they, too, were Germans, and at that point Strickler had no wish to alter the impression.

To get away from Hollange, the men had to wade a stream that turned out to be waist deep. So wet and cold that it was hard to keep moving, they reached another wood from which they could look down on Hollange. At daylight the village came alive with German soldiers, who mounted bicycles and rode away.

To Strickler, there was no question but that they had to do something to get dry. Drawing back deep into the woods, he took the chance, over the objection of several of the men, of lighting a small fire, and the men took turns drying their clothing.

During the break, one man pulled a K-ration packet from his jacket. He agreed to share it (he had little choice) and the ten divided it carefully. Each had five sips of bouillon, a nibble from a cracker, and a single bite of the egg-and-ham mixture that came with a breakfast meal.

Setting out again as the night of December 21 approached, they ran almost immediately into dense, briar-laced undergrowth that tore at their uniforms and their skin. Famished, exhausted, disgruntled, and frightened, some of the men were close to delirium, but Strickler pressed them on. When they finally emerged from the undergrowth, they were so fatigued that they took their chances in the open and marched down a dirt road until they came to a hamlet. They knocked on several houses before a man finally opened his door.

Strickler said his men had to have food, and the Belgian invited them in. Two days before, he told them, American troops had blown a bridge just beyond the hamlet, and he was expecting the Germans at any moment. He nevertheless produced ersatz coffee, milk, bread, butter, and jam.

An hour later, food in their stomachs and the warmth of the Belgian's fire a pleasant memory, they set out again. Some three miles away, American sentries challenged them. They had reached Vaux-les-Rosières astride a principal highway leading southwest out of Bastogne to the town of Neufchâteau. Having had to relinquish Sibret, General Cota and what

was left of the 28th Division's headquarters had paused there for the
night.

By daylight on December 20, men of the 5th Parachute Division controlled Wiltz. When they found an occasional American straggler, they
sent him to the old château in upper Wiltz to help with the wounded.
There the surgeons and technicians left behind by the 42d Field Hospital
cared both for the seriously wounded Americans left behind and for German casualties. Shouting that one of the surgeons, Capt. Harry Fisher,
was Jewish, the Germans took him away, leaving his colleagues to assume grimly that the Germans shot him. In reality, the Germans used
him to work at a front-line aid station just outside Bastogne at the village
of Marvie and employed him at other forward aid stations until the end of
the war.

There were two other Americans in Wiltz of whom the Germans had
no knowledge. One was Sgt. George Carroll, found, painfully wounded
in the shoulder, by an elderly couple in lower Wiltz, M. and Mme. Jean-
Pierre Balthasar. Reluctantly—for it was a terrible risk—the couple hid
him in their attic. The second was Pvt. Ralph Ellis, one of a few to escape
from the positions of the 110th Infantry's Company C and Cannon Company on the other side of the Clerve River.

Hiding by day and traveling by night, fording both the Clerve and
Wiltz Rivers, Ellis reached the fringe of lower Wiltz just at daylight on
the 20th. Exhausted, starving, half-frozen, his feet so numb that he had
to look down at them to make sure he was walking, he made his way to a
deserted house on the edge of town, found a half-empty container of
oatmeal, ate it raw, and climbed into a bed.

Madame Balthasar was deeply concerned about the wounded soldier
in the attic, and when German soldiers arrived to be billeted in the
house, she became even more worried. She decided to climb the hill to
upper Wiltz and the Clinique St. Joseph. There she found a sympathetic
volunteer nurse—she gave her name only as Mademoiselle Anna—who
agreed to bring some medicine and help Madame Balthasar's *invité* (her
guest).

Just over a week later, the number of Americans hiding in Wiltz increased by one more. As the Germans were evacuating the hospital in the
château, Sgt. Lester Koritz, a member of the 28th Division's G-2 Section
whom the Germans used as an interpreter in the hospital, hid in the
basement until everybody left. After dark he made his way to a tobacco
shop run by two spinster sisters, Mariechen and Elise Goebel, whose
acquaintance he had made earlier. They took him in.

Ralph Ellis by that time had begun to forage at night for food, but he
was becoming almost delirious, his feet dark, swollen, and pus-filled. Unless he could find help, he decided, he was going to die. One night he
made his way to another deserted house deeper inside lower Wiltz and

the next morning inadvertently showed himself at a window. A man saw him: Louis Steinmetz, who worked with the Red Cross and was also a member of the underground resistance. Steinmetz and his sister-in-law took Ellis in, and when Steinmetz went to the Clinique St. Joseph for ointment, Mademoiselle Anna deduced that he too was hiding an *invité* and offered to help.

In time, the civilians brought all three Americans to a common hiding place. They were still hiding and caring for them—Ellis's feet in critical condition—when in early January American liberators came for a second time to Wiltz.

CHAPTER FIFTEEN

Developing Crisis at St. Vith

The commander of the 106th Infantry Division, Alan W. Jones, was expecting to have at his disposal soon after daylight on December 17 a combat command of the 7th Armored Division. His corps commander, Troy Middleton, had told him so.

On the basis of that information, Jones had changed his orders to the 9th Armored Division's CCB, which had been preparing to attack into the Losheim Gap to block the open north flank of the two regiments of the 106th Division on the Schnee Eifel (regiments which Jones, on the basis of a misunderstood telephone conversation with Middleton, deemed he had no authority to withdraw). The assignment to help those two regiments was to pass instead to the 7th Armored Division, while the 9th Armored Division's CCB helped the 106th Division's third regiment, the 424th Infantry, farther south. Although the 424th Infantry was in no immediate danger of encirclement, its left wing appeared to be about to give way, which would open to the Germans a direct route to St. Vith, a route even shorter than that leading from the Schnee Eifel.

Although the contemporary U.S. Army field manual on the armored division specified no accepted rate of march, experience had shown that armor moving in convoy under semitactical conditions rarely exceeded ten miles per hour. When the commander of the 7th Armored Division, Brig. Gen. Robert W. Hasbrouck, received the order to move to St. Vith, his division was in the southern tip of the Netherlands, sixty miles and a minimum of six hours away from St. Vith; and not until close to 5 A.M. the next morning, December 17, were the first of Hasbrouck's vehicles to obtain road clearance and begin to march. Under the best of road conditions, that meant that not until well into the day of December 17 could any substantial part of the division reach St. Vith, and even then planning and deploying for an attack would consume additional time. Jones and Middleton should have had some appreciation of all that.

* * *

However far away the 7th Armored Division, General Jones already had one of the "big friends" that Middleton was sending to help him: General Hoge's CCB, 9th Armored Division. The leading vehicles of Hoge's convoy entered St. Vith just as day was breaking and halted close to Jones's command post in the St. Joseph's Kloster. Hoge and his staff were inside talking with Jones when small-arms fire rained down on the column of vehicles. It was coming from the second floor of a house. As machine gunners on half-tracks returned the fire, infantrymen broke down the door on the ground floor and raced upstairs. There they found spent cartridges littering the floor and three men in civilian clothes firing German rifles. The soldiers took no prisoners.

Inside the command post, General Hoge learned that before daylight, the Germans had mounted a heavy attack at Winterspelt against men of the 424th Infantry: Cannon Company, forced back the day before from nearby Eigelscheid, and the 1st Battalion, committed late the day before to help hold Winterspelt. Hoge was to use his armored infantry to seize high ground strengthening the position at Winterspelt, while his tanks remained behind the Our River for use as the situation developed.

On the way from St. Vith to the Our crossing at Steinebrück, Hoge got the impression that the situation at Winterspelt was worse than General Jones knew, for CCB's column came upon more than a hundred stragglers from the 424th Infantry retreating in disarray toward St. Vith. Hoge stopped to talk with the men, and at his urging, junior officers among them agreed to form a provisional company and reinforce CCB's 27th Armored Infantry Battalion.

As Hoge soon learned, the defenders of Winterspelt had broken, most of them falling back onto other positions of the regiment, although a platoon leader, 1st Lt. Jarrett M. Huddleston, Jr., had rallied a few men in front of the important bridge across the Our at Steinebrück. The Germans nevertheless held the high ground looking down on the bridge.

By noon, CCB's armored infantry, with the help of a platoon of the 14th Tank Battalion, had retaken that first stretch of high ground, and in mid-afternoon General Hoge decided to commit the rest of his tanks to retake Winterspelt. The tanks were ready to move when Hoge received a message from General Jones. Hoge was to attack if he wished, said Jones, but after nightfall he would have to withdraw. Having authorized the adjacent 112th Infantry of the 28th Division to retire behind the Our River, the corps commander, General Middleton, had told the 424th Infantry to do the same.

Rather than spill blood to take meaningless ground, Hoge called off the attack.

As daybreak approached on December 17, all that stood in the way of the 18th Volksgrenadier Division clamping a pincers around the two regi-

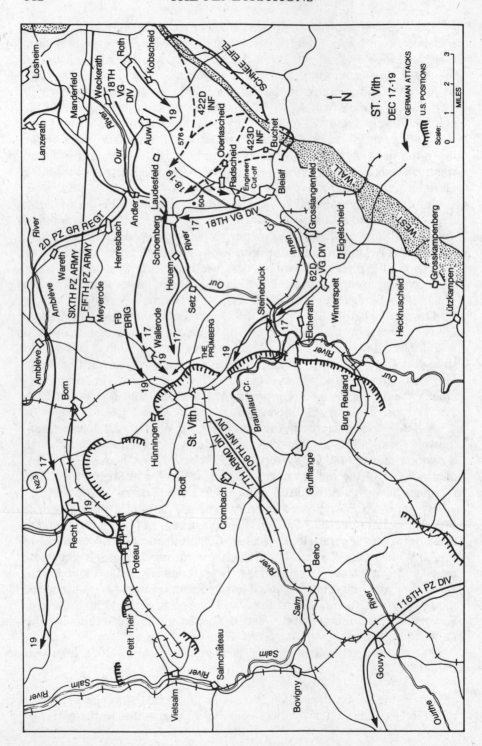

ST. Vith

DEC 17-19

GERMAN ATTACKS

U.S. POSITIONS

Scale:

0   1   2   3

MILES

ments of the 106th Division on the Schnee Eifel were two small forces. At Bleialf, at the southern end of the Schnee Eifel, waited the little conglomerate that the commander of the 423d Infantry, Colonel Cavender, had mustered the first day to retake the village; and at Andler, behind the northern part of the Schnee Eifel at a point of entry into the valley of the Our River, was a lone troop of the 32d Cavalry Reconnaissance Squadron with nothing more powerful in its arsenal than machine guns and 37mm. cannon mounted on thin-skinned armored cars. If either or both of those small forces collapsed, the Germans would soon be in Schoenberg, where the roads from Andler and Bleialf joined. That in turn would trap the 422d and 423d Regiments and their supporting artillery on the far side of the Our and open a direct route to St. Vith.

During the night of December 16, two of the U.S. artillery battalions were in immediate danger: the 589th, supporting the 422d Infantry, and the 592d, the division's general support 155mm. howitzers. The firing positions of both were just off the Auw-Bleialf road (the so-called Skyline Boulevard) down which the Germans had attacked southward from the direction of Auw. Although the arrival at midnight of Colonel Puett's infantry battalion from the division reserve provided some protection, the two battalions were still virtually in the front line. The division artillery commander, Brig. Gen. Leo T. McMahon, ordered both to displace, to be followed by the third battalion, the 590th, which supported the 423d Infantry.

The 155mm. howitzers of the 592d made it out except for one left stuck in the mud and another that missed the Engineer Cut-Off and was destroyed by German fire at 88 Corner, possibly from the assault guns Lieutenant Patton had encountered earlier. Before daylight the remaining howitzers assumed new firing positions near St. Vith.

The 105mm. howitzers of the 589th Field Artillery Battalion tried to displace to the vicinity of the battalion's Service Battery along the Bleialf-Schoenberg road just over a mile short of Schoenberg, which would still leave the pieces with a river behind them. Because the Germans blocked the only road leading out of Battery C's positions, none of that battery's howitzers was able to get out. Except for one piece whose prime mover ran off the Engineer Cut-Off, the other two batteries made it to the new positions. Yet there the crews soon discovered that they had merely exchanged one hot spot for another.

That was because at Bleialf—one of the two critical spots that had to be held lest the Germans gain Schoenberg—the German regiment comprising the southern arm of the 18th Volksgrenadier Division's pincer movement struck just before dawn on the 17th with the help of a few assault guns. The little provisional force in Bleialf folded, and as the first vestiges of a fog-shrouded daylight appeared, the Bleialf-Schoenberg road was open to German advance.

Not long after, so was the Andler-Schoenberg road, for there the 32d Cavalry Reconnaissance Squadron's Troop B had no chance of holding the village. For the first time in the offensive King Tiger tanks entered the fighting, the leading tanks of the 506th Heavy Panzer Battalion, big, slow, and cumbersome but also powerful and terrifying. A separate unit attached to the Sixth Panzer Army, the battalion had gone outside the army boundary in search of a road capable of handling the big tanks and merely stumbled into the fight for Andler.

Lest the entire troop be lost, the commander, Capt. Franklin P. Lindsey, Jr., asked permission to fall back and establish a roadblock on the road to Schoenberg, but that authority was still to come when fire from the tanks drove part of the troop to the west. Facing collapse, Lindsey ordered the rest to head for Schoenberg. Learning there that Bleialf had also fallen, Lindsey kept moving through Schoenberg to the village of Heum, two miles behind Schoenberg along the road to St. Vith.

The *Volksgrenadiers*—but not the big tanks—followed closely and at 8:45 A.M. stormed across the bridge over the Our River at Schoenberg, a critical bridge that nobody on the American side had made any plans to demolish. At that point the American troops to the east—two regiments and attached units, two divisional artillery battalions, and parts of three corps artillery battalions—had no way of getting out unless somebody came to their rescue, unless they could find some other escape route, or unless they could fight their way out. If their predicament needed any further confirmation, the experiences of the artillery battalions soon provided it.

Although the corps commander, General Middleton, had expected that in the event of trouble in the Losheim Gap or around the Schnee Eifel, he would get a lot of help from those powerful corps artillery pieces, that was not to be. Partly because there was little central coordination of fires by the newly arrived 106th Division, but primarily because the guns had a river at their backs.

The two surviving firing batteries of the 589th Field Artillery Battalion with their seven remaining howitzers reached their new positions along the Bleialf-Schoenberg road not long before full daylight. They had yet to begin firing when a truck tore down the road from the direction of Bleialf, the driver shouting that the Germans were right behind him. It was a truck from the battalion's Service Battery, located only a short distance up the road. In the absence of the battalion commander, Lt. Col. Thomas P. Kelly, Jr., who was still trying to save Battery C's howitzers, the executive officer, Maj. Arthur C. Parker III, ordered withdrawal behind the Our.

In the scramble to get onto the highway, the three remaining guns of Battery B bogged in mud and were unable to make it. So did one of Battery A's four howitzers. The other three raced downhill into Schoen-

berg, across the bridge over the Our, and through the village only minutes ahead of the *Volksgrenadiers* coming from Andler.

Close behind those pieces, a few trucks carrying men of Battery B
also got through Schoenberg, but not the last one. In that truck was the
battery commander, Capt. Arthur C. Brown, who delayed leaving the
battery's position until he could check for stragglers. As the truck in
which Brown was riding headed down the steep hill into Schoenberg, a
group of black American soldiers shouted and waved frantically; moments later Brown was to understand that those men were trying to warn
him that the Germans were inside Schoenberg, but Brown's instantaneous reaction was to step on it. So he told his driver.

A short distance beyond the bridge, Brown spotted a German assault
gun (he saw it as a tank) between two buildings. Brown emptied his pistol
at the observation slots, which provided just enough time for the truck to
get past before the assault gun fired. So close was the round that "the
canvas on the truck bellied in from the blast."

As Brown's truck passed the last houses and cleared a rise in the road,
another German assault gun sat full astride the narrow road. There were
dead and wounded Americans in the ditches, and others stood with arms
stretched overhead in surrender. Brown's driver brought the truck to a
screeching halt and all aboard dived for the ditches. Most were captured,
but Brown and a few others made it to a nearby wood. After a harrowing
seven days, they eventually reached American lines.

The black soldiers Brown had encountered near the bridge were men
of the 333d Field Artillery Battalion, a part of the 333d Field Artillery
Group, whose firing positions had been beyond the river. Their group
commander, Lt. Col. John P. Brewster, had begun the day before to
extricate his three battalions, all of which were east of the Our; but as
was evident from the presence of those soldiers in Schoenberg, not everybody made it out.

Shortly after the offensive opened, in mid-morning of the 16th, Colonel Brewster felt compelled to shift a battery of the 740th Field Artillery
Battalion from positions near Auw lest it be overrun. The battery joined
the battalion's other two firing batteries south of Schoenberg near the
village of Amelscheid. By mid-afternoon, Brewster was convinced that he
should displace all his batteries behind the Our; but at the request of the
106th Division's artillery commander, General McMahon, who assured
Brewster that his division was going to hold, Brewster agreed to leave a
firing battery of each battalion in place.

At daylight on the 17th, Brewster realized that was a mistake, for he
learned of the penetrations at Bleialf and Andler. He promptly ordered
the three remaining batteries to displace. That of the 740th Field Artillery
Battalion got through Schoenberg ahead of the *Volksgrenadiers*. Not so
the other two.

Battery C, 333d Field Artillery Battalion, was still in firing positions north of Schoenberg when at 8:15 A.M. *Volksgrenadiers* attacked. Seeing the situation as hopeless, the battalion commander, Lt. Col. Harmon S. Kelsey, who had stayed behind with the battery, ordered the howitzers abandoned. He and his troops headed for Schoenberg in three trucks, but once they debouched onto the Andler-Schoenberg road, they ran into Germans headed for Schoenberg. Kelsey ordered the trucks abandoned, every man for himself. He and most of the others were captured, but about a dozen men escaped, and later in the day a few others got away when an American fighter-bomber strafed as the Germans were marching them to the rear. Men of the 333d's Service Battery had much the same experience; only twenty-seven of them eventually made their way to St. Vith.

From positions just south of Schoenberg near Amelscheid, Battery B, 771st Field Artillery Battalion, was about ready to depart by way of Schoenberg when a truck that had already left came racing back with word that the Germans held Schoenberg. Having occupied the positions for several weeks, the battalion commander, Lt. Col. Mark S. Bacon, was more familiar with the terrain than were commanders in the 106th Division, and he knew a way out. He led Battery B along a woods trail to a narrow bridge across the Our downstream from Schoenberg at the hamlet of Setz. From there, having bypassed Schoenberg, the men and their guns got onto the road leading to St. Vith.

The last of the three organic battalions of the 106th Division, the 590th Field Artillery Battalion, waited through the night for word from General McMahon to begin its exodus; but communications with the division's command post were out, and not until daylight did the word finally come. Men of the battalion's survey section in the lead ran into a German roadblock on the Bleialf-Schoenberg road not far from the lower end of the Engineer Cut-Off, and the first howitzers to displace came under punishing German shelling just as they turned onto the cut-off. Those two events convinced the battalion commander, Lt. Col. Vaden C. Lackey, that he and his men stood a better chance by staying where they were until relief came. As he ordered all howitzers back to their original positions, the fate of the 590th Field Artillery Battalion was from that point tied inexorably to that of the infantry the artillerymen supported.

One more small group of the 598th Field Artillery Battalion had still to make an effort to get through Schoenberg. The group consisted of twenty-five officers and men, including the executive officer of Battery A, 1st Lt. Eric F. Wood, Jr., who had stayed behind to try to get his mired howitzer onto the road. At last they despaired and piled aboard three jeeps.

As the jeeps headed down the hill into Schoenberg, the men saw "men in greenish uniforms running back and forth in the main street." A burp gun fired. Bullets "zipped around" the men's ears, and they "dove off the jeeps into the ditch." Determining that the closest concealment was a wooded hill just north of the road (it was to figure prominently in later action as Hill 504), the men climbed laboriously to the top. As a heavy barrage of mortar rounds fell, they scattered, every man for himself.

It remained for Troop B, 18th Cavalry Reconnaissance Squadron, attached to the 423d Infantry, whose commander, Captain Fossland, had pulled back the day before into Winterscheid just outside Bleialf, to make the final try that day to get through Schoenberg. The 106th Reconnaissance Troop having collapsed at Grosslangenfeld and Bleialf having fallen, Troop B had no neighbors. When Fossland radioed his plight to the commander of the 423d Infantry, Colonel Cavender authorized him to try to withdraw through Schoenberg but warned him that the Germans might be in the village.

Along with thirty officers and men of the 106th Reconnaissance Troop, Troop B in mid-afternoon headed for Schoenberg. With no difficulty, the column reached the Bleialf-Schoenberg road near where the 589th Field Artillery Battalion had tried to establish new firing positions. Part of the column had turned onto the highway heading for Schoenberg when a jeep coming from the direction of Bleialf pressed into the column—a jeep filled with Germans. One of Troop B's armored cars fired its 37mm. gun, and the jeep crashed into a ditch, a mass of wreckage and tangled bodies.

Wary of what lay ahead in Schoenberg, Captain Fossland halted the column short of the first houses and sent a platoon under 1st Lt. Elmo J. Johnston to reconnoiter. With Johnston riding in the first of three armored cars, the men started out just at dusk, crossed the bridge over the Our without interference, and turned left along the road to St. Vith. Up ahead, Johnston could make out a long line of American 6×6 trucks filled with Germans. His first reaction was that they were prisoners headed for the rear, but if so, why were they carrying rifles and burp guns?

Shouting a warning over the radio to the vehicles following, Johnston told his driver to step on the gas, and the drivers of the other two armored cars did the same. As they raced past the column of trucks, the gunners on all three vehicles fired canister from their 37mm. pieces, and German soldiers tumbled from the trucks to find cover. Johnston's armored car got all the way past the German column before German fire knocked it out. Fire from an assault gun caught the other two armored cars, and of six jeeps with Johnston, only the last one got away.

When that jeep returned to Captain Fossland, he saw no alternative but to destroy his remaining vehicles and split his men into small groups to make their way out as best they could. (He knew nothing of the nearby bridge across the Our at Setz, used earlier by Colonel Bacon and his artillerymen.) A few of them, including Fossland himself, eventually succeeded.

The experience of Fossland's column along the last segment of the Bleialf-Schoenberg highway and of Johnston's men in the village demonstrated that the Germans had yet to establish a hold on that part of the highway or to prepare to defend the village against breakout attempts. The problem lay with the regiment of the 18th Volksgrenadier Division that was supposed to move from Bleialf to Schoenberg. The men of that regiment were slow to push through little groups of Americans they encountered along the road, so that not until nightfall did the German pincers actually close at Schoenberg. Yet that had little effect on the fate of those Americans trapped east of the Our, for even if only one arm of the pincers was in Schoenberg, the principal way out was blocked.

Yet as Colonel Bacon had demonstrated, that was not the only way out. Between Schoenberg and embattled Steinebrück, downstream from Schoenberg, there were four small yet nonetheless negotiable bridges over the Our. The one used by Bacon at Setz led onto the Schoenberg–St. Vith highway, which by late in the day was thick with German traffic; the other three led to woods trails that eventually joined the Steinebrück–St. Vith highway, which was under the control of the 9th Armored Division's CCB. Whoever tried to use those bridges would first have to get across the Bleialf-Schoenberg highway, but that would be a far easier assignment than trying to fight through Schoenberg.

Like most commanders of the trapped units, few of the men who tried individually or in small groups to infiltrate back to St. Vith were familiar with the general terrain or the roads. They had been there only a few days, and few knew any route other than that from St. Vith to Schoenberg by which they had arrived. Hardly anybody among the fleeing soldiers had a map and very few had a compass. Yet somehow over the next few days and nights, some managed to elude the Germans and make their way to safety. How many would never be known: perhaps two hundred or so on the 17th and 18th, probably another two hundred or so after that. Then again, many another failed, blundering into German positions or rounded up by German patrols.

One who reached the west bank of the Our but still failed to gain American lines was the executive officer of Battery A, 589th Field Artillery Battalion, Lieutenant Wood. When American troops swept back through the area in late January, they found Wood's body in the forest behind Schoenberg not far from St. Vith near the village of Meyerode. Wood was officially listed as killed in action on December 17, the same day that he and others from his battalion had come under mortar fire near Schoenberg and scattered. When his body was found in the forest near Meyerode, seven dead Germans lay close by.

To Wood's father, a brigadier general on General Eisenhower's staff, that was an indication that his son had died not on the 17th but weeks later after having conducted a heroic guerrilla struggle in the German rear. In support of that theory, Wood's father accumulated affidavits from civilians in the village of Meyerode.

While moving through the woods near Meyerode late in the afternoon on December 17, Peter Maraite came upon two American soldiers, one a young officer. After convincing them he was to be trusted, he invited them to his house in Meyerode, where he and his wife fed them and they spent the night. When the two departed the next morning, they said they intended to reach St. Vith, only three miles away, but failing that, they meant to collect American stragglers in the woods and harass the Germans.

Over the days and weeks that followed, civilians in Meyerode heard occasional small-arms fire in the nearby woods. Sometimes wounded German soldiers stumbled from the woods into the village, and from time to time civilians heard German soldiers complaining and swearing about resistance in the forest. Word spread in Meyerode that a small group of Americans was roaming the woods, ambushing German work parties and preying on supply columns, and that the leader was a young officer, "very big and powerful of body and brave of spirit."

Residents of Meyerode later found the body of a young American officer in the woods—a big man "with single silver bars upon his shoulders," and close around him the bodies of seven German soldiers. That officer, Wood's father maintained, was his son, and for his valor in the forest, he should be awarded posthumously the Medal of Honor.

If, indeed, Lieutenant Wood fought a small-scale guerrilla war in the thick forest between Schoenberg and St. Vith, he was a man of incredible intrepidity. Almost every U.S. soldier trapped behind German lines had but one goal, to reach American lines, and whoever those two men who spent the night in Peter Maraite's house were, they were only a relatively short distance from American lines. What kind of charisma enabled Wood to persuade other Americans to abandon that goal (so close at hand) and join him in a long-running, virtually hopeless vendetta in the frozen woods? Where was the food to be found to sustain themselves over days and weeks? And what about ammunition?

For the Belgian civilians, at any rate, there were no doubts. Whether Lieutenant Wood died on December 17 while trying to reach St. Vith or whether he did, indeed, fight on with a small band of men, the Belgians erected a monument to him in the forest where, they say, he for long continued the fight. Set at the edge of a patch of fir trees along an almost eerily silent gravel trail, it is a touching memorial.

After the 106th Division's field artillery battalions displaced before daylight on December 17, General Jones ordered Colonel Puett to withdraw his 2d Battalion and reconstitute a reserve at Schoenberg. Yet hardly had Jones issued that order than he learned of German success at Bleialf, and before Puett could make any headway in moving to Schoenberg, word came of the German breakthrough at Andler. A short while later the division's signal officer, Lt. Col. Earle Williams, tapped a telephone wire along the Schoenberg–St. Vith road to tell Jones that the Germans had taken Schoenberg. All Colonel Puett could do at that point was to join his parent regiment, the 423d Infantry, to become part of an all-around defense.

At 9:45 A.M., General Jones gave the two trapped regiments their first authority to pull back. "Withdraw from present positions," the message read, "if they become untenable." Yet the message reflected a continuing belief on the part of Jones that with the arrival of the 7th Armored Division, matters would be set right. The division expected to clear out the area "west of you," the message went on, during the afternoon.

Meanwhile, word from Captain Lindsey's Troop B, 32d Cavalry Reconnaissance Squadron, was that the troopers were trying to delay along the Schoenberg–St. Vith road at Heuem, but that little force was all that stood between the 18th Volksgrenadier Division and St. Vith. In midmorning, Jones told the commander of his 81st Engineer Combat Battalion, Lt. Col. Thomas J. Riggs, to throw together some kind of force to block the road as far to the east as possible.

Riggs had few of his own men available. Two of the line companies were still attached to forward regiments, and of the third, which the Germans had overrun the day before at Auw, there were only sixty-four men, making a total from the 81st Engineers and the division headquarters defense platoon of just over a hundred. Although corps headquarters had released the 168th Engineer Combat Battalion to General Jones, only the headquarters and a single company were immediately available, perhaps 175 men. There was also a platoon of the 820th Tank Destroyer Battalion, which had lost its towed guns while fighting with the 424th Infantry, but three replacement pieces arrived from an ordnance depot to the rear. The one bright spot for Riggs was the presence of ten of the original twelve 155mm. howitzers of the 592d Field Artillery Battalion, which had escaped the entrapment beyond the Our.

Riggs's instructions were to move down the road toward Schoenberg as far as Heuem to join Captain Lindsey's cavalry; but when the 168th Engineer Combat Battalion's reconnaissance officer, 2d Lt. Harry Balch, reached Heuem, he found Lindsey and his men withdrawing. They had orders, said Lindsey, to join a line the 14th Cavalry Group was trying to form north and northeast of St. Vith against Germans moving through the Losheim Gap, and nothing Balch could say would stop them. The Germans, said the cavalrymen, were just around the next bend in the road.

It took Balch little time to verify that. When he passed the information to his own commander, Lt. Col. William L. Nungesser, and to Colonel Riggs, the two agreed that it would be folly to try to hold Heuem. If the engineers were to have any time to dig in before the Germans were upon them, they would have to choose the last possible defensive position short of St. Vith itself. That was high ground, mostly wooded, a mile outside the town, known as the Prümerberg. From the Prümerberg, the ground dips down sharply—almost a bluff—to the town in the valley below. Choosing that position might afford the engineers precious minutes to get ready, but should their line fold, German guns would have a commanding position from which to fire directly into St. Vith.

The 592d Field Artillery Battalion provided the engineers a little time when around noon 1st Lt. George Stafford as pilot and 2d Lt. Alonzo A. Neese as observer took off in an observation plane from the 106th Division's airstrip. Flying low because of poor visibility, the plane picked up a German column along the highway about two miles beyond where the engineers were digging in. A first volley of 155mm. shells hit an assault gun in the lead, sending it up in flames, and accompanying infantry scattered.

Not quite an hour later, three German assault guns emerged cautiously around a bend in the road only a few hundred yards from where the engineers were digging in. Moving off the road into a field, one of the assault guns bogged down; and as the crew dismounted, the commander of Company B, 168th Engineers, 1st Lt. William E. Holland, killed everybody with a .50-caliber machine gun. A bazooka team knocked out a second assault gun, and the third withdrew. Moments later three P-47 fighter-bombers appeared and made several strafing runs along the road leading through the woods from Schoenberg.

The fact that the German probes along the main highway from Schoenberg to St. Vith were tentative reflected General von Manteuffel's plan for taking St. Vith. Since woods along the main highway sharply canalized an advance, he intended the final assault to come from the village of Wallerode, just over a mile and a half northeast of St. Vith, where more open ground would make it possible to bring more strength to bear. Consisting of a company each of assault guns and engineers and *Volksgrenadiers* mounted in half-tracks, the 18th Volksgrenadier Division's Mobile Battalion was to make the assault. Reaching Schoenberg at noon, the battalion had to toil along a woods trail leading to Wallerode, so that not until after nightfall did the battalion arrive.

The regiment of *Volksgrenadiers* that had taken Schoenberg nevertheless continued to probe up the main highway toward St. Vith. As patrols sought to determine the location of the American line, the little band of some three hundred American engineers on the Prümerberg kept glancing backward hoping to see reinforcements in the form of the men and tanks of the 7th Armored Division.

*   *   *

Bruce Cooper Clarke, forty-three years old, was a big man, well over 6 feet tall, with a heavy frame, broad shoulders, and a barrel-like chest. Raised on a farm in New York State, he enlisted as a youth in the National Guard, then received an appointment to the Military Academy at West Point. After spending most of his early military career with the engineers, he transferred to armor as the U.S. Army was forming its first mechanized units. He entered combat in Normandy as commander of the 4th Armored Division's CCA, but on October 30, he faced an unwelcome transfer. When General Bradley relieved the commander of the 7th Armored Division, he elevated the commander of the division's CCB, General Hasbrouck, to command the division and needed a strong replacement for Hasbrouck. That was to be Clarke.

On December 16, Bruce Clarke was dining with General Hasbrouck, who suggested that he should take a three-day leave in Paris. Clarke had been looking for a break so that he might have an operation for gallstones, an illness he was controlling only with constant medication, and three days was insufficient for that; but he welcomed the break anyway. He had had no rest since coming ashore in Normandy.

Back at his billet, Clarke pulled out his Eisenhower jacket and replaced the colonel's eagles on the shoulders with the single stars of a brigadier general. That was the only pair of stars he possessed, for he had received his promotion just nine days before.

He was about ready to leave for Paris when the telephone rang. It was Hasbrouck. The 7th Armored Division, he said, had received orders to move immediately to Bastogne. Why, he did not know. In any event, Clarke's CCB was to lead the march, and Hasbrouck wanted Clarke himself to head immediately for Bastogne: "Find out what you can from General Middleton. Take a radio jeep so you can let me know what's happening."

So much for the Eisenhower jacket and Paris. Within the hour Clarke was on his way to Bastogne, where he arrived at 4 A.M. on the 17th. Middleton, who had trouble sleeping because of bursitis, was awake in his sleeping van. Giving Clarke a quick rundown on the German attack, he said he intended using the 7th Armored Division to help the 106th Division at St. Vith; but first, said Middleton, he wanted Clarke to catch a few hours' sleep.

That Clarke did, and when he awoke, he radioed General Hasbrouck that the 7th Armored Division was to go not to Bastogne but to St. Vith. He suggested that the division assemble at the town of Vielsalm on the Salm River eleven miles behind St. Vith. During the conversation, he learned that because of difficulty in obtaining road clearance, the division had begun to march only at 5 A.M. It would be late in the day before even Clarke's CCB in the lead would be available for commitment at St. Vith.

After a quick breakfast, Clarke left for St. Vith, where he arrived at

General Jones's command post at ten thirty. By that time the German trap had closed on the two regiments beyond the Our River, and so effective was German jamming of radio frequencies that Jones received only an occasional message from them. Jones wanted Clarke to counterattack immediately with his combat command "and break that ring that these people have closed around the Schnee Eifel."

It pained Clarke to have to tell Jones that only he, his operations officer, his aide, and his driver had reached St. Vith. He had no idea when his combat command would arrive.

As *Kampfgruppe Peiper* prepared to start its drive for the Meuse before daylight on December 17, the other two columns of the 1st SS Panzer Division also prepared to begin their advance through the Losheim Gap. Except for Major Diefenthal's battalion of *SS-Panzergrenadiers* with Peiper, the columns included the division's two *SS-Panzergrenadier* regiments supported by twenty-two self-propelled tank destroyers and twenty Mark IVs and Panthers.

The roadnet assigned those columns was skimpy at best. Only three roads for the two columns, and all converging either at Manderfeld or on the ridge behind the village. From there the roads were even poorer— mainly woods trails—through a belt of forest two to three miles wide. Only beyond the forest did the roadnet open up.

Whoever drew the inter-army boundary paid scant attention to the route assigned to the southern column of the 1st SS Panzer Division, for from Manderfeld that route led through Andler and Herresbach, both within the Fifth Panzer Army's zone of advance, thence to Vielsalm, behind St. Vith even deeper within the Fifth Panzer Army's zone, and on to the Meuse at Huy. As soon as the skimpy roadnet within the Sixth Panzer Army's zone jammed with traffic, commanders of units in the southern column predictably said to hell with the boundary and moved through Andler. That produced traffic congestion of monumental proportions, which soon brought officers from both panzer armies fuming and swearing onto the scene, including the commander of the 66th Corps, General Lucht. Yet for all the fuming and swearing, nobody went very far very fast.

That difficulty with traffic was why few units of the 14th Cavalry Group—other than Captain Lindsey's Troop B, 32d Cavalry, at Andler— experienced any enemy pressure through much of the day of December 17. Yet the 14th Cavalry Group continued to retire nevertheless.

While Colonel Devine was waiting on the night of the 16th to see General Jones in St. Vith, the corps commander, General Middleton, telephoned with a complaint from the 99th Division that the cavalry had lost contact with the division's right flank. Promising to rectify it, Devine telephoned the commander of the 18th Cavalry Reconnaissance Squadron, Colonel Damon, to move what was left of his command back through the thick belt of forest stretching the width of the Losheim Gap to the village of Wareth, and from there establish contact with the 99th Division.

The departure of Damon and his command was what had left Lieutenant Reppa and his troop of the 32d Cavalry alone in the northern reaches of the gap and prompted Reppa to abandon his position and go to Honsfeld. Which put him the next morning right in the path of *Kampfgruppe Peiper*.

Those departures left only two components of the 14th Cavalry Group still forward in the Losheim Gap: Lindsey's troop at Andler and head-quarters and Troop B, 32d Cavalry, two miles to the northwest at Her-resbach, just in front of the wide belt of forest. There the commander of the squadron, Colonel Ridge, visibly shaken by all that was happening, had found an excuse to go back to Vielsalm, virtually abdicating his command in favor of his executive officer, Maj. John L. Kracke. Early in the evening, a passing artillery officer told Kracke that the unimproved trails leading west through the forest were impassable, and Kracke began to worry that he and the command might be trapped.

Around midnight, Kracke sent an officer to reconnoiter the only improved road through the forest, that leading northwest to Wareth. Somebody had blocked the route, the officer reported, by felling trees across it.

That left only the woods trails. Reconnoitering one of those, the squadron's motor officer, Capt. Samuel E. Woods, concluded that it was in good enough shape to warrant a try. At eight thirty on the morning of the 17th, with Colonel Devine's approval, withdrawal began. By that time a disparate array of vehicles had accumulated—at least two hundred—not only those belonging to the cavalry but others from tank destroyer, antiaircraft, and medical units.

It was fortunate for the men in that column that the Germans exerted no pressure, for even without it, the trek through the forest was a nightmare. Vehicles bogged down; others with chains on their wheels pulled them out. Then the same thing happened over and over again. At a sharp curve on the side of a steep hill, a shoulder of the road gave way, and Captain Woods had to form a work party to fell trees and keep it passable. Not until early afternoon was the last vehicle past that chokepoint.

At last returned from the fruitless wait in St. Vith, Colonel Devine had approved Kracke's withdrawal because it fitted with a new plan he had devised. All units of the 14th Cavalry Group—including Captain Lindsey's, by that time fighting a delaying action on the Schoenberg–St. Vith road—were to form a new line north of St. Vith extending from Wallerode northeast to the village of Born. To General Jones, Devine reported that he was withdrawing to "a final delaying position" and sent a map overlay depicting it. Jones approved, at least tacitly, for he had dire need of some kind of block north of St. Vith if the 7th Armored Division was to be able to get into the town.

In setting up the new line, Devine came into conflict with the commander of his artillery support, Lt. Col. Roy U. Clay. Clay was already piqued because Devine, unsure of the location of isolated American troops, refused to allow Clay's self-propelled 105mm. howitzers to fire on Schoenberg and villages in the Losheim Gap. When Devine told Clay to place his pieces in the new line in positions from which to employ direct fire, Clay refused.

Detailed to support the 14th Cavalry Group but not under Devine's command, Clay hurried to the command post of the 106th Division's Artillery, to which his battalion was attached. He was "mad as hell," he told the artillery commander, General McMahon, because there were "Germans all over the place" and Devine refused to allow him to shoot. Before McMahon could respond, a captain spoke up: As liaison officer from headquarters of the VIII Corps Artillery, he was attaching Clay's battalion to the 7th Armored Division. Clay could fire "anytime and any place" he wished.

When Clay returned to his howitzers, he found Colonel Devine abandoning the final delaying position so recently established from Wallerode to Born. He had learned that to the north, Germans were already farther west than Born and thus might cut in on the rear of the new line. He ordered everybody back to the vicinity of Recht, a crossroads village several miles behind Born. Having had no contact with the enemy except for Captain Lindsey's harsh encounter just before daybreak at Andler, the 14th Cavalry Group had nevertheless retired during the day a distance of more than ten miles.

The operations officer of the 38th Armored Infantry Battalion, Maj. Donald P. Boyer, moved with his jeep and driver about an hour in advance of his battalion, which was a part of the 7th Armored Division's CCR. Driving along the division's eastern march route through Malmédy and the road junction at Baugnez, Boyer was on his way to Vielsalm to pick out an assembly area for his battalion. Shortly after midday on December 17, he reached the hamlet of Poteau marking a road junction where the Ligneuville-Vielsalm road joined the principal highway connecting Vielsalm and St. Vith. Boyer found it hard to believe what he saw: "a constant stream of traffic hurtling to the rear (to the west) and nothing going to the front (to the east). We realized that this was not a convoy moving to the rear; it was a case of 'every dog for himself'; it was a retreat, a rout."

What Boyer saw was undeniably ugly. Here a 6×6 with only a driver, there another "with several men in it (most of them bareheaded and in various stages of undress), next perhaps an engineer crane truck, then several artillery prime movers," some of them towing howitzers, "command cars with officers in them," jeeps, "anything which would run and which would get the driver and a few others away from the front." He was "seeing American soldiers running away."

What Boyer failed to appreciate was that most of the people in those vehicles were moving away from the front under legitimate orders. Some of the vehicles were from the squadrons of the 14th Cavalry Group that mistakenly got onto the road to Poteau rather than to Recht. Others were from the 771st Field Artillery Battalion that had withdrawn from the vicinity of Schoenberg to Wallerode but had to displace again; still others were from the 740th Field Artillery Battalion, which was trying to move its 8-inch howitzers from positions near Schoenberg; and both battalions were following orders from the artillery officer of the VIII Corps, Brig. Gen. John E. McMahon, Jr., who had directed all of the corps artillery battalions in the vicinity of St. Vith, with the exception of Clay's 275th Armored Field Artillery Battalion, to fall back.

Do you leave precious general support howitzers and guns without infantry protection in positions so close to the front that they are likely to be overrun? Do you leave heavy engineer equipment in the same predicament? Do you leave ordnance, quartermaster, signal, and medical installations to be annihilated or captured?

The bulk of the traffic moving westward on the St. Vith–Vielsalm road late on December 17 constituted a legitimate exodus. That it had gotten out of control was another matter. At the order of the corps artillery officer, five of the retiring corps artillery battalions had avoided the St. Vith–Vielsalm road, taking other roads to the south, but the other two—the 740th and the 771st—had no choice. Anticipating problems, the 106th Division's Military Police Platoon had early moved into position to control the traffic, but the sheer volume overwhelmed the few MPs who were available.

When congestion inevitably developed, individual drivers, sometimes at the behest of their officers, broke out of the column and tried to push ahead in the eastbound lane. Since the road was twisting and narrow, little more than a hard surface poured onto an existing dirt road without first eliminating the bumps, rises, and sharp bends, the eastbound lane was soon as jammed as the westbound lane. And when the first vehicles of the 7th Armored Division arrived and tried to get through the road junction at Poteau, a traffic jam of epic proportions quickly developed. It took the commander of the 7th Armored Division, General Hasbrouck, five hours to negotiate the eleven miles from Vielsalm to St. Vith.

The American commanders might have taken some consolation from the fact that the same thing—only worse—was happening on their enemy's side of the front, and two of the senior German commanders got caught up in it. The commander of the Fifth Panzer Army, General von Manteuffel, was trying to get to Schoenberg, where he intended to pass

the night at headquarters of the 18th Volksgrenadier Division in an effort
to put some spark into that division's attack on St. Vith; but the roads
were so blocked that he eventually got out of his command car and began
to walk. The same thing happened to the commander of Army Group B,
Field Marshal Model, and each used his rank, with little success, to try to
get the traffic moving.

The two came upon one another in the night.

"And how is your situation, Baron?" asked Model.

"Mostly good."

"So? I got the impression you were lagging, especially in the St. Vith
sector."

"Yes," said von Manteuffel, "but we'll take it tomorrow."

"I expect you to," responded Model. "And so that you'll take it
quicker, tomorrow I'm letting you use the *Führer Begleit Brigade.*"

Inside the 106th Division's command post in St. Vith that afternoon,
staff activity could be considered hectic, but General Jones himself was
calm. At one point, on the telephone to General Middleton, he told the
corps commander not to worry. "We'll be in good shape. Clarke's troops
will be here soon."

Around 1:30 P.M., the door to Jones's office burst open and the cavalry commander, Colonel Devine, almost fell in. "General," he gasped,
"we've got to run. I was practically chased into this building by a Tiger
tank, and we all have to get out of here."

To General Clarke, Devine looked like a man who had been through
too much. "I suggest we send Colonel Devine back to Bastogne," said
Clarke. "Maybe he could give General Middleton a first-hand account of
the conditions up here." Devine saluted and left.

An hour later, the sound of small-arms fire emerged from the east.
Going to the third floor of the St. Joseph's Kloster, Jones and Clarke
could see a small group of Germans at the edge of the woods on the bluff
overlooking the town. "General Clarke," said Jones, "I've thrown in my
last chips. I haven't got much, but your combat command is the one that
will defend this position. You take over command of St. Vith right now."

Clarke accepted, the first step in what was to become a confused command arrangement destined to persist through much of the remainder of
the fight in and around St. Vith. Clarke was junior to three other brigadier generals on the scene: Jones's assistant division commander and his
artillery commander and the commander of the 9th Armored Division's
CCB, General Hoge. Furthermore, Clarke's division commander, General Hasbrouck, had one less star than did General Jones, and he, too,
was junior to Hoge. It remained to be seen how that confusion of stars
would work out.

In mid-afternoon, hoping that CCB would soon be arriving, Clarke sent his operations officer, Maj. Owen E. Woodruff, to the first crossroads outside St. Vith at the village of Rodt to guide the vehicles in and make sure the road was clear of westbound traffic. With little to occupy him at Jones's headquarters, Clarke soon joined Woodruff. He found the major looking dejected and part of a field artillery battalion without howitzers monopolizing the road. The artillery commander, said Woodruff, insisted on using the road and was threatening to shoot him if he interfered.

Clarke soon had the lieutenant colonel in front of him at attention. "You get your trucks off this road so my tanks can get up here," the imposing Clarke thundered. "If there's any shooting done around here, I'll start it."

Shortly before four o'clock the first vehicles of the 7th Armored Division's CCB arrived, those of Troop B, 87th Cavalry Reconnaissance Squadron. "Keep going down this road," said Clarke to the troop commander. "You'll run into a great big lieutenant-colonel named Riggs. Tell him that you're attached to him, and he'll tell you what to do."

Troop B was soon going into position with its armored cars, light tanks, and assault guns on the left of the thin engineer line on the Prümerberg, covering some of the open ground between the Prümerberg and Wallerode to the north. The Germans may well have heard the cheer that arose from the engineers when the reinforcements appeared.

General Hasbrouck reached St. Vith close behind Troop B. As he conferred with Jones and Clarke in the St. Joseph's Kloster, night was falling, and the main body of CCB was still toiling forward along the congested road from Vielsalm. Quite obviously, there could be no attack that night to relieve the men—including Alan Jones's son—who were trapped beyond the Our River on and in the shadow of the Schnee Eifel. Hope remained nevertheless for an attack by CCB early the next morning.

As other units of CCB filtered into St. Vith, so imperative was the need to reinforce the thin line on the Prümerberg that Clarke felt impelled to commit them piecemeal as they arrived without regard to their parent battalions. The first to follow the cavalry troop into the line were a company of the 23d Armored Infantry Battalion and a company of mediums of the 31st Tank Battalion.

The 38th Armored Infantry Battalion arrived soon after. Normally a component of CCR, that battalion had reached Recht, where CCR began to establish a headquarters, when Hasbrouck ordered it forward for attachment to CCB. General Clarke put the commander, Lt. Col. William H. G. Fuller, in charge of the critical defenses in front of St. Vith, which Fuller reinforced with two of his line companies (the third had been diverted by mistake to Vielsalm). The line on the Prümerberg received additional reinforcement with the arrival of another company of the 168th Engineer Combat Battalion.

By midnight of December 17, a fairly cohesive defense had been established in front of St. Vith with three companies of armored infantry, a company of medium tanks, and a troop of cavalry; and Fuller pulled the engineers who had first established the position into reserve for a time so that they might reorganize. The line extended from the vicinity of Wallerode in the north across the Prümerberg, there blocking both the main highway from Schoenberg and a secondary road leading less directly from Schoenberg. A few hundred yards south of that road, the line ended. Although the Germans probed the developing line several times during the night with strong patrols, they made no attack. They were planning to take St. Vith the next morning with a strike by the 18th Volksgrenadier Division's Mobile Battalion from Wallerode.

Hasbrouck also sent the rest of the 87th Cavalry Reconnaissance Squadron, which was normally a part of other combat commands, to St. Vith, and Clarke put the two remaining troops of the squadron to the north and northeast of the town to block two principal roads that had been exposed by withdrawal of the 14th Cavalry Group. That enabled Clarke to hold the remainder of CCB as a reserve behind St. Vith: three-fourths of the 23d Armored Infantry Battalion, all but a company of the 31st Tank Battalion, and a company of the 33d Engineers.

South of St. Vith, General Hoge's CCB, 9th Armored Division, and Colonel Reid's 424th Infantry, 106th Division, conformed to General Jones's retirement order and during the night of the 17th pulled back across the Our River. The combat command kept most of its strength in reserve along the road from Steinebrück to St. Vith, with outposts along the river and light tanks patrolling woods trails to the east. Hardpressed during the day only on the flanks at Winterspelt and near Grosskampenberg, the 424th Infantry got its supporting 591st Field Artillery Battalion out first, then leapfrogged its infantry battalions to the west bank of the Our. The regiment had to leave behind considerable equipment and supplies.

Arriving in late afternoon, the 7th Armored Division's Combat Command A moved into an assembly area southeast of Vielsalm, there to be in a position to block any enemy move from the south while at the same time serving as a division reserve. In view of the uncertainty of the situation everywhere around St. Vith, General Hasbrouck kept CCA on thirty-minute alert.

Headquarters of the 7th Armored Division third combat command, CCR, divested of its armored infantry but still in charge of the Shermans of the 17th Tank Battalion, was at Recht on the Ligneuville-Vielsalm road with the tanks in an assembly area nearby. Although Recht was to have been the center of the 14th Cavalry Group's latest defensive position, only three reconnaissance teams, made up mainly of armored cars, arrived there; the rest of the cavalry became entangled with the morass of vehicles on the St. Vith–Vielsalm road in and near Poteau. Colonel Devine had established his headquarters in Poteau, but when the cavalry's vehicles finally broke through the traffic jam, they continued to the next village of Petit Thier.

Artillery available at first in what was fast shaping up as a horseshoe defense of St. Vith was limited. The 424th Infantry still had its direct support battalion, but the other pieces that had made it back from beyond the Our (the three 105mm. howitzers of the 589th Field Artillery Battalion and the ten 155mm. howitzers of the 592d) had displaced from the vicinity of Wallerode and had yet to occupy new firing positions. The 9th Armored Division's CCB also had its usual support, the 16th Armored Field Artillery Battalion; but because of the necessity of a detour to avoid the road junction at Baugnez, only one of the 7th Armored Division's three battalions arrived during the night. Not until midday on the 18th were the other two to be ready to fire, and none of the three was close enough to St. Vith to provide support for the critical defensive line on the Prümerberg.

There were also a few batteries of corps guns still on hand south of Vielsalm, and close behind St. Vith was the 275th Armored Field Artillery Battalion, so recently attached to the 7th Armored Division. The commander, Colonel Clay, found General Clarke on the road near St. Vith and told him he was sick of retreating. "I want to shoot," said Clay.

When General Jones learned in mid-afternoon of the 14th Cavalry Group's withdrawal from the Wallerode-Born line, he ordered Colonel Devine to his headquarters in St. Vith. Dusk was approaching, around four o'clock, when Devine set out from his new command post in Poteau with three jeeps escorted by an armored car. Among the party were Devine's executive officer, Lt. Col. Augustine D. Dugan, and his operations officer, Maj. Lawrence J. Smith.

Because the main road to St. Vith was still hopelessly jammed, Devine and his party moved by way of Recht to a wooded crossroads known as the Kaiserbaracke, there to gain access to N-23, the Ligneuville–St. Vith highway. In St. Vith, Devine saw either General Jones or his operations officer, for he received orders to return his squadrons to the Wallerode-Born line.

On the way back to Poteau via the Kaiserbaracke, Devine and his party became aware as they neared the crossroads of what looked in the darkness to be German tanks a few hundred yards off the road. Just as the armored car in the lead reached the crossroads, a German sentry close beside it yelled, "*Halt!*" An officer riding erect in the commander's position in the armored car put the muzzle of his .45-caliber pistol full in the man's face and fired. As the gunner on the .50-caliber machine gun opened up, tracer bullets illuminated some fifteen lightly armored German vehicles just off the road.

The armored car backed up, forcing the jeep in which Devine and his operations officer, Major Smith, were riding into a ditch. Devine's driver quickly sensed trouble and climbed aboard the armored car. The other two jeeps also escaped, but Devine and Smith were left behind, eventually to crawl away until they gained a railroad right of way that Smith knew led to Poteau.

They reached Devine's command post in Poteau shortly before midnight. There Devine immediately summoned the commander of the 18th Cavalry Reconnaissance Squadron, Colonel Damon, told him to "take over," and "left the room and went to bed." Before daylight, his staff arranged his evacuation through medical channels.

Hardly had Colonel Damon assumed command when word came from General Jones reiterating the order for the cavalry to return to its former positions. Somebody managed to intercept the last troop of the 32d Cavalry Reconnaissance Squadron as it was passing through Poteau and get it turned around and facing back in the direction of Born. Yet in the darkness and amid all the confusion of heavy traffic through Poteau, all that accomplished was to bring the traffic through the road junction to a dead halt.

A short time later, a message arrived from headquarters of the 106th Division repeating an order from headquarters of the VIII Corps for "the commander of the 14th Cavalry Group" to report to Bastogne. That was the outcome of Jones's and Clarke's unhappy encounter with Colonel Devine that afternoon and was meant to bring Devine (not the current commander, Colonel Damon) to Bastogne. Yet Damon had no way of knowing that. Handing over the group to the commander of the 32d Cavalry Reconnaissance Squadron, Colonel Ridge, Damon left for Bastogne.

Within half an hour, Devine's executive officer, Colonel Dugan, returned following his escape by jeep from the encounter at the Kaiserbaracke. Senior to Ridge, he assumed command of the group, and Ridge promptly repaired to his accustomed post in Vielsalm. Like Devine, Ridge was evacuated through medical channels as a nonbattle casualty.

During the afternoon of December 17 at Recht, the acting commander of the 7th Armored Division's CCR, Lt. Col. Fred M. Warren (the regular commander was on leave in Paris), learned from a passing jeep driver that the Germans had captured Ligneuville, only three miles to the north. Warren and his operations officer, Maj. Fred Sweat, drove up the road and just south of Ligneuville came upon some of the men of the trains (supply trucks and troops) of the 9th Armored Division's CCB who had escaped from the town.

Assured that the Germans were, indeed, in Ligneuville, Warren and Sweat hurried to St. Vith and the 106th Division's command post to give the alarm. There they came upon their division commander, General Hasbrouck, who told them to return to Recht and hold the village as long as possible.

Having given up CCR's armored infantry battalion to the defense east of St. Vith, Warren was reluctant to use his tanks to defend the village without infantry protection. Although he appealed to the division headquarters for at least a company of armored infantry, word came back that none was available. The headquarters was as yet unaware that a company of CCR's own armored infantry battalion had been mistakenly diverted to Vielsalm.

In early evening, the driver for the 7th Armored Division's chief of staff, Col. Church M. Matthews, arrived on foot in Recht with the news that during the afternoon he and Matthews had happened upon a German armored column outside Ligneuville. The Germans had shot up the jeep and killed Matthews.

The Germans that Matthews and his driver had encountered were part of the tail of *Kampfgruppe Peiper*, which had no intention of turning south toward Recht, but Warren could not know that. Should the Germans take Recht, they might move on to Poteau and soon be in Vielsalm, only seven miles away, in the process cutting off all the American troops who were trying to build a defense of St. Vith. Overcoming his qualms about committing tanks without infantry protection, Warren called in a company of the 17th Tank Battalion.

Whatever the intent of *Kampfgruppe Peiper*, Colonel Warren was well advised to prepare to defend Recht, for the southernmost column of the 1st SS Panzer Division had at last gotten some troops and vehicles through the traffic jams to the rear and onto the assigned route through Recht and Vielsalm. Those were men of the 1st SS Panzergrenadier Regiment under Col. Max Hansen.

The defenders of St. Vith were about to face the first of what would turn out to be multiple crises. Unlikely heroes of that first crisis were to be the men of the 14th Cavalry Group.

CHAPTER SIXTEEN

Shaping the Defense of St. Vith

At Recht (*see map, Chapter Fifteen, p. 312*) the attack that CCR's head-quarters troops, the three reconnaissance teams of the 14th Cavalry Group, and the company of mediums of the 17th Tank Battalion were expecting came at 2 A.M. on December 18. Dismounted *SS-Pan-zergrenadiers*, strong on automatic weapons and *Panzerfausts*, penetrated the village and by the light of flares searched for the American tanks. After forty-five minutes of heavy fighting, CCR's acting commander, Colonel Warren, came to the conclusion that he was in danger of losing an entire company of medium tanks and ordered withdrawal.

The headquarters troops and the few armored cars belonging to the 14th Cavalry Group fell back on Poteau, while the tanks moved southeast toward the battalion's assembly area near the hamlet of Feckelsborn. From there, the tankers commanded an abandoned railroad underpass between the hamlet and Recht, and when daylight came, they drove back every German attempt to get through the underpass.

At Poteau, Colonel Warren and his staff found the highway through the hamlet blocked. They spent most of the remaining hours of darkness trying to get traffic rolling but eventually despaired and moved on foot down the Vielsalm road to Petit Thier. Had the Germans who captured Recht marched immediately on Poteau, they could have wreaked havoc on the stalled column.

The new commander of the 14th Cavalry Group, Colonel Dugan, found meanwhile that there was still fight left in the remnants of his group; it was a matter of exerting leadership to bring it out. The stub of an unlit cigar clenched between his teeth, Dugan was here, there, and everywhere, trying to get the clogged traffic under way and at the same time reorganize his command sufficiently to comply with General Jones's order to reoccupy the Wallerode-Born line. Damon the night before and Dugan in the early morning told headquarters of the 106th Division that any task force from the 14th Cavalry Group trying to reoccupy the Wallerode-Born line was doomed. Since it was obvious by that time that the Germans were already in Wallerode, Jones modified the order to require reoccupying only Born; but he was adamant on that.

Since the bulk of the 32d Cavalry Reconnaissance Squadron had already retreated all the way to Vielsalm, Dugan ordered the squadron to return, but the traffic jam precluded it. With the help of Major Mayes of the 18th Cavalry Reconnaissance Squadron, Dugan created a small task force from the remnants of that squadron reinforced by the 32d Cavalry's assault guns. Because the traffic jam blocked one of only two roads to Born, Task Force Mayes headed out the road to Recht. Although Dugan expected the task force to encounter Germans before reaching Born, he was unaware that *SS-Panzergrenadiers* had captured Recht. No matter what, he had to comply with his order from Jones.

In darkness and fog at 7 A.M. on the 18th, Task Force Mayes had gone only 250 yards beyond the last houses of Poteau when a rocket from a *Panzerfaust* struck the second vehicle, a 75mm. assault gun, setting it on fire, and German small-arms fire erupted. The task force had run head-on into an attack by troops of the 1st SS Panzergrenadier Regiment on Poteau. Fighting a delaying action, Task Forces Mayes's armored cars, half-tracks, and assault guns fell back on the road junction.

For the rest of the morning, those cavalrymen held the road junction at Poteau against a determined infantry attack supported by self-propelled tank destroyers. Typifying the élan the men brought to the fight, Staff Sgt. Woodrow Reeves clung to the outside of his light tank, the better to direct the fire of his gunner, and when an officer ordered him to get inside, Reeves replied: "Can't, Lieutenant; too busy shooting Germans." When a group of Germans set up a machine gun on a wooded hillock overlooking the road junction, a patrol of cavalrymen swarmed from Poteau to knock it out. Somebody got on the radio frequency of a battalion of the 7th Armored Division's artillery and brought in fire support. Through it all, Colonel Dugan, cigar still held between his teeth, circulated among the soldiers, grinning, encouraging, exhorting.

The fighting built a fire under the drivers of the vehicles clogged along the highway through the hamlet. Somehow the column at last began to move, but in some cases there was panic. The crews of eight 8-inch howitzers of the 740th Field Artillery Battalion abandoned their pieces (although the 7th Armored Division eventually recovered them). Some vehicles still on the St. Vith side of the road junction turned back to try to find another way out.

The cavalrymen, for all their valor, were nevertheless engaging in a markedly uneven fight. The Germans were closing in when Colonel Dugan soon after midday ordered withdrawal down the road toward Vielsalm. Reaching Petit Thier, Capt. William G. North, Jr., and Staff Sgt. Walter Gregory climbed into the steeple of the church, smashed a hole in the roof to afford observation, and adjusted artillery fire on Poteau. Probably as a result of that fire, the cavalrymen were able to continue their withdrawal under no pressure from the enemy.

From that point, all that was left of the 14th Cavalry Group was attached as a task force to the 7th Armored Division. Finally afforded an opportunity to fight rather than withdraw, and provided with firm leadership, the cavalrymen had performed at Poteau as they had on the first day of the German offensive. Unfortunately, the performance came too late to save the commander who rallied them, Colonel Dugan. In a general house-cleaning of senior commanders in the group, General Middleton summarily relieved Colonel Dugan of his command.

Because 1st Lt. Joseph V. Whiteman had worked his way through college selling Indian blankets, his colleagues called him "Navajo." A member of the 23d Armored Infantry Battalion, Whiteman acted as the battalion's motor officer during the trip south but fell behind the convoy when his truck developed engine trouble.

Arriving in Vielsalm late in the afternoon of December 17, Whiteman joined the crews of several half-tracks that for one reason or another had also fallen behind and headed for St. Vith to rejoin his unit. Because of the traffic jam, the half-tracks were able to get no farther that night than Petit Thier. Just as Whiteman and the others were preparing before daylight the next morning to continue, they heard "all hell break loose up the valley toward Poteau."

When the surviving vehicles of the 14th Cavalry Group fell back through Petit Thier, Lieutenant Whiteman made up his mind to defend the village, else the Germans might overrun the 7th Armored Division's artillery and move into Vielsalm. With the half-tracks, Whiteman established a roadblock in front of the first buildings in Petit Thier and began to corral reinforcements. He soon had two assault guns, two tanks, and two tankdozers that had become separated from the 31st Tank Battalion, as well as eighty-four men of the 106th Division's 424th Infantry, whose lieutenant said he was "out of ammunition, out of chow, and out of orders." Whiteman said he could provide all three. Before the day was done, Task Force Navajo had forward observers from all three of the division's artillery battalions, a platoon of self-propelled tank destroyers, and a company of engineers, to whose commander, senior to Whiteman, command of the task force passed.

Early on December 18, the commander of the 9th Armored Division's CCB, General Hoge, sent his liaison officer, Lieutenant Lewis, to St. Vith to learn the dispositions of the 7th Armored Division's CCB. As Lewis approached the St. Joseph's Kloster, one of General Clarke's staff officers stopped him in considerable agitation. German tanks were approaching St. Vith along the road from the north, he said, and all that stood in the way was a reconnaissance troop. Could General Hoge send somebody to help?

Climbing into Lewis's jeep, the two "drove like mad" to Hoge's command post in a beerhall along the road to Steinebrück. Hoge decided to go to St. Vith himself, but before departing he told Lewis to direct the commander of the 14th Tank Battalion, Lt. Col. Leonard E. Engeman, to get a strong task force ready to move out. Minutes later Hoge telephoned from St. Vith, telling Engeman to get under way.

Composed of two medium tank companies, a company of self-propelled guns of the 811th Tank Destroyer Battalion, a reconnaissance platoon, and a few antiaircraft half-tracks, Engeman's task force reached St. Vith shortly before noon to find not one but two German attacks moving against the town. The 18th Volksgrenadier Division's Mobile Battalion had debouched from Wallerode onto the highway leading from Amblève into St. Vith, while contingents of the 1st SS Panzergrenadier Regiment had reached a hamlet on N-23 not quite a mile outside St. Vith. Holding one of the tank companies in reserve on the fringe of St. Vith, Colonel Engeman sent the other up the Amblève road and the tank destroyers up N-23.

As the men in the tank destroyers soon learned, General Clarke had already sent a company of his own tanks and a company of armored infantry marching on the hamlet on N-23, while another company of tanks provided fire support. In less than an hour the *SS-Panzergrenadiers* were fleeing the hamlet, and the results were much the same along the road from Amblève. The 9th Armored Division's tanks knocked out four assault guns and drove the Mobile Battalion back on Wallerode. As General Clarke placed one of his tank companies in a position from which to cover the north flank, the 9th Armored Division's men and vehicles returned to their own command.

Early on December 18, the commander of the 7th Armored Division's Combat Command A, Col. Dwight A. Rosebaum, went to St. Vith in search of his division commander, General Hasbrouck, only to learn that Hasbrouck was in Vielsalm. En route there, Rosebaum laboriously threaded his way through the coagulated traffic at Poteau only minutes before the Germans attacked the road junction. At the division headquarters in the Middle School on the Rue de l'Hôtel de Ville in Vielsalm, he told Hasbrouck that in his view, there appeared to be no immediate threat to the division's south flank, certainly nothing comparable to the threat developing on the north. He recommended that Hasbrouck shift his combat command to Poteau.

With Hasbrouck's agreement, Rosebaum left his company of light tanks, a company of engineers, and some antiaircraft half-tracks to screen the division's south flank while he headed with the rest of his command for Poteau by way of St. Vith. Because the remnants of the 14th Cavalry Group had to abandon the road junction before anybody from CCA got there, the 48th Armored Infantry Battalion had to fight to gain a foothold among the houses. That was achieved by nightfall, and the armored infantrymen with tank support cleared the last *SS-Panzergrenadiers* from Poteau the next day.

The alleviation of the threat to Vielsalm was not attributable solely to the arrival of CCA at Poteau. It came about also because *Kampfgruppe Peiper* had run into trouble at Stoumont and La Gleize, and American countermeasures were threatening Peiper's line of supply. The commander of the 1st SS Panzer Division, Colonel Mohnke, had lost interest in propelling his own southernmost column toward the Meuse by way of Vielsalm. He instead turned everything available to him due west in an attempt to reach Peiper and with him continue the drive to the Meuse.

South of St. Vith, yet another threat loomed on December 18, though of less serious proportions. There, even as General Hoge was responding to the cry for help against German thrusts from the north, men of the 62d Volksgrenadier Division were trying to get across the Our River at Steinebrück and have at St. Vith from that direction.

At Steinebrück, the bridge over the fast-flowing little Our was still intact, intentionally left so after the withdrawal the night before in the outside hope that some of the troops trapped in the vicinity of the Schnee Eifel might fight their way to Steinebrück. By noon on the 18th, it was obvious that Germans infiltrating across the river were converging on the bridge in such numbers that General Hoge had to give the word to blow the bridge or risk the Germans seizing it. While a platoon of light tanks laid down suppressive fire, a platoon of armored engineers succeeded in blowing half the span.

Since the Our had ceased to be a barrier anywhere else, there was little point in the 9th Armored Division's CCB continuing to overextend itself to hold the low ground along the river. Better to fall back to the first range of hills and establish contact with the 7th Armored Division's CCB on the left and the 106th Division's 424th Infantry on the right.

Having first conferred with General Jones in St. Vith, General Hoge withdrew after nightfall on the 18th. He chose an area of high ground generally behind and commanding the Steinebrück–St. Vith highway, and at a point close to St. Vith barred the road. The new position also blocked access to the little valley of the Braunlauf Creek, which formed an avenue of approach into the rear of the defenders of St. Vith.

Although troops of the 62d Volksgrenadier Division were quick to build up beyond the Our, they made no immediate move against the new American line, for the regimental commander at Steinebrück, Col. Arthur Jüttner, wanted first to rebuild the bridge in order to get his assault guns across the river. For that, Jüttner had a company of impressed Russians who traveled with the regiment to perform such onerous tasks as peeling potatoes, digging entrenchments, and building bridges over icy streams.

Also on the south flank but well to the west, where the 7th Armored Division's CCA departed its assembly area to move to Poteau, the light forces left behind began patrolling in search of enemy buildup. On the way to check the village of Gouvy, half-tracks of the 440th Antiaircraft Artillery Battalion, along with a platoon of light tanks, came upon three Mark IVs serving as a flank patrol of the 116th Panzer Division, which was advancing on nearby roads toward Houffalize. The half-tracks and light tanks might have been in serious trouble had not the first round from one of the Mark IVs knocked out an air-compressor truck; its carcass blocked the road and kept the German tanks from getting at the American column. After firing a few rounds at long range, the Mark IVs withdrew.

Scouting about, the antiaircraft troops at a railroad depot a short distance from Gouvy found an American railhead containing, among other stores, great quantities of C- and K-rations. Thinking the Germans were closing in, the guards had set the depot on fire, but it was soon extinguished. The food was to prove a godsend for the men defending St. Vith.

At the railhead were also 350 German prisoners of war awaiting transportation to the rear. Since a highway westward from Vielsalm was still open, that was soon accomplished.

Among the myriad monumental problems facing the commanders and troops of the 422d and 423d Infantry Regiments and their attached units east of the Our River was that of communications with their division headquarters in St. Vith. Mainly because of German jamming, communications were at best erratic. From time to time messages got through to the 423d Infantry, and occasionally through the artillery net to the 590th Field Artillery Battalion, but almost every message had to be repeated over and over until finally received, usually several hours after the original transmission.

That was the case with the message that General Jones sent in midmorning of December 17 telling the two regiments to withdraw if their positions became untenable but explaining that the division intended to clear out the area to the west of them that afternoon. Colonel Cavender of the 423d Infantry received the message around 3 P.M. and finally got a copy of it to Colonel Descheneaux of the 422d Infantry just after midnight. By that time, the message was obviously out of date, for there was no indication that anybody had cleared out anything to the west.

Both commanders were nevertheless content to hold where they were. They had strong, well-prepared positions on the Schnee Eifel, and through the day of the 17th, their men had been adjusting them for all-around defense. If promised resupplies by air arrived, they were confident they could hold out long enough for a relief column to break through.

It was thus with something less than enthusiasm that the two commanders received a message sent by General Jones at 2:15 A.M. on December 18 directing the regiments to fight their way out and in the process destroy the enemy along the Schoenberg–St. Vith road. (Colonel Descheneaux bowed his head and almost sobbed: "My poor men—they'll be cut to pieces.")

The message was ambiguous: The two regiments were "to destroy [the enemy] by fire from dug-in positions S[outh] of Schoenberg–St. Vith R[oa]d." Cavender and Descheneaux took that to mean that they were to drive southwest across the Bleialf-Schoenberg road, draw up to the Our River downstream from Schoenberg in the vicinity of Setz, and there dig in to provide fire on that portion of the Schoenberg–St. Vith road running alongside the river, thereby to support a relieving attack by the 7th Armored Division. Then the two regiments might cross the Our to safety. Avoiding Schoenberg made sense, for the Germans would surely be strongest there, the obvious spot for the Americans to attempt a breakout; and although neither commander was aware of it, almost everybody who had escaped since the Germans closed the trap at Schoenberg had done so by crossing the Our downstream from Schoenberg.

Although General Jones designated no overall commander for the breakout attempt and Colonel Cavender made no attempt to assert his seniority to assume command, the two officers made every effort to coordinate their plans. That in itself was difficult, for they had no communication with each other except by patrols. They nevertheless made plans to attack the next morning with Cavender's 423d Infantry, which was closest to the Bleialf-Schoenberg road, in the lead in a column of battalions. At that point there was still hope of bringing out the regimental vehicles in the wake of the infantry, and even though the 590th Field Artillery Battalion was running short of ammunition, it would be possible to provide some artillery support for the 423d Infantry's attack.

At 10 A.M. on the 18th, Colonel Puett's 2d Battalion—the former division reserve—set off in the lead, heading west toward the hamlet of Radscheid along the Auw-Bleialf highway (Skyline Boulevard) to gain the entrance to the Engineer Cut-Off leading to the Bleialf-Schoenberg road. Puett's men made good progress, and the lead scouts were soon at the juncture of the Engineer Cut-Off with the Bleialf-Schoenberg road. But Puett was worried. Germans were pressing down Skyline Boulevard from the direction of 88 Corner into his left flank and rear. By radio, he asked Colonel Cavender to commit another battalion to block that threat.

Puett's message reached Cavender only minutes after Cavender received another from General Jones: There was to be no counterattack by the 7th Armored Division from St. Vith to Schoenberg, said the message. Cavender and Descheneaux were to shift the direction of their attack to take Schoenberg, then drive on to St. Vith on their own.

The message came as a jolt. The two regiments had left the cover of their prepared positions to meet and assist a relieving force, and now that they were in the open and exposed, they learned that there was to be no relieving force. Furthermore, they were to attack Schoenberg, a bridge and a road junction that the Germans obviously saw as critical. Yet because of the difficulty with communications, there was no way to debate the issue with General Jones, no recourse but to obey the order.

By that time, German fire had so increased that most of the men of Puett's battalion were pinned to the ground, unable to move in any direction. Sending a messenger to inform Colonel Descheneaux of the new order, Cavender ordered his 3d Battalion under Lt. Col. Earl F. Klinck to bypass Puett's battalion and proceed along a farm track that became a woods trail leading from Radscheid in the direction of Schoenberg. Klinck was to cut the Bleialf-Schoenberg road at the foot of a wooded height overlooking Schoenberg—Hill 504—and continue less than a mile into the village.

Klinck and his men crossed Skyline Boulevard near Radscheid without difficulty and had moved unimpeded into the wood a third of the way toward their objective when at the Ihren Creek they ran into small-arms fire. They nevertheless continued to advance until Company L on the left was within a few hundred yards of the Bleialf-Schoenberg highway. With that company halted, Klinck committed Company K to help, and the two companies plodded forward until Company L's left platoon cut the highway near the base of Hill 504. There Klinck consolidated his battalion for the night.

In response to continued pressure against Colonel Puett's battalion from Germans pushing down Skyline Boulevard from 88 Corner, Colonel Cavender at dusk committed his 1st Battalion; but as darkness fell, confusion set in, and the battalion made little progress. Late in the evening Cavender pulled the battalion back to Oberlascheid, just downhill from Radscheid, to prepare to join the drive on Schoenberg the next morning; but Company A, unable to disengage, had to stay behind.

Cavender at that point knew nothing about the success of Colonel Klinck's 3d Battalion in reaching the Bleiaif-Schoenberg road close to Schoenberg. Radio communications with the battalion had failed soon after the jump-off, and messengers sent back by Klinck never reached Cavender. At long last, a patrol from Cavender's headquarters located the battalion, and Cavender himself was preparing to go forward when another message got through from headquarters of the 106th Division:

> Attack Schoenberg; do maximum damage to enemy there; then attack toward St. Vith. This mission is of gravest importance to the nation. Good luck.

Cavender and his staff found the appeal to patriotism degrading; they were already trying to do what the order said in any case. Once Cavender had returned from talking with Colonel Klinck, he ordered his other two battalions to close up on the 3d Battalion and renew the attack on Schoenberg early the next morning. As far as he knew, he would be doing the job alone, for a messenger sent to notify Descheneaux of the change in plan had failed to return, and every effort to locate the 422d Infantry during the afternoon had failed.

Colonel Descheneaux and his regiment were actually close by. In keeping with the plan for the 422d Infantry to follow the 423d across the Bleialf-Schoenberg road, Descheneaux had attempted no attack but instead had assembled his units a mile north of Oberlascheid and just short of Skyline Boulevard. It was a slow, laborious march to the assembly area from the heights of the Schnee Eifel three miles away, but the men were nevertheless in fairly good spirits. Some grumbled about having to give up their prepared positions, and all were aware that before leaving their positions, they had drawn the last C- and K-rations available to the regiment. Yet on the morrow the 422d Infantry was going on the offensive, at last to do something about the predicament in which it found itself. The word was, too, that an armored division was on the way to help, and there would also be—so the word had it—resupply by air.

Having, in fact, learned of the new order to attack Schoenberg, Descheneaux that night called his battalion commanders together. The regiment was to attack the next morning with two battalions forward. The first objective was the wooded high ground overlooking Schoenberg known as Hill 504. Although there could be no artillery support, the regiment still had some ammunition for its 60mm. and 81mm. mortars. Descheneaux had no specific word as to the plans of the 423d Infantry, but he assumed that the regiment would be moving forward on his regiment's left.

By daylight on December 19, Colonel Cavender had all three of his battalions forward. Deep in the forest, he had just completed giving the attack order and told his battalion commanders to synchronize their watches. Said Cavender: "It is now exactly 9 o'clock."

As if his words were a signal, the woods erupted with bursting artillery shells. "It sounded like every tree in the forest had been simultaneously blasted from its roots." Everybody scattered, but for some it was too late, among them the commander of the 1st Battalion, Lt. Col. William H. Craig, who was mortally wounded. At about the same time, German infantry overran the firing positions of the 590th Field Artillery Battalion, whose guns had moved across Skyline Boulevard to support the attack.

Despite that disastrous prelude, the attack began as scheduled at 10 A.M. Farthest forward and on the left flank, Company L, commanded by Capt. John B. Huett, moved with two platoons abreast astride the road to Schoenberg; but the men had gone only a short distance when fire from assault guns and from flak guns mounted on half-tracks rained down. Hope stirred when a Sherman tank nosed around a bend in the road: Was that the start of the promised counterattack by American armor? Hardly. Not after the tank opened fire with its machine guns and the men could see German helmets protruding from the turret.

At the rear of the company came a deluge of small-arms fire from *Volksgrenadiers* moving down the road from Bleialf. What was left of Company L was in a vise. Although Captain Huett managed to pull the survivors onto the wooded lower slopes of Hill 504, in early afternoon, as ammunition was running out, *Volksgrenadiers* charged the position. Thirty-two men managed to surrender.

To Company L's right, the rest of the 3d Battalion, moving through the forest, gained a position on Hill 504 from which the men could look down on Schoenberg, but that was as far as they could go. Again deadly fire from assault guns and from flak guns mounted on half-tracks. Colonel Klinck pulled his men back slightly to gain some defilade and told them to dig a perimeter defense.

As for the 1st Battalion, Company C was the regimental reserve, and although Company A had finally managed to disengage and fall back on Radscheid, it happened too late for the company to participate in the attack. That left only Company B. That company got across Hill 504 and gained a clearing only five hundred yards short of the highway leading north out of Schoenberg to Andler. But there the omnipresent assault and flak guns cut the company to pieces.

Colonel Puett's 2d Battalion, advancing on the regiment's right flank, also gained a position on Hill 504 from which to look down on Schoenberg. Unable to contact Colonel Cavender by radio, Puett decided to drop down into the valley of the Linne Creek leading to the Schoenberg-Andler road and get into Schoenberg from that direction. In early afternoon, the men started to move, but hardly had they entered the valley when a blaze of small-arms fire struck them from the other side. Men of the 422d Infantry had taken them to be Germans.

Although the firing was soon stopped, the battalion, already reduced to 450 men, was badly disorganized. Out of contact with the regimental commander, Puett saw no alternative but to cast his lot with the 422d Infantry.

That regiment began its attack almost as inauspiciously as did the 423d Infantry.

The 1st Battalion on the right got virtually nowhere. As the men of Company C crossed Skyline Boulevard, they came under fire from assault guns and machine guns, and even though some of the men gained a bare knob beyond the road, continued fire broke up that group. As other men of the battalion were emerging from the assembly area up a draw leading to Skyline Boulevard, German assault guns were waiting. Almost all of the men of the two companies were either killed or captured.

Farther away from the German guns, men of the 2d Battalion on the left had considerably more success. They got across Skyline Boulevard with little difficulty and continued beyond the Ihren Creek to high ground occupied by the only surviving platoon of Company C.

Joined by Colonel Descheneaux, those men continued to advance and in early afternoon came out onto the forward slope of open ground leading down to the Schoenberg-Andler road. Below them vehicles lined the road bumper to bumper. Word spread that the vehicles were American, not to fire; but that was wishful thinking. Hardly had the men stood up and started down the slope when fire from machine guns and assault guns in the stalled column swept the hillside.

That was about the same time that Colonel Puett's battalion came under small-arms fire in the valley of the Linne Creek. The firing was from the 422d Infantry's 3d Battalion, which had come up in the woods to the left of the 2d Battalion. That mistake straightened out, Puett sent patrols up the creek valley in search of a covered route into Schoenberg, while he himself sought out Colonel Descheneaux, who was pulling his 2d Battalion back from the open slope into nearby woods.

To Puett it was obvious that Descheneaux saw no hope of continuing the attack, but he himself was determined to make one more try. He left to rejoin his battalion.

As for Descheneaux, it had become a question not of continuing the attack but of surrendering. What triggered his decision was the appearance of tanks behind him on Skyline Boulevard. For a brief moment there was hope that the 7th Armored Division had at last arrived, but when the tanks opened fire, that thin hope vanished. The tanks were from the *Führer Begleit Brigade*, on their way to participate in the attack on St. Vith but traveling by way of Skyline Boulevard to Andler in an effort to avoid the bottleneck of Schoenberg.

Descheneaux could move neither forward nor backward. Almost in despair, he called together his battalion commanders, including the commander of the 598th Field Artillery Battalion, Colonel Kelly, who had joined the regiment after failing to get out of the pocket with his battalion. All knew that little food remained, drinking water only from streams, virtually no medical supplies, only a few rounds of mortar ammunition, and small amounts of ammunition for the rifles and machine guns. The promises of relief by the 7th Armored Division and resupply by air had been empty.

"We're sitting like fish in a pond," said Descheneaux to the assembled commanders. Just at that moment men bearing a stretcher passed. On it was the young commander of Company M, Capt. James Perkins, one leg missing, blood pouring from the stump. As the litter bearers deposited

Perkins at the makeshift aid station nearby, Descheneaux could hear the moans of other wounded.

"My God," he said, "we're being slaughtered!" Asserting that he himself had no wish to die simply for glory, Descheneaux asked his commanders what they thought. All were reluctant to surrender but saw no choice.

The commander of the 589th Field Artillery Battalion, Colonel Kelly, protested. In little more than an hour, he pointed out, it would be dark and they could try then to get away.

Descheneaux rejected the suggestion. "As far as I'm concerned," he said, "I'm going to save the lives of as many men as I can, and I don't care if I'm court-martialled."

As men began to smash their weapons against the tree trunks, George Descheneaux broke down. Sitting with his feet in a slit trench, he "cried like a baby." Looking up, he saw several young officers staring at him. Their eyes looked cold. Was it pity, Descheneaux asked himself, or hate?

When Descheneaux requested a volunteer to go under a white flag to arrange surrender, it seemed to the executive officer of Puett's 2d Battalion, 423d Infantry—Maj. William J. Cody Garlow, a grandson of "Buffalo Bill" Cody—that Descheneaux was looking directly at him. "OK, Colonel," said Garlow, "I'll go." Borrowing two white handkerchiefs, he tied them together and set off alone, not thinking to take with him someone who spoke German.

Coming at last to a German position, Garlow waved the handkerchiefs frantically. German soldiers beckoned him in but then scrambled from their foxholes to strip him of his watch, a few bars of candy, and a pint of whiskey. Knowing no German, Garlow was unable to communicate that he had come not to surrender himself but to arrange his unit's surrender.

At last a young lieutenant with crew-cut hair arrived. When he spoke in English, Garlow explained his mission and demanded that the soldiers return his property. The lieutenant barked a command, and the men complied. Accompanied by a squad, the two officers were soon on their way toward the woods where Descheneaux and his troops, some of them in tears, were waiting.

There Colonel Puett had returned from his reconnaissance to learn of Descheneaux's decision. Puett found it unbelievable and told Descheneaux he intended getting his battalion out. No, said Descheneaux, he had already sent out a white flag. If Puett and his men tried to escape, it would go hard on everybody else. He specifically ordered Puett himself not to try it.

Going back to his battalion, Puett told his men what was happening. Anybody who wanted to try to make it out alone or in small groups could take off. About seventy-five men faded into the woods.

A few hundred yards away in the woods atop Hill 504, the commander of the 423d Infantry, Colonel Cavender, was arriving independently of Colonel Descheneaux at the same decision: that it would be best to surrender. Calling his battalion commanders together, he surveyed the condition of their units. The 1st Battalion had virtually ceased to exist; Colonel Klinck's 3d Battalion had lost well over half its strength, including all of Company L; and Colonel Puett's 2d Battalion had disappeared.

There was no ammunition left, said Cavender, except for the few rounds each man still had on his person. Nobody had eaten all day. The supporting artillery had already been overrun.

The officers detected what was coming. "I know it's no use fighting," said one of them, "but I still don't want to surrender."

"I was a GI in the First World War," said Cavender, "and I want to see things from the soldier's standpoint." He was silent for a moment. "Gentlemen," he said at last, "we're surrendering at 1600 [4 P.M.]."

One of those whom Cavender surrendered was the son of his division commander, Alan W. Jones, Jr.

The 422d and 423d Infantry Regiments, along with their attached and supporting units—the 589th, 590th, and 592d Field Artillery Battalions; Companies A and B, 81st Engineer Combat Battalion; Battery D, 634th Antiaircraft Artillery Battalion; Company C, 820th Tank Destroyer Battalion; Companies A and B, 331st Medical Battalion; the 106th Reconnaissance Troop; and Troop B, 18th Cavalry Reconnaissance Squadron —lost more than eight thousand men in the fighting atop and in the shadow of the Schnee Eifel.

Many men got out before the surrender, including almost all the 592d Field Artillery Battalion, part of the 589th, and some of Troop B, 18th Cavalry, along with a few men of the 106th Reconnaissance Troop; and still others had been wounded, captured, or killed before the mass surrender. Some made it out individually or in small groups after the surrender, notably forty men and two lieutenants, Harold A. McKinley of Company A, 423d Infantry, and Ivan H. Long of the I&R Platoon, 422d Infantry. Like most of those who escaped, men in that group hid in the woods by day and traveled by night, often guiding on the path of V-1 buzz bombs.

How many men surrendered en masse in late afternoon of December 19 would never be known exactly. The 106th Division lost 6,879 men captured, to which would have to be added those captured from attached units for a total slightly above 7,000. Assuming an average strength of the infantry battalions at the time Cavender and Descheneaux surrendered their regiments to be five hundred men—possibly an overestimate—approximately three thousand Americans surrendered in the two mass capitulations. Thus the oft-suggested spectacle of some eight to nine thousand Americans plodding into Germany with hands overhead was false.

There were men from both regiments who continued to fight even after the regimental commanders surrendered. For some the fight was brief, for a cruel rumor spread that the 9th Armored Division had recaptured Bleialf, and many men, including those left in charge of the 422d Infantry's vehicles, headed for Bleialf. The rumor being baseless, the men paid dearly for their desperate gullibility.

Meanwhile, fragments of the 422d Infantry began to coalesce on high ground a few hundred yards outside the village of Laudesfeld, Hill 576, not far from the old firing positions of the 592d Field Artillery Battalion. There half-tracks of the 634th Antiaircraft Artillery Battalion, originally emplaced to protect the artillery, had held their ground while the fighting surged around them. By midnight of December 19, some five hundred men had assembled on the hill, and under the overall command of the 2d Battalion's executive officer, Maj. Albert A. Ouellette, they organized for defense.

Almost every man had arrived with some ammunition, and on the antiaircraft half-tracks and a few other vehicles were some twenty .50-caliber machine guns. At least as important, there were enough rations for each man to have two meager meals for two days. The men with the antiaircraft half-tracks thought they still had radio communication with their battalion headquarters in St. Vith and reported that they were holding out. Even though they received no acknowledgment of the message, the fact that they had sent it provided hope that a relief column might eventually break through.

The next day, December 20, artillery fire began to pummel the position. German troops ringed it closely, as any attempt to move about the open hill in daylight quickly affirmed; but the Germans made no assault. The Americans, in time, obviously would have to surrender.

Late that day, a German reconnaissance car flying a white flag and carrying a German medical officer approached. He wanted to arrange a truce, said the officer, to assure safe evacuation of both German and American wounded in the vicinity; but while he was about it, he suggested that the Americans surrender.

At the invitation of the German, Major Ouellette sent with him a lieutenant who returned a few hours later with word that the Germans had artillery pieces trained on Hill 576 and infantry poised to follow an artillery preparation to sweep the hill. The lieutenant knew it to be fact, for the Germans had paraded their preparations before his eyes.

Although some of the junior officers still wanted to hold out, Major Ouellette saw no reason for further loss of life. On the promise of a cease-fire through the night, he agreed to surrender early the next morning. So closely ringed was the position that probably none of those who tried to sneak away during the night succeeded.

At 8 A.M. on December 21, the last organized resistance east of the Our River ended. It marked the conclusion of the most costly defeat for American arms during the course of the war in Europe.

Even as the men beyond the Our River surrendered, General Jones and his staff were still trying to get them resupplied by air. It was a task that had proven utterly frustrating.

Colonel Cavender had first asked for an airdrop early on December 17 and specified the most needed items. Somebody on Jones's staff contacted the air officer at headquarters of the VIII Corps, Lt. Col. Josiah T. Towne, and word went back to Cavender to expect a drop that night.

It never came. Towne relayed the request through the IX Fighter Command to the IX Tactical Air Command, which, in turn, had to refer it to headquarters of the First Army for approval. Not until early the next morning, December 18, did the request reach England and headquarters of the IX Troop Carrier Command, whose C-47 transport planes would have to fly the mission. Ground crews loaded forty planes of the 425th Troop Carrier Group with ammunition and medical supplies; but the weather was closing in, and only twenty-three took off.

Those planes arrived during the afternoon of the 18th over a base at Florennes, in Belgium, where they were supposed to land, but the controller waved them off. The base was too busy to accommodate them. Most of the planes eventually landed at a base in France. The commander himself did land at Florennes, only to learn that nobody knew anything about the mission and that no fighter escort was available.

During the early afternoon of December 19, somebody at the 106th Division's headquarters asked headquarters of the VIII Corps if supplies had been dropped. It was late in the evening—and men of the 422d and 423d Regiments were already trudging deep into Germany—before a reply came back: "Supplies have not been dropped. Will be dropped tomorrow weather permitting."

It never took place. As senior commanders had accepted awkward defensive positions on the Schnee Eifel in the belief that nothing ever happened in the Ardennes, so they had failed to provide adequate machinery for responding to a sudden need for resupply by air. For except in pre-planned airborne operations, nobody ever got surrounded.

Along the horseshoe-shaped defense protecting St. Vith, the Germans during December 19 made only reconnaissance probes. That was not what General von Manteuffel intended. He was counting on the arrival of the *Führer Begleit Brigade* and a strong thrust to take St. Vith on the 19th, but traffic conditions in the German rear were still appalling. Von Manteuffel himself went again to Schoenberg, where he found the traffic stacked up three abreast on the Schoenberg-Andler road. The 18th Volksgrenadier Division was still using two of its three regiments and all but one of its artillery battalions against the trapped Americans east of the Our and would be able to turn its full strength against St. Vith only after eliminating them.

During the day von Manteuffel met near Wallerode with the commander of Army Group B, Field Marshal Model, and the commander of the 66th Corps, General Lucht. There was little the three officers could do other than vow to get the attack moving early on the 20th. By that time the 62d Volksgrenadier Division should have the bridge at Steinebrück rebuilt, at least two of the 18th Volksgrenadier Division's regiments should be forward, and the *Führer Begleit Brigade* should be ready to make the principal thrust down the Amblève highway into St. Vith. Then again, that depended upon untangling the traffic jams on the roads in the rear.

During the afternoon of December 19, the commander of the 9th Armored Division's CCB, Bill Hoge, strode into a schoolhouse in the village of Crombach, two miles outside St. Vith, where Bruce Clarke had moved his command post. "Who do I work for?" demanded Hoge. "I was sent down here by First Army to be attached to Jones and the 106th Infantry Division. Where is Jones? Now I don't know what the situation is. Maybe I had better go back to Bastogne and find out."

Clarke tried to placate him. There was no need to deal with Jones; the two of them could work things out together.

On a map, Clarke noted that the positions occupied by Hoge's CCB the night before were for the most part forward of a railroad track built on a high embankment. He knew, said Clarke, that the Germans were going to hit him hard and that sooner or later he was going to have to give up the town of St. Vith, which would eliminate the only route of withdrawal for those of Hoge's troops forward of the embankment. When Clarke suggested that Hoge withdraw that night behind the embankment, Hoge agreed.

It was on that same day, December 19, that Colonel Nelson of the 28th Division's 112th Infantry reported to General Jones to announce the availability of his regiment and its supporting artillery battalion. Attaching the regiment to the 106th Division, Jones notified General Middleton, who subsequently approved. Jones told Nelson to tie his regiment's defenses to the right flank of the 424th Infantry and block the main highway leading to Vielsalm from the south, a road that was, in effect, an extension of the Skyline Drive.

By midnight of December 19, a horseshoe-shaped defense of St. Vith had taken form. No reinforcements were to be expected. The next move was up to General Lucht and his 66th Corps.

BOOK

IV

THE

SHOULDERS

CHAPTER SEVENTEEN

In Front of Luxembourg City

On the southern shoulder of the German offensive, amid the frontier villages, woods, and steeply rolling hills between the southern reaches of the Skyline Drive and the Our River, and below the confluence of the Our and the Sûre on either side of the Ernz Noire ("Little Switzerland"), the American troops at the start of the second day were having their difficulties. Yet they were considerably better off than many of their colleagues elsewhere, primarily because they were facing no German armor but only a parachute and three *Volksgrenadier* divisions of General Brandenberger's Seventh Army. Those German divisions were in fact having problems throwing bridges across the Our and the Sûre in order to bring forward such fire support as they did possess: horse-drawn divisional artillery and the equivalent of an under-strength battalion of self-propelled assault guns.

There, too, even though Brandenberger had assumed at the end of the first day that his adversary had committed all his local reserves, there were actually reserves still to make their presence felt. Although the 109th Infantry's Colonel Rudder had committed his reserve infantry battalion, primarily in an effort to rescue Company E, surrounded in Fouhren, he still had a company of medium tanks of the 707th Tank Battalion to add weight to a renewal of that effort. During the night, the 60th Armored Infantry Battalion, in the line to gain battlefield experience, had reverted to control of its parent command, the 9th Armored Division's CCA, and the bulk of that combat command's tanks and self-propelled tank destroyers were still to enter the fight.

On the high plateau east of the Ernz Noire, generally astride the highway linking Echternach and Luxembourg City, the 12th Infantry's Colonel Chance had committed the last of his reserve battalion; but the commander of the 4th Division, Tubby Barton, had arranged to borrow a company of medium tanks from the 9th Armored Division's CCA. Taking a chance that the German offensive would not expand to the south,

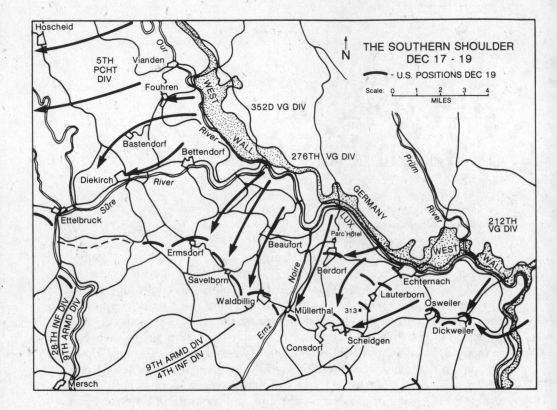

THE SOUTHERN SHOULDER
DEC 17 - 19

〜 - U.S. POSITIONS DEC 19

Scale: 0   1   2   3   4
MILES

Barton was bringing forward the reserve battalion of his southernmost regiment, the 22d Infantry. He also still had in reserve his organic reconnaissance troop and engineer combat battalion.

More important still was another reserve whose early commitment Brandenberger could in no way have anticipated. That was the 10th Armored Division's CCA, which at daybreak on December 17 began moving to Luxembourg from the sector of the Third Army in northeastern France. The combat command was to be available at the start of the third day, December 18.

American commanders intended on the second day, December 17, to use their local reserves to rescue surrounded units, strengthen threatened units, and block exits from the gorge of the Ernz Noire leading into the rear of the units on either side. Rudder of the 109th Infantry was to rescue Company E in Fouhren; Collins of the 60th Armored Infantry Battalion was to block roads leading into his rear from the Ernz Noire and maintain contact with his line companies on the wooded heights overlooking the Sûre River; and Chance of the 12th Infantry was to rescue the men of Company F in the Parc Hôtel outside Berdorf and the men of

Company E in Echternach and to reinforce the hardpressed men of the 3d Battalion southeast of Echternach in Osweiler and Dickweiler.

In the northern part of the 109th Infantry's sector, where the commander of the 85th Corps, General Kniess, was trying to break the 5th Parachute Division loose in order to lean on the advance of the adjacent *Panzer Lehr Division*, the Germans were content to bypass most isolated defensive positions in favor of pushing on to the Skyline Drive. Yet if they were to open a road for their drive to the west, they had to have Hoscheid on the Skyline Drive. That was what had led to the day-long fight for the village, ending after nightfall with American withdrawal. A road westward at last available, the 5th Parachute Division from that point became, in effect, an adjunct of the Fifth Panzer Army's drive for Bastogne.

The situation of the 5th Parachute Division at Hoscheid was similar to that of the 352d Volksgrenadier Division at Fouhren. The *Volksgrenadiers* needed the village in order to gain access to the valley of the Sûre River at Diekirch and their assigned road leading west; but without support from assault guns, it was difficult to force the 109th Infantry's Company E from Fouhren. Because of American artillery fire, it was late in the night of December 17 before a bridge was in place to allow assault guns to cross the Our. Yet even though two American companies trying to gain Fouhren had help from a platoon of medium tanks, the *Volksgrenadiers* managed to prevent them from breaking through to the village.

When Company E radioed in some desperation for food and ammunition, Colonel Rudder ordered a patrol to try to get through after nightfall, but again Fouhren remained out of reach. The last word from Company E came by radio an hour after midnight. When a patrol from the I&R Platoon, accompanied by a tank, got within two hundred yards of the village at daylight, the men could see that the house that had served as the company command post had burned to the ground. Company E, 109th Infantry, had ceased to exist.

The collapse at Fouhren meant increased pressure on the 109th Infantry's 3d Battalion close by in the angle formed by confluence of the Our and the Sûre, for it left that battalion's northern flank exposed. Eliminating that battalion was critical to the German advance, for it was forward observers with the battalion who were directing the shelling of the 352d Volksgrenadier Division's bridge site. At dawn on December 18, a German regiment hit the 3d Battalion's north flank and surrounded and captured a platoon of Company K, but the battalion held.

Despite that stand, the positions of the 109th Infantry were fast becoming untenable, for there was no way to halt German movement between the widely spaced American positions. By midday of December 18, German forces the size of companies and even battalions were moving almost with impunity behind the American-held villages. Here and there they overwhelmed little outposts trying to fill the gaps between villages: a brace of 57mm. antitank guns, a few men from Cannon Company fighting as infantry, a squad of engineers defending a roadblock.

As early as the pre-dawn hours of December 17, a battery of 105mm. howitzers of the 107th Field Artillery Battalion just behind the southern reaches of the Skyline Drive came under small-arms fire from German patrols; and in the early afternoon on the 18th, an entire battalion of *Volksgrenadiers* attacked that battery and a nearby battery of 155mm. howitzers of the 108th Field Artillery Battalion. While neighboring batteries took the Germans under fire, two half-tracks from the 447th Anti-aircraft Artillery Battalion raced up the Skyline Drive, their quad-50s blazing, and chased the Germans off the road. From the north, the platoon of tanks sent to try to break through to Hoscheid returned and helped drive the Germans away. The artillery pieces were for the moment safe, but it was obvious that all the artillery in support of the 109th Infantry would have to displace.

By that time, Companies F and G had fallen back on the 2d Battalion's headquarters village of Bastendorf, and remnants of Companies A and B, having failed to reach Fouhren, fell back under fire to a road junction less than half a mile from the road following the trace of the Sûre River into Diekirch. If the men of the 3d Battalion were to withdraw from their positions in the angle formed by confluence of the Our and Sûre, they would need that road.

Early that same afternoon, December 18, two assault guns supporting a battalion of *Volksgrenadiers* hit the road junction. With the first rounds, the German guns knocked out six 57mm. antitank guns and one of three medium tanks still fighting with Company A. For a moment it looked like a breakthrough; but with the help of the two surviving tanks, the infantry rallied and held.

To Colonel Rudder, the near disaster at the road junction underscored the need to pull his regiment back and consolidate along a new line. Although he had in mind eventual withdrawal behind the Sûre River, he asked authority at first merely to consolidate on high ground near Diekirch. The men were well dug in on the high ground by the next afternoon, the 19th, when German artillery, having at last crossed the Our, opened heavy preparation fire. Yet the attack by *Volksgrenadiers* was weak. In more than three days of fighting, the 352d Volksgrenadier Division had lost heavily, and in the attack that afternoon, the division commander, Colonel Erich Schmidt, was seriously wounded.

That night Colonel Rudder asked General Cota for permission to withdraw behind the Sûre. Cota suggested instead that Rudder fall back along the Ettelbruck-Bastogne highway, thereby rejoining the 28th Divi-

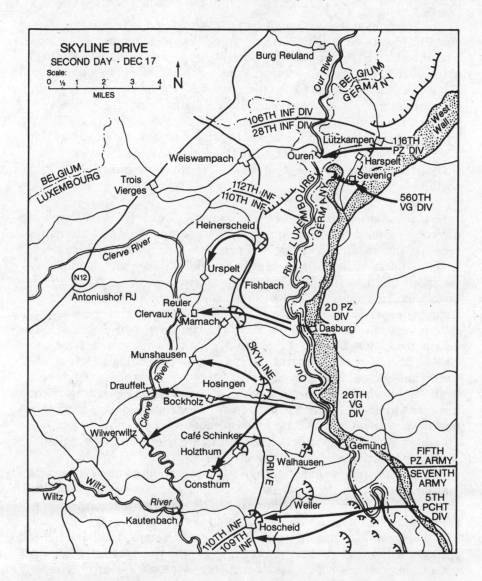

SKYLINE DRIVE
SECOND DAY - DEC 17

Scale:
0 ½ 1 2 3 4
MILES

N

Burg Reuland

BELGIUM
GERMANY

Our River

West Wall

106TH INF DIV
28TH INF DIV

Lützkampen

116TH PZ DIV

Ouren

Harspelt

Sevenig

BELGIUM
LUXEMBOURG

Weiswampach

Trois Vierges

112TH INF
110TH INF

GERMANY

River Our LUXEMBOURG

560TH VG DIV

Heinerscheid

Clerve River

Urspelt

Fishbach

N12

Antoniushof RJ

Reuler

Clervaux

Marnach

Dasburg

2D PZ DIV

Munshausen

SKYLINE

Our

Drauffelt

Clerve River

Hosingen

26TH VG DIV

Bockholz

Wilwerwiltz

Café Schinker

Holzthum

Walhausen

Gemünd

FIFTH PZ ARMY

DRIVE

SEVENTH ARMY

Consthum

5TH PCHT DIV

Wiltz

Wiltz River

Weiler

Kautenbach

110TH INF
109TH INF

Hoscheid

sion; but because of the 5th Parachute Division's advance, Rudder believed that would be less a withdrawal than an attack. "Use your own judgment," said Cota finally. "You are on the ground."

Under protective artillery fires, most of the troops left Diekirch before midnight along the road to Ettelbruck and before daylight the following morning were digging in on high ground south and west of Ettelbruck. From those positions they could cover both the Ettelbruck-Bastogne highway and the principal highway leading south from Ettelbruck to Luxembourg City. An attached company of the 28th Division's organic engineers blew bridges both at Diekirch and at Ettelbruck.

In Diekirch, at the first rumor that the Americans were going to abandon the town, the civilians erupted from their cellars into the streets. They had started to flee early on December 16, but in order to keep the roads open for military movement, local officials at the behest of officers of the 109th Infantry had halted the exodus. Over the next few days, the local *gendarmerie* had helped the Americans by housing German prisoners of war in the town jail. Fearing reprisals, the civilians were determined to leave, and with Colonel Rudder's approval, they followed the Americans out of town. More than three thousand men, women, and children set out in freezing cold and darkness along the roads leading south.

For the 60th Armored Infantry Battalion between the Sûre River and the gorge of the Ernz Noire, the basic concern was likely German movement up the undefended gorge and egress along one of the three roads leading into the rear of the American positions. There was also the possibility of envelopment from the north, where on the first day the Germans had eliminated a small outpost which the armored infantry battalion commander, Colonel Collins, had positioned there to give the alarm.

During the night of December 16, the commander of the battalion's parent unit, Col. Thomas L. Harrold of the 9th Armored Division's CCA, took a few steps toward blocking those possibilities. He sent the 19th Tank Battalion's company of light tanks to screen the northern flank; he attached a troop of the 89th Cavalry Reconnaissance Squadron to Collins to patrol the road from the Ernz Noire into Collins's headquarters town of Beaufort; and he sent another troop plus the 76mm. self-propelled guns of Company B, 811th Tank Destroyer Battalion, to block the other two roads leading up from the gorge.

Those were timely steps, but they were insufficient to prevent German infiltration. During the night of the 16th, troops of the 276th Volksgrenadier Division worked southward through some woods in the rear of Collins's companies, and others occupied a ridgeline between Beaufort and the forward companies. Although a counterattack by the attached cavalry cleared the ridgeline, the Germans in the woods remained, which meant that the line companies of the 60th Armored Infantry Battalion were cut off.

At the same time, a regiment of *Volksgrenadiers* moved unopposed up the gorge of the Ernz Noire to the settlement of Müllerthal, where the road along the bottom of the gorge met another bisecting the gorge, an intersection that soon became known to American troops as "the T." From Müllerthal, the Germans threatened the village of Waldbillig, not far behind firing positions of the 3d Armored Field Artillery Battalion.

Early that afternoon, a troop of cavalry reinforced by four self-propelled tank destroyers tried to drive the *Volksgrenadiers* from Müllerthal, but on a narrow, winding road leading down into the gorge, a German with a *Panzerfaust* knocked out the leading tank destroyer, blocking the road. Dismounted cavalry got nowhere, and as daylight waned, the American force withdrew to the top of the gorge.

As night came on the 17th, *Volksgrenadiers* at the other end of the gorge poured into Beaufort. Colonel Collins ordered his headquarters troops to withdraw while the attached troop of cavalry under Capt. Victor C. Leiker fought a rear guard action. Leiker's troop managed to hold for about two hours, just long enough for self-propelled pieces of the 3d Armored Field Artillery Battalion near the next village to displace.

During the night, the only radio still affording communication with the trapped companies of the 60th Armored Infantry Battalion, one belonging to an artillery forward observer, ceased to function. Yet that was of little concern for the moment in view of the fact that the commander of CCA, Colonel Harrold, was assembling a force to attack early the next morning to relieve the armored infantrymen and "drive the enemy into the river." And it was an impressive force: two companies of mediums of the 19th Tank Battalion, a company of the 9th Armored Engineer Battalion mounted in half-tracks to fight as infantry, a troop of the 89th Cavalry Reconnaissance Squadron, and the 60th Armored Infantry Battalion's I&R Platoon. The attack was to begin from what was fast becoming CCA's new defensive line, extending from Waldbillig northward along a ridgeline through the village of Savelborn and on to screening positions of the light tanks in Ermsdorf.

On the German side, the commander of the 276th Volksgrenadier Division, Generalleutnant Kurt Möhring, was at the same time preparing to attack the center of that line at Savelborn, from which Harrold's attack was to debouch. Möhring had a battalion of *Volksgrenadiers* and an anti-tank company with fifty-four *Panzerfausts*.

Unknown to General Möhring, his failure to build a bridge quickly across the Sûre, which had resulted in a slow buildup beyond the river, had prompted his superior, General Brandenberger, to call upon Field Marshal Model at Army Group B to send a replacement for Möhring. As it turned out, Möhring was riding in his command car that evening near Beaufort when fire from an American machine gun killed him.

The next morning, the steps Möhring had taken to assemble a force near Savelborn served the 276th Volksgrenadier Division well. Before daylight, as the Germans were preparing to attack Savelborn, the 60th Armored Infantry Battalion's I&R Platoon, in the vanguard of the attacking American force, entered the woods outside the village. German fire killed the platoon leader at the outset and in the end virtually wiped out the platoon.

After daylight, the main body of CCA's attacking force followed along the same road through the woods, and to men in the half-tracks and tanks, there appeared to be a *Panzerfaust* behind every tree. In what seemed to be only minutes, the *Panzerfausts* knocked out a light tank and six Shermans. The commander of the leading medium tank company, Capt. Arthur J. Banford, Jr., his own tank shot from under him, ordered withdrawal. Pleading insufficient foot troops to protect the tanks, the entire column fell back on Savelborn, an inauspicious first offensive action for those troops of CCA, and it left the men of the 60th Armored Infantry Battalion to fend for themselves.

In the beleaguered positions of that battalion, the artillery forward observer late in the afternoon of December 18 finally managed to repair his radio. By order of Colonel Harrold, the men were to make their way out by infiltration. That night and over the next two nights 400 men made their way to safety; but in the three-day fight, the 60th Armored Infantry Battalion lost close to 350 men, most of them during the withdrawal.

The new line to be held by the 9th Armored Division's CCA extended for more than seven miles, from Waldbillig alongside the Ernz Noire through Savelborn and Ermsdorf and beyond. Yet despite the length of that line, a gap between the combat command and the 109th Infantry of four miles still existed. That regiment's depleted 2d Battalion soon moved into the gap, a stopgap measure, at best, but as it turned out, all that was needed.

A new commander for the 276th Volksgrenadier Division, Col. Hugo Dempwolff, made it his first priority to reorganize his command, for casualties had been heavy. Still lacking a bridge over the Sûre, he arranged during the night of December 18 to pass his artillery and supplies over bridges belonging to the two adjacent divisions; and when his engineers at last completed a bridge late on the 19th, he was able to move forward three assault guns that the commander of the Seventh Army, General Brandenberger, had scrounged from some place. Only with the arrival of those guns was Colonel Dempwolff prepared for the 276th Volksgrenadier Division to return to the offensive, and by that time higher command had arrived at other plans.

By daylight on December 17, the slight superiority in numbers possessed by the commander of the 212th Volksgrenadier Division, Generalmajor Franz Sensfuss, over the 12th Infantry's Colonel Chance—five infantry battalions (one regiment served as the Seventh Army's reserve) against three—had disappeared. For the commander of the 4th Division, General Barton, had ordered the reserve battalion of his southernmost regiment to the threatened sector and his organic engineer battalion into the line as infantry. That made it five against five, and Barton had a decided edge in artillery, tanks, and tank destroyers, for Sensfuss had only four assault guns and as yet no way to get them or his horse-drawn artillery across the Sûre River.

Although Sensfuss's engineers had thrown a bridge across the Sûre on the first day of the offensive, American artillery fire knocked it out before the first vehicle could cross. That night the German engineers brought down searchlights close to the river opposite Echternach. They planned to build a bridge based on the stone piers of an earlier bridge that had served the town since the Middle Ages; but American shelling again interfered. Falling back, the engineers had to wait for daylight before building a bridge at another site downstream, and not until late afternoon of December 18 did that bridge begin to serve the division.

The first move General Barton made early on December 17 to meet the continuing German threat was to send the 4th Reconnaissance Troop and the 4th Engineer Combat Battalion, before daylight, to an obvious point of danger: the high ground above the gorge of the Ernz Noire not far from Müllerthal and the road intersection known as the T. When in the early morning *Volksgrenadiers* reached Müllerthal, Barton decided to reinforce by creating Task Force Luckett, headed by a former commander of the 12th Infantry, Col. James S. Luckett, then carried as an excess officer with the division headquarters. In addition to the reconnaissance troop and the engineers, Luckett was to have eight Shermans which Company B, 70th Tank Battalion, had by that time managed to put into some kind of operating order, the tank battalion's mortar platoon, and the reserve battalion of the adjacent 8th Infantry. Calling on that battalion was a risk, for the German offensive still might expand southward; but knowledge that the 10th Armored Division's CCA was on the way made Barton's decision easier.

When the eight Shermans arrived in mid-afternoon of the 17th, Colonel Luckett sent them to block the gorge of the Ernz Noire a half-mile upstream from Müllerthal, and when the 8th Infantry's reserve battalion reached the scene, the 2d under Lt. Col. George L. Mabry, he added the infantry to that block. Yet, ironically, General Barton had created a block against a German force that threatened not his 12th Infantry but rather the 9th Armored Division's CCA; for the Germans in the gorge were from the 276th Volksgrenadier Division, whose zone of advance lay on CCA's side of the gorge. Barton and Luckett would be left to wonder why the Germans made no effort to emerge from the gorge into the rear of the 12th Infantry.

Elsewhere the 12th Infantry spent the second day of the German offensive trying to rescue surrounded units and reinforce others.

The regimental commander, Colonel Chance, again sent Company B, reinforced by a platoon of light tanks and four mediums, to clear the village of Berdorf and rescue the men of Lieutenant Leake's Company F. That was no easy assignment, for Berdorf was an elongated village extending for more than half a mile along a spine formed by the highway leading from the 2d Battalion's headquarters village of Consdorf. Accompanied by the light tanks, half of the infantrymen worked house by house up the spine, while the rest of the men and the four medium tanks bypassed the village over open ground between the village and the Ernz Noire. That route led to Lieutenant Leake's little force in the Parc Hôtel.

As the four tanks neared the hotel, it looked to Lieutenant Leake as if they were maneuvering to get into position to fire on it. As indeed they were; for since Lieutenant McConnell had lost Company F's SCR-300 during his fracas with the Germans in Berdorf, Leake had had no way to report his position. How to reveal to the tanks that Americans held the hotel? Leake had no identification panels, no flares, nothing.

One man suddenly remembered that in rummaging through the drawers of a dresser in one of the rooms, he had come across an American flag. He rushed to find it, and a volunteer climbed to the shattered roof of the hotel and waved it frantically.

As the tanks and their accompanying infantry reached the hotel, the rest of Company B was pushing the Germans past the road junction a hundred yards away in Berdorf, but that was as far as the attack carried before nightfall brought a halt. Leake and his men continued to hold the hotel, for that provided good flank protection for the men in Berdorf.

In the center of the 12th Infantry's sector on December 17, Colonel Chance sent Company A to reinforce Company G in Lauterborn, astride the last high ground before the highway dropped down into Echternach, whereupon the two companies were to drive to the relief of Company E inside Echternach. Because the Germans held high ground on either side of the highway leading into Lauterborn, it took Company A the better part of the day to get into the village, and by that time it was too late to continue the attack. The men of Company E remained isolated in Echternach.

On the right of the 12th Infantry's sector, in Osweiler and Dickweiler, the third line company of Chance's reserve 1st Battalion, Company C, reinforced the defending companies of the 3d Battalion; and in mid-morning, the reserve battalion from the 22d Infantry, the 2d under Lt. Col. Thomas A. Kenan, detrucked behind the two villages. The men of one company climbed immediately onto the decks of a company of tanks borrowed from the 9th Armored Division's CCA and headed for Osweiler. On the way they flushed and routed a company of Germans in some woods alongside the road and in the process freed sixteen men of Company C, captured during the company's move to Osweiler.

In mid-afternoon, the rest of Colonel Kenan's battalion headed for Osweiler on foot. The column was nearing the crest of a ridge a mile short of the village when a column of Germans appeared. Taken by surprise, the men of both columns dropped to the ground and opened fire. The fight was a stand-off until darkness came, when the Germans disengaged, and the next morning Kenan's men resumed their march to Osweiler.

The Germans had been on their way to Scheidgen, close by Consdorf and headquarters of the 12th Infantry's 2d Battalion. There the Germans gained their only success of the day when a platoon of self-propelled tank destroyers abandoned the village without a fight. With only a few men from the headquarters available to defend Consdorf, the battalion commander, Maj. John W. Dorn, spent an anxious night, but the Germans made no effort to push beyond Scheidgen.

At the end of the second day of the German offensive, the trace of a new defensive line was beginning to take shape in the 12th Infantry's sector. Osweiler and Dickweiler on the right were firmly held (a fact soon recognized by the German commander, General Sensfuss, who made no further attempt to take those villages). So, too, on the left, Task Force Luckett had firmly anchored the line along the upper reaches of the Ernz Noire. The weakness was in the center, where there was a gap between Osweiler and Consdorf along the principal highway through the sector— the road from Luxembourg City to Echternach (which General Sensfuss also recognized and intended to try, with his limited means, to exploit).

Out in front were two projections. Company B and Lieutenant Leake's little band at Berdorf constituted one; Companies A and G in Lauterborn and Company E in Echternach constituted the other. Except for the danger to the men in those projections, the 12th Infantry at nightfall on December 17 was in fairly good shape, and reinforcements were arriving. They consisted of a corps engineer battalion, the 159th, which General Barton put in reserve near his left flank lest the enemy break through the adjacent sector, and the 10th Armored Division's CCA.

After conferring with General Middleton in Bastogne, the commander of the 10th Armored Division, General Morris, met with Barton in Luxembourg City and agreed on how to use CCA. Since the entire 10th Armored Division, except for CCB at Bastogne, was to be committed in Luxembourg, CCA was not attached to the 4th Division. The two commanders nevertheless agreed that the armor would attack the next day, the 18th, through the positions of the 12th Infantry, to drive the Germans back across the Sûre.

In early afternoon, Barton worked out the details of that commitment with CCA's commander, Brig. Gen. Edwin W. Piburn. One task force was to clear the gorge of the Ernz Noire; a second to push through Berdorf and thence into Echternach; and a third to retake Scheidgen, link with the infantry in Lauterborn, and continue into Echternach. Since Barton was most concerned about the possibility of the Germans debouching in strength from the Ernz Noire, the first of Piburn's task forces to arrive was to be committed there. It was unfortunate that the first task force contained the bulk of the combat command's medium tanks, for the gorge of the Ernz Noire was no place for tanks.

As the three task forces began to advance early on December 18, the Germans made their move to exploit the gap between Osweiler and Scheidgen. Two German battalions drove south along secondary roads close by the main highway leading to Luxembourg City, in effect cutting into the rear of the American troops at Osweiler and Dickweiler and, if the advance continued, into the rear of the neighboring 8th Infantry.

Fortunate it was for the Americans that those two German battalions had lost heavily in the first two days of fighting, for in the sector where they struck, the 12th Infantry had no prepared defensive positions. In both cases, the Germans bumped into forces that had to turn from other duties to fight back—in one hamlet, the 12th Infantry's Cannon Company, caught as the cannoneers were moving into new firing positions; in another, the rear command post of the 2d Battalion, 22d Infantry, whose headquarters troops had the support of only a platoon of towed tank destroyers. Yet in both cases the Americans held off the Germans long enough for a few medium tanks to get forward and enable them to withdraw.

The German commander, General Sensfuss, may not have realized it, but he had at last achieved a breakthrough, for in the hamlets ahead hardly anybody stood in the way. Yet both German battalions, already under strength, had taken heavy losses during the day and were in no condition to exploit their gains. Once General Sensfuss had learned of the arrival of American armor, he convinced General Brandenberger to release his third regiment from the Seventh Army's reserve, but it would be another twenty-four hours, at best, before that regiment got across the Sûre River.

Meanwhile, the attacks by the three task forces of the 10th Armored Division's CCA achieved little, particularly the attack aimed at clearing the enemy from the gorge of the Ernz Noire. Tanks of the 11th Tank Battalion entered the gorge upstream from German-held Müllerthal, but because the road at the bottom of the gorge was narrow and closely confined on both sides by woods, the width of the attacking front was the width of one medium tank. When a round from an antitank gun damaged the leading tank, it took considerable time to work the rest of the column around. It was late afternoon before the head of the task force reached Müllerthal, there to confront a strong German position.

CCA's second task force, composed of the 61st Armored Infantry Battalion and a company of Shermans, moved to Berdorf and there joined the 12th Infantry's Company B in clearing the rest of the village. Progress was slow. When night came, the Germans still held a few houses in Berdorf and the task force had made no progress on its second assignment of pushing beyond Berdorf into Echternach.

The third and smallest task force (composed of a company each of medium tanks and armored infantry) found only an enemy rear guard in Scheidgen and with the help of two companies of the 159th Engineer Combat Battalion soon took a commanding height overlooking Lauterborn. Once inside the village, the two companies of the 12th Infantry delayed their planned push into Echternach to await arrival of the tanks.

Yet when the tanks got there, the task force commander, Lt. Col. John R. Riley, considered it too late in the day to continue into Echternach. While the task force holed up for the night at the mill alongside the road to Echternach, where Company G had its command post, Riley sent two tanks accompanied by two squads of infantry into Echternach to ascertain how the 12th Infantry's Company E was faring.

Fairly well, as it turned out. The company commander, 1st Lt. Morton A. Macdiarmid, had established his headquarters near the edge of town in a hat factory along the road to Lauterborn, the Rue de Luxembourg, and his kitchen in the garage of the adjacent Hôtel de Luxembourg. The headquarters was under no particular enemy pressure, and Macdiarmid had withdrawn such men of the rifle platoons as could make it back to the command post; but others in outposts elsewhere in the town, including an entire platoon, were cut off.

What Macdiarmid wanted was not relief from the assignment of defending Echternach but tanks to help extricate the men who were cut off. Although the commanders of the two tanks were unwilling to risk the peril of *Panzerfausts* in narrow streets after nightfall, they promised to return along with additional tanks the next morning.

On December 19, the commander of the 10th Armored Division's CCA, General Piburn, changed his mind about employing tanks in the gorge of the Ernz Noire. To General Barton, Piburn proposed that the road forming the top of the T at Müllerthal could be neutralized by holding high ground on either side of the gorge, thereby freeing Piburn's tanks to constitute a reserve that would be readily at hand should the Germans try to emerge from the gorge. Barton agreed, an all-too-rare example of reconsideration of an ill-considered original commitment.

For a second day CCA's central task force continued to clear Germans from Berdorf, but slowly. The Germans made a bastion of every house, and from time to time the task force had to send tanks to the rear to clear German patrols from the supply route leading back to Consdorf.

All the while, Lieutenant Leake and his sixty men continued to hold the Parc Hôtel just outside the village. German artillery fire still ripped into the roof and rockets from *Panzerfausts* tore big holes in the east side. Maintaining a constant vigil at doors and windows, the American soldiers amused themselves by trying to pick off Germans who carelessly showed themselves in nearby houses. Not an American was killed and only one wounded, hit in the leg by a random enemy machine-gun bullet.

On the night of December 19, a dense fog descended. Under its concealment *Volksgrenadiers* inched close to the hotel, in some places no more than twenty yards away, and dug in so quietly that none of the sentries in the hotel detected them.

Before daylight the next morning, a crushing blast tore a great hole in the east side of the hotel, and the *Volksgrenadiers* attacked. Since it was too foggy and dark to make out the advancing Germans except when they fired their weapons, the defenders of the hotel relied for the most part on hand grenades. For half an hour "it was a desperate fight." Then almost as suddenly as the German firing had begun, it ceased.

With the coming of daylight, the Americans could see that during the night the Germans had also dug in on the west side of the hotel—the side facing Berdorf—apparently hoping the Americans would abandon the hotel and withdraw in that direction. The coming of daylight also revealed that the demolition preceding the German attack had blown open a sealed door in the basement leading to a room containing hundreds of bottles of liquor, liqueurs, and a barrel of beer, but Lieutenant Leake allowed nobody to touch it.

As it turned out, there would be little time for imbibing in any case, for Leake and his men soon had to abandon their sanctuary. Leaving behind their lone prisoner, the German sergeant who had been shot in the buttocks, they joined Company B and the armored task force in Berdorf just after nightfall for withdrawal to Consdorf. As on the German side, higher command had come up with a new plan for that part of the front.

On December 19, General Patton was beginning to turn more of the troops of his Third Army northward toward the southern shoulder of the German penetration. Command of the VIII Corps having passed to Patton, he created a provisional corps headquarters to control those troops of the VIII Corps still in Luxembourg and others coming in. Under the commander of the 10th Armored Division, General Morris, the headquarters controlled Morris's division (except for CCB at Bastogne), headquarters and CCA of the 9th Armored Division, the 109th Infantry, and the 4th Infantry Division.

Retaking the ground the Germans had seized in the first four days of the offensive no longer had a high priority. What mattered was holding a firm line to allow time for additional troops from the Third Army to arrive. With that in mind, General Barton was to form a line extending from Osweiler and Dickweiler through Scheidgen and Consdorf to the positions held by Task Force Luckett overlooking the Ernz Noire at Müllerthal, while the 10th Armored Division's CCA pulled back in reserve. Which meant withdrawal from Berdorf, from Lauterborn, and from Echternach.

On the German side on December 19, the commander of the 80th Corps, General der Infanterie Franz Beyer, was also ordering his troops to shift to the defensive. Although the 212th and 276th Volksgrenadier Divisions had failed to push the shoulder of the penetration as far south as plans called for, the two divisions, in Beyer's opinion, had gone as far as they were capable of going. The time for a major American reaction to the offensive, Beyer reasoned, was drawing near, and he needed to get his men dug in and ready for it when it came. That was tacit admission that the forces at the base of the southern shoulder—blessed from the start with more ambition than resources—had ground to a halt.

Two small offensive tasks remained. Beyer wanted the 276th Volks-grenadier Division to take the village of Waldbillig so as to afford those troops in the gorge of the Ernz Noire at Müllerthal a route of egress from the gorge. The Germans accomplished the takeover against cavalry of the 9th Armored Division's CCA during the afternoon of the 20th. The other task was to eliminate the Americans who were still holding in Echter-nach.

To that task the commander of the 212th Volksgrenadier Division, General Sensfuss, turned his personal attention, for to Sensfuss, that little band of Americans represented the height of impudence. They obviously could be eliminated at will and their presence had little effect on German operations, yet they persisted in sticking it out in the town. To wipe them out, Sensfuss called on his division's Fusilier Battalion and his four at-tached assault guns.

Arriving in Echternach from the dreadful carnage in the Hürtgen For-est, men of the 12th Infantry's Company E were delighted with their new assignment. The front was quiet, and they were in sole charge of a town where five thousand people normally lived and all had been evacuated, leaving the men free to plunder for whatever goodies the American troops who had preceded them had missed or left behind. That included ample stocks of wine, champagne, brandies, canned foods, apples, and potatoes. "Really, it was swell; the boys were getting rested up and they were showing signs of being able to smile again." Few were aware—and probably could have cared less—that they occupied a town that in peace-time was one of Luxembourg's premier tourist attractions, whose popula-tion swelled every spring for a folk festival honoring St. Willibrord, the town's patron saint, and featuring a "dancing procession," in which young men and women, linked by white scarves, did a kind of jumping jig through the streets and into the cobblestoned Place du Marché.

Although the men were widely scattered in outposts in various parts of town, reinforced in some cases by heavy machine gunners and 81mm. mortarmen of the 2d Battalion's weapons company, all were in buildings, warm, dry, relatively secure. Carrying details brought three hot meals a day from the company kitchen in the garage of the Hôtel de Luxem-bourg. If any Germans were inside the town during daytime, they never showed themselves; and at night no American stirred from his post or his billet, so that anything that moved in the dark streets was considered to be German and worthy of a few hand grenades.

Back at the 2d Battalion's headquarters in Consdorf, the operations officer, Capt. Paul H. Dupuis, learned that there was a 1937 Plymouth sedan in Echternach with low mileage but lacking a battery and with a hole in the gasoline tank. The battalion commander, Major Dorn, told Dupuis that if he got the automobile running, he could take it on a week's leave to Paris, and Dorn himself would go next. Late on December 15, Captain Dupuis went to Echternach to spend the night at Company E's headquarters and see what he could do the next morning to get the Plymouth running. That was why Dupuis was in Echternach when the enemy's artillery preparation began, and he elected to stay to provide such assistance as he could to Macdiarmid.

Germans were soon crossing the river at various points in rubber assault boats, sometimes driven back by the fire of Company E's outposts but at other sites unseen and undeterred by the defenders. By mid-afternoon, *Volksgrenadiers* were roaming parts of the town almost at will, taking the scattered outposts under fire, and in some cases surrounding them. Lest the outposts be picked off one by one, Lieutenant Macdiarmid ordered everybody to fall back on the hat factory and the Hôtel de Luxembourg. Yet some men were unable to break away, including the entire First Platoon.

At dusk on the first day, December 16, a small group of Germans tried to storm the company headquarters, but cooks with the help of fire from a .50-caliber machine gun mounted on a jeep in the doorway of the garage drove them off. For long after that, the Germans ignored the men in the hat factory and the Hôtel de Luxembourg, concentrating instead on knocking off the few outposts that had been unable to withdraw. The men of the First Platoon nevertheless held fast.

When the two tanks from Task Force Riley entered Echternach in late afternoon of December 18, hope rose for the First Platoon's rescue. It quickly fell again with the refusal of the tank commanders to move about the town after dark. True to their word, both tank commanders nevertheless returned the next morning, the 19th, with the rest of their platoon. Accompanied by riflemen from Company E, the tanks quickly broke through to the First Platoon and brought the men back to the hotel.

The commander of the 4th Division, General Barton, expected at that point that Company E would withdraw, for he had directed that a message authorizing withdrawal should go forward with the tanks. Yet no such message reached either Dupuis or Macdiarmid. As far as they knew, Barton's early order that there was to be "no retrograde movement" by any unit of the 12th Infantry was still in effect. Not that it bothered Dupuis, at least; he had been surrounded as a company commander in the Hürtgen Forest, and a relief force had broken through. As evidenced by two visits from American tanks, relief could be accomplished in Echternach at any time. Radio communications to the rear were sometimes in, sometimes out, but nobody ordered withdrawal, nor did Dupuis or Macdiarmid ask authority to withdraw.

It was during the afternoon of December 19, not long after the rescue of the First Platoon, that the German commander, General Sensfuss, turned his personal attention to erasing the American position in Echternach. In mid-afternoon, men of his Fusilier Battalion slipped into buildings facing those held by Company E and opened fire with burp guns, machine guns, and *Panzerfausts*. From a position alongside a building not three hundred yards away, an assault gun opened a systematic and destructive fire. If that kind of direct shelling continued, Company E would be unable to hold out much longer.

Just before dusk, Captain Dupuis told one of Company E's platoon leaders, 1st Lt. Richard L. Cook, to take a volunteer and one of the company's jeeps from the garage, make a dash up the hill to Lauterborn, and "for God's sake get the tanks." Accompanied by Staff Sgt. Michael J. Siscock, Lieutenant Cook left just before dark, pulling swiftly out of the garage, swinging into the Rue de Luxembourg on two wheels, and racing up the road toward Lauterborn. The German assault gun fired, but the shot was wild.

At Lauterborn, Cook encountered frustration. The commander of the armored task force, Colonel Riley, refused to venture his tanks in the streets of the town after dark, particularly under the foggy conditions prevailing that night, and the commander of CCA, General Piburn, upheld him. They understood, in any case, that Company E was to withdraw during the night to Lauterborn, and throughout the night the armored troops waited in vain for the infantrymen to appear.

Early that same evening, December 19, Company E did receive an order by radio to withdraw during the night, but unknown to Task Force Riley, Captain Dupuis had replied that it would be impossible to conform. In the darkness, he said, platoon leaders would be unable to make sure that every man received the order to pull back, and neither he nor Lieutenant Macdiarmid wanted to risk leaving somebody behind. They would have to wait for daylight.

When daylight came on December 20, nobody outside Echternach knew what was going on with Company E, and what was more, hardly anybody appeared to give a damn. Task Force Riley was getting ready to withdraw in conformity with the plan for the 10th Armored Division's CCA to constitute a reserve behind a new defensive line, and shortly before noon the bulk of the task force began to move. At the request of the commander of the 12th Infantry, Colonel Chance, a platoon each of medium tanks and armored infantry stayed behind to join the 12th Infantry's Company G in an effort to break into Echternach and rescue Company E; but there was no getting through. As darkness came, everybody fell back through Lauterborn all the way to the new defensive line.

For the men of Company E, it made no difference at that point in any case. Beginning at two o'clock that afternoon, four German assault guns opened a devastating fire on the buildings held by those men and by the machine gunners and mortarmen of Company H, and there was nothing they could do to stop the deadly fire. General Sensfuss himself led his fusiliers in the attack and was slightly wounded.

Among the defenders, Sgts. Daniel B. Stresow and John Redovian in the Hôtel de Luxembourg ran back and forth between floors in an effort to avoid the German shells. At long last, having ripped great holes in the front of the hotel, the German gunners turned their fire on the garage next door. From an upper story window, Stresow and Redovian could see the entrance to the garage and German shells bursting around it. They "heard groaning and an officer appeared, yelling to cease fire."

"Gee," said Stresow to Redovian, "the company commander is surrendering the company." Then the two sergeants "saw the kitchen crew and a few others line up outside with their hands in the air." Stresow had "an awful feeling" deep inside his stomach.

Twenty men of Company H and 110 of Company E surrendered, victims of a debacle that never should have happened. Captain Dupuis and Lieutenant Macdiarmid never asked if there had been a change in General Barton's order for no retrograde movement, which they clearly should have done before their situation grew critical. Even in the absence of such a request, commanders at battalion and regiment with broader knowledge of the overall situation should have ordered Company E out. By the time that finally happened, after dark on the fourth day, December 19, the reluctance of Task Force Riley to employ its tanks in Echternach in the dark left Company E to the mercy of the enemy.

The timidity of Task Force Riley reflected a similar timidity in all the 10th Armored Division's CCA and also in the 9th Armored Division's CCA. Neither combat command made any determined effort to exploit its marked superiority in armor, mobility, and firepower. With rare exceptions, the two combat commands had encountered nothing more formidable than *Volksgrenadiers* sometimes armed with *Panzerfausts*, and in almost every case they had recoiled in a kind of paranoid dread of what else might be out there.

Not until December 19 was anything else out there with the 212th Volksgrenadier Division, and then it was only four assault guns; and not until the next day was anything else out there with the 276th Volksgrenadier Division except three assault guns. Crews of American Shermans had legitimate concerns when they faced the superior armor of the Panther and even more so when they faced the superior armor and armament of the Tiger—but seven 75mm. assault guns against 102 Shermans?

In three days of fighting, the 9th Armored Division's CCA lost one light and six medium tanks—all to *Panzerfausts*—and in two days of fighting, the 10th Armored Division's CCA lost not a single tank. Did those statistics reflect clever deployment and maneuver or reluctance to close with the enemy? The crews of the Shermans of those two combat commands treated their tanks with the deference and protectiveness that an old-time cavalryman might have lavished on his horse.

Rightly or wrongly, foot soldiers, who seldom had anything between them and their enemy except the muzzles of their rifles, sometimes had a hard time understanding the concerns of men who rode behind several inches of armor plate.

CHAPTER EIGHTEEN

In Defense of the Twin Villages

At the designated rendezvous point for the German paratroopers near the Belle Croix road junction atop the Hautes Fagnes, Colonel von der Heydte eventually gathered not quite three hundred of his men, less than a fourth of those who jumped before daylight on December 17. The men had only their individual arms and the ammunition they brought with them, for the supply panniers were as widely scattered as the parachutists themselves. Although somebody found von der Heydte's radio, the drop had smashed it, which left no way to communicate with the Sixth Panzer Army.

When von der Heydte and his men saw the convoys carrying troops of the 1st Infantry and 7th Armored Divisions southward across the Hautes Fagnes, they dared not attack nor even harass them, so few were their numbers. Before daylight on the 18th, while a group of paratroopers was resting in the ditches near a crossroads, an American convoy was upon them before they had a chance to hide. As soldiers on the trucks waved sleepily—the German paratrooper's helmet resembled that of the American soldier—the Germans with immense relief waved back.

By noon on the 18th, von der Heydte had established a kind of base camp deep within a forest, from which small patrols moved to attack single American vehicles and to scrounge for food. Concerned about two men who had each broken an arm in the parachute jump, von der Heydte detailed six American prisoners to escort the men to the main highway and arrange to get them to a hospital. He gave the prisoners a note addressed to the commander of the 101st Airborne Division, General Taylor, against whom von der Heydte had fought in Normandy, asking that he "please treat my jump casualties as well as my regiment has treated casualties of your division."

By nightfall of December 20, von der Heydte was convinced that nobody was going to break through to him. (Because of American bombing, the big *Jägdtigers* with their 128mm. guns that were supposed to relieve

370

von der Heydte never got past a railhead in the northern reaches of the Eifel.) Although von der Heydte had no way of knowing how the offensive was going, it seemed clear from the failure of the Sixth Panzer Army to reach the Hautes Fagnes and from a continuing stream of American convoys moving south that the battle hardly could be going as planned. On the assumption that the Germans had captured Monschau, von der Heydte released thirty other American prisoners and headed there with his men.

Reaching a creek not far from the Eupen-Monschau highway, the paratroopers came upon an American outpost line designed to keep them cooped up in the forest. After a brief skirmish, the Germans withdrew; but when patrols could find no way out of the forest past the American blocks, some of them supported by tanks, von der Heydte despaired of getting through with his entire force moving together. He himself was growing desperate: His splinted arm was hurting, he feared his feet were frostbitten, and he had eaten not a morsel since before the jump early on the 17th. There would be a better chance of getting through, he decided, if the men broke into groups of three. In the end, only about one-third— a hundred men—succeeded in reaching German lines.

Traveling with his executive officer and his orderly, von der Heydte himself came upon a farmhouse, where he stopped to rest and learned that the Americans still held Monschau. Convinced that his condition was delaying his companions, he insisted that they go on without him.

That night, the 21st, von der Heydte finally reached Monschau. He had to knock at the doors of several houses before someone answered. When the owner let him in, von der Heydte asked for pen and paper, wrote a note in English, and asked the man's fourteen-year-old son to take it to the Americans. He was turning himself in.

On maps of Belgium, no Elsenborn Ridge appears. The commanders and staffs of the American units that fought against the northern prong of the German offensive arrived at that name to designate a high ridgeline on the German side of the town of Elsenborn and nearby Camp Elsenborn. It is shaped like a boomerang, with the highest point, at just over two thousand feet between Elsenborn and the village of Wirtzfeld, forming the southern prong of the boomerang and its slopes dropping off sharply to a reservoir, the Lac de Bütgenbach. To the northeast of the highest point, two other crests form the other prong of the boomerang. The ridge constitutes the watershed for the area, and while broad and sprawling rather than sharply defined, it is clearly the dominant high ground for miles around.

Shortly before seven o'clock on the morning of December 17, as Walter Robertson learned that German tanks were headed for Büllingen, it began to look as if the commander of the First Army, General Hodges, had waited too long to approve calling off the 2d Division's attack and withdrawing the division to the Elsenborn Ridge. As headquarters troops scurried to form a last-ditch defense of the division's forward headquarters in Wirtzfeld, Robertson finally received the word he had been so anxiously awaiting: Call off the attack and withdraw.

Yet with German tanks in Büllingen, the only way left for his troops and most of those of the 99th Division to get out was through Wirtzfeld over the back road to Elsenborn that his engineers had been working hard to make passable. Lose Wirtzfeld and that escape hatch would be closed. So too it would be barred if the Germans took the twin villages of Krinkelt-Rocherath just to the east of Wirtzfeld. If the 2d and 99th Divisions were to survive, they had to keep the Germans out of the twin villages and Wirtzfeld long enough for everybody to funnel through. Robertson saw the job of directing that fight to be his.

The most serious threat at that point appeared to be from the German tanks in Büllingen, which might drive north on Wirtzfeld or northeast on Krinkelt. Aside from ordering a last-ditch defense of Wirtzfeld, Robertson directed the only reserve still at his immediate disposal, a battalion of the 23d Infantry, to drop off a company at the southern edge of Krinkelt and the rest of the battalion to occupy high ground between Wirtzfeld and Büllingen.

There were two other routes by which the Germans might get into the twin villages: one led from the crossroads at Losheimergraben northwest through Mürringen, the other over the two trails through the forest from the International Highway due east of the twin villages. Because Robertson had lost communications with headquarters of the 99th Division, he had no way of knowing how well the troops of that division were blocking those approaches; but he could take some comfort in the knowledge that a battalion of his own 23d Infantry, attached to the 99th Division, was in a back-up position along each of the approaches.

Robertson could only hope that the defenses along the two approaches would hold long enough for him to get at least some of his battalions back from Wahlerscheid to hold Krinkelt-Rocherath and Wirtzfeld. Then when everybody had reached the twin villages, he would pull all his men back to the Elsenborn Ridge.

The withdrawal would be facilitated by the fact that Robertson had anticipated it and the night before had alerted the commanders of the six battalions at Wahlerscheid to plan for it. Under Robertson's plan, the 38th Infantry was to defend the twin villages, while the 9th Infantry, which had incurred the greater losses at Wahlerscheid, joined the battalion of the 23d Infantry that was defending Wirtzfeld. Once those defenders were in place, the 99th Division's 395th Infantry, which with two of its battalions and an attached battalion of the 393d Infantry had attacked in support of the 2d Division at Wahlerscheid, was also to pull back and cover the north flank of the defenders of the twin villages. Rob-

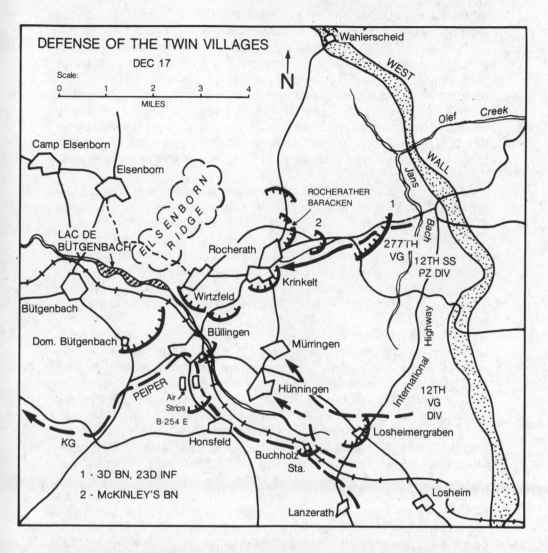

DEFENSE OF THE TWIN VILLAGES

DEC 17

Scale:
0   1   2   3   4
MILES

1 - 3D BN, 23D INF

2 - McKINLEY'S BN

ertson personally went to the command post of the regiment to inform the commander, Col. Alexander J. Mackenzie, and to tell him that on his own authority he was attaching Mackenzie's regiment to the 2d Division.

The first unit to withdraw was to be the 38th Infantry's reserve battalion, not yet committed, which was to defend the southern periphery of Krinkelt, at that point seemingly under the gravest threat. Two of the division's artillery battalions that were forward along the Wahlerscheid road were to follow, then the three battalions of the 9th Infantry and, finally, the two remaining battalions of the 38th Infantry. Three companies of mediums of the attached 741st Tank Battalion and two companies of self-propelled guns of the 644th Tank Destroyer Battalion were to find places in the withdrawing column. (The 741st's light tanks and the third company of tank destroyers were committed elsewhere.)

Having issued those instructions, Robertson left his forward command post and moved up the road leading to Wahlerscheid. Through much of the rest of the critical day to come he would be driving up and down that road, watching the men of his division execute one of the most difficult of all military maneuvers: withdrawal in broad daylight in close contact with the enemy and in the face of violent enemy attacks from another direction. The extinction or survival of the 2d Division and much of the 99th Division hinged in large measure on Robertson's actions along that road.

At the crossroads settlement of Losheimergraben, where Colonel Osterhold's 48th Regiment of the 12th Volksgrenadier Division was trying to open a path for the 12th SS Panzer Division, Osterhold had trouble again on the second day of the offensive getting fire support for his *Volksgrenadiers*. When an assault gun tried to move forward to help, an antitank gun concealed among the houses immobilized it, and not until midday did Osterhold finally establish radio contact with his supporting artillery. Only then could the *Volksgrenadiers* get up close to the first house.

In English, Osterhold called out for the Americans in the house to surrender, but he received no answer. "I want to talk with your commander," Osterhold yelled. "I warn you not to fire at me. May I come out?" When an American voice answered, telling him to advance, Osterhold and several of his men walked forward. He found thirty men and a lieutenant in the cellar, many of the men holding hand grenades from which they had already pulled the safety pins. They stood not a chance, Osterhold told the young officer; better they should give up. When the lieutenant assented, the Germans helped find the safety pins for the grenades.

The final conquest of the crossroads at Losheimergraben was strongly reinforced by another regiment, which exploited the American decision the night before to pull half the rifle strength from Buchholz Station to prepare a back-up position behind Losheimergraben. Early on the 17th, the men of that regiment passed quickly through the station and continued north into the rear of the defenders of Losheimergraben. Since that move jeopardized all three battalions of the 394th Infantry, the commander, Colonel Riley, in early afternoon ordered everybody to fall back on the prepared positions at Hünningen and Mürringen, where the attached battalion of the 2d Division's 23d Infantry was already in position at Hünningen.

The 394th Infantry had incurred heavy losses at Buchholz Station and at Losheimergraben, and the maneuver to pull back was not to prove easy. Yet what really mattered at the moment was that no Germans had gotten past Losheimergraben in time to interfere with the 2d Division's withdrawal from Wahlerscheid.

To twenty-two-year-old 1st Lt. Long Haley Goffigon, who grew up on a truck farm on Virginia's pastoral eastern shore and got his military training in ROTC at Virginia Polytechnic Institute, it seemed there was an occupational hazard in commanding a company's First Platoon. When it came to making assignments, it was easiest for the company commander to say: First, Second, Third, which meant that the First Platoon as often as not got more than its share of hairy tasks. That was what happened just before nightfall on December 16, when Goffigon's First Platoon of Company I and the rest of the 23d Infantry's 3d Battalion arrived at a road junction on the fringe of a dense fir forest due east of the twin villages of Krinkelt-Rocherath. As everybody tumbled from the trucks, sure enough, the company commander called out: First, Second, Third.

As it turned out, Goffigon and his First Platoon assumed a defensive position astride a road leading east through the forest. At first glance, it appeared to have its rewards, for there Goffigon found foxholes already dug, some with overhead cover—a back-up position prepared earlier by some supporting unit of the 99th Division. Although there were not enough holes for the entire platoon and the crews of two heavy machine guns that arrived later, the rest of Company I, extending the line in the woods to Goffigon's right, had no holes at all, and digging them in snow-covered frozen earth with small individual entrenching tools was difficult.

On the other hand, as Goffigon soon discerned, his position had major drawbacks. He was on the extreme left flank of the 3d Battalion with nobody on his left to prevent the Germans from pressing through the woods and getting in behind him. He was also astride the only road through that part of the forest, a road along which to the east, his company commander told him, a battalion of the 99th Division's 393d Infantry was fighting for its existence. If the Germans broke through that battalion and continued through the forest, that road would be the main axis of advance, and only he, the thirty-five men of his platoon, and his attached machine gunners stood directly in the way.

When Goffigon and Company I first arrived, defense was not the issue. The battalion commander, Lt. Col. Paul V. Tuttle, Jr., was under orders to attack to help the 3d Battalion, 393d Infantry, reestablish its positions along the International Highway; but during the night that changed. Since the commander of the embattled battalion, Colonel Allen, thought he could do that on his own, Tuttle's battalion was to form a back-up defensive position.

It was close to two thirty in the morning when that word came, so that nobody made any effort to readjust the battalion's positions to provide more strength along the road. The battalion was responsible in any case for another road that entered the right flank of its position, the road leading from the 393d Infantry's 1st Battalion. The Germans might come along either road or both. Thus Tuttle's battalion remained in a linear defense covering more than half a mile of thick forest with both flanks in the air.

Even aside from the poor position, the 3d Battalion, 23d Infantry, was ill prepared to defend for any length of time; for in keeping with orders, the battalion had left its former positions near St. Vith with only a basic load of ammunition, which meant just a few bandoleers per man. Since the battalion was attached to the 393d Infantry, supplying the battalion was that regiment's responsibility, but every appeal to that hardpressed regiment for more ammunition brought no result. During the night, the battalion's supply officer went to the rear to do the job himself, but before he could get back, *Kampfgruppe Peiper* cut the supply route at Büllingen.

The battalion was also notably weak in antitank defense. There were no antitank mines and only a few bazookas and rockets. As the battalion entered the woods, there were two 57mm. antitank guns from the 393d Infantry at what became Lieutenant Goffigon's position, but sometime during the night the crews of those guns hitched up and slipped away. The only hope Goffigon would have for stopping German tanks lay with two Shermans from the 741st Tank Battalion, commanded by 1st Lt. Victor L. Miller, which arrived just before daybreak on the 17th and took up positions in rear of Goffigon's platoon.

Deeper in the woods, early on December 17, the commander of the 393d Infantry's 3d Battalion, Colonel Allen, ordered his men and the company of the 394th Infantry that had joined the battalion late the day before to attack to regain the battalion's original positions. Hardly had that effort begun when the situation on the German side markedly changed. A second battalion of *SS-Panzergrenadiers* joined the fight and with it a platoon of what was eventually to be four companies of the 12th SS Panzer Division's tanks.

In the dense forest, bazooka teams were able to keep the tanks at some distance, but Allen's position soon became critical nevertheless. Almost everybody was running out of ammunition, and the wounded were piling up in the aid station with no way to evacuate them. Talking by radio with the commander of the 393d Infantry, Colonel Scott, Allen asked authority to withdraw, to which Scott—with General Lauer's approval—in mid-morning agreed. The battalion was to pull back through the 23d Infantry's 3d Battalion, reorganize behind those positions, and return to the line on the left of the attached battalion. At the same time, Scott ordered his 1st Battalion to withdraw down the other woods trail and extend the other flank of the 23d Infantry's 3d Battalion.

As Allen's men prepared to withdraw, they found places on vehicles for all but fifteen of the more seriously wounded. The battalion surgeon, Capt. Frederick J. McIntyre, and a few of his aid men volunteered to stay behind with those men.

Around eleven o'clock, while one company acted as a rear guard, the 393d's 3d Battalion began pulling out, machine guns on jeeps blazing away into the forest on either side of the road through the woods. As the men passed through Lieutenant Goffigon's platoon, Goffigon and his men begged them for their ammunition, and many donated what they had left. Two men dropped out of the bedraggled column to fight with Goffigon's platoon.

To everybody in the 23d Infantry's 3d Battalion, it was obvious that the Germans would be close behind the withdrawing column. How long the battalion could hold; how long its ammunition would last; and how well two Shermans might deal with accompanying German tanks—on all those factors might well depend the fate of those other men of the 2d Division who were beginning to withdraw through the forest from Wahlerscheid to the twin villages and Wirtzfeld. Indeed, the fate of everybody in the 2d and 99th Divisions who had yet to gain the twin villages or Wirtzfeld might well depend upon how long the 23d Infantry's 3d Battalion could hold—and when it got right down to it, upon how long Lieutenant Goffigon and the men of the First Platoon, Company I, could hang on.

For troops in close contact with the enemy in daylight, there could be no quick response to the word that they were to pull back, abandoning the positions they had won over four days at high cost. (They were later to call Wahlerscheid "Heartbreak Crossroads.") Withdrawal was easy enough for the 38th Infantry's uncommitted reserve battalion, which headed down the forest road to the twin villages around nine o'clock on the 17th and was soon digging in on the southern and southeastern fringes of Krinkelt. Not until over two hours later, at 11:20 A.M., was the first of the committed battalions of the 9th Infantry able to start back; and not until 1 P.M. would the last of the 9th Infantry's three battalions pull out.

That was the 1st Battalion under Lt. Col. William D. McKinley, which had made the first attack at Wahlerscheid. Around 3 P.M. the battalion finished reorganizing in the woods and began the long foot march down the road toward the twin villages. The men were cold, wet, exhausted from the four days in the line, their ranks reduced by shot, shell, and winter weather to four hundred officers and men, little more than the normal strength of two rifle companies.

As the men began to march, neither McKinley nor the commanders of the two battalions of the 38th Infantry that still had to begin their withdrawal were aware of what was happening in the woods east of Krinkelt-Rocherath, not far from the road into the twin villages that everybody had to use. Neither was General Robertson, who was still moving up and down the forest road, here lending a word of encouragement, there resolving a dispute over priority on the road; for when the 23d Infantry's 3d Battalion had become attached to the 99th Division's 393d Infantry, the battalion had passed out of the 2d Division's communications net.

Hardly had the last men from the 393d Infantry passed through the 23d Infantry's 3d Battalion when Lieutenant Goffigon spotted troops forming up in a wooded draw down the hill from his positions. For a short time, there was some doubt whether they were yet more withdrawing Americans or Germans; but as they headed up the road, unaware that the Americans stood in their way, Goffigon could make out their duckbilled caps and their *feldgrau* greatcoats. Goffigon, his men, and the attached machine gunners of Company M greeted them with a hail of fire. Company M's 81mm. mortars and Company I's little 60mm. mortars also fired, and Goffigon's company commander, Capt. Charles B. MacDonald, called for artillery fire. The result was depressing: only three rounds. As the afternoon wore on, that proved to be the only response to every request for fire, for the supporting battalion of the 99th Division's artillery was critically short of ammunition.

Those rounds and the fire from the rifles, mortars, and machine guns nevertheless drove the Germans back, but as they regrouped in the draw, Goffigon spotted something potentially more disturbing. Where the road crossed the forward slope of a ridge beyond the draw, he saw a cluster of tanks. One of the three-round salvos from the artillery dispersed them, but as the German foot troops began another assault, the presence of the tanks weighed heavily on Goffigon's mind. Particularly when he discovered that the two Shermans had withdrawn a considerable distance down the road behind his position, which the tank commander, Lieutenant Miller, said was to achieve better firing positions.

As the Germans returned to the attack, the assault lapped over against the rest of Company I and the left wing of Company K. To the defenders, the assaulting Germans seemed to be oblivious of casualties, fanatically so, as well they may have been, for they constituted two battalions of *SS-Panzergrenadiers* of the 12th SS Panzer Division, their ranks filled mainly with seventeen- and eighteen-year-old volunteers from the Hitler Youth.

The second assault nevertheless faltered, and again the Germans fell back to reorganize in the draw. Then once again came the shrill commands, the blowing of whistles, and a third assault.

Except for Goffigon's platoon, the defenders had little protection other than the trunks of the big trees. They nevertheless took few casualties, for no mortar or artillery fire accompanied the assaults; but squad and platoon commanders were soon reporting almost desperately that they were running out of ammunition.

By that time the assault had spilled over against the battalion's third unit, Company L, and MacDonald and the other company commanders were pleading with their battalion headquarters for more ammunition. They got only a reply that became maddening in repetition: "We're doing all we can!" Without more ammunition, MacDonald told the battalion's operations officer, Company I would be unable to hold much longer. The orders, the reply came back, were to hold at all costs.

The dwindling supply of ammunition soon became subordinate to another threat: German tanks. There were five of them, big Panthers. From his foxhole close alongside the road, Lieutenant Goffigon could see them waddling forward, their treads clanking noisily on the frozen surface of the road, infantry close behind them. Artillery fire dispersed the infantry, but the tanks kept coming.

Captain MacDonald sent a runner to tell the two Shermans to move forward, but as the runner discovered, Lieutenant Miller's tanks had fallen even farther back, all the way to the road junction at the edge of the forest. Although MacDonald appealed to his battalion commander, Colonel Tuttle, to order the tanks to return, Tuttle said no. The Shermans stood no chance against Panthers in a frontal engagement, and there was no place to maneuver off the road within the forest.

To MacDonald, that signaled the end. How could men in foxholes with nothing but their rifles stand up to tanks?

"For God's sake, Captain," Goffigon yelled over his sound-powered telephone, "get those tanks down here. These bastards are sitting seventy-five yards away and pumping shells into our foxholes like we were sitting ducks!"

Over the SCR-300 to battalion, MacDonald told Colonel Tuttle that without the two Shermans, he would be unable to hold. Tuttle said again that the orders were to hold at all costs, and if he ordered the Shermans forward, he was convinced the tank commanders would defy him.

MacDonald's light machine gunners, their ammunition exhausted, were filing rearward past the slit trenches of the company's command post. As MacDonald tried to stop them, Goffigon reported over the telephone that his position was collapsing. When he and his platoon runner, Pfc. John Welch, climbed from their hole, they realized for the first time that except for dead men in some of the holes, they were the only ones left of the First Platoon. In a hail of machine-gun fire from the German tanks, Goffigon and Welch took off through the woods alongside the road.

At that point MacDonald saw no chance for his company other than to try to form a new line along a firebreak a few yards to the rear of his command post. Unable to contact Goffigon, he told the other platoon leaders to fall back to the firebreak. There the men of the company headquarters and a machine gunner held briefly; but once the rifle platoons began withdrawing, they went to pieces under the German fire.

Company I's collapse left Company K's left flank exposed, and before the company commander, 1st Lt. Lee Smith, could get word to his left platoon to withdraw, the Germans overran one of the squads. As the riflemen scrambled through the woods, the German tanks passed undisturbed along the road until they neared the road junction at the edge of the forest. There the two Shermans of the 741st Tank Battalion gave battle. They knocked out two Panthers but in turn succumbed to return fire. Most of the crewmen died in the fight, including Lieutenant Miller.

As Company L also fell back, an American line in front of the twin villages ceased to exist. Although Company I had parried the *SS-Panzergrenadiers* for close to three hours, the German tanks decided the issue in less than thirty minutes. As the opposing tanks fought their duel at the edge of the forest, the time was 4 P.M., an early winter dusk was gathering, and along the road from Wahlerscheid to the twin villages, three of the 2d Division's withdrawing battalions had yet to pass.

Close to 4 P.M., Walter Robertson happened to stop by the command post of Colonel Mackenzie's 395th Infantry in the woods off the Wahlerscheid road. There he learned for the first time that Colonel Allen's battalion of the 393d Infantry had withdrawn from the forest and that "the Germans had broken through" his 3d Battalion, 23d Infantry.

With jeep and driver, Robertson hurried back to the Wahlerscheid road and at a crossroads a short distance north of Rocherath (the Rocherather Baracken) overtook the last company of the 9th Infantry's 3d Battalion, Company K, which had fallen behind during its battalion's withdrawal. Jumping from his jeep, Robertson found the company commander, Capt. Jack J. Garvey. Swiftly he ordered Garvey to move his company into a defensive position astride a complex of roads and farm trails near an isolated farmhouse, just over halfway between the woodsline to the east and Rocherath. Robertson also commandeered a platoon of heavy machine guns and the battalion's Ammunition and Pioneer Platoon and sent them with Company K.

Returning to his jeep, Robertson headed back up the road toward Wahlerscheid until he came upon the front of the column of the depleted 1st Battalion, 9th Infantry, Colonel McKinley's battalion. Appropriating ten 6 × 6 trucks belonging to the 395th Infantry, Robertson told McKinley to load as many men as possible onto them while the rest followed on foot, whereupon Robertson in his jeep led the way to the Rocherather Baracken, then turned southeast toward the complex of roads and trails and the farmhouse where he had sent Company K. McKinley was to hold the road network, said Robertson, "until ordered otherwise."

William Dawes McKinley, twenty-eight years of age, a grand-nephew of President William McKinley, grew up on U.S. Army posts and never considered any career other than that of an army officer. After graduation from West Point, he had long service with the 2d Division's 9th Infantry; and as the regimental executive officer in Normandy, he was personally leading a platoon in an attack when he took two machine-gun bullets in the stomach. He returned to the regiment in September. Friendly, cheerful, seemingly fearless under fire, McKinley was utterly devoted to his troops.

In fading light amid patches of unmelted snow, the men of McKinley's 1st Battalion, 9th Infantry, began wearily to dig in, bitter after four days and nights of hard fighting to be thrown back into the line to make up for some unit that had failed to do its job against (they believed) a local counterattack. McKinley put two of his depleted companies forward, tied in with Company K at the farmhouse, and held his third, which was down to just over fifty men, in reserve on what he thought was an exposed north flank. (Colonel Allen's battalion of the 393d Infantry was actually in position there but some distance away.)

Coming upon the commander of a detachment of three self-propelled guns of the 644th Tank Destroyer Battalion at the Rocherather Baracken, McKinley got from him a number of antitank mines, which McKinley's men stockpiled for use once they could be sure all American tanks and other vehicles had made their way out of the woods to the east. The commander of the tank destroyers also provided fifteen bazookas and ample rockets to go with them.

By 6 P.M. in murky darkness, "absolutely black," McKinley's battalion and Company K (totaling perhaps as many as six hundred men) had prepared a defensive position of sorts. It consisted mainly of hastily dug foxholes along thin low hedges marking the perimeters of fields, but since an artillery battalion had earlier occupied the area, there were a few log-covered dugouts, one of which McKinley used as a command post. For a time, "communication with the world outside of the battalion was non-existent." It was around six thirty when the artillery liaison officer, 1st Lt. John C. Granville, finally got his SCR-610 to work and established contact with the 9th Infantry's usual artillery support, the 15th Field Artillery Battalion.

Only minutes after Granville established that contact, Company B reported three tanks approaching. On the possibility that they might be American tanks escaping from the forest, McKinley told Company B to hold its fire; and by the time the men discovered that the tanks were German, to have revealed their positions by opening fire would have been suicidal. The tanks passed through the line and turned toward Rocherath along a road that ran behind the foxholes of Company A and in front of the farmhouse occupied by Company K's command group.

Hearing tanks approaching, two men from Company A, Sgt. William Floyd and Pfc. Herbert P. Hunt, left their foxholes to make sure they were American. The two men were standing alongside the road as the tanks and accompanying infantry neared. To Hunt, what followed was incredible: The German infantrymen (they were *SS-Panzergrenadiers*) passed by, some laughing and joking, scarcely looking in his and Floyd's direction. Then came the tanks, "splashing Billy and me with mud and slush. One of the tank commanders, standing in the open hatch of his tank, gave us the vulgar middle finger gesture as he passed."

As Hunt and Floyd hurried back to their company commander to ask for artillery fire, the tanks pulled off the road and cut their engines. Since the company's radio had failed, the two, accompanied by their platoon sergeant, Tech. Sgt. Charles Reamer, headed for headquarters of the battalion's weapons company, Company D, to use that company's radio; but as they were passing by, machine guns on the tanks fired. The first burst killed Reamer and Floyd. Hunt escaped and made his way to Company D's command post. Shells from the company's 81mm. mortars and artillery were soon exploding all about the tanks, and one went up in flames.

By the light of the burning tank, the men of Company A opened fire on the foot troops, but that fire revealed to the Germans for the first time that they were behind an American line. The two surviving tanks turned against Company A's foxholes, methodically showering them with machine-gun fire and grinding them with their heavy treads. To Hunt, it looked like the end of his company, but in the darkness the tanks failed to find many of the positions.

Aware at that point that anything that came down the road would be German, men of Company B hastily laid mines on three trails leading into their position. Hardly had they finished when four tanks accompanied by *SS-Panzergrenadiers* approached. The mines immobilized two of them, and as the other two turned off the road, bazooka teams stalked them and knocked them out. Their tanks eliminated, the *SS-Panzergrenadiers* went to ground.

Half an hour later, more tanks with *SS-Panzergrenadiers* approached in a column that looked in the darkness as if it stretched all the way back to the forest. Lieutenant Granville called for artillery fire close to Company B's foxholes, then called for the gunners to walk it back to the forest. As the German tanks dispersed, the men could hear the screams of German wounded.

At about the same time, seven German tanks passed along a road just outside Company A's positions. Artillery fire knocked out four of them, but three continued in the direction of Rocherath.

Although the Germans were taking heavy losses, that failed to stop them. The commanders of all three American companies were soon aware that individual German tanks were slipping past foxholes where the defenders were dead or wounded or had no way of coping with tanks. Bazooka teams from all three companies went in search of them. The commander of Company B, 1st Lt. John Melesnich, himself accounted for one tank with a bazooka; a man from Company K, Pfc. William A. Soderman, got three before machine-gun fire wounded him severely; and a machine-gun section leader from Company D, Sgt. Charles Roberts, and a squad leader from Company B, Sgt. Otis Bone, took a can of gasoline from an abandoned American half-track, poured the gasoline on the rear deck of an immobilized German tank, and set it on fire with a thermite grenade.

Not quite an hour went by before the Germans struck in strength again with three columns of tanks and infantry coming up all three trails leading from the forest. Lieutenant Granville screamed into his radio for fire on all three routes. "If you don't get it out right now," he shouted, "it'll be too goddamn late." Receiving no acknowledgment of his message, Granville "reached out for God to take him by the hand." Three minutes later the artillery responded with a deep-throated rumble. Nobody could survive such a shelling as that.

As Granville was later to learn, so vital did General Robertson consider Colonel McKinley's position that he afforded the battalion priority on all artillery under his control not engaged in some other essential mission. That included all four of the 2d Division's battalions and three corps battalions of 155mm. howitzers.

When the Germans fell back around midnight, a silence—"almost frightening"—descended over the American positions. In the hiatus, Colonel McKinley sent a message to the 38th Infantry, to which his battalion was attached: "We have been strenuously engaged, but everything is under control at present."

Even as General Robertson turned McKinley's battalion to the cluster of roads northeast of Rocherath, two battalions of the 38th Infantry were still marching down the forest road from Wahlerscheid, so that the defense of the twin villages had not fully formed. The 38th Infantry's reserve battalion, the 3d, was on the southern and southeastern fringes of Krinkelt; the regiment's Antitank Company had placed its nine 57mm. antitank guns at various points along the fringes of the villages; and the regiment's Service Company fighting as infantry held on the northeastern edge of Rocherath, where two of the roads leading from McKinley's position joined before entering the village. The regimental commander, Col. Francis H. Boos, established his command post in Rocherath at an X-shaped crossroads near the center of the village.

By that time all supporting units of the 99th Division had left the twin villages, but stragglers continued to pour in, including many men of the 23d Infantry's 3d Battalion, knocked from the woods to the east. Those men in most cases either attached themselves to units of the 38th Infantry or in small groups holed up in houses without knowledge of who else was near.

One of the units of that battalion, Company L, made it out of the woods almost intact except for one platoon caught by German shelling. The company commander, 1st Lt. Walter E. Eisler, Jr., still had 120 officers and men; and as he entered Krinkelt, he came upon the seemingly ubiquitous division commander, General Robertson, who attached the company to the 38th Infantry. Eisler and his men extended the north flank of the regiment's 3d Battalion along the eastern edge of Krinkelt. To their delight they found a house in their sector containing a ration of liquor intended for the officers of the 393d Infantry.

On the way to the twin villages, the 38th Infantry's 1st Battalion ran into a thunderous barrage from German artillery and *Nebelwerfers* at the crossroads north of Rocherath, the Rocherather Baracken. One rifle company had already passed, but the other two lost twenty-two men to the shelling, cutting sharply into ranks already depleted at Wahlerscheid. The concussion from one shell knocked the battalion commander, Lt. Col. Frank. T. Mildren, to the ground, but he arose unhurt. He hurried into Rocherath to put his lead company into position, but it was some time before the other two could reorganize and continue into the village.

Last to arrive from Wahlerscheid, the 38th Infantry's 2d Battalion also took some casualties from shelling at the Rocherather Baracken. The commander, Lt. Col. Jack K. Norris, left Company F to defend the crossroads; put Company E between the crossroads and Service Company's position at the road junction on the northeastern edge of Rocherath; and at the order of his regimental commander, sent Company G to defend the regimental command post.

The twin villages and the countryside between them and the forest were at that point "a scene of wild confusion." Artillery fire from both sides was pummeling the ground; German machine guns were firing at long range from the edge of the forest, their bursts liberally laced with tracer bullets that created arcs of what looked like dotted lines of neon; and a radar set abandoned by an antiaircraft unit near the edge of the woods was smoldering, a fiery concave skeleton. Men in the twin villages could see the burning German tank inside Colonel McKinley's position. Houses in both villages were on fire. Flares flickered eerily, burned out, and fell to the ground. As one officer saw it, "the night was ablaze with more noise and flame" than he had "thought possible for men to create." Into that cauldron the men made their way, cold, tired, miserable, stumbling, cursing the night, the misty rain, the unknown, their fate.

Toward the twin villages churned the three German tanks that had slipped past Colonel McKinley's Company A. With them was the tank battalion commander, SS-Lt. Col. Helmüt Zeiner, and forty *SS-Panzergrenadiers*. They bumped into the men of Service Company at the road junction on the northeastern edge of Rocherath but in the face of heavy fire, sideslipped around Service Company's flank into Rocherath.

By that time, the two companies of Colonel Mildren's 1st Battalion, hit by the shelling at the Rocherather Baracken, had worked their way into Rocherath and then to Krinkelt. They fanned out to houses and thin hedgerows east of a church that in normal times served parishioners of both villages and roughly marked an otherwise indiscernible boundary between the two. Most of the men dug in or took up firing positions inside the houses, but the company commanders pushed a few men farther to the east as outposts to give the alarm should the Germans approach.

Among those men was Pfc. John T. Fisher. He and the other men of two under-strength squads occupied two farmhouses on either side of a road on the fringe of Krinkelt, whereupon the sergeants posted several men, including Fisher, in ditches at a juncture of trails not far from the houses to serve as listening posts close to a 57mm. antitank gun. The men had been there only a short time when they heard the noise of tanks "just creeping along." As the tanks drew nearer, somebody threw a hand grenade and "all hell broke loose." The Germans fired a flare, a first round from a tank's cannon knocked out the antitank gun, and Fisher and the others ran back to the farmhouses.

In one of the houses, Fisher found himself with most of the men of his squad. German troops were soon milling around the building, and one man suggested that he drop a grenade from a window and open fire with his BAR, whereupon everybody was to take off. He had dropped the grenade and was about to fire when a round from a German tank exploded inside the house. The blast wounded Pvt. Donald Foulke in both legs, and before anybody could escape, the Germans rushed in, seized the men, and at gunpoint forced them outside, six of them, including Fisher.

Were they the only ones who had been in the house? Assuming the Germans would provide help for the wounded Foulke, the others told them about him. One of the Germans entered the house, fired a burst from his burp gun, and came back out.

Terrified, one American dropped to his knees, pleading obsequiously with the Germans to spare him and proffering cigarettes. A German knocked him down with his rifle butt. As the man began to weep uncontrollably, the Germans escorted him and two others to the far side of the house. Several bursts from burp guns, a scream, then silence.

When the Germans returned, they ordered Fisher and the other two remaining Americans to line up against a wall of the farmhouse. Three of the Germans raised their rifles, another a burp gun. Just as they fired, Fisher and one of the others dropped precipitately to the ground while the third fell to his knees, pleading in agonized tones: "Lord, have mercy!" A burst of fire from the burp gun knocked him to the ground.

As all three men feigned death, the Germans went away. After waiting what seemed like hours but was only a matter of minutes, Fisher asked if the other two were alive. Both said yes, but both were severely wounded, and the man who had dropped to his knees soon died.

When Fisher dared raise his head to look around, the other man had slipped away. Waiting a few more minutes to make sure no Germans were around, Fisher himself ran off into the night.

Less than half an hour after that encounter, the three German tanks, with some *SS-Panzergrenadiers* riding on the decks and others on foot, struck the men of the 38th Infantry's 1st Battalion. Having had time to dig in, Company A held fast, but the men of the other two companies went to pieces under fire from machine guns and cannon. Company B's commander, Capt. William S. MacArtor, his command group, and many of his men simply disappeared into the night. (They were captured.) The survivors of Company C joined men of the Antitank Company holding houses near the regimental command post.

As the tanks continued, they gained one of two main streets running through the villages, a street with the church on one side and on the other, a few yards up the road, a house occupied by Colonel Mildren and the 1st Battalion's headquarters group. With the approach of the tanks, officers and men alike rushed to the windows and opened fire with any weapon at hand.

Seizing a machine gun that had no tripod, Pvt. Grover C. Farrell stepped into the street in the path of the first tank. Firing from the hip, he marched straight for the tank. Possibly in concern for the *SS-Panzergrenadiers* on the deck, the tank commander pulled his vehicle back.

Colonel Zeiner's three tanks and what amounted to a platoon of *SS-Panzergrenadiers* were giving an impression of a German attack out of all proportion to the numbers involved. That was partly because of the heavy drumbeat of German artillery fire that pounded the twin villages, setting buildings on fire, and partly because the German force had bounced off opposition when encountered: Service Company first, then the 38th Infantry's 1st Battalion. The turn of the 38th Infantry's Company K came next.

As the tanks pulled back from Colonel Mildren's command post, they bumped into the positions of Company K, where the men were under orders from their battalion commander, Lt. Col. Olinto M. Barsanti (who was concerned for withdrawing troops of the 99th Division), to fire only if men or vehicles could be positively identified as enemy. That was why the men let the tanks through. When they at last opened fire, two of the tanks turned on glaring spotlights, blinding the defenders, and wailing sirens added to the confusion.

As that first spate of fighting for the twin villages began, many of the tanks and self-propelled tank destroyers available for the defense were scattered. Four platoons of the 741st Tank Battalion's Shermans were either in Wirtzfeld or in the extreme southern end of Krinkelt looking toward likely German advance from Büllingen, and two tanks under Lieutenant Miller had already been knocked out at the edge of the woods east of the twin villages. The battalion commander, Lt. Col. Robert N.

Skaggs, held his remaining tanks near his command post, ready to move to threatened sectors. He sent a platoon when Service Company came under attack, but when the German tanks bounced off the position, no direct encounter occurred. When word came later that Company K was under attack, Skaggs sent three tanks to help. Zeiner's tanks knocked out all three. Close to the church, the three tanks burned through much of the rest of the night.

By midnight, Colonel Zeiner had come to the conclusion that he faced vastly superior American strength in the twin villages. He, his tanks, and the little band of young *SS-Panzergrenadiers* went into hiding and before daylight sneaked out of town with eighty prisoners they had captured. They had given the troops of the 2d Division, most of them coming into the villages after nightfall under heavy shelling, quite a scare. It was with considerable relief that Colonel Boos reported to General Robertson around 2 A.M. on the 18th: "Action quieting; believe we can hold."

During the afternoon of December 17, in conformity with the decision by the commander of the 394th Infantry, Colonel Riley, and General Lauer's approval, the regiment had begun to withdraw to the vicinity of Mürringen and Hünningen. For two of the battalions, the 1st and 3d, which had fought at Buchholz Station and at Losheimergraben, it was far from easy. They fell back under fire from *Volksgrenadiers* dogging their footsteps. It was well after dark before remnants of the 1st Battalion —roughly 250 men—were sufficiently organized to occupy previously prepared reserve positions on high ground outside Mürringen. The commander of the 3d Battalion, Major Moore, had even fewer men (all of Company K was missing) and both battalions lost many of their vehicles.

In the woods north of Losheimergraben, the 2d Battalion was less severely pressed but continued to be handicapped by the presence of a battalion commander reduced to "a quivering hulk." Leaving a small covering force in place, the companies withdrew in orderly columns, carrying their mortars and machine guns by hand as they trudged uphill and down along snow-covered trails through the thick forest. In keeping with the plan, the covering force fell back just before dark but when unable to find the battalion's assembly area, continued into Mürringen.

The main body of the battalion was having problems because the command group lost contact—and communications—with the companies. Chancing upon Company C of the adjacent 1st Battalion, 393d Infantry, which had decided with the coming of darkness to wait until daylight to continue the withdrawal, the command group over a failing SCR-300 regained radio contact with the companies and talked them to Company C's position. By that time, daylight on December 18 was fast approaching. Unable to contact the regimental headquarters by radio, the command group decided to push on after daylight to Mürringen in hope that the rest of the regiment would be found there.

It would prove to be a false hope.

Under heavy attack in the reserve positions at nearby Hünningen soon after nightfall on the 17th, the commander of the attached 1st Battalion, 23d Infantry, Lt. Col. John M. Hightower—a great hulk of a man—asked Colonel Riley for authority to withdraw. Hightower's battalion—and Riley's regiment to only a slightly lesser degree—was stuck out beyond any other American force in a salient with but a single road out, that through Krinkelt. Only support from a battalion of the 2d Division's artillery and a battalion of corps guns was enabling Hightower's men to hold. Riley's supporting artillery battalion of the 99th Division was out of ammunition.

Yet Riley said no. He had so little knowledge of the location of his own troops—including his 2d Battalion still somewhere out there in the woods—and thus so little control over them, that he dared not risk withdrawal, and to permit Hightower to pull back would bare his southern flank.

A short while later, around ten o'clock, Hightower received a message relayed through his artillery liaison officer's SCR-610 telling him that his battalion was no longer attached to the 394th Infantry but instead to the 2d Division's 9th Infantry in Wirtzfeld. An hour later, a message from the commander of the 9th Infantry, Col. Chester J. Hirschfelder, told him: "Pull back to new positions or you will be cut off."

By that time, Hightower's men were so closely engaged with the enemy that Hightower considered an attempt to withdraw might prove disastrous. By means of the artillery liaison officer's radio, he told Hirschfelder so, but another message quickly followed: "Withdraw immediately. Hirschfelder."

When Hightower informed Colonel Riley of that order, Riley was still reluctant to see the battalion depart. Yet when he queried his division headquarters, General Lauer verified Hightower's attachment to the 9th Infantry and told Riley that he, too, was authorized to withdraw if he considered his position to be untenable. Still knowing nothing of his 2d Battalion in the woods, Riley remained hesitant. In view of the critical shortage of ammunition and no artillery support, he nevertheless came to the conclusion that he had no real choice. The two commanders agreed to coordinate their withdrawals to begin two hours after midnight.

Having heard that a fight was raging in Krinkelt, Colonel Hightower thought at first that he would have to abandon his vehicles, but he was yet to give that order when an ambulance driver appeared. He had just come through Krinkelt, he said, and he could guide the vehicles out. As worked out with Riley, the ambulance driver was to lead the way, followed by vehicles of the 394th Infantry, then by Hightower's vehicles. Men of the 394th Infantry were to move on foot along the east side of the road to Krinkelt, thereby affording some protection for the vehicles.

Hightower elected to bypass Krinkelt with his foot column and move cross-country to Wirtzfeld.

As Hightower had anticipated, withdrawing from Hünningen proved to be difficult. Two companies managed to break contact with little problem, but for the third, Company B, which had borne the brunt of the fighting, it was different. Because the company's little walkie-talkie radios had ceased to function, the company commander, Capt. Kay B. Cowan, had to get word to his platoons by runner, and two sent by different routes to the First Platoon never made it. Nobody heard anything more from that platoon, and of 175 men who had entered the fight in Company B, only 47 made their way out. Of 65 men in attached antitank and heavy machine-gun platoons with the company, only 19 escaped.

The withdrawal of the bulk of what was left of the 394th Infantry and of Hightower's battalion of the 23d Infantry began soon after 2 A.M. on the 18th. It was a black night, and the Germans, alerted to withdrawal by the departure of Hightower's troops, pounded Mürringen and the road to Krinkelt with interdictory shelling. As the men began the dismal march, nobody was really sure who held Krinkelt or even Wirtzfeld.

In deciding to commit the 12th SS Panzer Division against the twin villages, the commander of the 1st SS Panzer Corps, General Priess, missed his chance for a quick run around the flank of the 2d and 99th Divisions through Büllingen and Bütgenbach. Throughout much of the fateful day of December 17, only small detachments of towed tank destroyers, light tanks, and stragglers barred that route, mainly at Dom. Bütgenbach, the manor house and outbuildings astride the highway roughly midway between Büllingen and Bütgenbach. But then American reinforcements had arrived.

The reinforcements were from the 1st Infantry Division's 26th Infantry, which at the order of the First Army's General Hodges late on the 16th, had started south from an assembly area near Eupen where the entire division was recuperating from the terrible fight in the Hürtgen Forest. Although the 26th Infantry had been absorbing replacements and hospital returnees, few of the companies had more than a hundred men, many of them newcomers. In the 2d Battalion, the officers and men of two companies were almost all replacements, for those two companies had been cut off during the fighting in the forest and everybody in the forward positions either killed or captured.

In early morning of the 17th, the 26th Infantry reached Elsenborn, where the executive officer, Lt. Col. Edwin V. Van Sutherland (the regimental commander, Col. John F. R. Seitz, was on leave but would soon return), learned that his regiment was attached temporarily to the 99th Division. At the division's interim command post in a café in Elsenborn, Sutherland found the staff in "a state of shock," with little knowledge of the situation of either American or German forces. Yet it was obvious that somebody needed to block the principal highway leading from Büllingen to Bütgenbach. To do that, General Lauer sent the 26th Infantry to defend Bütgenbach.

At Bütgenbach, Colonel Sutherland held one battalion in reserve, sent another to high ground overlooking Büllingen about three-quarters of the way between the two towns, and sent his remaining battalion marching down the main highway to Dom. Bütgenbach. As the battalions moved out early on the afternoon of the 17th, the 26th Infantry's normal artillery support, the 33d Field Artillery Battalion, arrived.

The battalion that went to Dom. Bütgenbach was the 2d, commanded by Lt. Col. Derrill M. Daniel. During the night of the 17th, Daniel's men dug in on a reverse slope between Büllingen and Dom. Bütgenbach and put outposts on the crest. No longer was the way open for the Germans to exploit their early capture of Büllingen.

As darkness was falling, Daniel called his company commanders to his command post in the manor house. Many of the men, said Daniel, had heard tales of American troops surrendering or running away. That was not going to happen in the 2d Battalion, 26th Infantry, and he wanted every man in the battalion to know that he as their commander had adopted a motto for the battalion: "We fight and die here."

CHAPTER NINETEEN

To Gain the Elsenborn Ridge

Moving cross-country from Hünningen, the foot column of Colonel Hightower's battalion of the 23d Infantry encountered few problems. Before daylight on December 18, the battalion was occupying a reserve position behind the twin villages.

It was not so easy for the vehicular column. As the vehicles neared Krinkelt, so many houses were burning and so heavy was the shelling that the commander of the 394th Infantry, Colonel Riley, assumed the Germans held the village and ordered the vehicles abandoned. As the drivers and others on the vehicles started moving cross-country toward Wirtzfeld, they were soon joined by most of the men of the 394th Infantry who were making the exodus on foot.

Not so the commander of Company M, Capt. Joseph Shank, who as commander of a weapons company had a number of vehicles in the column. Why abandon the vehicles without at least some effort to get through Krinkelt?

With a few men, Shank proceeded into Krinkelt, where he found an American tank. From the crew he learned that the Americans did, indeed, hold most of Krinkelt and that the vehicles should have no difficulty passing through the southern edge of the village to gain the road to Wirtzfeld. Returning to the vehicles, Shank found enough men to drive them all (the drivers from the 23d Infantry had stayed with theirs), and the column got under way. Passing through Wirtzfeld before daylight, the vehicles continued to Camp Elsenborn, where General Lauer was in the process of assembling and reorganizing his division.

As daylight came on December 18, there were still considerable numbers of men from both the 393d and 394th Regiments in the woods, stragglers and men in organized units alike.

One of the units was the 394th Infantry's Company K, which had become separated from the rest of the 3d Battalion during the withdrawal

391

and had never reached Mürringen. With the coming of daylight, the men saw a few German vehicles between the woods and Mürringen, and the company commander, Capt. Wesley J. Simmons, decided not to risk trying to enter the village. He led the company along a wooded draw leading toward Krinkelt; but because of the noise of battle there, he avoided the village and passed instead along a draw leading to Wirtzfeld. Except for seventy men lost in the first two days of the offensive, Simmons brought his company out intact.

Company K had long since moved on when shortly after noon on the 18th, the 394th Infantry's 2d Battalion, its distraught commander still more a hindrance than a help, reached the woodsline overlooking Mürringen. With that battalion was all that remained of the 393d Infantry's 1st Battalion, which except for Company C was not much.

Since all appeared to be quiet in Mürringen, two companies advanced on the village, but as they neared the first houses, they met "a withering hail of enemy small arms fire." Still in radio contact with a corps artillery battalion, an artillery liaison officer with the 393d's 1st Battalion called for fire, which enabled the infantrymen to fall back to the woods.

By the time those two companies could reorganize and the withdrawal resume, it was growing late and a rapidly developing mist helped conceal the column. Much like the men of Company K, the remnants of the two battalions entered the draw short of Krinkelt and headed for Wirtzfeld. Somebody in the gathering dusk took them to be Germans and brought down heavy shelling. That split the column, some men heading for Krinkelt, others for Wirtzfeld. When at last there was time to count heads, it turned out that the 394th Infantry's 2d Battalion had emerged with almost six hundred officers and men, but the 393d Infantry's 1st Battalion had fewer than three hundred.

One more of the 99th Division's regiments was still in the forest: Colonel Mackenzie's 395th Infantry, minus the battalion that was at Höfen but with an attached battalion of the 393d Infantry. At the order of General Robertson, to whose division the regiment was attached, all three battalions had pulled back several hundred yards on the 17th to positions from which to protect the Wahlerscheid road as the units of the 2d Division withdrew. Then on the 18th, they withdrew farther to positions a thousand yards short of the Rocherather Baracken, there to provide flank protection for the defenders of the twin villages.

Late in the afternoon of the 18th, Colonel Mackenzie received a coded radio message from the 99th Division's headquarters ordering the regiment to fall back to the Elsenborn Ridge. To Mackenzie, that seemed odd, for he had received no order negating his attachment to the 2d Division, and he knew that the 2d Division was still holding Krinkelt and Rocherath. While conforming to the order by directing his battalions to

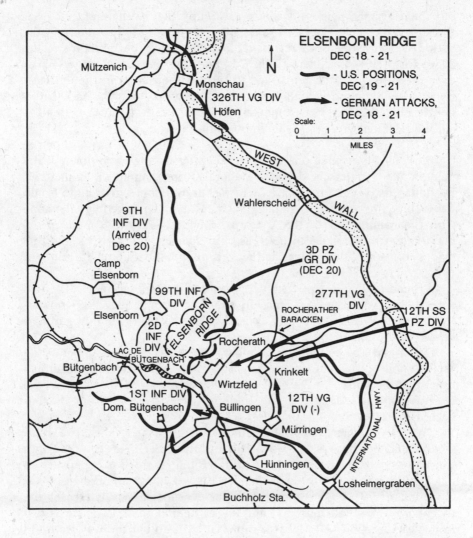

withdraw, Mackenzie went ahead of them to the division headquarters in Camp Elsenborn.

When Mackenzie arrived, an hour before midnight, General Lauer was shocked to see him. He had sent no such message, and the regiment was still attached to the 2d Division. Mackenzie had no choice but to turn his men around and go back.

The origin of the withdrawal order could never be determined. It could have been that the Germans had captured a copy of the American code and sent the message; yet that would appear unlikely, for if equipped with such a valuable tool, why would they use it only once? Nor did the Germans make any effort to occupy the 395th Infantry's positions. It could have been that somebody on Lauer's staff, aware that the 99th Division's other two regiments had withdrawn but unaware of the 395th Infantry's attachment to the 2d Division, sent the message. Whatever the case, the weary men had to retrace their steps in the darkness (when one battalion commander refused to order his men back, Mackenzie relieved him of his command), and before daylight on December 19, the regiment was once again in position.

Early in the evening of December 17, after having spent much of the day on the Wahlerscheid road, General Robertson finally joined his headquarters, which on his order had withdrawn from Wirtzfeld to Camp Elsenborn. From the new command post, Robertson talked by telephone with the commander of the V Corps, General Gerow. Robertson explained that he intended to hold the twin villages and Wirtzfeld until all troops forward of the villages had retired, then fall back to the Elsenborn Ridge.

Around midnight, Robertson conferred with General Lauer. The two agreed that while the 2d Division should continue to hold Krinkelt-Rocherath, all other troops of both divisions were to start preparing a new line on the Elsenborn Ridge.

Robertson also conferred that night with the operations officer of the 1st Division, Lt. Col. Clarence E. Beck, and learned with considerable relief that the entire 1st Division was on its way south. Other units of the division were to extend the 26th Infantry's line westward from Bütgenbach in the direction of Malmédy.

That development sharply diminished Robertson's concern for his south flank, but he was still worried about the other. Between the 395th Infantry and the detached battalion at Höfen, there was a gap of ten miles. Although the entire gap was densely wooded, the Germans could move infantry with light support weapons over logging trails to reach the Elsenborn-Monschau highway and get in behind the Elsenborn Ridge from that direction. All Robertson had at hand to bar the way were the 2d Reconnaissance Troop and the 15th Field Artillery Battalion, whose firing positions were astride the road. That open flank continued to perturb Robertson for two more days until units of the 9th Infantry Division began to arrive; but to his immense relief, the Germans made no effort to exploit the gap. Had the Germans been able to break through at Höfen or Monschau, thus opening the road leading south to Elsenborn to tanks, the situation would have been graver still.

Having failed on the first day of the offensive to penetrate either the American cavalry at Monschau or the 395th Infantry's 3d Battalion at Höfen, the 326th Volksgrenadier Division on the 17th concentrated an entire regiment with a company of assault guns against Höfen, but to no avail. In a pre-dawn assault, some Germans got into the village but were soon wiped out in confused fighting or ejected. After daylight, some of the *Volksgrenadiers* broke through, so threatening the battalion command post that the commander, Colonel Butler, called for artillery fire on it; but when the towed guns of the 612th Tank Destroyer Battalion held off the German assault guns, the *Volksgrenadiers* were unable to sustain their penetration.

That turned out to be the last German effort to break through in the north. Why the 326th Volksgrenadier Division desisted was evident from a quick look around the battlefield at Höfen. There on December 17, fifty Germans surrendered and more than five hundred died. As on the day before, the contrast with American losses—five killed, seven wounded— was striking.

Just before daylight on December 18, as Colonel Zeiner pulled out of Krinkelt with the three tanks that had created such a tumult in the twin villages through much of the night, he saw a formidable German force poised at the woodsline ready for a major assault to take the twin villages. While sending his three tanks to the rear for refueling, Zeiner himself joined the attacking force.

That force consisted of most of the surviving tanks of Zeiner's battalion—probably around eighty—and a dozen *Jädgpanthers* (tank destroyers) each equipped with an 88mm. cannon on a Tiger chassis, which probably accounted for numerous reports by American soldiers of Tiger tanks in the twin villages. In addition to two battalions of *SS-Panzergrenadiers* that were to accompany the tanks, an attached regiment of the 277th Volksgrenadiers was to cover the open northern flank. The commander of the 12th SS Panzer Division, Brigadier Krass, exhorted his subordinate commanders in no uncertain terms to make quick work of the twin villages and get on beyond the Elsenborn Ridge. Sharp messages to that effect from Model and von Rundstedt had been pouring into headquarters of General Dietrich's Sixth Panzer Army with increasing frequency, and Dietrich was quick to pass the vitriol down the chain of command.

During the night of December 17, Bill McKinley and his little band from the 1st Battalion and Company K, 9th Infantry, had done what their division commander asked of them: They had held at the cluster of roads and trails northeast of Rocherath long enough for the two battalions of the 38th Infantry that were still withdrawing from Wahlerscheid to reach the twin villages. By their stand, they had prevented the Germans from cutting the road into Rocherath at the Rocherather Baracken and had sharply restricted routes remaining to German tanks to get into the twin villages. Yet they still had a job to do. They were to continue to hold until the 38th Infantry's 2d Battalion could get firmly entrenched behind them.

Once the action died down at midnight, communications men laid a telephone line to that battalion, and squad, platoon, and company commanders took inventory of their ranks. Somehow the battalion's supply officer got a resupply of small-arms ammunition and bazooka rockets as far forward as McKinley's command post in a dugout a hundred yards behind the line of foxholes. Through the night, supporting artillery delivered interdictory fires on the open ground between McKinley's positions and the forest and on the two trails leading through the forest, the only avenues of approach for German tanks and half-tracks. (Such a morass had those trails become that only tracked vehicles could negotiate them.)

Shortly before 7 A.M. on the 18th, the battle erupted again. Tanks and tank destroyers poured machine-gun and cannon fire into the foxholes of McKinley's men, and *SS-Panzergrenadiers* were close behind. At Lieutenant Granville's call, American artillery quickly responded. Around the farmhouse and along the roads, trails, and spare little hedgerows, there was fire, noise, and confusion—a reprise of the melee of the night before.

Back and forth the fighting ebbed. Incredible the courage of men on both sides: Germans constantly pursuing the fight, climbing over their own dead, ignoring their losses; Americans holding fast in their holes, refusing to panic, resolved not to give in. In only one case did any defender break. Having run out of rockets for their bazooka, seven men from Company B's left platoon made a dash for the rear, but Colonel McKinley himself, stepping from his dugout, stopped them and ordered them back. The men turned and retraced their steps.

At close to nine o'clock the commander of Company A, 1st Lt. Stephen E. Truppner, radioed that tanks and infantry were all over his position and called for artillery fire on his own foxholes, the only chance, he said, for any of his men to survive. As Truppner requested, Granville put the fire of a full battalion of guns on the company's positions for half an hour, no doubt killing many Germans who were caught in the open; but when it ended, no further word came from Lieutenant Truppner.

Hard on that success, the Germans overran the positions of Company K in the vicinity of the farmhouse. From the basement of the house, the company commander, Captain Garvey, could see Germans prodding those few of his men who were still alive from their foxholes, while a German tank approached the house and halted with its cannon only a few feet from the front door. Aware that it would be a matter of seconds before the tank blasted the house to pieces, Garvey told a man who spoke German to call out that his company commander would surrender to a German officer. When a German lieutenant arrived, Garvey and his command group filed out with their hands above their heads.

Around 11 A.M., Colonel McKinley at last received the word he was anxiously awaiting: Beginning at noon, he and his men were to withdraw behind the 38th Infantry's 2d Battalion. Yet so closely were his men locked in combat that McKinley saw little possibility of extricating anybody without close fire support from tanks or self-propelled tank destroyers.

Almost as if by a miracle, the leader of the battalion's antitank platoon, 1st Lt. Eugene Hinski, spotted four Shermans of Company A, 741st Tank Battalion, that were patrolling near the Rocherather Baracken. Running to them, Hinski asked the platoon leader, 2d Lt. Gaetano Barcellona, if he wanted to fight. "Hell, yes!" Barcellona responded.

When Barcellona reported to McKinley, he learned that the greatest difficulty involved four German tanks located between the farmhouse and Rocherath that would be able to fire on the route of withdrawal. Barcellona was to split his platoon, two tanks maintaining concealed positions while the other two moved into the open to lure the German tanks from their hiding places.

The maneuver worked. Barcellona's tank destroyed one of the German tanks with a single shot and another with three. As the two others turned toward Rocherath, another of the Shermans disabled one with a shot in the rear, while the other escaped into the village.

With supporting artillery fire landing close to the American foxholes, two of the Shermans moved toward the left flank of McKinley's position and two toward the right, their machine guns blazing. Under cover of that fire, the infantrymen began to withdraw with, under the circumstances, "unbelievable control." As the men left their holes, the *SS-Panzergrenadiers* tried to close, but the machine-gun fire sent them to ground. Colonel McKinley and his operations officer, Capt. James Harvey, were the last to leave. As they headed down the road toward the Rocherather Baracken, they heard Germans shouting for them to surrender.

Counting Company K and other attachments, Colonel McKinley had gone into position with something like 600 men; he got out with 217. Among the survivors were only five men from Company A and twelve from Company K.

McKinley and the men of the 1st Battalion and Company K, 9th Infantry, had performed an incredible feat. By their stand, they had enabled two battalions of the 38th Infantry to reach the twin villages for a defense that otherwise probably could not have been mounted. ("You have saved my regiment," Colonel Boos told McKinley.) They had left the ground around the cluster of roads and trails and the farmhouse littered with German dead and the carcasses of seventeen tanks and tank destroyers.

For all the pertinacity and valor displayed by a number of other battalions of the 2d Division during the fight for the twin villages, none performed with more fortitude and sacrifice than the men of McKinley's battalion and Company K. And for all the heroic defenses of many another American unit during the German offensive, probably none exceeded and few equaled McKinley's battalion and Company K in valor and sacrifice.

Even as that terrible fight developed northeast of Rocherath, the main body of the attacking German force crept through the early morning darkness to the very edge of Krinkelt and Rocherath, and behind a heavy barrage of artillery and *Nebelwerfers* struck the twin villages. All day the battle raged and all that night.

To many an American soldier fighting for his life in what was fast becoming the rubble of the two farming villages, the big German tanks appeared terrifying and seemingly invincible; but that was far from the reality. Indeed, what happened to the German armor in the twin villages well demonstrated why armored commanders were reluctant to risk their big battle wagons among the houses and streets of villages and towns; for there they were particularly vulnerable to stalking bazooka teams and to tanks and tank destroyers lying in wait in concealed positions.

The German tanks became even more vulnerable under the pounding of the 2d Division's four artillery battalions reinforced by three corps battalions, for even when that fire failed to knock out a tank, it might break a track or a sprocket wheel, leaving the tank sitting "like a crippled goose in front of the hunter." So, too, once concern for the withdrawing vehicles of the 99th Division had eased, antitank mines on roads and trails might immobilize a tank and leave it immobile prey to intrepid men with bazookas. Even nightfall failed to end the searches, for the light from burning tanks and buildings enabled them to continue; and once the American infantrymen had gotten over the first shock of blinding search-lights on some of the German tanks, they used the lights to guide them to the tank's sides and rear.

As everywhere during the German offensive, the 75mm. guns on the American Shermans and the 76mm. cannon on both the towed and self-propelled tank destroyers were usually ineffective against the frontal armor of Panthers; but the experienced American crews knew they could deal a death blow with a shot in side or rear. Lying in ambush, with the darkness and fog helping them to avoid detection, they could wait for the advantageous shot at close range. Even crippled tanks still might be effective under those circumstances: two immobilized Shermans concealed in a lane in Rocherath accounted for five German tanks that incautiously passed in front of them.

Holed up in the houses, American infantrymen were in favorable positions to get in a shot from a bazooka from an upper story into an open turret or onto a rear deck. (From a house on the eastern edge of the village, Lieutenant Goffigon and his runner, Private Welch, had holed up with two other men from the 23d Infantry's 3d Battalion; when a German tank appeared in the street just outside the house, a single rocket knocked it out, blocking the street and any further movement there by

German tanks.) Seldom were the German crews able to escape a destroyed tank, for even if the vehicle failed to burn, Americans in the buildings picked them off as they emerged from their turret or the escape hatch.

In the center of the twin villages, where Rocherath and Krinkelt imperceptibly joined, no front line existed. Americans held some houses, Germans others.

When the tank of a platoon leader of the Third Company, SS-Sgt. Willi Fischer, reached the center of the villages near the church, the scene looked to be a "tank grave." Just ahead of Fischer, Beutelhauser's tank was knocked out; close beside it, Brödel's tank was burning, Brödel hanging lifeless in the turret. Still others were knocked out, some still aflame. To Sergeant Fischer, it was "a cruel sight."

As another platoon leader, SS-Sgt. Gerhard Engel, arrived at a house near the church where Colonel Zeiner had established his command post, the commander's face reflected "depression and resignation." Even as Engel reported to Zeiner, a Panther approaching the command post not a hundred yards away turned into "a flaming torch," knocked out by an immobilized Sherman whose crew still fought from the tank.

In the first surge into the twin villages, a force of *SS-Panzergrenadiers* seized a house alongside the main road through the villages just north of the church. All through the day and night those men held on, the deepest German penetration, and had not American troops continued to hold the houses across the road, the Germans would have cut the villages in half.

Just to the north of Rocherath, once McKinley and his men had withdrawn, the Germans moved in strength against the 38th Infantry's 2d Battalion in the vicinity of the Rocherather Baracken. Those were men of the attached regiment of the 277th Volksgrenadiers protecting the 12th SS Panzer Division's flank. Small-arms and artillery fire broke up two German assaults against the crossroads, but tanks approaching from the direction of McKinley's former position got in among the northern buildings of Rocherath. Five were within a hundred yards of the 38th Infantry's command post before tanks and tank destroyers knocked out four and the fifth withdrew.

Another tank approached the command post of Colonel Mildren's 1st Battalion close to the church. As it neared an intersection, two American soldiers in a jeep roared out of a side street. Coming to a precipitous halt, they dived for cover. The tank flattened the vehicle, but in the process its turret jammed and was unable to traverse. The driver headed for a concrete utility pole, banging it with his cannon in an effort to loosen the traversing mechanism, but the pole snapped. He hit a second pole; it too snapped but not before the turret broke free.

As the tank continued toward Mildren's command post, the battalion's communications officer, 1st Lt. Jesse Morrow, fired a bazooka into its rear. The tank brushed against a house and veered into a ditch, immobilized; but the crewmen still had fight in them. As Morrow prepared to fire a second rocket, the tank's cannon spat fire. Morrow collapsed, wounded only slightly in the neck but knocked unconscious by concussion. The tank might have finished him off had not another soldier thrown a thermite grenade into the turret.

In early afternoon, the Germans struck again at the Rocherather Baracken, swept across the Wahlerscheid road, and got in behind the crossroads, cutting a farm track leading to Wirtzfeld. Colonel Boos promptly committed the two companies of the 23d Infantry's 1st Battalion that constituted a reserve behind the twin villages. Those two companies—their strength still pretty much intact despite their earlier fight at Hünningen—drove the Germans back and dug in to extend the flank of the position at the Rocherather Baracken.

In a house on the eastern edge of Krinkelt, two men from the command group of Captain MacDonald's Company I, 23d Infantry (who with the rest of their company had fallen back from the woods to the east) had taken refuge the night before—Pfc. Hugh Berger, an eighteen-year-old who took comfort in reading his Bible every night, and Pfc. Willie Hagan, an older career soldier. Soon after the German attack began on the 18th, a tank came up beside the house. Finding a bazooka without a sight, Berger fired but missed. Hagan quickly shoved another rocket into the bazooka, and Berger fired again. "You got him," yelled Hagan; "you knocked hell out of the sonofabitch!"

As the hatch opened, only one German emerged, a hand blown off, his face "like fresh ground meat." The two men carried him into the house and put him on a bed; but as the German began to revive, he shouted loudly and seemingly irrationally. With all that noise, said Hagan, he was bound to give their position away.

"If I stop that noise," said Hagan, "you won't ever tell, will you, Berger?"

"No, Willie," said Berger, "I'll never tell."

Early in the day's battle, the commander of Antitank Company, Capt. James W. Love, came upon two men, both badly wounded, each supporting the other, who told Love that they had been captured, lined up against a wall, shot, and left for dead. Private Fischer and his companion in tragedy also told their story, and there were reports that in the forest east of the twin villages a squad of Company K, 23d Infantry, had been summarily executed. Others told of SS troops bayonetting American wounded.

Word of those incidents spread as only word can spread among men fighting for their lives. Men of the 2d Division had faced SS troops before, back in Normandy. As the fighting for Krinkelt and Rocherath continued, they gave no quarter.

To many an American and German alike, the battle for the twin villages was as close as they would ever come to Armageddon. Yet through it all the American supply routes leading back through Wirtzfeld remained open, so that lack of ammunition never became a general problem, and the wounded, when the fight in their immediate vicinity permitted, could be evacuated. Although losses among artillery forward observers were high, communications with the seven supporting artillery battalions remained constant, and the German artillery fire never came close to matching the American fire in volume or intensity. By late afternoon, senior American commanders in the twin villages were convinced that they could hold indefinitely, and Colonel Boos released the two hundred tired and battered survivors of Colonel McKinley's battalion to go back for rest at Camp Elsenborn.

Yet for all the confidence, withdrawal was in the offing. During the afternoon, General Robertson met with Gereral Lauer and the commander of the 1st Division, Brig. Gen. Clift Andrus, and worked out a plan for retiring to the Elsenborn Ridge to positions to be tied in with those of the 1st Division. The men of the 2d Division had done the job Robertson had asked of them, and there was no point in staying longer in the twin villages; for the villages constituted a salient forward of positions the 1st Division had begun to occupy and which the 9th Division was soon to move into farther north. Furthermore, the high ground of the Elsenborn Ridge was far more advantageous for a defense. To facilitate occupation of the new positions, the corps commander, General Gerow, early in the evening attached the 99th Division to the 2d, with Lauer acting as Robertson's deputy.

On the German side, commanders had to accept the fact that in quest of a quick route across the Elsenborn Ridge, they had stumbled into a deadly cul-de-sac. Although it was still vital to gain the Elsenborn Ridge, for the ridge controlled all three roads assigned the 1st SS Panzer Corps for the drive to the Meuse, the critical problem at the moment was the necessity to open the southernmost of those routes—that through Bütgenbach. The corps commander needed that road in order to get supplies and reinforcements through to *Kampfgruppe Peiper*, and it needed the high ground in the vicinity of Bütgenbach to cloud the eyes of American artillery, which was making a shambles of all efforts to succor Peiper along the lesser road Peiper himself had taken.

In passing through Bütgenbach, the 12th SS Panzer Division would pose a threat to the Elsenborn Ridge. That would assist a new thrust against the ridge to be mounted by a unit released from the Sixth Panzer Army's reserve, the 3d Panzergrenadier Division, with the help of the 12th and 277th Volksgrenadier Divisions.

Before daylight on December 19, those tanks of the SS panzer division that got the word and could still maneuver began withdrawing from Krinkelt and Rocherath. The American defenders were soon aware that the ratio of their strength versus that of the enemy had markedly changed. *SS-Panzergrenadiers* nevertheless made some attacks to cover the German withdrawal, but small arms and artillery fire took care of those with little difficulty. In early afternoon, the Americans began systematically destroying all American and German vehicles, weapons, and equipment that could not be extricated. General Robertson had decided that the time had come not to withdraw but, as his order put it, "to move to new positions" on the Elsenborn Ridge.

Once Robertson gave that order in mid-afternoon on December 19, all vehicles not essential for continuing defense began infiltrating in ones and twos to the rear; and at the hour designated for the withdrawal to begin—just after nightfall at 5:30 P.M.—the little road from Wirtzfeld that meandered back to Elsenborn, the road on which the 2d Division's engineers had worked so prodigiously, became one-way for traffic pulling out. While the 395th Infantry conducted its own withdrawal over logging trails and cross-country to an assigned sector on the Elsenborn Ridge, the 38th Infantry's units began to peel off a battalion at a time from north to south. Tanks of the 741st Tank Battalion and self-propelled guns of the 644th Tank Destroyer Battalion, plus the I&R Platoon and a contingent of engineers, formed a rear guard. Once all units of the 38th Infantry had passed through Wirtzfeld, the rear guard retired to that village while the 9th Infantry and the 23d Infantry's 2d Battalion withdrew.

Because the Germans were in close contact, there was no concealing the fact that a withdrawal was under way, and German artillery and *Nebelwerfers* soon took the twin villages and Wirtzfeld under fire. Under strict orders to walk, not run, most of the withdrawing troops obeyed the order despite the shelling, and medics were able to load men wounded by the shellfire onto departing vehicles. Some vehicles bogged on muddy sections of the withdrawal route, but there were enough men on foot nearby to get them moving again.

At 2 A.M. on December 20, the withdrawal was complete except for six men of the 38th Infantry's Headquarters Company, who had taken refuge from the shelling in Wirtzfeld in a cellar. There they fell into a sleep of exhaustion. When they awoke after daylight, all they could see from the cellar window were German boots. They waited until heavy concentrations of American artillery fell on the village and sent the Germans fleeing for cover, then ran for it.

Close behind the 1st Division's 26th Infantry, which reached Bütgenbach late on December 17, came another of the division's regiments, the 16th Infantry. While the division's third regiment hunted paratroopers near Eupen, the 16th Infantry began to extend the defensive line along the highway leading from Bütgenbach to Waimes, three and a half miles to the west in the direction of Malmédy. The first troops of that regiment arrived early on December 18.

It was none too soon for 2d Lt. Mabel Jessop, nine other nurses, a few medical and medical administrative officers, and the technicians of the platoon of the 47th Field Hospital in the schoolhouse in Waimes. Following the near collision with *Kampfgruppe Peiper*, the nurses had returned to Waimes and with the other medical personnel reopened the hospital, however limited the facilities. Although worried that the Germans might come, they were at a loss to know how to get to safety.

By the morning of December 18, the hospital not only had new patients but close to fifty able-bodied stragglers who still had their weapons. That disturbed the medics, for under terms of the Geneva Convention, no arms were allowed in a medical facility. They made the men deposit them in a remote part of the building.

In mid-morning, Lieutenant Jessop paused in her work to go into a corridor for a cigarette. As she looked out a window, she saw two soldiers enter the courtyard, weapons at the ready. One was a German captain; the other wore an American uniform with a sergeant's stripes and a shoulder patch denoting the 5th Armored Division. "Your hospital is under arrest," shouted the man in American uniform. "Everybody line up in the yard!"

As everybody conformed—the medical administrative officer in charge would allow none of the stragglers to go for their weapons—the German in American uniform announced that patients and all medical personnel were to load into American vehicles and head for German lines. The able-bodied soldiers were to walk.

As loading began, the soldier in American uniform embraced a middle-aged woman in the street. Word spread (rightly or wrongly) that the man was a native of Waimes and that the woman was his aunt.

Amid the confusion of loading, one of the ambulance drivers slipped away. On the fringe of the town, he found three half-tracks with quad-50 machine guns. In a matter of minutes, they were racing for the schoolhouse, and the German captain and his companion were on the run. Bullets chased them down the street, but they got away.

Less than an hour later, Lt. Col. Charles Horner arrived, wearing the shoulder patch of the 1st Infantry Division. A battalion of the 16th Infantry was on the way, said Horner, and the patients, nurses, and medics were to prepare for evacuation.

Derrill McCollough Daniel had commanded one or another of the 26th Infantry's battalions since the 1st Division's assault landing in North Africa in 1942 and the 2d Battalion since the landing in Sicily in 1943. At thirty-nine, he was one of the senior battalion commanders in a division that had long taken pride in a nickname derived from its shoulder patch, the "Big Red One." Born in South Carolina, Daniel obtained his commission through ROTC at Clemson, the state's agricultural and mechanical college, and then pursued advanced degrees, including a Ph.D. in entomology. By the time he entered the army as a reserve officer in 1940, he was a recognized authority on the biological control of insect pests.

As the men of Daniel's 2d Battalion dug in during the night of December 17 between Büllingen and Bütgenbach at Dom. Bütgenbach, the battalion had the support of four self-propelled guns of the 634th Tank Destroyer Battalion and five Shermans of the 745th Tank Battalion. Under strength by some two hundred men, Daniel nevertheless withheld a rifle platoon to serve as a counterattacking force with the tanks.

Daniel put the tanks behind a rise in the ground near Dom. Bütgenbach and concealed the tank destroyers among the hedges and buildings of the settlement from which they could cover both the main road from Büllingen and another road leading up from the south that joined the main one just short of Dom. Bütgenbach. He placed six 57mm. antitank guns within the line of forward foxholes. His regiment's 3d Battalion covered his left flank from high ground between Bütgenbach and Büllingen. Although his right (or western) flank was open, the regimental executive officer, Colonel Sutherland, had withheld the regiment's third battalion in Bütgenbach as a reserve.

All through December 18, while *SS-Panzergrenadiers* and tanks of the 12th SS Panzer Division tried to wrest the twin villages from men of the 2d Division, Daniel's men had time to dig deep, cover their foxholes with logs, and reinforce them with sandbags. Patrols probed toward Büllingen, determining that the Germans still held the town. Late that afternoon, when an armored car emerged from Büllingen and approached the line of foxholes, a 57mm. piece knocked it out, killing three of the crew and wounding a fourth. The men turned out to be from the 12th SS Panzer Division.

Despite heavy, almost continual American artillery fire on Büllingen (a civilian in the town noted 3,500 rounds in one day alone, and the town was virtually leveled), some two hundred *SS-Panzergrenadiers* and a dozen tanks assembled there and before daylight on December 19 headed up the road toward Dom. Bütgenbach. Fire from the 33d Field Artillery Battalion drove back all but three tanks. Those got past the line of foxholes and headed for the buildings of Dom. Bütgenbach, firing their machine guns as they went; but by that time the 1st Division's 5th Field Artillery Battalion had arrived, and a few salvos from its big 155mm. howitzers convinced the German crews to turn back. Once they had withdrawn beyond the line of foxholes, either the self-propelled tank destroyers or the 57mm. guns knocked out two of them. (For the only time during the German offensive, the 57mm. was an effective weapon against German tanks; somewhere the 26th Infantry had scrounged a few rounds of British Sabot ammunition, which had a high muzzle velocity, making the rounds capable of penetrating heavy armor.)

Two hours later the Germans were back, probing for a soft spot with a company of *SS-Panzergrenadiers* and two tanks, but again American artillery broke up the attack. The shelling sent the *SS-Panzergrenadiers* reeling back in disorder and knocked out one of the tanks.

Through the rest of the day, only occasional shelling hit the American positions; but during that time, Colonel Zeiner, the surviving tanks from Krinkelt-Rocherath, and the rest of the 12th SS Panzer Division's tanks reached Büllingen. Shortly after midnight, accompanied by *SS-Panzergrenadiers* and an attached regiment of the 3d Parachute Division, ten of Zeiner's tanks moved out along the road toward Dom. Bütgenbach. As one of the Germans later noted, "exceedingly heavy artillery and mortar fire" erupted. (By that time, all four of the 1st Division's artillery battalions were in place, along with a battery of 90mm. antiaircraft artillery, a corps artillery battalion with 155mm. howitzers, another with 4.5-inch guns, a battery of 8-inch guns, and a battalion of 4.2-inch chemical mortars.) The Germans "suffered most serious losses." Although a few tanks got past the line of foxholes, tank destroyers knocked out two of them, and the rest fell back.

A few hours later, shortly before daylight on the 20th, the Germans tried again, with eight Panthers in the lead. A shell from some source knocked out the company commander's Panther, setting it on fire, and three more fell victim to artillery fire.

Several tanks nevertheless broke into Company E's position. By the light of flares fired by 81mm. mortars, the crew of a 57mm. antitank gun put four rounds into one of them, sending it up in flames. The light from the flames enabled the gunner, Cpl. Henry F. Warner, to put four more rounds into a second tank, knocking it out; but after the fourth round, the breech block on the gun failed to open. As a third tank appeared, heading directly for the gun, all the crew but Warner dived for foxholes.

Staying with his piece, Warner tried desperately to free the breech block. When the tank was but a few feet away, the turret opened, and the head and shoulders of the German tank commander appeared. Firing his .45-caliber pistol, Warner dove into a foxhole. Still the tank advanced on an apparent collision course with the 57mm. piece and the foxholes of the crew; but just as it reached the first hole, it stopped and went into reverse. Stealing a quick glance, Warner could see the commander slumped over the rim of the turret.

In the fights for the twin villages and for Dom. Bütgenbach, Colonel Zeiner had lost so many tanks that he had to consolidate those that survived into a single company.

Inside Büllingen before daylight the next day, December 21, twenty young SS troopers of the 12th SS Panzer Division, quartered in a house belonging to a farmer, Albert Kohnenmerger, were sleeping in the cellar. Most were boys, fifteen to seventeen years old, and they had already participated in the attacks on Dom. Bütgenbach and experienced the dreadful wrath of the American artillery. Kohnenmerger was with them in the cellar when noncommissioned officers arrived to order them back to the attack. The Belgian farmer watched in silent pity as the boys began to weep. As they gathered their gear to move out into the cold night, tears streaked down their faces.

Those young Hitler Youth were on their way to participate in the strongest thrust yet to be launched against Colonel Daniel and his men. By that time, in the wake of repeated demands from the SS panzer division commander, Brigadier Kraas, the artillery and *Nebelwerfers* that had been ranged against Krinkelt-Rocherath had been relocated to fire on Dom. Bütgenbach, so that for the first time the attackers had powerful fire support.

The artillery and *Nebelwerfers* began firing three hours before dawn on the 21st and despite heavy counter-battery fire from American guns, continued until the first hint of light appeared in the sky. The shelling set three of the outbuildings at Dom. Bütgenbach on fire, including a barn used as an aid station, and tore great gaps in the line of foxholes.

As Colonel Daniel's men waited for the inevitable ground attack to follow, their position was slightly stronger than before because engineers had laid antitank mines on both roads leading into Dom. Bütgenbach. Daniel also had ten more 57mm. antitank guns and a company of infantry from the regiment's reserve battalion. He used a platoon from that company to reinforce his Company G, which had lost so heavily that he had had to use his lone reserve platoon to fill gaps in its line. On the other hand, the enemy's prolonged shelling negated much of that additional strength, for despite overhead cover on the foxholes, casualties were heavy.

As two battalions of *SS-Panzergrenadiers* approached under covering fire from at least thirty tanks and tank destroyers, each battalion taking one of the two roads leading into Dom. Bütgenbach, Daniel called on his supporting artillery to place "a ring of steel" in front of his position. A total of twelve battalions responded: all battalions of the 1st and 2d Divisions; a battalion of the 99th Division (the only battalion of that division within range); and three corps battalions, plus a battalion of 4.2-inch chemical mortars. Through the entire morning, German soldiers, displaying incredible courage (the Americans saw it as fanatical), tried to break through that ring of steel, but not a man made it. They died in droves.

The German tanks eventually found a weak spot: the battalion's open right (western) flank. There Colonel Daniel had placed three of his newly arrived 57mm. antitank guns. One of them scored a hit on the drive sprocket of a Panther, and as the tank backed up, exposing its thinner side armor, the gun knocked it out, setting it on fire. When a Mark IV appeared out of the fog, the same gun knocked it out, but a round from a *Panzerfaust* destroyed the American gun. A round from a Mark IV destroyed a second of the 57mm. guns, and machine-gun fire from another wiped out the crew of the third; but not far away was the gun for which

Corporal Warner was the gunner. Warner got in a shot against the rear of a Mark IV, sending smoke billowing from it. Then a burst of machine-gun fire from the dying tank mortally wounded Warner.

The German tanks were at that point free to roam up and down the foxhole line, shooting up the holes, crushing the occupants with their treads. As more tanks appeared, a U.S. self-propelled tank destroyer knocked out seven in rapid succession, but five others continued toward the buildings of Dom Bütgenbach. Two Shermans knocked out two of the German tanks before they themselves succumbed to the firing. Taking cover behind the one remaining barn, the three surviving German tanks began to blast Daniel's command post in the manor house.

Inside the house, Colonel Daniel appealed to his regimental commander, Colonel Seitz, for a fresh company of infantry armed with extra bazookas. Borrowing a company from the neighboring 18th Infantry, Seitz sent it forward; but that company could not arrive until mid-afternoon, and Daniel's need was immediate.

Daniel nevertheless got the help he needed: a platoon of self-propelled guns of the 613th Tank Destroyer Battalion had just reached Bütgenbach, and those were the new 90mm. pieces. Concealed by a smoke screen, the four guns of that platoon raced down the road from Bütgenbach. When the platoon leader reported, Daniel told him to place his guns in protected positions from which they could fire through the barn at the German tanks behind it.

Fire from the 90mm. guns soon prompted two of the German tanks to make a run for it, but as they came out of hiding, the big pieces knocked them out. The third tank remained in place until late afternoon, when rounds from the battalion's 81mm. mortars at last forced it to try to escape. An early evening mist enabled the crew to make it.

It was close to nightfall when the Germans finally abandoned their day-long attempt to ram through the defenders of Dom. Bütgenbach. It was a costly effort. American patrols later reported enemy dead beyond the main line of resistance "as common as grass." One patrol actually counted 300 bodies in one sector alone, and men of a Graves Registration unit in an early count found 782 dead. In addition, the Germans left behind the hulks of forty-seven tanks and tank destroyers. The defenders lost 5 57mm. antitank guns, 3 Shermans, a tank destroyer, and close to 250 men.

Impressed by the weight of the attack, Colonel Daniel briefly contemplated falling back to high ground closer to Bütgenbach, for his position constituted a distinct right-angle corner in the line, joining the positions of his regiment's 3d Battalion and those of the 2d and 99th Divisions, facing east, with those of the rest of the 1st Division, facing south. Yet when the reserve company from the 18th Infantry arrived, Daniel reconsidered. It was he who had coined the motto, "We stand and die here," and his men had fought by it, many of them dying in the process. There was to be no falling back.

As it turned out, the attack on December 21 represented the high-water mark of the German attempts to break through to Bütgenbach, outflank the Elsenborn Ridge, and succor *Kampfgruppe Peiper*. Not that the German command desisted. The next day, the 22d, the Germans attacked again, but as before they were unable to penetrate the deadly curtain of American artillery fire.

Again a few tanks broke through, not into the 2d Battalion's positions but into those of the 1st Battalion, which Colonel Seitz had committed to extend Daniel's line south to Bütgenbach. Those tanks got into Bütgenbach itself, but without infantry support, they were reduced to playing a deadly game of hide-and-seek with tank destroyers and bazooka teams. Some briefly took cover within the walls of the hospital for geriatric patients, whose inmates were still there, but the bazooka teams eventually knocked all the tanks out.

Like Bill McKinley of the 9th Infantry, Derrill Daniel attributed the success of his battalion to the big guns that backed him up. "The artillery did a great job," he noted later. "I don't know where they got the ammo or when they took time out to flush the guns, but we wouldn't be here now if it wasn't for them."

On that critical day of December 21, American artillery in support of the 2d Battalion, 26th Infantry, fired more than ten thousand rounds in an awesome display of firepower. It was no wonder that not a single *SS-Panzergrenadier* or paratrooper got past the line of foxholes. Yet the artillery would have been of little consequence had not intrepid infantrymen and antitank crewmen held their ground with incredible courage and pertinacity. Like McKinley's men, Daniel's had made one of the truly epic stands against the big German offensive.

By December 21, American troops opposing the northern prong of the German offensive had "knocked a part of Hitler's personal operations plan into a cocked hat." The division commanders, the corps commanders, Dietrich, Model, von Rundstedt, and eventually Adolf Hitler himself all had to face the fact that the Sixth Panzer Army and Hitler's beloved SS troops had failed to do the job Hitler asked of them.

At that point, the Sixth Panzer Army faced a formidable American line. In the north, the veteran 9th Infantry Division moved in to back up the cavalry at Monschau and the infantry at Höfen, and to extend the line southward to link with the 2d and 99th Divisions on the Elsenborn Ridge. Each of those battered but still viable divisions held only a regimental front, with a second regiment of each division manning a second line of defense, and the third regiment of each division in reserve. Separated from the positions of the 2d Division only by the Lac de Bütgenbach, the

1st Division extended the line to the west from Bütgenbach all the way to Waimes and a juncture point near Malmédy with another veteran division that had hurried south to oppose *Kampfgruppe Peiper*. Those four divisions, which included three of the most experienced in the United States Army, formed a solid shoulder against any expansion of the German offensive on its northern wing.

Not that the Germans would not try. Hardly had the men of the 2d and 99th Divisions entrenched on the Elsenborn Ridge than fresh troops of the 3d Panzergrenadier Division tried to penetrate the 99th Division's line. The attack came through the forest well north of the twin villages up the valley of the Schwalm Creek; but it got nowhere. When the spring thaw came in 1945, local civilians found German bodies stacked in the valley of the Schwalm three and four deep.

There the infantry could again pay tribute to its sister arm, the artillery, for in few places during the course of the war in Europe did the American command amass such a concentration of firepower. Word passed among the infantry on the Elsenborn Ridge that the artillery massed behind them was hub to hub, which was almost literally the case. There were sixteen battalions of divisional artillery, which included four 155mm. howitzer battalions, plus seven battalions of corps artillery: 155mm. howitzers, 155mm. guns, 4.5-inch and 8-inch guns. There were in addition the 105mm. howitzers of the Cannon Companies of twelve regiments. The total number of guns capable of firing in front of all or portions of the four divisions was 348, plus tanks and tank destroyers and a battalion of 4.2-inch chemical mortars. To control that tremendous collection of firepower, the corps commander, General Gerow, deputized the 2d Division's artillery commander, General Hinds, who was free to call upon any battalion other than divisional battalions that might be engaged in a priority mission for their own troops.

Once more, on December 26, the Germans would test the defenses of the Elsenborn Ridge with an attack against the 99th Division by a newly arrived 246th Volksgrenadier Division, but hardly had the attack begun before a deadly rain of shells broke it up. Nobody was going to get through the ring of steel those artillery pieces were capable of laying down.

Between December 13 and 19, the 2d Division had penetrated a heavily fortified section of the West Wall, then executed an eight-mile daylight withdrawal while in close contact with the enemy and assumed defensive positions at the twin villages facing in another direction. There they came immediately under heavy attack, held the villages for two days and nights while troops of the 99th Division streamed through, and then broke contact and withdrew to new positions on the Elsenborn Ridge. It was, as the division commander, General Robertson, noted, "a pretty good day's work for any division. Leavenworth [Command and General

Staff College] would say it couldn't be done, and I don't want to have to do it again." He was not alone in that assessment, for the commander of the First Army, General Hodges, told Robertson: "What the 2d Division has done . . . will live forever in the history of the United States Army."

What the 2d Division had done was to block an attack by Sepp Dietrich's Sixth Panzer Army constituting the main effort—the *Schwerpunkt*—of Hitler's offensive. With the exception of the push by *Kampfgruppe Peiper* and the 1st SS Panzer Division, that main effort had failed to get more than three to four miles beyond the German frontier and had failed to open three of the five routes assigned to the 1st SS Panzer Corps for the drive to the Meuse. And the fourth route, that taken by *Kampfgruppe Peiper*, was subject to a powerful array of American artillery; while a fifth, that through Vielsalm, was still blocked by other American troops.

Credit for sealing the third route belonged to Colonel Daniel's 2d Battalion, 26th Infantry, 1st Division. But for the heroic stand of that battalion, the 12th SS Panzer Division, foiled at the twin villages, might have broken through at Bütgenbach, outflanked the Elsenborn Ridge, and undone everything the 2d Division had previously accomplished.

So, too, part of the credit for stopping the drive belonged to the inexperienced soldiers of the 99th Division. From greatly overextended defensive positions, they had kept the Germans at arm's length for the first day and almost all of the second, which turned out to be—by a hair's breadth—the time needed to enable the men of the 2d Division to reach the twin villages. The Germans had expected to penetrate the 99th Division's line and commit their armor soon after daylight on the first day. Despite some disarray in command at the division level, the fighting men of the 99th Division had denied that expectation by many hours.

German losses were never determined with any degree of accuracy, but they were obviously tremendous. It was because of heavy losses that the 326th Volksgrenadier Division abandoned its attacks at Monschau and Höfen, and after only one day of attack, the 277th Volksgrenadier Division could contribute little to the continuing drive against the twin villages. After the fight at Losheimergraben and some assistance in the attacks at Dom. Bütgenbach, the commander of the 12th Volksgrenadier Division, General Engel, told his superiors that, without reinforcements, his division was incapable of attacking.

In the fight for the twin villages, the 12th SS Panzer Division started out with 105 tanks and self-propelled tank destroyers, plus a dozen *Jädgpanthers* of the 560th Army Tank Destroyer Battalion. Allowing for some duplication in counting, Brigadier Kraas lost sixty-seven tanks and tank destroyers in the rural streets and lanes of the twin villages and the surrounding landscape and at Dom. Bütgenbach, forty-seven more. The 12th SS Panzer Division had ceased to be a viable force.

On the American side, the stand at the twin villages amply demonstrated the importance to the infantrymen of tanks and tank destroyers. Without the three companies of Shermans of the 741st Tank Battalion and the two companies of self-propelled pieces of the 644th Tank Destroyer Battalion, the infantrymen, however determined, probably would have been unable to hold. A company of towed guns of the 612th Tank Destroyer Battalion and three guns of the 801st Tank Destroyer Battalion were much less effective. Lacking the Sabot ammunition employed by the 57mm. pieces at Dom. Bütgenbach, the 2d Division's antitank guns were virtually worthless; but bazookas were effective, and the artillery turned out to be the most effective antitank weapon of all.

When the 2d and 99th Divisions counted their losses, the totals were less than might have been expected. For the 2d Division, just over a thousand men killed and missing, and since the division had few men captured, most of those could be presumed dead. The 99th Division lost not quite one thousand four hundred men killed and missing, but a considerable number of those—perhaps five hundred—were captured. The total loss for the two divisions, including wounded, was close to five thousand men.

Stymied on the northern shoulder, the Germans had to swing their remaining weight southward to roads already overcrowded. Whether, despite the failure of their *Schwerpunkt*, they could still accomplish their goal—or at least reach the Meuse River—remained to be seen.

BOOK

V

DAMS AGAINST THE TIDE

CHAPTER TWENTY

Command Decisions

Bernard Law Montgomery was an ascetic. One of nine children in an Anglo-Irish family of modest means, he decided early that life was an unending struggle to be conquered only by hard work, integrity, and moral courage. After finishing the military academy at Sandhurst, he served a tour with the British Army in India, where he found the atmosphere conducive to furthering his asceticism: no late nights, no tobacco, no alcohol, little consort with women. Happily married to his profession, he nevertheless took a wife in 1927 and had a son, David, to whom he was devoted; but when his wife died ten years later, he once again dedicated himself almost exclusively to the military and his role in it. As he rose steadily in command and rank to become one of Britain's ablest soldiers, he made conscious, determined efforts to be seen and identified by his troops, who for the most part adored him. Yet at the same time he developed attributes of arrogance and imperiousness that irritated many of his colleagues and, when the time came, American commanders in particular.

Like his superior, the Chief of the Imperial General Staff, Field Marshal Sir Alan Brooke, Montgomery deeply resented the fact that British troops had to serve under American command, and he exploited every possible opportunity to broaden his own role. While acting as overall ground commander under Eisenhower in the invasion and the campaign in Normandy, he had been content; but when Eisenhower, according to plan, assumed personal command in the field on September 1, 1944, Montgomery launched his campaign to alter Eisenhower's strategy and send the bulk of the Allied forces under his command in a single grand offensive north of the Ardennes, which would well serve his ambition to become once again the overall ground commander. It was a campaign still going on in one form or another when the Germans launched their offensive.

Montgomery may well have seen the offensive as a heaven-sent op-

415

portunity to gain his goal. Within hours after learning of it, he sent teams of picked junior officers, known by the codename PHANTOM, who acted as his eyes and ears on the battlefields, hurrying to the Ardennes. Either they misinformed him of the extent of the American problem or he chose for his own ends to paint the picture in colors gloomier than actually warranted.

In a telegram to Field Marshal Brooke on December 19, Montgomery spoke of "great confusion and all signs of a full-scale withdrawal . . . a definite lack of grip and control . . . an atmosphere of great pessimism. . . ." "The command setup," he continued, "has always been very faulty and now is quite futile, with Bradley at Luxembourg [City] and the front cut in two." He had told Eisenhower's deputy chief of operations, the British officer Jock Whiteley, that Eisenhower should put him in command of all troops north of the German penetration. Somebody, Montgomery added, meaning either the Combined Chiefs of Staff, of which Brooke was a member, or the British prime minister, Winston Churchill, should give Eisenhower "a direct order . . . to do so."

By December 19, the broad shape of the German offensive and the altered form that American defense might impose on it had begun to become apparent, particularly on the shoulders of the penetration. In front of Luxembourg City, which some on the American side still saw as a possible German objective, the American troops had given little ground; and by the 19th, they were forming a line anchored near the German frontier and the Sûre River at Osweiler and Dickweiler and extending northwest toward high ground overlooking Ettelbruck, and that part of Erich Brandenberger's Seventh Army facing the line was going over to the defensive. On the north shoulder, by the 19th, Monschau, Höfen, and the twin villages had held; the 1st Division had arrived to extend the shoulder from Bütgenbach westward toward Malmédy; and the 9th Division was arriving to strengthen the line north of the Elsenborn Ridge. As events over the next few days were to demonstrate, nobody was going to get past the Elsenborn Ridge.

The center, on the other hand, was in a state of flux. Although American troops were coming in to try to bottle up *Kampfgruppe Peiper*, Joachim Peiper and his tanks deep behind American lines at La Gleize and Stoumont still posed a serious threat. It was late on the 19th that the trapped men of the 106th Division in front of St. Vith surrendered; but a surviving regiment of that division, a regiment of the 28th Division, CCB of the 9th Armored Division, and the entire 7th Armored Division, had formed a defensive peninsula, a kind of horseshoe, based on St. Vith, thereby forcing the German columns onto overcrowded roads on either side. So, too, a combat command of the 10th Armored Division and the 101st Airborne Division had won, by the slimmest of margins, a race for the road center of Bastogne.

Yet between St. Vith and Bastogne there was a gap measuring on the diagonal twenty miles. Through that gap had surged two panzer divisions, the 2d and the 116th; and by late on the 19th, they had reached the north-south highway connecting Bastogne through Houffalize to Liège. There the gap was somewhat narrower, about fifteen miles across, partly because the defenders of Bastogne had pushed their line out several miles north of the town and partly because the 82d Airborne Division was arriving a few miles north of Houffalize in the vicinity of Werbomont.

Between Houffalize and Werbomont were two highways leading to the east that American supply trucks were still using. Both led to the Salm River: one to Trois Ponts, where the little band of engineers that had blown the bridges there in front of Peiper was still holding, and the other to the rear of the horseshoe at St. Vith. Yet there was nobody to defend those roads other than a few outposts dropped off by the 7th Armored Division's supply trains.

Nor were there other than scattered units to oppose a continued advance by the 2d and 116th Panzer Divisions toward the Meuse. The commander of the VIII Corps, General Middleton, had managed to find a few engineer battalions and a Canadian forestry company to demolish bridges and cover crossing sites over the Ourthe River, which meandered across the gap; but that was all.

By the 19th, only four days after the start of the offensive, American strength in the Ardennes had grown to close to 180,000 men, double the numbers there when the offensive began. Instead of an armored and five infantry divisions, there were three armored and ten infantry (including two airborne) divisions, and another armored division, the 3d, was arriving. It was a display of mobility that German commanders would find difficult to believe. Although Eisenhower had no more reserves per se, he could, by shuffling the lines north and south of the penetration, produce three more divisions from the vicinity of Aachen and more than that from the Third Army.

The Germans at that point had committed four panzer and thirteen parachute and *Volksgrenadier* divisions, and the *Führer Begleit Brigade* was soon to appear at St. Vith. Sepp Dietrich still had two uncommitted SS panzer divisions, and Field Marshal Model at Army Group B had a reserve of a panzer, a *Panzergrenadier*, and a *Volksgrenadier* division. There were presumably other divisions in a so-called Führer Reserve; but apart from two divisions, the 9th Panzer and the 15th Panzergrenadier, the field commanders could never be sure that such a reserve actually existed. Those two divisions were for the moment earmarked for possible use in the projected supporting attack by the Fifteenth Army around Aachen.

What the Germans called Hitler weather—mist, fog, low-lying clouds, drizzle—was still holding, which meant that the heavy Allied advantage in airpower was yet to be brought to bear. While mounting a maximum effort by fighter-bombers against the attacking ground forces, the Allied air commanders wanted to turn their medium bombers against communications centers and railheads in the Eifel in order to shove German unloading and supply points all the way back to the Rhine; yet that would be impossible so long as the Hitler weather held. Tactical aircraft managed only a few sorties during the first four days with just one notable achievement—the dramatic intervention against *Kampfgruppe Peiper* during the afternoon of December 18—and mediums flew only one mission, a blind bombing attack through the clouds that probably did little damage.

While shielding the ground columns, the Hitler weather also worked against the Luftwaffe. German fighters made only a few appearances: over the northern shoulder as *Kampfgruppe Peiper* was breaking free early on the 17th; over Krinkelt-Rocherath that afternoon; and in the skies over St. Vith the same day. Most operations by the Luftwaffe were night bombing missions against American supply installations in the vicinity of Liège, but like the tactical missions, they did little damage. Nor was it likely that the Luftwaffe could maintain even that much effort for long, for on December 17 alone, American antiaircraft guns knocked down 54 German planes while Allied fighters destroyed 114.

As late as December 18, senior American commanders still saw the German offensive as a spoiling attack designed to disrupt American offensives north and south of the Ardennes and still thought the drive was aimed at the supply installations around Liège. Late on the 18th, for example, although General Bradley saw the situation as "worse than it was at noon," he still looked on the offensive as an opportunity for Patton "to rush the Siegfried Line and hurry our way to the Rhine." General Eisenhower was thinking much the same way: to take advantage of what appeared to be an imprudent move out of the West Wall fortifications by containing the Germans with minimum forces while simultaneously launching offensives all along the rest of the front other than the Ardennes to converge along the Rhine River. (That was paying no attention to the fact that the Germans north of the Ardennes still held the Roer River dams.)

Plans for moving troops of Patton's Third Army northward against the German penetration nevertheless proceeded. Meeting with Bradley in Luxembourg City early in the afternoon of the 18th, Patton said he could intervene "very shortly" with three divisions, including the 4th Armored Division. A combat command of that division and a corps headquarters began moving north that night, to be followed early on December 19 by the rest of the armored division and an infantry division and during the night of the 19th by a second infantry division. It appeared fairly certain, Bradley told Patton, that Patton was to assume command of Middleton's VIII Corps.

Having pretty well completed building a wall against expansion of the penetration at the northern corner—or "door post," as the Germans called it—Patton's counterpart in the north, Hodges of the First Army, was primarily concerned at that point with the big gap between the northern wall and the defenders of Bastogne. The 82d Airborne Division could fill a portion of the gap, as could the incoming 3d Armored Division; but Hodges felt compelled to withhold most of the armored division as a reserve. An infantry division, the 84th, was also soon to arrive, sent south from the Ninth Army.

Faced with German troops only a few miles short of the headquarters town of Spa, Hodges during the 18th moved his headquarters to the rear to another watering place, Chaudfontaine, just outside Liège, the site of his rear headquarters. There were lingering reports that headquarters of the First Army panicked, but those appeared more a misinterpretation of soldiers hurriedly packing and getting out of town than a reality. Hodges himself, for example, and the principal members of his staff waited around the Hôtel Britannique into the evening expecting a visit by the commander of the 82d Airborne Division, General Gavin. When Gavin failed to arrive, they left around 10 P.M. That hardly looked like panic.

In Chaudfontaine, Hodges moved into a room on the second floor of the Palace Hotel with an office across the street in the Hôtel des Bains. That street was a principal highway leading into Liège, and the noise of traffic on it plus the passage of buzz bombs overhead at all hours later prompted Hodges to move again, to Tongres, some fifteen miles on the other side of Liège.

By the morning of December 19, General Eisenhower had a better fix on his enemy than he had on the 18th, partly because of material provided by ULTRA. He had learned, for example, that the Germans were getting ready to commit two SS panzer divisions under the 2nd SS Panzer Corps, and there had been more calls for aerial reconnaissance of the bridges over the Meuse. By that time, Eisenhower also knew the identities of most of the seventeen German divisions thus far committed. The increasing German strength gave added meaning to the earlier intercept of von Rundstedt's hortatory order to the troops, which pointed to considerably more than a spoiling attack.

Eisenhower's thinking about how to meet the offensive thus had undergone considerable change when, at his summons, his senior commanders joined him and key members of his staff at 11 A.M. on December 19 at the 12th Army Group's rear headquarters in Verdun. The meeting took place on the second floor of a stolidly ugly French Army barracks in a room heated only by a pot-bellied stove. The commanders—Bradley, Devers, and Patton, along with a few members of their staffs, and Eisenhower's deputy supreme commander, Air Chief Marshal Arthur W.

Tedder—had assembled when Eisenhower's G-2, General Strong, and G-3, General Bull, at last arrived. "Well," said Eisenhower with a touch of irritation, "I knew my staff would get here; it was only a question of when."

As the generals took their places at a long table, Eisenhower admonished them. "The present situation," he said, "is to be regarded as one of opportunity for us and not of disaster. There will be only cheerful faces at this conference table." To which Patton responded: "Hell, let's have the guts to let the sons of bitches go all the way to Paris. Then we'll really cut 'em up and chew 'em up."

A new infantry division, Eisenhower revealed, had just arrived in France and would be moved forward swiftly. Three infantry divisions then in Britain were to accelerate their shipping schedules, and he was asking that divisions in the United States alerted for early movement ship their infantry regiments in advance. He was also asking authority to use artillery shells equipped with the super-secret radio-controlled proximity fuse. (He was unaware that Colonel Axelson of the 406th Field Artillery Group had already put the fuse to work with good results at Monschau.)

All offensive action, declared Eisenhower, was to cease. Although commanders were to be prepared to give ground, if necessary, to shorten lines and free reserves, there was to be no withdrawal beyond the Meuse River. General Devers was to shift the boundary of his 6th Army Group northward to free some of Patton's troops for a drive into the enemy's south flank, while Simpson's Ninth Army was to do the same to free divisions of the First Army. Because Hodges was too preoccupied at the moment with containing the German thrusts, there could be no counterattack immediately from the north, but Patton was to mount an attack to reach Bastogne and from there eventually drive northward to link with a later attack by the First Army. (The belief that Hodges was in no position for an early attack and the desire to link with the American troops in endangered Bastogne thus served to obviate the obvious possibility of cutting the Germans off at their base with simultaneous attacks by Hodges southeastward on St. Vith and Patton northward up the Skyline Drive; but unknown to Eisenhower, Hodges was even then contemplating an early drive on St. Vith.)

Turning to Patton, Eisenhower asked: "When can you start?"

Patton responded: "As soon as you're through with me."

Eisenhower wanted him to be more specific.

"The morning of December 21st," said Patton. "With three divisions."

That was only a little more than thirty-six hours away. "Don't be fatuous, George," said Eisenhower. "If you try to go that early, you won't have all three divisions ready and you'll go piecemeal. You will start on the twenty-second and I want your initial blow to be a strong one! I'd even settle for the twenty-third if it takes that long to get three full divisions."

The man who only a few hours earlier had argued vehemently with General Bradley over releasing any of his troops was at that point exultant. Having already drawn up three proposals with his staff, he had but to go to a telephone and give a codeword to put the plan to move on Bastogne into action.

Patton would have liked to have seen the Germans drive westward some forty or fifty miles, then chop them off and destroy them, but he recognized that he would never muster support for that kind of daring. As he set about directing a ninety-degree turn by one of his corps and shifting the troops more than 150 miles to the north for an attack to begin two and a half days later—a maneuver that would make Stonewall Jackson's peregrinations in the valley campaign in Virginia and Gallieni's shift of troops in taxicabs to save Paris from the Kaiser look pale by comparison—he remained supremely confident. To his wife, Beatrice, Patton wrote: "Remember how a tarpon makes one big flop just before he dies."

It was well into the evening when General Eisenhower and his party returned to Versailles. As the Supreme Commander went to his office in the Trianon Palace Hotel, his intelligence officer, General Strong, retired to his billets, which he shared with the deputy chief of operations, Jock Whiteley. Strong soon learned that Whiteley had been pondering the telephone call he had received early in the day from Field Marshal Montgomery suggesting that Eisenhower place Montgomery in command of all troops north of the German penetration.

Although Whiteley was no partisan of Montgomery's, the more he thought about the proposal, the more sense it made. Since General Bradley was determined to remain in Luxembourg City, how could he give the northern part of the front the attention it deserved? He was sure that Bradley's communications with the First Army's new headquarters in Chaudfontaine must be poor, for communications from Versailles to Chaudfontaine were poor.

When Strong agreed that the move was warranted, Whiteley telephoned Eisenhower's chief of staff, General Smith, and asked for an audience. Going with Strong to Smith's office, he made his proposal and in return got a taste of Bedell Smith's well-known hair-trigger temper. He had always counted on Whiteley, snapped Smith, to maintain "a completely Allied outlook," yet there he was "talking like a damned British staff officer."

Whiteley nevertheless stuck by his proposal. It was based, he said, strictly on military considerations. Smith could fire him, but he stuck by it.

Picking up the telephone, Smith got Eisenhower on the line and told him of Whiteley's proposal and Strong's concurrence. By that time, his flare-up of temper had passed, and when he put down the telephone, he told the two British officers: "General Eisenhower says we can decide this matter after our staff meeting tomorrow morning."

Although it was then close to eleven o'clock in the evening, Eisenhower was still in his office, a cavernous room normally used for meetings and banquets. Rising from his desk, he walked over to a big situation map that covered part of one of the walls.

As Eisenhower pondered the map, he noted to himself that Whiteley's proposal made sense. The critical battle might well be joined on the northern shoulder of the penetration, and Bradley was too far away to exercise close personal control. Before the German offensive was over, it might well be that all Allied troops north of the penetration would become involved. He needed a single commander to coordinate the four armies located there. Besides, Montgomery's 21st Army Group had the only considerable reserve then available on the Continent, the 30th British Corps, which had been out of the line getting ready to renew the offensive. Although Eisenhower as Supreme Commander had full authority to call on that corps, and if Montgomery objected to its use, he had no question but that the Combined Chiefs of Staff would back the Supreme Commander, it would be better, should British troops be required, that Montgomery himself commit them.

On the other hand, Eisenhower mused, some of the senior American commanders (particularly Bradley and Patton) would resent the move, primarily because it involved the imperious, abrasive Montgomery. However temporary the change in command, some would see it as a surrender to Montgomery's persistent arguments that he be made overall Allied ground commander, and some hotheads might even see it as a loss of confidence in Bradley.

Yet as Eisenhower continued to study the map, it became ever clearer that he had to do it. With a grease pencil, he drew a line across the map from Givet on the Meuse River eastward through the Ardennes and across the German frontier to Prüm. All forces north of that line—the First and Ninth Armies, the First Canadian Army, and the Second British Army—were to be temporarily under Montgomery; those south of the line—the VIII Corps and the Third Army—under Bradley.

Going to the telephone, Eisenhower told Bedell Smith to notify Bradley of his decision. As might have been expected, the news jolted Bradley. Indeed, he was "completely dumbfounded—and shocked." When he had left Eisenhower only a few hours earlier, the Supreme Commander had given no inkling of a change in command. Although there had been, in fact, some problems with telephonic communications to Hodges, his communications people were laying new lines, including one west of the Meuse. He thought the staff at Versailles was beginning to panic when in fact there was nothing to justify undue alarm. Although he failed to say so to Smith, he also believed it would be a loss of face for him and the entire American command; and it particularly rankled that he would have to relinquish his beloved former command, the First Army, which he had earlier tried to safeguard from Montgomery's clutches by inserting Simpson's Ninth Army into the line between the First Army and the British.

Bradley nevertheless felt compelled to admit that if it were anybody but Montgomery, even another British commander, and certainly if it were an American commander, the proposal made sense, was "the logical thing to do." Furthermore, should the Germans get across the Meuse, Montgomery's 21st Army Group would be in jeopardy. Against that possibility, Montgomery would want to hold onto the 30th Corps; but if he were in command of the northern front, he might be disposed to use his reserve to keep the Germans from getting across the Meuse. "There's no doubt in my mind," said Bradley finally, "that if we play it the way you suggest, we'll get more help from the British in the way of reserves."

Assured by Smith that the change was to be temporary, Bradley gave his consent, an act, he was to note near the end of a long life, that was "one of my biggest mistakes of the war." As Eisenhower personally notified Bradley the next morning, the change was to take effect at noon that day, December 20.

Unaware that a change was in the offing, Field Marshal Brooke had in the meantime responded to Montgomery's demand that he be placed in command in the north by going, not to the Combined Chiefs of Staff (there was no time for that) but to the prime minister, Winston Churchill. Late in the night of the 19th, Churchill telephoned Eisenhower. Whether Churchill intended to push Montgomery's candidacy would never be known, for early in the conversation, Eisenhower volunteered that he intended giving Montgomery temporary command in the north. In typical Churchillian fashion, Churchill assured him "that British troops will always deem it an honor to enter the same battle as their American friends."

As Eisenhower had anticipated, Patton, like Bradley, resented the decision. Patton thought Eisenhower did it either "through the machinations of the Prime Minister" or in the hope of getting help from British divisions. In any event, he saw Eisenhower as "unwilling or unable to command Montgomery."

Conscious of the pain caused to Bradley and the possibility of misinterpretation of the move as a loss of confidence in Bradley, Eisenhower suggested to the U.S. Army's chief of staff, General Marshall, that it "would be a most opportune time to promote Bradley." Although Marshall agreed, he noted that because the Congress had adjourned for Christmas, that was for the moment unfeasible.

As presented to Bradley, the basic reason for the change was the difficulty of Bradley's communicating with Hodges. Without question, face-to-face discussions between the two commanders would have been difficult. One or the other would have had to circle by road or by air far around to the west of the Meuse, and if the Germans crossed the Meuse, that might prove to be impossible. Although communication by telephone would be no real substitute for direct contact, Bradley was correct in that some telephonic communications—whether sufficient to the demand would remain problematical—still existed, but by circuitous and not always reliable routes. As early as December 22, the Germans forced men manning a repeater radio station at Jemelle, near Marche, to abandon their post; and the next day they cut the main telephone line, a buried cable, and two days later another, an open-wire circuit.

In the final analysis, Bradley himself was the author of his own discontent. It was he who located—or approved—a forward headquarters in Luxembourg City, only fourteen miles behind the front, considerably closer than any of his three subordinate army headquarters and most of the corps headquarters. Nor could it be argued that that location was central to his three army commands, for it was considerably closer to the headquarters of the Third Army than to those of the First and Ninth Armies. (Was that to keep close tabs on the impetuous George Patton?)

It looked like an affinity on the part of somebody for the creature comforts of a big town, that plus the general belief that the Germans were already beaten. Even so, Bradley's dogmatic refusal to relocate his headquarters reflected an undue concern for the reaction of the civilians of the Luxembourg capital. There were already thousands of refugees all over the Ardennes, and the withdrawal of Hodges's headquarters from Spa had generated others; furthermore, however miserable the plight of refugees, Europeans over the centuries had grown to live with the comings and goings of conquerors.

At headquarters of the First Army in the Hôtel des Bains in Chaudfontaine, the news of the change in command "created undercurrents of unhappiness." As Bradley looked on his former command with affection, so did the members of the First Army's staff on their former commander, and Montgomery with his "cocky mannerisms" would do little to ease the pain of separation. When Montgomery arrived at the headquarters around noon on the 20th with his chief of staff, General de Guingand, he had already received reports on the situation at the front from his PHANTOM couriers, and rather than consult the First Army's operations map, he referred to a small one of his own. To one of the members of his entourage, he seemed to stride into the headquarters "like Christ come to cleanse the temple."

The Americans had rebuffed Montgomery in happier times, but now, in their hour of trial, they deigned to call on him. In Montgomery's view, had they but listened to him, followed the strategy he advocated, made him the overall ground commander, no hour of trial would have arrived.

When it came time for lunch, Montgomery declined General Hodges's invitation, turning instead to eat alone from a lunchbox and Thermos. No matter that that was his usual practice when dining away from his headquarters, the Americans saw it as an affront.

Having been told by Eisenhower that he approved giving up ground if necessary in order to gain reserves, Montgomery proposed withdrawing from St. Vith and softening the angle of the northern corner by pulling back from the Elsenborn Ridge. Hodges and his staff saw that as a typical Montgomery maneuver, a step to "tidy the battlefield." In their view, what American blood had bought, American soldiers held onto. When Montgomery saw that they reacted as if he intended to strip them of their birthrights, he demurred temporarily, but the matter of withdrawal from St. Vith was to arise again.

While considering, as did Hodges, that Liège was a basic German objective, Montgomery believed that German ambition went beyond Liège. It looked to him as if the Germans intended swinging northwest and crossing the river between Liège and the bend at Namur, in which case Hodges needed to extend his retaining wall southwestward as far as Marche and assemble a strong reserve behind the Ourthe River between Marche and the Meuse to counterattack whenever the Germans had outrun their resources. To command that reserve, Montgomery insisted upon having the commander of the VII Corps, Maj. Gen. J. Lawton ("Lightning Joe")* Collins, whom he considered to be one of the more capable American corps commanders.

Courtney Hodges also thought highly of Collins; indeed, there were those who said that Joe Collins was Hodges's fair-haired boy. Hodges was already considering pulling headquarters of the VII Corps from the line east of Aachen and assembling enough troops to counterattack southeast from Malmédy on St. Vith in hope of linking with a drive by Patton up the Skyline Drive—a move advocated both by Gerow of the V Corps and Middleton of the VIII Corps.

To flesh out the VII Corps, Collins was to have the 84th Infantry Division, already under orders to move from the Ninth Army to the Ardennes, and the division that Eisenhower had remarked at Verdun as having just reached France, the 75th Infantry Division. At the suggestion of Montgomery's operations officer, Brig. David Belchem, Montgomery ordered the Ninth Army's reserve, the 2d Armored Division, to the Ardennes to provide Collins with a third division. The corps was to be employed not, according to Hodges's plan, to drive on St. Vith, but according to Montgomery's, as a reserve between the Ourthe and the

---

* Although Collins was an audacious commander, the nickname derived not from swift battlefield maneuver but from his having earlier commanded the 25th ("Tropic Lightning") Infantry Division in the Pacific.

Meuse. Whether the Germans would allow the Allied command the luxury of withholding a reserve remained to be seen.

Even before assuming command in the north, Montgomery ordered his 30th Corps with four divisions (a fifth was to follow later) to move to a deep reserve position some thirty miles north of the Meuse. That put the corps in position not only to counter a crossing of the Meuse but also to counter any German attempt to take advantage of the thinning of the American line around Aachen. Montgomery also sent detachments to secure bridges over the river between Namur and Liège.

As Montgomery left Hodges's headquarters, he was concerned about Hodges's health. To Montgomery, Hodges appeared to be exhausted, a candidate for a heart attack, and he thought he should be relieved of command. At the first opportunity, Montgomery telephoned Bedell Smith, telling him that as a British officer, he himself was unwilling to relieve an American general but he thought Eisenhower should relieve Hodges.

When Eisenhower learned of it, he thought he knew immediately what was wrong; Montgomery had failed to realize that God had given Hodges a face that always looked drawn and pessimistic. He promptly sent off a note to Montgomery advising him that Hodges was "the quiet reticent type and does not appear as aggressive as he really is. Unless he becomes exhausted he will always wage a good fight."

As early as December 18, the commander of the Fifth Panzer Army, Hasso von Manteuffel, had concluded that the German offensive had failed, that there was no hope of reaching Antwerp (which he had never anticipated in any case), and that even the Meuse River appeared to be out of reach. The only army commander who was enjoying any real success, he passed his pessimistic opinion on to the commander of *OB WEST*, von Rundstedt, and to the chief of the armed forces operations staff, General Jodl, both of whom had already come to much the same conclusion.

As von Rundstedt saw it, the way to salvage something from the offensive was to mount the projected attack by the Fifteenth Army to drive in behind the American forces in the vicinity of Aachen, thereby forestalling the shift of any more American divisions to the Ardennes. He ordered the Fifteenth Army to attack early the next morning, December 19.

Hitler promptly overrode him. Were his defeatist field commanders trying to set up conditions for shifting to their Small Solution? There was to be no attack by the Fifteenth Army. And to ensure it, he ordered the two divisions of the Führer Reserve that were earmarked for use with the Fifteenth Army—the 9th Panzer and 15th Panzergrenadier Divisions—to move to assembly areas in northern reaches of the Eifel. That put them beyond reach for unauthorized commitment with the Fifteenth Army, and Hitler reiterated that neither division was to be employed without his specific approval. With everything else remaining, von Rundstedt was to exploit the penetrations already achieved in the Ardennes.

Since the Sixth Panzer Army had failed to get past the Elsenborn Ridge, the commander of Army Group B, Field Marshal Model, with von Rundstedt's endorsement, ordered the main effort to shift on December 20 to the Fifth Panzer Army. At Hitler's order, General Dietrich nevertheless had to continue to hammer away for four more days in what turned out to be a continuing futile effort to get past the Elsenborn Ridge; but the Sixth Panzer Army's role was inexorably changing from getting across the Meuse to protecting the Fifth Panzer Army's north flank.

As a first step in that shift, one of the uncommitted SS panzer divisions, the 2d *(Das Reich)*, was to swing around to the south of St. Vith, follow the path of the 116th Panzer Division, and turn north against the line the Americans were building up along the north flank of the German penetration. Meanwhile the other SS panzer division, the 9th *(Hohenstaufen)*, was to move through the Losheim Gap, cross the Salm River upstream from the route taken by *Kampfgruppe Peiper*, and swing north against the developing American line close alongside the 2d SS Panzer Division. Vital to the new role of the Sixth Panzer Army was the necessity for the main body of the 1st SS Panzer Division to make contact with *Kampfgruppe Peiper*, and the new alignment could never be fully developed without the road network in and around St. Vith to take the place of the network denied by the American stand on the Elsenborn Ridge.

Although nobody told Adolf Hitler, the German field commanders were no longer thinking in terms of reaching Antwerp—if, indeed, they had ever thought seriously in those terms. Their long-range goal was to use the Sixth Panzer Army to pin the American forces along the northern flank while the Fifth Panzer Army crossed the Meuse in the vicinity of Namur, then swung northwest toward Aachen to trap those American forces facing the Sixth Panzer Army south of Liège and at the corner at the Elsenborn Ridge.

A variation on the Small Solution.

As was the case at Eisenhower's headquarters, realization of the portent of what was happening in the Ardennes was slow to come to the people in Allied capitals. That was basically because of a system of strict censorship imposed on all news by the headquarters, not only on news transmitted to Britain and the United States but also on what was aired or printed in Belgium and France.

Before the invasion, the exiled government of Belgium had agreed to voluntary censorship, while France had agreed to subject its press and radio to the same restrictions as SHAEF imposed on British and American correspondents. Although an occasional newsman violated the restrictions, retribution in the form of withdrawn credentials inevitably followed, and that might mean being sent home.

The official radios in Belgium, Britain, and France began transmitting some reports of what was happening on the second day, December 17, but most of the first newspaper accounts came only on the third. No Washington newspaper, for example, had any mention on the second day, although *The New York Times* carried a story on page 19 under a one-column headline: GERMAN ASSAULT ON FIRST ARMY FIERCE. The correspondent noted: "It was a new and violent move in the enemy's campaign to delay and harass us and make every yard of our advance as costly as possible." The banner headlines across front pages came only on the third day, December 18.

There was at first no particular concern among the people of Brussels and Paris. Neither the official radio nor the newspapers engaged in sensationalism, and only a few months earlier the people had seen with their own eyes a thoroughly defeated German Army limp back to the homeland. To most people it was unbelievable that such a crippled force could mount a really viable threat to Allied armies, whose power was plain for all to see. Most housewives were concerned less with what was happening at the front than with finding something special for Christmas dinner among the rationed stocks in the shops.

As the days passed and it was obvious that the weather was preventing Allied planes from operating, some concern began to arise. There were tales from refugees, reports by telephone from friends or relatives close to the front, and word that the British Army had established road blocks on the approaches to Brussels. Some even saw the possibility of a second occupation with inevitable reprisals, but for most the concern never developed into more than a gnawing worry. The Germans obviously were advancing with no such speed as they had displayed in 1940. Nobody in either Brussels or Paris took to the roads.

Seeing supporting units hastily falling back in the first days, newsmen at the front were shocked and dismayed by what they took to be panic. Many fled to Maastricht in the Netherlands, where they tried to send dispatches reporting wholesale flight, but the censor saw what they wrote as "sheer hysteria" and squelched it. At least one of the newsmen, Wes Gallagher of the Associated Press, was later grateful. "What could have been an unholy mess," he noted, "was saved by the good sense of front line field censors."

American newsmen in particular were nevertheless outraged at the little information SHAEF's press office provided and at the little the censor would pass. An "angry session" erupted at Versailles on December 19 with reporters demanding the release of more details. "May I say," shouted George Lyon of the Office of War Information, "that SHAEF's policy . . . is stupid?" Another said that "everybody across hell and forty

acres" knew what was going on, and the American people were entitled
to know.

Nothing remotely critical of the Allied command or the troops appeared in print in the early days. What had befallen "our troops" and
"our men" was obviously a result of the fortunes of war, and even though
Christmas would be "tinged by sorrow, anxiety, and a graveness of
spirit," all was sure to be set right in time. President Roosevelt and the
White House made no public comment, and a spokesman for the War
Department urged that "the situation should not be viewed with panic."
The American public would "do well to reserve its judgments and fears
until enough time has passed for a clarification of the situation." The
Germans, he said, were incapable of a decisive victory.

The military editor of *The New York Times*, Hanson Baldwin, made
one of the first criticisms. Writing on Christmas Eve, he noted that the
Allied command appeared to have been surprised threefold: with regard
to time, place, and size of the German forces. American intelligence officers appeared "to have made the same mistake they made before and
during the hedgerow fighting in Normandy," which was to underestimate
"the capacity and will of the enemy to fight."

Two days later *The Washington Post* noted editorially that "our command was caught napping." The blame clearly belonged to "the intelligence service," and the government should remember that and create a
strong intelligence arm in the postwar era. Yet except for British newspapers, which saw in the events an opportunity to push for a larger command role for their countryman, Field Marshal Montgomery, that was
about as sharp as the criticism ever became.

CHAPTER TWENTY-ONE

The War Against *Kampfgruppe Peiper*

As Joachim Peiper and his armored column descended into the deep valley of the Amblève River at Stavelot early on December 18, distance and terrain disrupted radio communications with headquarters of the 1st SS Panzer Division. Throughout the day, while American engineers at Trois Ponts and near Habiémont were frustrating Peiper, he knew nothing of what was happening behind him—whether the 3d Parachute Division was moving forward to hold his lifeline at Stavelot, whether the 12th SS Panzer Division had broken through to drive along his northern flank, whether the rest of the 1st SS Panzer Division was advancing to link with his rear. Nor did he have any information as to what steps the American command was taking to counter his drive. What he did know from the actions of the American engineers and from the attack during the afternoon by American fighter-bombers was that he had lost his principal ally: surprise.

Only near midnight, when a liaison officer managed to get forward with an ultra high-frequency radio, was he able to reestablish contact with his division headquarters. To his concern, he learned that two American divisions, the 7th Armored and the 30th Infantry, were moving into the Ardennes from the vicinity of Aachen. Although both those divisions had been in reserve and out of contact with German units, American radio security was so poor that German intelligence had quickly picked up their movements.

Having seen the bridge over the Lienne Creek near Habiémont blown in his face just at nightfall, Peiper had sent reconnaissance detachments with half-tracks and assault guns upstream and down in an effort to find another bridge. Although both detachments located bridges, they were in each case too fragile to carry his tanks. One of the detachments nevertheless crossed to the west bank of the Lienne, but there in the darkness ran into a company of American infantry supported by two self-propelled tank destroyers. Only one of the German vehicles escaped, an

430

armored car in which the detachment commander, Lieutenant Preuss, was riding.

As darkness deepened, Peiper saw no choice but to pull back to the north bank of the Amblève by way of the bridge he had taken intact near Cheneux. Leaving a strong force to defend Cheneux in the event he needed the bridge later, he assembled his command in and around the village of La Gleize. Up to that point, his losses had been relatively light, a total of thirteen tanks—three at Dom. Bütgenbach, four in front of Wirtzfeld, one at Ligneuville, four at Stavelot, and one at Cheneux—plus two flak tanks and a few half-tracks and smaller vehicles. During the night, seven of his attached Tiger tanks and the division's reconnaissance battalion joined him.

Peiper at that point considered that there were two ways he could continue the thrust to the Meuse. Beyond La Gleize and the next town of Stoumont, the road followed the valley of the meandering Amblève close alongside the river, with steep, clifflike wooded hills on the other side, so that a few men with antitank mines might block it at any number of places; only ten winding miles later did the road enter more open country at the Bastogne-Liège highway. Yet there was supposed to be a bridge not far beyond Stoumont, between the hamlet of Targnon and a railroad stop, known as Stoumont Station, that afforded passage across the Amblève and a return to the road he was trying to reach that led to Werbomont. Given the confined nature of the road beyond Stoumont Station, getting that bridge appeared to be Peiper's only real hope, and even that was dependent upon the great imponderable of gasoline.

What Peiper did not know was that he was practically within spitting distance of enough gasoline to take him not only to the Meuse River but to the North Sea and back several times. In the woods along a secondary road only a few miles north of La Gleize was the second and larger of the First Army's big depots with more than 2 million gallons of gasoline, guarded as night fell on the 18th by only about a hundred men of a rear echelon headquarters with five half-tracks and three assault guns reinforced by a few men of the Belgian Fusiliers. Although two 90mm. anti-aircraft guns and four more half-tracks with quad-50s arrived after nightfall, it was still a defensive force in no way capable of dealing with the strength Peiper might throw against it. Yet not until the next morning did any Germans move toward the depot; and then it was only a flank reconnaissance patrol of a few armored vehicles, under orders to fall back if encountering resistance, which it did.

Thus Peiper in his ignorance worried and fretted in La Gleize about the growing shortage of fuel. As his exhausted troops bedded down for the night, it was Peiper's second self-imposed delay, and it was to have consequences even exceeding those that followed the delay before Stavelot. For his patrols determined during the night that the road to Stoumont Station was not to be Peiper's for the asking.

*   *   *

Long weeks earlier, in Normandy, a battalion of the 30th Division's 120th Infantry had held onto a hill, although surrounded, for six days and helped frustrate a Hitler-ordered offensive aimed at cutting off American spearheads that had broken out of the beachhead. After that, a turncoat American radio propagandist for the Nazis known as "Axis Sally" referred to the 30th Division as "Roosevelt's SS," a name in which the men of the division took a certain pride. The division's true nickname was "Old Hickory," after President Andrew Jackson, which reflected the division's origin in the Carolinas-Tennessee National Guard.

Night had fallen on December 17 by the time most of the vehicles carrying troops of the 30th Division to the Ardennes got on the road. A few German planes flew over the column, dropping flares and an occasional ineffective bomb and making a few futile strafing passes, and there were reports of German paratroopers but no real difficulties. As the column started out, the plan was that the division would back up the defenders of the twin villages and Bütgenbach, but with news of *Kampfgruppe Peiper's* breakthrough, the massacre at Baugnez, and later Peiper's attack on Stavelot, all that changed. In the end, the 117th Infantry went to Stavelot, the 120th Infantry to Malmédy, and the 119th Infantry to Spa, there to be prepared to defend the First Army's headquarters town but also to be ready for commitment elsewhere, depending on which direction *Kampfgruppe Peiper* took from Stavelot.

Those assignments made, General Hodges asked the division commander, Maj. Gen. Leland S. Hobbs, to come to Spa.

As Hodges made that request, he already had a visitor, the temporary commander of the XVIII Airborne Corps, James Gavin, who had just made an all-night trip by jeep from his 82d Airborne Division's encampment in northern France. Gavin went immediately to the War Room, where he talked with Hodges, as well as the chief of staff, Bill Kean, and the operations officer, Tubby Thorson.

It was at that conference that Hodges, in concern for the threat posed by *Kampfgruppe Peiper*, decided to order the 82d Airborne Division to bypass Bastogne and move to Werbomont to stop Peiper, leaving the 101st Airborne Division to go to Bastogne. From the Hôtel Britannique Gavin drove to Werbomont, where at the bridge over the Lienne Creek near Habiémont, he talked with the engineer officer assigned to destroy the bridge, Lieutenant Edelstein. Then continuing on to Bastogne, Gavin made sure the acting commander of the 101st Airborne Division, General McAuliffe, understood the change in orders. He returned in the evening to Werbomont by way of Houffalize. (Only later was Gavin to learn that advance contingents of the 116th Panzer Division had already driven past Houffalize.) As Gavin reached Werbomont around 8 P.M., first troops of the 82d Airborne Division were arriving.

The regular commander of the XVIII Airborne Corps, General Ridg-

way, had in the meantime hurried back with his staff by air from England. He spent the night of the 18th at Middleton's headquarters in
Bastogne and drove after daylight to Werbomont, there to establish his
corps headquarters in a farmhouse across the road from General Gavin's,
which at that point became the headquarters of the 82d Airborne Division. That done, Ridgway drove to Hodges's relocated headquarters in
Chaudfontaine. There he learned that he was to have control of the 30th
Division's 119th Infantry, a portion of the 3d Armored Division, which
was on the way to the Ardennes from the Ninth Army, and the 82d
Airborne Division. It was a small force indeed with which to stop Peiper
and at the same time fill a gap between Werbomont and the Ourthe
River, a gap of some fifteen miles toward which other German armored
columns were driving. Yet that was Ridgway's assignment.

As Leland Hobbs entered the Hôtel Britannique around noon on December 18, many of the First Army's headquarters units were packing,
getting ready for the shift to Chaudfontaine. General Hodges had just
received word from pilots of cub planes flying from the First Army's airstrip just outside Spa that the big German armored column had turned
away from Trois Ponts and was heading up the valley of the Amblève
toward La Gleize and Stoumont. That obviously presented the enemy
commander with three choices. He could continue to follow the valley of
the Amblève; cross the bridge at Cheneux and head for Werbomont; or
turn north at one of several points on Liège.

In any case, the German column had to be stopped. When Hobbs left
the headquarters and found the commander of the 119th Infantry, Col.
Edward M. Sutherland, he had orders to send one of Sutherland's battalions to hold along the Lienne Creek in front of Werbomont until
troops of the 82d Airborne Division could assume that task. The rest of
the regiment was to block the German column in the valley of the Amblève. As part of the battalion that moved to the Lienne Creek, it was
Company F that devastated one of Peiper's reconnaissance detachments
along the creek that night.

Early the next morning, the commander of Company F, 1st Lt. Edward C. Arn, was astounded to see a jeep pull up outside his headquarters and a two-star general in the uniform of a paratrooper jump out.
"I'm Jim Gavin of the 82d Airborne Division," said the general. His men,
he explained, were soon to relieve Arn's, and if Arn had no objection, he
would "go on up ahead and have a look around." A few minutes later
one of Arn's platoon leaders, 2d Lt. Kenneth Austin, called over his
walkie-talkie radio. "I wish to suggest that you have me relieved," said
Austin; "I'm going nuts. There's a two-star general in a jeep . . ."

Meanwhile, the rest of the 119th Infantry had headed in late afternoon of the 18th for the valley of the Amblève River. Traveling behind a

reconnaissance screen that found the road clear of Germans at least as far as Stoumont, the leading 3d Battalion detrucked in that town.

Since it was well after dark, the commander, Lt. Col. Roy C. Fitzgerald, Jr., told his men to dig defensive positions for the night. The wisdom of that decision was soon revealed when patrols, sent probing in the direction of La Gleize, returned with word that they had seen Germans openly talking and smoking less than a thousand yards away along the highway near the imposing Château de Froide-Cour. As best the men could discern in the darkness, there were some thirty-five to forty tanks.

At about the same time, Peiper's patrols discovered that the Americans were near. Ordering an attack before dawn to seize Stoumont and push on to the bridge across the Amblève just short of Stoumont Station, Peiper spent much of the night moving among his troops, joking with them, bantering, encouraging them. He was concerned that fatigue and the day's frustrations were taking a toll of his men's enthusiasm and esprit.

Around mid-morning of the 18th, the 117th Infantry's 1st Battalion reached the gasoline depot in the woods above Stavelot. There just forward of the woodsline, Belgian Fusiliers were still maintaining a roadblock by burning gasoline in the road. Since the fire denied any use of the road, the battalion commander, Lt. Col. Robert E. Frankland, ordered a halt to the burning; but since it might be some time before vehicles could pass, he told his men to detruck and proceed on foot. His fire support—three assault guns and a platoon of towed tank destroyers—would have to wait until the fire died down. Nor would Frankland have artillery support, for his regiment's supporting artillery battalion had yet to arrive.

Having anticipated early reinforcement by troops of the 3d Parachute Division to hold Stavelot and the vital bridge over the Amblève, Peiper had left only a small security detachment in the town. As Frankland's infantrymen approached, men of that detachment opened fire. The Americans nevertheless gained the first houses and gradually worked their way farther into town. The towed guns of a platoon of the 823d Tank Destroyer Battalion finally bypassed the roadblock at the gasoline depot and assumed firing positions overlooking the houses.

Early that afternoon ten Mark IVs suddenly appeared, racing into Stavelot along the road from Trois Ponts. Those tanks might have done terrible damage had not the fighter-bombers that were attacking Peiper's column near Cheneux roared to the attack. They knocked out no tanks, but they drove them to cover.

By nightfall, the men of the 117th Infantry's 1st Battalion held half of Stavelot, the towed tank destroyers had entered the town, as had three Shermans of the 743d Tank Battalion, and the 118th Field Artillery Battalion was ready to fire. All that was fortunate, for the fight for Stavelot was only just beginning.

Soon after midnight, a Tiger, one of a number of the 501st Heavy Panzer Battalion following in Peiper's wake, approached the town square along the street leading up from the bridge over the Amblève. Men of a platoon of Company A under 1st Lt. Robert O. Murray, Jr., knocked it out with a bazooka fired at close range, and the great carcass blocked the narrow street. As two following Tigers tried to turn into even narrower side streets, they had to back and fill to make the turns, leaving them vulnerable to Murray's bazookamen. Well-placed rockets knocked them out.

By midday of December 19, Frankland's infantry had cleared all of Stavelot except for a few houses on the western edge along the road to Trois Ponts. Although the men had gained the buildings facing the river near the bridge, the bridge itself was still intact. Just across the river was a force of the 2d SS-Panzergrenadier Regiment, a contingent of one of the other columns of the 1st SS Panzer Division under orders from the division commander, Colonel Mohnke, to open a route to Peiper. With the *SS-Panzergrenadiers* were four Panthers. From an observation post on the high ground behind Stavelot, Colonel Frankland's artillery liaison officer called for such heavy fire beyond the river that the *SS-Panzergrenadiers* ran for cover, but the tanks continued to roll toward the bridge.

At first they had cover from a row of houses, but forty yards short of the bridge, the cover ran out. The crew of a towed 3-inch gun covering the bridge—Sgt. Clyde Gentry was the commander, Cpl. Buel Sheridan the gunner—could see the tanks pass behind the buildings and waited nervously for the first one to appear at the other end. It was a Panther.

Before the tank could turn toward the bridge, presenting the protection of its heavy frontal armor, Sheridan got in two shots. The first missed, but the second ripped the turret off. A second Panther made it to the center of the little stone span under a hail of rounds both from Sheridan and from the crews of other towed guns before a round so damaged the turret and the gun that neither could traverse.

When two more Panthers emerged, Sheridan hit one in a track; as the driver tried to back up, he ran into a ditch and there foundered helplessly. The other came to a halt behind the last house, the muzzle brake on its cannon visible, but it made no further effort to advance.

That ended the attack from the south bank of the Amblève. Yet even as that fight was going on, another developed at the western end of town, the work of the 1st SS Panzer Division's reconnaissance battalion. Commanded by Maj. Gustav Knittel, that battalion had passed through Stavelot the night before to reach Peiper at La Gleize. Once Peiper learned of the American capture of Stavelot, he summoned Knittel to his command post in a farmhouse near the Château de Froid-Cour and told him to retake the town.

That was Knittel's first chance to talk with Peiper since his arrival. As he got ready to depart, he paused. "They've killed a good few at the crossroads," he said.

"The crossroads?" asked Peiper.

Yes, Knittel responded. The one where the road turned toward Ligneuville. "There're a lot of *Amis* dead there."

That was the first indication Joachim Peiper received that anything untoward had happened at the road junction at Baugnez. At about the same time, his superior, the commander of the Sixth Panzer Army, Sepp Dietrich, was also receiving his first information on the massacre. His chief of staff, General Kraemer, handed him a piece of paper containing a report of a radio broadcast from *Soldatensender Calais*, a British propaganda station over which German prisoners of war beamed reports aimed at the German soldier. According to the broadcast, some sixty Americans had been "shot by the enemy as they were surrendering or had already surrendered."

A message went out almost immediately from headquarters of the Sixth Panzer Army to subordinate units to conduct "an immediate enquiry whether anyone knew anything about the shooting of some American prisoners of war." Otto Skorzeny was one who received the message, and he reported in the negative. To Skorzeny, "such a crime was quite unthinkable in the German Army." The commander of the 1st SS Panzer Division, Colonel Mohnke, also submitted a negative report.

For the attack against the western side of Stavelot, Major Knittel obtained three Mark IVs to strengthen his own force of light tanks, armored cars, and half-tracks. Dividing his force, Knittel sent the main body directly up the road from Trois Ponts and the other part up a back road through the hamlets of Parfondruy, Ster, and Renardmont, on high ground overlooking Stavelot. Knittel hoped to pass beyond those hamlets and get in behind the Americans at Stavelot.

Knittel's means in no way matched his ambition, nor did he take into account the gunners of the 118th Field Artillery Battalion. Against the two German attacks at Stavelot that afternoon, the cannoneers fired three thousand shells. So rapidly did they work their pieces that they had to cool the tubes with water. As night came on December 19, Colonel Frankland's battalion of the 117th Infantry still had a firm grip on Stavelot, and during the night the infantrymen all but sealed their hold when a contingent of the 30th Division's 105th Engineer Combat Battalion, working behind a smoke screen under the noses of Germans on the other bank of the Amblève, at long last blew the stone bridge over the river.

The engineers who blew the bridge made a major contribution to continued defense of Stavelot, but their accomplishment failed to put an end to German efforts to force a way through the town, for unlike Peiper, the follow-up force of the 1st SS Panzer Division, commanded by Lt. Col.

Rudolf Sandig, had bridging equipment. Before daylight the next morning, December 20, a hundred men of the 2d SS Panzergrenadier Regiment, covered by heavy fire from tanks and self-propelled tank destroyers, began wading the icy, swift-flowing little river. Theirs was an incredibly difficult assignment, for at that spot both banks of the river were steep concrete revetments.

By the light of flares, American soldiers in the buildings facing the river had little difficulty picking off the men struggling through the water. Some concentrated their fire on those carrying makeshift ladders and on anybody who looked to be an officer, while supporting tanks fired white phosphorus shells in an attempt to light the scene by setting fire to houses on the other bank. When that failed, Sgt. William Pierce swam the river with a can of gasoline, emptied it against the side of a house, and set it afire.

A few of the Germans nevertheless managed to get into the first row of houses near the bridge, but their presence masked the fire of their supporting tanks and tank destroyers. Lieutenant Murray's platoon of Company A had little difficulty retaking the houses, and the German attack collapsed.

The killing of Belgian civilians by soldiers of *Kampfgruppe Peiper* began early on December 18 as the first Germans passed through Stavelot. Along a street leading to the road to Trois Ponts, a machine gunner on a half-track fired into the kitchen of the house of M. Gengoux, killing his fourteen-year-old son José. Nearby, Joseph Albert and his daughter, Denise, hiding in their cellar, heard a noise upstairs, and when M. Albert went to investigate, a German soldier shot him dead. On the fringe of Trois Ponts, two soldiers engaged M. Warnier and his wife briefly in conversation, then killed them both.

The next day, also among the few houses of Trois Ponts standing on the north bank of the Amblève, five German soldiers entered the house of M. Georgin, where Georgin, his wife, and three young neighbors were in the kitchen. "They are hiding terrorists here!" shouted one of the soldiers. Another ordered young Louis Nicolay to follow him, and as soon as they got outside killed him. Yet another ordered M. Georgin to accompany him, but when they were out of the house, Georgin made a run for it. As the German fired his burp gun, Georgin pretended to be hit and fell to the ground. "*Kaput,*" said the German to his companions, but he made no effort to investigate. Inch by inch, Georgin crept toward the bank of the Amblève, then leapt to his feet and threw himself into the swirling waters. As he reached the far bank, the Germans fired, almost severing one of Georgin's arms, but he got away. Nobody else in M. Georgin's house survived.

That night, the 19th, on the fringe of Stavelot, Mme. Régine Grégoire was taking refuge in a neighbor's cellar with her two children (aged four and nine) and twenty-three other people, all women and children except for two elderly men. A hand grenade rolled down the steps and exploded, harming nobody, but a second one wounded Madame Grégoire slightly in the leg. Shouts came from the top of the stairs: "*Heraus! Heraus!*"

Since Madame Grégoire spoke German (she was a native of Manderfeld in the Losheim Gap), she called out that there were only civilians in the cellar. When the Germans insisted that she come out, she went upstairs with her children in tow, there to find a dozen German soldiers whom she recognized by their uniforms as SS. Although she insisted there were only women and children in the cellar, and the two elderly men, the Germans demanded that everybody come into the garden.

There the soldiers pushed Madame Grégoire and her children to one side but forced the others to stand or kneel alongside a hedge. One soldier with a pistol, another with a rifle, then executed them methodically. They ranged in age from four to sixty-eight. Only Madame Grégoire and her children were spared.

Those were but a few incidents in what became an orgy of killing in Stavelot, Trois Ponts, and the hamlets of Parfondruy, Ster, and Renardmont. Here an old man and his wife; there a farmer in his barn; elsewhere twelve people collected in ones and twos and brought together in a house, executed, the house burned; one woman lying in her bed.

Of a population of just under a hundred people in Parfondruy, twenty-six were murdered. As best the Belgian authorities could determine, 138 people died in brutal, senseless executions.

For defending Stoumont, the men of the 3d Battalion, 119th Infantry, had the support of eight towed pieces of the 823d Tank Destroyer Battalion, which took up firing positions on the forward edge of town covering the highway from La Gleize and open fields on either side of the road. Although the 119th Infantry's normal artillery support had yet to arrive, the regimental commander, Colonel Sutherland, had the promise of support from the 400th Armored Field Artillery Battalion, newly attached to the 30th Division, although whether the self-propelled 105mm. howitzers would arrive in time remained to be seen. As soon as Sutherland learned that the Germans were close, he obtained from General Hobbs a promise of a company of mediums from the 743d Tank Battalion, the 30th Division's usual tank support, to arrive at dawn. Sutherland held his 1st Battalion in reserve near his headquarters three miles up the valley of the Amblève.

Also present at Stoumont were two weapons seldom employed in a ground role: powerful 90mm. antiaircraft guns. Under the command of 1st Lt. Donald McGuire, the two guns belonged to Battery C, 143d Antiaircraft Artillery Gun Battalion, which only a few days earlier had arrived from the United States. Such was the concern at headquarters of the First

Army about Peiper that even before anybody knew troops of the 119th Infantry were going to Stoumont, the First Army's antiaircraft officer, Col. Charles G. Patterson, ordered Battery C to go there and block Peiper.

Around 7 A.M. on December 19, with the first indications of daylight but with a dense fog blanketing the valley, Peiper threw his *SS-Panzergrenadiers* and his company of paratroopers against Stoumont. As those troops, supported by tanks and assault guns, began to advance, Lieutenant McGuire's two big antiaircraft guns were moving into position near a farmhouse along the La Gleize highway where a platoon of the 119th Infantry's Company I had established a roadblock. The crewmen were so nervous about their first combat that in trying to maneuver one of the guns into position, they got the prime mover entangled with the gun, and both mired in a ditch. The crew of the remaining gun dug it in near the farmhouse.

As the Germans approached, the fog and darkness were such that the crews of attacking tanks and defending antitank pieces alike could discern few targets. Lieutenant McGuire had yet to see his first tank when an infantry lieutenant ran up asking for two men "to take care of a tank." Although neither Pfc. Roland Seamon nor Pvt. Albert Darage had ever fired a bazooka, they volunteered, and the lieutenant, giving them a quick lesson with the weapon, told them to aim for the rear of the tank. As the two crept warily through the fog, each with a loaded bazooka, they found not one German tank but four, two of them Tigers, two Panthers. Each man fired into the rear of one of the tanks. "Biggest Goddamned noise I ever heard," said Seamon later. As both tanks began to burn, machine guns on the other two raked the roadside, and Seamon and Darage fell back to the farmhouse.

A short while later, one of the other tanks—a Tiger—came into the vision of McGuire's remaining 90mm. gun. A first round hit near the tank's left front sprocket, while a second sheered off most of the barrel of the tank's cannon. "The escape hatch flew open, and the crew boiled out."

By that time, German foot troops were closing in on the farmhouse, and a half-track bringing ammunition to McGuire's gun went up in flames. Since the exploding ammunition was threatening the gun crew, the sergeant in charge ordered his men out and put a rifle grenade down the barrel. Moments later ammunition stacked close to the gun exploded.

Although the outpost at the farmhouse was fast collapsing, the men of the 119th Infantry at other places were turning Peiper's *SS-Panzergrenadiers* and paratroopers back, and Peiper was soon aware that the concern he had felt the night before was real: fatigue and frustration had taken something out of his men. As he himself rallied the foot troops, he saw the incredible spectacle of many of his tanks backing up. At Peiper's order, the tank commander, Major Poetschke, moved personally to get the vehicles moving forward again. Seizing a *Panzerfaust*, he went from tank to tank, threatening "every commander to shoot him down if he went back one more meter."

Just as the German attack picked up momentum, part of the promised defensive tank support—two platoons of Company C, 743d Tank Battalion, under 1st Lt. Walter D. Macht—arrived in Stoumont. Those ten tanks hurried to the fringe of the town, but they arrived scant minutes too late, for Company I astride the road to La Gleize was falling apart. As the infantry broke, a round from a German tank knocked out one of the towed tank destroyers, small-arms fire killed the entire crew of another, and most of the other crews, unable to manhandle their ponderous pieces, joined the flight.

Inside Stoumont, near Colonel Fitzgerald's command post in the schoolhouse, Company I's leaders managed to stem the hegira. There the tanks and a bazooka accounted for six German tanks, either destroyed or disabled, but *SS-Panzergrenadiers* continued to pour into town. After two hours of fighting, little of Company I remained (the company later counted twenty-four survivors). Since the advance into the center of Stoumont threatened the other two rifle companies to the southeast and northeast of the town, Fitzgerald ordered them to withdraw. The men of Company L had a covered route of retreat; those of Company K, on the other hand, had to join the survivors of Company I and Fitzgerald himself in flight down the main road toward Targnon and Stoumont Station while fire from German tanks and assault guns exploded all around them.

Fairly early in the fighting, word of the crisis in Stoumont reached the regimental commander, Colonel Sutherland, who promptly sent Company C of his reserve battalion forward in trucks. As the trucks reached Targnon, the men of Companies I and K passed them fleeing the other way. Five hundred yards beyond the hamlet, the company commander, Capt. Donald R. Fell, ordered his men to dismount and continue on foot.

As Fell drew closer to Stoumont, he came upon the commander of the American tanks, Lieutenant Macht, whose mediums were falling back by bounds, one group providing covering fire while the other withdrew, then repeating the process. Incredibly, Macht had lost not a tank, but all were rapidly running out of ammunition. Together, he and Fell agreed to conduct a fighting withdrawal until additional reinforcements arrived. That was already beginning to happen, for a battery of the 400th Armored Field Artillery Battalion had reached firing positions, but by that time there was little that artillery support could do to resolve the crisis.

With German foot troops and tanks close behind, Fell's infantry and Macht's tanks fell back through Targnon and thence down the hill toward Stoumont Station at the bottom of the valley. At a sharp bend in the road just short of the station, they gained some help from a 90mm. antiaircraft gun that the commander of Battery C, 1st Lt. Jack Kent, had been trying to move into Stoumont but, despairing of that, had put into position near the station. The big piece knocked out a half-track and two Panthers before pressure from the approaching *SS-Panzergrenadiers* prompted Kent to order his gun destroyed.

At Colonel Sutherland's command post, the commander of the 30th Division, General Hobbs, had arrived. He was swiftly in touch with headquarters of the First Army, asking for additional tank support. Without it, it appeared that Peiper would soon force his way out of the valley of the Amblève and—as the American commanders believed—turn on Liège. From one of Sutherland's staff officers, Hobbs had learned that the 740th Tank Battalion, newly arrived in Europe, was waiting to draw tanks and equipment from an ordnance depot at Sprimont, only a few miles from Sutherland's command post. When Hobbs asked for that battalion, General Hodges approved.

As it turned out, there were precious few tanks and little equipment at that ordnance depot. The battalion commander, Lt. Col. George K. Rubel, and most of his men had arrived at the depot the day before on the theory that they soon would be committed somewhere; but they had found that it was a repair depot with only about fifteen tanks that could be made operable. The crewmen worked through the night, robbing parts from other tanks to get those operating and in the end appropriating anything that would run and had some firepower—self-propelled 105mm. howitzers, self-propelled tank destroyers, nine light tanks, towed 75mm. pack howitzers, armored cars, whatever. Few of the vehicles had radios, so that the men in them would have to communicate by visual signals.

By the time word came for the 740th Tank Battalion to move to help the 119th Infantry, Company C, commanded by Capt. James D. Berry, had fourteen Shermans, five duplex-drive (amphibious) Shermans, and an M-36 (a self-propelled tank destroyer with a 90mm. piece). As Berry moved past Sutherland's command post, he told one of the staff officers: "They're bastard tanks but we're shooting fools."

When Berry and his bastard tanks neared Stoumont Station, Lieutenant Macht's tanks, down to only a few rounds of ammunition among them, and the 119th Infantry's reserve 1st Battalion, commanded by Lt. Col. Robert Herlong, had blocked the valley road a thousand yards behind the station at a point where the railroad and the river on one side and a steeply rising wooded cliff on the other sharply restricted passage. By that time, the 119th Infantry's normal artillery support, the 197th Field Artillery Battalion, was ready to fire, and any of Peiper's tanks coming past Stoumont Station would do so at their peril.

While Macht's tanks withdrew, Berry's took their place. At the order of Colonel Sutherland, Colonel Herlong and his infantry, with Berry's support, were to drive back up the road and gain a good line of departure for retaking Stoumont the next morning.

It was around four o'clock, with the evening closing in and fog swelling up from the river. A Sherman commanded by 2d Lt. Charles D.

Powers led the way. In the gathering fog and darkness, Powers knew that all might depend on his getting in the first shot. Hugging the cliff side of the road, he rounded a curve just short of Stoumont Station. Ahead of him, barely discernible in the haze, he made out the form of a Panther. When he fired, his shot ricocheted off the gun mantlet and penetrated downward into the driver's compartment, setting the tank on fire.

Continuing to advance cautiously, Powers made out another Mark V. Again he got off the first shot, but it ricocheted off the heavy front slope plate, and Powers's gun jammed. Standing in the turret, he signaled for help from Staff Sgt. Charles W. Loopey, who was close behind in the M-36 tank destroyer. The first round from Loopey's 90mm. gun set the German tank on fire. With Powers's gun at last cleared, the lieutenant continued forward. Finding a third Panther, he knocked off the muzzle brake from its cannon with his first round and with two more set the tank on fire.

With darkness descending and the three destroyed Panthers forming an effective roadblock, Berry's Company C, 740th Tank Battalion, in its first taste of combat, and Herlong's 1st Battalion, 119th Infantry, holed up for the night, blocking the road and the valley of the Amblève at Stoumont Station. As the commander of the 119th Infantry, Colonel Sutherland, knew, he was to get his 2d Battalion back that night from its assignment in front of Werbomont protecting the assembly of the 82d Airborne Division, so that on the morrow he would have two full battalions for retaking Stoumont. In response to persistent demands from headquarters of the First Army, Sutherland sent what was left of Fitzgerald's 3d Battalion to block a secondary road leading through woods north of Stoumont to Chaudfontaine and Liège.

What Berry, Herlong, Sutherland, Hobbs, Gerow, Hodges, and everybody else on the American side could not know was that Joachim Peiper had no intention either of driving on Liège or of continuing up the valley of the Amblève. What he wanted to do was get out of the valley by way of the bridge between Targnon and Stoumont Station. Although a patrol had discovered that that was only a footbridge, the original bridge having been destroyed as the Germans retreated in September, there was a ford nearby with firm footing.

Nevertheless, as night came on December 19, Peiper recognized that taking even that route was beyond his means. The day's fighting had left his gasoline tanks almost dry. (Peiper was still unaware that salvation in the form of 2 million gallons of American gasoline was to be found not far away in the woods just north of La Gleize.)

By radio, he asked permission to use his small amount of remaining fuel to turn around and fight his way back to the rest of the 1st SS Panzer Division, but the division commander, Colonel Mohnke, said no. Peiper was to hold where he was until the rest of the division broke through to

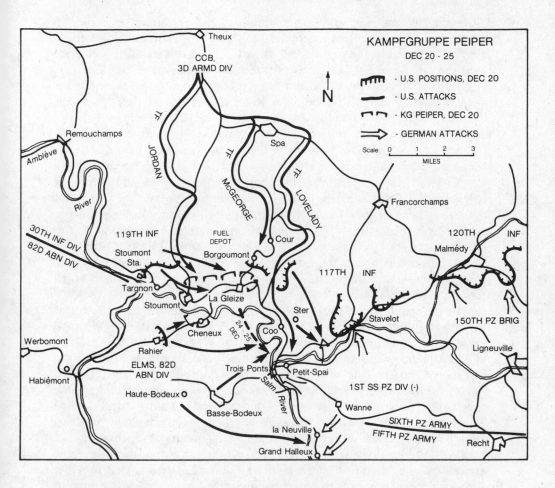

him, perhaps in two to three days, whereupon the entire division was to resume the drive to the Meuse.

During the night of the 19th, some help did reach *Kampfgruppe Peiper:* a battalion of the 2d SS Panzergrenadier Regiment, moving mostly on foot by way of a wooden span over the Amblève at the hamlet of Petit-Spai, just upstream from Trois Ponts and the railroad underpasses through which the road from Stavelot led to Trois Ponts. German engineers had been working on that little bridge since the previous night, and it was finally capable of carrying light vehicles. When the *SS-Panzergrenadiers* crossed, they were able to take a small amount of gasoline with them.

Yet even that makeshift supply route might soon be denied Peiper, for the net around him was tightening on both banks of the Amblève.

Early on the morning of December 19, the commander of the 82d

Airborne Division, General Gavin, knew little of the situation—friendly or enemy—in front of his assembling troops at Werbomont. His orders were to push out to the east and southeast in hope of establishing contact with the 7th Armored Division and the other defenders of St. Vith.

It turned out for the most part to be an uncontested march, for there were no Germans short of the Salm River except for the defenders that Colonel Peiper had left to hold Cheneux and the nearby bridge over the Amblève. By nightfall, one of Gavin's regiments was in Rahier, close to Cheneux, where civilians told the men that the Germans held Cheneux. Men of another regiment penetrated the next day, December 20, all the way to Trois Ponts. There, much to their surprise, they found the men of Company C, 51st Engineer Combat Battalion, who on the 18th had thwarted *Kampfgruppe Peiper* by demolishing the three bridges in and around Trois Ponts. (Said the engineer commander, Major Yates, to the paratroopers, "I'll bet you guys are glad we are here.") Patrols from that regiment, the 505th Parachute Infantry, were soon pushing up the valley of the Salm, where they established contact with patrols from the 7th Armored Division.

On the other side of the Amblève, early on December 20, a powerful force was joining the 30th Division for the fight against *Kampfgruppe Peiper:* the 3d Armored Division's Combat Command B. The 3d Armored Division was one of those two American armored divisions in the European Theater (the other was the 2d Armored) organized under a Table of Organization and Equipment, subsequently superseded, which called not for three separate tank and armored infantry battalions, as with later divisions, but for two tank regiments (four medium and two light battalions) and an armored infantry regiment (three battalions). Each of the two divisions had not quite 4,000 more men than the later armored divisions and 55 more medium tanks (232 as opposed to 177). Although there was no separate headquarters for a Combat Command Reserve, the division commanders usually held out portions of their commands as a reserve under the control of one of the regimental headquarters.

As the 3d Armored Division's CCB reached the scene, the combat command had two full medium tank battalions, a battalion of armored infantry, a company of armored engineers, and a battalion of self-propelled 105mm. howitzers. Ordered to clear the north bank of the Amblève between Stavelot and La Gleize, and in conjunction with Sutherland's 119th Infantry to clamp a vise on *Kampfgruppe Peiper*, Brig. Gen. Truman E. Boudinot divided his combat command into three task forces, all three to drive along woods roads leading into the valley of the Amblève from the vicinity of Spa.

The largest of the three, named for its commander, Lt. Col. William B. Lovelady, consisted of a battalion of tanks and a company of armored infantry. The task force passed without incident through the woods to gain the valley highway near the village of Coo, in happier times a center for tourists visiting a nearby waterfall. As Lovelady's tanks turned down the road toward Trois Ponts, a small German column appeared around a bend in the road. Consisting of a few self-propelled guns, some infantry, and a few trucks carrying gasoline, the column had crossed the Amblève over the wooden bridge at Petit-Spai. Lovelady's tanks quickly ripped it to pieces, and the presence of those tanks ended the little trickle of supplies reaching Peiper by way of Petit-Spai and split Major Knittel's reconnaissance troops at Stavelot from *Kampfgruppe Peiper.*

The central task force, commanded by Maj. Kenneth T. McGeorge and consisting of a company each of medium tanks and armored infantry, headed for La Gleize by way of the woods road leading past the big gasoline depot near the hamlet of Cour. And the third task force, commanded by Capt. John W. Jordan, which had a company of light tanks, a few mediums, and a company of armored infantry, moved toward Stoumont along the woods road blocked earlier by the 119th Infantry's 3d Battalion to prevent Peiper from turning north toward Liège. Since both of those task forces ran head-on into Peiper's strength, neither was able to get past the woodsline overlooking La Gleize and Stoumont.

Less than a quarter of a mile outside Stoumont, on a steep hillside overlooking the road to Targnon, stood the St. Edouard Sanitorium, a large four-storied brick building maintained by a Catholic order for convalescent children and young girls and the elderly. As the two priests and the sisters staffing the sanitorium learned of the German advance, they had no choice but to remain, for there was no way to evacuate their frail charges. They were immensely relieved when after nightfall on December 18, American troops arrived in Stoumont, and twenty of them established an outpost in the sanitorium.

Their relief was short-lived. In mid-morning of the 19th, as the sisters herded everybody into the basement—250 civilians all told—the Germans attacked, and the little band of Americans surrendered. "You have nothing to fear from us," a German noncommissioned officer assured the priests and the sisters, "if you do nothing. But we had to shoot some people in Stavelot who fired on our troops from the windows of the houses." It was the old rationale, noted the sisters, the shibboleth of *francs-tireurs* that the Germans had used as long ago as the Great War to justify the killing of Belgian civilians.

To the commander of the 119th Infantry's 1st Battalion, Colonel Herlong, it was obvious that if he was to pass along the highway below the windows of the sanitorium and retake Stoumont, he would have to seize the big building. With artillery support at last available and a company of the bastard tanks of the 740th Tank Battalion, some of them fitted overnight with radios, Herlong began his attack early on December 20 through fog swirling up from the river bottom.

Almost at the moment the attack began, a Panther covering the road opened fire, but the leading American tank, commanded by 1st Lt. John E. Callaway, knocked it out with a round that "opened its muzzle up like a rose." A few hundred yards farther along the road, Callaway knocked out two half-tracks, but it was soon evident that those vehicles were only outposts. The Germans had pulled back from Targnon, and beyond the hamlet they had liberally strewn antitank mines, covered by fire from infantry dug in on the steeply rising slope above the road. It took all day for Herlong's infantry and the supporting tanks to eliminate those Germans and get past the minefields.

As night was approaching and fog was again rising from the river bottom, Herlong's force had come within the length of a few football fields of Stoumont when a round from a German gun damaged the leading tank, commanded by 2d Lt. David Oglansky. Although Oglansky's gun was disabled, his motor still functioned. In view of the approaching darkness, the commander of the tank company, Captain Berry, with Herlong's approval, ordered the attack halted for the night and Oglansky's tank placed sideways as a roadblock. While one of the rifle companies dug in around the tank, the other two started up the hill to take the St. Edouard Sanitorium.

On the downhill side of the sanitorium was a stone retaining wall, a kind of glacis, some five feet high, sufficient to prevent a vehicle (even a tank) from climbing it but no real obstacle for men on foot. After a short artillery preparation, men of the two companies clambered over the embankment and under concealment of the fog and gathering darkness stormed the building.

As Father Hanlet, one of the two priests in the basement of the sanitorium, described it:

> Fighting raged around us and over our heads . . . and in the halls and the rooms. . . . Suddenly, a door to the basement opened and shots echoed on the stairway, evoking heart-rending cries: "Civilians! Civilians!" Some American soldiers descended: we were saved! What joy, what relief! The Sister Superior recited a dozen rosaries for the eternal rest of the soldiers killed in the battle . . . while the Americans set up their guns on the first floor and, in the kitchen, made hot water for tea, coffee, and chocolate. Our liberators were as happy as we were.

Although the Americans promised that they would evacuate everybody at daylight, that was not to be, for the strategic location of the St. Edouard Sanitorium was no less apparent to Joachim Peiper than it was to Robert Herlong. Supported by tanks firing from a road above the sanitorium, a hundred *SS-Panzergrenadiers* shouting "*Heil, Hitler!*" charged the building. The fight raged from room to room, and the German tanks moved in close enough to fire into the windows.

Down on the road below, Captain Berry's tanks tried to come to the rescue, but they were unable to get beyond the steep embankment. A *Panzerfaust* set one afire, and when German flares lit the landscape, German tanks from their positions higher up the slope knocked out two more.

Most of the Americans in the sanitorium eventually got out to form a line along a hedge only fifty yards from the building. Thirty-three surrendered, but in an annex to the building, Sgt. William J. Widener and eleven other men held out. Well into the night, Widener called out sensings to an artillery observer in the defensive line on the grounds.

Meanwhile, down in the basement Father Hanlet moved to help an American who was badly wounded in the arm and losing blood rapidly. Although Father Hanlet applied a tourniquet, he was so concerned the man still might die that he administered the last rites of the church. "Thank you," the man whispered. "I understand what you have said and done. My wife is very Catholic; should I die, she will be pleased. Thank you."

The Germans soon brought in another American, wounded in the knee, and two wounded Germans. The sole German medic was so busy that Father Hanlet, recalling that one of the American prisoners appeared to be a medic, suggested that the Germans enlist his help. Soon the two medics were working side by side.

Taking pity on the American whom the priest thought was dying, a German noncommissioned officer lit a cigarette and placed it between the man's lips. The man took a few puffs and seemed to revive. Fumbling in his pockets, he came up with a piece of chocolate and handed it to the German. The sergeant thanked him, but turning away, he whispered to the priest: "I can't eat it; it's covered with blood."

Outside, two hours before daylight, the Germans tried to expand their success at the sanitorium by a foray out of Stoumont along the highway to Targnon. When a round from a self-propelled gun knocked out Lieutenant Oglansky's tank, set in place as a roadblock, Oglansky told his crew to head for the rear while he took command of a nearby tank. He was hardly aboard when a *Panzerfaust* knocked it out, setting the tank on fire. Other *Panzerfausts* knocked out two more tanks, which also began to burn. Together with Oglansky's immobile tank, the three burning vehicles effectively blocked the road. The heat from the flames was so intense that nobody could get near, nor could the *SS-Panzergrenadiers* get past.

When combined with heavy shelling from supporting artillery, that put an end to the sortie from Stoumont; but Herlong's infantry and Berry's tanks were in no shape to renew their attacks on the sanitorium and Stoumont right away. The wild night had cost both forces dearly, including the loss of almost half the two rifle companies that fought at the sanitorium.

*　　*　　*

Only a few miles away on the other side of the Amblève River, the 82d Airborne Division's 504th Parachute Infantry during the afternoon of December 20 sent a patrol probing toward Cheneux. The regimental commander, Col. Reuben H. Tucker, was anxious to take the village, both because it was on higher ground than Rahier, where his troops were located, and because Cheneux and the nearby bridge in German hands posed a threat to the entire airborne division. As the patrol soon discovered, the Germans were in Cheneux in force: most of Peiper's light flak battalion with its self-propelled 20mm. flak guns and a company of the newly arrived battalion of the 2d SS Panzergrenadier Regiment that had crossed the wooden bridge at Petit-Spai the night before.

In mid-afternoon, with a heavy mist limiting visibility to two hundred yards, Tucker sent two companies in an approach march formation across open fields toward Cheneux. The mist made it impossible to bring down accurate artillery fire, so that the only real fire support the companies had was from a 77mm. assault howitzer mounted on a half-track that the Germans had left behind when they withdrew before the destroyed bridge near Habiémont. Men of both companies soon went to ground, punished by fire from machine guns and flak guns in Cheneux. As night fell, the company commanders pulled their men back to the edge of a small wood.

When Colonel Tucker learned of the withdrawal, he insisted that the companies resume the attack. Concealed by the darkness, the paratroopers made good progress at first, despite barbed-wire fences that tore at their uniforms and their flesh. They were within two hundred yards of a roadblock on the edge of the village before German gunners opened a withering fire. Again the men went to ground, but as the firing continued, Staff Sgt. George Walsh of Company B jumped to his feet and shouted: "Let's get the sons of bitches!" That got the attack moving again. Men fell left and right, wounded or dead, some left hanging on the barbed-wire fences, but the survivors plodded on.

Walsh and a few other men were soon atop the roadblock. Walsh himself tossed a hand grenade into a flak wagon, knocking out the crew. A second man jumped aboard another flak wagon and slashed the gunner's throat with his knife. Hand-to-hand fighting was still going on when two self-propelled tank destroyers, which Colonel Tucker had been trying to locate for hours, at last moved forward. With the help of those pieces, the survivors of the two companies soon had a toehold in the village, but so few men were left that they were unable to clear the rest of the buildings. Although the battalion commander, Lt. Col. Willard E. Harrison, came forward, he could provide no help, for his remaining company was on a separate mission elsewhere.

Colonel Tucker, meanwhile, decided on a wide encirclement of the village to get in behind the Germans at the bridge over the Amblève and soon had his 3d Battalion on the march. It was late afternoon of the next day, December 21, before that battalion gained high ground overlooking the bridge; but at that point the Germans in Cheneux were cut off, and Company G, sent to reinforce, attacked to clear the village. In gathering darkness, some of the Germans escaped to make their way across the Amblève. They left behind fourteen flak wagons, a battery of self-propelled 105mm. assault guns, six half-tracks, a few trucks and other vehicles, and mounds of dead *SS-Panzergrenadiers.*

In the attack on Cheneux, the two companies of Harrison's battalion lost 23 men killed and 202 wounded, including all the officers of Company B. That brought Company B down to eighteen men, and Company C to thirty-eight men and three officers.

The story of the attack of those two companies was another of those incredibly heroic actions. But however courageous, the unsupported infantry attack across open fields laced with barbed-wire fences was as ill-conceived and senseless as many of the herdlike German assaults, such as those against Lieutenant Bouck's I&R Platoon outside Lanzerath. Afforded time to mount an attack with accurate artillery support—or even with the support of just the two tank destroyers—those companies could have taken Cheneux at far less cost and with no great forfeiture of time.

CHAPTER TWENTY-TWO

The Last Days of *Kampfgruppe Peiper*

The stands by American troops in front of the Elsenborn Ridge and at Dom. Bütgenbach were having a marked effect on the fortunes of *Kampfgruppe Peiper*. First, they denied Peiper help from the 12th SS Panzer Division along his north flank. Second, because they made it necessary for the 3d Parachute Division to hold an elongated defensive front extending all the way from Bütgenbach to Waimes, they denied him help from the paratroopers in keeping his supply route open at Stavelot.

Meanwhile, in the Losheim Gap, the fitful but nevertheless time-consuming fight by men of the 14th Cavalry Group had delayed the advance of the rest of the 1st SS Panzer Division, trying to get through to Peiper and bring him gasoline. The massive traffic tie-ups in the gap had further delayed the follow-up force, as did brushes with the defenders of the developing horseshoe defense of St. Vith at Poteau.

By the time engineers supporting Colonel Frankland's battalion of the 117th Infantry had destroyed the bridge over the Amblève in Stavelot, only seven Tiger tanks plus Major Knittel's reconnaissance battalion of the follow-up force had come through, and Frankland's troops had repulsed two attempts by tanks and a battalion of the 2d SS Panzergrenadier Regiment to get across the river, once before the bridge was blown, once after. The remaining battalion of that regiment (one had been with Peiper from the start) had nevertheless crossed during the night of the 19th over the wooden bridge at Petit-Spai. Throughout December 20, a few men and light vehicles continued to cross that span; but early on the morning of December 21, when a self-propelled tank destroyer tried to cross, the bridge collapsed.

To the commander of the 1st SS Panzer Corps, General Priess, to try to continue to gain any advantage from *Kampfgruppe Peiper*'s breakthrough seemed sheer folly. It was time, in Priess's view, to cut the losses, to tell Peiper to fight his way out. Yet Priess's superior, Sepp Dietrich, disagreed completely, for Dietrich was determined to wring

450

every possible advantage from the one success his Sixth Panzer Army had achieved.

At Dietrich's order, Colonel Mohnke on December 21 was to employ every available resource to break through to Peiper. He was also to employ an additional resource, Otto Skorzeny's 150th Panzer Brigade, in order to take Malmédy and open up roads that might be employed to get through to Peiper, and also to get in behind the stalwart American opposition on the Elsenborn Ridge.

On the American side, senior commanders were sensing the kill, and as soon as *Kampfgruppe Peiper* could be eliminated, General Hodges intended driving through to relieve the troops at St. Vith and close the gap between Malmédy and St. Vith. To facilitate control of that attack, he placed the entire 30th Division and the 3d Armored Division's CCB under General Ridgway and the XVIII Airborne Corps.

Using the 150th Panzer Brigade as a regular ground combat force was the idea of Skorzeny himself, who had become convinced as early as the evening of the second day of the offensive, December 17, that his brigade would be unable to accomplish its mission of seizing bridges over the Meuse. When he made the suggestion at Dietrich's headquarters around midnight, Dietrich told him to report to Mohnke, who had established his headquarters in the Hôtel du Moulin in Ligneuville. The fact that the journey would involve Skorzeny's going beyond the German frontier, which Hitler had expressly forbidden, was of no concern to Skorzeny.

Part of the rationale in attacking Malmédy was that early in the offensive one of Skorzeny's operatives had reported entering the town and finding it lightly held. Unknown to Skorzeny, that had markedly changed. Although Colonel Pergrin's little band of 291st Engineers was still there, the engineers had been strengthened early by Colonel Hansen's Norweigians and by part of the 526th Armored Infantry Battalion, then by all of the 30th Division's 120th Infantry. Amid the hills and valleys behind the town there were six artillery battalions, and December 21 was the date on which American artillery was to be free—as authorized by the War Department at General Eisenhower's request—to use the VT or POZIT fuse on its shells.

Skorzeny's was "a motley crew." A few men had full American uniforms, including dog tags; others had American trousers and boots but German tunics; still others had American field jackets but German trousers; and some were in full German uniform. There were a few captured American jeeps and armored cars, but the ten tanks available to Skorzeny were either Mark IVs or Panthers, most of which had been fitted with sheet metal to create sloping sides in an attempt to make them look like American tanks, and painted with the Allied marking, a white star in a white circle. Along with a few assault guns and mortars, those would provide the only heavy fire support, for Skorzeny had no artillery at his disposal.

Three hours before daylight on December 21, as a dense fog blanketed the valley of the little Warche River, which runs through Malmédy, one of two German columns struck down Highway N-23 past the Baugnez road junction along the principal road into the town from the south (*see map, Chapter Twenty-one, p. 443*). Almost all of the 120 men involved wore all or some part of American uniforms, but they got nowhere. Late the previous day, the Americans had captured one of Skorzeny's men, who revealed that the Germans would attack at three thirty the next morning, and the defenders were on full alert. The leading half-track set off a mine and exploded, throwing vehicle parts, equipment, and human flesh high into the big ash trees lining the road, the same trees Pergrin's engineers had been planning to blow five days earlier but which still stood.

Men of the 120th Infantry's 1st Battalion stopped that thrust, and the artillery, making plentiful use of the new fuse that produced deadly air bursts, finished the Germans off. By the time daylight came, none other than dead Germans was to be found along the road from Baugnez.

Skorzeny's main force, which included all ten tanks, attacked by way of a dirt road leading along a winding route from Ligneuville to the Malmédy-Stavelot highway a mile southwest of Malmédy, then over a temporary but sturdy wooden bridge carrying the highway across the Warche River just before the little stream wends southward to join the Amblève. Since the highway and most of Malmédy itself were on the south bank of the Warche, the Germans had no need of the bridge in order to take the town, but they would need it to turn toward Stavelot or to use the road to Spa. Although the 291st Engineers had prepared the bridge for demolition, they had yet to connect the detonator, and as two American engineers arrived to do that, they were too late. Skorzeny's attack was already under way, signaled by a blaze of light as the Germans crossed a field and tripped wires the defenders had installed to set off flares.

Part of the infantry, accompanied by a single Panther, swung toward Malmédy, where the Norwegians of the 99th Infantry Battalion were dug in atop a railroad embankment. In the fog and darkness some of the Germans, shouting in English "Surrender or die!," made it to the foot of the embankment, but machine-gun fire and hand grenades rolled down from above finished them off. When the Panther tried to break through a roadblock where the Malmédy-Stavelot highway passed under a trestle, a round from a towed piece of the 825th Tank Destroyer Battalion damaged it and prompted the commander to pull back, and American artillery again took command of the field. Under the devastating fire of shells equipped with the VT fuse, some of the Germans panicked, running not away from the air bursts but full into them, all the while shouting "*Kamerad!*"

The going was rougher near the bridge, for there were to be found the other nine German tanks. One early set off an antitank mine and began to burn, but the others were soon shooting up the landscape. The tanks forced back a platoon of the 120th Infantry's Company K that was manning a roadblock in front of the bridge, partly because the crews of two towed tank destroyers were away from their pieces as the Germans struck. When one tank crossed the bridge and headed toward Stavelot, a forward observer for 81mm. mortars, 2d Lt. Arnold L. Snyder, knocked it out from the rear with a bazooka. Pfcs. Francis S. Currey and Adam Lucero hit the turret of another with a rocket from a bazooka, so damaging the tank that it was unable to fire, and the crew abandoned it.

From a steep bluff along the road to Spa, three towed tank destroyers drove several of the remaining tanks to cover behind a masonry wall beside a house. Two self-propelled tank destroyers then drove forward from a roadblock along the road to Stavelot, crumpled the wall with fire from their 76mm. pieces, and knocked out two of the tanks.

With the German tanks reduced to four, much of the sting passed from the attack, but fighting continued into the early afternoon, mostly around a paper mill and houses near the bridge where some of the Germans holed up. From a hill overlooking the battlefield, Otto Skorzeny could see the turn the fight was taking and ordered everybody to fall back, but none of the tanks succeeded.

That evening, as Skorzeny was driving to Colonel Mohnke's command post in the Hôtel du Moulin in Ligneuville, he came under artillery fire, and a fragment ripped the flesh over his right eye. Although he reported to an aid station, where medical officers removed the fragment and sutured the wound, he refused evacuation.

Except for minor defensive assignments, the attack on Malmédy marked the end of Skorzeny's participation in the offensive and that of the 150th Panzer Brigade. Neither of Hitler's two special units—von der Heydte's and Skorzeny's—had accomplished much of anything.

As part of the renewed effort to break through to Peiper, the battalion of the 2d SS Panzergrenadier Regiment that had twice tried to cross the Amblève at Stavelot tried again on the morning of the 21st. Again the *SS-Panzergrenadiers* attempted to wade the stream, their weapons held high above their heads; but they displayed considerably less spirit than on the day before, and they had no tank support. The attack quickly collapsed. Although a few men of the battalion were later to get across the river along an undefended sector between Stavelot and Trois Ponts, the presence of Task Force Lovelady prevented them from reaching Peiper. All they could do was augment Knittel's reconnaissance troops in the hamlets overlooking Stavelot, eventually to be mopped up along with Knittel's men by troops of the 117th Infantry supported by Lovelady's tanks.

The 1st SS Panzergrenadier Regiment, which had seen little fighting except for a brief encounter against the forming American line behind St.

Vith, made Mohnke's main effort, supported by self-propelled tank destroyers and tanks transferred from support of the other *SS-Panzergrenadier* regiment. The troops were to get across the Salm River at Trois Ponts and farther upstream.

By that time, a company of the 82d Airborne Division's 505th Parachute Infantry had established a small bridgehead beyond the Salm on the heights around the railroad station across from Trois Ponts, and the rest of the regiment had dug in at likely crossing sites upstream. At the hamlets of La Neuville and Grand Halleux, the paratroopers wired two bridges across the Salm for demolition but delayed blowing them in anticipation of the projected drive on St. Vith.

Trying to cover a front of close to eight thousand yards—more than four miles—the paratroopers were nowhere strong. Such a distance would have been a severe test for an infantry regiment, and parachute regiments were considerably smaller than infantry regiments. Their three battalions had only three companies as opposed to four in infantry battalions, and the companies even at full strength had only 140 men.

The main German thrust hit Company E around the railroad station on the high ground across the river from Trois Ponts. Commanded by 1st Lt. William J. Muddagh, the 110 men of the company fought back with determination, using one platoon as a counterattacking force whenever a penetration seemed about to develop, and making good use of the fires of the 456th Parachute Field Artillery Battalion. Yet it was a fight against markedly uneven odds. Although the battalion commander, Lt. Col. Benjamin V. Vandervoort, wanted to withdraw the company, his regimental commander, Col. William E. Ekman, had ordered the bridgehead established, and Vandervoort was out of communication both with Ekman and the division headquarters. Unwilling to order withdrawal without higher authority, Vandervoort sent first a platoon then all of Company F across the debris of the destroyed bridge in the heart of Trois Ponts to join the fight on the far bank.

Those two companies were holding their own, partly because the ground was so soggy that the German tanks and tank destroyers were unable to close, when in early afternoon the assistant division commander, Col. Ira P. Swift, arrived at Vandervoort's headquarters. Maintaining the little bridgehead, said Swift, was costing more than it was worth. Although conscious of the difficulty of withdrawing in daylight while engaged at close quarters, he saw that as preferable to having the two companies cut to pieces.

As the paratroopers began to pull back, a few men at a time, the Germans quickly sensed what was happening and launched a final charge. For the paratroopers, it became a case of *sauve qui peut*. Men raced down the steep hill, stumbling, falling; some jumped from the cliff into the river; others scrambled frantically over the debris of the bridge. Almost all the men of Company F made it to safety, but Muddagh's Company E left half its strength on the far bank.

Although the SS troops had eliminated the little bridgehead, they were still unable to cross the river. Major Yates's engineers covering the remains of the bridge with fire saw to that. And when the German attempts ceased, the engineers subjected what was left of the bridge to a second demolition, then withdrew to be committed elsewhere with the main body of their battalion.

Late in the day, upstream at La Neuville and Grand Halleux, the Germans mounted lesser attacks; but in both cases, as German vehicles drew near, the paratroopers blew the bridges. Through the night and into the next day, the 1st SS Panzergrenadier Regiment continued to try to cross the Salm, and in several places small groups made it, for there was no solid defensive line; but each time the paratroopers either killed the Germans or drove them back. Nobody was getting through to help *Kampfgruppe Peiper*.

Early on December 19, the commander of the 30th Division, General Hobbs, sent his assistant division commander, Brig. Gen. William K. Harrison, to command all the forces around Stoumont—Colonel Sutherland's 119th Infantry and Task Forces McGeorge and Jordan of the 3d Armored Division's CCB—in order to take Stoumont and capture La Gleize. He was under some pressure to get the job over with, for not only was the presence of *Kampfgruppe Peiper* holding up a drive to close the gap between Malmédy and St. Vith; it was also delaying a transfer of the 3d Armored Division's CCB elsewhere to oppose rampaging German tanks.

However unsuccessful the German sortie from Stoumont down the highway toward Targnon before daylight on December 21, it nevertheless delayed the start of what Harrison intended as a three-pronged attack on Stoumont; for Harrison had to afford the commander of the 119th Infantry's 1st Battalion, Colonel Herlong, time to get his troops into some kind of order following that foray and the costly fighting for the St. Edouard Sanitorium. In the interim, the 119th Infantry's Cannon Company joined the 197th Field Artillery Battalion in heavy shelling of the sanitorium and the town, while the 119th Infantry's 2d Battalion under Maj. Hal D. Mc-Cown began a long foot march through the woods above Stoumont to push downhill from the woods, cut the La Gleize-Stoumont highway, and have at Stoumont from the rear.

When Herlong's infantry soon after midday at last renewed the attack against the sanitorium—still a prerequisite for the drive on Stoumont—a few men managed to get inside the building; but when a German tank moved in close and began firing through the windows, those men fell back under the concealment of a smoke screen fired by mortars. Nor did an attempt by Task Force Jordan to drive into Stoumont from the woods north of the town fare any better, for again fire from German tanks denied exit along the narrow road leading out of the forest.

Only Major McCown's 2d Battalion achieved any success. Encountering no opposition during the long march through the woods, the battalion in early afternoon debouched into the open and quickly cut the highway between Stoumont and La Gleize. As soon as the Germans discovered the battalion's presence, tanks and assault guns began firing from both Stoumont and La Gleize, and Peiper started preparing a counterattack; for the cutting of the highway left only a meandering dirt road alongside the river linking his two forces.

Because Task Force Jordan's tanks were supposed to join McCown's battalion but failed to show, McCown set out with his orderly and radio operator to find them. The three were climbing a steep, wooded slope when a German soldier jumped from behind a bush. Although McCown killed him with fire from his grease gun, other Germans opened fire. As McCown and the other two dropped to the ground, a voice called from behind them: *"Kommen sie hier!"* Turning, McCown saw a line of Germans covering them, weapons at the ready. All three surrendered.

Although General Harrison was yet to learn of McCown's capture, he came to the conclusion in late afternoon that there was no point in subjecting McCown's battalion to enemy riposte along the La Gleize–Stoumont highway when the attack to take the sanitorium and Stoumont had gained nothing. He told the battalion to retrace its steps through the woods.

When General Hobbs telephoned Harrison for "the real picture down there," Harrison made no effort to mask his concern. Two of the 119th Infantry's battalions had been badly battered, even demoralized, and American tanks were no match for the big German tanks firing from dug-in positions. "That place [Stoumont]," said Harrison, "is very strong. I don't think those troops we have now, without some improvement, can take the thing. That is my honest opinion." The trouble was, Harrison went on, that he could "only get light artillery fire on the town, and the Germans can shoot at us with tank guns and we can't get tanks to shoot back unless they come out and get hit."

It was a rare display of candor that would have endeared Harrison to his troops had they but known of it. Since Hobbs had long worked with his assistant division commander and trusted his judgment, he agreed to delay further attack until he could explore alternatives.

One who was seeking some way to help break the impasse was the commander of the 740th Tank Battalion, Colonel Rubel. Having found a spot in Targnon from which direct fire could be poured into Stoumont, he sent a member of his staff foraging for a 155mm. self-propelled artillery piece. Shortly before dark, the officer returned with it—where he got it from was never recorded; it was just one of those incidents that happened often in the Ardennes when a tank, a gun, a small group of men came briefly upon the scene, did a job, then passed on without record. Before darkness forced a halt, the artillery piece fired some fifty of its big, ear-splitting shells into Stoumont.

Another member of Rubel's tank battalion, Captain Berry, was also seeking a way out of the impasse. Soon after nightfall, he reconnoitered around the fringes of the sanitorium in search of some way to get his tanks over or around the stone retaining wall below the building. Finding a spot where he thought he could construct a short corduroy road to enable his tanks to get past, he called for volunteers among the infantry to help. Using felled trees and empty shell casings, the men toiled re-lentlessly. Shortly before midnight, a road was in place.

As snow was beginning to fall, four tanks, including one in which Berry himself rode, headed for the sanitorium. Successfully navigating the cor-duroy road, the tanks—like the German tanks before them—drew up close to the building and fired point-blank through the windows. The Ger-mans found that as punishing as had the Americans and soon took off.

To Father Hanlet and the other civilians in the basement, the silence that followed was eerie, almost as terrifying as the incessant explosion of shells they had so long endured. One shell had even penetrated a wall of the basement and lodged among one of the supporting arches, but amid a loud chorus of rosaries, it had failed to explode.

Father Hanlet rushed upstairs. The Germans had gone! He was con-fident the Americans would soon arrive, and *merci Dieu*, not one of his charges, for all the harrowing ordeal, had been hurt. Furthermore, the seriously wounded American to whom the priest had administered the last rites was still alive and appeared to be holding his own. Stepping across the stiff bodies of fallen Americans and Germans, Father Hanlet paused to say a prayer for the dead.

It was close to mid-morning of December 22 when General Harrison, noting an apparent absence of German activity at the sanitorium, sent a patrol to investigate. With the sanitorium at last in hand, Harrison changed his mind about renewing the attack on Stoumont and prepared again to move up the highway and down from the woods to the north.

Unknown to Harrison, the Germans in the sanitorium represented a rear guard designed to conceal as long as possible the fact that Peiper had fallen back from Stoumont to concentrate his entire force in and around La Gleize. At noon on the 21st, Peiper had called his commanders to his headquarters in the farmhouse near the Château de Froid-Cour and told them his plan. Since the Americans had already demonstrated that they could cut the highway connecting La Gleize and Stoumont, and the American paratroopers on the other side of the Amblève might well cut the dirt road linking the two places, he intended to avoid the risk of having his force split by falling back on La Gleize. There he would await reinforcement by the rest of the 1st SS Panzer Division, or, if that failed, attempt to return to German lines.

In preparation for the withdrawal, Peiper ordered all American prisoners and German walking wounded to move from the Château de Froide-Cour to cellars in La Gleize. Seriously wounded Americans and Germans in the château were left in the care of a German medical sergeant and two American aid men. Also left behind on a whitewashed wall of one of the rooms in the basement was a charcoal drawing of Christ, thorns on his head, tears on his cheeks—whether drawn by a German or an American nobody would ever know.

Unfortunately for Peiper and his men, they had completed their withdrawal and the Americans had occupied Stoumont and pushed on beyond the Château de Froide-Cour when, during the night of the 22d, twenty transport planes of the Luftwaffe finally responded to strident demands from General Dietrich to drop supplies to Peiper, and almost all dropped their containers in and close around Stoumont. When daylight came, American fire stymied virtually every German effort to recover the containers. Among those few that were recovered were containers filled with such nonessential (however welcome) items as cigarettes and Schnapps, and one held nothing but Luger pistols.

Peiper got enough gasoline from the containers to move a few tanks to better defensive positions and to recharge the batteries of some of his vehicles so that the crews could operate their radios, but that was all. Nor was an effort to float gasoline cans down the Amblève River any more successful.

Hal Dale McCown, twenty-eight years of age, a native of Arkansas and an honor ROTC graduate of Louisiana State University, was one of Peiper's prisoners of war, captured during the course of the first offensive action conducted by the 119th Infantry's 2d Battalion since he had assumed command of the battalion a few weeks earlier. His captors took him to a farmhouse, where a German lieutenant colonel questioned him (McCown was unaware at the time that the officer was Peiper). McCown duly gave only his name, rank, and serial number.

Losing interest, Peiper told the guards to take McCown away. They conducted him to a cellar in La Gleize lit by a single unshaded electric bulb. A young officer seated him so that the light was full in his face and a noncommissioned officer toyed menacingly with a Luger. So obviously staged was it that McCown found it difficult to suppress a smile. He replied the same way to every question: name, rank, serial number.

Eventually tiring of the charade, the officer sent him to a cellar in a house adjoining the village schoolhouse and left him there with four lieutenants from his own regiment and four guards. In a bookcase, McCown found a book by a British novelist of the 1920s, E. Phillips Oppenheim,

The Great Impersonation, and began to read to pass the time, but darkness soon put an end to the diversion.

Late in the evening of December 21, a guard took McCown to Peiper's new command post in the cellar of a farmhouse on the fringe of La Gleize. When the two were alone, it became obvious that Peiper wanted to talk. His English, McCown found, was almost perfect, and the man appeared to be amiable and cultured. He also appeared to be supremely confident that Germany would yet win the war. A new reserve army that Himmler was raising . . . secret weapons.

Think of the good Hitler was accomplishing, said Peiper. "We're eliminating the Communist menace, fighting your fight." So, too, Europe united under the Führer would bring a new, productive era to the old Continent. "We will keep what is best in Europe and eliminate the bad." Yet it was soon clear to McCown that Peiper was engaging in bravado, that he was too intelligent not to recognize not only the immediate plight of his command but the inevitable fate awaiting Nazi Germany.

Aware that Peiper was holding more than a hundred Americans as prisoners of war, McCown's immediate concern was for their safety. Like almost everybody else on the American side by that time, McCown had heard of the massacre of American prisoners near Malmédy, and he felt fairly certain he was talking to the man whose troops had done the deed. As Peiper's senior prisoner, said McCown, he felt a responsibility for the well-being of the others whom Peiper held. Would Peiper give him his personal assurance that the prisoners would be treated according to the Geneva Convention?

"I give you my word," said Peiper.

La Gleize had already taken heavy shelling from American artillery, but with the 119th Infantry's occupation of Stoumont and the Château de Froid-Cour, forward observers had an unobstructed view of the village. By midday on the 22nd the village was under almost constant shellfire, but except for an occasional direct hit, Peiper's tanks were virtually impervious to it.

Soon after midday, the commander of the 740th Tank Battalion, Colonel Rubel, set up his borrowed 155mm. self-propelled artillery piece alongside the Château de Froid-Cour, and close by the 105mm. pieces he had found at the ordnance depot at Sprimont. With a clear view of La Gleize, the gunners wreaked havoc on the buildings in the village, and one of the rounds from the 155 chopped the top off the spire of the village church. From farther away, the 155mm. howitzers of the 30th Division's 113th Field Artillery Battalion added the fury of their fire, much of it shells armed with the VT fuse. Little would be left of La Gleize but rubble, and those German soldiers who survived the carnage would ever after have a name for the village: *Der Kessel* (The Cauldron).

In the little cellar alongside the schoolhouse, McCown's guards took cover beside their prisoners, McCown and the four lieutenants. In early afternoon, a shell hit a wall of the cellar, tearing a gaping hole in it and sending rubble cascading inside. Moments later, another shell burst near the hole in the wall, spraying the cellar with rubble and shell fragments, killing one of the American lieutenants, and wounding three Germans, one of them mortally.

On the eastern fringe of La Gleize, in the cellar of the farmhouse that served as Peiper's headquarters, Peiper was sharply conscious of the terrible pounding his men—and his wounded—were taking in the village. He was particularly concerned with what appeared to be a big artillery piece employing direct fire from (so he thought) a window of the Château de Froid-Cour, but he considered he could not spare the ammunition to try to knock it out. Like gasoline, food, and medical supplies, ammunition was virtually exhausted.

Despite an ultra high-frequency radio brought to him earlier, communication with his division headquarters was erratic. The day before he had radioed that all supplies were exhausted and asked permission to break out, but only on the afternoon of the 22d did a reply come, and it was infuriating: "If *Kampfgruppe Peiper* does not punctually report its supply situation, it cannot reckon on a running supply of fuel and ammunition." There were six Tiger tanks that belonged with Peiper located near Stavelot, the radio voice continued. What did Peiper want done with them? Send them, Peiper replied sarcastically, by air to La Gleize.

Composing himself, Peiper asked again for authority to break out. He could do it, he said, only on foot, without vehicles and without wounded.

As the operator signed off, apparently to consult with Colonel Mohnke, Peiper felt sure authority to fall back would come. Possibly because of what had happened at the Baugnez road junction, he was concerned about leaving his wounded and called for Major McCown to be brought to the command post. He wanted to make a deal, Peiper told McCown; he wanted McCown's assurance that the American commander who occupied La Gleize would return the wounded to German lines. In exchange, he would leave all the American prisoners behind except McCown himself, whom he would release once the German wounded were repatriated.

"Colonel," McCown responded, "that proposal is a farce. For one thing, I have no power to bind the American command regarding German PWs. All I can do is sign a statement that I heard you make the offer. I can do nothing more."

Peiper settled for that. McCown wrote the statement, and he and another captured officer, Capt. Bruce Crissinger, commander of Company A, 832d Tank Destroyer Battalion, signed it. Since Crissinger was to stay behind with the other prisoners, he retained the statement.

Returning to the radio, Peiper asked if approval had come to break out. "May we break out?" his radio operator asked. "I repeat, may we break out?"

The answer was yes, but only if vehicles and wounded were brought along.

Blow up the radio, Peiper told the operator. Without vehicles, without wounded, he was getting out.

Through much of the day of December 23, from a sandpit just outside La Gleize, big Karl Wortmann watched the shelling of the village. Having started out with *Kampfgruppe Peiper* as a gunner on a flak tank, he had become, in the wake of casualties, a section leader, but one of his two flak tanks had been knocked out near the sanitorium in Stoumont. He and the men of his surviving tank watched the shelling in dismay: white phosphorus shells, shells that burst in the air, shells that plowed the ground and ripped open the buildings. As Wortmann was wont to do late each day, he left the position and headed into the village for the *Kampfgruppe*'s command post to check on developments. Don't forget, his men called after him, as they did each day, "by all means bring back something really good to eat." At least, thought Wortmann, his men still retained their gallows humor.

Wortmann was unable to get to the command post, for the shelling was too intense. The men he encountered were dazed, numbed by it. He hastened back to his own men and his flak tank.

The night was bitterly cold, the ground covered with a deep snow. Wortmann had no idea of the time, but he knew it was well past midnight and he feared he had dozed off and was dreaming. Or was that a real voice calling out, "Merry Christmas, Merry Christmas"?

Jumping from the tank, Wortmann ran toward the sound. It was a messenger from Peiper's command post. Why, demanded Wortmann, was he saying Merry Christmas when Christmas was still a day away? It was the codeword, said the messenger; it meant "immediate escape— blow up your tanks and follow!"

By the time Wortmann and his men had implanted delayed demolition mines in their tank and made their way into La Gleize, the village appeared to be deserted. Wortmann had no idea of the route for the breakout. He was beginning to despair when one of his men found a trail of footprints in the snow, a track left by hundreds. Following it, he and his men soon came upon the tail of the withdrawing column.

Behind a small advance guard, Peiper himself led the column of some eight hundred men with Major McCown by his side and two men from the headquarters detailed to guard McCown. At a farmhouse, Peiper ordered two Belgians, Laurent Gason and Yvan Hakin, to join him as guides. They led the Germans to a small wooden bridge spanning the

Amblève underneath the remains of a demolished railroad bridge. As the men crossed, they could hear the first of the explosions of the demolitions placed in their vehicles, either with delayed fuses or by a small engineer detail left behind with the assignment. When the head of the column reached the crest of a wooded hill beyond the river, the men could see fires burning in La Gleize.

With the coming of daylight, Peiper released the two Belgians and ordered his men to conceal themselves in the woods. All through the day, Peiper, McCown, and McCown's guards trooped about the forest trying to determine the best route to take when night came again. Having had only four pieces of dried biscuit and two swallows of cognac, McCown was desperately hungry, but there were no rations for anybody. Late in the day an officer gave him a small piece of hard candy from a K-ration. That helped.

Shortly before nightfall—it was Christmas Eve—the column began moving again behind a strong advance guard. With such discipline did the eight hundred men move that McCown was convinced they could have passed within two hundred yards of an outpost without being detected. Over and over McCown heard the word that any man who fell behind the column was to be shot. Later in the night he saw some men crawling in an effort to keep up.

Karl Wortmann was a part of the advance guard when around 11 P.M. a patrol of American paratroopers tried to seize the leading men. Firing broke out, "fierce, wild shooting." There were casualties and cries for medics, and Peiper himself was grazed by a bullet.

As the Germans around Major McCown scattered for cover, McCown lay still, awaiting some order from his guards. When it failed to come, he arose cautiously and began to walk slowly at right angles from the direction of the firing, all the while glancing back to see if anybody was covering him or following. Sure at last that he was alone, he turned and headed directly toward where the firing had come from.

He was walking slowly and whistling "Yankee Doodle" as loudly as he could when a voice shouted: "Halt, Goddamn it!" McCown permitted himself half a smile. He had made it.

The German column meanwhile continued to withdraw, got across the highway paralleling the Salm River south of Trois Ponts, and took refuge in a gully long enough to give such first aid as was possible to the wounded. Although patrols searched for a bridge, none was to be found. There was nothing to do but wade or swim.

Some of the taller men, including Wortmann, formed a chain spanning the forty-foot width of the river, arms locked, every other man facing in the opposite direction. The others began to cross upstream from the chain, but despite that precaution, the swift current carried some men downstream to their deaths. No one could stand the icy waters for long, so that men forming the chain had to be constantly relieved and replaced.

It was well after daylight when the last man crossed, and as the column headed for the village of Wanne, where long days before Peiper's passing had interrupted a football match, American artillery opened fire. More men wounded, some killed, blood on the snow. When the survivors finally gained the barns and houses of the village, their uniforms were so frozen that it was a major task to get them off.

Of some 4,000 men who had started the attack with *Kampfgruppe Peiper*, plus about 1,800 men of Major Knittel's reconnaissance battalion and the additional battalion of the 2d SS Panzergrenadier Regiment that had later joined Peiper, only those 800 made their way out of the entrapment. A few wounded also made it, for while the wooden span over the Amblève at Petit-Spai still stood and while Peiper still had access to it, he had evacuated many of his wounded. He nevertheless had to leave behind 80 wounded in the Château de Froid-Cour and just over 300 in La Gleize. Unknown to Peiper, he also left behind fifty *SS-Panzergrenadiers* in the woods above La Gleize who never received the code word, "Merry Christmas," and subsequently fought to the death. Out of a force totaling 5,800 men, Peiper lost close to 5,000.

Just how many tanks and other vehicles *Kampfgruppe Peiper* left behind at Cheneux, La Gleize, Stoumont, and Stoumont Station was difficult to determine, for U.S. Army counts and later counts by civilians in the area differed. Based in large measure on tanks and other vehicles known to have started out with the column, the figures were probably sixty tanks, including seven Tigers; three flak tanks; seventy half-tracks; at least fourteen 20mm. flak wagons; twenty-five 75mm. assault guns and 105mm. and 150mm. self-propelled howitzers; plus trucks and smaller vehicles. To that total would have to be added others lost along the way: thirteen tanks, two flak tanks, and here and there a half-track, plus six mediums and three Tigers at Stavelot. The total number of tanks was eighty-seven, including five flak tanks and ten Tigers.

Although Peiper confessed to Major McCown that his men killed 7 American prisoners at La Gleize, when, according to Peiper, they tried to escape, the conduct of the SS troops toward 170 other American captives was satisfactory. So, too, apparently, toward Belgian civilians, for even though twenty-three civilians died at Cheneux, La Gleize, and Stoumont, in only one case, when an older couple died as a result of rounds fired from an automatic weapon through the window of their home, was there any indication of deliberate killing.

Peiper had fallen far short of his goal of reaching the Meuse, yet he had accomplished more than he probably realized at the time and certainly much more than Skorzeny's disguised infiltration teams or von der

Heydte's parachutists. Peiper had provoked genuine concern in the American command, and by his continued presence, he had so delayed an American drive to close the gap between Malmédy and St. Vith that by the time he withdrew, conditions were no longer conducive to making it. He had also kept a powerful American combat command tied up for almost five days when it was critically needed elsewhere.

A tragic and in some ways incredible postscript to the war against *Kampfgruppe Peiper* remained to be enacted.

Skies had yet to clear fully over the Ardennes on December 23 when twenty-eight medium bombers, B-26 Marauders of the Ninth Air Force's IX Bombardment Division, headed for the German town of Zulpich, site of a railhead for the German Army some thirty-three miles northeast of Malmédy. The pilots of most of the planes soon realized they were off course and either aborted their mission or bombed alternate targets; but six others, also thinking they were bombing an alternate target, dropped eighty-six 250-pound general purpose bombs on Malmédy. All six pilots reported "excellent results."

So they were. Someone at the 30th Division's headquarters telephoned frantically to headquarters of the First Army: "Planes are bombing Malmedy. We haven't a line left to anybody in town. Get them off." But by that time the damage was done. The bombs hit squarely in the center of town, destroying buildings, blocking streets with rubble, burying civilians and soldiers alike.

Adding to the destruction, fires erupted and for a time raged out of control, for the little town's fire-fighting equipment was never intended to cope with such a holocaust. Here and there men of the 291st Engineers dynamited buildings to create firebreaks, but it was well into the night before the fires were under control. By that time the school's playground was carpeted with dead civilians. Dazed survivors with tears streaking down dust-stained faces asked incredulously of the soldiers: "American planes?"

Twice before, in Normandy in July, American bombs on two successive days had fallen short on men of the 30th Division as they waited to participate in the big attack to break out of the beachhead. The division lost 138 men killed, hundreds more wounded, and for long afterward old-timers in the division spoke sardonically of the Ninth Air Force as the American Luftwaffe; and whenever American planes attacked in support of the 30th Division, General Hobbs always insisted on a wide margin of safety between the bomb line and his troops. Yet again American aircraft had attacked men of the 30th Division. And not once but twice.

In the early afternoon of December 24, Christmas Eve, Colonel Pergrin and men of his 291st Engineers were still digging survivors from the rubble created by the bombing the day before when a flight of eighteen heavy bombers, B-24 Liberators, droned overhead, and "what the medium bombers did the day before was nothing compared to what the eighteen B-24s did." They leveled the entire central core of the town. A desperate telephone call from the 120th Infantry went through to head-quarters of the 30th Division: "These planes are on us again; they are about to ruin us. Can you call them off?" Yet again the damage had already been done.

Just as the bombers approached, men of the 291st Engineers had fi-nally tunneled into a cellar to rescue a few men of the 120th Infantry trapped there, and Colonel Pergrin had squeezed through the opening. Then the bombs exploded, and a nearby freestanding wall collapsed, seal-ing the cellar again. It took the engineers an hour to dig Pergrin and the others out.

Fires again broke out. Entire streets were burning, and as night fell, "it looked as if the whole town could go up in flames." Dead civilians were once more laid out in rows in the schoolyard.

The struggle to dig out from the two bombings was still under way on Christmas Day when around 2:30 P.M. another flight of B-26 Marauders approached the town. Thirty-six planes were on their way to bomb St. Vith, which was by that time in German hands. Most of the planes found their targets, but four mistook Malmédy for St. Vith and dropped sixty-four 250-pound general purpose bombs.

In a town crammed with refugees, authorities in Malmédy never were able to determine exactly how many civilians died over those three terri-ble days, but the figure was probably at least 125. American losses were 37 killed and close to 100 wounded, and the center of the pretty little town was a ruin.

Many an American soldier long attributed the bombings to a map appearing in the soldier newspaper *Stars & Stripes*, which erroneously showed Malmédy to be in German hands. Yet that theory took no ac-count of the fact that big identification panels were prominently displayed on rooftops of the town. Through the years, surviving inhabitants tried to arrive at some explanation: Were the Americans expecting to lose the town and wanted to turn it into a chokepoint, as they did at such places as St. Vith, Houffalize, and La Roche? Yet why would they do that when their own troops were still there?

None of those theories explained the tragic bombings. It was, in fact, the human equation: pilot error. Nothing more, nothing less.

CHAPTER TWENTY-THREE

The Defense of St. Vith

Armor is an offensive weapon, created essentially to exploit a breakthrough achieved by infantry or armor or a combination of both. Few commanders of armored combat commands and divisions would endorse the use of their tanks, self-propelled tank destroyers, half-track–mounted infantry, and self-propelled artillery in a defensive role. Leave that to the separate tank and tank destroyer battalions whose basic assignment is support of the infantry.

Yet there are obviously times when a commander has no choice but to use his armor defensively. When that happens, no armored commander wants to be bound by the dictum (so often propounded by infantry commanders) to hold a static defensive line at all costs. Impose maximum delay but give ground rather than be overwhelmed, then counterattack, not necessarily to regain and hold the ground relinquished but to impose further delay. The object: to take full advantage of armor's mobility.

As the commander of the 7th Armored Division's CCB, Bruce Clarke, put it during the course of the fight for St. Vith: "This terrain is not worth a nickel an acre to me." Before an enemy in far superior strength, he could afford to give ground grudgingly, Clarke believed, because a few hundred or a thousand yards here and there was of no real value to his opponent. If his opponent was to succeed, he had to make great strides and make them swiftly, and only by outmaneuvering or by overwhelming and annihilating the defenders could he do so. As was demonstrated when Clarke urged his colleague, Bill Hoge of the 9th Armored Division's CCB, to pull back behind the railroad line southeast of St. Vith because Hoge's only route of withdrawal was through St. Vith, and Clarke felt sure he would in time lose the town.

Clarke's division commander, Bob Hasbrouck, thought the same way. When on December 17, for example, the acting commander of CCR, Colonel Warren, told Hasbrouck of a developing threat to the village of

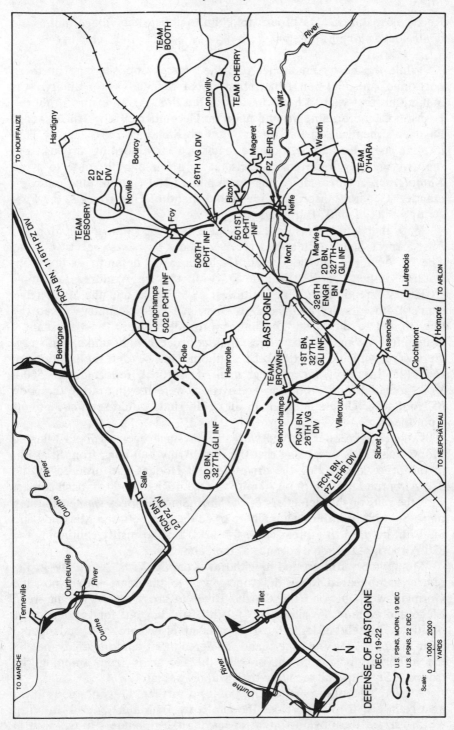

TO HOUFFALIZE

TEAM BOOTH

Wiltz River

Longvilly

TEAM CHERRY

Hardigny

Bourcy

26TH VG DIV

Mageret

PZ LEHR DIV

Wardin

2D PZ DIV

Noville

Bizory

Neffe

TEAM O'HARA

TEAM DESOBRY

Foy

501ST PCHT INF

Mont

Marvie

506TH PCHT INF

Longchamps

2D BN, 327TH GLI INF

Lutrebois

TO ARLON

502D PCHT INF

326TH ENGR BN

Hompré

Bertogne

Rolle

BASTOGNE

Hemroulle

Assenois

Clochimont

RCN BN, 116TH PZ DIV

TEAM BROWNE

1ST BN, 327TH GLI INF

Villeroux

Senonchamps

RCN BN, 26TH VG DIV

3D BN, 327TH GLI INF

Sibret

Salle

River

Ourthe

RCN BN, 2D PZ DIV

RCN BN, PZ LEHR DIV

TO NEUFCHÂTEAU

Tenneville

Ourtheuville

River

Tillet

Ourthe

River

Ourthe

TO MARCHE

DEFENSE OF BASTOGNE
DEC 19–22

N

U.S. PSNS. MORN. 19 DEC

U.S. PSNS. 22 DEC

Scale: 0   1000   2000
           YARDS

Recht, near Poteau, Hasbrouck told him to defend the village, not to the death, but as long as possible.

While the new commander of Allied forces opposing the northern portion of the German penetration, Field Marshal Montgomery, was making his first visit to headquarters of the First Army in the Hôtel des Bains in Chaudfontaine around noon on December 20, the 7th Armored Division's chemical warfare officer, Lt. Col. Frederick Schroeder, walked into the hotel. He had been on the road since early morning, driving from the division's headquarters in Vielsalm on a roundabout route to avoid *Kampfgruppe Peiper*. He brought with him a letter from his division commander, General Hasbrouck, for an old friend of Hasbrouck's, the First Army's chief of staff, Bill Kean.

With that letter, Hasbrouck provided the first solid information the First Army's headquarters had received about the situation at St. Vith. The 7th Armored Division, wrote Hasbrouck, was defending a line from Poteau southeastward to include St. Vith; the 9th Armored Division's CCB was extending the line southwest of St. Vith; and the 106th Division's 424th Infantry and the 28th Division's 112th Infantry curved the line around to the west. The infantry regiments were "in bad shape." Only a few reconnaissance troops, tank destroyers, light tanks, and stragglers were available to extend the southern flank beyond the positions of the 112th Infantry; and off that flank, Hasbrouck reported, the 560th Volksgrenadier and 116th Panzer Divisions were moving in the direction of Houffalize. Unless he got help, those divisions would soon cut him off from the rear.

Colonel Schroeder arrived with that message even as Field Marshal Montgomery was proposing that the First Army pull back from St. Vith, in the process canceling the drive General Hodges had ordered by the 82d Airborne Division to push up to the Salm River and establish contact with the rear of the defenders of St. Vith. Since Hodges wanted to hang on to St. Vith in order eventually to close the gap between Malmédy and St. Vith, he used the threat to Hasbrouck's rear to justify continuing the 82d Airborne Division's advance to the Salm.

Montgomery still wanted to withdraw from St. Vith. As he saw it, the real crisis appeared to be developing well to the rear, with a possible German sweep beyond the Ourthe River to cross the Meuse between Liège and Namur. A salient at St. Vith, sticking out far beyond other positions, merely absorbed troops needed elsewhere and endangered their existence. On the other hand, he agreed that continued advance by the airborne division might prevent the Germans from trapping the troops at St. Vith and facilitate their withdrawal later.

Although Hodges pursued the point no further, he continued, in his own counsels, to plan to close the gap between Malmédy and St. Vith, which carried the obvious intent of leaving the defenders of St. Vith in place. Furthermore, once the 82d Airborne Division gained contact with Hasbrouck's rear, the forces around St. Vith were to pass to the command of the XVIII Airborne Corps. The commander of that corps, Matthew B. Ridgway, was an airborne soldier not given to worrying about being surrounded and not accustomed to giving ground.

For the German command, December 20 was a day of disappointment around St. Vith. Model, von Manteuffel, and Lucht had been planning an all-out attack to take the town starting at daylight, a three-pronged envelopment with the 62d Volksgrenadier Division attacking from the southeast along the road from Steinebrück; the 18th Volksgrenadier Division attacking along the two roads from Schoenberg, which converged just behind the American defensive line on the Prümerberg, just short of St. Vith; and the *Führer Begleit Brigade* attacking from the north.

In releasing the *Führer Begleit Brigade* to General von Manteuffel—in effect, directing him to use it—Field Marshal Model thought he would gain quick access to the roadnet at St. Vith, whereupon he intended sending the brigade driving swiftly for the Meuse or cutting in behind the opposition on the Elsenborn Ridge that was stymieing the Sixth Panzer Army. Yet the monumental traffic jams in the Losheim Gap and at Schoenberg continued to delay both the 18th Volksgrenadier Division and the *Führer Begleit Brigade*, and not until after daylight on the 20th would a bridge be ready at Steinebrück for the 62d Volksgrenadier Division. Those factors dictated at least another twenty-four-hour delay before a major assault on St. Vith could begin.

Commanded by Col. Otto Remer, the *Führer Begleit* (Escort) *Brigade* had been built around the nucleus of a battalion which Remer had commanded with the mission of protecting Hitler at his headquarters on the Eastern Front in the Gorlitz Forest. A prompt reaction to the attempt on Hitler's life in July had brought Remer to the Führer's personal attention, propelling him into that small fraternity of relatively junior officers, such as Skorzeny and Peiper, whom the Führer especially favored. In the wake of the big Allied airborne attack in the Netherlands in September, Hitler had become so concerned lest parachutists drop on his headquarters and attempt to capture him that he summoned Remer to the *Wolfschanze* and told him to enlarge the *Führer Begleit* from a battalion to a brigade.

Remer was occupied with doing that when in late November Hitler revealed that he was moving his headquarters to Berlin and wanted Remer to reorganize his brigade as a combat force to be employed on the Western Front. (He failed to bring Remer in on his grandiose plan for an offensive.) As finally formed, the brigade was a powerful force, something like a strongly reinforced American combat command. Remer had three mobile grenadier battalions, an artillery battalion of 105mm. pieces, a flak regiment with twenty-four 88mm. guns (the regiment had provided antiaircraft protection for the *Wolfschanze*), and contingents of antitank troops and engineers and a panzer battalion with forty-five Mark IVs and thirty-five assault guns. Because the panzer battalion and some of the grenadiers came from the renowned *Grossdeutschland Panzer Division*, which was on the Eastern Front, prisoner identifications were later to cause considerable concern and bafflement to American intelligence officers.

So anxious was General von Manteuffel to get the drive going on St. Vith that even though he had lost all hope of mounting a major attack on December 20, he told Remer to use whatever he had on hand to get something moving quickly. Before daylight on the 20th, a company each of infantry and tanks tried to move from Wallerode on St. Vith, but by that time the overall commander on the Prümerberg, Colonel Fuller, had extended his line to cover that approach to St. Vith, and much of the 7th Armored Division's artillery had moved forward to positions close enough to augment the fires of the 275th Armored Field Artillery Battalion. The probe got nowhere.

An ambitious man, Otto Remer was actually less interested in helping to take St. Vith than in beginning a drive for the Meuse, for which he needed crossings of the Salm River at Vielsalm and a short distance upstream at Salmchâteau. Displaying some of the same independence as Skorzeny and Peiper, Remer decided, without consulting von Manteuffel, to shift the thrust of his effort away from St. Vith to the roads behind the town that led to those crossing sites. At midday on the 20th, he sent a battalion each of tanks and infantry to take the village of Rodt, where he intended to get on the highway leading to Poteau and thence to Vielsalm; but as the four leading tanks crossed the brow of a hill, 90mm. guns of the 814th Tank Destroyer Battalion knocked out all four with an expenditure of only seven rounds. Remer decided to call everything off until his full brigade arrived.

By that time, the commander of the defenses in front of St. Vith, Colonel Fuller, had assembled a fairly sizable force in an arc stretching from the main highway into St. Vith from the north across the heights of the Prümerberg to a draw southeast of the town near where the railroad and the road from Steinebrück entered St. Vith. Fuller had two companies of his own 38th Armored Infantry Battalion (the third company— armored infantry battalions had only three line companies—was with CCA at Poteau), two of the 23d Armored Infantry Battalion (the third was a part of CCB's reserve), a composite force of about four hundred men of the 81st and 168th Engineers, a troop of the 87th Armored Cavalry Reconnaissance Squadron, and a platoon of the 423d Infantry that had been the 106th Division's headquarters guard.

In support were a company each of the 31st Tank and 814th Tank Destroyer Battalions. Most of the tank destroyers were in reserve in St. Vith, but in recognition that the road from Steinebrück was a likely ave-

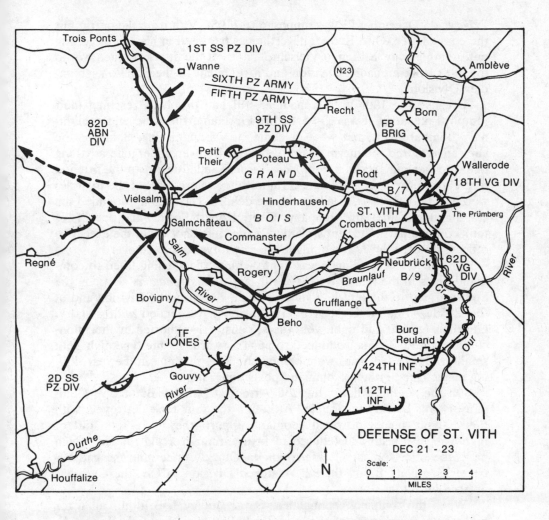

DEFENSE OF ST. VITH

DEC 21 - 23

nue of attack and because there was a six hundred-yard gap between Fuller's line and positions of the 9th Armored Division's CCB, four guns were in position on that flank with the 23d Armored Infantry Battalion's Company B. The eleven available medium tanks were positioned to cover open ground near Wallerode, the second and lesser highway leading from Schoenberg, and the main highway crossing the Prümerberg.

Fuller's position had three obvious disadvantages: a lack of unit integrity, for the troops had been committed piecemeal; the gap on the southern flank; and a lack of depth. The lack of depth was particularly serious for the men on the Prümerberg, since close at their backs the ground dropped off sharply—almost a bluff—which was much like having a river behind you.

On specific order from General von Manteuffel, the *Führer Begleit*

Brigade on December 21 was supposed to hit St. Vith from the north; but the commander, Otto Remer, nevertheless persisted in his aim of getting onto the highway leading to Vielsalm. That left the attack on the town to the 18th Volksgrenadier Division and a regiment of the 62d Volksgrenadier Division.

Because the 18th Volksgrenadiers still had problems reaching their jump-off positions, it was 3 P.M. before German artillery began a preliminary bombardment, but when it came, it was punishing. Some of the veteran armored infantrymen swore they had never undergone anything like it. Screaming rockets from *Nebelwerfers* added terror to the fire and tore gaps in the line, and on the Prümerberg, where most of the foxholes were inside the woods, tree bursts were deadly. The shelling wounded the commander of the tank company, Capt. Robert Foster, and one of his tank commanders, and sent a platoon leader into shock; but the executive officer, 1st Lt. John J. Dunn, made his way forward to take over.

At four o'clock, as dusk was approaching, the shelling lifted to command posts in the rear and to St. Vith, and *Volksgrenadiers* all along the line swarmed to the attack. Artillery of the 7th Armored Division and of the 275th Armored Field Artillery Battalion responded with alacrity. Germans fell left and right, yet others, constantly exhorted by their non-commissioned officers, continued to push forward. By the time night fell, small groups of Germans were behind the line, roaming in the rear, killing messengers, bringing command posts under fire.

On the southern flank, the 23d Armored Infantry Battalion's Company B was quickly in trouble. Although the four tank destroyers with their 90mm. pieces provided yeoman support, they were soon out of high-explosive shell and reduced to firing armor-piercing rounds, which had little effect on the *Volksgrenadiers*. Quickly discerning the gap between Company B and the 9th Armored Division's CCB, the Germans pressed into it.

When the company commander, Capt. Dudley J. Britton, called for tanks, the commander of the 31st Tank Battalion, Lt. Col. Robert C. Erlenbusch, told Lieutenant Dunn to send four that were in a concealed position behind the Prümerberg. The tanks started out, but one quickly broke down, and the commander of the 168th Engineers, Colonel Nungesser, who was roaming up and down the line watching for trouble spots, saw the peril where the main highway crossed the Prümerberg as too great and ordered the tanks back. When Dunn learned of the shift, he ordered his own command tank to join him; sent two tanks that were covering the open ground facing Wallerode to the southern flank; and ordered the other three to the highway on the Prümerberg. Thus five tanks were soon in position there.

On the southern flank, Company B was fast going to pieces. As infiltrating Germans approached Britton's command post in a house, they yelled in English: "Come on out!" To which Britton yelled back: "Fuck you, come on in!"

Although Britton's headquarters troops drove those Germans off, so thickly were the *Volksgrenadiers* surging through the gap on the company's flank that Britton saw no alternative but to withdraw. With his tank destroyers, he hoped to hold a few hundred yards back where the highway from Steinebrück passed beneath the railroad. Yet by that time two of Britton's platoons were surrounded and were unable to break away, and when Britton and his remaining platoon reached the railroad, events happening elsewhere made it impossible to form a new line.

On the Prümerberg, it was almost full dark, around 5 P.M., when six Tigers of the 506th Heavy Panzer Battalion, which had earlier appeared with devastating results at Andler, approached along the highway from Schoenberg. Lieutenant Dunn radioed his five tanks on the hill to get into positions from which they could cover a rise in the road, and when the Tigers crossed the rise, to open fire simultaneously.

The tankers were ready, but as the Tigers crossed the rise, they fired high-velocity flares which burst behind the American tanks with a brilliant light. That blinded the American gunners and silhouetted their tanks. In a matter of seconds, the German gunners had knocked out or disabled all five tanks, killing or wounding most of the crews. Having demolished the American tank support in one powerful blow, the German gunners began knocking out machine-gun crews as fast as they could be replaced. Nobody could long stand such a pounding, and the survivors along the highway broke for the rear.

Stunned by those events, the overall commander of the forces in front of St. Vith, Colonel Fuller, told the commander of the 81st Engineers, Colonel Riggs, to take over. He himself was heading for General Clarke's headquarters "to plan alternate positions." When he got there, he told Clarke he couldn't take it any more. Preoccupied with other events, Clarke told him to report to the medics, who subsequently evacuated him through medical channels. (Soft-hearted medical officers appeared predisposed to soft-hearted treatment of field grade officers.)

Back on the Prümerberg, despite the breakthroughs along the southern flank and the main road from Steinebrück, there was still an American line in front of St. Vith. In between those two roads, the infantrymen, cavalrymen, and engineers were still holding, along with two tanks guarding the other road from Schoenberg; and on the open ground facing Wallerode, both Company A, 38th Armored Infantry, and Company A, 23d Armored Infantry, although hardpressed, were still intact. The company of the 23d Armored Infantry had just been reinforced by sixty men of the 106th Division, consisting mostly of the men who had made their way out of the entrapment beyond the Our River with Lieutenants McKinley and

Long. Before returning to the fight, they had had a twenty-four-hour rest in the schoolhouse at St. Vith.

Inside St. Vith, on the other hand, confusion was rampant. The big Tigers, *Volksgrenadiers* clinging all over them, were soon lumbering down the steep hill along the highway, and even though an occasional group of Americans and a tank destroyer or two tried to make a stand, nobody could hold for long. In the darkness, vehicles of all types began streaming out of town toward the west, American soldiers clambering aboard on any available space.

Around 9:30 P.M., General Clarke got word to Colonel Riggs to withdraw to a new line to be formed on the first high ground behind the town. Riggs was able to get that order to few of the men, and with the Germans in St. Vith, it was impossible to withdraw in any case. A few got out individually or in small groups, but many, including Riggs, were captured.

It was close to midnight when the commander of the 38th Armored Infantry's Company A, Capt. Walter H. Austey, on the open ground facing Wallerode, finally established radio contact with his battalion's executive officer and learned of the order. With some seventy men, he began to withdraw in a heavy snowstorm, but many men lost contact in the snow and darkness, and only Austey and thirty-three others escaped.

Men of the 23d Armored Infantry's Company A got the word even later. Finally succeeding in making a field artillery radio function, Cpl. Harold Kemp contacted the 275th Armored Field Artillery Battalion. "What are our orders?" asked Kemp. After a brief delay, the word came back: "Go west! Go west!"

Well over a hundred men lined up in single file to begin the withdrawal, but in the darkness and blinding snow, the column soon broke apart and most of the men lost their way. Only twenty-one finally reached General Clarke's command post, among them none of the men from the 106th Division who had struggled to make their way back across the Our River to St. Vith.

The 7th Armored Division's CCB lost heavily in the defense of St. Vith: at least nine hundred soldiers who had stood in front of the town. Of eleven tanks, four survived (one of them commanded by 1st Lt. Will Rogers, Jr., son of the American humorist), along with most of the tank destroyers. The debacle left Clarke with only one full company of armored infantrymen.

As Clarke made the decision to withdraw from in front of St. Vith, he notified the commander of the 9th Armored Division's CCB, General Hoge, who would have to pull back his north flank to conform with the new line Clarke hoped to form a thousand yards behind St. Vith. Although Hoge's troops had sustained some pressure during the day from the 62d Volksgrenadier Division, they had handled it with little difficulty.

By midnight, Clarke's new line was forming. Officers stationed on roads and trails halted stragglers and directed them to the new positions, which in view of the shortage of infantry, would be porous at best. Clarke had his usual 31st Tank Battalion, a company of the 814th Tank Destroyer Battalion, and the bulk of the 17th Tank Battalion, which normally fought with CCR but which had become available after CCA took charge in the vicinity of Poteau.

Fortunately for Clarke and his men, the Germans were in no position to pursue their success in capturing St. Vith immediately. Most roads leading into the town converged along narrow streets at a traffic circle near the southern edge of the town, not far from the St. Joseph's Kloster, which quickly became a bottleneck with effects as stultifying as those already experienced at Schoenberg and in the Losheim Gap. Men of all three regiments of the 18th Volksgrenadier Division and one regiment of the 62d Volksgrenadier Division poured into the town, eager to get at the booty and the warmth of the houses, and units were soon almost hopelessly intermingled. Support troops raced down from the Prümerberg to join what rapidly became "a kind of scavenger hunt," and officers and men in captured American vehicles added to the confusion. Still searching for a way around the stalled traffic in the Losheim Gap, some contingents of the Sixth Panzer Army also entered the town; and as usual, SS officers among them were truculent and imperious, refusing to obey the orders of other officers or military policemen. Once again the commander of Army Group B, Field Marshal Model, had to get out of his command car and walk.

On December 22, after all of the *Führer Begleit Brigade* had at last arrived, Colonel Remer intended to get on with his self-appointed task of capturing Rodt and gaining the main highway to Vielsalm—a first step toward the glory of a drive to the Meuse. A strong infantry patrol had found a way around Rodt the day before. Remer sent an infantry battalion to follow that route and reach the highway, while his other two infantry battalions attacked the village itself. At the same time, twenty-five tanks were to bypass the village and attack it from the rear.

The juncture point for the defenses of Combat Commands A and B, Rodt was weakly garrisoned by Service Company of the 48th Armored Infantry Battalion. With strong support from the 275th Armored Field Artillery Battalion, the Americans of that company nevertheless turned back one German battalion and allowed only a few men from the other to get into the fringe of the village. The battalion that was following the route taken earlier by the patrol bumped into the 48th Armored Infantry's vehicle park, where drivers and mechanics manned the .50-caliber machine guns on the half-tracks to turn the Germans back. Remer's tanks nevertheless got behind the village. When they attacked, the few men of Service Company had no way to stop them.

In capturing Rodt, Remer drove a wedge between Combat Commands A and B, and with Germans in both Rodt and St. Vith, two troops of the 87th Armored Cavalry Reconnaissance Squadron between the two villages had to pull back to General Clarke's new line. At about the same time, men of CCA around Poteau captured prisoners whose identity told the American commander, Colonel Rosebaum, that he faced a strong new force: the 9th SS Panzer Division.

That division had finally threaded its leading units through the coagulated traffic in the Losheim Gap under orders from General Dietrich to cross the Salm River and drive westward and, if possible, rescue *Kampfgruppe Peiper* in the process. The division had no interest in Vielsalm other than to guard against interference by the American armor known to be in the vicinity and merely left a task force to guard the division's flank in front of Poteau.

That Colonel Rosebaum could not know. Confronted with possible attack by an entire SS panzer division that might cut off all American troops east of the Salm River by a drive through Poteau on Vielsalm, Rosebaum abandoned any further contest with the *Führer Begleit Brigade* and pulled back to form a close-knit semicircular defense of the vital road junction at Poteau.

That action further widened the rift between CCA and CCB, which in turn prompted General Clarke to fall back to a new line based on the village of Hinderhausen, southwest of Rodt, and his old headquarters village of Crombach. While Clarke's headquarters moved to the village of Commanster, deep in a vast expanse of forest (the Grand Bois) which screened the approaches to Vielsalm, the withdrawal proceeded with little difficulty. Except for the *Führer Begleit Brigade*, still consolidating at Rodt, most of the Germans facing Clarke were still involved in the disorganization and confusion that was St. Vith.

Unhindered by the bottleneck at St. Vith, two regiments of the 62d Volksgrenadier Division meanwhile continued to attack the 9th Armored Division's CCB, their goal being to gain the Salm River at Salmchâteau. In mid-morning of December 22, a company of *Volksgrenadiers* broke through the line of the 27th Armored Infantry Battalion, plodded through deep snow up the constricted valley of the Braunlauf Creek, and opened fire on the battalion's headquarters in a large farmhouse in the settlement of Neubrück. The commander, Lt. Col. S. Fred Cummings, Jr., his staff officers, and headquarters troops, firing from the windows, drove off a first assault; but with a second, a few Germans got into the basement, which at the rear of the house was on ground level. Since the defenders were almost out of ammunition, Cummings agreed to surrender.

Wounded in the attack, the German commander, a captain, insisted on medical treatment for himself, one of his lieutenants, and several of his men. Since the Germans had also overrun the battalion aid station in a nearby farmhouse, they brought the battalion surgeon, Capt. Paul J. Russomano, and several of his medics to treat their wounded. Pleading a shortage of medical supplies, Captain Russomano convinced the German officer to allow him to send an ambulance for more.

When the ambulance departed, the Germans ordered their prisoners to march toward German lines. They had gone only a short distance when they came under a crossfire from the machine guns of two platoons of American tanks. When the guards ordered everybody back to the farmhouse, the battalion's intelligence officer, Capt. Glen L. Strange, ducked under an abandoned half-track and eventually worked his way to one of the tank platoons.

At the farmhouse, in the meantime, the German captain insisted that he and the other German wounded be evacuated to German lines under a flag of truce. The ambulance having returned—but not before the driver had alerted General Hoge's headquarters to what was happening—the wounded Germans—and at the captain's insistence, Captain Russomano—departed in it.

By that time, a platoon of tanks under 1st Lt. David P. Duck, with twenty infantrymen rounded up by Captain Strange riding on the decks, was heading for the farmhouse. Duck's tank fired two quick rounds of high explosive, one into each floor of the house, then thrust its 76mm. piece through the front door. The Germans boiled from the windows, hands overhead. Colonel Cummings, his staff officers, and his headquarters troops followed, none of them injured. Although the Germans held onto Captain Russomano, two months later they sent him under a white flag into American lines.

The issue of who was in overall command of the conglomerate of American forces in the vicinity of St. Vith remained for long unsettled. In response to General Hasbrouck's message carried by his chemical warfare officer to the First Army's headquarters, General Hodges noted that Hasbrouck was to "retain" under his command the 112th Infantry; the 9th Armored Division's CCB; and the 106th Division. That disturbed Hasbrouck, first, because none of those units had been under his command and second, because he was a one-star general and the commander of the 106th Division, General Jones, was a two-star. Furthermore, Hasbrouck was also junior to the commander of the 9th Armored Division's CCB, General Hoge.

Hasbrouck promptly sent another message to the First Army's headquarters. He also sent a copy to Jones for his information and another to General Ridgway, for by that time, late on December 20, patrols of the 82d Airborne Division on the other side of the Salm River had established contact with patrols of the 7th Armored Division, and with that contact all forces in the vicinity of St. Vith passed to the command of

Ridgway and the XVIII Airborne Corps. Hasbrouck pointed out the differences in ranks and noted that Jones was still in command of the 106th Division and that Hoge's combat command and the 112th Infantry were attached to that division. The next day, Ridgway responded by "discontinuing" attachment of the 106th Division to Hasbrouck but directing Jones "to cooperate with 7th Armored Division to carry out corps orders."

Cooperation had been the order of the day in any case. What bothered Hasbrouck far more than who was in charge was the survival of his division, a question that came up shortly before midnight of December 21 after the defenses in front of St. Vith collapsed. Aware that Ridgway wanted to hold the St. Vith salient and attack to close the gap between Malmédy and St. Vith, Hasbrouck's old friend, Bill Kean, told Ridgway—even though he knew that his superior, General Hodges, also wanted to attack—that Hasbrouck was "not expected to sacrifice his command out there." Whether to continue to hold or to withdraw, said Kean, was a decision that should be Hasbrouck's alone.

Despite the loss of St. Vith, Ridgway still believed the troops beyond the Salm could hold; for the 82d Airborne Division was beginning to build a fairly firm line that should prevent the Germans from cutting off the salient from the rear, and he hoped that the 3d Armored Division soon might attack to remove all threat of encirclement. Not long after midnight, he ordered the forces in the salient to shorten their lines by withdrawing to an oval-shaped defensive position in front of and encompassing Vielsalm—a position that came to be known as the "fortified goose egg"—there to await relief by the 3d Armored Division. To resolve the command problem, he attached the 7th Armored Division to the 106th Division, which meant that General Jones was in overall command.

Hasbrouck, Hoge, Clarke, and Rosebaum were all decidedly unhappy with Ridgway's defensive plan. Although the shortening of lines would help, the goose egg would still have an extensive perimeter and would embrace the vast forest in front of Vielsalm, the Grand Bois. When viewed on a map, the roads looked extensive; in fact, all were dirt trails except for a gravel highway that cut diagonally across the forest. How could tanks—or even mounted infantry for that matter—be shifted to meet developing threats? What, too, if the airborne troops failed to keep the rear of the goose egg accessible? It was one thing to supply lightly armed airborne troops by air; but armor? Clarke called the plan "Custer's Last Stand."

Before daylight came on December 22, all commands were nevertheless beginning to comply with the order to form the fortified goose egg; but soon after dawn, Hasbrouck wrote out a long recital of the situation in the salient for transmission to Ridgway. First, he called attention to the dearth of roads and to the fact that all supplies would have to come over a single bridge at Vielsalm. Then he pointed out that even that bridge might be denied should the 2d SS Panzer Division, identified south of the salient, drive the airborne troops back even as much as three thousand yards. Hasbrouck also noted that Clarke's CCB had lost heavily in front of St. Vith, fully half the command. "I don't think," concluded Hasbrouck, "we can prevent a complete breakthrough if another all-out attack comes against CCB tonight."

Hasbrouck quite clearly wanted to withdraw. Just as he finished writing, word arrived of the *Führer Begleit Brigade*'s attack on Rodt and of the attack against the headquarters of the 9th Armored Division's 27th Armored Infantry Battalion. In a postscript, Hasbrouck told of those attacks; and lest any doubt of the seriousness of the situation still remained, he added: "In my opinion if we don't get out of here and up north of the 82d before night, we will not have a 7th Armored Division left."

Meanwhile, a British captain had arrived at Hasbrouck's command post in the Middle School in Vielsalm. He was a PHANTOM, one of Field Marshal Montgomery's junior liaison officers. Ushered in to see Hasbrouck, the captain asked what Hasbrouck thought should be done with the 7th Armored Division. If holding beyond the Salm was considered to be vital, said Hasbrouck, he would assuredly continue to hold, but he personally recommended withdrawal.

When that word reached Montgomery, he went to Chaudfontaine to confer with General Hodges. The time had come, said Montgomery, to withdraw. Reluctantly, Hodges agreed, and the order went out to the XVIII Airborne Corps.

Matthew Bunker Ridgway, forty-nine years old, was born into an army family, and the U.S. Army had been his life. He was a man of great personal courage (he wore a harness with a hand grenade attached to each of the front straps, not, he maintained, because he wanted to create a distinctive image but because he might need them). His airborne troops from as far back as the days when he had commanded the 82d Airborne Division admired his toughness and called him "The Eagle." He drove himself relentlessly and saw no reason not to drive others the same way. You won wars, in Ridgway's view, not by giving ground but by taking it and holding it.

In early afternoon of December 22, General Ridgway arrived at the Middle School in Vielsalm. Although he knew of Field Marshal Montgomery's order to withdraw and the fact that there was probably no way of circumventing it, he was reluctant to acquiesce until he had a feel himself for the situation on the ground.

In Hasbrouck's headquarters, Ridgway talked with Hasbrouck and with Jones, whose headquarters was also in Vielsalm, in a Belgian Army barracks built originally for the *Chasseurs Ardennais* close by the Salm River. In one hand, Ridgway held Hasbrouck's recent message urging withdrawal and fearing for survival of the 7th Armored Division. Holding aloft the message, Ridgway demanded in a scathing tone: "Did you read this before you signed it?"

Replied Hasbrouck: "Yes, sir, I most assuredly did."

With that reply, Ridgway's attitude changed. What, he asked, were the prospects for holding the fortified goose egg until a relief force arrived? In response, Hasbrouck cited all the things wrong with the position: the woods, the dearth of roads, the fatigue of the troops, the reduced strength. Jones, on the other hand, he who had remained rosily optimistic in the St. Joseph's Kloster at St. Vith even as two-thirds of his command was about to be lost, said he thought it could be done.

Although that was what Ridgway apparently wanted to hear, it obviously irritated him. Beckoning to Hasbrouck, he told him to come along; he was going forward to have a look for himself.

At General Clarke's command post in Commanster, the two met with Clarke and with the commander of the 424th Infantry, Colonel Reid, much of whose regiment was to form the reserve within the goose egg. What, Ridgway asked each commander, was the combat efficiency of his command? About 50 percent, said Reid; 40 percent, said Clarke.

There was one more commander Ridgway wanted to talk to, one who had been on the football team at West Point when Ridgway had been the manager, a man whom Ridgway knew from long acquaintance to be "calm, courageous, imperturbable" and in whom he had "absolute, implicit confidence." If Bill Hoge told him things were bad, he would know without doubt that things were bad.

Although Hoge was on the road, Ridgway contacted him by radio and arranged to meet at a farmhouse. There Ridgway tried a ploy.

"Bill," he said, "we've made contact with you now. This position is too exposed to try to hold it any longer." He had no intention he said, of leaving Hoge's combat command in place "to be chopped to pieces, little by little." Watching closely for Hoge's reaction, he said he intended to begin withdrawal that night. "We're going to get you out of here."

Hoge: "How can you?"

That terse response told Ridgway all he needed to know. "Bill," he said, no longer employing artifice, "we can and we will."

Back in Vielsalm after dark, Ridgway summoned General Jones to Hasbrouck's command post. He found Jones's attitude "strange." How could he be so optimistic when he seldom left his command post and knew so little about what was happening? He seemed to Ridgway to be "casual, almost indifferent, little interested in the fact that that night we were going to bring his people out of the trap."

In Hasbrouck's presence, Ridgway relieved Jones of his command and put all the troops in the salient under Hasbrouck. Apparently unaware that Hoge was senior to Hasbrouck (or ignoring the fact in view of the difference in the size of the forces the two commanded), he assigned

Hoge as Hasbrouck's deputy, although Hoge was too busy with his own combat command ever to assume the post. To soften the blow of relief for Jones, Ridgway made him deputy commander of the XVIII Airborne Corps.

The sudden relief added to the strain created by all that had happened to the fledgling 106th Division—which Alan W. Jones had so expectantly brought into the line not quite a fortnight before for an introduction to combat in a quiet sector—was too much for Jones, one of the more tragic figures in the events that occurred in the Ardennes. Shortly after midnight, he suffered a serious heart attack. Medics evacuated him to a hospital in Liège.

There were something like twenty thousand American troops in the salient beyond the Salm River, more than a hundred medium tanks, around seventy self-propelled tank destroyers, scores of half-tracks, trucks, and other vehicles, and the howitzers of nine field artillery battalions. There were only two ways out: either through Vielsalm or not quite two miles up the river to the south, through Salmchâteau.

Three principal roads led to the exits: the main St. Vith–Vielsalm highway passing through Poteau and entering Vielsalm from the north; the gravel road cutting diagonally through the Grand Bois and Commanster into Vielsalm from the southeast; and the highway following the valley of the Salm into Salmchâteau from the south. Because that highway was on the west bank of the river and accessible at points to the south, the bridge at Salmchâteau was not vital, but the town, which was also on the west bank, was, and the town was outside the defensive line established west of the river by troops of the 82d Airborne Division.

Getting onto any one of those three routes was the big problem, particularly for the heavy vehicles of the artillery and the armored units, for in many cases they would first have to feed their vehicles over narrow woods trails and farm tracks. Despite nearly a foot of snow, the ground underneath was still soft and with the passage of only a few heavy vehicles was soon churned into a morass. "The mud makes it pretty difficult," General Clarke told General Hasbrouck late in the night of the 22d. "I don't know how we're going to do it."

There was also an enemy to be reckoned with. Since early in the evening an intense combat had been raging for control of Crombach, and there was considerable doubt whether the Shermans of Colonel Wemple's 17th Tank Battalion could break away without incurring heavy losses. Soon after midnight, men of the 62d Volksgrenadier Division advanced up the valley of the Braunlauf Creek and again broke into the settlement of Neubrück, that time in numbers not to be denied. A few miles to the south *Volksgrenadiers* got into a village and overran a platoon of medium tanks.

In late evening of the 22d and on into the early hours of the 23d, the artillery battalions began a phased withdrawal along with a part of Colonel Reid's 424th Infantry that had moved into reserve near Commanster, but neither General Clarke nor General Hoge thought it possible to begin his withdrawal. It was close to five o'clock in the morning of December 23 when General Hasbrouck sent a message to both of them. Just beyond the river along the highway leading west from Salmchâteau, the 2d SS Panzer Division's reconnaissance battalion was attacking positions of the 82d Airborne Division; unless the withdrawal began soon, "the opportunity will be over." It would be necessary "to disengage whether circumstances are favorable or not," otherwise it would be impossible to execute "any kind of withdrawal with equipment."

During the night, a cold wind had begun to blow out of the east, bringing what weathermen call a "Russian high." Although both Clarke and Hoge noted it, they saw little hope that the ground might freeze in time to aid their withdrawals; but after receiving Hasbrouck's message, Clarke stepped outside his command post in a beerhall in Commanster and tested the ground. He could hardly believe it. Checking first with Hoge, then reporting to Hasbrouck, he was exultant. "That cold snap has frozen the road," he said. "I think we can make it now."

So did Hoge. First in the march table, his troops were unable to get under way until close to 7 A.M., and even before the first vehicles reached Vielsalm, full daylight had come. The last battalion of the 424th Infantry, which served as a covering force for Hoge's withdrawal, nevertheless soon followed but got out only under sustained small-arms fire. Provided covering fire by a platoon of 105mm. assault guns, Colonel Wemple's tanks in Crombach also managed to break contact and—thanks to the freeze—move cross-country, eventually to get on the route of withdrawal through Commanster. The crush of traffic was soon so great where the road narrowed to pass through the village that General Clarke himself took a hand in keeping it moving.

A short distance northwest of Crombach, at Hinderhausen, Colonel Erlenbush's 31st Tank Battalion and the two remaining troops of the 87th Armored Cavalry Reconnaissance Squadron faced Otto Remer's *Führer Begleit Brigade* less than a mile away across open fields in Rodt. Having churned the roads and trails around Rodt into a morass, Remer's vehicles had been unable to attack, but that too changed with the coming of the freeze. Putting a few tanks in the lead, Remer sent a battalion of infantry moving on Hinderhausen.

By that time, Remer had changed his objective. At the order of General von Manteuffel, he was to turn south and get on a road to Salmchâteau, there to join General Krüger's 58th Panzer Corps, which with the 2d SS Panzer and 116th Panzer Divisions was fast becoming the new *Schwerpunkt* of the German offensive.

The only route of withdrawal for the men and vehicles at Hinderhausen was a woods trail eventually leading to Commanster, a rutted track that General Clarke himself the day before had found almost impossible to negotiate even in a jeep. The tanks and a company of tank destroyers, infantrymen clutching for dear life to any handhold on the sides and decks, were forming for the withdrawal when the German column came into sight. While the cavalrymen deployed their vehicles as a rear guard, two of the tank destroyers knocked out the leading tanks with their 90mm. guns. The withdrawal began.

God bless the Russian high! The ruts were far from solidly frozen, but the footing was good enough for tracked vehicles. Although one tank threw a track, the driver managed to get it off the trail into a grove of seedling firs. The covering force soon followed with little attempt by the Germans to pursue, for Otto Remer had at last found an order to his liking: To turn the *Führer Begleit Brigade* south to Salmchâteau and join the 58th Panzer Corps in the drive for glory to the Meuse.

The next force to withdraw was Colonel Rosebaum's CCA in and around Poteau. At mid-morning the troops of the 9th SS Panzer Division that had been left to block toward Vielsalm attacked, but Rosebaum's tanks had little difficulty stopping them; and soon after midday, out of a sky that was at last beginning to brighten, a flight of P-38 Lightnings of the 370th Fighter Group appeared. Unable to establish radio contact with the unit they were supposed to support, the pilots chose a target of opportunity, the Germans in front of Poteau.

When word came shortly before 2 P.M. for CCA to withdraw, the Germans failed to react. Nor did they follow the withdrawal closely, which enabled the few men of CCR who were defending the village of Petit Thier to climb aboard their half-tracks and other vehicles and depart without a round fired at them.

The last troops scheduled to come out were those on the southern flank: the 112th Infantry and the task force that Hasbrouck had created to screen the open portion of that flank, named for its commander, Lt. Col. Robert B. Jones, commander of the 7th Armored Division's 814th Tank Destroyer Battalion. Jones had two companies of his self-propelled tank destroyers, his reconnaissance company, a company of light tanks, and the remnants of the 14th Cavalry Group.

Before daylight on the 23d, General Hasbrouck ordered the commander of the 112th Infantry, Colonel Nelson, to send one of his battalions to a village due east of Vielsalm, there to block trails leading through the Grand Bois to Vielsalm; that battalion thus eventually withdrew through Vielsalm. He ordered another battalion to provide close-in defense of the bridge at Vielsalm and with a company defend the bridge at Salmchâteau until the withdrawal was completed, then demolish it. That left Colonel Nelson with only one battalion, headquarters troops, and attached engineers and towed tank destroyers.

With that force, Nelson was to screen south of the village of Beho, where the route of withdrawal for Hoge's combat command joined the road to Commanster. Once the armor passed, the infantry was to fall back on the village of Rogery, there to block a secondary road (it fed into the Salm valley highway by means of a bridge over upper reaches of the river) and await General Hasbrouck's order to withdraw. That was supposed to come as soon as all but Nelson's men and Task Force Jones had departed, for Task Force Jones was supposed to be the last out.

Using a radio belonging to a liaison officer from Hasbrouck's headquarters, Nelson reported at 1 P.M. that everybody was out except his force and Task Force Jones, but no order to withdraw followed. A few minutes later, seven German tanks preceding truck-mounted infantry appeared in front of Rogery, an advance guard of the *Führer Begleit Brigade* on the way to Salmchâteau.

A towed gun of the 630th Tank Destroyer Battalion knocked out one tank, and one of two 90mm. guns loaned to Nelson by the 814th Tank Destroyer Battalion knocked out another. (The 112th Infantry's executive officer, Colonel Train, found himself caught between the tank destroyers and the German tanks; the shells passed over his head "like subway trains.") The other German tanks fell back, but the infantry dismounted and attacked.

Seeing no point in a last-ditch fight when withdrawal was in the offing—indeed, should have been under way had the order but come from Hasbrouck—Colonel Nelson in mid-afternoon decided the time had come to get out. Under cover of fire from the tank destroyers, he sent his vehicles across the nearby bridge over the Salm to gain the valley highway and his infantry cross-country to cross the stream on a railroad bridge.

It was well after dark by the time Nelson's troops reached the valley highway. To their amazement and dismay, they found the road blocked by vehicles two and three abreast—the vehicles of Task Force Jones, which were supposed to have followed their own withdrawal. Inching forward in a jeep on a shoulder of the road, Nelson learned that as the light tanks heading Jones's column had approached Salmchâteau, German tanks had opened fire, knocking out several of the light tanks and blocking the road. The *Führer Begleit Brigade*'s advance guard had hit Nelson's position at Rogery, then continued toward Salmchâteau along a farm track.

There were at that point no American troops in Salmchâteau. Just before dusk, the company of the 112th Infantry stationed at the bridge asked paratroopers of the 82d Airborne Division, who occupied high ground to the west of the town, to blow the bridge. That done, the infantrymen joined the paratroopers in their defensive line. Destruction of the bridge would have no effect on the withdrawal of Colonel Nelson and Task Force Jones, for they were already across the Salm; but the departure of the infantry company left the town open to German occupation, and the Germans soon moved in.

With most of the 2d SS Panzer Division immobilized while awaiting gasoline, the commander of the division's reconnaissance battalion, Maj. Ernst Krag, had set out on December 22 to prepare the way for his division's advance northwestward alongside the 116th Panzer Division by getting onto the main highway leading west from Salmchâteau. Having no success penetrating positions of the 82d Airborne Division along the highway (it was those thrusts that had prompted Hasbrouck's concerned message to Clarke and Hoge at 5 A.M. on the 23d), Krag sent a portion of his command to Salmchâteau. There he might at least establish contact with other Germans forces he knew to be advancing from the direction of St. Vith.

Although Colonel Nelson sent his I&R Platoon, a platoon of engineers, and a platoon of infantry to get into Salmchâteau, they had no success, and by that time the stalled column along the valley highway was feeling the wrath of an enemy sensing a kill. Tanks and infantry of the *Führer Begleit Brigade* followed up the American withdrawal from Rogery and continued toward the Salm and the bridge leading to the valley highway over which Colonel Nelson's vehicles had passed. A platoon of the 814th Tank Destroyer Battalion under 1st Lt. Hugh T. Bertruch, Jr., stood in the way.

A brilliant moon had risen. Lieutenant Bertruch's tank destroyers opened fire, using their machine guns to discourage the infantry and their 90mm. pieces to stop the German tanks. In a blazing firefight, the tank destroyers knocked out seven German tanks but lost all their own guns. As the survivors among the crews fell back down the hill into the valley, they found engineers ready to blow the bridge leading to the valley highway. The demolition stopped the *Führer Begleit Brigade* from driving full into the flank of the immobilized column along the road.

Only the bright moonlight prevented utter confusion from developing among that column. The men and vehicles of Task Force Jones and of the 112th Infantry were hopelessly intermingled; and a detachment of engineers from the 82d Airborne Division, under orders to blow a culvert near the end of the column to block the road, seemed determined to do their task and get back to their command. The 112th Infantry's executive officer, Colonel Train, stopped them; but once he turned away to other tasks, they did the job they were ordered to do and to hell with the consequences. That trapped a few light tanks and an ambulance, and the guns of the *Führer Begleit Brigade* dealt with them swiftly.

Somebody at last discovered a secondary road leading off the valley highway to the west. There was no choice but to take it, try to bypass Salmchâteau, and come into the 82d Airborne Division's lines along the highway behind the town. It took much of the rest of the night to do that, men and vehicles often moving cross-country (once again, prayers of thanks went up for the Russian high). Some of the first men to gain the airborne division's line found the paratroopers getting ready to bring down artillery fire on what they took to be an approaching German column.

Before daylight came on December 24, most of the men and vehicles of Task Force Jones and the 112th Infantry had escaped. Colonel Nelson estimated that he lost only eighteen out of more than a hundred vehicles. To his chagrin, at ten o'clock in the morning he at last received a copy of the order from General Hasbrouck for him to withdraw—an order sent at 1 P.M. the day before.

In Vielsalm on the night of December 23, a small detachment of airborne engineers, covered by a platoon of the 508th Parachute Infantry's Company A under 1st Lt. George D. Lamm, prepared to demolish rail and road bridges spanning the little Salm River. Early that evening, word came from the 7th Armored Division that everybody scheduled to withdraw through Vielsalm had passed; but unless pressed by the Germans, the engineers intended to delay until midnight to allow for stragglers. While the bulk of Lamm's platoon covered the bridges from the west bank, Lamm led an eight-man patrol to the far bank to discourage any Germans trying to reach the bridges.

A little after 10:30 P.M., Lieutenant Lamm and his men spotted a platoon of Germans coming along the street leading to the highway bridge. Lamm told his men to open fire, then to fall back while he covered their withdrawal. He then moved back over the railroad bridge, pulling the fuse to the demolitions there, while one of the other men did the same at the highway bridge.

To the dismay of all, neither charge went off.

While the airborne engineers rewired the charges, setting them for a thirty-second delay, Lamm led the patrol back to the west bank. Once the engineers pulled the fuses, the patrol rushed back. The railroad bridge went up with a roar; but again, at the highway bridge nothing happened.

Despite fire from a German tank on high ground inside Vielsalm, Lamm once more led the patrol forward, again engineers set the fuse, and again the patrol fell back across the bridge. Yet again, nothing happened.

For a fourth try, Lamm attacked across the bridge to drive Germans back from nearby houses. As the patrol withdrew, the engineers fired a bazooka into the demolitions to make sure they went off. They did, but they blew only the flooring from the bridge, leaving supporting joists intact.

From the west bank, Lamm and his platoon kept up a steady fire while engineers went back for more explosives. For close to an hour, the paratroopers held the Germans away from the remains of the bridge until at last new explosives were in place.

He had so much TNT under the joists, shouted the engineer officer, that Hitler was bound to hear the explosion in Berlin. Waiting nearby around a bend in the road, one of General Hoge's liaison officers, Lieutenant Lewis, allowed as how the lieutenant knew what he was talking about: "The earth shook and fragments went high in the sky."

Hasso von Manteuffel had intended taking St. Vith and its important network of roads by the end of the first day of the offensive, December 16. He got the town only at the end of the sixth day, December 21. Even then it was a bottleneck, and the roads beyond were still denied until the end of the eighth day, December 23. It was a critical, crushing delay, second in importance in disruption of German plans only to the stand of American troops on the northern shoulder in front of and along the Elsenborn Ridge.

It had not come easy nor without heavy cost. Because most of the troops involved immediately after the withdrawal went into action farther west, the losses east of the Salm were difficult to pin down. Probably as many as five thousand men killed, wounded, or captured. The 7th Armored Division alone lost fifty-nine medium tanks. Losses in the two infantry regiments, which on the south flank of the salient had been out of the mainstream of the action, were severe but less than might have been expected. Including the fighting in the first few days of the offensive, for example, the 112th Infantry lost seven hundred men.

For much of the late afternoon of December 23 and into the evening, Bob Hasbrouck was at the western end of the highway bridge in Vielsalm to welcome his men to a new lease on life. The Supreme Commander, General Eisenhower, promptly sent a letter of commendation to all the units. And the man then in charge of the troops along the northern edge of the German penetration, Field Marshal Montgomery, even as he ordered the withdrawal, sent a message saying: "They can come back with all honor. They come back to more secure positions. They put up a wonderful show."

It remained for the 30th British Corps, which by that time had assembled in watchful waiting behind the Meuse River, to forward the most terse and yet most moving tribute. All the message said was *"A bas les Boches!"*

For the rest of their lives, Robert Hasbrouck, Bruce Clarke, William Hoge, Dwight Rosebaum, Alexander Reid, Gustin Nelson, and many another commander who had fought in the salient beyond the Salm River would be grateful to Field Marshal Montgomery for getting them out of what they saw as a deathtrap for their commands. Yet to the credit of Matthew B. Ridgway, he had gone to the scene himself and for all his preconceptions to the contrary, had determined that withdrawal was imperative.

CHAPTER TWENTY-FOUR

The Defense of Bastogne

A market town with a population in 1944 of slightly over four thousand, Bastogne stands on a plateau at 1,600 feet elevation. The plateau lacks the vast expanses of forest and the turbulent terrain of most of the Ardennes; much of it is open pastureland amid rolling hills with occasional wood lots of coniferous trees. The town has no natural defense features other than the surrounding hills, but concentric circles of farm villages with sturdy brick and stone buildings provide solid anchors for defensive positions.

Until the late seventeenth century, when Louis XIV's troops demolished the town's fortifications, Bastogne had been a bastion of considerable military importance, primarily—as again in the winter of 1944—because of its central position astride the high plateau and its nexus of roads. In December 1944, five major and three secondary highways converged on a shop-lined square near the southern edge of town. It was those roads that made Bastogne important to Americans and Germans alike.

Early on December 19, the presence of what was left of the 9th Armored Division's CCR at Longvilly and of the 10th Armored Division's Team Cherry on the road between Longvilly and Mageret seriously interfered with efforts of the 47th Panzer Corps to get an attack under way against Bastogne. Throughout the day, their presence prevented the 26th Volksgrenadier Division from getting into position to attack the town from the northeast through the village of Bizory. The commander of the Panzer Lehr Division, General Bayerlein, was so intimidated that he made only tentative probes against the town from the east. (General von Manteuffel was furious with Bayerlein for getting off onto side roads and becoming involved at Mageret. If he was unable to read a map, why didn't he ask one of his staff officers to do it for him?) Even the commander of the 2d Panzer Division, Colonel von Lauchert, whose tanks were bypassing the town on the north en route to the Meuse, felt compelled to leave a few of his artillery pieces behind to counter the American tanks and artillery near Longvilly.

The delays thus imposed—plus the presence near Bastogne of the other two teams of the 10th Armored Division's CCB—would go a long way toward enabling the Americans to consolidate their hairbreadth victory in the race for Bastogne. One of the other two teams, commanded by Lt. Col. James O'Hara, was blocking the principal highway to the southeast in the direction of the Café Schumann crossroads and Ettelbruck; and since the Germans were trying to get into Bastogne along other roads, O'Hara and his men had only brushes with the enemy on the first day. Not so the team commanded by Maj. William R. Desobry.

William Robertson Desobry, twenty-six years old, grew up on army posts but considered himself a Texan. When it came time for college, he chose not West Point but Georgetown University in Washington, D.C., and entered the army through the ROTC. With the commander of the 10th Armored Division's CCB, Colonel Roberts, the veteran of the Great War, young Desobry had established almost a father-son relationship.

As Desobry came into Bastogne on the night of December 18, Roberts pointed on a map to the village of Noville, four miles northeast of Bastogne on the principal highway to Houffalize and Liège, Highway N-15, and told Desobry to go there. He had no way of knowing, said Roberts, who was there: Americans, Germans, or nobody. General Middleton nevertheless had designated the village as an outpost for Bastogne at the limit of artillery support positioned close to the town.

"You are young," said Roberts, "and by tomorrow morning you will probably be nervous. By midmorning the idea will probably come to you that it would be better to withdraw from Noville. When you begin thinking that, remember that I told you it would be best not to withdraw until I order you to do so."

Desobry's was a small force of around four hundred men, including a company of Shermans of the 3d Tank Battalion, a company of the 20th Armored Infantry Battalion, and a few engineers, medics, and reconnaissance troops. When Desobry and his men reached Noville, about all they could discern of the village without a map (hardly anybody had a map in the early days at Bastogne) and in darkness and fog, was that it was a collection of houses, barns, a beerhall, a church, and a schoolhouse. Most of the buildings lined the Bastogne-Houffalize highway. And the whole place stood on windswept ground, for only at a little cemetery in a depression off the highway were there any trees.

Establishing a defense to the east, north, and northwest, Desobry sent outposts onto three roads leading into the village. Anticipating stragglers from other units, he told his men to hang onto any engineers and infantry who appeared to be willing to fight (*see map, p. 467*).

It was close to four o'clock in the morning when the men on the road leading from the east and the village of Bourcy heard half-tracks approaching. Not certain whether they were American or German, a sentry yelled: "Halt!" As the leading half-track braked abruptly, someone shouted something in German. From an embankment above the road, the men in the outpost hurled hand grenades into the half-track, and a duel with more hand grenades ensued. To get away from the rain of potato mashers, the man in charge, Staff. Sgt. Leon D. Gantt, ordered the men to fall back a short distance toward Noville. As the Americans disengaged, the half-tracks turned and headed back toward Bourcy.

Silence was settling in again when the men in Noville heard a strange rumble in the distance that as it drew closer became a dull roar. German tanks and other tracked vehicles were moving west along a road bypassing Noville to the north. In the fog and darkness, it was an eerie sound.

Shortly after 6 A.M., the men in the outpost along the Houffalize road heard tanks approaching. Because American stragglers had been feeding through the outpost for some time, they held their fire. Then, as two German tanks came into view, their gunners opened fire, knocking out two Shermans in the outpost. At Desobry's order, that outpost and the other two fell back.

Daylight was slow to develop through the thick fog. Visibility was still meager when two more German tanks approached down the Houffalize road accompanied by *Panzergrenadiers*. Tanks, machine guns, bazookas, rifles—every American weapon within range opened up. The *Panzergrenadiers* scattered and disappeared in the fog, while the two German tanks went up in flames. From that time the two hulks served as a partial roadblock along the Houffalize road.

It was mid-morning, around ten thirty, when the fog suddenly lifted "as if it were a [theater] curtain" to reveal an awesome spectacle. For the first time the defenders could see that they were on relatively low ground dominated by ridgelines to the north and northeast. On the high ground to the north were fourteen German tanks arrayed in a skirmish line, and on the other ridge and at various other points around the landscape there were more, altogether possibly as many as fifty or sixty. Quite obviously, Team Desobry was facing the might of an entire panzer division.

Partly because Colonel von Lauchert had difficulty getting his *Panzergrenadiers* to accompany the tanks over the open ground, the fight quickly became a duel between armored vehicles, mostly at long range and often influenced by the vagaries of the fog, which swirled and eddied, sometimes rising, sometimes descending. Just as the duel opened, a platoon of self-propelled guns of the 609th Tank Destroyer Battalion raced into the village. Those guns and the Shermans drew some advantage in that the buildings of the village afforded a degree of concealment and protection.

In quick succession, the American pieces hit nine of the fourteen tanks on the ridge to the north, setting three on fire, and as another German tank headed down a farm track leading to Noville, a round from somebody's gun set it ablaze. With a 37mm. gun, an armored car scored a hit at some vulnerable point on a Panther and knocked it out; the gunner himself found it hard to believe.

In the flaming encounter, the 2d Panzer Division lost seventeen tanks, plus the two destroyed earlier on the Houffalize road. Team Desobry lost a single tank destroyer, four smaller vehicles, and thirteen men wounded.

However one-sided the victory, it left Major Desobry acutely conscious of the size of the enemy force he faced and of the vulnerability of his position. As was soon demonstrated, German tanks and assault guns could sit in defiladed positions on the high ground above the village and pour their fire almost with impunity on Desobry's defenses, gradually destroying the protection of the buildings in the process.

Desobry was thinking, just as Colonel Roberts had predicted, that it would be better to withdraw from Noville. He also remembered that Roberts had said he was not to withdraw without permission. Radioing Roberts, he requested that permission.

Shortly before midnight on December 18, Col. Julian J. Ewell led his regiment, the 501st Parachute Infantry, into an assembly area three miles west of Bastogne. His was the first contingent of the 101st Airborne Division to arrive from Camp Mourmelon. A few hours later he received a summons to report to what was left of headquarters of the VIII Corps in the Heintz Barracks on the northern fringe of Bastogne.

There Colonel Ewell—a wiry, blunt-spoken man, something of an iconoclast, little given to formalities and speaking with a mountaineer's twang—found the situation map so covered with red markings indicating German units that "it looked as if it had the measels." The members of the corps staff appeared to be punch drunk from fatigue, but General Middleton and the interim commander of the 101st Airborne Division, General McAuliffe, were alert and calm. Having little knowledge of what was going on east of Bastogne with Team Cherry and the 9th Armored Division's CCR, the two had agreed to husband the bulk of the airborne troops for defense of the town but to send a regiment to the east to develop the situation.

That job was to be Ewell's. Pointing to the highway leading through the hamlet of Neffe and then through Mageret and Longvilly—the road along which Team Cherry and CCR were soon to be fighting for their lives—McAuliffe told Ewell to move out along it, "make contact, attack, and clear up the situation."

It was still dark and foggy when at 6 A.M. Ewell's leading 1st Battalion, commanded by Maj. Raymond V. Bottomly, Jr., passed on foot through the Place St. Pierre at the northeastern edge of Bastogne and out onto the road leading to Neffe and Mageret. As the troops approached

Neffe, daylight had come, but a heavy fog still limited visibility to a few hundred yards.

The paratroopers had just passed the last curve in the road before it descended straight into Neffe when a German machine gun opened fire. Shells from German tanks soon followed. The only weapons available to Bottomly capable of dealing in any way with tanks were seven 57mm. antitank guns, and because of the straightness of the road, it was impossible under German fire to get those into firing positions. Until a battery of short-tubed 105mm. howitzers of the 907th Glider Field Artillery Battalion could arrive, there was little Bottomly could do to get his men into Neffe.

Just outside Neffe the commander of Team Cherry, cut off from his command by the presence of General Bayerlein's tanks and *Panzergrenadiers* in Mageret, had established his command post in a château; and in Neffe he had created a roadblock with the 3d Tank Battalion's Reconnaissance Platoon, equipped with armored cars and light tanks. Around six o'clock that morning, two of Bayerlein's tanks with two platoons of infantry had probed through Neffe in the direction of Bastogne.

That probe was nothing more than a tentative thrust conditioned by Bayerlein's concern for the armor to his rear, but it was strong enough to eliminate the Reconnaissance Platoon's roadblock, and with *Panzergrenadiers*, Bayerlein turned against Cherry's command post in the château. All through the morning, Cherry's headquarters troops ran from window to window, firing a few rounds from each to give an impression of strength. They gained some respite with the approach of Major Bottomly's paratroopers, for the Germans had to turn some troops in that direction; and in early afternoon a platoon of paratroopers worked around to the south to reach the château. Despite that reinforcement, Colonel Cherry decided, once the château caught fire from German shelling, to retrace the route of the paratroopers and get out. He was not driven out, reported Cherry, he was "burned out"; and he was not withdrawing, he was "moving."

In the meantime, the second of Colonel Ewell's parachute infantry battalions arrived. Since Bottomly was unable to advance on Neffe, Ewell decided that he might get at the hamlet by occupying Bizory, which stood atop high ground a few hundred yards north of Neffe. He sent his 2d Battalion to Bizory, which the paratroopers found was still being held by a few men of the 158th Engineers.

Hoping to eliminate the German opposition in Neffe by a drive from Bizory into Mageret, behind Neffe, Colonel Ewell ordered the battalion commander, Maj. Sammie N. Homan, to take Mageret. That effort ended near a woodlot on the crest of high ground between the two villages where Homan's men ran into the 26th Volksgrenadier Division's reconnaissance battalion, the only contingent of the division that had at last gotten past Longvilly to drive on Bizory. "For the time being,"

Homan reported laconically to Ewell, "I cannot think of taking Mageret."

The 501st Parachute Infantry's 3d Battalion was, in the meantime, having trouble getting forward because of the exodus from Bastogne of headquarters and logistical units of the VIII Corps. In the process, some of the men managed to cadge helmets, rifles, and ammunition from those troops, and as they passed through the main square in Bastogne, from headquarters troops of the 10th Armored Division's CCB.

When the battalion finally broke free of the congestion in early afternoon, Ewell told the commander, Lt. Col. George M. Griswold, to bring the bulk of his battalion to the hamlet of Mont, on the Bastogne-Neffe road, from which he intended coming upon Neffe from the south by way of the château that had been Colonel Cherry's command post. To protect the flank of that maneuver, he told Griswold to send a company farther south into the village of Wardin, where, so Ewell believed, the company would find a part of Team O'Hara, one of the three teams of the 10th Armored Division's CCB.

Team O'Hara was actually a thousand yards beyond Wardin astride the Bastogne-Ettelbruck highway, but since Wardin was close on the team's north flank, Colonel O'Hara had recently dispatched his S-2, Capt. Edward A. Carrigo, and one of his infantry company commanders, 1st Lt. John Drew Devereaux, to check out the village. As the two officers entered in a jeep, Devereaux driving, civilians rushed from their houses, obviously distressed.

Devereaux stopped his jeep and jumped on the hood. An actor who not many months before had been appearing on Broadway and a member of the august theatrical family, the Barrymores, Devereaux appeared to relish his role. "Don't be afraid," he called out in French. "We Americans are here to stay. Keep to your cellars, and don't be afraid."

Continuing through the village, Devereaux and Carrigo had just passed the last house when a projectile of some kind hit the bumper of their jeep. It failed to explode, but through the fog the two officers made out a German armored car and a half-track. Turning around quickly, they hurried back into Wardin. Slowing the jeep, Devereaux announced to the civilians: "The Germans are coming. Get back to your cellars."

As the two officers raced out of Wardin, the paratroopers of Company I, 501st Parachute Infantry, commanded by Capt. Claude D. Wallace, Jr., were plodding on foot toward the village. They got into Wardin just as the Germans were coming in the other side in strength, the second prong of the attack on Bastogne planned by General Bayerlein for his *Panzer Lehr Division:* a battalion of *Panzergrenadiers* supported by seven tanks.

The 130 or so men of Company I were no match for such a force. They fought bravely—one man knelt with a bazooka in the middle of the little dirt road that passed for a main street and knocked out the leading

German tank before return fire cut him down, and other men with bazookas accounted for three more—but there were still other German
tanks and too many *Panzergrenadiers*.

When Colonel Ewell learned that Company I was in trouble, he ordered Captain Wallace to pull back, but it was too late for many of the
paratroopers. The company lost all of its officers and forty-five men, most
of them killed or so badly wounded that they had to be left behind. Captain Wallace was among those who died. For all Lieutenant Devereaux's
high promises to the inhabitants of Wardin, their village at that point
belonged to the Germans.

The pattern of all that happened that day, December 19—repulse at
Neffe, occupation of Bizory but repulse in the thrust on Mageret, and
repulse at Wardin—convinced Julian Ewell that the offensive phase of his
commitment was over. Going to McAuliffe's headquarters, Ewell asked
permission to occupy a defensive line along high ground extending southward from Bizory. Although Ewell discerned that some people on
McAuliffe's staff thought him timid, McAuliffe approved; and Colonel
O'Hara soon received authority to fall back to a position astride the Bastogne-Ettelbruck highway just north of the village of Marvie, there to tie
in with Ewell's line.

At the same time, General McAuliffe afforded Ewell a battalion of
the 327th Glider Infantry to serve as a reserve behind that flank. The new
line was only just over a mile outside Bastogne, which would limit maneuver; but as doubters on McAuliffe's staff would soon learn, what they
had taken to be Julian Ewell's timidity was, in reality, the better part of
valor.

When Colonel Roberts in his command post in the Hôtel Lebrun on
the Rue de Marche just off the main square of the town received Major
Desobry's request for permission to withdraw from Noville, he was torn.
Desobry's position was obviously dominated by German-held high
ground, and there was a better defensive position atop a ridgeline a few
miles behind Noville at the settlement of Foy. Under the conditions of
the commitment of his combat command at Bastogne, Roberts considered that he had authority to approve the withdrawal of any part of his
command. On the other hand, they were not going to hold Bastogne
without steadfast defense everywhere. Before granting the authority,
Roberts left to have a talk with General McAuliffe in the Heintz barracks.

On the way, Roberts bumped into the airborne division's assistant
commander, Brig. Gen. Gerald J. Higgins. As he was explaining the situation at Noville to Higgins, Lt. Col. James L. LaPrade and the men of his
1st Battalion, 506th Parachute Infantry, appeared and with them their
regimental commander, Col. Robert F. Sink. Higgins promptly ordered
Sink to send a battalion of his paratroopers to reinforce Desobry, and

Colonel LaPrade and his men simply kept on walking in the direction of Noville.

Returning to the Hôtel Lebrun, Colonel Roberts radioed Desobry: "You can use your own judgment about withdrawing, but I'm sending a battalion of paratroopers to reinforce you." That settled the issue for Desobry. As soon as the paratroopers arrived, he intended to attack to take the high ground from which German guns were doling out such misery, and with the high ground in hand, he hoped to be able to hold on at Noville.

Like the other battalions of the 101st Airborne Division, LaPrade's was short of helmets, weapons, overshoes, coats, and ammunition. Learning of that, Desobry told his Service Company in Bastogne to try to do something for the men. Loading several vehicles with supplies, 2d Lt. George C. Rice drove through LaPrade's marching paratroopers and deposited them at the head of the column so the men could pick from them as they passed. He did that three times before the paratroopers got all the way to Noville.

As the paratroopers entered the village, German shelling was continuing. Desobry and LaPrade nevertheless mounted their attack against the high ground in early afternoon, but nowhere did it gain more than five hundred yards. The fire from German tanks on the ridges was devastating, and the attack coincided with a German thrust on Noville that Colonel von Lauchert had been trying to get under way ever since his tanks had absorbed such heavy losses that morning. Again the *Panzergrenadiers* deserted their tanks on the open ground, and again the 2d Panzer Division lost heavily in tanks; but the American attack came nowhere near gaining the high ground overlooking Noville.

Shortly before nightfall, McAuliffe's deputy, General Higgins, went to Noville for a first-hand look at the situation. As he was conferring with Desobry and LaPrade on the ground floor of a house that served as their joint headquarters, German shells exploded outside, prompting LaPrade to pull a big armoire in front of the most exposed window, which faced the highway just outside the house. Hardly had Higgins gone when the commander of the 506th Parachute Infantry, Colonel Sink, also arrived for a first-hand look.

Shortly after Colonel Sink left, the battalion maintenance officer parked his tank recovery vehicle just outside the house and came inside to report that he had completed his work and was returning to Bastogne. In the gathering darkness, gunners on German tanks made out the outline of the vehicle and began shooting at it. They missed the vehicle, but several rounds hit the house.

One tore through the armoire. Colonel LaPrade fell to the floor dead. Major Desobry also fell, unconscious, with one eye virtually torn from its socket and a serious wound in the back of his head.

Medics rushed Desobry by jeep to the 506th Parachute Infantry's aid station, then by ambulance to the airborne division's collecting station, set up in tents at a crossroads near the division's original assembly area west of Bastogne. There surgeons saved his eye and while he was still under anesthetic, put him in an ambulance ready for evacuation. But when the anesthetic wore off, Desobry was to find himself on the way into Germany, a prisoner of war.

Late that night, six armored vehicles—a mixture of tanks and half-tracks—approached the crossroads and opened fire on the collecting station. Just as the firing began, a twelve-truck convoy on the way to the rear for supplies arrived; although the drivers fought back with the .50-caliber machine guns mounted above the cabs of their trucks, their cause was hopeless. German fire soon knocked out all the trucks, setting some of them alight, which clearly illuminated the big red crosses on the nearby tents. Everybody in a truckload of wounded waiting to be moved into the collecting station was killed.

After fifteen minutes of firing, a German officer entered the main tent and ordered the senior officer, the division surgeon, Lt. Col. David Gold, to surrender. All medics and all patients were to load on American vehicles.

Three medical officers and a few men managed to slip away into the night and tell their story in Bastogne. Most of the attackers, they said, wore civilian clothes, and when a patrol reached the site, the men found no American dead or wounded, only dead men of military age in civilian clothes.

There was some speculation later whether the raid on the collecting station might have been the work of Belgian Nazis who accompanied German units in the offensive. (They included the Belgian quisling, Léon DeGrelle, whom the Germans intended to head a new government in Belgium.) Although the Germans may have staged the raid to look like the work of civilians, there was no question that the officer who demanded Colonel Gold's surrender was a German, and the dead in civilian clothes wore the identification discs of German soldiers.

Back from Noville, General Higgins told General McAuliffe that the men in Noville were "way out on a limb" and in his judgment "had better get out." While the two were still talking, Colonel Sink arrived. He wanted his battalion of paratroopers out.

Although McAuliffe reckoned he had the authority to pull back his own troops, it was the corps commander, General Middleton, who had ordered that Noville be held; and at that stage, McAuliffe had no command authority over troops of the 10th Armored Division's CCB. (Nobody apparently thought to consult with Colonel Roberts, who considered he had authority to pull his troops back.) Instead, McAuliffe telephoned Middleton at his new corps headquarters seventeen miles away in

Neufchâteau. "No," said Middleton. "If we are to hold on to Bastogne, you cannot keep falling back."

That night in Noville, December 19, in the same dense fog that blanketed every corner of the Ardennes, the paratroopers, the armored infantrymen, the crews of the armored cars, medium tanks, and tank destroyers stood to their posts. Early in the evening, McAuliffe sent forward five self-propelled guns of the 705th Tank Destroyer Battalion, long-barreled 76mm. pieces—less powerful than the 90mm. but considerably more powerful than the regular 76mm.—which had just arrived in Bastogne with the rest of the battalion following a run from the Ninth Army. Also early that evening, another battalion of the 506th Parachute Infantry moved into Foy, just over a mile down the highway toward Bastogne.

All through the foggy night, small groups of *Panzergrenadiers*, sometimes accompanied by a tank or two, probed the perimeter, leaving the defenders praying for the coming of daylight. When it came, they wished for the night again, for the German shelling increased and two German tanks raced at full speed along the shoulders of the Houffalize road, fire from their machine guns keeping American troops pinned deep in their foxholes.

As the tanks drew up alongside the first building in Noville, the crews failed to note in the fog that they were within ten yards of an American bazooka team. The first rocket from the bazooka set one of the tanks on fire.

A short distance up the highway, Staff Sgt. Michael Lesniak dismounted from his tank, had a look, returned to his tank, and moved into the center of the road. Before the Germans knew what was happening, Lesniak's gunner fired and with his first round knocked out the other German tank. Yet a third tank that had stayed some distance behind the others threw a few shells into the village before falling back. One of those hit Lesniak's tank, damaging the traversing mechanism on the turret.

That was but the start. For the next two hours, groups of *Panzergrenadiers* supported by a few tanks probed at various points. Here and there a fight would flare and as defending tanks or tank destroyers lent a hand, would diminish, only to spring up again at another spot. Fog and smoke from burning buildings obscured the scene.

Again a German tank, a Panther, got through along the Houffalize road and came to a halt in front of a house serving as the command post for the company of the 20th Armored Infantry Battalion. As the tank swung its cannon toward the front door, the company commander, Capt. Omar Billet, said a silent prayer. He got a quick answer: only twenty yards away, Sergeant Lesniak was able to traverse the damaged turret on his tank just far enough to enable his gunner to get a bead on the Panther.

The gunner fired three quick rounds from his 75, which did no apparent damage, yet that was enough for the German crew. The driver put the tank in reverse, only to run over a jeep, crushing it and fouling one of the tracks on the tank. Dragging the jeep with it, the tank continued to back up but next collided with a half-track. The collision tipped the tank precariously far over to one side; the crew bailed out and raced from the village under concealment of the fog.

As on the day before, the fog in mid-morning suddenly lifted. In a reserve position near the rear of the village, the crews of the guns of the 705th Tank Destroyer Battalion could see on the high ground to the east a skirmish line of fifteen German tanks. With the first salvo, the gunners knocked out four and, as the crews tried to flee, took them under fire with .50-caliber machine guns. The other tanks turned back beyond the crest of the hill.

As the fog lifted, the two officers who had succeeded LaPrade and Desobry—Maj. Robert F. Harwick of the paratroopers, Maj. Charles L. Hustead of the armor—verified something they had long suspected: The Germans had moved in on their rear and cut the road to Bastogne. The situation was actually worse than they knew, for the Germans had also driven back the battalion of paratroopers that had occupied the settlement of Foy, forcing them to retire to high ground just to the south.

Again unknown to Harwick and Hustead, for all communications had failed, General McAuliffe was trying to send help. He ordered a battalion of the 502d Parachute Infantry, which had assembled as the division reserve around the village of Longchamps, not quite three miles southwest of Noville, to push through. The battalion got as far as a village about a mile from the Foy-Noville stretch of the main highway, but there ran into some of the Germans who had cut in behind Noville.

By that time, McAuliffe had decided that it was no longer a matter of reinforcing the defenders of Noville but of getting them out. That time he made no reference to General Middleton, for in mid-morning Middleton had attached Colonel Roberts's CCB to McAuliffe's division, which afforded McAuliffe command authority over the troops of CCB, and he had come to the conclusion that if he tried to continue to hold at Noville, every man there would perish. McAuliffe planned at first an attack by two parachute infantry battalions to open a way out, but the commander of the 506th Parachute Infantry, Colonel Sink, argued that there was no time for that.

When at last, around 1 P.M., radio contact was reestablished through the artillery net, the order went out to the two majors in Noville to fight their way out. The battalion of paratroopers on the high ground behind Foy was to help by retaking Foy; when the men in Noville heard the noise of that attack, they were to take off.

To Majors Harwick and Hustead, the chances of a successful withdrawal looked bleak. The road from Noville to Foy ran straight as a ruler, open fields on either side, not a single tree, the only cover or concealment a lone farmhouse on the left of the road some five hundred yards short of Foy. Since the lifting of the fog in mid-morning, the atmosphere had become almost clear so that for the German gunners visibility was close to perfect.

The two officers nevertheless prepared to depart. A company of paratroopers on foot, supported by three tanks, was to lead, followed by four half-tracks and five tanks providing an armored escort for vehicles carrying more than fifty wounded. Most of the rest of the men were to follow in vehicles of some kind, while another company of paratroopers on foot, supported by four tank destroyers, formed the rear guard.

As if acting as a signal for the withdrawal to begin, the curtain of fog descended again. The foot troops in the lead made the march with few problems, and all might have gone well for everybody except for a freak incident. As the first half-track preceding the vehicles carrying the wounded came abreast of the farmhouse outside Foy, the armored shutter over the slit through which the driver looked out to drive fell shut. When the driver raised his arm to lift the shutter, an officer thought the man had been wounded and pulled the hand brake. As the vehicle came to an abrupt stop, the half-track behind it rammed into the rear. In accordion fashion, every vehicle along the entire column came to a halt.

At that moment, small-arms fire struck the head of the column, some coming from the ditches on either side of the road, some from the farmhouse. As machine guns on the leading half-tracks blazed, men all along the column took to the ditches.

In time, the drivers of the half-tracks got their vehicles moving again and with machine guns still blazing, were soon inside Foy; but wary of what lay ahead in the fog, the driver of the first of the five U.S. tanks preceding the vehicles with the wounded was reluctant to push forward. He stalled until the armored commander, Major Hustead, arrived and ordered him to take the farmhouse under fire and get going.

The house was soon ablaze, and all five tanks began to move, only to be caught broadside by fire from three German tanks firing from somewhere beyond the farmhouse. Rounds hit the two leading tanks, setting the first on fire and disabling the second, in the process seriously wounding the driver.

Amid the confusion, the tank company commander, Capt. William G. Schultz, who had been riding in the fifth tank, walked up to the third tank and climbed aboard. On the theory that if he advanced, the rest of the column would follow, Schultz started off and got all the way through Foy before a round from a German tank knocked his tank out. Schultz and the crew nevertheless made it on foot into Bastogne.

Back near the farmhouse, nobody had followed Captain Schultz's example; for as the fourth tank started forward, a round from a German tank set it on fire and knocked the turret off into the road, blocking it. Only one tank was left, that in which Captain Schultz had been riding. Its driver, having learned that the driver of the second tank had been wounded but not that the tank was disabled, had gone forward to drive that tank. Major Hustead tried to find him, but without success, so he looked around for another driver from among the crews. Nobody professed to be able to drive a tank. That may well have been true, for there were specialists other than drivers in the crew of a tank; but nearby paratroopers and armored infantrymen refused to believe them. They swore at them and called them yellow bastards.

Far back in the column, everybody was growing restive. Swinging off the road to the west, a large group of paratroopers moved through the fields and gained Foy with no difficulty. The four tank destroyers with the rear guard followed and like the paratroopers, reached Foy without incident.

As the tank destroyers moved beyond Foy, an officer with the paratroopers who had retaken the settlement stopped one of them and told the driver, Pfc. Thomas E. Gallagher, to come with him. He had spotted the three German tanks that were firing at the withdrawing column. When Gallagher said he was short of crew and had no gunner, two other paratroopers climbed aboard. With a paratrooper doing the firing at a range of two hundred yards, Gallagher's tank destroyer knocked out one of the tanks, and the others turned away.

Delivered from the damaging fire of the German tanks, the remaining men and vehicles—including those carrying the wounded—worked their way off to the west of the road. The vehicles included the fifth tank, manned and driven by paratroopers, who climbed aboard swearing that somehow they would learn how to drive "the son of a bitch."

Darkness was near when the last of the survivors from Noville pulled into Bastogne. Team Desobry had gone to Noville with fifteen medium tanks; only four came back. The team also lost five tank destroyers and approximately half its 400 officers and men, while the 506th Parachute Infantry's 1st Battalion lost 212 killed, wounded, and missing.

Team Desobry had nevertheless imposed telling losses on the 2d Panzer Division, at least thirty tanks and perhaps as many as six hundred to eight hundred men. Ironically, while fighting in defense of Bastogne, Team Desobry had made its greatest contribution in delaying the panzer division's drive for the Meuse River by at least forty-eight hours—two days that were to have a telling effect.

For the attack on Bastogne on December 20, each of the attacking German divisions was short a regiment. Only with American withdrawal from Wiltz during the night of the 19th was Colonel Kokott's third regiment freed of the task of screening the corps flank before Wiltz, too late for the regiment to join the attack the next morning. So, too, one of the *Panzergrenadier* regiments of the Panzer Lehr Division had been delayed by the steadfast defense of men of the 110th Infantry on the other side of the Clerve River at Consthum, and as daylight came on December 20, that regiment was still toiling over roads turned by churning vehicles into a morass of mud.

The obstacle posed by Team Cherry and the 9th Armored Division's CCR at last eliminated by a combination of German guns and American withdrawal, Colonel Kokott was finally free to drive with one regiment on Bizory, the other on the Houffalize highway to get into the town from the north. But by that time both those routes were blocked: the one through Bizory by Major Homan's battalion of Ewell's 501st Parachute Infantry; the Houffalize highway by a battalion of Sink's 506th Parachute Infantry; the 3d under Lt. Col. Lloyd E. Patch. That battalion was preoccupied through much of the day with the drive to retake Foy and facilitate withdrawal of the troops in Noville. Partly for that reason, a problem developed along a railroad that served as a boundary between the two regiments.

Down the line of that railroad late on the 20th, a battalion of *Volksgrenadiers* supported by seven assault guns headed toward Bastogne, the way barred only by a patrol from Homan's battalion. That patrol nevertheless delayed the German advance long enough for both Colonel Ewell and Colonel Sink each to send a company to plug the gap.

The *Panzer Lehr Division* had no more success against the line that Colonel Ewell had formed on the eastern approaches to Bastogne. As two battalions of *Panzergrenadiers* supported by tanks attacked after nightfall from Neffe, fire from every artillery piece engaged in the defense of Bastogne converged on the hamlet. The Germans lost three tanks, and the attack got nowhere, while fire from the machine guns of five of the 705th Tank Destroyer Battalion's self-propelled pieces helped stop a second thrust. Only with the coming of daylight did the gunners learn why their fire was so effective: The Germans had been trying to advance in the darkness across a field laced with barbed-wire fences forming feeder pens for cattle. Bodies lined the base of every fence, and many hung on the wire.

Late on the night of December 20, the commander of the 47th Panzer Corps, General von Lüttwitz, could point to only two successes in the fight for Bastogne. The Americans had withdrawn from Noville, and well after nightfall, a task force built around the 26th Volksgrenadier Division's reconnaissance battalion and commanded by Maj. Rolf Kunkel skirted the town on the south and without opposition reached the Bastogne-Neufchâteau highway at the town of Sibret. There *Kampfgruppe Kunkel* found that a company of the Seventh Army's 5th Parachute Division had arrived first and was trying to drive headquarters of the 28th Division out of the town. When Kunkel's men joined the fight, General Cota again had to displace his headquarters; and the highway to Neufchâteau, the main supply route for the troops in Bastogne, was at that point severed.

Yet there was little joy that night in the headquarters of any German commander involved in the fight for Bastogne. To try to break the impasse, von Lüttwitz begged General von Manteuffel to allow the 2d Panzer Division to continue from Noville into Bastogne, but mindful of Hitler's insistence on getting to and over the Meuse, the commander of the Fifth Panzer Army said no. ("Forget Bastogne and head for the Meuse!") Made fully aware of his superiors' priorities, von Lüttwitz during the night ordered General Bayerlein to leave a *Panzergrenadier* regiment to help Kokott at Bastogne and send the rest of the *Panzer Lehr Division* skirting the town on the south and heading for the Meuse.

By December 20, virtually all the forces that were to participate in the defense of Bastogne had assembled, and as General Middleton had notified both General McAuliffe and Colonel Roberts during the morning, McAuliffe was in overall command. The principal component of the defensive force, the 101st Airborne Division, had left some men behind for housekeeping chores at Camp Mourmelon, but most of those who had been on leave when the division hurriedly moved out had come forward. At that point the division had just over ten thousand men in three parachute infantry regiments, a glider infantry regiment, an engineer battalion, four artillery battalions, and the usual technical support units. Because casualties in the Netherlands had been heavy, there were many replacements, but the division as a whole was a veteran outfit with high esprit.

By the 20th, Colonel Roberts's CCB, 10th Armored Division, had already lost heavily, Team Cherry having been almost annihilated and Team Desobry at Noville having taken severe losses in men and tanks. Yet Team O'Hara still had a full company of medium tanks, and Colonel Roberts found eight new tanks in Bastogne with their ordance crews, who had been on their way to deliver the tanks at the front. Thus CCB still had about thirty tanks, and the 420th Armored Field Artillery Battalion was intact.

Since Colonel Roberts had come under McAuliffe's command and thus no longer had full control of his armor, his basic concern was to see that the airborne commanders made proper use of it, that once tanks and tank destroyers did a job, they were not held as forts among the foxholes but returned to Bastogne, there to be ready for quick commitment at some other spot as trouble developed. With that in mind, Roberts virtually abandoned his command post in the Hôtel Lebrun to spend most of his time at McAuliffe's side.

The 9th Armored Division's CCR was no longer a viable fighting force. Only its supporting 73d Armored Field Artillery Battalion had emerged from the fighting at Longvilly in any way intact; the battalion still had eight howitzers. Nine tanks that had escaped the disaster attached themselves to Major Homan's battalion of the 501st Parachute

Infantry at Bizory, and some enterprising officer, finding fourteen of the combat command's mediums far to the rear at Neufchâteau, led them back. Under a tank company commander, Capt. Howard Pyle, those tanks, supported by sixty armored infantrymen, were to fight as Team Pyle. Other men of CCR—armored infantrymen, tankers without vehicles, whomever—became part of a makeshift force, Team SNAFU, acronym for a popular soldier expression of the time, "Situation Normal, All Fucked Up."

Conscious that there would be many stragglers in any big battle, Colonel Roberts early prepared a net to catch them; a junior officer among the stragglers suggested the name; and an officer from the 110th Infantry, Capt. Charles Brown, commanded the team. Roberts set up a detail in the town square to assign the men—many of whom were hollow-eyed, semi-coherent—a place to sleep and to feed them a hot meal. Within twenty-four hours, most were sufficiently recovered to join Team SNAFU.

The stragglers were mainly from CCR and the 28th Division. During the morning of December 20, that division's assistant commander, Brig. Gen. George A. Davis, with General Middleton's permission, took three hundred of the men who wore the red keystone shoulder patch to rejoin the division. Team SNAFU nevertheless numbered about six hundred men, used to man close-in roadblocks on the edges of Bastogne, to form small task forces, and to serve as individual replacements.

Given the losses sustained by the two armored combat commands, the arrival of the 705th Tank Destroyer Battalion was a godsend. On the way from the Ninth Army, the commander, Lt. Col. Clifford Templeton, had dropped off eight guns to hold a crossing of the Ourthe River at the village of Ourtheuville on the Marche highway until his supply vehicles got past, and he lost a gun at Noville; but he still had thirty-six with their powerful long-barreled 76mm. pieces.

The defenders were strong in artillery. Like the howitzers of an infantry regiment's Cannon Company, the pieces of the 101st Airborne Division's 105mm. howitzer battalion had short barrels, which limited their range but not their power. The division's other three battalions had 75mm. pack howitzers. There were also CCB's and CCR's support battalions. Most of the 28th Division's 109th Field Artillery Battalion reached Bastogne too, and there were four battalions of corps guns with 155mm. pieces. (A fifth, the 58th Armored Field Artillery Battalion, with only four guns following the fight at Longvilly, passed through the town before anybody thought to stop it.) There were stragglers among the artillery pieces as well, such as three guns of the 687th Field Artillery Battalion that had escaped the fate of the rest of the battalion at the Café Schumann crossroads. That made eleven battalions of artillery—about 130 pieces.

*   *   *

Both General Middleton and General McAuliffe were anticipating that the defense of Bastogne would soon be augmented by the Third Army's 4th Armored Division. During the night of December 18, Middleton had learned that the division was on the way northward, one of the early shifts of troops of the Third Army even before General Eisenhower's conference with his senior commanders at Verdun on the 19th. The 4th Armored Division, Middleton understood, was to be attached to his VIII Corps.

Around midnight on the 19th, the 4th Armored Division's Combat Command B under Brig. Gen. Holmes E. Dager arrived at the village of Vaux-les-Rosières, astride the Neufchâteau-Bastogne highway approximately halfway between the two towns, there to become a part of the VIII Corps. Yet that day at Verdun, General Patton had promised Eisenhower to mount a major offensive on December 22 to push through to Bastogne; and Patton had sent headquarters of the III Corps under Maj. Gen. John Millikin to prepare for the offensive at Arlon, well south of Bastogne on the principal highway leading into the town from the south, many miles from Vaux-les-Rosières. Millikin understood that the entire 4th Armored Division was to be his for the attack on the 22d.

Before daylight on the 20th, somebody on General Middleton's staff ordered General Dager to send a task force from CCB into Bastogne along the highway from Vaux-les-Rosières, the Neufchâteau-Bastogne highway—a company each of tanks and armored infantry and a battery of self-propelled artillery. Although Dager resented having his command whittled away like that, the force set out at ten thirty that morning under Capt. Bert Ezell of the 8th Tank Battalion with orders "to aid CCB of the 10th Armored Division."

In Bastogne, Captain Ezell talked with General McAuliffe, then reported, at McAuliffe's order, to Colonel Roberts in the Hôtel Lebrun. Roberts sent Ezell to a reserve position not far from the town of Sibret on the Bastogne-Neufchâteau highway, there to await, as both Roberts and McAuliffe thought, the arrival of the rest of the 4th Armored Division.

In the meantime, General Dager established radio contact with headquarters of the division and protested the diminution of his command. After having been Patton's chief of staff, Maj. Gen. Hugh J. Gaffey had only recently assumed command of the 4th Armored Division and was incensed that somebody appeared to be making off with a third of his new command. With Patton's approval, he ordered Dager to recall Ezell's little force and bring all of CCB back to the vicinity of Arlon to join the rest of the 4th Armored Division for the attack on the 22d.

By such quirks are battles and sometimes even campaigns decided. Had Middleton been allowed to hold onto the 4th Armored Division's CCB and with it keep open the Neufchâteau-Bastogne highway, Bastogne probably never would have been surrounded. Even if the Germans had cut the Neufchâteau-Bastogne highway, the 4th Armored Division might have capitalized on the location of CCB and attacked from Vauxles-Rosières instead of from Arlon. Which would have spared many officers and men of the 4th Armored Division a great deal of misery and, in some cases, death.

The arrival of many of the paratroopers without their personal gear foretold that there would long be supply shortages in Bastogne. Nor did an airborne division travel with the big supply trains to be found with infantry and armored divisions. Yet Colonel Roberts had arrived with his trains full and would be able to share, and most of the artillery units (other than those of the airborne division) had fairly ample supplies of rations and ammunition.

Scrounging supply officers soon found that many of the units attached to the VIII Corps had left behind large stocks of supplies, including a Red Cross depot with great amounts of flour for doughnuts, so that pancakes appeared on everybody's breakfast menu. So, too, the town of Bastogne had some reserves of food, and the poultry, pig, and cattle population in the surrounding farm villages was a resource not to be ignored.

Nevertheless, should the town be surrounded and subjected to siege, there was bound to be hardship and concern, in particular, for ammunition and gasoline. A further problem quickly developed when the 101st Airborne Division lost its collecting station, along with most of the surgeons and other medics, creating a severe shortage of surgeons and medical supplies.

During the afternoon of December 20, General McAuliffe left Bastogne for a talk with General Middleton at his new headquarters in municipal offices in Neufchâteau. How long could he hold Bastogne? asked Middleton. For at least forty-eight hours, replied McAuliffe, possibly longer. Middleton said he was determined to hold the town, but he was none too sure it could be done. In any event it was critical to keep the Neufchâteau-Bastogne highway open. As McAuliffe departed, Middleton admonished him with a smile: "Now don't get yourself surrounded."

Climbing into his command car, McAuliffe told his driver to gun it. He was none too sure that Bastogne was not already surrounded. A half hour after he got back there, the Germans cut the Neufchâteau-Bastogne highway at Sibret.

For the civilian population of Bastogne, the first day of the German offensive, December 16, was calm. Since it was a Saturday, the shops along the Grand' Rue were doing a bustling business. Not until the next morning, as the congregation in the Church of the Franciscan Fathers spilled out after mass into the Place St. Pierre, was there anything other than rumor to indicate that something unusual might be happening. A long column of refugees from Luxembourg, among them the fathers from the Benedictine abbey on the heights behind Clervaux, was trudging through the square.

Around noon on the 17th, electricity all over town went off, but everybody assumed it was simply a malfunction and temporary. There was still no indication that the fighting was approaching the town, but at 5 P.M. an American staff officer passed to the acting mayor, Leon Jacqmin, an order for a curfew. Yet as always happens when civilians get caught up in battle, nobody told them much of anything. They were expected simply to take to their cellars and stay out of the way.

By the morning of the third day, December 18th, there was no mistaking the sound of artillery fire, and American stragglers began to enter town. By midday, some of the people were leaving, pushing carts, pulling children's wagons piled high with possessions; but some three thousand people remained.

One who departed was Abbé Jean-Baptiste Musty, head of the Bastogne Seminary on the Place St. Pierre. He was anxious to get his fifty boys to safety. Early on the 20th he accompanied them on foot out onto the highway leading northwest across the Ourthe River toward the village of Bande and the town of Marche.

As the fighting closed in at Bastogne, some people stayed in their own cellars, while others joined neighbors whose cellars were sturdier. More than six hundred—including a hundred students—crowded into the underground corridors of the Boarding School of the Sisters of Notre Dame, others nearby in a shelter beneath the choir in the Franciscan church, and others again under the thick vaults of ancient cellars in another monastery, the Récollets. One who lived in a cellar among strangers was the woman from Bivels, Luxembourg, whom American intelligence officers had brought to Bastogne to tell her story of a German buildup beyond the Our River: Elise Delé.

Facing the possibility that the town might be surrounded, M. Jacqmin called for volunteers to take stock of available resources. There was considerable coal, they found, at the railroad station. Somebody discovered stocks of German drugs and dressings in Father Musty's seminary. More than 7 tons of flour and 2 tons of tinned biscuits turned up. There was a central abattoir for butchering pigs and cattle from nearby villages, and the boarding school had bakery facilities. There were also two doctors.

The people of Bastogne were facing a long, tedious, uncomfortable, hazardous underground existence, which some of the elderly would not survive, but nobody was to lack for essentials. They would live "in a sort of dream," having little way of knowing how serious their plight, how went the battle, whether the Germans would finally take the town, and if they did, what would be their fate. Yet their plight was easier than that of the people in surrounding villages, for those people sometimes got caught up in the actual fighting and felt the terrible blows of the powerful American artillery. (Within the town and the defensive perimeter, 115 civilians were killed.)

Renée Lemaire, thirty years old, was a beautiful young woman with strikingly blue eyes and a thick cascade of brown hair. She had studied and trained for four years at the Brugmann Hospital in Brussels to become a visiting nurse and then worked under the auspices of the Ixelles Hospital in Brussels.

Close to Christmas, 1943, Renée met Joseph, the son of an elderly widower for whom she was providing nursing care. They discovered mutual interests—both adored playing the piano, and Renée loved to sing while Joseph played—and soon they were in love and planning marriage.

Near the end of February, 1944, Renée was on night duty at the hospital for a week, and when it ended, she went to Joseph's house. The doors and windows were locked. From neighbors she learned that the Gestapo had taken Joseph and his father away. They were Jews.

Devastated, Renée nevertheless continued her work. But after the liberation, in late fall of 1944, she obtained permission to spend a month with her family in Bastogne, where her father, Gustave, had a hardware store in the Grand' Rue. Her mother, an older sister, Gisèle, and a younger sister, Maggy, were also there.

Like others in Bastogne, the Lemaires welcomed American soldiers to their home, and Renée was swiftly caught up in the glories of the liberation, the laughter of the Americans, the delights of their K-rations, their coffee and chewing gum, their kindness "made in U.S.A." Soon Renée was laughing again, her eyes sparkling. She played the piano in the living room while the soldiers sang, and she learned their songs: "Mexicali Rose," "I'll Walk Alone," "Paper Doll." One of the soldiers, Jimmy, tall and handsome, started coming often to the house, and the two went for long walks together.

On December 17, Jimmy came once more. His unit had sudden orders to leave. "Don't forget, Renée," he said. "I'll be back. I promise you."

As the fighting drew close, the Lemaires retreated to their cellar, which they shared with neighbors and from time to time with American soldiers. One was a medic, Frank, with the 10th Armored Division's CCB. When Frank learned that Renée was a nurse, he asked if she would help at his aid station in a large store near the railroad station, the "Sarma."

Beginning the next day, Renée worked long hours at the aid station together with another young woman, an immigrant from the Belgian Congo, Augusta Chiwy, and each night they returned to their cellars exhausted. But their presence, noted the surgeon, Maj. John T. Prior, was "a morale factor of the highest order."

*   *   *

Word that the Germans had cut the highway leading from Bastogne to Neufchâteau during the night of December 20 was quick to pass among the troops around Bastogne. Most men assumed that at that point, they were surrounded.

Among the American commanders, the news of the cutting of the highway stiffened their resolve to hold Bastogne, for at that point what was the alternative? They might not have to hold for long, in any case, for the attack General Patton had promised General Eisenhower at Verdun was to begin early on December 22, and the expectation was that Patton would have little difficulty in breaking through swiftly to Bastogne.

Strictly speaking, Bastogne was not yet surrounded. At last free to pass through Noville, columns of the 2d Panzer Division were soon swinging around the town to get onto the Bastogne-Marche highway, in the process cutting all roads to the northwest; but it took longer for the *Panzer Lehr Division*, swinging around Bastogne to the south and heading for the Meuse by way of St. Hubert, sixteen miles due west of Bastogne, to cut all roads leading west.

Both those divisions were, in any case, en route away from Bastogne, so that any buildup west of the town was the responsibility of the 26th Volksgrenadier Division. Having despaired of getting into the town from east or north, that was what the division commander, Colonel Kokott, intended doing. While the attached regiment of *Panzergrenadiers* of the *Panzer Lehr Division* struck from the south, Kokott's third regiment, which had just arrived, was to attack along with *Kampfgruppe Kunkel* from the southwest and west. Yet it would take some time to get the regiment into position, so that the job of cutting the roads and completing the encirclement of Bastogne fell to Major Kunkel.

On December 21, as Kokott accompanied his third regiment along the path taken earlier by *Kampfgruppe Kunkel* south of Bastogne, he became optimistic that the town would soon fall. In the villages along the route, he found no defenses, and here and there he saw small groups of Americans fleeing. Those were the last escapees from Wiltz or somewhere else to the east, but Kokott took their presence to mean that the defenses of Bastogne were falling apart.

Field Marshal von Rundstedt also thought Bastogne would soon fall. Through Field Marshal Model at Army Group B, he directed General von Manteuffel to proceed immediately to reduce the town, but still under the mandate of doing nothing to interfere with the drive of the panzer divisions for the Meuse. At headquarters of the 47th Panzer Corps that night, von Manteuffel found General von Lüttwitz optimistic, primarily because the leading force of the Seventh Army, the 5th Parachute Division, had at last begun arriving on the south flank of his corps. With the parachute division blocking the highways from Arlon and Neufchâteau, von Lüttwitz would no longer have to keep looking over his shoulder for fear an American relief force might be advancing on Bastogne from the south.

Colonel Kokott found no defenses in the villages south of Bastogne because there were none, for General McAuliffe had first concentrated on the obvious threats from east and north. Only the 326th Airborne Engineer Battalion stood south of Bastogne, manning roadblocks on the Arlon highway, astride a secondary road facing the village of Assenois, and on the Neufchâteau highway, and Kokott had passed south of those roadblocks. German movement there nevertheless prompted McAuliffe to send two battalions of the 327th Glider Infantry to augment the engineers and build a line facing south.

It was the attempt by *Kampfgruppe Kunkel* to get in behind Bastogne that produced the heaviest fighting on both the 21st and 22d. There most of the heavy American artillery battalions were to be found, with nothing more than little clumps of infantry to protect them, and only the fourteen tanks of Team Pyle to serve as a mobile defensive force.

As a first step in completing the encirclement, *Kampfgruppe Kunkel* early on December 21 set out from Sibret on the Bastogne-Neufchâteau highway for the village of Villeroux, a mile beyond the highway. Unknown to the Germans, in the vicinity were three of the American 155mm. artillery battalions. The Germans quickly came upon the 771st, and the gunners abandoned their pieces and fled; but before the German column could continue, the tanks of Team Pyle appeared. Although the Germans forced the tanks back on the village of Senonchamps, the brief engagement afforded time for the gunners of the other two corps artillery battalions, the 755th and the 969th, to pull their pieces back to Senonchamps.

At the edge of Senonchamps, Team Pyle made a stand. Helped by the quad-50s of a battery of the 796th Antiaircraft Artillery Battalion, the tanks inflicted such losses that Major Kunkel called off the attack for the night.

Senonchamps was of considerable importance to the defense of Bastogne, for from it ran two secondary roads leading to the Bastogne-Marche highway, one of them joining the highway only a mile from the first buildings of Bastogne. In and around the village, in addition to Team Pyle, was the 10th Armored Division's 420th Armored Field Artillery Battalion, whose commander, Lt. Col. Barry D. Browne, had collected a few light tanks, three mediums, and thirty infantry stragglers to create a force that became known in time as Team Browne.

As elsewhere in the Ardennes before daylight on December 22, snow began to fall in and around Bastogne. In mid-morning, *Kampfgruppe Kunkel* renewed its attack, but fire from the American tanks quickly broke it up. Three more times during the afternoon the Germans tried to break into Senonchamps while infantry worked through nearby woods to get at the American howitzers; but nowhere did they succeed. As night began to fall, General McAuliffe sent a company of the 327th Glider Infantry and a hundred men from Team SNAFU to help protect the artillery pieces.

The remnants of yet another corps artillery battalion were farther west near the village of Tillet, the 58th Armored Field Artillery Battalion with four guns salvaged from the fight near Longvilly. As the battalion fell back from Bastogne, the artillerymen encountered men of the 101st Airborne Division's Reconnaissance Platoon, who had been trying to find a road open to St. Hubert. They reported that the Germans were in Tillet in strength.

As the two forces linked to try to find a way around the village, trucks attempting to transport unneeded impedimenta of the 501st Parachute Infantry away from Bastogne joined them. The column soon encountered a roadblock, which the Reconnaissance Platoon attacked and eliminated, but behind it was a far stronger German force. Forming a perimeter defense, the commander of the artillery battalion, Lt. Col. Walter J. Paton, radioed Bastogne for help. General McAuliffe could send none, and as Paton tried to turn back to Bastogne, he found that the Germans had moved in behind him.

Soon after daylight the next morning, the 22d, a contingent of the *Panzer Lehr Division*'s reconnaissance battalion attacked. By noon, assault guns had disabled all but one of the four howitzers, and Paton saw no alternative but to try to break out on foot. With fire from the last howitzer, the men destroyed the 501st Parachute Infantry's trucks and the other vehicles. Screened by falling snow, they set out. Not quite seven hours later, they trudged into Neufchâteau, having lost not a man.

By nightfall on December 22, the rough outline of a perimeter defense of Bastogne—characterized by Colonel Kinnard, the 101st Airborne Division's G-3, as "the hole in the doughnut"—was beginning to emerge. The defensive line was closest to the town on the east and the south, just over a mile off. And in the still unsettled portion of the perimeter west of town, a finger-like projection held by a battalion of the 327th Glider Infantry extended for almost six miles along the Bastogne-Marche highway. That projection obviously would have to be withdrawn.

Except at Villeroux and Senonchamps, the enemy's jockeying for position had provided a welcome respite. That cheered McAuliffe and his staff, but another development dampened the cheer: the matter of supplies. There had been some hope on the 22d for resupply by air, but the snowstorm had squashed that. Supplies of small-arms ammunition were running low. Most critical of all, they were short of shells for the artillery pieces, without which the defenders would have little hope for survival.

All the gunners had dug pits that enabled them to switch their pieces to fire in any direction, which was essential, but it quickly ate deeply into the stocks of ammunition. By nightfall on the 21st, it was obvious that the gunners would have to conserve their shells for crises; and German trucks, half-tracks, and tanks bypassing the town to north and south moved almost with impunity, while infantry commanders and artillery forward observers swore in frustration.

By noon of December 22, all four of the artillery battalions of the 101st Airborne Division were down to two hundred shells each, and General McAuliffe was contemplating imposing a ration of ten rounds per gun per day. The man who had succeeded McAuliffe as the division's artillery commander, Colonel Sherburne, lied through his teeth whenever men and officers asked him how the ammunition was holding out, but to McAuliffe he told the grim truth.

Within the town, all aid stations had become makeshift hospitals, and since nobody could be evacuated, the wounded piled up. The few exhausted surgeons shook their heads sadly as men died who with proper medicines and operating facilities might have lived. In the Sarma, where Renée Lemaire and Augusta Chiwy were helping as nurses, Major Prior had close to a hundred patients, thirty of them seriously wounded. There were no beds; the men lay on blankets on the floor, and even blankets were scarce.

In a church near the center of town, patients in the 501st Parachute Infantry's aid station lay in rows on the floor with scarcely enough room between them for the medics to walk. In front of an altar in an alcove, two surgeons worked steadily, hour after hour. So crowded did the church become that the regiment had to open another aid station in a garage, where the men lay on their blankets on top of sawdust. Against a back wall the surgeons placed those men who under the existing conditions had no chance of surviving.

Yet all that misery might soon come to an end, for at mid-morning on the 22d, McAuliffe's headquarters received a brief but encouraging message: "Hugh [General Gaffey of the 4th Armored Division] is coming."

Around noon on December 22, near a farm belonging to Jean Kessler, not far from the Arlon highway, men of a platoon of Company F, 327th Glider Infantry, watched in astonishment as four Germans, one of them carrying a large white flag, appeared in front of the foxhole line. Two sergeants left the platoon's command post in the farmhouse to see what was afoot, Oswald Y. Butler and Carl E. Dickinson, accompanied by a medical aid man, Pfc. Ernest D. Permetz, who spoke German.

Amid falling snow stood two German enlisted men and two officers: a major and 1st Lt. Hellmuth Henke, of the *Panzer Lehr Division*'s operations section, who spoke English. "We are parliamentaries," said Lieutenant Henke, "and we want to talk to your officers." At a few words in German from the major, Henke corrected himself: "We want to talk to your commanding general."

Butler and Dickinson conducted the four to the farmhouse. Leaving the enlisted men under guard, the platoon leader, 2d Lt. Leslie E. Smith, blindfolded the officers and led them a few hundred yards to the rear to the company command post. There the Germans handed the company commander, Capt. James F. Adams, a typed message, one page in German, the second in English, apparently done on an American or English typewriter, for the diacritical marks over some of the vowels in the German had been inserted in ink.

It was an ultimatum from "The German Commander" addressed "to the U.S.A. Commander of the encircled town of Bastogne." There was "only one possibility," read the message, "to save the encircled U.S.A. troops from total annihilation: that is the honorable surrender of the encircled town." The American commander was to have two hours in which to consider the ultimatum, whereupon, if he rejected it, German artillery was prepared "to annihilate the U.S.A. troops in and near Bastogne." Serious civilian losses from that fire, the message concluded, "would not correspond with the wellknown American humanity."

Captain Adams promptly contacted headquarters of the 327th Glider Infantry. The commander, Col. Joseph H. Harper, was away; but the operations officer, Maj. Alvin Jones, alerting General McAuliffe's command post to what was happening, drove to Company F's command post. Leaving the German officers, still blindfolded, with Captain Adams, Jones hurried with the message to the Heintz Barracks, while along the line of foxholes, men took advantage of the unaccustomed quiet to get out of their holes, stretch, build fires, shave, go to the latrine.

At the barracks, where in response to German shelling, McAuliffe had moved his command post into a cellar beneath the main building, Major Jones asked to see McAuliffe personally. Saluting, he said he had a message from the German commander, an ultimatum, and passed the papers to McAuliffe's chief of staff, Lt. Col. Ned D. Moore.

"What does it say, Ned?" asked McAuliffe.

"They want you to surrender," said Moore.

"Aw, nuts!" said McAuliffe.

When McAuliffe got around to composing a reply to the ultimatum, he was at a loss as to what to say.

"That first crack you made," said his G-3, Harry Kinnard, "would be hard to beat."

"What was that?" asked McAuliffe.

"You said 'Nuts!'"

With a pen, McAuliffe wrote: "To the German commander: Nuts! From the American Commander."

By that time, the commander of the 327th Glider Infantry, Colonel Harper, had arrived at the headquarters and insisted on taking the reply back himself. When he reached Company F's command post, he ordered the German officers to be put in a jeep and driven, still blindfolded, to

Lieutenant Smith's platoon headquarters at the Kessler farm. To the immense relief of the Germans, their blindfolds were at last removed.

Lieutenant Henke told Harper that he and his companion were authorized to negotiate details. Would he be so kind as to give them the answer from the American commander?

"The answer," said Harper, "is 'Nuts!'"

Although Henke had spent years in the import business and spoke excellent English, the reply perplexed him. He translated literally for the major, but neither of them understood. Was the reply, asked Henke, negative or affirmative?

"The reply," answered Harper, "is decidedly not affirmative, and if you continue this foolish attack, your losses will be tremendous.

"If you don't understand what 'Nuts!' means," Harper continued, "in plain English it is the same as 'Go to hell!' And I will tell you something else; if you continue to attack, we will kill every goddamn German that tries to break into this city."

The German officers came to attention and saluted. "We will kill many Americans," said Henke. "This is war."

"On your way, Bud," said Harper, then to his everlasting regret added: "And good luck to you."

The surrender demand was the work of the commander of the 47th Panzer Corps, von Lüttwitz, who sent it without consulting his superior. When General von Manteuffel learned of it, he was furious, for quite clearly he lacked sufficient artillery to make good on the threat. Lest the lack of retaliation should make the German command appear ridiculous, von Manteuffel put in a call to the Luftwaffe to bomb Bastogne.

CHAPTER TWENTY-FIVE

To Relieve Bastogne

By late 1944, George Smith Patton, Jr., at fifty-nine years of age, was already something of a legend in the United States Army and a darling of the American press. It had not always been so. After word had leaked out that in Sicily Patton slapped two American soldiers whom he suspected of malingering, newsmen had gone for his jugular. An impolitic remark before a ladies' club in England before the invasion had set the jackals to howling again, but General Eisenhower had stuck by Patton, confident of his ability on the battlefield.

His dash across France from the Normandy beachhead in late summer appeared to justify Eisenhower's loyalty; and a fickle press, suddenly adoring his posturing, his profanity, his flashy uniforms, glistening helmet, pistols on each hip, nicknamed him "Old Blood and Guts" and turned him into an idol of the American public. Soldiers who had hated him in Sicily came to love him. All they needed to say was that they were in "Patton's army"; everybody knew which army that was.

A man of independent means, married to a woman of even greater wealth, George Patton had no economic need to devote his life to the United States Army. He did so because he loved it, lived and breathed it, and in it he could fulfill a deep emotional need to excel, to star. An avid student of military history, he "wrote knowingly on the phalanxes of Greece, the legions of Rome, the columns of Napoleon, and the mass armies of World War I. He could compare the tank to the heavy cavalry of Belisarius." Nobody loved the profession of arms more than did George Patton.

He was a man given to extreme ups and downs. Thus he could kick and scream like a child deprived of a toy when on December 16 General Bradley ordered him to relinquish an armored division to the First Army in the Ardennes, then three days later enthusiastically embrace the sending of a major portion of his army into the Ardennes. The difference was that in the second case, he, George Patton, was to be the star.

514

* * *

On December 20, Patton summoned General Middleton to meet him in Arlon. "Troy," Patton greeted him, "of all the goddamn crazy things I ever heard of, leaving the 101st Airborne to be surrounded in Bastogne is the worst!" Well accustomed to Patton's outbursts, Middleton merely pointed out patiently the importance of the network of roads at Bastogne.

"All right, Troy," said Patton, "if you were in my position, where would you launch the attack? From Arlon or from Neufchâteau?"

Middleton replied that he would make the main attack along the Arlon highway and east of it, "to cut off the Krauts instead of pushing them straight ahead." On the other hand, to get to Bastogne as quickly as possible, he would send the 4th Armored Division up the highway from Neufchâteau, which was seven miles closer to Bastogne than Arlon. He might have added that from where the American line had stabilized along the two roads, it was twelve miles to Bastogne on the Arlon highway, nine miles on the highway from Neufchâteau.

No, said Patton, he wanted to keep his divisions concentrated. He would send the 4th Armored Division up the highway from Arlon, the infantry divisions through the countryside east of that road.

Patton's decision may have been based on nothing more than the fact that he had earlier approved General Gaffey's recalling General Dager's CCB from the Neufchâteau-Bastogne highway to Arlon. On the other hand, to Patton, relieving Bastogne was as irritating as a burr under the saddle to a horse, for Patton was not after Bastogne but St. Vith, thereby hoping to cut off the German forces that had penetrated far to the west and destroy them. Yet he had his orders to relieve Bastogne.

It hardly appeared to be a momentous decision in any event, for as an officer in the 4th Armored Division summed up the view held in the division's command circles: "The general impression was that we could just cut our way through." It would turn out to be an unfortunate decision, nevertheless, for as might have been anticipated, there were far fewer Germans along the Neufchâteau highway than there were along the highway from Arlon.

George Patton made good on his promise to attack on December 22, not only in the direction of Bastogne but also farther to the east, to remove any lingering threat to Luxembourg City. As early as December 19, the commander of the Seventh Army's 80th Corps, General Beyer, had recognized that an American reaction would soon be coming and had ordered the bulk of his troops to dig in and hold what they had gained. Yet the American attack there involved at first only one regiment, for not until late on December 23 did the commander of the Third Army's XII Corps, Maj. Gen. Manton S. Eddy, get his supporting artillery in place and all the veteran 5th Infantry Division forward. Thus it was not until the morning of the 24th that an attack began in earnest to drive the Germans back across the Sûre River.

The 5th Division advanced northward on both sides of the Ernz Noire, while the 10th Armored Division's CCA and a task force from the 9th Armored Division's CCA extended the attack to the west. The advance moved across ground and through villages recently relinquished by men of the 4th Division's 12th Infantry and the 9th Armored Division's 60th Armored Infantry Battalion: Müllerthal, Lauterborn, Berdorf, the Parc Hôtel, Waldbillig, Beaufort.

By nightfall of the first day, the armor reached that part of the Sûre River that flows from west to east and forms the angle at the juncture with the Our where men of the 109th Infantry had defended at the start of the German offensive. The infantry in the meantime had slower going but on Christmas Day reached high ground at various points overlooking that part of the Sûre that forms the boundary between Luxembourg and Germany. Late that day and all the next, artillery forward observers called down heavy concentrations, many of them aerial bursts with the POZIT fuse, on hapless Germans trying to get to the other side of the river, whether across a lone remaining vehicular bridge or the few footbridges, in rubber boats or by swimming. By that time the two defending German units, the 212th and 276th Voldsgrenadier Divisions, were shattered, infantry companies down to twenty-five or thirty men, a few reduced to no more than ten.

In Echternach, the first patrols of the 5th Division's 10th Infantry to enter the town searched in vain for any trace of Captain Dupuis, Lieutenant Macdiarmid, and the men of the 12th Infantry's Company E. The relief force that Dupuis had counted on with such trust had at last arrived—as Dupuis had said it would—but six days too late.

In addition to the 4th Armored Division, charged specifically with breaking through to Bastogne, Patton's main attack employed two infantry divisions, the 26th and 80th, both experienced and both fairly well rested after brief periods out of the line. All operated under headquarters of the III Corps, commanded by General Millikin, but the commander and his staff were engaging in their first operation. The zone of attack encompassed twenty-four miles, from the Alzette River inside Luxembourg (Ettelbruck is near the juncture of the Alzette and the Sûre) to the Neufchâteau-Bastogne highway.

The task assigned to the infantry divisions was essentially to clear territory between the Alzette River and the Arlon-Bastogne highway, thereby protecting the right flank of the 4th Armored Division and advancing the line so that when relief came to Bastogne, there would be no narrow corridor leading into the town but a broad expanse of American-controlled territory extending eastward. That also conformed with Pat-

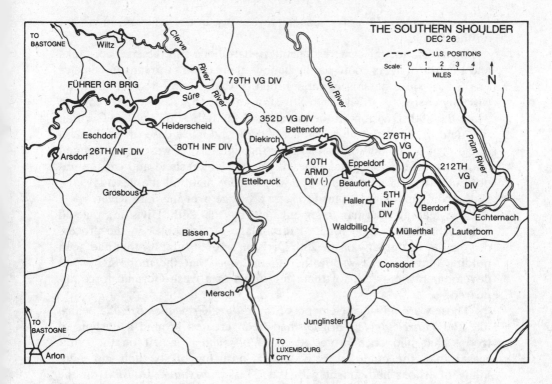

ton's ambition to proceed beyond the relief of Bastogne with a general movement of the entire southern flank in a drive on St. Vith.

In the vernacular of the foot soldier, whoever picked the terrain over which the 26th and 80th Divisions advanced had a taste for shit. It was like a roller-coaster; it had deep hollows and ravines; it was heavily wooded; and it had a roadnet that Charlemagne's knights would have complained about. The obvious first phase line for the advance was the deep, meandering, generally wooded gorge carved by western reaches of the Sûre River.

Fortunately for the men of the two divisions, the Germans were not only ill-prepared but totally unprepared to meet an attack. Except in front of the American armor, where the 5th Parachute Division had arrived, nobody was manning the ramparts. The commander of the Seventh Army's 85th Corps, General Kniess, was still trying to get his other division, the 352d Volksgrenadier Division, forward from Ettelbruck over a road that turned off the Ettelbruck-Bastogne highway a few miles outside Ettelbruck and meandered westward through little farm villages for an eventual connection with the Arlon-Bastogne highway. As the American infantrymen began plodding through the snow before daylight on December 22, the 352d Volksgrenadiers were not in defensive positions but on the march.

Observers for the American artillery battalions and the crews of tanks and tank destroyers could hardly believe their eyes: Germans in vehicles or on foot were passing in column before them, unaware that their foe was anywhere near. The 26th Division caught the head of the column while the 80th Division hit the middle and the tail. Although the German regiment bringing up the rear quickly deployed in defense of Ettelbruck, a regiment of the 80th Division broke through farther west and continued under a bright moon to take the village of Heinerscheid and cut the important Ettelbruck-Bastogne highway. Before nightfall the next day, the 23d, a company pushed ahead to seize a bridge over the Sûre River.

The leading German regiment, hit by the 26th Division, reacted quickly, making a fight for it at the village of Grosbous, in the process driving out a company of the 28th Division's 109th Infantry that had been holding there. Yet it was farther to the west that the more significant development occurred, for there first units of a fresh German force appeared.

Those were advance elements of the *Führer Grenadier Brigade*, which like the *Führer Begleit Brigade* had been created around a nucleus of troops that had once protected the *Wolfschanze*, albeit on the outer rather than the inner protective rim. Consisting of six thousand men, many of whom had fought with the *Grossdeutschland Division* on the Eastern Front, the brigade had two battalions of infantry mounted on half-tracks and trucks, an assault gun battalion, and a battalion of forty Mark IV and Panther tanks.

The going through the rugged country between the Alzette River and the Arlon-Bastogne highway was no longer to be easy. To add to the newly acquired strength of the *Führer Grenadier Brigade*, the commander of the Seventh Army, General Brandenberger, received from the Führer Reserve the 79th Volksgrenadier Division. With those forces, Brandenberger—who had established his headquarters in nearby Wiltz—intended to counterattack south of the Sûre River to drive the Americans back and regain control of the Ettelbruck-Bastogne highway.

From that point, both the 26th and 80th Divisions had a brutal slugging match on their hands. As it opened, the commander of the 80th Division, Maj. Gen. Horace L. McBride, had to relinquish at his corps commander's order two of his infantry battalions to help the 4th Armored Division. And in view of the presence of the *Führer Grenadier Brigade*, General Millikin told the commander of the 26th Division, Maj. Gen. Willard S. Paul, to advance with caution.

That brigade turned out to be less of a threat than it might have been, for the American advance forced piecemeal commitment, and the German commander, Col. Hans-Joachim Kahler, was seriously wounded by artillery fire while on reconnaissance the night of December 22. So, too, the venom of American fighter-bombers, at last released by the clear weather on the 23d, seriously interfered with the arrival of all units of the brigade and of the 79th Volksgrenadier Division, for the planes made a bottleneck of the bridges to the rear over the Our River.

It was a grim fight, as bitter in the brutal cold as any that occurred anywhere during the battle in the Ardennes. Men died by the score on both sides, but by the day after Christmas the two American infantry divisions had carried the field. Except at a few points, they controlled all the rugged countryside south of the Sûre River, held two small bridgeheads over the river, and had regained Ettelbruck. There the attack came to a halt to await General Patton's pleasure in continuing the drive northward to erase the bulge the Germans had created in American lines.

During the drive across France the 4th Armored Division had established a reputation as a slashing, freewheeling outfit, and it was George Patton's favorite; but as the division prepared to drive on Bastogne, there were problems. The division was short of tanks, and many of those that remained had clocked so much mileage that breakdowns were frequent. The division had also recently lost its veteran commander, sent home for medical reasons; and for the new commander, General Gaffey, it was to be a first fight with a division command. There were also many replacements among the tank crews and the armored infantrymen.

The armor began its advance in two columns, one combat command up the Arlon-Bastogne highway, another up secondary roads just west of the highway. Demolitions executed earlier by engineers as a precaution against German advance delayed both columns.

It was mid-afternoon of the 22d before CCA on the main highway approached the town of Martelange and the deep gorge of the Sûre River, not quite half the distance from Arlon to Bastogne. There a company of the 5th Parachute Division denied access to the sites of two demolished bridges, and not until well after midnight did a company of armored infantry succeed in getting to the far bank. Engineers then discovered that the banks were too steep for either pontoon or treadway bridges. They would have to take the time to erect a Bailey Bridge, which would not be ready until mid-afternoon of the second day, December 23. Patton had charged the 4th Armored Division to "drive like hell," but it wasn't working out that way.

Progress was better with CCB on the secondary roads west of the highway. Only after coming abreast of Martelange did that column encounter enemy fire, and then only small-arms fire from outposts that quickly fell back. By nightfall on the 22d, CCB had reached the village of Burnon, just seven miles from Bastogne; but that column, too, had to pause to replace a demolished bridge.

Before daylight on the second day, CCB resumed its advance, only to find the next village of Chaumont defended by a company of the 5th

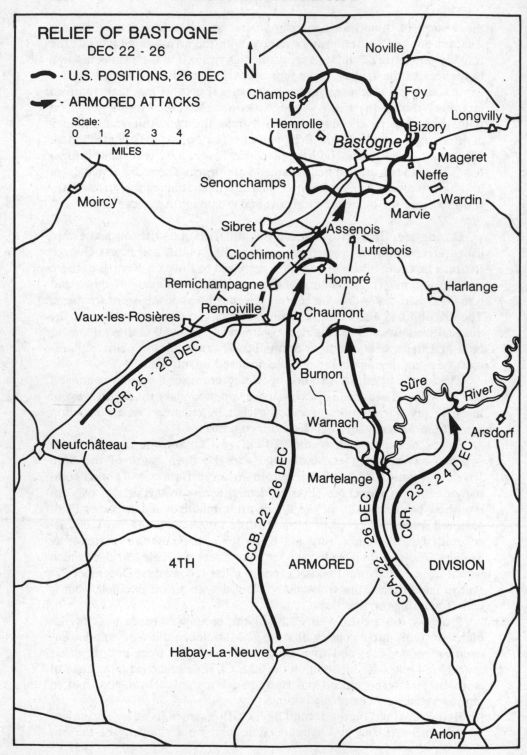

RELIEF OF BASTOGNE
DEC 22 - 26

- U.S. POSITIONS, 26 DEC
- ARMORED ATTACKS

Scale:
0   1   2   3   4
MILES

Noville

Champs

Foy

Longvilly

Hemrolle

Bizory

Bastogne

Mageret

Neffe

Moircy

Senonchamps

Wardin

Marvie

Sibret

Assenois

Lutrebois

Clochimont

Hompré

Harlange

Remichampagne

Remoiville

Chaumont

Vaux-les-Rosières

Burnon

Sûre

River

CCR, 25 - 26 DEC

Warnach

Arsdorf

Neufchâteau

Martelange

CCB, 22 - 26 DEC

CCA, 22 - 26 DEC

CCR, 23 - 24 DEC

4TH   ARMORED   DIVISION

Habay-La-Neuve

Arlon

Parachute Division. In a combined tank-infantry assault in the afternoon, CCB's tanks bogged down on slopes turned soft by the sun, but the armored infantrymen rooted the paratroopers out alone. Yet hardly had the infantrymen reported their success when ten German assault guns and what the Americans took to be five Tiger tanks with paratroopers clinging to them opened a deadly fire.

That morning at headquarters of the 26th Volksgrenadier Division near Bastogne, five *Ferdinand* tank destroyers, which had long-barreled 88mm. guns mounted on a Tiger chassis, had arrived. They were part of the 653d Heavy *Panzerjäger* Battalion, which had recently come from Italy and was scheduled for commitment in Alsace; but somehow those five *Ferdinands* had been diverted to the Ardennes. The division commander, Colonel Kokott, cared not where they came from nor how they got there, for they seemed heaven sent to prevent the American drive from the south from cutting into the rear of his division at Bastogne.

Kokott promptly sent the tank destroyers southward along with ten of his assault guns. They arrived just in time to enable the paratroopers to retake Chaumont, and the German guns exacted a heavy toll of the American tanks mired on the hillside outside the village.

That night General McAuliffe sent an obviously concerned message from Bastogne to the 4th Armored Division: "Sorry I did not get to shake hands today. I was disappointed." A short while later, somebody on his staff sent another: "There is only one more shopping day before Christmas!"

During the afternoon briefing of December 22 at headquarters of the Ninth Air Force in a big office building in Luxembourg City across the Place de Metz from headquarters of the 12th Army Group, Maj. Gen. Hoyt S. Vandenberg listened in gloom to the prediction of his chief meteorologist, Maj. Stuart J. Fuller. A low front, said Fuller, had settled in the general vicinity of the Rhine River, and he could see no break in the clouds for at least four more days. After the briefing was over, the two talked in Vandenberg's office. There were high pressure areas both to the west and to the east, Fuller noted, but he saw no possibility of either arriving quickly.

At breakfast the next morning in the nearby Hôtel Kons, Fuller was happy to acknowledge that he had been wrong. The cold winds of the Russian high had at last driven the clouds away. All morning officers and airmen lined the windows of the big headquarters building, gaping at the sky, and by noon the streets of Luxembourg City were full of people craning to see the show: One parade after another of medium B-26 Marauders, and seemingly everywhere, the fighter-bombers, P-47 Thunderbolts and P-38 Lightnings "like shoals of silver minnows in the bright winter sun." By nightfall, the Ninth Air Force had flown almost 1,300 sorties.

*　　*　　*

Nobody was more jubilant over the break in the weather than the men in and around Bastogne. At nine thirty that morning, teams of path-finders landed to mark a drop zone between Senonchamps and the town. Shortly before noon came the unmistakable hum of vast numbers of motors, then the big C-47 transport planes lumbered into view, looking for all the world like pregnant geese against the sky, and the hum became a thunder. As the big planes slowly plowed through the air at little more than a thousand feet above the ground, out of their bellies plunged para-packs with parachutes of red, yellow, orange, blue, and white.

Men watched in awe from their foxholes, others from windows and the streets of the town, and crowds of civilians emerged from their cata-combs for what seemed to be a miracle, "resupply coming from the sky." They "applauded, shouted with joy, cried"; they were saved, "lost hope rekindled." To at least one paratrooper, Capt. Laurence Critchell of the 501st Parachute Infantry, it was difficult "not to feel a sentimental pride of country."

As the planes followed their low course, German antiaircraft gunners, ignoring the presence of hordes of fighter-bombers flying cover, opened fire. A few planes came in trailing smoke, but not a single pilot veered from his course.

One of the planes had dropped its load and was gaining altitude when antiaircraft fire knocked out its controls. Having often flown in the cabin of a C-47, Captain Critchell was able to imagine the scene inside: "the two American youngsters struggling with the controls, the cockpit win-dows showing nothing but uprushing earth, the instinctive start back-wards toward the cabin, and then—."

Before it was over, 241 planes had dropped 144 tons of supplies in close to 1,500 packets. A few fell inside German lines, but not many, and some fell in the town itself. (The next day, Christmas Eve, one of the soldiers gave a white silk parachute to the nurse, Renée Lemaire, who planned to take it home that night and eventually make it into a wedding dress.)

The resupply failed to meet all needs, particularly for medical supplies and ammunition for the 75mm. pack howitzers of the parachute artillery battalions; but that might be remedied on other days. What mattered was that even as a supply crisis was beginning to grip the defenders, the skies had cleared and relief had come. Informed that the troops had recovered 95 percent of the packets, McAuliffe's G-3, Colonel Kinnard, allowed as how that was "close enough for government work."

That day and over the next four days, with a hiatus on Christmas Day because of unfavorable weather over air bases in England, 962 C-47s dropped 850 tons of supplies. On December 26, there were in addition eleven gliders, some of which brought in surgeons. During the five days, the Germans shot down nineteen planes and badly damaged fifty more.

None the less welcome were attacks by fighter-bombers, directed to their targets by Capt. James E. Parker of the Ninth Air Force, who had come into Bastogne on December 19 and scrounged a high-frequency radio from Colonel Roberts's CCB. Parker directed the first planes, which were on the scene by 10 A.M. on the 23d, to the northwest and west, in front of the positions of the 502d Parachute Infantry and a battalion of the 327th Glider Infantry. The Germans had been building up heavily there, and because of the ammunition shortage, the artillery had been unable to do anything about it.

The snow helped the pilots tremendously, for German vehicles left telltale tracks leading to assembly areas in the forests. Against those the fighter-bombers used Napalm, setting the forests on fire. Before the day ended, there were fires all around the circle of American positions so that the smoke made it seem "almost as if the fog was closing in again." Either with explosive bombs or with Napalm, the fighter-bombers hit every village within a mile or two of the perimeter, some of them numbers of times. They flew more than 250 sorties each day.

The clearing weather enabled the commander of the Ninth Air Force, General Vandenberg, to put in motion a plan of aerial reaction he had devised soon after the start of the German offensive. The first priority was to blunt the enemy's armored spearheads and the motor transport supporting them by every available means while at the same time knocking out his railheads and communications centers in the Eifel—Prüm, Nideggen, Bitburg—and the bridges he was using to bring supplies and reinforcements across the Rhine.

The two objectives were in a way contradictory, for in order to provide the necessary fighter escort for the mediums that hit the targets inside Germany, many fighter-bombers had to be withdrawn from the primary goal of blunting the spearheads. Vandenberg solved it by calling on the Eighth Air Force in England to send two groups of P-51 Mustangs to the Continent to provide escort.

Partly as a result of the shift of American forces north of the German penetration to Field Marshal Montgomery's command, British fighter-bombers became readily available in accord with needs discerned by American air commanders. With the shift, the IX and XXIX Tactical Air Commands passed to operational control of the British Second Tactical Air Force; but on the theory that the IX Tactical Air Command's General Quesada had a better feel for the support needed, the commander of the Second Tactical Air Force, Air Marshal Sir Arthur Coningham, sent a liaison officer to Quesada's headquarters and put British planes at Quesada's disposal. At Quesada's request, most British fighter-bombers flew escort, attacked German airfields, or flew armed reconnaissance along the Rhine. Yet whenever Quesada needed British planes for close support of the ground troops, the liaison officer called them in.

On December 23, Colonel Kokott struck again at Bastogne, using the fresh regiment of the 26th Volksgrenadier Division along the Marche highway northwest of the town and the attached *Panzergrenadier* regiment between the Ettelbruck and Arlon highways to the southeast. In conjunction with the attack from the northwest, the *Volksgrenadier* division's *Kampfgruppe Kunkel* renewed its thrust against Team Browne at Senonchamps.

They were strong attacks, but Team Browne stopped *Kampfgruppe Kunkel* a third time. Then, rather than risk being cut off in the projection along the Marche highway, the commander of the 327th Glider Infantry's 3d Battalion, Lt. Col. Ray C. Allen, withdrew by phases to an arc-shaped line conforming to the shape of the defensive perimeter on either flank. To the southeast, the *Panzergrenadiers* in a night attack wrested half the village of Marvie (just off the Ettelbruck highway) from Team O'Hara, but they seriously depleted their ranks in the process.

At that point neither von Manteuffel, von Lüttwitz, nor Kokott held out much hope of taking Bastogne without considerable reinforcement. When Hitler on the 23d released two divisions from the Führer Reserve—the 9th Panzer and the 15th Panzergrenadier Divisions—von Manteuffel hoped to get both. Instead, Field Marshal Model sent all but one regiment of the *Panzergrenadier* division to bolster the drive for the Meuse. While awaiting the arrival of that regiment, which had artillery and tank support, Colonel Kokott on the 24th held fast at Bastogne.

Early that day, General von Manteuffel attempted to force the issue of Bastogne. In a message that—as he intended—soon reached General Jodl and Hitler himself, he asked what he should do: Turn all resources to capture Bastogne, or continue to emphasize the drive for the Meuse? Having insisted in advance of the offensive on the utmost importance of Bastogne, Hitler at that point appeared to have lost interest in it. The answer came back: Use all available forces to gain the Meuse.

Hitler nevertheless remained ambivalent about Bastogne, for he found it galling that what was apparently a small American force could hold onto the town. That night he ordered an aide, Maj. Johann Mayer, who was at the front, to go to headquarters of the 47th Panzer Corps to find out what was wrong. By the time Mayer left the headquarters, General von Lüttwitz had convinced him of the stiffness of the American resistance, which Mayer promised to pass on to the Führer; but, said Mayer, Hitler insisted that Bastogne must be taken the next day, Christmas Day.

That conformed in any case with what General von Manteuffel was planning. For an experienced military man, continuing enemy holdout astride the nexus of almost all roads in the area was unacceptable. Since the regiment of the 15th Panzergrenadier Division was arriving that night, he ordered an all-out attack for the following morning. Attacking on Christmas Day might take the Americans by surprise, and in the wake of the bombing of Bastogne, which was scheduled that night, provide the Germans with a psychological advantage.

That Christmas Eve along the perimeter of foxholes surrounding Bastogne, men grew pensive and quiet. Some for the first time "felt fearful," as if "the end was at hand." They shook hands, wished each other a Merry Christmas.

In command posts and in cellars, wherever there was light, men could read a Christmas message from their commander, General McAuliffe. "What's merry about all this, you ask? We're fighting—it's cold—we aren't home." Yet, wrote McAuliffe, every man in the Bastogne perimeter could take comfort from the fact that the defenders of Bastogne had "stopped cold" everything thrown at them from every direction. They were writing a page in "world history" and in the process "giving our country and our loved ones at home a worthy Christmas present." The 101st Airborne Division's G-2 Periodic Report that night depicted a circle of enemy positions and activity around Bastogne in red ink and in the center (the hole in the doughnut), in green ink, the words "Merry Christmas."

Early in the evening, as McAuliffe was walking past the police station, he heard German prisoners inside singing carols. He paused to listen: *"Stille Nacht," "O Tannenbaum."* On an impulse, McAuliffe went inside. "We'll be in Antwerp in a few weeks," shouted one of the prisoners in English. "We'll soon be freed," shouted another, "and it is you who'll be the prisoner." And still another: "You'll like it there, General; it is most comfortable and cozy."

McAuliffe waited for them to quiet down. He had come by, he said at last, to wish them all a Merry Christmas.

Earlier in the day, McAuliffe had received a message from General Patton: "Xmas Eve present coming up. Hold on." Yet there was to be no Christmas Eve present. When McAuliffe returned to his command post that night, he spoke by radio with Middleton in Neufchâteau. "The finest Christmas present the hundred and first could get," said McAuliffe, "would be relief tomorrow."

As Middleton was aware, there was little chance of that. Indeed, in view of all the problems the 4th Armored Division was encountering, General Patton was ill-advised to send his message, for it raised false hopes. It had taken CCA until midday on December 24 to clear the first village beyond the Sûre River on the Arlon-Bastogne highway, the village of Warnach, still nine miles from Bastogne. Although CCB on the secondary roads west of the highway was less than five miles from Bastogne, that combat command was still battling the assault guns and *Ferdinands* that had appeared the day before with such effect at Chaumont. And the threat posed east of the highway by an arriving *Führer Grenadier Brigade* had prompted General Gaffey to commit CCR there to protect the division's flank. Hopes of a quick, bold thrust to Bastogne had faded.

The basic problem was the stubbornness of the German paratroopers. Whenever the tanks gained ground or a village, the paratroopers would counterattack or infiltrate back, and it took time to clear them out. That was what had prompted General Millikin to call for two battalions of the 80th Division's infantry to help; they were to join the fight on Christmas Day. At midnight he also shifted the boundary of the 26th Division to the west, to give that division full responsibility for the *Führer Grenadier Brigade*, and ordered CCR back to Neufchâteau to make a supporting attack along the Neufchâteau-Bastogne highway.

Inside Bastogne, around eight thirty on Christmas Eve, men heard the approaching drone of a swarm of big planes, their motors throbbing in a manner uncharacteristic of American planes. For almost all the Americans in the town, the bombing that followed was a new and terrifying experience. First came magnesium flares that made the night seem brighter than day and anybody caught in the open feel naked; then the bombs.

The first fell near a railroad overpass close to the Heintz Barracks. Inside the cellar of the camp's main building, it seemed to the only newspaperman in Bastogne, Fred MacKenzie of the Buffalo *Evening News*, that "an all but imperceptible movement swept along the passage"; it was men "drawing their physical parts into tight knots to resist shock." Then a "thin, shrieking whistle and a thunderous roar beat down their senses."

In a building next door to the department store, the Sarma, which served the 10th Armored Division's CCB as an aid station, the medical officer, Major Prior, was preparing to go to the aid station to write a letter for a young lieutenant who was dying of a chest wound. As he started to step out the door, one of his men reminded him that it was Christmas Eve and suggested they open a bottle of champagne. The two had just begun to drink when they detected "the screeching sound" of the first bomb either of them had ever heard. It sounded as if it was heading straight for them. They threw themselves to the floor.

In the aid station, along with a number of the medics, Renée Lemaire was in the kitchen. At the screech of the bomb, she either dashed into the cellar or somebody pushed her there for safety. As the bomb hit, it seemed to those who survived as if it came straight down the chimney. The blast blew those in the kitchen out through a large plate glass window. It buried those in the cellar.

What remained of the building was soon in flames. As Major Prior and others gathered in the street, they pulled anyone they could from the ruins, their work hampered by two strafing runs from a German plane. Several men volunteered to be lowered through a window at sidewalk level into the cellar and succeeded in rescuing three wounded men before the entire building collapsed.

Twenty of the wounded in the aid station died in the bombing. Also Renée Lemaire. Many days later men dug the bodies from the debris, and Prior himself carried Renée Lemaire's remains to her parents, encased in the silk folds of a white parachute, like the one she so treasured for her wedding dress.

In two runs over Bastogne, German bombers—most of them Junkers 88s—dropped approximately 2 tons of bombs, low in terms of what American bombers usually delivered (seldom less than 20 tons), but enough to do heavy damage to a town the size of Bastogne. One bomb hit the command post of CCB's Team Cherry, killing four junior officers, among them Captain Ryerson and Lieutenant Hyduke who had figured so prominently in the fighting along the Longvilly-Mageret road. The chief damage was to buildings around the main square, and when the fires had burned themselves out, most were charred skeletons. A town that had hardly been touched earlier in the war at that point "wore that ghastly air of desolation" that had come to so many other places in Europe.

For the all-out attack on Bastogne on Christmas Day, Colonel Kokott had been counting on the entire 15th Panzergrenadier Division. He got instead a *Panzergrenadier* regiment with only two of its three battalions forward, plus two battalions of self-propelled artillery and eighteen Mark IV and Panther tanks. Although the commander, Col. Wolfgang Maucke, protested the lack of time for reconnaissance and proper preparation, his was a powerful force, and to it would be added one of Kokott's *Volksgrenadier* regiments and the bulk of his divisional artillery.

Wearing white camouflage capes to match the snow, their supporting tanks painted white, the *Volksgrenadiers* and *Panzergrenadiers* moved forward shortly after three o'clock on Christmas morning, seeking to puncture the American line west of Bastogne in two places: that of the 502d Parachute Infantry at the village of Champs, a little over two miles north of the Marche highway; and that of Colonel Allen's battalion of the 327th Glider Infantry between Champs and the highway. In the darkness, *Volksgrenadiers* quickly got inside Champs. Such intense fighting at close quarters developed that the battalion commander, Maj. John D. Hanlon, was reluctant to send reinforcements until daylight would enable them to tell friend from foe. He nevertheless sent two companies marching toward high ground close by, to which the company inside Champs might retire if forced from the village.

At the same time, a battalion of *Panzergrenadiers* on foot and another riding the eighteen available tanks struck Allen's glider infantrymen. Midway between Champs and the Marche highway, the tanks broke through and headed for the village of Hemroulle, between Champs and Bastogne. In the darkness, several of the tanks passed through the firing positions of the 755th Field Artillery Battalion. As soon as the artillerymen made out the distinctive muzzle breaks on the cannon, they opened fire with machine guns, but the tanks were too close for the 155mm. howitzers to be brought to bear.

Just outside Hemroulle, seven of the tanks, *Panzergrenadiers* still aboard, swung west in an attempt to cut into the rear of the American lines. They were soon approaching the command post of the commander of the glider infantry, Colonel Allen. The commander of Company C, Capt. Preston E. Towns, telephoned Allen to warn that the tanks were approaching.

"Where?" Allen asked.

"If you look out your window now," said Towns, "you'll be looking right down the muzzle of an eighty-eight." So he was. Allen and his staff took off, fire from the tanks following them closely in growing daylight.

The same tanks were soon nearing the command post of the 502d Parachute Infantry in the Château Rolle, a thousand yards behind Champs, where at midnight a Belgian priest had celebrated mass for American soldiers and for civilians who had taken refuge in the château. The headquarters troops, soon joined by walking wounded from the regimental aid station in the stables, rushed to man a position where a tree-lined road leading to the château joined the Champs-Bastogne road. Inside the château the regimental commander, Lt. Col. Steve A. Chappius, his executive officer, and his radio operator, the only three left, could see the German tanks approaching.

German tanks were also heading toward the two companies of the 502d Parachute Infantry that at Major Hanlon's order were marching toward beleaguered Champs. Two self-propelled guns of the 705th Tank Destroyer Battalion fired on them, but German gunners quickly knocked those out. Retiring to a nearby woodlot, the paratroopers fired on the *Panzergrenadiers* riding the tanks, prompting them to seek such cover as they could find in ditches and folds in the ground.

Two other guns of the 705th Tank Destroyer Battalion fired, knocking out three of the tanks; the paratroopers accounted for another with a bazooka; and the scratch force from the 502d's headquarters got another, also with a bazooka. One continued toward Champs, but there the paratroopers, still in command of the village, knocked it out. The seventh turned back toward Hemroulle, but there the crew surrendered, for at Hemroulle the other German tanks had encountered a maelstrom of American fire.

The commander of the German tanks had early radioed Colonel Kokott's headquarters that he had reached the western edge of Bastogne. Although Kokott for long believed the report and thought he was at last about to achieve the success that had so long eluded him, the tank commander had confused Hemroulle with Bastogne. The eleven tanks that entered the village quickly ran into an intense fire from a variety of sources: four of the 705th's tank destroyers, tanks supporting Team Browne, the 463d Parachute Field Artillery Battalion, and bazookas manned by foot troops from whatever formation. Each tank sustained such a variety of hits that it later proved impossible to determine just what kind of fire had delivered the *coup de grâce*.

At Hemroulle, the Germans had again come within just over a mile of Bastogne, as they had in the opening engagements on the other side of the town outside Neffe, at Wardin, and along the railroad between Bizory and Foy; but once again they had failed to get through. Under pressure from Generals von Manteuffel and von Lüttwitz, a dispirited Colonel Kokott launched, as he himself termed it, a last "desperate effort," before daylight the next morning, but to no avail. For all that the all-out attack on Christmas Day accomplished, Kokott, von Lüttwitz, and von Manteuffel might as well have formed a trio and stood in the snow singing *"Tannenbaum! O Tannenbaum!"*

The knowledge that American armor was driving up from the south to relieve Bastogne had long plagued Heinz Kokott. That was why he earlier had dispatched assault guns and the heaven-sent *Ferdinands* to retake the village of Chaumont, and as early as December 23 he had turned some of the attached *Panzergrenadiers* of the *Panzer Lehr Division* and some of his own *Volksgrenadiers* to face south along the highway to Arlon. That and the highway from Neufchâteau were his principal concerns. But late on Christmas Day, when he learned that an American armored column had entered the village of Hompré, less than four miles from Bastogne, a secondary road leading north from Hompré through the village of Assenois became of intense concern. That night he hurried a depleted battalion of his *Volksgrenadiers* to Assenois.

Unlike most American armored divisions, the 4th Armored Division seldom employed its CCR as an integral tactical unit but instead shuffled tank and armored infantry battalions in and out as CCA or CCB needed them and used the headquarters to control battalions requiring rest and replacements. The basic components of the reserve combat command on Christmas Day—the 37th Tank Battalion under Lt. Col. Creighton W. Abrams and the 53d Armored Infantry Battalion under Lt. Col. George L. Jaques (pronounced Jakes)—had nevertheless worked together frequently, but both were under strength. The armored infantry battalion was short 230 men, and Abrams had only 20 medium tanks. Also available to CCR were a platoon of self-propelled tank destroyers, the self-propelled 94th Armored Field Artillery Battalion, and an attached battery of 155mm. howitzers of the 177th Field Artillery Battalion.

Ordered to Neufchâteau at midnight on Christmas Eve, CCR began to advance along the highway leading to Bastogne shortly before noon on Christmas Day. The first objective was Vaux-les-Rosières, from which the 28th Division's headquarters had recently been rudely ejected. At that point only a replacement engineer battalion was holding the village as an outpost for the town of Sibret farther along the highway. As CCR's tanks raced into Vaux-les-Rosières, their machine guns crackling, the German engineers dived for cover and at the first opportunity surrendered.

Rather than come at what were apparently strong German defenses at Sibret frontally, CCR's commander, Col. Wendell Blanchard, turned the column off the main highway at Vaux-les-Rosières onto a secondary road that he trusted might be less strongly defended and from which he could later turn to drive on the defenses of Sibret from the flank. A demolished bridge delayed the column for an hour until a bulldozer arrived to push the debris of a stone wall into the stream, and at the village of Remoiville, the column paused to allow four battalions of artillery to pummel the buildings. That proved to be a prudent decision, for when tanks and armored infantry rushed into the village, they routed an entire battalion of the 5th Parachute Division from the cellars.

By that time it was dusk, and a crater in the road barred further advance until it could be filled. That was to be done during the night. The next day Colonel Blanchard intended to continue along the secondary road until he had come abreast of CCB at Hompré, then swing back against Sibret for what obviously would be a major engagement.

With help from sixteen P-47s of the 362d Fighter Group, CCR during the morning of December 26 took the next village of Remichampagne and cleared nearby woods. Around 3 P.M., the leading tanks reached a road junction just short of the village of Clochimont where, according to Colonel Blanchard's plan, the column was to swing northwest on Sibret.

The tank battalion commander, Colonel Abrams, was at that point becoming wary, for he knew that there were strong German forces in Sibret, and by turning in that direction he might be exposing a flank to other German forces beyond Clochimont in the vicinity of Assenois. Before moving out, he sent tanks scouting in both directions.

As Abrams and the infantry commander, Colonel Jaques, were standing at the road junction discussing their next move, they saw C-47 aircraft dropping supplies at Bastogne. That so vividly underscored the plight of the men at Bastogne that Abrams took an ever-present cigar from his lips and proposed that they say to hell with Sibret and barrel-ass through to Bastogne by the shortest route, a secondary road from Clochimont through Assenois. Jaques agreed, but as the two officers made their decision, they neglected to tell their commander, Colonel Blanchard.

Abrams radioed his operations officer, Capt. William A. Dwight, to come forward with what was known as the C Team: Company C of the 37th Tank Battalion and Company C of the 53d Armored Infantry Battalion. He also radioed for assistance from three battalions of artillery in support of CCB. When Captain Dwight arrived, Abrams told him his objective and the plan and put him in charge. Said Abrams: "This is it."

It was 4:20 P.M. and dusk was fast approaching when six Shermans under 1st Lt. Charles P. Boggess moved out in the lead, followed by the armored infantrymen in their half-tracks. At 4:35, Boggess radioed that he was nearing Assenois and asked for artillery fire. Abrams himself radioed the artillery: "Concentration Number Nine; play it soft and sweet."

Four artillery battalions and the separate battery of 155s opened fire. The 155s and three of the light battalions fired ten volleys each on the center of the village, while one battery of the 94th Field Artillery Battalion hit the forward edge in hope of knocking out antitank guns, and the other two fired on woods flanking each side of the road just beyond the village. It was an intense bombardment, a total of 420 rounds, "soft and sweet."

At a dip in the road just before the village, Lieutenant Boggess called for the artillery to lift. Not waiting to make sure Abrams had received the message, he gunned his tank and was soon beside the first buildings. "Smoke from burning buildings and dust caused by the artillery . . . made the center of Assenois almost as dark as night," but not a German was to be seen. Two tanks took a wrong turn into a side street, and an infantry half-track strayed into the tank column behind the third tank.

As planned, one battery of artillery was still firing into the center of the village to keep the Germans under cover. Those shells were no real problem for the thick-skinned tanks, but they were for the Americans in the open-topped half-tracks. A round knocked out one of the half-tracks, killing four men, and the armored infantrymen in the others jumped down to find whatever cover they could.

At that moment at least a hundred Germans, a mixture of paratroopers and *Volksgrenadiers,* surged up from the cellars. While most of the American tanks and the lone half-track continued past the last houses of the village and up a hill beyond, the fight for control of Assenois raged between the foot troops, fierce, close-in combat.

The advancing column consisted at that point of three medium tanks in the lead, the stray half-track, and two more Shermans bringing up the rear. As Lieutenant Boggess in the leading tank neared the woods beyond the town, where the trees were close to the road on both sides, his machine gunners maintained a steady fire to keep any Germans pinned to their holes. So fast were the tanks moving that the half-track and the other tanks following it soon fell behind. That afforded time for Germans in the woods to put a few antitank mines on the road. The half-track hit one and exploded.

Riding with one of the tanks, Captain Dwight directed them onto the shoulders of the road, and while they pinned down the Germans in the woods with fire from their machine guns, surviving armored infantrymen removed the mines. Then with the infantrymen hanging on, the tanks raced ahead to catch up with the others.

Meanwhile, as Lieutenant Boggess emerged from the woods, just over a hundred yards ahead of him, at a point where a farm track crossed the road, he saw a small pillbox (an old Belgian fortification) and American troops nearby, seemingly getting ready to assault it. With a quick round from the tank's 75, Boggess's gunner knocked out the pillbox and sent the American troops diving for cover. Standing in his open turret, Boggess shouted: "Come here! This is the 4th Armored!"

As the men emerged, their commander, 2d Lt. Duane J. Webster of the 326th Airborne Engineer Battalion, came forward, and Boggess leaned down from his perch to shake his hand.

At 4:50 P.M. on December 26, Boggess and his men lifted the siege of Bastogne.

At first sight of the three tanks, someone in the 326th Airborne Engineer Battalion reported—with some error—to General McAuliffe's headquarters the approach of "three light tanks believed friendly." That brought McAuliffe hurrying to an observation post nearby. There Captain Dwight found him and saluted.

"How are you, General?" asked Dwight.

"Gee," said McAuliffe, "I'm mighty glad to see you."

Meanwhile, as Colonel Abrams prepared to go forward, he received a radio message from the commander of CCR, Colonel Blanchard. What did Abrams think of the possibility, asked Blanchard, of breaking through to Bastogne that night?

Not until an hour after midnight did the 53d Armored Infantry Battalion clear all Germans from Assenois and from the woods behind the village, thereby ensuring at least a minimally secure route into Bastogne. In the process, the armored infantrymen took 428 prisoners.

Yet even before the route was minimally secure, 260 of the most seriously wounded men in Bastogne departed in 22 ambulances and 10 trucks. The others were soon to follow, and the next day, December 27, the first supply convoy entered the town with tanks of the 4th Armored Division providing escort. Having arrived in Paris from the United States on the 26th, the commander of the 101st Airborne Division, General Taylor, declined an offer from General Gaffey to send him into Bastogne in a tank and with his driver made the trip in a jeep.

The siege of Bastogne was over. It had cost the 101st Airborne Division 1,641 casualties; the 10th Armored Division's CCB, 503; the 9th Armored Division's CCR considerably more; others among the artillery and Team SNAFU; and from the 4th Armored Division, 1,400.

As the men in and around Bastogne soon learned, the end of the siege spelled no end to the fighting. Bastogne was no longer a hole in a doughnut but a balloon on the end of a string, and the string was vulnerable. In the days ahead, the defenders of Bastogne were destined to face their most severe test; for the failure to capture Bastogne and events taking place elsewhere in the Ardennes had at last convinced Adolf Hitler that he had to alter the objective of his offensive. Under a new plan, taking Bastogne was more important than ever.

CHAPTER TWENTY-SIX

In Front of the Ourthe River

The Ourthe River has two sources. An east branch rises in the high ground near St. Vith and flows westward past Houffalize, while a west branch rises in the high plateau near Bastogne and joins the other branch five miles west of Houffalize, whence the river cuts a wriggly swath through the center of the Ardennes and eventually flows into the Meuse at Liège. Although the river is small and in many places shallow, the banks are often steep. The west branch and the main course form the last military obstacle of appreciable importance in front of the Meuse; for beyond them is a high plateau, the Condroz, with rolling farm and pastureland and, in comparison with the rest of the Ardennes, relatively little forest cover.

After the 7th Armored Division reached Vielsalm and St. Vith on December 17, the division commander, General Hasbrouck, had seen no point in risking his supply stocks and trucks that far forward. Instead, he ordered the commander of his trains, Col. Andrew J. Adams, to displace nineteen miles to the rear to the town of La Roche astride the Ourthe River. A good direct highway, bisecting the Bastogne-Liège highway (N-15) several miles north of Houffalize at a crossroads called Baraque de Fraiture, connected La Roche with Salmchâteau and thus with the division headquarters at Vielsalm.

As the units of General Krüger's 58th Panzer Corps—the 116th Panzer and 560th Volksgrenadier Divisions—finally broke through the 28th Division's 112th Infantry, they faced a gap created when the 110th Infantry fell back toward Bastogne and the 112th Infantry moved northward into the developing St. Vith horseshoe. The only Americans in that gap were men of the 7th Armored Division's Trains, the 9th Canadian Forestry Company, and the 51st and 299th Engineer Combat Battalions. At the order of the corps commander, General Middleton, those forces were preparing bridges for demolition along the west branch of the Ourthe and

534

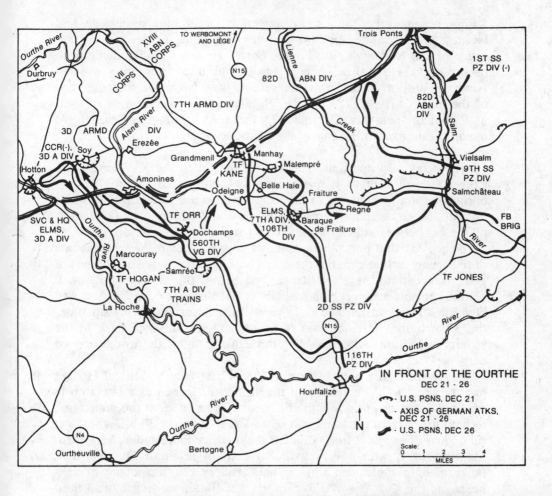

IN FRONT OF THE OURTHE
DEC 21 - 26

⌒ - U.S. PSNS, DEC 21

⌐ - AXIS OF GERMAN ATKS, DEC 21 - 26

◣ - U.S. PSNS, DEC 26

N

Scale:
0 1 2 3 4
MILES

along the main course of the river at La Roche and farther downstream, with particular attention to a major crossing site ten miles from La Roche at the village of Hotton.

By early morning of December 19, General von Waldenburg had sufficiently reorganized his 116th Panzer Division to send his reconnaissance battalion scouting to the west. Since the word was that Houffalize was stoutly held (in reality, it was only an outpost established by the 7th Armored Division's Trains), the reconnaissance troops bypassed the town to the south and early that afternoon drew up to the west branch of the Ourthe, only to find the bridge demolished. When patrols reported a Bailey Bridge a few miles upstream at the hamlet of Ourtheuville, von Waldenburg told the reconnaissance troops to seize it.

The corps commander, General Krüger, countermanded the order. A cautious commander—which was why General von Manteuffel afforded two of his three panzer divisions to von Lüttwitz instead of to Krüger—

Krüger reasoned that the Americans were bound to blow the bridge, and besides, the reconnaissance troops were trespassing in the zone of advance of von Lüttwitz's 47th Panzer Corps. He told von Waldenburg to backtrack to Houffalize, where patrols had discovered only a small American outpost in the town, and resume the advance on the other side of the main course of the Ourthe. Because of that decision, it was not until noon the next day, December 20, that the 116th Panzer Division got moving again toward the goal of the Meuse River.

The delay afforded time that the commander of the XVIII Airborne Corps, General Ridgway, sorely needed. Having ordered the 82d Airborne Division to move up to the Salm River in the rear of the troops at St. Vith, he was anxiously awaiting arrival of the 3d Armored Division to fill the gap between the airborne division and the Ourthe River.

Nobody at that point knew much of anything about the whereabouts of the enemy in that gap; but there had been reports from truck drivers of a German column near Houffalize, and before the day was out, small German patrols were probing roadblocks established by the 7th Armored Division's Trains at La Roche. In view of the uncertain enemy situation, the 3d Armored Division was to assemble some distance back in the vicinity of Hotton. After traveling through the night, the troops arrived early on December 20.

It was only part of a division, for the First Army's General Hodges had detached CCA to remain in the vicinity of Eupen as a backstop in case the Germans got across the Elsenborn Ridge (and, at the same time, to hunt for parachutists) and had sent CCB to help the 30th Division get rid of *Kampfgruppe Peiper*. That left the division commander, Maj. Gen. Maurice Rose, with only a battalion each of armored infantry, light tanks, medium tanks, and armored field artillery, plus a company of engineers and the 83d Armored Reconnaissance Battalion—not quite a third of Rose's usual strength.

With that small force, Rose was to occupy a thirteen-mile segment of the Bastogne-Liège highway extending north from Houffalize as far as the village of Manhay, where the highway from Trois Ponts to Hotton cut across. If the Germans intended moving north on Liège, that highway— N-15—was vital for them. If they intended moving west, it was still vital, for from it roads led west from the crossroads at both Baraque de Fraiture and Manhay. General Rose's broader mission was to provide a screen for the assembly of General Collins's VII Corps as a counterattacking force on the plateau beyond the Ourthe, the Condroz.

In view of the dearth of information on the enemy, the width of the zone of advance, and the paucity of forces, General Rose tried to maintain flexibility by creating three task forces and a fairly sizable reserve. Consisting of four hundred men, each task force had a company of medium tanks, a battery of self-propelled artillery, light tanks, and reconnaissance troops. The reserve included a company of medium tanks and a battalion of armored infantry.

The advance toward the Bastogne-Liège highway began in early afternoon of December 20. That was only a short time after the leading troops of the 116th Panzer Division, their countermarch at last completed, set out along their new line of march, designed to take them over the Ourthe both at La Roche and downstream at Hotton, the same sector through which two of the 3d Armored Division's task forces were headed.

On the left, outside that sector, a task force under Lt. Col. Matthew W. Kane encountered no enemy and soon reached the crossroads at Manhay. On the right, it was much the same at first for a task force under Lt. Col. Samuel M. Hogan, heading for La Roche, in normal times one of Belgium's more popular tourist attractions. Entering the town's picturesquely narrow streets nestled deep in the valley of the Ourthe beneath the ruins of an eleventh-century castle, Hogan found with considerable relief that men of the 7th Armored Division's Trains and assorted stragglers held the town. Because it had appeared earlier that the Germans were approaching La Roche from the south, where most of the supply stocks were located, the trains commander, Colonel Adams, had shifted the bulk of them to the village of Samrée, a few miles up the Salmchâteau road.

Continuing along the river road beyond La Roche, Hogan's reconnaissance platoon ran into a roadblock. German fire knocked out the leading armored car, setting it on fire and blocking the road. When Hogan reported that development to the rear, word came back to hold fast for the night; Hogan himself was to return the next morning for a possible change of orders. As the men settled down in La Roche, they loaded their vehicles with rations and cigarettes from the 7th Armored Division's stocks.

The center task force under Lt. Col. William R. Orr had in the meantime headed down the valley of the little Aisne River, a tributary of the Ourthe, to gain the La Roche–Salmchâteau highway at Samrée, then continue to the crossroads on Highway N-15 at Baraque de Fraiture. In early afternoon, as the head of the column reached the village of Dochamps two miles short of Samrée, the 7th Armored Division's quartermaster, Lt. Col. Andrew A. Miller, raced into the village in a jeep. He needed help, said Miller, to protect his supplies at Samrée.

German patrols preceding the main body of the 116th Panzer Division had entered Samrée, but since Miller gathered that a task force of the 3d Armored Division was coming, he believed he could hold them off until the armor arrived. As supply troops continued to load trucks with rations, ammunition, and gasoline, Miller went to look for the U.S. tanks.

Hardly had Miller returned with the promise of help than German tanks and *Panzergrenadiers* attacked in force, quickly knocking out Miller's only heavy weapons, a light tank and four half-tracks mounting quad-50s. When Miller ordered everybody out, most made it, in the process evacuating all remaining ammunition but leaving behind 15,000 rations and 25,000 gallons of gasoline. As the evacuation was in progress, two armored cars and six Shermans from Task Force Orr appeared, but the German tanks quickly knocked out all six Shermans. Picking up survivors among the tank crews, the armored cars fell back on Dochamps.

Although the fight at Samrée further delayed the 116th Panzer Division, it paid off with the acquisition of rations and precious gasoline. That was only the second occasion (the first was at Büllingen) when the Germans captured appreciable amounts of fuel. Aware that an undetermined number of Americans were in La Roche, General Krüger saw no need to fight for that town when little seemed to stand in the way of continuing to the Ourthe at Hotton. Once he had a crossing of the river there, he could proceed southwest to Marche, gaining excellent roads emanating from that town toward the Meuse, and any Americans left in La Roche would be cut off. He told General von Waldenburg to send a task force composed of four Panthers and a company of *Panzergrenadiers* marching through the night to grab the bridge at Hotton.

At Hotton, the valley of the Ourthe is wide. The village was on generally flat ground with most of the buildings on the south bank, but a few houses, the schoolhouse, and the little Hôtel de la Paix stood on the north bank. Most of the 120 or so support troops of the 3d Armored Division that were there—clerks, signalmen, mechanics, medics—were billeted in the schoolhouse. At a sturdy two-way bridge erected by U.S. Army Engineers to replace a permanent span demolished by retreating Germans in September, a platoon of the 51st Engineer Combat Battalion was on guard. There were two tanks in the village, a light and a medium, both stragglers awaiting minor repairs.

At 7:30 A.M. on December 21, the men were eating breakfast when mortar shells began falling in the schoolyard. Minutes later, two Panthers appeared on a trail leading from a finger of wooded high ground overlooking the village and rolled toward the bridge over the Ourthe. Moving out to meet them, the lone Sherman got in the first shot but in vain, and return fire from the leading Panther knocked it out.

A rocket from a bazooka fired by Sgt. Vern Sergent and Pvt. Hugh Lander hit the Panther near its gasoline tank and ignited spilled gasoline. Thinking the tank doomed, the crew jumped out and ran, but the fire quickly dissipated. Although the second Panther knocked out the light tank, a rocket from another bazooka manned by Cpl. Phillip Popp and Pfc. Carl Nelson hit the turret, and again the crew bailed out and ran.

The loss of the two tanks discouraged further German attack for the moment, but the *Panzergrenadiers* began digging in on the high ground, which commanded not only the village but also the highway leading from Soy, the location of General Rose's small reserve. That highway followed the forward slopes of a narrow ridgeline, the last before the ground dropped away to the wide valley of the Ourthe and beyond it, the broad plateau of the Condroz. To German tankers so long confined amid the woods and gorges of the eastern Ardennes, the view of the open ground—tank country—was tantalizing.

After radioing division headquarters for help, the senior officer in Hotton, Maj. Jack W. Fickessen, organized a defense. At Rose's order, the commander of the 36th Armored Infantry Regiment, Col. Robert L. Howze, Jr., doubling in brass as commander of the reserve, tried to send tanks and infantry down the road from Soy, but the Germans commanded the road. Only after nightfall was Howze able to send two platoons of tanks and a company of armored infantry along back roads to Hotton.

The Germans before Hotton were awaiting reinforcements, which General von Waldenburg was doing his best to send; yet instead of the weak opposition General Krüger had anticipated, the Germans had to contend with Task Force Orr at Dochamps. That interfered with the movement of German reinforcements, and not until near nightfall was the German armor, with the help of a battalion of the 560th Volksgrenadier Division, able to force Colonel Orr to abandon Dochamps and pull back to the hamlet of Amonines, only three miles short of Colonel Howze's reserve position in Soy.

Samuel Mason Hogan was a small-town Texan who grew up hunting, fishing, and riding horses. After two years at a local junior college, he obtained an appointment to West Point and finished with the class of 1938. Whatever vehicle Hogan rode in flew the Lone Star flag of Texas.

Daylight was beginning to break on December 21 when Sam Hogan downed a quick cup of coffee and with his driver and orderly set out, as ordered the night before, to check in at his division's headquarters. Hogan's operations officer, Maj. Travis M. Brown, and the leader of his reconnaissance platoon, 1st Lt. Clark V. Worrell, were to come along in another jeep and lead the way.

After traveling four miles, Travis and Worrell spotted a group of soldiers in the road ahead, gathered around a jeep and two half-tracks and eating K-rations. Two of the soldiers were wearing American overcoats, but as the officers drew closer, they made out in the growing light that the others were unquestionably Germans. The driver brought the jeep to a halt little more than ten yards from them. As Hogan and his jeep closed up, Worrell whispered as loud as he dared: "They're Germans, Colonel!"

Jumping from their jeeps, Hogan and the others began to run, which sent the Germans scurrying for their weapons. Hogan was sure he would be hit, for he was wearing fleece-lined British flying boots and they were made neither for walking nor running. He nevertheless reached a clump of bushes moments after the others—only the driver of Brown and Worrell's jeep was missing—and after catching their breath, they continued running. They escaped, Hogan believed, because the booty in the jeeps diverted the Germans: cigarettes, K-rations, and two good old Texas fruitcakes Hogan had received for Christmas.

On the theory that they were closer to Hotton than to their starting point in La Roche, Hogan headed for Hotton, but at every turn they ran into more Germans. In escaping from one group, Brown and Worrell became separated from Hogan, his driver, and his orderly.

After all three spent the night huddled in the woods under Hogan's trench coat, Hogan decided he might make better progress returning to La Roche. In a hamlet, civilians told him there was an American force in the next village of Marcouray. It was Task Force Hogan.

In Marcouray, Hogan learned from his executive officer, Maj. W. Stewart Walker, that a medical sergeant going back for supplies had come upon the driver of Brown and Worrell's jeep, and from him Walker learned something of what had happened to Hogan. When he radioed that information to division headquarters, he received orders to bring the task force out. Walker had gotten as far as Marcouray, on the upper reaches of a slope overlooking the Ourthe, when at dusk a *Panzerfaust* knocked out the lead tank. Walker had holed up in the village for the night.

Although the orders were still to break out, patrols soon determined that a sizable German force blocked the way. Since Marcouray had some forty solidly built stone houses and good fields of fire in all directions, Hogan decided to hold in the hope that somebody could break through to him.

Afforded a battalion from the 517th Parachute Infantry—a separate regiment that had been resting in northern France when the German offensive opened—Colonel Howze early on December 22 again tried to break through from Soy to Hotton. Yet again the attempt got nowhere, for the Germans still held the high ground overlooking the highway. The defense of Hotton would be left to the little band of original defenders and the tanks and armored infantrymen that had gained the village during the night.

It was late afternoon of the 22d before the Germans attacked once more at Hotton, to meet, as a German commander noted, "a hailstorm of fire." *Panzergrenadiers* got into some of the houses, splitting the defenders, but fire from the two platoons of Shermans and the threat of bazookas kept the German tanks at a distance. Night had fallen and a crisis was approaching when the German firing inexplicably died down, and with incredulity the Americans became aware that their foe was falling back. They could only wonder why.

As the result of the resistance at Hotton, an apparently strong American presence in Soy, armor at Amonines, and armor again (albeit surrounded) at Marcouray, General Krüger had come to the conclusion that he faced a powerful American force and would be unable to get across the Ourthe at Hotton without a hard fight and a long delay. Krüger had learned that the Americans had abandoned La Roche and also that the 2d Panzer Division of the 47th Panzer Corps had gained a crossing of the west branch of the Ourthe, and there was something to be said for advancing close alongside another panzer division.

Once again Krüger, master of the countermarch, ordered General von Waldenburg to backtrack. While the 560th Volksgrenadier Division continued to seek a crossing of the river at Hotton, the panzer division was to cross at La Roche and continue the thrust to the Meuse.

Although General Rose had far less strength than his adversary imagined, he did enjoy a brief hope of sizable reinforcement when the army commander, General Hodges, released CCA from its back-up position near Eupen. By daylight of the 22d, most of the combat command had arrived, but orders soon followed to send the bulk of CCA to form a screen along the west branch of the Ourthe to protect the assembly of the 84th Infantry Division at Marche, a part of the counterattacking force to operate under General Collins's VII Corps. All that was left as reinforcement for General Rose was a company of armored infantry and a battalion of medium tanks.

With the departure of the 116th Panzer Division, Rose's position improved. Nevertheless, as he and his men soon found out, the 560th Volksgrenadiers still had a lot of fight in them. So, too, the sharply compartmented, hilly, heavily wooded countryside with few roads better than farm tracks favored infantry far more than it did armor, and Rose was particularly short of infantry. There was also a real possibility that the Germans might break through along Rose's north flank, for there, at the crossroads known as Baraque de Fraiture, a crisis was developing.

To the men involved, it seemed light-years ago. In reality it had been only a few days since the executive officer of the 598th Field Artillery Battalion, Maj. Arthur C. Parker III, had brought three of his battalion's 105mm. howitzers out of their positions beyond the Our River in the shadow of the Schnee Eifel and through Schoenberg and St. Vith. Two days later, on December 19, the commander of the 7th Armored Division, General Hasbrouck, had arranged with the commander of the 106th Division's artillery to send Parker and his howitzers back along the supply route leading to La Roche to help keep that route open at Baraque de Fraiture.

An X-shaped crossroads, Baraque de Fraiture stands on high, windswept ground where the snow was soon to be deep. At an elevation of just over 2,200 feet, it is the second highest point in the Ardennes, and much of the countryside nearby is wooded and marshy, much like that on the Hautes Fagnes. There was no village, only three farmhouses with their outbuildings; the village from which the crossroads took its name was a thousand yards to the northeast. The roads crossing at Baraque de Fraiture were the generally east-west Salmchâteau–La Roche highway and the major north-south route—Highway N-15—linking Bastogne, Houffalize, and Liège. Although the ground close about the crossroads was cleared, thick fir forests closed in on all sides.

To the American commanders, who still saw Liège as a primary German objective, Baraque de Fraiture and Highway N-15 were obviously of critical importance. Although the crossroads was the objective assigned by General Rose to his Task Force Orr, the task force had failed to get past Samrée.

Highway N-15—and Baraque de Fraiture—was roughly in the center of what turned out to be the sector of the XVIII Airborne Corps, which extended for some thirty miles from Trois Ponts to Hotton. To the east of the highway, the 82d Airborne Division had to defend the line of the Salm River, a long stretch of the Salmchâteau–La Roche highway., and, so long as *Kampfgruppe Peiper* remained a threat, much of the south bank of the Amblève River as well. Thus General Gavin had nothing left with which to block Highway N-15. Once the small available portion of the 3d Armored Division got involved between the Ourthe and the little Aisne River, neither did General Rose, even though according to the interdivisional boundary the highway was Rose's responsibility. Thus, at first, Major Parker's three artillery pieces and their crews, plus a few men of the 589th Field Artillery Battalion's Service Battery, who had also escaped from the shadow of the Schnee Eifel, were all that stood in the way of German advance past Baraque de Fraiture. A total of 110 men.

The next morning, December 20, a detachment from an antiaircraft battalion with three half-tracks mounting quad-50s and a self-propelled 37mm. gun joined Parker. When at noon an order arrived from the 106th Division for the three artillery pieces to be moved well to the rear where the 598th Field Artillery Battalion was to be reconstituted, Major Parker recognized that if he left, the little band of antiaircraft troops would have no hope of holding the vital crossroads. He ignored the order.

As an indirect result of the Sixth Panzer Army's failure to get across the Elsenborn Ridge, a threat to the crossroads was soon building. In keeping with Field Marshal Model's order of December 20, the Sixth Panzer Army's uncommitted 2d SS Panzer Corps under General der Waffen-SS Willi Bittrich began to move forward in pursuit of the new mission of protecting the north flank of the Fifth Panzer Army, which at that point was making the main effort.

One of the two divisions under Bittrich's command, the 9th SS Panzer Division, began the difficult task of negotiating the jammed roads through the Losheim Gap and crossing the Salm River, while the other, the 2d SS Panzer Division, circled behind St. Vith and entered the gap through which General Krüger's 58th Panzer Corps had begun to pass early on December 19. (The 2d SS Panzer Division and its commander, Generalleutnant Heinz Lammerding, were infamous for one of the war's worst atrocities. In June, the troops had destroyed the French village of Oradour-sur-Glâne and murdered 642 of the inhabitants, including women and children.)

When the 2d SS Panzer Division reached the gap southwest of St. Vith, it was out of gasoline. Only during the night of December 21 did enough fuel arrive to enable Major Krag's reconnaissance battalion to try to open the Salmchâteau–La Roche highway for the division's advance; but Krag had achieved nothing and had eventually turned on Salmchâteau. Not until the morning of the 22d did enough gasoline arrive to move a *Panzergrenadier* regiment, some tanks, and an artillery battalion, and even then, to stretch available fuel, each vehicle towed at least one other and in most cases two. Because outposts of the 82d Airborne Division still denied the Salmchâteau–La Roche highway, those troops had to trudge through the day's heavy snowfall over back roads to reach Highway N-15 at Houffalize and there turn north to Baraque de Fraiture.

By that time, the night of December 22, the little American force at the crossroads had received some reinforcement. Sent to guard the 7th Armored Division's supply route at Samrée, a troop of the 87th Armored Reconnaissance Squadron had found the enemy there and joined Parker's force, and the 3d Armored Division's Task Force Kane sent two self-propelled 105mm. assault guns.

Parker himself was no longer around. Late on December 21, a fragment from a mortar shell wounded him seriously; he refused evacuation, but when he lost consciousness, that was no longer his to say. Another officer of the 589th Field Artillery Battalion, Maj. Elliott Goldstein, took over. To Goldstein it was fairly obvious that the crossroads was soon to come under attack by the 2d SS Panzer Division, for the men repulsed a reconnaissance patrol from that division and captured the leader of the patrol.

The commander of the 82d Airborne Division, General Gavin, was in the meantime growing increasingly concerned about Highway N-15. If the Germans drove up the highway, they might either trap the airborne division in the angle formed by the Amblève and Salm Rivers or at least force the division's withdrawal, in either case preventing Gavin from accomplishing his mission of covering the exodus of American troops from the St. Vith salient. During the afternoon of December 21, in company with the commander of the regiment closest to the highway, Col. Charles Billingslea of the 325th Glider Infantry, Gavin went to see the 3d Armored Division's General Rose. He found him on the second floor of a house at the crossroads behind Baraque de Fraiture at Manhay.

Since the highway was Rose's responsibility, Gavin asked what Rose had available for blocking it. Not much, responded Rose. He had had to send Task Force Kane, which had earlier been at Manhay, to help Task Force Orr near Dochamps; his CCB was still fighting Peiper; and although CCA was at last on the way, he had the impression he was going to have to send the bulk of that combat command to the other side of the Ourthe River to screen the assembly of the 84th Division. He would nevertheless try to hold part of CCA at Manhay.

Little encouraged by that visit, Colonel Billingslea moved a platoon into the hamlet of Regné, astride the Salmchâteau–La Roche highway, which extended his line to within two miles of Baraque de Fraiture. Yet he was still unhappy and asked Gavin to release his 2d Battalion, which Gavin had withheld as a division reserve. When Gavin agreed, Billingslea sent a company to Baraque de Fraiture and the rest of the battalion to high ground overlooking the crossroads at the village of Fraiture itself. Both forces moved into position during the heavy snowfall of December 22.

That night, men and tanks of the 2d SS Panzer Division moved into attack positions in front of both the crossroads and the village. Just before daylight on the 23d, seventy-five *SS-Panzergrenadiers* hit the 2d Battalion, 325th Glider Infantry, at the village, coming close to carrying the position when they caught most of the glider infantrymen out of their foxholes eating breakfast in the houses. A counterattack led by the battalion commander, Maj. Richard M. Gibson, restored the situation.

All morning the Germans kept up a drumbeat of mortar and artillery fire against Baraque de Fraiture. In quest of help, Major Goldstein, taking with him a captured German captain and sergeant as proof that he faced attack by the SS, went by jeep to the crossroads at Manhay. There he found a newly arrived task force of the 3d Armored Division's CCA under Lt. Col. Walter B. Richardson, the only part of CCA remaining for General Rose's use. Richardson agreed to send a platoon each of armored infantry and medium tanks to help and added a company of paratroopers from a separate parachute infantry battalion, the 509th, the U.S. Army's oldest, whose men had fought in one place or another since North Africa, and, like the 517th Parachute Infantry, had been moved forward from a rest area in northern France.

Shortly after midday, as the tanks and infantry started down the highway toward Baraque de Fraiture, they ran into a roadblock the Germans had established behind the crossroads. While the platoon of armored infantrymen and company of paratroopers dismounted to take out the roadblock, the commanders of the five tanks buttoned their hatches and kept going. They reached Baraque de Fraiture around 1 P.M.

Dusk was approaching when at four o'clock German mortars and artillery began a heavy shelling. For twenty minutes the guns pounded, then as the fire lifted onto the highway behind the crossroads, eight Mark IVs accompanied by what looked to the defenders to be hordes of *SS-Panzergrenadiers* attacked up the road from the south, while other *SS-Panzergrenadiers* accompanied by half-tracks attacked along the road from the west, the direction of Samrée.

Except for one tank, which found cover behind a masonry wall, the Shermans were in the open on flat ground, fully exposed to enemy fire. Pausing at the woodsline, the Mark IVs quickly knocked out two of them; but the Shermans also got two Mark IVs and one of the 598th Field Artillery Battalion's howitzers accounted for two more.

Because the Mark IVs had yet to close in, the defenders were holding their own against the *SS-Panzergrenadiers* when two Panthers appeared along the road from the east, the direction of Salmchâteau. Fire from the Panthers quickly knocked out two more of the Shermans. The one taking cover behind the wall would drive into the open, fire a shot at the Panthers, then return to its cover. Yet for all the effect the rounds had on the heavy frontal armor, it was "like throwing peas at a plate glass window." Once again the Sherman emerged from its hiding place to get in another shot, but that was one time too many. A round from one of the Panthers blew it apart.

It was fully dark and *SS-Panzergrenadiers* were swarming over the crossroads when the commander of Company F, 325th Glider Infantry, Capt. Junior R. Woodruff, radioed his battalion commander, Major Gibson, that the defense of the crossroads was falling to pieces and asked permission to withdraw. When the request reached Colonel Billingslea, he refused in the hope of getting other reinforcements from the 3d Armored Division. Moments later, Woodruff radioed again: German tanks were grinding down the foxholes. That time Billingslea said, OK, get out.

As the Germans engulfed the crossroads, small bands of men tried to make stands in barns and farmhouses. In one farmhouse, Major Goldstein's operations officer, Capt. George Huxel, although wounded, tried to hold with a few men; but when the attached barn collapsed, Huxel saw no choice but to run for it. As three cows dashed bellowing from the barn, Huxel and those with him took advantage of the confusion to escape.

Men in another house holed up in the cellar until the building caught fire and forced them out, hands overhead. German shells and small-arms fire cut down others as they tried to gain the woods.

All three of the 589th Field Artillery Battalion's howitzers were lost, as were the two assault guns of Task Force Kane, the antiaircraft half-tracks, and all the vehicles of the troop of the 87th Armored Cavalry Squadron. The total of men who died or were captured would never be known, but of the 116 glider infantrymen of Captain Woodruff's company F, only 45 got away. In tribute to the officer who first established a defense at Baraque de Fraiture, the men who survived the fight renamed it Parker's Crossroads.

With news of the collapse at Baraque de Fraiture, General Gavin risked pulling out one of the battalions of the 504th Parachute Infantry that was watching *Kampfgruppe Peiper* and sent it to regain the crossroads. Yet on second thought Gavin decided that a counterattack by a single battalion would be an exercise in futility. (Said Major Gibson: "I wouldn't attack that damned place with a regiment, not to mention a battalion.") It would be wiser, Gavin decided, to use the parachute infantry to help Major Gibson protect the division's ruptured flank.

Gavin had nothing left with which to try to block the critical highway behind Baraque de Fraiture, and General Rose had little more. Rose did order Colonel Richardson at Manhay to send a platoon each of armored infantry and medium tanks under Richardson's executive officer, Maj. Olin F. Brewster, to join the armored infantry and company of paratroopers that had earlier tried to get through. That force dug in astride the highway inside the forest, roughly midway between Manhay and Baraque de Fraiture, at a spot that on the maps had a name, Belle Haie.

Although General Ridgway had been pressing General Hodges for release of the 3d Armored Division's CCB from the fight against *Kampfgruppe Peiper*, he had yet to succeed. That meant that the only uncommitted troops left to him were those that had begun withdrawing early that morning from the salient near St. Vith. Those men were disorganized, scattered about in various villages, and obviously in need of rest. Although reluctant to call on them, Ridgway considered that he had no choice.

General Hoge's CCB of the 9th Armored Division had been the first unit to get out of the salient as an integral force. Early in the afternoon of December 23, even before the Germans hit Baraque de Fraiture, Ridgway ordered Hoge to back up the 82d Airborne Division's western flank. To cover the assembly of the combat command, Hoge sent a company of tanks to Manhay and the 27th Armored Infantry Battalion to Malempré, a village two miles southeast of Manhay, which was off Highway N-15 but on ground that looked down onto the highway.

Ridgway and the other American commanders fully expected the 2d SS Panzer Division to exploit its success at Baraque de Fraiture by continuing without pause up Highway N-15 to Liège. That city was indeed the formal objective of Bittrich's 2d SS Panzer Corps, for under the changed mission whereby the Sixth Panzer Army was to protect the Fifth Panzer Army's northern flank, that might be best accomplished by pushing the Americans back across the Meuse at and around Liège. In fact Field Marshal Model saw that as beyond the capabilities of the Sixth Panzer Army at the moment. He indicated instead that he would be happy establishing a line along the Amblève River and on high ground north of Manhay, thereby uncovering the Trois Ponts–Hotton highway. Then the 2d SS Panzer Division was to veer northwest to get across the Ourthe River and onto the Condroz plateau, there to provide the Fifth Panzer Army with flank protection for the continuing drive to the Meuse.

Yet even to gain that line was for the moment beyond the means of the Sixth Panzer Army, for only on December 23 with the American withdrawal from the St. Vith salient had the road network there become available. It would take time to reposition divisions to assist the 2d SS Panzer Division. Indeed, not until the next day, December 24, was Hitler to agree to end the futile battering against the Elsenborn Ridge; and shortages of gasoline, aggravated by the break in the weather that turned loose Allied fighter-bombers, complicated the task of shifting units.

Kampfgruppe Peiper by that time was reduced to a shell, its commander intent only on getting his men out of their trap on foot; and the rest of the 1st SS Panzer Division had been so punished that the division was capable for the moment of nothing more than holding a defensive sector facing Stavelot and Trois Ponts. The other armor of the 1st SS Panzer Corps—the 12th SS Panzer Division—had also lost heavily and would need several days to re-form into any kind of an effective fighting force. Freed by the American withdrawal from the St. Vith salient, the two *Volksgrenadier* divisions of General Lucht's 66th Corps were to defend along the lower reaches of the Salm River, between Vielsalm and Trois Ponts, thereby enabling the 9th SS Panzer Division, which had made no headway in crossing the river, to shift upstream and cross in the vicinity of Vielsalm and Salmchâteau.

The 2d SS Panzer Division thus might anticipate help soon from that division operating on its right flank; more immediate help was meanwhile to come at Field Marshal Model's order from Colonel Remer's *Führer Begleit Brigade*. Remer was to follow the trace of the 2d SS Panzer Division and attack close along the division's right flank near Baraque de Fraiture.

Even had the division commander, General Lammerding, not wanted to await that brigade's arrival, he had other reasons for delaying an attack up Highway N-15 beyond Baraque de Fraiture, not the least of which were the mounting swarms of P-38 Lightnings and P-51 Mustangs that seemingly pounced upon anything moving in the open by daylight. (General Dietrich complained that the pilots showed no respect for general officers.) Because of the dense forest on both sides of N-15, an attack directly up the highway would be restricted, as far as tanks were concerned, to twenty-two feet of macadam, and Lammerding wanted no part of that. He intended instead to move through villages off either side of the highway, then converge on Manhay at a point close to the crossroads where the woods ran out.

To prepare the way for his maneuver, *SS-Panzergrenadiers* during the night of the 23d infiltrated through the woods and attacked the village of

Odeigne, just west of the highway and roughly parallel with Major Brewster's position at Belle Haie. In the darkness, the Germans quickly routed a platoon of light tanks protected by only a squad of riflemen. Yet Lammerding would be unable to exploit that gain until his engineers could improve a dirt track leading to the village to enable his tanks to get forward. Not until near nightfall on Christmas Eve—December 24—were the engineers to complete that task.

For the American command, it became increasingly unfortunate that Highway N-15 represented the approximate boundary between the 82d Airborne and 3d Armored Divisions. Although General Ridgway had tried to ease the problem by assigning responsibility for the highway to one division, the 3d Armored, his superior, General Hodges, in late afternoon of the 23d, introduced a complication. Because the bulk of the 3d Armored Division was screening the assembly of General Collins's VII Corps and was eventually supposed to form a part of Collins's counterattacking force, Hodges transferred the division to Collins's command. Highway N-15 lay close at that point not only to an interdivisional but to an inter-corps boundary; but responsibility for the highway remained with Ridgway's XVIII Airborne Corps, which meant that it was no longer a responsibility of the 3d Armored Division, which was no longer a part of that corps. Since the highway was also the approximate boundary between two German corps—Bittrich's 2d SS Panzer and Krüger's 58th Panzer—Field Marshal Model solved the problem by placing the 2d SS Panzer Division under Krüger's command. As events were soon to demonstrate, Hodges would have been well advised to adopt a similar solution.

Even though Major Brewster's little task force at Belle Haie belonged to the 3d Armored Division, nobody moved immediately to order Brewster to withdraw. Indeed, a second company of the 509th Parachute Infantry Battalion reinforced Brewster, but the task of finding a force capable of prolonged defense in front of Manhay remained Ridgway's. Ridgway turned to the commander of the 7th Armored Division, General Hasbrouck, just back from the St. Vith salient. Hasbrouck in turn called on Colonel Rosebaum and CCA, which had emerged from the salient in considerably better shape than had General Clarke's CCB.

As a defensive position, the village of Manhay suffered from the fact that it was dominated by high ground to the south in the direction of Baraque de Fraiture. Thus Colonel Rosebaum prepared to push his defenses out beyond the crossroads to block the road linking Odeigne to Highway N-15, to cut the main highway itself, and to relieve armored infantry of Hoge's CCB, 9th Armored Division, at Malempré. That done, Hoge's CCB was to become General Ridgway's reserve, and Major Brewster's task force at Belle Haie was to withdraw.

Late on the morning of December 24, as Rosebaum's troops moved to their positions, a contingent of tanks and infantry from the *Führer Begleit Brigade* attacked Regné, the hamlet on the Salmchâteau–La Roche highway only two miles from Baraque de Fraiture. The lone platoon of glider infantrymen in the hamlet was no match for the German tanks. General Gavin was considerably concerned about losing the village, for from it led a road into the valley of the little Lienne Creek to both Gavin's and Ridgway's command posts. Afforded a company of medium tanks from Hoge's CCB, Gavin in early afternoon used parachute infantry riding on the tanks to retake Regné.

Much to the delight of the commander of the *Führer Begleit Brigade*, Colonel Remer, who still nursed the ambition of garnering glory by driving to the Meuse, Field Marshal Model ordered his brigade to disengage. He needed it more, Model had decided, to help the Fifth Panzer Army reach the river.

Not long after that, the 82d Airborne Division also relinquished Regné. Gavin's division was getting ready to withdraw.

Hardly had the 82d Airborne Division moved up to the Salm River and the Salmchâteau–La Roche highway than the officer known for his dislike of withdrawals, General Ridgway, told Gavin to reconnoiter for a defensive line to his rear that might be occupied once the troops had pulled back from the St. Vith salient. Like Ridgway, Gavin also disliked withdrawals and protested. Ridgway nevertheless insisted, pointing out that the Germans might threaten the 82d Airborne Division's western flank (which was in fact what had happened). The line Gavin chose ran generally along the highway linking Trois Ponts and Manhay.

Early on December 24, Ridgway issued a warning order to Gavin to prepare for possible withdrawal to that line. Despite Gavin's concern for his western flank, the possibility of withdrawing still disturbed him. He prided himself on the fact that his division had never relinquished any ground it had gained. More important, the spectacle of tired and in some cases dispirited troops from the St. Vith salient passing through the airborne division's positions was fresh in Gavin's mind. To withdraw so soon after his men had gone through that experience, and while belief was widespread that the Germans were using American vehicles and men in American uniforms, might lead to panic.

As it turned out, Gavin would be unable even to argue his case, for in mid-morning of December 24, General Ridgway had a visitor at his farmhouse headquarters in Werbomont who insisted on withdrawal: Field Marshal Montgomery. Arriving in an open car without escort, Montgomery jauntily acknowledged the salutes of the guards and went inside. It was essential, he told Ridgway, that the First Army build a solid northern flank by shortening the line in preparation for counterattack by General Collins's VII Corps. The new line was to be a southwestward extension of the solid positions already established on the Elsenborn Ridge and at Malmédy and Stavelot.

As worked out with Ridgway, the line was to extend from Trois Ponts along the road leading to Manhay, the line that General Gavin had previously reconnoitered; but at Manhay, Colonel Rosebaum's CCA, 7th Armored Division, was to leave only an outpost at the crossroads and occupy high ground behind it. To the west of Manhay, the 3d Armored Division was to continue to defend generally along the Trois Ponts–Manhay–Hotton highway.

The choice of the night of December 24 for the withdrawal and re-shuffling of the line—the same night that *Kampfgruppe Peiper* was withdrawing from La Gleize—proved to be unfortunate, for it coincided with a renewed attack by the 2d SS Panzer Division. Task Force Brewster and the 7th Armored Division's CCA were destined to pay the consequences.

Not until well after dark, around 6 P.M., did Colonel Rosebaum receive the order to withdraw. His men were still making their preparations when at 9 P.M., in bright moonlight glistening on a frozen snow cover, *SS-Panzergrenadiers* supported by tanks began moving from Odeigne toward Highway N-15 and Manhay.

The Americans standing in the way astride the little road from Odeigne consisted of under-strength companies of the 48th Armored Infantry Battalion and the 40th Tank Battalion, the latter with only seven medium tanks. Tankers and infantrymen were both on the alert, but as a column of tanks approached, quite clearly the first was a Sherman. It had the silhouette, the characteristic engine noise, and an unmistakable blue exhaust.

They all knew that contingents of the 3d Armored Division were in the vicinity, and nobody wanted to be guilty of firing on a friendly column. A call to the rear failed to clarify anything, for in the confusion resulting from the shifts in boundaries and from the fact that the units that had withdrawn from the St. Vith salient had yet to establish viable communications, there was no communication between the two American armored divisions.

Before anybody could discern that it was no friendly column but Mark IVs and Panthers that were approaching, *SS-Panzergrenadiers* opened fire with *Panzerfausts*. They knocked out four tanks with the first rockets and crippled two more. After six days in the embattled salient near St. Vith, the American crews had had all they could take. The crippled tanks and the one that had escaped damage took off. They fled toward Manhay, leaving the armored infantrymen to plead for authority to fall back. Denied that, they broke in disorder.

In the attacking force, SS-Sgt. Ernst Barkmann of the 4th Panzer Company commanded a Panther, Panzer 401. In the confusion, Barkmann and his tank became separated from the others and soon emerged alone on Highway N-15. Thinking the rest had gone ahead of him, Barkmann continued along the highway until he reached a small clearing. Fifty paces ahead he saw a tank, its commander's upper body visible in the turret. That was his platoon leader SS-Sgt. Maj. Franz Frauscher, thought Barkmann, but as Barkmann's tank drew abreast and Barkmann started to speak, the man in the turret disappeared and slammed the hatch shut. For the first time Barkmann noticed that the tank had not the green panel lights of a panzer but dark red lights. It was a Sherman.

Over the intercom, Barkmann shouted for the gunner to fire, but as the turret swung in the direction of the American tank, the barrel of the cannon slammed against the Sherman's turret. Discerning immediately what was wrong, Barkmann's driver needed no orders to back up. That freed the panzer's traverse and at a distance of precisely one yard, Barkmann's gunner slammed a round into the rear of the Sherman.

Still convinced that SS-Sergeant Major Frauscher and the other tanks were ahead, Barkmann continued along the highway. Rounding a sharp curve, he came again to a clearing. Then he gasped. Ahead of him he counted nine American tanks partially dug in. To stop or to turn back would be suicide. "Keep driving," Barkmann ordered the driver. "Full speed." As they passed the American position, nine turrets turned as if in unison, but nobody fired.

Once past those tanks, Barkmann halted and tried to raise his company on the radio but without success. Quite obviously, he was ahead of Frauscher and the rest of his platoon; but if he tried to withdraw, he would have to pass the dug-in American tanks again. *Wenn schon, denn schon!* (What the hell!) Barkmann decided to keep going.

As the forest again enveloped each side of the highway, he saw American infantrymen falling back along both sides of the road. Swearing as only foot soldiers can swear at men who ride, they made way for the tank, obviously unaware in the darkness that it was German.

Then came a broad clearing and Panzer 401 was inside Manhay. American tanks and other vehicles were parked alongside the buildings. At a café, such was the activity that Barkmann was convinced it was a command post, but nobody paid his tank any heed other than to get out of the way.

Reaching the crossroads in the center of the village, Barkmann wanted to turn left, toward the west, which he knew to be the direction the attack was to take from Manhay, but down that road three Shermans were approaching. Barely pausing, he told his driver to continue straight up the highway in the direction of Liège.

Moments later, Panzer 401 was passing one American tank after another, all pulled over to one side of the road, their crews standing outside, talking and smoking. Again there was no choice but to keep moving. And again American soldiers leaped aside to allow the tank to pass, but that time some of them recognized it for what it was. Jumping into their own tanks, the crews swung their turrets; but being in column, one tank masked the fire of another, and Barkmann dropped a smoke grenade onto the highway to cloud their vision further.

Up ahead a jeep approached, somebody standing in it and shouting over and over to halt. When the driver at last realized he was approaching a German tank, he screeched to a halt and tried to back up. "Roll over it!" ordered Barkmann.

The impact of crushing the jeep threw Barkmann's tank against a Sherman parked alongside the road, and the treads of the two behemoths interlocked. Panzer 401's motor choked and stopped. Small-arms fire erupted, forcing Barkmann to close his hatch. Unless the driver could restart the motor quickly, some American gun was sure to do the tank in. Again and again the driver tried, and Barkmann was beginning to despair when at last the motor caught.

Back up! Barkmann commanded. With little difficulty, the Panzer broke free and again headed up the highway.

However brief the delay, it provided time for the Shermans to organize a pursuit. Although Barkmann dropped another smoke grenade onto the road, the pursuing Shermans came on. Swinging the turret all the way around to the rear, the gunner fired, hitting the first American tank and setting it on fire, which blocked the highway.

A few hundred yards down the road, Barkmann saw a trail and ordered the driver to pull onto it. There the crew found a sheltered position affording a view of the highway, and Barkmann permitted his men to dismount for a breath of air.

Back at the sharp curve in the highway overlooking Manhay where Barkmann and his Panther had passed dug-in American tanks, an experience similar to that at Odeigne occurred. There the American commanders and men of another under-strength rifle company supported by ten tanks also hesitated to fire on what looked to be an American column, for again a Sherman was in the lead with its characteristic silhouette and blue exhaust. The delay proved fatal. As on the Prümerberg outside St. Vith, the German tanks fired high-velocity flares, blinding the American crews. They knocked out most of the tanks. All the crews fled, and when *SS-Panzergrenadiers* closed in, so did the armored infantrymen.

Beyond the highway, in the village of Malempré, men of another task force of armored infantrymen and tanks could see the fight along the highway taking place. Their orders were to withdraw to the new positions behind Manhay at 11 P.M. and to do so even should communications fail. Since it was almost that hour, the infantry and tank commanders, unable to reach their battalion commanders by radio, moved the timetable up by fifteen minutes. Close behind them, a column of *SS-Panzergrenadiers* occupied Malempré.

In Manhay, there was no real contest. An American platoon leader got two tanks into position for a brief stand at the crossroads, knocking out two German tanks, but in what became a general hegira, they failed to stand for long.

Every commander who has ever executed a planned withdrawal has worried lest his enemy should strike while the withdrawal was in process. That was what happened at Manhay, and it happened along a unit boundary where responsibilities were ill-defined, to exhausted, battle-weary men who had yet to get a good night's sleep after six days in the line in the St. Vith salient. Predictably, a rout ensued, possibly abetted by the knowledge of many men that at least one German tank had already penetrated the village.

From their hiding place north of Manhay, SS-Sergeant Barkmann and his crew could discern that German tanks were firing inside Manhay. It was "like music to their ears." As the noise of battle at last faded in the darkness, Panzer 401 inched back onto the highway and returned past burning American vehicles to the village.

The debacle at Manhay left a small American force standing alone astride Highway N-15 at Belle Haie: Major Brewster's task force, composed of seven tanks and a platoon of armored infantry of the 3d Armored Division and two companies of the 509th Parachute Infantry Battalion. The German advance on Manhay had cut off the force from the rear, and *SS-Panzergrenadiers* were thick and close in the woods.

Early in the evening when Brewster's superior, Colonel Richardson, had learned that the 7th Armored Division was to withdraw to a new line behind Manhay, he himself had received no orders to pull back. Thus he radioed Major Brewster to stand fast. Even when Brewster reported that German tanks had cut the road behind him, Richardson still ordered him to hold. "Don't give an inch unless I approve it," said Richardson.

In less than an hour Manhay was a scene of confusion and panic, and Richardson realized that it was pointless for Brewster to continue to hold at Belle Haie. By radio he told him to get out fast. If it was necessary, to save his men, he was to destroy his remaining vehicles, including the tanks.

Although Brewster tried to move down the highway to gain a secondary road leading to Malempré, German tanks knocked out a tank at each end of his column, making it impossible for the remaining vehicles to move either backward or forward off the constricted road. Brewster ordered all vehicles to be damaged and left behind: a half-track, a 6 × 6 truck, a jeep, and five Shermans. Moving on foot through the woods, Brewster and his men reached positions of the 82d Airborne Division beyond Malempré not long before daylight.

When Brewster later in the day reported to his division commander, General Rose, he was startled to find Rose antagonistic. "Why did you destroy government equipment?" demanded Rose. Brewster replied that he had authority from his commander, Colonel Richardson, and that he had thought it better to save his men rather than lose everybody trying to salvage a few vehicles. "Major," said Rose, "I call that misbehavior."

A strict disciplinarian, Rose ordered court-martial charges prepared against Brewster for cowardice before the enemy. Neither Colonel Richardson nor the commander of CCA, Brig. Gen. Doyle A. Hickey, would endorse them, and nothing had come of the charges when three months later, beyond the Rhine River, General Rose died in battle.

That Christmas Eve yet another surrounded American force was seeking a way out: the 3d Armored Division's Task Force Hogan, which since December 21 had been trapped near the Ourthe River in the village of Marcouray. The rest of the 3d Armored Division had been too hard-pressed to attempt a rescue, and an attempt at firing medical supplies in artillery shells had gone awry.

Close to noon on Christmas Eve, a German jeep approached under a white flag with a lieutenant who, when ushered before Colonel Hogan, demanded that he surrender. The American troops were surrounded by three panzer divisions, their situation hopeless. He was authorized, said the lieutenant, to take an officer on a tour of the German positions to verify the Americans' plight. Hogan responded that he had orders to fight to the death, and as a soldier, he would obey his orders.

That afternoon seven C-47 aircraft attempted to drop supplies, but German flak shot down all but one. Some of the airmen tried to parachute, but so low were the planes that Hogan and his men feared none would survive. Two pilots, nevertheless, entered Hogan's perimeter that night, their falls having been checked by the treetops.

Reconnaissance that same night revealed that there was no way out of Marcouray for vehicles other than the main road, and that was thick with German troops and vehicles. Hogan radioed the news to the rear. The next day, he and his men had just finished a Christmas dinner of K-rations when a message arrived from General Rose directing Hogan to destroy his heavy weapons and vehicles and get out on foot.

Through the afternoon, the men drained the oil from the tanks and other vehicles, put sugar in the gasoline, then ran the motors a few at a time until they froze. Just before leaving, the crews of the tanks and artillery pieces were to drop their breech blocks into a well. The surgeon, Capt. Louis Spigelmann, and several of his medics volunteered to stay with the wounded and the next day were to attempt (unsuccessfully, as it turned out) to pass through German lines under a white flag. Some of the less seriously wounded were to guard German prisoners until the Germans arrived. A detail buried the only one of Hogan's men killed at Marcouray and a German prisoner whom an impetuous lieutenant had shot in the back of the head before anybody could knock his weapon away.

After nightfall, faces blackened with burnt cork, steel helmets left behind to cut down on noise, a force that the American press had by that time come to call "Hogan's 400" started out. A reconnaissance platoon led the way, followed by the rest of the men in groups of twenty with an interval of thirty seconds between each.

Much to Colonel Hogan's regret, he was still wearing those fleece-lined British flying boots. Struggling uphill in the dark over rough terrain, it seemed to Hogan that he slid two steps backward for every step forward, and going downhill was like "a modified ski slide." His orderly and his driver helped, but so slow was Hogan's progress that in time the three ended up at the tail of the column. Daylight was about to break when Hogan felt he had no choice but to rest. Once again the three huddled together under Hogan's trench coat.

It was well after daylight when they resumed their march, eventually coming upon a company of infantry from a newly arrived unit of the 75th Infantry Division. By jeep they traveled to the 3d Armored Division's command post and there found that everybody else had arrived safely except for one man killed by a nervous sentry.

When General Rose saw Hogan, he wanted to know why he was the last man out. Hogan thought of several heroic answers he might give but decided finally to stick with the truth, even though for a stalwart, outdoors Texan, it was a difficult admission.

Said Hogan: "My feet hurt."

For the German drivers of the 2d SS Panzer Division's 2d SS Medical Company and their wounded, traveling in a convoy of sixteen ambulances, Christmas Eve was a nightmare. In fourteen regular and two high-capacity ambulances, with SS-Capt. Hans Winkler riding in the last vehicle, the convoy started off at 1 P.M. from the division's main field-dressing station near Houffalize. Because American fighter-bombers sometimes attacked individual ambulances, the medical company had grouped its ambulances in convoy on the theory that that would minimize the chance of pilots failing to spot the Red Cross markings. Their goal was a hospital a few miles inside Germany at Neuerburg.

The convoy had gone only a few miles when at the edge of the village of Sommerain one of the ambulances had a flat tire. As all the vehicles halted briefly, the walking wounded took advantage of the pause to stretch their legs and grab a smoke.

At that moment a P-38 Lightning flew over, buzzing the column at such a low level that Winkler could make out the pilot's features. As that plane soared away, another approached. For a moment Winkler thought the pilots were playing a game of nerves, but it was more than that. The second plane opened fire with all its machine guns, strafing the column. Five more Lightnings followed closely, and all came back for a second run.

The two high-capacity ambulances immediately burst into flames. Ignoring continued strafing, the drivers, assistant drivers, and walking wounded braved the flames to enter the vehicles, cut the straps holding the patients to their litters, and throw the wounded outside, where other men seized blankets and overcoats to try to smother their fiery uniforms. "Despairing, pain-filled cries for help" filled the air. Despite every effort, many of the wounded burned to death, "black and ashened."

As the Lightnings flew away, everybody able to help redistributed the wounded among those vehicles that could still operate. The less seriously wounded, including two American prisoners whose faces appeared to be white from fear that the Germans might take revenge on them, sat on fenders or held onto the tops of the ambulances. At a nearby headquarters, Captain Winkler left the two Americans and his less seriously wounded to be taken to the nearest field-dressing station.

It was near midnight when the convoy reached the hospital at Neuerburg, but the hospital was already overtaxed with patients. At the direction of the officer in charge, Winkler continued another fourteen miles to Bitburg. Once again there was no room. It was the same at the next hospital in Bad Bertrich.

By that time it was daylight, and the wounded had been on the road for almost seventeen hours in unheated ambulances with little to eat or drink. When a lieutenant said there was no room, Winkler seethed with anger. As he left the building, he noted that the rooms did, indeed, appear to be full; but there were no patients in the corridors, and the corridors were far warmer than the ambulances. Once the patients were there, thought Winkler, the doctors and nurses could hardly ignore them.

Winkler and his drivers had deposited most of the wounded in the corridors when a senior officer ordered Winkler to either remove the patients or face arrest. "Neither I nor one of my comrades," said Winkler defiantly, "is going to be arrested here, and we will depart only when our wounded are cared for."

The confrontation attracted a crowd of surgeons, nurses, and visiting civilians, and the senior officer departed. People began to mutter, and nurses hurried to find hot drinks and cookies for the wounded. My God, thought Winkler, Christmas cookies! What a Christmas!

Accompanied by two guards, the officer in charge came back, but again Winkler refused to return the wounded to the ambulances. He did agree to bring in no more but to take those who remained to a Luftwaffe hospital in the nearby town of Andernach. With that, the officer let him go. Although Winkler heard later that his division headquarters intended charging him with "refusing orders and unsoldierly conduct," nothing ever came of it.

For long Captain Winkler pondered which had been more traumatic: the enemy's attack upon the convoy or "the refusal to admit our wounded in the homeland."

*   *   *

At headquarters of the First Army in a Belgian Army barracks at Tongres, the situation on the night of December 24 looked "if anything, worse than before." There were reports of armored columns of the Fifth Panzer Army nearing the Meuse, and the G-2, Colonel Dickson, was convinced that the Germans at Manhay were intent on taking Liège.

Yet despite the debacle that occurred later that night at Manhay, the situation was in fact brighter than General Hodges and his staff realized. The 82d Airborne Division had withdrawn to new positions with little interference from the enemy, and the 7th Armored Division had begun to form a new line north of Manhay astride N-15 leading to Liège. A battalion of the 106th Division's 424th Infantry, which had been in the St. Vith salient, was sufficiently reorganized to become a part of that line. Other battalions of that regiment, plus those of the 28th Division's 112th Infantry, also might be called on in an emergency; and as part of the readjustment of the line, General Hoge's CCB, 9th Armored Division, had retired to afford the XVIII Airborne Corps a reserve.

Along that part of the Trois Ponts–Hotton highway between Manhay and Hotton, the 3d Armored Division was soon to receive reinforcements. Seriously short of infantry from the start, General Rose had already received help from the separate 509th Parachute Infantry Battalion and from two battalions of the separate 517th Parachute Infantry (a third had joined the 30th Division for the mop-up of *Kampfgruppe Peiper*). On the morning of December 24, the 290th Infantry of the 75th Infantry Division—the untried division only recently arrived on the Continent— had begun to attack to help drive the Germans back from the highway between Soy and Hotton. That night a second regiment, the 289th Infantry, arrived and was able to help the armor on the other flank near Manhay. On Christmas Day, Rose was also to get help from his own CCB, released at last from the fight against *Kampfgruppe Peiper*.

On Christmas morning, one message after another reached General Ridgway from the First Army's headquarters insisting that the crossroads at Manhay be retaken. They reflected the continuing concern of Hodges and his staff that Liège might fall and imperil all American positions south of the Meuse, but they failed to take into consideration the fact that Field Marshal Montgomery had ordered the new line behind Manhay.

Contingents of the 2d SS Panzer Division did make a stab up Highway N-15 from Manhay early on Christmas morning, but after meeting heavy fire, the Germans turned back. General Lammerding's goal was not Liège but a turn to the northwest, to get across the Ourthe River and onto the Condroz plateau where he could protect the flank of the Fifth Panzer Army. For Lammerding, Manhay was but a pivot for that turn.

Goaded by the messages from Hodges's headquarters and unaware of Lammerding's intentions, General Ridgway ordered the 7th Armored Division to retake the village, but General Hasbrouck had precious little with which to do the job. Furthermore, retreating tankers the night before had felled trees across the highway to block a German advance, and they just as effectively blocked American tanks trying to go the other way. Not until two nights later with the help of a battalion of the 517th Parachute Infantry was Manhay retaken and then primarily because the village had ceased to be important to the 2d SS Panzer Division.

General Lammerding's first objective after making the turn at Manhay was to move down the highway toward Hotton to take two villages— Grandmenil and Erezée—from which roads led northwest to a crossing of the Ourthe River at Durbruy, six miles downstream from Hotton. No sooner were the Germans in control of the crossroads at Manhay than Lammerding sent an under-strength company of Panthers moving on Grandmenil, just a mile away, with *SS-Panzergrenadiers* following closely. Only a platoon of self-propelled tank destroyers of the 3d Armored Division's Task Force Kane, without infantry support, stood in the way at Grandmenil; and when the *SS-Panzergrenadiers* closed in under darkness, the tank destroyers retired along the highway toward Erezée.

Meanwhile, the 75th Division's 289th Infantry, commanded by Col. Douglas B. Smith, which had arrived the night before, was in an assembly area near Grandmenil. The commander of the 3d Armored Division's CCA, General Hickey, whom General Rose had put in charge of the division's eastern flank, ordered Smith to block both the main highway between Grandmenil and Erezée and a secondary road leading northwest toward the Ourthe.

Although a roadblock was soon in place on the highway, the inexperienced U.S. infantrymen manning it succumbed to the same ploy that earlier had tricked the veterans of the 7th Armored Division's CCA: An American tank appeared first. Followed closely by eight Panthers, the Sherman continued past the roadblock. Even as the German tanks shot up the main body of the battalion, somebody got off a round from a bazooka, which knocked out one of the tanks at a spot where the road ran along the side of a cliff. Unable to get past, the remaining German tanks fell back on Grandmenil.

For General Hickey, it was too much to ask the green infantrymen to retake Grandmenil without armored support. That came in early afternoon with the arrival of a first contingent of the 3d Armored Division's CCB, Task Force McGeorge, which had a company each of armored infantry and medium tanks.

Task Force McGeorge was getting ready to attack when eleven P-38 Lightnings of the 430th Squadron, flying a mission for the 7th Armored Division, mistook the formation for Germans and bombed and strafed the assembly area. Although the American tanks were displaying orange identification panels, they were just outside the no-bomb line designated by the air control officer with the 7th Armored Division, and the airmen took the panels for a ruse. Task Force McGeorge lost thirty-nine officers and men killed. It was near nightfall the next day, December 26, when the task force, assisted by a battalion of the 289th Infantry, finally retook Grandmenil.

As that happened, it was becoming clear on the German side that General Lammerding's 2d SS Panzer Division had gone about as far as it could go. The *SS-Panzergrenadiers*, in particular, had lost heavily in the opening attack at Baraque de Fraiture, and by Christmas Day there were eighteen American field artillery battalions (more than two hundred guns) in position to crush any movement along the roads in the vicinity of Manhay and Grandmenil. Because of the seemingly omnipresent fighter-bombers, little of Lammerding's artillery had come forward.

Nor was Lammerding getting the promised help from the 9th SS Panzer Division, which was to have attacked up the valley of the Lienne Creek along the 2d SS Panzer Division's eastern flank. Beset by air attacks and short of gasoline, only a few of that division's tanks had arrived. In the end, only one of the division's *SS-Panzergrenadier* regiments, composed mainly of ethnic Germans from the Black Sea region of Russia, posed any real problem for the 82d Airborne Division.

The fighting along the northern shoulder of the German penetration was to continue for several more days, but by nightfall of December 26 the worst was over. The next morning, the commander of the Sixth Panzer Army, General Dietrich, ordered Lammerding to turn over the sector around Baraque de Fraiture to the 9th SS Panzer Division, then join what was left of the 560th Volksgrenadier Division and of the 12th SS Panzer Division (at last brought forward from the vicinity of the Elsenborn Ridge) in a new attack to break through Hotton and Soy onto the Condroz plateau. That too was to turn out to be futile, an exercise accomplishing nothing but to prolong the agony for both sides.

All four of the once-proud SS panzer divisions had been reduced to little more than shells and were to have little impact on the continuing battle. At least as important for the Americans at the moment, none of the German divisions had succeeded in crossing the Ourthe River, which meant that the troops of the Fifth Panzer Army struggling for the Meuse had no protection on their northern flank.

CHAPTER TWENTY-SEVEN

Crisis Before the Meuse

One of the principal waterways of western Europe, the Meuse River rises in northeastern France, meanders past Sédan, where the Germans in 1940 made their principal crossing to drive triumphantly to the sea, and enters Belgium near the French town of Givet. Along much of the course downstream from Givet, the banks are steep, sometimes cliffs up to 300 feet high; but there are level stretches, as at a point near Dinant where in 1940 the first Germans to cross the river used a weir. Within Belgium, the river in most places is about 120 yards wide, the current swift. At Namur, where it absorbs the waters of the Sambre River, it becomes wider still for the northeastward flow past Liège and the turn north into the Netherlands, where it is known as the Maas. So critical is the trench of the Meuse to the defense of Belgium that in the years between the two world wars, the Belgian government limited the number of bridges spanning the river. There were a number of crossing sites, nevertheless, mainly at the towns of Dinant, Namur, and Huy, and at Liège.

On the second day of the German offensive, General Eisenhower charged the commander of the Communications Zone (the Services of Supply), Lt. Gen. John C. H. Lee, with defending the bridges over the Meuse. Although they were to be prepared for demolition, none was to be blown except on specific order.

To do the job, General Lee called for the most part on general service engineer regiments. Within France, he used six French light infantry battalions, only recently organized and equipped with a diverse collection of small arms and makeshift uniforms. For the bridges considered to be most critical, Lee had a separate regiment, the 29th Infantry, which had long provided the demonstration troops for The Infantry School at Fort Benning, Georgia. At the time, the 29th Infantry was guarding railroads in France and searching for what constituted a small corps of AWOL American soldiers engaged in a lucrative black market business in rations, cigarettes, and gasoline.

During the first days of the offensive, some American commanders—particularly General Middleton of the VIII Corps—were concerned that the Germans might turn south along the valley of the Meuse toward Sédan and Paris. The route was wide open, for the western flank of the VIII Corps between Neufchâteau and the Meuse (a distance of thirty miles) hung in the air. Although there was hope of filling the gap with the 11th Armored and 17th Airborne Divisions, which General Eisenhower on December 18 ordered to move from England to the Continent, those divisions would not be available for several days.

Thus General Lee ordered the 29th Infantry to cover not only the bridges in Belgium but those in France as far south as Verdun. Starting on December 18, the regiment sent small contingents to all the bridges and a platoon to the radio repeater station at Jemelle, near Marche, with orders to defend the station against paratroopers and patrols. If threatened by a large attack, the equipment was to be sabotaged before falling back.

Even before assuming command in the north, Field Marshal Montgomery had hurried a scratch force of three hundred men to the bridges from Huy to Givet with an assignment to delay the Germans as long as possible, for the thinking at that point was that the Germans would get across the Meuse, whereupon the 30th Corps—assembled under Lt. Gen. Brian G. Horrocks as a reserve behind the Meuse northwest of Liège—was to counterattack. By the 20th, when Eisenhower gave Montgomery command in the north, the staunch American stand at various points—particularly in front of the Elsenborn Ridge—led General Horrocks to conclude that "the enemy's hopes of bouncing the Meuse crossing have almost vanished." The line of the Meuse was to be held.

Montgomery ordered the 29th Armoured Brigade, consisting of three regiments (the equivalent of American battalions), to defend the principal crossing sites from Huy to Givet; and by nightfall on December 21, the 23d Hussars was in position at Givet, the 3d Royal Tank Regiment at Dinant, and the 2d Fife and Forfar Yeomanry at Namur. Patrols from yet another British unit, the 2d Household Cavalry, crossed the river and probed as far east as the road center of Marche. Those deployments freed the bulk of the 29th Infantry to move to Liège, there to guard the bridges and defend supply installations.

With those dispositions, the chance of the Germans getting a bridge across the Meuse by a *coup de main* was remote. There remained, nevertheless, a real possibility that German armor might reach the river and force a crossing.

Despite the despair over the prospects for the offensive that senior German field commanders had begun to voice as early as December 18, Field Marshal von Rundstedt's staff on December 22 prepared an optimistic estimate of the situation. Not until January 1, the staff predicted, would American reserves be able to mount major attacks from north and south, and not until near the end of December would the Americans be capable of defending the Meuse in strength. There was apparently still time for the armor of von Manteuffel's Fifth Panzer Army to get across the Meuse. That was in Hitler's mind the next day, the 23d, when he released the 9th Panzer and 15th Panzergrenadier Divisions to the Fifth Panzer Army.

The German estimate came on the very day that General Patton launched his attack from the south, and an American force to attack in the north was already assembling. Under General Collins and the headquarters of the VII Corps, that force was scheduled to consist of the 4th Cavalry Group, the 75th and 84th Infantry Divisions, the 2d Armored Division, and at least a part of the 3d Armored Division.

On the other hand, whether those units, as Field Marshal Montgomery had ordered, could stay out of the defensive battle to get ready to attack was problematical. When the vanguard of the 3d Armored Division arrived early on the 20th, the troops were fighting before the day was out. So, too, the leading regiment of the 84th Division had been in Marche only a few hours when the likelihood developed that not only that regiment but the entire division soon might be engaged.

Early on December 21, the commander of the 84th Division, Brig. Gen. Alexander R. Bolling, having established his headquarters in Marche, learned of the German attack against the bridge over the Ourthe River nearby at Hotton. Aware from talking with the commander of the 51st Engineer Combat Battalion, Lt. Col. Harvey R. Fraser, that only Fraser's men guarding bridges and manning roadblocks stood between the enemy and Marche, Bolling felt compelled to position his leading regiment in a semicircular defense of the town.

That same morning, December 21, General Collins arrived at Hodges's command post in the Hôtel des Bains in Chaudfontaine, where he learned his mission and the divisions that were to make up his corps. The big question before the two commanders was whether in assembling as far forward as Marche, they risked getting Collins's troops drawn into the fight prematurely. They were still conferring when at 11 A.M. General Bolling telephoned. It looked, said Bolling, as if he might be involved in a fight for Marche. Should he pull back and await the rest of his division or should he hold the town?

"Yes," replied Hodges, "hold." With that decision, whatever Field Marshal Montgomery's orders, another portion of the troops earmarked for the VII Corps was bound to be caught up in the defensive fight.

When a second regiment arrived just before nightfall on the 21st, General Bolling adjusted the defense of Marche to put two regiments in the line, leaving his third as a reserve behind the town. The 334th Infantry dug in forward of the highway connecting Marche and Hotton, while the 335th Infantry defended in front of the town and bent its line back to protect the division's open southern flank.

The next morning, December 22, as motorized patrols of the 84th Division probed in search of the enemy, General Collins again visited General Hodges, concerned lest the Germans penetrate the undefended sector south of Marche and get behind the town, thereby threatening the assembly of the rest of the VII Corps on the Condroz plateau. In reaction to that concern, Hodges told Bolling to push out a screen well to the south and southwest of Marche.

That deployment increased the chances of the 84th Division becoming involved in the defensive battle. Yet when Montgomery visited Hodges early in the afternoon, the mission of the VII Corps remained unchanged: Avoid battle and prepare to attack. To allow time for the last of the 2d Armored Division and corps artillery to arrive, the attack was to be delayed for two days. The 2d Armored Division was to form the right—or southern—wing, the 84th Division the center, and the 3d Armored Division the left—or northern—wing, while the untested 75th Division was to constitute a reserve.

As General Bolling readily deduced, the Germans needed Marche, for the town was as much a road center as was Bastogne. The most important routes were a highway leading north to Liège and the Bastogne–Marche–Namur highway, N-4, from which lesser roads ran west to the Meuse at Dinant. It was Highway N-4 that General von Manteuffel was after. Not only did it afford access to the tank country of the Condroz plateau but also to the Meuse at the bend in the river at Namur, the most direct route to Brussels and Antwerp. To a commander who from the first had seen Antwerp as beyond reach, it would hardly go unnoticed that gaining the Meuse at Namur would position his army if not for implementing the Small Solution, then at least for trapping those Americans still holding south of the Meuse and Liège.

Failure to gain Marche and its roads would force von Manteuffel onto a much less desirable route to the Meuse in the vicinity of Dinant, a route running along the southern rim of the Condroz through what geologists call the Famenne Depression. That is an extension of the rugged country of the main body of the Ardennes, with steep-sided ridges and deep-cut, meandering streams, including that of the Lesse River, which joins the Meuse near Dinant.

Even as Colonel von Lauchert's 2d Panzer Division engaged Major Desobry's force at Noville just north of Bastogne during the night of December 19, patrols from the division's reconnaissance battalion were exploring the roads leading west. Just before dawn on the 20th, some of the reconnaissance troops, supported by a few light tanks, approached the bridge over the west branch of the Ourthe at Ourtheuville. It was a

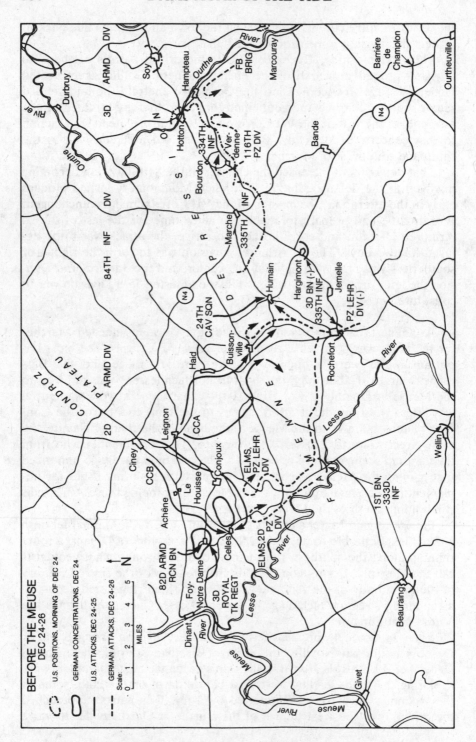

BEFORE THE MEUSE
DEC 24-26

U.S. POSITIONS, MORNING OF DEC 24

GERMAN CONCENTRATIONS, DEC 24

U.S. ATTACKS, DEC 24-25

GERMAN ATTACKS, DEC 24-26

Scale:

MILES

0   1   2   3   4   5

sturdy Bailey Bridge, the bridge that General Krüger of the 58th Panzer Corps had assumed the Americans would demolish before troops of the 116th Panzer Division could seize it.

There a platoon of the 299th Engineer Combat Battalion and a company of the 158th Engineer Combat Battalion, hurried to the bridge after having screened in front of Bastogne until the airborne troops arrived, had prepared the span for demolition. They had support from the eight tank destroyers of the 705th Tank Destroyer Battalion, which their commander, Colonel Templeton, had dropped off to cover the move of the rest of his battalion to Bastogne.

As the Germans reached the bridge, the engineers pushed down on the detonator to set off the explosives, but nothing happened. Although a light tank started across the bridge, one of the tank destroyers knocked it out. With that, the Germans fell back, and the rest of the day passed quietly. Some motor traffic going to and from Bastogne resumed, and several groups of civilian refugees crossed the bridge, among them the Abbé Musty and his fifty boys from the Bastogne Seminary.

That night the Germans came back. After mortars and artillery shelled the defenders intermittently for two hours, *Panzergrenadiers* at midnight waded the shallow river. Again the demolition charges on the bridge failed to go off.

With Germans ensconced in houses around the bridge, the commander of the 1128th Engineer Combat Group, to which the engineer defenders were attached, authorized withdrawal. To the surprise of a handful of men of the 51st Engineer Combat Battalion, who were manning a roadblock just three miles from the bridge at a crossroads known as Barrière de Champlon, the Germans made no immediate effort to exploit their success. The engineers had no way of knowing it, but the 2d Panzer Division had run out of gasoline.

It was that delay—all through the 21st and 22d—that afforded time for the 84th Division to reach Marche, whereupon, once the engineers at Barrière de Champlon had further blocked the highway by felling trees and blowing a big crater in the road, their battalion commander, Colonel Fraser, ordered them to retire. The delay also afforded time for General Bolling to send a rifle company seven miles southwest of Marche to the town of Rochefort, a first step in implementing General Hodges's order to push out a screen beyond Marche. It also provided time for a task force of the 3d Armored Division's CCA to come forward to bolster the defensive screen in front of Marche.

By nightfall of December 22, enough gasoline had at last arrived to enable the 2d Panzer Division's reconnaissance battalion to resume its advance. Bypassing the felled trees and crater in the highway behind Barrière de Champlon by using trails in the woods, the light tanks and armored cars then returned to Highway N-4 and soon swung west to avoid Marche to the south. At the highway connecting Marche and

Rochefort, the column hit a screening force of the 3d Armored Division's CCA and lost five vehicles, but it bounced off along a side road to reach the highway at the village of Hargimont.

General Bolling in the meantime reinforced the screen south of Marche by sending two motorized infantry battalions, one to augment the company already sent to Rochefort, the other to continue six miles to the west to block a crossing of the Lesse River. Both columns ran into German fire at Hargimont but backtracked, swung well around to the west, and reached their objectives without further difficulty.

The next day, December 23, the main body of the 2d Panzer Division had hardly begun to advance when the leading *Kampfgruppe* came to a halt. The commander reported a roadblock, heavily defended. Doubting the report, the corps commander, General von Lüttwitz, went forward himself and found only a light barricade, no defenders in sight. He relieved the commander on the spot, and at last, in mid-afternoon, the advance began, only to come to a halt again at the crater in the highway behind the Barrière de Champlon. It took four hours to construct a route around it capable of handling the medium tanks.

Based on the progress of the reconnaissance battalion south of Marche, von Lüttwitz decided for the moment merely to block in the direction of Marche with a *Panzergrenadier* battalion while turning the rest of the division westward in the wake of the reconnaissance troops. Before halting for the night, the head of the column got as far as Buissonville, five miles beyond the Marche-Rochefort highway; but the rest of the long column was still toiling forward.

As the 2d Panzer Division began its advance in earnest, the bulk of the American 2d Armored Division had reached the division's assembly area on the Condroz plateau. During the morning of December 23, the commander, Maj. Gen. Ernest N. Harmon, a man noted for his gravel voice and his swearing, who had commanded the division long ago in North Africa and then rejoined it in Normandy, called on his corps commander, General Collins, at the corps command post in the Château de Bessines ten miles north of Marche. The 84th Division, said Collins, was fast being drawn into the battle, but he still hoped to keep the arrival of Harmon's division secret long enough to mount a surprise attack.

Returning to the armored division's headquarters in a small château a few miles away at Havelange, Harmon had lunch with his staff and senior commanders. All were relaxing over coffee when a lieutenant, Everett C. Jones, arrived, a bloody bandage on his head.

At a village ten miles to the south near the town of Ciney, he explained, his patrol from the 82d Armored Reconnaissance Battalion had received fire from several German armored vehicles, including what Jones saw as two Mark IV tanks. Although his armored car had been hit and burned, he and his crew had escaped.

It would be determined later that Jones's patrol had tangled not with Germans but with a British patrol probing east from Dinant. Yet it appeared to Harmon at the time that the engagement had compromised the attempt to keep the 2d Armored Division's arrival secret and that the German spearhead, avoiding a fight at Marche, was headed for the Meuse, only nine miles beyond Ciney.

Running across a field to a grove of trees where a tank battalion had bivouacked, Harmon asked a company commander, Capt. Charles B. Kelley, how long it would take him to get on the road. If he could break radio silence, said Kelley, five minutes. So be it, replied Harmon. "You get down that road to a town called Ciney . . . block the entrances and exits and start fighting. The whole damn division is coming right behind you."

With all of CCA soon following Kelley's tank company, Harmon reported to General Collins what he had done. Having already received reports of German armor bypassing Marche and of another column heading for Rochefort (it was the *Panzer Lehr Division*), Collins not only approved but ordered Harmon to attack immediately to take Buissonville, thereby securing the 84th Division's open flank, and to continue forward to help the battalion of the 84th Division that had occupied Rochefort. Quite clearly, Collins believed, his VII Corps would be unable to "remain aloof from the defensive battle."

Under orders from Harmon, the commander of CCA, Brig. Gen. John H. ("Pee Wee") Collier, left half his command to block the roads around Ciney until CCB could arrive and sent a task force under the commander of the 66th Armored Regiment's 2d Battalion, Lt. Col. Hugh O'Farrell, southeast toward Buissonville. A skirmish delayed the column at the first village of Leignon, so that it was close to midnight before the column got going again. Made cautious by the skirmish, O'Farrell put Company F of the 41st Armored Infantry Regiment in the lead on foot. The armored infantrymen marched in single file on either side of the road; the night was bright, with light from a full moon reflecting off a thin cover of snow.

The men were nearing a farm close to the village of Haid, where Lieutenant Jones had encountered fire that afternoon, when the company commander, Capt. George E. Bonney, who was moving up and down the column in a jeep, heard vehicles approaching. Riding slowly back along the column, he told his men to pull off the road into the shadows of big trees lining either side. They were to fire only after the first vehicle of what was apparently a German column reached the rear of the company.

Germans in two American jeeps led the column, followed by three-quarter-ton American trucks, an American ambulance, and German scout cars, motorcycles, and two half-tracks towing 88mm. guns—twelve vehicles in all. Who started the firing remained unclear, but "all hell broke loose." As the riflemen fired, so did the .50-caliber machine guns on their half-tracks at the rear of their column. Wounded Germans "screamed in agony." Some Germans tried to break away across the fields, but the machine guns on the half-tracks cut them down. Others raised their hands above their heads and tried frantically to surrender.

Only minutes had passed when Captain Bonney shouted as loud as he could to cease fire. It took some time for the firing to die away, and even then, as the infantrymen began to march some thirty prisoners toward the rear (another thirty Germans were dead), somebody opened fire with a machine gun on a half-track. Two .50-caliber bullets almost severed Captain Bonney's right leg.

It was not until December 22 that the main body of the *Panzer Lehr Division*, which had left behind a *Panzergrenadier* regiment at Bastogne, began moving in the direction of the Meuse. Following an encounter with an American artillery unit near the village of Tillet, the head of the column entered the road center of St. Hubert after nightfall without further delay or fighting. Not until noon on the 23d was there sufficient gasoline to continue the march along two roads leading in the direction of Rochefort.

Soon after nightfall on the 23d, a *Kampfgruppe* under Lt. Col. Joachim Ritter von Porschinger approached the town and paused to send out patrols. The patrols returned with word that the town was undefended.

The word was wrong. The 335th Infantry's 3d Battalion, commanded by Maj. Gordon A. Bahe, was in Rochefort, albeit short two of its companies. One had been left behind on the Marche-Rochefort highway to face the Germans at Hargimont, and the other had left Rochefort to scout villages farther south. Yet Major Bahe also had two platoons of 57mm. antitank guns; a platoon of the 51st Engineer Combat Battalion, sent to Rochefort to repair a bridge damaged earlier; and a platoon of the 29th Infantry that had been defending the radio repeater station at Jemelle but had conformed with orders to sabotage the equipment and withdraw. Once fighting began, Bahe was to recall the company that was reconnoitering to the south.

Just before the road from St. Hubert entered Rochefort, it passed between two commanding hills. Going forward to supervise the attack personally, the *Panzer Lehr*'s commander, General Bayerlein, recognized the danger of passing through such a defile without first securing the hills; but in view of the reports from the patrols, he decided to make a dash into the town. "OK," he shouted, "let's go! Shut your eyes and go in!"

As if on cue, heavy fire from small arms and antitank guns rained down on the road. Several vehicles caught fire. Quickly ordering withdrawal, Bayerlein sent a platoon of tanks circling the town to cut the highway beyond it while he prepared for a deliberate assault to begin at midnight.

Since Rochefort was a sizable town, Major Bahe had no hope of defending all the buildings, so that in the darkness the Germans had little trouble gaining entry. Fighting proceeded from house to house until by daylight the American infantrymen were confined to buildings on one side of the town square with a strongpoint in the Grand Hôtel de l'Etoile.

Early in the morning, word arrived from the commander of the 335th Infantry, Col. Hugh C. Parker, to withdraw, for Bahe's mission was delay, not last-ditch defense. Yet most of the men were so closely engaged that only the battalion headquarters and the weapons company managed to reach trucks waiting beyond the damaged bridge. Endangered by German fire, the trucks had left when the rest of the men threw smoke grenades into the square and made a break for it on foot. All but a few were eventually to make their way back to Marche by roundabout routes, many of them going as far south as Givet, then traveling back along the west bank of the Meuse.

At that point the *Panzer Lehr Division* would have been free to continue toward the Meuse, its route blocked only by another of the 84th Division's battalions sent to delay in the valley of the Lesse River (and that battalion withdrew under orders during the night), but General Bayerlein, conscious of the utter fatigue of his troops, nevertheless decided to delay in Rochefort. Although he sent reconnaissance patrols up the valley of the Lesse, he wanted his men to enjoy "the success of the day" and "special rations" that had arrived for Christmas.

On the night of December 23, Generals von Manteuffel and von Lüttwitz conferred. Quite obviously, noted von Manteuffel, the Americans held Marche in strength, thereby barring access to Highway N-4 onto the Condroz plateau and to the Meuse at Namur. On the other hand, the 2d Panzer Division had already bypassed Marche to the south, and the *Panzer Lehr Division* should soon have access to the valley of the Lesse River beyond Rochefort. While not the most desirable route to the Meuse, because it cut across the grain of the Famenne Depression, it was the shortest: from Rochefort to the Meuse at Dinant was only fourteen miles.

Continuing the thrust in that direction was not without peril, for the two panzer divisions—as von Manteuffel put it—constituted nothing more than "a pointed wedge" with both flanks open. Both divisions would have to drop off troops, as indeed they had already begun to do, to guard the flanks. Still there was some hope that the 9th Panzer Division would arrive if not the next day, the 24th, as promised, then soon afterward, and that division could protect the 2d Panzer Division's north flank at Marche, probably taking the town. There was also hope that the 15th

Panzergrenadier Division would soon arrive, and even though von Manteuffel had already designated a sizable portion of that division for Bastogne, the presence of the rest of the division would alleviate a chronic shortage of infantry in the panzer divisions.

Furthermore, von Manteuffel intended to go personally to visit the commander of the 116th Panzer Division, General von Waldenburg, to prod him into getting on with cutting the Marche-Hotton highway and Highway N-4 beyond it. That would prevent the Americans from pouring reinforcements into Marche to hit the army's north flank. That done, and entry gained to the Condroz plateau, von Waldenburg was to drive westward to Ciney, thereby extending the flank protection.

Neither von Manteuffel nor von Lüttwitz saw the plan as ideal, particularly in view of the fatigue of German troops, who had been fighting almost without respite for eight days. Yet to both it appeared to be the only way any German force was going to reach the Meuse River. They would have considered it even less ideal had they been aware of the presence of General Harmon's 2d Armored Division, part of which had already gone into action against the foremost troops of the 2d Panzer Division.

On the day before, December 22, General von Waldenburg had begun conforming to the order from his corps commander, General Krüger, to pull the 116th Panzer Division back to La Roche and there cross the Ourthe River and proceed to cut the Marche-Hotton highway. Von Waldenburg noted, not without a touch of bitterness, that that would put the division almost exactly where it would have been had Krüger allowed him to try for the bridge over the west branch of the Ourthe at Ourtheuville. He had a point and more, for had his troops crossed the west branch on the night of December 19, they could have beaten the Americans to Marche. As it was, they had lost "three important days."

While the bulk of the 116th Panzer Division was toiling through the narrow streets of La Roche and over a single bridge which men of the 7th Armored Division's Trains had damaged as they left, reconnaissance troops pushed ahead. Soon they reported a thin American line on high ground just forward of the Marche-Hotton highway. As along the Hotton-Soy portion of the highway, which von Waldenburg's troops had so recently left, that high ground commanded the highway behind it and represented the last major obstacle before German tanks might debouch onto the more open ground—tank country—of the Condroz.

When the approach of darkness brought relief from Allied fighter-bombers, two companies of *Panzergrenadiers* pushed ahead of the main column in half-tracks and captured American trucks. During the night, while German artillery shelled a line of hamlets on the ridge, those two companies—120 men—infiltrated on foot through a thin line of foxholes outside the hamlet of Verdenne and holed up in a fir forest between the hamlet and the Marche-Hotton highway.

Just before daylight on December 24, Pfc. Frank A. Carroll of Company I, 334th Infantry, awakened to find his foxhole mate, Pvt. Eddie Korecki, on full alert. "A bunch of people," said Korecki, had come through the line during the night; he assumed they were men of mine-laying details that had been at work in front of the line, but he thought it might be a good idea to check with their platoon leader.

The two Americans found the foxholes of both their platoon leader and their platoon sergeant empty. Although there were no signs of blood or a struggle, footprints in the snow revealed that a large body of men had been there during the night. Going to the company command post, Carroll gave the alarm, and a patrol following the trace of the footsteps into the forest came under heavy small-arms fire.

When the commander of the 334th Infantry, Col. Charles E. Hoy, learned of the presence of the German force, he ordered an immediate attack to clear the Germans out. In mid-afternoon of December 24, the 3d Battalion's reserve company, supported by two platoons of Shermans of the attached 771st Tank Battalion, moved toward the woodsline. There they found the Germans in skirmish formation, ready to plunge from the woods toward the houses of Verdenne in support of a frontal attack against the hamlet. Fire from the infantrymen and tanks prompted most of the Germans to surrender (there were almost a hundred of them) while the others either were killed or fled back into the forest.

The attacking force those men were to have helped was nearly an hour late in reaching its line of departure. With the support of five Panthers, two half-tracks, and an armored car, a company of *Panzergrenadiers* broke into Verdenne and continued as far as an imposing edifice, the Château de Verdenne, three hundred yards beyond near the edge of the forest.

The commander of the 84th Division, General Bolling, called on his reserve regiment, the 333d Infantry, to send a battalion to retake Verdenne. One of that battalion's rifle companies was away on another mission, and the other two were considerably under strength; for like the rest of the infantry companies of the 84th Division, they had recently undergone a severe and costly baptism of fire in an attack near Aachen. Company K, for example, had four officers and little more than a hundred men.

The two companies rendezvoused late in the evening at the village of Bourdon, behind Verdenne astride the Marche-Hotton highway. As they left Bourdon to gain a line of departure at an escarpment along the edge of the woods overlooking Verdenne, a guide sent from the company that had relinquished the hamlet put them on the wrong route. Instead of taking a trail leading directly through the woods, Company K in the lead began to move up a circuitous woods road.

Inside the woods, the night was black. Plodding up the steep road, the men came upon a stationary column of tanks. Those, thought the company commander, 1st Lt. Harold P ("Bud") Leinbaugh, were Shermans from the 771st Tank Battalion that were to support the attack on Verdenne. Leinbaugh told his communications sergeant, Donald Phelps, to tell the tankers to hitch onto the tail of Company K.

Feeling in the darkness along the side of one of the tanks, Phelps pounded on the turret with his rifle. "Hey, you guys, open up!" He pounded again. The hatch opened slowly, and the head and shoulders of a man appeared. "*Was ist los*?" a voice demanded. "*Was ist los*?"

As machine guns on the tanks blazed, Leinbaugh and his men plunged into ditches alongside the road. They had stumbled upon a column of Panthers, some thirty to forty, operating under their battalion commander, Maj. Gerhard Tebbe. Earlier in the evening, Tebbe and his tanks had pushed through a burning Verdenne and entered the woods. Although under orders to cut the Marche-Hotton highway and continue to the west, Tebbe had halted to allow *Panzergrenadiers* and artillery to catch up and to await reports from patrols sent to investigate the terrain just beyond the Marche-Hotton highway, which from Tebbe's map appeared to be marshy. Since his men were exhausted, Tebbe had told them to button up and get some rest. It was, after all, Christmas Eve, and over a radio in Tebbe's tank he could hear the bells of the cathedral in Cologne tolling the approach of the Yuletide.

Although the drivers of the Panthers started their motors, they made no effort to move, and the gunners, unable to depress their 75s low enough to hit the Americans in the ditches, fired into the surrounding woods. Recovering from his surprise, Sergeant Phelps grabbed a bazooka and got in a shot at one of the tanks, but before he could fire again, shell fragments mangled his left hand.

Over the company's SCR-300, Leinbaugh reported to his battalion commander that he had run into German tanks. "Get that stuff out of your way and get moving," came the reply. Snapping off the radio, Leinbaugh said to the men around him: "Let's get the hell out of here." Company K fell back and once out of sight of the tanks, dug in to block the road to Bourdon and the Marche-Hotton highway.

The mishap that befell Leinbaugh's Company K delayed the attack to retake Verdenne for an hour; but at 1 A.M. on Christmas morning, the company of the 333d Infantry that had been following Leinbaugh teamed with a company of the 334th Infantry and behind heavy artillery fire, got into the hamlet. Clearing it was another matter. All through Christmas Day the men fought, dodging under covering fire from house to house, digging Germans out of cellars only to see others take their places.

The Château de Verdenne—where the owner, a Belgian nobleman of Polish origin, Baron Charles de Radzitsky d'Ostrowick, his daughter,

Elizabeth, and fifteen other civilians took refuge in the cellar—changed hands several times. The baron and his companions learned to tell who controlled the floors above them by the sound of the footsteps: soft thuds meant Americans in rubber overshoes; loud clicking, Germans in hob-nailed boots.

On one occasion, when the baron ventured upstairs to get water for a wounded German tanker who had taken refuge in the cellar, he found that only the dead controlled the upper floors. The once beautiful grand salon was a shambles, ancestral coats-of-arms along the staircase riddled with bullet holes, tapestries and draperies sagging and shredded, and a billiard table (one leg missing) matted with blood. Moonlight streamed through holes cut by artillery fire in the roof, and dead men littered the floor.

Even with Verdenne reduced to rubble at last in American hands, the German threat to break across the Marche-Hotton highway and onto the Condroz remained. All through Christmas Day and the day after, the 116th Panzer Division's tanks and *Panzergrenadiers* tried to retake Verdenne and seize adjacent hamlets, while Colonel Remer's *Führer Begleit Brigade* entered the fight close along the Ourthe River to try to get past the hamlet of Hampteau and at last seize the bridge across the Ourthe at Hotton. So, too, Major Tebbe's Panthers in the woods behind Verdenne might at any moment break out to cut the highway.

That the infantrymen gave no ground was attributable in large measure to their valor and determination, but almost to a man they paid tribute to the fire support behind them. As on the Elsenborn Ridge and in the vicinity of Manhay, the array of artillery pieces was overwhelming. All the 84th Division's 48 pieces were able to fire into the sector, plus the 334th Infantry's Cannon Company, 18 pieces of armored artillery of the 3d Armored Division's CCA, and 72 pieces of VII Corps artillery, which included a battalion of 8-inch howitzers, a total of 150 pieces.

It was the artillery that eventually crushed Major Tebbe's Panthers. From the positions of Company K, 333d Infantry, near the German tanks, Lieutenant Leinbaugh adjusted the fire of one of the battalions, which set a Panther to burning. Once that firing data had been passed to other battalions, all of them fired in one tremendous Time-on-Target, a cascade of deadly shells such as Leinbaugh and his men had never witnessed before. "Whole trees were blown into the air, tanks and trucks exploded, and as the rain of shells slackened, the screams of dying Germans carried clearly to the watching men of Company K."

Those Germans who survived, including Major Tebbe, had no intention of staying in the woods to await more of that kind of punishment. Although patrols had determined that Americans held the nearby hamlet of Marenne, Tebbe hoped that in the darkness he might be able to sneak through. American vehicles, including tanks, lined the road through the little village, houses so close on either side that the German tankers would have been unable to rotate their turrets to open fire; but all was quiet.

At a house just beyond Marenne, a few men of the 333d Infantry had been detailed, upon the approach of German tanks, to pull a daisy chain of seven antitank mines across the road. Although the men were alert, the approach of tanks from their rear disconcerted them, and they made no effort to pull the mines into the road. One of the Panthers nevertheless blundered onto the pile of mines and blew up in a tremendous explosion.

The carcass partially blocked the road, forcing the remaining tanks and other vehicles into a field which turned out to be laced with antitank mines. As one vehicle after another hit mines, American artillery fire, some of it shells fitted with the POZIT fuse, descended on the field. Noting a bright moon in the sky to the east, Major Tebbe over his radio ordered all the drivers to "head for the moon." Many of the tanks and other vehicles made it, but seventeen stayed behind in the field.

Although General von Waldenburg continued for several days to try to gain the Condroz plateau, the final outcome of the engagement had been determined by the end of the day after Christmas. There was to be no protection on the Condroz for the north flank of the 2d Panzer Division.

Late on December 20, the Abbé Musty and his fifty students from the seminary in Bastogne reached the village of Bande on Highway N-4 between the Ourthe River and Marche. Exhausted from the long hike, the Abbé accepted invitations from the villagers to pass the night. The next day he decided to discontinue his flight and take his chances with the people of Bande.

By Christmas Eve, Germans were all over Bande, mainly support troops of the 2d Panzer Division, but there was also a group wearing the black and white shoulder patch of the *Sicherheitsdienst*, the SD, the security service of the SS. Those soldiers camped out in the ruins of the buildings along Highway N-4, the Grand' Rue, which the Germans had put to the torch back in September in retaliation for the attack by the *Armée Secrète* on German troops in the nearby St. Hubert Forest.

During the morning of December 24, which was a Sunday, the Abbé Musty celebrated mass in the stone church among the farmhouses on the hill above the Grand' Rue. As he emerged after the service, he learned that the SD had been going from house to house arresting all men of the village age seventeen and over, and they quickly seized those who had attended the mass. Among them were four of Abbé Musty's students. To the Abbé and disturbed relatives, the Germans insisted that they were merely conducting a check of identity cards. Everybody would be home for Christmas dinner.

Other SD soldiers were doing the same in the neighboring hamlet of

Grune. They brought all the men together at a sawmill alongside the Grand' Rue and through most of the afternoon questioned them, some alone, some in groups. They were looking for information about the *Armée Secrète*.

Worried that the men were to be deported to Germany, Mme. René Tournay headed for the sawmill with two overcoats, one her husband's and the other belonging to her landlord's son. An officer stopped her, promising to deliver the coats and demanding that Madame Tournay bring him some cognac. When she returned with three bottles, she begged the officer to release her husband. "Don't bargain with me," snapped the officer. "I'm not a Jew!"

Inside the sawmill, an interrogator learned that Albert Schmitz ran a soft-drink bottling plant and sent him to bring back a hundred bottles of lemonade. (Schmitz seized the opportunity to escape.) Another learned that Armand Toussaint was a farmer and sent him to bring back twenty bottles of wine, promising that when he brought them, he would free Toussaint and his son. To Toussaint's amazement, the German held to his promise.

As the afternoon wore on and people gathered outside the sawmill with coats and food, the Germans finally allowed them to deliver their gifts and speak briefly with the men. In that way, Mlle. Marthe Picard had a short talk with her fiancé, twenty-one-year-old Léon Praile.

Dusk was approaching and a few flakes of snow were falling when the interrogators divided their captives into two groups, those who were over thirty-two in the first, those under that age in the second. They ordered the younger men outside, thirty-three of them, including the four seminary students from Bastogne, lined them up in three rows, and stripped them of such personal belongings as pocketbooks, money, rings, watches, rosaries.

There were six guards armed with rifles and burp guns and three officers, everybody wearing the shoulder patch of the SD. Ordering the Belgians to put their hands over their heads, they marched them down the highway. At the ruins of a house beside the Café de la Poste, which had also been burned but had been replaced by a one-story wooden building, they halted them and still in three rows, made them turn their backs to the house.

One of the guards put a hand on the shoulder of the last man in the front row and led him to the door of the damaged house. A shot rang out. The man tumbled through the door into the cellar. Another guard executed the last man in the next row, then another the last man in the third row. Then the next man in row after row. When the Germans fired, some of the victims cried out, but a second round silenced them.

As the executions proceeded, Léon Praile, tall, solidly built, broad shoulders, whispered to those near him. They stood no chance unless they fought back, said Praile. If they all turned on the guards, surely some of them would escape. Several nodded agreement, and Praile was about to act when he felt a heavy hand on his shoulder.

As the guard—a sergeant—led Praile toward the door, Praile perceived that the man was weeping. Praile made up his mind: There was no way he was going to submit docilely to execution. They were three paces from the door when Praile wrenched free and with every ounce of his strength jammed a fist into the sergeant's face. The German fell.

In the gathering darkness, Praile dashed across the road, jumped a hedge, plunged into a little stream, and ran into a field beyond it. Although the Germans fired, none of the bullets found him. Beyond the field he penetrated deep inside a forest before at last daring to pause for breath. Despite his wet clothes, he spent the night in the forest and the next day tried to gain American lines; but there were too many Germans. That night he crept back to the edge of Bande and hid himself in the hayloft of his uncle's house.

Praile's flight did nothing to stay the other executions. When they were over, the bodies of thirty-two young men lay in the cellar, crudely concealed by planks torn from burned houses nearby. The next day the Germans released the older men at the sawmill to return to their homes.

When the massacre at Bande became known, many of the villagers recalled the departure of the Germans in September as American troops approached. The Germans had brandished their fists and shouted: "We'll be back!"

During the night of December 23, as Colonel O'Farrell's task force of the 2d Armored Division's CCA was moving toward Buissonville under orders to continue to Rochefort, the reconnaissance battalion and a leading *Kampfgruppe* of the 2d Panzer Division passed through the village on their way to the Meuse. Composed of forty Mark IV and Panther tanks, twenty-five self-propelled guns, and *Panzergrenadiers* in half-tracks, both the reconnaissance troops and the *Kampfgruppe* had gone before O'Farrell's task force, having paused for the night after ambushing the German vehicles, resumed its advance. That was shortly before daylight on December 24, and since CCB had begun to arrive at Ciney to hold that town, the rest of General Collier's CCA joined the advance on roads paralleling that taken by O'Farrell's tanks and armored infantry.

After an occasional brush with antitank guns and a few tanks left behind to guard the 2d Panzer Division's flank, both task forces of CCA in the early afternoon approached Buissonville. As O'Farrell's tanks and armored infantry entered the village, the other task force reached the crest of a ridge looking down over it and much of the surrounding countryside.

Below them the men could see a long German column approaching Buissonville. Tanks and self-propelled pieces of the 14th Armored Field Artillery Battalion opened a devastating fire. Those Germans who survived the first salvo tried to flee, leaving behind four antitank guns, six artillery pieces, and thirty-six vehicles, most of which were destroyed. A few Germans escaped; many were killed and a hundred captured.

With Buissonville in hand and Rochefort by that time abandoned by the troops of the 335th Infantry, CCA holed up around Buissonville while patrols scouted in the vicinity. Nearby, the commander of the 4th Cavalry Group, Col. John C. MacDonald, moved his 24th Cavalry Reconnaissance Squadron into the village of Humain, between Buissonville and the 335th Infantry's open flank. The presence of American forces in the two villages effectively blocked the route the 2d Panzer Division had been using to toil toward the Meuse. Unless the Germans swung far to the south, the only road left to them was the highway from Rochefort up the valley of the Lesse River.

Before daylight that morning, as the 2d Panzer Division's reconnaissance battalion reached the village of Celles, the commander paused at the main crossroads for a look at his map. As he was studying it, his leading Panther hit a mine in a daisy chain that a squad of American engineers had placed across the road.

The explosion awakened a Belgian woman, Mme. Marthe Monrique, who was the proprietress of an inn, the Pavillon Ardennais, just across the road from where the German commander was standing. Although Madame Monrique's neighbors had fled to the woods, she had stayed behind to try to prevent the Germans from destroying her inn, hopeful that the fact that she spoke German would help. With the noise of the explosion, she turned on a light and pulled back the blackout curtain to see what was happening.

Seeing the light, two Germans knocked at the inn. "How many kilometers to Dinant?" one of them asked. Aware that there was a signpost just across the road, Madame Monrique saw no point in trying to deceive them. "Ten kilometers," she said in German. "How's the road?" the German came back. At that point, a lie seemed credible. "The Americans mined the whole road," said Madame Monrique; "they've been working night and day burying mines in the road—for miles."

The loss of the leading Panther to a mine gave credence to what the Belgian woman said, but her stratagem failed to delay the Germans for long. Because the *Kampfgruppe* bringing up the rear had had to halt two miles back at the village of Conjoux, almost out of gasoline, the commander of the reconnaissance battalion was under considerable compulsion to push ahead, for his was the only force that might quickly gain the Meuse. It was still dark when the battalion resumed its march.

Although the Germans encountered no more mines, trouble lay ahead in the form of five British-operated Shermans. Part of the 3d Royal Tank Regiment, commanded by Col. A. W. Brown, which was defending the west bank of the Meuse at Dinant, each tank covered a road leading to

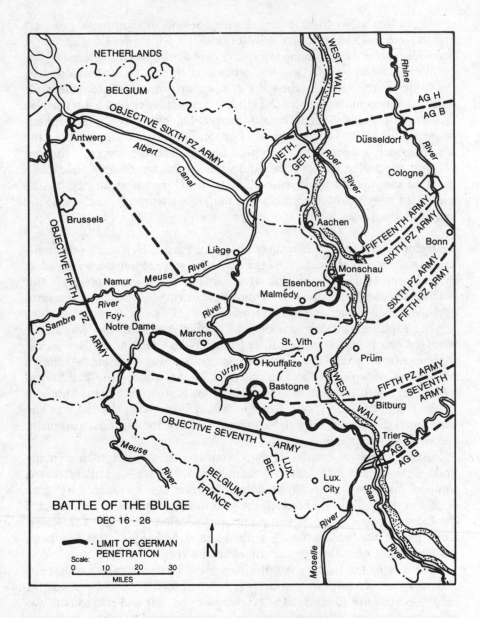

BATTLE OF THE BULGE
DEC 16 - 26

▬▬▬ - LIMIT OF GERMAN PENETRATION

N

Scale:
0   10   20   30
MILES

the highway bridge at the town. The tanks were to delay long enough for the bridge to be blown, then form a roadblock for a last-ditch defense. The thinking was that nobody would come back.

Along the road that the main body of the German reconnaissance battalion was taking, everybody in a Sherman covering the road—including the commander, Sgt. F. ("Geordie") Probert—had fallen asleep. They awoke with a start to "the sound of straining engines and the clank of tank tracks." In gathering light, Probert saw a long column of German vehicles along a twisting road below him.

In the excitement, Probert's gunner failed to lower the range on his sight. When he fired, he hit not the leading vehicle for which he aimed but another far down the column, a truck apparently loaded with ammunition, for it exploded and burst into flame. A second truck behind it, loaded with gasoline, also caught fire. When a Panther pushed past the burning vehicles and headed toward the British tank, Probert ordered the driver to pull back behind the ridge.

Discouraged by the unexpected resistance and almost out of gas, the German commander ordered his vehicles to cover among the houses of a nearby village, Foy–Notre Dame. There they holed up, precisely three miles from the Meuse. Although an order eventually filtered down from Field Marshal Model to continue to the Meuse on foot, nobody paid any heed. By that point—Christmas Day—it had become a matter not of the Meuse but of survival.

Early in the afternoon of December 24, Field Marshal Montgomery, seriously perturbed about what the Germans still might accomplish, visited the First Army's headquarters at Tongres. As Montgomery had notified General Eisenhower two days earlier, he had little confidence that General Patton's attack into the southern flank of the German penetration would be strong enough to deter the advance of the Fifth Panzer Army, in which case he would be left to deal "unaided" with both the Fifth and Sixth Panzer Armies. It was Montgomery's broad concern about the enemy's next move that had prompted him that morning to direct General Ridgway to pull back the 82d Airborne Division from its salient along the Salm. Montgomery was so worried that he attached the British 51st Highland Division to the First Army to assemble as a reserve south of the Meuse near Liège.

As to the threat to Collins's VII Corps, Montgomery told Hodges that he was releasing Collins from his mission to attack. Instead, "if forced," Collins was authorized to pull back the 2d Armored and 84th Divisions all the way to a line extending from Hotton northwest to the Meuse at the town of Andenne, twelve miles downstream from the bend in the river at Namur.

As Hodges noted with concern, that would allow the Germans to occupy almost all of the Condroz plateau and a great stretch of the eastern and southern banks of the Meuse, thereby driving a deep wedge into the First Army's western flank. He was not advocating such a withdrawal, Montgomery assured him, merely authorizing it if the Germans forced it, and that line from Hotton to Andenne was to be a final defensive position. Whether to fall back was to be up to Collins.

Hardly had Montgomery left Hodges's headquarters when in mid-afternoon General Harmon telephoned headquarters of the VII Corps. He wanted permission to attack immediately against panzer formations in the vicinity of Celles. He knew they were there because Belgian telephone operators and police in the towns through which the Germans had passed were reporting to the Belgian police in Harmon's headquarters town of Harvelange.

Since General Collins was away from the headquarters, his artillery commander, Brig. Gen. Williston B. Palmer, a curmudgeon and a perennial bachelor (he had no time, Palmer told friends, for both the army and a wife), took the call. Aware of the effort to keep troops of the VII Corps out of the defensive battle, Palmer told Harmon to wait, that he expected Collins to return soon. "Furious," Harmon unleashed a few of the expletives for which he was noted.

To Palmer, it seemed that he had hardly put down the telephone before Harmon called again. As aggressive a commander as Harmon himself, Palmer considered for a moment giving Harmon the permission he sought, but he thought better of it. Wait, he said again, for Joe Collins to return.

A few minutes later Palmer was again called to the telephone. That time it was the First Army's chief of staff, General Kean. Montgomery had visited Hodges, said Kean, with new instructions for Collins. To make sure Collins understood them, he was sending an assistant G-3, Col. R. F. ("Red") Akers, Jr., to Collins's headquarters. In the meantime, he wanted to make sure that Collins understood that he had "unrestricted use of all of his troops" and, if necessary, authority to alter his defensive positions.

Unwilling to talk openly on the telephone, Kean asked Palmer if he could find on his map a town beginning with the letter A and another with the letter H. Studying the map, Palmer picked out the towns of Achêne and Le Houisse, both southwest of Ciney in the direction of Celles—the direction in which Ernie Harmon wanted to attack. Yes, said Palmer, he saw the two towns. Collins was authorized, said Kean, to change his defensive positions to a line between those two towns.

Palmer was jubilant. That meant Harmon could attack.

Having learned that General Collins had arrived at Harmon's command post, Palmer sent his aide with a written message (Harmon's telephone was out) passing on what Kean had told him, including the word about the two towns, Achêne and Le Houisse.

The lieutenant had been gone only a few minutes when General Kean telephoned again to say that, on reflection, he doubted whether Palmer had understood him correctly. Colonel Akers was on the way, he reiterated, with a full explanation. In the meantime: "Now get this. I'm only going to say it once. Roll with the punch."

Viewed in the context of rolling with the punch, Palmer realized that his identification of the towns A and H southwest of Ciney, forward of the 2d Armored Division's positions at Ciney, made no sense. Looking again at the map, Palmer spotted Andenne and Huy, both on the Meuse well over thirty miles to the rear. On a carbon of the original message to Collins, he explained that he had misconstrued the double-talk about the towns A and H. Calling a liaison officer to take the message to Collins, Palmer quickly added a note: "I think you had better come home."

When General Collins received the second message, it was too late in the day in any case for General Harmon to attack. Telling Harmon to prepare for attack early the next morning, Collins returned to the Château de Bessines.

While awaiting the arrival of Red Akers, Collins discussed the situation with his staff. To a man they agreed with Collins: They should attack. When Akers did arrive—"his lips blue with cold and his face almost frozen"—Collins gave him a drink of rum, then listened "a bit aghast" as Akers told of a possible withdrawal to the line Andenne-Hotton. On the other hand, noted Collins, he was only authorized to withdraw to that line, not obligated to. He also had unrestricted use of all his divisions, no longer having to withhold them for a counterattack, and the decision to withdraw was his alone.

Having lectured as an instructor at The Infantry School on events of World War I, Collins was well aware of the incident in which an emissary of von Moltke's, Lt. Col. Richard Hentsch, acting on oral orders, directed premature withdrawal of the German First Army, which contributed to a French victory. Wanting no part of the kind of recriminations that later befell Hentsch, Collins directed Akers to put his instructions, as derived from Montgomery by way of Hodges, in writing.

With that piece of paper in hand, Collins told Ernie Harmon to attack.

A survey on December 24 of the German order of battle in or near the eastern end of the bulge that the Germans had driven into the American line would lend some credence to Field Marshal Montgomery's immense concern. Five panzer divisions were already in action and a sixth on the way: the *Panzer Lehr* and the 2d Panzer pushing past Marche for the Meuse; the 116th Panzer trying to get across the Marche-Hotton highway onto the Condroz plateau to assist that push; the 2d SS Panzer and the 9th SS Panzer on the other side of the Ourthe River also trying to get onto the plateau; and the 9th Panzer on the way to help at Marche. There was also the *Führer Begleit Brigade* and such as was left of the 12th SS Panzer after its futile efforts to get past the Elsenborn Ridge. It was that formidable array that convinced Montgomery the Germans were getting ready for a powerful, concentrated effort—perhaps the most powerful blow since the start of the offensive.

The array was actually more formidable on a G-2 map than in reality, for except for the 9th Panzer Division, all the panzer formations had already incurred heavy losses. Allied aircraft sharply curtailed their maneuvers by day; and the men still fighting were close to exhaustion, their supplies (including gasoline) sharply diminished. The goal of the Meuse River was nevertheless close at hand.

In quest of that goal, the commander of the 47th Panzer Corps, General von Lüttwitz, early on Christmas Day sent contingents of the *Panzer Lehr Division* from Rochefort to retake Humain and Buissonville, hoping thereby to reopen the shortest route westward and secure the north flank at the base of what von Manteuffel called the "pointed wedge." At Humain, the light tanks and armored cars of the 24th Cavalry Reconnaissance Squadron were no match for the German tanks and relinquished the village; but the loss made little difference, for General Collier's CCA maintained a firm hold on Buissonville. With Collier's powerful force on the north flank, neither von Lüttwitz nor von Manteuffel was willing to send anybody else marching for the Meuse until at least a portion of the 9th Panzer Division arrived to hold that flank.

In the countryside close to the Meuse River near Dinant, Christmas Day dawned with a light cloud cover, but that cleared early and both American and British fighter-bombers were soon overhead. There were at first few targets, for the tanks and other vehicles of the two advanced forces of the 2d Panzer Division—one in and around Foy–Notre Dame, the other in woods between Conjoux and Celles, both with gasoline tanks almost dry—kept under cover. It remained for the 3d Armored Division's CCB under Brig. Gen. I. D. White to flush them.

CCB began to advance shortly after daylight on Christmas morning with two task forces marching down roughly parallel roads from assembly areas outside Ciney with plans to link at Celles. Neither task force had any great difficulty. One moving from Achêne on Celles dug a few Germans from a forest alongside the road and beyond the forest came under fire from tanks concealed among the buildings of a farm, but American fighter-bombers drove the tanks out (four Panthers), and the American tanks and tank destroyers quickly destroyed them. The other task force had a brief engagement near Conjoux, then pushed on in the face of fire from an occasional tank or antitank gun.

In mid-afternoon, the two tasks forces linked on high ground overlooking Celles and continued down into the village without resistance. Near the Pavillon Ardennais, the men saw a Panther that had been disabled by a mine, but that was the only sign of the enemy.

Covering the western flank of the advance, the 82d Armored Reconnaissance Battalion approached Foy–Notre Dame. Seeing German vehicles in the village, the commander of Company A, Capt. James Hartford, sent a platoon to reconnoiter. When the Germans fired on the platoon, Hartford committed the rest of his company, then called on another company to help. Once the men knocked out an antitank gun near the center of the village, the rest was mop-up. Just under 150 Germans surrendered.

In the attack, the reconnaissance troops were helped by the five Shermans of the 3d Royal Tank Regiment, whose crews were relieved that the arrival of the American armor eliminated the requirement for them to make a last-ditch stand in front of the highway bridge at Dinant. Unfortunately, in the first meeting, the crew of an American tank mistook one of the British-operated Shermans for a German tank and knocked it out.

As night fell on Christmas Day and General White made plans for mopping up the German pockets the next day, the only hope for the trapped Germans lay in relief forces breaking through. When a *Kampfgruppe* of the 9th Panzer Division arrived at last near Marche, General von Lüttwitz could send help, but not much. Through the night a *Kampfgruppe* of the 2d Panzer Division—all that was left—and another of the *Panzer Lehr Division* toiled up the valley of the Lesse River toward Celles. Each force had not quite a company of tanks (about fifteen), a few *Panzergrenadiers* and engineers, a light artillery battalion, and part of an antiaircraft battalion.

The *Kampfgruppe* of the 2d Panzer Division was the first to arrive. As the column came within two miles of Celles, it seemed to the Germans that the ridge ahead of them was "crawling with tanks." Before they could disperse into an attack formation, fire from American tanks and from artillery directed from spotter aircraft began to riddle their ranks. By way of the British tanks at Foy–Notre Dame, General White called in a squadron of British Typhoons, but since the Americans had no radio contact with the planes, the little artillery observation aircraft had to dive dangerously low to point out the German column, whereupon the British pilots went to work with deadly rockets.

When the *Kampfgruppe* of the *Panzer Lehr Division* arrived, it received much the same reception. Learning of the disasters, General von Lüttwitz ordered both columns to fall back on Rochefort, leaving the trapped men of the 2d Panzer Division's spearhead to fend for themselves. That night General von Manteuffel authorized them to break out on foot.

Around six hundred Germans eventually escaped. They had to leave behind all the vehicles and equipment of an entire *Panzergrenadier* regiment, a battalion of tanks, three artillery battalions, and the bulk of an antiaircraft battalion. In the whole engagement, including the fighting at Buissonville, the 2d Armored Division knocked out or captured 82 tanks, 83 antitank and artillery pieces, and 500 other vehicles of various types; the division captured 1,213 Germans and killed at least another 900. The American division lost 28 medium tanks (26 of which were soon back in action), 201 men wounded, and 43 killed.

The day after Christmas marked if not the absolute end, then at least the beginning of a precipitous end to the German offensive as Adolf Hitler had originally planned it. On that day, December 26, the American defenders on the Elsenborn Ridge were still holding firm; the big attack on Christmas Day at Bastogne had failed; General Patton's attack against the southern flank was still under way and a relief column entered Bastogne; the attempt by the 2d SS and the 9th SS Panzer Divisions to break past Manhay failed; so, too, did the 116th Panzer Division's attempt to push beyond the Marche-Hotton highway.

Many long, bitter days of combat were to pass before Hitler would finally admit that his grand offensive had failed. Indeed, that same day he was to announce new, grandiose plans to salvage something from it. Yet saner heads recognized that the Führer's desperate ambition, like a lone panther in the garden of the curé of Foy–Notre Dame three miles short of the Meuse River, lay broken in the snow.

BOOK

VI

***

THE
ROAD
BACK

CHAPTER TWENTY-EIGHT

Crises in Command

In the underground concrete chambers of the *Adlerhorst* near Ziegenberg Castle, Alfred Jodl, chief of *OKW*'s operations staff, received a telephone call on the night of December 24 from General von Manteuffel. On the eve of the all-out attack to take Bastogne—to be launched just a few hours later on Christmas Day—von Manteuffel said it was impossible for him to continue driving for the Meuse River and still hope to take Bastogne. The time had come, he said, for a completely new plan. Upon nearing the Meuse, he would wheel north and drive between the Ourthe and the Meuse. That would bring him in on the flank and rear of the American forces fighting south of Liège, at Malmédy, and on the Elsenborn Ridge. Such a plan clearly inferred abandoning Antwerp as an objective, and that, Jodl responded emphatically, the Führer would never countenance. He nevertheless promised to pass along von Manteuffel's recommendation.

On Christmas Day, when Hitler finally arose, he appeared to be cheerful. Late in the day he joined his staff around a candlelit Christmas tree and to everyone's surprise drank a glass of wine and seemed to enjoy it. Yet his physical appearance continued to disturb everybody: "his face was haggard and his voice quavered. . . . His handclasp was weak and soft; all his movements were those of a senile man."

Late that night his military advisers, along with Field Marshal von Rundstedt, joined him for a review of the military situation. There was immense concern about Russian advances in Hungary and speculation as to why the Russians had failed to open a new offensive in Poland.

When the discussion turned to the Ardennes, there was a late report from Field Marshal Model. His chief of staff, General Krebs, had drafted it while Model was visiting the front. Yet for all the gloom Model had encountered there, he made no effort to alter the optimistic tone of Krebs's draft. Even though Model often still spoke frankly to the Führer, he saw little point in inviting Hitler's wrath.

Although the Fifth Panzer Army would soon reach the Meuse, noted Model, the Sixth Panzer Army had been unable to get across the Ourthe so that von Manteuffel's north flank was exposed. Meanwhile, the Seventh Army was under heavy attack from the south. The Fifth Panzer Army might be able to seize some "unoccupied crossings" of the Meuse (he failed to elaborate on what he meant by that), but Model considered it essential for von Manteuffel to turn his main force northward and in conjunction with the Sixth Panzer Army eliminate the Americans fighting south of the Meuse and Liège. And Bastogne would have to be taken. Once all those goals were achieved, Model concluded—but merely as a sop to the Führer's ambition, not through any personal conviction—the drive for Antwerp might be resumed.

After reviewing Model's report, General Jodl, who was another of the few still able to speak candidly to the Führer, paused for a moment. "*Mein Führer*," he continued, "we must face the facts squarely and openly. We cannot force the Meuse River."

Hitler refused to accept that. "We have had unexpected setbacks," he said, "because my plan was not followed to the letter." On the other hand, "all is not yet lost."

As Hitler continued, it became clear that he had accepted von Manteuffel's and Model's recommendation to concentrate on eliminating the Americans south of the Meuse in the vicinity of Liège; but as a prerequisite, to remove the threat to the rear of the two panzer armies, he insisted on capturing Bastogne. Rejecting a proposal to seize Luxembourg City so as to bolster the morale of the troops, he also turned down a proposal from von Rundstedt to return to the earlier plan for the Fifteenth Army to drive down the valley of the Meuse behind Aachen and link with the forces in the Ardennes. That, he said—no doubt thinking of his field commanders' espousal of the Small Solution—would be too costly and would take away resources from the final objective, which he still intended to pursue: Cross the Meuse and capture Antwerp.

Three days later, on December 28, Hitler admitted that the situation in the Ardennes was serious, even desperate, but then added: "As much as I may be tormented by worries and even physically shaken by them, nothing will make the slightest change in my decision to fight on until at last the scales tip to our side." By attacking in the Ardennes, he said, he had forced the Americans to withdraw 50 percent of their strength from other parts of the front, which left those sectors "extraordinarily thin."

Jabbing a finger at a large map on the wall, he indicated the province of Alsace in the northeastern corner of France. There, on New Year's Eve, he announced, he was launching a new offensive (it had been in preparation since December 22) to be known as Operation *NORDWIND*. It would force the Americans to pull back the divisions that were threatening the southern flank in the Ardennes, and with the collapse of that threat, the main offensive in the Ardennes would "*then be resumed* [he stressed the words] with a fresh promise of success."

Field Marshal Model, said Hitler, was "to consolidate his holdings and reorganize for a new attempt on the Meuse." He was also to "make another powerful assault on Bastogne. Above all, we must have Bastogne!"

At Field Marshal Montgomery's invitation, General Bradley flew on Christmas Day (by a roundabout route avoiding the bulge in the American line) to confer with Montgomery. When Bradley landed at St. Trond, northwest of Liège, nobody from Montgomery's staff was there to meet him, which Bradley took to be "a calculated insult." He was tempted to turn around and go home; but when General Hodges's aide-de-camp, Maj. William C. Sylvan, arrived in a staff car, he decided to proceed.

Montgomery's headquarters was in a modest house in Zonhoven, a few miles north of Hasselt. Montgomery offered neither food nor drink (Bradley had had only an apple for lunch) but began immediately to lecture his guest. "I was absolutely frank with him," Montgomery reported later to Field Marshal Brooke. "I said the Germans had given us a real 'bloody nose'; it was a proper defeat, and we had much better admit it." It was, said Montgomery, "entirely our own fault" for trying to advance in two columns rather than putting everything behind the thrust north of the Ardennes. "The enemy saw his chance and took it. Now we were in a proper muddle."

Montgomery told Brooke he felt sorry for Bradley; he "looked thin, and worn and ill at ease." According to Montgomery, Bradley agreed entirely with everything he said. "Poor chap; he is such a decent fellow and the whole thing is a bitter pill for him. But he is man enough to admit it and he did."

Bradley saw it quite differently. He found Montgomery "more arrogant and egotistical" than ever, lecturing and scolding him "like a schoolboy." Bradley was "so enraged and so utterly exasperated" that it was all he could do, while "seething inside," to keep silent.

Most disturbing of all to Bradley was Montgomery's view on attacking to erase the German bulge. Convinced that the Germans were still capable of another major blow, Montgomery said he had no intention of attacking until "he was certain the enemy had exhausted himself." The First Army was too weak to go on the offensive, and the Third Army's attack would accomplish little. The proper course was for everybody to go on the defensive and in the south to withdraw to a shorter defensive line (possibly as far back as the Vosges Mountains) in order to free divisions to strengthen Hodges's First Army. As Bradley understood him— although Montgomery subsequently denied it—he believed it would be three months before Hodges would be capable of a major offensive.

The meeting lasted only half an hour, and Bradley flew back to his headquarters in a mood to match the gathering blackness of the night. Late that evening he had a talk with George Patton, who found Montgomery's ideas "disgusting." If ordered to fall back, Patton thought he would "ask to be relieved." Montgomery was just "a tired little fart."

The next morning, Bradley telephoned Eisenhower's headquarters, talked with the chief of staff, Bedell Smith, and "let him have it with both barrels." Montgomery, he said, was throwing away "an opportunity to inflict a devastating defeat on the enemy." He wanted the First and Ninth Armies returned to his command immediately, whereupon he would move his headquarters to Namur to assure proper coordination and "get some action in the north."

Still seething, Bradley took "the extraordinary step" of writing to one not then under his command, Courtney Hodges. While making it clear that his letter should in no way be considered a directive, he said he failed to view the German situation "in as grave a light" as did Montgomery. Although conscious that the First Army had absorbed a heavy blow, he believed the Germans had lost much more heavily and were so weak that an attack by the First Army would force them "to get out in a hurry." He urged Hodges to look for an opportunity to attack "as soon as the situation seems to warrant."

That night, December 26, aware of the death blow that Ernie Harmon's 2d Armored Division was administering to the spearhead of the German offensive near Celles, Bradley again telephoned Bedell Smith. "Damn it, Bedell," he said, "can't you people get Monty going in the north? As near as we can tell, the other fellow's reached the highwater mark today."

Before daylight on Christmas Eve, two small converted cargo ships— one British, the SS *Cheshire*, the other Belgian, the *Léopoldville*—set sail from Southampton across the rough waters of the English Channel, bound for the French port of Cherbourg. Each carried 2,200 American soldiers of the 262d and 264th Infantry Regiments, the vanguard of the 66th Infantry Division, scheduled to relieve the 94th Infantry Division that was containing Germans holding out in ports in Brittany and so release that division for commitment in the Ardennes. Three British destroyers and a French frigate served as escort.

A German submarine, *U-486*—one of a new class equipped with a snorkel—lay on the Channel floor five miles outside the breakwater at Cherbourg. As part of the German Navy's support of the offensive in the Ardennes, *U-486* and a number of other submarines had received orders early in December to begin operations in the Channel. Under the command of 1st Lt. Gerhard Meyer, *U-486* had assumed its station the night before, December 23.

As the Allied convoy reached open waters, the sea was running heavy. It was bitterly cold. All through the day most of the soldiers aboard the two troopships were seasick. In the crowded compartments below decks on the *Léopoldville*, the air was fetid.

By 5 P.M. it was dark enough for Lieutenant Meyer to chance bringing his craft to the surface. Some thirty minutes later, a lookout picked up the approaching convoy. Slightly before six o'clock, Meyer gave the order to fire a torpedo, which headed unerringly for the *Léopoldville*.

The torpedo struck the vessel starboard side aft and exploded in number four hold. At least three hundred soldiers died from the explosion or drowned in the water that swiftly flooded two of the troop compartments.

All lights went out, and the ship's engines stopped. Among the troops, there was no panic; they took their places on deck as they had learned to do earlier in the day in a lifeboat drill. While some helped carry injured to the ship's infirmary, word passed among the men that tugs were coming to tow the ship into the harbor at Cherbourg. That seemed logical, for the lights of the port were clearly visible—to shore-trained eyes, only a short distance away.

There were indeed plenty of tugs at Cherbourg and many another vessel that might be used for rescue, but for a long time nobody notified American Army and Navy headquarters in the port about the disaster. The senior British commander, Lt. Comdr. John Pringle, captain of HMS *Brilliant*, had no radio communications with Cherbourg, and even though he notified authorities in Southampton, they failed to pass the word along. Not until 6:25 P.M., almost half an hour after the torpedo hit, did anybody notify Cherbourg, and then it was a blinker message from HMS *Brilliant* stating only that the *Léopoldville* had been hit and needed assistance.

That message mystified officials at the port. What kind of assistance? Every request by blinker message for additional information went unanswered. That contributed to the delay in sending help. Even greater delay stemmed from the fact that it was Christmas Eve and every man who could be spared was on leave. It was close to 7 o'clock, a full hour after the torpedoing, before the first rescue craft left the harbor.

Meanwhile, HMS *Brilliant*, along with the other British destroyers and the French frigate, was looking for the German submarine and dropping depth charges. All the while, *U-486* lay on the bottom of the Channel, its motors silent. Neither Lieutenant Meyer nor any of his forty-eight-man crew felt any elation. They knew they had scored a hit but thought they had only grazed their target.

The big problem aboard the *Léopoldville* was that nobody knew how extensive was the damage. The skipper, Capt. Charles Limbor, made no attempt to check it, and somebody (nobody would ever determine who it was) kept announcing over the public address system that there was no danger of sinking. Several times the word went out that tugs were coming to tow the *Léopoldville* into port. At other times, that all passengers were to be transferred to other ships. Yet always, no danger of sinking.

To the soldiers, that made the behavior of the Belgian crew—mostly men from the Belgian Congo—incomprehensible. The entire crew except for the four senior officers early made for the lifeboats, climbed aboard, and launched them. A few U.S. soldiers joined them, and others filled one of the boats until an officer ordered them out. There was no danger of sinking.

As the powerless *Léopoldville* began to drift, Commander Pringle aboard the *Brilliant* ordered Captain Limbor by blinker signals to drop anchors. Learning finally that there were many wounded aboard the troopship, Pringle stopped his search for the U-boat and came alongside the *Léopoldville*. Although he intended only to remove the wounded, the British sailors encouraged other soldiers to come aboard.

In the rough seas, getting anybody across from the *Léopoldville* to the *Brilliant* was more than perilous, it was death-defying. With virtually no crew left aboard the troopship, hardly anybody knew how to moor the two vessels. It took considerable time before British sailors manning the *Léopoldville*'s antiaircraft guns and American soldiers accomplished the task. Even then the lines broke constantly, and others had to be secured to keep the two vessels close together.

They were never exactly parallel. Over and over again, both vessels rose and fell in the heaving seas, came together with a grinding, crushing noise, pulled apart, then came together once more. Many men nevertheless heeded the cries of the British sailors: "Jump, Yank!" Some mistimed their jumps and fell between the two ships, there to be crushed when next the two vessels surged together. That discouraged many others from jumping, and even though the *Léopoldville* had developed a strong list, there was still no word from anybody in authority that it was sinking. Was it safer to stay with the ship or jump?

As 2d Lt. Harry Peiper saw it: "It was like trying to jump on a big, bobbing cork on a rough pond. . . . At one second, [*Brilliant*] was crashing the side of our ship some fifteen feet below me, then it was at my level but fifteen feet out. There was no telling where it was going to be at the next second." A former football player at the University of California, Peiper finally jumped and just managed to grab a handhold on the lifelines of the destroyer's deck. Seconds before the two ships crashed together again, he swung his feet over the railing.

They tried at first to transfer the wounded by means of lines and pulleys, but there was no way to keep the stretchers flat, and even though strapped down, men slipped off into the sea between the two vessels. One soldier with both arms in splints began slipping while halfway across, slowly, headfirst, "desperately but futilely clutching the sides of the litter with his feet."

The better way seemed to be to throw the wounded across, either on their stretchers or in wicker basket sea litters, sometimes in a sheet or a blanket. Aboard the *Brilliant*, British sailors and American soldiers who had made the jump tried to catch them, to cushion their fall, but some hit the deck hard.

There was still no word to abandon ship. Although Captain Limbor ordered the few of his crew who were still aboard to leave, nobody told the soldiers what to do. Again, why make that perilous jump when there was no danger of the *Léopoldville* going down? Nor did anybody tell Commander Pringle that the *Léopoldville* was mortally wounded.

For the better part of an hour, the *Brilliant* remained alongside; but as boats from Cherbourg began to arrive, Captain Pringle pulled away. He had already taken on a heavy load, he needed to get the wounded to Cherbourg for medical attention, and he presumed that the arriving craft would be able to take the other troops off, should that prove necessary. Had he realized that the *Léopoldville* was sinking, he might have considered towing the vessel; but that would have been difficult because the *Léopoldville*, at his order, had dropped anchors, and no crewmen remained to hoist them.

Not long after the *Brilliant* departed, word began to pass among the soldiers that the *Léopoldville* was doomed. The ship's list was becoming "more pronounced every minute."

When two small tugs came alongside, some soldiers got aboard. Others turned to nine remaining lifeboats, which they managed with great difficulty to launch, but none carried its full capacity. (In lifeboats with a total capacity of 590 men, 300 got away.) There were still many men who made no effort to leave the ship, for as a battalion commander, Lt. Col. J. Ralph Martindale, later noted: "Until one minute prior to sinking, all indications and all information indicated that the ship would stay afloat."

At close to 8:30 P.M., the ship gave a sudden lurch. Then came "a rumbling, like the beating of drums in a serious symphony . . . the drums getting louder and louder." Hatch covers blew off. The ship began to upend, going down by the stern while at the same time rolling to one side. Life rafts broke loose, crashing among the soldiers. Steel helmets careened about the decks. Some men fell overboard; others threw themselves into the water. Almost to a man they still wore their heavy woolen overcoats beneath their little life jackets. When waterlogged, those pulled many a man to his death. Some still refused to enter the icy water, but as the ship assumed the vertical, they had no choice. Others were still trying to climb the rapidly rising decks when the ship plunged beneath the water.

Once in the water, panic at last engulfed many of the men. They grabbed at other people, dragging them under. They fought for positions on the small life rafts, to be first to be pulled aboard lifeboats, tugs, PT boats, destroyers. Many a man hefted aboard one of the craft was already dead from hypothermia or drowning; the crews threw their bodies overboard to make room for the living.

When the ghastly ordeal was finally over, five hundred more men from the *Léopoldville*—plus Captain Limbor, who went down with his ship—were dead. Counting the three hundred who died at the start, that made a total of eight hundred or more, the worst disaster to befall a troopship carrying American soldiers during the course of the war.

Between the time the torpedo struck and the *Léopoldville* went under, two and a half hours elapsed. At least five hundred men went to their deaths in the cold waters of the English Channel who should have lived; yet in view of the delay in communications with Cherbourg, the bungling and indecision, the early departure of the Belgian crew, and the lack of information or direction from the bridge, it was incredible that the toll was no higher.

Like General Bradley, General Eisenhower was anxious for Field Marshal Montgomery to attack; but in one respect he was thinking like Montgomery. Because of the slowness of General Patton's advance on Bastogne, Eisenhower saw a pressing need for more divisions. The 17th Airborne Division had yet to arrive from England, and the tragedy at sea meant that the 94th Infantry Division would have to continue the task of containing Germans in the ports of Brittany. That left him with only two divisions not yet committed: the 11th Armored Division, just arrived from England, and the 87th Infantry Division, which the Seventh Army had pulled from the line by extending the sectors of other divisions. Yet so long as the Germans continued to attack, Eisenhower was reluctant to commit those two divisions. At his daily staff conference on December 26, he ruled that the commander of the 6th Army Group, General Devers, would have to withdraw from the Saar and Rhine Rivers back to the Vosges, thereby shortening the line and freeing two or three divisions.

That decision taken (although yet to be implemented), Eisenhower prepared to meet Montgomery in Brussels. Even though telephone communications were functioning satisfactorily, Eisenhower found the telephone no substitute for face-to-face conversation. Because of his staff's continuing concern for his safety, he agreed to go by special train, planning to depart that night, the 26th; but before anybody boarded the train, the Luftwaffe bombed it, and it was noon the next day when Eisenhower finally got under way. At a staff conference before leaving, he learned that Montgomery was at last contemplating attack, to which Eisenhower responded: "Praise God from Whom all blessings flow!"

Partly because of security precautions, which annoyed Eisenhower, the journey was slow, and the roads were so icy that he headed not for Brussels but for Hasselt, which was considerably closer to Montgomery's forward headquarters. It was near midday on December 28 before the train reached Hasselt and Montgomery came aboard.

Eisenhower found Montgomery still convinced that the Germans had one more full-blooded attack left in them. He apparently based that belief on the estimates of his G-2, Brigadier Williams, who like most Allied intelligence officers was at that point living by the adage, once burned, twice cautious. An aerial reconnaissance report of a concentration of five hundred German vehicles led Williams's staff to speculate that the Germans might be moving up one, perhaps two more SS panzer divisions to assemble a corps behind the SS panzer divisions on the northern flank, "to deliver next breakout." The British Joint Intelligence Committee was also being cautious, noting that the Germans had failed to reach either their intermediate or long-range objective and thus "might well release additional reserves for a final lunge."

That kind of caution failed to meld with the intercepts that ULTRA was producing. Most intercepts pointed to the Germans' being in serious straits, with heavy tanks losses, and suffering from an acute shortage of gasoline. Although there were indications that they were shifting some formations already committed toward Bastogne, there was none indicating a buildup in the north.

Montgomery told Eisenhower that while he awaited the expected blow, he was beginning to replace General Collins's troops at the tip of the bulge from Rochefort to Hotton with British troops, thereby enabling Collins finally to assemble for an attack. When Eisenhower raised the possibility that the Germans might not in fact mount another major thrust, Montgomery promised that if it failed to develop, he would start General Collins's attack six days later, on January 3. With that assurance, Eisenhower telephoned his headquarters to direct release of the 11th Armored and 87th Divisions to General Patton.

Before Eisenhower departed, Montgomery raised the issue that had so long complicated Allied command relationships: When the Allied armies renewed the drive into Germany, Montgomery insisted that he be designated overall ground commander and in particular that he have command over Bradley's 12th Army Group. As Eisenhower left, Montgomery thought he had won his point. So he reported to Field Marshal Brooke; but Brooke thought otherwise. "It looks to me," Brooke confided in his diary, "as if Monty, with his usual lack of tact, has been rubbing into Ike the results of not having listened to Monty's advice!"

Nevertheless emboldened, Montgomery the next day wrote Eisenhower a letter that if not insubordinate, was at least insolent and arrogant. Because of Eisenhower's failure to designate an overall commander for a principal Allied thrust north of the Ardennes, he inferred, they had already had "one very definite failure," so that the time had come for Eisenhower "to be very firm on the subject . . . no loosely worded statement" would do. He proceeded even to write Eisenhower's directive for him: "From now onwards full operational direction, control and co-ordination . . . is vested in the C.-in-C. 21 Army Group, subject to such instructions as may be issued by the Supreme Commander from time to time." He considered it essential that "*all* available offensive power" be assigned to a northern thrust and that "one man" should direct and control that thrust, without which, he concluded, "I am certain that . . . we shall fail again."

In view of all the earlier disagreements over ground command and a single thrust into Germany, that letter in itself would have been enough to submit the Supreme Commander's patience to rigorous testing. As it happened, it came at a time when the voice of the British press had become strident, maintaining that Montgomery "had saved the Americans from the consequence of their follies and that he would rightly go on to lead all the Allies to victory."

Once General Marshall in Washington learned that the British press was predicting that Eisenhower was to name Montgomery as overall ground commander, he cabled Eisenhower that in his opinion, there should "under no circumstances" be "any concessions of any kind whatsoever," for that would create "a terrific resentment" in the United States. (At that point there were forty-two American divisions on the Continent as against nineteen from Britain and the Commonwealth countries, and the margin was bound to increase.) "You are doing a fine job," Marshall concluded, "and go on and give them hell."

As for Eisenhower and many senior members of his staff, Montgomery's letter generated deep resentment. They saw it as an ultimatum. Almost everybody, including Eisenhower's British deputy supreme commander, Air Marshal Tedder, considered that the time had come for a showdown. Either Eisenhower or Montgomery had to go; and given the preponderance of forces that the United States was contributing to the alliance, quite clearly it would not be Eisenhower.

Through a PHANTOM liaison officer at Bradley's headquarters in Luxembourg City, Montgomery's chief of staff, General de Guingand, learned of the deep resentment the reports and editorials in the British press had generated. That prompted him to telephone Walter Bedell Smith at Versailles, from whom he learned that Montgomery's message had upset everybody. An "extremely dangerous situation" had developed.

Despite de Guingand's position on Montgomery's staff, the Americans trusted him, and he knew it. If he could get from Brussels to Versailles in time, thought de Guingand, perhaps he could head off a showdown. Yet throughout the morning of December 30, abominable flying weather appeared to forestall that. Not until early afternoon did the weather clear sufficiently to risk takeoff; even then it was a hair-raising ride, and several times the pilot contemplated turning back, until at last he got a glimpse of the Seine and followed it at treetop level to Orly Airfield outside Paris.

At the Trianon Palace Hotel, de Guingand learned from Bedell Smith that he might be too late. Together, the two went to a small house in a nearby forest where Eisenhower's security officers had insisted that Eisenhower stay until the apparent threat to his life passed. "In a somberly lighted room, full of smoke from [Air Marshal] Tedder's pipe but made somewhat more cheerful by a healthy blaze in the fireplace," Eisenhower explained the intolerable position in which the British press reports and Montgomery's insistence on overall command placed General Bradley.

Eisenhower said he was "tired of the whole business" and had concluded that it had become a matter to be decided by the Combined Chiefs of Staff. He had already drafted a message to be sent through General Marshall to the Combined Chiefs, stating explicitly that they would have to choose between him and Montgomery. Should the Combined Chiefs decide in favor of Eisenhower, the British commander in Italy, Field Marshal Sir Harold Alexander, would be an acceptable substitute for Montgomery.

Well aware that it would be Montgomery who would have to go, but wanting no showdown in any case, de Guingand insisted that his chief had no inkling of the resentment his letter had fostered. He was convinced that once Montgomery understood, he would back down and cooperate. Withhold the message to Marshall for twenty-four hours, implored de Guingand, to afford him an opportunity to talk with Montgomery.

To both Eisenhower and Tedder it seemed that the damage had already been done, and neither was inclined to agree. Only when Bedell Smith took de Guingand's side did Eisenhower relent. He would sit on the message for a day.

Back in General Smith's office, de Guingand sent a message to Montgomery, saying that he planned to fly back the next day and come to Zonhoven to discuss an important matter; but because of continued bad weather, it was 4:30 P.M. before he reached Montgomery's headquarters. Since Montgomery was just sitting down to tea, de Guingand joined him. Neither man interrupted the ritual to discuss business. Rising, Montgomery said: "I'm going upstairs to my office, Freddie. Please come up when you have finished your tea."

When de Guingand came upstairs, he put the matter bluntly. "I've just come from SHAEF and seen Ike," he said, "and it's in the cards that you might have to go." Explaining the hard feelings at Eisenhower's headquarters in some detail, de Guingand told of the message Eisenhower was planning to send to Marshall. He "believed the situation could be put right," de Guingand concluded, but "it required immediate action."

To de Guingand, Montgomery seemed "genuinely and completely taken by surprise" and "found it difficult to grasp" what he was saying. He "looked completely non-plussed—I don't think I had ever seen him

so deflated. It was as if a cloak of loneliness had descended upon him."
Asked Montgomery: "What shall I do, Freddie?"

De Guingand pulled out a message he had already drafted, and with a
few changes, Montgomery approved it. He had "seen Freddie," the message began, and understood from him that Eisenhower was "greatly worried by many considerations." He had given Eisenhower his "frank
views" because that was what he believed Eisenhower wanted, but he was
"sure there are many factors which have a bearing quite beyond anything
I realize." The message concluded:

> Whatever your decision may be you can rely on me one hundred
> per cent to make it work and I know Brad will do the same. Very
> distressed that my letter may have upset you and I would ask you to
> tear it up. Your very devoted subordinate Monty.

Over icy roads, de Guingand drove to the 21st Army Group's rear
headquarters in Brussels, where he spoke candidly to four prominent
British news correspondents. Montgomery's command of American
forces, he explained, had been a temporary expedient, and in view of the
overwhelming number of American troops in Europe, pressure for an
overall British ground commander was not only self-defeating but dangerous. With the newsmen promising to consult their editors, de
Guingand telephoned Versailles. Bedell Smith told him that Eisenhower
had received Montgomery's message, had been "most touched," and the
signal to Washington "now reposed in the waste-paper basket."

The next day, Eisenhower forwarded to all three army group commanders an outline plan for future operations, which he had just finished
drafting when the crisis with Montgomery arose. In it, he proposed to
reduce the bulge in the Ardennes "by immediate attacks from north and
south" with Montgomery continuing to command in the north until the
First and Third Armies linked, whereupon Bradley was to resume command of the First Army. As he explained to Montgomery in a covering
letter, also written before he received Montgomery's apology, he was
leaving the Ninth Army under Montgomery for reasons of "military necessity," a decision, he said, that "most assuredly reflects my confidence
in you personally. Yet in the matter of command, he could "go no further."

That crisis between Eisenhower and Montgomery was as close as Adolf Hitler came to precipitating a break in the Western alliance, and it
was nowhere near a break. However heated and serious, it remained
merely another difference of opinion between field commanders, a controversy in large measure generated by a mercurial press always ready to
champion dissension and preach disaster. (Not just the British press; for
the American press was complaining vehemently that Montgomery had
committed no British troops to help in the Ardennes.) The insensitive
Montgomery was destined to provoke controversy again a few days later,

and the Chief of the Imperial General Staff, Field Marshal Brooke, who constantly lamented the inexperience of senior American commanders in "handling large masses in battle," would for long persist in raising the issue of "a more effective overall control of the ground forces"; but it remained an intramural issue among military men that in the end had no appreciable effect on conduct of the war by the Anglo-American alliance.

The bulge in the American line was forty miles wide at its base, sixty miles deep at the apex. The problem was how to eliminate it.

To George Patton, who had disliked the assignment of relieving Bastogne because it diverted him from the obvious solution, the answer was simple—the same as that taught between wars at the Command and General Staff College—cut it off at the base. ("If you get a monkey in the jungle hanging by his tail," said Patton, "it is easier to get him by cutting his tail than kicking him in the face.") He wanted to assume the defensive at Bastogne and with a reinforced XII Corps under Manton Eddy in the lead attack northeastward across the Sûre and Our Rivers into Germany to Bitburg and Prüm, there to link with a drive by the First Army southeastward from the Elsenborn Ridge. Those drives would penetrate deep into the enemy's rear and trap all the forces that had plunged into the Ardennes.

The First Army's Courtney Hodges agreed, but only "in principle." Hodges saw the roadnet leading southeast from the Elsenborn Ridge to Prüm as too limited to support a major advance, a view that the German commanders who had had such a task toiling through the Losheim Gap would certainly have seconded.

The man whom Montgomery had designated to spearhead the attack from the north, Joe Collins, had a proposal that would eliminate that problem and still cut the base of the German salient: Move his corps behind Malmédy and drive southeast on St. Vith while Patton drove north up the Skyline Drive.

When Montgomery visited Collins in the Château de Bessines on several occasions after the stopping of the 2d Panzer Division near Celles, Collins pressed that plan while at the same time urging Montgomery to get on with the attack before the Germans could consolidate their gains. Yet every time, Montgomery reiterated his concern for still another major German blow, which might well pierce the First Army's lines. Nobody, replied Collins, was going to break through "such top-flight divisions" as the 1st, 2d, 9th, and 30th, the 3d Armored, and the 82d Airborne. When Montgomery insisted it would be impossible to supply a corps over "a single road" (that from Malmédy to St. Vith), Collins responded: "Well, Monty, maybe you British can't but we can."

On December 27, Collins presented his plan to drive from Malmédy to St. Vith to General Hodges, but in view of Montgomery's objection, he proposed two other possibilities, both aimed at Houffalize for link-up with troops of the Third Army advancing north from Bastogne. Hodges chose to endorse one of those.

On the same day, before Eisenhower left by train for his meeting with Montgomery, Bradley visited him with his own proposal for eliminating the bulge. Patton, said Bradley, should attack with Middleton's VIII Corps from Bastogne on Houffalize and with Millikin's III Corps northeastward on St. Vith. (To ensure that Patton did not shift instead to the drive he wanted on Bitburg and Prüm, Bradley specified that the two new divisions afforded Patton, the 11th Armored and the 87th, had to be employed with the VIII Corps in the vicinity of Bastogne.) Hodges was to drive with Collins's VII Corps on Houffalize and with Ridgway's XVIII Airborne Corps push southeast on St. Vith. Again Bradley urged Eisenhower to return the First and Ninth Armies to his command and again he said that he would shift his headquarters to Namur.

While disapproving any immediate change in command, Eisenhower approved Bradley's plan of attack. When Montgomery subsequently agreed—at last persuaded by Joe Collins not to strike at the tip of the German salient, not to kick the monkey in the face—it became the Allied plan. It was no drive to cut the enemy's feet from under him and trap him in the Ardennes; it was instead a conservative push against his waist, combined with drives not unlike two windshield wipers sweeping the enemy back like raindrops toward St. Vith. When von Rundstedt learned the nature of his enemy's riposte, he called it, not without a touch of irony, the "Small Solution."

In ordering a diversionary attack against the 6th Army Group to force the Americans to pull some of their divisions from the Ardennes, Adolf Hitler displayed considerable prescience; for in taking over much of the Third Army's front to allow Patton to attack and in releasing the 87th Division, General Devers's command had become gravely overextended. Devers's Seventh U.S. Army and First French Army held a line 240 miles long, which included a big reentrant known as the Colmar Pocket that afforded the Germans a sally port west of the Rhine. General Eisenhower constantly worried about that extended line and told Devers on several occasions that he had to be prepared to give ground rather than endanger the integrity of his forces.

By Christmas Eve, it was already apparent that the Germans were planning an attack of some kind in the south. "Excellent agent sources [for which read ULTRA]," noted Devers's G-2, Brig. Gen. Eugene L. Harrison, "report enemy units building up in the Black Forest area [just east of the Rhine] for offensive."

That was one consideration behind General Eisenhower's decision two days later, on December 26, for Devers to pull back to the Vosges Mountains; but Devers interpreted that not as a directive but as another warning of what he might be called upon to do. On New Year's Eve the

6th Army Group was still in place along the German frontier and the Rhine in the sharp angle that is the extreme northeastern corner of France and around the periphery of the Colmar Pocket.

By that time indications of a German buildup and probable attack were clearer still. As before the attack in the Ardennes, ULTRA was telling nothing specific but was providing considerable information on the assembly of German troops. Several reports provided fairly accurate indications of the enemy order of battle. Another noted that replacements for the 17th SS Panzergrenadier Division were being rushed forward, and yet another revealed that the 21st Panzer Division was moving south. Those intercepted messages, when combined with prisoner interrogations and aerial reconnaissance, made it clear that an attack was coming, either on New Year's Eve or at the latest on New Year's Day.

In response to Eisenhower's warnings about possible withdrawal, General Devers—the only senior American commander whom Eisenhower had had no hand in selecting and thus one in whom he was never fully confident—had designated three fall-back positions, the last being the line of the Vosges; but he had ordered no withdrawal. One reason was Devers's concern for French sensibilities, for any large-scale withdrawal involved relinquishing the city of Strasbourg.

The French, Devers knew, saw Strasbourg symbolically as the capital of Alsace and Lorraine, the two provinces lost to the Germans from 1870 to 1918 and again from 1940 to late 1944. No Frenchman could forget that it was in Strasbourg in 1792 that Rouget de Lisle had composed what became the revered national anthem, *La Marseillaise*. Nor was there a French schoolchild who had not been moved to tears reading *"La Dernière Leçon"* ("The Last Lesson"), a touching short story by Alphonse Daudet about a schoolmaster's last class in the French language before German authorities in 1871 took charge. To abandon Strasbourg meant exposing thousands of Frenchmen to cruel German reprisal. More than that, to abandon Strasbourg was to serve up a part of the very soul of France.

When the German First Army attacked an hour before midnight on New Year's Eve with five divisions and with two panzer divisions in reserve, the importance of Strasbourg to the French either escaped General Eisenhower or else he deemed military considerations to be overriding. At the first word of the attack, Eisenhower told Bedell Smith to "call up Devers and tell him he is not doing what he was told." He wanted Devers to leave light screening forces on the plain between the Rhine and the Vosges and fall back on the mountains. That was as much as to say: Abandon Strasbourg.

As soon as the head of the French provisional government, Charles de Gaulle, learned of Eisenhower's directive, he promptly sent the chief of staff of the French Ministry of Defense, General Pierre Juin, to Versailles to protest. In a fury, Juin told Bedell Smith that France would never relinquish Strasbourg. Already de Gaulle had ordered the commander of the First French Army, General Jean de Lattre de Tassigny, to take responsibility for defending the city.

General Smith's well-known temper flared, for de Gaulle's action not only represented defiance of Eisenhower as Supreme Commander but unilateral alteration of an interarmy boundary. You go through with it, said Bedell Smith, and not one more bullet, not one more gallon of gasoline would the French Army receive.

In that case, responded Juin, the French government might deny American use of French railroads. If Eisenhower persisted, de Gaulle was prepared to withdraw the First French Army from his command.

It sounded like an argument in a school yard. It was in fact a clever ploy. Juin departed knowing that he had left General Smith visibly shaken and that Smith would tell his chief everything. That would afford Eisenhower time to reconsider before he met with de Gaulle at de Gaulle's request the next afternoon. Lest the stratagem miscarry, de Gaulle that night cabled President Roosevelt and Prime Minister Churchill for help. Roosevelt declined to intervene in what he considered to be a military matter. Scheduled to fly to Paris on January 3 to lunch with Eisenhower, Churchill withheld his judgment.

When the prime minister, delayed by bumpy flying weather over the Channel, reached Versailles around 2 P.M., General de Gaulle had already arrived, and at Eisenhower's invitation, Churchill sat in on the conference. Explaining the vital symbolic importance of Strasbourg to the French people, de Gaulle said that unless Eisenhower defended the city, he himself as head of state would be compelled to act independently. Of such importance was Strasbourg that he was prepared to risk losing the entire First French Army rather that relinquish the city without a fight.

Losing his temper, Eisenhower repeated Bedell Smith's threat to deprive the French Army of supplies; but in reality, even before opening the conference, he had begun to reconsider. The crisis in the Ardennes was past, and although Operation *NORDWIND* was a heavy blow, troops of the Seventh Army by nightfall of the second day had almost brought the main effort to a halt. Besides, there must be no threat by the French to the U.S. Army's lines of communication across France.

He would instruct General Devers, said Eisenhower, to withdraw only from the tip of the salient in the extreme northeastern corner of France back some twenty miles to the little Moder River. He would adjust the interarmy boundary to give responsibility for defending Strasbourg to the French. As de Gaulle departed, immensely relieved, Prime Minister Churchill, who had said not a word during the deliberations, remarked quietly to Eisenhower: "I think you've done the wise and proper thing."

So did the commander of the 6th Army Group, General Devers, and the commander of the Seventh Army, General Patch, for both saw Eisenhower's order to withdraw as premature. Fighting in bitter cold and heavy snow continued until January 25. One column advancing out of the Colmar Pocket got within thirteen miles of Strasbourg while another north of the city got within nine miles; but Operation *NORDWIND* ended with the Germans gaining nothing more than twenty miles of flat landscape of no tactical or strategic importance.

The offensive cost the Germans 25,000 casualties; the Americans, 15,600. Contrary to Adolf Hitler's goal, it produced no diminution of the American effort in the Ardennes. Lest the German operation should expand to the north, Eisenhower and Bradley on January 10 ordered Patton, over his strenuous objections, to send a division to back up his overextended XX Corps in defensive positions facing the Saar; Patton chose the 4th Armored Division, which was down to forty-two medium tanks and badly needed a rest in any case. That was all.

CHAPTER TWENTY-NINE

Erasing the Bulge

Once burned, twice cautious. Having perceived no intruders at all before December 16, Allied commanders and their intelligence officers in the days that followed saw a burglar under every bed. Their alarm persisted even after the Germans in front of the Meuse on Christmas Day and the next day suffered "one of the most serious things that can possibly happen to one in battle"—as Tweedledee explained it to Alice—getting one's head cut off.

At the height of the battle on December 22, General Eisenhower had issued an order of the day in which he noted that "By rushing out from his fixed defenses the enemy may give us the chance to turn his great gamble into his worst defeat." Everybody was to hold before him "a single thought—to destroy the enemy on the ground, in the air, everywhere—destroy him!" Yet when it came down to how to do that, the specter of all those burglars dictated caution. Not as much caution as Field Marshal Montgomery had urged, but caution nevertheless. As von Rundstedt put it: the Small Solution.

Concern for burglars was also evident in other actions of the Supreme Commander. Near the end of December Eisenhower suggested raising Belgian, Polish, and more French divisions, and plans were soon under way for equipping eight French divisions and close to 500,000 men— mostly Frenchmen—to guard lines of communication. In Washington, at Eisenhower's request, the Joint Chiefs of Staff stepped up the sailing dates of an airborne, three infantry, and three armored divisions to Europe. They also allocated to Eisenhower three more infantry divisions not previously scheduled for his command. General Marshall began to comb out support units in the United States, Alaska, and Panama to provide infantry replacements.

What about transferring divisions from Italy? asked Eisenhower. Perhaps 100,000 U.S. Marines? He set his staff to work on a plan for obtaining volunteers from segregated Negro support units to join the infantry.

On the theory that Hitler might be shifting divisions from the Eastern Front to the Ardennes, Eisenhower asked Marshall to obtain from the Russians "at the earliest possible moment some indication of their strategical and tactical intentions." The Red Army had been lying low since late summer; when would the Russians begin their long-awaited winter offensive?

On December 26, General Marshall notified Eisenhower that the Russian dictator, Joseph Stalin, would be pleased to confer with any senior officer whom Eisenhower might send to Moscow. Eisenhower promptly sent his British deputy, Air Marshal Tedder, but because of delays caused by bad weather in both Naples and Cairo, Tedder reached Moscow only in the middle of January. Said Eisenhower: "His trip is of the utmost importance," but by the time Tedder saw Stalin, events had overtaken his mission.

Even before visiting Versailles on January 3, Prime Minister Churchill had directed his service chiefs to find another quarter of a million men from somewhere, a perplexing requirement in view of the heavy levies already imposed on limited British manpower over six long years of war, and he wrote President Roosevelt urging more American troops. On January 6, Churchill, with Eisenhower's approval, wrote personally to Stalin: "The battle in the West is very heavy. . . . I shall be grateful if you can tell me whether we can count on a major Russian offensive during January. I regard the matter as urgent."

Stalin answered promptly, to explain that bad weather had held up the Red Army's offensive, but "taking into account the position of our Allies on the Western Front," the Russian high command had decided "to accelerate the completion of our preparations" and regardless of the weather, "open an offensive along the entire Central Front no later than the second half of January."

Whether Stalin would speed up his offensive remained problematical. In terms of his long-range goal of dominating as much of Europe as possible, he had no need to help his Western Allies, but he did have a need to get the Red Army moving westward to occupy as much territory as possible before the armies of America and Britain got there. Whatever Stalin's motivation, fourteen infantry divisions and two tank corps attacked across the Upper Vistula River on January 12, the start of what was to become a mammoth offensive.

The offensive did nothing to ease the situation for American forces in the Ardennes; for by that time the issue was no longer in doubt, and in any case, the Germans had shifted only one unit from the Eastern Front, a *Volksgrenadier* division that had been in reserve in Hungary. Born out of an unjustified concern (not far from panic), the call for help from Stalin was ill-considered and unnecessary. It was to help put Stalin in a strong bargaining position a few weeks later at Yalta, where, in response to an invitation long sought by Churchill and Roosevelt but issued only three days after Churchill's plea for help, the Allied heads of state came to discuss the postwar face of Europe. The Red Army's drive, proclaimed Stalin in an order of the day in February, "resulted in breaking the German attack in the West." At Yalta, he would play that for all it was worth when, in reality, Hitler's ill-starred adventure in the Ardennes actually eased the task of the Red Army.

Although Hitler insisted that the drive to gain the Meuse was to continue even as General von Manteuffel reduced Bastogne, the commander of the Fifth Panzer Army, with Field Marshal Model's tacit approval but without notifying the *Adlerhorst,* went on the defensive at Rochefort and Marche and directed full attention to Bastogne. It was essential to attack quickly, before the Americans could broaden their thin corridor into the town. Yet von Manteuffel could not be ready until December 30, and on the 27th, the 9th Armored Division's CCA, shifted hurriedly from Luxembourg, retook Sibret to open the Neufchâteau highway into Bastogne.

Von Manteuffel put much of his hope for severing the corridor in Colonel Remer's *Führer Begleit Brigade*, shifted from its brief commitment near Hotton, for the brigade had incurred nothing like the heavy losses in men and machines incurred by the panzer and SS panzer divisions. The brigade was to attack the corridor from the west to seize Sibret and cut the Neufchâteau highway, while another force struck simultaneously from the east across the Arlon highway.

That second force consisted of the *Führer Grenadier Brigade*; the 3d Panzergrenadier Division, its numbers sharply reduced after battering futilely against the Elsenborn Ridge; and the 1st SS Panzer Division, Joachim Peiper's outfit, which had enough repaired and replacement tanks to form a *Kampfgruppe* with the strength of a separate American tank battalion, perhaps forty to fifty tanks. The second force also had a powerful fresh unit, the 167th Volksgrenadier Division, hurried from a reserve position in Hungary.

Aware from radio intercepts that it would be several days before the American First Army attacked from the north, von Manteuffel assumed that General Patton would delay a renewed attack until the First Army was ready. In fact, Patton was already widening the corridor into Bastogne and was preparing for a major attack on December 30, the same day as von Manteuffel, in the direction of Houffalize.

Close along the Arlon highway an experienced 35th Infantry Division had entered the line between the 4th Armored and 26th Infantry Divisions, and an experienced 6th Armored Division was on the way. With the 9th Armored Division's CCA and the two divisions that Eisenhower released on the 28th (the 11th Armored and 87th Infantry Divisions), General Middleton's VIII Corps was to pass west of Bastogne and head for Houffalize.

On both sides of the corridor, the opposing attacks ran head-on into each other just as a foggy day was dawning, and predictable confusion ensued. Predictably, too, the inexperienced 11th Armored and 87th Infantry Divisions lost heavily, particularly in junior officers, but so did the Germans. Fighting with far greater determination than had been exhibited in a first commitment in Luxembourg, the 9th Armored Division's CCA brought the *Führer Begleit Brigade* to a halt well short of Sibret and the Neufchâteau highway. As the fighting resumed the next day, the Americans began to gain ground—however laboriously—toward the highway leading west out of Bastogne to St. Hubert.

On the night of December 30, the Luftwaffe returned to Bastogne with a raid far heavier than that of Christmas Eve. Since there was by then a way out of the town, many of the civilians grabbed a few personal belongings and took it.

Southeast of Bastogne, the veteran 35th Infantry Division stood full in the path of the German attack. A bloody melee ensued, and before the day was done the Germans had trapped and wiped out three American rifle companies. Although the 35th Division had arrived without its customary supporting tank battalion, communications were good to the adjacent 4th Armored Division, and General Gaffey's tanks lent a hand. The heaviest fighting was for the village of Lutrebois, only two and a half miles from the little road through Assenois over which supplies were moving into Bastogne. By early afternoon the weather had cleared sufficiently to bring American fighter-bombers to the scene, and the 35th Division's artillery made liberal use of the POZIT fuse. Even so, as night came, the *Volksgrenadiers* held Lutrebois.

There the German attack stalled. Although the day's gain extended what was already a salient in the American line to a depth of three miles and a width of four, a firm line sealed it on all three sides. The 26th Division attacking in the direction of Wilz threatened one flank of the German salient, while the 6th Armored Division passed through Bastogne and on New Year's morning attacked northeast, threatening the other flank. The fresh armored troops quickly took three places that had figured prominently in the early fighting for Bastogne: Bizory, Neffe, and Mageret.

The failure to sever the corridor into Bastogne convinced General von Manteuffel that he stood no chance of taking the town and that the time had come to abandon all thought of continuing the offensive in the Ardennes. Lest the troops in the tip of the salient be trapped, he appealed to Field Marshal Model on the night of January 2 for permission to fall back to a line anchored on Houffalize. Von Lüttwitz, who still had troops in the tip of the bulge, lent his voice to the appeal. He was convinced the British were soon going to hit the tip, a possibility lent credence by the identification near Rochefort of a British division.

Although Model agreed professionally, he had no authority to sanction withdrawal or even to desist in trying to take Bastogne. For his troubles in asking, von Manteuffel received merely another order to attack. What was left of the 12th SS Panzer Division was on the way, along with a *Volksgrenadier* division transferred from the vicinity of Aachen. With these reinforcements, von Manteuffel was to try once again to capture Bastogne on January 4.

On January 3, Hitler at last admitted that his original plan to cross the Meuse and capture Antwerp had failed. Yet he was convinced—or so he said—that the bulge forged in the Ardennes could be turned to German advantage. In launching the offensive, Hitler reasoned, he had forced General Eisenhower to employ almost all his resources; was not the use of elite airborne divisions to do the brutal defensive work of infantry proof of that? By holding the bulge, he might keep the Allies spread thin elsewhere while he assembled divisions for spoiling attacks, such as Operation *NORDWIND*. That way he could prevent Eisenhower from concentrating for a renewed offensive to gain the Ruhr. Yet if the bulge was to be held, he had to have Bastogne, both to anchor the southern flank and to deny the town's roads to his enemy.

Hitler by that time had already demonstrated how much he wanted Bastogne—enough to risk what remained of the Luftwaffe to prevent Allied fighter-bombers from intervening in von Manteuffel's efforts to take the town. At his order, the Luftwaffe mustered every available plane to strike British and American airfields in the Netherlands, Belgium, and northeastern France. In the hope that Allied pilots and antiaircraft gunners would be less than alert in the wake of New Year's Eve, the Luftwaffe struck early on New Year's Day.

Over the Netherlands that morning, the pilot of an artillery observation plane yelled unbelievingly into his radio: "At least two hundred Messerschmitts flying low on course 320 degrees!" What he saw was the vanguard of three groups of planes, a total of 1,035 Focke-Wulf 190s and Messerschmitt 109s coming in on the deck to hit twenty-seven Allied airfields where row after row of fighter-bombers stood in close formation.

No source of intelligence, including ULTRA, had provided any warning. In what Allied airmen would later call the "Hangover Raid," the Germans destroyed 156 planes, 36 of them American, most of them hit on the ground or while trying to take off. The losses included Field Marshal Montgomery's personal C-47.

They were heavy losses, but they could be quickly replaced (Eisenhower sent Montgomery his own C-47). The Germans paid with over three hundred planes and as many irreplaceable pilots, their heaviest losses in a single day during the entire war. As a senior German air commander noted, it was the Luftwaffe's "death blow."

The snow was deeper than ever in the Ardennes, the temperatures lower, the fog thicker, the chill winds more penetrating when early on

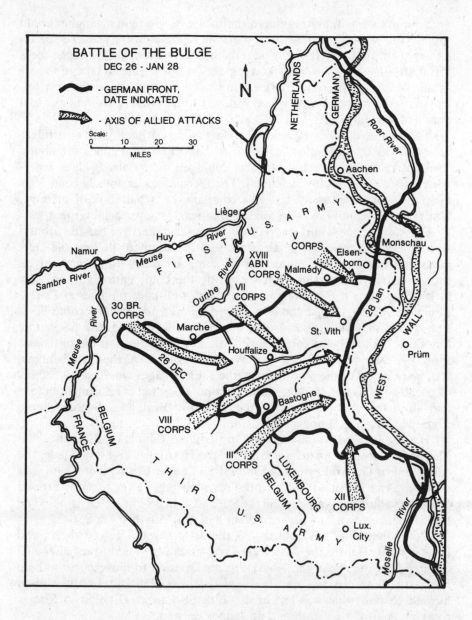

BATTLE OF THE BULGE
DEC 26 - JAN 28

- GERMAN FRONT, DATE INDICATED
- AXIS OF ALLIED ATTACKS

Scale:
0   10   20   30
MILES

N

NETHERLANDS

GERMANY

Roer River

Aachen

Liège

Huy

Meuse River

Namur

Sambre River

F I R S T   U S   A R M Y

V CORPS

XVIII ABN CORPS

VII CORPS

Malmédy

Elsenborn

Monschau

28 Jan

W E S T   W A L L

Prüm

30 BR. CORPS

Ourthe River

Marche

Houffalize

St. Vith

26 DEC

Bastogne

VIII CORPS

III CORPS

Luxembourg

BELGIUM

FRANCE

BELGIUM

T H I R D   U S   A R M Y

XII CORPS

Lux. City

Moselle River

January 3, Joe Collins sent the 2d and 3d Armored Divisions driving southeast from the Hotton-Soy-Manhay highway toward Houffalize. Three old adversaries—the 12th and 560th Volksgrenadier and the 2d SS Panzer Divisions—stood in the way. The *Volksgrenadier* divisions had only three thousand men each, the SS panzer division six thousand; yet that was sufficient, when added to the cruel terrain and weather, to impose a crablike advance.

So murky was the atmosphere that not a single fighter-bomber could support the attack, and sorties by artillery planes were possible for no longer than an hour. It was a pattern that underwent little change for a fortnight. On only three days were fighter-bombers able to take to the air at all. Much of the time the men advanced through snow flurries, followed on the fourth day by a heavy snowfall that piled drifts in places to a depth of several feet.

Tanks stalled on icy hillsides. Trucks towing antitank guns or artillery pieces skidded, jackknifed, collided, and blocked vital roads for hours. Two trucks towing 105mm. howitzers plunged off a cliff. Bridges everywhere were out, the sites defended. The Germans occasionally counterattacked—a brace or so of tanks, a company or a battalion of infantry. Under those conditions, two miles a day was a major achievement.

For men of the Third Army, it was even rougher, for the foe around Bastogne was himself trying to attack and represented the best the Germans still had to offer. Bitterly cold, stung by biting winds and driven snow, nostrils frozen and lungs seared by the cold, Patton's troops saw little change in a pattern long familiar. Such well-known names as *Panzer Lehr*, the *Führer Begleit* and *Grenadier Brigades*, the 5th Parachute Division, the 26th Volksgrenadier Division, the 1st, 9th, and 12th SS Panzer Divisions. Not the elite formations that had plunged out of the mists and snow on December 16, but worthy adversaries nevertheless. Familiar, too, were many of the place names, the same villages where small clumps of paratroopers, armored infantrymen, and a few tanks a fortnight before had thwarted the Germans in the race for Bastogne; Senonchamps, Champs, Mageret, Longvilly, Noville.

Having had no success against the corridor south of Bastogne, von Manteuffel struck from the north astride the Houffalize highway. Under the command of General Priess and the 1st SS Panzer Corps, there were four divisions: the 26th and 340th Volksgrenadier, the latter recently arrived from the vicinity of Aachen, and the 9th and 12th SS Panzer Divisions. The two SS panzer divisions between them had only fifty-five tanks.

Von Manteuffel anticipated that the attack would get nowhere, and he was right. Before the day of January 4 was out, Field Marshal Model ordered him to release the 9th SS Panzer Division to move north to help the Sixth Panzer Army, and the next day von Manteuffel took it upon himself to pull what was left of the 12th SS Panzer Division to form a reserve. A threat to Bastogne no longer existed.

Three days later, on January 8, Hitler finally agreed to a limited withdrawal from the tip of the bulge. It was not to go all the way back to Houffalize, as his field commanders wanted, but to a line anchored on the point where the two branches of the Ourthe join five miles west of the town. That was Adolf Hitler's first grudging admission that the offensive in the Ardennes had failed utterly.

*   *   *

Freddie de Guingand's appeal to four senior British newsmen in Brussels failed to stop the British newspapers from praising Montgomery and criticizing Eisenhower for not giving him overall command of the Allied ground forces. In an effort to quell it, SHAEF's public relations office on January 5 made the first public announcement of the shift of command in the Ardennes, noting that it had come about "by instant agreement of all concerned" and only because the German thrust had severed communications between Bradley's headquarters and the First and Ninth Armies. Yet far from quieting the British press, the announcement fueled the outcry.

At Luxembourg City, General Bradley was furious that SHAEF's announcement made no mention that the shift in command was temporary, and he and his staff saw the furor in the British press as "a cataclysmic Roman Holiday." So much of the comment involved either direct or implied criticism of Eisenhower that Prime Minister Churchill felt impelled to write President Roosevelt that "His Majesty's Government have complete confidence in General Eisenhower and feel acutely any attacks made on him."

According to Montgomery, he too was "perturbed. . . about the sniping at Eisenhower which was going on in the British press." He informed Churchill that he intended holding a press conference to explain "how the whole Allied team rallied to the call" in the Ardennes and "put in a strong plea for Allied solidarity." Churchill approved.

Most of what Montgomery had to say to newspapermen at his headquarters on January 7 reflected that purpose. He paid high tribute to the American soldier, who was "basically responsible for Rundstedt not doing what he wanted to do." He would "never want to fight alongside better soldiers" and singled out three particularly heroic stands: the Elsenborn Ridge, St. Vith, and Bastogne.

So, too, he praised Eisenhower. He was "absolutely devoted" to him, and it grieved him when he saw "uncomplimentary remarks about him in the British press." Eisenhower bore "a great burden," needed "our fullest support," and had "a right to expect it." "Let us all rally round the captain of the team."

Had that been all Montgomery said, no repercussions would have occurred; but some of his other remarks were imperious, after the manner of "St. George come to slay the dragon." Von Rundstedt, he said, had driven "a deep wedge into the center of the United States First Army and the split might have become awkward"; but "As soon as I saw what was happening I took certain steps myself to ensure that if the Germans got to the Meuse they would certainly not get over that river." He took "precautions," he was "thinking ahead." Nevertheless, "the situation began to deteriorate." Yet "the whole Allied team rallied to meet the danger; national considerations were thrown overboard; General Eisenhower placed me in command of the whole Northern front." (No mention of why.)

Then: "I employed the whole available power of the British Group of Armies," bringing it "into play very gradually" so as not to interfere with American lines of communication. "Finally, it was put into battle with a bang and today British divisions are fighting hard on the right flank of the United States First Army." Thus British troops were fighting alongside "American forces who have suffered a hard blow. This is a fine Allied picture."

Much of that was patently untrue. For a legitimate reason—so low were British manpower reserves that Montgomery had to husband the 30th Corps for the renewal of the drive into Germany—Montgomery had moved British troops only into reserve positions, sparing them the heavy casualties they were bound to incur if he sent them east of the Meuse. As he talked, "British divisions" were not "fighting hard on the right flank of the United States First Army," only the 29th Armoured Brigade, two battalions of the 6th Airborne Division, and the 53d Welsh Division, under orders to push the Germans back from the tip of the bulge, but cautiously, in order to avoid undue losses. Hardly "the whole available power of the British Group of Armies." Was that commitment "with a bang"?

The battle, Montgomery continued, had been "most interesting . . . possibly one of the most interesting and tricky" he had ever "handled." The first step, he said, was to "'head off' the enemy from the tender spots and vital places," then "rope him in and make quite certain that he could not get to the places he wanted, *and also* that he was slowly but surely removed away from those places."

Yet how much of that had Montgomery actually done?

- He wanted to pull back from the Elsenborn Ridge even as the battle there was almost won, but bowed to Hodges's objection.
- He wanted to pull back immediately from St. Vith, which would have afforded the Germans early use of a vital road network but again bowed to Hodges's objection; and by the time he specifically ordered withdrawal, Hodges had already specified that the decision on withdrawal was to be up to the man on the ground: Hasbrouck.
- He ordered the 82d Airborne Division to withdraw from the Salm River to the Trois Ponts–Manhay line, but Ridgway had already directed Gavin to prepare for such a withdrawal.
- He ordered relinquishing the Manhay crossroads, but in recognition that that opened to the Germans another route to the Ourthe River, Hodges ordered the crossroads retaken.
- He ordered Joe Collins to assemble for an attack, but when most of Collins's force became involved in the defensive battle, authorized with-

drawal. Collins attacked instead and stopped the Germans short of the Meuse.

• When it came to reducing the bulge, Montgomery moved so slowly—however "surely"—that the Germans were able to regroup undisturbed by the First Army for new assaults on Bastogne.

What, then, had Montgomery accomplished? His presence assured what conceivably might not have been possible with Bradley remaining in Luxembourg City: one hand at the helm. Yet Hodges and Simpson of the Ninth Army were old friends from the days of the Great War, and every division that moved to the Ardennes from the Ninth Army, with the exception of the 2d Armored Division, was on the way when Montgomery assumed command. Even without Montgomery's request for the 2d Armored Division, which was the Ninth Army's reserve, there was hardly any likelihood that Simpson would have withheld it; and even before Montgomery asked for Collins and the headquarters of the VII Corps, Hodges had already alerted Collins to move to the Ardennes and prepare to attack.

Montgomery's contribution rested in those "certain steps," the "precautions," the "thinking ahead," essential to positioning the divisions of the 30th Corps as a reserve behind the Meuse, which made it possible for Simpson to release divisions without undue concern that the Germans might take advantage of a thinned front. Yet as a loyal member of the Allied team, as Montgomery professed to be and was, he had already made that move even before Eisenhower put him in command.

There was no question but that Montgomery was highly complimentary on the achievements of American troops (wrote *The New York Times:* "No handsomer tribute was ever paid to the American soldier"), and the appeal for solidarity behind Eisenhower rang of sincerity. Yet the other remarks left the impression, as de Guingand noted, that Montgomery was saying: "What a good boy am I!" That as Montgomery himself later noted, he "appeared, to the sensitive, to be triumphant—not over the Germans but over the Americans."

For one as sensitive as Omar Bradley over the transfer of the Ninth Army and, most especially, his beloved First Army, probably anything Montgomery said would have rankled. ("Not only should I not have held the conference," wrote Montgomery later, "but I should have been even more careful than I was trying to be.") Bradley learned of Montgomery's remarks by what he took to be a broadcast by the BBC. In fact an Australian newsman, Chester Wilmot, believed what Bradley heard was his own dispatch to the BBC which the Germans had intercepted, altered, and rebroadcast over a propaganda station in the Netherlands. Whatever the case—and Bradley was as livid in later years, when he had had time to read accounts of the press conference, as he had been at the time—Bradley was "all-out right-down-to-his-toes mad."

He quickly telephoned Eisenhower, protesting both Montgomery's remarks and SHAEF's failure to note in its announcement that the transfer of command was temporary. Although fairly certain that Eisenhower would never make Montgomery overall ground commander, Bradley wanted to make his position unmistakably clear. "After what has happened," he said, "I cannot serve under Montgomery." If Eisenhower put Montgomery in overall command, he "must send me home." He added that Patton too had told him he would refuse to serve under Montgomery.

Without consulting Eisenhower (nor had Montgomery), Bradley called his own press conference, in which he defended his decision to hold the Ardennes lightly. Describing the circumstances of Montgomery's assuming command, he used the word "temporary" three times. He also said that as soon as the forces of the First and Third Armies joined hands, he was to reassume command of both the First and Ninth Armies. Although he knew that Eisenhower had already decided to leave the Ninth Army with Montgomery, he hoped his misstatement might prompt Eisenhower to reconsider.

A fortnight later Winston Churchill entered the arena to set matters right. Before the House of Commons on January 18, he noted that the battle in the Ardennes was primarily an American battle. "The Americans have engaged 30 or 40 men for every one we have engaged and they have lost 60 to 80 men for every one of us." It was, Churchill continued, "the greatest American battle of the war and will, I believe, be regarded as an ever famous American victory."

With that, the tempest was over. Adolf Hitler may well have learned of it and taken some comfort from it, but it was again no more than an intramural issue among proud military commanders and posed no threat to the Anglo-American alliance. Indeed, when Bradley told Eisenhower that if he had to serve under Montgomery, he would forfeit "the confidence of my command," he was overrating the importance of the issue. They read British newspapers and listened to the BBC at Versailles and Luxembourg City, but down in the foxholes, nobody read newspapers other than the *Stars & Stripes* (usually a day or so late) and nobody had radios.

Did it really matter to the American soldier, fighting for his life in the harsh cold and snow of the Ardennes, who commanded him at the top? Who was this Montgomery? Who was Bradley? Who, even, was Hodges or Gerow, Collins, or Ridgway? (Patton was another matter.) A front-line soldier was immensely well informed if he knew the name of his company commander, who had just arrived the day before to replace that other one who had lasted only a week.

As British units—the 29th Armoured and 34th Tank Brigades, the 6th

Airborne, 51st Highland, and 53d Welsh Divisions—left the tip of the bulge to regroup for a renewed drive to the Rhine, troops of the First and Third Armies plowed slowly but inexorably toward Houffalize. As juncture neared, a division in each army set out to achieve the honor of making the link-up.

In the First Army, that was the 84th Infantry Division, which formed a thirty-three-man patrol representing all battalions of the 334th Infantry. Shortly before noon on January 15, the patrol crossed the Ourthe near the confluence of the two branches of the river and settled down in a village to await arrival of troops of the 11th Armored Division. Word came late that night that the patrol was to move closer to Houffalize. At two thirty in the morning, cold and exhausted, the men holed up in a Belgian farmhouse, where the owner and his family welcomed them with bread, butter, and coffee.

At nine thirty the next morning, January 16, the second-in-command of the patrol, Pfc. Rodney Himes, spotted a soldier outside the farmhouse. Since all the men were under orders to stay inside, Himes beckoned the man in order to chew him out. He wasn't from the 84th Division, said the soldier; he was from the 41st Armored Cavalry Reconnaissance Squadron, 11th Armored Division.

That man had apparently strayed from his unit, which on orders from the commander of the 11th Armored Division, Brig. Gen. Charles S. Kilburn, acting on word from General Patton, had started out on January 15 to establish contact with the First Army. Because the squadron commander, Lt. Col. Miles Foy, was at the moment away, his executive officer, Maj. Michael J. L. Greene, led the advance.

Early on the 16th, Greene and his men reached high ground overlooking the east branch of the Ourthe and the rubble of a town nestled in the valley, which a sign along the road indicated was Houffalize. Some of Greene's men spotted soldiers moving along a crest on the far side of the river—they could be Americans, they could be Germans—and Greene sent a six-man patrol to investigate. When the squadron commander, Colonel Foy, arrived in his jeep, he set off in the wake of the patrol.

On the north bank, a motion picture cameraman, Staff Sgt. Douglas Wood, arrived in mid-morning at positions of a task force of the 2d Armored Division's CCA commanded by Colonel O'Farrell. Wood said he thought juncture between the American armies was imminent and he wanted to be on hand to film it. Having paid little attention to the possibility of a link-up and expecting relief momentarily by another unit, O'Farrell discouraged him. Wood was on the point of giving up when the commander of Company F, 41st Armored Infantry Regiment, asked Wood to film his men.

As Wood began filming the infantrymen in their foxholes, a figure emerged from a nearby wood. The men waved him forward, but the soldier paused briefly to beckon others behind him. They were from the 41st

Armored Cavalry Reconnaissance Squadron, 11th Armored Division, said the men, and having waded the river, they were goddamned wet and cold.

Close behind the patrol came Colonel Foy with his driver and radio operator, their jeep left down at the river. When Foy said he wanted to make contact with a senior officer, Sergeant Wood took him to find Colonel O'Farrell.

As they approached O'Farrell's tank, Wood called out: "There's a colonel here from the 11th Armored to see you, sir."

O'Farrell's head and shoulders emerged from the turret. "Well, Jesus Christ," blurted Foy, "if it isn't O'Farrell . . . Haven't seen you since Fort Knox."

That night the 2d Armored Division moved into Houffalize, and the next day, January 17, the First Army went back to the open arms of Omar Bradley.

On January 12, Hitler ordered the four SS panzer divisions pulled from the line to reserve positions near St. Vith, ostensibly to guard against an American attack along the base of the bulge, but in reality a first step in extricating the Sixth Panzer Army and leaving responsibility for what remained of the bulge to the Fifth Panzer Army. To von Rundstedt, that indicated that Hitler was at last facing reality in the Ardennes. Upon arriving at the *Adlerhorst* two days later and receiving no long lecture, he was sure of it. He seized the opportunity to ask not only for an immediate withdrawal behind Houffalize but for authority to withdraw by stages all the way to the Rhine, whose broad moat provided the only hope of stopping the Allied armies.

Even though Hitler had, indeed, accepted the inevitability of losing the ground gained in his offensive, von Rundstedt was asking too much. Approving withdrawal behind Houffalize, Hitler also authorized further withdrawal, when forced by American pressure, to the frontier and the West Wall. There the German armies were to stand. Soon after that he left the *Adlerhorst* for Berlin, and a week later, on January 22, he ordered the SS panzer divisions with the two SS corps headquarters shifted to the Eastern Front.

Although the soldiers of the German Army in the Ardennes deeply resented the withdrawal of the SS divisions, thinking they were to get a rest, they continued to resist with a tenacity that to American soldiers and their commanders defied explanation. For the most part, their resistance centered on occasional key high ground, at road junctions, and in villages. The villages were of importance to both sides, for only there was to be found protection from the cold. In most cases, it took direct fire from tanks and tank destroyers to blast the Germans out.

As the days passed, von Manteuffel and his corps and division commanders began to exceed the authority granted them by Hitler and sometimes authorized withdrawal even without American pressure, for it was vital to begin getting men and such vehicles as had gasoline back across the few tactical bridges spanning the Our River. When that happened, American units might advance for an hour or even half a day without a shot fired at them. Then, suddenly, at a stream bank, a farmhouse, the edge of a wood or a village, a flurry of fire from automatic weapons or shelling from mortars and artillery would erupt. Again a slow, costly fight to dig the Germans out, and then they almost always counterattacked with a company or a battalion.

Most of the American divisions that fought in the defensive phase joined the drive back. As a part of the First Army were the 1st, 30th, 75th, and 84th Infantry Divisions; the 82d Airborne Division; the 2d Division's 23d Infantry; the surviving regiment of the 106th Division; the 4th Cavalry Group; the separate 517th Parachute Infantry; and the 2d, 3d, and 7th Armored Divisions. As a part of the Third Army, the 4th, 5th, 26th, 35th, 80th, and 87th Infantry Divisions; the 101st Airborne Division; and the 6th and 11th Armored Divisions. Joining them were four units new to the Ardennes: with the First Army, the 83d Infantry Division; with the Third Army, the 6th Cavalry Group and the 17th Airborne and 90th Infantry Divisions.

Back to places with bitter memories: Baugnez, where the 30th Division found grisly snow-covered evidence of murder; Vielsalm, Salmchâteau, St. Vith, where a new commander of the V Corps, General Huebner, afforded the honor of entering the demolished town to the 7th Armored Division and General Hasbrouck in turn afforded it to Bruce Clarke's CCB; the Café Schumann crossroads; Wiltz, Clervaux, Consthum, Marnach, Diekirch, Fouhren.

On January 18, General Patton at last got a drive going—as he had always wanted—along the base of the bulge, an attack by General Eddy's XII Corps across the Sûre River and up the Skyline Drive. It was too late at that point to hope to trap large German forces, but the thrust speeded up an already frantic German scramble for the tactical bridges across the Our. On the 22d, as leaden skies finally cleared, pilots were early in the air, jubilant to find German vehicles stalled bumper to bumper waiting their turn to cross ice-encrusted bridges. Astride the Skyline Drive, infantrymen cheered to see the carnage that air and artillery wrought. By January 26, 1945, only a few small German delaying detachments remained, and they were all eliminated by the 28th, the official date set by the U.S. Army for the end of the Ardennes campaign.

Adolf Hitler in his desperate gamble had failed not only to reach Antwerp, which his generals never expected to gain, but he also fell short of his interim objective, the Meuse River, which his generals saw as a reasonably realistic goal. However it might be argued that Hitler had no alternative to ultimate defeat except, as von Clausewitz put it, "to regard the greatest daring as the greatest wisdom," to concentrate his forces in "one desperate blow . . . employing the assistance of subtle stratagem," all he accomplished was to assure swift success for the Red Army's renewed drive in the East and, possibly, to delay the Allied advance by a few weeks. In the end, he probably speeded his country's ultimate collapse.

Among 600,000 Americans eventually involved in the fighting—including 29 divisions, 6 mechanized cavalry groups, and the equivalent of 3 separate regiments—casualties totaled 81,000, of which 15,000 were captured and 19,000 killed. Among 55,000 British—2 divisions and 3 brigades—casualties totaled 1,400, of which just over 200 were killed. The Germans, employing close to 500,000 men—including 28 divisions and 3 brigades—lost at least 100,000 killed, wounded, and captured.

Both sides lost heavily in weapons and equipment, probably as many as 800 tanks on each side, and the Germans a thousand planes. Yet the Americans could replace their losses in little more than a few weeks, while the Germans could no longer make theirs good. Only foul weather, German ingenuity, and American recourse to the Small Solution prevented the Germans from losing even more men and machines.

The German soldier in the Ardennes amazed his adversary. Short of transport, short of gasoline, short of artillery because of the lack of transport and gasoline, his nation on the brink of defeat, he nevertheless fought with such courage and determination that the American saw him as fanatic. What motivated him to such ends? Was it the tradition of discipline dating from Frederick the Great? Unit loyalty? Personal honor? Fear of what defeat held in store for his country? Harsh discipline? Threats to his family? A pistol at his back? Whatever his motivation, he performed with heroism and sacrifice, marred only by the excesses of a few, primarily by the SS.

The victory in the Ardennes belonged to the American soldier, for he provided time to enable his commanders—for all their intelligence failure—to bring their mobility and their airpower into play. At that point the American soldier stopped everything the German Army threw at him.

A belief would long persist that when the Germans first struck, some American troops fled in disarray. In a book published as late as the fortieth anniversary of the battle, one historian noted that "during the early stages . . . hundreds of American troops fled to the safety of the rear in sheer panic."

That was patently false. Some individuals deserted, often getting as far back as Liège or Dinant before being apprehended. Yet with the possible exception of the conglomerate group of infantrymen hurriedly thrown together from men in a rest center to hold Honsfeld against Peiper's tanks, no front-line American unit fled without a fight. After hard fighting—out of ammunition, overwhelmed by tanks—some fell back in disorder, and there was indeed brief panic within the 9th Armored Division's CCR at Longvilly; but anybody with any knowledge of what it is like to confront the enemy would recognize that exigent circumstances were involved.

There were many cases where retreating troops, halted and thrown back into the line with some other unit, quickly melted away. Yet that is not an uncommon occurrence on the battlefield, for the individual lacks unit loyalty, his own noncommissioned and junior officers are no longer there either to inspire or to discipline him, and he has nobody to let down but strangers. On the other hand, those same men, again afforded unit identity, almost always rallied. A case in point was Team SNAFU in Bastogne.

What many did see—including Major Boyer on the road behind St. Vith—were supporting units hastily falling back. Yet in most cases those units had authority to withdraw. Why expose corps artillery pieces, big antiaircraft guns, ordnance and quartermaster depots, hospitals, replacement depots, whatever, to devastation or capture? Was anything gained by delaying withdrawal of the platoon of the 47th Field Hospital from Waimes so long that 2d Lt. Mabel Jessop and nine other nurses almost became victims of the massacre at Baugnez? Only when the withdrawing units clogged the roads did any form of panic develop. Anybody who has difficulty differentiating between hurried (even harried) withdrawal and panic should read Ernest Hemingway's *A Farewell to Arms*.

Except for a few individuals, the front-line American soldier stood his ground. Surprised, stunned, unbelieving, incredulous, not understanding what was hitting him, he nevertheless held fast until his commanders ordered withdrawal or until he was overwhelmed. If nobody ever achieved sufficient superiority on the battlefield to overwhelm his enemy and compel him to surrender or flee, nobody would ever win. It happens to one side or another in every battle, else there is stalemate, and it is folly to think that in every case the American soldier will be the one who wins.

Hitler saw the American soldier as the weak component (the "Italians") of the Western alliance, the product of a society too heterogeneous to field a capable fighting force. Bouck, Crawford, Tsakanikas, Umanoff, Moore, Reid, Descheneaux, O'Brien, Jones, Erlenbusch, Goldstein, McKinley, Mandichak, Spigelman, Garcia, Russamano, Wieszcyk, Nawrocki, Campbell, Barcellona, Leinbaugh. Black men, too, although their color was hardly to be reflected in their names. The heterogeneity was indeed there, but at many a place—at Krinkelt-Rocherath, at Dom. Bütgenbach, in the Losheim Gap, behind the Schnee Eifel, at St. Vith, atop the Skyline Drive, at the Parc Hôtel, Echternach, Malmédy, Stavelot, Stoumont, Bastogne, Verdenne, Baraque de Fraiture, Hotton, Noville—the American soldier put the lie to Hitler's theory. His was a story to be told to the sound of trumpets.

Epilogue

Well before the final victory in Europe, the U.S. Army began canvassing prisoner-of-war compounds in search of German soldiers who might have been involved in war crimes against soldiers and civilians in the American sectors, with particular attention to a search for the perpetrators of the Malmédy Massacre. Not until several months after the war ended was the search completed and five hundred former members of *Kampfgruppe Peiper*, along with their superiors, assembled for interrogation.

Among them was the commander of the Sixth Panzer Army, Dietrich; his chief of staff, Kraemer; the commander of the 1st SS Panzer Corps, Priess; and Peiper himself. All four were charged with an illegal order in regard to treatment of prisoners or with transmitting on illegal order and Peiper, in addition, with failing to give instructions on the disposition of prisoners of war.

Along with sixty-nine other suspects winnowed from the five hundred, the officers were transferred in the spring of 1946 to a detention barracks at the site of one of the most notorious Nazi concentration camps at Dachau. The trial began at Dachau on May 16, officially designated as *U.S.* v. *Valentin Bersin, et al.* (after a tank commander whose name came first alphabetically among the defendants). The prosecution charged that the defendants as a group

> did willfully, deliberately, and wrongfully permit, encourage, aid, abet and participate in the killing, shooting, ill treatment, abuse and torture of members of the Armed Forces of the United States of America, and of unarmed allied civilians.

There was a separate bill of particulars for each of twenty-four officers and forty-nine noncommissioned officers or enlisted men.

Among survivors of the massacre who testified for the prosecution either in pre-trial depositions or at the trial were Lieutenant Lary and Sergeant Zach; and among the Belgian civilians, André Schroeder on the

620

killings at Honsfeld and Madame Grégoire on the killings of civilians at Stavelot. Major McCown testified in defense of Peiper, basically to the effect that there were no killings of American prisoners at La Gleize and that Peiper and his men exhibited high military competence and treated their prisoners humanely.

During the course of the trial, the prosecution freely admitted gaining confessions through the use of hoods (as if the man was to be executed), false witnesses, and mock trials. All seventy-three defendants were nevertheless convicted. On July 11, 1946, they were sentenced:

> to death: 43, including Peiper.
> to life imprisonment: 22, including Dietrich.
> to prison for 10, 15, or 20 years: 18, including Priess (20 years) and Kraemer (10 years).

The prisoners were transferred to Landsberg fortress, where Adolf Hitler served time following his abortive *putsch* in Munich in 1923. An exhaustive review process then began. Each of two review boards recommended reductions in some of the sentences, citing irregularities in pretrial investigations and the trial itself, including a number of questionable procedural rulings by the bench. As finally recommended by the Theater Judge Advocate for War Crimes to the commander of the American Zone of Occupation, General Lucius Clay, Dietrich's sentence of life imprisonment should be confirmed, but thirteen convictions should be disallowed, and only thirteen of the forty-three death sentences (including Peiper's) should be carried out.

Those recommendations came only in the spring of 1948, by which time a Cold War had begun, and many Americans had come to look more kindly on their erstwhile enemy. Returned to civilian life, the chief defender, Col. Willis M. Everett, Jr., began a fervent campaign in behalf of the defendants. Like the review boards, Everett deplored both the methods used in the pre-trial investigation (two of the principal interrogators were German Jews who had emigrated to the United States upon the rise of Hitler) and the trial itself. Although Everett had never been in combat, he was convinced that the SS troops had acted without premeditation in the heat of battle and maintained that many an American soldier had killed prisoners under similar circumstances. Everett appealed to the Judge Advocate General in Washington, to the Supreme Court (which declined to hear the case), to the newspapers, and to a friend in Congress, who succeeded in getting the allegations before Secretary of the Army Kenneth Royall.

Royall created a three-man commission to review Everett's allegations (the commission upheld the thirteen death sentences) and called on General Clay in Germany for yet another review. Religious leaders and others in Germany began to appeal to the American Congress and to air their distress in the German press. More stories—not always substantiated—of ill-treatment of the prisoners emerged: broken teeth, blows to the genitals. Some American newspapers were soon expressing doubt about the findings of all war crimes trials and deploring the depths to which American military justice had sunk. A strange alliance of pacifists and right-wing, anti-Semitic groups joined the din; on the other side were the veterans' organizations.

In March, 1949, the Senate Armed Services Committee appointed a subcommittee to investigate the trial and Colonel Everett's allegations and invited the participation of a member of the Senate Investigations Subcommittee, who had tried unsuccessfully to obtain the investigation for his subcommittee. He was a junior senator, eager to distract attention from his own indictment for unethical conduct as an attorney and judge in his home state and equally eager for exposure to establish himself on the national scene. Since some of his constituents were wealthy, right-wing, and pro-German, the case was tailormade for him: Joseph McCarthy of Wisconsin.

McCarthy made a circus of the hearings. To demonstrate that he knew what was meant by the heat of battle, he paraded his own dubious war record as a pilot in the Pacific. It was pitiful, he shouted, that "16- or-17-year-old boys" should be "kicked in the testicles, crippled for life." So often did McCarthy raise the subject of genitals that "It sometimes seemed that [he] believed the quality of postwar American military justice to hinge on the condition of the sexual organs of German prisoners." He viciously attacked one of the pre-trial interrogators, a German-Jewish immigrant, and bluntly accused him time after time of perjury. He wondered if the officer would submit to a lie detector test; there would be, he said snidely, "no kicking in the groin or anything like that."

On May 20, 1949, McCarthy issued a press release, then took the floor before the subcommittee to accuse the U.S. Army of "Gestapo and OGPU tactics" and the subcommittee of attempts to "whitewash" the army's conduct in the Malmédy case. Declaring the hearings a "shameful farce," he stalked out of the room, soon to find another *cause célèbre* through which to project himself into the national limelight.

The final report of the Senate subcommittee proved or disproved nothing, but the widely publicized hearings put additional pressure on General Clay in Europe. Even as the hearings were under way, he commuted six of the thirteen remaining death sentences to life imprisonment. All the while furor was mounting in the German press, which, with the end of military government, had markedly increased. (Poor Peiper—his wife, his three blond children.) Yet another review board conducted a continuing examination of all cases of war crimes, and before long, the seven remaining death sentences for the Malmédy Massacre, including Peiper's, were commuted to life imprisonment.

As the Federal Republic of Germany neared full sovereignty and acceptance into the European family of nations, custody of the remaining prisoners passed to the Germans, and a board composed of three Germans and a representative each of the United States, Great Britain, and France was empowered to make recommendations for clemency and parole. In 1954, the board reduced Peiper's sentence to thirty-five years. In 1955, Dietrich was paroled; and shortly before Christmas, 1956, the last prisoner still in the Landsberg fortress, Joachim Peiper, having served (including pre-trial determent) eleven years, departed a free man.

Despite the campaign in Germany for the release of the Malmédy prisoners, Peiper found the environment hostile. He soon moved to Alsace to the village of Traves, where he supported himself and his family by translating books. All seemed to be well until in the summer of 1976 a sensational article on the notorious resident of Traves appeared in the French Communist newspaper *L'Humanité*. Two weeks later, fire bombs destroyed Peiper's house and killed the sixty-year-old former commander of *Kampfgruppe Peiper*.

Author's Note

At twenty-two years of age, I fought in the Battle of the Bulge as a rifle company commander and subsequently wrote an account of my wartime experiences, *Company Commander,* which led me to a career as a civilian historian with the United States Army.

During the forty years since the battle, there have been four histories by American authors, including a superb official military history by my friend and former mentor, Hugh M. Cole, which is the essential starting point for any research on the battle. Although I admire the three general works, I eventually became convinced that only someone who knew the fighting firsthand could capture the special aura of the battle, one who knew what it was like to live in a frozen foxhole under German shelling, to see German soldiers in greatcoats charging toward you like—it seemed to us—men possessed, to experience the numbing horror of mammoth tanks clanking toward you, their long cannon preceding them like something obscene.

I was further convinced that whoever that person was should also be able to bring to the story knowledge of military factors at the command level, what it meant to senior commanders to face the greatest crisis to hit the Western Front during the course of the war. At the same time, he should provide an interpretive account of the military campaign sufficiently interesting and understandable to attract the general reader.

With the encouragement of my friend John Toland, who wrote one of the early books on the battle, I concluded upon my retirement in early 1979 that I should attempt the assignment. I approached the work with a kind of messianic zeal, for I wanted to tell the story to my own satisfaction (the battle had shaped my life, and I have always felt that I left a little something of me in the Ardennes). I also wanted to tell it for the veteran of the battle, who in many cases knew little of what went on beyond hand grenade range of his foxhole, the veteran whose attention would surely be refocused on the battle upon its fortieth anniversary in

1984. And I wanted to tell it in terms understandable to the generations who have come after us, to demonstrate that we were no cardboard figures of history but young men with human frailties like everybody else, suddenly involved in a terrible struggle with which we somehow coped, almost always with fear, sometimes with cowardice, sometimes with courage that we never knew we had.

During my five years of research and writing, I returned to the Ardennes four times for months at a time. I traveled what seemed to me every way and by-way of what is today a beautiful region, found old foxholes (including my own) in fir forests, dug from them spent cartridges and corroded fragments of shells. I talked with many civilians who shared our ordeal, and I became closely acquainted with local historians and in particular with a group of men and women in Luxembourg who are dedicated to studying the battle and unearthing previously undisclosed information, the *Cercle d'Etudes sur la Bataille des Ardennes.*

Although considerable material exists on the actions and decisions of senior German commanders, I wanted to find out from soldiers of lesser ranks what it was like to fight us. Thus I arranged to interview many German veterans, corresponded with others, and obtained more than a thousand pages of published and unpublished materials, both personal accounts and unit histories.

In pursuit of fresh material from American veterans, I placed notices in veterans' publications and received a heart-warming response. I was particularly touched by the responses of two men who survived the dreadful Malmédy Massacre, who told me that they had never before talked publicly of their experience but were persuaded to do so in the belief that the man who wrote *Company Commander* would understand.

I can only trust that I have fulfilled their faith and my assumed responsibility to other veterans, as well as to readers from later generations.

Acknowledgments

Many people helped make this book possible. Credit to some is provided in the documentation by chapters, but there are others—Americans, Belgians, British, Germans, and Luxembourgers—to whom I owe special tribute.

United States: In the U.S. Army Center of Military History, Carol Anderson, Jefferson Powell, Mary Sawyer, John Wilson, and Hannah Zeidlick; in the National Security Agency, Wallace Winkler (now retired); in the Modern Military Records Branch, National Archives, John P. Taylor; in the Cartographic Branch, William Cunliffe, and Robert Richardson; in the Washington Federal Records Center, Victoria Washington and Fred Pernell; in the Office of Air Force History, William Heindahl; and in the Navy History Center, Dr. Dean Allard.

For diligent help in unraveling events on the northern shoulder, Ralph G. Hill, Jr., Wyomissing, Pa.; for assistance with events of their former divisions: Haynes W. Dugan, Shreveport, La., 3d Armored Division; Brig. Gen. Hal C. Pattison, Fairfax, Va., 4th Armored Division; Walter Berry, Falls Church, Va., 4th Division; Ken Danielson, East Point, Ga., and Generals Robert W. Hasbrouck, Washington, D.C., and Bruce Clarke, Arlington, Va., 7th Armored Division; Raymond L. Lewis, San Diego, Calif., CCB, 9th Armored Division; Robert H. Phillips, Springfield, Va., 28th Division; John Campbell, Rockville, Md., and Harold Leinbaugh, Fairfax Station, Va., 84th Division; Dr. Lyle J. Bouck, Jr., St. Louis, Mo., and Joseph C. Doherty, Alexandria, Va., 99th Division; and Francis H. Aspinwall, Ponchatoula, La., 106th Division.

For an order of battle and for commenting on the entire manuscript, a knowledgeable student of the battle, Danny S. Parker, Helena, Mont,; for German translation, Greg Kitsock, Ashland, Pa.; for the loan of unit histories, Fleming Fraker, Arlington, Va., and David Ruby, Pitcairn, Pa.; for permission to use Colonel Dickson's papers, Mrs. Benjamin Abbot Dickson, Paoli, Pa.; for the use of General Sibert's papers, Mrs.

Edwin Sibert, Martha's Vineyard, Mass.; for loan of research materials gathered for earlier books, my friends John Eisenhower and John Toland; and for maps, of which I am proud, my longtime friend Billy C. Mossman, and Robert Love and Harry Bruenhoefer of Blair, Inc., Falls Church, Va.

Belgium: For access to his voluminous files on events around St. Vith and for commenting on the entire manuscript, my friend Dr. Maurice Delaval, Vielsalm; for a conducted terrain study of the site of the gasoline depot near Stavelot, Lt. Col. Roger Hardy, Blankenberge; for help with interviews, Joseph Scholzen, Büllingen; for guiding me through the forests around Krinkelt-Rocherath, Paul Droesch, Büllingen; for unsurpassed Belgian hospitality and help with interviews, Sanny and Nicolas Schugens, Lanzerath; for help on events near Celles, Comte Jacques de Villenfagne de Sorinne; for the tragic story of Renée Lemaire, her sisters, Mmes. Gisèle Lemaire and Jacques Bourlet (Maggy Lemaire), Brussels; in the Syndicat d'Initiative, Bastogne, Simonne Schmitz; in the Bibliothèque de Stavelot, Maria DuBois and Marie-Louise Lejeune; in the Syndicat d'Initiative, Rochefort, Maria De Leeuw; at the Château de Froid-Cour, M. and Mme. Charles-Albert de Harenne; at Spa, George R. de Lame and members of the *gendarmerie;* at La Gleize, Gerard Grégoire; and as a host, guide, research assistant, and long-suffering consultant, a British subject currently living in Hedomont, my friend William C. C. Cavanagh.

Great Britain: In the Cabinet Office Historical Section, London, Eve Streatfeild and Mrs. H. E. Forbes; for help with ULTRA, Peter Calvocoressi, London, and Ralph Bennett, President, Magdalene College, Cambridge; for help on events at the tip of the bulge, historian and former Troop Sergeant, 3d Tank Regiment, Peter Elstob, London; and for incidental assistance, Roger Bell, Goodmayes, Essex, and Patrick Hargreaves, Keighley, Yorkshire.

Germany: For finding materials in German veterans' publications and locating veterans, Günter von der Weiden, Stolberg, and for a mammoth task of translation, Heino Brandt, Stolberg; and to both, my appreciation for traipsing about their country with me to help with interviews and to find Ziegenberg Castle and the site of the *Adlerhorst;* appreciation also to Dr. Adolf Hohenstein, Höfen, and Prof. Dr. Jürgen Rohwer, Bibliothek für Zeitgeschichte, Stuttgart; and to those who granted interviews which I was unable to use, particularly Fritz Schmäschke, München-Gladbach.

Luxembourg: For serving as a guide and reviewer of chapters, Pierre Eicher, Marnach; for interview and research assistance, Jean Milmeister, Tuntange; for locating headquarters sites, Jean Welter, Luxembourg City; and for hospitality and general assistance, President Camille Kohn and members of the *Cercle d'Etudes sur la Bataille des Ardennes (CEBA)*, Clervaux.

Special thanks to my agent, Carl D. Brandt, and my editor, Bruce Lee, both of whom displayed faith in this book long before they probably should have, and to one who should receive a campaign star, my superb copy editor, Ann Adelman. Special appreciation also to my editor with Weidenfeld & Nicolson in England, John Curtis.

U.S. INFANTRY REGIMENT
Strength: 3,257

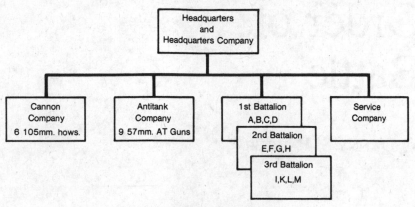

U.S. INFANTRY BATTALION
Strength: 836

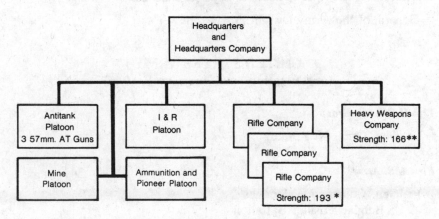

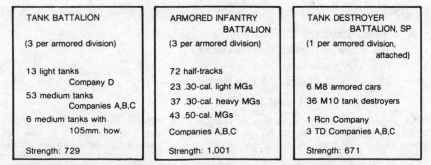

* (each with 3 rifle platoons of 3 squads each and weapons platoon with 2 .30-cal. light MGs and 3 60mm. mortars)

** (8 .30-cal. heavy MGs and 6 81mm. mortars)

Order of Battle

BY DANNY S. PARKER*

Supreme Headquarters Allied Expeditionary Forces (SHAEF)

General of the Army Dwight D. Eisenhower

UNITED STATES ARMY
(organization as of January 1, 1945)

12th U.S. Army Group

Lt. Gen. Omar N. Bradley

First U.S. Army

Lt. Gen. Courtney H. Hodges
    5 Belgian Fusilier Battalion
    143 and 413 AA Gun Battalions

V Corps

Maj. Gen. Leonard T. Gerow
    102 Cavalry Group, Mechanized
    613 TD Battalion
    186, 196, 200, and 955 FA Battalions

* With appreciation for the assistance of Michael Cox, Winston Hamilton, Victor Madej, William F. Murphy, Jr., Bruno Sinigaglio, Shelby Stanton, and Charles V. P. von Luttichau. Material is drawn from the author's war game, *The Last Gamble* (Tokyo: Hobby Japan, 1984).

254 Engineer C (Combat) Battalion
187 FA Group
   751 and 997 FA Battalions
190 FA Group
   62, 190, 272, and 268 FA Battalions
406 FA Group
   76, 941, 953, and 987 FA Battalions
1111 Engineer C Group
   51, 202, 291, and 296 Engineer C Battalions
134, 387, 445, 460, 461, 531, 602, 639, and 863 AAA AW Battalions

1st Infantry Division ("Big Red One") *

Brig. Gen. Clift Andrus
   16, 18, and 26 Inf Regiments
   5, 7, 32, and 33 FA Battalions
   1 Engineer C Battalion
   745 Tank Battalion †
   634 and 703 TD Battalions
   103 AAA AW Battalion

The division fought in North Africa, Sicily, Normandy, Aachen, and the Hürtgen Forest.

2d Infantry Division ("Indianhead")

Maj. Gen. Walter M. Robertson
   9, 23, and 38 Inf Regiments
   12, 15, 37, and 38 FA Battalions
   2 Engineer C Battalion
   741 Tank Battalion
   462 AAA AW Battalion
   612 and 644 TD Battalions

9th Infantry Division ("Octofoil")

Maj. Gen. Louis A. Craig
   39, 47, and 60 Inf Regiments
   26, 34, 60, and 84 FA Battalions
   15 Engineer C Battalion
   38 Cav Rcn Squadron (attached)

---

*In most cases, nicknames came from shoulder patches; some units had no nickname.
†Tank, TD, and AAA AW (Automatic Weapons) Battalions in infantry divisions were attached.

746 Tank Battalion
376 and 413 AAA AW Battalions

The division fought in North Africa, Sicily, Normandy, and the Hürtgen Forest.

78th Infantry Division ("Lightning")

Maj. Gen. Edwin P. Parker, Jr.
309, 310, and 311 Inf Regiments
307, 308, 309, and 903 FA Battalions
303 Engineer C Battalion
709 Tank Battalion
628 and 833 TD Battalions
552 AAA AW Battalion
CCR, 5th Armored Division (attached)
2 Ranger Battalion (attached)

The attack in support of the 2d Division's attack on the Roer River dams was the division's first action.

99th Infantry Division ("Checkerboard")

Maj. Gen. Walter E. Lauer
393, 394, and 395 Inf Regiments
370, 371, 372, and 924 FA Battalions
324 Engineer C Battalion
801 TD Battalion
535 AAA AW Battalion

The division had held a long defensive front in the Ardennes since mid-November, its only action.

VII Corps

Maj. Gen. Joseph Lawton Collins
4 Cavalry Group, Mechanized
29 Inf Regiment
French Light Inf Brigade
509 Parachute Inf Battalion
298 Engineer C Battalion
740 Tank Battalion
18, 83, 87, 183, 193, 957, and 991 FA Battalions
18 FA Group
188, 666, and 981 FA Battalions
142 FA Group
195 and 266 FA Battalions

188 FA Group
    172, 951, and 980 FA Battalions
342, 366, 392, 1308, and 1313 Engineer Gen Service Regiments

2d Armored Division ("Hell on Wheels")

Maj. Gen. Ernest N. Harmon
    41 Armored Inf Regiment
    66 and 67 Armored Regiments
    14, 78, and 92 Armored FA Battalions
    17 Armored Engineer Battalion
    18 Ren Battalion
    702 TD Battalion
    195 AAA AW Battalion

The division fought in North Africa, Sicily, Normandy, and in the vicinity of Aachen.

3d Armored Division ("Spearhead")

Maj. Gen. Maurice Rose
    36 Armored Inf Regiment
    32 and 33 Armored Regiments
    54, 67, and 391 Armored FA Battalions
    23 Armored Engineer Battalion
    83 Rcn Squadron
    643 TD Battalion
    486 AAA AW Battalion

The division fought in Normandy, the pursuit across France, and costly fall battles in the vicinity of Aachen.

83d Infantry Division ("Thunderbolt")

Maj. Gen. Robert C. Macon
    329, 330, and 331 Inf Regiments
    322, 323, 324, and 908 FA Battalions
    308 Engineer C Battalion
    772 TD Battalion
    453 AAA AW Battalion

The division fought in Normandy and at Brest, then after having rested briefly in the Ardennes, moved to the Hürtgen Forest.

84th Infantry Division ("Railsplitters")

Brig. Gen. Alexander R. Bolling
    333, 334, and 335 Inf Regiments

325, 326, 327, and 909 FA Battalions
309 Engineer C Battalion
771 Tank Battalion
638 TD Battalion
557 AAA AW Battalion

The division underwent its baptism of fire in November in the vicinity of Aachen.

XVIII Airborne Corps

Maj. Gen. Matthew B. Ridgway
14 Cavalry Group, Mechanized
254, 275, 400, and 460 FA Battalions
79 FA Group
153, 551, and 552 FA Battalions
179 FA Group
259 and 965 FA Battalions
211 FA Group
240 and 264 FA Battalions
401 FA Group
187 and 809 FA Battalions

7th Armored Division ("Lucky Seventh")

Brig. Gen. Robert W. Hasbrouck
CCA, CCB, and CCR
23, 38, and 48 Armored Inf Battalions
17, 31, and 40 Tank Battalions
434, 440, and 489 Armored FA Battalions
33 Armored Engineer Battalion
87 Rcn Squadron
814 TD Battalion
203 AAA AW Battalion

The division arrived in time to participate in the pursuit across France, encountered heavy fighting near Metz in September, and had another costly encounter in October in Holland.

30th Infantry Division ("Old Hickory")

Maj. Gen. Leland S. Hobbs
117, 119, and 120 Inf Regiments
113, 118, 197, and 230 FA Battalions
105 Engineer C Battalion
743 Tank Battalion
823 TD Battalion

99 Inf Battalion (attached)
517 Parachute Inf Regiment (attached)
526 Armored Inf Battalion (attached)
110 and 431 AAA AW Battalions

The division began fighting in Normandy in June, figured prominently in repelling a German attack at Mortain, and fought in November near Aachen.

75th Infantry Division

Maj. Gen. Fay B. Prickett
    289, 290, and 291 Inf Regiments
    730, 897, 898, and 899 FA Battalions
    275 Engineer C Battalion
    750 Tank Battalion
    629 and 772 TD Battalions
    440 AAA AW Battalion

The division's first action was alongside the 3d Armored Division in front of the Ourthe River.

82d Airborne Division ("All American")

Maj. Gen. James M. Gavin
    504, 505, and 508 Parachute Inf Regiments
    325 Glider Inf Regiment
    551 Parachute Inf Battalion (attached)
    376 and 456 Parachute FA Battalions
    307 Airborne Engineer Battalion
    80 AAA AW Battalion

The division made combat jumps in Sicily, Normandy, and Holland.

106th Infantry Division ("Golden Lions")

Maj. Gen. Alan W. Jones
    422, 423, and 424 Inf Regiments
    589, 590, 591, and 592 FA Battalions
    81 Engineer C Battalion
    820 TD Battalion
    634 and 563 AAA AW Battalions

The division's first action was in the Ardennes.

Third U.S. Army

Lt. Gen. George S. Patton, Jr.

109, 115, 217, and 777 AA Gun Battalions
456, 465, 550, and 565 AAA AW Battalions

III Corps

Maj. Gen. John Millikin
6 Cavalry Group, Mechanized
179, 274, 776, and 777 FA Battalions
193 FA Group
177, 253, 696, 776, and 949 FA Battalions
203 FA Group
278, 742, and 762 FA Battalions
183 and 243 Engineer C Battalions
1137 Engineer C Group
145, 188, and 249 Engineer C Battalions
467 and 468 AAA AW Battalions

4th Armored Division

Maj. Gen. Hugh J. Gaffey
CCA, CCB, CCR
10, 51, and 53 Armored Inf Battalions
8, 35, and 37 Tank Battalions
22, 66, and 94 Armored FA Battalions
24 Armored Engineer Battalion
704 TD Battalion
25 Cav Squadron
489 AAA AW Battalion

The division first saw action in Normandy in July and during the fall experienced heavy fighting in Lorraine and with the Third Army's drive to the Saar River.

6th Armored Division ("Super Sixth")

Maj. Gen. Robert W. Grow
CCA, CCB, CCR
9, 40, and 50 Armored Inf Battalions
15, 68, and 69 Tank Battalions
128, 212, and 231 Armored FA Battalions
25 Armored Engineer Battalion
86 Cav Squadron
777 AAA AW Battalion

The division entered combat in Normandy and exploited the breakout into Brittany, then fought through the fall in Lorraine.

26th Infantry Division ("Yankee")

Maj. Gen. Willard S. Paul

101, 104, and 328 Inf Regiments
101, 102, 180, and 263 FA Battalions
101 Engineer C Battalion
735 Tank Battalion
818 TD Battalion
390 AAA AW Battalion

The division experienced heavy combat near Verdun in September and had only recently been pulled from the line to absorb replacements when sent to the Ardennes.

35th Infantry Division ("Santa Fe")

Maj. Gen. Paul W. Baade
134, 137, and 320 Inf Regiments
127, 161, 216, and 219 FA Battalions
60 Engineer C Battalion
654 TD Battalion
448 AAA AW Battalion

The division entered the line in Normandy in July and figured prominently in stopping the enemy attack near Mortain, then fought through the fall in Lorraine.

90th Infantry Division ("Tough Hombres")

Maj. Gen. James A. Van Fleet
357, 358, and 359 Inf Regiments
343, 344, 345, and 915 FA Battalions
315 Engineer C Battalion
773 TD Battalion
537 AAA AW Battalion

The division took heavy losses in its first engagements in Normandy in June and through the fall fought in the vicinity of Metz and in the drive to the Saar River.

VIII Corps

Maj. Gen. Troy H. Middleton
687 FA Battalion
174 FA Group
965, 969, and 700 FA Battalions
333 FA Group
333 and 771 FA Battalions
402 FA Group
559, 561, and 740 FA Battalions

422 FA Group
    81 and 174 FA Battalions
178 and 249 Engineer C Battalions
1102 Engineer Group
    341 Engineer Gen Service Regiment
1107 Engineer C Group
    159, 168, and 202 Engineer C Battalions
1128 Engineer C Group
    35, 44, and 158 Engineer C Battalions
French Light Infantry (six Metz Light Inf Battalions)
467, 635, and 778 AAA AW Battalions

9th Armored Division

Maj. Gen. John W. Leonard
    CCA, CCB, CCR
    27, 52, and 60 Armored Inf Battalions
    2, 14, and 19 Tank Battalions
    3, 16, and 73 Armored FA Battalions
    9 Armored Engineer Battalion
    89 Cav Squadron
    811 TD Battalion
    482 AAA AW Battalion

The Battle of the Bulge was the division's first action.

11th Armored Division ("Thunderbolt")

Brig. Gen. Charles S. Kilburn
    CCA, CCB, CCR
    21, 55, and 63 Armored Inf Battalions
    22, 41, and 42 Tank Battalions
    490, 491, and 492 Armored FA Battalions
    56 Armored Engineer Battalion
    602 TD Battalion
    41 Cav Squadron
    575 AAA AW Battalion

The division's first action was west of Bastogne.

17th Airborne Division ("Golden Talon")

Maj. Gen. William M. Miley
    507 and 513 Parachute Inf Regiments
    193 and 194 Glider Inf Regiments
    680 and 681 Glider FA Battalions
    466 Parachute FA Battalion

139 Airborne Engineer Battalion
155 Airborne AAA AW Battalion

The division entered the line for the first time in late December west of Bastogne.

28th Infantry Division ("Keystone")

Maj. Gen. Norman D. Cota
 109, 110, and 112 Inf Regiments
 107, 108, 109, and 229 FA Battalions
 103 Engineer C Battalion
 707 Tank Battalion
 630 TD Battalion
 447 AAA AW Battalion

The division's first action was in Normandy in late July, followed by an attack into the Siegfried Line near St. Vith and heavy combat in the Hürtgen Forest.

87th Infantry Division ("Golden Acorn")

Brig. Gen. Frank L. Culin, Jr.
 345, 346, and 347 Inf Regiments
 334, 335, 336, and 912 FA Battalions
 312 Engineer C Battalion
 761 Tank Battalion
 549 AAA AW Battalion

Although committed briefly in the Saar region, the division's first major action was west of Bastogne.

101st Airborne Division ("Screaming Eagles")

Brig. Gen. Anthony C. McAuliffe
(Maj. Gen. Maxwell D. Taylor)
 501, 502, and 506 Parachute Inf Regiments
 327 Glider Inf Regiment
 1 Battalion, 401 Glider Infantry
 321 and 907 Glider FA Battalions
 377 Parachute FA Battalion
 326 Parachute Engineer Battalion
 705 TD Battalion
 377 Airborne AAA AW Battalion

The division jumped on D-Day in Normandy and later in Holland.

XII Corps

Maj. Gen. Manton S. Eddy

2 Cavalry Group, Mechanized
161, 244, 277, 334, 336, and 736 FA Battalions
177 FA Group
    215, 255, and 775 FA Battalions
182 FA Group
    802, 945, and 974 FA Battalions
183 FA Group
    695 and 776 FA Battalions
404 FA Group
    273, 512, and 752 FA Battalions
1303 Engineer Gen Service Regiment
452 and 457 AAA AW Battalions

4th Infantry Division ("Ivy"—for IV)

Maj. Gen. Raymond O. Barton
    8, 12, and 22 Inf Regiments
    20, 29, 42, and 44 FA Battalions
    4 Engineer C Battalion
    70 Tank Battalion
    802 and 803 TD Battalions
    377 AAA AW Battalion

The division landed on UTAH Beach on D-Day, fought in Normandy, helped liberate Paris, penetrated the Siegfried Line on the Schnee Eifel, and fought in the Hürtgen Forest.

5th Infantry Division ("Red Diamond")

Maj. Gen. S. Leroy Irwin
    2, 10, and 11 Inf Regiments
    19, 21, 46, and 50 FA Battalions
    7 Engineer C Battalion
    737 Tank Battalion
    818 TD Battalion
    449 AAA AW Battalion

The division entered combat in Normandy in July and took heavy casualties in the fall fighting for Metz.

10th Armored Division ("Tiger")

Maj. Gen. William H. H. Morris, Jr.
    CCA, CCB, CCR
    20, 54, and 61 Armored Inf Battalions
    3, 11, and 21 Tank Battalions
    419, 420, and 423 Armored FA Battalions

609 TD Battalion
55 Armored Engineer Battalion
90 Rcn Squadron
796 AAA AW Battalion

The division entered the line in Lorraine in late September and participated in the encirclement of Metz and the drive to the Saar River.

80th Infantry Division ("Blue Ridge")

Maj. Gen. Horace L. McBride
317, 318, and 319 Inf Regiments
313, 314, 315, and 905 FA Battalions
305 Engineer C Battalion
702 Tank Battalion
610 TD Battalion
633 AAA AW Battalion

The division began fighting in Normandy in August, had a hard fight for a crossing of the Moselle River in September, and in November participated in the drive to the Saar River.

U.S. ARMY AIR FORCES

U.S. Strategic Air Forces in Europe

General Carl Spaatz

Eighth Air Force (strategic)

Lt. Gen. James H. Doolittle

Ninth Air Force

Lt. Gen. Hoyt S. Vandenberg

IX Bombardment Division

Maj. Gen. Samuel E. Anderson

IX Troop Carrier Command

Maj. Gen. Paul L. Williams

IX Tactical Air Command (supporting First Army)

Maj. Gen. Elwood R. ("Pete") Quesada

XIX Tactical Air Command (supporting Third Army)

Brig. Gen. Otto P. Weyland

XXIX Tactical Air Command (supporting Ninth Army)

Maj. Gen. Richard E. Nugent

BRITISH ARMY

21 Army Group

Field Marshal Sir Bernard L. Montgomery

30 Corps

Lt. Gen. Brian G. Horrocks
     2 Household Cavalry Regiment
     11 Hussars and Cavalry Regiment
     73 Antitank Regiment
     4 and 5 Royal Horse Artillery Regiments
     7, 64, and 84 Royal Artillery Regiments
     27 Light AA Regiment

6th Airborne Division

Maj. Gen. Eric L. Bols
     3 and 5 Parachute Brigades
     6 Airlanding Brigade
     53 Light Royal Artillery Regiment
     3 and 4 Airlanding AT Battalions
     6 Royal Armoured Car Regiment

The division jumped on D-Day in Normandy.

51st Infantry Division (Highland)

Maj. Gen. T. G. Rennie
     152, 153, and 154 Inf Brigades
     126, 127, and 128 Royal Artillery Regiments
     2 Derby Yeomanry
     61 Antitank Regiment
     40 Light AA Regiment

A veteran division that had been fighting since Normandy.

53d Infantry Division (Welsh)

Maj. Gen. R. K. Ross

71, 158, and 160 Inf Brigades
81, 83, and 133 Royal Artillery Regiments
53 Rcn Regiment
71 Antitank Regiment
25 Light AA Regiment

Another veteran division that had seen heavy fighting in Holland.

29th Armoured Brigade

Brig. Gen. C. B. C. Harvey
23 Hussars Regiment
3 Royal Tank Regiment
8 Rifle Brigade
2 Fife and Forfar Yeomanry

A veteran brigade that had been scheduled to draw new tanks and equipment when ordered to the Ardennes.

33d Armoured Brigade

Brig. Gen. H. B. Scott
144 Royal Armoured Car Regiment
1 Northamptonshire Yeomanry
1 East Riding Yeomanry

A veteran brigade that had seen hard fighting in Normandy.

34th Army Tank Brigade

Brig. Gen. W. S. Clarke
9 Royal Tank Regiment
107 and 147 Royal Armoured Car Regiments

Having no infantry, the brigade fought closely with the 6th Airborne Division.

(In reserve, 43d and 50th Infantry Divisions and Guards Armoured Division.)

ROYAL AIR FORCE

Bomber Command

Air Chief Marshal Sir Arthur T. Harris

Fighter Command

Air Marshal Sir Roderic M. Hill

Second Tactical Air Force

Air Marshal Sir Arthur Coningham

GERMAN ARMY
(organization as of December 28, 1944)

OB WEST

Field Marshal Gerd von Rundstedt

Army Group B

Field Marshal Walter Model

Fifth Panzer Army

General der Panzertruppen Hasso von Manteuffel
    19 Flak Brigade
    207 and 600 Engineer Battalions
    653 Heavy Antitank Battalion
    669 Ost (East) Battalion
    638, 1094, and 1095 Heavy Artillery Batteries
    25/975 Fortress Artillery Battery
    1099, 1119, and 1121 Heavy Mortar Batteries
    3 Todt Brigade (paramilitary engineers)

47th Panzer Corps

General der Panzertruppen Heinrich von Lüttwitz
    15 Volkswerfer Brigade
    182 Flak Regiment
    766 Volksartillerie Corps

2d Panzer Division

Col. Meinrad von Lauchert
    3 Panzer Regiment
    2 and 304 Pzgr Regiments
    74 Artillery Regiment
    2 Rcn Battalion
    38 Antitank Battalion

38 Engineer Battalion
273 Flak Battalion

Reorganized after heavy losses in Normandy, the division had more than a hundred tanks and assault guns and many veterans still in its ranks.

9th Panzer Division

Genmaj. Harald von Elverfeldt
    33 Panzer Regiment
    10 and 11 Pzgr Regiments
    102 Artillery Regiment
    9 Rcn Battalion
    50 Antitank Battalion
    86 Engineer Battalion
    287 Flak Battalion
    301 Heavy Panzer Battalion (attached)

A veteran division recovering from losses incurred in Normandy when ordered from Holland to the Ardennes; with attached Tigers, the division had just over a hundred tanks.

Panzer Lehr Division

Genlt. Fritz Bayerlein
    130 Panzer Regiment
    901 and 902 Pzgr Regiments
    130 Rcn Battalion
    130 Antitank Battalion
    130 Engineer Battalion
    311 Flak Battalion
    559 Antitank Battalion (attached)
    243 Assault Gun Brigade (attached)

Virtually destroyed in Normandy, the division had been rebuilding when hastily committed to counterattack the Third Army in the Saar region. With no time to replace men and tanks before commitment in the Ardennes, the division was beefed up with attachments.

26th Volksgrenadier Division

Col. Heinz Kokott
    39th Fusilier and 77 and 78 VG Regiments
    26 Artillery Regiment
    26 Rcn Battalion
    26 Antitank Battalion
    26 Engineer Battalion

Often destroyed on the Eastern Front, the division was rebuilt for the Ardennes offensive under the old organization of three infantry battalions per regiment and had a strength of over 17,000 men.

Führer Begleit Brigade

Col. Otto Remer
102 Panzer Battalion
100 Pzgr Regiment
120 Artillery Regiment
120 Rcn Battalion
120 Antitank Battalion
120 Engineer Battalion
828 Grenadier Battalion
673 Flak Regiment

Built around a cadre of troops from Hitler's headquarters guard, the brigade included a tank battalion from the *Gross Deutschland Panzer Division* (still on the Eastern Front) and some infantry fillers from that division. It was strongly reinforced with assault guns and 88mm. and 105mm. pieces.

66th Corps

General der Artillerie Walter Lucht
16 Volkswerfer Brigade
86 and 87 Werfer Regiments
244 Assault Gun Brigade
460 Heavy Artillery Battalion

18th Volksgrenadier Division

Col. Hoffman-Schonborn
293, 294, and 295 VG Regiments
1818 Artillery Regiment
1818 Antitank Battalion
1818 Engineer Battalion

Formed in September in Denmark around a cadre from a Luftwaffe field division with many fillers from the Luftwaffe and the Navy; at full strength and with two months of experience on the defensive in the Eifel.

62d Volksgrenadier Division

Col. Frederich Kittel
164, 193, and 190 VG Regiments
162 Artillery Regiment

162 Antitank Battalion
162 Engineer Battalion

Rebuilt almost from scratch from a division destroyed on the Eastern Front with many Czech and Polish conscripts who spoke no German.

58th Panzer Corps

General der Panzertruppen Walter Krüger
    7th Volkswerfer Brigade
        84 and 85 Werfer Regiments
    401 Volksartillerie Corps
    1 Flak Regiment

116th Panzer Division ("Greyhounds")

Genmaj. Siegfried von Waldenburg
    16 Panzer Regiment
    60 and 156 Pzgr Regiments
    146 Artillery Regiment
    146 Rcn Battalion
    226 Antitank Battalion
    675 Engineer Battalion
    281 Flak Battalion

The division had strong unit pride. Although losses were heavy in Normandy and the Hürtgen Forest, replacements of fairly good caliber filled the ranks, and the division had over a hundred tanks and antitank and assault guns.

560th Volksgrenadier Division

Col. Rudolf Langhauser
    1128, 1129, and 1130 VG Regiments
    1560 Artillery Regiment
    1560 Antitank Battalion
    1560 Engineer Battalion

Formed from occupation troops in Norway in late summer of 1944, the division was poorly trained and was at first missing the 1129th Regiment; but the troops quickly gained battle experience and fought effectively in front of the Ourthe River.

29th Panzer Corps

Genlt. Karl Decker
(Brought forward at the end of December to control some of the troops at Bastogne: 1st SS Panzer Division; 901st Pzgr Regiment, *Panzer Lehr Division;* and the 167th Volksgrenadier Division.)

167th Volksgrenadier Division

Genlt. Hans-Kurt Höcker
    331, 339, and 387 VG Regiments
    167 Artillery Regiment
    167 Antitank Battalion
    167 Engineer Battalion

Virtually destroyed on the Eastern Front, the division was reformed in Hungary with replacements mainly from a Luftwaffe field division.

Sixth Panzer Army

Oberstgruppenführer der Waffen-SS Josef ("Sepp") Dietrich
    Von der Heydte Battalion
    506 Heavy Panzer Battalion
    683 Heavy Antitank Battalion
    217 Assault Panzer Battalion
    394, 667, and 902 Assault Gun Battalions
    741 Antitank Battalion
    1098, 1110, and 1120 Heavy Howitzer Batteries
    428 Heavy Mortar Battery
    1123 K-3 Battery
    2 Flak Division
        41 and 43 Regiments
    4 Todt Brigade

1st SS Panzer Corps

SS-Gruppenführer Hermann Priess
    4th Volkswerfer Brigade
        51 and 53 Werfer Regiments
    9th Volkswerfer Brigade
        14 and 54 Werfer Regiments
    388 Volksartillerie Corps
    402 Volksartillerie Corps
    501 SS-Artillery Battalion

1st SS Panzer Division ("Liebstandärte Adolf Hitler")

SS-Oberführer Wilhelm Mohnke
    1 SS-Panzer Regiment
    1 and 2 SS-Pzgr Regiments
    1 SS Artillery Regiment
    1 SS Rcn Battalion
    1 SS Antitank Battalion
    1 SS Engineer Battalion
    1 SS Flak Battalion

501 SS Heavy Panzer Battalion (attached)

The division had a reputation for daring and ruthlessness; with 22,000 men, it was one of the more powerful German divisions.

3d Parachute Division

Genmaj. Wadehn
    5, 8, and 9 Parachute Inf Regiments
    3 Artillery Regiment
    3 Rcn Battalion
    3 Antitank Battalion
    3 Engineer Battalion

Practically destroyed in Normandy, the division had been rebuilt in Holland, mainly from rear echelon Luftwaffe ground troops. Both troops and commanders were inexperienced.

12th SS Panzer Division ("Hitler Jugend")

SS-Standartenführer Hugo Kraas
    12 SS-Panzer Regiment
    25 and 26 SS-Pzgr Regiments
    12 SS Artillery Regiment
    12 SS Rcn Battalion
    12 SS Antitank Battalion
    12 SS Engineer Battalion
    12 SS Flak Battalion
    560 Heavy Antitank Battalion (attached)

The division had been rebuilt following heavy losses in Normandy and had approximately 22,000 men but was short of experienced junior officers.

12th Volksgrenadier Division

Genmaj. Gerhard Engel
    27 Fusilier and 48 and 89 VG Regiments
    12 Artillery Regiment
    12 Antitank Battalion
    12 Fusilier Battalion
    12 Engineer Battalion

After heavy losses in the summer of 1944 in Russia, the division was hastily rebuilt and hurried to halt American attacks around Aachen, where it earned the honorific *"Volksgrenadier."*

277th Volksgrenadier Division

Col. Wilhelm Viebig

289, 990, and 991 VG Regiments
277 Artillery Regiment
277 Antitank Battalion
277 Engineer Battalion

The division had only about a thousand veterans, many of the others being ethnic Germans from conquered border regions. A weak division.

150th Panzer Brigade

Obersturmbannführer der Waffen-SS Otto Skorzeny
    Two panzer cos., two Pzgr cos., and two antitank cos.
    A heavy mortar battalion (two batteries)
    600 Parachute Battalion
    Kampfgruppe 200 (Luftwaffe ground unit)
    An anti-partisan company

A makeshift formation hurriedly assembled to meet the special requirements that Hitler imposed on Skorzeny.

2d SS Panzer Corps

SS-Obergruppenführer Willi Bittrich
    410 Volksartillerie Corps
    502 SS Heavy Artillery Battalion

2d SS Panzer Division ("Das Reich")

SS-Brigadeführer Heinz Lammerding
    2 SS-Panzer Regiment
    3 and 4 SS-Pzgr Regiments
    2 SS Artillery Regiment
    2 SS Rcn Battalion
    2 SS Engineer Battalion
    2 SS Flak Battalion

A division with a reputation for brutality, it had experienced heavy fighting in Russia and then in Normandy. Rebuilt during the fall with replacements considered better than average.

9th SS Panzer Division ("Hohenstaufen")

SS-Oberführer Sylvester Stadler
    9 SS-Panzer Regiment
    19 and 20 SS-Pzgr Regiments
    9 SS Artillery Regiment
    9 SS Rcn Battalion
    9 SS Antitank Battalion

9 SS Engineer Battalion
9 SS Flak Battalion
519 Heavy Antitank Battalion (attached)

Rebuilt after heavy losses in Normandy and Holland, the division had many ethnic Germans from border regions and few veterans, but ethnic Germans from the Black Sea region of Russia were excellent soldiers. The division was badly short of transport.

67th Corps

Genlt. Otto Hitzfeld
    17 Volkswerfer Brigade
        88 and 89 Werfer Regiments
    405 Volksartillerie Corps
    1001 Heavy Assault Gun Company

3d Panzergrenadier Division

Genmaj. Walter Denkert
    8 and 29 Pzgr Regiments
    103 Panzer Battalion
    3 Artillery Regiment
    103 Rcn Battalion
    3 Antitank Battalion
    3 Engineer Battalion
    312 Flak Battalion

Transferred from Italy in the summer of 1944, the division lost heavily in fighting around Metz and later around Aachen. Refitted hurriedly for the Ardennes, the division lacked 20 percent of its strength in troops and 40 percent in equipment.

246th Volksgrenadier Division

Col. Peter Koerte
    352, 404, and 689 VG Regiments
    246 Artillery Regiment
    246 Antitank Battalion
    246 Engineer Battalion

Virtually destroyed on the Eastern Front, the division also lost heavily in the fall fighting around Aachen. Scheduled to attack at Monschau, the division arrived late.

272d Volksgrenadier Division

Col. Georg Kosmalla

980, 981, and 982 VG Regiments
272 Artillery Regiment
272 Antitank Battalion
272 Engineer Battalion

Virtually destroyed in Normandy, the division had been hastily rebuilt and committed in the vicinity of Monschau, where it was scheduled to attack but instead fought defensively against the American 78th Division.

326th Volksgrenadier Division

Col. Erwin Kaschner
751, 752, and 753 VG Regiments
326 Artillery Regiment
326 Antitank Battalion
326 Engineer Battalion

Rebuilt following the withdrawal from France with generally inexperienced and poorly trained troops.

Seventh Army

General der Panzertruppen Erich Brandenberger
657 and 668 Heavy Antitank Battalions
501 Fortress Antitank Battalion
47 Engineer Battalion
1092, 1093, 1124, and 1125 Heavy Howitzer Batteries
660 Heavy Artillery Battery
1029, 1039, and 1122 Heavy Mortar Batteries
999 Penal Battalion
44 Machine Gun Battalion
15 Flak Regiment
1 Todt Brigade

53d Corps

General der Kavallerie Edwin von Rothkirch
(Brought forward on December 22 to command the 5th Parachute— see 85th Corps—and 15th Panzergrenadier Divisions and the *Führer Grenadier Brigade* at Bastogne.)

9th Volksgrenadier Division

Col. Werner Kolb
36, 57, and 116th VG Regiments
9 Artillery Regiment
9 Antitank Battalion

9 Engineer Battalion

After heavy losses in Romania in the fall of 1944, refitted and moved to Denmark for training. First committed in the Ardennes on December 28.

15th Panzergrenadier Division

Col. Hans-Joachim Deckert
104 and 115 Pzgr Regiments
115 Panzer Battalion
115 Artillery Regiment
115 Rcn Battalion
33 Antitank Battalion
33 Engineer Battalion
315 Flak Battalion

Transferred from Italy in late summer of 1944, the division during the fall served as a kind of fire brigade, fighting both around Aachen and in the Vosges. Not fully refitted for the Ardennes.

Führer Grenadier Brigade

Col. Hans-Joachim Kahler
99 Pzgr Regiment
101 Panzer Battalion
911 Assault Gun Brigade
124 Antitank Battalion
124 Rcn Battalion
124 Engineer Battalion
124 Flak Battalion
124 Artillery Regiment

Formed from a nucleus of troops who provided the outer rim of defense for Hitler's headquarters, the brigade had a brief and costly commitment on the Eastern Front before arriving piecemeal in the Ardennes.

80th Corps

General der Infanterie Franz Beyer
408 Volksartillerie Corps
8 Volkswerfer Brigade
2 and *Lehr* Werfer Regiments

212th Volksgrenadier Division

Genmaj. Franz Sensfuss
316, 320, and 423 VG Regiments
212 Artillery Regiment
212 Antitank Battalion

212 Engineer Battalion

Despite heavy losses on the Eastern Front, the division retained a large cadre of experienced officers and noncommissioned officers, and its replacements, largely from Bavaria, were above average. It was the best division in the Seventh Army.

276th Volksgrenadier Division

Gen. Kurt Möhring (later Col. Hugo Dempwolff)
986, 987, and 988 VG Regiments
276 Artillery Regiment
276 Antitank Battalion
276 Engineer Battalion

Formed from the shell of another division destroyed in Normandy, the division had a number of hospital returnees but not enough to make up for other poorly trained replacements and inexperienced leaders.

340th Volksgrenadier Division

Col. Theodor Tolsdorff
(committed in late December at Bastogne under the 1st SS Panzer Corps)
694, 695, and 696 VG Regiments
340 Artillery Regiment
340 Antitank Battalion
340 Engineer Battalion

Having absorbed the remnants of another division, the division had more veterans than most, but since it had only recently come from the line near Aachen, it was considerably under strength.

85th Corps

General der Infanterie Baptist Kniess
406 Volksartillerie Corps
18 Volkswerfer Brigade
21 and 22 Werfer Regiments

5th Parachute Division

Col. Ludwig Heilmann
13, 14, and 15 Parachute Inf Regiments
5 Artillery Regiment
5 Rcn Battalion
5 Engineer Battalion
5 Flak Battalion

11 Assault Gun Brigade

Virtually destroyed in Normandy, the division had been refitted over the fall and had close to 16,000 men. Both the division commander and the regimental commanders were inexperienced in combat.

352d Volksgrenadier Division

Col. Erich Schmidt
  914, 915, and 916 VG Regiments
  352 Artillery Regiment
  352 Antitank Battalion
  352 Engineer Battalion

Reconstructed almost from scratch with a great influx of Luftwaffe and Navy replacements to a strength of 13,000, the division was poorly trained and lacked experienced officers.

79th Volksgrenadier Division

Col. Alois Weber
  208, 212, and 226 VG Regiments
  179 Artillery Regiment
  179 Antitank Battalion
  179 Engineer Battalion

Totally destroyed in the summer of 1944 on the Eastern Front (one man survived), the division had men culled mainly from rear area headquarters.

LUFTWAFFE

II Fighter Corps

Genmaj. Dietrich Peltz

III Flak Corps

Genlt. Wolfgang Pickert

Notes

PROLOGUE

For events at Bande: Commission des Crimes de Guerre, Ministère de la Justice, Royaume de Belgique, *Les Crimes de Guerre—Bande* (Liège: Georges Thone, 1950).

"I have made a momentous decision" (p. 11), Cole, *The Ardennes*, p. 2.

For the story of Elise Delé-Dunkel, author's interview (assisted by Jean Milmeister) with Mme Delé, Bivels, Luxembourg, 24 Aug 81; corrections of an early draft by Mme Delé, 30 Aug 82; and G-2 journals as noted.

CHAPTER I: THE DECISION, THE SETTING, AND THE PLAN

For "knocked from Britannia's hand" (p. 17), MS # C-065i, *Ministerialrat im OKW* Dr. Helmut Greiner, "Operation *BARBAROSSA*."

"Probing the Soviet attitude" (p. 19), Irving, *Hitler's War*, p. 773.

"Ultra-capitalist states on one side" (p. 20), Stenographic Account of Staff Conferences of Adolf Hitler and German High Command, Fragment No. 39, S. L. A. Marshall Military History Collection, University of Texas, El Paso.

Von Rundstedt at the *Wolfschanze* (p. 21), Warlimont, *Inside Hitler's Headquarters*, p. 477.

Marshall Foch and "If you go into that death-trap" (p. 23), Charles B. MacDonald, "The Neglected Ardennes," *Military Review*, Apr 63.

Oshima's conference with Hitler (p. 25), War Dept—ACofS G-2—No. 897, 8 Sep 44, RG (Record Group) 457 (Records of the National Security Agency), Box 10, "MAGIC" Diplomatic Summary, 1944, NA (National Archives).

"One of the most important tasks in this offensive" and following quotations (p. 32), Otto Skorzeny, *Special Mission* (London: Futura Publications, no date but c. 1958), p. 145.

For "excessively modest, too reserved" (p. 33) and following quotations, MS # B-344, Gen der Inf Günther Blumentritt, "Three Marshals, National Character, and the 20 July Complex."

"His manner was rough" and "My dear Bayerlein" (p. 33), Brett-Smith, *Hitler's Generals*, p. 200, citing von Manteuffel to B. H. Liddell-Hart.

"A field marshal does not become a prisoner" (p. 34), MS # B-593, Genmaj Carl Wagener, "*Army Group B* (22 Mar–17 Apr 45)."

For "to change the guards" (p. 34), Elstob, *Hitler's Last Offensive*, p. 36n, citing von Rundstedt to B. H. Liddell-Hart.

For "correct but not cordial" (p. 34), Cole, *The Ardennes*, pp. 23–24.

For "a stroke of genius" and "all, absolutely all" (p. 35), Rundstedt Testimony, *Trial of the Major War Criminals Before the International Military Tribunal*, Vol. XXXI, p. 29.

"This plan hasn't got a damned leg to stand on" (p. 35), Charles V. P. von Luttichau, Report on the Interview (14–19 May 52) with Thuisko von Metzsch (one of Model's staff officers) on Operations of *Army Group B* and Its Role in the German Ardennes Offensive 1944, CMH (Center of Military History).

For "unalterable" and "In our present situation" (p. 36), ltr, Jodl to Westphal, 1 Nov 44, *OB WEST, KTB Anlage 50*, Vol. I. pp. 30–31, as cited in Cole, p. 28.

"I think under your plan" (p. 36), Eisenhower interv with von Manteuffel.

"Preparations for an improvisation" (p. 37), msg, Jodl to von Rundstedt, 22 Nov 44, *OB WEST, KTB Anlage 50*, Vol. II, p. 12, as cited in Cole, p. 31.

"All Hitler wants me to do" (p. 37), Elstob, p. 56.

For "continue this battle" (p. 38), Gilbert, ed., *Hitler Directs His War*, p. 106.

CHAPTER II: THE DECEPTION AND THE INTELLIGENCE APPARATUS

For "there can be no doubt" (p. 40), *OB WEST KTB*, 6 Nov 44, as cited in MacDonald, *The Siegfried Line Campaign*, p. 394.

"Miracle of the West" (p. 43), MacDonald, p. 392.

For "a broken man" (p. 47), MS # B-151a, von Manteuffel, "The *5 Pz Army* and the Offensive in the Ardennes."

"Our thoughts wandered" (p. 48), ltr, Stiegeler to Günter von der Weiden, 18 Jan 82.

For Oshima's report on conference with von Ribbentrop (p. 49), War Dept—ACofS G-2—No. 970, 20 Nov 44, RG 457, Box 10, "MAGIC" Diplomatic Summary, 1944, NA, and additional msg No. 79712, 22 Nov 44.

"Monty's suggestion is simple" (p. 50), Kay Summersby, *Eisenhower Was My Boss* (New York: Prentice-Hall, 1948), p. 170.

"Two and a half months of bitter fighting" (p. 51), SHAEF Weekly Intelligence Summary 22, 27 Aug 44.

"The defeat . . . is complete" (p. 51), Diary, Office of the Commander-in-Chief, 5 Sep 44, SHAEF files.

For political upheaval within Germany (p. 51), FUSA (First U.S. Army) G-2 Estimate 24, 3 Sep 44.

For "deliver the original in thirty days" (p. 51), Bradley, *A Soldier's Story*, p. 426.

For Colonel Koch's G-2 estimate (p. 52), TUSA G-2 Estimate 9, 28 Aug 44.

"The dwindling fire brigade" (p. 53), SHAEF G-2 Weekly Intelligence Summary 30, 15 Oct 44.

For large-scale surrenders (p. 53), FUSA G-2 Estimate 36, 20 Nov 44.

"It is now certain" (p. 53), 12th AGp (Army Group) G-2 Summary 18, 12 Dec 44.

"I wonder what is wrong with him" (p. 54), Pogue interv with Sibert, 11 May 51. (All Dr. Pogue's interviews conducted for his volume *The Supreme Command* are in the U.S. Army Military History Research Collection, Carlisle Barracks, Pa.)

For personality conflict between Dickson and Kean (p. 55), Pogue interv with Adolph G. Rosengarten, Jr., ULTRA officer in G-2 Sect, FUSA, 22 Dec 47, and author's intervs with various members of the FUSA staff.

For "hated Sibert and the latter reciprocated" (p. 55), *ibid.*

For Dickson visits to Williams (p. 55), Pogue intervs with Williams, 30–31 May 45, and with Sibert, *op. cit.*

"Monk's shrubbery" and a man who sometimes had to be sat on (p. 55), Pogue intervs with Williams. See also Pogue interv with Rosengarten and ltr to the author from Rosengarten, 4 Jun 82.

"I don't want a man from OSS" (p. 56), Pogue interv with Sibert and Col. William H. Jackson, Sibert's deputy, 11 May 51.

"He fools some of the people" (p. 56), Baldwin, *Battles Lost and Won*, p. 363.

For not a single OSS agent (p. 56), CIA, memo to Sibert by Luman B. Kirkpatrick, subj: Operations of OSS with 12th Army Group, no date, Sibert papers.

For "absolutely no indication" (p. 57), Histories of Radio Intelligence Units European Theater September 1944 to March 1945, Vol. I, NA.

"No confirmation" (p. 57), 106th Div G-2 Periodic Rpt, 12 Dec 44.

"A sonnet written by a machine" (pp. 57–58), Lewin, *Ultra Goes to War*, p. 20.

For "the unpredictable waywardness of genius" (p. 58), Lewis, p. 40.

For "long hair . . . dirty clothes" (p. 58), Garlinski, *The Enigma War*, p. 69.

For "a large copper-coloured cupboard" (p. 58), Garlinski, p. 68.

CHAPTER III: WHAT DID THE ALLIES KNOW?

All direct quotes from German messages are either from Bennett, *Ultra in the West*, or from the messages themselves as found in the Cabinet Office Historical Section. For uses of ULTRA in American headquarters, see: American Embassy, London, Memorandum for Colonel Taylor, subj: Report of Lt. Col. Munane and Lt. Col. Orr on Use of Ultra at 12th Army Group, and subj: Report on Ultra Intelligence at First U.S. Army, Lt. Col. Adolph G. Rosengarten, Jr., both in NA; and Lt. Col. M. C. Helfers, unpublished MS, "My Personal Experience with High Level Intelligence," Nov 74, courtesy of the author.

Strong's G-2 Rpt of 1 Oct (p. 62), SHAEF Weekly Intelligence Summary 28, 1 Oct 44.

Strong's G-2 Rpt on *Fifth Panzer Army* (p. 63), SHAEF Weekly Intelligence Summary 33, 5 Nov 44.

Sibert's report (p. 63), 12th AGp Weekly Intelligence Summary 9, 7 Oct 44.

For "a truly colossal effort" and "final showdown" (p. 64), SHAEF Weekly Intelligence Summary 34, 12 Nov 44.

Summary of Allied intelligence view (pp. 64–65), Lt. Col. Harry L. Dull, Jr., Classified Annex to Addendum to U.S. Army War College Military Research Program Paper, "The Ultra Study," 25 May 77, NA.

For "a calculated risk" (p. 68), Bradley and Blair, *A General's Life*, p. 373.

For "the First Army is making a terrible mistake" (p. 68), Blumenson, *The Patton Papers*, p. 582.

For "to launch a spoiling . . . offensive" and "We'll be in a position" (pp. 68–69), Brig. Gen. Oscar W. Koch with Robert G. Hays, *G-2: Intelligence for Patton* (Philadelphia: Whitmore Publishing Co., 1971), p. 86.

For "to mount a spoiling offensive" (p. 69), TUSA G-2 Periodic Rpts 186 and 188, 13 and 14 Dec 44.

Skorzeny's order (p. 69) is reproduced in a preliminary draft of an unpublished MS by Dickson in Toland files, LofC (Library of Congress). See also Eisenhower, *The Bitter Woods*, pp. 165–166.

For "desperate men" (p. 69), Pogue interv with Rosengarten.

For Mendenhall's study (p. 69), see Col. B. A. Dickson and Ivan H. Peterman, unpublished MS, "We Wouldn't Be Warned in the Bulge," Toland files, LofC.

For "deft, sure hand" (p. 70), Dickson, unpublished MS known as Monk Dickson's Journal and entitled "Algiers to the Elbe," Dickson papers.

For "when anyone attacks" (p. 71), Bradley, *A Soldier's Story*, p. 454.

For "we could chew them up" (p. 71), Sibert, unpublished MS, "Military Intelligence Aspects of the Period Prior to the Ardennes Counteroffensive," Sibert papers.

For "get Dickson straightened out" (p. 72) and "stressed the optimistic picture" (p. 73), Pogue interv with Sibert and Jackson, *op. cit.*

"We cannot really feel satisfied" (p. 73), SHAEF Weekly Intelligence Summary 38, 10 Dec 44.

For "at least a fortnight" (p. 73), Pogue, *The Supreme Command*, p. 365n, citing ltr from Strong, 31 Aug 45.

For "a nasty little Kasserine" (p. 73), Pogue, p. 361.

For "aware of the danger" (p. 73), Pogue citing ltr from Strong, p. 365n. See also Pogue interv with Sibert and Jackson, *op. cit.*

For "to make a fighting withdrawal" (p. 74), Bradley and Blair, p. 354.

"The enemy's present practice" (p. 74), Eisenhower, *The Bitter Woods*, pp. 174–175. Judge Malcolm R. Wilkey, Washington, D.C., formerly a member of the G-2 Sect, VIII Corps, provided the author with an unpublished MS prepared over the period January–March 1945, "Summary of G-2 Estimates re Battle of the Bulge, 15 November 1944–9 March 1945."

"Whereas previously the Germans" (p. 75), Hanson W. Baldwin, "The Battle of the Bulge as a Case History in Battlefield Intelligence," *Combat Forces Journal*, citing ltr from Simpson, 29 May 46.

For "the relief is now complete" (p. 75), 2d Div G-2 Periodic Rpt, 10 Dec 44.

"Go back to sleep, Robbie," (p. 75), author's interv with Maj. Gen. Ralph W. Zwicker, CofS, 2d Inf Div, 4 Mar 82.

For "in towns close to the front" (p. 75), V Corps G-2 Periodic Rpt, 15 Dec 44.

For "a major counterattack" and "probable" (p. 75), 2d Div G-2 Periodic Rpts, 11 and 12 Dec 44.

For "many PWs" and "between the 17th and 25th of December" (p. 76), FUSA G-2 Periodic Rpt 189, 15 Dec 44, which reflected information available to Dickson on the 14th.

"It's the Ardennes!" (p. 76), Dickson draft MS, Toland files, *op. cit.*

For the "black propaganda" incident (p. 76), Bradley, *A Soldier Reports*, pp. 426–427; Dickson's involvement provided by Rosengarten.

"A very interesting report" (p. 77), FUSA G-2 Periodic Rpt 189.

For Tasker's prediction (p. 77), see Lt. Gen. Lewis H. Brereton, *The Brereton Diaries* (New York: William Morrow, 1946), p. 387.

For "visiting galaxy" (p. 77), unpublished diary kept by Hodges's aide, Maj. William C. Sylvan, CMH.

Allied air commanders' conference (p. 78) and for "the enemy could still do something" and "had looked in a mirror" (p. 79), Cole.

CHAPTER IV: THE LAST FEW HOURS

For "had more forces hidden" (p. 85), Eisenhower interv with Von Manteuffel, 12 Oct 66.

For "strong enemy forces" (p. 85), MS # B-151a, von Manteuffel.

"There will be no deviation" (p. 86), Eisenhower, *The Bitter Woods*, p. 161.

On the wearing of enemy uniforms (p. 87), Skorzeny, *Special Mission*, p. 149. For a more studied analysis of the subject, see Eisenhower, p. 124n.

For "deceive very young American troops" (pp. 87–88) and "Well, go and think it all over" (pp. 88), Skorzeny, pp. 155 and 158–159.

For "more fit for bicycles" (p. 89), ETHINT (European Theater Historical Interview) 10, Peiper.

For "not necessarily a great victory" (p. 90), author's interv with Wortmann, 16 Oct 82.

For "perhaps in the process" (p. 90), author's interv with Osterhold, 16 Oct 82.

"There is a general feeling of elation" (p. 90), Merriam, *Dark December*, p. 37.

"I write during one of the great hours" (p. 90), Annex 3 to 1st Div G-2 After Action Rpt, Dec 44, "Captured Letter" ('We March'). See observations on morale in MS # B-151a, Von Manteuffel.

For "a temper when tested" (p. 91), ltr, Col. Ralph V. Steele, Exec O, 9th Inf, to Joseph C. Doherty, 8 Apr 82.

For "in a large-scale offensive" (p. 94), Royce L. Thompson, "American Intelligence on the German Counteroffensive," prepared in support of Cole, *The Ardennes*, CMH.

For "sound of vehicles . . . barking dogs" (p. 94), 106th Div G-2 Periodic Rpt, 15 Dec 44.

For "much saluting" (p. 94), Thompson, *op. cit.*

For "large enemy formations in Bitburg" (p. 94), author's interv with Barton, 10 Jun 54, CMH.

"Don't worry" (p. 94), author's interv with Col. Léon Kimmes, Luxembourg Army, 21 Aug. 81.

For "a more active participant" (p. 95), ltrs to the author from Allard, 17 May and 9 Jun 82. Allard's twin brother survived as a prisoner of war.

"Tomorrow the heavies'll start firing again" (p. 95), Charles Whiting, *Death of a Division* (New York: Stein and Day, 1980), p. 4. Whiting has some new material from interviews with Belgian civilians but depends almost entirely for the tactical story on Cole. His analyses and criticisms of the 106th Division are ill-considered.

For "didn't have the chance of a snowflake" (p. 96), Combat Interv with men of Troop C, 18th Cav Rcn Sqdn.

"Soldiers of the West Front!!" and "Tomorrow brings the beginning" (p. 97), Thompson, *op. cit.*

CHAPTER V: IN FRONT OF ST. VITH

Combat Interviews for the 14th Cav Gp are many and detailed but under-standably less so for the 106th Div, although the division has an excellent unit history by the distinguished military historian Col. R. Ernest Dupuy, *St. Vith: Lion in the Way* (Washington, D.C.: Infantry Journal Press, 1949).

For "in the true Prussian tradition" (p. 101), Brownlow, *Panzer Baron*, p. 62.

"You remember our conversation" (p. 102) and "How do you know" (p. 102), Eisenhower interv with Von Manteuffel.

"Surrender, Americans" and "Take a ten-minute break" (p. 106), Combat Intervs with 14th Cav. Gp.

The story of Sanny Schür (pp. 106–107), author's interv with Mme Susanne Schür Schugens, Lanzerath, 5 Aug 81.

"If they can't sign off" (pp. 107–108), Eisenhower, *The Bitter Woods*, p. 185.

For "seventy-five yards from CP" (p. 109), Combat Intervs with 14th Cav Gp.

For "a volcano about to erupt" (p. 110), author's interv with Col. Pierce Timberlake, who knew Devine well, 21 Oct 83.

"I'll stay" (p. 111), Combat Interv with Co A, 81st Engr Bn.

For "a major offensive in this sector" (p. 115), 2d Div Ltr of Instructions, 132400A Nov 44, in 2d Div G-3 Jnl file, 13–14 Nov 44. Cole, *The Ardennes*, says that in the event of enemy attack, the 2d Division intended withdrawing the two regiments from the Schnee Eifel to the Auw-Bleialf road and using one to counterattack into the Losheim Gap. The author finds no evidence of such a plan. Robertson in a letter to Dr. Delaval, Vielsalm, confirmed the possibility of withdrawal but mentioned no counterattack plan, and neither the former division CofS, General Zwicker, nor the G-3, Maj. Gen. John H. Chiles, nor the artillery commander, Maj. Gen. John H. Hinds, recalls such a plan.

"If you can't hold" (p. 118), Combat Interv with Troop B, 18th Cav Rcn Sqdn.

"Subject: Undertaking *GREIF*" (p. 119). The order is reproduced in Dupuy, *Lion in the Way*, p. 235. Differing from Dupuy's account of the findings of the order, the author's account is based on ltr to *The Cub* (106th Div. Ass. newsletter), 24 Jan 47, from Lt. Col. Charles F. Girand (copy in Robert C. Ringer, unpublished MS, "The End Is Not Yet.")

"*Marschiert schnell!*" (p. 120) and "Somebody's got to stay here" (p. 121), Combat Interv with Cannon Co., 424th Inf.

For "might go half-way to Paris" (p. 123), Combat Interv with Middleton in ETO Historian's file, NA.

For "not to get heavily engaged" (p. 123), Combat Interv with Puett.

"*Bonn hier*" (p. 128), ltr, Hill to Joseph C. Doherty, 15 Oct 80 and author's intervs with Hill, Jul 82.

For "two keys . . . two big friends" (p. 128), Hill, unpublished MS, "The Battle of the Bulge."

"You know how things are" (p. 128), Toland, *Battle*, p. 32.

For "but I agree" (p. 129), Hill MS, *op. cit.*

"Well, that's it" and "I just talked to Jones" (p. 129), Toland, p. 33. See also Combat Interv with Middleton and accompanying ltr, Middleton to Theater Historian ETO, 30 Jul 45.

Additional sources: ltr, Col. Joseph F. Puett to author, 7 Apr 83; extensive correspondence between the author and Ralph G. Hill and Francis H. Aspinwall; ltr, Col. Joseph C. Matthews, Exec O, 422d Inf, to Hill, 7 Jul 82; tp intervs by the author with Maj. Gen. John H. Hinds (CG, 2d Div Arty), Aug 82; author's interv with Zwicker, *op. cit.;* and ltr, Maj. Gen. John H. Chiles (G-3, 2d Div) to author, 18 Dec 82.

CHAPTER VI: THE SKYLINE DRIVE

Combat interviews are detailed for the 109th and 112th Inf Regts but probably because so many men were lost, few for the 110th Inf. Robert H. Phillips, *To Save Bastogne* (New York: Stein and Day, 1983), filled the lacuna with interviews he himself conducted.

"Get them when they cross" (p. 133), Combat Interv with Cannon Co., 112th Inf.

"Nobody able to sleep" (p. 134), Cole, *The Ardennes*, pp. 198–199.

"What do you make of it?" (p. 138), Maj. Gen. Daniel B. Strickler, unpublished MS, "The Battle of the Bulge," Toland files, LofC.

For "in friendly fashion" (p. 139), Cole, p. 184n.

Additional sources: author's interv with prof. Dr. Joseph Maertz, Clervaux, 22 Aug 81; Maj. Georg Loos, "The Operations of *Army Engineer Battalion 600* during the Battle of the Bulge."

CHAPTER VII: THE SOUTHERN SHOULDER

Combat interviews with all units are extensive, and there is an excellent regimental history: Col. Garden F. Johnson, *History of the Twelfth Infantry Regiment in World War II* (privately printed, 1947).

For "a good-looking blonde" (p. 149), and action (pp. 150–151), James V. Christy, unpublished and untitled MS written for the author.

For "fanatically hopped up" and following quotations (p. 151), Maj. Harry M. Kemp, "The Operations of the 3d Battalion, 109th Infantry, in the Vicinity of

Diekirch, Luxembourg," monograph prepared for Advanced Infantry Officers' Course, Ft. Benning, Ga., 1949–50.

For "very bloody fighting" (p. 151), MS # A-876, Brandenberger, "*Seventh Army* in the Ardennes Offensive," vol. II.

For "no cause for alarm" and following quotations (p. 152), Combat Interv with Rudder.

For quotations and action at the Parc Hôtel (pp. 156–158), Combat Intervs with Leake, *et al.* and "Notes on Parc Hôtel," Toland files, LofC.

For "no retrograde movement" (p. 159), 12th Inf AAR, Dec 44.

For "a matter of making the breakthrough" (p. 159), MS # A-876, Brandenberger.

CHAPTER VIII: THE NORTHERN SHOULDER

Combat Interviews are detailed and comprehensive for all units of the 2d and 99th Divisions. Unit histories: *Combat History of the Second Infantry Division in World War II* (Baton Rouge, La.: Army & Navy Publishing Co., 1946); Maj. Gen. Walter E. Lauer, *Battle Babies: The Story of the 99th Infantry Division* (Baton Rouge, La.: Military Press of Louisiana, 1951); and *741 Tank Battalion D-Day to V-E Day* (privately printed, 1982).

For "attached to him perpetually" (p. 160), Cole, *The Ardennes*, p. 76.

For "decent, but stupid" (p. 160), Merriam, *Dark December*, p. 18.

For shooting of Russians (p. 160), Brett-Smith, *Hitler's Generals*, p. 157.

For "an earth-shaking inferno" (p. 163), Frühbeiser, "The *9th Parachute Regiment* in the Offensive Against the Americans," *Der Deutsche Fallschirmjäger*, No. 12, 1964.

For "all hell broke loose" (p. 163), Nawrocki, unpublished MS, "Battle of the Bulge, 99th Infantry Division, December 1944, Co B, 393."

For "thunderous" (p. 163), Combat Interv with Kempton.

For "a terrifying experience" (p. 163), Ronningen, unpublished MS, "The Battle of the Bulge," courtesy of William C. C. Cavanagh.

For "the earth seemed to break open" (p. 163), Holz, "*Panzerjäger 12* in the Battle of the Bulge," Part II, *Der Alte Kameraden*, No. 12, 1972.

For "could see them against the skyline" (p. 164), ltr, Macay to Cavanagh (no date).

For "in swarms" (p. 164), Maj. Keith P. Fabianich, "The Defense of Höfen, Germany," *Infantry School Quarterly*, Jul 48.

The definitive work on the proximity fuse (p. 165) is Ralph B. Baldwin, *The Deadly Fuze: Secret Weapon of World War II* (San Rafael, Cal.: Presidio Press, 1980).

For "headlong retreat" (p. 166), 38th Cav Rcn Sqdn AAR, Dec 44.

For "every weapon" and "practically swept" (p. 166), Fabianich, *op. cit.*

For "just as startled" and "didn't know and didn't care" (pp. 172–173), ltr, Newbrough to Cavanagh, 7 Oct 79.

All material on Adolf Schür (pp. 176–178), author's interv with Schür, 10 Aug 81.

"What shall we do then?," "Hold," "No, I have orders to hold" and "hanging limply" (p. 178), Eisenhower, *The Bitter Woods*, pp. 188, 190, 191. Dr. Bouck confirmed the story as written by Eisenhower.

"Can't we go to your CP" (p. 179), ltr, Hinds to Cavanagh, 2 Feb 82, and author's tp intervs with Hinds, 20 and 22 Nov 82.

"Go slow and watch your step" (p. 180), Robertson, "Operations 2nd Infantry Division—6-20 December 1944," attachment to 2d Div AAR, Dec 44.

For "entire front was practically reestablished" (p. 181), Lauer, *Battle Babies*, p. 25n.

For "could be decisive" (p. 182), Skorzeny, *Special Mission*, p. 166.

For "gone to bed" (p. 182), ltr, Peiper to Lyle Bouck, 9 Dec 66, courtesy of Bouck.

Additional source: Hubert Meyer, *Kriegegeschichte der 12 SS-Panzerdivision (Hitlerjugend)*, Vol. II (Osnabrück: Munin Verlag, Gmb H., 1982).

CHAPTER IX: REACTION AT THE TOP

For "might be the answer" (p. 185), 12th AGp Briefings, 16 Dec 44, 12th AGp files.

"Well, Brad" and "A counterattack, yes" (p. 186), Bradley, *A Soldier's Story*, p. 450.

For "send Middleton some help" (p. 186), ibid., p. 451.

"Tell him" (p. 186), Eisenhower, *The Bitter Woods*, p. 215.

"I hate like hell to do it" (p. 186), Bradley, p. 475.

For "cracked a bottle of champagne" (p. 186), unpublished diary kept by Bradley's aide, Lt. Col. Chet Hansen, entry of 17 Dec 44 (copy in U.S. Army Military History Research Collection).

Signal to *Jadgkorps II* (p. 186), Ultra files.

For "do whatever they wish" and "I wish everybody could see them" (p. 187), Sylvan Diary.

"God gave him a face" (p. 188), MacDonald, *The Mighty Endeavor*, pp. 406–407, citing author's interv with Eisenhower.

For "implicit faith" (p. 188), MacDonald in Parrish, ed., *The Encyclopedia of World War II*, p. 282.

For "the heaviest artillery fire" (p. 188), First Light Rpts, 160645 Dec 44, FUSA G-2 Jnl file.

For "in large patrol strength" (p. 188), Sylvan Diary, entry of 16 Dec 44.

"This call to arms" (p. 189), tp msg from V Corps, 161244 Dec 44, FUSA G-2 Jnl file.

For "the situation for the division" (p. 189), msg, 161415 Dec 44, VIII Corps G-3 Jnl file.

For "neither optimistic nor pessimistic" (p. 189), Sylvan Diary, *ibid.*

"These documents indicate" (p. 190), Annex 3, VIII Corps G-2 Periodic Rpt, 162400 Dec 44.

For "by 1130 hours" (p. 190), msg from 99th Div, 161300 Dec 44, V Corps G-2 Jnl file.

"The sudden attacks" and "Until the magnitude" (p. 190), 12th AGp G-2 Periodic Rpt, 162300 Dec 44.

For "did not come up to expectations" (p. 191), MS # B-151a, Von Manteuffel.

"Hold on as long as possible" (p. 191), Nobécourt, *Hitler's Last Gamble*, p. 186.

On the German parachute drop (pp. 191–192*ff.*), see Willy Volberg, unpublished MS, "Operation STÖSSER," a personal experience account prepared for the author (translation by Maj. Dieter Kopac, Würselen).

For "crush everything" (p. 192), Nobécourt, p. 152.

"Balck! Balck!" (p. 193), Toland, *Battle*, p. 39.

For "the Italian" (p. 194), Irving, *Hitler's War*, p. 741.

CHAPTER X: *Kampfgruppe Peiper*

An essential source is Giles, *The Damned Engineers*. Immensely helpful also were the correspondence and interviews with Col. David E. Pergrin and Ralph Hill, Jr.

For "well bred . . . resourceful" (p. 197), Weingartner, *Crossroads of Death*, pp. 21, 88.

For "the decisive role in the offensive" (p. 197), ETHINT 10, Peiper.

For "the decisive hour," "wave of terror," and without "humane inhibitions" (p. 197), sworn statement by Dietrich, 22 Mar 46, in Royce L. Thompson, "The ETO Ardennes Campaign: Operations of the Combat Group Peiper, 16–26 December 1944," prepared in support of Cole, *The Ardennes*, CMH.

For quotations from Peiper (pp. 197–198), sworn statement by Peiper, 21 Mar 46, in *ibid.*

For "fight in the old SS spirit" and following quotations (p. 198), prosecution exhibits in Case No. 6-24, *U.S. vs. Valentin Bersin, et al.*, NA.

For "biggest damn tank" (p. 201), Toland, *Battle*, p. 47.

For "in wild scramble," (p. 201), Combat Interv with 14th Cav gp.

Material on Karl Wortmann (pp. 202*ff.*) from author's interv with Wortmann, 16 Oct 82.

"Those don't sound like ours" and following quotations (pp. 202–203), Toland, pp. 46–47.

For war crimes at Honsfeld (pp. 203–204), see affidavits in SHAEF War Crimes files.

For the story of Erna Collas (p. 204), author's interv with André Schroeder, 14 Aug 81, and ltr, Schroeder to author, 10 Sep 81.

"The Germans are coming!" (p. 206) and the actions oJ Meads, Yager, Rapp, Paul J. Rutka, and Charles W. Smith, ltrs to Ralph Hill and the author, 3 Jun, 2 Jul, 15 Aug, 1 Sep, and 11 Dec 82.

"My God! They shot Pappel" (p. 207), ltr, Yager to Ralph Hill, 2 Jul 82. See also Case 6-107, SHAEF War Crimes files.

"The enemy had the key to success" (p. 209), Cole, p. 91.

For "a last ditch defense of the CP" (p. 210), personal diary provided the author by Matt F. C. Konop.

For "the usual cold, tasteless mixture" (p. 211) and expected "to be blown up" (p. 212), Mabel Jessop, "The Teams of Majors Hurwitz and Higgenbotham," in Dr. Clifford L. Graves, ed., *Front Line Surgeons* (San Diego: Frye and Smith, 1950).

"Hey, why don't you ride with me" (p. 213) and Bechtel's story, Bechtel, unpublished MS, "Untold Story of Battery B," and ltr, Bechtel to the author, 7 Jun 82.

"We're going to blow" (p. 215), Giles, p. 92.

"There's a big Kraut column" and "That little FAOB outfit" (p. 215), Giles, pp. 93–94.

For "those beautiful trucks" (p. 217), Peiper testimony in Thompson, *op. cit.*

For "almost like a lowing" (p. 219), James P. Mattera (with C. M. Stephan, Jr.), "Murder at Malmédy," *Army* magazine, Dec 81.

For "for a few minutes" and following quotations (p. 219), prosecution exhibits in *U.S. vs. Valentin Bersin, et al.*

Lieutenant Lary's account (p. 220), 1st Lt. Virgil P. Lary, Jr., "The Massacre at Malmédy," *Field Artillery Journal*, Feb 46.

"Let's go!" (p. 220) and "Forget the password" (p. 222), Mattera, *op. cit.*

For Lieutenant Lary's story (p. 220) see Hugh Mulligan, article based on interviews with Mesdames Martin, *Ohio State Journal*, 16 Dec 69, copy with Ringer MS, *op. cit;* also interview with Mesdames Martin by William C.C. Cavanagh, 9 Mar 84.

"There is absolutely no question" (p. 222), Sylvan Diary, entry of 17 Dec 44.

Additional sources: Richard Gallagher, *Malmédy Massacre* (New York: Paperback Library, 1964); Charles Whiting, *Massacre at Malmédy* (London: Leo Cooper, 1971); Gerard Grégoire, *Les Panzers de Peiper Face à l'U.S. Army* (privately printed, n.d.); Charles A. Hammer, ed., *History of the 285th Field Artillery Observation Battalion* (privately printed, n.d.); 81st Cong., 1st Sess., Report of the Subcommittee on Armed Services, United States Senate, Malmédy Massacre Investigation (13 Oct 49); Steven P. Kane, *The 1st SS Panzer Division in the Battle of the Bulge* (Bennington, Vt.: International Graphics Corporation, 1982); Kenneth C. Parker, "More on the Massacre at Malmédy," *Field Artillery Journal*, May 46; Marshall Andrews, "10 Years After, Malmédy Massacre," *Washington Post*, 16 Dec 54; Sgt. Ed Cunningham, "Massacre at Malmédy," *YANK* magazine, Jan 44; Maj James B. Kemp, "Operations of the 612th Tank Destroyer Battalion, Second Infantry Division, in the Battle of the Bulge, Vicinity of Elsenborn Corner," Advanced Infantry Officers' Course, Ft. Benning, Ga. 1949–50; author's interv with Haley Marshall, 394th Inf, 17 Jul 82; unidentified CO, Co B, 2d Engr Bn, "Diary of a Prisoner of War," in *The Checkerboard* (newsletter of the 99th Div Assn), Dec 82; author's interv with Samuel M. Barrett, Btry B, 285th FA Obsn Bn, 10 Aug 81; ltrs to the author from Albert M. Valenzi, 20 Jan 83, William H. Merriken, 24 Jan 83, and Michael Sciranko, 8 Feb 83; Statement of Pfc Homer D. Ford in ETO Historians' file; and ltr to the author from Ralph A. Logan, date missing but late 1983.

CHAPTER XI: "THE DAMNED ENGINEERS"

Many of the sources for Chapter X also apply for this chapter, particularly Giles, Grégoire, and Pergrin.

"They're Krauts!" (p. 225). Giles, *The Damned Engineers*, p. 293.

"German tanks," (p. 227), "If anything happens" (p. 228), and "Murderer!" (p. 229), Toland, *Battle*, p. 58.

"The people of the village" (p. 231), Giles, p. 53, and with the exception of the next entry, all following quotations.

"Go to the devil" (p. 234), author's interv with Schugens, 8 Aug 81.

Additional sources: Charles Foley, *Commando Extraordinary* (London: Longmans Green, 1954); Howard R. Bergen, *History of the 99th Infantry Battalion* (Oslo: Emil Moestueas, n.d.); Cecil E. Roberts, *A Soldier from Texas* (Fort Worth, Tex.: Branch-Smith, 1978); Raymond L. Lewis (CCB, 9th Armd Div), unpublished MS, "Eight Days at St. Vith"; Ken C. Rust, *The 9th Air Force in World War II* (Fallbrook, Cal.: Aero Publishers, 1967); testimony of Marie Lochem in SHAEF War Crimes files; and Roger Hardy, *Le 5e Bataillon de Fusiliers Belges Durant L'Hiver 1944–1945* (privately printed, 1983). A photograph of a German officer at the Kaiserbaracke, a crossroads between Ligneuville and St. Vith, was for long mistakenly identified as Peiper, which led a number of writers (including Giles) to conclude that Peiper split his column. That was not the case. The editors of the British periodical *After the Battle* have conclusively proven that the photograph is not of Peiper. See No. 4, Nov 74.

CHAPTER XII: THE RACE FOR BASTOGNE: THE FIRST PHASE

A basic source is Phillips, *To Save Bastogne*. Unit histories are: *History of the 110th Infantry Regiment, United States Army, World War II*, and *The 28th Infantry Division* (both Atlanta: Albert Love Enterprises, 1945 and 1946).

"I don't know any details" (p. 262), Hewitt, *Workhorse of the Western Front*, p. 173 (full citation under Chapter XXI).

"I'll put it up to Ike" (p. 262), Eisenhower, *The Bitter Woods*, p. 226.

"Pardon my French" and "I will never move backwards" (p. 262), Hansen Diary, entry of 17 Dec 44.

For "considered the situation . . . critical" and "prepared for any eventuality" (p. 263), Gavin, *On to Berlin*, pp. 204–205.

"Get all your boys together" (p. 267) and "From now on" (p. 268), extract from a ltr from Col. Gustin M. Nelson to his father, written in May 45, Toland files, LofC.

For "the sharpshooter of Munshausen," "swinging a souvenir American bayonet," and "measures would be taken" (pp. 272–273), Toland, *Battle*, p. 79, and ltr to the author from Pierre Eicher, 22 Aug 83. Eicher corrects Toland's identification of the village as Marnach.

"We've blown up everything" (p. 274), Combat Interv with Company K, 110th Infantry.

For "no more time to talk" (p. 277), Col. Hurley Fuller, unpublished MS, "Report of Operations of the 110th Infantry Combat Team, December 16–18, 1944," Toland files, LofC.

"This switchboard is now closed" (p. 278), author's interv with Malcom R. Wilkey, G-2 Sect, VIII Corps, 20 Jan 83.

Additional sources: Prof. Dr. Joseph Maertz, *Luxemburg im Der Ardennenoffen-*

sive 1944/45 (Luxembourg City: Sankt-Paulus-Druckerei, 1969); Richard V. Grulich, Hq Co, 110th Inf, unpublished MS, "Three Days Plus 102"; John B. Allard, unpublished MS, "A Replacement in the 'Bloody Bucket,'" prepared for the author, and ltrs to the author, 17 May and 9 Jun 82; ltr to the author from John E. Peiper, Co I, 112th Inf, 18 Apr 82; and author's interv with Jean Servais, 22 Aug 81.

CHAPTER XIII: THE RACE FOR BASTOGNE: THE SECOND PHASE

Phillips, *To Save Bastogne*, was again highly useful, and some other sources cited for Chapter XII also apply.

For "already imperiled" and "could seriously endanger" (p. 280), MS # B-151a, Von Manteuffel.

For "flowing to the west" (p. 281), MS # B-040, Genmaj. Heinz Kokott, *"26th Volksgrenadier Division* in the Ardennes Offensive."

For "go find your regiment" (p. 284), ltr, Seely to Marshall S. Reid, no date, but published in the newsletter of the Southwest Chapter, 3d Armd Div Assn, Mar 82, courtesy of Haynes W. Dugan.

"My God, this is the sort of thing" (p. 285), Charles T. Johnson, unpublished and untitled MS prepared for the author and ltr, 10 Sep 82.

"There's a tank coming" (p. 287), Seely ltr, *op. cit.*

For "a fantastic aspect" (p. 289), MS # A-942, Genlt. Fritz Bayerlein, *"Panzer Lehr Division* (15–22 Dec 1944)."

"How many teams?", "Three," and "Sir, I want authority" (p. 290), Combat Interv with Roberts.

For "cut the column in the middle" (p. 294), CCR, 9th Armd Div AAR, Dec 44.

For "young, blonde, and beautiful" and following quotations (p. 295), B. H. Liddell-Hart, *History of the Second World War* (New York: G. P. Putnam's Sons, 1971), p. 651n, and Marshall, *Bastogne: The First Eight Days* (full citation under Chapter XXIV), p. 185. Both historians received their information from Bayerlein himself.

For "mischance and confusion" (p. 297), Cole, *The Ardennes*, p. 303.

Additional sources: History of the 58th Armored Field Artillery Battalion (privately printed, n.d.), provided by Raymond T. Summers; Lt. Gen. William F. Train, unpublished MS, "My Memories of the Battle of the Bulge," prepared for the author, Dec 82; and Lester M. Nichols, *Impact: The Battle Story of the Tenth Armored Division* (New York: Bradbury, Sayles, O'Neill Co., 1967).

CHAPTER XIV: THE DEFENSE OF WILTZ

See again Phillips, *To Save Bastogne*, and for the Americans hiding in Wiltz, Toland, *Battle*.

For "like autumn leaves" (p. 303), Phillips, p. 240.

For "mud, fields, streams" (p. 306), Col. Daniel B. Strickler, "Action Report of the German Ardennes Breakthrough as I Saw It from 16 December 1944–2 January 1945," in *History of the 110th Infantry Regiment*.

Additional sources: G. Martin, "Fighting Around the 'Schumann Café,'" *Der Deutsche Fallschirmjäger*, No. 2, 1976; and "The Second Platoon of the 42d Field Hospital at Wiltz" in Graves, ed., *Front Line Surgeons*.

CHAPTER XV: DEVELOPING CRISIS AT ST. VITH

Combat Interviews for the 7th Armored Division are extensive. Unit histories are Dupuy, *op. cit.; The Lucky Seventh: History of the Seventh Armored Division and the Seventh Armored Divison Association* (privately printed, 1982); and *The Valiant 275th Armored Field Artillery Battalion* (privately printed, 1978). Correspondence conducted with veterans by Francis H. Aspinwall was most helpful.

For "the canvas on the truck" (p. 315), ltr, Brown to Aspinwall, 24 Aug 81.

For "men in greenish uniforms" (pp. 316–317), Aspinwall, unpublished MS, "Memorandum of Personal Experience, 589th FA Bn."

For "very big and powerful" and following quotation (p. 319), Dupuy, *Lion in the Way*, p. 153, citing affidavits from civilians in Meyerode obtained by General Wood.

"Withdraw from present positions" (p. 320), Cole, *The Ardennes*, p. 165.

"Find out what you can" (p. 322) and "break that ring" (p. 323), Eisenhower, *The Bitter Woods*, pp. 227, 229.

For "a final delaying position" (p. 324), Cole, p. 163.

For "mad as hell" and "anytime and any place" (p. 325), *The Valiant 275th Armored Field Artillery Battalion*, p. 13.

Quotations from Boyer (pp. 325–326), Eisenhower, *The Bitter Woods*, pp. 231–232.

"And how is your situation, Baron" and following quotations (p. 327), Toland, *Battle*, p. 66, and confirmed in Eisenhower interv with Von Manteuffel, 12 Oct 66.

"We'll be in good shape" (p. 327) and following quotations, Eisenhower, *The Bitter Woods*, pp. 229–230. See also Toland, pp. 54, 62.

"I want to shoot" (p. 330), Eisenhower, p. 233. '

For "take over," "left the room," and "the commander of the 14th Cavalry Group" (p. 331), 14th Cav Gp AAR, Dec 44.

Additional sources: The Armored School, *The Defense of St. Vith, Belgium, 17–23 December 1944*; Lewis, "Eight Days at St. Vith," *op. cit.*; William Donohue Ellis and Col. Thomas J. Cunningham, Jr., *Clarke of St. Vith: The Sergeant's General* (Cleveland: Dillon/Liederbach, 1974); ltr, Col. Charles C. Cavender to Toland, 13 Mar 59, and day-by-day account by Cavender, Toland files, LofC; ltrs to the author from Cavender, 20 Jun and 3, 14, and 16 Jul 83; interv with Col. George Descheneaux, Toland files, LofC; Maj. Gerald K. Johnson, "The Black Soldier in the Ardennes," *Soldiers* magazine, Feb 81; Capt. Alan W. Jones, Jr., "The Operations of the 423d Infantry (106th Infantry Division) in the Vicinity of Schoenberg during the Battle of the Ardennes," Maj. Lewis M. Keyes, "Operations of the 106th Infantry Division in the Battle of the Bulge," and Maj. John C.

Hollinger, "The Operations of the 422d Infantry Regiment in the Vicinity of Schlausenbach, Germany," Advanced Infantry Officers' Course, Ft. Benning, 1949–50; *The Lion's Tale—Short Stories of the 106th Infantry Division* (limited edition by Seventh Annual 106th Division Convention Committee, 1953); Thomas J. Riggs, "An Engineer's Seven Day War," (published article but journal not identified) in Ringer, unpublished MS, *op. cit.*; ltr to author from Lawrence J. Smith, 14th Cav Gp S-3, 22 Oct 83; and ltr to the author from Lt. Col. Levin L. Lee, 14th Cav Gp, 7 Sep 83.

CHAPTER XVI: SHAPING THE DEFENSE OF ST. VITH

Most sources for Chapter XV also apply to this chapter.
"Can't, Lieutenant" (p. 334), Combat Interv with 14th Cav Gp.
For "all hell break loose" and following quotations (p. 335), Combat Intervs with Whiteman and 1st Sgts. Frederick J. Mabb and Andrew J. Ellmer.
For "drove like mad" (p. 336), Lewis, "Eight Days at St. Vith."
"My poor men" (p. 339), Dupuy, *Lion in the Way*, p. 121, citing ltr, Tech. Sgt. T. Wayne Black, 422d Inf.
For "to destroy by fire" (p. 339), *ibid.*, p. 104, and Cole, *The Ardennes*, p. 167.
"Attack Schoenberg" (p. 340), "It is now exactly," and "It sounded like" (p. 341), Dupuy, pp. 128, 137.
"We're sitting like fish in a pond" (p. 343) and following quotations, Toland interv with Descheneaux, Toland files, LofC.
"OK, Colonel, I'll go" (p. 344), Eisenhower, *The Bitter Woods*, p. 293.
"I know it's no use" and following quotations (p. 345), Toland, *Battle*, p. 122.
"Supplies have not been dropped" (p. 347), Dupuy, p. 134.
"Who do I work for?" (p. 348), Eisenhower, p. 285.

CHAPTER XVII: IN FRONT OF LUXEMBOURG CITY

Combat Interviews are extensive and have valuable covering narratives.
"Use your own judgment" (p. 355), Combat Interv with Rudder.
For the evacuation of Diekirch (p. 356), Lt. E. T. Melchers, "Rapport sur l'Activité de la Gendarmerie Grand-Ducale du Bombardment et de l'Evacuation de la Ville de Diekirch," courtesy Lt. Col. Melchers.
For "drive the enemy into the river" (p. 357), FO 3, CCA, 9th Armd Div, in CCA AAR, Dec 44.
For "it was a desperate fight" (p. 364), Combat Interv with Leake, *et al.*
"Really it was swell" (p. 365), Daniel B. Stresow, unpublished MS, "E Company's Last Stand," Toland files, LofC.
Barton's sending a message (p. 366), author's interv with Barton.
For "for God's sake get out the tanks" (p. 367), Combat Interv with Cook.
For "heard groaning" and following quotations (p. 368), Stresow MS.

Additional information on the stand in Echternach obtained in author's tp interv with Paul H. Dupuis, 15 Aug 83.

CHAPTER XVIII: IN DEFENSE OF THE TWIN VILLAGES

Most sources cited for Chapter VIII apply.

"I want to talk with your commander" (p. 374), author's interv with Osterhold, *op. cit.*

Lieutenant Goffigon's story (pp. 375–376 and 378–379), author's interv with Goffigon, 11 Mar 82, and Charles B. MacDonald, *Company Commander* (Washington, D.C.: Infantry Journal Press, 1947; current edition Bantam Books).

"We're doing all we can!" (p. 379), Walter E. Eisler, Jr., CO, Co L, 23d Inf, unpublished MS, "The Breakthrough, 16–19 Dec 1944, L Co, 23d Inf, 2d Inf Div," prepared for the author, Sep 81.

For "the Germans had broken through" (p. 380), Combat Interv with Robertson.

For "until ordered otherwise" (p. 380), Combat Interv with McKinley, *et al.*, 1st Bn, 9th Inf.

For "absolutely black" and following quotation (p. 381), Combat Interv with Maj. William F. Hancock, Exec O, 1st Bn, 9th Inf.

For "splashing Billy and me" (p. 382), Herbert P. Hunt, unpublished MS, "A Rifle Company That Would Not Budge: The Sequence of Events," prepared for the author, fall 81.

"If you don't get it out right now" and two following quotations (p. 383), Combat Interv with Hancock.

For "a scene of wild confusion" (p. 384), Combat Interv with McKinley, *et al.*

For "the night was ablaze" (p. 384), MacDonald, *Company Commander*, p. 139.

The story of Private Fisher (pp. 385–386), is from SHAEF War Crimes files and ltr, Fisher to author, 10 Sep 81. Fisher's testimony was corroborated by that of Staff Sgt. Charles Hunt.

The actions of Colonel Zeiner's tanks (pp. 386–387), Meyer, *Kriegegeschichte der 12 SS-Panzerdivision, op. cit.*

"Action quieting" (p. 387), historian's narrative of 38th Inf action in Combat Interv files.

For "a quivering hulk" (p. 387), Maj. Ben W. Legare, "The Operations of the 2d Batallion, 394th Infantry, in the German Counteroffensive, Vicinity of Losheimergraben, Germany," Advanced Infantry Officers' Course, Ft. Benning, Ga., 1949–50.

"Pull back to new positions" and "Withdraw immediately" (p. 388), Combat Interv with Capt. Frank W. Luchowski, S-3, 1st Bn, 23d Inf.

For "a state of shock" (p. 389), ltr, Sutherland to Joseph G. Doherty, 18 Oct 81. See also taped remarks, Col. Oscar A. Axelson, CO, 406th FA Gp, for William C. C. Cavanagh, no date, but in 1981.

"We fight and die here" (p. 390), Maj. Thomas J. Gendron, "The Operations of the 2d Battalion, 26th Infantry at Dom. Bütgenbach, Belgium," Advanced Infantry Officers' Course, Ft. Benning, Ga., 1949–50.

Additional sources: Royce L. Thompson, "Tank Fight of Rocherath-Krinkelt, 17–19 December 1944," prepared in support of Cole, *The Ardennes*, CMH; "The *12th Division* in the Battle of the Bulge 1944," *Der Alte Kameraden*, No. 11, 1975, and Nos. 2, 6, and 11, 1976; ltr, John W. Reid, 3d Bn, 393d Inf, to Toland,

18 Jan 58, Toland files, LofC; ltr, Lee Smith, CO, Co K, 23d Inf, to author, 26 Mar 82; ltrs, Daniel W. Franklin, Co K, 38th Inf, to author, 21 May and 2 and 17 Aug 82; and ltr, F. G. Prutzman, Hq, 2d Div Arty, to John H. Hinds, 2 Jul 47.

CHAPTER XIX: TO GAIN THE ELSENBORN RIDGE

See sources previously cited for Chapters VIII and XVIII.

For "a withering hail" (p. 392), historian's narrative in Combat Interv file.

"Hell, yes!," "unbelievable control," and "You have saved my regiment" (p. 397), *ibid*.

For "like a crippled goose" (p. 398), Cole, *The Ardennes*, p. 125.

For "tank grave" and "a cruel sight" and following quotations (p. 399), *"Die dritte Kompanie"* (unit history, *Co C, 12th SS-Pz Regt, 12th SS-Pz Div*, 1978).

"You got him" and following quotations (p. 400), ltr to author from Hugh Berger, Co I, 23d Inf, 28 Dec 81.

For "to move to new positions" (p. 402), historian's narrative.

"Your hospital is under arrest" (p. 403), Jessop, "The Teams of Majors Hurwitz and Higgenbotham," *op. cit.*

For "exceedingly heavy artillery" and following quotations (p. 405), Captured Combat Report, *3d Bn, 12th SS-Tank Regt*, in 1st Div, Annex 4 to Monthly Intell Activities Rpt, Dec 44.

For "a ring of steel" (p. 406), Gendron, *op. cit.*

For "as common as grass" (p. 407), Combat Interv with Daniel, *et. al.*

"I don't know where they got the ammo" and "knocked a part of Hitler's personal operations plan" (p. 408), Cole, pp. 132, 135.

For "a pretty good day's work" (pp. 409–410), Combat Interv with Robertson.

"What the 2d Division has done" (p. 410), historian's narrative of 1st Bn, 9th Inf, in Combat Interv files.

Additional sources: Maj. Gen. Derrill M. Daniel, unpublished MS, "The Operations of the 2d Battalion, 26th Infantry, at Dom. Bütgenbach, Belgium," Toland files, LofC; ltr, Daniel to Joseph C. Doherty, no date but in 1982; ltrs, Daniel to author, 23 Jun and 2 Jul 83; ltr, William Boehme, G-2 Sect, 1st Div, to Joseph C. Doherty, 16 Jan 82; Capt. Donald E. Rivette, "The Hot Corner at Dom. Bütgenbach," *Infantry Journal*, Oct 45); Diary, Col. Robert E. Snetzer, CO, 2d Engr C Bn, 12 Dec 44–20 Jan 45, courtesy of Tom C. Morris; ltr, Robert L. Dudley, plat ldr, 741st Tk Bn, to Joseph C. Doherty, no date but in 1982; and author's intervs with Joseph Scholzen and Albert Kohnenmergen, 14 Aug 81.

CHAPTER XX: COMMAND DECISIONS

For a heaven-sent opportunity (pp. 415–416), Sir Francis de Guingand, *Generals at War* (London: Hodder and Stoughton, 1964), p. 106.

For "great confusion" and following quotations (p. 416), Bryant, *Triumph in the West*, pp. 270–273.

For "worse than it was at noon" (p. 418) and "Well, I knew my staff would get here" (p. 420), Hansen Diary, entries of 18 and 19 Dec 44.

"The present situation" and "Hell, let's have the guts" (p. 420), Eisenhower, *Crusade in Europe*, p. 350.

"When can you start?" and following quotations (p. 420), Eisenhower, *The Bitter Woods*, pp. 256–257.

"Remember how a tarpon" (p. 421), Blumenson, *The Patton Papers*, p. 603.

For "a completely Allied outlook" (p. 421) and "General Eisenhower says" (p. 422), Eisenhower, *The Bitter Woods*, p. 368.

For "completely dumbfounded" (p. 422), Bradley and Blair, *A General's Life*, p. 363.

For "the logical thing to do" and "There's no doubt" (p. 423), Bradley, *A Soldier's Story*, p. 276.

For "one of my biggest mistakes" (p. 423), Bradley and Blair, p. 363.

For "British troops will always" (p. 423), Eisenhower, *The Bitter Woods*, p. 270.

For "through the machinations of the Prime Minister" and following quotation (p. 423), Blumenson, p. 601.

For "would be a most opportune time" (p. 423), Chandler, ed., Vol IV, *The War Years*, p. 2367.

For "created undercurrents of unhappiness" and "cocky mannerisms" (p. 424), Monk Dickson journal.

For "like Christ come to cleanse the temple" (p. 424), Wilmot, *The Struggle for Europe*, p. 592.

For "the quiet reticent type" (p. 426), Chandler, ed., Vol IV, p. 2369.

Material on public reaction (pp. 427–428) provided by J. Vanwelkenhuyzen, director, *Centre de Recherches et d'Etudes Historiques de la Seconde Guerre Mondiale*, Brussels, and Mme. Gracie Delépine, *Bibliothèque de Documentation Internationale Contemporaine*, Nanterre.

For "sheer hysteria" and "What could have been an unholy mess" (p. 428), Phillip Knightley, *The First Casualty—From the Crimea to Vietnam: The War Correspondent as Hero, Propagandist, and Myth Maker* (New York: Harcourt Brace Jovanovich, 1975), p. 324.

For the "angry session" (p. 428), *New York Times*, 20 Dec 44.

For "tinged by sorrow" (p. 429), *Washington Post*, 25 Dec 44.

For "the situation should not be viewed with panic" (p. 429), *New York Times*, 21 Dec 44.

CHAPTER XXI: THE WAR AGAINST *KAMPFGRUPPE PEIPER*

Most sources for Chapters X and XI are applicable. The 30th Division has an excellent unit history, Robert L. Hewitt, *Workhorse of the Western Front* (Washington, D.C.: Infantry Journal Press, 1946), and each of the regiments has a published history. See also *Spearhead in the West: The Third Armored Division* (compiled by the division staff in Germany, 1945), and Lt. Col. George Kenneth Rubel, *Daredevil Tankers, The Story of the 740th Tank Battalion* (privately printed, no date). Although there were detailed interviews for the 30th Division, they were combined into a general narrative, Capt. Franklin Ferriss, "The German Offensive of 16 November: The Defeat of the *1st SS Panzer Division Adolf Hitler*." Interviews with CCB, 3d Armored Division, and the 82d Airborne Division are extensive.

"I'm Jim Gavin" and following quotations (p. 433), Edward C. Arn, CO, Co F, 119th Inf, unpublished MS, "The Saga of a Civilian Soldier," and ltrs to the author, 17 Sep 82 and 30 Jan 83.

"They've killed a good few" and following quotations (p. 436), Whiting, *Massacre at Malmédy*, pp. 96–97 and 137–138.

For "such a crime" (p. 436), Skorzeny, *Special Mission*, p. 177.

All quotation reference to the killing of civilians (pp. 437–438), Commission des Crimes de Guerre, *Les Crimes de Guerre—Stavelot*, p. 16.

For "to take care of a tank," "Biggest Goddamned noise," and following quotation (p. 439), "AAA Units in Ardennes Battle," ETO Historian's file.

For "every commander to shoot him down" (p. 440), Peiper testimony, Thompson MS, *op. cit.*

"They're bastard tanks" (p. 441), Ferriss MS.

"I'll bet you guys" (p. 444), Giles, *The Damned Engineers*, p. 279.

"You have nothing to fear" (p. 445) and subsequent quotations from L'Abbé Hanlet from "La Tragédie de la Maison St-Edouard," courtesy William C. C. Cavanagh.

For "opened its muzzle up like a rose" (p. 446), Ferriss MS.

"Let's get the sons of bitches!" (p. 448), Combat Interv with officers of 1st Bn, 504th Prcht Inf.

CHAPTER XXII: THE LAST DAYS OF *KAMPFGRUPPE PEIPER*

Most sources for Chapters X, XI, and XXI are applicable.

For "a motley crew" (p. 451) and "*Kamerad!*" (p. 452), Cole, *The Ardennes*, p. 361.

"Surrender or die!" (p. 452), Giles, *The Damned Engineers*, p. 312.

"That place is very strong" and following quotation (p. 456), 30th Div Tp jnl 21 Dec 44.

"We're eliminating the Communist menace" and "We will keep what is best" and "I give you my word" (p. 459), Toland, *Battle*, p. 178. For McCown's story, see also ltrs to the author from McCown, 15 and 27 Jul 83, and Annex 3 to XVIII Corps (AB), G-2 Per Rpt No. 11, Observations of an American Field Officer Who Escaped from the *1st SS Panzer Division "Adolf Hitler."*

"If *Kampfgruppe Peiper* does not punctually report" (p. 460) and "May we break out?" (p. 461), Toland, p. 211.

"Colonel, that proposal is a farce" (p. 460), Eisenhower, *The Bitter Woods*, p. 278.

For "by all means bring back," "Merry Christmas," and "immediate escape" (p. 461) and "fierce, wild shooting" (p. 462), Karl Wortmann, "Password: 'Merry Christmas,'" *Der Freiwillige*, No. 12, 1978 (translation by Hans Holtkamp).

"Halt, Goddamn it!" (p. 462), Toland, p. 243, and ltrs to the author from McCown.

For the bombings of Malmédy (pp. 464–465), Royce L. Thompson, "Malmédy, Belgium, Mistaken Bombing, 23 and 25 December 1944," prepared in support of Cole, *The Ardennes*, CMH; 120th Inf AAR, Dec 44, and 30th Div G-3 Jnls, 23–25 Dec 44.

CHAPTER XXIII: THE DEFENSE OF ST. VITH

See previous citations for Chapters XV and XVI.
"This terrain is not worth a nickel" (p. 466), ltr, Clarke to author, 6 Apr 83.
For "in bad shape" (p. 468), Hasbrouck msg as cited in Cole, *The Ardennes*, pp. 394–395.
"Come on out!" and "Fuck you" (p. 473), Combat Interv with Britton, *et al*.
For "to plan alternative positions" (p. 473), Riggs, "An Engineer's Seven Day War."
"What are our orders?" and "Go west!" (p. 474), Combat Interv with 1st Lt. Roger W. Cresswell, Exec O, Co A, 23d Armd Inf Bn.
For "a kind of scavenger hunt" (p. 475), Cole, p. 411.
Hasbrouck msg (p. 477) and unless otherwise noted, messages exchanged between Hasbrouck and the First Army and the XVIII Airborne Corps are in 7th Armd Div Combat Interv file.
For "not expected to sacrifice his command" (p. 478), tp conv, Ridgway and Kean, 212350 Dec 44, Ridgway papers.
"Did you read this?" and "Yes, sir" (p. 480), author's interv with Hasbrouck, 20 Aug 83.
For "calm, courageous, imperturbable" and following quotations (p. 480), Ridgway, *Soldier*, pp. 119–120.
"The mud makes it pretty difficult" (p. 481) and "That cold snap" (p. 482), Eisenhower, *The Bitter Woods*, p. 302.
For "the opportunity will be over" and quotations following (p. 482), Cole, p. 415.
For "like subway trains" (p. 484), Train MS.
"The earth shook" (p. 487), Lewis MS.
"They can come back with all honor" (p. 487), Cole, p. 413.
"*A bas les Boches!*" (p. 487), MacDonald, *The Mighty Endeavor*, p. 386.

CHAPTER XXIV: THE DEFENSE OF BASTOGNE

The historian for the European Theater, Col. S. L. A. Marshall, assisted by Capt. John G. Westover and 1st Lt. A. Joseph Webber, conducted detailed interviews with the 101st Airborne Division, CCR, 9th Armored Division, and CCB, 10th Armored Division, whereupon Marshall wrote a narrative summary, which is in the Combat Interv files. The author has been unable to find the original interviews with the 101st, although it is evident from the interviews with the armored units that Marshall adhered scrupulously to the interview material. His narrative was subsequently published semi-officially as *Bastogne: The First Eight Days* (Washington, D.C.: Infantry Journal Press, 1946). In an appendix, "The Enemy Story," Marshall provides valuable material obtained through postwar interviews with von Lüttwitz, Bayerlein, Kokott, and von Lauchert. Any direct quotation without a citation is attributable to Marshall.

One of the better unit histories is Leonard Rapport and Arthur Northwood, Jr., *Rendezvous with Destiny: A History of the 101st Airborne Division* (101st Airborne Division Association, 1948). For the first days at Bastogne, the authors reprinted Marshall's account, but where they developed additional material, inserted it and marked it with an asterisk.

For "as if it were a [theater] curtain" (p. 490), Combat Interv with officers and men of Team Desobry. Maj. Gen. William R. Desobry provided detailed corrections to an early draft accompanying ltr to the author, 24 Aug 83.

For "it looked as if" (p. 491), Eisenhower, *The Bitter Woods*, p. 311.

"Don't be afraid" and "The Germans are coming" (p. 493), Toland, *Battle*, p. 129.

For "the son of a bitch" (p. 500), Combat Interv with Desobry.

For "to aid CCB" (p. 504), Cole, *The Ardennes*, p. 514.

For civilians in Bastogne (pp. 505–507), see Joss Heintz, *In the Perimeter of Bastogne* (Kiwanis Club, Bastogne, 1975), and Nobécourt, *Hitler's Last Gamble*.

For the story of Renée LeMaire (p. 507*ff.*), the author is deeply indebted to her two sisters, as noted in the acknowledgments. See also Dr. John T. Prior, "The Night Before Christmas—Bastogne, 1944," *The Bulletin*, Dec 72.

For "the hole in the doughnut" (p. 510), Fred MacKenzie, *The Men of Bastogne* (New York: David McKay, 1968), p. 151.

Most published accounts of the demand for surrender (pp. 511–513) are similar, and Rapport and Northwood (pp. 510–511), reproduce the German and English versions of the demand. New material is from Mme Simonne Schmitz of the Syndicat d'Initiative, Bastogne, and an account by one of the parliamentaries, Lt. Hellmuth Henke, provided by CEBA (with special thanks to Jean Milmeister). Although there has been speculation that instead of "Nuts!" General McAuliffe used a vulgarity, he assured the author in an interview in 1949 that he did indeed say "Nuts!"

Additional sources: Robert J. Houston, *D-Day to Bastogne: A Paratrooper Recalls World War II* (Smithtown, N.Y.: Exposition Press, 1980); and Rudolf Siebert, *2d Pz Div Rcn Bn*, "Die Schlacht in den Ardennes," *The Bulge* (CEBA), No. 2-81.

CHAPTER XXV: TO RELIEVE BASTOGNE

Sources listed for Chapter XXIV are applicable, particularly Marshall; and again no quotations from that source are cited. There are good Combat Intervs for the 4th Armored Division.

For "wrote knowingly" (p. 514), Martin Blumenson, *The Patton Papers 1895–1940* (Boston: Houghton Mifflin, 1972), p. 15.

"Troy, of all the goddamned crazy things" (p. 515), Eisenhower, *The Bitter Woods*, p. 333.

"All right, Troy" and "to cut off the Krauts" (p. 515), Price, *Troy H. Middleton*, p. 262.

"The general impression" (p. 515), Combat Interv with Lt. Col. Hal C. Pattison, Exec O, CCA, 4th Armd Div.

For "to drive like hell" (p. 519), "Sorry I did not get to shake hands," and "like shoals of silver minnows" (p. 521), Cole, *The Ardennes*, pp. 515, 531, and 468.

For "resupply coming from the sky" and following quotations (p. 522), ltr to the author from Mme. Jacques Boulet (Maggy LeMaire).

For "not to feel a sentimental pride" and following quotations (p. 522), Laurence Critchell, *Four Stars of Hell* (New York: The Declan X. McMullen Co., 1947), p. 267.

For "close enough for government work" (p. 522), Mackenzie, p. 189.

For McAuliffe at the police station (p. 525), Heintz, *In the Perimeter of Bastogne*, p. 67

"Xmas Eve present coming up" (p. 525), Cole, p. 475.

For "an all but imperceptible movement" (p. 526), MacKenzie, p. 212.

For "wore that ghastly air" (p. 527), Critchell, p. 274.

For "desperate effort" (p. 529), and "three tanks believed friendly" (p. 532), Cole, p. 480.

"This is it" (p. 531) and two following quotations, Combat Interv with Abrams, *et al*.

"Come here!" (p. 532), Toland, *Battle*, p. 264.

"How are you" and "Gee" (p. 532), Eisenhower, p. 345.

Additional sources: Capt. William A. Dwight, "Events Preceding Entry into Bastogne," in 4th Armd Div Combat Interv file; ltr, Maj. Gen. Joseph H. Harper to William C. C. Cavanagh, 3 Aug 69; and Lt. Col. Joseph A. Wyant, historian, Ninth Air Force, "Battle of the Ardennes," Office of Air Force History.

CHAPTER XXVI: IN FRONT OF THE OURTHE RIVER

"They're Germans, Colonel!" (p. 539), Samuel M. Hogan, unpublished and untitled MS, courtesy of Dr. Maurice Delaval; also ltr to the author from Hogan, 13 Nov 83.

For "a hailstorm of fire" (p. 540), Cole, *The Ardennes*, p. 379.

For "like throwing peas at a plate glass window" (p. 545), ltr to the author from Frank Evans, Trp D, 87th Cav Rcn Sqdn, 7th Armd Div, 22 Oct 83.

For "I wouldn't attack" (p. 546), Combat Interv with Billingslea.

SS-Sgt. Ernst Barkmann's story (pp. 550–552) is from Otto Weidinger, *Division Das Reich (The Path of the 2d SS Panzer Division 'Das Reich'—The History of the Backbone Division of the Waffen-SS)* (Osnabrück Verlag, 1982), Vol. V, Chapter V (translation by M. Trevor Shanklin).

"Don't give an inch" and "Why did you destroy" (p. 553), Toland, *Battle*, pp. 230, 251.

For the story of SS-Capt. Hans Winkler (pp. 555–556), Weidinger, *op. cit.*

For "if anything, worse than before" (p. 557), Sylvan Diary, entry of 24 Dec 44.

Additional sources: "Action at Samrée, Belgium: The Role of the Division Quartermaster in Defense of Samrée," *The Lucky Seventh, op. cit.*; William R. Breuer, *Bloody Clash at Sadzot: Hitler's Final Strike for Antwerp* (St. Louis: Zeus Publishers, 1981); Gert Schmager, *"Regiment 'Der Führer'—22d until 27th December 1944," Der Freiwillige*, Vol. 12, 1964; Committee 3, Officers Advanced Course, The Armored School, 1948–1949, Armor Under Adverse Conditions (2d and 3d Armored Divisions in the Ardennes Campaign, 16 Dec 44–16 Jan 45); and XVIII Abn Corps, Rpt of Investigation, CCA, 7th Armd Div, Manhay (Dec. 24–25, 1944).

CHAPTER XXVII: CRISIS BEFORE THE MEUSE

Combat Interviews are good for both the 2d Armored and 84th Divisions. Both have excellent unit histories: Donald E. Houston, *Hell on Wheels: The 2d Armored Division* (San Rafael, Cal.: Presidio Press, 1977), and Theodore Draper, *The 84th Infantry Division in the Battle of Germany, November 1944—May 1945* (New York: The Viking Press, 1946). See also Perry S. Wolff, *Fortune Favored the Brave: A History of the 334th Infantry, 84th Division* (printed in Germany, 1945). For British operations, see in addition to the official history, Operations of 30 (Br) Corps During German Attack in the Ardennes, December 1944–January 1945, in ETO Historian's file.

"Yes, hold" (p. 562), Sylvan Diary, entry of 21 Dec 44.

"You get down that road" (p. 567), Maj. Gen. E. N. Harmon (with Milton MacKaye and William Ross MacKaye), *Combat Commander: Autobiography of a Soldier* (Englewood Cliffs, N.J.: Prentice-Hall, 1970).

For "remain aloof" (p. 567), Collins, *Lightning Joe*, p. 285.

For "all hell broke loose" and "screamed in agony" (pp. 567–568), "The Battle of Eastern Belgium" in 2d Armd Div Combat Interv file.

"Ok, let's go!" (p. 568), Cole, *The Ardennes*, p. 437.

For "the success of the day" and "special rations" (p. 569), Helmut Ritgen, "The Battle of the Ardennes" in *Die Geschichte der Panzer-Lehr-Division im Westen, 1944–1945* (Stuttgart: Motorbuch Verlag, 1979) (translation by Maj. Dieter Kopac).

For "a pointed wedge" (p. 569), MS # B-151a, Von Manteuffel.

For "three important days" (p. 570), MS # A-873, Genmaj. Siegfried von Waldenburg, "Commitment of the *116th Panzer Division* in the Ardennes (16–26 Dec 1944)."

Story of Carroll and Korecki (p. 571), Eisenhower, *The Bitter Woods*, p. 363.

"Hey, you guys, open up!" and "Let's get the hell out of here" (p. 572), and "Whole trees were blown" (p. 573), Harold P. Leinbaugh and John D. Campbell, "Christmas in Verdenne," *The Washington Post Magazine*, 23 Dec 79, p. 7. Also intervs with Leinbaugh and Campbell; Videotape interv, Leinbaugh and Campbell with Gerhard Tebbe; and F. Memminger, "As the Law Demanded—In Remembrance of the Breakthrough of the Combat Group Bayer North of Verdenne and of 1st Lt. Hans Joachim Weissflog," Journal of the *116th Panzer Division*, No. 1, 1958 (translation by Hans Holtkamp).

"Don't bargain with me" (p. 575) and the crime at Bande, Commission des Crimes de Guerre, *Bande, op. cit.*

The story of Madame Monrique (p. 577) is from Toland, *Battle*, pp. 217–218. See also Nobécourt, *Hitler's Last Gamble*, pp. 237–238.

The story of the British tanks (pp. 577–579) is from Elstob, *Hitler's Last Offensive*, p. 393, and ltr to the author from Elstob, 20 Dec 83.

For "unaided" (p. 579), Montgomery to Eisenhower, M-389, 22 Dec 44, Eisenhower personal file, as cited in Pogue, *The Supreme Command*, p. 382.

For "if forced" (p. 579), Baldwin, *Battles Lost and Won*, p. 347. See also Baldwin, "Great Decisions," *The Infantry Journal*, May 47.

"Furious" (p. 580), Houston, *Hell on Wheels*, p. 341.

For "unrestricted use," "Now get this" and "I think you had better come home" (pp. 580–581), Brig. Gen. Williston B. Palmer, "Narrative from Memory of Actions and Orders at CP VII Corps on 24 December 1944," 7 May 47, in 2d Armd Div Combat Interv file.

For "his lips blue" and "a bit aghast" (p. 581), Collins, p. 289.

For "crawling with tanks" (p. 583), Cole, 562.

CHAPTER XVIII: CRISES IN COMMAND

For "his face was haggard" (p. 587), Irving, *Hitler's War*, p. 821.

For "unoccupied crossings" (p. 588), Von Luttichau and Bauer, "Key Dates During Ardennes Offensive," Pt I, p. 39.

"*Mein Führer*" (p. 588), Merriam, *Dark December*, p. 151.

"We have had unexpected setbacks" (p. 588), "As much as I may be tormented," *then he resumed*," and "to consolidate his holdings" (p. 589), Toland, *Adolf Hitler*, pp. 837–839.

For "a calculated insult" and "more arrogant and egotistical" and following quotations, (p. 589), Bradley and Blair, *A General's Life*, pp. 369–370.

"I was absolutely frank with him," "entirely our own fault," "looked thin" and "Poor chap" (p. 589), Bryant, *Triumph in the West*, p. 278.

For "he was certain" (p. 589), Bradley, *A Soldier's Story*, p. 481.

Montgomery's denial (p. 589), John Eisenhower interv with Montgomery, 1 Oct 66.

For "a tired little fart" (p. 590), and preceding quotations, Blumenson, *The Patton Papers*, pp. 606, 608.

For "let him have it" and following quotations, "the extraordinary step" and "Damn it, Bedell" (p. 590), Bradley and Blair, pp. 370–371.

For the story of the troopship *Léopoldville* (pp. 590–594), Jacquin Sanders, *A Night Before Christmas: The Sinking of the Troopship Léopoldville* (New York: G. P. Putnam's Sons, 1963). Additional German material provided by Prof. Dr. Jürgen Rohwer, Bibliothek für Zeitgeschichte, 16 Apr 82. There are detailed interviews with survivors in 66th Div Combat Interv file.

"Praise God" (p. 594), Cole, p. 612.

For "to deliver next breakout" and "might well release" (p. 595), Weigley, *Eisenhower's Lieutenants*, pp. 541–542.

"It looks to me" (p. 595), quoted in Bryant, p. 279.

For Montgomery's letter to Eisenhower (pp. 595–596), Montgomery, *Memoirs*, pp. 284–285.

For "had saved the Americans" (p. 596), Weigley, p. 543.

For "under no circumstances" and three following quotations (p. 596), Marshall to Eisenhower, W-84337, 30 Dec 44, Eisenhower personal file, as cited in Pogue, *The Supreme Command*, p. 386.

For "extremely dangerous situation" (p. 596) and following quotations, unless otherwise noted, de Guingand, *Generals at War*, pp. 106–115.

"In a somberly lighted room" and "tired of the whole buisness" (p. 597), Eisenhower, *The Bitter Woods*, p. 383.

"Whatever your decision" (p. 598), Montgomery, p. 286.

For "handling large masses" (p. 599), Bryant, p. 287.

"If you get a monkey" (p. 599), Weigley, p. 566, citing Patton news conference, 1 Jan 45.

For "in principle" (p. 599), Cole, p. 611.

For "such top-flight divisions" and "Well, Monty" (p. 599), Collins, *Lightning Joe*, p. 292.

For "the Small Solution" (p. 600), Cole, p. 605, citing *OB WEST* War Diary.

"Excellent agent sources" (p. 600), John Frayn Turner and Robert Jackson, *Destination Berchtesgaden: The Story of the United States Seventh Army in World War II* (New York: Charles Scribner's Sons, 1975), p. 106.

For "call up Devers" (p. 601), Ambrose, *The Supreme Commander*, p. 577.

"I think you've done" (p. 602), Eisenhower, *Crusade in Europe*, p. 363. Nobécourt, *Hitler's Last Gamble*, has more detail on the encounter, particularly from the French viewpoint.

CHAPTER XXIX: ERASING THE BULGE

A detailed account of the fighting around Bastogne is in Cole, *The Ardennes*, and more detail on erasing the bulge in MacDonald, *The Last Offensive*.

For the allusion to Tweedledee and Alice (p. 604), the author is indebted to Strowson, *The Battle for the Ardennes*, p. 115. Eisenhower's order of the day is in Pogue, *The Supreme Command*, p. 547.

For "at the earliest possible moment" and "His trip" (p. 605), Irving, *The War Between the Generals*, p. 362.

"The battle in the West" and "taking into account" (p. 605), Elstob, *Hitler's Last Offensive*, pp. 445–446.

For "resulted in breaking" (p. 606), Cole, *The Ardennes*, p. 676.

For "death blow" (p. 608), the head of the German fighter forces, Lt. Gen. Adolf Galland.

For "by instant agreement" (p. 611), Bradley and Blair, *A General's Life*, pp. 380–381.

For "a catacylsmic Roman Holiday" (p. 611), Hansen Diary, entry of 7 Jan 45.

"His Majesty's Government" (p. 611), Eisenhower, *The Bitter Woods*, p. 386.

For "perturbed . . . about the sniping" (p. 611), the press conference, and "appeared to be sensitive" (p. 613), Montgomery, *Memoirs*, pp. 278–282.

For Chester Wilmot (p. 613), Wilmot, *The Struggle for Europe*, p. 611n.

For "all-out . . . mad" (p. 614), Bradley and Blair, p. 383, citing Ralph Ingersoll.

"After what has happened" (p. 614) and "The Americans have engaged" (p. 614), Pogue, p. 389.

"There's a colonel here" and following quotations (p. 616), historian's narrative with 2d Armd Div Combat Intervs.

For "during the early stages" (p. 618), Carlo D'Este, *Decision in Normandy* (New York: E. P. Dutton, 1983).

EPILOGUE

All quotations from Weingartner, *Crossroads of Death*. Professor Weingartner is kinder to the defendants than one who lay on the ground that dreadful day would be, but his is a careful, detailed, scholarly account, focusing primarily on the trial and subsequent events.

Bibliography

PUBLISHED WORKS

Articles and books, including unit histories, applicable to only one or two chapters are listed with the appropriate chapter documentation.

Stephen E. Ambrose, *The Surpreme Commander: The War Years of General Dwight D. Eisenhower* (Garden City, N.Y.: Doubleday, 1970).

Hanson W. Baldwin, *Battles Lost and Won: Great Campaigns of World War II* (New York: Harper & Row, 1966).

Ralph Bennett, *Ultra in the West: The Normandy Campaign of 1944–45* (New York: Charles Scribner's Sons, 1980).

Martin Blumenson, *The Patton Papers 1940–45* (Boston: Houghton Mifflin, 1974).

Omar N. Bradley, *A Soldier's Story* (New York: Henry Holt and Co., 1951).

——— and Clay Blair, *A General's Life* (New York: Simon and Schuster, 1983).

Richard Brett-Smith, *Hitler's Generals* (San Rafael, Cal.: Presidio Press, 1977).

Donald Grey Brownlow, *Panzer Baron: The Military Exploits of General Hasso von Manteuffel* (North Quincy, Mass.: The Christopher Publishing House, 1975).

Arthur Bryant, *Triumph in the West: A History of the War Years Based on the Diaries of Field-Marshal Lord Alanbrooke, Chief of the Imperial General Staff* (Garden City, N.Y.: Doubleday, 1959).

Peter Calvocoressi, *Top Secret Ultra* (London: Cassell, 1980).

Alfred D. Chandler, Jr., ed., *The Papers of Dwight David Eisenhower,* Vol. IV, *The War Years* (Baltimore: Johns Hopkins Press, 1970).

Hugh M. Cole, *The Ardennes: Battle of the Bulge,* US ARMY IN WORLD WAR II (Washington, D.C.: Government Printing Office, 1965).

J. Lawton Collins, *Lightning Joe, An Autobiography* (Baton Rouge, La.: Louisiana State University Press, 1979).

Wesley Frank Craven and James Lea Cate, eds., *Europe—ARGUMENT to V-E*

Day, Vol. III, *The Army Air Forces in World War II* (Chicago: University of Chicago Press, 1951).

David Downing, *The Devil's Virtuosos: German Generals at War 1940–5* (New York: St. Martin's Press, 1977).

Dwight D. Eisenhower, *Crusade in Europe* (Garden City, N.Y.: Doubleday, 1948).

John Eisenhower, *The Bitter Woods* (New York: G. P. Putnam's Sons, 1969).

Maj. L. F. Ellis, with Lt. Col. A. E. Warhurst, *Victory in the West,* Vol. II, *The Defeat of Germany* (London: Her Majesty's Stationery Office, 1968).

Peter Elstob, *Hitler's Last Offensive* (London: Secker & Warburg, 1971).

Jósef Garlinski, *The Enigma War* (New York: Charles Scribner's Sons, 1980).

James M. Gavin, *On to Berlin: Battles of an Airborne Commander 1943–1946* (New York: The Viking Press, 1978).

Felix Gilbert, ed., *Hitler Directs His War* (New York: Oxford University Press, 1950).

Janice Holt Giles, *The Damned Engineers* (Boston: Houghton Mifflin, 1970).

David Irving, *Hitler's War* (New York: The Viking Press, 1977).

———, *The War Between the Generals: Inside the Allied High Command* (New York: Congdom & Lattés, 1981).

John Keegan, *Waffen-SS: The Asphalt Soldiers* (New York: Ballantine Books, 1970).

Ronald Lewin, *Ultra Goes to War* (New York: McGraw-Hill, 1978).

Charles B. MacDonald, *The Mighty Endeavor: American Armed Forces in The European Theater in World War II* (New York: Oxford University Press, 1969).

———, *The Siegfried Line Campaign,* US ARMY IN WORLD WAR II (Washington, D.C.: Government Printing Office, 1963).

———, *The Last Offensive,* US ARMY IN WORLD WAR II (Washington, D.C.: Government Printing Office, 1973).

Robert E. Merriam, *Dark December* (Chicago: Ziff-Davis, 1947; current edition: *The Battle of the Bulge,* Bantam Books).

Bernard L. Montgomery, *The Memoirs of Field-Marshal the Viscount Montgomery of Alamein, K.G.* (Cleveland: World, 1958).

———, *Normandy to the Baltic* (Boston: Houghton Mifflin, 1946).

Jacques Nobécourt, *Hitler's Last Gamble: The Battle of the Bulge* (New York: Schocken Books, 1967).

Thomas Parrish, ed., *The Simon and Schuster Encyclopedia of World War II* (New York: Simon and Schuster, 1978).

Forrest C. Pogue, *The Supreme Command,* US ARMY IN WORLD WAR II (Washington, D.C.: Government Printing Office, 1954).

Frank James Price, *Troy H. Middleton: A Biography* (Baton Rouge, La.: Louisiana State University Press, 1974).

Matthew B. Ridgway and Harold H. Martin, *Soldier: The Memoirs of Matthew B. Ridgway* (New York: Harper & Bros., 1956).

John Strowson, *The Battle for the Ardennes* (London: B. T. Batsford, 1972).

John Toland, *Battle: The Story of the Bulge* (New York: Random House, 1959).

———, *Adolph Hitler* (Garden City, N.Y.: Doubleday, 1976).

Walter Warlimont, *Inside Hitler's Headquarters 1943–1945* (New York: Praeger, 1964).

Russel F. Weigley, *Eisenhower's Lieutenants: The Campaign of France and Germany 1944–1945* (Bloomington, Ind.: Indiana University Press, 1981).

James J. Weingartner, *Crossroads of Death: The Story of the Malmédy Massacre and Trial* (Berkeley: University of California Press, 1979).

Chester Wilmot, *The Struggle for Europe* (New York: Harper & Bros., 1952).

OFFICIAL RECORDS

During periods of combat, each headquarters from army down through regiment and separate battalion submitted a monthly narrative after action report, along with such supporting documents as G-2 and G-3 daily journals, daily periodic reports, G-2 estimates, messages, and overlays. Although use of the after action reports is essential, commands often put the best possible light on their activities; for that reason, the G-2 and G-3 journals are vital, for in the manner of a ship's log, no entry in the journals was to be erased or altered. It would take a score of years to study every unit's journals in detail, but I have used them where something was unclear, where something appeared to have been covered up, and for such critical periods as the days immediately preceding the German attack.

After action reports of the V Corps, First and Third Armies, and the 12th Army Group were published officially. Copies may be found with the World War II unit records in the National Archives. The raw files of the First Army and the 12th Army Group are nevertheless important, particularly for G-2 estimates and periodic reports.

COMBAT INTERVIEWS

Soon after an important action, teams of historians in uniform working under the European Theater Historical Section descended upon the units involved, interviewed commanders and men at various levels, and sometimes provided an overall covering narrative based on the interviews and the historians' own observations. The materials are in rough typescript with the World War II records in the National Archives, filed by division or corps. They provide much more human interest material than do the official records, and, like the G-2 and G-3 journals, can sometimes be used as a corrective for after action reports.

AUTHOR'S INTERVIEWS AND
UNPUBLISHED MANUSCRIPTS

In response to notices in veterans' publications, more than a hundred veterans of the battle provided information on their experiences and some provided unpublished manuscripts. I corresponded at length with some of the veterans and interviewed others. Where I have used the material, identification is provided in the chapter documentation; to all who responded, I am grateful.

Through the kindness of John Toland, I used interviews he conducted for his earlier work on the battle, located in the Library of Congress, and through the kindness of John Eisenhower, his interviews with Field Marshals Montgomery and von Manteuffel, located in the Dwight D. Eisenhower Library.

Credit for interviews with civilians in Belgium and Luxembourg is included in the chapter documentation.

SPECIAL MATERIALS

MAGIC files in the National Archives and ULTRA files, September 1944–January 1945, normally in the Public Records Office, London, but temporarily withdrawn for the use of official historians in the Cabinet Office Historical Section, London, where I was premitted to use them.

Other special materials are noted in the chapter documentation.

GERMAN MATERIALS

Under the auspices of the European Theater Historical Section, German generals in captivity immediately after the war prepared narrative accounts of their experiences. Every German general who was involved in the Ardennes at division level and above (with the exception of General Dietrich) wrote an account. They vary in quality but are essential to telling the German story; they are stored in the National Archives. Although I have used all the manuscripts for the Ardennes, citations are provided only for direct quotations.

In support of the official histories, historians in the U.S. Army Center of Military History prepared detailed studies based on the German manuscripts and official German records. Identified by the letter R and a number, the studies are also in the National Archives. Of particular value for my work were three studies by Charles V. P. von Luttichau—R-12, "Ardennes Offensive—Preliminary Planning"; R-13, "Framework of *Wacht am Rhein*"; and R-14, "The Strategic Concentration"—plus another by von Luttichau in collaboration with Magna E. Bauer, R-15, "Key Dates in the Ardennes Offensive."

With the help of Günter von der Weiden and Heino Brandt, I traveled the length and breadth of West Germany interviewing German veterans who served at regimental level or below. Again with their help, I obtained well over a thousand pages of published German material, including unofficial unit histories and personal accounts. Since my work is focused on the American view, I was able to use only portions of that material where it dovetailed with the story from the American side; the use is reflected in the chapter documentation. I am nevertheless grateful to all who consented to interviews.

Index